THE
SACRED
HUNT
DUOLOGY

The Finest in Fantasy from
MICHELLE WEST:

The House War:
THE HIDDEN CITY
CITY OF NIGHT
HOUSE NAME
SKIRMISH
BATTLE
ORACLE
WAR*

The Sun Sword:
THE BROKEN CROWN
THE UNCROWNED KING
THE SHINING COURT
SEA OF SORROWS
THE RIVEN SHIELD
THE SUN SWORD

The Sacred Hunt:
HUNTER'S OATH
HUNTER'S DEATH

* Coming soon from DAW

MICHELLE WEST

THE
SACRED
HUNT
DUOLOGY

Hunter's Oath
Hunter's Death

DAW BOOKS, INC.
DONALD A. WOLLHEIM, FOUNDER
375 Hudson Street, New York, NY 10014
ELIZABETH R. WOLLHEIM
SHEILA E. GILBERT
PUBLISHERS
www.dawbooks.com

First Printing, August 2016

1 2 3 4 5 6 7 8 9

DAW TRADEMARK REGISTERED
U.S. PAT. AND TM. OFF. AND FOREIGN COUNTRIES
—MARCA REGISTRADA
HECHO EN U.S.A.

PRINTED IN THE U.S.A.

Hunter's Oath

Chapter One

25th day of Corvil, 396 A.A.
King's City, Breodanir

A NEAR-SKELETAL BOY PEERED OUT from around a shadowed corner. His face was the color of winter; white, muddied by the dark hollows of wide eyes. Those eyes examined the thin crowd in the lower city streets.

Only one there caught his attention—a man dressed in audacious furs and bangles, with a thick, new purse attached to his wrist and a belt heavy with winter supplies girding him round his midsection. His cap alone would fetch a good price and guarantee food and shelter besides.

The boy was hungry and tired. That he was cold as well had ceased to bother him; the winter had been harsh enough that the icy bite of nearing spring felt something akin to warm. It had been a very bad season.

It would be worse still if he didn't go back to the den armed with some display of money or barter goods. Marcus, self-proclaimed den leader, had already made that perfectly clear; the bruises still showed on the boy's face. Fear set him to shivering and the cold joined in. A ragged cough that would not be ignored scraped at his throat. He needed a warm place to stay, and soon. Twice this winter he had seen cold kill.

The rich man stopped every so often to tsk-tsk at the state of the buildings. His purse bounced and jangled, even at this distance. The young boy swallowed nervously. He would have already made his mark, but for the dogs. Not even the most ignorant of children could claim not to know what their presence meant.

One of these dogs stayed at its master's heels, lifting its proud, wide head. Its eyes, circled on both sides by patches of black, darted back and forth, but it didn't stray far. The other dog, a bitch by the look of it, was a little more testy, but its fur was clean and it was an almost even gray. Its low-throated growl could be heard when anyone approached. These were no city dogs, rough and mangy after winter's scavenging. They were obviously well fed—on what, the boy didn't care to speculate. But their jaws, their teeth . . .

Stephen, the boy thought to himself, as his hands shook, *he's a Hunter Lord. Find someone else.*

But he'd looked; Luck knew it well and had obviously seen fit to curse him. There was no one else that was even likely, and if he waited in the shadows like a dithering rat, he'd lose his entrance ticket and—he coughed, retching—any chance for a meal this day.

Hunger and cold decided him. He moved forward, his worn shoes squelching in the slush. Thin shoulders came up, as did his chin. Seen this way, he was a stick of a lad, but not uncomely, and not particularly dangerous. Only poor—and that, in the King's City, was danger enough.

Soredon, Lord Elseth, smiled softly at the sound of light steps. It was about time; how long did the urchin think to keep him out in this dismal weather? Corvil was a chill month; one to be avoided if at all possible.

Maritt growled and began to swivel her head. Her jaws were open, and her teeth, cleaner than the snow, were also whiter.

Easy, easy, Maritt. Stay at heel. Stay calm.

She heard his Hunter's command and shifted on her hind legs. Her growl didn't really diminish, and Soredon sighed, shaking the purse he carried with renewed vigor in an attempt to drown out Maritt's voice. It was his own fault, and he knew it. Maritt was his prize bitch, and he coddled her overmuch.

Ah, well. At least Corwel was behaving. Absently, he dropped one gloved hand to rest upon the alaunt's broad head. Corwel was young yet, but still the best dog that Elseth had ever produced. He tousled those flopped ears with genuine pride and pleasure.

Good. The boy was behind him, sauntering gently forward. Lord Elseth carefully positioned his broad back and began the inner search for the Hunter's trance. He was experienced enough to have earned the rank of Master Hunter at the King's pleasure. The trance came quickly and easily, fitting him better than these awkward, fine clothes. The crisp bite of the air grew keener still; the colors of the street faded into sharp, clean outlines. Everywhere, life ground to a slower, subtler movement.

He reached out from the trance, found Maritt's eyes, and looked carefully through them, feeling the background thrum of her deep-throated growl as if it came from his own chest.

The boy approached his back slowly. Through Maritt's vision, he examined the young thief. The boy was all bones and sallow skin, with a thatch of pale hair that might be paler still when less filthy. Lack of height and weight made his age hard to guess, but Lord Elseth was certain he was somewhere between seven and nine. A good age; one that suited the Hunter Lord's purpose fully. But would the little thief continue to linger in the half-melted, filthy snow, or would he at last make his move?

Please, Lady Luck, smile on me now. I've seen enough of your frowns for this ten-day.

Her answer was beneficent and sudden.

The boy darted, like a pale shadow, flickering at his side. He saw the gray flash of what once might have passed for a dagger and lifted his wrist in a snap of motion, carrying the purse strings easily out of the boy's reach. His turn was so smooth and deft that the child's knife didn't have time to stop its motion.

With a smile that was all white teeth, Lord Elseth grabbed the boy's wrist and hauled him off his feet.

"What have we here?"

He'd moved so quickly that Stephen still wasn't sure when the broad, fur-covered back had suddenly changed into the man's front—but he didn't like it. Thievery had its own penalty in the King's City—and the punishment was far worse when the victim was one of the Hunter Lords or Ladies. Hunger and fear were forgotten now, as was breathing; he saw instead the shadow of the knife at his thumbs. If he'd had the chance, he might have taken a swing with his dagger—but it was the dagger hand that the Lord held, and the Lord showed no signs of loosing his grip.

He swallowed a deep breath, lost it to coughing, and choked. His wrist was firmly trapped in the larger man's hand. *Think, damn it. Think.* He cleared his throat. "You've got no call to hold me, sir, I was just—"

"I know well what you were doing, whelp. And it has its price. Come along; your thieving days are over."

Stephen struggled as the tips of his toes brushed the ground. He kicked out with his feet and found the ribs of the large black-and-white dog. It snarled and snapped to the side, avoiding its target by turning at the last second.

"That's enough," Lord Elseth said, his voice remarkably similar in tone to that of the dog's. "You will *be still.*"

Gulping, Stephen nodded, and found the flat of his feet. What he did next was born of instinct and terror—but it was also unexpected. His small jaw found the inside of the Hunter Lord's wrist and clamped down.

The Hunter Lord cursed and pulled back, and for a moment, Stephen was free. It was all that he needed. He had had to become good at running. In a blur he was gone into the sanctuary of the alleyways and warrens that he knew so well.

Blood dripped down to the snow, mingling with dirt and water to become another murky patch of ground. Soredon smiled and shook his head. He bound his wrist carefully; it took him only seconds.

"Well, Corwel, Maritt. What shall we do?"

Maritt was straining at the invisible leash that held her at his side.

Lord Elseth reached down. From the left side of his belt, he lifted a silver-mouthed horn. He held it to his lips, feeling the chill press of metal and the thrum of the silent demands the dogs made. Ah, he had chosen well, even though it had taken too much time. The child had spirit and not a little cunning.

The long, loud lowing of the horn announced the Hunt in the King's City. Twice it blew long, and a third time, short. Corwel waited until the last note had died and then placed his nose to the ground. His tail, short and stumpy though it was, began to crisscross the air.

"Yes, Corwel. Find him."

Stephen heard the horn. It cut across the sound of his feet and the horrible rasp of his breath. He had not heard its like before, but now that he had he would never forget it.

They followed by scent. He knew this because he always remembered the old stories, even when he no longer believed in them. He hoped that this part, at least, was true; nothing else had been.

Hunter dogs ran fast, and they were smarter than most normal dogs, but Stephen was certain he knew these alleys and buildings better than they knew their kennels and forests. His life depended on it.

His breath was quick and sharp with cold. He wanted to look over his shoulder, but he knew it would slow him down; that much he'd learned over the last year of running.

Please, Lady, smile. Let it work. I'll make my offerings. Please.

He made a sharp right past the building that was called the Stonemason's, cutting it close enough that he could use the wall as a balance while he pivoted.

If the dogs followed by scent, he was going to give them something to smell.

Soredon ran, keeping pace with his dogs. He was deep into the Hunter's trance and running came easily to him now. The boy, like any animal that knew it was being pursued, didn't flee along a straight path. It was another good sign; fear didn't make the boy stupid.

There was no question at all in Lord Elseth's mind that the boy was afraid.

Stephen lost time to the doubled doors of Benny's Tavern; they were tall and heavy enough to take the damage of a good sized brawl. His hands were shaking because he'd balled them into fists that were too tight, but he still managed to pull the doors open. Sunlight streamed in at his back, making a silhouette of his height and girth.

"Hey!"

He wasn't allowed into the tavern, but he moved quickly enough so that no one had time to stop him as he rushed into—and through—the sparse crowd. It was early yet, but lunch would soon be served, and the regular patrons had already filled the air with a steady stream of smoke, sweat, and salty language.

"HEY, YOU! STOP!" The bartender's bellow carried with an ease that spoke of too much experience. Next would come the slam of the wooden countertop as it was raised too quickly, and the heavy-soled tread of a large, angry man.

Stephen missed it all. He bolted past the last of the bar's patrons and into the kitchens. If the smell of this place didn't stymie the dogs, nothing would. It probably wasn't cleaned more than twice a year, and at that, only when Benny's mother visited.

The kitchens, of course, weren't empty.

"Hey!"

Stephen dodged a ladle—Benny's wife wasn't quite as slow and large as Benny was—ducked under the lunge of Benny's oldest son, and avoided sliding on a piece of something that had probably once been bread. He didn't even pause at the woodstove, although he almost smiled at the fleeting warmth.

The kitchen door exited into another alley. Stephen managed to yank it open and get through it before Benny's son caught up with him. Then his feet hit the snow and his lungs filled with clean, cold air.

Let them figure that out.

He had no intention of waiting to see whether or not they could. He ran.

Lord Elseth rarely cursed; his Lady found vulgar language ignorant and acutely embarrassing—and she exacted a high price for the latter. Nonetheless, he had just enough time to do so before his dogs leaped up at the closed doors of the tavern, growling.

Through the trance, the boy's scent passed from Corwel to Lord Elseth; it was strong and distinct. *Corwel, Maritt—away from the door. Come.*

Corwel obeyed gracefully, Maritt with a growl. But they both came to stand by his side, fur bristling, eyes trained on the closed doors.

Stay.

With a grimace of distaste, Lord Elseth pulled open a single door, and attempted to blend into the ambience of Benny's Tavern. Silence radiated outward from him like a wave as each and every patron in the large, beamed room stopped to stare at this newest customer.

"Good day to you, sir," Benny said. His voice, pitched out of long habit to travel over a crowded, noisy room, was uncomfortably loud. He ran out from behind the counter, wiping his hands almost fastidiously on his large, heavy apron. "Is there anything at all that I can do for you?"

Soredon was a tall man; Benny was short and somewhat rounder. It was not because of height alone that Lord Elseth looked down. "Yes." He reached into the pouch that jangled so obviously at his belt and pulled out a gold coin that bore the impression of a stag's antlers astride the King's Crown.

Benny reached for it, and Soredon snapped his open hand into a large, gloved fist. "I'm following a young thief. Slip of a boy, pale hair. I believe he came in here."

"Couldn't have," Benny said promptly. "No kids're allowed." He looked pointedly at the gloved hand.

Soredon growled. It was a feral sound, not a human one, and Benny took a step back as he realized—for the first time—that he faced a Hunter Lord.

"Uh, that is, no kids can come in and stay, your lordship." The bartender ran a hand over his forehead and tried not to look at the fist that held a small fortune. "He ran out through the kitchen."

"Good." Lord Elseth opened his palm and tossed the coin into the air.

Benny was still scrabbling for it when the dogs came in through the door Soredon held open.

Stephen ran, holding his side as the cramps started. Let Luck only smile, and he'd never thieve again. He thought, for a moment, that she'd heard his prayers and had chosen to grant them. For a moment. Then a new sound started, worse than the horn. The dogs were baying.

He thought of their teeth, and had no doubt as to which would give first: his skin or their jaws. The alleys that towered above him in faceless, near windowless walls, became distant, unfriendly terrain. He searched in vain for stairs, for anything that would take his feet off the ground and give the dogs another pause.

The baying grew louder and closer, filling his ears completely, obscuring his shallow breaths. He bounded around a corner, sliding in the muddied snow. His hands scraped a wall and came away splinter-filled and bleeding as he continued to run.

The alleys opened up as he crossed a deserted street. Buildings flashed by, and he recognized them: The Tern, its board flapping in the breeze; the butchers', the one baker's. He hesitated a moment in front of the butchers' and caught a glimpse of the bitch as she rounded the corner down the street.

There was only one place to go. His teeth bit through his lower lip as he put on a burst of speed—probably the last that was left him. The fear of the dogs was greater than the fear of Marcus and his retribution.

There. Ahead, in a nook that the restructuring a century ago had created, stood the door to the den. As always, it was closed. He ran at it full tilt, skidding at the last moment to give a first knock with his entire body.

A flap of wood, at an eye level that cleared his head by at least a foot, scraped open. Above the bridge of an oft broken nose, two dark eyes squinted in the sunlight.

"Marcus, it's me! Let me in!" Stephen began to bang frantically at the wood; the dogs were closing fast.

"What've you brought for me?"

"Marcus, please! I need to get in—they're coming!"

The flap shut. Stephen stood in the silence for a heartbeat before the dogs started again. He was shaking and gasping as he looked from side to side. There wasn't any place else to run; the den had been chosen because it stood in the middle of an alley that had no escape to either side.

He lifted his hand to strike again, and then let it drop. Steadying himself, he turned, his dagger shaking as much as his thin arms did. He would have to face them. Maybe, if he was careful, he could injure the dogs enough to get away.

The large black and white bounded around the corner and lifted its broad, triangular head. It came to a stop but didn't take its eyes from its quarry. At its heels came the bitch. The Hunter Lord could not be far behind.

If he'd had food, he might have tried to bribe the dogs, or at least distract them. It was an idea. But he wouldn't be in this situation if he'd had anything to eat, and he suspected that the dogs ate well enough so they wouldn't even look at the scraps he could throw them.

He crouched, holding the knife out as if it were a shield. Why hadn't the dogs come forward?

As if in answer, the Hunter Lord joined them, following the same trail that both Stephen and the dogs had left in their hurried race through the snow; he wasn't even breathing heavily. His cap was gone now, although he didn't appear to be carrying it. All he held in his hand was the horn that had sounded the chase. The dogs moved apart, and he came to stand between them, placing one hand on either of their heads. The bitch bridled at the feel of the hard, cold horn but stayed her ground anyway.

Everywhere there was silence.

Stephen met the eyes of the Hunter Lord; they were brown to his blue, and narrowed as if in thought. He waited, wordless, until the waiting itself was as fine a torture as the running had been.

"Don't—don't you move!" He waved his dagger, swordlike, through the air in front of his face. "I'm telling you, stay where you are! I don't want to hurt you!"

"Oh, indeed," the Lord replied. "I can assure you, my boy, that you needn't fear that. And I have no wish to harm you; you've led a fine chase. Better than I would have guessed. Come. Cease this nonsense. We have far to go." The hand that wore the thick, cloth gauntlet rose. "Come."

Stephen backed into the door, shaking his head firmly from side to side. How stupid did this Hunter Lord think he was? "I ain't going nowhere. Go away, or I'll have to use this." He waved the knife wildly, loosing a startled cry as the door gave way behind him.

Before he could react, he was jerked off the ground by the back of his collar. His dagger went tumbling into the snow. He didn't have to look back to know who held him.

"Well, fine sir," Marcus said, raising Stephen higher. "It seems that you've had trouble in our fair city streets."

"Let the boy go," the Hunter Lord replied. "I have no business with you."

"Don't you just?" Marcus looked down at Stephen, noted the creeping purple tinge to his skin, and slammed him to his feet. "Well, I've got your thief, at no small risk to myself. I think that's worth something." The convivial smile Marcus wore was so out of place on his face that the Hunter Lord couldn't even manage a similar expression. Lip curling, he said, "Let the boy go."

"Not from around here, are you?"

"No." The one word made clear what the Lord thought of that.

"Well, maybe I'll explain a few rules of the King's City. This," he shook Stephen, who was too stunned to struggle, "is a thief."

"I'm aware of that."

"I," once again he used Stephen as punctuation, "am the man who caught him."

The black and white answered with a low, warning growl.

"In my books that makes me the one who gets the reward. But I ain't a greedy man. I'll share it with you."

"Marcus—please. . . ." Stephen's voice was a rasping choke.

"Shut up." No openhanded slap, this. When Marcus' hand drew back, it was bloodied.

Lord Elseth stared hard at Marcus for a moment. When he moved his mouth, it formed no words, and the lift of his lips was no smile. "Corwel." The Lord took a step back. "Yours."

He lifted the horn to his lips.

The dogs sprang, their feet covering the short distance as if they needed no ground to run on. Marcus' eyes grew wide, and with a loud cry, he threw Stephen at them. He ran into the old building, yelling as if they had already reached him.

Corwel's voice joined his in the music of hunter and hunted. Without pause, he followed through the open door.

The Hunter Lord ignored the sounds that came out of the building. Quietly, he walked over to the huddled bundle of youth that lay at Maritt's feet.

No, Maritt, he sent softly. *Go and join Corwel.*

She needed no other word. Like the breeze, she passed them by, leaving almost no trace.

The Lord knelt, unmindful of the snow that immediately began to melt into his knees. He reached out with one large hand, saw the horn that it held, and stopped to return it to his belt.

Stephen was too tired, too weak, to offer any more resistance. He lay on his side, his face covered by hands that showed red. What Marcus had done had taken the last of his spirit and guttered it. It had been stupid to come here. But even if Marcus wouldn't let him in, he didn't have to—didn't have to . . .

Lord Elseth reached down gently and drew Stephen's hands away from his face. "Come, boy. Let me see it."

His lips were already swelling. Very gingerly, Lord Elseth probed at the bruised jaw. Stephen gasped.

"It may be dislocated. Can you walk?"

Nodding, Stephen tried to rise. His eyes were dark, their blue lost, as he glanced furtively up at the larger man.

"We don't go to the Justice-born, lad. We go to the Mother-born. There's a temple not far from the lower city. I'll make the offering." Lord Elseth rose and put his hands under Stephen's arms. He set the boy on his feet, saw that he wobbled dangerously, and lifted him up instead.

The child weighed almost nothing.

"Boy?"

Stephen shook his head, flailing weakly, although he had almost no strength for it. Then he sank into the furs that surrounded the Lord. They were soft, and so very, very warm.

"Dogs?" He muttered, an edge of fear in the solitary word. His lids were already too heavy and he missed the expression on the Hunter Lord's face, which was just as well.

"They'll be along soon. When they've finished here."

The silver mists rolled in over the scene like fog across the lowlands. She sat in an inn half a continent away, in Everani, a fishing village downcoast of Averalaan, her palms cupped around a glowing, crystalline sphere.

At her back, she heard the whispers: *seer-born*. She did not disillusion them; it gave her privacy for the moment, and besides, it was not altogether untrue. But she was more, and different, than simply talent-born.

Stephen of Elseth, she thought, as she pushed strands of hair back into the privacy of her hood. *You're so young. We don't meet yet.* But she knew where she was, and more important, knew *when* she was.

The mists obscured the young boy completely before she looked away. She was Evayne a'Nolan, and quite alone. She straightened her shoulders, took a deep breath, and rose. It was time for work now, not for dalliance, and she had lost precious minutes watching.

And remembering.

Chapter Two

THE BROAD-SHOULDERED, AUBURN-HAIRED NOBLE who rode beside the Hunter Lord was not in a good mood. He spoke gently enough to Stephen, but every time he turned his attention to the lord, his lips whitened around the edges. The Hunter Lord was also angry.

Stephen did his best to shrink into the saddle and avoid the notice of either of the two large men. It was hard; his legs ached, first from walking and then from riding. Horses had been, at best, a thing to dream about until three days ago. Now, they were incredibly wide, large, and frightening animals that he could, just barely, sit astride.

The dogs were still the dogs, and if the bitch looked up and growled periodically, she was a good few feet out of range. When the Hunter Lord wasn't looking, he took the opportunity to sneer at her.

He'd been fed, clothed in warm furs, and given a real bed to sleep in as they'd traveled along the road to Mother only knew where. But his own mother had told him once that they fed sheep and cows before they slaughtered them, too.

He stared at his breath as it misted.

The red-haired man in gray and green glowered at his Hunter.

"Let it be, Norn," Lord Soredon said, his voice low and grating.

Norn of Elseth snorted.

Late snow fell in a thick, wet blanket that made travel difficult. Inns were cold and not well provisioned to deal with a Hunter Lord's disgruntled dogs, and Lord Elseth was never capable of dealing with ruffled innkeepers. In fact, Norn thought, as he walked his horse around a particularly tricky bridge—which had iced in the evening and was only visible at all because he knew the roads here well—Soredon wasn't capable of dealing with people. Period.

As a prime example, he took the waif who had walked, or ridden, listlessly between them for the better part of the journey. Fright was still upon him and he answered any question with a monosyllable or a silent nod. His winter legs had finally given out two days ago, and he rode now on the packhorse. The four-legged one. Of course the horses couldn't be further burdened down, not with Lady Elseth's commands for purchases in the King's City, and Soredon, stubborn idiot that he was, had refused to take a proper wagon. Norn, huntbrother to Lord Elseth, carried one half of the boy's weight in goods, and Soredon, grumbling, took the rest.

An argument was brewing between the two men, but Norn didn't wish to have it out in front of the boy. The boy was just too vulnerable and too isolated to have to deal with the tempers of the nobility. And Norn didn't trust him not to try to effect some sort of escape during such an argument, which would probably kill him in the end.

Norn glanced over his broad shoulder, shifting so the pack frame didn't block his sight. Stephen sat sidesaddle across the horse, clutching at the braided manes for dear life. They had had a coat and mittens for him, but the latter he'd removed when he'd been deposited on the beast. His fingers were reddened by cold; Norn feared the bite of frost there.

He exhaled a fine, billowing mist and looked at the sun's crisp shadows. Soon, he was certain, they would see the village that sprawled around the manor grounds. And once the boy was safely inside, he had a word or two to say to Soredon.

In winter, the light was gone too early from the sky. For the villagers and the farmers, dinner was an afternoon affair. The cost of tallow and wick was high enough that they were perfectly happy to see their hours dictated by the sun. Solstice had passed, and the day was lengthening. Enough so that the Lady Elseth, along with her two small children, took dinner amid the fading pinks that showed through the towering bay window that was the manor's pride.

A fire burned merrily against the two walls, and servants busied themselves tending to it; it was warmer here than in their quarters. All was as it should be in the manor of Elseth.

"Lady."

Elsabet looked up from her plate as the door opened and the keykeeper walked in. Boredan was an older man; the oldest of those who served the Hunter Lord. He wore his age as he did his fine, tailored robes: perfectly.

It was unusual for him to interrupt the Lady Elseth at her dinner, and she rose at once, fearing some accident or mishap. "Boredan?"

"My apologies for interrupting your repast, Lady." He gave a low bow. "It appears that the Lord and his huntbrother are home."

"Already? We weren't expecting them for at least three . . . Where are they?"

"If I should be so bold as to hazard a guess, I would say in the kennels, Lady. They have, however, left a guest, and Norn was most insistent that he be attended to."

"Father's home?" The older of the two children leaped out of his chair, food forgotten. His linen napkin tumbled to the floor, a crumb-covered, gravy-stained heap.

"Gilliam."

"But—but Father's—"

"Father is busy." Her tone made it clear that she was in no mood to indulge him.

He sat, disgruntled.

"Maribelle, do remember how you were taught to use a fork." Lady Elseth carefully pushed her chair in, folded her napkin, which was spotless, and left it on the table. "Why don't I see to the guest?"

"It would be appreciated, Lady."

She was certain of it. "Boredan, I know you're very busy, but do you think you could stay with the children?"

Boredan nodded as Gilliam rolled his eyes in despair. Mother was bad enough, but no one else in the house compared to the keykeeper for strictness of manners and demands on behavior.

"Most certainly. It looks as if Master Gilliam has forgotten everything I've taught him about dining habits."

She could hear the shouting before she reached the wide, grand hall that opened out from the vestibule. The words were muffled by distance, and the voices were raised so much that she couldn't distinguish them, which was for the better. On the other hand, the manor had been quiet since her Lord and his huntbrother had left. This would give the servants at least a three-day's worth of amusement.

And it was good that somebody was going to be amused by it. Certainly, from the set of lines in her otherwise smooth forehead, and the faint creases around her thinned lips, it was clear that she was not.

Now, Elsabet, she told herself. *I'm certain things could be worse.* She stopped in the hall, found it empty, and saw that both sets of doors were firmly closed. The shouting, obviously, carried through them. Biting her lip, she reminded herself not to think that in the future—it invariably turned out to prove true.

So annoyed was she that she walked to the door and tested the handle with a sharp yank before she saw the guest that the keykeeper had spoken of. He sat, his knees curled beneath his chin, against the banister of the stairs. His eyes were wide and ringed with the dark of sleeplessness or illness, and his clothing . . . best not to think about the dreadful state of that. Yet even though it was oversized and quite thick, she could see that he was mostly skin and bones; his cheeks were sunken, his fingers almost skeletal.

She knew why he had been brought here, and what he would become. It was quite clear that he did not.

If she had been angry before, it was forgotten; she was furious now. That two grown men couldn't set aside their differences for long enough to see to a cold, starving boy. . . .

The child looked up to meet her eyes. His knees came down, and he straightened up, away from the banister. His effort to be more alert only made him seem more frail.

"Hello," Lady Elseth said softly. "I see that you've been left quite alone."

He nodded, not daring words in front of so grand a Lady. She couldn't see her reflection in the dark of his eyes, but she knew that he was well aware of the contrast her fine dinner clothing made with his winter wear.

"You must be starving. And cold."

He nodded again.

"Well, come then. You are a guest in our house, and I won't do our hospitality a disservice by leaving you here any longer." She held out a hand and he stared at it as if it were a weapon. There was no mistaking the fear that lurked beneath the wary surface of his eyes.

In all, it was probably a good thing that Norn and Soredon were outside. Had her Hunter Lord of a husband been within the walls, and within her reach, Lady Elseth might have killed him. In an instant, she forgave Norn—for she knew them well enough to understand the nature of their dispute after having met the boy.

"Come," she said again. "There is no fire here, and no food. I shall see that you have rooms set aside for you, but dinner is already served." She made her voice softer still, and lowered her hand gently, capturing the blue of his eyes with the hazel of hers. "Don't you want to eat?"

She saw him struggle with hunger and fear, and was thankful that hunger won out; it was a near thing. He stepped forward and she began to move toward the dining room, taking great care not to crowd him.

He didn't know what to think of the Lady. He was certain he had never seen anyone so lovely—she looked as if she'd stepped out of a story just to meet him. Her dress was so fine and so long, the skirts full and rustling, the sleeves soft and draped. Her hair was darker than his, and pulled back from her face to fall in curls at the nape of her neck. Her eyes were hazel, not as cold as blue or gray. She seemed friendly.

He looked away from her, disgusted at himself. Stories. At his age.

"Come and sit here. Boredan, this is . . ."

"Stephen."

"Stephen. I'm Elsabet, and this is my daughter, Maribelle."

Maribelle looked up and sniffed, but Stephen couldn't be angry; she was almost a baby. Her face was still sort of fat and chubby, and her hair, like her mother's, fell long at the back, but in finer, softer ringlets.

"This is Gilliam, my son."

Gilliam made to rise, and no one stopped him. He looked Stephen up and down and then shrugged, his young lips turning up in a curl that reminded everyone of his father.

"Gilliam!"

"Pleased to meet you."

Stephen didn't bother to answer. This Lord's son was his own age at least, and probably thought too much of himself, given the way he'd answered. Well, fine clothes didn't make a person—his mother used to tell him that—and this Gilliam wasn't so much bigger than he.

"Why don't you take that seat, Stephen. The servants will bring dinner in a moment, and I shall join you when they arrive. I have a few things to attend to first, but I hope you won't hold that against our hospitality." Lady Elseth smiled, nodded, and turned almost in one motion. She was used to being obeyed, and even though her voice was friendly and warm, Stephen heard the command in it.

He paused to watch her retreating back. She couldn't be real, but just the same, she reminded him of old words and voices that he could barely put faces to.

"Are you going to stare, or are you going to eat?"

"Master Gilliam."

"I was just asking." Gilliam picked up his fork and began to cut away at the meat on his plate.

Meat. Something white nestled underneath a blanket of gravy, and something green sat beside it, untouched. Stephen looked self-consciously at his clothing and then straightened out. He'd be damned if that boy would make him feel uncomfortable. "I'm going to eat," he replied curtly, pulling the chair out.

"Aintcha gonna change?"

"Maribelle."

"Well," the child said, tilting her head to one side and looking seriously at Boredan. "Ma always makes *me* change."

"Yes, and your Lady mother also tells you that you mustn't question guests."

She shrugged and faced Stephen. "Want my peas?"

"No, he doesn't," Boredan said, quite severely. "You do. Please, Master Stephen."

Master?

Servants came into the hall carrying trays and plates and an endless amount of food. They began to serve Stephen at Boredan's curt nod as Stephen stared. Still, it was obvious that the food was meant for him, so he didn't bother to ask. He was hungry.

Into his third mouthful of meat, he froze at the sound of Gilliam's unwelcome snicker.

"Don't you even know how to use a fork?"

The fork, curled in his left hand, stopped moving as Stephen stared down at it, embarrassed in spite of his best intentions.

"Master Gilliam, it isn't an art that you are a master of yourself. Your manners, if you please." The last three words were as pointed and cold as any that Stephen had ever heard.

Gilliam's cheeks purpled in a flush, but he doggedly continued. "Well, why don't you tell *him* how to eat?"

"Because *he* is a guest. *You* are a rude little boy."

Stephen waited until just the right moment. Boredan's attention was still upon the Lord's son, but the Lord's son was glaring at him. He smiled, stuck out his tongue, and bent down to his food.

He decided right there that he hated Gilliam. But not enough that he wouldn't eat at the table with him.

"What do you mean, you didn't even ask?"

Soredon rolled his eyes, "Elsa, don't you think we might—"

"Don't change the subject."

He could tell by the familiar flash of her eyes that he wasn't about to enter his domicile without satisfying her anger. He might be cold, hungry, and already bone-weary with arguing, but it wouldn't likely budge her an inch from her place in front of the doors.

And Norn, curse him, wasn't being much help at all. He stood to the side, his arms crossing his broad chest, his mouth turned down in a frown that had only half the severity of hers.

"I didn't have time to ask."

"You had time to *hunt him* in the King's own city and you didn't have time to ask?"

"Elsa, I—"

"He thinks he's here for some sort of punishment, no doubt. The boy's positively terrified!"

"Before you get carried away with motherly sentiment, do remember that he was trying to rob me."

If she'd had an ounce of common blood, she would have spit. Instead, the line of her usually full lips disappeared further into the white set of her mouth. The stone that framed her was less hard and cold than she. Certainly less dangerous.

"Why wouldn't he try? He's cold, he's probably starving, and you were dangling enough money to feed him for a few years."

"What does it matter? The boy's here, he'll have better clothing, enough food, and any education you can force on him. Let's just drop it, shall we?"

"The 'boy,' as you call him, is here, but he doesn't have to stay if he doesn't choose to. Don't forget it."

"Elsa, the dogs have just been bedded down, and I'd like the chance to do the same. We've been traveling hard these last few days just to reach home."

"I should feel sorry for you, is that it? You're used to hard travel. The boy isn't."

"Elsabet," Norn said quietly.

She met his eyes, and he shook his head in response, mouthing a silent *later* that Soredon couldn't see.

Still she hesitated another moment before stepping out of the way. Soredon heaved a grateful sigh and inched past her.

"If we have another son, Soredon, I will never trust you to find a huntbrother for him. Is that clear?"

"Perfectly."

"Good."

"Oh, Elsabet?"

"What?"

"I missed you, too."

She didn't even bother to answer as he opened the door and walked through it. "And what are you smiling at?" But part of her anger was stemmed, and Norn didn't feel any sting in the words.

"You, Lady." He shook his head. "If the boy makes the choice and the vow, he'll be blessed in you. He couldn't ask for a better mother." He walked over and put an arm around her shoulders to shield her from the night's chill. "I think it will be fine. I had a similar experience with Soredon's father, after all." He felt her shoulders relax slowly. "It's the Elseth way. I don't know why they choose among the young thieves in the King's City; the Valentin custom of choosing local orphans seems much more intelligent."

"They enjoy the challenge of catching a likely thief, I suppose," Elsa answered as she walked with Norn to the door. "Or they like hunting in the King's City." She lowered her head, briefly, to his shoulder. "My husband has the best huntbrother in the kingdom of Breodanir, so I shouldn't argue with Elseth custom." Her lips grew thin as she raised her face. "Only with the execution of that custom."

"Elsa," Norn said, pulling against her arm. "It's cold. Shall we enter?"

She linked an arm with his and shook her head again, struggling free of temper. "Sometimes I think huntbrothers are more of a blessing to us than the Hunters we marry. But next time, Norn, keep a better eye on him. I am trusting you, after all, with my family's name."

He had a bed. A real one, with tall, thick posts and a headboard that disappeared into curtains. Those curtains were deep green—Hunter colors—with tasseled edges of harvest gold.

Better, he had pillows. Three, all thick and soft and fluffy. At the table by his bed, someone had left some sort of clothing, all neatly folded into a careful pile.

He had enough food in his stomach to last days, he had a fire in the grate that was burning merrily, and the comforter that he sank into was at least as good as the pillows.

He was in the Heavens, he was certain of it. Either that, or he was about to embark on a journey to the Hells proper, and this was the price that they offered him. He didn't much care.

Not until the knock came at the door. He leaped to his feet and jumped away from the bed, glancing around the room for some place to hide. They must have realized that they'd made a mistake, sending him here. At least he hadn't touched the clothing.

"Hello?"

He recognized the voice. It was the huntbrother's. Norn's.

"Hello, Stephen. I've ordered a bath for you. Do you mind if I come in?"

Yes. He thought it, but the wariness hadn't left him at all, so he said, "No."

The door opened and Norn, carrying a small lamp, walked over the well-lit threshold. "Ah, I see you won't be needing this." The wick flickered and went out in the noisy gust of his breath. He stepped out of the way, and three people carrying a large tub entered in his wake. They put the tub down in the room's center and disappeared, only to return with buckets that appeared to be steaming.

Stephen didn't much hold with bathing and water—especially not in the winter. He eyed the servants with a suspicion that bordered on fear.

"It's a bath, boy," Norn chuckled. "You're not afraid of it, are you?"

"No," Stephen answered. The word was far more resolute than his face. "It's just water."

"And a good deal of soap, which you could use. Ah, Terril, that's quite enough of the hot for the moment."

Terril, a dark-haired younger man, nodded briskly, although he seemed dubious. He stepped aside and looked at Stephen.

Stephen stared back.

Norn cleared his throat. "Stephen, you're supposed to sit *in* the tub."

Stephen still hesitated.

"And you're to give your clothing to the servants. They'll see to its cleaning."

"I'm supposed to get undressed in front of everybody?"

"That's the way it's normally done. Come on, boy. There aren't any women about."

Gritting his teeth, Stephen submitted himself to the first bath of the year. He was fine; he didn't even yowl when his feet hit the water that he was certain would boil flesh.

The servants were gone, and Stephen sat on the side of his bed—his, as Norn had assured him—in the soft flannel of newly acquired nightclothes. He couldn't stop touching them, and occasionally his hands would fall to the comforter as if to make sure it was real.

Norn didn't miss any of this as he sat in the room's sole chair. Cleaned up, the boy looked much less like a street orphan—a little food and a little sleep, and no doubt the child would begin to look human.

"Well, Stephen, what do you think of our home?"

"You live here?"

"Yes.

"My apologies for the way you were found. We were overdue and Soredon was anxious to return home." It was a lie, but a harmless one. "It's Master Gilliam's birthday in two short months, you see."

That didn't mean much to Stephen, as was obvious by his lack of response, so Norn found another tack.

"Do you enjoy living in the streets of the King's City?"

Stephen's shrug was answer enough.

"Would you like to return to them?"

"Why're you asking?"

"Because you don't have to." Ah, now he could see the suspicion that had dogged the boy for the entirety of their journey. It was natural enough; hadn't he been suspicious when he'd first come to the manor? "Do you know what a huntbrother is?"

"Maybe."

"Because," Norn continued, as if Stephen hadn't replied, "if you so choose, you could be one."

"I ain't Hunter-born."

"No. Neither am I." Norn edged closer. "None of the huntbrothers are."

Stephen looked at Norn's fine clothing with obvious skepticism. But he was interested, that was clear.

"This would be your room. You would eat at the Lord's table, wear clothing as good as this, and take lessons. No one would expect you to thieve just to have a place to stay in the winter. No dens would try to kill you or force you to join. You wouldn't have to worry about running with, or from, a street pack."

Stephen's hands drummed the side of his bed as he stared past Norn's shoulders. Reflected firelight flickered in his eyes as if trapped there. It was warm here, and the food, like the Lady, had been something out of story or dream. It was almost too good to be true, and anything like that had its price.

"What do I have to do?"

"Perform the duties of a huntbrother."

It was a trick. Stephen was certain of it; Norn was a huntbrother. "Why me? Why not a real brother?"

"Stephen, no huntbrother is Hunter-born. No huntbrother is noble-born. Don't you know any of your stories?"

"Stories are for kids," Stephen replied, sullen at the implication that he was stupid.

"Not all stories are," Norn said softly, remembering another time, a different boy. He shook himself as the silence lengthened, and then continued. "Hunter Lords are like Lord Elseth—closer to their dogs and their hunts than they are to their people. Huntbrothers are supposed to balance that; to remind them of the rest of humanity."

Stephen nodded in quick agreement. "Why do we need 'em anyway?" he asked, warming to the subject. "Why're they worth more than the rest of us?"

"You don't know your history," was Norn's quiet reply. "And I don't have the time to teach you everything you'd need to know. But let me tell you quickly about the Betrayer, the Doomed King."

In spite of himself, Stephen leaned forward intently.

"You know that to kill your parents is a crime against the Mother," Norn said softly.

Stephen nodded. Everyone knew that.

"Over fifty years ago, the King of that time—the current King's grandfather—was challenged by his son, Prince Aered, to a duel in the Hunter's see. The King's Queen, Leofwyn, stood by her son, and the King's Priest stood by the Prince as well.

"Under the eyes of the Hunter God, Prince Aered killed his father, and saved all of Breodanir in the doing. But the Prince had still committed a crime in the eyes of the Mother, and he died after only a short reign."

"What do you mean saved Breodanir?"

Stories are for children, Norn wanted to say—but he knew that the time for teasing Stephen, if there ever was one, would come much later. "The King whom we do not name was a weak-willed man who wanted to please too many people. He made his court of foreign men and women, not the Breodani, and he belittled his Hunters.

"These foreign lords and ladies felt our customs barbaric and foolish, and over the years they convinced the King that they were right. Do you know what the Sacred Hunt is?"

Stephen flushed. "Everyone knows that!"

"And?"

"Once a year the King and all of the nobles go into the royal forests and call a hunt. And once a year, one of the nobles dies. Always."

"Yes," Norn said quietly, seeing the question in Stephen's eyes. "It's true. Always. The Hunter Lord, or huntbrother, is taken by the Hunter's Death—the Hunter God made flesh. It's a gruesome death, Stephen. The death we all fear." He shivered even as he spoke, and then shook himself again. "Where was I? Ah, yes.

"The Doomed King did not call the Sacred Hunt as it had always been called.

The Hunter Lords pleaded with him, as did their Ladies, the Priests, and even the Queen—but to no avail. He was tired, he told them, of being laughed at by greater men than they, and the foolish custom of the Hunt would end with him.

"But the Sacred Hunt is called for a reason, Stephen, even if you do not believe in it. The Hunter God made his covenant with the Hunter-born: that he would help them hunt and feed his people every day of the year; that crops would be bountiful and game plentiful; that the forests and fields would be green and grow well. But in return for this, the Hunter Lords and their huntbrothers must, one day a year, allow the God *His* Hunt.

"After the first year with no Hunt, the crops failed, and the game became scarce. The King's fine foreigners said that this was coincidence, but the Breodani knew better and they redoubled their efforts to reach their King.

"He was a weak man, as I've said, and having made a mistake, he would not acknowledge it for fear of seeming weak. So the next year, he again refused to call the Hunt."

"Why didn't another noble call it?"

"Because," Norn said quietly, "only the King can call the Sacred Hunt; it is part of our covenant with God. Now, save your questions and let me finish.

"Each noble must keep granaries full in case of drought or a very bad harvest. The second year emptied the last of the granaries, and people began to starve. Without the Sacred Hunt, the lands became parched and dry. The crops did not take at all.

"The King's oldest son, Prince Aered, knew that the Breodani could not survive a third such year. In anger and sorrow he took counsel with the Queen and the King's Priest.

" 'The Sacred Hunt *must* be called,' he told them both, and they both agreed. All of them knew what this meant, because only a King can call the Sacred Hunt. The Priest prayed to the Hunter God, as did the Prince, and the next day, the Prince killed his father in combat, by the grace of the God, and became King.

"He called the Hunt, and we knew the wrath of the Hunter God betrayed. Two-thirds of our number perished that day." Norn was silent again, contemplating deaths he had been too young to witness, but could imagine just the same. "But that year the harvest was the richest it had been in ten, and the hunting, for those of the Hunter Lords who still remained, was also good.

"This is why we need Hunter Lords, Stephen."

"Then what are huntbrothers good for?"

"Huntbrothers?" Norn cleared his throat. "They must be both protectors and friends to their Hunters. They must train in all things to do with the Hunt, and hunt by their Hunters' sides in the Sacred Hunt, dying if that is the will of the Hunter God. They must become well schooled and must deal with the Ladies and their laws.

"We are the common people whom the Hunters are supposed to protect and feed, Stephen—and our very presence, as decreed by the God, is meant to remind them of that, so that they never misuse the powers that God has granted them."

Stephen was silent; Norn wasn't certain that he understood all that had been said. But he'd understood enough of it.

"If you can vow that you will do all of this, you will be accepted as hunt-brother. You will live with our family, and become Stephen of Elseth."

Oh, yes, it was a trick. Had to be. But Stephen's hands were sinking into soft down, and the warmth of the fire was pulling his eyelids down. Why shouldn't he say yes? Even if he didn't like the stupid boy, why shouldn't he lie? He could take the oath and pretend—and he'd have all this for his own. If he'd been born to the right person, he'd have had it anyway.

But Norn's words about the Hunter's Death had been true: Stephen could tell that Norn was afraid of it. "Are they afraid of this Hunter's Death?" he asked, before he could stop himself.

"No," Norn replied. "The Hunter Lords are not. But they die it, just the same. I've seen it, Stephen," he added in a somber voice.

Stephen waited for Norn to continue, but the older man would not speak further. They were quiet for a few moments. *What difference does it make? I can die of cold or hunger, or I can take a chance that I might die once a year.*

"Yeah. I could do that."

"You'll take the huntbrother's vow?"

"Didn't I just say yes?"

"Then I will inform Lady Elseth."

Stephen froze, and his fingers became fists. "Tell the—the Lady?"

"Yes. It was she who provided the choice of room and clothing. I think she'll be quite pleased at your decision." Norn rose then, and made his way to the door.

Stephen wanted to stop him. He opened his mouth, and shut it forcefully enough that his teeth snapped. He didn't mind lying to Norn, and he especially thought he'd enjoy lying to the Lord's son—but the Lady was a different matter. She was—she must be—really nice. Special. And he wasn't certain that he wanted to lie to her.

His face hardened and he was disgusted at himself again. So what if she was special? She was a Hunter's Lady, after all. She'd had an easy life.

Even so, he was glad that he wasn't going to be the one to deliver the lie.

"Stephen?" Norn said, his hand on the door frame.

"What?"

"I hated Soredon when I first met him." That, and Norn's chuckle, lingered in the room long after he'd left. Norn was no fool, after all.

Four days into his stay at Elseth Manor, Stephen silently cursed his decision. If it hadn't been winter, he'd have taken the road back to the King's City on a minute's notice.

Oh, the food was everything that the first dinner had promised, and there was always a fire in the grate as proof against the cold. He'd clothing to spare, although where it came from he didn't know, and Lady Elseth was like a walking miracle. Better than that, Lord Elseth was never really home, except at dinner for one evening, and Norn was often out with him. The servants didn't even seem to notice that he'd grown up in the streets, and they were always polite, even when he was deliberately rude. After the first week, he stopped trying to provoke them out of frustration and shame.

No one pried into his past with unwanted questions, so he didn't have to tell them about the last year of his life. Didn't have to remember in detail the start of it: Three days alone in the small room he'd shared with his mother, after which he fully realized that he was alone. He didn't know what happened to her body; he didn't want to know. He didn't tell them about how he'd learned to steal things, about how many times he'd almost been caught, about how many packs he'd had to run from. He was alone here without being lonely, and he almost liked it.

The manor house was wonderful. It was so big and grand, he could get lost forever in it. The servants' wing was bigger than the den had been, and even their rooms were fine in comparison with what he'd lived in for most of his life.

He didn't even hate the lessons as much as he'd thought he would. Hours spent sitting in front of a rectangular slate with a piece of chalk while some "lessons-master," as Lady Elseth had called him, droned on and on actually became interesting. And he could put up with Maribelle, who followed him around every minute he wasn't busy, babbling at him and spilling things on his clothing.

What he hated was Master Gilliam.

"I don't have all day, Stephen." Just at the moment, said Master was trying to look down his broad nose. "Are you coming or not?" The side door that led to the outside from the empty kitchen let a draught of cold air into the room.

Stephen locked his eyes into place so they wouldn't roll. Unfortunately, his jaw also locked, making his smile more rigid than usual.

"Well?"

"It's sort of cold, don't you think?"

Gilliam snorted. "I don't care if it's cold. The kennels aren't." His brown eyes narrowed, and he drew himself up to his full height in unconscious imitation of his father. It wasn't very impressive. "Besides, you're the huntbrother; you have to follow. And I say we're going."

And that was that.

It isn't worth it, Stephen thought, as he took deliberate steps into the snow and the wind. *Food and a home isn't worth this.*

No? His breath came out in clouds that wreathed his thin cheeks; his cheeks grew pink under winter's weakening fingers. The sky was bright, the sun blazing, and both conspired to cast his shadow forward in a long, thin line. He walked it, delicately balancing between two bad choices.

He swallowed and started to jog. The kennels, as Gilliam said, were warm. He had almost decided again, but biting back the words that anger gave him was difficult.

The kennel opened up around him. It was the longest building Stephen thought he had ever seen, and it was dark. It smelled of wood and straw and dogs. In both stone—stone, of all things!—walls, the east and west, two large fires burned merrily. The heat of their light put the house fires to shame. The north and south walls were wood, but not the dovetailed, clumsy work of many of the poorer shacks he'd seen in his life. Whole families in the King's City would be proud to call this home. And what lived in it? Dogs.

There were, at the moment, twelve here; the others were in their runs. Gilliam called them six couple, and Stephen had learned that a couple was just another word for a leash that held two dogs. Each of these dogs had a heavy, oaken bed, with boards carved out in the simple stark letters of their names. Stephen couldn't read them yet, although it would be one of his duties. He didn't need to. These dogs lived like kings. They even had a second story in the kennel which was built solely to give them more protection from the cold.

Well, at least they didn't have mattresses, and the blankets on them were rough wool, not down. Straw surrounded them, and Gilliam had told him a huntbrother's duty was to see to its turning at least once a day.

Closest to the west wall was the grandest of beds, and in it, head perched on two crossed paws, lay Corwel, the leader of the pack. Both eyes were patched black, and the rest of his face was white, but his eyes, where they caught the fire, were a peculiar red shade.

Stephen thought it suited well; these dogs, the Hells would be proud to own.

As if hearing this, Corwel raised his massive head and opened his jaws, displaying his teeth as if they were regalia. Stephen flung himself back, coming to rest in time to feel foolish: the dog was only yawning. He smiled nervously, but stayed where he was.

Corwel sat up, shrugging the blanket off. He bounded to the floor, shook himself, stretched, and then padded forward, head up.

Lady Luck wasn't frowning; she was shouting in anger.

If he could have run, he would have—but his legs didn't remember how. He opened his mouth and didn't recognize the squawking that came out.

Corwel's jaws opened suddenly, closing on a snap that seemed to break the air. He jumped forward, forelegs extended, and caught Stephen's jacket in his teeth, bearing him to the floor.

Stephen screamed.

Corwel barked.

Five sleepy dogs suddenly joined him in a hideous cacophony of sound. But worse than that was the sound of laughter. Master Gilliam's.

"You idiot!" He was bent over, as if laughter were a burden that was heavy. "You should see your face! What did you think he was going to do? Eat you?"

Corwel's tongue, wet and decidedly smelly, washed over Stephen's face.

"Maybe you're too stupid to be my huntbrother."

"I'm not too stupid," Stephen said, giving Corwel a vicious shove. He rose, straightening out his clothing. "I'm too *smart*." And on that last word, he lashed out, his thin fist all sharp knuckles.

"Mommy! Mommy! The dogs're barking!" Maribelle skidded to a halt around the corner, slipped on the carpet, and rolled knees over head, sending her carefully starched skirts into a wrinkled blue spray.

Lady Elseth rose immediately from the long chair, her lips turning ever so slightly in a delicate frown. "The dogs?"

The discovery was too important to be forgotten in tears, and Maribelle hastily pulled herself to her feet, any scratch or injury ignored. "Barking and barking."

"Oh, dear. Where is your father?"

"Don't know."

Norn, who had been sitting beside Lady Elseth while she practiced her stitches, rose also. "He's at his letters. Lord Poreval requested his presence on a Hunt in a two-month."

"Well, I hate to interrupt him," Elsabet said softly, "but this might be important." Her regret was completely genuine; it was nigh impossible to get Soredon to sit down with quill and ink, even when the correspondence related to the one true love of his life: The Hunt. And a two-month meant boar or bear, so it was a more serious business.

"Maribelle, why don't you wait here while I find your father."

Norn followed his Lady out of the sitting room. He could tell by her gait that she was worried; the dogs seldom barked for no reason. To be truthful, he was slightly worried himself.

They walked the halls to Soredon's study, and Lady Elseth knocked firmly at the door before entering. It was habit; Soredon rarely paid attention to formality, and was never insulted when one just walked into his chambers. That was, when he noticed the interruption at all.

True to form, he sat facing the window, his eyes captured by the winter world outside and its dreams of coming spring. Winter was not the best hunting season, but it was a fact of life, and Soredon never railed against the inevitable.

"Soredon," Lady Elseth said softly. She, too, knew better than to wait for his notice.

"Hmmmm?" He turned, and his eyes brightened on seeing her. "Elsa." He pushed the parchment aside and stood, thankful for the excuse to leave it.

"Maribelle says the dogs are barking. Can you see to them?"

He was up in an instant. Household squabbles and small emergencies couldn't command his attention or concern—but the dogs were his domain alone, and Gods help any who troubled or injured them. He was halfway out the study door when he paused.

"Where is Gilliam?"

Lady Elseth's brow creased in mild concern. Her brief shake of the head answered the question.

Her husband stopped inches away from her hands. He closed his eyes, pulled his chin up, and looked into the distance of eyelids and darkness.

Norn recognized the Hunter's trance at once. He, too, became silent and intent as he watched the blank lines of Soredon's face. He could see the subtle shift of lips and eyes that spoke of contact. He was, even bounded by walls and windows, with his hunting pack.

The contact lasted for seconds. It was over before the Hunter Lord opened his eyes and brought himself back to his study.

"Well?" Norn said softly.

Lord Elseth turned to him and smiled. The surface of the smile broke, and laughter welled up from beneath it.

"In the kennels," he said, as he managed to fit the words between breaths. "With Stephen." The laughter ended, leaving affection and memory in its wake.

Norn's expression lost its worry, and he shook his head wryly. "He's not as patient as I was. This is what, four days? Five?"

"If I might interrupt this?"

They both turned to stare at Lady Elseth, losing the privacy of their moment. "Elsa?"

"What is going on in the kennels?"

"Stephen and Gilliam are at fist play."

"I see."

"Elsabet, where are you going?"

"To the kennels."

"Wait a moment, then. You know the dogs don't like—"

"I don't care what they like," she said icily. Nonetheless, she stopped.

"You're learning too much from Boredan," Soredon said, shaking his head in mock disapproval. "Why don't I go to the kennels and bring them."

"Why don't you?"

"Norn."

"With you," was the swift reply. Norn, brave and steadfast as he was, had no wish to be left behind with Lady Elseth's decidedly ill humor.

"And gentlemen?"

They turned warily.

"If you can stop congratulating yourselves for the Mother only knows what, you can bring both boys to me." Fist play indeed.

Silver mist obscured the reminiscing grins of Lord Elseth and his huntbrother, leeching them of color and warmth until they looked like ghosts within the confines of the sphere.

Evayne a'Nolan had been a young woman when she first walked the Hunter's wood—the King's Forest, as the Breodani called it. That was years past; more years than she cared to remember, although she was not, by the standards of the empire of Essalieyan, old now.

She shook her head softly and put aside her seer's ball, folding it into sleeves of midnight blue until its glow could no longer be seen or felt.

Gilliam of Elseth. I remember you.

She knew when she was.

But it was not the time for memory, whether fond or painful. She began to study the periphery of the wood itself, walking with great care, searching with the vision that was by now second nature: seer's sight.

She found what she sought. It was hidden from normal magic and normal sight, and it was subtle enough that she almost missed it at first. But interwoven with leaves, roots, and blades of wild grass was a net: a shadow-snare. Shadow-magic was the province of the demon-kin and the priests of Darkness; they were at work here, now.

Lifting her arms, she waited for the path, certain that she had seen what she had been sent to see; as she stepped onto it, the forests faded from her view. She dared not linger, for fear of being spotted.

Chapter Three

"GILLIAM, STOP FIDGETING."

"I'm not."

Lady Elseth sighed before she stepped back to look at her oldest child. The robes that the Elseth Hunters were confirmed in looked odd and empty on the shoulders of their youngest heir. They hung low, and although pains had been taken to belt them, they looked awful.

But Gilliam, on the eve of his eighth birthday, did not, through no merit of his own. The blackened eye that had been the start of his friendship with Stephen had given way from yellow to pale pink. On the other hand, the large scrape on his cheek from their enterprise at the mill remained a thin mess of scabs and flaked skin. What, by the Mother's grace, had possessed them to try to climb the mill wheel, she didn't know—and at three days from his ceremony, not much could be done to aid him; the nearest of the healer-born was sixty miles away. Worse still, Stephen had quietly come forward, and in private no less, to take the blame for the escapade.

Elsabet was not a stupid woman; how could she be, and occupy the seat of judgment for her lands? She knew a lie when she heard it, but the heart beneath the lie was sound, and the reason for it unquestionable. Before he had even given his oath, Stephen had truly declared himself huntbrother. She wondered if he knew what those words and that false confession had meant, and did mean, to her. Of course, she had still had the duty of meting out just punishment for both the lie and the escapade, but the doing had not made her heart heavier.

She didn't understand completely how the friendship of her son—her two sons—had come about; the only time she had ever been caught at fist play herself still smarted as an episode of humiliation. She and Lady Eveston had never become friends, although age and experience had lent their rivalry a patina of civility.

Now was not the time to think of it. Her oldest child was about to enter the Hunter's rites and swear the Hunter's Oath. And he looked like an underfed urchin. Her own gangly son, with hints of his father's temperament already showing in all the little ways. Her son.

"Well?"

Boredan sniffed. "I think he will have to do. The Hunter Lords have already gathered, and they only wait on the final preparations of the Priest."

"Are you nervous, Gil?"

"Of course not!"

Ah, age. Lady Elseth smoothed the lines of teasing smile from her face, already regretting the loss of the small child her son had so recently been. Maybe, years from now, she would tease him again and he would smile. Maybe not.

Still, just as her mother had warned her when Gilliam was first born, the time would come to let go a little. She stood, smoothing out the simple linens of her own white robe. Her hair was one long, burnished braid that slid down her back, giving her dress its only color. Tonight, the only finery one could carry was in the heart. Not even the band of the wedding was seen upon her fingers; they were smooth and unadorned.

We are all the Hunter's people, she thought, and knew it for truth.

But only the huntbrothers and their Hunter Lords faced the Hunter's Death.

"Lady?"

"I'm all right, Boredan. It is . . . chilly this eve."

Ah, Elsabet, her mother had said, *it is hard when the first child is a son. When you let him go, you give him to the Hunter God, and the life and death of the Hunter's Oath. You gave him life, but it is not your province, or even his father's, to protect that life. It is in the hands of God.*

And the hands of the Hunter God were red indeed with the blood of his loyal servants.

She wanted to hold her son, one last time. Wanted to, but knew by the proud little thrust of his chest and chin that he would have been humiliated by it. Children could be so cruel in their race and struggle to grow. But they could be crueler still, by dying.

Elsa, you may love your sons for their youth, for their strength—but love them as the sacrifices they might become. Love your daughters more.

Yet she remembered her mother's wet, red eyes, and her trembling lips well.

They are all our children.

Yes. Her mother had answered, although her eyes had never left her son's bier.

For the first time, Elsabet understood why mothers of the Hunter-born looked so pale and quiet at the first of the ceremonies. And for the first time, she understood the folly of the Doomed King, who had attempted to halt the Sacred Hunt—and the deaths it always caused.

But the land had paid for it; the people had learned anew the lessons that had almost become fable and story. And the Hunter still claimed his blood in return for the life of the land. She looked quietly at her son, seeing only an eight-year-old child, like unto any of the Mother's children. How could he understand duty? How could he understand death?

The knock that came at the door was soft and insistent. It rescued her from the sadness of her musings. She knew who it would be.

"Elsabet?" Norn didn't enter. "Is he ready?"

"As much as we can make him," she answered. "Stephen?"

"I've been waiting hours. Gil's always late."

"It wasn't my fault!"

"Was too. *I* said we shouldn't go to the kennels."

"Would have been fine if you'd cleaned them."

"Maybe we could finish this argument later?" Norn's large hand fell to rest on Stephen's thin shoulder. Green cloth, bordered in gray, slid down Stephen's short arms and trailed upon the ground at his feet. Like Gilliam, Stephen wore the robes of what must have been a much larger, or older, person. They were worn and simple, but the weight of a proud history was carried in each thread of woven cloth.

Elsabet smiled. *Do you know what you wear, Stephen?*

Perhaps he did. He carried himself with pride and a quiet awe as he touched his hem. Or maybe it was just her imagination; he had to lift the robes to walk.

"Well, Gil?"

Gilliam nodded smartly and stepped out into the hall. His eyes were wide and his breath was fast; flags of excitement colored his cheeks. He took his place beside Stephen, and stopped to whisper something to the boy who would become his huntbrother.

Norn placed an arm around his Lady's shoulders. He didn't ask her how she felt. He had lived with her for years, and knew well her mother's fears. But he knew what this night meant for both Stephen and Gilliam, and he almost pitied her, for she would never fully understand it.

Her smile faltered as she looked into his familiar face.

"Strength," he whispered.

"Pride." But instead of taking the arm he offered, she grasped his hand and held it tightly as she had once held her dead brother's. They followed in the wake of the two young boys, stepping cautiously into the unknown future.

Outside, the ground was wet and soft; new shoots of green leafed out over damp earth that threatened to turn muddy. The stars were out, and the moon as well; clouds had fled the sky. Torchlight glowed on the faces of those who waited, chief among them the Lord of Elseth.

He, too, wore only a simple robe. It seemed almost black in the scant light, but Lady Elseth knew it for the dark green that the Master Hunters were entitled to wear. At his left stood Lord Samarin, at his right, Lord Stenfal. They were older than he by at least ten years, but each had attained the rank of Master Hunter; Lord Samarin had even been named Huntsman of the Chamber two Hunts ago.

As witnesses, none could be found finer or stauncher than these two. Lady Elseth felt a warm glow of pride, and smiled at her husband from across the green. He saw her and smiled back, the expression no less warm than the torch he carried aloft.

The villagers, holding torches and wearing their normal clothing, also stood on the green in an uneven circle. These, too, were witnesses that the ceremonies decreed. They were of the land; they were the Hunter's responsibility and support.

It was late, but even so, Elsabet was heartened to see small children standing at their parents' sides. The youngest were held in arms, although one or two of the most precocious were being chased down by very embarrassed villagers.

Perhaps the children knew best. Their understanding of life gave no pause to the solemnity of ceremony and oath—they laughed or cried as if all of life were encompassed moment by moment.

She had long since lost the ability to do so, but tonight she would not begrudge it to others, only envy it a little.

The circle opened to allow her to pass; she walked to its center, where the twin pillars stood flanking the simple altar of rough-hewn stone. It was weathered with time, and had stood here long before the borders of Elseth existed. She paused to bow low. Her hands came to her lips, held together in a solitary private prayer. When she rose, she looked to the east and west, at each of the stone pillars. Words were written there in row upon row; none could now read them, they were so old.

Will you take my only son?

Her lashes pressed against her cheeks, and she bowed again, unable to ask for mercy in the face of so much history. She was Elsabet of Elseth; she would be as the pillars—solid, strong, a testament to this moment.

She took her place in the foreground in front of her husband, and waited for Norn. Norn walked to the altars and drew a silver knife from his belt. This he laid before him, bowing as Lady Elseth had done.

He joined his Hunter, nodding quietly.

The priest came next. He knelt on the wet ground, unmindful of the robes that would bear the dirt's soft traces; in the darkness they would not be seen. He lifted the knife that had been left for him and pressed its cold length to his lined lips. He was old, the Priest, and by his colors, a Hunter also.

Greymarten, Elsabet thought. She was reminded again of how well-respected her husband's family was. It was no small matter to journey from the King's side to the Elseth village, but even aged as he was, he had chosen to make the trek.

The Priest rose, knife still in hand.

Only Gilliam and Stephen still stood outside of the circle.

"Breodani, we are gathered here to witness and to receive. We are the people of the Hunter. Who stands for the Hunters?"

Lord Samarin stepped forward and bowed, his robes flapping in the chill breeze. "I do."

The Priest nodded and gestured; Lord Samarin came to stand at his side. "Who stands for the people?"

An older woman, the village head, walked forward. She bowed, and her bow was held long. Elsabet recognized Corinna with a quiet tilt of the head; more would disturb the ceremony.

"I do." And she came to stand to the left of the Priest.

Greymarten nodded, satisfied. "Let them come through."

A pathway appeared on the green; the circle broke into a passage that Stephen and Gilliam could walk along. It did not close behind them.

Gilliam came first, and knelt at the feet of the Priest. Stephen started to follow, and one of the villagers gently placed his hand upon Stephen's shoulder. It was not yet time.

"You have chosen to walk the Hunter's path," Greymarten said to the young supplicant.

"I have."

"Do you understand what that path is, and where it might lead?"

"I do."

"You are young yet to know it." The words were ritual, but Gilliam bristled anyway. "Tell me."

The young boy looked up into the old man's face; torches held aloft revealed only shadows and lines.

"In the time of hunger," Gilliam began, "we followed our God. But few children were born, and many died too young. There was no game, and we did not know the ways of the growers." He took a breath, and then his brow wrinkled.

Greymarten looked down benignly, waiting. After a few minutes, he whispered something.

Gilliam blushed and continued, knowing he should have studied his lines harder. "Near death, we called out for aid to any who would hear us. God in the Heavens answered our plea. He came to us and showed us all of the ways of the Hunter, and promised that we would know the full—uh, um—use of it. Them."

It came as no surprise to the Priest that the boy knew the lines so poorly. Very few Hunters had the patience for scholarly work, so it was not a bad sign.

"He showed us this gift and more, for the dogs at his side came to stand before us in silence. He fed us from the fruits of his labor." This line, Gilliam didn't understand at all. It sounded stupid. "Grateful, we accepted what he offered.

"For these gifts, we swore to become his people and follow all of his ways." And if he could just remember the rest, Gilliam would happily do that. "Ummm . . ."

"The Price?"

"But the Hunter demanded of us the one Price that those who accepted his gifts must face: the Hunter's Death. For to give us his skills, he must use them, hone them. Once a year, before the harvest, he asked that we call the Sacred Hunt in his name."

"Very good, Gilliam of Elseth." Greymarten placed a hand on either arm, and raised the boy to his feet. He had said enough, and besides, it was painful to hear all of the awkward pauses of ritual poorly understood, but it was warming as well. Year after year, such mangled words were offered as the young entered into the beginning of their full promise. "The people of Breodanir agreed, and the Hunters swore their oaths. And once a year, the Hunter Lords must gather, to be Hunted in turn by the God who has given us our lands. One of these Lords must face the Hunter's Death, or the lands will die around us, and the game will flee."

There was silence; all eyes were upon Greymarten. But only the oldest remembered the famines of the King's folly. Only the oldest knew that when the Sacred Hunt was finally called three years after its promised time, the Hunter God had been angry indeed. Fully two-thirds of the Hunters had died that grisly death. But the lands and the game had returned, paid for by noble blood.

"Then, Gilliam, do you swear by the Hunter's Oath?"

"I do."

"Will you promise to hunt in the people's stead, and to feed them your kills?"

"I will."

"Will you protect them from outsiders, defending them by force of hounds and weapons if necessary?"

"I will."

The Priest turned to Corinna. "Do you accept his word?"

Corinna remembered witnessing Lord Elseth's first majority—although she had been no headwoman then. Tonight was a window into her youth, so like to the father was the son. "I do."

"Will you succor him and his heirs in times of need?"

"I will."

"Gilliam?" The Priest held out one hand, and Gilliam placed his own into it. The knife very gently came down; it was cold and sharp, and left a well of red in its wake.

Greymarten nodded, satisfied, and then looked up, his eyes seeing both this darkness, and every other darkness that made this ritual endless. "Who comes from the people?"

Stephen was given a little shove forward now, and he walked quickly across the cool green. He knelt at the feet of the Priest, beside Gilliam.

"I do."

"And why do you come?"

"To pledge my oath, under the Hunters' eyes. The Hunter God knew well the foibles of his people, for he knew all. He saw that those who labored under his gift might be driven too far from the people they had sworn to feed and protect. I have come, from the people, to take my place as huntbrother. To hunt, as my Lord will hunt, without use of his gift. To guard him and protect him and see all dangers by his side; to face the Hunter's law so that we may remain strong. To remind the Hunter, always, of the people he must defend."

"Rise, Stephen," Greymarten said, well pleased. The words, wrapped as they were by youth, had lost none of their power to move him.

Stephen did, holding out one hand just a little too soon. The Priest took it anyway, and gave it the kiss of the knife.

Stephen turned to face Gil, and the two clasped hands, right to left. Their grip was tight, and they ignored the blood that fell at the Priest's feet.

"I'll be your Hunter," Gil said. His grip grew tighter. "You'll be my brother and my friend." He looked at Stephen's shadowed face, and remembered the mill. "Everything I've got, I'll share with you. I'll defend you and listen to you—" He grimaced. "—in all things."

"I'll be your huntbrother," Stephen said quietly. He saw the half-healed cut across Gil's cheek and smiled suddenly, lowering his voice to a whisper, "even if you're an idiot."

Greymarten coughed, and Stephen blushed.

"I'll be your huntbrother," he began again. "I'll stay at your side for all hunts, even the Final One." On impulse, he added, "I'd face the Hunter's Death for you." His grip grew tighter also. His hands felt warm and sticky, but they didn't hurt at all, and he wondered if it was his own blood he felt, or Gilliam's. Something began to change slowly.

He forgot about hunger, and forgot about the cold. He forgot all of the people who stood in a circle around him, watching and listening intently. There was only Stephen and Gilliam, and that was right.

"I call the Hunter God to witness." Greymarten's words echoed oddly in the stillness. They were full, low, loud—as if said by a throat that was no longer merely human. He reached out, placing a hand on either supplicant's shoulder.

"This is the last rite," he said formally. Neither boy looked at him. "From here, there is no turning back. Understand this."

As one, they nodded solemnly.

"Breodan, Hunter, accept this pledge." His hands grew suddenly warm as they rested against the robes of the two boys.

Stephen saw Gilliam's eyes widen in the same instant that his own did. He opened his lips to speak, and they froze as he felt a warmth, a heat that he had never felt before.

It burned like fire relieved of malice; it was hot, but it brought no pain. It was darkness, ringed with a light that grew brighter and stronger as he watched. His lids grew heavy, but he would not close his eyes.

From within, something rose to greet the warmth. Wings, invisible, unfeathered, spread out in awkward first flight. The warmth took him, and he soared to its heart, giddily at first, and then more surely.

Darkness was there; he heard the low rumble of a growl that even a dog could not produce. It was loud. It touched more than his ears. The horns he heard also—but they were dim and distant in their musical plea. This was the spirit of the Hunt, and he knew it fully.

Without fear. *This* was his home, his place.

Stephen?

Gil?

Gilliam laughed; the feel of it resonated with Stephen's sudden triumph.

This, he knew, would be his for life. Not even Marcus could change that, or take it away. The boy who had lived in the King's City, eking out a meager existence as a petty thief, had known little of friendship or trust, except in his stories or dreams.

But he'd remembered enough that he'd yearned for it. This was his answer. For just a moment, he could *see* as Gil saw, feel what Gil felt. The heart of the darkness was the unknown, and its shadows fled Stephen's approach. He could see Gilliam's fears and hopes; could touch the web of his dreams. He knew that Gilliam was even now seeing the same of him, and he didn't care; the past meant nothing. The two of them would stand together, no matter what the future held.

Greymarten let his hands slide from the shoulders of the two who were no longer mere children. He lifted his arms, bringing his palms to touch either of the henges at his side.

The circle on the green closed at his gesture.

"It is done," he said softly. He reached forward and grasped the two young hands that remained locked.

Both boys turned to stare at him, a shadow of doubt in their eyes. He knew well why. Although his own huntbrother had long since perished, he had never forgotten his oaths and their special meaning: the bond that had been forged.

"It is real," he said quietly.

As always, he wanted to tell them of the risks; of the emptiness that waited in the hands of death. "Stephen," he said gently, as he touched the boy's hard fingers, "Gilliam, nothing but death will take from you what you have been granted. Do not fear to let go." The words were the truth, but the simple message, so slight and so soft, was almost a lie compared to the pain of the loss that Greymarten—and many a Hunter—had experienced in his life. More, he would not offer.

Gilliam relaxed his grip immediately; he had lived with the Hunter's Priests all his life, and knew the value of their word.

Stephen hesitated.

"Stephen, trust me. The oath has been accepted by God. No simple unfasting of hands can expunge it."

Clenching his jaw, he followed Gilliam's lead. Best to start now what would have to be continued. His hand slackened and he let it fall to his side, waiting for the loss to come, fearing it.

Minutes passed in his silence, and then tears came instead.

What his oath—his choice—had given, did not fall away. It remained securely inside him, a warmth and a wholeness upon which a new life would be built.

He wanted to stop the tears, but they wouldn't be caught, not even by his will. Gilliam reached out and grabbed his shoulders gently. He understood Stephen now, and he knew what fears Stephen had faced in those minutes.

"Let him be, Gilliam of Elseth. It has been hard for him to trust his choice; it is not pain that moves him now."

If Stephen had been afraid of laughter, none came. In turn, each of the villagers that was old enough to know how came to offer their thanks and best wishes. They did all in silence, at the foot of the altar that signified the Hunter's Death.

Then the Master Hunters brought their previous day's kill. They placed it upon the altar with the help of the villagers, and Greymarten set about portioning it with the silver knife; the heart for the God, the hides for the Hunter, and the meat for everyone present. For this one special Hunt alone, the dogs were not allowed their portion of the felled beast; this stag was given in celebration of the coming-of-age of a new Hunter. A fire was already sparking to life in the pits to the south of the manor, and ale and wine were now brought in heavy, earthen mugs by manor servants.

Corinna was given an old harp, and she played it with both gusto and warmth. Several of the villagers, emboldened by wine, began to dance at her feet, and the blacksmith even approached the Lady Elseth, who was kind enough to join him in his jig. Truly, tonight, they were all the Hunter's people, and they lived in the moment of his blessing. The cost and the Price was a shadow made distant by merriment and celebration. Even Soredon, the most dour and grim of men, chose to catch a young girl in the circle of his arms and spin her about on the green. His son was Hunter-born, and by God accepted; this made a magic of the evening, and brought his past momentarily to light in the fires of his eyes and the warmth of a smile that was so seldom given it was truly special.

Stephen, too, was caught in the play of the rough country music, although not by any maiden; Norn grabbed him from behind and placed him deftly upon broad shoulders. Their robes blended together, becoming one moving tapestry of times past and times present. Of all the burdens this huntbrother had carried, this slight, small boy was among the most precious.

"Welcome," Norn roared above the laughter and out of tune singing of the crowd, "to Elseth!"

*   *   *

The following week, Gilliam was inducted into the Hunter ranks, albeit at the very lowest station: He was made a Page of the Running Hounds to the kennels of Lord Elseth. He was full of pride and happy pomposity until he discovered that he would fail at the first of his duties unless he paid more mind to the lessonsmaster.

Soredon was both amused and sympathetic to the young boy's reaction, but, as he said, it was important to take the roll of the dogs. Which meant, of course, writing and spelling, as well as better reading.

There were two things that made this onerous chore bearable. The first was that Hunter Maradanne of Corinth would board at Elseth and begin the rudiments of weapon lore, and the second was that Gilliam would have every reason and excuse to be in the kennels with the dogs that he loved.

Stephen was at his side for every moment of the lessons, although he took better to reading and writing than Gilliam would ever do. They learned to spar together, and although Gilliam was the stronger of the two, he was also more quick of temper, and bore the bruises of it more often than his huntbrother did.

They walked the dogs, tended them, and learned to write the letters of their names, but as promised at the binding, only Gilliam could feel their presence and know their minds. He shared this with Stephen, as he did all that he was given.

But they rarely stopped their fighting. Indeed, it became as much of an annoyance to Lady Elseth as Norn and Soredon often were.

Four months after Gilliam's birthday, he became a Page of the Scent Hounds, and he was given his first horn. It was not so fine or grand as his father's, being simple silver, but he wore it proudly, and even in sleep would not be parted from it.

Both he and Stephen learned the use of it; the different calls that comprised the Hunter's canon were intricate and necessary. Winding the horn was easier for Gilliam than for Stephen. The music came naturally to his lips, and he rarely forgot the use of a single note. He willingly prompted his huntbrother in the rote of the huntbrother's calls, which were different, but harmonious, with his own. Another source of conflict and companionship.

He learned the use and making of nets, as well as the coupling and uncoupling of the dogs. But he was still not yet old enough, at eleven, to be allowed out on the hunts. He did not bide his time with patience.

When they were twelve years old, just before they gained the rank of Varlet of the Running Hounds, they were called to the Valentin estates.

Lady Elseth was always quiet at this time of year, although there was enough to occupy her. It was the week that preceded the planting season, when the farmers were at their busiest and their requests had to be attended to immediately.

It was also the time of the Sacred Hunt.

Winter's chill was almost gone from the air; it lingered only in the face of the Lady and her most senior of staff. She counted the days in busy silence, watching the turnings and visiting the solitary altar on the green in the morning before her children rose. What had looked mysterious and almost forbidding on the night of the Hunter's Oath now looked like a thing of mourning and silence. And why should it not? It served to bind boys on the verge of manhood, and it served to lay them to their last rest.

It served the women differently.

This morning prayer was a custom of the women of Breodanir during the time of the Sacred Hunt. The Lords did not see it; how could they? They served their King and their country in the great forests that were reserved for the God's purpose. They found their prey, they loosed their dogs, they gave in to the wildness of the Hunter's trance.

A pained smile tugged at the corners of her lips as she waited at the stones for a response that never came. Next year Gilliam would begin his real training; he would come to know the Hunter's trance, and the greatest of all of the God's gifts. He was already growing into the role that the God decreed; the dogs, even though they were not his own, loved him and obeyed him; his use of weapons, if not words, had progressed immeasurably, if one were to listen to Norn. He talked of nothing but the Hunt, yearned for nothing but the ability to join his father.

To join his father. . . .

The smile dimmed and was lost for the day. Here, now, the price to be paid for the gift was writ large.

Where are you, Soredon? Is Norn still with you?

She no longer prayed for her father or her brother; the one had been lost through age, and the other the God had already claimed. But she knew the time was coming soon when two more names would be added to her small ritual. Why was it that all of the men she loved would always face this risk?

Duty. Responsibility.

She shook herself and rose, bending at the knee to lift the mat she'd brought with her. The sky told the time, and the sun's shadows beyond the henges bid her return to the manor.

"Mother?"

She froze at the sound of the familiar voice and lifted her head, her lips already straightening. Stephen stood, just outside of the green, as if aware that he should not disturb her here. His hands were behind his back, and his chin was close to his neck; it lent him that peculiar air of vulnerability that her blood-born son never showed. She was glad to see he'd worn his jacket; it was chilly without the full light of sun. She hoped one day that his common sense would rub off on Gilliam, but it was a small hope; Norn had never managed to have that effect on Soredon.

Norn. Soredon. "What are you doing out here so early?"

Stephen looked down at his feet. "I—I'm taking a walk."

"On the Hunter's green?" Elsabet left the altar. Stephen's shrug told her more than his words. "Are you going back to the house?"

He nodded.

"Walk with me, then. Is Gilliam awake?"

"No. And Maribelle's with Maria." He fell silent, matching the stride of her step. In a few years, it would not be he who needed to stretch.

They walked quietly until the altar was at a safe distance. Then Elsabet stopped and turned to Stephen, thinking him very like Norn at this moment. She couldn't explain her prayer, but felt that it wasn't necessary; she could see his worry, and a little of his understanding, at play around his eyes.

Stephen faced her squarely. "They're late this time, aren't they?" He held out a hand; it was still fine and slim. Growth wouldn't change this.

She wondered if he did so because he had seen Norn make a similar offer on many occasions. And she didn't care. Holding the heavy mat awkwardly in one hand, she accepted his solace with the other, gripping just a little too tightly.

"Not very late. The roads are poor."

Stephen nodded encouragingly, and she didn't speak again. They both knew that she was lying. But he held her hand as she walked. He understood fear and loss very well.

The Hunter God was kind, this season, to Lady Elseth.

Norn and Soredon returned in a ten-day, worn by the rigors of the Hunt and the journey by road. They came by horse toward the darkness of the turning, and the manor house flared to life at their approach.

Soredon dismounted and barely had time to place his feet upon the ground before he was nearly swept off them by his Lady's embrace. He returned it, hugging her tightly and burying the length of his face in her neck. Not even Maribelle sought to disturb their reunion—although it was more due to Boredan's heavy glare than her own consideration.

"Gil, the dogs," Soredon said, glancing up over his wife's shoulder. Gilliam nodded immediately and went to Corwel's leash; the care of the dogs after the Hunt was something not lightly entrusted to anyone. That the dogs were not his father's very first consideration worried him.

"You were late," Elsabet said, when she at last drew back.

He nodded heavily. "I'm sorry to worry you, Elsa. But we had the duty to perform." He watched her grow still.

"Who?"

"Bryan." He shook himself. "We're called to Valentin in haste. We must leave in the morning."

Norn joined them, looking just as weary as his Lord. This was only the second time in their long years of hunting that they had been called upon to guard the dead on the road with full honors.

"How is Lord William?"

"Shattered." Norn hadn't the strength to be diplomatic, nor, surrounded only by his Lady and her Lord, the need for it. He rested his head against the side of Soredon's horse before the servants came to stable it.

Soredon gripped his shoulder tightly. "Norn?"

"Fine."

"Have you eaten?"

"Some. Not much."

It was always this way—the joy of a safe return was marred by the shadow of another woman's loss. Lady Elseth nodded quietly to Boredan, who disappeared back into the house. "When the boys return from the kennels, I'll tell them."

All of the Hunter-sworn within a four-day's travel were honor-bound to make the trek to the Valentin estates. Lady Elseth, well aware of her own responsibilities at such a time, oversaw the wardrobe for all four of her men, although Norn was quite capable of dressing for ceremony on his own.

She, too, was well prepared for such an emergency, and left Boredan in charge of the house and Maribelle, who was very much put out at being left behind.

One day, Elsabet thought, as she hugged her stiff, rebellious child, *you will be glad of the times you were spared this.* She bade her daughter be good, which didn't help, and then mounted to her seat in the carriage she would share with Stephen and Gilliam.

They knew well why they were going, and all of their arguments or enthusiasms were as subdued as their clothing. Bryan of Valentin had been huntbrother to Lord William, heir to the Valentin Duty. It was he, this year, who had faced the Hunter's Death, and paid the Hunter's Price. No Hunter, or aspiring Hunter, could do anything else but honor that sacrifice.

Still, the days were long, and after the first, Gilliam and Stephen grew undaunted by the shadows that haunted their elders. In the evenings, they shared a room, and during the day, a coach. Corwel and Maritt also traveled with them by wagon, and they spent each evening kenneling them properly, as was their duty. They argued, they spoke of their future as Hunters, and they played their learning games.

Until they arrived at the Valentin estates.

Black was the color of death in Breodanir, and it was everywhere in abundance. When they approached the manor road, the post that held the family crest was swathed in long ebony panels that bore only the crossed spear and sword of the Hunter God's dominion. The villager who met them at the fork in the road was also dressed in black. He directed the two carriages and accompanying wagon without so much as a word.

The guest houses were in readiness for the nobles who had come; the Elseth family was the last, waited for by three others.

Lord Valentin met Lord Elseth as they approached the manor house. He gave a low bow, his black cape skirting the ground.

"You honor my son." He was pale, his eyes darkened by rings that spoke of care and sleeplessness. His face, always long and thin, looked near-skeletal now.

"Your son has done all honor to us." Lord Elseth also bowed, but when he rose, he reached out and gripped the older man's forearm. "Eadward."

"William would be here to greet you," Lord Valentin said, "but he has his duties upon the green. Please, feel free in the use of the House. Ah, Lady Elseth. Corwinna is also at the green, if you wish to greet her."

Lady Elseth curtsied, lifting her skirts with the ease of long practice. She looked long at Lord Valentin's strained face, seeing that the age in it had suddenly come to rest. She wondered if he would shake it later, or if, like a scar, its mark would always be seen. "Yes," she answered, taking his hand, "I would dearly love to speak with Corwinna. If it isn't too rude, I'll leave you now."

He nodded, working at a smile. Elsabet shook her head slightly, acknowledging much she knew must be left unsaid by him. She knew the path to the green, and took it, leaving her own two sons—her living, breathing sons—behind in her husband's care.

As promised, Corwinna was at the altars. So was her blood-son, and the Priest they had called for the last rites. No servant lingered there, and the three nobles who had gathered were conspicuous by their stillness.

Corwinna wore the black as well, a long old robe that had been passed from grandmother to granddaughter for years. Her hair was bound back in a knot of graying brown, and around her neck she wore the medallion of the Death. It caught the light and flashed in the high sun like the fall of a sword.

Elsabet approached her quietly, sparing a glance for the Priest. She paused before she reached Corwinna and looked at Lord William. He, too, wore the blacks, but they seemed to cover all of him in the heaviness of their shadows; his normally active, friendly face was sunken and pale. He heard her approach, she was sure of it, but did not stop to acknowledge it in any way. He had eyes only for the altar, which was empty.

"Corwinna?"

Lady Valentin turned at the sound of the voice "Elsabet."

Between the women, there was no formality at a time of such loss. Grief took too much of a toll to be pushed aside for social niceties, and although the women were separated by twenty years of age and experience, in this there was understanding and common ground.

They moved away from the green in silent mutual consent, walking arm in arm. When they were far enough away that words would not carry on the wind, Corwinna looked back.

"He doesn't eat," she said softly. "He doesn't sleep. He doesn't cry." Her own eyes were pink and wet. "He won't even speak of it to Eadward." She looked down at her hands. "I don't know what I can do to help him."

Elsabet put an arm around her shoulders and drew her close, saying nothing.

"I'm sorry, Elsa. I've—I know you lost your brother. You must know what it's like. But I—the Hunter God has passed over my family until now." She struggled with words, lost them for a moment, and then lifted her chin. "I hate Him," she whispered, her eyes wide and red. "And I see all the people gathered here, all the villagers, my farmers—and I hate them, too."

Again, Elsabet said nothing. The words, she knew, were like water in a vessel that had fallen. They needed to run their course.

"Bryan died for them. And I don't know if William will recover." She shivered, and turned her gaze upon her companion. "He won't see the Priestess of the Mother, and I know he was injured. He doesn't want to live."

Quietly, Elsabet prayed that neither of her two would ever know a day such as this one. Prayed that she would not be there to see it, if they did.

"He was young. He was . . . he had so much to offer us. And it's gone now. So that we can eat."

"He won't eat, Elsa."

She waited with Corwinna, offering her silence and the strength of her presence when both could never be enough.

In the morning, the rites were called. Three Hunter Lords and their Ladies joined the procession to the green. Elseth was there, as was Samarin and Cormarin. The sun cut between the henges to shine its light upon the altar that would not remain empty for long.

Everyone wore black, except for the Hunter Priest; he wore his colors and his crest grimly as he said the final words above the stone.

The circle of villagers, dark and still, had no children within it. There was no laughter, no anticipation, no joy—and not many eyes remained dry. They had come to witness, these people; to see the cost of their lands and lives in the blood that was paid to keep it. To honor, one last time, the sacrifice. It was hardest for the older people; each of them had also witnessed the ceremony that had joined Bryan and William to the mysteries of the Hunt.

Stephen and Gilliam were not the only young Hunters present, and like the others, they stood to the side of Lord Elseth, waiting and watching. They did not yet know what to expect; neither Soredon nor Norn would speak of it.

They had not yet reached their full height, so they did not see William until he was already within the confines of the circle. At first, they did not recognize him; he wore only black, and no horn or sword adorned his robes. His hood covered his fair hair, and his head was bent so that cloth hid his face. But two dogs followed behind him, and they knew him then.

Beside William walked another man; one old, judging by the length of his beard and the stoop of his shoulders. He also wore black, but not comfortably, and he did not bother to hide his face with a hood. Although it wasn't hot, he was sweating.

"Stephen, there." Gil pointed, even though it wasn't necessary; Stephen knew at once what held his Hunter's attention.

Five feet from the old man, suspended in midair at shoulder height, lay Bryan of Valentin. He was gray and stiff, wrapped round in a long, white cloth that was his only accoutrement in his final journey home. No hands touched him at all; the old man was one of the mage-born. How long he had held Bryan thus suspended no one knew, but all understood the strain he showed; Bryan had not been a small man.

The Priest, aware of this, moved immediately from his place by the altar, bowing low to Lord William. The mage-born stopped at center circle, and managed a bow of almost equal grace. From here on, Lord William, Cadfel, and Sorrel would walk by Bryan's side alone, as they had often done while he lived.

William stepped into place and held out his arms, bracing his legs against the ground. Bryan's body floated toward him, untouched by breeze, and was lowered slowly and carefully into the two arms that awaited his burden. The Hunter staggered under the sudden weight as the mage released his care. The body went slack.

William drew strength from the Hunter's trance, and the trembling of his arms left as he cradled Bryan's head against his chest. His hood dipped, brushing what remained of Bryan's cheek. For a moment, he gripped the body tightly to his chest, and all watching wondered if he would have the strength to let go. No one moved.

"Hunter William," the Priest said softly, "it is time for his rest. Come."

Still William hesitated, and his grip grew even tighter. The Hunter Lords, almost as one, turned away; they did not need to see his face to know what was writ large upon it. Lady Valentin started forward, and her husband's huntbrother, Michaele, caught her shoulder firmly, shaking his head.

Then Cadfel, the leader of William's pack, darted forward with open jaws. His teeth snapped at air and the hem of the rustling black robe that William wore. William jerked his leg back, lifting his head. His face was pale and gaunt, too empty even for tears.

No one heard the words that he sent to Cadfel, but all knew, from the dog's sudden growling, that there was to be a testing here. Cadfel's hackles rose, and his throat rumbled in growling. Sorrel, the pack's bitch, suddenly lunged for William's other leg, catching the robe between her teeth. She began to back up, her growl higher than Cadfel's, but no less defiant, as she sought to drag William forward.

The villagers were surprised. They murmured indistinctly among themselves. The Hunter Lords were worried. In silence, they lent their strength to the dogs. The dogs who, in their animal way, understood a truth that only Hunters knew: William walked too close to Bryan, and his voice would be lost to them all if he could not be called back to life.

William's foot came up, connected with Sorrel's side, and then found the ground again as he staggered. His white cheeks took on flags of color; his eyebrows, fair though they were, could be seen to rise into the folds of cowl that framed his face.

Sorrel yelped, let go, and then started anew.

"Cadfel, Sorrel, go!"

Cadfel backed up a step, and then growled, hesitating. Sorrel grabbed wet robe in her jaws and started to tug again.

"Leave us alone!" William's face was suffused with red now—the most color that he had shown since the end of the Sacred Hunt. He kicked out, harder this time, and Cadfel caught the blow on the length of his face. He rolled, whining, to start at his master anew.

"What is this?" William shouted. His face had lost the peculiar tension of the Hunter's trance. "*I* am your Hunter. Do as I order!"

The dogs did not listen.

Stunned, William stared down at them as they worked at his feet. And then his eyes narrowed, and when he spoke his voice was low, deep-throated; his eyes were flashing. "And will you leave my command? Will you forsake your Hunter?" He bent all of his will outward, throwing it against the dogs' testing. "What was Bryan to you, but another commoner? You will not take him from me. *Let go!*"

This time, the dogs did as bid, growling all the while. They stopped when they touched the first of the gathered crowd. Stopped at Stephen's feet. He stepped back even as the growls changed, becoming the whining and whimpering that the pack offered only to its Hunter.

"And will you leave them?" The Priest asked softly, his voice breaking the silence. He did not move as William turned to face him. "They are yours as much as Bryan was. Must they pay the price of his loss too?"

William's eyes widened again. He stumbled and dropped to one knee, still clutching Bryan to his chest. Aware now.

"William, you have committed no crime. Your huntbrother made his oath at his own choice, or it would not have been accepted. Remember the King's folly. Remember what has always been the Hunter's Price."

"It should have been me," William said.

"The Hunter God did not choose, this year, to take your life—although you may well have your wish in another Sacred Hunt. You live. This is what your brother would have wanted. Bryan was no child. He knew the Price."

William closed his eyes and nodded, but bitterly, bitterly. He tried to rise and staggered again, but would not let Bryan touch the ground. No one moved to help him; they could not. Bryan was his huntbrother and his friend; to him fell the last task of rest. He was aware of it, even as he struggled; his pride, his duty, would not let him ask for any aid.

What aid, after all, had Bryan had, facing the Hunter's Death?

He rose and walked the last few feet to the altar. Then, very carefully, he laid his burden down. He started to stand once, but his arms would not release Bryan's body to the stone.

Now the Priest came. Now it was allowed. He gently but firmly caught William's shoulders and pulled him away.

William's eyes flared again, but he nodded and stepped back. He fell to one knee in front of the altar and bowed his head into his hands. Then he raised it, seeing the gray of sky and the sun. Silent, he called for the one thing that remained.

Cadfel and Sorrel bounded up to stand at his side. He reached out with a shaking hand to touch Cadfel's neck. Cadfel turned to lick his master's face. The bond between Hunter and dogs, tested so harshly, had not, and would not, be broken.

The ceremony started. The Priest spoke. And William, dogs at his side, paid his respects to his huntbrother, offering at last to share the emptiness and loss with the one who could never answer it, or comfort it, again.

Thus it was that Gilliam and Stephen first understood that the Hunter's Oath had two edges. They stopped by the body to pay their respects and looked long at the damage that the Hunter God had done; it had been no easy death, and not a painless one.

Stephen lingered longest, looking at the ruins of what had been a strong face. He touched the white cloth with one small, shaking hand. Death was no stranger to him—but this death . . . it was his. He felt certain of it.

Gilliam, who had almost left, came back to him. In silence, in awe of a loss he was old enough to fear, he put an arm around his huntbrother's shoulder and pulled him away. He knew what Stephen felt; he couldn't help but know.

"I won't let this happen to us," he whispered. "I'll protect you."

But Lord William could have meant to do no less, and even now he stood by the stone's side, the dead's side, a grim shadow of death and empty longing.

Chapter Four

EVAYNE A'NOLAN WAS a young woman in search of truth in the libraries of House Terafin. Her hair was a perfect black sheen, her eyes were a pale, cool violet, and her clothing, if somewhat provincial, suited her perfectly.

She had been escorted into the grand array of domed rooms by The Terafin herself, and given leave to peruse any of the volumes that the librarian guarded so jealously.

"This is the first time you've met me," The Terafin said quietly. "But it isn't the first time I've met you. You saved my life, Evayne of no House."

Evayne was surprised, but she nodded gracefully and allowed herself to be led by the powerful, older woman. She could not imagine that a woman in her prime, with so much power and such a force of personality, could need help.

"Did I tell you about myself?"

"Yes," the older woman replied. "But I would have guessed. It isn't often that a woman's age changes so drastically in the space of two days. Even I could hardly fail to notice it."

"She must have trusted you," Evayne replied.

"She?"

"I."

"Perhaps she did. Perhaps she still does. I confess that I do not understand how you walk your path. But come. The libraries are yours."

The doors opened, and Evayne saw, for the first time, the vaulted ceilings and multiple catwalks that were the pride of The Terafin. Books, many of them older than either of the women who stood before them, lined the walls in perfect rows.

"I hope you find what you seek."

Evayne bowed low.

And then she began her search into the rites of old Weston. Three days later—she was almost never in one time for three days—she found what she sought, and to the librarian's rage and sorrow, borrowed a volume bound in midnight blue with gold trefoil stamping for the next twenty years.

By the time she had finished reading it a third time, she met a man who could give her the truths of the knowledge that time had buried.

Had buried for everyone but Evayne.

On the tenth day of Fabril, the second month, Gilliam of Elseth entered his fourteenth year.

The Hunter's green became a place where festive poles and decorations, and pitched, painted tents in the Elseth pavilion, proclaimed the day a celebration. It was still cool, and the rains fell frequently, but the green showed the color of the new year well. Musicians of varying quality brought out harp and fiddle, and impromptu dances sprang up like wildflowers as the sun began to wend its way to its rightful place of rest.

Stephen's birthday was also celebrated on the tenth of Fabril because he told Lady Elseth that he didn't know when his real birthday was. He lied; he remembered well the frugal celebrations he had had with his mother when he was five and six on the fifth of Lattan, when there was no cursed snow.

Here, while the shadows lengthened across the faces of slowly tiring celebrants, he remembered his mother's long, gaunt face, her dark-ringed eyes, her shaking hands. She'd been two-thirds the age Lady Elseth was now when she died, but to his mind she seemed twice as old, her face sagging into tired lines. He wanted to remember loving her, but he felt nothing at all except unease and a little pity. She had been—they had been—very poor.

"Stephen?"

At fourteen, he was far too old to run into Elsabet's arms, but he was not so old that he couldn't, with dignity, allow her to put an arm around his shoulder.

Stephen? It wasn't so much his name, as the sense of his name. He looked into the crowd and caught Gilliam's eyes. His brother's concern and curiosity comforted him. He leaned back into Elsabet's arms, thinking only that he wanted no other brother, and no other mother, than these two.

She said nothing, but although no oath bound them, he felt her concern just as keenly as Gilliam's. They took a few moments of silence in the midst of the cacophony before duties took them, once again, to the middle of the Hunter's green.

It was the one time of year that the Hunter's altar was not forbidding or foreboding.

Soredon of Elseth was the only principal to escape the festivities almost before they'd begun. He was proud of his son, yes, and proud of his choice of hunt-brother; he was proud of his people and the festivities that had been planned, and executed, in his heir's name. He was proud of Norn, and Norn's ability to deal with inane chatter. He was even proud of Elsa, although he knew that, come evening, he would feel the sharp barbs of her words for his irresponsibility.

But his pride in people had never been worth very much to him, and on the eve of Gilliam's fourteenth year, it was worth less than usual. This year, Gilliam would finally be taught the Hunter's trance. If he could master it in the next season, he would finally answer the King's call. That would make him a Hunter proper, a Hunter Lord in his own right. He could choose and bind his own pack, and he could know, fully, the joy of the hunt.

The sun was indeed low; the foliage bore a faint, pink tint as the rising dew reflected it.

Corwel, sensing his master's mood, calmly placed his lower jaw into his Hunter's outstretched palm. Soredon smiled down at the leader of his pack. He would not be so for much longer.

The big black and white whined a little and placed a warm, wet nose against weathered skin.

I can't even hide that, can I? Not from you, old boy. He tried anyway, allowing the pride he felt in this, the best of his hunting dogs ever, to overwhelm the sorrow he felt at his aging.

I shouldn't hunt you this season. You've become slower while I wasn't watching. But he knew he would hunt Corwel this year, as he had done the last. And he knew that he would continue to hunt him until he couldn't track, couldn't run, or couldn't catch the running beasts beneath his jaws.

You're the best hunter in Breodanir. You're Bredari-born—you could have run with the first hunter in the first pack at the dawn of the best age. The stub of a tail wagged happily. Soredon rested his left hand against Corwel's neck.

This was the hardest part of being a Hunter Lord. Not the risk of your own death, but the certainty of your pack's. The first pack was special, always special, and rare indeed was the Hunter Lord who didn't hunt that pack until it was too old and a little sorry. Rarer still was the Lord who didn't go into nearly open mourning at the death of his first leader.

One learned better, of course, over the stretch of years. One learned how to say good-bye, to look at the births and deaths of so many friends, so many true companions, as the Hunter's Way.

Soredon's hand tightened briefly as it rested against Corwel. He thought of another time, a different fourteen-year-old boy, a smaller dog. *Conner,* he thought, with a pained smile. *I ran with you until you were what, nine?* If there was any justice in the world, Conner was still hunting in the deep, rich forests of the Hunter's Haven.

As Corwel would be.

Again his hand tightened. He could hunt for his people, feed them, protect them, provide for them. But he could do very little for his dogs in the end, and it was their loss that pained him most. They understood him better than any person ever could, with the exception of Norn, and they were loyal to the point of certain death. Only the loss of Norn would inflict a greater injury.

Out of the merriment of the celebration came a single voice. "Soredon?"

"I'm all right." He didn't look up. He knew Norn's voice better than he knew his own—he certainly heard more of it.

"It's Corwel." Norn's square hand came to rest on the black-and-white head.

"It's all of them." Norn could feel his Hunter's loss, but he couldn't understand why; no one could, who didn't make the bond with their pack. "I tire of watching my friends grow old and die while I do nothing. Go back to the celebration. Distract Elsa for me." He felt Norn's broad smile as it accompanied a gentle affirmative, and he returned to his brooding.

Tomorrow, Gilliam, Soredon thought, as he stared at the horizon, seeing not the sun but the roster of long-dead hounds, *you'll begin to understand the Hunt's glory. And a few years from now, you'll know the Hunter's loss.*

Corwel nuzzled his master's hand.

"It never ends, Corwel," Lord Soredon said softly. "And it always does."

Stephen was lost in the earliest of the myths and legends of the empire of Essa-lieyan—Morrel's final ride against the Lord of the Hells. The Shining City was before him, and at his side, the Princes of the First-born; his sword was raised above him in the darkness of unnatural night, and the hooves of his horse strode above the broken, blasted plain.

He knew this story well, of course. It was the one that had first revealed the true purpose of reading: ancient glories. Morrel's ride would take him to the very foot of the Lord of the Darkness, and the blow he would strike there would end evil's reign and bring the Shining City down.

It would also kill him.

For in the time of such greatness as Morrel, the very gods walked the world, changing it and shaping it to their pleasure and their whims.

In the act of turning a page, his fair hair falling almost into his eyes, Stephen of Elseth looked up.

Seven books were spread out before him in disarray; the long table was covered by slate, quill, and parchment. The shadows cast by the tall eastern window were long, hatched lines; it was early yet.

He sent his curiosity to his Hunter and waited.

The answer came back in a giddy rush that couldn't be contained by words. Gilliam of Elseth was more than happy, which was very rare.

Stephen stared up at the broad-beamed ceiling, and then slowly lowered his gaze to the shelves along the northern and southern walls. Lady Elseth's library was not the grandest, but it was by no means the least. Gilliam, at what distance Stephen didn't yet know, snorted in disgust. Of all the rooms in the manor proper, he hated this one most.

Stephen closed his eyes and saw in return a desk, an empty shelf, and an open window, which told him nothing. The vision shifted; he saw a fireplace with a closed grate, and above it the insignia of the Triple Hunt. Gilliam was in Lord Elseth's study.

After six years of practice they had learned this short form, a type of speech without words. The oath-bond wouldn't carry words between them, but pictures and emotions had a visceral quality that words alone could never convey.

Especially, Stephen thought, as he reluctantly set aside the last great ride of Morrel, when those words were uttered by a Hunter. He made haste to reach Lord Elseth's study. The Lord was not a patient man, and six years had done nothing to improve his disposition.

Gilliam met him at the halfway point between library and den of doom.

"Stephen! It's finally time! Get ready, and meet us at the kennels!"

Time? "Time for what?" Stephen shouted, at Gilliam's retreating back.

"Time," a much softer voice said in an icy, quiet tone, "to remember the rules of indoor behavior."

Stephen muttered a very quick "Yessir" to the keykeeper and retreated to his rooms, there to prepare to meet Gilliam at the kennels.

He found Norn before he found his Hunter.

The kennels formed a neat, almost tidy rectangle behind Norn's broad, green-clad back. It was cool, but both of the Elseth huntbrothers had dressed well for it, Norn in the green of the Hunter and Stephen in the gray-edged brown of the Varlet.

"Congratulations," Norn said, extending a hand. "As of today your Hunter is elevated to rank of first; if you do well, at year's end you will be huntbrother to a Hunter proper."

"He's calling the trance?" Stephen said, lowering his voice to a whisper.

Norn continued to speak in a normal bass. "He's trying." Without further pre-amble they both began to stroll toward the enclosed runs near the west side of the kennels. Some of the puppies were at play in what could best be described as mud under the supervision of two of the village girls. Out of these dogs, or perhaps the next generation, Gilliam of Elseth—and Soredon, Lord Elseth—would choose their packs. They seemed diminutive, these pups; hardly the hounds and alaunts that would terrify the forest animals in their time. None of them showed the promise that Corwel fulfilled, but they were young yet; one might, again, resemble the Bredari of old.

"My part in the hunts won't change."

Norn laughed. "They will, and then they'll ease off again, all your lessons aside. Gilliam's able to call a trance—but that doesn't mean he's able to control it." There was a glee in Norn's eyes that Stephen was glad he wasn't the target of.

"Norn—"

"I remember when Soredon first called trance, the idiot. After all we'd been taught, all we'd been forced to memorize, he tried to run the full hunt on his first outing."

"But—"

Norn laughed again; it was a bark, not unlike a dog's. "He paid. Gilliam will, as well."

"Gilliam wouldn't be so stupid."

"Let us wager, Stephen. A huntbrother's bet."

Stephen grinned back. "I'd rather it were a Lady's bet; I want real money when I win."

"I don't think I can take advantage of you in good conscience. Watch, and be amazed at what your elders know."

Stephen started to reply, but the world spun in double vision and the words were forgotten. He stopped walking, blinked, and raised both hands to his eyes to rub them clear of whatever it was that was making them water.

"Stephen?"

Eyes closed, he could still see everything in a doubled, hazy way. *It's Gil*, he thought. *What in the hells is he doing?*

"Walk slowly, Stephen," Norn said, all gaiety gone from his voice. "They've started sooner than I thought. Remember your lessons."

"He's—he's called trance." Stephen opened one eye, testing his vision. It held, and he took a tentative step forward. Light flashed; color diminished. Images flickered by before he could properly identify them.

"Yes."

"But—" His vision altered and flipped again. "He's moving around all over the place; I can't even tell how many dogs he's trying to see with."

"It's too new to him. Remember what you were taught," Norn said again. "Or you'll pay the same price he does, and you won't be in any position to take care of him."

Remember? Oh, yes. Blocking. Stephen winced.

"You don't have to block everything," Norn said. "But block the vision well."

Very carefully, Stephen did as he was told. It was almost as if, in the darkness, he had to struggle to find each of a multiple set of open eyes and firmly pull the lids shut. But it eased the confusion and the tingling that he felt with each successive move.

"They can hunt like that?" he asked Norn, the lines of his brow bunched together.

"No." Norn shook his head. "But they've all tried it, and Gilliam won't be an exception." He shook his head as Stephen's expression changed. "You can try to talk him out of it if you want, but you'd have as much luck trying to talk Corwel out of eating his portion of the kill. Gil's *with* the dogs."

"I know," Stephen said, almost sadly. Although his visual link was gone, the emotional one remained. "He's—he's happy. It's like—"

Norn waited for five minutes and then looked at his pensive companion. "It's as if he's suddenly discovered that he's been alone all his life—and he never has to be alone again." The older man began to walk again. "They don't forget us, Stephen; they never will.

"But never try to compete with the dogs," Norn added. "The dogs are the hunt; they and your brother were born and bred to it, and they cannot be separated."

There were eight hounds in total; Corwel, Absynt, Terwel, Vellas, Sanfel, Tannes, Solsha, and Browin. They had been wet down, dried, and brushed, and the sheen of their fur caught the sun and slanted it along ripples of gray and brown. Corwel alone was white with his black bandit's mask, but he would have stood out anyway; he was a full hand taller than the next largest dog and his carriage was almost regal.

Of the eight, Corwel was the oldest, and he relied on his experience and wit to keep his place in the pack. Corwel had found extreme favor in Lord Elseth's eyes, but not even Soredon would interfere with the instinctive natural laws his dogs obeyed. The hounds were the Hunter's method of pitting nature against nature, and there were some things that not even a Hunter Lord could judge as wisely, or as harshly, as was necessary.

These eight stood on the edge of the great, greening forests of early spring. Elseth Lords hunted here, for practice, pleasure, and duty. The ground was wet, almost too much so, and the trees were only beginning to show their leaves.

Both Gilliam and Soredon were quiet, which was usual. Norn and Stephen were also quiet, which was less so. Eight dogs was the minimum that was ever taken out for a proper hunt.

Gilliam's forehead was creased in a frown of concentration mingled with a little unease. In this, the first of his trance-run hunts, he was not the leader of his pack, not the Lord; he was Soredon's son, and a distant second to him. Only with Soredon's word and interior voice behind him did the dogs deign to obey Gilliam's commands, and they obeyed with obvious reluctance.

Get used to it, Gil, Stephen thought. *You'll hunt the full season with your father's dogs, and they'll always be your father's. Period.* He didn't say it out loud because he didn't want to embarrass Gilliam in front of his father and Norn, but also because he'd already said it at least ten times.

"Yes," Gilliam had said. "But at the end of this season, I'll be a Hunter Lord, and I'll have dogs loyal to me for the rest of my life." The implication that he would never give the key to *his* pack to anyone, son or no, was obvious.

Corwel suddenly moved, a restless lunge that ended with a distinct snapping of strong jaws.

"Gil," Soredon said, softly and sternly, "better control."

Gilliam nodded, lowering his chin slowly until his eyes were on a level with the pack's leader. "Will they do this to me?"

"Your own dogs?"

A fierce nod of dark, sweaty hair.

"Oh, aye. And more: If you don't exert your control from time to time, they'll test you—and they might win."

"And if they win?"

"They'll lead, Gilliam. You never want that to happen." He dropped a hand to Corwel's head. "If you're injured, they'll protect you; if you're fighting, they'll guard you. If you are upset, they will not leave your side unless you send them away. In all things, they will do as you say—but they *must* know that you are master." Soredon's sudden smile was a gleam of teeth; he looked not unlike Corwel. "And of *these* dogs, I am master. But you do well enough."

Stephen was surprised. In his life at Elseth, he hadn't heard Soredon say so many words at one interval. Gilliam, however, was not impressed or surprised. His eyes appeared to be all pupil, all blackness, as he swung his head to face the forest.

Absynt, a stately, fine gleam of gray, trotted forward. He met Gil's eyes, growled softly—and very, very quietly—and began to follow an invisible scent that a well-trained *lymer* could practically see.

Gilliam's lips moved, although he gave no voice to the command, and Absynt was swallowed by the Elseth forests. Gilliam of Elseth nodded curtly to his hunt-brother, and Stephen bent down to the doubled leads. He raised a brow in Gilliam's direction, but Gil didn't seem to notice.

"Should I uncouple them?" Stephen's hands hovered above the eyelets of chain that held Terwel and Vellas together.

"Wait for his command," Norn replied.

"What if he doesn't give it?"

Norn shrugged. "The Hunt is hard; it's best he learns it now, rather than at the King's call."

Gilliam did not forget. But the dogs were more disarrayed than Stephen had ever seen them when they finally moved in on the chosen stag's trail. Gilliam was already pale and breathing heavily from exertion when he disappeared from view.

Stephen was glad that he had placed no bets. He tightened his belt, securing water and dagger, and then nodded formally to both Norn and Soredon. It was time to join his brother in the hunt.

The first thing Stephen heard was the baying of the dogs. It was a bad sign; the Hunter's call should have been sounded first. He raised his own horn to his lips, knowing the Hunter's refrain. Both he and Gilliam had practiced calls with their silvered horns since they had reached the age of eleven.

"Late," Norn said, as the horn's triple notes—two long and one short—faded.

"And not," Soredon added grimly, "called by Gilliam."

Gilliam ran with his father's pack, almost as one of it; it was impossible for

Soredon not to know who did what, and how, during the hunt's course. Norn felt something akin to sympathy for the cocky young man who was as much a son to him as he was to Soredon.

After fifteen minutes, Stephen thought he needn't be too concerned for Gil. It was obvious that Gilliam had called the second measure of the trance; Stephen could see, in the spring earth, the sudden widening of Gilliam's stride. He had been taught the art of tracking by Norn, and now understood why it was necessary. The dogs at full run, with Gilliam in trance, left him behind, and he didn't dare follow with a similar burst of speed. It would exhaust him before the hunt was properly finished.

He felt a sudden surge of panic—Gilliam's, not his own—followed by a sharp determination.

Oh, no. Gil, don't do anything stupid, please. But even if Gilliam could have heard it, he wouldn't have listened. Stephen's jog picked up incautious speed. A jog, even a quick one, could be maintained for hours if necessary; running just so, Stephen could find his stride—the perfect combination of footwork and breathing—and when he did, he was certain he could run forever.

But breathing was control and rhythm; Stephen lost track of both it and the even, steady pace of his feet when he felt Gilliam's sudden despair.

He found Gilliam and the dogs across a stream so swollen with the last of winter's runoff that it was almost a river. There were stones and fallen trees that made passage possible, but Stephen ignored them; they took time to navigate, and too much caution.

He plunged into the stream, wading up to the far bank and pulling himself out of water and mud with the aid of an exposed tree root.

The dogs were trembling, their sides heaving. Almost as one creature, their faces were turned toward the woods, and Stephen could see the evenly spaced hoofprints that were imprinted into the dirt. He didn't have to search for them. Gilliam's fallen body, his outstretched arm, lay in a perfect line with their retreat. An unhindered line. The hunted had escaped the hunter.

He ran the rest of the way, and then crouched down, unmindful of the dirt, to touch his brother's throat. The pulse was far too rapid, but it was there.

"Gil?"

Gilliam didn't stir.

"Gilliam!" He turned his hunter over and tried to lift him. Corwel suddenly came to life with a loud series of barks. "Shut up, Corwel!"

"No," another voice said.

Lord Elseth came up from the stream's bank. He gestured, and Solsha broke away from the pack, heading back over the trail he had made. "Gil's fine, Stephen."

"He's not even conscious."

"Well, no. And he's barely fine. But he stopped in time." He walked over to his son and held out his arms.

Stephen met his eyes squarely. *He's my Hunter*, he wanted to say; his arms tightened around Gilliam's limp, dead weight.

"Yes, he is," Soredon replied, although Stephen had not spoken. "And you ran a good hunt until the end. You were slow." But he didn't really look at Stephen as he spoke; his eyes were on Gilliam's closed lids and flushed cheeks. "Norn will be coming; let's get Gilliam home."

Soredon waited, quiet, at his son's side. It had been hard to pry Stephen from it, which was as it should be, but irritating nonetheless. Sunlight tinged pink came in through the uncurtained window. Gilliam had still not stirred. Nor would he for at least the next eight hours. The Hunter's trance granted speed, endurance, rapidity of reflex—but it demanded its due when the Hunt was over. If the hunt were extraordinarily long, and the Hunter Lord weakened by some previous injury or illness, it could demand that due during the Hunt when the Lord's body couldn't answer it. Only a few had died this way, but they were lesson enough.

I never thought you would make it this far. You will be a Hunter Lord who will do Elseth proud.

Smile turned to grimace; he knew that Gilliam would be sick for the better part of a week. But that sickness was natural, part of the history of the Hunter. Very, very few had come as close as Gilliam had to owning that title proper on his first hunt. Pride made Soredon gentle, where very little else could.

You truly are my son.

The thought gave him a peace that not even the annoyance of the waiting pack could quell.

Gilliam was a good patient for the first three days of his convalescence only because he slept through it. He managed to retain a grip on alertness for long enough to eat before sliding back into sleep and dream. Stephen, Norn, and Lady Elseth took turns watching over him. Soredon, with duties to the Hunter title and its quotas, came in the evenings but did not tarry long.

On the fourth day, Gilliam woke in a quiet mood, and on the fifth, that mood turned sour. He hated being confined to bed, and his thoughts were not only with the dogs, but within them as well. Lord Elseth made clear to his sole heir how pleased he was with the hunt's progress, but the taint of failure clung to the whole venture and as Gilliam's memories of his first hunt were a patchwork of motley scenes at best, he wanted to be up at once and leading the pack again. This time, he swore, he would do much better.

Lady Elseth kept him confined for a full week, and Stephen was certain that had she been able to tolerate more of her son's surly behavior, it would have been longer. Stephen wished it so, but Stephen's temper was easily the better of the two brothers', and in the end Gilliam won out.

Suddenly, all of the duties of the huntbrother took on their full, and often irksome, meaning. No longer was Stephen allowed to spend time in his beloved libraries, learning the intricacies of history and language that had become his love. Instead, he was called to hold couples, and the hounds, in the forested lands. Months stretched to winter, and the busy Lady Elseth lost her evening reading with Stephen to the demands of the mill and the farmers of her demesne.

But the hunts, of course, never ended—and Stephen was obliged to follow Norn, Soredon, and Gilliam wherever it was that the season dragged them in search of food and prey. In the winter, they would spend days or even weeks away from Elseth Manor.

Stephen hated the cold. The dangers of winter had been ingrained by childhood into his reactions, and even though he was bundled in warm clothing with a hat, scarves, mittens, boots, and layers of sweaters and furs, none of these made up for the comfort of his own bed and the security of a place that was home.

But he had made his oath, and some small part of him—one that was firmly committed to silence—found satisfaction in tending both the dogs and Gilliam when they returned from their long hunts, exhausted and weary. Sometimes they succeeded, and sometimes they failed, but Stephen usually didn't move quickly enough to catch the hunt's end—or Hunt's glory, as Lord Elseth called it.

He was glad of it. He could barely stand the unmaking of the poor beast that the hunt caught. He was certain he would have no stomach to watch the beast's struggle as it was brought down.

But at least after the second hunt, Gilliam didn't return home ill. After the fourth, he didn't suffer from the headaches and nausea that always seemed to come with the trance.

And after the eighth, both he and Stephen were brought before the Hunter's Priest, and there they were given their full rank of Assistant Huntsmen, while Norn, Soredon, Lady Elseth, and Maribelle looked on with pride.

From there it was only a matter of time before Stephen and Gilliam completed the Hunter's triple: On their own, and with the use of Soredon's dogs over the months to follow, they brought back stag, bear, and boar.

The boar was the last, and the hardest, and Norn and Soredon both waited at the periphery of the chosen forest during their sons' four attempts. Two dogs, Vellas and Browin, were felled there, and their bodies joined the boar's on the silent return home.

But it was the third, and come the spring of their fifteenth year, Gilliam and Stephen were ready to be called by the crown to take the rank of Hunter.

Chapter Five

HIGH ON THE SUMMER POLES, wind curled round the flags of Cormaris, Lord of Wisdom, lifting them lightward. Rays of sun glinted off the gold in embroidered beams of the light that signified knowledge, sparkling as if on water. Multihued ribbons were entwined down the length of the poles, and later in the afternoon the young men and women of the King's City would choose their colors and begin their dances. Ironic, really, that this dance occurred under the watchful eyes of the Lord of Wisdom, for the young women and men in their light, summer colors were often anything but.

Wine, provided by the King's cellars, flowed perhaps a little too freely, and ale more freely still, but the Breodani had a knack for handling their drink, and they'd do nothing to embarrass themselves here, at the edge of the King's Forest.

It was the eighth of Lattan, the longest day of the year; it was always celebrated thus. Farther down the hill, toward the clear, cold waters of Lake Camrys, the Priestesses of the Mother were weaving willow wreaths; the unsuspecting were crowned with them to the amusement of their elders.

The Hunter's green was the only area that seemed almost unoccupied by comparison, but the Hunter's Priests and the Hunter Lords took no slight from it. It was the summer solstice, after all, and the time for death and mourning had passed with the chill of early spring and the land's renewal. Although the Lords did not join in many of the festivities, their Ladies did, adding color, grace, and a cunning wit to the proceedings.

First among these was the Queen of Breodanir; she held her court at the center of the fair, and everyone, from the greatest of the Ladies to the least of the children, made their way there to bend knee and bow head at her feet. Yet for all that, it was not a somber or stately affair. There was a genuine joy in the air that no formality could stifle.

Into this day, she came.

She was tall, slender, pale; her hair, dark and straight, fell down her shoulders past the spill of her midnight-blue hood. Where the celebrants gathered to glory in light and summer, she was ice and night; obviously not one of the Breodani.

Evayne a'Nolan, in the cover of shade made stronger by a touch of violet mage-light, watched and listened to the gathering throngs. There were games being played that had lost all of the significance that once made them ritual; there were songs being sung that had lost all magic; there were prayers being whispered that had lost all power to invoke. Yet for all that, they were imbued with life, with an enjoyment of the moment, that they had not possessed at their beginning.

She knew what this celebration had once been, and what it no longer was: High Summer's Day, when the hidden paths of the First-born briefly touched the world of man. Twelve years of study had given her knowledge that had been lost to all but the most dedicated of the Order of Knowledge. Birth gave her the ability to use it.

And she knew, the moment that she appeared beneath the ancient trees, that that knowledge had been gleaned and gained for a reason. It was High Summer's Day, and she was to invoke the power of it. Why, she did not yet know.

When am I? She knew it was the eighth of Lattan, but did not know which year. Very slowly, with care to avoid the scattered rays of sunlight through the leaves, she reached into the hanging folds of her robes. The robes had been a gift from her father, and they sheltered many things, but none more precious than this: the soul-crystal; the seer's ball.

At faires and carnivals throughout the empire of Essalieyan, men and women who claimed mystical insights carried crystal balls. With light and smoke and mirrors, they huddled in darkened tents and wagons, mumbling cryptic nonsense and touching the edge of their customers' beliefs. The intellects among the Order knew that crystal balls were balderdash and children's nonsense.

But the wise knew that some children's rhymes held hidden and deeper meanings than the adult world could remember.

Evayne knew it well. She held in her hands the proof of that. *When am I?* She thought again and looked into the ball itself. It was smooth and hard as glass, but the light that struck it was absorbed, not reflected. *And where?*

Mists caught the sun's rays and turned silver as they rolled in on themselves. She looked into them, waiting for the visions to come. Resolving themselves out of formless clouds, they obeyed her silent supplication.

At first, all she saw was the faire itself, but it was closer and clearer than her cautious distance otherwise allowed. She studied the faces that drifted quickly by, searching for one woman, or one man, whom she might know. There were none—not directly.

But there were the Hunter Lords and their huntbrothers, and she recognized their green uniforms, although she did not know what the gold, gray, and brown embroidery signified. She knew she was in Breodanir, and as her vision scanned further, and she saw the Queen's pavilion, she knew that she was near the Sacred Wood, the King's Forest.

Her heart quickened; her teeth bit her lower lip. She scanned the crowd more intently, half-hoping. But no; minutes passed, and there was no sign of him. Stephen of Elseth was not here.

You aren't a girl anymore, she chided herself bitterly, *you're twenty-eight; you've work to do. Get to it.* But she looked a little longer. It had been years since she'd last seen Stephen, but she did not forget.

When?

But this time, at this place, she knew where to look. The mists rolled, resolving themselves into pale gray ghostly images. There. Stephen of Elseth was with Gilliam. They were hunting in the woods of the southern Elseth demesne. The corners of her lips turned up as she watched them. The ball gave them no voices, but it was clear that they were arguing.

She thought that they might be fourteen or fifteen; it was hard to tell. Certainly, they were not the men that she had met years ago, but there were traces of those men in the lines of their jaws, the width of their shoulders, their height. She lingered over the vision a little longer and then let it fade. It was costly to maintain it, and she still did not know what her purpose in this time was.

The mists shifted; she felt her hands tingle in a rush of dangerous warmth. She was no longer in control of the crystal. It caught her attention and held it fast, whether she willed it or no. White light sparked like lightning across the clouds; the silver mists folded and then folded again, moving at an unfelt gale.

Then, suddenly, they flew apart like curtains pulled too quickly. At the heart of the ball, creeping through the undergrowth, was a shadowy figure. Evayne watched in silence as the figure rose and became clearer. It was a young woman with dark, wild hair. She was perhaps five feet in height, with a round face and pointed chin. Her lips were thinned over teeth that seemed a little canine, and her eyes were so dark a brown they appeared black. Her hair was a black, burr-infested tangle, and her skin was darkened by sun and dirt. She wore no clothing.

She had seen this girl before, as wild and unkempt, but almost never alone. There was something strange about her, something that Evayne couldn't quite place—until she realized that, in fact, she had seen *exactly* this girl; there was no change between the then and the now.

It can't be time yet, she thought. *In the now, Gilliam of Elseth is too young.* But the ball never lied, although it was never completely clear, and she knew her task was urgent by the color and immediacy of the vision itself. She had to do something for or about the wild girl whose name she had never thought to ask. But what? The mists began to creep in; the girl was slowly obscured.

She almost set the ball aside, for there were dangers associated with its use, but some instinct held her back for a few seconds longer. Because of this, she was prepared for the second vision—and the second vision explained the first too clearly.

In the shadows of the forest, cloaked in a seeming that shimmered when seen through the soul-crystal, was a tall, lean figure. It ran, catlike, on all fours, and then paused to stand and test the air with a flick of a sliver-thin tongue. Its eyes were obsidian, its teeth long and sharp where opened lips revealed them.

Demon-kin. Her fingers whitened as they clenched the crystal sphere. Not all of her journeys through the otherwhen were dangerous; this had just become so. Although she had studied enough to discipline her magery, her mastery of it was uneasy—it would be years before she had the power necessary not to feel so threatened.

The image began to slide away, and she concentrated on the fading details. *Tracker.* She had not yet encountered one, but knew them to be deadly—even the least of the kin posed a threat to the unwary, and the trackers were by no means the least.

Where?

The ball's light flickered; what had been warm against skin was now cool, calm blue. Her face went blank as she stared; her eyelids slowly closed. The answer to her question was not given in pictures or words, but rather in feel. She *knew* where she must go, although she couldn't have given a simple direction other than the word "follow," had there been others to speak with.

Before the last of the sense-light faded, the ball vanished into the folds of her sleeves. She murmured a word, and the sleeves retracted toward her body.

Evayne a'Nolan, seer, mage, and historian, began to run.

The leaves that grew closest to the sunlight were thick and plentiful enough to make the forest a place of shadows, which suited Ellekar perfectly. Hunting in shadow was his specialty, his existence. No matter that the scents were strong and oversweet in these mortal woods; the scent of his prey was unmistakable and singular. She was a light thing, with clumsy feet, but she was faster than most humans her size.

He had to be careful, cunning. Less than a mile away the humans who styled themselves the Breodani were playing the games of High Summer. Against High Summer, only the rites of Winter held sway. Shadows meant nothing, and shadow-magic was at a nadir that made it virtually powerless.

None of the demon-kin would willingly allow themselves to be without power, but today Ellekar's power was weak indeed, and his ability to track was lessened. He had to rely on things physical not things magical, and he cursed High Summer as he hunted, for this was not a pleasure hunt, and the consequences of its failure would be extreme. He twisted around the trunk of a tree, head snapping at air as he ran.

The girl must not be allowed to leave the forest.

* * *

There are demons in Breodanir. Evayne tried to remember the canon of the kin, but she could not recall it without the aid of the seer's crystal, and she had no time to coax the information from the mists. *How did it get here? Who's the fool who plays at demonology?*

It was supposed to be a lost art, although there were mages—there would always be mages—who studied its lore and practiced it. In the debate in Averalaan's Order of Knowledge, there were always those who felt that the study of the lost arts—demonology, necromancy—should be allowed to come out into the open, if for no other reason than the fact that knowledge was a weapon against the dangers of misuse. The motion was always brought forward by the younger members of the Order, and always defeated by the elder.

Evayne, on the rare occasions when she was present for debate, always counseled the vote against. *You cannot control them all of the time, and it only takes one slip, one mistake, to begin the end of everything.*

"Evayne Doomsayer," she had been called. "Evayne Truthspeaker," was her reply.

She almost tripped over a tree root that had been exposed by the spring runoff. Cursing, she righted herself, leaving some of her skin on the bark. She had no time to lose.

The demon must not be allowed to reach the girl.

There is a wild keening that only animals can make. Part howl, it holds the essence of the forest nights, the sparse winters, the fires, and the storms that nature knows and accepts.

The seeress froze as that cry filled the wood. It was low yet loud, the tremor before the quake.

Evayne realized just how much noise and life there was in the forest when it suddenly ceased to be. There was a silence so encompassing that she thought, for a brief instant, it might go on forever. Into that silence, the howling started in earnest. Where there had been three in the forest, there were now four.

She raised a hand to her mouth and whispered a quiet prayer to the Hunter God. She had seen death, but the Death that he granted was one that she prayed never to witness again—certainly not to experience. Balling both hands into fists, she began to run once more.

Ellekar's hair would not come down; it rode the back of his neck and arms like iron spikes. He, too, felt the reverberations in the silence.

It cannot be. It is not the right time.

But correct time or no, when the second such cry came, Ellekar knew it for what it was: the Death of the human Hunters. Such a howling was almost akin to the Great Beast of Allasakar—and what made it could not be faced down. Not by a tracker.

He froze in place, becoming more rigid and still than the trees that surrounded him. Ears pricked, he listened as the silence returned, trying to gauge direction and distance. What he heard instead was the sound of snapping twigs and shaking leaves. The sound of human breath.

It was not his quarry, and it was not the Death. But it was human, and it was approaching him quickly. He'd listened to the sounds of their clumsy feet through the forests for decades, and he knew it well. He now had three problems; one, he could not face and survive; the other two he could not allow to survive.

He growled, but the sound was almost entirely contained by his throat.

The seer-born had instincts that they learned quickly not to question. Evayne a'Nolan suddenly leaped between two maple trees to her right, responding physically to the instinct before she realized it was there.

A claw shredded her hood, grazing the back of her neck.

She wheeled, crouching behind the broad back of a rotting log. A second later, she was rolling again—a controlled thrust of leg and turn of shoulder that ended with both of her feet firmly planted.

Ten feet away, staring at her with an expression of surprise that was already fading into determination, stood the demon-kin. He was tall, almost preternaturally slender; his head was roughly human in shape, except around the jaw. The skin there was extended around teeth that came out in a long wedge.

She moved again as he pitched forward, dropping his hands onto the earth. Trackers ran best on four legs, not two, and they never chose to be slow in the chase.

Only in the kill.

She rolled, dodged, ran in short bursts. He followed, slashing and snapping at empty air or the occasional fold of cloth that just barely slid out of his grasp.

Neither spoke a word, as if, by mutual agreement, they chose to make their combat as quiet as possible. The Hunter's Death was close, and even fighting for their lives, they had no wish to attract it.

But Evayne was tiring rapidly, and the tracker was not; the kin didn't feel physical exhaustion when on the mortal plane.

He's too fast, she thought, as she rolled again. *I'm not going to*—No. She bit her lip and took a second to catch his moving shadow. Jumped out of his way. Then, lifting one arm in a rigid line, she began the incantation.

As Evayne watched, a thin streak of lightning crossed the clearing in a blink of the eye. It wasn't going to work. The demon-kin had a way of protecting themselves against the weaker magics, and her strongest elemental spell was considered unworthy of note by the Collegium and the Order.

Crackling blue light struck the demon's chest, transforming into a thin, erratic cage an inch from its skin. The creature screamed.

It was a cry of rage and of pain; there was no fear in it. Evayne didn't stop to marvel or wonder. She ran. And as she ran, she smiled crookedly, remembering what day it was. High Summer. She intended to make the most of it, although she knew it wouldn't last.

Come on, girl, she thought as she nearly flew between the trees, *where are you?* In the distance, the demon was once again silent. Evayne knew what it meant, and she cursed the Hells for it, for all the good it would do. She was tired, and she didn't have the energy necessary to contain the creature magically; she wasn't even certain that she had the skill.

Where are you?

Evayne paused behind the smooth, barkless wood of a stripped cedar. Breaths were shallow and slightly painful; she forced herself to inhale slowly and deeply. Standing thus, she found the girl.

Or rather, the girl found her. She came out of the woods in a sudden rush. The movement barely caught the corner of Evayne's eye before she was overrun.

Where the demon and Evayne had fenced in silence, the girl had no fear. She let out a strange, keening noise that was halfway between a child's whine and a dog's. Before Evayne could move, the girl bounded up to her, throwing her arms around the seer's waist.

Evayne pulled her arms free, and placed a hand on the girl's shoulders. "We don't have time for much," she said, her voice light with relief. "Hold on tightly and walk when I say walk."

The girl said nothing at all, but she watched Evayne with unblinking eyes as the seer reached into her robes and pulled out three things: a pale, speckled robin's egg for spring, a diamond—symbol of eternal beauty—for summer, and grains of the coming harvest for autumn. She placed them on the ground and traced three concentric circles that enclosed them both, whispering quietly as she did. Then she placed the robin's egg in the outer circle, the diamond in the middle, and the grains at her toes. The sun was still high, the day was still strong. Fingers of light illuminated the forest floor.

The girl growled; Evayne looked up. A breeze blew strands of her hair into her eyes, but she saw nothing else. The growling intensified, and Evayne began the High Summer chant.

Reaching into her robes a second time, she pulled out her dagger. An amethyst caught the light and sent it scuttling down the perfectly balanced blade. It was an old piece, this dagger, and the getting of it had cost her much.

But it was not the time for memory. With a quick blade stroke, she drew her own blood, and then with another, the girl's. The girl stared down at her forearm as blood dripped earthward, but she made no new complaint; growling seemed to require all of her attention.

The breeze grew stronger and then died down. It felt nice to let the sweat evaporate in the summer heat. The wind reminded Evayne of Callenton in her youth. The wind . . . downwind . . . she looked down at the girl and realized why she was growling.

Evayne lifted her knife-hand skyward in supplication.

"I have drawn the circles, and I have paid the price. In darkness, and against darkness, have I fought and will I. *On this day, shadow shall have no dominion.*" She let her knife drop to the ground within the smallest of the circles. The outer circle began to shimmer.

The girl shifted restlessly. Evayne continued to chant. "Let the light be cast wide enough that I might see the paths hidden, the paths perilous. *For on this day, darkness shall have no dominion.*"

She raised her voice so that it carried over the sudden crashing in the undergrowth. She did not turn her face to see the tracker as he ran. The girl did; Evayne's one-handed grip grew pincer-like.

"As we see by the light, let the light see by us; on this day, let us be judged worthy to walk; we are supplicants, we will abide without fear. *On this day, evil shall have no dominion.*" The second circle began to shimmer.

Now, Evayne turned to see the demon-kin. She felt no fear and no exhaustion. She threw her shoulders back and felt the light of the High Summer circles warm her throat, her chin. The girl, she drew against her chest and held tight.

The demon's smooth skin glistened in the sunlight. She could see his muscles as his hind legs propelled him forward. Even as she watched, they locked; he froze as he reached the outer periphery of the High Summer Circle. His eyes were darkness and shadow, and these Evayne had already denied.

"You are," she said, raising her empty knife-hand, "too late. The path is open. I see what the darkness hides. Your name is clear." The demon began to back away. He gestured, but it was futile. He had no defense against the season, and none whatsoever against his name. "You are *Ellekar-sarniel* of the kin, and by the light of the High Summer Circle, I bid you begone!" And the last circle flared to life, glowing so brilliantly it hurt the eyes. Golden light bathed the clearing, the very essence of the sun at High Summer.

The creature screamed in rage and pain. He struggled against her knowledge and against her control. But the circles glowed brighter, glowed stronger, and he raised his hands to his eyes as he fell. His face sought the dirt as his skin began to burn.

"On this day, you shall have no dominion." Evayne felt the thread of his resistance snap. As quickly as that, he was gone; only the gouges in the ground were left to prove he had been there at all. She looked away as her charge stirred restively against her.

"Come," she said, in a voice full of strength and hope. "Can you see the path? We must walk it." She lifted one arm and held it wide; a fine, beaded mist seemed to trail from her sleeve toward the circles on the ground.

Evayne thought that this conjunction might resemble the path of the otherwhen, but in this she was mistaken. She watched as, for the first time in centuries, the hidden path was revealed.

The forest did not fade from sight. Instead, it became, by slow degree, older and grander. The trees became wide and wider still; they stretched skyward until their tops could not be seen. The forest floor became darker and softer, but where sunlight cut through the tree cover, it was distinct and golden.

"Come." She spoke quietly to her companion; the forest seemed to demand it. "We must be clear of the path by the end of High Summer's Day or we will not leave it for another year." Her hand, she placed upon the girl's bare shoulder. She felt a shock of kinship then, a recognition that words could not express.

The girl looked up at Evayne and uttered a soft, little bark. Evayne returned the girl's regard, and then shook her head softly. "You cannot speak?"

Silence was enough of an answer.

"It doesn't matter here. We will find another way to talk. Are you cold?"

The girl said nothing, and after a moment, Evayne reached out and gently took one of her hands. "Follow me, child. We will be off the road and in safe surroundings soon enough."

Her robe began to heal itself as she walked. It was a gift from her father, and it could not be easily destroyed. The same, she thought, in quiet reflection, could not be said of its wearer.

They came out of the forest so abruptly they were almost hit by a passing wagon on the crowded city streets of Averalaan. What made matters worse, and a reasonable apology on either side difficult, was the fact that Evayne's companion had not, magically, become well-clothed, or even clothed at all, during their walk on the hidden path. Averalaan was the capital of the empire of Essalieyan, but although a more cosmopolitan atmosphere could not be found on the continent, or off it for that matter, nude, disheveled young women were not a common public sight.

It was one of the few times that Evayne did not wonder when she was before she wondered where—exactly—the path she traveled had taken her. She had friends in Averalaan scattered across at least five decades, and one of them was certain to be able to help her. One of them could guard and protect a girl who was important enough that some mage had risked the forbidden arts to conjure one of the kin to hunt her.

Calm down, she told herself, taking a deep breath. *Where and when am I?* She looked around as people continued to shout or point, and the chaos of the crowds in front of buildings that overhung the street in a tight, disorderly fashion told her what she needed to know.

Of course, had the path not led them to the heart of the city's largest market square, life would have been less complicated. Or perhaps more so.

"You aren't going anywhere." Grabbing the girl's shoulder with her left hand, Evayne held her in place as she searched through the pockets of her robe, looking for coins. She carried gold solarii and silver lunarii, but coppers and half-coppers were not of interest to her; they weighed too much and proved, always, to be of too little value in her travels.

The dates of the coins were as early as 387 AA, and as recent as 433 AA. She took, as always, the oldest coin first and began to push her way through the crowds. Several people tried to stop her, whether to lecture her or show their concern, she didn't take the time to discover. She met their gazes with her now impenetrable violet glare, and they moved aside.

The girl was content to be pulled through the crowd, although she herself did not seem to feel any of the acute embarrassment that Evayne did. *I do not understand*, the seer thought, as she turned onto Crafting Street, holding fast to her charge. It was clear that her mind was not quite right, and Evayne worried about adding a fey child to the struggle—although she knew instinctively that this "child" was no helpless pawn, no easy victim.

We're all part of it, child, adult, weak or strong. One way or another we win or we die, and if we die, does it matter how the death's met?

It mattered, of course. But what was done was done; the girl had come to Essalieyan, and safety. Together, they entered the long, open stall of a clothing merchant.

The year was 402 AA, and evening was closing in on the eighth of Lattan. She would not be able to leave the city the same way she had arrived in it, but she was glad of it—the High Summer road, while quiet, was not peaceful, and it was said that there was always a price to pay for the traveling of it. Superstition, of course, but Evayne herself was proof that superstition was not always wrong.

The girl at her side did not seem to notice the strangeness of their transit. She did, however, seem to notice the oddity of her clothing, which was a simple, sturdy dress that could be pulled over the head and gathered at the waist. The color was a rusty brown with fringes of green and ivory, none of which suited the wearer—but it had been late enough in the day, and the buyer had been desperate enough, that aesthetics were not in question. Scratching and pulling at the dress, the girl kept an eye on Evayne as if to say, "You see, I'll wear it, but I don't have to like it."

The market square was a mile from the merchant's port, but in Averalaan the city streets near the dockside were orderly, clean, and most important, very well patrolled. Evayne led her charge along the open roadways until she reached the boardwalks. They were the pride of Terralyn ASallan, master builder. He said they could keep back the very tides of time, and if no one believed him, they were still impressed at the length and breadth of the builder's work.

"If we hurry," Evayne said, speaking more to herself than to her companion, "we'll be able to cross by the bridge. Otherwise it's the ferry for us." She caught the girl's hand and began to walk more quickly, listening to the thump of her feet against the planks.

They made the bridge, although they almost missed the hour; Evayne's pockets contained coins too large for the toll required, and the guards, after a long shift, were not in the mood to be lenient. Neither was Evayne, and after the ensuing debate, in which they implied that she wasn't fit to cross the bridge to the High City and she implied that they weren't fit to bear the emblem of the Twin Kings, she was at last granted passage across.

She let the wind across the open water play with stray strands of her hair. *Be calm*, she thought, *and as quiet as possible. He hates noise and bustle.*

Holding to that thought, she made her way through the High City streets toward the Order of Knowledge.

Before she entered the grand, four-story building, she took the time to pull her hood up and arrange it so its shadow covered all but the tip of her nose.

"Come," she said softly, taking the girl by the hand again. "But be as quiet as possible." The warning wasn't necessary; the girl hadn't seen fit to utter more than an outraged squeak since their arrival.

Together, they walked between the pillars of the entranceway and into the grand foyer. Here, the ceiling was one large arch that stretched from wall to wall. Sun, when the sun was high, streamed in through the slightly slanted windows above, giving the Order a sense of lightplay that otherwise dour mages would never see. There were guards lined up as they walked, one per pillar for a total of six, but they were less a matter of utility than show. As show, they wore the Order's colors quite well; their black shirts, white pants, silver-embroidered sashes, and gold shoulder plates were of a quality made only by the High City seamsters.

The girl seemed to find them quite interesting, and Evayne stopped to let her wander around both pillars and guards. When she returned, she wore a very quizzical expression.

"They're at attention," Evayne said. "They aren't allowed to move. Now, come." The doors were opened by doormen who also wore the colors of the Order but without the dramatic weaponry that the guards bore. Evayne nodded politely, although she knew they couldn't see her face, and walked up to the gleaming, stately desk that barred would-be curiosity seekers from the Order proper.

A rather bookish man looked up from his paperwork. His face was as sour as

the foyer was grand. Evayne wondered what mistake he'd made that had incurred the wrath of the Magi. Very few of the members ever manned this particular desk themselves. "What do you want?"

Obviously, there was a good reason for the lack. Evayne's hood hid her smile.
"I've come to see Meralonne APhaniel."

"You've got an appointment, have you?"

"I don't usually require appointments to see him."

"You don't usually see him, then. He *always* demands appointments be made.
It's a question of being orderly." The man returned to his notes with something
just short of a sniff.

"Excuse me."

He looked up balefully. "Are you *still* here?"

"Yes. I've come to see Meralonne APhaniel, and I'm afraid I can't leave until I
have."

"Well, we'll see about that," the man replied.

"GUARDS!"

Meralonne APhaniel was one of the Magi, the council of twenty, and one that directed the business of the Order of Knowledge. He was not a young man, and
Evayne often wondered if he had ever been one. He was tall, but somewhat gaunt,
his skin lined and pale, his hair a platinum and gold spill that crept down the
middle of his back when exposed. As one of the Magi, he was not only entitled to
wear the colors of the Order, he was expected to.

But, as common wisdom held, the Magi were all a little insane—certainly,
they were no ordinary men and women—and when Meralonne was forced from
his room in the study tower by two of the Order's guards, he came down the stairs
in his favorite bathrobe, and very little else.

The man at the desk—Jacova ADarphan—was consigned to desk duty for another three weeks, and there was every sign, from the mutinous expression on his
face, that that stay would have cause to be extended. Evayne, however, was removed with extreme pointedness from that list of future causes by a rather irate
Meralonne.

"You really shouldn't have been so hard on him," she said, as she climbed the
tower stairs. "No, we want to go *up*." The girl gave her a look best described by the
word *dubious* and then began her four-legged crawl up the carved, stone stairway.

"If I'm to be disturbed," he replied, his brows still drawn down in one white-
gold line, "it had better be with good reason. ADarphan wouldn't recognize a
good reason if it spitted him." He frowned. "And come to think of it, neither
would you. What are you doing here, anyway?"

"I've come to ask a favor."

"What, another one? I've wasted years of precious research time with your education—for free, at that!—and you've come to ask me for *more?*" A head bobbed out from around the corner of the third-story landing. "This is a private conversation, ALandry—get back to your books!"

"Sir!" The head vanished.

Meralonne had a tendency to have private conversations that the entire High City had no choice but to hear. Evayne's forehead folded into delicate creases. "My Lord APhaniel, might I remind you that in return for your time, I've—"

"'My Lord,' is it? Don't talk back to your master," he snapped. "I know perfectly well what we agreed to at the time, but if I weren't an honorable man, I'd demand more."

They reached the wide sitting area near the window of the fourth floor's gallery. Evening had almost fallen, and the curtains to the window had been drawn. Lamps, with a nimbus of light that seemed a little too strong be natural, gave the paintings and sculptures of the gallery of the Magi a preternatural glow; it was almost as if, at any moment, any one of the images, invoked, would come to life. Meralonne walked past them briskly, taking the time to reknot his bathrobe's belt as he did. Evayne glanced from side to side, wondering if anything the gallery contained was new to her. And the girl trotted—there really seemed no other way to describe her motion—from picture to sculpture to picture again, her eyes wide with wonder or curiosity.

But at last they passed the gallery completely, and entered into the chambers of Meralonne. As one of the governing council, he was permitted to keep a residence within the Order itself, and if it was small and suited only for living in and not for entertaining, no mage yet had been heard to complain.

"You realize," he said over his shoulder, "that I'm liable to be called upon to explain this public disruption?"

"Yes, Meralonne."

The door swung open into a chaotic jumble of papers, books, slates, and the occasional scrap of clothing.

"When you were a young girl," the mage said, "you knew how to be properly respectful. Of all the traits to grow out of, Evayne, that one is least pleasing. Well, don't just stand there gawking. I was in the middle of something important when you barged in."

"Yes, Meralonne." Evayne walked into the room, very carefully pulling the hem of her robes well above her feet in order to make sure she didn't step on anything vital. The girl followed with considerably less restraint, something that was not lost on the mage. He did not seem nearly as annoyed at the girl as he did at his student.

"Don't be condescending. It doesn't suit you." Meralonne found a chair beneath a small pile of clothing. He took it. "Now, what it is this time?"

"The girl," Evayne replied. But as her master sharpened the steel-gray focus of his eyes, she found herself watching him. It was hard, with Meralonne, to tell what age he was, he aged so well. His hair was perhaps a touch whiter, and his eyes slightly more creased than the last time she'd seen him; he was clean-shaven and ill-dressed as always.

And yet. And yet. At sixteen, she had found his curmudgeonly ways almost a comfort; at twenty-eight, she was not always certain how much was affectation, and how much genuine. There were times when she could catch a glimpse of something darker, something far more somber, in his words. Then, the lines of his body would alter subtly.

Only once had she seem him called to the private duties that were his, by right, to take on. He set aside his poor clothing for dress that could only be described as magical, pulled back his hair in a long braid, and girded himself as if for battle. She had asked him, then, where he was going, and the expression, distant and cool, frightened her more than his temper, his growling, or his pointed unkindnesses. He hadn't answered. She never asked again.

Meralonne was the teacher that the otherwhen had taken her to when she had started walking the path twelve years ago. For the first eight years, it had brought her to him every other day. He was the only living person that she had seen so regularly, so . . . normally. He aged as she did, and he remembered her almost as she remembered herself.

Not, Evayne mused, as every other person that she met did. They might be old yesterday, and a child tomorrow; they might remember meeting her ten years ago, when she would not meet them again for decades; they might be dead or dying, but live on in the otherwhen, compromised by the vividness of their end in her memory. They might have information for her that she could not use in any future she could see, but that she could not afford, ever, to forget. Evayne did not forget.

And they might gaze at her with awe and fear, and no understanding whatsoever.

"Evayne," Meralonne said, catching her attention with the flat of his hand against the crowded top of his desk. "I'm speaking to you!"

"I'm sorry. I was thinking."

Meralonne snorted. "And you do it rarely enough I shouldn't complain. But you can think on your own time. Give me explanations instead. What is this girl, and why did you bring her here?" He reached into his desk and pulled out a leather pouch so worn that it shone from years of accumulated oil and sweat. Evayne grimaced as he pulled a pipe dish from it. Of all his habits, this was the one that she found most odious. And, of course, the one he would take no criticism of.

She lifted her shoulders delicately and let them fall in a graceful shrug. "I don't know who she is. But as to why I brought her—let me show you." She let her hands tumble in the air in slow free fall, and as she did, she spoke.

The words had all of the rhythm of language, but none of the sense; their cadence deliberate, evocative, and elusive. No man or woman, be they mage or merely mortal, could repeat what she said, even if they heard it all, and listened with a mind devoted to that purpose. She knew that if she were a better mage, she wouldn't need the words or the gestures to find her focus.

Meralonne knew it as well, but he nodded gruffly as the spell progressed, because it was a difficult spell—a subtle one, and not a spell for the warrior-mage.

Any idiot, he was prone to say, *can learn how to throw fire and lightning around. Look at nature—how much thought and purpose does nature show? But I'm not about to train just any sentient mammal. You'll learn* magery, *not some trumped-up sword-substitute.*

Yes, Meralonne.

And she learned as if her life, or more, depended upon it. Because, of course, it did.

As the last of the spell-words echoed against the sturdy stone walls of his chamber, Evayne lifted her hands as if to embrace the empty air. Light the color of her irises showered in sparks from her fingers, dancing across the air and leaving multiple trails. She looked directly ahead, her focus short, her violet eyes wide. Slowly, as she concentrated, an image began to form between her outstretched arms.

He uttered an oath under his breath, in a language that Evayne did not understand. "You're losing your focus, girl. *Concentrate.* Have you learned nothing?" But his heart wasn't in the complaint, and the words had no sting, no real energy.

He stood, lifting his pipe arm, and walked over to Evayne's illusion. Smoke wreathed his face, his hair. Carefully, he began to examine the details. "It ran like this?" He asked in a tone of voice that was almost subdued.

Evayne nodded.

"I see." He turned to look at the girl, who remained silent. "Well, little one, it seems you've attracted the wrong person's attention." He studied her more intently, steel-gray eyes meeting near-black ones. "Evayne, how did you see that creature and still escape with your life?" His voice was soft now, even quiet. There was no inflection to the words.

"High Summer rites," she said. It was hard to speak, think, and hold the image static.

"High Summer rites." The words were stilted.

"I—I walked the hidden roads."

"You did. And who taught you this skill?"

"You did! We studied them in the—"

"We studied their theory, Evayne. Trust the master to know when the pupil has been properly tested."

She swallowed. It was true.

"Still, if you managed to use the *theory* to escape such a creature, I will do my best to be grateful at a quickness of thought that you rarely reveal." He lifted his finger, and the room flared with an angry orange light. The image of the demon was torn into beads of spell-light that faded before Evayne could piece them together. "Very well. You've shown me what you had to show me. You will not image that in my presence again. Is that clear?"

"Yes, Master."

"Good." He passed his hand over his eyes. "You were the best student I ever had the hardship of teaching. You know what this will mean. Demonology is being practiced again; keep it quiet until we find the source, or we'll have widespread panic." His gaze narrowed. "Where were you?"

"Breodanir. In the King's hunting preserve."

"You think that the Breodani—"

"Absolutely not."

Meralonne raised a pale brow. "You aren't usually this defensive, Evayne. Are you reacting instinctively or because of experience?"

She said nothing, but blushed; both were as he expected.

"Still, Breodanir. There's something about it that seems vaguely familiar. There's certainly an Order there, if small. Let me see." He walked over to his desk, and began to search—sift, really—methodically through the papers and journals there. It was quite clear that the chaos represented some form of order to the mage, but what exactly it was, Evayne couldn't say. When she had studied more intensively under his tutelage, her desk had always been meticulously tidy and well-organized. "Ah, here it is."

Evayne held out one hand, and Meralonne gave her a piece of paper. It was a letter from Zoraban ATelvise. Something about the name was familiar; it nagged at her thoughts, holding knowledge just out of range of her immediate memory. "Who is he?"

"Zoraban? The head of the Order in Breodanir."

"The head of the—" She went pale. "I remember now."

"Remember what?" It was a sharp question, sharply worded. Meralonne's steel-gray eyes were narrowed to a dangerous edge; they glinted like blades. It was clear, from the color of Evayne's face and the momentary twist of her features, that the memories were not pleasant ones.

She fell silent; it was her only defense against the mistake she would otherwise make. The otherwhen held its secrets, and her life was hostage to them. She remembered, as she always did at times like this, the first step that she had taken on the path. She stood beside a figure whose features shifted so regularly and so completely she could not describe him at all. He spoke with a voice that was a multitude of voices, and gestured with an arm that was an infant's, an old man's, a brash youth's. *For the sake of the world,* he said, *I will let you walk my path at your father's behest. But it is* my *path, and I share it with only you, child. You will share it with no other. Remember this: that what is, is; what will be, will be. You are your own time, and you must live as if your time is all there is. You will never be able to change your actions, once taken. What you choose to do now, at forty you must abide by, as any other mortal; you cannot reverse it by use of the otherwhen, no matter how hard you try. And if you try . . .* He lifted a hand, and the path became molten, bubbling and hissing inches away from her toes. *There will be no path, and no future for you. After all, time will still exist, no matter who wins the war.*

And will I control this path?

He laughed. She could still hear it, a mixture of anger and sorrow. *Who claims control of his own destiny? Not I, not you. The path will take you where you need to go, little sister.*

Meralonne hated her silence. It was these impenetrable spaces that had driven distance between them and kept it there over the years. He watched her still face, her opaque eyes, the way she bit her lower lip. He saw the struggle in her rigid stance.

Perhaps, had he not given his word at the outset of his tutelage, he would have forced the issue; he did not. But he returned silence with silence, and the distance between them grew a little larger still.

At last, she started, and turned to face him.

"What would you have of me, Evayne?"

"If you would, I would have you watch the girl. She is safer here than anywhere in Essalieyan, and until we understand what the demon-kin want with her—until we know which mage summoned it—I think she must be kept safe."

"Agreed." A thin stream of smoke trailed out of the corner of his mouth. For a moment, he resembled a dragon in the center of his messy hoard. "And you?"

"I don't know." She turned to face the blank wall of the mage's study; it was the only clear space in the room. "This has something to do with the Breodanir God. The Hunting God."

"Evayne, it hasn't been proved to the Order's satisfaction that such a god even exists."

"If he doesn't," she said, her voice sharp with sudden pain, "his avatar most certainly does." She bit her lip as the words left her in a rush. She wasn't thinking clearly, but she never did where Stephen of Elseth was concerned.

"I see." Meralonne raised both pipe and brow in unconscious unison. "Very well. I will see to the girl's safety. But you, student, you look peaked. I recommend something foreign to your nature: sleep."

She smiled bitterly and nodded. "I'll take my old room, if you don't mind."

"Evayne?" She turned back, framed by the door. Her eyes were shadowed with fatigue that was not feigned. "One day, I demand an explanation."

"One day," she said, as she always did, "I will give you everything you demand." It was as much an apology or explanation as either was willing to give.

"Tomorrow, then."

"Tomorrow."

Chapter Six

THE FOLLOWING MORNING, when Evayne returned to her master's study, she was forty years old.

It was not immediately obvious, for she wore the same robes that she always did, and the hood was pulled high and hung just over her forehead. But her stance had altered, and her gait had a surety that at twenty-eight she had not possessed. Her voice was a touch lower, her words, when she spoke at all, direct.

She did not speak now. The familiarity of the study returned to her slowly, as if from a great distance. Her hands shook as she touched the outer frame of the door through which she had passed, day after day, in her youth. The otherwhen had been kinder then, although she had not appreciated it.

She had seen—

Closing her eyes, she drew breath, finding the familiar question. *When am I?* But the answer was slow to come; the past that was, for her, hours old, held fast and would not easily be dislodged. Soul-crystal warmed her hands; familiar shadows, scattered with silver light, began to roll. Peace. Time.

Now?

402 AA. Espere.

She slipped the ball back into the safety of her robes. The otherwhen did not take her into horror without reason. Somehow, the wild girl, whose name she now knew was Espere, and yesterday's vision were linked, although any who lived at the time of the coliseum were less than dust.

The rings.

She had not been to Meralonne's study for well over ten years. She remembered their final argument clearly; the heat of their discussion still had the ability to burn old scars. *But I should have known better,* she thought sadly. *To come to a member of the Order and expect him to put aside all curiosity without an adequate explanation was a child's dream.* When she had stopped being a child, she didn't know, didn't remember. But she wasn't one now.

She knew where she was in the otherwhen, and knew that the argument had not yet taken place. But she also knew, now, why he had started to increase his pressure and his curiosity; knew what had spurred him and piqued him too greatly.

She had.

She had never expected to be here; not like this. She put her hands in her pockets and felt the curve of the seer's ball as it pulsed against her palm. It was time. With an outward calm that she didn't feel, Evayne a'Nolan pressed her fingers against Meralonne's outer doors and whispered three distinct words. They crept open.

It was not her way to try to sneak, and indeed she knew that she would have no success—what had happened had happened—but she tried anyway. She always tried. Time—how could it be immutable, and she able to walk between the here and now of so many different lives?

But it was. And as she crossed the threshold, she saw the orange-white glimmer of Meralonne's spell as it flared to life along the seams of stone blocks and oak planks, seeking her identity, her mission, her reason for intrusion.

"Evayne," she said, giving it what it sought. "I have come for the girl that I left here last eve. We have far to travel." She saw the spell shiver as her words hit it, and she smiled in spite of herself. The years had given her knowledge and experience. She had learned to hone her sight so that it might be used without spell and focus. Meralonne had always said he was a mage of no small power.

At sixteen, she thought he was the most powerful wizard in Averalaan. At thirty, she believed him one of the more mediocre. At forty, she knew better than to guess—but she was aware that the spell of protection woven here had very few equals.

She took a chair—the old, orange leather that had seen the use of three previous members of the Order—and wedged her elbows and forearms along the winged rests. Her breath, she stilled. The otherwhen had never before taken her to him out of time; he was the one presence that had been steady—until their break.

He had nothing left to teach me, she thought bitterly, hating the path, hating Time, and hating her father. She waited, counting seconds. Stared at the room, eyes lingering longest over the scattered mess of books and papers nestled in with the dirty clothing. Meralonne, although he would never admit it, must have come from a family of means to treat so much of value with such casual familiarity. At least, so she had always thought.

Did you have to bring me here today? Wasn't yesterday punishment enough? But the path had no voice and no sentience that she could discern. It had never answered her, and she had raged, cried, and pleaded with it in her time. *Evayne. You are not a child. If you are here, it is for a reason; even a good one.* She reached into her robes and touched the seer's ball, pulled it, luminescent in the shadow-darkness, from her sleeves. She gazed into the silvered mists that she knew so well, and in but a few seconds, coaxed a distinct image.

The wild girl, indeed. She shook her head. Her life was a series of loose ends, things half-finished because the otherwhen took her from them in mid-stride. The wild girl, in this place, was one such thing. It was clear that they were to walk the same road today—an echo of the past. She shuddered, and took a breath to steady herself. *Think about yesterday tomorrow. Think about Meralonne today.*

When the door to one side opened, she was ready for him. Or so she thought.

"Who are you?" It was his voice, and not his voice. She had heard him in many moods and in many tempers before, but this was new. She turned in surprise to find him quite alone; the girl was not at his side. She would have spoken, but silence came in the wake of surprise as she looked upon the man who had been her teacher.

Standing just inside the door's frame, he was taller than he had ever been. He wore his bed robes loosely about his body, but she could see the very threads crackling with energy, with magery. Some of it was the orange threads of protection and cancellation, some of it was the white of discernment, and some of it was a deep, steady violet, so calm she might once have missed it. His hair was white and very wild, as hers was dark and wild, and his eyes were the color of a sword blade, but less friendly.

"*Who are you?*" He did not lift a hand or utter a word, but she could see the colors ebb and flow around him as a spell took shape.

"I am Evayne," she whispered, against her will. There was a command in his words that was almost bardic.

"So you've said," he replied. "And you are telling the truth, as you believe it." A little of the ice seemed to leave his eyes, but they were still hard, still keen. "But you are not the Evayne that I know, or that this room knows."

"No," she said, "I'm not." She rose, pulling her robes more tightly to her body.

"Those are the same robes. That much, I can see." He took another step into the room, and the door swung shut at his back. It surprised Evayne. He was not usually a man given to display, and the use of magic for the triviality of shutting a door was quite unlike the Meralonne that she knew. "Very well, Evayne," and his voice was quiet. "Why have you come?"

"I have come," she replied, as carefully neutral as she could be, "to take the girl that I left in your keeping."

"I see. And where exactly would you take her?"

"I'm afraid that is not a concern of the Order, and it is best left so."

"That," he said, his voice so soft she almost missed the word, "is not for you to decide. You intrude here. You are the stranger."

She started to speak when she saw his power flare again. It was quick; there was no hint of word-focus, no gesture, to presage the spell itself. Gray mage-light touched her cheeks, her chin, her eyes, as her hood was yanked back. She smiled grimly as the midnight-blue material struggled free of Meralonne's spell and settled around her face once again.

But he had seen enough.

"You are Evayne," he whispered. "What's happened to you?" He took a step toward her, and she a step back, although she could not have said why.

"We do not have time," she said. "Bring me the girl that I left in your care, and I will leave."

"We don't have—" His eyes narrowed. He walked the length of the room to his desk and pulled his chair free from the debris that inhabited it. Then he sank back, his fingers a steeple before his eyes. "Your age is not the effect of spell."

She said nothing.

He gestured; that single fact told her he used a greater magic. She needed to conserve her power. She let the rings of coruscating light spring up from the floor to the ceiling around her still body without raising a finger in her own defense. The circles flashed by so quickly it was impossible to discern their color, but she could guess what the spell conveyed to its caster. She knew that he wouldn't harm her.

When at last he finished, his eyes were slits, he was stiff, and his face, long and thin, had never looked so unusual. "You have great power," he said at last. "And more. You have walked hidden ways, Evayne."

"I walked," she pointed out, "the hidden path to bring the girl to you."

"You walked it," he countered, "but it did not change you. You invoked it on High Summer. No, you've walked in the Winter, along the dark road. I can see the scars."

She offered him no answer; he spoke the truth.

"What you've learned, I didn't teach you."

"Experience is a good teacher, Meralonne—but in magery, indeed, you were my only master."

" 'Were?' "

"Are."

He smiled, but the expression was neither friendly nor pleasant. Not for the first time, Evayne wondered who he was, and who he had been before he joined the Order. She did not ask.

"You have learned to cross time. It is not an art I would have thought possible."

"It is not an art," she agreed. "It's an accident or a curse. Meralonne, you must know that if I could share this with you, I would. But in no wise am I able; indeed, I am compelled to do otherwise. I ask your forgiveness and your indulgence in this, but even if you do not grant it. . . ." She let the words trail off into uncomfortable silence.

"Yes?" He would not let the silence lie.

"What do you think I was going to say? Why do you seek to force my words?"

"Why are you afraid to give them?"

She lowered her chin. *Why, indeed? We will argue, and we will part. Nothing I say or do can prevent it. It has happened.* "There is nothing you can do to take the information from me. If I have to, I will die to protect it."

"I . . . see."

"There are forces at work that even I do not understand. Meralonne—"

"You deny me this—this spell. And yet, you had not learned it, Evayne. Not . . . not yesterday." His eyes changed color and shape. "I would give much to be able to travel time; to correct old wrongs and old crimes." There was a hunger to the words. Evayne wondered if it had always been there, lurking behind the mercurial, peculiar man who had been her master, and would never be again.

I never came to you as an adult, she thought, *until now. I do not even know who you are.* "I would as well, Master APhaniel of the Magi. I would give more than you could possibly imagine. But I do not choose where I walk, and I can change *nothing* of what has been."

"I see." He spun round on the chair, showing her his slender back. "And what if I do not choose to release this girl to you?"

"Then you doom us, for she is part of what we need to face the demon-kin. The darkness is coming, Meralonne, and whether we are at hand to fight it or merely to be trampled underfoot is our choice."

"You ask me to make a choice without facts, without knowledge."

"I ask you to make the same choice that I have had to. Do you think I know what will happen, or why, or how?"

"You know more than I."

"Yes. But I have paid for that knowledge."

"There is always a price to be paid for knowledge!" He wheeled, sudden in his rage; his face was transformed. Then he lifted his hands to his face and fell silent, kneading his forehead with his pointed fingers.

"Yes," she said bitterly, although this blaze of anger was something that she had never seen from him. "There *is* always a price. But you would pay it, even knowing what that price was. I—" Bitter smile. She cast her gaze groundward, offering him silence.

"I am," he said at last, "nothing if not a judge of character. Whether I was willing to pay your price or no, you would not give me the answers I seek."

"No."

"What, then, do you know of the demon-kin?"

"Too much, Meralonne, and I have not the time to tell you all. Suffice it to say that they hunt the girl that you keep, as we surmised years—no, yesterday."

He did not blink as he met her eyes. "Evayne."

She looked away. "I don't know," she whispered. "I see glimpses, Meralonne, but never the whole picture. I see the facets, but not the gem; the trees, but not the forest." It was as much a plea as she was willing to make. She turned. "The girl?"

"She comes." He sank back into his seat, the fire gone from his gaze. "I know you well, Evayne a'Nolan. If you say it's important, it's important—that much I trust. But can you tell me where you go?"

"I'm not sure." As a pupil, she had always been a child; even in their final argument, their break, she had been a willful, headstrong girl to him. Not now.

He raised a brow, and then shook his head. From out of his bed robes he pulled his pipe. He lit it, and only when he did did Evayne realize that the room was covered in shadows. Smoke wreathed his face like a halo gone awry. "You . . . don't know." He smiled, but it was the veneer of an expression.

"Meralonne, I—" She drew her shoulders up and lifted her chin. "I am not a child any longer. We are equals, or we are nothing. My word that I will explain all will have to suffice."

"When will you tender this explanation?"

"When it does not threaten our future."

He chuckled and brought the pipe to his lips again. "I will accept your word."

But he wouldn't. She knew it, and knew that his inability would shame him. "Thank you, Master APhaniel. I've—I've always done my best to be true to your teachings."

His eyes shone with a genuine pride, and for a moment his expression was soft, almost gentle. "You are an odd student, but easily the best I have had."

The door to the study swung open. In the shadow of the door frame, lit by golden spell-light and not by day, stood the girl. She cocked her head to one side and gave Evayne a puzzled look.

"Come," Evayne said. "We have far to go today, if I have guessed correctly." She walked toward the girl, and then stopped to look back.

It hurt, suddenly, to leave his study as a stranger. She had never done it before. *Never look back*, she told herself bitterly, as she turned away for the last time. *Especially when there's nothing you can do but mourn.*

Meralonne APhaniel watched her leave, his lips tightening around the stem of his long, ancient pipe. When she was gone, he nodded and the door swung shut. On her. On their discussion.

But other doors had opened. A past that he rarely thought about, and never spoke of, had been recalled by the strangely aged Evayne's visit. Smoke wreathed the air again, eddying in the currents of his breath, his silent words. He brushed long, ivory strands out of his eyes as he stared into a past that he had thought lost forever.

He did not move. Were it not for the smoke that continued to curl in an upward spiral, he could have been mistaken for one of the statues in the gallery.

Sunlight, filtered by exterior glass and interior shutters, worked its way into the room. He had work to do; things to see to. Perhaps it was time to investigate the findings in Breodanir.

A rock skittered across cobbled stone as a sulky young man let fly with a kick. His hands were jammed into his pockets, and his hat was pulled down over his forehead; stray, unkempt curls jutted out to either side. Were it not for his expression, he would have looked quite pleasant. He was slim, with a fine-boned face and large eyes. His limbs were slender and his skin pale. It was obvious that his day was not taken up with hard physical labor, or perhaps any labor at all. An elderly woman, walking by with two attendants, gave him a distinct frown. He met it with a scowl, but moved out of her way.

Kepton Crescent was lively enough for an off-market street, and it would become more lively still as Korven's Drinking Establishment opened for the day. The public baths kept the morning traffic brisk, especially when the day was bright, warm, and reasonably clear. Today was just such a day, and the outdoor springs—although they were no more than trumped-up fountains—meant that the baths would be in great demand.

The young man found it hard to loiter without being nudged off the road by any number of parties who were making their treks toward the baths. Finally his patience ran out and in a fit of pique and surly annoyance, he stood his ground, glaring at a young woman and her attendant, a rather stiff, plainly attired matron.

The older woman in the mottled dress looked down the bridge of her nose out of stern, violet eyes. "Excuse me, young man, but you impede our passage." Before he could reply, she turned to the young girl who walked behind her and took her hand, both protectively and forcefully.

The young man lifted the corner of his hat, and then mumbled something under his breath. "Ma'am."

"Kallandras." Evayne a'Nolan, dressed in the matronly, severe style of decades past, inclined her head slightly. Her voice very soft, she said, "Are you almost ready?"

He shrugged, and then fell into step beside her as she continued to walk down the street. His tone and his words belied each other; the casual listener would have no reason to suspect anything other than wheedling ill humor. "Where do we go?"

"I'm not sure. Not precisely."

He nodded as if he expected no more and then glanced casually at the young girl who was fidgeting with her skirts. "Who is she?"

Evayne was certain that although he had only just met the wild girl, Kallandras was more likely than she to be able to answer questions about her height, her weight, her age. He would know, if he never looked at her again, what she wore, what its colors were, where the style of the dress originated. "She is a rather un-usual young lady."

"Which means you won't say." He shrugged. "You're old, this time. Does this mean trouble?"

"I'm *not* that old," she replied. "And, yes, it does." Evayne at forty still did not understand the otherwhen, but she could begin to see a pattern to the course the path chose for her. She was a mage now of no little power; her knowledge was up to the test of the best of the Order; her ability to protect both herself and any she chose to champion had never been greater.

It was not a coincidence that, as she aged, the dangers she found herself facing grew more potent and more deadly. At least, it did not appear to Evayne to be so.

She glanced out of the corner of her eyes and saw that Kallandras was watching her intently. He was young, this time, but his youth was not the liability that it would have been for any other.

"Which is why you summoned me."

"Yes," Evayne said softly. She looked up at Kallandras. His eyes were, in youth, the same piercing blue that they would always be; meeting them, she could al-most forget to notice the rest of his face. His attention always seemed entirely fo-cused, entirely absorbed. "You won't be missed?"

"Evayne—Lady." He frowned a moment, and then smoothed the expression from his face. "When you forced me to make the choice, I was already one of the best of my number. It's important to your mission that I not be missed; I will not be missed." He fell silent as they walked to the end of the street. "I've arranged," he said, waving his arm, "for transport—but it would've helped to know where we are going."

Evayne let herself relax a little bit as a single-horse cab pulled to the side of the road. As always, Kallandras had looked to the details of their meeting. He offered her companion an arm, and the girl looked at it dubiously before scampering up into the body of the carriage. He shrugged, offered Evayne his arm, and then joined them. "I've told the driver we wish to go to the northwestern quarter. Will that be out of our way?"

"No. You've done well." Evayne sat back in the padded chair and let the city begin to move by.

"Good." He gazed out of the windows as well, his face losing all signs of surli-ness or aimlessness. Then, after a moment, he turned to her and met her gaze. She knew what he would ask next, but it always unnerved her to hear it, especially on occasions when he was young. *But in youth*, she reminded herself, *we have less com-passion and more of a will to absolutes, to brutality. When you are older, Kallan, even you will mellow.* But not much, if she was being honest; not much at all. The Ko-vaschaii took their members very young and trained them well.

"Who do you wish me to kill?" His expression was completely neutral; there was no judgment in it, and no curiosity whatsoever. He became, for the moment, just another weapon; one to be held with care and used with confidence.

She did not wish him to be such a thing. "Kallan," she began. "How has Senniel fared?"

"The college fares well, with me and without."

"And Sioban?"

"As far as I know, she's fine. She's still the headmaster of the college, if that's what you mean. I haven't seen her in a month, but I've been avoiding it. She means to give me my papers and my route and have me travel the empire between Attariel, Senniel, and Morniel."

They were three of the five bardic colleges in Essalieyan; Senniel was oldest and foremost. Evayne nodded as if the conversation were a normal one. "And training of the voice?"

"She says that she hasn't seen a talent as strong as mine in all of her years at the college. She also says that she can't train it further; it will grow with experience or not at all." The reply was smooth and without inflection. Kallandras took no pride or joy in being bard-born. It was a fact, like the weather, only slightly more relevant. His very detachment made it hard to envy him. It also made it hard to like him much.

"Kallan, do you enjoy the music?"

He shrugged. "It's music, like any other skill." But she thought his expression just a touch softer. "You haven't answered my question."

She grimaced. "I don't want you to kill."

"You want me to kill, or you would not have summoned me." He turned his gaze back to the city streets.

She grimaced. "You leave me no illusion, do you?"

"You aren't a woman in need of illusion." He shrugged, and she thought she caught a glimpse of anger and impatience in the motion. It was hard to tell; all of Kallandras' public displays were dramatic and not genuine. "You came to me because I was an assassin. You showed me what you needed me to see. I gave up the brotherhood for you, but I took my skills with me.

"Who, Evayne?"

Evayne looked at her hands, stiffly clasped in her lap. How long had it been for Kallandras? She counted the years at three. She did not often see him as a youth anymore, and she had forgotten how the choice she had forced upon him could still sting.

For she had taken him from the brotherhood of the Kovaschaii shortly after she herself had been forced to give up her own life to walk the path of the otherwhen, and she had not been gentle.

I was younger then, she thought. *And youth is always cruel.*

"I play no game with you, Kallandras. I do not know if we will be called upon to kill or to hold our hand. But we travel in search of our history, and I do not know exactly how long it will take."

"What do you hope to find?"

"Nothing. But that's not what I think we *will* find."

"You've been walking again."

She nodded. Kallandras was so different from Meralonne. He knew that she traveled in time, but he never asked her what she had seen, or where she had seen it. The past was not his concern, nor was the future. The present was the time for action, and he concentrated his considerable power upon it.

"It was yesterday," she said softly. But she could not tell him what she had seen, although she greatly desired the freedom to do so. The dictate of the maker of the otherwhen was absolute. "But what I saw there is not what we will see today."

He nodded. "Today?"

So unlike Meralonne. "As I said, I'm not sure—but I think, if we see anything, we will see the kin."

"Servants of darkness," Kallandras whispered. "So soon. Do you think it will be over with this?"

She did not answer because she knew the answer was not the one he wanted—yearned—to hear. "Be ready," she said softly.

"What do you know of the history of Vexusa?" Evayne's robes had fallen back into their familiar shape. She did not regret the loss of the matron's dress, as perhaps she had regretted other gowns in the past.

She let the curtains fall back into place and turned from the window of the Imperial State's hotel room. Her eyes were light, yet somehow dark, as if they reflected both the aurora and the night sky.

Kallandras shrugged. He sat stiffly in one of three high-backed chairs. Both of his feet were planted against the floor, and his hands rested in his lap.

"You would have made a terrible mage," she said, and smiled.

"I never wanted to be anything but Kovaschaii," he replied. "And you cost me that."

It had been long since she had seen him in his youth, and she had forgotten how much his words could cut. At twenty, he did not view her as the ambivalent friend he would know her to be when he became forty. She remembered, as well as she was able, what she had been like at twenty. Meeting Kallandras as an older man had been a shock, then. *We circle each other, Kallan. Will we never walk the same path?*

"I'm sorry," she said, and she meant it. "I would not have taken you from your life of death had I another choice."

"So you've said." He did not relent.

"Kallan—"

"Tell me what we seek, Evayne."

She turned back to the window, looking for a way out. To come straight from Meralonne to the intense chill of Kallandras . . . "History, as I said."

"If you seek history, then you have far to go. Vexusa exists in legend and lore, but the annals of the wise have very little to offer in the way of truths. If you remember," he added coldly, "the city was destroyed by the combined wrath of the god-born; it was razed to the last stone."

"Vexusa existed in far more than the fancy of beautiful voices and children's tales." Her voice became remote. "You know the old Weston bardic lays?"

"Some."

"Do you know the *Fall of Light?*"

"Yes." Grudgingly, he added, "It was about the loss of the Wizard Wars, when the Dark League destroyed the last of the Dawn Rose."

"And do you know the *Hand of Myrddion?*"

He nodded again. "Shall I get my lute?" His voice was tinged with a trace of sarcasm, but his fingers began to flex where they rested against his thighs.

"If you wish it, yes."

He looked down at his hands and then back at her; he stayed his ground. He knew what compassion was although the learning of it had been difficult, but he would not lay it at her feet; not yet. "Myrddion was a mage of the Dawn Rose. He fought and failed against the Dark League when he was betrayed by Ancathyron, his apprentice. Carythas, who led the Dark League, stripped Myrddion of his power, and put him on display in the coliseum in Vexusa, the capital of the mage-state. They cut off his right hand, and then they set him to fight.

"He died."

Evayne raised an eyebrow. It was hard to believe that Kallandras was so good a bard that he had already built a reputation for himself. She almost said as much, but she knew what his response would be, and she did not wish to hear it again. Instead, she said, "And the hand?"

"Myrddion's right hand had five rings. After his death, Carythas had the hand brought to him and attempted to claim the rings for his own use. He set them upon his hand, and they began to burn him.

"He died, as well."

"He did not understand their nature," Evayne said.

"No one did," Kallandras replied. "Or do you?"

She shook her head, and pulled the curtains, briefly, away from the window again; the sky above was darkening. With Kallandras, she walked a tightrope; the spirit of the law of the otherwhen had been violated on a dozen occasions, but never the letter—the letter, through no choice of her own, was kept and would always be kept. She discussed "known" history, of course. She did not discuss whether or not she had been present at its unfolding. And Kallandras, so unlike

Meralonne, never cared to ask. "Not fully, no. They were a set, and they operated as a set, at a particular moment. Myrddion—he *knew* that he was going to be betrayed; I'm certain of it. He *knew* that those rings would be taken from his body by no less a mage than Carythas. It was a trap."

Her voice broke on the last word. "It must have been a trap." She closed her eyes, and prayed that it was so—because he had died such a hideous, demeaning death to lay it. In the end, although he had been a strong man, he had screamed and pleaded, and eventually, after the hours had whiled away and the crowds had their fill of their greatest enemy's torment, they granted him his death. And she had watched; all she had done was watch. Even prayer had been beyond her.

It was the third time that the otherwhen had taken her to so distant a past. She prayed that there would be no fourth visit. "What happened to the rings?"

Kallandras shrugged. "After Carythas' death, three mages attempted to touch the rings. They also perished, although less hideously and less slowly than Carythas. Carythas fought Myrddion's trap to the end."

Evayne nodded. There was a grim satisfaction in both his death and the time it took him to surrender to it.

"The fourth mage attempted to lift them by spell, but they would not be coaxed by any magic he could cast. There was no fifth mage; no one was willing to touch them. The lays do not make clear what the eventual fate of the rings was, but it is believed, in legends associated with the lays and contemporary to them, that the rings remained a part of the coliseum—that they could not be moved, although they did not serve an active purpose after the death of Carythas." He stopped. "You think they're still in the coliseum in Vexusa."

"I don't know. But . . . yes, I do. If they could not be moved by the greatest of the mages of the League, the enchantment on them was one that defies description." She would not look at Kallandras until she could school her face. "Therefore, the coliseum in Vexusa is important—and it still exists, although Vexusa does not."

"Averalaan." His voice was almost hushed, "You think it *here* somewhere, or you would not be here."

"Yes," she said, and this time, pale but steady, she turned away from the support of the window ledge. "It stands near the heart of Averalaan." She was on safe ground again, for she could always speak of the here and the now.

He was silent a long time, absorbing her news. She thought him pale, and the arrogant ice of his expression was chilled for a moment by something other than his great anger toward her.

His lips moved over a single word as he bowed his fair head. "Where, Evayne?" he said at length. He knew the city better than any but another member of the brotherhood. "The coliseum for the King's Challenge was built after the founding. There is no other coliseum in Averalaan."

She slid her hands into the sleeves of her robes. Kallandras frowned with mild distaste as the orb of the seer appeared between her palms.

She did not notice the grimace. Her attention was absorbed by the silver mist as she stared into the world that only the seer-born could see. "It exists, Kallan. It exists in darkness, but it is part of the here and now." He did not ask her how she knew; he never did.

"You think our mission is to find these rings."

"I don't know."

"Assume it's so. What of her?" He pointed to the figure that slept, with her knees curled up to her chest, in the center of the crimson counterpane.

"It's important that she travel with us," Evayne's voice was a study in neutrality. "Our road is the same road for the time being—and I believe that only she can set us upon that road." The ball she held cast light against her face like a shimmering web.

Kallandras looked away. "Where is the coliseum?"

"I don't know. It's hidden." She smiled grimly. "Even the seer-born would have trouble piercing the darkness that surrounds it."

"And you?"

"I have trouble. If I did not know exactly what to look for, I would see nothing out of the ordinary." She lifted the soul-crystal high; the web across her face pulsed suddenly, a lightning mask. She walked over to the bed. "Child." She took a deeper breath. "Espere. Come. It is time to find the legacy that your father's people have long forgotten. Can you feel it? We are close."

The girl's eyes flickered open. She lifted her head and rested her chin upon the backs of her wrists as she gazed quizzically up at Evayne.

Evayne lowered one hand to touch the girl's upturned forehead. The girl flinched, and the seeress paled. The orb spun; the clouds within it grew murky and dark for a moment. "Let me lend you what you do not have, child. We cannot wait for your proper time. Tonight we must hunt in the city streets." Silver sparkled in a web of mist and light. It covered them both, melting like snow against skin.

The girl's eyes began to change color; the alteration gradual enough that an observer might miss the transformation completely. She frowned and then looked up at Evayne, meeting violet eyes with golden ones. She looked around at her surroundings: the bed, the curtained window, the empty desk, and the unused grate. Then she nodded almost gravely and rose, sliding her legs toward the carpets beneath her bare feet. Those feet were callused and padded; the stones and pebbles of the city streets made no impression upon them.

"We will follow as we are able," Evayne said, as the wild girl approached the door and reached for the handle.

Kallandras rose from the chair he occupied. He was tense, the line of his jaw hard and sharp. "Evayne—what did you do?"

"It's an old healing spell," she said quietly.

He met her weary gaze with narrowed eyes before nodding grimly. They both knew he knew she was lying.

Averalaan at night was the shadow-twin of its daylight self. The moon's light across the open bay was high and full, but it shone on an empty stage; the city's streets were almost deserted. In isolated wells of light and noise, people gathered for entertainment and company.

Evayne, Kallandras, and Espere avoided them. They each used the shadows in their own way. Evayne drew them up like a cloak, with a touch of magic to seal them; Kallandras used them as a wall to hide in and behind; Espere used them as a guide.

They did not speak. They felt no need of words, and indeed, words would have been more of a barrier than a bridge. Here, with night come and darkness a friend, silence was a shield and a weapon, and the better armed they were, the more confident they felt in their companions.

Espere moved with a purpose that was singular and new; her steps were lighter and her eyes quicker than they had yet been. She paid attention to the buildings that she passed in and around, staring at them in wonderment. Children gazed at the new and the unfamiliar in just such a way. She did not linger, though; her hunt drew her on.

Kallandras watched her dart back and forth. He saw her stop once or twice in the long stretches of cobbled road, turning her face to the breeze as if it bore a scent she could follow. He could make no sense out of what she was doing, and that annoyed him, but he knew better than to interrupt or break the silence with questions.

The hotel that Evayne had chosen was in the most sensible part of Averalaan; merchants patronized it, and many foreign to Essalieyan were also quartered there, with their followers or their companions. Among them, three people of any description were unlikely to stand out, and any business that had to be done could be done almost freely. Espere led them out of the quarter, which was unfortunate.

What was worse was where she led them. The roads narrowed; the buildings began to close in on the street. Here, the moon's light was blocked by the height of narrow, closely spaced buildings that housed whole families. Averalaan was as safe as any city could be—but it was a city, still, and even at its heart there were darknesses that wise men did not trespass upon.

He watched as the wild girl began to lead them to the most dangerous of the hundred holdings.

"What's wrong?" Evayne said softly, her voice coming out of silence and leaving no echo in its wake. Magery.

He had a like way of answering her, and wrapped his own reply in bardic tones, precise and cool. "She's leading us to the thirty-fifth."

"Thirty-fifth?"

"There are two holdings in the hundred that are dangerous. The thirty-fifth is the worst." If he thought it odd that she did not understand the shorter reference, he kept his own counsel.

"Why?" Again, the word carried in an unnatural stillness.

His shrug was answer enough. "It is known," he said.

"Not to the Kings." She lifted her head as Espere caught the shadows and came sliding between them to stand before her.

Above them, the bowers of trees older than the city let the moonlight through in a dappled, dark pattern. The freestanding circles were planted throughout the old city in a pattern that not even the wise understood. They were tended by the Mother's children, and hidden behind the bases of their broad, dark trunks, one could often find those who made of the night a private affair.

Beneath the height of their highest branches, the rooftops sheltered—and these roofs were three stories and more above the ground.

"If it were winter," the seeress said gravely to the young girl, "I would not have been able to pull you this far back."

The girl cocked her head a moment, as if listening to the wind. Then she lifted a slender arm and pointed. To the ground.

"Where, wild one?" Evayne said softly.

Again, the wild girl lifted her arm, but this time, in the shadows of buildings that blocked the full moon, it was clear that she pointed not to the door of the tall building, in, at best, a questionable state of repair. No, she pointed instead to the trapdoor in the street beside it, where wood was placed by cutters' wagons, for the course of the cooler season. In Averalaan, winter was mild nine seasons out of ten.

Kallandras stepped forward. Dressed for the street and the night, he wore no lute—and the lute was the only thing that softened him in Evayne's eyes. His hair was pulled back so tightly it showed no evidence of the curl and bounce that was the envy of many a young court lady.

He raised a pale brow at Evayne, and she a dark one in return. If the stuff of dark legends stood here—in any age—it was in an age so long forgotten that nothing at all remembered it. Shrugging, he began to walk toward the closed trap.

Evayne watched as he unlocked and unlatched the banded, wooden door. It creaked on heavy hinges, but he lifted it as if it weighed nothing. Opening the slender, slight pouch strapped to his hip as part of his clothing, he pulled something out and held it for a moment in the flat of his palms. By it, the underside of his jaw was illuminated.

Curling his fingers around it, he let the darkness obscure him again. "I'll be back," he said softly.

He did not return.

Chapter Seven

A N HOUR PASSED.

Evayne could feel it as clearly as she could see it; the moon moving across the sky, changing by slow degree the texture of the shadows the buildings cast against the dark road. The wait was difficult, and not only for her.

Espere looked up at the seer, and then away again. She had repeated this motion every few minutes since Kallandras had gone down into the darkness that the trapdoor covered.

"He's gone," Evayne said softly. The wild girl edged forward toward the trap itself, sniffing at the air before turning to face the seer.

It had gone on for too long already.

Sliding her hands into fabric that moved obligingly out of her way, she brought the round orb into the darkness, where she might better see its depths for the light it cast. The line of her hood fell forward, obscuring her eyes and her expression. Her palms cradled the sphere to either side, as gently as if they held another's upturned face. *Kallandras. I have searched for you before, and you are never easy to find, curse your training.*

To push the silver mists away was, after these many years, a trivial matter. To hide behind them, to see glimpses without revealing one's self to the vision of another seer who might be searching—that was a challenge, and one that a seer almost never faced. It took skill, but more than that, it took power. She spent that power; instinct alone made her cautious, and a seer never ignored her instincts.

Kallandras, trained and nurtured by those schooled in the arts of the hidden ways, was never an easy presence to find—not even with seer's vision. Unlike Stephen of Elseth, or Gilliam, or any of the other people whom Evayne had had cause to seek in the otherwhen, Kallandras was a shadow, someone who conformed to the mists instead of standing apart from them.

Her jaw tensed; it always did when she exerted herself in silent concentration. She did not tell the wild one to guard their backs because she knew it to be unnecessary.

Already, Espere tested the scent the breeze carried and watched the flicker of light and dark—an interplay of shadow and moonlight. The stars were there as pale companions to the moon's pensive face; the evening was clear, the breeze gentle. None of the Essalieyanese walked along these streets; nor did a walking patrol of the magisterial guards come by to disturb the silence, which was in itself unusual.

They stood, two lone women in the folds of magic-imbued shadow, in safety—the safety of the tightrope, or the razor's edge.

Time passed.

Espere looked up, but Evayne was still draped in silence and shadow; she had not moved. The girl hesitated, and then she reached out and grabbed the seer's arm.

Evayne cried out in shock as one palm fell away from the seer's ball. She fumbled and the crystal teetered precariously in the air before she caught it again and pulled it close. "What are you doing?" she said, eyes blazing silver. There was majesty to her anger, and power, and danger.

It faded as she met the gaze of the wild girl. The urgency and fear she read there made Evayne's anger seem as unreasonable as it was. She slid the crystal into the folds of her robes. "He is hidden," she told her companion.

"Yes. By us."

Evayne looked up, and up again as the moon cast a shadow across her face. Feet planted apart against the roof edge of the tenement, a tall, slender creature looked down upon them. His lips were turned in a smile, his arms were crossed. At his elbows and along the line of his shoulder blades, twin spikes jutted out to either side, and two long horns adorned his forehead. He wore no clothing and no armor—and he needed neither.

Evayne used a word that she hadn't spoken since a childhood she barely remembered had passed. She threw her hands up and light leaped from her fingertips, sparking and dancing in the shape of a translucent, orange dome.

The demon laughed and launched himself into the air, drawing his hands into fists above his head so that the elbow-spikes pointed down toward Evayne. His laughter died abruptly as they struck the barrier. Where they had broken through, they burned. Lightning ran up and down their length, snapping and arcing.

Snarling, the creature pulled himself away. Evayne staggered backward as her spell buckled. Underestimating one of the demon-kin usually had only one result.

Evayne was not the only person who could use the shadows to her advantage. Moonlight dimmed; starlight vanished completely. The demon sprang up, twisting in the air as if parts of it were solid to his touch. He was *fast*. Evayne had battled the kin before, but she didn't remember this speed.

At twenty-eight, she would have died.

At forty, she barely managed to resurrect her mage-shield before the demon was upon her again. She was no fool. There was no comparison between them on a purely physical level, and she had no intention of allowing the creature to prove it. Her shield crackled as he forced it; he snarled, she grunted.

It was Evayne who was pushed back.

He saw her eyes widen and laughed. "This night, mage, you face a lord, and not a lackey. You will serve us well."

Demon lord. Evayne met his eyes without flinching. "I face one of the kin, no more, no less." But she paled, and he saw it clearly. From a demon, the darkness hid nothing.

"The Priests call me Lord Caraxas. You may call me master." Almost casually, he reached up and tore a branch from one of the freestanding trees. It was old, and the branch itself was the width of his arm. "I do hope you won't consider surrendering."

Lightning struck the branch. Wood cracked and shivered; splinters drove themselves into the demon's hands. He laughed and threw the branch away. "Ah, little human—you remind me of days long gone. The world was ours, and we had time to enjoy our distractions." He gestured suddenly, and the ground around Evayne's feet erupted into stony spikes.

Not one of them struck her. "Morrel rode," she replied.

"Morrel died." But he spat; the amusement gone to anger. "And Morrel had what you do not—strength and power. I am bored."

"And I." She threw her arms wide and spoke a single word. Pale fire roared up around him in a golden, glowing circle. Reflected off his teeth and his almost metallic skin, it grew stronger and brighter.

"I *am* impressed," the demon replied. "You are stronger than you appear. You will make our lord a fitting sacrifice."

She smiled, and for the first time, the hood of her robes fell away from her face, although she did not lift her hand to move them. "I think your lord would find me most unpalatable."

"You will have a chance to be proved wrong," the demon replied. "We've been searching for you." He smiled. It was the most threatening thing he had yet done.

Evayne looked at the fires, and at the demon. He was contained within her circle, and it burned brightly. "What—"

The wild one howled.

Evayne turned to see the young girl's dark, strained features. They were pale with fear, raised toward the open sky in near panic.

The moon was slowly fading from sight.

"I am contained," Caraxas said, and his smile darkened. "But I'm not alone."

She looked up. Espere was right, but wrong; the moon stayed where it was. *They* were the ones in transition. The shadows above grew darker and more solid; the moon became a ghost, and then an afterimage against her eyes.

She knew what the spell was, and as the sky above her grew completely solid and shadowed, she turned white. There were perhaps five mages in existence who could cast this spell—and only one of them could cast it on more than one person without paying the ultimate price.

She looked up. There was rock above her head—something dark and convex. There was no sky, no open air, no breeze. To either side of her, shadows slowly thinned as her eyes adjusted to darkness. She stood upon the steps of a building that took shape and form as she stared.

It was black and seemed to rise forever, gleaming in the light of her spell of containment. The steps went up to doors that were thrice her height. Towers stood astride the door, and a circular window above it. Only the building's face was visible in the poor light, but she recognized the style of architecture. It was a cathedral to rival that of Cormaris in the High City. And she knew it well. Having seen it once, she would never forget its dark face.

"Welcome," Caraxas said, his voice the purr of a demonic feline, "to Vexusa."

"Vexusa—Vexusa was destroyed in the cataclysm." Her voice was tense and strained; she could barely speak at all.

Caraxas laughed, the sound low and rich with pleasure. "So your histories have said—but the lords of the Hells know the truth of the matter. What was built here could not be destroyed by mere humanity." He threw his arms wide; light shone off skin. "No, when Vexusa fell to the Legion, the Dark League turned its hand to the city's heart—and they buried it, mage.

"Like a seed, it has bided its time, growing within the depths of the earth and waiting for its proper season. We tend it, we feed it.

"The City of Gold will rise again." The amusement warmed his voice. He raised a finger to his chin and shook his head, a very human gesture. "But you will not be here to see it." He lowered his hand and walked through the ring of fire without even flinching.

Evayne called light, and light came; a miniature sun burst into being in front of the demon lord's eyes. He cried out in shock and anger. "Espere—run!" she commanded.

"To where, little mage?" The voice was soft, feminine—and quite cold.

Of course, Evayne thought. *He would not be alone here.* Standing beneath the arched stone frame of the cathedral doors, a figure in perfect stillness commanded the seeress' attention. Her hair was pale as platinum, her skin alabaster, and her eyes very red. Her nails were long and iridescent, and her clothing was . . . magical in nature. Beneath the walls and windows of halls hallowed by death, she looked every inch the High Priestess.

"To freedom," Evayne replied.

"There is only one freedom in Vexusa for you or your companion," the woman replied, stepping out from beneath the hard, curved arch. "And we call it Myrddion's escape." She raised her arms and a black, coruscating light shimmered up them.

Evayne swore. She did not need the sight to know that this demon was more powerful than any she had ever encountered. She could feel the presence of darkness, could see it as a fog, not a mist.

"You will be staying with us for a short while, mage. And after we have spoken, you will have the privilege of meeting a God."

"Thank you, but I fear I must decline. I have been in the half-world before and I don't find it very interesting."

The demon smiled softly. Evayne had never seen so attractive, so sensual an expression. "You don't have the option, I'm afraid."

"You can't force a person to the half-world."

"No."

Silence. The demon was patient enough to let Evayne figure it out for herself; it didn't take long. "By the Mother," she whispered softly. *It started here. Father— why?*

"Oh, yes. He's here, seeress. In this world. And the Shining City, when it rises and obliterates Averalaan above, will be his capital and the beginning of his dominion."

Evayne saw the black-light billow out in five distinct tendrils. It closed round her like a fist. She had magic, yes—but against the trail of demon-magery that her enemy used, it would not last. She was not a fool; as bad as things were, they could get much, much worse before the end.

She knew it, having seen the coliseum of Vexusa in use once before.

"Very good. You will come with us now."

The hand of darkness lifted Evayne off the ground.

"And you, silent one. You, too, will have the privilege of suffering for the company you keep. Come."

Espere was surrounded by darkness, and by darkness lifted. Her arms were pinioned to her sides, but her head was free to move. She twisted it and stared at the seeress.

Evayne could think of no reply.

They began to move up the stairs of the cathedral as Caraxas joined his mistress. The doors swung open, creaking rather than gliding smoothly.

Evayne passed through them, head up, eyes focused.

As did Espere—but not in the manner the demons had intended. With a snarl that lengthened to a growl, she tore her arms free of the shadow that bound her. Her feet hit the ground, and she rolled along glistening black marble. The dark interior of the open cathedral swallowed her; she was gone.

Caraxas shouted in surprise. Fire leaped from his fingertips, leaving a molten trail in a thin, red stream in the wake of the fleeing girl.

"Sor na Shannen, you fool!" he cried, as Espere avoided flame and shards of rock. "Why didn't you warn me?"

"I had her!" The demoness snarled back. "There's no possible way she could escape that spell—she wasn't even a mage!" She scanned the darkness. "There!"

"She moves quickly," Caraxas said. "Leave her to me." He lifted his arm again. Fire flayed the darkness like a whip.

"No. If she could break that spell, she—" And then the demon called Sor na Shannen suddenly became quiet. "There is a way." She turned to Evayne and grabbed her chin, piercing her flesh with the tips of her delicate claws. "Mage, where was she from?"

Evayne said nothing. The claws touched bone in three places, but the process was slow, like a caress gone awry. "You *will* tell me. Caraxas, go to the orbs. Get Ellekar's report, and get it quickly."

"He's not due to report—"

"Send the message. We will use the power. *Now.*"

"But the girl—"

"I will deal with the girl, but I need that information."

Caraxas nodded and vanished. Sor na Shannen turned her attention back to her hands. Blood ran down her fingers and dripped onto her wide skirts. "You are quite clever," she said conversationally, "and skilled. It's a pity that you chose to interfere here.

"But you are not the only mage that has come across Vexusa in the past several centuries. Perhaps, if you offer us your cooperation, you might be allowed to join their ranks, rather than join my lord."

It was hard to speak with talons embedded in the lower jaw. Evayne spoke. "I'll cooperate. How?"

"First, tell me about your companion."

"I met her on the road." Evayne spoke quickly, as if aware that her time was very limited. "She—she's strange; looks very unusual under a magical scan. I convinced her to return with me to the Order, where I could study her properly, but she would only do so if I accompanied her here."

"What did she hope to find here?" The demon spoke softly and slowly, but the tone made a mockery of gentleness.

"I don't know—*I don't know!*" Blood fell faster. Evayne's face was white.

"It's a pity that I don't believe you. Come along. You will meet a better interrogator than I, and we will have answers."

Evayne slumped forward as Sor na Shannen released her jaw. "You are an attractive woman," the demon said. "I hate the waste, but I fear we do not have the time." Very gently, she planted a kiss on Evayne's bloodied lips.

"**Do not move.**" The words were command embodied.

Sor na Shannen froze, her lips locked in a predatory smile. And then she cried out in pain, clawing at her back as she stumbled to the side. The shadows that held the seer began to unravel as their mistress lost focus and control.

"You should learn to lie," Kallandras said, as he stepped out of the shadows. "Or at least to negotiate with conviction." He watched, arms crossed casually against his chest, as Evayne's gesture burned the last of the darkness away.

Evayne cradled her jaw in her palm for a moment. "Where have you been?" Kallandras was bard-born, but he rarely demonstrated his power, relying instead on what the Kovaschaii had given him: assassin's skills. *I'd almost forgotten that you were this strong, so young. Thank the Mother. Sioban must be anxious indeed to have you travel the empire in Senniel's service.*

"I met—a demon. It brought me here." He shrugged.

She did not have to ask the demon's fate. "Come on."

Kallandras seldom showed surprise. Even now, he raised an eyebrow, no more. It was enough. "Evayne—where are you going?"

"To the coliseum—it's here; it's almost a courtyard, of sorts, to the cathedral proper."

"The priests and the mages sat in the galleries or watched the entertainment from their rooms."

"Didn't you hear anything she said? We can't afford to—"

"We don't have a choice!" Her eyes were flashing violet; her cheeks were flushed. There was a pain in her eyes that had nothing to do with the injury Sor na Shannen had inflicted. She raised a hand to point. It was slick with blood. "Espere went there."

"Espere seems to be able to take care of herself."

But Evayne wasted no further time in argument. She ran down the grand hall of the empty cathedral. The vaulted ceilings echoed her hasty steps, but Kallandras made so little noise that the sound of one person, and one alone, filled the hall as they ran.

She wanted to tell him the truth. She wanted to tell him that it wasn't Espere she was afraid for; that it wasn't Espere that drove her, half-crazed, into the heart of a cathedral that had once served the Lord of the Hells. She wanted to tell him, simply, that yesterday—in her life, if no one else's—she had seen Myrddion die the most hideous of deaths; that she had had to endure it, because to leave would have been to draw attention to herself; that she had had to pretend to enjoy the spectacle, for the same reason; that she had counted each second of each minute until, at last, he was granted peace. She could not let that experience mean nothing. The path of the otherwhen had taken her there for a reason.

And she needed to see the coliseum again. To see it, empty and unused; dusty and cracked with the passage of time, locked away underground in the darkness. It would bring her a measure of peace.

Or so she prayed.

The halls were long and dark. She had sight enough to pierce the shadows. She slowed down for a moment to listen for signs of pursuit; there were none. Her robes retreated a little higher above the ground, giving her feet room to take longer strides.

She pointed, Kallandras followed; words became secondary to breath, to breathing. The hall became a T, and she turned to the right, catching the wall as an anchor and pivoting lightly on one foot. She did not forget her way to the cloisters, and through the cloisters, the edge of the arena was visible.

She ran, her feet pounding stone, her throat growing drier. Her right hand kept touching the wall at her side. It provided her with sensation, with direction. Here and there, her fingers ran over large cracks, places where the walls had settled poorly after the cataclysm.

Evayne, she thought, *stop. You've got to be rational. You can't—*

Thought stopped as the slaves' and combatants' entrance to the coliseum came fully into view.

Kallandras pulled up at her back; she sensed him stop. He made little noise as he turned, scanning the darkness at her back as she gazed at Darkness in front of her.

The floor of the arena was no longer dirt; it was marble, of the same texture and consistency as the stairs to the cathedral had been. Gold and silver runes were writ large across the marble's face. The letters were almost as tall as she, and there was a pattern to them, and a magic, that defied her immediate understanding. Nor was this the only change.

In the center of the arena, there was an arch, a single, solitary structure. It was, at first sight, simple stone, but glints of iridescent light shot through it, concentrated at the arch's keystone. To either side, there was a pillar, each the width and height of three large men.

She froze in place, her hand gripping the edge of the wall.

"Evayne?"

She could not speak, her attention absorbed by the runes on the floor. They encircled the pillared arch in a permanent ring, radiating darkness; Winter power. She did not know the full arts of demonology, but she knew enough to be certain of two things. It was a summoning, and the kin were not its target.

In the center of the arch, suspended as if in air, was a growing darkness that curled in on itself in hunger. It was large; easily the size of two grown men.

"What—what is it?" Kallandras' question was hushed. For the first time in her life, Evayne heard a trace of fear and nervousness in his question. And her life encompassed many more ages of Kallandras than a mere youth of nineteen.

"It's—" But she could not speak the name. Because the name had power now. Because the saying of it could attract attention that they both desperately wished to avoid. She swallowed and very gingerly began to back out of the opening to the arena.

No. She stopped. *I am not done here, not yet. The path has not opened; the way is not clear.* Her jaw ached. She bunched up midnight-blue cloth and folded her sticky hands into fists around it. This she hadn't done since she was a youth not fully Kallandras' age.

She drew herself up to her full height, lifted her chin, and stared into the darkness. Her skin was white, her jaw clenched. Kallandras came in behind her, still watching their backs.

Very slowly, they made their way along the outer periphery of the arena. Evayne took care not to touch any of the symbols and wards that covered the marble floor. She swallowed. She never forgot anything important, but it was hard to remember in the face of the arched gate.

No. I was sitting . . . there. Carythas sat on his throne . . . there. The throne was gone; at another time she would have been grateful for it. *Myrddion died . . . there.* It was the very spot over which the gate had been erected. A sudden anger displaced some part of her fear.

Kallandras sensed the shift in her mood. She could almost feel him relax. *Don't,* she thought, but did not say it aloud. She kept her concentration, forced herself to remember every detail of Myrddion's death—because she knew, if she remembered it well enough now, she would never have to think about it again.

Myrddion lost his hand there. And Carythas came to the pit itself and burned—there. There. She pulled down the hood of her robe—when it had risen to cover her face, to protect her expression, she couldn't say—and walked, with purpose, to the spot.

There, an orange, glowing ward pulsed in the shadows. It was not the same type or of the same magical texture as the runes surrounding the gate; it was older, and its power was not of darkness, but of a magery so strong she had only twice seen its like.

She could almost hear Meralonne's voice. *The knowledge here, the history, Evayne! Think of all that we could discover about the past!* She did not spit, but only because of the noise it might make.

Touching Kallandras very slowly on the shoulder, she pulled him to her right side. She lifted her finger to her lips and then lowered it toward the ground. He raised a brow, pointed to his feet, and then pointed a little distance off. She shook her head, no. He nodded.

She reached into her robes, found the cool, hard surface of the seer's ball, and then froze in place.

The lights went out.

"Welcome," a velvet voice said. "Welcome to the dominion of Allasakar."

There were ways to sense that did not involve the light. Hearing: the change of a voice's tenor and volume; its direction; and its strength. Touch: the movement of air as a door swings open and then shut. Smell: the nearness of bodies; of sweat. Of death.

Kallandras had trained in the arts of the night. Darkness was an efficient tool—not a weapon in and of itself, but an augmentation, an advantage. He was not a master of the night kill, but he was an able student.

With ease, he pivoted, crouching, toward the sound of the voice. He recognized it, of course. It belonged to the demoness. Somehow, he had failed in his mark. Shame warred with fear. Fear won. Caution moved him now. He recognized the name.

Allasakar.

Lord of the Hells. God of the Darkness. Reaver of the Chosen road.

"Yes, you were clever, boy. And foolish; you might have bought yourself time, had you run in any direction but this one."

He rolled at once. The ground erupted in a spray of shards and splinters. They bit into his neck, his back, and his arms, but not very deeply. He steadied himself as he rocked back to his feet.

"You missed. Have care." Another voice; male. Not Caraxas.

"I know what I do," Sor na Shannen replied, the velvet gone from her voice. "Do you think inconsequential magics like this could break the gate?" Kallandras rolled again, but this time the spell that struck ground was not dark; it was a sizzle of angry red lightning. Instead of shards, there was a spatter of molten rock.

"No—but the mage is the danger here; you waste time on the boy."

"Then, my lord," the sneer belied the title, "deal with the mage as you see fit."

She didn't understand why they chose not to use the darkness; Sor na Shannen's ability to weave it was greater than Evayne's ability to weave spellfire. But she did not suggest, and she did not complain.

In the stands, at the exact spot Carythas had once occupied, Sor na Shannen and a demon of more formidable stature stood side by side. Sor na Shannen was naked; all pretense of clothing and civility were gone. Her skin, like the light around the arch, was vaguely iridescent to Evayne's eyes; her body was distinctly nonhuman. The demon at her side was taller. At seven feet, he towered over his companion. His hair was almost white, and his eyes an unnatural black; he had no horns, no spikes, no fangs—indeed, he seemed to be a tall, very forbidding man.

Which was ill indeed.

There was an old Weston adage. *The more human evil's face, the more dangerous the threat.* It was, more often than not, true.

She was already prepared with a countersign when he leaped into the arena, a combatant assured of victory. It was a long drop, but he made no more noise than a cat would have when he landed.

"Greetings, mage."

She waited, ready for combat, but he did not try to approach her, and in a moment she understood the error of her assumption. He walked quickly, his arrogant demeanor melting into near subservience. He crossed the border of runes and wards, taking care to step between the golden lines, not across them. Then, in front of the pillared arch, he knelt.

"My lord," he said, his words the loudest that had yet been uttered in the arena. "We bring you two more." He bowed his head; Evayne could see, in the shimmering light of the keystone, the reflection of his face in black marble.

"Kallandras!" Evayne shouted. It was a command.

He heard the demon's words as he rolled, once again avoiding Sor na Shannen's strike. The hair on the nape of his neck stood on end as she readied herself for another.

It faded.

"Kallandras!"

He could not see Evayne, not clearly, but he could hear the command in her words. Taking care to avoid the arch, he began to make his way back to her. His feet made no sound; he held his breath as he moved, and stopped only to renew it.

But there was no further attack.

She reached out for him as he approached; he heard the familiar rustle of her sleeves. He hated to touch her. He took her hand.

Together, they stood in silence.

The darkness confined by the pillars began to convulse. The demon remained as he was, head bowed to floor, shoulders curved to ground. Shadow shot over his head, a living bloom of writhing tentacles—the twisted version of a giant human hand.

Evayne had no time to draw breath. The tentacles wrapped themselves around her body and lifted her above the ground. Kallandras was likewise taken, but he was silent.

She screamed as the darkness pierced her flesh. It left no mark, but it burrowed, searching her body for the spirit it contained—for the shard of immortality that only the gods themselves could touch. She wanted to fight, but she couldn't; she couldn't concentrate. She was a mage, but the center of her power had been distorted and shifted; it was unreachable.

Only the reaving was real.

Somebody uttered a piteous cry in the distance. It wasn't Kallandras, but she didn't know the voice—she had never heard herself scream so. She reached out with one hand, then with both, trying to touch something that was not darkness or torture.

Her right hand found Kallandras again. Their fingers locked tight, their hands became rigid. Her left hand brushed against cobwebs, or dust; something light, but definitely real.

The cries that continued piteously in the background were distant, the whisper that touched her left ear was not.

Daughter of destiny, you have been long in coming. It was a quiet, strong voice, the whisper of an older man who had lived his life assured of his power. It was Myrddion's voice; having heard it once before, she would know it anywhere. *I have been waiting for you, and now that you are arrived, my travail is at an end.*

I was, as you are, a seer-born. The future came in dream and vision, and I saw the end of the world—but so far ahead of my time that only by becoming fell or dark could I hope to survive to fight it. I could not chance it, for once the Winter road is walked, who can say what will become of the walker? Yet I could not turn away.

I went to Fabril, and to the houses of the Unknown lord called guardian of man. Guardian of Man. It was not a name that Evayne had heard before, but she would remember it later. *And between us, we forged the five. Some part of our power is in them, and in this way, we give our legacy to those who must be mankind's warriors.*

I give into your keeping that which you seek. They are not yours, but they are your responsibility. You are their guardian, and I trust you to know when your guardianship is at an end. Do not attempt to remove them, or once they are removed, to retain them.

I give you earth, air, fire, and water; the elements that you know. But I give you a fifth ring as well. It is not meant for this world. It is haven on the darkest of roads, comfort in the most evil of places.

And now, I have kept my vow; I have fulfilled my responsibility. May you one day know the peace that I will now know. For I do not think I could have traveled your road.

I have one last gift to offer: Be free!

Evayne lurched forward at the force of the words—and the magic inherent in them. She looked down at the darkspell around her and saw the shadow streaked with fissures of light. The screaming stopped as the fingers of Allasakar lost purchase. Suspended in air by the crumbling remnants of the dark lord's spell, Evayne could see again.

The marble just below her feet was buckling and heaving. The solitary ward above it was a green, mottled glow. It twisted, resisting the movement beneath it.

"NO!" The voice was Sor na Shannen's and the demon lord's combined. "My Lord!"

But it was too late. A fissure cut across the glow, darkening and lengthening as the rock struggled to cast off the ward's magic. Another crack joined it, and another, and another.

Evayne watched. Everything moved slowly. Even the shadow that bloomed once again like a flower of darkness from the arch grew sluggishly as it crept toward her. She watched, and as the last of the pain receded, she saw a glint of silver light. The mists.

The path was opening beneath her feet.

She could not turn quickly enough to see Kallandras. She didn't have to; her hand still clutched his. *Mother,* she thought, *have mercy; we are all your children, no matter to whom we make our pledge.*

The marble shattered, but its shards turned to vapor before they touched her unprotected legs. A small, sharply edged pit opened up beneath her, and it was filled with light.

Five stars rose, and behind each, a trail of magic seared itself into her vision; Myrddion's brand. Two were blue, one green, one red, and one a silver that stung the eyes. They came, across the shadow itself, to rest upon the fingers of her outstretched hand. Warmth tingled against her skin.

She did not look. Instead, she called upon her magic, upon the core of the power that she had used little of this eve. She could not take Kallandras with her; the path opened only for her, and no other living being, be they god or mortal. But she could see him to safety if he was not already consumed. That much power, she had.

Lowering her chin, she focused her will. Rings of gray light rippled down her right arm in a wave. They grew in number, in speed, in intensity, and as they touched Kallandras, they began to converge. Unlike all else, they moved quickly. Time's gift.

She whispered a benediction as the mage-rings connected and the spell's power fled her body in a cold rush. Shadow-magic collapsed in on itself and she heard the roar of an angry god as Kallandras vanished into Averalaan.

The otherwhen opened around her. Her feet touched the path and the silver mists shot up like impenetrable walls. Her legs began to tremble. As did her arms, her back, her lips. She couldn't control them.

You pushed too hard, she told herself reprovingly. *Called too much.* Her knees and her palms struck the ground. Nausea hit as the shaking got stronger. She gave in to it—she hadn't the will left to do otherwise.

Slowly, and with great difficulty, Evayne began to crawl along the path. The road could only take her someplace if she journeyed along it. The distance didn't have to be great—it just had to be measurable. She threw up twice and gagged continuously, but concentrated on keeping her tongue flat against the roof of her mouth. The seizures were dangerous, otherwise. Her right hand moved. Her left. Her right leg. Her left.

The path delivered her slowly into the world. The mists cleared; day came, with a sun far too bright, and a season too cold. Her face was three inches above stone steps, and that distance grew less very suddenly.

Chapter Eight

WHY DID YOU HAVE TO bring me to this particular house? Evayne asked of the otherwhen in a tone of mild disgust. She received the usual answer: silence.

She was still in the year 402, although it was later as the seasons went. She didn't understand why she was in this particular time, but was certain that she would come to. When she had the strength.

The roof in the house of healing was adorned by only a single, fine crack in the plaster between the large, darkly stained cross beams above Evayne's bed. She knew it well. During the past week, between intermittent seizures, she had done little but stare at it. The walls were a shell-white, and the sill of the single window was the same dark stain as the cross beams.

"Lady, can I get you anything to drink or anything to eat?" The voice of the slender young woman contrasted with the severity of her starched, stiff uniform. Her smooth, uncallused hands and her pale skin identified her as an apprentice healer, and not just an orderly.

"No. But thank you." She turned her head to the side to see a look of disappointment cross the young attendant's features.

"Will—will you be staying much longer?"

"That," she replied dryly, "is probably a decision best made by Healer Levec. You could ask him."

The girl's face told her just how useful that would be. She dropped an almost courtly bow, and then wandered out of the room, lingering a moment in the doorway as if hoping to be recalled.

The orderlies and the attendants of the house were, for the most part, young men and women with romantic notions. The idea of a mysterious, wealthy woman, who was no doubt a mage given her unusual form of dress, spoke to their imaginations.

Evayne smiled, wondering what the truth would do. She propped herself up gingerly and tried to look out the window. The curtains were drawn; it was probably dark. Her elbows began to shake, and she sank back. Ruefully, she looked at her wrists. They were thin and fragile to the eye. She had come rather close.

Lamplight played off her fingers, glinting over gold.

It's no wonder they think I'm wealthy, she thought, as she turned her hand slowly in front of her face. On her forefinger was a thick, golden band. It wasn't plain, but rather delicately veined, as if a leaf had been pressed into the mold when the gold was being poured. At its heart was an emerald that flashed with the green of the first forest, cut in a rectangle with a flat, perfect face.

On her second finger was a band that seemed somehow orange in the light. Although it, too, was gold, it looked like liquid caught beneath crystal—molten precious metal. It held a ruby that was bright, not dark; the color of fire, not of blood.

Where fire stirred, water stirred also. The third ring, on her ring finger, was fashioned of white-gold. It almost looked as if the band were ice, for frost seemed to have covered the ring as if it were glass in a cold climate. The sapphire looked like the heart of the north wind, but no matter how long she stared at it, she could not see its depth. She stopped trying and turned her gaze to the last ring she had.

For some reason, it drew her attention away from the others, although it was a simple, rounded band, with no gems and no intricate design to mark it. She thought it made of white-gold, at first—but the weight was wrong. Later, she would have it properly identified. If she could find someone willing to do so when she couldn't take the ring off her finger.

This ring was the fifth that he had spoken of.

She was enough a member of the Order of Knowledge to feel a sharp curiosity. But she shook her head and let her hand fall back to rest against the simple, un-dyed woolen counterpane.

She had four rings, but she was not concerned; she knew where the fifth was. She had seen it many, many times throughout the years. She had even asked about it once, although Kallandras, at thirty-eight, hadn't provided her, at twenty, with much of an answer.

No, not true, she thought. A rare and genuine smile of pleasure touched her face in the privacy of her room. He had said, *It was the gift of a friend, and you will come to know her well in time.*

You would never have said that that eve. What changed you?

"Ah, I see rumors of your alertness aren't exaggerated this time." A dark-haired, dark-skinned man entered the room. It was obvious that he was the healer on duty, and equally obvious that he was the senior member of the house. He wore around his neck the open-palmed symbol of the healer-born. Upon his face, he wore an expression of distinct disapproval.

The healer-born could not affect someone suffering from mage-fever. Nothing— be it herb, spell, or potion—could. But there wasn't a healer alive who could accept that gracefully, or if there was, Evayne hadn't met her.

"You weren't terribly careful, this time."

"No, Levec," she replied meekly.

"You're never careful. Never."

"No, Levec."

"What's the excuse? Years ago, you could at least blame it on youth—but you aren't a child, or even a wayward, serious young woman, anymore—and it seems to me that you are often more severely injured or at risk than you ever were.

"If the young do not gain in wisdom as they age, what sort of example are they?" His fingers rapped the bedpost as he spoke, and his brows, which were lovely and thick, drew down into a single, fierce line. Levec was not a man who appeared, at first glimpse, to be of the healing persuasion. Nor, for that matter, at any glimpse.

The path had a cruel sense of humor at times; Evayne, exhausted but recovering, could do nothing to stem the flow of the healer's pointed tirade.

She knew that Espere survived, because she had seen her, years ago, in the other-when—an older woman, if no less dangerous. She didn't know how she had managed to escape the cathedral in Vexusa; "how" was often the single question that she hadn't the luxury of asking.

Well, forest sister, I hope you found what you hunted; with your aid, I found what haunted me. Light bubbled in the ball she held between her palms. The room itself was dark; the curtains drawn, the door closed. It was a pity that it couldn't be locked, because she desired no interruption. The use of the ball often made her more vulnerable.

And if Healer Levec saw it, he would almost certainly feel compelled to attempt to remove it from her keeping—a task which would see them both involved in . . . too severe a disagreement.

Don't push, Evayne. You've been here for a week already—you can't afford more time.

But ignoring her own advice was a habit of youth—one that she had not entirely lost with wisdom and experience. She searched the mists again and again, but they gave her no answers.

They did give her another glimpse of Stephen of Elseth. He was fighting with his huntbrother—did they do nothing but argue?—over the apportioning of a hunt's kill. Youth robbed his features of their ability to sting. He was fair-haired, slender of build, and graceful in carriage—but he was not yet adult, even if he hovered on the brink.

She watched him for a while before sleep took her away from the vision.

And it was in sleep that her answer came.

The ball was a deliberate use of her birthright. She summoned the mists and the strands of her soul's history, her soul's light, and they came. They bore her examination, if not willingly. Not all seers were gifted with the creation of such a ball. Evayne thought she might be the only living seer to walk the Oracle's path, although in the distant past, those seer-born had made the trek to the Oracle's hidden testing ground as a matter of course. If one could survive the Oracle's path, the Oracle would create the soul-crystal. If one died, it was no longer necessary. Many had died.

But before they walked the Oracle's path, they knew themselves seer-born because of their dreams and their visions. The dreams of the seer had a texture and a reality that a return to the waking world could not force one to surrender.

She had such a dream now.

It was brief, but unmistakable. In it, two men she did not recognize met in a well appointed room. One appeared to be a messenger; he handed the older gentleman a scroll. Their conversation had no bearing on the information it contained.

It wasn't important to hear their words; they were obvious. For one of these men wore a symbol of the Order of Knowledge—a bad sign, but not, unfortunately, a unique deviation. The other man wore, seared into his left ear, the mark of the chalice.

The mark of the Kovaschaii.

Their discussion was irrelevant; the name of the target was *never* spoken. But in the seer's vision, warped and guided by an unknown twist of fate, a face was superimposed, like a ghost, over the two men.

It was Stephen's face. He wore a green cape, Hunter's green, with gold, gray, and brown edges, and a cap that covered his hair and shadowed his face. The cap itself was embroidered with a crest: against a field of green, a sword, crossed over a spear, beneath the horns of a stag in full season.

He was fourteen.

She woke with a start; the ball was already clasped between her palms. She didn't remember falling asleep, but sleep had provided her with the answer that had proved so elusive during her waking hours.

You never take me anywhere without a reason. Her hands were shaking. With determination, she began to search the mists of the now for sight of Kallandras. *Think, Evayne. What did the crest mean? When is it?*

The ring was made of gilded crystal. On his hand, it seemed to fade into nothing but a diamond's flash in the right movement of light. It was a marvel of craftsmanship, with a history that rivaled that of his—of the Kovaschaii. It was the only piece of jewelry that he had ever worn outside of the ceremonies of the brotherhood.

It would not come off of his finger. He had only tried to remove it once, and even then only for curiosity's sake. It was not small—indeed, it fit him as if crafted for his use—but it would not budge. It remained on the thumb of his right hand.

And that was of significance to the brotherhood's ceremonies. On that finger, he had worn, for the minutes of the calling, the ring of the Lady. By it bound, he made his oaths.

His right hand became a fist. He stared at his thumb, seeing, through the crystal, another ring, donned in a smoke-wreathed, darkened hall. His eyes grew opaque in the seeing. It was the one memory that any of the Kovaschaii could call at will—for it was the ceremony that made them one with the brotherhood, and no longer separate from it.

Light flashed; he stiffened and raised his left hand to shield his eyes. The diamond, large and well-mounted, had obviously caught a flicker of sunlight.

Eyes watering, he shook his head and relaxed both hands. Evayne waited for him in the house of healing in the northwestern quarter on Lowell Street near the boardwalk. He didn't know who she would be, this time. He had seen her very young and very old; she was never quite the same person as the woman who had forced him from the Kovaschaii almost four years ago.

He looked at the ring, swallowed, and started to whistle as he walked in a jaunty, purposeful way. The whole of his body was a mask right up to his calm, still eyes.

"I'm sorry, sir," Kallandras said, for perhaps the hundredth time.

"Her brother, are you?" Levec's raised brow bordered on open disbelief, but he shook his head. "Well, I guess you'd have to be."

"Have to be?"

"If I weren't of the same family, *I'd* never claim her as blood-kin." He led the young man down the hall to the steps, and then began to climb them. "But I don't recall Evayne ever giving a family name."

Kallandras shrugged. "She's the boss." It was as close to truth as he'd yet come.

Levec raised a brow again. "Not," he said darkly, "in *this* house, she isn't. She's not well enough to travel—so if you've got any intention of taking her with you, I'd strongly advise you to think again."

"Yes, Healer Levec," Kallandras replied. He opened the door. "Evvie—you *are* here!"

"Evvie" raised a brow in a fashion that made her look quite similar, for a passing moment, to Healer Levec. "You took your time," she finally said dryly. "Are you going to stand there warming the door?"

"You've got an hour, because I'm feeling generous. Don't abuse it. Is that clear?"

"Yes, sir."

"Yes, Levec."

"Good." He was not a rude man, and left them to their discussion, drawing the door firmly shut behind him.

Kallandras half-expected to hear the door lock at their backs. He tensed, and then relaxed when Levec's heavy tread took him away from the door. "I don't think I've ever seen Healer Levec quite so . . ."

"He doesn't approve of my condition," Evayne replied. Then she sat up in bed, straightening her shoulders and raising her chin. *It's good to see you*, she wanted to say. But she didn't. Kallandras was still young and still very angry.

She watched as all show of friendliness slowly fell away from his face. It took a few seconds, but she always found it disconcerting. One instant he was alive with the gestures and habits of life, be it rural, urban, courtly—and the next, he was one of the Kovaschaii, cold and distant in his disdain for the lives that he could so effortlessly mimic—and take. "You summoned me."

"Yes."

"Why?"

"I have to ask you a few questions."

"Ask."

"Why don't you take that chair and pull it up."

He did as she asked; he often did. He could follow a command to the letter, yet still radiate an aura of hostility. Or contempt. "Ask," he repeated, as he sat, placing his hands casually in his lap.

"If you were Kovaschaii—"

He lifted a hand; his right hand. "I will not answer questions about the brotherhood. You know this, Evayne."

"It's not a specific question."

"It's a question. Of yours. I will not answer it."

"Very well. You know me—not as well now as you probably will in the future. Tell me what my chances against you would be if you were sent to kill."

"Kill who?"

"Anyone."

"Evayne—"

"Let me make it clearer. I would know, in advance, who the victim would be."

"Impossible," he said flatly. "You could not know."

"Just answer the question."

"If you knew, your chances would be better than if you didn't. But I wouldn't say they'd be high. Against what you fight, Evayne, we are not sent. You wouldn't be at your strength if you chose to fight me."

"No," she said quietly, and turned away.

"Is that all?" He rose.

"No," she said again. "I have a mission for you."

"And it is?"

"Go to Breodanir. Be there for the Sacred Hunt."

"The what?"

"The Sacred Hunt; it is the festival of the greatest import to the Breodani, and one of their number is always killed in it. It occurs, without fail, on First Day, although preparations leading up to it start weeks in advance. Go to the King's City, and there you will be able to find out all that you need."

"That is the whole of your order?"

"No. There will be a boy there. Stephen of Elseth. He must be protected against any threat. Tell him—tell him that I sent you." Her voice dropped, but she did not turn to face Kallandras. Instead, she waited.

"Evayne." She heard him rise. He pulled the chair slightly on purpose, because when he chose to be, he was completely silent.

"Yes?" She stared at her hands. The room was suddenly too small for both them and their memories.

"Your question. Why did you ask it?"

She didn't answer.

"Evayne."

She wouldn't answer.

It was answer enough for Kallandras. She heard the door open and close with force before she turned to look. Kallandras was Kovaschaii, and even young, he hated to show emotion.

Will you do it, Kallan? Will you do as I direct? She raised her palms to her cheeks and closed her eyes. When she opened them again, the silver-misted walls of the path rose to her right and left. She did not turn back, but a smile helped to erase some of the lines from her face.

Healer Levec was going to be most angry.

Kallandras the bard sat in the darkness of the empty theater, his harp in his lap. His lute was at his side; he always traveled with both. The wind from the sea was moist and cool in the open stands.

Two hours ago, the stands had been full. Every eye in the audience was turned toward him; reckless, he had used a touch of the voice to assure that. The stage lights, protected by large shells, cast a glow beneath him. At times like this, surrounded by light, he could almost forget his loss.

Music helped. The old lays, with their history and their grim tales of sacrifice to duty, were both a goad and a balm. But words, while they had their lovely cadences and intrinsic harmonies, were not necessary. The lute and the harp in isolation had their tales to tell, their sorrows to speak of.

Without words, he let his music weep for him. He offered the audience, in their ignorance, his fear, his self-loathing, and his final determination. He knew it disturbed them, but he had to release his burden—and no member of the brotherhood would now stand to witness or comfort the only member, in all of the

Kovaschaii's long history, to betray them. Sioban might ask about his concert choices, but he doubted it. After the musical play, he had once again returned to the more traditional performance arts.

The audience offered him their left hands, palm out—a gesture of the highest approval. He accepted it gracefully and then melted into the stands to better hear the next performer. Two hours after the end of the set, both audience and performer were gone. He remained.

How could she ask this of him? His fingers strummed the strings of the harp rhythmically, seeking solace, not answers. He shifted the smooth, unornamented frame in his lap and stared into the darkness.

I have not seen my brothers for almost four years, Evayne. Am I to see them now as an enemy?

The air rippled with the dissonance of the chord that he struck. He was, to them, a traitor, but they were his family, his friends. Only for their sake, in the end, had the words of Evayne held sway. For in the end, even the brotherhood could not face a god.

It was a bitter fact: He would willingly have given his life to save the brotherhood—but giving up the brotherhood to save the brotherhood. . . . What was done, was done. But he could not say with certainty that, had he the choice again, he would choose as he had.

Silence surrounded him; the strings were absolutely still. His left hand held the harp, his right was curled into a fist so tight his nails cut the skin of his palm. *I won't do it. I* can't *do it. I will not confront a brother. I—*

Golden light flared in the darkness, half-blinding him. He recognized it as the flash of a diamond reflecting sunlight at an awkward angle.

Except there was no sunlight; not even the fires along the stage still burned. A mile down the boardwalk, near the docks proper, the lights were clearly haloed by the coming sea mist, but they hadn't the power to wake the gem.

He stared at his right thumb in bitter silence.

Chapter Nine

"STEPHEN?" LADY ELSETH SMOOTHED out the wrinkles her hands had put in the folds of her gray skirts.

"I kneel first, and if Gilliam doesn't remember, I knock his knees out from under him." Stephen's gaze was not upon Lady Elseth, but rather upon the head of the stairs.

"Yes, but do it surreptitiously."

Her tone of voice caught him, and he gave up watching for Gilliam. Gilliam wasn't late, after all. On this occasion it was Stephen who had finished packing and preparing early. He stepped over his single, modest trunk and made his way to Lady Elseth's side.

"Do you think Gilliam will remember—"

"I packed it," he said, placing an arm around her shoulders just as Norn would have done had he not been busy with Soredon. "With mine. If he forgets his trunk, we'll still have our uniforms, don't worry." He smiled, but it was only half real, and it vanished as she met his eyes.

"You'll know soon enough that I'll never stop worrying. Not now. This is the first year you won't be here when Soredon goes off to the Sacred Hunt. You'll be with him." Her hands had returned waywardly to the skirts, and were already kneading new creases into them before she caught herself.

Maribelle turned around a corner, catching their attention as she made her way down the stairs. At eleven she'd lost both curls and lisp, and she no longer tried to worm her way into the kennels at her older brother's heels. She could read better than Gilliam, which wasn't saying much, and she could write better, too, which said even less. Numbers were one of her stronger points, and already she had shown her willingness to take part in Elseth duties at her mother's side.

Still, her face hadn't lost all of its baby fat, and when it came right down to it, she was a full four years younger than Stephen, so he rolled his eyes at the tilt of her chin, a movement that she didn't fail to catch.

"Mari," her mother said, gently pulling away from Stephen's arm. "I was afraid you would miss the farewells." Her skirts rustled as she moved to her daughter and caught her in a hug.

Maribelle's arms returned her mother's embrace, and Stephen felt a twinge of envy.

But there's only so much comfort you can offer the Lady, Norn had said, *and it's very little when it comes time for the Sacred Hunt. You'll go with the men, now—and you'll have your chance to die like the rest of them. You can't do anything to make her feel good about it, Stephen, but if it helps you, you can try.*

He sighed as he watched his mother and his sister pull apart, wondering which was harder: to stay and to worry, or to go and be at risk. Loss or death? He shivered, feeling a morning chill that the fires couldn't protect him from. The nightmare image of Bryan's corpse warred with the empty hollowness of William's loss: his first funeral. Bryan was horribly dead, but William . . . even after five years, William was barely alive. He had his dogs, which helped—and he hunted without benefit of huntbrother—but even among Hunter Lords, William was withdrawn and silent. The glory had gone out of the hunt. The loss of Bryan would never be lessened with time; Stephen was certain of it.

"Stephen?"

He spun to face the open door, aware that he hadn't heard its hinges at all. Norn peered in. "We're almost ready. Is the young master down?"

Maribelle snorted. "Gilliam?" Her mother very quietly whispered something that neither Stephen nor Norn could hear, but the meaning of the words was made plain by the flush they engendered in the young girl's cheeks.

Soredon joined them before Gilliam did. He walked over to Elsabet's side and draped an arm across her shoulders. Her expression, as she leaned into his embrace, was one of resignation and fear. Stephen knew it well; for seven years he had waited quietly while Norn and Lord Elseth embarked upon their duty: the Sacred Hunt. This day marked the beginning of Stephen's adulthood in Breodanir, and he, too, would add to the burden of her worry from this moment on.

"Can someone help me with this?"

All eyes looked up to see Gilliam teetering at the railings. A large chest, one double the size of Stephen's modest choice, was precariously caught in a grip that was faltering even as they watched.

"Gilliam!" Elsa shouted, as Norn began to run up the stairs. She had been worried about whether or not he would show up in appropriate dress, but her eyes slid off the heavy gray jacket and the brown pants that were folded haphazardly into leather boots without comment. "Why didn't you send for the servants?"

He answered her by dropping the chest. It clattered down the stairs, narrowly missing Norn. Everyone scattered as the large, heavy box came to rest. That the lock held surprised them all.

Not an auspicious beginning.

* * *

"I don't suppose it will do any good to tell you all to keep an eye on each other?" Lady Elseth stood on her toes to give her son a kiss on the forehead. He was a boy for these few days more; not until the King called and accepted him would he be a Breodani Hunter.

"Mother."

"I'll take care of him," Stephen piped up. He held out his arms and caught Lady Elseth in a very tight hug. If Gilliam had become too self-consciously grown up for this sort of display, Stephen had not. He was going to have a few words with Gilliam on the subject once they were under way. "I'm sorry I won't be staying."

"So am I." Their foreheads touched. "You'll be back, though. I keep telling myself that."

"And you don't really believe it until you see it," Norn added. "Now enough of your time with the whelp—what about the real Hunters?" Breathing and being hugged by Norn were mutually exclusive activities; Lady Elseth couldn't have talked had she wanted to. She caught his beard in her fingers and yanked almost playfully.

He set her down without comment. He had been through this routine for so many years, he knew there was nothing to be said. It would wait until they returned, because it had to.

Last, she turned to Soredon.

"This is his first Hunt," he said quietly, a hand on either of her shoulders. "Try to be as proud as he is, Elsa."

"I am." Her voice was soft. "The Hunters have their risk, and all of Breodanir depends on it. But we Ladies have our risk as well. I am proud for Elseth. I am worried for Elsabet."

He kissed her quietly, holding her face in the palms of his hands. Then he stepped back, still staring into her red-rimmed eyes. She wanted to cry; he knew it, and knew she would not.

"I love you." He turned. "Is everything ready?"

Norn nodded.

"The dogs?"

Gilliam nodded.

"Then we're off!"

The roads were very quiet for most of the journey. This year, because Stephen and Gilliam were to be presented to the Master of the Game, they had to arrive two weeks before the Sacred Hunt, rather than the usual four days.

Gilliam was in good spirits—this was the pinnacle of his youthful dreams. He would walk into the King's court with his huntbrother by his side, kneel, and be given the dress cloak and horn of the Hunter. He would be allowed to take part in the Sacred Hunt, and there he would further prove himself.

And on his return home, he would finally be able to form his own pack. Corwel's newest brood looked promising, and although Corwel was now too old to be the pride of Elseth, he was still capable of breeding true.

Soredon was happy as well, especially when he contemplated the arrival in the capital of his son and heir. Gilliam was everything that one Hunter-born could aspire to. He was young, strong, fast—and his ability with the trance had grown so quickly Soredon half-regretted that they hadn't had time to choose a proper pack for Gilliam's first appearance. Gilliam would hunt with a select number of Soredon's dogs.

Corwel would be at the head of the pack that Soredon had chosen for himself. He wasn't pack leader anymore, but he was second, and if Terwel was separated from him, Soredon was certain that Corwel would still make a good show of himself.

He knew it was foolish to take Corwel along; any of the younger dogs would be better for show. He was becoming sentimental. Well, yes, but what of it? He would hunt Corwel just this one last time, and they would face the Hunter's risk together, as they had for so many years.

We're both getting older, he thought with wry affection. He turned to look at Gil, who was positively impatient as he sat astride his horse, and shook his head with a smile. *It may well be time soon; the younger generation will eclipse us both.*

But we're not doddering and useless yet.

"They aren't worried, are they?" Stephen wrapped another scarf around his throat, and fastened the highest button of his jacket. It was chilly here; the wind across the plain had few trees or rocks to break its passage.

"Them?" Norn looked over his shoulder. "No, probably not." He, too, wore an extra scarf for warmth, but the color of his jacket was deep, warm green. Hunter's clothing. "I've rarely met a hunter who was. Not an oath-bound Hunter, at any rate. Why?"

"Are you?"

"Worried?" Norn nodded. "Of course. I always am. I have to be—I've got two people to worry about, since one of us isn't worrying about himself. Why?"

"I'm worried." Stephen's voice was quiet. "I'm worried that Gilliam will make a fool of himself in front of the King. I'm worried that we'll do something wrong before the Sacred Hunt. I'm worried that I'll forget all of my horn calls—it isn't as if they're used anywhere but the Sacred Hunt." He took a breath and shadowed his eyes although the sun wasn't sharp, and the light was muted. "But mostly I'm worried about . . ." The words stopped, trailing into the quiet rush of wind against the ears. All of a sudden he didn't want to say them. For Stephen, words had always had a special magic, a feel of permanence, a ring of truth. To give voice to his fear was more than acknowledgment; it was empowerment.

"The Hunt is always a risk," Norn said quietly. He glanced at his companion, seeing an odd echo of the boy he had once been, traveling to the King's City and the duty of the Sacred Hunt for the first time.

If Soredon felt a pride and continuity in the legacy of his blood as he contemplated Gilliam, Norn felt something equally strong as he rode beside Stephen. They were not related, but in the end, they were bound by a choice and a purpose that made them unique in Breodanir. Hunters were chosen by birth and by blood, with all of the abilities that the Hunter God could grant. Huntbrothers were the link between the Hunters and the rest of the populace, and they chose the same risk as their sworn oath brothers, without any of the God-granted advantages.

But they chose anyway, and they held true to their vows. If a brotherhood like this could extend forever outward, in all of the facets of Breodanir society, miracles could be achieved, he was certain of it. And proud of it as well.

"Why aren't they afraid?"

"You wouldn't want them to be," Norn answered. He shifted in his saddle, keeping an eye on the road. It was muddy, even with the chill, and the horses were not always as watchful as they could be. "Well, maybe you do now. But it isn't a pretty sight, and it feels wrong. Like a little breaking of the vow."

"But why aren't they afraid?"

"I don't know. Have you asked Gilliam?"

Stephen shook his head curtly. No.

Norn knew that Stephen would never ask. "Ah, well. I've never asked Soredon either. But I think it's because they live for the Hunt, those two and the others like them. You and I live for more because we can't feel what they feel—no matter what the Hunt or the conditions of it, we'll always be strictly human, strictly normal. The God-touch—the Hunter's trance—it's not for us. We'd never be able to attain it. So we want what other people want. Family, friends, a little knowledge outside of nets and couples and boar spears and dogs."

"You've never married outside."

"No." Norn closed his eyes for a moment. "And I won't either. Don't ask, Stephen; it's silly enough, and it isn't relevant. You may well marry as you please and find those who will be happy to accept your troth." His lips turned up in a smile, and his eyes softened.

"I don't know." Stephen shot a glance at Gilliam's straight, gray back. "I don't know how I could have a family and Gilliam at the same time."

Norn's laughter caught the attention of their brothers. He waved them on, still laughing into his beard. "Aye, there's truth in that. But he isn't your life, even though he may be your death in the end. You'll find a life that calls you yet, and you'll have to balance your vows with your aspirations." His laughter left a red glow at his cheeks. "It's the life of a huntbrother, Stephen. And it's true: When you're young enough to make the vow, it's always the easiest. Growing into it gets harder year by year." He shook his head. "Perhaps you will make the choice that we did, Soredon, Elsa, and I."

Norn's voice, full, deep, and tinged, every word, with affection, told no tale of regret at the choice he had made. Stephen gripped his own reins firmly and tried not to think of the Hunter's Death. He didn't want to die it, and he didn't want Gilliam to die it either. But he was certain that it was for him; so certain that he could not speak to Norn of it for fear that the speaking would make it real. Still . . .

"What does it look like?"

"What?"

"The Hunter's Death."

"No one really knows, Stephen. And it's better so—although, when we reach the King's court, you'll see at least five artistic depictions of it. The only thing these artisans agreed on is size: It's big. Everything else—fangs, claws, number of legs, number of heads, color, shape—that changes depending on the artist. But the finest artists in the kingdom have turned their hands to the subject more than once—you'll even find a sculpture by Ovannen himself in the grand foyer."

It wasn't the answer he'd hoped for. He was silent, and after a moment, Norn continued.

"What does it look like? That's a question that every Hunter, and every hunt-brother, asks. But the only way to get an answer is to die the Hunter's Death, and no one rushes eagerly into that. Well, no huntbrother. The Hunters . . . I'm certain that each and every one of them dreams about facing the Hunter's Death and taking it in the full glory of a called Hunt.

"But say that it looks like this: Nightmare, fear, and a very dark desire. This is what the artists have done. When we arrive, I'll show you."

It gave Stephen a very odd feeling to pass through the gates of the King's City. Years had passed since last he'd walked these streets, and they were no longer snow-covered or cold. It was almost spring, almost First Day, the time of renewal when the new year began. Even this close to the city gates he could see the brown and greens of the Mother's followers as they set up their banners to line the main thoroughfare beside the banners of the Hunter Lords. He felt young again, in the worst possible way, as the arches of the gate trailed fingers of shadow down his back.

Since leaving the King's City with Lord Elseth and Norn, Stephen had never had cause to return. He wished that he had never been given cause, and then felt ashamed of the impulse. Gilliam glanced up, and steadied his horse into a waiting step as Stephen approached. He couldn't just bring the horse to a stop, no, not Gil.

"Something wrong?"

Stephen shrugged. He could say no, but there was really no point. If Gilliam hadn't known something was wrong, he wouldn't have stayed his horse. "Just nervous."

"Why?" It wasn't the Hunt, and Gilliam knew it. Stephen's fears about the Hunt were crystal clear and completely unique in feel. Gilliam ignored those because it had been made clear, by a succession of heated arguments, that Stephen wished them to be ignored.

"I keep expecting to see Marcus come pounding down the road looking for me." He said it sheepishly, and placed a hand firmly on the pommel of his sword. "Not that I wouldn't be able to defend myself now."

"But you couldn't then." Gilliam shrugged. "Maybe we should leave Father and Norn at the castle. We can go looking for this Marcus ourselves and teach him a lesson."

"Don't even think it, Gil." Norn's voice was crisp and clear. Not a hint of amusement gentled it.

Unfazed, although the interruption was unexpected, Gilliam whirled in his saddle. "But it's just—"

"Nothing." The older man replied, just as crisply. "You're here in your official capacity as Hunter-aspirant of Breodanir—you don't have time to settle some petty score from bygone years. You hunt for the land's blood, not for the blood of a den warden. Clear?"

"Yes, Norn."

"And you, Stephen. You aren't a child anymore, and you aren't a den rat. No den could claim you now, even if one were foolish enough to try. You're of Elseth, and you *will* leave your fears of childhood behind. Is that clear?"

"Yes, Norn." Of the two, only Stephen's quiet acknowledgment held any conviction. Norn hesitated a moment, and his hands bunched the reins in fists. Stephen could practically hear the older man's inner dialogue as he weighed Gilliam's impulsive determination with Stephen's ability to rein it in.

At last he nodded. He swung his horse around and sidestepped Gilliam's black gelding before looking back over his shoulder.

"Gilliam, you are here as an Elseth Hunter. If you embarrass your father or do anything to disavow the responsibility of that title, Lord Elseth will be furious. Rightly so."

Sullenly, Gilliam nodded. But he was too used to arguing with his own hunt-brother to just let the matter drop into silence, even though the conversation had already drawn the ears of passersby. He glared rudely at an elderly matron who was obviously on her way to market. She blushed, pulled at her kerchief, and began to fiddle with the straps of her basket.

"Gil!" Stephen whispered, as he reached for Gilliam's shoulders. Gilliam ducked his hand.

"But we've got rights, Norn! We protect our own!"

Weary and annoyed, Norn shook his head. "You're your father's son!" He didn't even look back over the broad green of his shoulders to acknowledge Gilliam's shout.

Stephen didn't feel uneasy about Marcus anymore. Norn's words had penetrated deeply enough to drive that ghost away. Instead, he settled into the familiar worry about ceremony and custom.

Gilliam felt the change in his huntbrother's mood, and it only incensed him more. He knew what Stephen was worried about—but did *everyone* he was traveling with have to assume he was an idiot? With a very curt nod, he yanked at the reins of his horse and sent it cantering down the city streets.

Stephen sighed as an echo of Gilliam's anger flittered past. With more concern for his own mare—and her mouth—than Gilliam had shown, Stephen brought up the rear and followed the thoroughfare to where the King's castle lay in wait.

The castle did little to still Stephen's fears; it was a grand old building—and the work of the maker-born was in evidence everywhere, from the solid, sheer surface of the outer walls, to the high balustrades and buttresses of the twin towers. A stag seemed to leap in white, hard life, from the very heart of the gate; beneath it, the poles of the portcullis cast evenly spaced shadows.

The gate shadowed them, and it was not plain either, for above their heads in the archway was the bold relief of a Hunter and his *lymer* as they sought out prey in the quiet alabaster of the King's wood.

If he had just come to visit, Stephen would have been tingling with excitement and joy. Past the second portcullis, rearing on two legs, was a bear—but so ferocious a bear, and with such large teeth, that Stephen knew for a fact the artist had never truly seen one hunted. Yet even in ignorance, the sculptor had managed to portray nature's primal anger and defiance—thus did the hunted become, momentarily, the hunter.

"It's a fine work, isn't it?"

Stephen looked down at the voice, and realized that a man in royal livery was waiting patiently at the reins. He blushed and looked around; all three of his companions were unhorsed and waiting. Soredon looked annoyed—which meant, of course, that the dogs had been kenneled by someone other than a "real" Hunter. Gilliam was bored and impatient, and Norn was smiling quietly.

He slid off Dapple's back with a mumbled apology. The man in brown, green, and gold only smiled. He was older than Stephen, and his long thin forehead was obviously bereft of hair, although it was capped in gold-rimmed brown. "We don't mind it ourselves. It takes the eyes of a newcomer to lend a little life to the courtyard—and you've the right sort of eyes. Makes me remember how I felt when he," and he gestured at the stone bear, "was first dragged in here."

"Were you here then?"

"I've been here a long time. I'm good at what I do." The man bowed, his hands still firmly upon the reins. "I don't know if I'll be on shift to see you off, but if I'm not, we're pleased to have you. This your first?"

It was pleasantry, nothing more, for the warden knew that Stephen and Gilliam had arrived at the correct time for aspirant Hunters. Still, Stephen nodded quietly.

"We serve our King—and the whole of our country—in the ways that we can. But your way, huntbrother, is hardest; our thanks and our welcome to you." So saying, he turned and led the horse away from the flagstones.

Norn's voice cut across the quiet grandeur of the courtyard. "Don't worry about looking around for a bit. We've got a little wait ahead of us. The keeper of the outer estate is seeing to the Hausworth family, and we won't get our lodgings until he returns. Besides, the first time you cross these gates, they're significant. Do what you can to fix it in memory; it'll all become commonplace soon enough." Norn smiled, his eyes crinkled at the corners. "I did it myself when I first came." He turned, whispered something to Soredon, and left Gilliam in the care of his father. It wasn't necessarily a completely wise choice—two Hunters alone without the wisdom of a huntbrother to guide them—but they couldn't do much damage to their reputations, or each other, here.

"Did the maker-born do this?" Stephen asked, his voice hushed and muted.

"Aye. You can see their touch where their hands have been. Some little, perfect magic. Some quiet impressions. There—do you see the awnings with the ivy creepers? By the fountain."

Stephen nodded.

"They're stone. Solid as my wrist. But don't they seem to move with the breeze?" Norn shook his head in an echo of Stephen's wonder. "That's the maker-born though; if they can't have the raw materials they need, they'll force what they want out of the ones they do have."

"Have you met them?"

"Them?"

"The maker-born."

"Aye, some. Why?"

"What are they like?" Stephen reached out gently to touch the claws of the bear.

"Like anyone else with a mission or a talent. The Hunter-born live for the Hunt, the healer-born live for the healing—and the maker-born live for the making. Of course, they've got a little more leeway, and a little less similarity of personality, but that's to be expected. They choose what they learn to make, after all.

"The maker-born who worked upon this castle was a foreigner at one time. He came here to create a residence worthy of any king, and he stayed. You'll see his hand in the upper city as well. The maker-born who sculpted the bear—she's an artist. No buildings or carpentry for her; she works from different impulses. But the gift is the same in either." His arm caught Stephen's shoulders companionably.

"You and I, we don't have talent to drive us. Makes you wonder, doesn't it? Why do we do all of this? Why do we take our oaths?"

"I don't know about Stephen," Lord Elseth said, coming out of nowhere to stand at his huntbrother's elbow, "but in your case it was probably just another chance to talk."

"Aye," Norn's eyes sparkled, "and at that, a chance to do it without your interruptions. Are we ready to go?"

"*We* are." Soredon stood aside, the tilt of his brow bringing shadowed lines along his square forehead.

"Stephen?"

"Hey! Don't touch that! What are you doing? Get out of here! OUT!"

The raised voice was unmistakably Gilliam's. Stephen recognized it, muffled though it was by two doors and a wall.

Oh, no. The lid of his small chest fell with a bang, crunching dress breeches that were halfway out. He had no time to put his boots on. In the seconds that he considered it, he heard another shout.

He wasn't worried for Gilliam; Gilliam wasn't frightened, just angry. Well, not even really angry. But very, very annoyed. He wasn't quite out of his room when he heard Gilliam's door slam shut. As he peered out, he saw the flying brown, gold, and green of heavy skirts. Wisps of dark hair trailed beneath a golden cap and down a smocked back.

Lady Elseth was going to kill him.

Angry, he walked over to Gilliam's door and wrenched it open. "Gilliam, what in the Hells did you just do?"

Gilliam looked up from the mess of clothing and Hunter's wear on his bed. His face was red, and his brows dovetailed neatly; his hands were curled around his horn and hat. "What did *I* do?"

"That's what I asked." Stephen took a deep breath, crossed the threshold into the room itself, and closed the door behind him.

"I got back here from Father's room and found that—that girl snooping through my things!" He threw the hat down and pushed his dark hair out of his eyes. "So I asked her to leave."

"Asked? Gilliam, half the hall must have heard you!"

"So? Is it my fault if they were listening?"

"Gil . . ."

"Look, you aren't my mother, you're—"

"I'm your huntbrother. She was a *maid*, Gilliam, not a 'girl,' and she was doing her duties. You *don't* throw a maid in the royal service out of your room as if she were a common thief!"

As the full import of Stephen's words hit home, Gilliam had the grace to blush. "I was surprised."

"Great. And what are you going to do three days from now? Demand that the Queen get out of your way because she's looking at your sword?"

"I'm not an idiot."

"You're worse than an idiot."

"She shouldn't have been going through my things!"

"Did you leave them in that mess on the bed?"

"I had to find my horn." Gilliam let his hair fall as he picked up his hat again. "And this."

"So you left these rumpled things all over the bed, and it was her fault that she saw them and assumed they were to be put away?"

"She's got no business being in my room."

"Then don't leave things here like that—it's begging for her help." Stephen stomped over to the set of drawers against the wall beside the cherrywood headboard. He grabbed ornate brass handles and yanked so hard the drawer itself came off its rails and fell to the floor. Luckily the carpet muted most of the impact.

"Put them in here," he said, without bothering to pick it up. "Put the drawer back into the dresser when you're finished."

"This is my room, and I'll do what I like in it."

"Oh, really?" Lord Elseth leaned against the door frame with his left shoulder. Both boys gave a guilty start, and both cursed the fact that the door hinges were so well-oiled. Soredon's arms were folded neatly and tightly across his chest.

"Thanks, Stephen," Gilliam whispered as he straightened up and faced his father.

"It's your own fault, you idiot," Stephen replied, his voice as quiet as possible.

"I'm glad to see," Lord Elseth said, looking anything but, "that you've both decided to make yourselves at home here. But in case you weren't aware, this is the *King's* castle, and you are expected to behave like polite, happy young men while you're in it. I don't care if you want to squabble outside of his gates; it's expected from huntbrothers. But do not do it here. Understood?"

"Yes, sir."

"Yes, sir."

They cast very dark looks at each other, and Stephen, barefoot, stomped back to his room. Why, indeed, did anyone choose to take the Hunter's Oath?

"That was careless."

The woman knelt in the center of the golden mandala that had been worked into the large, dark carpet. Her hair, brown and straight, cascaded down her back and cheeks, obscuring her pale face. Her hands, palms out, lay before her; her knees were shaking slightly. The King's colors, caught in the common dress of a chambermaid, looked drab and unseemly in the room's light. She had removed the cap, but had not had time for any other changes.

"Yes, Lord."

The man so addressed nodded quietly. His eyes were hooded by frosted brows; his face lined by the long thin winter of a beard. His nose was his most pronounced feature, and he made the most of his height by looking down it. Silently, he let her fear take root before deigning to speak.

"Still," his fingers curled around a platinum medallion. Four symbols stood in shining relief along quartered lines beneath his hand; one each for earth, air, fire, and water. "The circumstances could have been worse. Are you certain it was only one of the children?"

She nodded without looking up. He had not given her leave to rise. "T-two."

"Two children? Ah, yes. I suppose one was the huntbrother." He let the medallion drop, and it nestled quietly against a black field with a white fur border; the robes of moneyed nobility. "Rise, then."

She lifted her head. Her pretty face, her widened eyes, met his.

"Did you find anything?"

"No, Lord."

"Are you certain?"

"Yes." She swallowed. "You said that I was to look for a very simple horn, with odd markings along the mouthpiece."

"Well, then. I think we can rest in peace for the moment." He smiled. "Our duty to God is done, and we may now consider our duty to less lofty principles."

She froze; her outstretched hands grew pale. Licking her lips, she turned only her eyes away. "I must—must return to my duties, Lord."

"Duties?" His voice deepened. "Ah, yes. But little Linden, that *is* what I spoke of."

"W-what do you mean?"

"Don't you know?" He gestured suddenly, and her whole body stiffened as the air crackled. The door that led to his sleeping chambers flew open and rocked on its hinges. "Your duty to the King of Breodanir means nothing. But your duty to Krysanthos, Priest of Allasakar, may well save your life in the end. Or do you recant?" Even the mention of the Dark God's name was enough to ensure her loyalty. Still, it was a risk to speak it aloud.

Silence again, heavy on her tongue, and the ashen gray of her face. This was always the moment he loved best in these little charades: the sinking anchor of realization, the loss of hope.

He gestured again, with the slightest twist of his fingers, the merest syllable. Her hair fell away from her face, and the golden strings that kept tight the forest-green bodice were suddenly undone.

With magic he held her still, although he knew she would not be foolish enough to run. Her breath, short and sharp, was nearly silent in its panic.

"Come, Linden. Surely others Priests have called upon your services before me."

He did not allow her to answer, but instead raised her to her feet. She walked past him stiffly and almost blankly into the waiting room, to the bed with sheets already turned back.

He would have to kill her sometime, but that was weeks away. Now, he indulged in the luxury of the moment. He would have to finish in hours and send her back to the castle. The Hunter Lords would be arriving within the week, and he still had need of her special access to their rooms.

But he was certain that he would not find the thing that the Dark God feared. After all, his coven had been watchful, and they had seen no reappearance of the cursed Horn that had somehow been stolen from their keeping. Neither had they seen the Spear, although it was less of a concern. It was harder—much—to hide, and had little use without the sounding of that Horn.

Anger lined his face and he turned away from it to view instead the ivory lines of a young maid's body. Soon, very soon now, the wait would be over—and the Hunter's Kingdom would be just another vassal for the Dark Lord's coming empire.

Allasakar would walk, whole, upon the face of the world, as no God had truly done in all of mortal memory. And Krysanthos, the mage-born Priest, would be there at His side, to reap the benefits of years of service.

Chapter Ten

GILLIAM AND STEPHEN WAITED nervously at the side entrance to the King's Hall. Although they were impeccable in their dark-brown velvet jackets, shadow-black pants, and gold-trimmed sashes, they were not nearly so ornate, so full of history, as even the door that lay closed before them. At a distance, that door seemed plain compared with the inlaid and wreathed great hall entrance that the nobles were using now to crowd the halls. But this close, one could see the fine quality of the darkwood beneath the cast-iron band; one could touch the cold stone frame, with its plain, gray surface free of any detailing or sculptor's fancy. This door stood as it had always done since the first day of its making—the passageway for those who would step between youth and adulthood.

"Stop it." Stephen's whisper came from the depths of a carefully placed smile which faltered only as he watched Gilliam fidget.

"When are we going in?"

"When they call us." Sighing, Stephen caught Gilliam's collars and straightened them, as much to soothe his own nerves as to clear away any wrinkles. "Do you know what we've got to do?"

"Walk down the side path to the—"

The door swung open, and a green-robed Priest of the Hunter nodded to them both. Like the door itself, there was a deceptive elegance and age to the man. His robes, although simple, were the purest green of the Hunter; they needed no ornamentation. "Who are you who seek to enter?"

"Gilliam of Elseth and his huntbrother Stephen." Gilliam bowed low, and remembered to keep his arms stiffly at his side.

"And what is your business?"

"We have come to offer our service to the Master of the Game." It was the King's Hunter title, and as such, the only one of many titles that Gilliam found easy to remember. "We have hunted together and we've completed the Triple Hunt."

"And your proof?"

"Here." Stephen stepped forward and held out a small, plain chest. He flipped it open; the rounded and well-oiled lid rested briefly and coolly against his chest as the Priest examined the stag hoof, bear claw, and boar horn carefully displayed therein.

The Priest passed his steady, large hand over the open box. The air tingled around the three for a moment before the Priest nodded to Gilliam. Gilliam left the rigid stance of his bow behind.

"You have done as you have claimed. Come, then. You are judged worthy to seek His audience." The door swung fully open, and the dais which led to the King's throne, and to the Master of the Game, came into full view. The throne itself was inset too far back to be seen without actually entering the room. It bothered neither Stephen nor Gilliam, for they had no intention of turning away.

Gilliam went first, as was his right and duty. He walked calmly, if a little quickly, and he looked neither to the left, with its long, floor-to-ceiling tapestry depicting all of the greatness and glory of the Hunt, nor to the right, at the row of men clad in greens and browns, with their horns at their belts, and their weapons at their sides. They were not young men, not any of them—and they wore the scars caused by both prey and the passing years across their silent features. Stephen could not resist glancing at both the wall and the men, and it was Stephen who would remember it in detail. Quieted by the sight of so much finery and so much experience, he followed in Gilliam's wake, his hands still clutching the box that the Priest had viewed. The effort kept him steady.

He had thought that Gilliam would be the nervous one, because Gilliam hated both public occasions and the crowds that came with them. But Gilliam, in bearing and stride, was already one with the Hunters that he had come this far to join; he didn't falter or misstep.

Stephen did, but only once, when the dais opened up and the throne came into view, and he saw the King upon it. He had never seen the King before, although he had seen his likeness several times on most of the coinage of the realm, both in the lower city as a child and in Elseth as a youth. What he had expected, he did not know, or perhaps it just fled his mind, leaving only the reality behind.

The King was not a young man, but not as old as Soredon either. His hair was black shot through with a glimmering of gray that would one day overtake it all. His eyes, even from this distance, were a deep brown and seemed preternaturally large. He was not overly tall, but even seated he gave the impression of height, although the back of the throne dwarfed him, its simple wood edge bearing the horns of the very Stag itself above him. He wore a circlet of plain gold, yet without it he would still have been known as Master of the Game.

"Not yet," someone whispered with amusement, and Stephen spun around to meet the crinkled corners of gray Hunter's eyes. "You'll be kneeling soon enough—make sure that you do it at your brother's side."

Embarrassment drove awe back to its proper place. Stephen walked briskly up the aisle, closing the distance between Gilliam and himself. His hands stopped their shaking; his pace grew measured and seemingly more confident. But he did not look at the King again. Instead he fastened his gaze neatly at the point on Gilliam's back where shoulder blades bracketed spine.

He's only a man, he thought, but the words were a tickle at his ear. He could not believe them, not when the very air seemed to glow in the perfect, silent hush. During the long trip to the King's City, Stephen had been filled with many fears, most nameless—but among those had not been the fear of failure. He felt it keenly now. Although he knew his hunting craft as well as any huntbrother of his age, he felt raw and inexperienced. His hands began to tremble as doubt dwarfed the significance of the contents of the small Elseth chest.

Gilliam stopped walking and knelt three feet away from the King's throne. Stephen made haste to join him, dropping to one knee as he opened the box and placed it before them both in supplication. He bowed his head.

"Who are you and why have you come?" The Master of the Game spoke at last, his voice as deep and purposeful as any fancy could have made it.

"I am Gilliam of Elseth. In my father's name, I have hunted the Elseth preserves to feed her people and prove my worth." Gilliam's head, bowed, shadowed his legs in the flicker of torchlight and the sky seen through stained glass.

"And what have you hunted there?"

"The three."

"When have you hunted them?"

"In their proper time."

"And who will speak for you?"

"I will." Stephen started slightly at the words; they were distant enough that they offered scant comfort, although he recognized Lord Elseth's booming voice. "While Gilliam of Elseth has hunted in my name, I have hunted in yours."

"So be it. Look at me now, Gilliam of Elseth." The tone of the King's voice changed slightly, a hint of amusement warming its depth. "You have the look of your father about you—and his father before him, if the portrait gallery indeed holds truth." The voice cooled again. "But it is not in seeming that the Hunter judges. Who stands beside you?"

There was an eerie moment of silence before Stephen realized that his voice was meant to fill it. He remembered to keep his head bowed, and found fascinating creases in the dark folds of his tunic to hold his eyes. "Stephen," he said, and his voice grew steady. "Stephen of Elseth."

"And have you hunted at Lord Gilliam's side?"

"I have."

"What have you hunted?"

"The three."

"And when have you hunted them?"

"In their proper time and at the need of the people of Elseth." He almost looked up then, but he stopped himself; no permission and no order had been given. Still, the speaking of the words brought the comfort of an old truth, well understood by both speaker and listener.

"Who speaks for you, Stephen?"

Norn answered from a distance exactly as far as Lord Elseth's. "I do. Stephen of Elseth has hunted at his brother's side at the call of Elseth and her people."

"So be it. Rise, Stephen of Elseth. Rise, Gilliam of Elseth. Come stand before me."

Gilliam stood without effort and paused to offer Stephen a hand up. Stephen took it, leaving the chest behind. It had served its purpose and he did not think he could carry it.

"You have come to offer me your services, and I have seen that you are worthy to hunt with the Master of the Game. But I am also a worthy master. I will tell you of the risk and the Death that you face if you choose this path. There will be no other choice, and you cannot turn from it once you have begun—for all of Breodanir rests upon the choice once made." The King rose then, discarding the finery of his throne. Behind his head, the antlers drew level with the circlet of gold, and he looked like the heart of the living forest.

"You will hunt in my name from this day forward, and I—I hunt in the name of the Hunter. This is my pledge to Him: that once a year I will call the Sacred Hunt, that *he* might Hunt, in return, those who serve him. You will hunt in my name, and perhaps in that Hunt you will earn Breodanir's life by giving your own. But you might choose, in the King's Forest, your own prey, your own hunt; you might bring, on that one day, your own dogs into domains that are otherwise solely mine.

"I accept your service, Gilliam and Stephen of Elseth. Do you choose now to honor your offer?"

Stephen thought that Gilliam would answer immediately and be done with it. Instead, Gilliam turned to him, one eyebrow lifted in question. There was no doubt at all in Gilliam's mind, and no fear; this was the pinnacle of his years of training and hunting. He waited nonetheless on Stephen's word and Stephen's gesture—for no hunter came to the King without a huntbrother, and none left in his service without one by his side.

"We will serve the Master of the Game," Stephen said, his voice very small.

The King raised his hands, and from the recess behind his throne two Priests emerged, each carrying a heavy green cloak. In silence they came to stand, one in front of Gilliam, the other in front of Stephen.

"This is the color of your office. Wear it proudly, Lord Gilliam of Elseth, in my name."

Gilliam smiled and nodded as the gold leaf was fastened across his shoulders; the folds of deep, heavy green fell about his back like a perfect wave.

"And you, Stephen of Elseth, you share in your brother's office. Wear these colors, as befits your station, in the name of the people of Breodanir."

"And in your name, son of the Hunter."

Pleased, the King smiled, and his smile deepened his face, revealing the warmth that lay beneath severity. He nodded again to the attending Priests. Simple horns, with mouths of silver, appeared in their hands. These were offered in turn to Gilliam and Stephen.

Stephen's hands shook as he placed the horn in his sash. He could feel Gilliam's pride and excitement, but when he snuck a glance, no sign of it showed. Gilliam stood a little taller, and perhaps his chest was farther forward than normal posture allowed, but that was all.

"Turn," the King said quietly. "You wear the green of the Hunter now, and you have the blessing and approval of the Master of the Game. From this day forth, at this time, you will journey to the King's City at my behest, and you will hunt in my forest. If you fail to do so, you will be stripped of your title and the honors that you have accepted this day; you will be shunned by the Hunter Lords and cast out by the Priests. No Hunter will speak your name, and your deeds will be forgotten. Your children, should you have issue at that time, will inherit in your stead if you hold the preserves of your family. If you do not, your lands will return to the crown, to be given to others who have proved themselves worthy." The words were harsh, but the King's tone made it clear that they were strictly a formality; he did not doubt those who had become Hunters in his name. "You are among equals now. Go into Breodanir in pride and with determination."

Stephen did not gasp as he turned, but only because he lost his breath for a moment. The ranks of the Hunters that had formed a human wall from the side entrance of this chamber to the foot of the King's dais had somehow changed shape and form. Leading directly to the double doors the Hunter Lords had entered by was a dark, green carpet with a border of gold filigree nestled around brown. On either side of it stood Hunter Lords and their huntbrothers in three evenly spaced ranks. They carried spears by their sides, and they were now unhooded as they all looked, as one man, to the two who had passed the final test.

"Go now. I will call you again within the ten-day for the Sacred Hunt."

Neither looked back; they had no choice, and no inclination, to do other than obey. Slowly, they began their silent procession, and as they did, banners unfurled above their heads. The first, a leaping stag on a white field, held by Hunter Lords, and older ones at that, on either side of the carpet. The second was a golden bear on a green field, held likewise. The third was a boar, black as pitch, again on a green field. And beyond it there was darkness; a field of ebony with a single, broken spear, a solitary broken horn.

Stephen paused before it; he had but to pass beneath it and he would gain the door. But he understood well what it was: the Hunter's Death. Gilliam didn't even seem to notice the way it hung like a pall above the day's ceremony. He walked until its shadow covered his head before he realized that Stephen was no longer in step.

"Yes, Stephen of Elseth," someone said, but although Stephen strained his eyes searching through the ranks closest to him, he could not see the speaker, "you see truly. But you will have no freedom now. You have accepted the path and must pass beneath this shadow, or it will hold you back forever."

"Stephen," Gilliam hissed, before his huntbrother could come up with an answer to that strange voice, "it's just a bloody banner."

A breeze blew in through the open doors, and the spear and horn disappeared in the sheen of moving black cloth. Stephen shook his head and grimaced in sudden embarrassment. "Sorry," he whispered, as he walked quickly to join his brother.

"Doesn't matter," was the terse, but happy reply. "We did it. We're in." He crossed the threshold and waited patiently for Stephen to follow. "And do you know what it means?"

From the seriousness of the expression, anyone other than Stephen might have thought Gilliam had somehow managed to be affected by the ceremony. Bound by more than blood, Stephen couldn't make that mistake, although he might have been happier had he been able to.

"You get to choose your dogs."

"I get to choose my dogs!"

His father came out of the doors and into the nearly empty hall just in time to catch the echo of the words rebounding off beamed ceiling and walls. He arranged the hood to frame his head. "Gilliam!"

Gilliam turned and stopped. "Father?"

Soredon laughed. "Yes, there is the matter of your first pack. We'll have to discuss it now, you and I—after this Hunt, you won't be able to use my dogs anymore."

They started to walk, and Stephen hung back by the doors, waiting for Norn to come out. It was only a few minutes, but long enough to lose sight of the Elseth Hunters as they turned the bend in the hall.

"Stephen, you did well." Norn's hood was a fold of cloth against his shoulder blades. "Where's Soredon?"

"With Gilliam. Ahead. Talking about Gil's hunting pack."

"A bit premature, isn't it?"

Stephen nodded.

"But you didn't say anything?"

"No. He already knows. He doesn't see his death in any of this." His frustration was evident in more than the tone of his voice; his forehead was wrinkled, his brows gathered at the bridge of his nose.

Norn said, "I told you, they never do. Come on, let's get a drink. I'll take you to the Hunter's garden."

"The Hunter's presence was strong today," the King said softly, as the last of his Hunter Lords filed out of the hall. The banners that had formed a ceremonial rite of passage had been curled neatly against their poles. Servants would clear them away soon at the direction of Priests, and they would be held in keeping until next year's passage.

"Yes," was the quiet answer.

"And I gather from your tone, you've a feeling why." The King rose carefully and walked away from the throne, sparing a backward glance for the antlers that rose like white shadow above him. "I'm too old for this, Iverssen. Tell me what it was." He knelt, a solitary man on the dais used when he served as Master of the Game.

What a deadly game.

Iverssen's square jaw tightened as he pulled his brown hood away from his face. A single, white scar that sun and time would never remove ran from his upper right eyelid to the point of his chin. Only a miracle had preserved his sight.

"What it was?" came the testy answer. "Hunter's touch, I'd say." He walked over to where the King knelt and stood before him. The King bent his head a moment, both to hide his irritation and to murmur the Hunter's prayer—the one said only by the King.

Iverssen joined him with a counter-cadence. Their words mingled, at cross-purposes to begin, but in harmony at the end.

"They grow younger every year," the King said, as he slowly removed the gold-trimmed green greatcoat that the passage ceremony demanded. It was followed by the rest of his finery, of which there was little enough: cuff links; two rings; his crown.

"Yes." Iverssen took the coat and folded it, showing as much reverence as he ever did. He snorted as the rings hit his palm, and squinted as light circled the crown. "And not much smarter."

"Iverssen."

"Majesty."

The King rose, clad now in a fine tunic that simply bore his colors in a crest above deep brown; his leggings were even plainer, and of the same color. "I have almost never felt His touch so strongly."

Iverssen nodded gruffly. With a little twist, he made a bundle out of greatcoat and valuables that would set the seamstress screaming. "Almost never?" The question was grudgingly given.

"Maybe never," the King answered, his thoughts turning inward. "You are no younger than I; you know that memory is never a trustworthy truth keeper."

"I don't think I want to hear this," Iverssen said, but he stopped walking so his robes wouldn't rustle.

"It was when I was a boy," the King said quietly.

Iverssen's face became a set study of rigid lines. "Majesty, you—"

"I was four." The King's voice grew distant as he faced a memory that was never very far away. "It was the day I watched my father and my grandmother kill my grandfather for the sake of all Breodanir. I saw what my father was that day, and I never doubted that he would succeed. He looked older, more powerful, and more harsh than I ever saw him before or after. He came to the throne room. I followed him. And he stood," the King turned, "there. In front of the antlers. He was the very Hunter."

Iverssen knew the "he" the King spoke of. "Your father was of the blood, and it ran true. Your grandfather was a foolish and weak man."

"Was he?" The King's voice was soft. "He was a man of great heart."

"What great heart destroys the very people he is meant to rule and protect?" Iverssen's words were cutting; they spoke seldom of this, for this very reason. "Your father was Breodani."

"My father," the King replied, with only a trace of bitterness, "was still judged by the Mother for the crime of patricide. He ruled a scant ten years."

"Majesty," Iverssen said, conveying perhaps less respect than the word demanded, "we are all judged for the crimes we commit, and I believe the judgment was not the Mother's, but rather, Aered's."

"Yes." The King shook his head. "As heir to the Breodani, my father had little choice. I know it. I've been told no less for the entirety of my life—and I believe it's truth. But . . . I remember my grandfather, although not well. He was a gentle man.

"It broke my grandmother and my father. Killing my grandfather was the worst thing that either of them ever did—and they did it for the Breodani.

"My grandfather hated sending the young to their deaths. He listened to the foreigners, and I believe—if no one else does—that he wanted to end the Hunt to save his people. Not more, and not less. If it would not weaken our people, I would make that truth known."

Iverssen's pursed lips and lined brow made his thoughts on that revelation quite clear.

"As I get older, Iverssen, I understand my grandfather's folly too well." The King shook his head, his voice very soft as he spoke what was almost heresy. Iverssen was disquieted, but he had seen the King in many moods. During the ceremonies of the Sacred Hunt—or those leading up to them—that mood was often the most bleak, the darkest. It was not easy to sentence your followers to death. Still, he was King, and the mood must be put aside. They would leave these chambers soon, and melancholy was not a public sentiment. "But the Hunter's power was strong today."

"Yes," Iverssen nodded.

"The Elseth brothers."

"Yes."

"You're being very agreeable," the King said wryly. "It's unlike you, and I'm not sure that I favor the change."

Iverssen snorted. "Agreeable, is that it?" But he started to walk again, absently swinging his precious bundle. "It was those two, yes. I don't know why. But did you see the huntbrother? I didn't think he'd make it to the throne."

"I saw him. And I saw what he did as he left."

"Aye, and I as well. The Death stopped him cold." Iverssen shook his head quietly. "Think he has a touch of the seer-born?"

"Not unheard of," was the equally quiet answer. "But I'm not sure that this is the case here. The Hunter God has some plan that requires one, or both, of them."

"You're certain?"

"As much as I can be. But time will tell, as always. Come; we have barely enough time to change and present ourselves for the festivities. Some young bard has journeyed all the way from Senniel College in Averalaan in order to woo the ladies of the court. I heard his song last eve, and it was . . . pleasant."

"From Averalaan?" Iverssen's frown made clear what he thought of that.

"He's not a dignitary, Iverssen—he's a bard, and a bard-born one at that. You know that the bards form no allegiances or alliances political. They travel with news and music, no more."

It was obvious that the Priest felt the presence of an outsider improper just days before the most important ritual of the Breodani. He started to say as much, when the King held out a hand.

"He makes the Queen laugh, Iverssen. And almost nothing does before the Hunt. I've accepted the young man in the court for that reason. Do you question it?"

"No, Majesty," Iverssen replied, bowing low. To that tone of voice, and that expression, there was no other answer.

"Good," the King said. He turned and continued to walk until he reached the closed door. Iverssen opened it for him, just as the lowest of servants might, and the King passed him by, stopping at the last moment to meet the eyes of his closest friend. The matter of the bard was forgotten, as was his momentary irritation. Only things Breodani remained. "I ask you to pray to the Hunter, Iverssen. I know what happened the last time I felt His presence so clearly. Let there not be so terrible a price associated with it, this time."

"No," Norn said, as he adjusted Stephen's jacket. "The King has no huntbrother. The closest he has is Priest Iverssen. Sometimes Priest Greymarten."

Stephen looked at himself in the long oval mirror; his face was pale, his hair brushed back and drawn up around it. "Why not? He's a Hunter, isn't he?" It was a question that he had often wondered about, but had never pressed until now.

"Not just 'a' Hunter, no. You might have seen the difference today?" Stephen didn't answer the question; Norn shrugged. "The King is *the Hunter* personified, when the Sacred Hunt is called. In the beginning of time, it was the King of our people to whom the Hunter God appeared. And it was with the King that the covenant between the Breodani and their God was forged. The King is the living vessel of the God at the time of the Hunt proper, and that vessel need not be reminded of . . . commonality. Not in the way the nobility must. Because *the Hunter* is *not* common in any way.

"Hold still; I'm beginning to think you've caught Gilliam's jitters."

Stephen waited patiently until Norn drew out of the mirror's vision. "But the King hunts, doesn't he?"

"Yes—" Norn shook his head. "I forgot. You've never hunted with the King. Yes, he hunts. He has his pack, just as Soredon does, as Gilliam will. But he never hunts without the Priests. They tend to him, as you tend to Gilliam. There are also the Huntsmen of the Chamber; when they hunt, they hunt in the King's party. They offer him counsel and they offer him protection.

"Should you become such a one, you will learn an entirely new set of horn calls and obediences and services. The worst of which will be forcing Gilliam to conform to royal protocol.

"With all of that, a King doesn't need a huntbrother. A King has to be closer to God than he does to the commoners, I'd imagine." Norn shrugged. "Doesn't make a lot of sense to me. If the Betrayer had had a huntbrother, we'd never have had the famines and plagues."

"Why not? The Betrayer didn't listen to the Priests either. Why would he listen to a huntbrother?"

"How easy a time does Gil have when he's set on ignoring you?"

Stephen smiled.

"Well, and maybe there you have it. A huntbrother's bond is strong—maybe stronger than the sworn oath the King gives when he takes the crown. You and Gilliam will have Elseth as a responsibility, but you'll have the luxury of watching over each other as well. The King can't afford that partiality; he is sworn to all of Breodanir for his term."

"Do the Kings die in the Sacred Hunt?"

"Stephen, you think too much of death," Norn said quietly. He looked at Stephen's still face in the mirror, and then relented. "A King died once. Harald the Second, if I recall correctly," Norn answered as he walked to the window to see where the sun sat. "It was . . . it was not a good time for the kingdom; his son was too young. The Hunt wasn't called the year after the King's death."

Stephen knew what that meant.

"And you'd know it, too, if you'd more time for our history. That'll come, now that Gil is a Hunter proper and both of you have less to prove. The King's vows are more complicated and subtle than ours were. One day, Stephen, you'll be witness to them, for they must be taken at a gathering of the Sacred Hunt, and the Hunter Lords."

"You've seen them?"

"Aye, but I was young and impressionable. Now come; these festivities are paid for by the crown—do you think to make me miss them?"

"It's a fine new generation of young Hunters, isn't it?" Lady Alswaine looked out at the crowd with a predatory sparkle in her eyes. She had two daughters of marriageable age, and had every intention of pressing their interests with a suitable family. She had been quite the beauty in her time, and even now, with the spark of youthful verve faded, she was still one to catch and command the attention. She lowered the powder-pink fan and turned her gaze upon her companion.

"Indeed," he replied softly. From long habit, his fingers strayed to his beard as he smiled across at her. Few women were his equal in height; she was one.

"What is this, Krysanthos? Have the mage-born become dullards with words in some vain attempt to equal the Hunter Lords?" Her smile was warm and only a trifle edged as it glanced off the back of her husband. There, from the gallery, she could see him surrounded by his hunting companions. They were involved in an animated discussion which no one not born to the Hunt could possibly have any interest in.

"Ah, your pardon, Lady. I was merely looking at the young Hunters. It is, after all, their occasion." He leaned slightly over the edge of the gallery railings. "Who are those two?"

"Which ones? I'm afraid my sight is not as good as it used to be."

He knew that her sight was as poor as an eagle's, but smiled and indulged her; it cost him nothing. "The young, fair-haired one; he's smartly attired—or rather, he wears his clothing like a huntbrother. I believe his Hunter is the dark-haired boy with his hands in the canapes, standing beside Astrid of the maker-born guild."

"Ah, those two." Her voice took on a lilt of interest. "I don't know, but I believe they're from Elseth. Come, why don't we go down and congratulate them on their passage? It is why we're here, after all."

"Why not?" Krysanthos replied, offering Lady Alswaine a perfectly accoutered arm. She smiled as she slid her fingers around the black velvet of his sleeve. They took the stairs carefully and crossed the main floor with ease. The Hunter Lords didn't notice their passage, and the other guests usually made way for Krysanthos; he wore the emblem of the Order of Knowledge, after all, and all who saw it, save perhaps untutored children, knew him for one of the mage-born. Vivienne, Priestess to the Mother, nodded coolly at his passing before turning again to listen to the words of a shy young man.

All of the nobles and all of the noteworthy people of the kingdom came to this feast and this festival of celebration. There—heard more than seen—the bard-born trilled some ageless, deathless melody of a Hunter's bitter rite of passage. At the doors, priests of other orders could be seen making their entrance, chief among them Vardos, justice-born, with his gold-irised eyes, and his grim, severe face.

Lady Alswaine and her escort did not appear to notice their arrival; they were seeking other prey. "Hello," Lady Alswaine said, as she released Krysanthos' arm and walked up to one of the two young men.

Stephen looked up at her and smiled brightly. The hand that she offered, he took, holding it for exactly the right length of time. His hands were dry, and certainly not food encrusted. She would not have offered her hand to Gilliam.

"I'm Lady Alswaine. My husband is a Huntsman of the Chamber."

"I met him earlier. I've heard that he's a Hunter without match, except perhaps for the King himself."

Clearly pleased, Lady Alswaine bowed her head, tipping her fan in Stephen's direction. "You've been listening to him speak, then?"

A little "o" of shock came out before Stephen recovered himself. "He would never admit the truth of any of the tales, Lady." Especially not while she was present.

Lady Alswaine was a tall woman. This was made clear to Stephen when she bent down to whisper in his ear. "Gilliam of Elseth has found himself a fine hunt-brother. You will do Lady Elseth proud—you already have tonight."

"Don't monopolize the young man, Lady."

Stephen turned at the words and stiffened. Years of etiquette lessons took over, and he held out his hand with a smooth smile as he performed the half-bow of equals. The bow was awkward. Stephen's gaze was drawn and held by the platinum medallion that clung round the stranger's throat. A slender crescent, a half moon, and the moon in full circle were raised in a triad that spoke of mystery and the light in darkness. Quartered in the moon at zenith were the symbols of the elements.

"Yes," the man said quietly. "I am of the Order of Knowledge. Let me welcome you to our city."

"Thank you, sir." The words were formal, as stiff as Stephen himself. His fingers and legs tingled with the urge to be gone. The matters of the mage-born were not the concern of common men, and Stephen knew well the folly of trying to bridge the gap. All children, no matter whether they lived as unparented thieves in the lower city streets, or as wealthy scions of the highest families in the land, had heard many of the tales that surrounded the mage-born.

"Let me introduce myself. I am Krysanthos of the second circle. You are?"

"Stephen of Elseth." He looked up and met the mage's eyes. They were brown, palely tinted with flecks of gold and green, and they were clear and unblinking. In stories he had often read about how hair stood on end at the nape of one's neck—and now he was certain it was no fanciful bardic wording.

"You've heard of Elseth, surely?" Lady Alswaine said, as she once again reached for the mage's arm.

"Lord Elseth is a Master Hunter, I believe—and Elseth is a well governed preserve." He did not raise his arm, or otherwise acknowledge Lady Alswaine's unspoken request. Instead he stared at Stephen.

Stephen couldn't look away. He froze as the eyes of the mage-born man came to life with a luminescent flare of blue. He could not even gasp as that light flashed forward toward his defenseless face.

"Stephen?"

Gilliam was there; suddenly Gilliam was at his side, instead of at the tables. His voice was quiet, concerned. He reached out quickly to place a hand on Stephen's paralyzed shoulder.

The white mage-light sprang forward and fell short, dripping into nothing like an awkward spray of shining water. Stephen felt warmth for a moment, a familiar heat that radiated outward from a center no mage-light could reach. He caught Gilliam's hand in his own and met the mage's gaze squarely.

The mage shrugged; there was no hostility at all in his expression. "It's been a pleasure to meet you, young man. May you fare well in the Sacred Hunt." He turned, moving neither too quickly nor too slowly, and left Stephen to wonder if his fear had grown fangs from his imagination.

"Who was he?" Gilliam asked, as he watched the velvet robes retreat.

"Krysanthos. Of the Order of Knowledge."

"Mage-born." Gilliam sounded as if he'd just swallowed something bitter. "I don't like him."

"Neither do I." Stephen shivered. "I—I don't know why."

"He's a mage."

Which was as good an answer as any. Stephen shook off the shadows, but he stayed as close to Gilliam as possible for the rest of the evening. Which meant, of course, that Gilliam was remarkably well behaved for a young Hunter Lord.

Krysanthos was concerned. Although he had tried several times throughout the course of the evening, he had not been able to come close to the young Elseth huntbrother. He had made a cursory scan of all the rest and found them to be common, uninteresting young men; certainly not eager to go to the Hunter's Death, but also caught up in their Lords' pride.

But this Stephen worried him slightly. No other boy had reacted so strongly to what was a completely invisible use of magic—it was almost as if the youth had seen the flare of power, which was impossible.

The mage-born recognized the mage-born; it had always been so. And Krysanthos had seen no kinship, no like spark, in Stephen of Elseth. But he was certain the boy knew that a spell had been cast on him.

Angry, he paced the length of his chambers, pausing when he reached the carpet's edge and turning on the ball of his heel. He hated Breodanir and longed to be quit of the place. Give him Essalieyan, and the most dangerous of missions there, and he would be content.

But no. He was here, with a mission that bordered on ludicrous for all its import, and a mystery that was not to his liking. For not only had the boy apparently been aware of his spell, he had also, somehow, negated it.

He pulled a tasseled bell. He would call the maid back and have her search, as thoroughly as she dared, the young man's chambers. Some sort of protection spell, perhaps a maker-born amulet, was obviously behind this.

Yes. Of course. And when he found it, he would conveniently replace it with one less . . . potent. That done, he could catch the boy and mask out the memory of white-light and mage-spell. If that failed, he would have to resort to a common assassination—which might anger the Lord if any grew suspicious.

He walked over to the curtains and drew them aside. He had done it so often the finery of gold, brown, and green was beneath his notice. The sun was gone, the moon a crescent against the sky. Clouds ate away at the stars in blackness. It was time.

He let the curtains fall and left off tracing his impatient path into the carpet. The mirror in his bedchamber, perfectly dusted and gleaming in the light of his lamp, watched him like a sightless eye. That would change. He stood before it, saw the lines of concern around his lips and the corners of his eyes, and forced himself to smooth them into a cold, noncommittal expression. Pride made him pull his medallion from the folds of his shirt so it stood out as a proclamation of what and who he was.

The crackle of white mage-light came readily. It shot out and surrounded the mirror's surface, dancing against it as if the silvered glass were liquid. He felt the pull of power as it left him; the cost of communication from Breodanir to the heart of the city of Averalaan was high. He was glad that he performed this spell so seldom. Unfortunately, recent casting times had come relatively close together and it took him some weeks to recover.

The mirror grew murky as it lost his reflection. The light without dwindled, and the light within grew, taking shape and substance until once again the mirror's surface looked polished and reflective. It did not show his image.

"Sor na Shannen." His bow was indolent, at best half-respectful—but he bowed.

"Krysanthos."

He saw her back, and felt a flash of annoyance. She knew the time and the hour, and had had enough warning to comport herself with dignity. But no; the pale luminescence of her skin was completely uncovered. Her perfect shoulders rippled as she turned, slowly, to face him.

"You must be early." She was seated on a low divan. Her hair was a spill of finespun night that trailed around exposed breasts and perfect torso. Her lips were red and full, her teeth a pale glimmer.

Against his will he felt himself responding. Annoyed, he cast a distancing spell with his personal power; it robbed some of the glamour of its strength—but not all. Sor na Shannen was a powerful demon, and she held her demesne in the Hells with an absolute strength that many of the demon lords admired. No others of her kind had made the climb to such a height.

"You've been long away from the Hells," he said quietly. "Do you trust your lieutenant?"

Her smile fell away from sharp, white teeth. "I will return in good time." But she was cold now, and in coldness, quite safe. "You have a report to make; make it. I have waited until now to feed, and I am impatient to be out."

"It is as it has been for the last four years."

He knew what she would say, and she did not disappoint him. "Are you certain?"

"I am certain."

"The last four years and the last three months differ greatly in circumstance." Her voice grew sharper. "You saw no sign of the Horn?"

"I have seen no sign of it."

"The Spear?"

"The Spear is useless without the Horn," he said, through teeth that were already clenching. "But no. I have seen no sign of the Spear either."

She relaxed, and her eyes once again grew liquid and lazy. "I don't need to remind you of their import."

"No." He smiled, as cold as she had been. "Had they been in my keeping, I would not have been required to waste precious energy to speak about them."

She hissed, and his smile grew warmer. "Enough. The priests that were responsible have perished, and I, too, grow tired of this game."

"Then let me return."

"No. We know that the agent who stole the Horn and the Spear came from the King's Forest in Breodanir; Ellekar perished there. We know that the girl was not a Hunter, and we know that the Horn's power resides with the 'Hunter-born.' It *must* be there. We are less than ten years from the completion of our plans—the gate-spell goes well, and our Lord should soon have free access to the mortal lands. Find the Horn. Do *not* let it be winded."

Krysanthos cut the connection before his annoyance built beyond tolerable levels. As soon as he knew the succubus' personal name and sigil, he would send her back to the Hells—and into the demesne of her worst enemy. But for now he needed her, as she did him.

Another decade. Of this.

Chapter Eleven

"STEPHEN?" THE WORD WAS muffled by carpets and curtains, but it was still conspicuous in the wide-open spaces and hollows of the King's library. The King's colors—the colors of Breodanir itself—had been deemed too loud for this particular wing of the palace, and were in evidence only in the banners that hung from the ceiling at the library's entrance. Wide, long tables and sturdy chairs were grouped in the center, surrounded by the library's many shelves; those shelves, lined with row upon row of books, rose up to the heights of the roof. Ladders and single-person walkways provided access for the many librarians who worked here. Norn could see one or two deftly pulling single volumes from their places.

"Stephen?" The single word was louder, an obvious affront to the quiet dignity the setting demanded.

"May I help you?" An elderly man appeared at Norn's elbow. The lines of his round face were heightened by a disapproving frown, the tone of his voice one that only respectable age could wield.

Norn gazed down his nose at the brown-robed man who stood with his arms folded. His clothing was rumpled, if clean, and he looked as if he lived within the bowels of the stacks.

"I'm looking for someone."

"I'd guessed. Who are you shouting for?"

It was hardly a shout, but the librarian's expression made it clear that any correction of facts would only be seen as an argument. Norn sighed. "Stephen of Elseth. Young man, about this tall. Fair hair, bluish eyes."

"You're with him?" Faint disbelief colored the words before the librarian's face relaxed. "Well, at least one of you understands the concept of quiet study."

"Is he here?"

"Yes. You'll find him reviewing the Mythos of the Essalieyanese culture, or perhaps more properly, of the Weston culture the empire eventually supplanted. If you wish to converse, the sitting room beyond the east doors is appropriate." The librarian turned and started to walk away.

"Uh, excuse me?"

"What?"

"Where is that?"

"Beyond the east doors." The frown was back in place.

"I mean where would he be researching these myths?"

"Oh." The man shook his head. "Of course. I forget that it isn't obvious to everyone. If you'd care to follow me?" He was short, but for all that he seemed to shuffle, his pace was both brisk and silent.

Stephen sat with his legs curled beneath him, in the center of a chair with arms. It didn't fit under the desk, but it was clearly quite comfortable. A book was open in his lap, and he studied its pages intently. On the desk, a dozen books in various piles made an impromptu fortress.

"Stephen?"

Stephen looked up. "Norn? Is it dinner already?"

"Not yet."

The librarian cleared his throat. "The east room," he said, in a long-suffering tone. But he spared Stephen the ghost of a smile before he walked off.

Stephen nodded at the librarian's back and gently closed his book. He placed it on one of the piles with such care it became obvious to Norn that the stacks had their logical order. Standing, he stretched his legs, and then led Norn to the discussion chamber that lay to the east of the collection.

He stepped in, held the door for Norn, gestured at a chair, and closed the door—with great care to be quiet—behind him.

"What are you doing here?" Norn's voice was still hushed. "This is what, the third or fourth day in a row? You've missed most of the festivities—and the food, mind—just to read religious texts?"

"I haven't missed them all," Stephen replied, with quiet dignity. "I dined yesterday eve with the Ladies Alswaine and Maubreche, and the day before, with Lady Devenson and the King's clerk for the Hunt. I had lunch with Lady Morganson and her two daughters, Lianor and Lylandra, and two days ago—"

"All right, all right—you've made your point. You've certainly kept up your end of the Elseth duties. But you've missed anything that might be fun in between."

"I've been doing research."

"I'd guessed. And I thought you didn't have time to study Breodanir history. I didn't realize that it was merely lack of inclination."

Stephen winced, and because it was the festival and the first Hunt, Norn relented. "What's so fascinating that you study it here?"

"God."

"The Hunter God?"

Stephen frowned as he nodded. "But there's so little here about Him. They have volumes about every other god, and more than just volumes about how the gods interact. But about the Hunter God . . . almost nothing. When the pantheon is discussed at all, there's never any mention of Him. Can He be that minor?"

"Not to us, no. But He *is* Breodanir's God; the only people outside of Breodanir who worship Him are envoys from our country. Why are you so curious?"

"The King," Stephen answered quietly. "And the ceremony afterward. I felt God. I know it." He shook his head, although Norn said nothing mocking. "But I don't understand why. The Hunters call themselves Hunter-born, but they aren't. Not really. Here—oh. It's outside. Well, I can tell you what it said. The god-born—they're obvious. First," he raised a finger, "they have golden eyes. Every one of them. Doesn't matter which god. Second, they have powers associated with their god. Third, if they study it, they can talk to their god. And fourth—most important—they're the *children* of a god."

"Yes?"

"So the Hunters *aren't* Hunter-born, not in the way that someone's Mother-born, justice-born, or wisdom-born."

"And?" Clearly Norn was not enlightened by Stephen's discoveries.

Stephen was a little crestfallen, but he continued anyway, showing the determination of his age. "All right. No god is involved here, not that way. Which leaves the talent-born. Normal people without gods for parents, who somehow have power. The bard-born, the healer-born, the seer-born, the mage-born, the maker-born." His forehead wrinkled as he tried to remember the others. "Never mind."

"And you think the Hunter-born should fall in with the talent-born."

"No!" But he smiled, and his cheeks flushed. He was sharing the fruits of days of labor with someone who was willing to listen. "Because talent doesn't breed true."

"And the Hunter-born always have children who are Hunter-born."

"Yes."

"So?"

"Don't you see? The Hunter-born aren't god-born, but they aren't talent-born either."

"And what does that mean?"

Stephen's face fell, and his shoulders drooped forward a little. "I don't know. I've been trying to find out, and I'm not the only one. The Order of Knowledge first opened its Collegium in Breodanir when the mage-born came to study the Hunter-born. They call it a talent, but . . . well, they don't know why it works the way it does either. Andarion was first circle in the Order, and he spent a long time trying to figure it out. He didn't."

"Maybe," Norn said, rising, "it's just the power of God—it doesn't have an explanation to those who won't take the oath and be affected by it, the arrogance of the mage-born notwithstanding."

Stephen frowned. "We'd have all the answers, you know."

Norn nodded and reached out to grip Stephen's shoulder. "If not for the fire that destroyed the Hunter's temple over three hundred years ago."

Stephen's widening eyes made Norn smile. The arrogance of the mage-born was as nothing when compared to the arrogance of the young. "Yes," he said, trying to keep the amusement from his voice, "you aren't the only one to ask questions, Stephen, nor the only one to notice the Hunter's touch in the King's face at the ascension." He helped Stephen to his feet. "Let's put the books away for today."

"You knew about the fires?"

"In my day," Norn said, with the mock severity of a much older Lord, "we had to take *real* lessons; study history as well as weapon use and hunting. Of *course* I knew about the fires."

"That's Tallespan you're imitating!"

"Indeed. A man who knew much about everything—except perhaps enjoyment and relaxation. Now come; the library doesn't hold the answers that you're searching for. If you're really determined, you might petition the Collegium of the Order, and they might allow you to peruse the treatises that have been written on the Hunter-born."

Stephen nodded sheepishly, and remained in the library just long enough to make a neat stack of the books he'd been studying. Norn waited, and then made sure that Stephen was ushered to yet another dinner with the various Hunter Lords. The Hunt was gathering.

The temple walls were stone: solid; square; and obviously the work of competent masons—but no more. There were windows, long and open to catch as much of day's frugal light as possible, but the window seats were rough and lacked the greater dignity of most of the King's palace. A fireplace the width of the great hall lay blackened and silent; as silent as the temple itself. No one was there.

Stephen knew he was dreaming. He looked down upon leathered feet and saw the edge of real robes brushing the ground around them. The robes were simple and practical brown. He liked them, and after a moment realized that they reminded him of those worn by the Mother's Priesthood. There was no green here, no gold, no fanciful embroidery. He liked that, too.

But he was dreaming. He knew it. The world around him seemed imprecise, as if seen through morning eyes. He wiped at his to see if it helped. Felt his face and froze; it was strange, bristly, harder. He pulled his hands away and saw that they, too, had changed. They were lined, thicker, older—and covered in blood. Some of it was new; it was warm and liquid. Some was older, though; red flakes caked the crossed spears of his Order's ring.

He remembered then why the halls were silent, remembered what had filled them minutes—hours?—before. All of those voices were stilled now. There were no throats left for screaming or shouting or crying. A sudden pain flared up in his side and at his forehead. He was running, or he should have been running. He had stopped to listen for the little noises that spoke of pursuit. There were none.

He began to run.

It's a dream.

It hurt. He felt a trickle leave his lips and knew it for blood by the warmth along his tongue. He tried a window, for the third or fourth time, and found it sealed as the others had been; an invisible barrier protected the glass and soft lead that might have been his one escape. It was magic. The mage-born were here in force.

Yet it was not the mage-born that frightened him.

It's only a dream.

He began to run; he did not know where, but the feet did as they beat a steady, quick rhythm against the stone. The hall passed as did the great fireplace and the fading pinks of the coming evening. Torchlight caught his shadow, trapping it and making it seem more substantial in his wake. Worse, the winking torches began to go out.

They knew where he was, but if he moved quickly they would not be able to stop him before he reached his destination. He prayed, the silent vowels cracking his dry lips, although he knew it would do no good. They were at the year-end and the Sacred Hunt was mere days away.

Ah, the darkness; the darkness terrified him. The mages who bore it, who sheltered it and used it and fed it—they were the sword in the expert's hands. He heard the crackle of blue-light behind his back and leaped around the corner. The wall, inches away from where he had been, flared to life in a cloud of energy that shattered the torch holders.

The two ribs that were cracked pressed against his lungs as he drew breath and winced with the effort. It was a dream. A dream. A dream.

His hands were bleeding; the old blood had been completely superseded by the flow that trailed his arms from the height of his shoulders. His hands shook as he reached the doors and struggled to swing them open.

And then, for a moment, he was clear again. Into stone and silence; the steady quiet of temple life and its security. There, at the center of the room against the tiled inlay of gold and wood and marble, a small altar rose from the ground.

Against green cushions, the perfect edge of a well-oiled sword glinted silver in the light of the eternal flame that sat, like a miniature sun, in the flat, beamed ceiling above. The spearhead, silver also, topped a hardwood pole that had to be replaced every few generations, as it rested against the floor. The couples and leads were perfect, undisturbed, the very icons of the temple's inner life.

These were symbols of comfort and continuity; the regalia that went with the oath. But they were not what he sought. He ran to the altar. The wound had opened enough so his hand's quick passage above the cushions left a telltale mark.

Shaking, he brought away the last of the Hunter's hold in his hands; a simple, carved horn that defied time, temperature, and moisture to remain as perfect now as it was on the day of its making.

His fingers covered the only marking upon it as he brought it to his lips and called upon lungs that might not draw breath strong enough to wind it. Cold caught him in his midsection; cold and the heat of fire. He cried out in agony, and his hands closed rigidly.

He could not let go of the horn.

Wheeling, staggering, he turned to face the open doors that held his enemy. He reached out and gripped the altar's edge with one hand, needing to steady himself. He caught a glimpse of scorched brown cloth and the blistered flesh beneath it before he turned once again to the horn.

But the door held none of the mage-born, and none of the darkness. Instead, in the center of the frame, a slender figure robed in midnight blue stood. A hood was drawn over its face, and in silence it regarded him.

It's only a dream, he thought, and felt his shoulders sag in relief. The dream was turning. He saw his hands shift as age and blood reversed themselves and vanished into nothing.

"Yes," the figure said, in a voice that was soft and low. "It is a dream, but not only. The darkness waits without, but does not wait idly. Will you not sound the horn, oathtaker? Will you not fulfill your ancient pledge?"

Around the figure's feet, shadow pooled and began a slow crawl across the ground. Where it passed, stone began to smoke like kindling.

It's only a dream. But he could not escape it, and the darkness was drawing closer still. Shaking, he lifted the horn to his lips and his now beardless face. The horn had not changed at all.

It transformed the air in his mouth to a sound that he had never heard before. No horn, no simple hunting device, had ever made a sound so lovely and so full. It echoed in the air, filling the chamber and stretching ever outward. His body shivered and resounded with the single, low note.

The room blurred; he lifted his sleeve—now Hunter green and whole—and brushed his eyes free of tears. The figure in blue bowed low and stepped slowly out of the doorway.

Behind waited the Beast. It snarled, its voice as terrifying as the horn's note had been beautiful. The great, shaggy throat uttered no words—how could it?—yet Stephen understood its meaning clearly.

It had been summoned, and finally it had arrived. Its fangs, its claws, its very size defied his ability to absorb details.

"Yes," the figure in blue repeated, "it is just a dream, Stephen of Elseth. But it is the first dream."

He had no time for horror or fear at the words; all of his attention was upon the Hunter's Death.

Stephen woke in the morning with the webs of the dream still around him. He struggled out of bed, leaving a trail of sheets and counterpane in his wake. The curtains were heavy and stiff as he dragged them away from the window. Light, muted and diffuse, relieved the room of its dark edges. He peered up, saw the gray clouds above that moved at the wind's whim.

It was cool. The fire no longer burned in the grate. Hands shaking, he began to dress. He did not want to call servants to start the flames burning. He wanted to be free of his room.

He met Gilliam in the breakfast hall—a hall that was mostly empty. The Hunter Lords had reveled and discoursed for most of the previous evening and were still abed. Here, in the King's City, scant days before the calling of the Sacred Hunt, candles and oil were in plentiful supply. If any thought the expense frivolous, very few could be heard to comment on it.

"What's wrong?" Gilliam said, from halfway across the hall. He pushed himself away from the table and strode across the solid, cold floor. For a moment, as he crossed the path of the fireplace, he looked like a slender shadow surrounded by tongues of flame. "Stephen?"

"Why are you awake?"

"Same reason you are."

Stephen really wished that Gilliam would lower his voice. The few Lords and—much worse—their Ladies who had graced the hall so early were clearly listening. In a whisper, he said, "Did you have a nightmare?"

"No." Gilliam frowned. "But you did. Woke me up and kept me awake." His eyes narrowed. "You look awful. What's the matter?"

"Nothing." He tried to brush past, and Gilliam caught his elbow.

"It isn't nothing. You feel as if you've seen the Hunter's Death."

Stephen couldn't lie to Gilliam. It was always brought home this way. He would try, and Gilliam would refuse to let him be. The oath-bond between them was strong, even for huntbrothers.

"You aren't wearing your colors," Stephen said lamely.

"And you're wearing yours. Now what is wrong?" Gilliam caught Stephen's shoulders. "No. Don't say 'nothing.' Don't shrug your shoulders at me. We *promised*, and we're bound by it."

He might have added that he couldn't eat, couldn't sit still, and couldn't concentrate; might have pointed out that Stephen's fear was so strong that it overwhelmed everything else. But he was Gilliam; he didn't. It seemed too obvious a truth.

Stephen sighed and nodded; his throat caught and tightened. He gestured toward the nearest corner of the room, and they both turned in silence.

When they were as far from the hearing of others as possible, Stephen turned to Gilliam.

"I had a dream."

Gilliam nodded, waiting.

"I was in the temple. The temple that was here before the palace. I told you about it last night." He stopped a moment, and looked at Gilliam. Gilliam's brown eyes were unblinking, and unmocking, as they met his. "Everyone else was dead. All the Priests, the servants—everyone. It was three days before the calling of the Hunt.

"I was alive—I was a Priest."

At this, Gilliam snorted. "You'd make a rotten Priest."

Stephen nodded, as if he'd heard the words without understanding them. "I was the only one. There were mages. There was fire and darkness. I was afraid. But I—I *knew* it was a dream—I knew it. I just couldn't wake up." He brought his hands to his face and examined them closely. "I was injured. Bleeding."

"What happened?"

"I ran to safety. A room in the temple with an altar. There was a sword, a spear, couples, leads—but the most important thing was a horn. I picked it up. I sounded it." He closed his eyes, remembering the only peaceful thing that had happened. "And someone came, someone in blue."

"Who?"

"I don't know. The face was covered by a hood. But I couldn't ask—because the Hunter's Death came, too." Shaking, he lowered his hands.

"It was only a dream," Gilliam said quietly. But he waited; Stephen was not yet finished.

"I think I might have said that. And the person in blue—he said, 'It is the first dream.'"

"The first?" Gilliam shook his head and slowly sat down. It didn't bother him that there was no chair to catch him; he was quite comfortable on the floor.

Stephen nodded. He knew he should at least tell Gil to get a chair, but he didn't have the energy. Saying the words aloud had made them more real than the silence of fear did.

The first dream.

The Unnamed God dealt in dreams and visions, and if he visited these upon you thrice in three nights, you were his subject, you bore his wyrd.

"'One dream is a dream.'" It was a quote, and Gilliam offered it to Stephen knowing that it wouldn't be any help. Stephen didn't answer in words, but after a moment he, too, lowered himself to the floor. They sat facing each other as they might have done on a normal day in the kennels.

Gilliam reached out, caught his huntbrother's hand, and held it very tightly. "You believed him, didn't you?"

Stephen nodded.

"Wait. We'll know in two days."

He nodded again.

"And it doesn't matter. If we've got the wyrd of the Unnamed on us, we'll face it together—and we'll beat it. I promise."

The knot in Stephen's throat eased, but only a little.

Lunch went well, and dinner was another festive affair. The ladies and their eligible daughters were now out in force—a force to be reckoned with. Twice, Stephen had to rescue Gilliam before he said enough to earn his absent mother's wrath. Norn was even busier with Soredon, and it soon became clear to Stephen that all of the huntbrothers present watched over their Hunter Lords with an eye to social details.

The Elseth preserve was not a small one; indeed, compared to many it was quite sizable. But it was close to the eastern boundary of the kingdom, and farther from the capital, so in the early marriage-seeking forays, Gilliam was not besieged. He did speak with one or two of the young Ladies—and Stephen winced when Gilliam began his earnest, passionate discussions about how he was going to build his hunting pack to any who could hear.

The Ladies listened politely of course, as any huntbrother would. Unfortunately, Gilliam could offer no like polite response when they attempted to steer the conversation to less specific topics. True to his class, he found it intensely uncomfortable to talk about the "weather," and it was impossible to draw more than a grunt or a nod from him about anything but the Hunt.

It was up to Stephen to fill the awkward silences, and again he did Lady Elseth proud. He talked, or rather listened intently, to matters of trade and governance; bowed with exactly the right amount of deference—forcing Gilliam to do the same by dint of a glare they both understood the meaning of—and complimented the women on their finery. That last was not hard to do. Any time a Lady, dressed in full evening wear, walked across the ballroom's threshold, he felt a hint of awe. The Hunter Lords had a grace that was born of agility and aggression, and honed on the Hunt; the Ladies had a grace born of the same, but honed on the dance floor, or in odd etiquette lessons—and Stephen found the mixture of delicacy and swift, sure steps the more entrancing of the two.

As well, although he didn't bother to say so to Gilliam, he found the colors that the Ladies wore much more pleasing to the eye; he'd had enough of Hunter green, brown, and gray to last a lifetime. Pale blues, azures, brilliant magentas, crimsons, golds—each dress as unique as the clothing of the Hunter Lords was uniform.

The only time he lost sight of Gilliam was when Lady Alswaine began her discourse on the problems with the seat of judgment in her preserve. For Stephen, to whom the law was still absolute and carved in stone, her ambivalence was both shocking and fascinating.

"There are mitigating circumstances for many crimes," she said, speaking more to the young women present than to Stephen. "For instance, Veralyn, what would you do if one of your villagers was caught stealing from the manor house?"

Lady Veralyn's cheeks clashed with her dress as she flushed. She opened her mouth to speak, and then closed it slowly, wondering at the game that Lady Alswaine, older and wiser, was playing, for Lady Alswaine asked no idle questions. Lady Veralyn was a year older than Stephen, and not yet pledged to any Lord or Lord's son. "I would—I would have to know more."

Lady Alswaine's smile held a glimmer of approval. "Indeed, and when you occupy your seat, you will have that opportunity. In this case, it was winter, and a harsh one." She tilted her head to the side and glanced at Stephen. "What of you, Stephen of Elseth?"

Stephen flushed, wondering whether or not Lady Alswaine knew of his origins. He was certain she must, and his response, defensive, was also a completely correct recitation of the laws of Breodani. "Fine, work edict, or finger. It would depend on what he'd stolen."

"Pigeons."

"Fine."

"He had no money." Lady Alswaine's lips turned up in a smile that was both friendly and annoying.

"Then work edict."

"Would you trust him in your manor?"

"Finger." It was the most severe of the sentences that could be meted out, and Stephen said it reluctantly, remembering his own fears, his own days in the lower city, surrounded by his hungry den mates.

"And what would his family do come spring and the common season? Death, I think, would be kinder—and death is not an option. Come, Stephen. I am the person who metes out justice, with the aid of the village head. In this case, the man committed a very real crime—but for foolish reasons, nay, stupid ones."

"But he committed a crime."

"Of course." She folded her arms very delicately. It made her look as fragile as a rock. "But the why of it was interesting. He was young, and had just taken a wife the previous summer. His wife was the pride of her parents, and the desire of many of the younger men—and he was still not comfortable in her choice of him. He considered the gift of her acceptance the whim of luck, and was afraid that if he failed her, she would revoke it. The house that they dwell in is simple, and was, of course, built with the aid of the village as a whole—but in order to impress her,

152 ◆ Michelle West

he foolishly bartered and used supplies that were to have seen them through the winter."

Stephen shrugged uncomfortably, but did not look away from Lady Alswaine. She waited a moment before continuing, to judge both his expression and his temper. Satisfied, she nodded and went on.

"What would you have done, were you in his position?"

"Gone to the village head," Stephen replied promptly. "If the village head wasn't prepared to deal with the shortage and arrange for repayment, they could go to the manor proper and ask for the reserves."

"Yes. That is what's supposed to happen. But if he went to the village head, his young bride would be sure to know. So instead, he came to the manor at night." Lady Alswaine held out her cup as a signal to a passing servant. The young man bowed and carefully refilled it before moving on. "He was caught, of course, and his case was brought to me immediately. Now, Stephen, Veralyn—place yourself in my position, and more important, place yourself in his. He committed a crime against Alswaine, yes, but that was only a symptom.

"The real wrong was done to his wife."

For a moment, Stephen's brow furrowed; his face grew intent, and his eyes less focused. The lessonmaster would have known the expression immediately and approved of it. As the Lady Alswaine commanded, Stephen tried to place himself in the young man's position. He found, to his surprise, that it was easy. He was in the King's City, after all; the place of his birth and the first eight years of his life.

He remembered, although the memory was blurred and fuzzy now, how he had spent those eight years. Luck had smiled often on him, and he had escaped the notice of the King's guard—and therefore, of the Queen's judgment—but he remembered how the fear felt.

"Did he steal wood?" he asked quietly.

She chuckled. "The city isn't out of you entirely, is it? No, wood is not a problem in Alswaine. He took only food, and it was near the end of the season."

He nodded, and continued to furrow his brow. Lady Alswaine spoke of the thief's crime against his wife, but clearly there wasn't one. First, she had nothing to steal, and second, he probably only wanted to feed her. Of course, if he had wanted to feed her, and he'd had half a brain, he'd have just gone to the village head, admitted his need, and been done with it.

But then he'd have to tell her that he'd wasted all of their winter supplies, and she'd be angry and leave him.

Or would she? He stopped, and the lines in his forehead melted away. "He didn't trust her," he said quietly.

"No, he didn't. And if you see that, you might know what I demanded as restitution." Clearly pleased, she turned her full attention upon him, her gold-fringed skirts rustling as she moved.

"You made him tell her."

"Very good!" She almost clapped, but the goblet she held prevented it. "Yes, but more; I had her called to the manor. I'm afraid I was rather cruel to the young man, which certainly suited the nature of both of his crimes. I didn't tell him that I had summoned her, for I believed that I understood his motives. Instead, I had her wait behind a screen with the various servants who attend the judgments. When he told me, at length, of the reasons for the theft, she could hear every word.

"I must say that I had always thought her sweet and relatively even of temper." Here she smiled, but the smile was one that Stephen couldn't understand at all. "She knocked the screen over and stood with her fists by her side. I thought she was going to hit him in front of all of us." She was laughing; wine swirled over the rim of silver and slid in droplets down her fingers. It was some minutes before she could speak again. Stephen didn't understand what was funny about it at all.

"She didn't kill him—I mentioned that I thought it was rather too severe for his crime—but she made her displeasure quite clear." And here, her eyes softened. "And when he understood that she was angry, not because of the theft or the shortages, but because he hadn't trusted her . . . well, they left together, and in the end I think she was glad that she hadn't killed him." She set her glass aside when the servant next passed by. "So there you have it. Not everything is clear, especially to those of us who must judge. And before you think that you learn more with age, I've news for you both—you unlearn much. Things become more complicated and less clear."

Stephen nodded attentively before he chose to speak again. When he did, his voice was quiet. "But, Lady," and he bowed, "what would you have done if the thief's wife was exactly what he was afraid she was?"

"Your point, young Stephen." Her smile was sad. "But you've ruined my little story for the evening. Even the unclear becomes more unclear with time. What would I have done? As I did, I think, but I wouldn't remember it fondly, nor as a triumph. And I would have grieved for the foolish young man in the privacy of my rooms. It is difficult for the young when their dreams die.

"Now. Enough. Where is your Hunter? You've left him long enough that he's bound to embarrass your House; go, quickly."

Stephen showed her a hint of the man he might become. Although he did not understand her sudden change, and the loss of her little smile, he asked no further questions. Instead he bowed, low and formal in his respect.

"Wisdom," she said, as he rose from his bow, "is not knowledge. It is experience. You will find, as you grow older, that you are capable of many wrongs which you consider evil now; you will also understand much about people that you dismiss. You may even understand the fear that comes with love, and the love that transcends fear."

*   *   *

That night he returned to the temple. This time there was no silence and no isolation, and the air was full of smoke and ash—the rewards of fire. He was standing in the pews which were only half full when the wall uttered a roar and suddenly crumbled.

He saw four men in dark robes, and behind them saw soldiers with raised swords, and crossbows that were already loosing quarrels. Because he was spinning, he was spared. A wooden bolt grazed his forehead, leaving a red trail but no death in its wake.

He ran; he was closest to the doors that led to the inner temple. The sounds of slaughter had already started before he crossed the threshold, but he spared no backward glance. He knew that there was nothing he could do. This was a dream, after all.

But he couldn't shake it and couldn't defeat it. His feet carried him where his will could not prevent it; already the halls and the torches were familiar, as was the pursuit. He reached the inner sanctum, threw the doors wide, and ran for the altar. The passage of time did not slow; he could feel darkness and hear the approach of the mages. Gone was the moment where each item laid out for the Hunter could be studied and appreciated—only one artifact was of any import.

His hands curled around the horn. He lifted it, shaking. He sounded it and the call was clear.

And once again, the midnight-blue robes that concealed and presented at the same time appeared. He was bent now, as if from some great work, or great injury; he seemed older and more diminutive. Behind him, the darkness was held at bay—and beyond that, a glint of unnatural light on divine fur and fangs began to grow.

"But it's only a dream!" Stephen shouted.

"Yes," the figure said, and it sounded just as it appeared—older or weaker. "But this is the second dream."

Stephen had breakfast brought to his room the next day. Although he woke early, he could not bear to enter the dining hall. He tried to think on other things; caught the strand of Lady Alswaine's lesson, and held it firmly. He even prayed to the Mother. It was foolish, but in the privacy of his room, there was no one to laugh or call him a child.

It was the last day of festivities; tomorrow, the hunters would leave the King's City—and the King's palace—to enter the royal preserve. There, when the Master of the Game called the Hunt, he and Gilliam would face the creature of nightmare: the Hunter's Death.

Before they could do that, there was the packing to attend to. In silence, Stephen rose and began to empty his drawers and closets of the things he would need: sword, spear, horn. Norn had, for the moment, the couples and leads; he would hand them over with the part of the pack that Gilliam would lead in the Hunt.

The dress jacket and cloak, the breeches and shirt—all of these would be carefully set aside, to be worn during the great feast that followed the Sacred Hunt. He started to hang them properly, when the door creaked open.

It was Norn.

"I heard you had words with Lady Alswaine last eve," he said jauntily. Then he stopped, hand still on the door. "Stephen—what's wrong? Too much drink?"

"No," was Stephen's reply, but it held little indignation, little fire.

"You've not been swept off your feet by a young lady, have you?"

"No!"

"Well, good, then. The Hunter Lords are oblivious when it comes to the ladies, almost the entire lot of them—but the huntbrothers are sometimes a little foolish at their first Hunt. About the ladies, that is." He walked into the room and shut the door. "Gilliam didn't do anything really bad, did he?"

Stephen shook his head. "Spilled ale on Lady Marget's dress; I apologized."

"You're sure that's all?"

"Yes."

"What's wrong?"

"Nothing."

"Then if it's nothing, you'd better snap out of it." Norn's voice grew harder. He sat down on the bed, resting his elbows against his knees. "You're having your effect on your Hunter, Stephen—and he can't afford it now. Any other time of the year, yes—but not before the Sacred Hunt. He'll need his wits about him; he'll need to be sharp and focused, not distracted and exhausted."

Stephen said nothing.

"You're having an effect now," Norn said, pressing on. "Gilliam was up early this morning, looking for you in the hall. I caught him on his way back up here. He's out with the dogs—as his duty demands—but he's not paying attention. He wanted to find you, and only a direct command from Lord Elseth prevented him." He paused as the last of this sank in. Stephen's eyes widened; when Norn called Soredon "Lord," it was a fair indication of what Soredon's mood had been at the time: bad.

Norn's voice became quieter, but no less sharp. "Whatever it is that's bothering you, it's too strong. It interferes with Gilliam's concentration, his ability to call a good trance. Later—three, four years—he'll be able to do it without pause. But *not now*. You're here in the name of Elseth as well as in the name of the King. You've got to do well at this Hunt. It's your first—every eye in the kingdom will be upon you.

"Both Lord Elseth and I are willing to help you in any way possible, if you need help. But you have to admit to that need, Stephen, or we'll assume the worst. What is bothering you?"

"I—" Stephen swallowed and looked away. His feet were particularly interesting, clad as they were in slippers that clashed with the carpet. Maribelle's gift, as he recalled. "I had the second dream."

"Pardon?"

"The second dream." He looked up, almost met Norn's eyes, and looked away again.

For a moment the older huntbrother wore a mask of confusion. When it fell away, it was replaced by a mixture of shock and amusement. "Hunter's Oath, Stephen—do you mean to tell me that you're bothered by a dream?"

"It's the second dream," Stephen said, but his voice was less steady, less sure.

"I don't care if it's the tenth! Of all the things I expected to hear—" He stood quickly and shook his head. Relief was evident in his smile. "Do you think that nightmares are uncommon for the Hunter folk? We have them all the time— especially before the Sacred Hunt."

"But," Stephen's word could barely be heard, "it's the second dream, on the second night. It was the same."

"Stephen, you sound like an impressionable child. A dream's a dream. The wyrd of fate, the Unnamed, was invented by old men who had nothing better to do with their time than terrify the gullible. Is that clear?"

Stephen nodded.

"I didn't hear you, lad."

"Yes, Norn."

"Good." Norn walked over to the door. "I see you've started packing—be done by lunch if you can. I'll come up then."

Stephen nodded again; his cheeks were bright red circles. For want of anything else to do, he started for his dresser.

"Dreams, indeed." Norn snorted. He was a very practical man, as all huntbrothers inevitably strove to be.

It was only a dream, a phantom of childhood and fear and gullibility. And like a phantom, it returned in the evening, when Norn's jaunty condescension wasn't there to keep it at bay.

The temple was on fire now; the flames crackled loudly as they split wooden beams, doors, and joists. Whole sections of the twisted maze in the inner temple were no longer passable. A carpet of dead bodies, fallen stone, and blackened wood barred the way.

Stephen ran, but each step he took was painful. His robes were not dark enough to hide the spread of blood. He was certain his ribs were cracked or broken; each breath, hurriedly and deeply taken, was agony. But one hall, familiar now, was still standing. Nearly empty, it awaited his passage.

He turned and glanced over his shoulder. He knew it cost him speed and time, but fear forced him to it. The darkness moved like a sluggish wave, destroying the light and leaving fire in its wake. Yet as the darkness spread, he saw one of his many enemies. She stood quite tall, robed in shadows and very little else; her hair, a sheen of pale, white gossamer, flared round her shoulders like a ceremonial collar; her eyes—he could not see them well enough to know their color, and he was glad of it. At her throat, before all light was lost, he saw a large, gold medallion, with a tower against the midnight black of moonless sky. She smiled; he felt the tug of her lips over teeth as a command, and turned in desperation. He was almost upon the sanctum. He would not be stopped now.

The doors opened inward with no difficulty; the sanctum was not locked or barred. Who among the Breodani would seek to steal or destroy the sign of their God's favor?

And who would be foolish enough to use it? Hands damp with a mixture of blood and sweat, he reached out, running all the while. He caught the horn, felt it tingle in his hands, and drew it to his lips. It hurt to take the breath that was necessary; he coughed, tasted salt, and lost vision for a brief second.

Then, somehow, the pain was gone; his hands were clean, his arm steady. He sounded the horn. Its note was long and lasting.

And the blue-robed figure stepped over the threshold, while darkness surged beneath its feet. Stephen lowered the horn slowly as he looked at the hood, trying to see a face, a person, within its confines. Hands rose and reached for the edge of the fabric, rolling it gently back.

"Stephen of Elseth, forgive us."

He looked into the face of a woman; she was older than he, but younger than the Lady Elseth. Or so it seemed at first. Her skin was pale, her hair darker than her robe—darker than any black that he had seen, save for the shadows without. Her eyes seemed gray, then blue, then violet, and last an icy, pale gold—they flickered and changed so quickly he couldn't say which was the true one. But he knew that none of the colors were warm.

"Some of what you have seen these past nights is real. History has folded it into a secrecy that even the Hunter's Priests cannot break. But some of what you have seen is yet to pass."

"Which?"

She shook her head, and seemed for a moment almost sad. "I do not know, fully—and if I did, my given oath would prevent me from explaining it." She lowered her hands and stood before him. "I am Evayne." She gestured suddenly, throwing her arms wide.

Warmth filled the room, different from the heat of the fires. A drowsy peace descended upon Stephen as Evayne brought her hands down, palms up, as if holding something precious.

"The world changes more than you know, Stephen. If I can be of aid to you, I shall—and you will need aid and more if the promise of all oaths is to be realized at last.

"This is the third dream."

Chapter Twelve

O N THE MORNING AFTER the third dream, Stephen woke before the dawn. He turned the counterpane neatly down and rose. It was chilly. The fire had burned down during the evening and the room smelled faintly of wood made ash. The curtains were pulled shut to keep the night out. He opened them quickly to give the sunlight that would soon come free passage.

He was afraid, but the fear had turned into something strange over the length of the dream, and he still felt a hint of the warmth that the woman, Evayne, had made manifest. Fear, he thought, remembering everything that Norn and Lord Elseth had struggled to teach him, was a type of wisdom. Terror was different; fear run rampant, with no control. He was no longer terrified.

He could not tell Norn of the third dream, of course. Norn's laughter still echoed in the bedchamber, reddening his cheeks. He began to dress. Breakfast today was important. It might be his last meal. When he was finished, he packed his small chest and left it beside the door for the porter.

Then he walked out of his room and down the hall to Gilliam's. He knocked quietly at first, listened for an answer, and then knocked more loudly. The sound that came through the door was Gilliam's attempt to make words. Stephen snorted and knocked, very loudly, before throwing the door open and marching in.

Gilliam's face was a bulge under the pillows. From the stretch of the bedsheets, Stephen could see that his back was to the door. He walked up, grabbed the pillow, and placed it gently on the chair beside the bed. As he expected, Gilliam's hands were over his ears.

"It's not even light yet—go away."

"Gil," Stephen said, as he reached for the rather rumpled clothing that Gilliam had stuffed, with nary a thought to proper folding, into the drawers of his dresser. "We were told that we had to be up before dawn proper. We've got to eat breakfast, and we have to join Norn and Lord Elseth in the courtyard. Or have you forgotten that we've got to find the right trail before we can hunt at the Master of the Game's call?"

Gilliam mumbled something that was inaudible. Stephen sighed, stepped over to the bedside, and grabbed the counterpane and the blankets beneath. With a quick, efficient tug—years of practice at work—he yanked them off. The cold would eventually force his lazy Hunter to find real clothing.

It worked; Gilliam yowled and scrambled up, taking the clothing that Stephen held out when he discovered the blankets were permanently out of reach.

"Are you packed?"

"Hmmmm."

"Good." Just to be sure, Stephen checked the contents of Gilliam's chest. He cringed at the rolled up jacket and the inelegantly folded pants. It was a good thing that couples and leads didn't require any forethought or care to stow away.

"Stephen?"

Stephen let the lid bang shut and looked up without rising.

"You didn't wake me."

He knew that Gilliam was speaking of the dreams. "No."

"Did you have it?"

"What?"

"Don't 'what' like that. You know damn well I mean the third dream."

"If I'd had it, you'd probably know, don't you think?"

The set of Gilliam's lips told Stephen very well what he thought. Prevarication was not Gilliam's strong point, but Stephen had learned the art from observation—and Gil knew that as well. Stephen hesitated anyway, although he could feel Gilliam getting more annoyed as the seconds passed.

He had wanted to wait until after the Sacred Hunt before seeking his Hunter's advice. He still did. It was something that he could keep to himself now. The terror was gone—and the Sacred Hunt, as Norn had pointed out, was indeed more important. But he knew, looking at Gilliam's face, that it wouldn't be right. He suddenly thought of the pathetic, stupid young thief of Lady Alswaine's odd story—and the lesson that had peered, half-formed, from the corner of his understanding, came fully to light.

I have to trust you. "Yes. I dreamed the third."

Gilliam exhaled, and his face lost the black expression that always brought an argument and often meant the fist play so despised by Lady Elseth. "But you aren't afraid of it now."

"Just a little. I—it was different, this time. The figure in blue removed the hood—and it was a she. She said her name was Evayne. She looked, I don't know, sad." He felt his stomach start to rumble and glanced at the door. "She said she'd help me if she could."

"Help you what?"

"I don't know." He shrugged. "And if we don't get downstairs for breakfast, we won't be around to find out. Norn's—"

"I *know* what Norn's been saying." Gilliam shoved his feet into his boots, and Stephen made sure that his breeches were neatly tucked in.

"We can talk after the Sacred Hunt—if we're both still alive." He smiled then, and it was genuine. "I mean, wouldn't it be funny if I died? The wyrd—and all the worrying I've done—would mean nothing."

Gilliam didn't think it was funny at all.

Krysanthos rose early as well. He often liked to rise and be fully awake by the coming of the dawn, but on this occasion it was more a matter of necessity than one of preference. The court would be ready to begin its long procession through the city streets, and he had to be among them.

He had had little opportunity, for the entirety of the two-week festival, to speak with the young Elseth huntbrother alone, and that worried him. It seemed too much of a coincidence that someone—or something—had consistently contrived to prevent his access. This single fact would have annoyed him, but it did not stand alone. The little maid had searched the boy's rooms at all hours, and found nothing that would give either magical vision or magical protection. The huntbrother had obviously managed to protect himself—which meant that he was dangerous.

Very well; he was a danger. Krysanthos smiled. Today, during the Sacred Hunt, the boy was, by law, placing his life at risk. There was always at least one death—but on occasion, there were more.

He managed to finish the onerous task of dressing well before the knock at the door sounded. It was precise, soft, and timely. Unlike many of the visiting dignitaries, Krysanthos traveled without a valet. He was forced to answer the door himself.

A slender young man in the blue and gray of messenger's garb bowed low. "Your pardon, sir, for this early interruption, but I bear a message that is most urgent."

"Please, come in," Krysanthos replied, holding out a hand.

The man rose and entered the room as Krysanthos stepped out of the way. The rolled sheet of vellum he placed in the mage-born's hand had no seal or distinguishing marks, although it was tied with black ribbon. Krysanthos gestured and the door swung shut.

The messenger nodded and stood, hands behind his back, waiting for a reply.

"You're almost early," Krysanthos' voice was casual as he looked at the message that slowly unfurled in his hands. One peppered brow rose, and he looked up. "This is more than your usual fee."

The messenger shrugged, neither affronted nor nervous. The long, thin lines of his face were like a mask; even the gray eyes were cold and still. "You've given little notice, and less chance to prepare."

Little notice, indeed. And he was exhausted with the effort of that sending, too soon after his discussion with Sor na Shannen. "Ah, well. It was worth comment." Krysanthos rolled the sheet into a tight curl. The Kovaschaii were the best at their craft; whole lives had been spent in the training and perfection of their art. "You won't mind if I ask to see your mark?"

Without a change of expression, the man complied, pulling white-blond hair away from the left side of his face. There, shadowed by the arch of his ear, was the small chalice that had once been burned into flesh.

Krysanthos gestured briefly, although by now it was a formality. At once, his sight shifted into the odd haze of magical vision. The room went gray and misty. In the background, the mirror he used for communication shone out, a stark, bright beacon. Beneath the bed, he could also see the halo of a walking stick. These were not his concern. Instead, he examined the mark of the Kovaschaii.

It, too, glowed softly and elegantly with magic's fire. Light silvered it and rounded it, giving it the appearance of a tiny, perfect chalice, which contained the Kovaschaii strength.

"Very well," he said, and the lights went out. He stood in silence for a few moments, considering the fee. There was no argument to be offered. He could accept it or reject it. The Kovaschaii did not negotiate.

"Very well," he said again. "I accept the conditions. Ten thousand Essalieyanese solarii. Success only."

"Who?"

This part of the operation was the one which Krysanthos hated most. Were it not for this, he was certain he would utilize the services of the Kovaschaii more frequently. As it was, only situations of urgency could force him to it. Gritting his teeth, he let one of his unseen magical shields drop.

The nameless man stepped forward and reached out for Krysanthos' forehead. He placed the flat of his palm against it and closed his eyes.

Krysanthos knew the routine well. He needed—and would suffer—no instructions. Luckily, the Kovaschaii were excellent at observation about human nature, and the young man did not make this mistake. The mage-born concentrated until he forced a perfect mental picture of Stephen of Elseth to the fore of his thoughts. With it came all of the rest of the details; the first meeting, the several attempts, the growing frustration.

And the Kovaschaii drank it in, searching through the undercurrents of associated thought until he was satisfied with the answer he'd received.

The moment the pressure of his hand was gone, Krysanthos slammed his shields into place.

"The other?"

"Other?" It was said too quickly; Krysanthos forced his hands to stroke the length of his beard to still their shaking. Nowhere in his long studies had he found any sensation so distressing as this: another man, rummaging through the privacy of his thoughts. Ten thousand solarii? He would have paid double to have been able to avoid the intrusion. It was never an option.

"The Hunter."

"Ah—him." With care born of experience, Krysanthos did not mention the name that leaped to mind.

"They will be together."

"Yes," the mage replied. "But the mission you've accepted is to make the death of the huntbrother seem an entirely natural occurrence. Surely the Hunter is your problem."

Kovaschaii shoulders moved up and down in a graceful motion that was almost feline. He asked no further questions; he had no need to. He now knew everything that Krysanthos knew about the intended victim. Krysanthos handed him the scroll that he had arrived bearing and saw him out the door.

Only the matter of the maid was left to be dealt with, and that was relatively simple—certainly less costly.

If Stephen had thought that two weeks of festivity showed the Breodani Lords and Ladies at their finest, he was quickly proved wrong. From the moment he set foot in the dining hall, until the moment he left it, he observed everything in the near-silence of awe.

The Hunter Lords were properly dressed in clothing that was well crafted but serviceable; this was expected. What was not was the added finery of capes and greatcloaks and strangely plumed hats that somehow managed to be multicolored without ever looking ridiculous against the background of green, brown, and hints of gold that comprised the Hunter's uniform.

Of course, after a few minutes of standing in their midst, the glitter of their wear vanished beneath the tense excitement of the soon-to-be-called Hunt. Conversation revolved around dogs, goals, battle plans. There was camaraderie, yes, but also competition, which had remained, until this moment, unspoken. One or two, younger Hunters to be sure, even mentioned the Hunter's Death as a type of prey. The older Hunter Lords said nothing, but a shadow passed over their faces, stilling them a moment before anticipation returned—the remembered costs of each passing year.

It was the Ladies and the attendants who lost none of their aura. When they entered the hall, whether on the arm of their Hunter, or attended by other companions, it was clear where the power in Breodanir lay. The older women, especially, walked with a grace and confidence that spoke of experience and easily accessible knowledge. They were comfortable talking of the Sacred Hunt, but equally comfortable arranging the last few bits of trade and barter, giving the final words of judgment advice or supping frugally on what was placed before them.

Gilliam had to elbow Stephen twice, hard, in the ribs when his attention strayed to the less relevant members of the huge hunting party.

Norn had looked sharply at Stephen when they finally appeared in the hall, but Stephen's curt and controlled nod seemed to satisfy him. The edge of the anger the older huntbrother had shown the day before—had it only been one day?—was blunted and put aside.

Stephen was keenly aware of the fact that Elseth put on no fine display. Both Norn and Soredon—heads of the Elseth responsibility—wore good, solid, serviceable spring cloaks. They were also incredibly dull.

Well, he'd talk with Lady Elseth about it when they got back to the manor, and if it could be afforded, they'd look better next year. He consoled himself with the fact that all of the finery would vanish the minute the King's horn was sounded. Then the Hunters would be measured by their true worth, not by their clothing. Still . . .

The drums sounded in the distance, and the hall quieted as all eyes turned to the doors. No horn sounded to announce the coming of the King—no horn would be winded this day until the start of the Hunt.

But the drums did their work, beating in time like an unnatural heart. The doors rolled open, and the King entered the room, the Queen by his side. He was clothed in the colors of Breodanir, all dark greens and browns, but his cloak and jacket were emblazoned across chest and back with gold thread. He wore no cap, and his hair hung in a single braid, beneath a simple circlet. Behind him, pages carried two spears, one long and slender, one thick with protrusions near its iron point.

The Queen had left behind the greens and browns; nor did she choose a simple dress for the outdoor occasion. She walked, in full skirts, like sunlight made human. Gold brocade danced just above her boots, and lit around her shoulders and arms like spreading fire. Where the King wore a circlet, she wore a crown, and the jeweled work, even from the back of the hall, bore the mark of the maker-born. It was perfect.

The King raised his Lady's hand and stood facing the gathered nobles. "We welcome you to the King's City," he said softly. "On this day we are called upon to prove our ranks, and their worth, to our people. Will you follow?"

The hushed susurrus of assent filled the room, as did the King's grave smile. He paused only once, his eyes scanning the crowd, until he found the one he was searching for. Stephen met his gaze and bowed; it obscured his eyes.

They left the palace, perhaps not in as orderly a fashion as one would wish; there was subtle jockeying for position between the various landed Hunters. But it was kept to a minimum, and by the time the procession, with carriages and footmen, banners and flags, reached the palace gates, the dignity of the occasion prevailed.

The streets were lined. It seemed that everyone, whether gainfully employed or not, bore witness to the passing procession. Some merchants had even taken the time to set up stalls and displays, although they didn't attract the nobles. The smell of food and ale was in the air, and the musicians that led the royal procession carried tunes that even the children here could sing; cradle songs, school songs—tunes of youthful fear and hope.

The dogs were growling in the wagons that carried them. Small children, whose age gave them some excuse, and large youths, whose age did not, approached the wheels and peered cautiously in to see snapping, white teeth.

Through dint of will, the Hunter Lords kept their packs contained—but as they prepared for the Sacred Hunt, with all of its little competitions, so, too, did the dogs.

Gilliam didn't have to worry about it for this hunt. Later, he would understand why the Hunter Lords grew testy and snappish as they rode by in their carriages, past plain small buildings, stalls, and real storefronts. Stephen, fulfilling the function of the absent Lady Elseth, reached out of his window and waved, keeping both his hands and his smile stiff and formal. One or two people waved back, but these were mostly the young, or the parents of the young who wished to teach them a friendly example. The oldest among the watchers only inclined their heads gravely, standing as if in salute, which, indeed, they were.

It was a bright, clear day—crisp and cool, which was to be expected. Some of the lords and ladies rode in open carriages and smiled as if they little minded the chill bite of the cold breeze. They had furs, mind, and cloaks that were up to spring's test.

Stephen thought an open carriage would be splendid, but knew that it would have to wait until Maribelle was of age and she and Lady Elseth came to the court in person. Hunters just didn't have the necessary pomp and circumstance about them to merit it on their own.

But he thought better of it when he realized just how exposed the lack of a roof above his head would make him; one open side window was enough. He waved until his arm was sore, and then continued to wave, thinking that it couldn't be much farther. To his amazement, the line of gathered well-wishers continued right up to the city gates that led north—and beyond that, as farmers and those who did not dwell within the King's City also lined the road to pay their respects.

The villagers, for such they were, were old-fashioned and not so prone to the casual ways of the city dwellers. The older folk bowed, hatless, and held their bows until the last member of the procession rode by.

Of course, the younger children tailed after the last carriage with happy little yowls of delight, until caught by their grandparents, which didn't happen in the city either.

*   *   *

Outside of the preserve, gardeners had been at work since the snows had melted, clearing away dead branches, old leaves, and the occasional remains of winter food the forest's predators had left behind. There were no trees here. They had been cut down and uprooted centuries past, and none were allowed to encroach. Seedlings which were lucky enough to survive the northerly climate's snow and wind did not escape the gardeners and the wardens.

The ground was soft and damp, and tended toward mud in some places, but the King's servants were up to the task they excelled in. New grass had already been laid—at great expense—and the King's pavilion, with its flat planks and colorful tents, was visible the moment the road came to an end. Flowers, carefully tended to indoors in the off-season, had been planted and arranged so as to be in their glory for the arrival of the nobles. The pits were ready, and would not remain empty past the late afternoon. Stones lined them, and the spits that served to grill meat for the feast were already set up.

A dais that was neither simple nor new had been erected. Only one throne sat upon it, not the customary two, and it was clearly not meant for the King.

The King and Queen were the first to disembark, as they led the procession. The King dismounted first, setting both feet on the ground before turning to offer his Lady his hand.

The Queen came out like the sun, and if her smile was slightly sad, only the footmen saw it, and they never commented. They bowed, and held their bows as their monarchs walked by, her hand on his stiff forearm. The King led her up to the dais and to the throne. There, he withdrew his arm, and as she sat—with the help of two attendants who managed to stay in the background while they arranged her billowing skirts—he, too, bowed, falling to one knee. She reached out, and placed the tips of her fingers against his velvet hood, pushing it back and away from his hair.

For a few moments, in the silence of the cool dawn, she was all of the waiting Ladies, and he all of the Hunters at risk—both of whom had seen too many deaths to make any promises or any wishes known.

And then their somber silence was rudely broken by the thrum of harp strings struck badly for just that purpose. Without so much as a by-your-leave, a very young man holding a harp at his hip as if it were a comfortable sack, leaped up onto the dais, singing. His hair was soft, burnished gold, which fell in ringlets past his shoulders in such a perfect way that some of the younger Ladies watched with envy—and interest. He moved with grace, surety, and speed, and somehow managed to toss the edge of his pale gray cloak over his shoulder without interrupting the music.

Unfortunately, he was singing the song that most peasants knew as "The Drunken Hunter," a ribald and silly little ditty that one didn't sing around one's mother. His voice, perfect in pitch and sweet in tone, carried so that even those farthest from the King and Queen could hear it clearly. This was the talent of the bard-born, and by his brazen act, rather than by any symbol of any college, Kallandras the bard made himself known.

Shock kept the Lords silent, and the Ladies kept straight faces, although one or two of the younger girls shook silently behind spread fans, which made it impossible to tell whether they were crying or laughing.

But the Queen laughed gaily, and the sparkle in her eyes made it clear that the cheek of the young bard did no damage to her good opinion of him. The King raised an eyebrow, but made no comment as he gained his feet. Kallandras' voice was so buoyant and cheerful, it was a delight to listen to, even wrapped as it was around such a questionable series of stanzas.

For his finish, he coaxed from his harp a series of notes that seemed impossible, and then bowed with a flourish, drawing his small cap down and across his chest in the manner of those from the East. A smattering of applause followed, mostly from the Ladies and the servants.

"Kallandras, why have you come?" The Queen held out one slender hand, her expression making clear her welcome, as the question did not. He took it gracefully, brought it to his lips, and smiled.

"Did you think I would miss such a festive occasion without just cause? I've decided to accept your invitation, Majesty. What other opportunity have I," he added, lowering his voice, "to spend so much time surrounded by such elegant and powerful Ladies—without the interference of their husbands?"

"Have a care, young minstrel," the King said, mock-sternly. "You give the studious and serious bards a poor name."

"Indeed I do, Highness," was the reply. "But it's not half so bad as the names they give—well, call—me."

Stephen, who had edged as close to the dais as he dared, realized that the stories the servants told of the bard-born were true: They would say anything at all, no matter how improper or inappropriate, and give no offense. Kallandras' voice was filled with a warmth and friendliness that permeated every word he spoke in the presence of the highest powers in the land. And they, King and Queen, could not help but respond.

"And who is the young eavesdropper?" Kallandras said quietly. The voice changed; it still held warmth, mixed now with curiosity—but beneath that there was something as cool as steel.

Stephen started as the bard turned to look directly at him. Then he cringed as the gazes of the King and Queen followed.

"The young man? He's huntbrother to Lord Gilliam of Elseth. Stephen?" The word, from the King's lips, had the force of command.

Stephen walked to the side of the dais and quietly mounted the steps. He took care with his cloak—the last thing he wanted, in front of personages such as these, was to trip or stumble.

"Stephen. Of Elseth." The bard came forward as Stephen hesitated, too aware that he had the attention of all of the Hunters and their Ladies. "I'm Kallandras of Senniel." He frowned when it was obvious that the name of the most illustrious of all bardic colleges meant nothing to the young huntbrother. That frown rippled and deepened; it became distant and cool once again.

This close to the bard, it was clear to Stephen that that coolness was not directed at him. He waited because he had nothing to say, and after a moment, Kallandras smiled wistfully. "I'm pleased to make your acquaintance, Lord Stephen." His voice was full, his bow, low. "I've heard about you."

Stephen's mouth formed a half "o" of surprise. He opened his mouth to speak, and the bard's ringlets shifted with the shake of his head. "Not now, huntbrother— you and I have other duties at the moment, or so the King's glare tells me."

The King was not glaring. "Duties? You?"

"Ah, yes. Didn't someone tell you?"

"Tell me?" The King turned his head to meet his wife's gaze. She smiled a little ruefully and nodded. "Tell me what?"

"It is almost the call of the Sacred Hunt. I join the drummers, Your Highness." Now, for the first time in the King's presence, Kallandras fell to one knee. "I will sing the Hunt's beginning with your permission, Master of the Game."

"And will your bard-born voice soothe the Hunter's Death and stave off the fulfillment of our promise?" It was said in jest, or at least it appeared so, but Stephen could see that the King's eyes did not smile with his lips.

"No. But perhaps I will give heart to your Hunters."

"And perhaps to our God." The King looked up to meet Iverssen's gaze. They locked stares for a moment, and then the Priest looked away. "Yes, if you will. Sing the Hunt's beginning." He reached up and unclasped his cloak. Before it left his shoulders, two attendants were behind him to smooth and preserve the folds of green velvet. "But, Kallandras?"

"Yes, Highness?"

"I charge you to do at the end what you claim you will do at the beginning. Lend heart to my Hunters."

To this, Kallandras had no reply. He nodded again, and bowed his head low until the King passed by him. When he heard the royal feet upon the stairs, he looked up to meet the solemn eyes of the Queen.

He mouthed a few words, and the Queen's eyes rose.

"No," she whispered. "*Not* 'The Drunken Hunter.'"

The drums began their sonorous roll at the edge of the clearing farthest from the preserve. The Hunter Lords had returned with their lymers—the best of the scent hounds in the kingdom. They had chosen their quarry well, if quickly, and all that remained was the Hunt. The huntbrothers coupled the dogs while their masters prepared as the drums beat on. It was an odd sound; steady and yet somehow almost musical. If the forest had a pulse, this was it: wild and primitive and endless.

The Ladies, those present, gave tokens to their Lords and wished them well—but it took mere minutes. The Lords were already in trance, and too far away from anything that was not either dog or huntbrother.

Stephen held the couples and every so often nudged a dog in the ribs with his boot. Terwel was the worst of the lot and could barely be kept from springing the leash and dragging his companion with him. He had sighted a competitor he dearly wished to test himself against—the big, red-brown hound that Lord Alswaine boasted as his pride.

Alair. That was his name.

Gilliam turned to stare wide-eyed at the leader of his borrowed pack. Terwel's growl grew stronger, but he settled back into the lead; the Hunt was close, he would soon be allowed to run and track and feed. Today was not the time to test the son of the master.

The strain in Stephen's upper arms and shoulders lessened. Freed from the intense worry and concentration the large gray alaunt demanded, he looked up to watch Gilliam's face. What he saw was the Hunter in trance. It was time, now, to join him.

He closed his eyes, and as sight left him nothing but the faint red-black beneath his eyelids, sound grew stronger. The drumbeats grew louder and more insistent, although they remained steady and rhythmic. He felt his own pulse racing to catch time, and felt one other join it. He could almost hear the whisper of the dogs, almost taste the absolute necessity to be free of the couples, hunting the running, jumping, cloven-hoofed, frightened prey. He felt energy, excitement, overweening pride—and none of it was his. Shaking his head, he pulled back. His eyes flew open and he saw the clearing as it was: full of dogs and men, the former gray and brown, black and occasionally white—the latter, green, brown, and gold. He did not understand, in that moment, how Gilliam could live in the Hunter's trance; just the taste of it, seen through their oath-bond, alarmed him, and if he regretted not being born to the Hunter God's service, he also felt relief.

And then he heard it: the single, haunting note of the King's horn. It shattered the noise that Stephen had barely been aware of and, before silence could settle, continued with three shorter ones.

In answer, the Hunter Lords drew their horns, and lifted them as one man. Stephen was no musician, but he knew that the absolute perfection of timing, of inhale, start, and stop, should have been impossible. He waited until the drums commanded the air once again before fumbling at his belt. The horn the King had given him was cold to the touch against both fingers and lips. He drew breath around the mouthpiece and expelled it forcefully. One short note. One long. Two short notes. One long.

In the forest, the shadows stirred; the leaves rustled, unusually loud with the force of the wind and the morning. Stephen felt something *snap* into place as the notes died away. Almost reluctantly, he tied the horn to his belt once more.

The tenor of the drumming changed; single strikes became staggered and flew faster and faster against the skins until, at the unseen hands of the Hunter Priests, the clearing was filled with the roar of thunder. The sun and the clarity of sky were anomalous; the Hunters of Breodanir entered the storm.

And behind them, almost at one with them, flowed dogs and huntbrothers alike.

Chapter Thirteen

SOREDON WALKED THE PRESERVE with the ease of familiarity. At his side, unleashed and barely collared, walked Corwel. Even with his nose to the ground and his bandit's mask flecked with mud, his gait was regal.

The Lord of Elseth had chosen his quarry well enough; without the need to discuss the Hunt with any but Norn, it had been a gentle and quiet operation. He was certain that he would have a good, brisk walk ahead of him. Again, familiarity told him that the northern preserve was where he would find his stag.

Corwel was peaceful as well, if quick, but every so often he would stop and look up at his master, the glint of curiosity in his black eyes.

"This is your last hunt, old boy," Soredon whispered sadly. "Let's make it count." He used words, instead of trance-speaking. Corwel wouldn't understand them, but he needed the release of saying them anyway.

Norn's familiar footstep, not as quiet or as sure as his own, was gaining ground. He shook his head, scratched Corwel's ears affectionately, and then gave himself completely to the Hunt.

It was going to be hard to fulfill the Hunt's promise. The sound of the horns and the beat of the drums had pierced the forest's stillness, an absolute warning to any who heard it, whether they'd listened for it or no. The sounds lingered, caught in Stephen's chest and inner ears.

Gilliam moved quickly and, after the initial exhilarating run into the undergrowth, slowly. Absynt walked in front of him, nose to the ground, a single collar around his gray throat. He was older now, but the most important of the senses were still his to claim; he followed Gilliam's chosen trail without wavering once. Indeed, he pulled at the leash as if it vexed him, and after a few moments, Gilliam gave him his head. He made no sign to Stephen to uncouple the rest of the dogs; his concentration had to be reserved for Absynt alone.

The tracks, deep and evenly spaced in the soft ground, spoke of the size and unworried pace of the stag. They were fresh, which was more important. Absynt followed them without any difficulty at all.

Now that the other dogs were out of sight, and for the moment, out of hearing, Terwel had settled back into his couple. He wasn't graceful about it, and every so often he shouldered Stephen almost hard enough to knock him over—but not quite. He knew he could make his displeasure known to a point, but not beyond that, before he brought the anger of his young master, and although he was a dog, he remembered the one time that he had been forcibly denied the Hunt.

Stephen felt Gilliam tense and looked up. He felt a ripple of dismay and knew its cause at once: the tracks had widened suddenly; the stag had already bolted.

Hard? he thought, as he picked up his pace. It was going to be impossible. And today, of all days, they dared not fail. He nodded at Gilliam, caught Gilliam's return nod and the flash of his back as the Hunter and Absynt ran on ahead.

The Kovaschaii was also a hunter, and if his lessons had been in the labyrinths of Melesnea, and his training had been in the city streets and parlors of Averalaan, it would have been hard to tell. He wore Hunter's colors, less the gold, and he moved with his back to the shadows and an eye to the light. Birds saw him pass without comment or movement, treating him as just another predator who was not interested in their mates or their growing nests.

He had seen the huntbrother enter the sacred preserve on the heels of his Hunter, and he trailed them quietly. The dogs, coupled and held, were upwind; with care, they would not catch his unfamiliar scent and give warning. He had to make sure that they were run in the Hunt proper before he approached his target—he made a practice of disarming his victims before a kill. The Kovaschaii were cautious.

The sun was barely above the horizon, but the trees here were thin and too new to provide good cover; his shadow was long and moved against the forest's patterns. He disliked it. But more, he disliked the sound of the other Hunters who had entered the forest at nearly the same point as his target. He had to avoid being seen by any. It was not the optimum situation.

Ah. There. He stopped when a flash of green, surrounded by four-legged browns and grays, came into view. His chest stopped moving; he stood as the trees did, but without their little rustles. Then the Elseth huntbrother was gone again, but he waited five minutes before picking up the trail. Timing was of the essence.

They jogged. The dogs weren't bothered by it, and Gilliam didn't notice at all. Stephen took deep and even breaths, forcing his feet into a steady rhythm. He held the dogs to his pace, knowing it dangerous to let them gain control here. They strained at the leads, testing his strength. Gilliam had vanished; the thin line of trees hid him from Stephen's vision. But the hounds knew where he was, and they followed unerringly.

Perhaps half an hour passed in the forced and silent jog before Gilliam appeared. He spoke no word, but by the signal made clear that all was well. Once again, the stag had slowed to a less frenetic pace. They could follow and hope to catch it at harbor.

Stephen breathed a sigh of relief—it was all the breath he could spare.

Ten minutes later, they came to the river.

From the cover of trees that were a little too thin for comfort, the Kovaschaii watched the Elseth huntbrother at the river's edge. Silt and mud were carried by the water's rush, and the banks were completely covered in the swell caused by melted snow.

It would be a good place to drown, if one slipped. The single bridge across the river was nothing more than flat slats; there were no railings, no way to grab hold. And it was almost ideal. The young Hunter was far enough ahead that he could not be seen. Certainly, he would not be able to interfere.

But the boy still held the dogs.

The wind shifted, and the Kovaschaii shifted with it as if caught in the breeze. He lost his moment as the boy, dogs still in hands that appeared to be shaking, crawled his way across the bridge. Another passing minute brought the Hunter; he spoke, but the words could not be heard naturally, and the Kovaschaii wished to preserve his reserves of power. The meaning of the words became obvious soon enough. The young huntbrother uncoupled two of the dogs, and unleashed the only animal that did not share a lead. These three went immediately to the banks and began to nose around.

He crossed his arms, watching with interest. He could wait. The Hunt, or the running of it, had not yet started—and once it had, the huntbrother would bring up the rear in a very vulnerable position.

What?

Corwel's ears were twitching, and the hair on his neck seemed to stand on end. He raised his head, stopping astride the tracks that had led him this far. The scent was strong enough to linger in his nostrils, but it was . . . odd.

Soredon moved into Corwel, following the lines of his trance until their two senses were all scent-hound. The green and brown of forest, with its interplay of shadow and light, became gray shades. The ripple of muscles that gathered around neck and jaw hurt.

Yes. Something was strange. In the familiarity of this Hunt, a new element had appeared. Soredon tried to place a finger on it—he was certain that he had felt it before—but it eluded him.

"Soredon?"

He shook his head, calling for Norn's silence and receiving it at once. He tested the air, touched the tracks, and then slid out of Corwel's viewpoint.

"We hunt," he said softly, as his hand fell once again to the wide, rounded head of his pack's leader. The words, a motto of the life he best loved, came out as if they were suddenly too large for his mouth. They were not for Norn, but Norn heard them anyway.

"Maybe we should leave this trail," he said, his voice quiet. "There were many that bore our interest."

But Soredon shook his head once, fierce in the motion, and urged Corwel forward. There was a light in his eyes, a ferocity in his step, that even Gilliam in the flush of first youth couldn't match. Budding leaves played against his face with their shadows, blocking the light; it made a phantom mask appear against his pale skin.

He looked not unlike Corwel as they continued along the track.

The stag was not young enough to be foolish, but not old enough to lose a seasoned hunting pack, and although it took time—and a backtrack across the river—Absynt found its trail again. His ears pricked up, his breath changed subtly, and he looked back at Gilliam with guileless pride. Gilliam wanted to leap with joy; he was wet from the river's edge, and cold as well, but at least it had not been without cause.

Stephen knew, of course. His sigh was louder than Absynt's, but just as unmistakable. "Gil?"

"What?"

"You'll be okay?"

Gilliam nodded. He had had to hold four dogs, jumping between them as they searched. It had been tiring, and would only get worse. The dogs had not yet been unleashed, and he would have to run at their head when he finally set them baying.

Stephen grimaced and hit himself in the side of the head for Gilliam's benefit. It had been a stupid question. If Gilliam were dropping from exhaustion, it wouldn't have made a difference; the Hunt had to be called, and it had to be run. This one day, no excuses would be tolerable—or tolerated.

The sun was well up by now, which warmed the ground and made it less pleasant to traverse. Stephen slipped once, but even that didn't slow them down. He jogged along, mud caked and drying along his back. His breath, short and sharp, came out in a mist that wreathed his face.

And then, in the distance, they saw it: a brown, fur-covered creature that had suddenly frozen in the wind, the white underside of its tail twitching. Its head turned in three-quarter relief, and large brown eyes met smaller ones unhindered by thin strands of trees.

Gilliam gave a wordless cry of excitement mingled with relief. His nervous fingers fumbled with his horn before it could be brought to his lips. The stag was gone in the blink of an eye. It left its tracks and the sound of its passing as evidence of its presence.

It was late to start the call, but the dogs lost all trace of exhaustion. They came to the Hunt as called, fresh and new—eager to prove themselves.

Stephen knelt, mud ignored, and uncoupled the dogs. His fingers trembled, not with cold—he'd barely removed mittens that practically made his hands sweat—but with anxiety. This was their first Hunt, their first act as real adults. They had to make it count.

Absynt was last to be freed, but he made way for Terwel, as did the other dogs that had gathered. Gilliam kept them in, but barely—they strained against his trance-voice as if it were merely the noise a groom made.

Stephen saw a flash of anger in his Hunter's eyes and bit his lip. *Not now, Terwel*, he thought, half-savagely. *We don't have the time.*

But the time had to be taken. Gilliam made them sit a full quarter-minute in order to show his control. He had no choice, this close to the quarry. Anything else ran the highest risk of an improperly finished Hunt. Not catching a beast was bad, but not portioning it properly was nearly as big a crime; it showed the Hunter's lack of control and will.

If we fail at this, Terwel, Stephen thought, as his hands formed fists in harmony with his thoughts, *I'll kill you myself.*

But the seconds passed, ending abruptly with Terwel's high, short whine. Gilliam's eyes shifted and changed; they grew strange even to his huntbrother.

The horn was winded. At last. Stephen had time to draw breath and brace himself before the pack was off and running, Gilliam at its head. He could barely hear, over the baying of the running dogs, the sound that left Gilliam's throat. It was a poor twin to their call, but he knew that Gilliam wouldn't notice.

He twined the leads carefully and shoved them into his jacket as he ran, trying to keep pace with dogs held back too long and a Hunter in trance. The gap widened between them, but Stephen had training to make up for the lack of blood-granted abilities—he lost ground perceptibly, but was not left behind.

Now.

The Kovaschaii felt the moment coming. He heard the horn call, and almost rolled out into sight before the notes had faded. Almost. Instinct whispered no, and he listened carefully, snapping his joints to a stop and drawing, finally, upon his many talents.

The terrain in the preserve was not always flat; indeed, small hills and short outcroppings that could almost be dignified by the name cliff abounded. The ground was slippery in places, more mud than dirt, and the undergrowth was new. A careless, anxious huntbrother, back from his Hunter and pack, might slip and fall in unfortunate foot play.

He came out upon the trail and began to jog in Stephen's wake. He kept pace with the boy, his eyes scanning the distance between his prey and the dogs. The gap was widening, but not as quickly as the Kovaschaii had hoped. Still, that couldn't last—the Hunter-born were known for their speed and endurance while hunting. Huntbrothers, such as the young Elseth one, were merely trained commoners.

The Kovaschaii had drawn no weapon, although by custom he carried three; he needed none for his chosen accident. He only need wait and strike quickly; it was that simple. But the boy was still too close to his Hunter.

The tenor of the dogs' raucous calls changed in pitch and frequency. He saw them disappear suddenly on their run, and realized that the time had come. They had crested a hill of some sort, and the huntbrother was due to follow.

A surge of energy, of otherworld calm, sizzled through his body. He heard its tingle with his inner ear, and rejoiced. It was time for silence, swiftness, accuracy; the carefully hoarded reserve was drained as he put on his last burst of speed and cloaked himself, momentarily, from normal sight. It required no gesture, no mantra, no foci—he was Kovaschaii, perfectly trained and aimed.

A foot from the boy's back, he raised his hand; it was hard, flat—as much a weapon as a sword might have been.

"HOLD!"

The arm stopped in midair, but not by the will of the Kovaschaii. Pain shot up through elbow and shoulder at the speed of his response. Anger, mixed with a foreign emotion, danced in lines across his pale face. He tried to force the hand down, to follow through on the imperative of his given mission, and failed. The fair-haired youth was already turning. His victim's motions were so painfully slow—a gift of the Kovaschaii magics—they stoked the fires of the assassin's anger. His plan had been perfect. There had been no interference, no followers, no witnesses. It was ash now, burned as if touched by the anger that had momentarily shorted control. He watched as the boy threw himself—again, slowly, slowly—off the trail and out of reach of the fatal strike.

Defeat, then.

The Kovaschaii spun on his feet in the direction of the single inimical word, casually relocating the joint in his arm. Only the voice of one bard-born and bard-trained had such raw and immediate power. He felt it still, although he could now deny its strength. He struggled to cast anger aside, and this time succeeded. Implacable, his face once again the cool, seamless mask, he met the eyes of Kallandras the bard.

The fair-haired man in Hunter's garb was inches away. His arm trembled awkwardly, like a branch in a stiff wind, but Stephen barely noticed this; his gaze was caught by a face of sharp, pale lines. It was calm, almost still, but its eyes were a gleam of light over steel—inhuman and dangerous. With a cry, Stephen threw himself to the side, forgetting the stag, the Hunter, and the pack. He rolled through the mud and came to his feet a little way off the track, his hands the color of dead bark and dirt. He looked wildly over his shoulder, as he had done many, many times as a thief in the lower city. Fear brought back memory, and made of it a sharp, clear weapon. There was no pursuit. He tensed further, brought himself around, and saw why.

Kallandras the bard stood astride the trail, hands on his hips, head tilted in the chill breeze. His hair, shoulder-length curls of gold-flecked brown, rustled and blew round his cheeks. Stephen thought it singularly stupid; long hair, especially in a fight of any note, was an idiotic risk.

But if there was any fear of risk in Kallandras, it was buried well beneath a jaunty, arrogant smile.

"Well met, Estravim." His voice, rich, deep, and warm, performed an invisible bow.

"It *is* you, Kallatin," the young man answered quietly. The tone of voice made a curse of the words in its intensity.

"Oh, yes," Kallandras answered, still in the same friendly tone. Stephen's eyes could only see the blur of white sleeves—billowing, more fool the bard—and Kallandras was suddenly armed. His weapon was a sword, of sorts—it was long and seemed far too thin to be dangerous. "I have your name." He whispered, but the bardic voice carried the words easily.

The smooth lines of the pale man's face rippled uncertainly. Stephen thought he saw fear until he heard the young man's words. "You *cannot* take a name now, traitor." He moved, and he, too, carried a sword that was, in shape if not in guard, the twin of Kallandras'.

"I have your name." The answer was implacable. The bard moved suddenly, covering yards of trail in long strides that barely left time for feet to touch ground.

And this, too, Stephen understood. The other man was moving easily as quickly—toward Stephen. The blade that he carried suddenly seemed a significant weapon. Stephen reversed himself, using the tree for interference as he ran. His cloak caught a branch, and he heard an awful tearing at his ankles. If he had the chance to explain it later, he'd consider himself lucky.

The Kovaschaii was furious. He followed the huntbrother, quickly catching up with him. As the boy dodged behind a tree, he corrected his path. It took no time and no thought; pursuit was the earliest teaching.

He knew that if he reached the boy now and managed to kill him, he would still fail in his taking. It was bitter knowledge; he would dance the death spiral yet, and it would be his own. But he also knew that Kallatin—the blackest name in the history of the Kovaschaii—was here to protect his victim. If he were to fail in his taken name, Kallatin, also, would fail. That much he would see to. Kallatin the traitor had barely completed the first—and the lowest—tier of training before he had disgraced the brotherhood by refusing a kill—and by vanishing into complex shadows and magic that even the Masters could not follow.

Estravim the Kovaschaii was of the third tier, and proud of it; he was young to be so skilled. But pride was not foolishness. He knew that the voice of the bard-born, from the throat of one Kovaschaii trained, would soon be his death.

He called on the last of his reserves, called up a power that he was never meant to touch, and used it. The boy's progress slowed to near-halting; even strands of flailing hair ceased their struggle with the breeze. A second passed, maybe two, and the sword was raised above the back of the huntbrother's neck, just as the arm had been earlier.

It came down in stillness and silence.

The clang of metal against metal was unmistakable as it reverberated to fill his ears. Time started to turn again; the boy's back began to retreat. Estravim stared into the eyes of Kallatin the traitor. He spat.

Spittle, completely ignored, ran down the cheek of Kallandras the bard as he pulled back his blade and twisted it in the air.

Signal: now. Gesture, respect from one of lower tier to higher.

Estravim stepped into position with grace and deadly ease. He should not have granted the bard that respect, and he knew it—but it was automatic.

Kallandras held his blade in his right hand. His fingers shifted beneath the guard, his grip changed, and in a flick of motion, the tip of the sword cut his forehead, leaving a scant trail of blood in its wake. With his free hand, he gestured, a snap of motion from wrist to elbow that drove the cuff of his shirtsleeve momentarily up his forearm, revealing a slender bracer. Gold melded with silver glinted in the dull light; each termination of the ten-point star—the symbol of the Kovaschaii—glittered. The sword fell slowly, point to ground, and wavered in the wind—but Estravim knew that Kallandras drew the foci of the ten-point star in the air like a sigil. Challenge. And it was a challenge that Estravim could not avoid.

No Kovaschaii of the first tier would have been able to draw this sigil. A grimace tugged at the corners of his mouth, and he spoke, although this, too, was foolish. "How?"

"Second tier," Kallandras whispered, his eyes remote.

"No master would train you. . . ." Words failed him, and his anger, stiff to the point of breaking, shattered. He saw the star traced, could not help but see the beads of blood that struggled waywardly down a nose that had been broken at least once. With a motion twin to the bard's, he snapped his wrist. He also wore the golden manacle of the Kovaschaii—but he had the right to bear it. He wanted to decry the bard's use of the symbol, but again the words would not come. For he looked at the eyes of his enemy; they were very blue, very pale. Beneath their slate surface was a hint of sorrow, a touch of shame. Estravim grimly traced the ten-point star, taking it from memory and engraving it in the air. His response. "How could you choose treachery? We were brothers."

At the use of the familiar term, Kallandras winced. "I am wyrd-ridden. I was shown what the death of the woman would bring us to: the end of the Kovaschaii—and the end of the world."

"You were shown lies."

"I was shown truth. For nothing less would I have left you." His blade came up and he lunged.

"Even so—what of it? We are guaranteed to the Lady." Estravim dodged and blocked, the movement turning to a thrust at the halfway mark. He felt steel against his skin before it entered; it was a cool, clean pain. He smiled anyway. He could see the spread of crimson across the bard's cheek. They had each called blood; each touched in the step of this intricate, ancient dance.

Kallandras nodded grimly and began in earnest. Beads of sweat had time to line his brow and cheeks as he fought. Estravim was good—had always been good—and he attacked like one possessed. Because, of course, he was.

Here, in the open spaces of sparse woods and flat ground, Estravim gave in to his training; his sword grew wings, and the wind ran down the runnels along the crescent in a sibilant song that the Kovaschaii were trained to listen for. There was art in his movements, and in his attack; he chose the grace of line and action that was only displayed among equals. It didn't change the ferocity of his weapon-play, but rather, made an art of it.

Kallandras, in defense, could not come up with half of the beauty and artistry that Estravim displayed in attack.

But that grace couldn't last; the man who had once been called Kallatin knew it. Estravim had exhausted reserves of power that no Kovaschaii not resigned to death could call. That he could attack so perfectly spoke of his skill and his determination.

Estravim knew it, too—and his attack was a dance, almost a farewell. One second, he was dodging in midair, his feet clearing the ground by a good twenty inches, and the next, he was looking down the blade of the sword that ended—or started—in his chest.

"So soon?" His eyes shuttered and dimmed immediately; his face twisted in a pain that had nothing to do with the physical.

"I will remember. You had no equal here."

A smile broke through the pain before his eyes rolled up. Kallandras stared down at him as he started to fall.

The clash and clang of swordplay stopped abruptly; the silence that followed was chilling. Stephen watched, his face at knee level, his body obscured by the trunk of the largest tree he had found.

The assassin had just stopped in mid-step, as if asking for a deathblow. Kallandras' sword appeared out of nowhere to grant the man his request. The pale man sank to the ground, his knees bending and giving under his weight. Kallandras watched for a moment and then suddenly cursed. He yanked the sword free—sending a spray of red droplets across the ground—and threw the sword, hard.

It landed inches away from Stephen's hand.

He barely noticed. Rising slowly, he began to retrace his steps, twice tripping over small inclines. His eyes were upon the bard.

Kallandras, in an odd mimicry of the assassin's slow crumple, knelt to the ground and stretched out his arms to catch the body. Where the wound was open, blood splashed his breast. He ignored it as he gathered the body close, and cradled it against his chest. He heard Stephen coming and looked back. Only the trail of drying crimson across his forehead colored his face at all; even his eyes were flat and colorless.

"Go," he whispered. "This is not for you."

Stephen heard the anger in his voice and stopped moving. "I—thank you for—"

"Don't say it." Kallandras rose, still holding the body. "This is not for you, young huntbrother. Go."

Stephen swallowed.

"It's been minutes," Kallandras said, as he lay the body down. "You won't have lost them if you run." He stiffened as Stephen hesitated. "**Go.**"

This time, confused or no, Stephen had no choice; the meaning of the word was made manifest in a way that no other spoken word had ever been. His legs were moving, his feet following the trail broken by dogs and Gilliam both—without his guidance.

And he was weeping. Tears coursed down his cheeks, warming them before wind turned them to ice.

It was how he knew that Kallandras' smooth, pale face really was a mask over private pain; the bard hadn't been able to keep the grief out of his command.

He was ashamed. To use the voice on the boy was inexcusable; a poor display of self-control if ever there was one. But he had no time; the Kovaschaii spirit awaited its death dance, and there were none here but he to give it.

None here yet, he reminded himself. The Kovaschaii knew when one of their number had fallen. They would come as soon as possible unless the dance was done. Cradling the head gently, he stroked the hair out of the slack face. He sat thus a moment, contemplating. Then he shook himself. He had no right to dance the death, but he wanted to anyway.

The arms and legs he arranged properly, until they formed four points of a star, to the fifth point Estravim's still face made. Then he rose lithely, for all that he was out of practice, and hesitantly began to trace the five secret points—the five that completed the ten. His movements grew more sure as he progressed, his feet leaving shadows across Estravim's body without ever disturbing his rest. He opened his lips and began to sing.

Singing was common, and part of the death dance—and if Kallandras, who had been Kallatin, had never been particularly graceful at the challenge or the attack, none had sung a better death than he. Wordless sorrow, endless loss, a blackness the night fled from—all these rose in him, contained by the thrum of throat and the shape of lip.

Faster and faster he flew, his arms like wings, his face the Kovaschaii mask. But the mask was cracked, imperfect; tears fled it, leaving the face unchanged in their passage.

Come, Lady, come. He danced.

Set my brother free; grant him passage.

He danced, and the world shifted; the forest fell away into mist and gray softness that humans had no words for. He sang, and the mist took shape on the periphery of the ten-point star.

"Who calls?" a toneless voice whispered. "Who wishes to meet me in the half-world?"

He spun to a standstill, one foot on either side of Estravim's face. "I do."

"And you?"

He squinted but the mists fogged his eyes, becoming both solid and less substantial. "I am Kallatin. Lady, you hold my name."

And suddenly, the mist unraveled and fell away from his eyes like gauze too thin to trap sight. He saw *her*, and she him. Hair, so dark a black that ebony would seem faded beside it, flowed around her thin, long face and past her shoulders. She was not tall, but height made no difference to her; she was majesty, a royalty that only the other gods could contest.

Upon her shoulder perched a raven, wings glossy black, beak pale orange. At her feet, where her flowing cape parted, a small, dark shape curled around her ankles and stared out through unlidded eyes.

"You are no longer Kallatin."

He bowed.

"But I know of your wyrd. I have not . . . forgiven you, little son. But I have not ordered your death either. I have heard your dance, and I accept it, although you have killed your brother, who served me truly." She stepped forward. "No, do not offer me your tears or your sorrow; they are not finished yet."

So saying, she lifted one hand, and her fingers curled up in calling. Estravim's pale eyes blinked open, the white sheen of lashes resting against dark, slack circles.

"I heard the music," Estravim said softly, and made to rise. His arms, weak and suddenly thin, would not move from the points of the star. Kallandras touched his forehead, which was still wet and sticky from the challenge. His fingers came away reddened, and he looked at them a moment before he knelt, taking care not to leave the points of the star that his feet formed. He placed his hands beneath Estravim's shoulders and concentrated.

Very slowly, Estravim rose out of his body. His face took on the color and the vibrancy of life that the corpse would never again have. But he did not look back to see who aided him.

"Have you come to give me back my name?" he said quietly to the Lady who waited.

"Yes," she answered. "You will find your strength soon; do not be concerned. When we walk, I shall guide you and protect your path. You are Estravim nee Soldaris Corasin. You have served me well."

He caught her hand, and with her help gained his footing. Before she could speak again, he was on one knee in front of her. Her smile was dark, but not cold, and her own hand rested gently upon his forehead as her pale, pale fingers stroked his hair. "Rise."

He did. And then he turned to see which of his brothers had danced his death, called the Lady, and lifted him from his prison.

"You." There was no anger in the word; only confusion lingered behind his otherworld eyes. "Why?" Before Kallandras could answer, he spun around to face his Lady. "Why did you come at his call?"

"Do you question me already?" She asked, but not harshly. "Very well. I hold his name still."

Estravim's smile was grim. "Then he will be trapped fully when he dies; none will call you to release him."

"It may be so," she answered quietly. "Come."

"Wait!"

They both turned to see Kallandras standing perfectly still. "What I saw— Lady, what I saw was truth."

"A truth." But she heard what lay beneath the words and the perfectly controlled tone. She nodded, ever the regal monarch.

"If I had killed her, we would have perished in time—each of my brothers, each of my teachers. Only for love of them could I make my choice; I have been as true to my Order as any. And I have lost all." He hated to plead.

"All?" One slim line of frosted black rose over a dark eye. What he left unsaid, she knew. Her expression grew remote as she stood, hand upon one of her chosen. "I have not forgiven you, bard. But you served me in your time, and I am not without compassion.

"Estravim of my Kovaschaii, this bard who was once Kallatin spoke the truth that he believes—yet even so, his actions were a betrayal of his oath. You have done me nothing but honor; therefore I will leave your response at your discretion. Recognize him, or not, as you choose. I will make no judgment."

Estravim turned with eyes of death and looked long at the bard.

The bard stared back, unblinking, his face a mixture of apprehension, longing, and bitterness. He opened his mouth and lifted his hand, as if to start another explanation; silence fell as he bit it back. It was not his choice—it was Estravim's, brother, and lost.

"I could not have made your decision," Estravim said at last. "Truth or no. The loss would have been too great. I loved none but the Kovaschaii, and none but the Kovaschaii have mattered to me, save the Lady.

"You danced my death," he bowed. "None among us could dance a death so perfectly. We all know it, even though we do not speak your name. I thank you. You have honored me, Kallatin." Stiffly, as if movement were no longer natural, Estravim touched his forehead and fell to one knee.

"Thank you," the bard whispered; the name that was lost lingered in the air. "It is I who am honored." As the mists faded and the half-world went with the Lady, the tears rolled down Kallandras' cheeks. He reached out blindly and ran his fingers across Estravim's face; it was still warm.

Stephen did not know the exact moment when he regained control of his feet, but he thought it was when he heard the dogs baying. The tenor of their voices, the precision of their cacophony, drove away all images of the bard save one: the way he knelt, heedless of mud, to cradle the body of the strange, pale man.

Stephen was near the end of his running breath, his throat raw and dry. The bardic voice had left him little choice but to sprint full out up the trail.

Please, please, please, he thought, when his breath refused him even a whisper, *finish the Hunt, Gil.* The baying stopped suddenly. The sides of his throat clung together. He gagged, but kept moving.

This one moment was safest for worry, fear, and anger. Gilliam was with the dogs—so completely given over to the hunt that his huntbrother's voice was the slightest of tickles in his inner ear.

Don't let the dogs eat, Gil. Don't please please please don't join them. He'd seen that once, and it was an ugly, horrible sight. Soredon had thought it funny, and even Norn had worn a grim, tired smile as they had pulled Gilliam away from the carcass of the boar he'd been hunting. But not even the smell of roasting flesh and boiling broth at the end of the long, cool day could entice Stephen to eat any meat that night—or for weeks afterward.

The ground at his feet became a blur of gathered tracks and gouged mud; he was close.

Gilliam, please, please—

The call of a horn answered his frantic litany. Nine notes, nine perfect, fully winded notes, came back to him, carried downwind by a faint breeze. Hunt's end had been called. He pulled out his horn and leaned his back against the smooth bark of the nearest tree. His hand shook as he carried the horn to his mouth and blew back the proper response. It sounded like a strangling duck. On any other Hunt, he would have laughed at the pathetic noise the horn made.

He started to cry.

"Stephen?"

"What?" He wiped viciously at his eyes with the cuff of his jacket.

"I heard it." Gilliam looked exhausted but content; sweat ran down his forehead, matting thin dark curls to his face. "Come on, we're waiting for you."

"You didn't let the dogs—"

"No." Gil held out a hand, and after a moment, Stephen took it and crushed it as hard as he could. Gilliam grunted and returned the grip, and they stood that way a moment before Stephen suddenly surrendered and let his hand go limp.

"You fell behind," the young Hunter said as they started to walk.

"I'm sorry," Stephen answered. "Someone tried to kill me."

It took the better part of half an hour to convince Gilliam that the danger was past, and even convinced, the young Hunter wanted his enemy's blood. Stephen thought it the aftereffects of being so long at the Hunt, and did his best to put out the odd, reddish light in Gilliam's eyes. Only afterward did he realize that the tone of voice and the simplicity of repetitive words he had chosen to use with Gilliam were like those he would speak to the dogs.

They had made the initial cut the length of the stag's proud throat with a blade that Gilliam pulled from a long pouch at his back, one carried for only this purpose. The flaps of wet, supple skin were pulled back almost to the neck, and the dogs were given their reward for the baying of the hart—a few mouthfuls of flesh and blood that had not yet cooled.

Stephen coupled the hounds, treading with care around the muddy ground. The hounds' tails whapped against his thighs, and the occasional dog tried to knock him over with a none-too-subtle shoulder-check—but he was used to this.

While Stephen worked, Gilliam played out the nine again, slowly and surely calling a triumphant close to his first Sacred Hunt. The sun was not yet upon the horizon, and the day not yet too cold. He carried the last note with what little breath remained in his lungs. The dogs looked up at this and joined him in their own fashion.

Stephen knew that Gilliam would make—and break—the last trance-connection with each of his hunting dogs. He would praise them and feed their animal egos before he set the horn aside and began the onerous task of carrying the stag back to the Queen's pavilion.

Carrying? Stephen grunted as he tied the front and back legs of the carcass together. Dragging, more like. At any other Hunt, there would be aides to help with the task of returning the kill. But, no, on the one day when the Hunter was most at risk, everything had to be done "independently." He grunted as he pulled.

Gilliam came to help him, and the dogs, tired from their run and satisfied with their master's praise, obeyed his terse commands. They followed at heel, and only occasionally got into the little territorial scrapes that so annoyed their master.

The Hunter Lord only called a stop once as they followed their trail backward, but the ground was clear and marked only by the many feet of the passing animals and their human masters. Stephen could not find the body of his would-be killer anywhere. He knew that he hadn't gone mad because the dogs found the scent—but even Absynt thought it weak and almost directionless, more like the scent of a place than like the trail of any living quarry.

"The thing I don't understand," Gilliam said between grunts, "is why anyone'd want to kill you."

"How should I—Terwel!—know?"

"Maybe he thought you were someone else." Gilliam stopped long enough to kick Terwel in the shoulder with the flat of his boot. Terwel whined and rolled over, and Gilliam started to lug again. "I mean, we're all dressed the same."

"I think he knew what he was doing."

"Oh. Maybe we should just ask Kallandras."

Kallandras had knelt by the body and gently cradled the corpse. There had been no anger in his eyes, in fact, no expression at all upon his face. But Stephen had had much experience with masking emotion, and he knew the sorrow the bard's stooped shoulders had spoken of. He felt that they were somehow cohorts in a very strange crime, and he didn't want to expose Kallandras to anyone else. Yet. "I will."

"We will."

"I will."

"Look, you're my huntbrother, and it's my responsibility to protect you. *We* talk to him."

"*I* talk to him."

"Oh right," Gilliam said, dropping the legs of the stag. "So you talk to him, and maybe someone else tries to kill you, and no one else is around to help. Forget it. I forbid it."

"If someone else tries to kill me, Kallandras'll probably handle him the same bloody way." Stephen's arms crossed his chest as his jaw tightened. "And what the hell do you mean, 'forbid it'?"

"*I'm* the Hunter Lord."

"You're an idiot!"

"An idiot. Right." Gilliam's shoulders tensed. "Idiot enough to finish the Hunt on my own."

Stephen drew breath sharp enough to cut his tongue; it meant he didn't have to bite it. *How dare you?* He thought, his face flushing. *You know damn well why I missed the last leg!* Red-faced, he spoke with anger's voice and anger's words. "What's the matter, Gil? Are you upset that Kallandras was a better protector than you'll ever be?"

Bull's-eye. Stephen had just enough time to recognize the hit before Gilliam answered anger with anger. Of course, Gilliam didn't answer with words, and the dogs watched in curious concern as their master and his closest ally began to roll around in the dirt, shouting, spitting, and punching each other with the happy abandon of sibling fury.

They were both so enraged that Stephen didn't stop to think about what Lady Elseth would say, which was just as well.

An hour later, they emerged from the King's preserve. The dogs, even Terwel, were quiet as they followed Gilliam's terse commands, walking to heel so perfectly that there was hardly any need for leads. Stephen's left eye was blackened, and his lip was swollen. Gilliam's lip was split and smeared with dried blood. Both of the young men were covered with dirt and the remnants of the previous year's fall; the careful crafted green velvet of Hunter's cloaks looked entirely brown at a distance. Blond hair and brown hair were a mass of knots and wild tangles, but at least the Elseth Hunters had come back successful.

Lord Maubreche, Lord Valentin, and Lord William of Valentin approached them in silence; the bare head of the eldest lord, framed in a ring of white tufts of hair, bent low. His huntbrother, Andrew, came to his aid, and together they lifted and dragged the carcass away to the center of the King's impromptu court—it would be unmade there, according to all of the proper rituals.

Lord Valentin bowed low; his peppered hair fell forward around his thin, lined cheeks. "Your Hunt," he said gravely. His huntbrother, rounder and shorter than he, also bowed. Michaele was not known for polite deference to either Hunters or huntbrothers, although he was still quite capable when it came to the politics of the Ladies.

Stephen was acutely conscious of the mess he presented. He glanced surreptitiously at Gilliam and cringed at what he saw.

But none of the Hunters or their huntbrothers seemed at all concerned—and not one of them was amused. No, their faces were grave, almost gray, in the afternoon light. He started to say something, and then his jaw stopped moving at all. All of the lords had removed their hats, and all of them wore the black sash of the Hunter's Death; it traveled across thin midriff and thick alike, clinging like a web.

Lord William of Valentin approached last; he fell to one knee and held out his hands. There, cradled carefully in the thin, scarred palms of the Hunter Lord were the three knives of unmaking; one to cut flesh and muscle, one to cut bone, and one to remove hide.

Each of these were much older than he—than any of the Hunter Lords who stood in silence before them—and they bore the crest of a stag over a field of stars in gold relief.

"The unmaking, Lord Elseth," William whispered with bowed head.

No one moved for a moment. William raised his head and caught Gilliam in the light of his gray eyes. They were red-rimmed and murky with held tears. "These are yours, Lord Elseth."

Stephen felt Gilliam's confusion turn. He knew a stab of fear so sharp, he wasn't certain whether it was his own, or his Hunter's. It twisted at him, doing more than a blade's damage. He bit his lip and looked at Gilliam's face. Gilliam didn't notice. He stared down at the three knives.

"Norn?" he said at last, and his voice was perfectly composed.

"Alive." William's response came quickly and easily—it was the only good news he carried.

The new Lord of Elseth swallowed and accepted Lord William's burden. His hands were sure and certain as he took the weight of the unmaking and the responsibility of his father's lands.

But Stephen of Elseth cried. Tears streamed down his cheeks, and his eyes were so full that the world blurred and moved incomprehensibly. He wanted to speak, but words couldn't escape the closed wall of his throat.

And he knew that it wasn't his pain alone that drove him to such an improper display. He was huntbrother, and linked to a Hunter Lord—and Gilliam had never been good at expressing pain; the only emotion that came easily was anger, and Stephen was certain he would see that later.

Chapter Fourteen

SOREDON LAY IN DEATH'S REPOSE atop an ornate altar ten feet from the Queen's dais. The King's Priest stood beside him in the silence of the Sacred Hunt, his brown robes flapping at his legs like crippled wings. He did not speak, not yet, but rather attended to the body with the ease of experience. The blood had been washed away, and the vital organs—what was left of them—were now bound to the body in a skein of pale green. Soredon's face was slack; whatever pain had been felt in the dying had left him with his life.

At the foot of the rough-hewn altar lay Corwel; his spine had been snapped, but he had not otherwise been savaged. The great white hound, with his bandit's black mask and a history of successful, even enviable, Hunts behind him, still attended his Lord.

No one watched the Priest at work. The Hunter Lords, drawn now and silent, went about the final responsibility of the Hunt. Beside the burning braziers that were meant as an offering to the Hunter God, they unmade their kills, working with sleeves pushed up past the elbows and cloaks discarded on the ground. It was cool, but warming as the season yearned toward summer. The meat had to be cut, cured, and hung if it was to serve as food for the people in the various demesnes of the kingdom.

Only the kills of the King and the Huntsmen of the Chamber were for the nobles who now waited, and even these were properly unmade with the quiet respect for the hunted that the Hunter knows.

Gilliam worked in silence, first anchoring the stag by his horns, then widening the cut along the throat until it traced the whole of the stag's underbelly. He removed the heart with care, and Stephen stepped quickly in to catch Gil's sleeves before they became blood-sodden. It was the only way he was allowed to help.

The heart was offered to the fire; there was no formal prayer, no formal thanks to accompany the sizzle of flesh that would soon char. But the beast's spirit would be free when the heart was ashes—he would go to the Hunter, and dwell in the afterlands in peace and plenty.

Maybe, Stephen reflected quietly, as he watched the heart burn, there were no formal words because the Hunter Lords, too new from their losses here, could not have been trusted to say them with the proper amount of pride and strength. Smoke, made heavy and dark with blood and flesh burning, wound its way up in a spiral of air, darkening the landscape and dimming the sun. He shivered as he watched, and then turned back to Gilliam.

A familiar figure barred his way. The pale, drawn face of the bard was a mirror to those of the Hunters, and any of the Lords who had thought his bawdy ballad a disgrace were mollified by the sorrow he now offered as his sole expression.

Only Stephen knew that the sorrow was not for Soredon's death, and he was surprised at the anger this brought him.

Kallandras saw the shift in Stephen's face and shook his head, smiling wryly. "It won't do, you know," he said softly. "You're too transparent by half, and it won't serve your House well in the company of the Hunter Ladies. They're all sharp and cold as hunting falcons—but only twice as deadly."

It was meant, Stephen knew, as a friendly comment; he smiled stiffly.

"Walk with me?"

"I can't. I have to attend to Gilliam—Lord Elseth."

Kallandras nodded and threw the folds of his newly donned cloak aside. Cradled like a child in the crook of his arm sat his small lute. "Salla," he said, naming her. "I wish to speak with your Lord, if he will allow it."

"About what?"

"I would—I would sing his father's death."

Stephen started to sidle away, and Kallandras caught his shoulder with his free hand.

"I offer it," he said quietly, "because it is the only thing I can offer. And not a bard in the kingdom, not even the foremost of the Masters of Senniel, could sing a better death than I."

"Why?"

"Why? Skill, perhaps. Too much practice."

"I meant, why did you save my life? How did you know?"

"Ah." Kallandras grew quiet. "If I answer your question—and I must say that you don't seem grateful for the saving of it—will you take my request to your Lord?"

Stephen nodded. Grudgingly, he added, "I'd ask him anyway."

"And honest, too." Kallandras shook his head, and ringlets glinted with firelight and dying sun. "Evayne sent me."

"Evayne?" The lady, robed in midnight blue and surrounded by shadows and dark hair, who had stalked his sleep for three nights.

"Yes. You are under the wyrd of her father."

"F-father?"

"She is god-born; that much I've been able to discover about her in the few years that we've . . . known each other. She calls me when she needs me, and I do what I must to help her."

"Why?"

"Too many questions," Kallandras answered gently, but the distance had returned to his eyes. He stepped back, bowed, and then looked up again; Stephen's eyes had not left his face. "You are young," he said, relenting a little. "I help because I'm committed to it. She fights the darkness in ways I don't understand, but she fights it with everything at her disposal. I fight because I, too, am under Fate's wyrd." He lifted Salla and began to idly strum her strings. Without thought, he pulled melody and harmony from her; a pensive, wordless tune. "It always costs. Always."

Costs? Stephen's dream came back, an echo too sharp to be just memory. Suddenly, he didn't want to ask any more questions. "Let me go find Lord Elseth. I'm sure he'd be happy if you'd sing his father's death. But—but don't make any jests, please?"

"No jests," Kallandras said gravely. "In mourning, young huntbrother, we are closer than you will ever understand." But the last words were a whisper, and Stephen, already searching for Gilliam's back, missed them.

The ring of torches and glass lamps and fires strove to capture the dying daylight when at last the Hunter Lords were entirely finished and ready. Their Ladies joined them in their bitter silence, offering them comfort and support by merely taking, and leaning on, the arms held out to them. Each Lord was allowed the presence of four dogs for the ceremony, and the clearing was warm and crowded.

Seventy-seven Hunter Lords stood at attention as the Hunter's Priest walked to the altar, accompanied by the King, four of the King's hounds, and four of the Priesthood. He carried a burning brazier on a link of chain that hung from a dark pole. The smoke from it smelled sweet and pungent as it rippled through the crowd. Two feet from the altar, he took the pole and drove it, hard, into the soft ground.

That done, he knelt before the King.

The King wore black; gone were Hunter greens and browns, gone the bow and the spear. Only black remained; emptiness, an absence of color, warmth, and light. For one instant, Stephen could see great tined antlers rising from the King's forehead into the night sky above the deep, calm wilderness of his eyes.

"Master of the Game, is the Hunt over?" The words, firm and strong, were ritual. But they were also sincere; a question that began and ended without a surety of the answer.

The Master of the Game walked over to Soredon, Master Hunter, and formerly Lord of Elseth. He stared down at the slack, still face as if searching for signs of life; nor did he give off this quiet, desperate search until minutes had passed.

Then, with infinite care and a respect that was tangible and not begrudged, the King reached down and gently closed his Hunter's eyes. "It is over."

He held out one hand, palm up, and curled his fingers tightly around the horn the Priest gave him. The drums started as the four who had accompanied the King and his Priest took their places on the green and began to play. Their faces were hooded by more than the night, but their pain came out in the throbbing of the skins. The horn sounded the end of the Hunt, and before the first note had died, every Hunter in the realm, Gilliam and Stephen included, had joined in.

The dogs, aware of their masters' grief, began to howl in time of sorts—and together, men and beasts, they made enough noise to be heard even by a God.

The King stepped away at last, and silence was allowed to return. He gestured to the Priest, and the Priest took over while the King stood by his side. He began a quiet incantation over Soredon's body. The hems of his sleeves brushed pale white cheeks and shuttered eyes.

"Hunter," he intoned, and it was clear that he spoke to the God. "We are no oath-breakers; we have come, and we have hunted at your behest, in your lands.

"And you, too, have hunted; you have taken, with skill that we cannot imagine or match, one of the greatest of our number.

"Keep him in peace, and keep our lands whole and healthy for another year. Feed the very land as we feed our people, and we shall return again to renew our vows."

The silence that followed was also part of the yearly ritual—but it, too, was full and heavy with genuine emotion and a grief too deep for words.

Only one man moved in the gathering. He came from the shadows at the farthest edge of the clearing in silence, carrying no torch, no horn, no weapon. He caught the King's eye, and the Priest's, but instead of gently remonstrating with him, they bowed their heads and looked away as he approached the body, to give him what privacy they could in such a public circumstance.

Norn of Elseth knelt in the dirt, his back to the gathered mourners. His broad shoulders seemed so shrunken they barely supported his bulk; the red lights of his hair were extinguished. His fingers moved blindly over Corwel's cold fur before they reached for the edge of the altar.

He rose. The drums stopped their beating, the breeze stilled. In silence, the huntbrother joined the Hunter Lord.

Loss. Stephen understood it well. There had been many deaths and disappearances in his past, in the years with the den, and even those leading up to them. Lord Elseth had changed all that—and now he lay as dead as any commoner. The magic of his presence, the force of his words—with their harsh anger and their prickly comfort—had been given to the Hunter and His Death. It hurt.

But not as much as it hurt Norn.

He knew that Norn shouldn't be alone. Gilliam caught his shoulder as he started forward, and he shook him off, quietly determined to go to Norn's side.

No doubt the death had been awful—it was hard to tell from the body—but at least, dead, Soredon was spared Lord William's fate. Norn was not. He had nothing now; unlike his Hunter Lord, he couldn't hear the voices of the dogs, and he couldn't anchor himself to their needs.

But when Stephen reached Norn, he found himself without words to say or comfort to offer. He reached out and placed one hand on Norn's stooped shoulder, but the larger man shrugged it off.

"Norn of Elseth," the King said softly. "Lord Soredon made his choice years before—as did you. All loss, whether of life or of companionship, was accepted then. We are Hunters and huntbrothers, and the Death takes one of our number, always."

Norn said nothing, nor did the King expect a response. The choice made as a child was bitter solace indeed for such a moment as this. They waited—King, Priest, and huntbrother—but Norn did not touch the body at all. He stared long into the frozen face and then turned away with a whisper. "It should have been me."

Only Stephen heard it. He trailed alongside the older man, afraid of disturbing him, but more afraid of leaving him alone.

Kallandras was true to his word. When at last the King, a wounded Hunter Lord in his own right, retired to his place at the foot of the Queen's dais, when the Priest and the drummers quietly paid their final respects to their fallen and withdrew into the shadows, when the Hunter Lords were finally free to mourn as they chose, he rose, his small lute cradled gently and formally in his arms, and took his place before the altar. He bowed, a sweeping, serious motion, first to Corwel and then to Soredon.

The Hunter Lords looked askance at Gilliam, but as Gilliam did not demur, they kept their thoughts to themselves and waited.

He sang.

His voice was full with the emotion that the Hunter Lords kept carefully masked. They, who had always been strong, had no way to weep but through him—and his voice, accompanied by the sweeping range of lute strings that seemed too small, too inadequate to convey such sound, washed over them all.

There were tears on his cheeks; the fire from the brazier caught them and made pale rubies of their fall. His voice broke over words more than once, but that too became part of his song.

Stephen cried, and after a few minutes, Gilliam joined him. It was safe, after all; no one noticed. Their attention was fixed upon the bard.

Time passed, no one knew—or cared—how long, and Kallandras' song began to slowly change. Strains of grief and utter despair, of loss in the most primal sense, were joined by a thin strand of hope. The death of the Hunter Lord became a green, unfolding life for the land of Breodanir; the fields became fertile, the ground soft and rich. The children, untouched by sorrow and death, played in the peace of Lord Soredon's sacrifice, instead of dying in drought or famine.

All of this, they knew—but they had never *felt* it so clearly, and so cleanly, as at this moment. As Kallandras sang, the ghost of Lord Soredon moved slowly, and with purpose, before them. He smiled, if smile it was—it was hard to tell with Soredon—and reached for his weapons. He frowned down, and Corwel suddenly joined him; Corwel remade, young and perfect and a little too eager. Together, they passed into shadow and were gone with the last strain of music.

In an hour, Kallandras had done what time would take months to do. A sweet, sad peace filled the clearing and spilled out into the forest. Hunter Lords and Ladies watched him quietly, seeing other deaths, other losses, from the perspective that peace allows.

They did not know that it was not the death of Lord Elseth alone that he spoke of; they didn't know that it was not the hope of the Breodani alone that filled the clearing. But they didn't have to; what they felt was Kallandras' emotion, and it was genuine, one with their own.

He bowed, first to Lord Elseth and Stephen, and then to the crowd at large. Their silence was their applause.

Only one man remained unmoved. He was like a lamp empty of flame. There was nothing at all left, not even for tears. Kallandras bowed to him as well, the third bow and the last of the evening. Norn nodded, but the nod, like the man, was empty.

Krysanthos, mage-born, was not proof against the magic of Kallandras' talent. He wept as freely as any of the Hunter Lords, although he felt only contempt for their loss. Only when the bard stopped singing did the spell fade, and Krysanthos was left with anger, and not a little fear. He wanted to approach the Hunter Lords proper, but did not dare. Observers—the gifted and exalted of the realm who were not blessed by the Hunter's gift—had a small area on the green that could not be abandoned until the full and proper end of the Sacred Hunt. As always, surrounded by Priests of various orders, and the official heads of many guilds, Krysanthos kept to custom. But magic augmented his vision as he watched.

The pale, muddied hair of the Elseth huntbrother, who stood shoulder to shoulder with his Lord in the gloom, was a taunt and a question that he had no answer for. The Kovaschaii had gone out in the morning, trailing the hunt in silence. He had not returned, which Krysanthos had expected—but the boy had. What had happened?

He felt certain that the boy could not have destroyed the assassin; or rather, he wanted to feel certain of it. But the boy's life was evidence against the assumption.

He didn't understand why more had not been made of the attempt, didn't understand why the boy had not mentioned the assassin at all. Unless the assassin had never even made the first attempt.

But, no, that was unthinkable. The Kovaschaii were almost a legend, and for very good reason. Krysanthos had called upon them twice before, and both times they had offered success and silence in return for their very high fee.

What a waste of an opportunity. He would have to hire again, or attend to the deed with his personal resources. He shivered; it was cool. The boy that had dealt with one of the Kovaschaii was not an opponent that Krysanthos was willing to challenge, however cunningly, without further study. None of the mage's plans took into account his own death.

Ah, the feast was starting. Perhaps food and a little wine would warm him. He began to walk over to the banquet tables set up for the perusal of hungry guests. Yes, he would eat, and then he would arrange for surveillance of the huntbrother to the new Lord Elseth.

Eadward Lord Valentin, his huntbrother Michaele, and Lord William of Valentin formed the honor guard. One of the mage-born—not Krysanthos, he was too highly placed—was called from the Collegium of the Order of Knowledge. He came with the dawn and attended to the body, with spells and potions made to preserve it on the long journey home.

Lord Maubreche and his huntbrother Andrew also honored the dead with their presence. They held the preserve closest to Valentin, and slowed their journey home to lend the strength and dignity of numbers to Soredon's last journey.

Norn rode, in black robes with a hood that showed little of his face, at Soredon's side. Michaele and Andrew tried twice to speak with him or offer their comfort, but he declined all human contact—and he shunned the dogs as well.

The young Lord Elseth proved himself to be the model of restraint; he held the dogs in check throughout the two-week journey, and never once let tears be shed in public. In all things, he was his father's son, but especially in this. Stephen knew how important the appearance of strength was to his Hunter, and he said nothing at all about it, pretending, as the other Lords did, that all tears had already been shed in the closing of the Sacred Hunt.

Lady Elseth saw the procession coming; she must have. When they arrived, she had food and rooms ready for the Lords who had served as guards. Dinner, for it was late afternoon, was hurriedly rearranged, and a Priest from the village was called for. He arrived within minutes, and showed sorrow more openly than did any of the Elseth clan save Maribelle, who, while on the verge of adulthood, had not completely left the fields of childhood's open grief and sorrow.

*   *   *

Stephen heard Lady Elseth crying the evening before the funeral. He stopped outside of her drawing room doors. They were closed, and the rules of the house, made when he and Gilliam had been younger children, were quite strict: One did not disturb Lady Elseth if the doors were shut.

But he lingered in the hall, the lamplight flickering beneath his chin like ghostly fingers. He wanted to enter and offer her comfort, but didn't know how. If he hadn't been wandering the halls, he would never have heard her—and it was obvious that she didn't want to be heard, just as it was obvious that Gilliam did not.

In the end, he chose to knock.

The crying stopped; he heard the rustle of cloth behind the doors before they were opened. In the darkness, the redness of her eyes and the slight puffiness of lids and cheeks were not so obvious.

"Stephen," she said, and tried a smile.

He held the lamp higher, so that its light touched them both. "Can I come in?"

"What are you doing awake at this hour? The funeral's tomorrow, and both you and Gilliam have to participate."

"I couldn't sleep."

"No." She stepped back and held the door open. He glided past the inlaid panels and into the room. She didn't wait for him to close the doors. Instead, she returned to her seat at the writing desk in the bay window. "I was—I was just working on accounts." She picked up a quill and set it to paper that was blotched and sodden with a liquid other than ink.

"The lamp is low," he offered.

She nodded. "I won't be up for much longer." But the quill trembled uselessly in her hands, and she set it aside. Gaining her feet, she turned to stare out of the windows. The curtains were pulled, and the moon, laced with clouds, glared down. Her feet, against the wood of the floor, must have been cold, but she didn't notice.

Stephen went through the drawing room and into her sleeping quarters, picked up the old knitted woolens and brought them out, offering them silently. She took them and bent down to place them on her feet, but her shoulders began to shake, and she left them in a messy pile on the floor.

"It isn't—it isn't for Soredon," she said, although it was hard to hear the words. "It's Norn. I can't reach him at all."

"He's lost his Hunter," Stephen replied.

"I don't care why," was her equally quiet answer. It showed him, again, how different their lives had been, because it told him clearly how poorly she, who had loved Soredon, understood the depths of his loss to Norn. "I can't reach him at all."

She opened the right-hand drawer of her desk and pulled out a crumpled handkerchief. She blew her nose, a most unladylike and inelegant gesture, and then rubbed her cheeks clean of tears with the sleeve of her night robe. "I'm so sick of the Hunter God," she whispered. "I'm so sick of all of it. He won't even talk to me. He only said, 'Lady, I'm sorry.' That was all. I called for him; he came and he just sat here, saying nothing." The tears fell harder, and her voice became raw. "I've tried everything in the last day, Stephen. But he's lost."

"He'll come back," Stephen said awkwardly. "Lord William did."

Her laughter was harsh and heated, a curse, not an expression of mirth. "Watch," she said bitterly, "and learn. The Hunter has no mercy. It is not enough that I lose husband; I must lose huntbrother as well."

"What do you mean?"

"Norn—he's—" And then she dropped her face into her hands. "Go away, Stephen. I'm sorry, but I can't be what I should. Go *away*."

He left.

And in the morning, the Lords and their Ladies gathered to stand witness as the body of Soredon of Elseth was laid to rest in the cemetery of the Elseth estate. A headstone would follow soon enough, one as fine and unornamented and strong as Lord Soredon himself had been.

Norn accompanied the body into the Priest's circle, and Norn stood beside it as it came to rest upon the Elseth altar. He knelt in the mud and the dirt, and clung tightly to Soredon's lifeless hands as if afraid of being parted.

And six months later, at the height of the harvest season, Norn of Elseth joined his Lord. He never recovered from the loss, it was said. What was not said, and what Stephen learned only with the passage of time, was that huntbrothers left alive after the Sacred Hunt were left alive in body only, a shadow of what they had been, until even the body, like an echo, paled and faded into nothing.

Norn's funeral was quiet but well-attended, and Lady Elseth was the gracious hostess throughout. She had wept what tears she had had on the nights after they had brought her husband's body home.

Stephen cried as he stood beside Maribelle; she, too, offered her tears. But Lord Elseth was as grim and silent as his mother. It was the best display of strength he could offer as his last sign of respect to the man who had been a second father for all of his life.

Chapter Fifteen

IN THE GLITTERING HALLS of Maubreche, beneath a flood of light made sharp and faceted by three huge chandeliers, Stephen of Elseth began to search for a quiet place to hide. It wasn't easy; the press of moving bodies and alert Ladies—many of whom wished his aid in cornering the Elseth title for either themselves or their offspring—created an eddy in the social currents that threatened to pull him under. To make matters more complicated—which was only barely possible—he could sense that Gilliam, lost to view somewhere in the ever-changing, ever-moving crowd, was angry with him. That was the last thing he needed at the moment. He felt as if he were eight again; the surety, poise, and skill of his twenty-two years were about to abandon him to a room full of strangers.

Luckily, recessed along the gold-foiled west wall of the ballroom, there were balconies, curtained heavily to close out the night and all hint of darkness. In the chill crisp air, he found his refuge. Lady Elseth would be disappointed, no doubt, and he would hear about it in the morning, but he needed the respite badly.

He shrugged himself out of his dancing jacket, taking care to hold tight to cream ruffles and lace as they tried to follow green velvet and satin. Better. The jacket he slung over the stone balcony before he turned to face the night. Music—the opening strains of Coravel's *Revelry* played with spice and skill by the small orchestra—reached above the din of conversation and tickled his ear. He knew, without checking his card, that he listened to the beginning of the fourth dance.

It was a three-step waltz, simple enough to maneuver through without demanding much of the Hunter Lords who would always be too busy to learn the grace and skill a more difficult dance would require. And Lady Cynthia of Maubreche, the center of the evening's celebration, would no doubt be dancing with one or another of the louts who'd been told to court her. He ground his teeth in frustration.

Lady Cynthia had come late into her majority—she'd seen the turn of eighteen, when many young Ladies had already married into the fold of a Hunter Lord. She even had the grace to look—and act—her age; her long, slender body and her sharp, serious face had rarely been found in gatherings such as these. No, until now, Stephen had been likely to find her in the temple libraries—or the King's libraries, if the time of year was proper.

His fingers tried to dig holes in the balcony, and his mood was such that he wouldn't have been surprised had the stone not resisted. But even that satisfaction was denied him.

The music of the dance went on and on. He closed his eyes and saw more clearly the sweep of her emerald-green gown as it flew above the floor; saw the twinkle in her eye, the smile on her lips, the pale, pleasing blush along her cheeks. Which Lordling held her made no difference to him; he had not even tried to reserve a dance for the evening.

"Stephen?" The curtains rustled and flew open, and Gilliam stepped out into the night. He was Lord Elseth now, which meant more to the Ladies than it did to the Lords, and he wore the title the same way he wore his clothes.

Had Stephen not been so moody, he would have stopped to yank the lace out of the stranglehold the collar of Gilliam's jacket had on it. He didn't even have the energy to comment on the crumbs that had been crushed into the pile of the pleats above Gilliam's left thigh. "Something bothering you?"

"No."

"Dogshit."

Gilliam was angry; had been angry for most of the last fortnight. His huntbrother hadn't been in the mood to deal with it, and frankly, he thought it would do Gilliam some good to deal with his tantrums on his own.

Stephen drew a breath and turned to face his Hunter. Air hissed out as his jaw stiffened. "Gil, now is not the time. All right?"

" 'Now is not the time.' " Gilliam shoved his jacket back and sat down, hard, on the stone. "It's been the same damned story for the last month."

"Gil . . ."

"You've come hunting, what, twice? If you can call what you were doing hunting."

"Fine." Stephen bent down, picked up his jacket, and shoved his arms into the sleeves. Even angry, he was careful with both linen and lace. "What did you want of me?"

Gilliam shrugged in turn, and his face, broader and harsher than Stephen's, set in exactly the same lines. "Nothing."

For a moment they glared at each other, and temper tightened their fists. But they were twenty-two now, no longer boys, or even adolescents, to be forgiven for fist play in public. Stephen, as always, turned away first. If Gilliam wanted to play out a stupid game, he could damned well do it on his own.

"It's her again, isn't it?"

Only the huntbrother's head turned. "Her?"

"Cynthia." No honorific, no title, and certainly no respect in the word. Stephen opened his mouth, but before he could answer in kind, Gilliam continued. "Why don't you do something about it, instead of fretting here like a bitch in heat?"

The color drained out of Stephen's face. His jacket slid to the stonework in a messy pile that also covered his boots.

"It's Cynthia, Cynthia, Cynthia! You think of nothing but Cynthia!"

"I—"

"Maybe you'd rather be her lover than my huntbrother—but you aren't doing both!" He slid to his feet and walked past Stephen, taking a moment to shove him to the side.

"Gil, I swear—"

"What?" Gilliam's voice was low as he stood, half in the light, half out. Already a quiet hush had built around the recess.

"You understand *nothing*! All *you* ever think about are your dogs and their kills! Maybe that's enough for you—who knows what—"

"Stephen." The voice was soft and feminine. The chill in the word had nothing to do with the air. "Gilliam. You do your House no honor by this . . . display." Her voice was not raised, and indeed her lips were turned up in the semblance of a perfect smile, which fooled no one. The Lady Elseth had grown in power over the years; if age had weakened her at all, none were there to witness it. She stood tall, although her cheekbones didn't clear her son's shoulders, and the regal fall of a perfect, night-blue dress made her face seem all the whiter.

"Lady," Stephen murmured. He dropped his shoulders and his head in a bow, and held it long enough for the flush to leave his cheeks.

"Good. Gilliam!"

Stephen looked up to see the back of Gilliam's head disappearing—none too politely—through the crowd. He was heading toward the doors.

"What was that about?" Lady Elseth asked softly.

"A private matter, Lady. Nothing important."

"Good. If you need a few minutes, take them, but you might consider making the social rounds soon." She nodded quietly to the alcove, and Stephen retreated as the curtains closed out the room once again. He picked up his jacket and brushed out the folds before they became wrinkles. All the while, his hands were shaking. In darkness, anger warred with pain; neither won.

For as Stephen stood alone again, under the eye of the moon, he felt a familiar tingle, an odd rush of warmth that surged through his skin and ran along his limbs. He cried out, but his throat passed a whisper, no more, and once again the jacket spilled to the stone like a liquid with no vessel to hold it. His hands found the balcony railing, for strength and stability's sake, as his vision floundered in the darkness like a wild, hunted thing.

He stood in the glow of the Hunter God's presence. And for just a moment, glimmering like fireflies near the perfectly kept lake, two golden, glowing eyes stared back at him. He blinked; they were gone. But the touch of God remained to sing its urgent, incomprehensible message.

He turned and the terrace became a spinning, unstable outcropping on the side of the larger building. His hair stood on edge, and his skin tingled so much it hurt. If the Sacred Hunt had ever threatened his life, he forgot it. Nothing had ever felt so full of danger as this moment.

Instinct, not any sure knowledge, guided his steps. He had to find Gilliam, and quickly.

Gilliam, Lord Elseth, was indeed an angry Hunter. His hair was a wild, dark mess, and his clothing, created at the behest of Lady Elseth, and chosen specifically for an occasion such as this, fit him both perfectly and poorly. Ashfel, the pride of his hunting pack, was safely kenneled at the Elseth Manor, as were the rest of his dogs; there was no release at all to be had in the streets of the King's City.

The fact that none of the other Hunter Lords had traveled with their dogs did nothing to still his temper. They, at least, had the attention and fealty of their huntbrothers, whereas he—

He swore, a steady stream of words that the Ladies would have heartily disapproved of—if they condescended to hear them at all. What was so bloody interesting about Lady Cynthia anyway? He kicked at a clod of dirt and overturned the edge of the flower bed that had been newly planted. A long green stem, topped by a stiff oblong bulb, keeled over into the cold air.

Oh, he supposed she was pretty enough, if you cared for that sort of thing; she was certainly quiet and not given to loud displays or political games; she dressed well and spent little time powdered and primped as so many of the younger Ladies did. So what? Any of her so-called good points were negatives; she wasn't like most of the other Ladies. And she still couldn't hold a candle to the glory and the stress of the Hunt.

He kicked something else that got in his way, a rock of some sort that lined the garden path. Hurt his toe, too, although his boots were heavy. He didn't really notice.

If Stephen wanted to mope around after Lady Cynthia, he could bloody well do just that. But if he thought that Gilliam would stand around and plaintively watch, he was an idiot. Gilliam, Lord Elseth, had far better things to do with his time—and anyway, he hated coming-of-age balls with all their attendant frippery and stiff-lipped good manners.

Shoving his hands into pockets that were not designed for a bulge made of fists, he stalked off down the street under the watchful eye of the ever present moon-in-glory.

"Stephen?" Lady Elseth's fingers were gentle as they curled around the crook of his arm. "What is it?"

He shrugged her off as gently as possible, and once again donned the jacket that now seemed impractical and gaudy. "Did you see which way Gilliam went?"

"Out." Her voice made clear what she thought of his departure. It was enough to give Stephen pause, but not enough to stop him.

"I—I'm sorry, Lady Elseth. You'll have to give our regrets to Lady and Lord Maubreche."

She raised one graying brow, but her hands fell idle and disappeared into folds of blue velvet. "Why?"

"Gilliam's in danger." As the words rolled off his tongue, he felt them to be both true and false; later, perhaps, he'd have the time to wonder why. "I've got to find him."

She caught his face in her hands then, searching his eyes thoroughly—but quickly—before releasing him. His cheeks were warm with the imprints of her fingers as he bowed his head. "Oh, Stephen?"

"Lady?"

"We need to speak about Lady Cynthia when you return."

"Lady." But he felt no dread, and little embarrassment; the urgency of his brush with God had put his life in perspective again. Gilliam, had he known, would have been pleased.

The guards at the door were not completely useless; they pointed to the damage that Gilliam had done to both the flower bed and the rock garden on his way out of the west gate. The keeper of the house was less helpful; he stopped Stephen once to comment quietly upon the state of the grounds, and twice to assure himself that Stephen needed no carriage. Stephen only barely managed to shake the man off before he made his way to the stables.

Gilliam was walking; Stephen would soon be mounted. Surely it wouldn't be that difficult to catch up to his Lord and bring him back to the estate. Whatever there was to be faced, they would face it together in the company of other Hunter Lords and their huntbrothers.

But the stables were shadowed and dark, and the stable boys too slow for Stephen's liking. He demanded a horse, and they brought out three that he deemed less than useless; they were fine-spirited, high-strung animals meant to be ridden by those with the time for odd tempers. They pranced about, evading bit and saddle and nickering their displeasure and their anxiety.

As if speaking in their tongue, he snorted to make his annoyance plain, and the fourth he chose himself: Greysprint, a horse used for riding that might as easily have pulled a great carriage without aid. He was steady, or so the stable boys vowed, but as Stephen mounted, he felt the beast shudder.

"Not now," he murmured, the words at odds with the soothing tone of his voice. He caught the reins, waved the hands off, and cantered out into the open air. The night, even with the moon to lessen it, was dark and shadowed. And unlike her sister sun, the moon gave off no warmth.

Gilliam had had enough of the social circus to last a long lifetime. He hated the odd dress and foreign mannerisms deemed necessary to interact with either the Ladies or the other Lords, who undoubtedly felt as dubious about the privilege as he. He hated the food, bits of ridiculous portions and equally ridiculous methods of preparation; hated the tinkling music and the constricting form of the few dances he knew; hated the milling servants with their stiff voices and perfunctory bows that so reminded him of his own manor's keeper, Boredan. He was angered by the strict adherence to the dogs-stay-at-kennel rule, angered by the idiotic velvet and silk that his mother insisted he wear, and annoyed by the fact that Maribelle, born of the same father and mother, fit so smugly into the whole charade.

But mostly, he was angry at Stephen.

The night was indeed cool now, and he'd left his jacket over the rails of the grand central staircase that pointed the way out of Maubreche Manor, so he walked briskly to keep the chill at bay. He had no idea where he was going; destination was not so important as escape.

Buildings, grand and recessed from the streets, loomed like hard shadow with hearts of orange flame where lamps were lit at entranceways. Guardhouses also contained a hint of light and movement all along the wide, cobbled streets. No one stopped him or attempted to challenge his passage; he strode the thoroughfare like a man with angry purpose.

But as he passed the last of the Lord's circle and left it at his back, the lights grew dim and intermittent. The buildings crowded in on the streets, as if no longer held back by gates or fences; they rubbed shoulders in a compacted, awkward way, and only garbage and refuse took up residence in the open air between them.

The scent—the awful, dank smell of the place—told him, more clearly than his limited vision, where he had come: the lower city. He slid his hand down to his sword belt, and smiled with just a hint of vindication. The Lords were allowed swords—not spears or axes or any other useful weapon—and daggers, but many of the older men chose to leave this formality in the comfort of their quarters. Or rather, many of the older men chose to let their Ladies direct them. Gilliam didn't have this problem, and as he refused to dance at all, the sword had been no hindrance.

He was glad to have it now. Out of habit, he checked his stride and glanced warily about. The wind rattled shutters and sent a hint of spoiled food from the mouth of an alley. He squinted, and the darkness settled in around his eyes.

He should go back. He knew it, but the moment he thought about returning, tail between his legs like any sorry dog, to the Maubreche estate—and to Stephen—the hairs on his neck stood on end. Stephen had no bloody time for anyone but Cynthia of Maubreche—and Gilliam had no time for Stephen.

He felt the raspy tickle at his throat before he realized that the sound he heard was himself. He was growling. He wanted a hunt. He began to breathe more deliberately. He knew of one way to make his vision clearer.

With moon full and at quarter height, Gilliam, Lord Elseth, called Hunter's trance in the lower city.

Stephen felt it.

He had spent fifteen minutes asking guards if they had seen his Lord's passage, and another five following their directions as he kept his horse on a tight rein. At least the streets had been empty; no steady stream of people, no farmers' wagons or merchants' train had slowed his passage with their right-of-way.

He was thankful. He forgot it. For the odd tingle, the strange and terrifying warmth that had been riding just above his shoulder, descended with a lurch. His fingers curled around the reins as if for support; Greysprint's mouth took the brunt of the shock.

The hand of God. But not God's alone; he felt something familiar, something raw and impatient and angry. Gilliam.

The Hunter's gift, he thought, as he urged Greysprint forward. *Gil, where are you?*

As if in answer, the feeling grew stronger as he rode. He concentrated on it, and on the horse, trying desperately to ignore the fact that they'd left both the Hunter's and the Priest's city circles. *I don't have my sword.* His shoulders stiffened. This one eve, Gilliam had probably been right to be stubborn and graceless.

The dagger would have to do—but the dagger seemed small and insignificant compared to the menace the lower city contained as Greysprint crossed its lip.

The world grew more distinct; the breeze slowed from a wispy brush to a gentle billow; the smell of the streets assailed his flared nostrils. Here and there, cedar burned in the fireplaces of those who had money to waste on that sort of warmth. These were few in the lower city.

There were shadows everywhere; deep and darker than the night. But they were still, and when Gilliam moved in near silence to confront them, he found them empty as well. The faces of houses and squat, tired buildings became so much scenery; he wanted to find something that moved.

The stories he'd been told of life in the lower city had made every dark alley a danger. Gilliam had half expected to see roving bands of thieves and cutpurses, each of whom carried glinting daggers as a substitute for fangs. He was to be bitterly disappointed as he stalked the city streets. Even the breeze seemed to die into stiff, unnatural silence.

*   *   *

The darkness brought back the dreams. Six years of quiet and relative peace had all but buried the wyrd. Although he walked in no faceless stone halls and heard no tortured screams or splintering of wood and stone, the three returned to him sharply. He shivered; Greysprint pulled at the reins in an attempt to turn around and head back.

"It's all right," he whispered, but his hands were shaking. Above his head, perched like vultures, the second stories of the street's buildings crowded out the sky. The road was narrow and poorly kept; weeds made new by spring were already claiming their territory.

These did not trouble him. But the shadows did. Even darker than he remembered, they seemed to have become a solid presence—one that absorbed both sound and light. And with every step that Greysprint took, each more grudging than the last, these living shadows grew substantial.

Stop it, he told himself firmly. *You're just being nervous about the past.* But Marcus' voice did not return to him, and the days that he'd lived in the den were far, far behind. The wyrd was not.

Greysprint came to a halt, and Stephen realized that he'd reined the horse in. Taking a deep breath, he forced the horse forward again. *Gilliam, where are you?*

He hated the answer.

He heard it before either his eyes or his nose could alert him. A loud, high-pitched keening threw off the silence of the city streets. Even the shadows seemed to shudder with the force of a wail that was either mournful or fearful. It was hard to tell; the voice was no human voice.

Gilliam froze, straining to hear as his eyes sought the shadows. Sound came before scent or sight did; the cry was either louder or closer. His hand dropped to his side; his fingers found the curved metal hilt of his sword. He drew it, and for a moment the ring of steel against the lip of the scabbard hid the sudden sound of running feet.

The Hunter's trance had set his heart to racing; he felt the pulse at his neck beat in time to steps that were many. Something was coming in his direction— and someone was following it. If he had heard the horns, he would have set his sword aside—the horn calls would have declared the hunt another Lord's preserve.

But blessed silence answered him; he had no reason not to interfere. His entire body tingled with the anticipation of action. All thoughts of Stephen vanished as a pale blur escaped the shadows. From an alley. Perhaps the stories had not all been lies.

It was a woman, or maybe a girl—it was hard to tell in the poor light, even in trance. She was wrapped in shadow, and her hair, from this distance, seemed knotted and dirty. Her face was long and thin, her jaw slender but angular, her forehead short. Whether or not she was pale or dark was impossible to tell; her skin was made blotchy by dirt and sweat. She saw him, but instead of halting, swayed her course. It should have surprised him. It didn't.

In silence, he waited to see what would follow her; she was headed directly for him. But she was at least a minute ahead of her pursuers, and in trance a minute is a long time. He watched her lips as they stretched thin over her teeth, and saw the lids of her eyes flutter down over irises so black they seemed to be all pupil. He waited to hear what she had to say.

And the long, thin sound left her lips. There was no mistaking it: it rose in the air like a howl in a throat not built to utter one. But there was no mourning or fear in it any longer—in fact, her expression was one of recognition. His eyes met hers and pressed against them across the distance as he struggled to remember who she was and how he knew her. He felt a tingle, an odd lurch, and a dizzy, spinning warmth. The moon changed position.

Suddenly, he saw himself, standing with his sword at the ready, his feet planted slightly apart, his knees gently bent. He wore no jacket, and he could see the sweat of the Hunter's trance along the linen of his shirt. His face was set and grim, but that expression slowly changed into one of astonishment.

With a cry part curse and part fear, he pulled himself out from behind her eyes.

Not since his very first Hunt, with his father to supervise and guide his steps, had he felt so disoriented and out of control. He staggered as she knocked against him, butting him in the center of his chest. Righting himself, he reached down to place a hand on her shoulder; he missed—it was unnaturally high. Her lips parted; this close he could smell her stale breath and hear the low growl in her throat. She wore clothing, but it was poorly made, an ill fit, more remarkable for the fact that it covered her at all, it was so torn and frayed. He couldn't say what the color of the shift had originally been, but hoped it wasn't white. She looked at him, as if asking for guidance. No, not as if. She was.

Stand left side. Be ready. The thought was automatic, but he shook slightly as she snapped to attention, just as Ashfel would have done, and turned her face to the shadows. Her lips drew up over her teeth; her eyes narrowed.

The shadows burst out of the alley's mouth.

Greysprint's mouth was flecked with foam; his eyes were wide and whitened. He stepped stiffly, his hooves so heavy against the ground Stephen thought they might take root in the cobbled stone and dirt. Still, he coaxed and gentled the horse as he tried to move forward. He knew, now, that the fear of the beast this eve was a natural and understandable fear, and he almost regretted his haste in cursing both the stable hands and Lady Maubreche's choice of riding beasts. For if Stephen, both rider and a huntbrother used to facing death, was terrified of the darkness in the lower city, could more be expected of a mount?

Greysprint didn't throw him and didn't flee in panic, but his breathing grew more labored and his sides began to heave. Stephen knew that more time would be lost trying to ride forward—he'd be faster if he dismounted and walked. But then he'd have feet in the shadows and no sense of motion and life beneath him.

What choice did he have? He felt Gilliam's trance, like a delicate pulse, unseen but still a light in the shadows. Gripping the saddle, he relinquished the bridle and slid down the left side of the horse. The buildings, with their second and third stories overhanging the street, closed in like a poorly made roof; he felt them keenly although he was now closer to the ground.

Greysprint nickered softly, and Stephen gripped the reins once more. He led the horse in a half-circle, and then gave him a forceful slap on the rear. "Home," he said softly, although the word wasn't necessary.

The moon, where it breached the top of densely packed buildings, cut a path in the darkness. Alone in the twilight world of sleeping dens and hidden bars, Stephen of Elseth began his search. He moved slowly at first, but whatever power rode him became less kind and more demanding. Without realizing it, he began to stretch his stride into a near-silent run.

Three men came out of the shadows. They were in clothing that was dark—near-black—in color, but light of weight. No dress jackets or odd robes impeded their progress. They wore masks that darkened their faces and left only their eyes visible. They carried long, slim knives, but no swords, no obvious scabbards. And they ran, in step, like a single man.

The wind blew at their backs, a soft huff of night's breath. It carried a scent back to Gilliam and his companion—one unlike any he had ever encountered. It was faint, pungent, and repulsive. He was reminded, although he couldn't say why, of the perfumes and heavy oils that were applied to a corpse to hide the stench of death. They were never completely successful.

He felt the heat of her anger flare up and mingle with anxiety. He felt, rather than saw, her gaze turn to his profile. *Not now.*

The three stopped in a web of shadows as they saw Gilliam Lord Elseth, and the woman who stood a foot behind and to his left. In silence, they gazed at one another, but the mouths beneath their taut cloth masks didn't move.

Kovaschaii. Who else could speak without speaking; which others could move so precisely and so perfectly? He knew a moment of fear, then; against even one of the Kovaschaii, he would have had difficulty. But the breeze blew their scent to his nose, stronger and less cloying, in denial of his fear. These were not Kovaschaii.

The Kovaschaii were human.

Fear—what fear a Hunter Lord allowed himself to know—gave the shadows form and substance; they roiled up, thicker than mist in the season before the snows came, and lapped at the knees of Gilliam's newfound enemies. He blinked his eyes and saw that the darkness had moved, did move. Four enemies then, and he wasn't sure which was most dangerous.

Until the man in the middle lunged forward, knife held flat and to the side in his left hand. Gilliam brought his sword up to deflect the long knife's passage. He missed, or rather, the knife stayed on its unaimed course. But the man's right hand, black as the shirt he wore, shot out, fingers forming a v. The edge of Gilliam's blade met the fold of skin between the second and third fingers—and the sound of metal against metal rang out. The man twisted his hand, and Gilliam's grip faltered. The sword spun out into shadow, and all sight of it was lost, although Gilliam could hear it skitter to stillness against the uneven stone. The man had worn no mailed glove—in fact, no glove at all; his skin was ebony.

Gilliam didn't pause to wonder or gape; instead he spun low, into a roll that carried him away from both knife and attacker. He felt the whistle of air as something cut into the ground a fraction of an inch from his back. They were fast, these creatures.

By the time he gained his feet, he had his dagger in hand. He could see two of the enemy and their shadow; the third was beyond him. Without thinking, he slid behind the girl's eyes, and saw what she saw; an arm, disappearing into shadow near the ground, biceps and shoulder blades taut. She was close; too close for the details of the cloth-covered face to be made clear. He felt, through their connection, the rough, hard skin between her teeth—and heard, with his own ears, the low, pained grunt that his attacker made. If there was blood, he tasted none. Which was probably for the better; he needed his wits about him, and even that would have been a distraction.

The moon suddenly disappeared; he leaped to the side, and something brushed against his ribs. Sharp, cold pain cut along the nape of his shirt, exposing the side of a rib. He pushed the trance, prayed for speed, dodged again; this time, only the shirt was abraded. He faced two, and he had no idea how the girl fared.

Stephen knew the shadows now. Even though there was no burning temple and no dying Priests surrounding him, he knew what they presaged. The dreams had returned, and they were his only reality. Blackness and death came under the cover it chose. What chance had he? The lower city held no sacred chamber, no hidden retreat—and none of the regalia of the Hunter God. But it held Gilliam; perhaps that would be enough.

He rounded the corner, and found that it was the final one. In the moonlit street, with shadows as carpets and flooring, he found Gilliam, Lord Elseth, as his Hunter struggled for his life.

He didn't recognize the two who attacked him. They were enemies; that was enough. His dagger slid out of his sheath, and he crouched into the nearest wall, trying to keep even with the shadow, and at the same time trying to stay out of its reach. His breath came heavily; his throat felt raw.

One of the men dressed in black turned suddenly. In the moonlight, his dark fingers were gloved by a red, liquid sheen. He moved so quickly, Stephen thought of the Hunter in trance, and involuntarily, his gaze found Gilliam. Lord Elseth was injured; the night couldn't disguise it.

He had never wondered, in all the years since the wyrding, why he ran in those dreams; he didn't wonder now. The assassin—what else could he call it?—leaped through the air, both hands extended. He carried no weapon, and took no time to dance the intricacy of mage-spell through the air. Just the same, his presence was death. Stephen used the wall to push himself into the ground. The hands of his attacker splintered wood above his head as they drove themselves into the exterior of a building.

They were stuck there for seconds; long enough for Stephen to raise the dagger and slash out at the man's neck. Steel grated as if being sharpened; the dagger hilt shook in his hand as he drew the edge against stone, or perhaps something harder. The only damage his single, free strike had done was to cut away the lower edge of the mask.

Black cloth rolled up, revealing another layer of darkness—ebony and a glint of white that overhung obsidian lips.

Gilliam didn't know the exact instant that he became aware of Stephen; certainly his huntbrother shouted no greeting or warning. But he felt a sudden surge of fear that was neither his own nor his strange new companion's. And where two had attacked him, one stood alone.

The knot in his chest tightened. He fumbled for his dagger, but without any hope; the hand that had twisted his sword from his grasp was not likely to be affected by the smaller, thinner blade. The attacker lunged low; Gilliam jumped high, and dragged the blade across his back. He heard again the scraping of metal against stone, and felt it rumble up his arm. The black cotton shirt was split from collar to waist. There was no skin beneath it.

Yet there had to be some way of injuring these assassins; the girl had done it. The taste of cold, hard arm, alien to him, lingered in his mouth. His mouth. She'd *bitten* down.

It meant something, he was certain—but he had no time to think what; he was moving, at the farthest reach of his trance, while the creature kept up its attack. He felt pain along his back, and his skin split as easily as the black shirt had done along his enemy's.

They were not going to survive this. From the moment wood splinters had cleared his head, he knew it for fact. He didn't have Gilliam's speed or skill; there was no Hunter's trance to draw on for protection. The dagger, dragged across an exposed throat, had done no damage. Were it not for the fact that the assassin's hands were caught in the wood for a few seconds longer, Stephen wouldn't have been able to avoid its next strike. He just moved too damned slowly.

He had to run; he knew it.

But he couldn't leave Gilliam behind.

Frantic, he began to race across the street, out into view of the silent moon and the cold, pale stars. The shadows roiled at his feet, growing more substantial as they tried to impede his progress. His heart wouldn't still; it filled his ears with its beating, although he needed to listen for any sign of his pursuer.

The cold, full laughter that suddenly broke the silence told him more than he wanted to know. Like a rabbit, he froze and looked over his shoulder. The assassin had not bothered to follow in his steps; he had waited, timing the perfect, deadly leap that would carry him to his quarry.

Stephen's knees unlocked. He tried to throw himself to the side, but too late, and far too slowly. The assassin fell like a perfectly aimed sword strike.

And the lightning that suddenly flared in the street answered his attack, an equally perfect shield.

Laughter was dwarfed by sudden screams, the sickly smell of death replaced by the scent of charred and charring flesh. The impact of the strike sent the creature flying in a direction, and with a speed, that mirrored its attack. The shadows reached up, caught it, and appeared to consume it; the screams halted suddenly.

The remaining two assassins stopped and drew back; the one that had attacked Gilliam without cease now threw up its arms and spat out syllables that no one could understand. Together they sprinted out of sight, back the way they'd come. The shadows seemed to pull in around them.

"No!" Gilliam shouted, and a small, dirty girl skidded to a stop. Her lips were black, as were her teeth, and the growl in her throat was feral, inhuman. "Stephen?"

Stephen rolled to his feet. His forearm was bruised, but he'd managed to keep hold of his weapon; it glinted with a light that had proved too pale to pierce the darkness. "Gil." His voice was shaky. "Who?"

"I don't know. I found her. Maybe she found me." He drew closer to his hunt-brother; close enough to give Stephen a full view of the various bleeding gashes he'd suffered. Stephen reached out automatically, but instead of pulling back, placed one hand on his Hunter's shoulder. They took two seconds to gain their breath as the smoke slowly cleared in the breeze.

"Hunter's power?" Gilliam asked quietly, as much awe in his voice as there had ever been.

"I don't know."

"No."

Two heads turned at the voice; only the girl seemed intent on her enemies to the exclusion of any interruption. Another shadow stood in the darkness.

And Stephen of Elseth recognized her voice.

"Well met, Lord Elseth. Well met, Stephen. You must follow me now. We have no time for explanations. The demon-kin will be back in minutes—and I do not have the power to strike again. Not from here. I am late, and the spell was . . . costly."

"Where?"

"Back," was the soft answer. Stephen squinted into the night, but the figure stayed out of moon's reach. He saw the hood pulled low, and the sleeves, long and flowing, that entirely covered her hands. "To Maubreche."

A cold, shrill cry rode on wind.

"Not yet!" Her words, soft and urgent, were not spoken to Gilliam or Stephen. "They return too soon." She gestured, and white hands broke free, for a moment, of concealing cloth. A light flared in her palms; it was a pale orange, beaded like fine mist as it trailed to the ground. "Follow the path the light reveals. Do not stray from it, or the lower city will not let you escape."

Gilliam turned to the girl, met her eyes, and gestured. Without further question, he stepped upon the path this stranger had created.

Stephen hesitated at the last moment, caught perhaps by strands of dream, or perhaps by the great weariness in a voice that still held power and decisiveness. "What of you?"

"I will join you if I am able. Now go!" So saying, she turned to face the darkness, shoulders slightly stooped, hands shaking but infinitely strong, as those she had named demon-kin burst once more from the night, wielding shadow that was edged in bright lines of shining blue.

Stephen ran. He followed Gilliam's lead, aware of the fact that Gil slowed his pace in order not to leave him behind.

Chapter Sixteen

BLOOD MINGLED WITH MIST as it made a wet, slick trail down Gilliam's exposed flesh, but acknowledgment of the injuries would wait; the path, faintly luminescent as it cut a trail beneath their feet, wavered and flickered like a lamp run low of oil. It was safety. It would not remain so. All around it—and it was not wide—shadows reared up like small garden hedges. Even the buildings that had seemed so tightly packed to Stephen's eyes now seemed a river away; they no longer blocked the moon's vision, but they offered no sense of comfort or familiarity.

The streets were still empty—or almost.

Stephen thought he saw people at the shadow's edge, but before he could give warning, they screamed with their young, terrified voices and melted away. It stopped him by stopping his breath; he turned as if to reach out, and faltered.

Gilliam caught him firmly; Gilliam, unperturbed by the shouts and the awful silence that followed. Like any Hunter Lord, his concern was first for his hunt-brother and his pack, second for the people in his demesne and preserve. For street urchins and thieves, as these must have been, he might have spared either pity or contempt had he time—but he did not. Tonight, he, Stephen, and the odd, dirty girl were being hunted. No matter that the methods of the hunt were foreign and heretofore unknown—it was still a hunt, and he had no intention of falling prey to demon-kin.

Demon-kin.

He pulled Stephen more squarely onto the path. The lower city circle was almost breaking; he could see the perimeter of the merchant's circle—and beyond that, Maubreche lay nestled in the highest circle in the land.

Stephen's shoulder trembled. He was still fit and trim, used to the rigors of accompanying Gilliam while the Hunter's trance was deep, so the shiver had nothing to do with exhaustion.

"You're injured," he said.

Gilliam nodded. There wasn't much else to do. "We're almost there."

"Great. What are we supposed to do when we get there? We can't lead those—those—into the ball; they'll kill everything in sight!"

As if talking to a testy child, Gilliam replied. "Lord Maubreche has his pack on the grounds."

"His pack?" Stephen laughed hysterically. "Gil, our daggers couldn't touch the God-cursed things at all—what the Hells good will a bunch of hounds do?"

Their situation was too urgent to allow Gilliam the luxury of bridling; he did anyway. "Maybe teeth have more of an effect—she bit them!"

It was difficult enough to argue and run, but they'd made a practice of it, and become near-experts. Throwing a third person into the process put Stephen off his stride, and for the second time that evening, he looked at the dirty girl. He also chided himself, very briefly, for being so unkind in his appellation. Except that she *was* dirty; filthy. She smelled rank and stale, even though the breeze and the pace pushed her scent away from, not toward, him. She looked at him with only a faint trace of interest in her eyes, and those eyes were all of a single color; either black or a very dark brown.

If they ever reached safety and light again, he would have to look more closely. "Who in the Hells is she?"

Gilliam shrugged, and Stephen felt him turn and shy away from the question. It wasn't like Gilliam; he was usually direct to the point of rudeness.

Not the time for arguments: not yet. Stephen swallowed, and asked a different question. "Why is she with us?"

"They," Gilliam said, motioning with his head toward the darkness behind, "were hunting her. She found me."

Again, Stephen felt an odd shifting.

"I had to help—you would have."

I would have, yes.

A scream broke the night again, shattering the conversation. Cold, long, with a hint of sibilance to underpin its ringing clarity, it gave the shadows more force as they crowded the path.

It certainly made it easy to remain with the light.

Maubreche Manor was still brightly lit, and even as the path brought them racing across the threshold of the grounds, the strains of orchestral music joined the rustle of leaves. There were guards at the front gate; Stephen saw them as he ran past, at Gilliam's heel.

Perhaps they were enchanted, or perhaps they were sleeping—although, with Lady Maubreche as their commander, he very much doubted that was the case— but for reasons that he did not understand, they did not stop or challenge the newcomers. Indeed, they stared straight ahead, like the Queen's guards at attention, rather than stooping to notice the noise and the scramble that passed yards away from their torchlit vision.

"Something's wrong," Gilliam said, breathing hard.

"You mean, beside the fact that demons from the Hells are hunting us?"

Gilliam didn't answer, and Stephen gave up—but he had a feeling that what he had said in sarcastic jest was, in fact, true. Any hunt, no matter who the intended victim and who the hunter, was "natural" to a Hunter; it probably felt somehow natural to Gil. Mouthing a quiet, heartfelt curse at Hunter Lords in general, Stephen dropped his eyes down to the misty path and continued to run along it.

To his great relief—or perhaps just to his relief—the path veered away from the grand manor, with its lovely lights and the carriages that stood as stately emissaries in the long, cobbled drive. He had no idea at all where they were running, but as long as the path still arched on ahead, he didn't worry.

Until he heard the screaming again, keen and icy. Until he heard the human voices that followed, and quickly died into stillness. The guards. Gilliam slowed; Stephen felt the sudden lurch of tension that revealed itself only in the squaring of Gilliam's jaw. The thieves had been prowling the lower city on their own, and their death was inconsequential to him. But he had led the demon-kin to Maubreche, where the two guards would never have met them otherwise.

It was Stephen who pushed him on this time; they had exchanged roles, as they sometimes did under duress. For if the demon-kin were so close on their trail, it meant that Evayne—if the ghostly, hooded apparition had indeed been the woman of his dreams—would no longer be there to offer them her protection.

And solid steel had availed them nothing.

The path never forked and never faltered; it remained wide enough to follow easily by foot, and straight enough to follow with eye. And although the moon was at her peak, with no buildings to hide her open face, she cast no shadows to bleed the light from the mystical road.

Stephen wasn't sure exactly when it all changed; he was too concerned with running, and too certain that their flight would soon be halted by the demon-kin. He had seen how quickly they moved, and was certain that they were mere inches away, waiting and preparing. They didn't come, but the hedges did, springing up like dark life on either side, with a scent of dirt and water, of leaves and bark—of green. In the night, they had no color, but they had shape and height, and they were so perfectly kept, so solid in appearance, they seemed to be walls.

Looking down at his feet, Stephen saw the only shadows there were the ones the moon cast. He took a deep breath, tried to hold it, and winced as his lungs expelled air, seeking more.

"Stephen?"

He shook his head and kept running.

They came at last, through a maze of dark hedges and perfect new grass, to light's end. The hedges stood at a respectful distance in an almost uninterrupted circumference. There was only one way in—and one way out—from this center. The light crawled the last leg of the journey, and ended abruptly at the base of a tall, solemn statue. Even in the poor light, it was obvious that this was carved in the likeness of a man—one tall and proud, perhaps a little severe. He stood, completely straight, and a simple robe fell gently to his feet. His face was long, his chin rounded gradually to a point; his hair, long as well, fell away from his face and forehead, trapped only by a circlet across his brow. It was hard to read his expression, and Stephen would not have been surprised to find that that expression was both changeable and changing. One hand was raised, palm out; the other held a spear or like weapon that ran from his feet past the height of his shoulder. Stephen had no doubt that one maker-born had fashioned the likeness, and he wondered who the original model had been; something about the man was familiar.

"This is it," Gilliam said, softly and irrelevantly.

Stephen barely heard him. He walked quietly, his steps gentle and almost hesitant, his right hand outstretched. "Is it a King, do you think? Maybe the founder?"

"It's no King," was the quiet reply.

And hearing the voice, Stephen lost his own. He spun in the darkness, his heart ice. Hidden, until this moment, by the folds of the robe and the base of the statue's pedestal, was Lady Cynthia of Maubreche.

She was pale, white even in shadows and moonlight. Her dress was of a simple and pleasing cut—but its make was no such thing; it had cost a fortune. Stephen had, many times, bought the bolts of cloth and the reams of lace that Lady Elseth and Maribelle required, and he knew how dear they could be.

"Stephen?" She stepped out and away from the statue; her finger trailed along its hem before pulling away. "What are you doing here? I wouldn't have thought you could navigate the maze on your own—not in this light."

He swallowed; the sides of his throat formed a neat trap for words—none came. Her smile faltered; her eyes widened, and even though he couldn't see their color, he knew how brown, and how deep, they were. Then they narrowed; her shoulders straightened, her jaw came up. Even her voice changed subtly. "Is that Lord Elseth, then? And who is your companion?"

"It's—"

The shrieking of demon-kin rescued Gilliam from a rather large social crime. A plume of fire flared up into the sky, dampening the light of the moon with its brilliance and its harshness. It burned itself into Stephen's vision, lingering until the very slight breeze, carrying the smell of burning leaves and wood, arrived.

"What was that?" Cynthia said softly. Her voice was steady and very cold.

"What are you doing here?" Stephen's words overlapped hers, but where she had chosen ice, he held fire. She was no Hunter Lord, trained to death or dying—she was a Lady, skilled in lore, history, politics, and the management of the Maubreche preserve, which would one day be her own. He felt certain she would die here, because she had been rude enough to leave a gathering held in her honor alone. A few short hours ago, he would have been overjoyed.

Another person would have taken a step back from the force in his voice. Her nostrils flared, and perhaps her cheeks grew a little more red. "I could ask the same of you, Lord Stephen. This is a private area of the Maubreche Estates, and is *never* open to the . . . public."

"Ask later!" Gilliam snarled. He had no sword, but his dagger was readied—and useless. He hated it.

Silence reigned a moment. The moment stretched.

"Why are they waiting?" Gilliam muttered at last. "They're fast enough to have followed."

Fire answered, stronger and closer. The smoke that the hedges surrendered drifted up in a thick, pale cloud. During the day, it would have been darker; now it wended its way on the thin breeze, the ghost of flame.

Cynthia's eyes widened. "They're—they're burning the *maze!*"

"Maybe they can't follow," Stephen offered quietly. "There's no shadow here, Gil. Look at the ground." It was a faint hope, but better than none.

Gilliam nodded; the shallow dip of chin told Stephen that his Hunter wasn't really listening. He was testing the wind, seeking the unfamiliar scent, readying himself for quick action and quicker response.

Slim fingers, strong and firm for all their lack of size, closed tightly around Stephen's forearm. "Stephen, who are they?"

He swallowed, fear for himself and fear for her becoming so tightly entwined they were inseparable. "Demons."

"Demons?" She laughed in astonished disbelief; her eyes seemed to sparkle.

"Damn it, Cynthia—demons! Look at Gil—I know he's barbaric, but he usually doesn't run around in bloodied rags!" She didn't have the chance to follow his command; Stephen caught her shoulders.

Angry, she wrenched herself free. He reached out again, but his hands met the invisible wall of her icy wrath. They fell, shaking. "Maybe," she said, and for a moment she reminded him of Gilliam—her jaw was clenched, and the tone of her voice walked the thin, tight line between anger and all-out fury, "they're of the mage-born."

Another scream, chill and loud. Yet another bolt of flame. Smoke and the smell of fire had become so common they barely noticed it.

"Oh?" He turned away, feeling a helpless anger of his own. "And what gives you that idea?"

"This is the Hunter's Hallow." Her lips curled up in what might have been a smile; it was an unpleasant expression. "The mage-born have no easy entrance here."

"It doesn't have to be easy," Stephen snapped back. "If they get here, we're lost. We met them in the lower city. We tried to fight. Steel doesn't affect them at all. Does that sound like the mage-born to you?"

"Not immediately, but mages are cunning and capable creatures." Her voice lost a bit of its edge. "Why did you call them demon-kin?"

"It's what she called them."

"She?" The edge returned, redoubled.

"Will the two of you shut the Hells up?"

Both Stephen and Cynthia spun, their mouths open in angry unison. The odd, dirty girl sprang suddenly to life, half-leaping and half-running to stand between Gilliam and his huntbrother. Her throat seemed to grow larger and thicker; the sound she made was unmistakable and loud. She was growling.

Cynthia took a step back; she couldn't help it. The black tongue, darkened teeth, and wild, wide eyes made the girl look mad, and dangerously so.

"No!" Gilliam shouted. "Get out of the way!"

Stephen's bond with Gilliam was strong enough that his shouted warning was unnecessary; he was already flying through the air with the force of his leap.

But Lady Cynthia did what a normal person would do in the face of just such a command. She spun around to see where the danger lay, her hand already falling to a well-adorned hip, and a lovely, functional dagger.

The hedge-wall erupted.

She would never laugh at Stephen again. It was absolutely clear, from the moment the strangers burst into the maze-heart, that they weren't mage-born. They weren't even human. Shreds and scraps of dark clothing barely clung to their arms and legs; their faces, in all their dark glory, were obsidian, ugly masks. But the teeth that rimmed their lips like serpent fangs were white and gleaming.

The demon-kin were children's games and children's fears. Cynthia was suddenly a child again. But not a foolish one. Her knees bent into a roll; her shoulders and upper thighs provided the necessary momentum. The long, plush skirts she wore were heavy and impeding, but she didn't take the time to fuss with them.

"CYNTHIA!"

Gilliam, Lord Elseth, had his dagger to hand in the shadows. His breath was harsh and heavy; he had pushed the Hunter's trance almost to its upper limits, and once his endurance flagged, not even the benefit of consciousness would be left.

He knew it; he even considered it on an instinctual level. But he showed no sign of doubt or hesitation as he leaped forward, dagger extended like a claw. He had pushed himself to survive to reach the center of the maze; he pushed harder, finding new strength. He was terrified, yes—terrified that it would not be enough.

The first of the demons touched earth, slamming its hands into the ground;

catching folds of velvet and embedding them in the dirt. Lady Cynthia jerked, hard, to a stop; the demon's obsidian hands came up.

Cynthia raised her pale hands to her face; they were white in the moonlight and shadows. A ring glinted as her fingers trembled. She opened her mouth; her lips parted as if in a scream. But the scream held a word, and the word held command.

"Sanctuary!"

The demon's hand sliced down in the darkness; Gilliam cried out, a rush of air against a raw throat. But before the lethal blow could cut across Lady Cynthia's face, another shadow met the first, snarling in dark fury.

Stephen had his dagger as well; he gripped it tightly, his fingers almost molding themselves to the bound twine of its hilt. He had no words at all, and very little breath; his knees were weak with momentary relief as the dirty, wild girl—somehow at the heart of this conflict—hurled herself at the demon who stood, like a death, over Cynthia's fallen body.

He was four feet from her spilled, torn skirts, but the distance seemed immense, uncoverable. Whatever anger or pain he had felt at the beginning of the evening was gone, a victim of the fear of her death. He ran, his free hand outstretched.

He was not gentle as he pulled her to her feet; even less so as he shoved her, hard, toward the statue in the maze's center. If he'd had voice or time, he might have broken all etiquette and commanded her to hide—but he had none. Gilliam's sudden terror, bright and clear, hit his throat through the Hunter's bond. He jumped, wheeling, and felt a sharp sting at his back.

Without thought, he struck out, his dagger only an extension of his hand.

Against hope, the demon growled. Stephen drew back. In the dim light the moon cast—if it was dim; it seemed now, to his eyes, bright and luminescent—he could see the trail of dark liquid that ran the runnels of his knife.

What he knew, Gilliam knew; in danger, their bond had always been strongest. He did not need to shout or gesture or otherwise catch his Hunter's attention. Instead, he began his dance across the grass and the flower beds, his pale eyes narrowed, his attention upon the demon.

But if the demon was somehow vulnerable now, it had not lost its great speed; lunging in, in off-step to Gilliam's attack, all concentration bent upon his opponent, Stephen almost lost his arm.

He screamed as something wide and sharp scraped bone.

Even had she been so inclined, Cynthia could not hide; the cry that Stephen uttered, his voice barely recognizable, pulled her forward. She saw him fall; saw it clearly, as she saw all things in the Hunter's Hallow. She saw Gilliam's desperate lunge; heard his low-throated, guttural snarl, and saw his dagger deflected.

Demon-kin. She took a breath, trembling. Let her eyes flicker off the second demon. He was shadow, tall and narrow, to the red-tinged back of the wild child who attacked him. She, too, growled—like a Hunter boy, too new to his pack, gone feral. There was none of Gilliam's control or concentration about her—yet somehow, she still stood.

Somehow.

Slowly, the shock began to drain out of Cynthia. She took a deep breath, and leaned back, gripping the pedestal of the Hallow's single statue in tight white fingers.

She was the heir to the Maubreche demesne, with its country preserves and its near-legendary labyrinth in the very heart of the King's City. And although she had never been given to the care of a weaponsmaster, never run or linked with a pack of Hunter dogs, never faced the truth of the Hunter's Death and all its implications—she had nonetheless learned to fight.

But her voice was thin and young and vulnerable as she began to speak.

"I am of Maubreche," she whispered, her voice slowly gathering strength, "and I am of your line. We have kept this garden and this maze and this mystery that is the Hunter's Hallow."

Stephen cried out again, and sudden tears welled up in her eyes, filming their surface without falling. Her throat grew tight. She struggled with the words, won, and continued to speak. But she closed her eyes, flinching and turning from his cries; she could no longer watch.

"We have kept our pledge and our word, and now I turn to you, Keeper and Lord of the Covenant. Grant me your Sanctuary!"

Stephen heard her pale, trembling words; heard them above the din of his own pain and his own cries. He looked up weakly, his eyes seeking hers in the shadows, as her words rippled through him with the force of an oath made, an oath kept. What she had said sunk roots and became planted in memory. He would not forget it.

Only twice before had he felt so.

But never so strongly and so completely. Dawn came to the clearing, springing like life into the heart of the labyrinth. A nimbus of light touched leaf and branch and bent, sticky blades of grass, spreading outward. He felt it along his upturned face, and his lips turned in a smile of sudden, inexplicable jubilation.

And the demon-kin screamed, both at once, their fight momentarily forgotten. Stephen rolled, almost drunkenly, to his feet, clutching his wounded arm, his shredded jacket. He glanced up, and up again, to the very height of the skies; they were dark and clear.

The dawn that prevailed in the Hunter's Hallow had nothing to do with the turning. His eyes followed the light as it grew stronger and clearer, and at last his eyes found its source: the statue at the center of the maze.

No light this bright should be easily viewed, and Stephen raised his hands automatically to shield his eyes, before he realized that he felt no pain, saw no searing intensity. As the demons screamed, and the dark smoke of burning flesh reached his nose, Stephen gazed into the stone face of an angry God.

Angry? No. Or rather, not angry alone.

Stephen stumbled forward, staring now and trying to understand what his eyes saw. Before him, upon a perfect pedestal, surrounded by the greenery of the maze and the broken silence of night, stone robes seemed to flow in the wind. A man— no, the very God—stood, one hand held fast to a Hunter's spear, and the other, palm slightly extended, as if in welcome. And then stone *moved.* The lips of the God formed near-silent words.

Help us.

He felt each one as a blow, and his knees collapsed, first the right and then the left, beneath him. He reached out with one hand, palm up, as if he could somehow bridge the distance between them. But even Stephen could not say, at that moment, whether his gesture was one of supplication or comfort.

Lady Cynthia of Maubreche squared her shoulders. The stone at her palms felt warm, almost living; the light at her back shone like a beacon and haloed her stiff form, growing stronger. She wanted to turn, then, and study the face of the God; but some instinct stopped her motion, and instead, she watched the demons as if from a great distance.

They burned. Just as the hedges had burned, shriveling and dying as the breeze blew their scent across the whole of the maze. It was hard to imagine, as they writhed and shrank in on themselves, that they had ever been a danger.

The wild girl, her lips black and wet, stood snarling as her enemy burned; she seemed leashed somehow. Cynthia heard the growl that came from this stranger's lips and shivered. Had she been in any other place, she might have felt fear—but under the watchful eye of the God, she had none to offer.

And then Cynthia saw Stephen, and even the deaths of her enemies were forgotten. She left the comfort of warm stone and crossed the grass quickly toward him, wondering why he knelt, frozen in position, upon the grass.

The look on his face was more than she could bear, and without a second thought, she lifted her overskirt, pulling both her dagger and a swath of thick cotton from her petticoats. These, she cut into long, wide strips.

Gilliam appeared at her side; it was clear that he, too, had suffered—but none of his wounds were as dangerous as the one Stephen had taken.

"How is it?" Lord Elseth asked bluntly.

"Take these," she murmured, handing him her newly made bandages. "Wash them in the fountain basin and bring them back. Quickly."

He followed her orders; she had known he would. Kneeling, she touched Stephen's face, one palm to either cheek, as she had never dared do before. He was cold; ice had settled beneath his skin. She closed her eyes, suddenly unable to look at the expression on his face.

"Stephen," she whispered, and then, pulling him out of his kneel and toward her shoulder, "*Stephen.*"

He came, as if suddenly released, a heavy weight. His arms, both the injured one and the whole, found her shoulders and held them, convulsively; his face, he buried in the side of her pale, white neck.

He was shaking. She rocked him gently, wondering how the minutes could stretch so unbearably. At last she heard movement across the grass and pulled her head up, turning it in the direction of the noise. Stephen would not let go.

Instead of Gilliam, she saw the girl. This close, the blackness at her lips resolved itself into more than just liquid. Even Cynthia, raised on the unmaking of the Hunter's kill, flinched. The girl did not seem to notice. Instead, she shuffled in, her head forward, her nostrils flared.

Like a dog.

"Not now," Cynthia said, her voice quavering slightly.

Stephen raised his head.

"Stephen?" Cynthia turned, forgetting the girl. But Stephen's eyes, wide and round, caught and distorted that feral child's expression. The girl darted forward suddenly, butting Stephen's shoulder with her head. He bit his lip on a cry and winced; the arm she had struck was the injured one.

"Go away!" Cynthia shouted.

The girl came forward again and began to nuzzle Stephen; there really wasn't another word for it. Cynthia, caught by Stephen's arms, nonetheless tried to physically shove the girl backward.

"What's wrong?" Gilliam said, and then, as he saw the three of them huddled upon the ground, "No." It was to the girl that he spoke. She looked up at him, guileless, and then began to whimper.

That whimper stretched out into a full whine.

Gilliam did not look away from the open darkness of her eyes. "Cynthia," he said, holding out the dampened strips of cloth.

She took them and eased herself out of Stephen's grip. "Who is she?" Her voice was soft; she did not look up at Gilliam.

"I don't know," he answered, each word measured.

"What is she?"

"I don't know."

But she heard, as she began to bind Stephen's wound as tightly as possible, the quiver in Gilliam's voice. Had she been in the seat of judgment, she would have called him forward and asked for the truth. She did not.

Instead, she worked in silence, aware that Gilliam had not turned or wavered at all. The girl's whine grew higher and sharper, but at least the girl was somehow contained, for she did not approach Stephen again.

"It's all right," Stephen said softly.

"Shhhh." She touched his fingers with her lips. "Lord Elseth, will you aid me? I do not think Stephen will be able to walk."

"I can walk," he said, ever so faintly. He started to prop himself up on one elbow. "I can walk; I will walk for you, Lord." His eyes were wide, almost glassy; Cynthia knew, as she stared at his face, that they did not see her. She paled.

Gilliam was at her side at once.

"What is it?" she asked him, grabbing his arm and holding it tight, as if to somehow shake the answer out of Gilliam. "What is he feeling?"

Gilliam pulled himself out of Cynthia's grip and bent down, placing a hand under each of Stephen's shoulders.

"Gilliam!"

He looked at her, over the pale thatch of Stephen's hair. "I can't answer that," he replied evenly. "He'll tell you himself, if he wants to."

Lady Cynthia, heir to the Maubreche responsibilities, was a very tired young woman. Her hair, carefully coiffed and secured at the evening's start, had come loose from combs and pins, and curled in darkness around her dirt-stained face. Her gowns were askew, and the very lip of her undergarments, cut so jaggedly with her personal dagger, hung loosely at her feet. Her body ached; her head felt so heavy, it hung with the weight of exhaustion.

And none of this mattered as she met Gilliam's suddenly shuttered face. She spoke, although she knew it was unwise.

"Lord Elseth," she said, her voice very cold, "we are not enemies, or even rivals, in this."

Gilliam's jaw set as he hoisted Stephen to his feet and draped one strong arm under Stephen's shoulders. "I never said we were." If possible, his voice was colder than Cynthia's.

Cynthia snorted. "You didn't have to say it. For the past two months you've been barely civil—and this evening you were a positive disgrace to Elseth!"

"Cynthia," Stephen said weakly. "Gil."

They ignored him. "That isn't for you to decide," he said, grinding his teeth. "Lady Elseth will make her opinion known, and I answer to her alone."

"Gil—"

"He isn't yours," Gilliam continued, brushing aside Stephen's weak plea. "He'll never be yours. You've got no right to interfere with the huntbrother's bond."

As Gilliam bristled, so did the wild girl.

Cynthia heard the snarl, turned, and snapped. "Be quiet!" The girl took a step back, but her growl grew tighter and lower.

"I'm not trying to interfere with what you and Stephen share," Cynthia said

222 ◆ Michelle West

evenly, her cheeks suddenly crimson. "I know full well that I'll never have it—or anything else of his, besides. I was—concerned for him. That's all."

Gilliam made no reply. They stood, in the darkness of moonlit sky, their faces shadowed by more than night.

"Gilliam," Stephen whispered. "You idiot."

Gilliam bridled; he always did. But he did not let his brother fall. "Come on," he said, to no one in particular. "Let's get inside. We'll have to call healers."

Cynthia nodded stiffly and turned to lead the Hunter and his brother out of the damaged maze. As she did, the girl darted forward. Gilliam shouted wordlessly, and the girl whined—but she continued forward until she could butt her head against Stephen's bloodstained chest.

Stephen staggered; Gilliam caught him in both arms.

The girl shoved her hands into her dirty, torn shift, still keening softly.

Gilliam shook his head, but the girl ignored him. Hands trembling, face quite still, she watched Stephen. After a second, she shoved her head into his midsection again, demanding some attention, some gesture.

Stephen put his hands out to gently push her aside. Before he could so much as brush against her shoulders, she pushed something into his shaking palms and jumped back, skittish. His fingers closed reflexively against something smooth and cool.

Gilliam, Lord Elseth, felt his huntbrother's sudden lurch of terror. "Stephen?"

Stephen shook his head. Even in darkness more complete than this, he would have known what it was that the wild, strange girl had given into his keeping. He could not look. He did not have to.

The wyrd of Fate and mystery, so long suspended, settled heavily upon his frail shoulders, contained as it was by the deceptively simple form of the Hunter's Horn.

Chapter Seventeen

"GILLIAM," LADY ELSETH SAID softly. "What happened?"

Gilliam knew that his mother's soft-spoken question was nothing short of a demand for information. Unfortunately, he also knew that Stephen did not wish that question answered. As he hadn't Stephen's faculty for words, he shrugged instead. A poor substitute.

The Mother-born Priestess, Vivienne of the King's City, had come as quickly as the night roads and travel allowed. She had said nothing at all as she entered the room that was to be Stephen's sick chamber. But she quickly cleared it of idle spectators—even, and including, Gilliam of Elseth. As always, he bridled.

"A shrug," his mother said quietly, "is not an answer that I find acceptable."

Lady Cynthia, newly changed, and now much more simply attired, stepped forward and placed a gentle hand on Lady Elseth's shoulder. "May I? Gilliam is also exhausted; the doctors prescribed rest for him."

Elsabet's eyes narrowed as she glanced at her son. Her son wisely refused to meet her eyes, but made a display of a yawn that was only part act.

"Lord Elseth, why don't you tend to your other guest?"

"Other guest?" Lady Elseth's voice was even softer.

"What a good idea," Gilliam said lamely. He knew it would spark his mother's curiosity further—but that was unavoidable now. Grudgingly, he nodded his thanks to Lady Cynthia of Maubreche and slunk out of the room, figurative tail between his legs.

"Lady Elseth, please forgive us for allowing this tragedy to occur on Maubreche lands. We've prepared rooms for you, should you wish to stay in the manor."

Elsabet nodded almost absently. "Yes, I'd appreciate that."

"Then let me show you to your rooms."

Lady Elseth was a shrewd and perceptive woman. For that reason, Cynthia had always both admired and feared her. As she walked now by her side, fear was the stronger emotion. She felt Lady Elseth's keen gaze upon her face. In silence, and without turning once to meet her elder's eyes, Cynthia led the way to the manor's west wing.

There, she paused in front of the door.

"Why don't you join me, Cynthia?"

It was not a request, no matter how politely worded. Swallowing, Cynthia nodded assent, and together they entered Lady Elseth's rooms. A fire was already burning in the grate, and a cozy tea had been newly set in the sitting room. Lady Elseth took the chair closest to the fire and motioned for Cynthia to join her.

But if Cynthia had thought to be questioned about the events of the evening, she was mistaken.

"Tell me," Elsabet said softly, "about Stephen."

Cynthia swallowed again. "You know him better than I ever will," she replied. "Tea?"

"Yes, please. And as for the other, I'm not so certain."

Cynthia poured slowly and let the liquid, still steaming, reach the gold rim of the cup before she passed it on. She poured for herself as well and then sat, cup between her hands, staring at her reflection upon the clear, brown surface of the liquid. Silence stretched widely between them before she ventured to speak. "Why do you want me to talk about Stephen?"

"Because," Elsabet said quietly, "you talk to no one else of him—and perhaps you need to speak."

"Am I so obvious?"

The smile that touched Lady Elseth's face was a wry one. "Perhaps only to me. Certainly not to Stephen."

Cynthia lowered her gaze to stare moodily at the table-top. "It won't make any difference. We both know that."

"Yes."

The word hurt; it still hurt.

"But it already has, Cynthia. You are eighteen now, and not even at the start of your year. You have met and been courted by many of the younger Hunters, although that should more properly have waited until you came out."

"I know," Cynthia said, her voice surprisingly bitter. "And I know that I'll marry the younger son of some Hunter Lord, and both he and his huntbrother will forsake their family name for Maubreche. Because, of course, the line must continue."

Lady Elseth said nothing at all.

"But that's not what I want." There. It was said.

"No," Elsabet replied. "And you have less choice than most of us had when we searched for our husbands. We had plans to tend to their estates; you are hampered by the fact that your estate will be—can only be—Maubreche. If you were not the only child, Cynthia, I would have happily recommended you to either of my sons. But Gilliam *is* Elseth; he cannot take Maubreche responsibilities as his own. And Stephen is no Hunter Lord, to offer Maubreche's services in the Sacred Hunt."

Cynthia set her tea down on the table; her hands were trembling. "Do you think I don't already know this?" she asked, her voice too low. "Do you think that I've thought about anything else for the last two years?" She rose, upsetting her chair; her cheeks were flushed and dark.

Lady Elseth did not move.

"Why are you asking me this? Why do you want me to speak openly about the impossible?"

"Because only by admitting it openly will you ever truly dismiss it. You parents are concerned; this you know well. Let me tell you that I, too, am concerned. For the sake of Stephen. Between you and I there is no pretense. What we do, we have little choice in, if we are not to abandon our responsibilities and our birthrights." This voice, these formal words, were those that Lady Elseth used when she sat in judgment. "If we are lucky, then we will have love; if we are not, then we will have duty. Love is for children, Cynthia."

Cynthia drew a sharp breath, but before she could frame a reply, Lady Elseth continued, sitting very, very still as she did.

"I was a child, too. I listened to the musings of the bard-born, and I dreamed. The man I chose was no Hunter Lord. He was a student, an academic in the King's City seeking admission to the Order of Knowledge. We met by accident at the Sacred Hunt in the year I came out."

Cynthia was silent now, watching the pale, neutral cast of Elsabet's calm face.

"After the Sacred Hunt, when death and loss were in the air, I went to him. I don't know why." She smiled, briefly, and shook her head. "I do know. I wanted no taint of loss or death; I wanted someone whose life was living. Or so I tell myself now.

"I contrived to stay in the King's City for three weeks, Cynthia. I met with Ladies and their sons, and began to search in earnest for the Lord of my future— during the days. But in the evenings, I went to him, stayed with him."

"You didn't—"

"No; I asked for the intercession of the Mother-born to aid me in my cycle."

Lady Elseth set her tea aside and closed her eyes, remembering. The fire crackled; not even breath was loud enough to be heard.

"Was it—was it worth it?"

"I thought so for those three weeks. For the next two years, I regretted it."

"And now?"

"Now? I regret nothing."

Cynthia met Lady Elsabet's gaze; their eyes locked; the room vanished around them. "But what if I want more than three weeks? What if I want forever?"

Elsabet knew what the question would be before it was spoken. There was no softness in her when she answered. "What if you have a choice between nothing and three weeks?"

Silence again; the evening had been measured by the quality of their silences, rather than the force of the words spoken. Cynthia's eyes were watery and red, but she allowed no tears to fall. "What if three weeks aren't enough for Stephen?"

Lady Elseth looked down at her skirts; she brushed them out carefully and methodically, almost automatically arranging them into the most pleasing drape. "I cannot speak for Stephen. Perhaps you should let him decide." She stood, then; the work on her skirts was undone. "I am fatigued by the evening, Lady Cynthia; I must retire. Perhaps we shall speak more of this tomorrow."

Stephen feigned sleep under Vivienne's gentle ministrations. It was only a partial act. Although the pain had receded, and the bleeding had stopped, he was exhausted. To be nursed and tended by the Mother-born was a balm, but it had its price. For to heal the body, the healer had to understand it, and to understand it well, she had to become, however briefly, a part of it. She brought warmth with her, sure knowledge, a deep understanding of all pain, all sorrow, all fear.

And when the healing was done, she left. His body, whole, let him feel the ache of the Mother's passing, as he had done only one other time in his life. It hurt.

She knew, of course. She could feel his pulse, unnaturally quick, at her fingers. But she, too, was weary. She had asked no questions about the injuries when she had first arrived, as Stephen had not been in any condition to answer them. Now that he was, she felt too weak to ask.

"Stephen," she said quietly, as she rose from his bedside. "If you feel the need to ask any questions, I will still be in the Maubreche estate on the morrow. Summon me, if you will."

He did not open his eyes; did not move or nod, or in any way acknowledge her offer. Trembling, he saw the shadow of her passing against his eyelids. She paused once; he heard the rustle of her robes. The lamps in the room were doused, and Stephen lay back against his pillows in the darkness.

He had not allowed them to take away the horn. He reached for it now, as it sat completely vulnerable upon the table beside his bed. As his eyes adjusted to the moonlight filtering in through the uncurtained window, he stared at his new burden.

He could still see the eyes of the girl in the moment that the horn had passed into his hands. And he did not understand what he saw there; a flicker of desperation, fear—something else. It had not lasted; her dark eyes had darted away, horn forgotten, to seek Gilliam.

The horn was smooth and curiously unadorned. It was simple bone or antler, but from what beast, upon close inspection, he couldn't say. Around the horn's lip, burned there as if by a brand, were two interlocked circles; they were perfectly round, unbroken.

Three times he had lifted this very horn, and three times—in dreams—he had sounded it. He pressed its mouth to his lips; both were cold. He could not draw breath to wind it.

Evayne, he thought. But this was no dream; she did not appear in the doorway to answer his questions or offer her unfathomable pity.

In the morning, he woke to a knock at the door. The sun was high; higher than it should have been. He began to scramble out from under the covers when the room spun back into focus. Maubreche. Not Elseth.

"Hello?" He expected breakfast, or lunch, judging the hour; neither came. Cynthia opened the door quietly and entered the room.

Speechless, he pulled the covers up to the tip of his chin.

"I see that your arm is better." She smiled, hesitant, her hands behind her back. Gone was the unfamiliar young Lady who had danced in fine silks and velvets; gone was the proud and beautiful solitary heir to the Maubreche estates. She wore a simple brown dress, and her hair, no longer combed and jeweled, rested at her back in single braid.

"It's—it's much better." He swallowed and sank farther back. "I—if you—"

"I brought you a book," she said, too quickly. She started to step forward, stopped, and pulled the volume from behind her back. Advancing upon him, she held it as if it were a shield.

He held out his hand; she placed the book in it. Neither of them so much as glanced at the title. Their fingers touched, and Cynthia pulled back. The book tumbled to the floor.

She blushed, bent, picked it up, and shoved it firmly into his hands. "I'll speak with you later," she said, and turning, fled.

On the third day of his recovery at the Maubreche estate, Stephen accepted Lady Cynthia's rather formally worded invitation to a tour of the grounds. He did so because he was curious; he wanted to see, in daylight, what night had shadowed. But he also wanted to see Cynthia, unwise though he thought it might be.

She met him in his rooms after breakfast had been served, and waited at the doors while one of the Maubreche valets helped him dress. Then, in near silence, she led him along the corridors and down the stairs of the wing. Only when doors opened into sunlight did she seem to relax.

Wind swept the strands of hair not caught in braids up along the sides of her cheeks; it ruffled the pale brown of her stiff, heavy skirts. She closed her eyes a moment, took a deep breath, and then accepted the arm that Stephen offered almost hesitantly.

"Is there anything that you'd like to see?" she asked. Her voice was soft, almost a whisper.

Several answers came to mind, but when he finally spoke, all he could say was: "The labyrinth."

She seemed to be expecting that, or perhaps that was what she had intended to show him. She nodded and began to lead him toward it.

Even from the house, the neatly kept sweep of tall, green wall dominated the perfect landscape of the Maubreche gardens. In their foreground, there was a tall stone slab, cut deeply across the middle, as if by a sword. Water trickled from the edge of the gash.

"What is it?" Stephen questioned quietly.

She didn't answer; instead, she approached the fountain to let the monument speak for itself. It seemed to be marble, shot through with hints of smoky gray and green. Etched into the grained pattern of the marble were names; Stephen recognized very few of them. But he knew them for Maubreche ancestors. Cynthia bowed very quietly to both the monument and the names it housed; after a moment, Stephen did likewise.

"Corason built the maze," she said, pointing to the very first name on the list. "Let me show you his work."

Stephen looked at the hedges as they approached. On first sight, they were not so different from any other shrubbery that he had seen—they were carefully tended, carefully pruned.

"The outside face," Cynthia said, as if she could hear his thoughts. She led him slowly around the circle of greenery. They came, at length, to a gap between the circumference. It was too narrow for them to walk through abreast, and Cynthia relinquished her hold on Stephen's arm to precede him.

"Where is the damage?"

"Damage? Ah. Around the other side." The momentary darkening of her features told him, clearly, what the hedge meant to her. "It was . . . not so bad as we first feared. Later, if you'd like, we can inspect it, but I want you to see what the labyrinth looks like when it's whole."

Stephen barely heard her answer. For as he stepped clear of the labyrinth's one entrance, he saw what the outside face hid. The walls of the maze were alive. Captured in green, as if the shrubs were stone, all manner of creatures stood. There, to his left, an elderly woman sitting upon a rock; to his right, an elderly man bent over some task that the leaves swallowed.

"These are the pride of the master gardener. He tends them every day he can. Every year the maze changes, very slowly and very subtly. I used to come out with him and try to guess what was different, when I was younger. I asked him once why he didn't sculpt—real stone, I mean. He laughed and walked off. It was two days before he decided to answer the question."

There, in the wall just ahead, one figure caught Stephen's attention. He almost missed it, it was so slight, but perhaps the light caught the figure at just the right moment, or perhaps Cynthia guided him toward it. He saw the face and hands of a young child, peering out of the greenery. Green eyes, branched limbs, wavering in the wind the way a child shivers in surprise or fear.

"These walls—that child . . ." He felt acutely aware of his lack of words, although words had never been his weakness.

"I know." She walked toward the leafy child. "He was so much younger the first time I thought I saw him. So much more hesitant. Just his nose, and his chin, and a couple of fingers. He only came up to here—" She motioned toward her waist. "He's coming out a bit, sort of escaping whatever life he has on the other side of that wall."

"I wonder what he's looking at."

"So do I."

"Cynthia?"

She nodded, reaching out at the same time to touch the small hand of the boy.

"You said the master gardener answered your question."

"Eventually." Her lips were curved in the same delicate smile as those of the green child.

"What did he say?"

"He said 'Look in my garden, child. Come back and tell me what you see.'" Her smile didn't change, but her eyes did, although Stephen could never afterward describe the difference. "I went out and spent the day wandering in the maze. I spent some time sleeping under the arms of the God, and some time talking to the rabbits—they were like the boy, but they're gone now—and when I came back, I'd almost forgotten the question. But he hadn't. He asked me what I'd seen there, and I told him."

"And?"

"He told me that it would change. He said stone is lifeless, cold, hard—you have to fight it and once you've finished, it's still stone. But life—he said life was the best material because it changed, and grew, and surprised one."

They were silent a moment, thinking on it. "I'd like to meet this gardener of yours someday," Stephen said finally.

"Perhaps we will see him today." By the forced lightness of her tone, he knew that she didn't mean it; he did not know why. "Come; let's go to the heart of the labyrinth." She released her tentative hold upon the green child. As she did, Stephen felt a sudden, sharp loss. He let it pass silently as she moved away; in a few seconds, he joined her.

As he did, Stephen's full attention returned to the hedges; he barely stopped to offer Cynthia his arm. If she begrudged him this rare breach of etiquette, none of her disapproval showed on her face; indeed, she was slow to place her hand upon his arm.

These bushes, they were like any other. There was no way they should have been so much of a presence. But try as he did to tell himself that, he still felt that they were more than alive—they were life, in expression, in intent, and in the odd quirkiness of their design. Every so often he would point out something that caught his eyes—the carved representation of birds nesting, of a sly fox darting for cover, of a group of men gathered around it with a clumsy sort of grace. There were people sitting under carved boughs; they were green but he could feel flesh, breath, and a slow, stately movement about them that more than wind through their tiny, delicate leaves could explain.

"This master gardener," Stephen said softly—for no loud words, he was sure, could be uttered in this maze, "he's maker-born, isn't he?"

She did not answer. "Here," she murmured softly. "You must look at this one. It will be gone very soon, unlike the others."

Stephen followed her obediently, and as he turned a corner, he came face-to-face with a stag leaping out of the hedge. Only half its body could be seen, and that half well above the ground, its front legs straining for height and speed. Its head was held high and crowned with strong, branching antlers. Its face was determined, noble, and touched by a sadness that almost overpowered his silent watchers.

Not until he was forced to exhale did Stephen realize that he'd been holding his breath. He pulled back, without a word, and they continued on, allowing the proud animal to continue undisturbed and untouched.

But to Stephen the stag crystallized what he felt in the hedges, and why. They were like forest, like hunting grounds in an inexplicable way; teeming with hidden and silent life, undisturbed by common human interaction. They were more than that, though. He knew, with a profound sense of loss, that were the animals in the hedges real, were he to encounter them at the side of his Hunter, he could no more allow them to be hunted than he could hunt in a ballroom. For the first time in his life, hunting felt almost profane. It disquieted him deeply.

Cynthia, not born and bred to the actual, physical hunt, could not know all of what he felt, but she sensed his silent mortification. "Here, Stephen," she said, as if to distract him. "Now we come upon the only thing that interests most of our visitors. The tapestries."

He shook his head; the stag slowly receded. The walls to either side were teeming with scenes from life, in different reliefs; they had none of the quirky reality that the other hedges had—they indeed seemed to be, as Cynthia had named them, tapestries. In green.

Acts of war were carved there, war and the heroism it often evoked; acts of sacrifice, love, pain. Figures melded in and out of one another, giving the whole a feel of continuity. Of Maubreche's lineage.

"These are the exploits of the Maubreche line," she said, although it wasn't necessary. "That"—she pointed almost reverently—"is Harald of Maubreche." She shivered, and Stephen came to stand at her side, wondering what in the young man's countenance could cause her reaction. The figure could not have been older than Cynthia. He stood on the edge of a cliff, looking outward insensibly upon his audience. His face was an open expression of grief, shock, and loss, but beneath that was a determination seldom seen in any his age. Stephen did not know the history of the family, but he knew that somehow, somewhere, this young boy had given up more than his life to protect something he loved. It radiated outward from him.

Cynthia bowed low and pressed her fingers against her lips. Then she stood and moved on. The scenes changed. Some of them featured women, some men, and some children. In one or two, the pride of the Maubreche hunting packs long past came to bristling life. But none of those had the resonance, and the sense of bitter, inevitable loss, that Harald did. Stephen was afraid to ask the story.

They walked together in silence until at last the tapestries ended. To Stephen's surprise, the hedge that preceded them into the heart of the maze seemed wild and untended. He turned to glance at Cynthia, and she smiled, as if she expected his reaction.

"These wait for the future deeds of the Maubreche family. We know that one of our line will be greater than any who have come before—and this whole wall will be his. Or hers. I hope I live to see that day." She swallowed, and, for a moment, her eyes were stripped of pride and assurance. She hoped for that day, but Stephen saw fear there, also.

And he wondered, as she did, whether that greatness would exact more of a price than Harald had paid—whatever that price had been.

"Come," Cynthia said, shaking herself. The moment—and the vulnerability—passed. She was again the adult heir to the Maubreche demesne. "We're almost upon the center. I want you to see the God in daylight."

Stephen stopped walking, and Cynthia noted this because her hand was upon his arm. "Stephen?"

He did not want to see the God in daylight. He realized, suddenly, that he did not want to see the God at all, even if it was a statue, a representation, no more. He opened his mouth, but he found that he could not tell her why; the horn at his side, hidden in the folds of his jacket, weighed heavily upon him.

But heavy or no, he walked with it, at Cynthia's side. The last of the wild hedge fell away, and in the center, as Cynthia had promised, the God stood in daylight.

But in daylight, the God was different; without darkness, some of its frightening mystery had been stripped away, concealed by the sun. There was a fountain that bubbled at his back, and although this maze was a testament to life, the fountain and the statue were both of stone.

There are some things, Stephen thought, *that do not change with time.* He stared up, following the lines of the statue's stone robes, until he could clearly make out the details of the God's face. There, his eyes stopped. For what he saw in this un-changing representation, he had also seen in the Maubreche living tapestries. In Harald's face. Sorrow, deep and profound, as well as determination and a measure of peace, were evident in the solemn line of jaw and forehead.

Without thinking, he dropped to one knee and bowed his head—just as he would have done in the presence of the Master of the Game.

"He doesn't look so horrible, does he?" Cynthia asked softly. "It's hard to imag-ine that he hurts us so badly each and every year." She walked past Stephen's bowed form, and came to rest both hands upon the pale stone, as if seeking warmth.

"Why did you ask for sanctuary here?"

She looked back, met Stephen's raised eyes. "Because here, there is no Hunt." She looked away. "And because here, in this hollow, we have promised to keep the Hunter's word in return for his peace."

"His peace?"

"It's an old custom, Stephen. A family custom. I don't understand it well, my-self; I won't until my father dies."

It didn't make any sense. "But if your father's dead, how can he tell you any-thing?"

She did not choose to answer, and although he was curious, he lost the desire to push her. Instead, he stared at the pale profile of her face. Her eyes were closed.

"Cynthia?"

"Yes?" She did not open her eyes.

He hesitated, and then rose, treading carefully across the grass to stand before her. "Why are we here?"

"Ever?" she returned softly. "Or now?"

"Now."

She swallowed, and to Stephen's surprise, her cheeks reddened. She opened her eyes, searching his; they stood very close. Words started, half-audible; words stopped. They were both afraid, and the fear was an old one, a common one.

"You know I'm going to have to marry soon," she said at last, uncomfortable and uncertain.

It was Stephen's turn to look away. "Yes. Do you—do you know who?"

She shrugged, an elegant rustle of cloth against skin. "One of three. It doesn't matter."

He wanted to tell her that it mattered to him, but he couldn't bring himself to say it. Awkward in silence, he matched her shrug.

"I would—I would have married you, if we had held different positions."

He had always thought it was what he wanted to hear, until he heard it in truth. But hearing the pain behind the words, hearing the farewell, he took no pleasure in them. "Cynthia—"

"Stephen," she cut off his question, her voice low. "Must I say everything?"

"What do you want from me?"

"Everything." Her face was pale and stark. "But I cannot have it; you cannot give it. Ask me a different question."

"What can I give you?" He reached out; traced the line of her cheek with his fingers.

"It's a better question," she said, not withdrawing. "Only you can answer it. I've asked it of myself, and I know my own answer. I brought you here."

He kissed her then, gently and hesitantly. She stiffened, and he pulled back, bumping her nose and the line of her forehead. She laughed shakily and reached up to encircle his neck with her arms.

They kissed again, less awkwardly, their nervousness blending with something else. And then, when Stephen pulled back, he caught her face in his hands and met her eyes. She did not look away, did not avoid him, nor make any move to leave.

He buried his face in the nape of her neck and pulled her close, hugging her as tightly as he dared. In awe, almost, at what she had asked, what she had decided. He knew that nothing that happened today, in this labyrinth, was permanent; knew, no matter how much he thought and planned and plotted, that Cynthia of Maubreche would go on to marry—and bear children to—a lesser Hunter Lord. None of it mattered. He held her close, closer; he lifted his head and found her mouth, still clutching her tightly.

Something sharp pressed into his hip.

He pulled back, as did she, and then looked down to see the plain, carved horn. And he remembered, clearly and suddenly, the last time he had been in the maze with Cynthia. He saw the eyes of the wild girl, as she had shoved the horn into his hands, and felt once again the presence of God.

He knew that he could not stay or accept what Cynthia offered; the time was poor for it, and dangerous.

But he bit his lip until he drew blood.

She knew. He did not have to speak. Her eyes filmed and then snapped shut; water glistened at her lids and along her lashes, but did not grace her cheeks. "I— I understand. I'm sorry to have troubled you."

He caught her by the shoulders, then. "You don't understand, Cynthia. I'm— I'm under wyrd; I would stay with you if I could. But that girl—that wild creature that Gilliam brought with him four evenings past—she gave me this." He lifted the horn at his hip.

"What of it?"

"It's the God's."

She did not believe him, or else she thought him mad. She turned her face to the statue and once again gripped the edges of its pedestal. "Then give it back to God." Her voice was shaky, angry.

"Cynthia," he said, but she would not turn. "Let me see to the horn and the girl; let me solve the problem they present. I'll return then."

"And what if you return too late?" Her voice was proud, almost haughty.

He swallowed. She was right; he was a fool to lose this one day, this one chance. He took a step toward her, and then another, but as he reached out, he felt *power*. The clearing glowed with it. Cynthia, unmoved, still kept her back to him.

The face of the God moved. His lips formed a single word or perhaps a snarl; it wasn't clear. Its meaning was *Go*. Cynthia had not seen it, and Stephen doubted that she would.

"If I return late?" he asked, determined to at least answer her. "Then I'll curse myself for a fool until I die."

She turned in an awkward rush. "Stephen—"

He pressed his fingers against her lips. "I'll return, Cynthia. I'll come back to you. We'll meet here again." But even as he said it, he felt the shadows growing. The wyrd was upon him, and in each of the three dreams, he had called his own death.

She had always been aware of him, or of part of him; she saw the shift in his face and the shift in his promise immediately. "Swear it," she said, her voice suddenly hard. "Swear it, Stephen."

"I so swear."

"No—not like that." She bent down and lifted her skirts in trembling hands. He watched as she removed the small knife that all Hunter Ladies carried. Before he could stop her, she dragged it across her hand, as Gilliam had once done, years ago.

"Cynthia . . ."

"You did it for him, when you were a child. Do it for me now." She was crying, her eyes almost as red as her palm. He took the knife.

"Tell me that you'll return to me, Stephen."

"I'll return to you. I swear it." His hand shook as he placed the knife against his palm.

"No matter what happens."

"No matter what." His blood flowed then. Before he could offer her his hand, she had taken it. He pulled her close, and she let him, although it was awkward; she did not release his hand.

"Lord," she whispered softly, her lips and eyes swollen. It was not until she continued to speak that Stephen realized she did not speak to him. "We've kept our oath and your lands. Bear witness to this vow; give it your blessing and your curse."

They were no Priest's words, but in their choked rhythm, Stephen felt a stir-ring. He could not identify it, could not name it; it was almost as if a different God's approbation drifted past on the quiet breeze.

But Cynthia stopped crying almost at once, and he held her in his arms for as long as he dared, thinking that not once had they spoken of love.

Chapter Eighteen

THE FIRST PERSON THAT Stephen met, when he returned to Elseth Manor, was Lady Elseth herself. She had had word of his coming, and perhaps contrived to meet him upon his return. Gilliam was nowhere in sight, and Boredan was also about his duties.

He was not tired from the journey; indeed, he had chosen a leisurely pace along the road. He had wanted time and privacy in which to think—and these would best be obtained in the company of complete strangers at the inns or along the roads.

"Stephen," Elsabet said, coming down the long hall, her skirts rustling, as always, in her wake. Fashions had changed since he was eight, and with those fashions had gone the plain, long skirts. Now, there were thin hoops, and panniers that reminded him, oddly, of saddlebags, around Lady Elseth's legs and petticoats. He thought them ugly, and hoped that fashion would be kind and turn again.

"Elsa," he said, grabbing her hands firmly in his own, and leaning down to kiss her cheek. "What news?"

"I was about to ask you that," she said, smiling. She pulled back, although she did not let go of his hands, and her eyes were distinctly appraising. "You didn't stay long."

"No."

"I'd sent word that you wouldn't be needed."

"You lied."

She met his eyes and the lines around hers deepened. Then she smiled, almost shyly; a hint of the young girl she might once have been. "I didn't," she said dryly, "realize that it was a lie at the time." She leaned forward into his chest, and he let go of her hands to place arms around her shoulders. "But I'm worried."

"About Gilliam?"

"Who else?" She laughed, but the laugh was too high, and a little too brittle. Then, as if remembering herself, she said, "You look well, Stephen."

He felt her shiver, and he smiled broadly. "Vivienne could raise the dead. But, yes, I'm well. I apologize if I frightened you."

She played at batting the side of his head. "Frightened me? The very thought of being left alone with Gilliam—say that you terrified me instead, and all will be forgiven."

They hooked arms together, but instead of entering into the house, Lady Elseth led Stephen out the front doors. She ambled along the kept area of their grounds, and to any watching servants, there was little out of the ordinary. Except that Stephen had not yet bathed, or even seen to the accoutrements of his travels.

"Stephen, what is happening?" Elsa said, when they were far enough away from the manor so she could be certain no servant's ears would hear her. All playful banter was gone from her voice, and the very set of her eyes and lips were exactly those she wore when she sat in judgment.

"Happening?"

"You did not see fit to explain your injuries; neither did Gilliam or Cynthia. I can understand, perhaps, your reluctance." It was, of course, a lie. "But the girl that Gilliam brought home with him—she's not normal."

"No," Stephen replied gravely. "But . . . how has she been?"

"I don't know." The words were clipped and cold. "She hasn't spoken a single word. Not just to me, Stephen. To anyone. Gilliam is constantly with her—or rather, she is constantly with Gilliam. She does not eat at our table, and . . . she cannot be made to dress in an appropriate fashion."

"Do you fear madness?" he asked, hoping that she did.

"No," Lady Elseth replied. The women of Breodanir were far too perceptive. "Not madness. She's possessed of a certain cunning, and a certain intelligence. I have seen it before, often."

"In the dogs."

"But surely only a madwoman—"

"Stephen, enough! I am the Lady of Elseth, and all who dwell on Elseth lands answer to me. This is a matter of safety for our people and our responsibilities, and I will have the truth. Now, if you please."

"Elsa—"

"*Now.*"

He told her, of course. And she knew that he would. Gilliam could turn her aside with a word or a dismissive gesture, but his huntbrother understood too well her cares and concerns.

He hesitated before he told her of the wyrd, but with her gentle prompting, he found it impossible to be afraid of her derision. He told her of the dreams first, and when she nodded gravely, he found himself speaking next of Krysanthos, the mage-born, and Kallandras, the bard-born. When he told her about the man who had tried to kill him in his first Sacred Hunt, she stopped him briefly.

"Why didn't you tell us?"

"I—it didn't seem important after Soredon's death." It was half-truth, but Soredon's death, even at years' distance, could still stop her in her steps, and she didn't question further.

Last, he told her of the creatures who had hunted them in the lower circle of the King's City. "She called them demon-kin," he said softly.

"She?"

"Evayne. The mage who saved our lives."

"The woman of your wyrd."

He nodded.

"And this girl?"

"I don't know. But—" But very gently, he reached for, and opened, his belt pouch. Hands shaking, he pulled the simple horn out, into the light of day. When she reached to touch it, his hands curled up reflexively. She drew back. "She gave it to me."

Sun touched the horn, casting little shadows in the palms of Stephen's hand. For a moment, it looked too simple, and too real, to be the cause of such concern. He expected Lady Elseth to laugh—if only a little—or to demur. She offered him neither comfort.

But her face was very pale, almost gray. "Stephen?"

He had to lean down to catch the word; the wind, weak and playful, pulled it from her lips.

"Walk me to the Hunter's altar."

He offered an arm, and without hesitation, she took it. Together, in silence, they made their way to the Hunter's green. There, at its edge, she let go of his arm. "Leave me," she said softly. "I need time to think."

"Elsa—"

"Leave me." There was no anger or rancor in her words; there was hardly any emotion at all. But her chin was set a little too high, and her lips were a little too thin.

"Elsa—" he tried again.

But she would not hear him. Instead, she drifted over the invisible circle, a quiet vision of deep blues and bright reds across the open green. She did not look back; she walked like a ruler who needed, and wanted, no aid. Stephen did not know what to offer, although Norn might once have, had he lived. Instead, he watched until she approached the altar itself. Then, abruptly, he turned, knowing what he would see, and unwilling to watch it.

Elsabet, Lady Elseth, knelt in the grass, unmindful of dirt or insects; she had brought no rolled carpet with her to protect her skirts. She pressed her forehead to the cool stone of the altar's edge, forced it, just to feel and to know that it would not give at all.

What must I do? she thought, afraid to even whisper the words, afraid to give them solidity, grant them reality.

She did not lie to herself, did not try—especially not here, in the sight of God. What she had heard, she felt as truth. *It is never over, is it?* She lifted her face, then, to look up at the henges, with their ancient, impassive runes.

The women of the Breodanir were never trained in the Hunt; they were trained, rather, to face its wake. They were not trained, or rarely so, to fight with the weapons that the Hunters bore—although they each had some knowledge of dagger play—yet they granted death, on rare occasions, from the seat of judgment in their demesnes. They did not face the Hunter's Death—but not a single one of them, upon becoming mothers, would have hesitated to face it if their children might be spared.

And if they were not fighters in the Hunter's scheme, they were warriors in their own. Elsabet, Lady Elseth, was tired—but she still held her title, and all of the responsibilities that went with it. She longed to find Gilliam a wife; she longed to leave, just for a moment, the duties that had shaped and scarred her.

But she would never hurt her line and her people by stepping aside to let them pass untended. She did not cry; she had long since learned that tears were a language that the Gods did not understand. Instead, she raised her face, looking almost serene in the dying light.

"What will you have of my sons?"

Grass rippled in the breeze; nothing else stirred.

"Very well, Lord. But I will not let them go lightly. What I can offer them, even in your game, I will."

She rose, and her pride settled upon her shoulders like an honorable, ancient mantle.

Stephen saw to his horse; he wanted the time to think about all that he had revealed to the woman who was his mother and his ruler. The stable hands, used by now to the moods of quiet and business that Stephen sometimes displayed, stayed out of his way; they did not even offer him brush or blankets.

When he had finished in the stables, he turned to the house. He greeted the keykeeper with studious politeness—he was still, at his age and station, measured and too often found wanting in Boredan's eyes—and then retreated to his rooms to wash and change.

But he did not sleep, and he did not eat. When he had finished, he left to search for Gilliam. It was not hard to guess where he would be found.

The sun was low, and the sky had given way to pinks and tufted clouds; the air was cooling rapidly. Stephen did not bother with a heavier jacket; the kennels, he knew, would have a fire burning in two places. He paused only to light the lamp he carried before he opened the small door at the kennel's side.

There, haloed by the light that he carried too tightly to his chest, he stopped in silence.

He understood, in an instant, the concern that Lady Elseth had failed to make completely clear. The dogs lay in their beds, resting before their final evening meal. Although he could not make them out clearly, he could read the names graven in plaques at the foot of each bed; he knew which ones woke to sniff the air before they settled their heads back down against paws and straw. Although Gilliam was Lord now, and master of the Elseth kennels, there were no younger brothers or cousins to tend the dogs, and the responsibility remained Gilliam's.

Ashfel, at three years of age the leader and pride of Gilliam's alaunts, growled softly and gently; a warning to Stephen, but not a threat. Stephen met the dog's eyes, reddened in the lamp's glow, and nodded, as if to quiet the dog. He did not have the kitchen scraps that he most often brought as a bribe—and had he carried them, he would have forgotten them in an instant.

For in a bed that should have been disused, the wild girl lay upon her stomach, her cheek to a pillow that looked incongruous upon the bed of straw. She wore a pale shift—one that was dirty and torn—of indeterminate color, and her hair was a tangle of darkness and shadow.

And beside her, in the tunic and vest that Gilliam wore when he tended the dogs in their kennels, Gilliam himself lay sleeping.

Stephen blinked rapidly, as if to clear away the fog from his vision. He even closed his eyes and bit his lip, something he had done only rarely since his Ascension, but when he opened his eyes again, Gilliam still lay in repose at the girl's side.

Mother's breath, he thought, as he leaned back against the wall. *I'm not seeing this. This isn't real.*

The girl suddenly raised her head, squinting against the light. She opened her mouth, and something midway between a bark and croon left her lips.

Stephen felt Gilliam stir, and wake, as he watched. He didn't know what he would say, didn't know what he wanted to say. Gilliam saved him the trouble.

"What in the hells are you doing here?"

Elsabet heard the kennels as they erupted into cacophony. A tight smile fixed itself to her lips; she did not so much as pause as she made her way to the house. The dogs were howling, and no doubt the litter that Gilliam's best bitch had recently whelped had joined their elders. She shook her head, glad that Stephen had at last arrived home, if not to set things right, than at least to argue sense with Gilliam in the way that Hunters knew best.

She was not surprised to see them come into the house. Bits of straw and dirt clung to their jackets, and it was clear that Gilliam's shirt had lost buttons. She could see, even down the stretch of the hall that held her sitting room, that they were both still very red-faced and angry—and that one, if not both of them would have bruises around their eyes. She held her peace, but an echo of the children they had once been touched her heart, and she almost smiled.

Until she saw that Stephen's arm was bleeding, and he held it close to his chest. With an ease that spoke both of custom and unquestioned authority, she pulled the rope that would summon the keykeeper, and then set off down the hall at a quick stride.

They both looked up, as if seeing her for the first time. "It's all right," Stephen said quickly. Gilliam said nothing, but he would not meet his mother's eyes.

"What on earth—Gilliam, did the dogs do this?"

"No!" They both said it in unison.

"Did you?" Lady Elseth said, her voice high.

"No."

She knew, then, what she thought might have happened, and she paled. But on this one point, she was too weary to press Gilliam. Stephen was his huntbrother, and on Stephen's shoulders, she would let it all rest.

"Elsa—we haven't finished talking yet," Stephen said, smiling rather dryly. "We'll be in the side room if you need us."

She nodded, but very, very stiffly. "Your arm?"

"It's not as bad as it looks," he said, but he winced.

"When you've finished this, you will see Boredan." It wasn't a question. Stephen grimaced and nodded. Then his face tightened as he looked at his brother.

"Come on," he said.

"Gil," Stephen said, the moment the door had closed, "what in the Hells is going on?"

"I told you, it's none of your damned business."

Stephen stiffened. "Why is the girl sleeping in the kennels? She isn't one of your damn hounds!" But looking down at his arm, he wasn't so sure. He tried not to remember the night of the demon-kin, and failed.

"She doesn't like sleeping in the house," was Gilliam's stiff reply.

"You said that already."

Gilliam turned. His jaw was set, and his face was nearly purple—and not just from their fist play.

"Don't start it again, Gil. What the *Hells* were you doing sleeping there?"

"I don't answer to you, Stephen!"

"You goddamned well do! You might have forgotten this, you flaming idiot, but you aren't a dog!"

Gilliam, never as good with words as his huntbrother, took two steps forward.

"There's no excuse for this—this sort of behavior. You're not fourteen anymore, and you aren't with your first pack. Remember who you are, Gilliam—you're the Lord of Elseth, for the Mother's sake!"

" 'This sort of behavior?' " Gilliam's eyes narrowed, and Stephen felt a sudden pull along the bond that they had shared since they were eight. Then Gilliam's eyes widened, before narrowing again, this time dangerously. "You think I've— you think that she and I—you think that *of me?*"

There was not, and there never could be, any lie between a Hunter and his huntbrother. Stephen said, "What the Hells am I supposed to think? You want to!"

And those last three words were the truth, too. But if there was honesty, there was also incredible anger—and that was never easily hidden either.

"You son of a bitch!" Gilliam roared.

Stephen didn't bother with words; the time for them had passed. He had time to dodge the full force of Gilliam's furious charge before they connected again. This time, free from the dogs and the need to control or confine them, they tried, as brothers sometimes will, to beat each other senseless.

"Look at the two of you," Lady Elseth said, as she picked up her napkin. Breakfast had been set and served, and the sun that filtered in through the windows of the breakfast room was bright and unforgiving.

Stephen did not reply, but looked across the table at his Hunter. Gilliam did not look up from his plate. Neither of them had gotten much sleep during the previous evening.

"You do realize," Lady Elseth continued, her frosty voice belying the warmth of the early day, "that the servants haven't had this much cause for gossip in years?"

"Mother." Gilliam's single word was a warning. His face was set and etched in lines of sullen anger.

Lady Elseth was not to be put off, but she did not ask, as she had every previous breakfast, where Gilliam's guest could be found. "I think, Gilliam, that both Maribelle and I have been tolerant enough."

Maribelle, following her mother's lead, had seen to her napkin and her serving, but her eyes, openly curious, followed her brother's face. Gilliam was bruised; there was a cut just under his eye, probably caused by Stephen's signet ring.

Stephen looked no better, although it was a wonder, given his smaller stature, that he didn't look worse. His arm was bandaged and hung in a sling across his chest. The servants that had just been mentioned had been called to help him dress, and although on one other occasion he had likewise been tended to, that had had the excuse of a hunting accident behind it.

He ate stiffly and awkwardly, and although he made polite conversation with both of the Ladies, he never once looked at his Hunter.

Lady Elseth did not have a good morning. For that matter, lunch was no better, and by the end of the day's second meal, only Maribelle dutifully tried to keep conversation light and pleasant. The only boon to Elsabet's day was the fact that Gilliam, whom she subtly kept watch over, did not once go down to the kennels after seeing to the dogs' morning run and feeding.

When dinner commenced, weighted down by the same heavy silence, she finally put both her fork and knife to the side—setting them down so heavily, the wine in her glass sloshed over the brim.

"I have had enough of this," she said, the anger behind the words so forceful that for a moment the similarities between mother and son were obvious. "Stephen, Gilliam—both of you have things to discuss."

Stephen, ever obliging, rose. He knew a dismissal when he heard one, and he wasn't particularly hungry.

Gilliam looked at his mother. "There isn't much else to discuss," he said. His voice was not quite the match for hers.

"Then discuss nothing," she replied evenly. "But do it like civil adults. And do it now."

He looked as if he might speak, but enough of his anger had played itself out the past evening that he had the sense to be cautious. He rose, scraping his chair against the floor and dumping his napkin, in an unceremonious white pile, on the floor.

They approached the closed door at the same moment, and stopped, neither willing to open it first and allow the other to precede him.

For a moment, Lady Elseth wished she had never had sons. She rose, her cheeks reddened by a sudden wash of color, and walked evenly to the door. Her dark eyes were wide as she cut both of the Elseth men with her glare. Stephen had the grace to blush and look away; Gilliam did not even meet his mother's eyes.

She opened the door. "Out," she said. That one word contained as much anger as she ever showed.

But in the face of it, neither Stephen or Gilliam dared to offer a word of resistance. They went—Gilliam first, and Stephen in his wake.

"I hope you're happy," Stephen said softly, as he leaned against the fence that kept the Elseth horses at pasture. His arm hurt, although Boredan had done what he could to insure it would not become infected, and he took care to favor it.

Gilliam said nothing. Instead of leaning forward, he let the rough-hewn wood of the fence cut into his back. He stared ahead, in the growing darkness, to the walls and runs of the kennels.

They were uncomfortable; it was rare that anger between them lasted this long. But Stephen tested the bond, and he felt the anger, mixed and folded into every other emotion, that lay between them. He would have been proud if he could have said that the anger was solely Gilliam's. It was not.

244 + ♦ Michelle West

"You took your time getting back," Gilliam said at last.

"Yes," Stephen said, equally quietly.

"Did you spend the time with her?"

Stephen's hands tightened into fists at the tone in his Hunter's voice. "Hunter's Oath, Gil—let it lie!" He could see clearly the glint of Gilliam's bitter smile; there was triumph in it. "You might recall," he said, his voice cold and sharp, "that I nearly died. Unlike the Hunters, I'm merely human. I was abed four days."

"You didn't want to come back." It wasn't a question.

"No."

Gilliam started to speak, and bit back the words in disgust. He was silent a moment; the air felt heavy, was made heavy, by what he said next. "Go back to her, then. We don't need you here."

It was meant as a slap. Stephen shut his eyes and clenched his fists. He exhaled slowly. "What of the girl?"

Gilliam did not reply.

"What about the girl, Gilliam?"

"What about her?" His voice was low; deep. Stephen had heard him speak just so before, although it took him a moment to remember when. He paled.

"Gilliam, she isn't yours. You can't keep her here. She's not right. She needs help."

The low rumble at the back of the Elseth Lord's throat was a growl. He turned toward Stephen, and then away, slamming his fist into the fence post.

Stephen reached out through their bond, pulling at Gilliam, urging him to understand. He felt an echo of the strangeness that drove Gilliam—and then he felt a terrible lurch as Gilliam leaped forward into the night. Anger was forgotten; pain and the bitter taste of betrayal vanished like morning mist. All that was left was panic and a desperate drive to action.

Stephen knew why an instant before it would have become obvious to any other observer.

The kennels burst into sudden flame, a symphony of night fire.

There were men on the grounds.

In the sudden flare of light—a light that burned and crackled with the faintest aurora of blue haze—Stephen could make out their shapes as they ran across the grass. He had not marked the setting of the sun, but although the edges of the sky were still bright, darkness had settled, and these intruders sought to take advantage, or cover, in it. They moved lightly on their feet, but he saw the glint of weapons; they wore no armor, or very little of it.

Gilliam, no! He did not shout; he did not want the attackers aware of his position or his place. Indeed, they moved so quickly, and with such a determination, he wasn't certain that either he or his Hunter had even been seen.

Gilliam's panic ebbed. He took a breath, and then another, deeper one. His heart was beating too quickly. He was frightened—terrified—for the dogs. It was never fear of his own mortality that drove him; it was fear, always, of the loss of things loved.

The dogs.

And the girl.

Stephen felt the shift as Gilliam called Hunter's trance. And he felt Gilliam recoil as the dogs began to whine.

Steady, Gil, he thought. He had no time for more. Passing his hunter, he made a direct line to the kennel doors that faced the pasture. For good measure, he drew his sword, and felt its weight settle comfortably into his hand. He tried to ignore the throb of his arm as he threw off the sling that Boredan had been so insistent upon.

Gilliam joined him in seconds, weapon likewise drawn and ready.

"Hold the dogs," Stephen said tersely, as he struggled, in a light blackened with tendrils of smoke, to free the latch and open the door.

Gilliam nodded, his eyes almost glazed. "She felt it," he whispered.

"Felt what?" Stephen did not pause until the latch had been lifted.

Gilliam shook his head, frustrated; Stephen knew, from his expression, that the thing felt could not be put into words that a human could understand. But he had a very bad feeling that he knew what that word would be, if Gilliam could find it.

Then he heard, through the door, the change in the tenor of the dogs' voices.

Gilliam cursed, and the anger that had been replaced by concern flared up, just as the fire had. "They're in through the other side!"

"Mother!"

Lady Elseth rose at once as Maribelle's high voice broke the silence of her sitting room. She left her papers, and the month's numbers, in an even, neat pile, and although she rose with both haste and force, not even the inkstand was upset.

The hall was empty, although Maribelle's single, imperative word had certainly come from outside of her doors. Lady Elseth looked around, concern growing. She began to walk down the hall when one of the younger boys threw open a door and came careening into the hall, his arms full.

"Talbet!"

He skidded to a stop, stumbling into the closest wall. "Lady?" His breath barely forced the word out.

She stepped forward to see what he carried, and her face paled. "Where did you get these?"

"Maribelle sent me, ma'am. The kennels're on fire and there are intruders on the ground." His pale hair was matted to his forehead with sweat, and his eyes, normally bright and crinkled, were a deep, wide green.

Without another word, Lady Elseth helped to lighten the boy's burden: She took from him one of the several crossbows he carried and began to wind its spring as she walked. "Run," she said softly. "I'll catch up with you."

Almost before the door was fully opened, Gilliam wedged his body through the darkened gap. His face gleamed with sweat, and the dirty smoke had added grime and circles to his eyes. The fire was eating the wood of the building; Stephen had expected that.

What he had not expected was the destruction of the stone walls. He bit his lip, narrowing his eyes as something—not human—shrieked in pain. Gilliam's back, and the clouds of smoke were all he could see—and in seconds he lost sight of his Hunter as well.

But he heard the sudden clash of steel against steel; heard a grunt and a scream.

Send the dogs out, Gil, he thought, as he dropped to his knees and began to crawl, sword still at hand, into the heart of the kennel.

"There," Maribelle whispered softly, pointing into the night sky.

Her mother nodded quietly as she followed Maribelle's finger. Three men stood, near the cover of the great trees that alone had not been cleared when their ancestral manor had been built. They carried a light, but only a small one. Even during the day, the distance would have prevented any recognition on Elsabet's part.

She had sent out an urgent request for the aid of the villagers, but the rising flames that encompassed the kennels were probably beacon enough. Soon, the wagons, with sand and what little water there was available for such an enterprise, would begin to wend their way up the roads.

She had two questions. The first she could not give voice to; the second she concentrated on. But Maribelle did not have her mother's sensibilities.

"Where are Gil and Stephen?" Maribelle scanned the horizon even as she asked.

Swallowing, uncertain of her voice, Elsabet lifted a perfectly steady hand and pointed. To the kennels. She heard Maribelle's sharp intake of breath—but Maribelle offered no argument to her mother's silent answer. It was obvious, after all. Where else would Gilliam have gone?

As if in taunt, the fires suddenly blazed again, becoming a solid, near-white wall.

Young Talbet jumped back; this far away, the surge of heat could still be felt. Elsabet remained steady. Maribelle, at eighteen the youthful pride of her mother's training, did likewise—although if she betrayed herself by starting, no one noticed.

But she looked to Lady Elseth for commands.

Lady Elseth closed her eyes, weighing and deciding all actions. "Are these three the only intruders?" she asked at last.

"The only ones we've seen," Talbet volunteered.

But Maribelle shook her head. "I think there are others," she said softly. "The kennels."

You have, Elsa thought, *your father's vision.*

The fires there were so bright and so high that the kennels were out of the question. Lady Elseth narrowed her eyes and shaded them as she turned, rigidly, to examine those very flames. The stone itself was on fire. Which was impossible, unless . . .

Stephen's words came back to her. Grimly, she looked back to the great trees. Those trees would not serve as shelter to enemies of Elseth for one moment longer. She took a breath, deeply, to steady herself. "This is my judgment," she said, and for a moment she might have been sitting in the ancient, Elseth seat. "Kill them."

"But the kennels—the Lord!" Talbet's eyes widened.

"We cannot go to them through those fires; they will not be banked by sand or water." Lady Elseth's voice was ice. "But we may find another method of putting the flames out." *Stephen. Gilliam.*

Maribelle nodded grimly. "Your judgment," she said, lifting her bow, "is accepted in the eyes of God, Lady of Elseth." Turning, she nodded to Talbet.

But Elsabet was not to be left behind. Not if one—or all—of these isolated three were, as she suspected, mage-born.

She had thought, one day, to lose either of her sons to the God. She had been born to it; she accepted it with the sorrow that was the burden of every noble mother. But if her sons were lost to her this eve, through unnatural fire and human malice . . . she struggled, holding her anger, tightly confining it. Control, especially in crisis, was everything.

"Approach them by the pastures," she said. That was all. She did not need to mention speed or silence.

Five feet into the kennels, the smoke vanished. It had not dispersed; indeed, Stephen could feel the heat and see the blackness that the flames shed. But some wall, some sort of barrier, had been erected here; he could mark the circle of it very clearly.

He knew what it was, and in silence he named it. Magic. He stayed low to the ground as his eyes adjusted to the muted, unnatural light.

There were four men in the kennel's confines. Four men, all of the dogs, the girl—and Gilliam. The intruders wore black—why was it always black?—masks and clothing; they had shoes of soft leather, and each carried a sword and small buckler. The smoke, and the magical absence of it, did not deter or bother them at all.

But the hounds did.

For once, Stephen was glad that he had no bond with the dogs. Through his link with Gilliam, he could feel an echo of their pain and their confusion, their anger and their determination—and that echo sent him reeling, his back to the smoke and charred embers of wood. Eyes stinging, he looked away and down; upon the rushes strewn along the floor he could see three of Gilliam's pack. Two at least would never rise, or hunt, again; in the darkness and smoke, he could not tell who.

He shook himself, and started to rise; he wanted to be at the side of his Hunter in this most dangerous of fights. Then he stopped, and let himself sink back into the ground, unnoticed. This was no Hunt, and these no animals; the danger that they presented could not be met by force of spear or hounds alone.

Swallowing, Stephen began to trace the perimeter of the smokeless circle in the hope of getting behind those who attacked.

Gilliam had never been so close to insanity in his life. Each and every voice, from the youngest to the most experienced of his hounds and lymers, clamored for attention. Only Piper and Vorel were silent, and their silence filled him with a bitter rage.

The kennels were dark, and the space in them far too confined, to be used to advantage. As well, the intruders were very good at what they did. He had almost misjudged their skill—and his arm, cloth and skin split by the same swift stroke, bore witness to that stupidity.

He had never before fought men with his hounds. He could not count on their fear, as he did with stag, or bear, or boar; nor could he predict their rages. He needed the dogs now more than he had ever done, but he did not—quite—know how to use them to their full advantage.

The girl fought at his side. Her, he had ordered back, and of all times, she had chosen this one to test him. She remained at his side, spitting fury, although his mental shout should have given her little choice but to flee. He did not dare to see from her eyes, for fear of being lost behind them.

But it was she that they wanted. Although they might cut at his hounds—at he himself—they had eyes for her, and her death.

Snarling, Gilliam rushed forward in a barely controlled frenzy of flickering swordplay.

If smoke could not fill the inner circle, the snap of crackling fire could. Stephen tried to ignore the splintering sound of wooden beams and tried not to think about the rushes on the floor and the way they would soon catch fire. They were damp now, damp and warm—but they would not remain so.

Stop it. He took a breath of the air closest to the floor; it was acrid, but it did not hurt his lungs. He listened again to the noises that came with fire. Against them, his movements were hidden and silent.

Straw scraped his cheeks and chin and clung to his jacket and pants as he moved. He felt little, sharp ends against his shins as his boots caught and held them. But he moved, struggling with Gilliam's anger and fear; afraid to let it in, but terrified to let go of it.

And then he saw the backs of the intruders, black-clad and wraithlike through the smoke.

Don't look, he whispered, his eyes turned up in supplication as he tightened his grip on his weapon. *Don't look back.*

Trembling with tension, he rose in the poor light, a multicolored, rush-strewn shade. Hands shaking, movements precise, he brought the edge of his blade down in a tight, forceful arc that ended with the back of the closest man's knees.

Maribelle moved, just a shade more quickly than her mother, through the tall grass. Elsabet could see her by the movements of the tops of the grass, but that was all. She counted three and then saw the grass move again, a little more forcefully, at Talbet's passing. They did well, although they had not been trained to this.

For that matter, neither had she. And if she had, she would certainly not have chosen the long, formal skirts of the evening meal for such an enterprise. Every crinoline rustled as she crept along. She swore, then, that she would forsake fashion entirely after this night's work. But she did not stop.

When she came at last to the old, slanted fence post that marked the farthest reach of the horses' pastures, she dared to glance up, dared to attract the attention of the three who waited.

And she saw, although she only looked up for an instant, that they were three men, all oddly garbed, with a light at the center of their triangle. They wore robes that were darker than the sky, with hoods drawn up and around their faces. The light that hit their cheeks made them appear skeletal, threatening.

She crawled beneath the fence, gently disentangling her skirts. Maribelle's head bobbed up; she bit her lip, and then exhaled slowly into the passing breeze. These men stood downwind—but they had no dogs to guide or warn them. Good.

And then, at last, they came to the edge of the tree's farthest roots. She saw her daughter's face in the moonlight, and she nodded quietly. They exchanged no words; none were needed. Maribelle's posture told Lady Elseth everything that she needed—or wanted—to know.

You have never killed a man, she thought, as she saw the silhouette of her almost-adult daughter shiver, *but you will be called upon to do it. We are those who sit in judgment, Mari—and when we judge a crime worthy of death, that weight is upon our shoulders. It is time to learn.*

Still, she hesitated. She herself had never learned this bitter truth so completely bare of pretense or tradition. Perhaps this was something to spare her daughter— Maribelle would, in the end, prove true to her lessons.

Or perhaps not. She realized, as she slowly brought her bow to bear, that she did not know which of these three, if not all of them, were mage-born. Taking a deep breath, she made the only quick decision she could: to trust her daughter's speed.

She crept as far away from the base of the tree as she dared before she rose to add her silhouette to the night.

"Hold!" Her voice was strong and clear in the darkness. As one, the three turned to face her. But only the man in the middle, bereft of all of the insignia of the Order of Knowledge, moved. His hands cut upward in a sharp steeple, his movements graceful, precise, controlled.

But before he could speak one word, utter even the beginning of a syllable, Maribelle of Elseth fired. The small lamp, carried by the man farthest from her, guttered suddenly.

As did the fires that surrounded the kennels like an impenetrable wall.

Lady Elseth fired into the night; heard a sharp cry followed by the sound of stumbling, running feet. She herself did not dare the darkness to pursue. Instead, she began to rewind her bow.

"Damn," Maribelle whispered softly, coming to stand at her mother's side. "I didn't kill him."

"Your aim was off," her mother agreed.

Stephen's entry into the fight proper changed the balance of the game—and Gilliam was quick enough, instinctive enough, to take advantage of it. The dogs found their openings, and moved from a defensive crouch and snap into full leaps beneath the swords of their attackers. Gilliam's strike was less lucky, or less deadly; the moment he stepped forward, his dark-robed assailant suddenly snapped back into the present, and the very real threat to his own survival.

They had scant minutes before the smoke, dark and thick, suddenly began to cross what had been an invisible boundary. The smoke changed everything again, for with it, came fear. Gilliam could almost smell it rising.

It was then that he knew he would win. One of the standing men suddenly broke and ran—an obvious, stupid mistake. Ashfel took off in pursuit, the embers and little flames disregarded. *This* hunt was Ashfel's territory and strength. Gilliam cursed, but let him go; he renewed his attack with ferocity and the last of his Hunter's strength.

Fear did not make his enemy a more tenacious fighter, and in the end, he fell. As did the man that his dogs now savaged. He waited a few seconds before calling them, sharply, back. It was bad to let the dogs eat flesh outside of the confines of the Hunt's end.

Only when he was certain that they would not test him further did he lead them out of the kennels, calling them quickly and giving them their positions. Ashfel also waited, angered.

"Gilliam," someone said, and Gilliam squinted into the darkness to see his mother's stiff form.

At her feet, unmoving, lay the one man who had seen fit to run. "Your work?" he asked softly.

She nodded. "Stephen?"

"I'm here, Elsa," Stephen said, emerging from what remained of the kennels. He was shaking and pale.

"What of the girl?"

Stephen twisted his head sharply to the side in denial. "She's—she's safe." But his color, if possible, became worse. He tried to close himself off, tried to keep the disgust and fear from Gilliam. This time, the Hunter Lord didn't need to test their bond. He turned sharply.

Stephen caught his arm. "Gil—"

But Gilliam shook him off without a word and returned to the kennels to call the girl out.

"Gilliam, you don't want to see her."

"Go away, Stephen. I'll—"

The light in the kennels was poor; moonlight came through the walls with barely perceptible rays of light. It was enough. On the rushes of the kennel's floors, the girl sat crouched over the twitching body of one of her assailants. Her eyes were narrowed, and her lips, where they could be seen, were flecked with blood.

Her teeth were planted firmly in the throat of the man; her jaw muscles were tense, and the high rasp of a growl filled the silent air.

Stephen closed his eyes, reaching for his dagger. He expected Gilliam to interfere—to say something, do something. But Gilliam was frozen, his mouth open in surprise.

As Stephen approached, the girl's wary eyes followed his movements. Her hands tensed, flexing as if they were the claws of some wild, dangerous beast. He hoped that Gilliam could hold her. He didn't care if he couldn't. With a soft, decisive strike, he planted his dagger firmly into the would-be killer's heart.

He left it there, his hands suddenly too weak to hold the hilt. The body stilled.

Sickened, Stephen walked away, past Gilliam and the sounds the girl made at his back.

Chapter Nineteen

IN THE MORNING, Lady Elseth rose early, refusing to feel her age. She called for the village head and saw to the burying of the bodies that remained. Sourly, she noted that the mage-born man, and one of his associates, was not among them.

She had seen the dead before; had, indeed, seen deaths much worse than these. She didn't flinch when it came time to inspect the bodies. Letters would have to be written, and some dispensation from the Queen's Justice would have to be granted. She also made a note to begin her own investigations into the Order of Knowledge within the King's City. She did not, however, expect to find the mage harbored there any longer.

"Lady!"

She looked up from her musings and saw one of the caretakers of the dead approaching her. He carried something that glinted in the sunlight, cupped carefully in hands held away from his body, as if he bore a serpent. "Kelset?"

Kelset was obviously tired; there was much to be done, and quickly; the air was warm, and there were many dead. He wore a hat to protect himself from the sun's light, and had she desired to do so, she could have pretended the shadows in the hollows of his face were cast by the hat's wide brim. "Look. On one of the dead."

She held out her hand, and after a minute's hesitation, the older man gave over what he held. It was a pendant on a long, thick chain, by its coloring platinum. She knew this because she knew that silver warmed with age and wear; this metal was still a cold, shining gray. The pendant itself was simple; a deep obsidian held by a platinum circle. No design, no engraving or carving, marred its black surface.

"Do you recognize it?" she asked, glancing up to see Kelset's intense gaze.

"No, Lady," he said hesitantly. He reached up to massage the growing knots of tense muscle along the top of his neck.

"But?"

"What good can come of it? It's black; blackness. And the man was wearing robes of some sort."

"Was he god-born?"

"No. Wrong eyes for it."

"Good news, then," she replied lightly. "It wouldn't do to anger any one of the Gods." But she held the pendant more carefully.

Stephen knew that he'd overslept when he heard the knock at his door. He had closed the curtains, just before he'd come to bed, as a precaution against the night. Unfortunately, it had served as a shield against the dawn as well. He swung quickly out of bed, sliding his feet into the slippers that stuck out beneath the wrinkled counterpane and reaching for his robe.

The knock came again.

Before he could walk the length of the room to answer the door, it opened. The servant that he had expected was nowhere in sight, but Gilliam of Elseth filled the door's frame for a moment as he lingered between the hall and the room.

There was no anger at all left in him, but Stephen didn't need their connection to know it. The night, with its fire and death, had killed the rage in them both.

Hesitant, perhaps a little too quick to offer, Stephen said, "Come in, Gil."

Gilliam nodded stiffly. He entered the room, closed the door at his back, and then used it as a support. His face was lined—creased almost as deeply as Stephen's sheets—and his eyes were circled and dark. It was obvious that he had had no help dressing; the buttons of his shirt were askew.

"Mother's seen the bodies," Gilliam said at last, when it became clear that Stephen would not speak first.

"Does she have any information?"

Gilliam shrugged. "She's waiting to speak to both of us. After lunch."

They stared at the carpets and walls in uncomfortable silence. It was Gilliam who, at length, broke the silence again. "I slept in the house last night."

Stephen started to speak, but with Gilliam's words came the image of the girl as he had last seen her. He paled. But he did not keep his queasiness away from his Hunter.

"I know," Gilliam said. His voice was low and unsteady. Had he been a dog, he would have been halfway between whine and growl, were it possible. "Stephen?"

Stephen nodded.

"The girl—she's part of my pack." There was no anger and no possessiveness in his words; his voice was even, but his hands shook where his words did not.

"Part of your pack?"

"I can see behind her eyes," Gilliam replied. "I can call her; I can command her. I know when she's near." He turned away. "It happened the night we were first attacked."

At once, Stephen understood everything. It happened like that, sometimes—information gathered in bits and pieces suddenly coalesced to form a whole that could never again be forgotten. His shoulders sagged slightly, and he thrust his hands into his pockets; they were fists. "How?"

"I don't know. I—I didn't think about it."

He hadn't wanted to think about it. Stephen didn't point it out; they both knew it, so there was no need.

"And I don't know how to find out." Gilliam turned again, his hands, palms up, before him. It was as close as he would come to asking for aid.

Stephen could not demand more. "I think we can help her," he said quietly, mind racing. He swallowed. "Does she—does she feel different than the hounds do?"

His Hunter nodded, hesitant. "She—she's more than an animal. But less than—than you and I. And I hear her all the time. Even now." His voice dropped. "She's unhappy. She knows I'm upset. Knows it's because of her, but doesn't understand why."

"Gil—has she ever spoken to you?"

"Never. I thought that she didn't know how. At first."

"I'd still say she doesn't know how," Stephen said mildly.

Gilliam shook his head. "It's there. Somewhere. If I get close enough to her, I can almost hear the *words*. She's more than a dog. She's stronger, too."

"Then maybe you can—"

"I can't. Don't ask me, Stephen. I can't."

This, too, Stephen suddenly understood. He looked across the room to his Hunter, and then bowed his head. He was proud of Gilliam, but he would never say so in words that would only embarrass them both. Instead, he let the feeling thrum down their Hunter's bond.

"Is Elsa waiting?"

Gilliam smiled. "Impatiently."

"Then I'd better finish dressing."

"Well?" Lady Elseth looked up across the length of the table as her luncheon dishes were finally cleared away. She had eaten little—but that was in keeping with her three companions at the meal.

Stephen met her gaze first. "They were after the girl," he said quietly.

She raised one slightly frosted brow. "The girl?"

"We think so."

"Do you know why?"

"No." Stephen shrugged.

"I've taken the liberty of sending for a member of the Order of Knowledge. No, not that one." Her own lips turned up in an imitation of a smile. "I don't believe that Krysanthos will be found within the Order's walls after last night's work."

"I'm not sure that we want one of the mage-born here."

"I'm certain that you don't," Lady Elseth said, a little too pointedly, "but in this case, I think it wise. A mage wanted the girl dead, Stephen; it only makes sense that a mage would be able to explain her . . . condition."

In matters of difficulty, it was Gilliam's custom to let Stephen speak for them both. He did not even venture a syllable now.

"Elsa, is that wise?"

"Perhaps." It was her turn to shrug. "Perhaps not. But truthfully, Stephen, it is not just because of the girl that I summoned a member of the Order. I want answers—and some restitution—for the attack last evening. And answers, I *will* have."

Stephen nodded; when the Lady of Elseth used that particular tone of voice, the matter was already settled. He tried to change the direction of the conversation. "Did you find anything of interest this morning?"

"On the corpses?"

Maribelle's eyes widened slightly at her mother's bluntness. Stephen didn't even blink. "Yes."

Lady Elseth closed her eyes and raised a hand to her forehead. "I'm sorry, Stephen. That was uncalled for. But I like these affairs no more than you, and I'm not in the best of moods for delicacy." She smiled wanly. "Yes. I did find something that may be of significance." She rose. "If you wait, you can look at it and tell me if it has more significance for you than it does for me."

They waited, still uncomfortable, while Lady Elseth left the room. Stephen did not even try to keep up light or pleasant chatter, and Gilliam certainly wasn't about to start what he had avoided for most of his life. Maribelle's silence was unnatural—but Maribelle looked very much like Gilliam; sleepless, dark-eyed, haunted.

Lady Elseth's return was a relief.

Until she stopped at Stephen's side and very gently unfurled one hand. Like liquid, the pendant she carried fell free, stopping to swing as the chain pulled tight against her thumb and finger. "This," she said, studying Stephen's face.

Stephen stared at the pendant in fascinated horror.

"Stephen?"

He shook his head, reached out to touch the obsidian surface of the flat oval, and then pulled back sharply before his fingers made contact.

"You recognize it." She put her free hand around his shoulder, as the pendulum continued its gentle swing. "Is it your—from your dreams?"

He nodded quietly. "But I also recognize it from my studies. In the King's library."

"Yes?" Her voice was gentle, but the question demanded an answer nonetheless; Lady Elseth had that kind of voice.

"It's the emblem of the Priests of Allasakar." Stephen glanced up and met the eyes of his Lady. "The Lord and ruler of the Hells."

Lady Elseth was silent a moment, absorbing the news. "Well," she said at last. "I think this merits a visit to the King's City. And perhaps even a visit to the Queen herself." She caught the pendant firmly in a tight, solid grip. "If I guess correctly, that religion has been forbidden practice in Breodanir."

"And in every other civilized land since the birth of the Twin Kings," Stephen replied. "But so has thievery, and thieves have never died out in the history of *any* people."

"True," Lady Elseth said, her gaze remote. "But it is not the habit of the seat of judgment to ignore those infractions that are brought to its attention. Especially not when that seat is the High Seat. I have work to tend to here, and accommodations to arrange in the city itself.

"We will wait upon the arrival of the member of the Order of Knowledge before you set out."

"How do we know they'll send one?" Maribelle asked.

"They'll send one," her mother replied grimly. "And quickly."

She was right, of course. She was the Lady of Elseth.

The Hunter Ladies had an informal messenger service and route that they used in circumstances of great urgency only. Elsabet had deemed this to be such an occasion, and had ordered her courier out on the roads with a horse and the writ of summons that bore her blood-red seal. She knew that once the messenger reached Valentin, he would turn his horse in to the Valentin stables in return for a fresh one; this operation would continue along the straightest path to the King's City. Therefore, a messenger that might normally travel for weeks would take perhaps five days to arrive. She expected one of the mage-born to arrive at the month's end.

He arrived two days after the earliest possible moment of the message's receipt.

His arrival was not an auspicious one to start; he walked, unhorsed, up the long and half-tended path to Elseth Manor. He was met by villagers who carried the long, wooden planks that were necessary to frame the second story of the half-completed kennels, and given the stories of attempted murder that had been whispered at the hearthside of each and every cottage and shanty in the Elseth village, his arrival was greeted with suspicion and worry.

Were it not for the fact that he arrived at midday, looking tired, travel-worn, and not a little exhausted, they might have been tempted to take matters into their own hands. Instead, the village head ordered him contained—much to his obvious chagrin—and marched, in the center of the village's most able young men, to Elseth Manor proper.

Elsabet discovered this oversight in her people's hospitality when a very harassed-looking keykeeper all but barged into her study. He knocked, yes, but entered without giving her the grace of time to give him leave to do so.

"Lady," he said, his face pale and lined, "an emergency that requires your attention has arisen. If you would be so kind?"

"Is it Gilliam?" she asked, rising immediately.

"No. I believe it is a visitor that you've been expecting."

"That hardly seems an emergency, Boredan." But she followed him quickly down the long hall and out to the manor's wide doors. Stephen met her in the hall.

"What's upset Boredan?" he whispered.

She shook her head, and he let the matter drop, but did pause to offer his arm. She took it.

When they at last went through the doors that the keykeeper held open for them, they found most of the village gathered at their steps.

"Lady!" Corinna said, her voice a rather hoarse shout. She was dressed in the daywear of a busy village headwoman, and her sun-lined, darkened skin was covered in a fine mist of wood dust and dirt.

Lady Elseth surveyed the crowd quietly. "What has happened, Corinna?" she asked at last.

"We've brought another robed intruder. He came with no papers and no letters, and we thought it best you dealt with him."

"I . . . see." Lady Elseth had turned a very becoming shade of white. Unconsciously, she put an unadorned hand to her throat as she searched the crowd more thoroughly. Then the color returned to her cheeks in a blush. "You've done well," she said, her voice so faint it could barely be heard. "But I believe all is as it should be. Have the men release him."

Corinna raised a peppered brow. "You're sure?"

"Yes," Elsabet said, her voice, if possible, weaker. "I had a summons that has been answered rather earlier than I thought possible." She was furious with herself for the oversight. "You haven't—he hasn't been hurt, has he?"

The tightly knotted crowd pulled back, and the intruder in question, a slender reed of a man in rather wrinkled traveling clothing, was given leave to speak for himself.

"No," he said wryly. "He hasn't."

Stephen felt Elsabet sag against his arm in relief. He, too, felt some relief—but that was understandable. One did not anger the mage-born often and survive it. Or so legend said.

This particular mage did not even look annoyed, although his smile was perhaps a bit thin at the edges. "I give my apologies for arriving without the proper seals and writs, Lady." He bowed, low, to her, and then to the amazement of all, also bowed courteously to the head-woman. She frowned at this and turned her back.

"Well?" she asked the waiting crowd. "What are you all hanging about doing nothing for? You heard the Lady—she's safe enough. Get back to work!" For good measure, and as an emphasis to the command, she whacked the nearest strong-arm on the side of his bronzed face.

Nobody argued with her, just as nobody argued with Lady Elseth—but it was always a wonder to Stephen how two such powerful women could carry themselves so completely differently. The villagers trickled away until only the mage was left standing at the foot of the Elseth steps.

"Where is Gilliam?" Lady Elseth whispered to Stephen.

Stephen rolled his eyes. "Out running the dogs."

"The girl?"

"With him." He started to speak, and then shook his head. He did not want to discuss his Hunter, and his Hunter's situation, in front of a stranger.

"I see." She turned back to the member of the Order of Knowledge. "Please accept my apologies—"

"Zareth. Call me Zareth if you don't consider that to be too informal." He bowed again, brushing his dark hair from his face as he straightened. In the light, the medallion that swung against his brown tunic glinted perfectly clearly; the quartered circle was obvious, although the elements each quarter contained could only be imagined.

"Very well. Please accept my apologies, Zareth. My people are not normally this . . . cautious."

"Given the circumstances—and the fact that I remain uninjured—I'm inclined to forgive and forget." He came up the steps, his stride both weary and long.

"Come in, then. You might appreciate the chance to rest. You arrived here at better speed than I would have thought possible."

If the mage heard the question in her voice, he ignored it politely. "Yes, I would appreciate it. I'll be ready to speak more properly in perhaps a few hours."

The few hours stretched out to encompass most of the next day. Stephen was well aware of the servants' gossip, as each and every one of them who had time to be interested in such affairs made guesses—most wrong—about the status of the stranger who had arrived with such indelicate fanfare. He busied himself with the dogs and his Hunter, trying his best to keep away from the stranger's rooms.

The kennels were not yet complete, and although Stephen was no carpenter, he spent time as an unofficial overseer while the villagers worked their shifts. The sun was free from clouds, and the peak of the day hot and dusty, but he heard no word of complaint pass any man's lips. These villagers, perhaps better than any, knew how important their task was; the Lord of Elseth was, in some ways, in their care. Gilliam kept his dogs away from the rising frame of their new home—but he kept that building in sight as well, almost as nervous as a new mother. Stephen thought it funny; no other building, no other structure, could command this amount of Gil's attention—not even the magnificent arches of the King's castle had moved him. He watched his Hunter, chuckled, and became aware that he was not the only person to notice Gilliam's anxiety. He was just the only one to think it amusing.

Still, in watching, he noticed that Gilliam's relationship with the wild girl— the still unnamed visitor—had markedly changed. Although the girl accompanied them in the runs, Gilliam took care to keep his distance. But he was stiff and a little awkward with the new effort. Stephen almost felt sorry for him. He did pity the girl, though; she whined and fretted in her inarticulate way, and her eyes rarely left her master. No—not her master; not that. Gilliam.

Stephen had to admit that it was hard, watching her, not to think of her as one of the hunting pack. It was clear that the rest of the dogs did. They nudged her, butted her, and even snapped at her, depending upon their own pack standing— and she returned their attention in kind.

It was after dinner—a dinner still awkward with tension and worry—that the mage-born visitor finally made his second appearance.

Lady Elseth, clothed in the near-finest of her apparel, rose at once to greet him; Maribelle and Stephen quickly followed her lead. Only Gilliam remained seated in blissful ignorance of custom and required manners. Had it not been a public first meeting, Stephen would have spoken with him.

Stephen noticed that Lady Elseth had forsaken the odd, ugly panniers for a skirt that was more easily maneuvered, and therefore more practical. It was odd; he wondered if perhaps Elsabet did not trust the mage. Still, in the formal, dark greens of her station, with a sash of burgundy and golden velvet to give brightness, she was a commanding figure.

The man who had named himself Zareth was not nearly so striking a presence. He wore clothing that was a cut above common, or so it seemed; the robes of the Order of Knowledge allowed only a glimpse of what lay beneath. Those robes didn't suit his coloring; they were smoky-gray, and fell heavily, like ill-hung drapery, over his gaunt frame.

For all that he cut such an odd figure, he was above ridicule. Perhaps the pendant, much clearer now in the light of the hall, was enough of a signification of power that clothing mattered little. Or perhaps it was his eyes; they burned with a striking intensity, even though they were dark and ringed.

"Zareth," Lady Elseth said, approaching him. "Have you eaten?"

"I don't require food," he said, and his smile was wan. But he bowed and held that bow longer than strict etiquette demanded. "What I do require—what we both require—is an exchange of information." He glanced around the room, noted Stephen, Gilliam, and Maribelle, and raised one eyebrow in question.

"Yes," Elsabet said quietly. "Anything that you have to say can be said freely here."

"Would you not rather retire to someplace where we might be less likely to face interruptions?"

She thought a moment. The servants would be clearing the table soon. "Yes. Follow."

Stephen watched the mage as he walked down the hall. It was clear that exhaustion still marred his step, and he placed a hand upon the wall to serve as a crutch. Whatever magics he had used to travel so quickly had obviously cost him dearly. The thought comforted Stephen.

They retired to the parlor, and Zareth chose the seat closest to the fire. Only after watching the mage press his hands tightly together did Stephen realize that he felt chill. Rather than call the servants, Stephen began to build up the small fire himself.

"Thank you," said Zareth, a trifle dryly. "I'm sorry to be so obvious in my infirmity."

"I'd rather see an infirm mage than an active one," Stephen replied, equally dryly.

Zareth laughed softly. "I imagine you would. You're Stephen?"

"Does it show?"

Zareth spoke much more softly. "Yes. I was told there would be a Hunter and his huntbrother—and I've rarely heard of a sullen and suspicious huntbrother."

Stephen smiled and turned back to the fire. He had surprised himself—he hadn't thought to like the mage that the Order would send.

Lady Elseth, however, had not apparently warmed to the visitor at all. While she was polite, even solicitous, and certainly a graceful hostess, her face was very set, and her eyes were free from the lines that bespoke a genuine smile. She waited until Stephen took a seat before she began to speak, and it quickly became clear that she intended to do all of the talking for the Elseth contingent.

"Let us come immediately to the matter at hand." She rested her elbows upon the arm of her chair, and rested her chin upon the tips of her pale fingers. "Ten days past, my estates were invaded by unknown men—led by a member of the Order of Knowledge."

Zareth nodded intently. "So you said in your letter."

"That member's name is Krysanthos."

"Are you certain of that?"

She nodded, not even glancing to the side to look at Stephen's face. "He is not, I assume, still in the capital?"

Zareth glanced down at the ground between his feet. "No, Lady. A summons was sent for him, but I do not believe it will be answered."

"How convenient."

This time, Zareth flinched. "I have come with an offer of restitution for any damages caused; the Order will cover your costs."

"That is acceptable," Elsabet replied. It was her turn to wait.

"You haven't brought this to the attention of the Queen's court?" Zareth asked softly. His hands, resting also against the arms of his chair, now gripped the rests almost convulsively.

"Is there any reason why I should not have done so?"

"No, of course not."

She watched him, her face set in the lines of judgment. After a moment, unblinking, she added, "But, no, I have not yet notified that court."

His relief was obvious, although his stance changed very little. "We appreciate your forbearance in this, Lady. As you well know, the mage-born are feared by the populace at large. We wish to avoid panic or any hasty reactions."

At this, the lines of Elsabet's mouth curved into a sardonic smile. "Such as the reception my villagers gave you?"

"Such," he said, returning her smile cautiously, "as exactly that."

"Perhaps if the mage-born were more open about the limits to, and extents of, their powers, they would be less feared. The Hunter Lords are not feared."

Zareth raised one dark brow. "Are they not?"

"Not in general," she said, conceding a small point. "But, yes, I have no wish to upset the Breodani for no reason. There *is* no reason?"

Zareth moved his head restively.

"Master Kahn?"

His eyes widened in surprise. Then he shook his head, and this time, he did laugh out loud. "I'm not of Breodanir," he said apologetically. "I constantly underestimate the Hunter Ladies. Yes, Lady Elseth, I am Zareth Kahn. Do you know the names of the rest of our Order?"

"Only its foreign members."

"Which are almost all. Very well. There is no reason to worry. Let me be blunt."

"Will you be?"

"As blunt as is prudent. Krysanthos is of Essalieyan, and a mage of the second circle. He has power. In Breodanir there is only one mage to match him, although they are generally considered to be equals in magecraft. The Order of Knowledge cannot explain his attack upon your manor; there is no reason—nothing at all to be gained—by such an obvious assault.

"The very fact that there were no casualties is suspicious. We did not understand why, given the fact that he had chosen to mount such an attack, he did not proceed with more force."

"More force?"

"He is capable of far, far worse than he showed. If the man you saw was indeed the same mage. We assume that he was."

"Explain."

Zareth glanced away, to the fires that burned in the wide, open hearth of the room. His eyes were lambent orange; a reflection of heat. "I cannot," he replied at last. "Forgive me."

Stephen was surprised when Elsabet returned a shrug for the mage's refusal. "Very well. Continue."

"There is little else to say. I have come, at your summons, to ascertain what it was that would attract a member of the mage-born to this household. This information will be reported to the head of the Order. You have our word," the mage added, "that we will pursue our investigations to the full extent of our combined power."

She listened. Her expression had only changed once in the course of the interview—and that small change could hardly be considered encouraging. Slowly, she folded her hands and let them settle into her lap. The fire crackled; breaths were drawn. No one moved.

At last, she nodded. "Gilliam. Stephen. Bring in our visitor."

Aside from an argument that threatened to delay them long past Lady Elseth's tolerance, Gilliam and Stephen obeyed her command. The subject of the argument made it clear that she would be presented, as she was, to the mage. Gilliam, of course, could see nothing wrong with it—but Stephen, taking in the torn, dirty fabric of her shift, and the matted tangle of straw and darkness that passed as her hair, shuddered.

He would have pressed his point had the mage not been at a disadvantage with Elsabet. As it was, he gave in to Gilliam's insistence, and together they returned to the manor, the girl trailing Gilliam in the wide, happy circles that the dogs usually did.

". . . and here she is," Lady Elseth said, as they made their way into the parlor.

Zareth looked up immediately. His eyes, shadowed now as the sun crept down the horizon, were wide and unblinking. "This one?"

Gilliam bristled at the incredulity in the voice, but held his tongue. Which was, considering his mother's mood, the only wise option possible. The girl, catching Gilliam's anger, bristled as well. Her growl, lower than a pup's, but certainly high compared to a full-grown hound, filled the room as she raised her lips over bared teeth.

"I see," the mage said. "May I?" Without waiting upon an answer, he rose.

Gilliam placed a hand firmly on the girl's shoulder. She didn't seem to mind, although it was perfectly clear that the hand was meant to restrain. "Hold," he said softly.

"You're certain that the girl was the object of the attack?"

"Stephen?" Lady Elseth said, looking quietly across the room.

"Yes, sir."

"Why?"

Stephen shrugged. "I don't know why he attacked her."

"Why," the mage said again, his voice less soft, "are you so certain it was the girl he sought?"

Stephen did not answer. The mage looked up, his eyes leaving the girl for the first time since she had entered the parlor. "Stephen of Elseth, the question is not idly asked. I would have you answer it."

"I understand," Stephen answered. "But I can't."

The mage drew himself to his full height and lifted a hand. For a moment, the hand played against the air. Stephen felt the faintest tingle of something odd, something wrong. It had been many, many years since he had last encountered this strangeness, but he knew it at once—it was not something he would ever forget, no matter how he might desire to. His hand was on his weapon at once; he fell back two steps, his midsection folding into a defensive crouch.

Zareth Kahn's eyes widened in surprise. In haste, he dropped his hand. "Your pardon," he said softly and bowed his head.

"You may have his pardon," Lady Elseth said, and her voice was undisguised ice. "It is not the pardon of Elseth. What has happened here?"

The mage looked warily at the Lady, suddenly reminded of where he was and why he had come. He met her eyes, unflinching beneath her cold regard, and then bowed his head again. When he raised it, his face was free of all conviviality; his eyes were dark and unblinking.

"I attempted to use my magics," he said softly. "To compel Stephen to speak more freely."

Even Elsabet was surprised at the bold frankness of this confession. Words left her; she once again raised her hands to her chin.

"You arrogant son of a—"

"Gilliam." Lady Elseth raised one hand, calling for silence. Not even her son dared gainsay her gesture, and although he bristled, he waited her word. As did Zareth Kahn. "I don't like the mage-born," she said at last, as if coming to a decision. "And I do not like foreign dignitaries. Twice in our history they have almost been our ruin."

Zareth Kahn nodded, offering no argument. His face, bland and expressionless, showed nothing.

"I particularly dislike the way both of these groups assume that because we are not of their number, we are ignorant or savage."

At this, the mage opened his mouth; she waved him to silence.

"But I imagine that our own opinions are worn just as gracefully by either of these two parties: mage-born or foreigner. Stephen, if it pleases you, you may speak freely without regard to the Elseth fortunes. The Order of Knowledge will likewise speak freely—through its representative—without regard to its reputation. If the one is hurt, I give you my word that the other will suffer."

The mage bowed. "You are gracious, Lady."

"No. I am pragmatic."

At this, the mage laughed again. "When you retire from the running of your demesne, you might consider foreign service—you would do well abroad."

She did not warm to his compliment, but did incline her head. "I have considered this. Stephen?"

Stephen, straight and once again composed, nodded and bowed to his Lady, with all the formality due her office, and not their relationship. "Zareth Kahn. We know that it is the girl who came under attack, because less than a month ago, on the eve of the majority of Cynthia of Maubreche, we found and saved her. She was beset by three creatures that we know for a fact were not human."

Zareth raised a pale hand; it was shaking slightly. "Hold. What do you mean, you know they were not human?"

"They could not be cut by our swords. They had blades for fingers. They had skin of stone. Is that enough?"

"There were three of these?"

"Three."

What Zareth Kahn said next could not have been repeated in the company of Ladies—should not have been even whispered in the parlor. "I will take my seat again," he said quietly, and proceeded to almost stumble back until the chair caught and held him. "How did you survive this?"

"Through the intervention of a mage," Stephen said shortly.

At this, Zareth Kahn's dark eyes narrowed. "Who? And how did you know for certain that this person was a mage?"

"Because the non-mage-born don't usually call lightning and have it answer."

"Stephen," Elsabet said, her voice quiet. He took the warning from it.

"She said her name was Evayne. She saved our lives, and lit a path for us to follow. They pursued the girl to the gardens of the Maubreche Estate. There, we finally managed to defeat them. I was injured and spent some time recuperating in the King's City.

"When I returned home, this same girl was attacked again, or, rather, her . . . rooms were." Even given leave and command by Elsabet, Stephen could not say everything to this stranger. "And this time, we found one other item of interest. You might know it, but let me describe it."

"Please do."

"It's a platinum chain with a simple oval obsidian stone at its end. The stone is ringed by platinum as well."

"I see," the mage said, very, very quietly. "Come, then. Let me examine the girl. I will use magic," he added, the words tentative.

"You will not!"

"Gilliam!"

"Gil . . ."

The girl began a low growl; it was almost as if she spoke the words that Gilliam had been forbidden.

"I will cause her no harm, Lord Elseth," the mage said, swiveling his head to meet Gilliam's angry glare. "If you wish, you can stand behind me with your sword. I seek answers only."

Gilliam nodded curtly, and strode across the room, his hand on his sword hilt. Stephen cringed.

"Gilliam. *I* have seen fit to trust this visitor, who has come at *my* summons."

"Lady," the visitor in question broke in. "I made the offer in all seriousness. It appears clear that the girl . . . responds to her master's unease. If this will make him feel more easy, I'm willing to submit to it without calling your hospitality into question."

She frowned, but grudgingly nodded her acquiescence. Gilliam did indeed come to stand behind the mage's chair, sword drawn. He was a dark shadow—the only one that didn't flicker with the fire and the lamplight. Steady in his defense, poised for some unforeseen battle, he looked more at ease—although the mage could not see this—than he had in the last three weeks.

A hush formed in the air, part magic, part shadow, part absence of sun. Zareth Kahn, instead of reaching out, settled back into his chair, striking a pose not dissimilar to the Lady Elseth's. Lines settled into the circles beneath his eyes; his forehead creased. Only the fire snapped and crackled as it burned away at the wood.

And then, growing so slowly it was hardly visible, came the faintest hint of blue light, as if lightning had indeed been harnessed and forced to stay its quick strike. Strands of the mage's dark, long hair began to rise.

Stephen drew breath and held it. He was uncomfortable, and as the blue light grew, his sense of unease increased. The gaunt contours of the mage's face drank in shadow until he looked skeletal; the horrors of a young boy's nightmares. For just an instant, Stephen was glad that Gilliam could not see the mage's face.

The mage gestured; the light leaped suddenly from his fingers. His fingers danced heavily, but certainly, through the air, like a drugged athlete. When they were again still, perfect blue rings surrounded the girl's body.

Stephen did not understand why she did not move, or snarl, or fight them. His hair, much like the mage's, stood on end at the back of his neck, and he was only an observer, not a participant.

The rings began to move, but Stephen saw that they cast odd shadows; they did not touch her skin, or even what remained of her ruined clothing, at all. He exhaled slowly, caught by the strangeness of the spectacle. For a moment, he could see an eerie beauty played out in her features, the perfect smoothness of her skin, her suddenly closed eyes. And then it was gone.

The lights vanished, and the mage sagged forward, visibly exhausted.

"Zareth Kahn?" someone said.

He looked up to meet Elsabet's concern. "It cost much to arrive here in such haste," he said softly. "But I think I have an answer for you." His forehead creased; his lips tightened. "Although I admit that I don't understand it."

"What answer?"

"The girl is god-born."

"God-born?" Stephen's brows vanished beneath his hair. "But that's impossible! Look at her eyes!"

"I know," the mage replied, and his sourness grew. "I don't claim to understand it either. But she *is* god-born. I have tested that to the limits of this spell—information is *my* specialty." He sat back heavily against the chair. "And the study of historical magics was one of Krysanthos'." He raised a hand to his brow. "Apparently, Mother watch us, summoning was one of those magics."

Chapter Twenty

THE ROOM WAS AWASH in the heat of flame; the fire had been piled high, and quiet servants tended it at the mark of each hour. But Zareth Kahn still felt the chill. Blankets, pulled from winter storage, were piled high around him; he shivered against them, pulling them closer and higher.

This was the mage-fever, the result of pushing too hard with too much power and too little energy. He contained what he could of it in the presence of the Elseth family. But the act of examining the god-born girl had been madness, a symptom of the disease of insatiable curiosity.

He would pay for it; was paying for it now.

Yet even as his body was racked by shudders in the moon-touched room, his mind was elsewhere. On the girl. On Krysanthos. On Stephen of Elseth. It was not possible that Stephen was mage-born; a talent as strong as his sensitivity to magic indicated would have destroyed him, untrained as he was, before he left puberty behind. And he was certainly not god-born.

Or was he? The girl, to everyone's surprise, had proved to be just that. But the girl was mad, not nearly so human as Stephen showed himself to be. It was a puzzle. Zareth Kahn hated puzzles, and lived to defeat them. The puzzle of the Hunter God had brought him to Breodanir—and years later, the God's mystery remained unsolved. The mage was certain that Stephen and the girl were somehow involved in it.

Answers come from strange places. He told himself this, as the cold attacked again. It was bad tonight. But not nearly so bad as it had been when he first crossed the Elseth threshold.

Krysanthos was also a dire portent—of what, Zareth Kahn could not say. But although he had not concentrated on it during the course of the eve—had barely acknowledged the Elseth huntbrother's words—he recognized the medallion that Stephen had described.

Allasakar, the Lord of the Hells, was the only God to claim such an insignia.

Krysanthos, you fool, what have you done?

And why are you interested in the girl? Is she hells-born?

The question was rhetorical; the magical scan that Zareth Kahn had slowly and deliberately completed ruled out that possibility. Ah. The cold subsided further; perhaps sleep had a chance to claim him, should it move quickly.

But even as his lids flickered down over his eyes, he felt annoyed. Not at Krysanthos' involvement—although that had consequences for the Order that he did not have the strength, or desire, to fully contemplate now—but rather at the fact that the mage of the second circle somehow had answers that he, Zareth Kahn, did not himself possess.

He would change that. He would bring the girl to the King's City.

"Elsa," Stephen said lightly. "Aren't you here early in the season? The time for the Sacred Hunt has passed us."

Lady Elseth looked up from her prayers. She was simply dressed this morning, favoring the practical over the fanciful. Her dress was a crisp brown, with long, plain sleeves that were wide enough to give her elbow play, but narrow enough not to be a nuisance. The skirts were wide and split at the hems; it was obvious that she planned some sort of physical labor this day. Perhaps the overseeing of the kennel's construction.

"Stephen. Is it that time so soon?"

He nodded and approached her, crossing the soft green to do so. "Will you come to see us off?"

She offered him a hand, and he took it, helping her to her feet. She rolled up her mat and handed it to him; he caught it carefully and placed in under the crook of his free arm. "Gilliam's excited about this, isn't he?"

Stephen drew a slow breath. "Yes. But worried, as well. And the mage tells us little, for all that he asks."

"You tell him less, Stephen. You failed to mention the horn the girl brought— and I think we both know that it is important. Perhaps important enough to launch such an obvious assault on our grounds for."

He nodded. "Later, if he proves trustworthy."

Lady Elseth inclined her head. "I will not gainsay you; if you do not see fit to trust a mage—especially one who has attempted magics in my presence—I will trust your judgment." She fell silent. Her lips were set, and her chin was tilted; she looked severe, or tired, or both.

"Elsa," Stephen said, placing an arm around her shoulders. "This isn't the Hunt. We'll be fine."

"You tell me that?" she said, turning sharply. "When you don't even believe it yourself?" Her voice was taut, like a rope pulled so tight and fine it might snap if touched.

"We don't have to go," Stephen said, leaving his convivial—and hollow—smile behind. He caught her cheek in his hand. It was cool to the touch.

She met his eyes; hers were filmed. For a moment, it seemed that she wavered; she lifted her own hand, and pressed it lightly against his, seeking either warmth or comfort. Then at last, she said, "Don't lie to me, Stephen. I have not lied to you." But her voice was softer than the words she spoke.

Stephen released a breath he did not know, until that moment, he was holding. He felt weak, as if her answer were not the one he had expected—or, rather, hoped for.

"It's the 'farewells' that I hate the most. Until I've said them, I can pretend that everything is, or will be, fine. But once you've gone, I can do nothing but wait."

"Should I have left you with the Hunter?"

"No." Her eyes were watery again; she looked away. "Because if I don't grasp the chance to say farewell, I might never have it again. This is the Hunter's land," she added bitterly. She bowed her head a moment. When she raised it, her expression was once again calm. "Shall we go? I didn't mean to keep you waiting."

Zareth Kahn was impatient to be off. Although still fatigued, his face was less hollowed, less dark; his eyes darted back and forth, as if he were trying to make sure he missed nothing, not even the most trivial of details.

The horses, saddled, were restive; the villagers—those that had the time— gathered in a quiet ring outside of the manor. They did not offer Zareth Kahn any friendliness, and for his part, he did not demand it.

"Are we ready to take our leave?" he asked, for perhaps the fourth time.

"We will be, momentarily," Stephen answered. "Lady Elseth said she'd something she wanted us to take to the King's City. She's gone to her rooms for it; she'll be down shortly."

"I suppose it won't wait?" The mage drummed his fingers against his leg.

Stephen watched, out of the corner of his eyes. It was hard to imagine that this slim, almost nervous man was the same one who had questioned them all two nights past. "It will only be a few more minutes," he said.

The mage nodded, and began to pace.

Gilliam, Lord Elseth, might have been annoyed at the mage's insistence— but he had his hands full. While the strange girl had, in the end, consented to ride within the confines of a carriage, she made it quite clear that she wanted nothing to do with horseback. Her incredulity at being asked to do so still made itself felt.

He was determined to try, but equally determined not to force the issue. Because, as Stephen said, she wasn't one of his dogs. His word was not—could not be—her law. He tried to tell himself this as he felt her press her disobedience. As he felt her test him, in a way that only the dogs ever did.

"Gilliam?"

"She won't ride," he said, the words clipped and uneven.

"Then let her walk. She'll change her mind." Stephen turned to face the girl, who was already half out of the tunic and breeches they'd managed to dress her in. "Then again, perhaps she won't. We aren't on the message relay," he added. "It won't make a difference."

Gilliam nodded curtly. He did not want to speak; the words would have added nothing. But he glowered at the girl more effectively than he could have shouted.

Stephen cringed. The girl did not. The mage politely inquired whether or not they could leave. And the manor door opened quietly.

It was the door that everyone looked to. Lady Elseth stood framed by it. Almost casually, she threw one bag to the ground; the other, she carried over her shoulder. Gone was even the practical dress of the morning; she wore dark pants, a loose, cream-colored shirt, and a large woolen vest. A hat covered and contained her hair, and on her feet she wore boots of thick leather.

"Mother?" Gilliam asked, contest with the recalcitrant girl forgotten.

"Yes?" She tilted her head to one side, raising a brow. One of the villagers ran up the stairs, and very carefully relieved Lady Elseth of her burden. "To the horse," she said, and he nodded.

Maribelle, quiet until that moment, suddenly seemed to appear from nowhere. "Mother?" In the word was the same question that Gilliam had asked, but without his harsh incredulity.

"Yes," Elsa said softly, answering the unasked question. "And I trust the keeping of our responsibility to you, Maribelle. You are old enough, and learned enough; my people will follow your commands."

Maribelle's forehead creased; watching her, Lady Elseth knew that those lines would one day become etched in her smooth brow. But in front of the villagers, she had the sense not to argue with her mother.

It was a cheat, of course. Elsabet had never had any intention of allowing her youngest the room or the space to argue with her sudden decision. She acknowledged it quietly when she hugged her daughter.

Maribelle said only, "Do you have to go?" But it was not the question of a child; it was the ambivalence of someone who had entered the twilight between childhood and adulthood, and stood on that line, for an instant, almost understanding all of the emotions of either.

"I have to go," Elsa whispered. "It's my duty and my right as Lady Elseth." Still, she felt oddly weak; her stomach was clenching, and her head felt a little too light. "No," she added, "that's not all of the truth. I—I have to be there. I have had to wait through so many Sacred Hunts." She swallowed, her voice tight and heavy. "But it isn't my duty to wait through this. They're my sons, Maribelle."

"And sons are always the most important," Maribelle said, her voice a whisper too, but a very, very flat one.

Lady Elseth felt her daughter's words as a blow. She held more tightly to Maribelle's shoulders. "No," she said, knowing that Maribelle would understand it one day, but not this one. "Sons are always the ones who die."

Her youngest surprised her. She returned the tight warmth of her mother's hug; held her longer than she should have in so public a circumstance.

"I wouldn't go," her mother said, again in the softest of whispers, "if I couldn't trust you here."

"I don't want them to die either," her daughter replied. And that was her apology. She pulled away, her clear eyes wide, her chin tilted, her shoulders squared. She was dressed to her station in a deep blue frock, and looked more the Lady than her mother, although no one who knew them would have mistaken the station of either. She curtsied, low, and held that gesture. "I will watch over Elseth in your stead, Lady." Her voice was strong, young, and rather loud.

"Thank you," Elsabet said. "You do our line proud." Then she looked at her still silent companions. "Well, gentlemen? Shall we ride? Or shall we rather gawk all day?"

Stephen shook his head in wonder, and then began to laugh. His body shaking, he caught the reins of his horse, and led it forward for his mother's use. Gilliam, still gaping, was nudged in passing.

"Yes, Lady Elseth. We ride." But the mage looked singularly less amused than Stephen did.

It shouldn't have been a grueling trip; it was. Zareth Kahn, himself exhausted and barely fit for the rigors of saddle, pressed the party hard. Lady Elseth accepted this prompting mildly, even docilely, Stephen and Gilliam accepted it gracelessly. But they did ride.

The girl, almost tireless, kept both feet on the ground, and circled Gilliam's horse whenever he paused. Still, she was quiet and caused little difficulty, perhaps understanding that there was urgency in their journey.

So it was that they came at last to the gates of the King's City, travel-worn, tired, and very much in need of sleep and bathing.

Stephen had thought to stay in an inn, but Zareth Kahn would not hear of it, and in the end they came to the grand halls of the Order of Knowledge, leading tired horses and a wild girl who never seemed to feel the exertion.

They were not an impressive delegation. Only Lady Elseth seemed to remember her bearing, although her clothing was not suitable for an embassy. She made certain that the horses were tended to, and quietly whispered a prayer of thanks to the Hunter—for Gilliam, pressed to move quickly, had elected to leave his dogs behind. The Order, of course, had no kennels for their keeping, as any normal inn would have.

Zareth Kahn, on the other hand, perked up almost the moment his feet crossed the grand threshold into the towering hall. Lady Elseth could well understand why. Her breath stopped a moment as she arched her neck back. Her eyes rose up, and up again, until they rested upon the very peak of the ceiling's stone arches. They were unadorned, but grand in their simplicity; a shout could be caught and echoed forever without losing any of its strength, or so she thought.

Stephen's eyes never reached the ceiling. He took in the rich red and gold of the carpeted stairs, glanced at the deep, dark wood that formed railings and borders, and then lighted upon the walls themselves.

They were not plain, although no tapestries or frescoes lined them. Where a statue or two was common in any such building, and an alcove dedicated to either a God or a relative should have been in evidence, these halls had neither. Instead, in row upon row, they had heavy, perfect shelves, with beveled glass in leaden frames, and ladders on wheels to walkways that rose four stories. And in each of these shelves, there were books.

Those books held voices, all silent now, that nonetheless called to him. The silence, the hush in the halls through which people could be seen moving, made perfect sense. This was a library that not even the King could boast. He reached out, pressed his fingers against the glass, and forgot about the complaints of a long and arduous journey.

"It is not so grand," Zareth Kahn said, his voice soft. "Our library in Essalieyan is by far superior." But he smiled almost fondly. "There is a library of older and more delicate works farther down the hall; it is the grandest of all of our rooms."

Stephen nodded, wordless. It made sense that the Order of Knowledge would have such a collection; it even made sense that mages would. Books, after all, were a hint of magic in Stephen's life.

"Wonderful," Gilliam snorted. "Do you have kitchens as well?"

As one person, they both turned, and their faces bore very similar expressions. Zareth Kahn recovered first. "Yes," he replied shortly. "We have kitchens. We also have rooms and wings for visiting . . . dignitaries. If you follow me, I'll see that your needs are attended to. Forgive me for forgetting the hospitality of the Order."

He began to walk the halls briskly, leaving their wonder to Stephen. Stephen's frown deepened, aimed as it was at the spot between Gilliam's shoulder blades.

The rooms they were given were grand, even by noble standards. They were both larger and better equipped than the rooms in the King's castle and on his grounds, in which the Hunter Lords lived until the Sacred Hunt. The ceilings, tall, were not arched; they were flat, and crossed by magnificent beams. There were paintings hung above the fireplaces that bore artist's signatures that even Gilliam could recognize. Attached to each sleeping chamber was a small, simple room with a stylized, but serviceable altar for votive offerings, prayer, and meditation. The Order had taken pains to ensure that these altars could be used by worshipers of many different faiths, although it was equally obvious that the altars themselves saw little use.

There was a sitting room, a small parlor, and a large study. The study was equipped with shelves, although these were empty, and two desks, either of which dwarfed any that the Elseth Manor claimed. It was clear that whoever visited these chambers came to both work and live.

"Do these rooms meet your approval?"

"Indeed," Lady Elseth replied, before either Stephen or Gilliam could speak. "They do. If this is the hospitality of the Order, Zareth Kahn, than we of Elseth are deeply grateful."

"Will you require anything? I shall send up servants and water for the baths, unless you would prefer to use the more public ones."

She raised a brow. "No, the small ones will do."

He nodded. "When would it please you to dine?"

"After our baths, I think." She lifted a hand to forestall Gilliam, and caught him in mid-word. "Is there a hall for the Order, or will we dine in our rooms?"

He hesitated a moment, and then bowed. "If it would not trouble you, Lady, I would prefer that you remained in your rooms until I have had time to confer with my colleagues."

Her shoulders relaxed. "It would be no trouble at all." Then she smiled, and although she looked weary, her smile was completely genuine—the first such one with which she had graced the mage. "My thanks."

". . . and that," Zareth Kahn said, sinking to rest in his chair, "is the whole of it, Zoraban."

The light in the room was low; although it was full day, and Zoraban's chambers had windows aplenty, the curtains had been drawn. They were a subtle, soft weave that allowed a whisper of light, no more, to pass through, but they were also magical in nature—a gift of creation from the Order in the capital of Essalieyan. What was spoken in these rooms when the curtains were drawn would be caught by no magical eavesdroppers, should any try to listen.

Zoraban nodded softly, and even in the poor light, the pale twinkle of his golden eyes was clear. He wore his age like a mantle, letting it suggest both wisdom and the power of gathered knowledge. It had been so for fifteen years, and if any thought it suspicious that Zoraban had not noticeably aged in those fifteen, they were wise enough not to voice their doubts. His long white hair gleamed softly, a halo around his slender features. His beard, thick and heavy, fell like milk into his lap.

Zareth Kahn raised his head idly, after minutes had passed in silence. Zoraban was not the most powerful of the mages that the Breodanir Order boasted—but he was easily the most learned of their number, and for that reason, held the seat of the Order. None had tried to gainsay him. After all, rare indeed was a god-born child of Teos, God of Knowledge—and when Zoraban had proved himself such a one, the Order had all but begged to receive him.

What are you thinking, Zoraban? What do you know that you've not seen fit to share with us?

As if he could hear the thoughts—and at times, Zoraban was uncannily, uncomfortably perceptive—the Master of the Order met Zareth Kahn's ringed eyes. Against all odds, the Teos-born man smiled; his face lit up with a deep, quiet joy.

"Have they eaten?"

"Pardon?" It was not the question he had expected.

"Have your companions eaten? Would they be willing to speak now, at my request?"

Almost, he said yes—but then he remembered two things. The first was the sour expression of Lord Elseth, and the second, that only Lord Elseth seemed to be able to communicate with the strange girl. Still, one did not easily say no to the Master of the Order. Zareth Kahn reflected on the wisdom of this, weighing the one against the other, before he sighed regretfully. "No, Zoraban. They will eat soon, and if you will it, I will bring them to your chambers the moment they have retired from their table."

Zoraban raised a frosted brow almost airily. "I see," he said, his words dry. "Then I will wait here in reposed patience." He smiled again. "There are answers here, Zareth—I can almost taste them."

"Answers?" Zareth Kahn asked mildly.

"To the questions the Gods ask," Zoraban replied. "Not to the questions of impertinent mages, even be they as exalted as to reach the second circle."

It was a matter of ease and custom to acknowledge a graceful defeat when the opponent was Zoraban; Zareth Kahn inclined his head elegantly. But his curiosity was piqued; it burned and flared to a life that hovered above his state of exhaustion, waiting. "If it won't trouble you, I will also sup quickly." He rose, without waiting a reply. In such a fey mood, Zoraban was unlikely to find a reason to protest.

Stephen found the very spartan simplicity of Zoraban's rooms almost shocking. Unlike almost every other inch of the sprawling order, it was unadorned by either paintings, shelves, or carpets. The floor was constructed of simple, well-oiled wooden planks, and the desk against the wall was small. It had two drawers, one on either side of the empty chair, and an inkstand that appeared to be empty.

There was a fire grate, but no mantle, and the only piece of finery in evidence anywhere was the expanse of draperies against the west wall. The drapes were closed and hung in a rippling cascade of oddly colored material; Stephen didn't like them, but he couldn't say why. Still, if not for those, he might have thought they'd been tricked into entering a confinement cell.

Zoraban did not seem to notice the shock of his visitors. "I bid you welcome to the Order of Knowledge," he said, rising. He wore simple robes, but dark ones; they were unbelted, and fell to his feet in a clean full-circle drape as he bowed, quite low. "I am Zoraban, Master here."

Lady Elseth, attired in a dress both simple and of obvious quality, returned his bow in kind; she knew that he was not, originally, of Breodanir, and left behind the formal curtsy that she would have otherwise offered. She was bathed and fed, a much renewed person, and as she rose, it was hard to imagine that she had been forced to the capital at such a harrowing pace.

"I am Elsabet, Lady Elseth," she said softly. "This is Gilliam, Lord Elseth, and his huntbrother, Stephen of Elseth. The girl is unfortunately afflicted and has been unable to give us her name."

"So I've heard," Zoraban replied. "But, please, those of you who will, be seated." He gestured to the walls, where four chairs were unceremoniously placed. The chairs, unlike the rest of the chamber, were finely ornamented; the hardwood of the arms and legs were worked with carvings and symbols, and laced liberally with gold.

Even Lady Elseth raised an eyebrow in question as she accepted the mage's offer.

"Bring the chairs in closer if you prefer; I don't usually have this many guests in my rooms, so I had the chairs brought and left to the side. I should have placed them more hospitably."

Lady Elseth was first to comply, although Zareth Kahn went to her aid; the chairs were heavy and not easily carried. Stephen followed his Lady's lead, and at length, so did Gilliam.

The girl sat at his feet, resting her chin on his knee. He stiffened, and she lifted her face, her expression almost a parody of hurt. Gilliam looked up then, at Stephen, as if for permission.

Stephen grimaced and then nodded quickly. He watched the girl's head settle back into Gilliam's knees, and after a moment, saw Gilliam slowly stroke her hair.

"Why have you come?" the Master of the Order asked suddenly. He rose, as if he had no need of a chair, but stayed his ground, surveying them all from the advantage of his height. And he was in truth tall, if not in seeming; the lamps at his back cast a long shadow, and the windows were allowed no chance to provide light. For a moment, light at his back and perfect, ivory hair against the black background of his robes, Zoraban seemed the maker-born image of a God.

Stephen drew breath sharply. Golden eyes seemed to flare, like the sun, in the pale face of the Master of the Order. At once, the Elseth huntbrother bowed his head.

The man laughed suddenly, and the shadows resumed their normal, everyday dimensions. "Yes, I'm of the god-born," he said. "Who else could hope to keep order within this Order of mages and knowledge-seekers?" Still, it was obvious that the chuckle was a pleased one, and although the fleeting aura of otherness vanished with the laugh, Zoraban did not choose to take his seat again.

"We want answers," Gilliam said abruptly. "We wouldn't have come had your mage not insisted."

Zoraban raised an eyebrow. "I would have known you as Hunter Lord with no introduction." His voice was grave. "But perhaps you will be glad of your journey, Lord Elseth. For I see that Zareth Kahn was correct in his appraisal. At your feet sits one god-born."

The girl looked up then, shaking her hair free of Gilliam's fingers. She met the mage's golden eyes with her dark ones, and then smiled and bobbed her head up and down, as if in greeting. Or agreement.

"Gil?" Stephen's eye were wide.

So were his Hunter's. "Yes," he said, half-whisper, half-word. "She says, yes." And he, too, looked up to meet the eyes of the god-born mage. He put a hand on the girl's shoulder, as if to draw her back—then realized what he was doing, and even had the grace to blush.

"The god-born can speak to the god-born," Zoraban said, his eyes gentle. "No matter what their language, no matter who their parents. But I have never seen such eyes on one so blessed—or cursed—among our number. Come, girl."

The girl rose and walked the length of the floor to stand before Zoraban. But she did turn—once—to glance back at Gilliam.

There were so many questions that Stephen wanted to ask—but as the mage lifted both of his hands and gently cupped the girl's upturned face, he forgot them. He could not speak; there was something about the scene that felt almost too private to watch. Yet it was compelling, magical. For a moment, the bright edge of mystery pervaded the room, and all of time seemed to whirl around the two who stood with the blood of the Gods in their veins, without ever eclipsing them.

The mage's eyes glowed; gold turned to sunlight, bright and crackling. The girl's face was turned away from them; they could not see her reaction, but she did not move or pull away.

"Yes," Zoraban said, in a voice too deep and too low for a human throat, "you are of the god-born. But I do not know your parent." He let his hands drop, slowly, and raised his head to face the spectators until now forgotten. "I will walk in the half-world for you—and for my own curiosity. I will call my father. Will you wait?"

Zareth Kahn's eyes widened in obvious surprise; Stephen, Gilliam, and Elsabet did no more than nod. What else could they do but wait? They had come this far seeking answers.

"He has only done this one other time," Zareth Kahn whispered, for Stephen's ears alone. "You are honored." Then he, too, fell silent, as Zoraban lowered his hands completely, until the long black sleeves melded with the drape of robes and his fingers curved loosely. His face, he lifted to some point beyond the ceiling, searching upward, and up again, as if the heavens themselves were visible to the golden aurora of his gaze. His lips parted, his beard rustled as if at wind.

The air before him began to sparkle; clouds rolled in, heavy and thick, like low-lying mist on the moors.

"Stand your ground; stay your place."

Stephen heard Zareth Kahn's command as if from a distance. He gripped the arms of his chair and looked rigidly down as the ground gave way to clouds and a lattice of darkness and light such as he had never dreamed.

"Gil!" He shouted, as he felt his brother begin to rise. "Stay seated. The half-world is not for us." He pressed his bond with his brother with more force than he had ever done; he could hear the distant screech of wood against wood as Gilliam sat back, hard.

"Trust him. He . . . has forgotten himself in his call. Let me explain. The half-world will open easily for the god-born—they speak with their parents in ways that normal mortals cannot. But humans were not meant to meet with Gods, and without a sure and certain guide, they cannot enter the realm. If they enter it, they can be lost until a God sees fit to return them—but no God can compel them there," Zareth Kahn said again, his tone calmer, his words slower. "The half-world will not consume us if we stay in our place. Lady?"

"I am . . . here. This is interesting, Zareth." Her voice was dry, with just the edge of a quiver. "What is this patchwork on the ground?"

"What do you see?" the mage replied.

"I see the golds and yellows of the harvest," she answered, measured, calm. "I see the shadows of the villagers in the fields; I see the foot of the seat of judgment. I see . . . I see my children—all of our children. The winter. It moves."

"What else?"

But she had fallen silent, and did not answer further.

"I don't see it," Gilliam said. "I see the hunt. I see stag and bear and boar; I see wolf and fox and hound. I see the spear and the sword and the bow. And Stephen."

"Stephen?" Zareth Kahn said softly.

"What do you see?" Stephen asked.

The mage laughed. "I see wind and rain and fire. I see the earth buckling, the heavens opening. I see books and lore and even a little death. More, but you wouldn't understand it. You?"

"I see darkness and light," Stephen replied.

"What?"

"Darkness, light—like the clouds here."

The mage was silent; his thought made the air heavy. "Stephen," he said at last, in a tone that was devoid of expression. "You are rare. What the half-world shows, no one fully understands—but not even I see it as it is; I see it as my hopes, my life, my dreams, my fears—but it is always connected with the everyday."

"Earthquakes happen every day, do they?" Stephen shot back. But he shivered. And then he felt it: the presence of God. It crept into his body slowly; started as a tingle, the vaguest hint of something familiar that teases the memory. It did not stop there. Instead, it grew stronger, brighter; the clouds at his feet closed over the lattice until there was mist, no more.

Still, he felt it. And as it grew more persistent, he found himself moving, as if to escape, all of his warnings to Gilliam forgotten. First one foot, then the other, fell firmly against what had been planked oak, and then his hands left the confines of his armrests.

Unanchored, and alone, he stood in the mists of the half-world. He could not even hear Gilliam's shout—but he felt it clearly along their bond. It was comforting to know that not even this place where man and God might meet could sever what they had made together.

He sent his peace back to Gilliam. *Stay, Gil. I'm safe.* Then he began to walk forward. He thought he might walk forever, lost. Thought, without the guidance of Zoraban, that he might pay for his foolishness the way that the fools in the children's stories that Lady Elseth told always did.

But if he had to walk, he did not walk alone.

Gilliam, Lord Elseth, appeared beside him, a shadow with substance in a strange world that seemed to have none.

"Gil! I told you to stay!"

Gilliam smiled grimly, and punched his huntbrother, hard, in the shoulder.

Stephen laughed and offered no further demur; what he had said and what he felt were two very different things, and Gilliam rarely paid attention to the said thing when the felt thing beckoned.

"Where are we?" Gilliam said, looking around.

"In the half-world," someone answered. The ground, if ground it was, rumbled and buckled slightly. They both looked up, and up again, following the strange echo of the voice.

And thus is was that the Elseth Hunter Lord and his huntbrother first met a God in the half-world.

Chapter Twenty-One

GILLIAM SAW A SLIGHTLY bent old man, leaning against a smooth, dark staff with one hand, while in the other he carried a heavy tome with a thick brass latch and two cracked leather covers. He wore robes, those dark and gray ones that the Priests of the Hunter often wore, and his head, hands, and throat were unadorned. His hair, long and white, fell past his shoulders, gathering in the hollows of his stooped shoulders, and a beard trailed into the mist.

But his eyes were not gold, not any living color; they had a depth to them that eyes should not have. Were it not for the towering height of the God, Gilliam might have mistaken him for Zoraban, Master of the Order.

Stephen saw differently.

Age was a thing for mortals, and this tall, inscrutable Lord of the Heavens bore no such taint. He wore robes, yes, long and fine, but they had no colors and all colors as they shimmered to the unseen ground. His perfect forehead was cut by a circlet of light; his face was smooth, his hair drawn tightly, completely back. In Stephen's vision, the staff was no staff, but rather a fine and perfect blade, edged along both sides, pointed into rising fog. But he carried a book, and in it, Stephen was certain that the knowledge of the cosmos was writ.

He met the God's eyes for a second, no more, and then looked away. He did not trust the ground beneath his feet, and so bowed instead of dropping to one knee in deference.

"You are not the ones who called me," the god said, his voice filling their ears, although it was mild, even soft.

"No, Lord," Stephen said. His voice was quiet as the God's was loud.

"Then follow," the God replied. "We are close to the one that did." He raised a delicate brow and looked down his straight, slender nose. "You walked without him."

To that, there was no answer. Stephen nodded.

"Brave," was the only reply. The God began to walk, and as he did, the mist cleared behind him, forming a path wide enough for two men to walk abreast. In grateful silence, the Hunter and the huntbrother did just that.

They did not have long to walk; ahead, standing on what appeared to be a little hill or groundsheet, stood Zoraban; at his side stood the girl.

"Lord," Zoraban said, his voice oddly resonant.

"Zoraban." To Stephen's surprise, the God bowed low. "It is good to see you again so soon. Why have you called me?"

"To ask the right question," the mage replied gravely. He bowed as well, although there was nothing as majestic or grand in his gesture. Then he straightened, and his eyes widened. "Lord Elseth, Stephen."

"I found them wandering the mists," the God said. "Will you take them in?" The words were formal, almost ritualistic.

"I will, as my responsibility," Zoraban replied.

"Then they are your care." He looked down and then lifted the arm that held the sword. "Go and stand beside him." Although there was no light above, or anywhere in sight, the blade cast a cutting shadow.

They reached the side of the mage, chastened but unbowed. "You will let me speak," Zoraban said. They nodded, and Gilliam didn't even show rancor at the severity of the tone. "Teos, it is your light and your labor that has granted man vision beyond the seen. To you, all knowledge is eventually brought, and from you, the desire for knowledge is kindled and burns yet.

"I come to you with information; it is my hope, my supplication, that that information will return to me as understanding, if you will it.

"And if you do not will it, Lord, I will be content, and I will continue to seek information in both your name and my own."

Gilliam rolled his eyes. "Why can't he just say 'I've got a question?'"

Stephen planted his elbow sharply between the two ribs his reach was most familiar with. He did not speak his disapproval, for fear of interrupting either Zoraban or Teos, the Lord of Knowledge—but he sent it sizzling along their bond.

The girl raised her head and looked back at Gilliam while the mage continued to intone the prologue that the Hunter Lord found of such little interest. Then, at last, Zoraban stopped.

Teos, meditative, looked down upon the four with his endless eyes. Then, if possible, the corners of his lips turned up as if in a smile. "Yes," he said softly, "you may present your case and ask your question." The mists curled up around him, becoming thicker and more dense. They took on shape and form, like water hardening to ice, until they at last held the appearance of a huge, if simple, throne. The god sat, laying his sword across his legs, and his book across the sword.

"This is an echo," Zoraban whispered, "of all that he is in the heavens." Golden eyes met endless ones without so much as flinching. If there was affection between the immortal and his son, it was not obvious, not noticeable.

"My lord, I bring you a mystery. This woman."

Teos studied the girl for a moment, and then inclined his head. Unlike a human monarch, he was not at all distressed by the state of her clothing, hair, or skin; these things rarely interested the Gods.

"She is god-born, Lord—but I do not know the God who was her parent, mother or father."

"Her place of birth?"

"She does not know it in a manner that I can repeat to you." He paused. "And she does not speak."

"I see." The God lifted a hand. "Come, girl." And on those two words, his voice changed. For a moment, it was indistinct, not a single voice, but a multitude of voices—high, low, deep, thin—all blended into a precise harmony of sound. Each syllable held the power and the mystery of command.

Stephen understood then that the bardic voice was an echo of the voice of the Gods. He was not certain that, had he wished it, he could have disobeyed Teos. The girl did not, but she did not seem troubled or even awed by the presence of the deity. The mists moved and parted at her feet; she traced a path cleanly and quickly, raising her face as she approached.

Teos reached down for her, and placed one hand upon her upturned head. Light lanced out from his fingertips, crackling in the silence.

"Lord Elseth," Zoraban said, his voice even, "stay your ground. She is not harmed."

But Gilliam had made no move, nor would he. Although he did not understand why, the girl was not afraid; had the God's magic harmed her in any way, he would have known it the moment she felt any pain. Still, his breath was tight and loudly drawn between clenched teeth.

Stephen did not even look at his Hunter; his eyes were drawn and bound to the hand of the God, the eyes of the God, the face of the God. Even the girl, straight and supple, with no taint of fear or awe, and therefore none of mortality, was barely a flicker in the field of his vision. He did not know that he held his breath until he was forced to expel it, and even then, he would not look away. He did not know why.

The God looked up. "She is god-born," he said, his voice once again a storm of voices. "But her mortal parent was no human."

"Ah," Zoraban said. "Which of the Gods was she born of?"

Teos' brow furrowed. Minutes passed; his eyes flickered gray and then flashed light, the essence of storm. "The Hunter God."

Gilliam closed his eyes and nodded. Stephen dropped to one knee; the mist rose to his chest. Only Zoraban dared to speak, and the word held only incredulity. "WHAT?"

"The God of the Breodani."

"But—but, Lord," Zoraban sputtered. "There is no Hunter God!"

"So we thought," Teos replied, while both Gilliam and Stephen gave way in turn to incredulity, if for very different reasons. "So I thought. But she is that, Zoraban." The God smiled suddenly, and the smile was a terrible, sudden change. "Ask the right question, my son."

"What do you mean, there is no Hunter God?" It was Stephen who asked the question, and he didn't care if it was "right" or not.

"Not a single Lord of Heaven has ever seen or met this God that Breodanir claims as its own," Zoraban answered tightly. "Not a single one of the so-called Hunter-born, *not one*, has ever manifested any signs of the god-born. Breodanir is a mystery to the Order—why else do you think so large a group would live in your King's City, away from the heart of Essalieyan, and the Order proper? But we have studied for years, and received no answers, found no records.

"Until now."

"There were answers," someone said. Stephen was almost shocked to find that the words were his own. "I have dreamt of them. Three times."

Very slowly, the God's gaze left the mystery of the girl and came to rest upon Stephen's face. Stephen tried to look away. "Three times, Stephen of Elseth? Tell me of your dreams, then. I would hear them."

"And may I then ask a question?"

"You are bold, but I am curious. Yes; you may ask."

Very quietly, Stephen began to tell the God of the dream that, three times, had troubled his sleep. He spoke of darkness, and as he did, the mists shifted, the ground rocked. He spoke of the destruction of the temple, the killing of the Priests, and the appearance, each of the three times, of Evayne.

"Evayne?" Teos said, lifting a hand.

"It was what she named herself," Stephen answered.

"You are wyrded."

Stephen nodded. "But upon each of these occasions, I found this, and winded it. And the Hunter's Death came." So saying, Stephen reached into his jacket, and very carefully pulled out the Hunter's horn.

In the half-world, it crackled with light and energy. Stephen nearly dropped it as it outlined his hand with its aura of power.

"Will you wind it for me now?" Teos asked softly.

Stephen lifted the horn to his lips at the command inherent in the God's request. But before his lips made contact with the mouthpiece, the girl shrieked. His hands froze in midair.

For in that shriek, he heard two words: *Not yet.*

Eyes wide, he met the girl's agonized stare, and saw what he had never seen in her eyes: a human sentience, and a very human fear.

"I see," the God said. "Very well, put it aside, Stephen of Elseth. Guard it well. It is your answer."

"It's what the followers of Allasakar seek."

Teos lifted his fair face; the lines of his lips tightened; his pallor grew dark, and his eyes, darker still. "Why do you speak that name in my presence?"

"Because," Stephen replied, "Zareth Kahn, a member of your Order, recognized the pendant that only Priests of the Dark God wear. Or so he named it."

"I see." Teos' face became calm once again. "And yes. I do not know what credence to lend your dreams; they are Mystery given, and not even the Gods," here he frowned delicately, "may know Mystery's plans."

"Mystery?"

"He is called the Shadowed One in the East, the Unnamed One in the North; to the West, he is called Teiaramu, and in a time long past, he was called the God or the Guardian of Man. We of his brethren call him Mystery, and not even the Mother claims to know his purpose. But his wyrd may have shown you a truth. The darkness hunts that artifact." The God fell silent a moment, but lifted his hand for peace; it was clear that he had not yet finished. His eyes grew gray, and more dangerous, his brow furrowed. "Yes," he said at last, although it was a reply to none of the four. "We must trust you with this information. Hold.

"The Lord of the Darkness is not in his seat in the Hells."

"Not in his seat? Is he in the half-world?" Again, Stephen surprised himself, for the God was obviously used to a different ritual when receiving the questions of the merely mortal.

"No, Stephen of Elseth. This is what troubles us."

"Then where?"

"We do not know. No, do not fear that. The Covenant of God of Man forbids the mortal lands to the Gods. But I fear that his absence is a danger to all."

"Covenant of God of Man?" Stephen's eyes narrowed. Something about those words felt familiar; he wondered if, in one or the other of the books he had read as a child, he had touched upon this covenant, this agreement.

And then Zoraban suddenly turned, his face pale, his hands clenched tight in fists. "Stephen," he said, his voice low and urgent. "That pendant. The one you said Zareth Kahn recognized. What became of it?"

Stephen shrugged. "We brought it with us. Lady Elseth is its keeper; she has it for your inspection."

Zoraban spoke in a language that Stephen did not recognize, and then met the eyes of his parent. "My lord, Stephen's question to you, and my own, must remain unasked for this evening."

"Understood," Teos said, rising. The throne vanished as both of his feet touched the ground once more. "But what I have allowed, I will still grant." Before either of them could move, he lifted his sword and swiftly brought it down upon Stephen's shoulder. Stephen cried out as the flat of the blade pressed against his jacket.

A net of color sprang to life around him; the world spun, the mists grabbed at his ankles. He gave a strangled cry as he felt the Sword of Knowledge pass *through* him.

"Heed me, Stephen of Elseth. Although you are rash and impetuous, you have of me one question to ask, and I will answer it to the best of my ability. But you cannot ask it now; indeed, you cannot ask it at all if you travel to the halls of judgment. The darkness is gathering.

"But if you have the time, or the need, or the right question, you will be able to call as if you were, in blood, my own son. And I grant you the gift of vision in your fight against a most ancient enemy, even if you do not yet understand what it entails.

"Now, go. *GO!*"

Zoraban lifted his arms, and the mist began to flee him, almost scurrying in its sudden roll away from the swell at his feet. The girl scampered forward to join him, and held fast to the hem of his sleeve. The sky, if sky it was, darkened and grew indistinct and hazy.

Zoraban's face grew troubled. He cast his hands wide, curling his fingers into his palms as if grasping at something invisible.

"What is it?" Stephen asked, raising his voice to be heard, although there was no other sound.

"I don't know," Zoraban said. He motioned for silence, his lips growing thin as the seconds passed.

And then, the mists exploded outward, fraying into air and nothingness. Above them, instead of endless gray, was a flat, stone ceiling; around them were those fine, well crafted chairs. Lady Elseth sat slightly forward in hers, and Zareth Kahn was likewise tense.

"Stephen, Gilliam!" She relaxed.

Zareth Kahn did not.

Without pause to greet them, Zoraban raced across the room and stopped only when he towered over Lady Elseth. "Lady, you carried a pendant with you to the King's City. Where is it?"

Her brows furrowed, and her eyes widened as she glanced at his face; his tone was not one she was used to hearing. But it was clear that worry drove him. "I have it with me," she replied, and sank her hands into the folds of her skirt. "Here."

Zoraban stared at the pendant as if transfixed, and then his eyes caught fire. Burning with the heat of liquid gold, they flared so brightly that all in the room saw it.

The obsidian that formed the pendant's heart began to melt. Lady Elseth gave a cry and dropped the chain, but it was not pain that moved her; the platinum remained cool against her fingers. "What are you doing?"

"Destroying a beacon," the mage replied gravely. "I was careless; I was too absorbed with your question and not with your plight. I pray that I've not been too slow to act." He drew his hand across his brow.

The door to his chambers buckled.

The wood warped in, as if some strange force had turned it to a thick, heavy liquid. For a moment, a fist far too large for a human hand could be seen pressing against the fabric that the door had become.

"Lady's frown," Zareth Kahn whispered. He rose, toppling his chair, and gripped the medallion of the Order in his right hand. His left weaved a complicated pattern in the air, his fingers deft, deliberate.

Zoraban joined him, although he wore no medallion.

Gilliam and Stephen rose as well, unsheathing their swords and waiting. Their movements were so dissimilar it was hard to see that the same hand had trained them, for Stephen was graceful, economical, and elegant; Gilliam wrenched his sword free with so much force, he stumbled back a step. But they acted in unison.

Even the girl fell to the ground in a low crouch, a feral growl in her throat.

"We—have the door." Zareth Kahn spoke through gritted teeth. "Lady, you might wish to move to the far wall."

Lady Elseth rose and drew a dagger. "If you have the door, it shouldn't be a—"

The stones around the door suddenly cracked. An unseen hand pushed against a part of the wall, hard; it fell forward into the room. Shadow, although there was no light to cast it, began to spill in through the hole.

"I see," Lady Elseth said. She moved. Quickly.

Something stepped into the hole in the wall. The shadows fell away from her, settling around her knees as if in homage. All that remained lingered against her body, supple, living raiment. Her hair was darker than the shadows, her eyes completely black. But her skin was pale and perfect, her chin a delicate point, her lips, unlined and full. She was not tall, yet even so there was nothing diminutive about her.

Before anyone could react, she lifted her hands, and the walls that framed her melted away, joining the darkness in velvet silence. Only the door, crackling blue, remained standing beside her, and it was not a fit companion.

"Zoraban," she said, inclining her head gently. "You are known for your wisdom and your learning, even in my circles." She smiled, and although there was no light upon her, her teeth glinted. "I bid you show it now. We have no interest in your Order, or any of your business. We want only the girl and her two companions."

"I'm afraid I will have to disappoint you," Zoraban replied. His eyes flashed, the rippling of almost liquid gold, and he added, "Giver of gentle death. Succubus."

A perfect brow rose in a perfect line, and she inclined her head in approval.

"But perhaps, Zoraban, that choice should not be yours." She looked at Stephen, and her smile deepened, becoming at once full and soft.

Although only her face moved, Stephen felt a sudden lurch; he was at the core of her attention, her focus; everyone else in the room seemed to vanish. The shadows that curled around her feet and slid up her calves no longer seemed menacing; they were velvet, they were a midnight of promise and mystery. She stood at their heart, waiting. He knew then that he had never seen—and would never see again—so beautiful a woman.

His lips moved; he shook his head, as if in denial, but the sibilance of the single syllable shook the air. He knew, then, that he must look away; knew it, but could not bring himself to lose sight of her face, her eyes.

"Stephen!"

Lady Elseth's voice came to him at a great distance; he stopped walking, aware then that he did so, but did not look back. The woman of the shadows raised one hand, palm up, and then raised her second, cupping them together as if she held something precious. He wanted to lower his face into those hands and rest there.

At his side, he felt a sudden flare of magic; the tingling, the uncomfortable ache, passed quickly, melting into the distance, just as Lady Elseth's voice had.

"Stephen!"

It was a male voice this time—one he did not recognize. Distracted, he brushed it aside, lifting his hand in a gesture of annoyed impatience. He was almost there.

"Do something!" Lady Elseth said, her voice shaking. Mist left her lips; the tower was full of Winter night air, although the season would not come for months.

Zareth Kahn raised his hands in gesture, and once again, a crackle of blue light snapped against Stephen's side, only to be swallowed by the darkness.

"Zareth," Zoraban said. "Leave it be. She has called, and he has come."

"What?" The outrage in the younger mage's voice was unconcealed.

"The lore of the summoned," Zoraban continued, his eyes glinting. "He has ceded some part of himself to her keeping. Only he can disentangle it."

Zareth Kahn turned his attention upon the Master of the Order. Something passed between them then, and the younger mage bowed his dark head. "As you will it, Master," he said, but each word scraped against his throat.

"Gilliam?" Elsabet said, turning away from the mages.

"I can't," Gilliam whispered, his face pale, his sword shaking. "I can't reach him."

The shadows in the room grew thicker at the base of the wall, but they came up against a barrier a mere foot away. If Zareth Kahn and Zoraban were powerless to act in Stephen's defense, they nonetheless had power. They used it now.

Light limned the walls not shadow-claimed, sealing out the darkness, sealing in what little warmth remained. It flared, brilliant and harsh, as it sought to take the walls and failed.

"There are others," Zareth Kahn said softly.

"Are there? My power does not see them. How many?"

"Only one."

Zoraban sagged against the nearest wall. "Its shape?"

The younger man's brow creased as he concentrated. "I do not know it," he said at last. "But this is its echo." And he gestured, drawing light into a spiral that began to twist, ever faster, in the air before him. Like water draining into a deep hole, it swirled faster, and faster still, but instead of vanishing, it took shape; something hard and strange. It had arms and legs, and a head of sorts, but these were obscured by the spines that covered its body. Even its round, flat face was ridged with small, precise blades. Where fingers might have been, there were daggers or small swords.

"A blade-demon," Zoraban said, and closed his eyes. "What does it do?"

"Nothing. I assume it's waiting."

"Don't. Guard the walls well, if you've the power for it. Mine is spent." He turned wearily and offered Lady Elseth a pained smile. "It's not easy to enter the half-world," he said, and that was all the explanation he offered.

"Come, Stephen. Rest. If you serve me, I will protect you; if you surrender unto me all things that I claim, I will even give you a measure of peace. Come." She had not moved from her place in the wall, but now the shadow framed her, clothing that had almost, but not quite, fallen aside. He felt it, thick and cold, at his feet.

Run, run, huntbrother.

He was trying to. She was close. But each step was harder to take; he had almost forgotten the feel of his feet as they moved, one in front of the other, like leaden, awkward things.

But her hands were close. Only a foot more, an inch more.

Run!

Yes. He drifted into the shadows; felt them sting him with their icy, invisible teeth. He didn't care. Very gently, and with infinite satisfaction, he rested his chin in the cup of her palms.

"Very good," she said, and her voice was a benediction that kept the cold at bay. She shifted her fingers, tracing his chin softly and gently with the sharp edges of her hands. Then, still holding his face, she lifted her left hand. Blood—where had it come from?—trickled down her forefinger.

"Shall you serve me? I am Sor na Shannen. I will be your master."

He tried to nod, but he could not move his head; tried to speak, but found his tongue heavy and swollen. There was only Sor na Shannen. There was only her.

And her smile, beatific, languorous, was the most beautiful thing in the world. She brought her finger down upon his forehead and began to trace a sigil there, with his blood as bond.

He heard her scream.

He screamed as well as a golden flash of light struck his face and sent him hurtling back across the room.

"It's not possible!" The demon shouted, lifting her arms in fury. She snarled, and for a moment, although she was still beautiful in a way that only immortals can be, the glamour, with all its heavy sensuality, was gone. *"Oath-bound!"*

Zoraban's eyes widened and he turned to stare at Stephen's crumpled body. "Oath-bound?" His voice was a whisper. "That's it!" And his eyes were like the sun suddenly stripped of clouds by a strong wind; they shone bright, completely eclipsing all memory of gray or night.

They were the last words that he ever spoke.

For although Sor na Shannen was succubus, she had not raised her arms for show; shadow limned them suddenly, and with shadow came an arc of icy blue. Mage-power, focused and tightly drawn, flared from her hands, thrown like expertly wielded daggers that left a bright trail across the air.

They took the Master of the Order in the eyes.

Stephen rose in time to hear Zoraban's electric scream. He shook his head, clutching at his ears as if to halt the flow of noise.

Stephen!

Gilliam's voice, carried by bond and urgency, jerked Stephen to the side as the walls shattered. Chunks of stone crashed to the floor; shards, thin and hard, embedded themselves into the wood. Stephen looked up and saw nightmare standing beside the woman who had almost been his death. He saw her clearly; she was still strikingly beautiful, still unearthly in her glory. But her glory was shadow and darkness, and in three dreams he had seen what these forces, twinned, had wrought.

At her side was a creature that not even Stephen could mistake for anything other than demon-kin. It was tall, and covered in what appeared to be shadow-tipped blades. Frantic, Stephen reached for his sword—and then saw it. It lay, only yards away, at the feet of Sor na Shannen; already shadow was rolling over it like mist in the lowlands. He could not remember dropping it, and as the blade-demon tensed to leap, he stopped trying.

It was almost unthinkable that something so large could move so quickly or so gracefully. But the demon-kin were not bound by the laws and the forms of the mortal; Stephen felt his jacket, shirt, and skin give way to three steel tines as they whistled past, brushing his back. He clamped down on a cry and reached for his dagger, staggering and turning on the same pivot.

The shortest of the creature's fingers, if fingers they could be called, were double the length of Stephen's dagger; as the demon flexed his hands, those blades rippled, incredibly supple although they must have been heavy. It leaped, Stephen dodged—and this time, the blades pierced his left shoulder.

Someone screamed in the distance. The demon stiffened before it could leap again, and then threw both of its arms back, exposing its chest. Stephen found no opening there, no way to attack—his dagger did not have the reach of the blades that bristled, more effective than plate armor, across the creature's midsection.

He threw himself back as the arms came round again, reaching for him. Blood glistened on the blades that were fingers, and Stephen wasn't sure whether or not it was his. He fell to the ground as the creature drove its fist through the wall. Rolled, as it kicked out, attempting to separate Stephen's head from his shoulders.

Zareth Kahn's forehead was beaded with sweat and human endeavor. His dark eyes were narrowed; the muscles along his thin jaw could be counted as they stood out in relief. He knew the "Givers of gentle death," or knew of them, better than any of the order here would have guessed.

And he knew that this one, this Sor na Shannen, was no ordinary succubus. Her ability to wield magic, her uncanny threading of shadows and blue mage-fire, even the demon-lords did not always possess.

He had not acted in time to save Zoraban, and later—if there was one—he would mourn. He pressed his barriers, hard. They shimmered as he struggled to make them solid, more sure. Light crackled, describing their surface; shadows huddled, deeper and darker with each passing second, just at their edge. But through both of these, the light and the dark, he could see her eyes clearly.

A scream cut the air; he ignored it. If the blade-demon came for him, he would have no choice but death; he dare not let these barriers down for even a second. Where had she learned such power?

Lady Elseth was stiff against the wall; she made no move to aid either of her two sons, although she had traveled here to protect them. She saw the folly of that now. Her dagger, clutched tightly in white fingers, trembled against her skirts.

She had never looked at a death so certain, so close.

Is this what you send for our sons? She mouthed the words, eyes turned up to the heavens that the roof cut from view. *Is this your Death, oh, Lord?*

But no; this creature, whatever it was, was not natural—and it was obviously under the control, or command, of the woman in the wall.

Biting her lip, Elsabet lifted her arm, trying to look like stone, like wall, like anything that was beneath notice. All ladies were taught some weapon-skill. Hers had been dagger. Very carefully, she reversed her grip, seeking balance, narrowing her eyes as she tried to get the best possible view of her target. She hesitated a moment. If she threw this, she would have no weapon, no method of defense at all.

But if she did not try . . .

The dagger sailed, bolstered by the force of her throw. She bit her lip and froze in place, forgetting even to breathe. The demon didn't seem to notice her.

Until the blade was a foot away, maybe two. A hand shot up, so quickly that its movement was invisible. The dagger changed trajectory in mid-flight. The shadows that pressed Zareth Kahn back faltered; the blade gathered momentum and speed.

It found its target, but it was not the target that Lady Elseth had intended. Horrified, she watched it strike and sink into Zareth Kahn's shoulder.

Chapter Twenty-Two

IN ALL OF THE FIGHT, the wild girl had been forgotten. Certainly Stephen did not notice her; nor did Elsabet or Zareth Kahn as the barriers he had so carefully built faltered for a crucial second. And her master, Lord Elseth, lay where he had fallen when the blade-demon had thrown his arms back in a wide, deadly circle.

He was still alive.

She would have known of his death. But his thoughts were gone from her; they had fled into patterns of pain so alien that she lost the ability to follow.

It was the only ability she lost. She crawled along the ground, nuzzling his neck with her nose, her cheek. He stirred, but he did not move or speak. The scent of his blood filled her nostrils.

She rose, leaving the floor, and planted a foot on either side of her master's prone body. She felt his consciousness flicker, and then felt it gutter as his breathing slowed.

What she did next, only she understood. And she knew that Gilliam, had he been conscious, or even sleeping, would have prevented it—without ever being aware that he did so. He could not do it now. No one could.

She began to change. Her hair, wild and tangled, stretched down in a sudden flash of brown; it widened, lengthened, and grew thick and hard. Then, in the pale crackle of the blue-light that was the contest of two mages, it became iridescent. Scaly. Her nose widened and lengthened, her jaw grew, and grew again in a sudden lurch. Her shoulders doubled in width, her arms and legs became larger, more muscular. Where there had been fingers and broken, dirty nails, there were claws of gold. Where there had been flat teeth, with canines perhaps a little too sharp, there were fangs and the jaws of death.

She roared, and the tower shook.

She roared again, and the blade-demon spun, heavy and certain in movement, its quarry momentarily forgotten. Even Sor na Shannen was surprised enough to falter in her attack.

Zareth Kahn, struggling against pain, did not; he could no longer afford to let anything come between him and his concentration. He heard Sor na Shannen's frustrated curse with great satisfaction. Hands touched his shoulder, his side. He did not acknowledge them at all, but he knew that they belonged to Lady Elseth. She could not help, of course, but if she remained close to him, so much the better; his circle of protection had become exceedingly small and was unlikely to widen again.

Bleeding, dazed, his sight obscured by the blood that would not stop dripping into his eyes, Stephen of Elseth looked up, transfixed. The blade-demon had been a thing of nightmare. The creature that challenged it was a much more personal dread. He recognized its shape, its form; recognized its size and the death of its claws and fangs. Three times he had dreamed it, and once he had passed beneath its banner in the halls of the King.

He knew what must be done. He was certain of it. Fumbling, he reached for his belt, his inner pocket. His hands trembled as they closed around the horn that the girl had given him.

The girl.

He opened his mouth, but no sound came out. Shuddering, he tightened his grip upon bone and silver.

No—not now, not yet! This is not the death that you dreamed, Stephen of Elseth. Heed me.

He hesitated, and then shook his head; the words were a buzzing at his ears, and with a little effort, he hoped to drive them away. The time for action was—

Now. The beast lunged, jaws wide and snapping; the blade-demon countered with a strike. But those long, fine, deadly tines that pierced cloth and flesh with such grace and ease, met resistance in the hide of the beast; the force of the demon's lunge was enough to score scale, perhaps tickle flesh. No more.

Then the demon opened its mouth, and for the first time in the darkened, broken room, its voice was heard. It spoke with shadow in harsh, guttural syllables. Stephen did not understand them; he didn't want to. Transfixed, he held to the horn without pulling it from his jacket.

The beast snapped at air again; the demon was slightly faster, slightly smaller. It could not roll, but somehow, through some undulation that such a creature should have been unable to perform, it managed to drive a fist up and under the beast's belly.

There was pain in the answering roar—but Stephen barely understood it. For in the wake of the demon's attack, he could see what lay, unmoving, beneath the bulk of the beast. Gilliam.

Later, he would not understand what he did, or why; he could not have explained why the horn and the sounding of it became for a moment only dream. He moved along the wall, circling the blade-demon's heaving back, cringing just out of reach of those blades and those hands.

Gilliam!

There was no answer.

If a heart could be stopped and its body still live, Stephen would have had no heart. The shadows became cold and complete, and against them he sheltered only his fear. *Gil—Gil, are you alive?* Again, there was no reply.

He took a breath; it was heavy with dust and shadow. He scrambled across the ground, with an eye to the blade-demon's feet. He traveled near the wall, as far from Sor na Shannen as he could be in the small room.

Small? There were only two people in the room. Even the monsters, these living nightmares brought to life by magics and gods and the dreams of minds not mortal, had become as the shadows: dangerous, death-giving, and not quite real. The blood that still ran the course of his face, and the wounds that burned at back and arms, didn't change this.

There was Gilliam. There was Stephen.

He tried to speak, but he had no voice; tried to push the bond that had been theirs since he became of Elseth. Instead of Gilliam's answering voice, he heard William of Valentin. Saw Bryan, dead and lost. Saw Norn, lowered into a waiting grave, before Elsabet's cold, stony silence.

He crawled, and the ruptured wood beneath his fingers reminded him of Soredon of Elseth. Hunter Lord. Dead. Stephen was no longer twenty-two; he was eight—and without Gilliam of Elseth he had no life; he was empty.

Stephen was afraid. But he moved.

Gilliam, damn you, answer me! Are you dead?

But no, no, he couldn't be dead. Surely Stephen would know if he were dead; he would feel it. *GILLIAM!*

Splinters cut his wrists; sharp, small bits of rock dug into his skin. He crawled. Blood touched his eyes, but he let it run. He didn't want to lose sight of Gilliam and the shadow that lay across his back. If he could see his face, even his face, it would help.

But his face was buried against the floor.

Two feet. Three feet. Above him, as if in the heavens, this clash of beast and demon, two titans in a battle that Stephen wanted no place or part in. Four feet. Five. He could not look up now, although the feet of the beast, like the feet of the great, jeweled dragons that were myth and legend, had not left their perch on either side of his Hunter Lord. Gilliam was her—it's—treasure. But he was more than that to Stephen. Not master, as he was to the girl, and not lover, as Cynthia was to Stephen, but brother.

Huntbrother.

The tenth foot. The last inch. Stephen reached out with the tips of his fingers and touched Gilliam's hand. A shock rippled up his arm, lending him strength.

He prayed that the beast would continue its fight without looking down, but even had it done so, he would not have let go. He inched forward, and forward again, until his grip on Gilliam's hand was as solid as he could make it. Then he inched up the slack arm. Taking a breath to steady himself, planting his knees against the ground as a brace, Stephen *pulled*.

Gilliam had always been the heavier of the two, but Stephen had never felt it as a solid truth until now. He pulled again, harder, gained more height as he was forced to find leverage. He cried out loudly, furiously—and silently to any person in the room that was not Gilliam of Elseth. But he did not let go.

And the beast did not stop him. Instead, although Stephen barely realized it, it moved to interpose its body fully between the blade-demon and the Elseth Lord and huntbrother, as Stephen at last managed to drag Gilliam away from the fight, and to the safety of the farthest wall.

He did not know what Gilliam's injuries were. Could not tell if his limbs or ribs were broken, if his vital organs had been pierced. Blood was everywhere along Gilliam's chest, arms, and legs. Stephen tried to think, but he could not; all he could do was pull Gilliam close and hold him, tightly as William had held Bryan's body on the green before the altar.

Elsabet saw them at last, huddled against the rock of the wall that faced the demon, the shadow, and Sor na Shannen. Her face, already white, could pale no further, and she had no breath for words. She began to move, and Zareth Kahn caught her arm, restraining her.

"Don't break the circle, Lady," he said, his voice tight. "I cannot protect you."

But what of my sons? She wanted to shout it; she didn't. The fingers that dug into her arm were solid, strong. As she hesitated, he grunted. The barriers that lit the room gave ground, closing more tightly around them. Zareth Kahn cursed, unmindful of manners and propriety. She cursed with him, but silently, silently.

The barriers fell back again, bowing to the greater pressure of the less-exhausted mage. All of her life, Elsabet had known of magic, and magic's existence—but it had been as real as any God save the Hunter God. It would never be so comfortably distant again.

Zareth Kahn turned to her. She could see the dark circles beneath his narrowed eyes. The line of his jaw was thin and tense; his dark hair clung to his face in damp, thin curls. "I'm sorry, Lady," he whispered.

She had no weapon with which to aid him. Although her dagger was within easy reach, she did not dare to pull it from its sheath of flesh, and had she done so, she wouldn't have thrown it again. That had cost them much; perhaps this battle itself.

So she did what any intelligent person would have done in her place. She prayed.

First, to the Hunter God, that merciless scion of death and fertility that had so marked her land and her people; that had succored those in her care while destroying the two men who had become entwined with each root of her strength. Her eyes were drawn by the flash of blades and scales; by the roar of a beast and the dissonant syllables of a demon. Perhaps He had already answered a prayer that had not yet formed; it was not enough. Without pause, she continued, one hand now near-burrowed into Zareth Kahn's shoulder, one pressed firmly against her lips. She prayed to the Mother, for she knew of the Mother's mercy; she begged Luck to turn a smile upon them; she pleaded with Justice to intervene.

She was good at prayer; she had prayed just so, once a year, for all of her adult life—and for much of her childhood as well, a shadow at her mother's side. She knew how to draw strength from pleas; knew how to lose her fears, for a moment, in their intensity, although fear was the base of her whispers by the altar-side. And she knew that though the fiercest of prayers remain unanswered, the time taken to utter them gave her the space in which to find the dignity to face all travails as the noble Lady that she was.

But this one time, she was wrong.

Mercifully, gloriously wrong.

There was the sharp song of a crackle, and above them all, human, demon, and god-born beast, the fierce blue of cloudless sky destroyed the darkness of shadow. It was so total, so complete in its presence, that Elsabet of Elseth only recognized it as mage-light when it began to shimmer.

"The Order!" Zareth Kahn whispered, as his eyes began to shine. "The Order is here!" Hope gave him strength, and with a great sweep of his uninjured arm, he strengthened his barrier, pushing it in one great jolt to the foot of the wall. There, illuminated briefly by a power that was not hers, Sor na Shannen's face was a study in dismay. And then, the shadows roiled about her feet, drawing up and ever up, until she was consumed by them.

Zareth Kahn cursed and surged forward, only to be halted by Elsabet's strong grip. The tines of the blade-demon whistled past, an inch from his chest. "She escapes!" he shouted.

Light struck the shadows, hard; it was not the multi-layered wall that Zareth Kahn had built, but rather the thick, sudden blast of lightning. Rock sprayed up in answer to that strike. The shadows cleared as if by gust of strong wind, and beyond them, for the first time since the hole in the wall had been made, Elsabet could see the halls, and the stairs, beyond. They were full now; men and women in the robes of the Order—and some perhaps less formally clad, stood arrayed there, arms held out, hands twisting in an incredibly complicated dance.

Zareth Kahn could see this as well, but he did not let his barriers drop. Instead, he pulled in just the smallest filament of their power, draining the light above him at their unspoken consent.

"The blade-demon," he said, his voice quiet, although the words resounded like a shout in Elsabet's ears, "must be destroyed. The beast that fights it must not."

The sky of their magic began to twist in a spiral of blue and crackling white, a pool being slowly stirred. It gained momentum, moving more quickly with each turn, each spin, until it was dizzying to gaze upon.

And then, in a sudden surge, it came *down*, funneled by the will of the mages of the Order. The blade-demon, arms extended, body rippling in mid-leap, was struck. It screamed and froze. The light intensified until it could not be gazed upon by any of the untrained; eyes watering and narrowed, Elsabet looked away.

But she heard its cries, smelled the charring of demon flesh. And she heard one other cry, wordless, that she recognized: Stephen's voice. Her heart froze, and all danger, all magic, all unnatural combat, were forgotten in that instant. Wheeling, she let go of Zareth Kahn's arm and stumbled toward the wall. Her eyes still watered, and only the glow of the mage-light penetrated the darkness that same light had left her for vision. But she knew where the cry had come from. Knew what it must mean.

"Stephen!"

He didn't answer; she didn't expect him to, although she had hoped that he might. Her fingers trailed against cool stone as she groped along the wall. Her sight began to clear, and as it did, she saw someone huddled against the floor, rocking under the weight of an unwieldy burden. She dropped to her knees as she approached; felt the crisp fabric of her crinoline brush against her legs.

"Stephen?" Her voice was a whisper now.

He looked up. "We won," he said, whispering as well. But his arms were tight, and had her vision been just a little clearer, she would have seen that his fingers were white and shaking.

"Yes," she said gently. Her eyes clouded, but this time there was no magic to blame. "Gilliam?" She reached out, slowly, and touched her son's still face. "Gil?"

"He won't answer," Stephen said, his voice as flat as his eyes. But he allowed her to touch his Hunter, and she found, against the side of his neck, the thing that she sought.

"Stephen—he's still alive."

Stephen looked at her blankly.

"You can carry him, but we have to see a doctor or a healer. Quickly. He's—he's still here."

"But he won't answer."

"I don't know if he can. Are you so certain that he's dead?"

Stephen looked down at the blood that was set and sticky, no longer sure that it was Gilliam's and not his own. "I don't know."

"Then he *is* alive," she replied, standing. "You would know if he were not, Stephen. There wouldn't be any question, any doubt. Now, come!" She straightened her shoulders, and the tilt of her chin held the power of long years of authority. She did not expect to be disobeyed, and Stephen, exhausted by loss of blood and near-frantic worry, responded automatically, and although he lifted Gilliam at Lady Elseth's command, the weight he carried was diminished by the force, the absolute surety, of her words.

It was the beast that stopped him, swinging the wide trunk of its neck forward. Its eyes were dark, almost entirely black, but as it studied Stephen, he felt the last of his fear drain away. If this was the Hunter's Death, he had labored years under a nightmare that would not become reality.

It snuffled a little, and then brushed its snout against Gilliam's chest.

"We have to go," Stephen said softly. "To take care of your master."

The gleaming, iridescent head bobbed uncertainly to one side, its eyes flickering in the darkness, even as the last of the shadow faded. It turned, suddenly and swiftly, although so large a creature should have been slower, more cumbersome in movement.

Stephen followed its gaze as it surveyed the ruined wall, and the men and women that seemed to go on past torches and lamplight down the winding staircase. "It's over," he said, equally softly.

The beast growled; the air around Stephen's ears buzzed with the sound of that throaty voice. And then, before Stephen's eyes, it began to change. He watched in wonder, and almost in terror, as the scales seemed to dwindle and gather in a cowl around its neck. It lifted its forepaws from the ground, and reared up on its hind legs, and the golden claws, now rimmed with darkness that might have been demon-blood, became flat, dull, and smaller. The jaw shrank, the head altered, and in a minute a naked, dirty girl stood before him, her head still cocked in an odd, questioning angle.

For the first time, Stephen felt no resentment and no unease as he gazed upon her. Her body was small, almost delicate, and were it not for dirt, and one or two long scratches, it would have been perfect, if a little boyish. Her hair was still a messy tangle, but its deep brown-black framed her silent face. She opened her mouth, and spoke.

In a whine.

He nodded, although he did not understand what she said, and began to walk, quickly now, as urgency grew, toward the open wall and the magicked door, still closed, that stood in its frame.

Before he reached it, the mages made way, and two women stepped out of the gathered, silent crowd into what remained of the Master's study. Stephen was the only person present who recognized both of them. He would have bowed, but that would have meant letting go of Gilliam.

Evayne, the mysterious woman of the wyrd and the night of demons, came first. Her dark blue cloak was draped around her, like the shadows had been around Sor na Shannen, but her cowl rested along her shoulders, and the blackness of her hair, drawn back, still framed her white face, her violet eyes.

At her side, lips pressed into a thin line, and eyes circled by weariness, stood Vivienne, the Priestess of the Mother. She was dressed in brown and gold and white, and her hands, as she lifted them, palm up, were steady.

"Lady," Stephen whispered. He took three steps, and stopped when he reached her side.

Her dark eyes widened. "Lay him down at once," she said, her voice almost harsh.

He did, but gently, placing Gilliam of Elseth at the feet of the Priestess. White, ringed hands touched Gilliam's neck carefully, and then moved out to span his chest. "You were right," she said, speaking over her shoulder to the woman in midnight blue who had not moved or spoken. "And I apologize for the harshness of my temper. He would not have survived the journey to the temple. Do not move him further, Stephen of Elseth. I have him now, and I will help as I am able."

Stephen nodded, and knelt by her side.

"I should have known," Vivienne added, in her slightly sharp tone, "that it would be one or the other of you. The night had that darkness about it. Breathe easy, huntbrother. If he can be saved at all, I will save him."

He recognized a dismissal when he heard it and made to rise. The girl did not, and one other came to kneel at the Priestess' feet. It was Lady Elseth.

This is the first time, she thought, head bowed, body stiff with control, *that you have answered my prayers*. She wanted to cry now, for the first time in years, but dignity and station forbade it. She could almost feel the warmth and heat that radiated from Vivienne's hands, and she was grateful for it, although she longed to touch her son and feel for herself the strength of his pulse, the beat of his heart, the tickle of his breath.

She knew better than to interfere with the healer's communion, and clasped her hands in her lap instead. She was not going to lose her son this night. She let that sink in, let herself believe it. Glancing up, she saw the eyes of the strange woman who had led the Priestess in. They were fixed upon Vivienne and Gilliam with such intensity that Elsabet could not help but notice it.

There was something odd about the stare, though; something strange about the woman. She was, to look at her, very young—no older than Maribelle, and perhaps younger—but her face was hard, emotionless, and her lips were drawn in a line that held no mirth, nor ever seemed likely to.

Then she turned, ever so slightly, and met Lady Elseth's gaze. They locked eyes, and for a second Elsabet caught a glimpse of something younger in the woman's face. A hint of wistful envy. Before she could even name it, it was gone, and the ice was back in place.

"Lady Elseth," the woman said, and bowed. "I am Evayne."

*　　*　　*

"Zoraban is dead," Zareth Kahn said flatly, wincing as the dagger was at last pulled from his shoulder. He felt the warmth of blood and the sting of the cut; it was deep.

The older man who attended him nodded grimly, although it had not been a question. "We know. Sela attends his body now, with Jareme. Sit *still*, Zar. You only make it worse, and I fear that the Priestess will have neither the time or the energy to attend to you."

"She wouldn't have had to," the mage said, clenching his teeth and attempting to sit still, as Elodra so quaintly put it, "had you deigned to notice the shadow-magic and arrive less tardily."

Elodra raised a frosted brow, and tugged tightly at the bandages he manipulated by hand. His was a slender, almost arch face. "Zareth," he said softly.

Zareth Kahn flushed heavily and looked away. "You didn't deserve that," he conceded.

"We didn't feel the shadow-magic," Elodra said. "Until we came to the tower's height itself." He knotted the bandage and then examined it more closely. Satisfied, he stepped back. "Is this to do with Krysanthos?"

"I don't know. He wasn't here, if that's what you're asking, and I didn't feel his signature." Free from Elodra's fussing—it was something that Elodra did well, and did constantly, which was why he also handled most of the Order's financial dealings—Zareth Kahn flexed his shoulder, winced, and then sagged. "But if you didn't—"

"The woman," Elodra replied, turning his gaze upon the diminutive figure who stood in the isolation of her midnight-blue robes and her unearthly strangeness. "She came, with the Priestess of the Mother, and bade us hurry for the sake of your lives. I started up on my own, but she insisted that we gather the brethren before we made our ascent." Elodra shivered. "I well understand why, now."

Zareth Kahn nodded, and then slid his hands over his face. It was safe, now, to shudder; to feel pain and the hint of a loss that the Order might never fully recover from. And in scant days, perhaps hours, he would also begin to question, to dissect, to understand, treating the events of this night as all things, in the end, were treated by the Order of Knowledge.

But here and now, his mage-power guttered, and the chill already beginning to set his teeth on edge, he had only questions with no depth and no force behind them. Shivers turned to shudders; he curled into the floor, bringing his knees to his chest.

Elodra was at his side at once, offering help. No, not offering, not precisely. Few indeed were the mage-born who resisted any of Elodra's assistance for long. And one caught by mage-fever had less chance than most. Almost docile, the second-circle mage allowed himself to be pulled to his feet, braced, and led out of the ruins of the tower.

*   *   *

Although Gilliam's injuries were healed, he had suffered much blood loss, and over his loud objections, was taken by mages out of the tower's rooms. The girl accompanied him, circling his carriers in an odd hop and jump step, and Lady Elseth walked, shivering and pale, at the side of his stretcher. Vivienne, Priestess of the Mother, was wan and pale. Only with the Hunter-born and their brothers was the cost of the healing—physically and emotionally—so one-sided. She was glad of it, or she would be, later.

But Stephen remained in the room until the last of the stragglers had left it. Then, and only then, he bowed once, deeply, to Evayne.

Evayne's smile was a bitter one. "Stephen of Elseth," she said, her voice soft and alien. Where, in the dreams, she had been power and mystery, in this room, at this moment, her words were no different in strength than the words any woman might speak. In such a situation. Indeed, perhaps because his vision of her had been the object of fear and confusion for so long, he found her almost disappointing.

"Evayne," Stephen said, stepping forward. "Twice now you've saved our lives. I should thank you for it."

The smile became more edged, the eyes colder—violets hit by a sudden, deadly frost. "But you won't, Elseth huntbrother."

The vehemence in the words took Stephen by surprise; he stepped back a pace, although she had not so much as lifted a hand. Then, before he could speak, she passed a hand over her eyes. The folds of her robes changed and fell as she moved, and he thought of shadow again. Natural shadow, of the kind that occurred only upon the clearest of nights, with the moon in her glory.

"I am sorry," she whispered, as her hand fell away over shut lids. "That wasn't necessary. I have never been good at beginnings, Stephen. Let us try this again."

He nodded, although he didn't understand. "This isn't the beginning," he said tentatively.

"No," she replied. "And, yes. I will not leave you when sleep does, and I will not leave you to flee. You have questions, and I carry news; we will share these together before I depart." She shivered again and seemed to shrink inward.

Stephen moved slowly forward, and held out his arm as stiff support. He looked down at his sleeve, wondering why it was so dark, when it had become so, and whether or not the shadows of her fingers would pass through his forearm instead of resting there.

"Don't." Once again, she was ice as she pulled back, staring at his proffered arm as if it were a sword. "I am not so weak, or so old, to require your aid."

"You don't have to be weak or old to be weary," Stephen said, but he stepped back and lowered his hands to his side. "Evayne." His voice was soft. "If you do not wish help, I won't offer it again."

She shook her head, looking down at her feet in silence, as if suddenly aware of her poor manners—if manners and the politenesses of society could be an issue in the ruined tower of a dead mage. "You have questions to ask me. Why don't you ask them now?"

"The questions I have I can't ask without Gilliam."

"No?"

"No. He is my Lord, as you are my wyrd."

"Don't," she said again, but less sharply. She lifted a hand as if in surrender.

"Come," he was gentle, as if he spoke soothing nonsense to a wild creature that stood petrified just out of reach. "It's dark here. There will be light in the morning, and perhaps we both need it."

"Before the morning, there's always the dreaming," she said, and then bit her lip. Her teeth trembled there for a moment, and then her expression flowed into a still, stately mask; she looked older, more regal—a thing of vision or wyrd. "Lead the way, then, Stephen of Elseth."

He did, although he had to force himself not to offer her his arm again. He stepped carefully over rubble and dust, lifting his hand to cover his head as he passed below the edge of the ruined wall closest to the ceiling.

Evayne watched him go.

Why, she thought to herself, for she was very, very weary, *can you never choose someone I can hate?*

There was no answer, of course, and she expected none as she followed Stephen's awkward gait. But she prayed as she walked, that he would be the last.

She knew that this, too, would not be answered.

Chapter Twenty-Three

EVAYNE DID NOT DISAPPEAR with the troubled dreams of the short night. By the time that dawn had cleared the remnants of darkness from the sky, she was awake and waiting.

Or so it appeared to Stephen of Elseth, as he entered the long hall that served as both study and library to the wing of the building that only the mages were called to. He saw her by the large arch of a window, as the sun streamed in through pale yellow panes of thick, perfect glass. She stood, facing out into the gardens, positioned beneath the peak of the window's height. The sun cast her shadow in a thin dark line against the empty tables at her back.

"That's her?" Gilliam said quietly, catching Stephen's attention.

"Yes."

"She doesn't look the same as she did when she saved us from the demon-kin."

"No," Stephen replied, as he began to move again. Still, it comforted him to hear it—because until Gilliam had spoken those words, in this place, he had not remembered it. A shadow lifted, perhaps a hint of the doubt that Stephen had not even felt strongly enough to place into words. "Sit still, Gil."

But Gilliam, not used to this odd contraption of a chair and wheels, could not. The girl who walked on his other side suddenly reached down and butted her head into his shoulder playfully.

"And keep your arms away from your sides."

"Yes, Priestess," Gilliam replied smartly. He cursed when Stephen whacked him suddenly on the top of the head. "Stephen," he began, as he grabbed the girl's arm before she could retaliate on his behalf.

"Gilliam," his huntbrother countered. "This is not the time or place. We've come to speak with—"

"Me." And the dark-robed figure at the windows turned.

She was hard to look at; the sun at her back made a shadow of her, a figure of darkness. Stephen could make out the outline of her chin and brow; he could see the light pass through stray strands of her hair, so he knew her hood was back and at her shoulders. But her hands were at her sides, and she was so perfectly still she could almost have been a dark statue, an ornament in a library for scholars and students, to be remarked upon and then forgotten as part of the daily surroundings.

"I am here," she said quietly, "and I have much to tell you both." She stepped into the room, away from the frame of blinding light that kept her obscured. "Shall we start?" She lifted a hand and curved her fingers gently in summons.

"We should wait for Lady Elseth and Zareth Kahn," Stephen replied, rolling Gilliam, with a grunt, over the edge of the carpet. "The Priestess will be here, too, I think. She's been tending Gilliam, but says she hasn't recovered enough to finish until this eve."

Evayne continued to walk toward them, and as Stephen's eyes grew used to the normal light of the room, he froze. For although her face was familiar, she was not the same woman who he had tried to comfort the evening before.

No, her chin was harsher, more defined, and her brow was lined; her eyes, although still violet, were lined as well. She walked, and carried herself, as Lady Elseth did, and would do in the future—as a woman who wears age and wisdom as tokens of power.

He recovered quickly, although the words did not return as easily as they might have. Instead, he busied himself, arranging Gilliam's chair at Evayne's dark side.

"None of your companions will arrive," this Evayne replied, with just a hint of bitter amusement to turn her lips at the corners.

"None?" It was said quickly; harshly. Stephen frowned as he met Evayne's eyes directly for the first time that day.

"No, Stephen of Elseth," she said, dropping her smile and her voice, "but not because I have magicked them or caused them any harm."

He had the grace to blush, and she, to look away.

"Go," she said, "and look outside for only a moment. You will understand, then, as much as I can explain to you. Do not ask me questions about what you see, Stephen. Even if I wished it, I could not answer them."

Reluctantly, he let go of Gilliam's strange chair and turned to the window that towered above him, stretching for the ceiling and the sky. The girl, as ever, stayed at Gilliam's side; Stephen might not have left his Lord otherwise. But whatever it was that Evayne thought he might see escaped his notice, and he almost turned away in disappointment.

The sky was blue and lightly clouded. The grass was perfectly cut, and rolled into distinct, velvet flatness—even around the base of the trees that topped the building's height by many, many feet. Flowers, in precise rows, grew against the base of the walls, gates, and walkways. Small animals, with more temerity than wit, ran across the green, and birds of all sizes cut across the air between ground, tree, and fountain.

And then he knew what the subtle strangeness was; knew why Evayne thought that none, after he and Gilliam, would arrive. One of those birds was frozen in the air, iridescent wings stretched wide, feet forming an outward strut inches away from the nearest fountain's ledge. It did not land; it did not move. As he shifted his focus, he saw that nothing did.

Not even breeze disturbed the Order's garden.

He turned slowly to face her and noted that she did not squint into the sunlight. But her face, with sun to light it, was still as pale as it had been last night, her eyes still as brilliant.

"I . . . understand." He bowed.

"Good. Explain it to me," Gilliam said. He shifted in the chair, winced, and settled back into his former position.

"I think—I think that time doesn't turn outside."

"Very good, Stephen. But within this room, it does, and we have little of it. This is costly, even if necessary, and I cannot hold it long; the world here is already too hectic and too busy."

He wanted to ask her why she needed to perform this magic, if magic it was, at all. Why not just speak with Zareth Kahn and Lady Elseth and the Mother's Priestess? He did not ask; her glance strayed.

"Hello, wild one," Evayne said quietly. She held out one hand, and after a moment, the wild girl—Gilliam's only packmate in residence—stepped forward almost timidly. "You found them, I see." Although the girl wore a simple shift—one loose enough not to be immediately discarded—she was hardly decent. Evayne, if she noted this at all, did not remark upon it.

The girl opened her mouth in a whine and bark.

"You are well. Don't worry; we will not fail."

"You—you know her?"

Evayne nodded. "I do now." She turned away from the girl. "And I know you, Stephen, quite well. I apologize if I confused you last night. It was—the first time I'd met you, and I am not good at first meetings, even though many years have passed." She raised a hand, looked at it carefully, and then let it drop.

"Years?"

"It hasn't been years yet, has it?" she said, almost to herself. "No, never mind it. As I said, I cannot hold us above Time forever; already I tire."

"Who are you?" Stephen asked softly.

"Evayne."

Exasperated, he opened his mouth; she raised a hand and gently swatted his words away, as if they were insects.

"You said, last night, that you would answer our questions," he said, undeterred by her cool gesture. His arms, clothed in the velvet that told his station, he crossed against his chest. Gilliam recognized the look on Stephen's face.

"I was young then, Stephen. If you prefer to think so, call me liar. But I am not what I was, and I cannot answer the questions that I know you will ask."

"Time?" he asked, but it was almost a sneer, he was so frustrated.

Her face lost the last of its warmth, and there had been little enough of it. "Would you become as I, Stephen of Elseth?" Her shoulders fell back, and her chin, proud and harsh, came up. "Would you walk a separate path, a separate time, from any other?"

He didn't understand the question.

"Tomorrow," she said, "you will wake and your Hunter will wake; you will go and breakfast and speak of the things that concern you, the worries you share.

"Next year, you will marry the woman you choose—should you choose—and you will eventually father children. You will watch them grow, and you will love them as you are able, regardless of how they change. You will understand them because you will have had the time to share, the time to form the bond.

"Tomorrow," her voice grew cooler, but softer, and her eyes became eerie in their remoteness, "I will wake to the clamor of war on a distant plain. People that I have not yet met will die there—and perhaps ten years from now I will have seen enough of them to mourn their passing in some human fashion.

"For I have walked away from Time's path, and forged a path of my own. None can walk it, Stephen; none can follow it with me.

"If you ask me questions, perhaps I will prove too weak to turn them aside, and you may find yourself above Time's path—and quite alone."

He did not doubt the threat, but doubted the weakness; in her voice there was ice, and that ice was not brittle.

"I'm sorry," she said suddenly, although she did not sound at all contrite. "There is no time. Let me tell you what I must. Come, child, sit—either at my feet or at your master's. Do not distract him until I have finished."

The wild girl tilted a head until her ear was almost level with her shoulder. Then she nodded, which looked even more peculiar, and folded up into a quiet little ball at Gilliam's feet.

Without further preamble, Evayne said, "You must leave Breodanir and travel to Essalieyan."

Gilliam's eyes narrowed.

"Essalieyan is the heart of the world," Evayne continued, serene now. "In it, there is much knowledge, much that is old, much that is wise or powerful. It is there you must find what you seek."

"What do we 'seek'? Why in the Hells would we travel to Essalieyan?" To say that Gilliam growled would have been inaccurate, but he did convey the sense of a growl by the curl of his lip and the lowering of his head.

"Because in Essalieyan, Lord Elseth, you will find a cure for the ailments of your companion."

Involuntarily, Gilliam looked down at the brown—and for the moment, un-
tangled—hair of the wild girl. He had not yet named her, and although he felt,
no, knew her to be of his pack, he could not bring himself to do so. He reached
down and stroked her fine hair. Answers. Essalieyan.

Prejudice—for no one from Breodanir could ever forget the damage done by
foreign nonbelievers—hope, and fear struggled within him. It was Stephen who
spoke next, and he spoke to break the silence, after contemplating her directive.

"Lady, you ask much without explanation."

"Yes," she said, bowing her head. Her brow wrinkled; she massaged it gently
with her fingertips. "Stephen, you will be free from your wyrd only in Essalieyan.
The demon-kin will hunt you, and only in Essalieyan is there any hope of refuge."

"Why will they hunt me? What do they seek?"

Silence answered him, silence and the remote chill of her expression. She
watched his face; he felt her eyes, unblinking, scrape across his brow. His skin
tingled as if he had endured a great cold before entering warmth. *Essalieyan.* It was
a whisper of a word, a youthful dream, a story. He looked down and met Gilliam's
eyes. Gilliam nodded. "Evayne, Lady, what you offer us, we accept. We will travel,
if possible, to Essalieyan. Shall we venture to the capital, Averalaan?"

"Yes," she answered softly. Then, her eyes narrowed as if the light from the
window had grown too intense. "But you must leave at once."

"At once? Impossible."

"Is it so?"

Stephen looked away. He had known, somehow, that she would ask them to
leave immediately; he had his answer prepared. "We cannot make the trek and be
guaranteed to return in time for the Sacred Hunt; it's a journey of two or three
months. We will have to wait until the Hunt is called before we take our leave, or
we lose our lands, our titles, and our people."

"If you wait for the Hunt," Evayne said, turning her back upon him, "you
doom Breodanir."

Silence reigned in the wake of her words. The words themselves seemed to re-
verberate with a life of their own; they had a truth to them that Evayne was conduit for, no more.

"Will you go? I cannot travel with you," she added, a little bitterly, "but I will
see you on the road, and in the city itself."

Stephen looked back at his Hunter.

Gilliam was silent, almost brooding. For it was Gilliam who held the title and
the lands that were forfeit if they did not return in time to Hunt at the King's—
and the God's—call. "Could we make it?" he asked, his voice a whisper.

"If traveling conditions are good; if there are no bandits and no problems in the
free towns; if the mountain pass is not heavy with snow—don't forget, it's late
enough in the season. That would leave us with scant weeks, maybe two in total,

in the city of the Twin Kings before we had to retreat. And once again, we depend on perfect conditions of travel if we are to return to the King's City and the Sacred Hunt."

"And how long will this thing take?" Gilliam said speaking directly to Evayne's dark back. She turned slowly, glancing over her shoulder, showing the perfect profile of her face.

"I do not know."

"And what exactly must we do?" Gilliam said, bringing his hands down hard on the armrests of his chair.

"I am not certain; I can't see it clearly."

"That's what I thought." He was silent again. Almost brooding. Stephen felt his Hunter's anger and his fear, his hope and his unease, as they braided themselves around the bond that he and Gilliam shared. And then, almost at once, they went slack as Gil raised his head, and his voice, again.

"Evayne."

"Yes?"

"What is her name?"

The question was unexpected, even to Evayne, who stared a moment in confusion before she realized who Gilliam was speaking of. Then a smile shadowed her face for the briefest of instants. "Her name is Espere."

The wild girl, so named, suddenly raised her head and barked. If she had had a tail, Stephen was sure it would be thumping away at the carpet.

Gilliam started to stand, which galvanized his huntbrother into action. That action, unfortunately, was to offer an arm as support, rather than to force an errant Hunter back to his seat. Gilliam would stand, and Stephen, knowing that this was not a point that he could win without a protracted and public argument, gave in gracefully.

"Evayne, mage, or whatever you are, we will go to the city. With Espere."

At this, Evayne laughed, although the laugh was a gentle one. Then the laughter faded, and she turned to face them both, fully. "He chose Espere's protectors well, when he sent her to you. Listen, both of you. Listen well. What I speak here will not be repeated." Her arms, she raised to either side; stiff and dark-robed, she became a mortal cross. Her eyes, violet, became darker still, irises spreading across the whites until nothing human remained.

When she spoke, her voice was a chorus.

Just as Teos' voice had been.

"The Covenant has been broken in spirit; the portals are open; the Gods are bound. Go forth to the Light of the World, and find the Darkness. Keep your oath; fulfill your promise. The road must be taken, or the Shining City will rise anew."

"What oath?" Stephen shouted, for the voices were a storm; even when the words had finished, the air was heavy with their texture. Pain and peace, age and youth, love and hatred called out through Evayne's lips, and then lingered a moment in her eyes. *"What oath?"* His words were heavy; sharp. The Shining City was a thing of legend—and a legend so fell and so dark that in the end, it claimed Morrel's life at the dawn of time.

Violet eyes cleared as Evayne lowered her arms; she had offered him no answer. "I thank you both," she said softly, her voice once again her own. "But I must travel now." Speaking had diminished her somehow.

"That was a God's voice," Stephen said.

"Yes. I am your wyrd, Stephen. You know which God speaks through me. And if you do not, I cannot speak of it. I must leave."

"What in the Hells did it mean? What oath are we supposed to keep? What is the darkness and what is the light?"

"I don't know." Bitterness returned to her face. "I only know from my own experience that my advice to you is sound—you must go to Essalieyan." When his eyes narrowed, she added, "I am no more god than you, Stephen of Elseth. Do you think that my God will grant me permission to enter his counsels, any more than yours does?" She turned, then, and began to walk away.

"Wait!" Stephen said, swiftly following her. He caught her shoulder in a tight grip, and she drew herself up to her full height. She did not pull away, but instead pivoted to face him.

"Yes?"

"Last night—last night you . . ." He didn't know what he wanted to say, and looked away from the pale violet of her steady glance. "Did you know, last night, what would happen to us? What we would choose?"

Her brows drew together into a peppered line; the wrinkles there deepened enough that it was clear what expression had formed them. "Yes," she answered at last, as if the words had been dragged from her. "But I did not know that now you would ask me of it. I was bitter in my youth," she added, and her lips turned up in a simile of a smile, and of wisdom. Neither reached her eyes. He saw her age clearly, but more clearly saw the weakness and the fear that he associated with only the very youthful.

"And not now?" He pressed her.

"I don't know. Am I?" Before he could answer, she reached up and touched his cheek, trailing its hollow with her fingers until they trembled off the line of his jaw. As he opened his mouth in shock, she withdrew her hand. There was an intimacy, a knowledge, a familiarity in her touch that Stephen was afraid of. She started to speak, and then shook her head and pulled away. He did not stop her.

But she turned again as she reached the door. "Time will start the moment I leave."

Gilliam, Lord Elseth, Stephen of Elseth, and the newly named Espere, watched her with wide, unblinking eyes.

It was to Stephen that she spoke, and the next words were so odd they were almost incomprehensible, although they were simple and plain.

"Stephen—when I was young, you were kind to me. Will you—can you—" She looked away. Drew herself up. Smiled ruefully, and shook her head. "We will meet again, you and I. Be as merciful as you can."

"She's gone," Stephen said quietly when Zareth Kahn pushed the door open and lightly stepped into the room. The scene that greeted his eyes was almost cozy; wood burned in the curtained fireplace in the room's northernmost wall, and around it, Gilliam and the wild girl sat, eyes drawn to the flame, attention absorbed by what they saw flickering in its heart.

It was late enough in the season to be chilly here, but the mages rarely burned wood at this time; they chose instead to don heavier robes and save the heat for more dire need. Zareth Kahn opened his mouth to mention this, then shut it again on the words.

Gilliam was quiet and pale, and the girl, not touching her Lord, but still by his side, even more so. Were it not for the windows, with their open view of birds and greenery, he might have thought it winter.

He cleared his throat, but before he could speak, the door at his back opened rather awkwardly. Navigating its wide, heavy swing, he stepped quickly out of the way as Lady Elseth entered the room.

She was severely dressed in heavy wool skirts and a rather stiff jacket; it was as if she, too, felt the cold here. "Well?" she said quietly, as all eyes turned to face her.

"Evayne is gone," Stephen replied.

Lady Elseth nodded mildly, as if to say that she had expected as much. She walked over to her sitting son and inspected his ribs with all the nonchalance of a worried mother. "What did she have to say?" she asked in a casual tone of voice that fooled no one.

"We're to travel," Gilliam replied, leaving off the preamble that would have been Stephen's opening, "to Essalieyan and the city of Averalaan. We leave within the week."

Lady Elseth had twice undertaken that trek on matters of commerce and trade before Gilliam's father had passed away and the duties of the Elseth demesne demanded her attention and her presence. It took her less than a minute to pale. Her eyes grew round and her hands fell to her sides as her fingers began to curl into the heavy, thick wool of her skirts. But her voice didn't waver. "Why?"

"I don't know," Gilliam said, and looked to Stephen's back.

"What did she say?" Zareth Kahn stepped between Lady Elseth and her adopted son. "What did Evayne say?"

"That Breodanir will fall if we fail to leave." Stephen stared into the fire, seeing in the flames neither warmth nor comfort. "I believe her," he added softly.

"Does she know what this may mean to Elseth?" Elsabet's eyes narrowed as she waited for the answer.

"She knows."

"And you know it," Lady Elseth said. "Very well." She swallowed and then pulled her hands from their nervous dance. "A week is not long enough to see to all of your needs. But—"

"It has to be long enough," Stephen said, and turned then to face her. His eyes were ringed, his face pale.

"This has to do with the . . . the demons, doesn't it?"

"What else can it possibly be?"

"Stephen." Gilliam, hand on either wheel, rolled his chair forward until he could touch his huntbrother's hand. "We faced them last night, and we won."

Stephen nodded, but it was clear that he took no strength from his Hunter's words. He was afraid. Time had begun, as Evayne had promised, the moment she left the room. Time turned; the birds touched branches and left the ground, the wind bobbed in leaves, teasing them away from their trees.

The shadows grew darker, although the sun was bright. The Hunter's Horn hung, heavy, at his side. He had the uncanny sense that if he left this city, this kingdom, he would never return to it again.

And everything that he loved was in Breodanir.

"Lady," he said, and bowed to the woman who was his mother. "We will have two weeks in the city of the Twin Kings to see to our task."

"What is your task?" the mage asked, crossing his heavily clad arms, daring to interrupt their discourse. Stephen had expected that Zareth Kahn would be irritated, but instead the mage seemed peculiarly intense and intent. His thin face, shadowed by lack of sleep, looked sharp—the edge of a personality, honed and pressed a little too close for comfort.

"Find the Light of the World. Find its darkness. Keep our oath."

"In other words," the mage replied, "you haven't the barest of notions." He shook his long dark hair, and his eyes became very bright. "But I may have, at the end of this week. With your leave, Lord Elseth, Stephen, I will travel with you at the end of the week—at least as far as Corason."

Stephen had never thought to be grateful for the company of a mage— especially not one who had attempted to force words from him by dint of a spell. He was grateful now. "She said—she said one other thing," he told Zareth Kahn in the quiet of the library.

"And that?"

"We must stop the Shining City from coming again."

"The Shining—"

Silence.

*   *   *

Elsabet watched as her two sons left the King's City. She knew that they would stop in the Elseth demesne; Gilliam would not be parted for months on end from all of his dogs, and had elected—against the quiet, restrained objections of Zareth Kahn—to take six of his dogs on the road with them.

The girl—Espere, he had called her; she wondered if he knew what it meant— still walked, pranced really, by the side of Gilliam's horse. She could not be forced to mount, but Gilliam insisted that this would not slow their progress. She did not believe him. Still, she had no choice but to believe Stephen when he solemnly backed his Hunter's word.

Time, she had told the more serious and studious of her sons, *is everything now. You have two and a half months, Stephen—don't tarry.*

If the Hunter's Death was a loss that every mother feared, Hunter's Disgrace was a life that they feared more. The Sacred Hunt would be called, and if her sons failed in their oaths . . . She clutched the locket at her throat as tightly as she dared and exhaled. There was no greater crime in all of Breodanir.

Then, squaring her shoulders and drawing her long, woolen overshawl tightly about her body, Lady Elseth began her short trek back to her rooms in the Order of Knowledge. She would have liked to travel with her sons; she was not certain when she would see them again, or in what circumstances.

But she had much to do; letters to write to Ladies Morganson and Faergif, a Queen to make a plea before, and a number of different Priests to see. She could not travel with her sons, but she could help them best without ever leaving the King's City.

Smoke was in the air; there was fire, dust, and the smell of rotting flesh. The sun had come and gone, but there had been too many casualties for the victorious troops to deal with all at once. In the morning, the rest of the bodies would be gathered and buried. Or burned.

Evayne began her quiet search in the darkness. She did not know yet when she was; nor did she know where. She did not know what battle this was, between what armies, over what disagreement. In the shadows and the muted hub of campfires in the distance, the banners hung like slack shadows against their poles, withholding all information. She had hoped, just for a moment, that this would be the end; the point at which, briefly, her path and the path of the rest of the world would finally coincide in a solid way, a meaningful way.

But that was the end of it; she knew it. And this was not the time. There was too much left to do. Who?

She traveled by mage-light and masked her coming, hid the sounds of her retching when the smell or the sight of the not-quite-dead overpowered her. Drawing the folds of her robes well above her knees, she continued to search. Who?

And then she saw the dirty thatch of long blond hair; curls crushed into shoulders and dirt and a tangle of arms. Her breath was sharp; she was never certain—never—that this time would not be the one in which she would find him dead. He alone, of all of her servants—her victims, as she had once called them in her youth—she had no ending for; no death, no finish. She did not understand Time, or his working, and he didn't understand her motions; they existed, uneasy, as allies of the unnamed God that they both served.

She knelt; felt someone's chest give beneath her left knee. Shuddering, she brushed the heavy, wet hair away from a face. His face. She looked at the lines of it, thinking, *we are almost in the same time.* Then, carefully, she dabbed the dried blood at the corners of his mouth.

He stirred. "Is it you?"

"Yes," she replied, cradling his head against her chest as she summoned her power. "Where are we?"

He shook his head, and struggled to sit up; grimaced in pain, but did not leave off his attempt.

"Kallandras," she said, more urgently. "Where are we?"

"I will not tell you," he replied, his breath a wheeze. "It hurts me; it will hurt you, no matter when you come from." He coughed; she lifted a hand and danced his noise away with her fingers and a little spark of blue-light. "Come, help me away."

She nodded in the darkness, brushed the top of his head with the tip of her chin. He froze, and she blushed and pulled away. She blushed—at her age, with so much death and darkness behind her.

But he was gentle, at this age, where he had been cruel in his youth; his anger was softened, although his lined eyes spoke of loss and a yearning which nothing could ever fulfill. No, not nothing. She grimaced as she thought of the Kovaschaii. Stiffened.

"Evayne," he said, and caught her arm. "Not here. I know now that we made the right choice."

She nodded and drew herself up. "To safety, then. I cannot stay."

"No," he whispered. "And I cannot leave." He caught her hand in his, let her support his weight with her shoulder, and followed her lead from the field of death.

And she remembered the first time she had met him at this age—she had been much, much younger then. And he had been almost kind.

"Where were you?" he asked, after they had passed through a circle of trees and over a wide lake, their feet never touching the ground in the moonlight, their bodies casting no shadows.

"I was with Stephen. Of Elseth."

"Ah." He put an arm around her waist, and drew her closer, offering her silence without the pain of words.

* * *

There was no light in this darkness. Even the brightest of magical light guttered like a tired torch when it crossed this threshold. There was shadow, thick and heavy, and then there was a cold, cold night.

But Sor na Shannen needed no pathetic mortal light, magical or no, to see into the depths of this growing chill. She stayed at the edge of the arena, and knelt low, brushing perfect marble with strands of her hair. Her head, she pressed into the floor, as countless numbers of humans had done before her.

But there was no blade above her neck, and no punishment to follow at the hands of a Priest. There was only the demon and the Gate.

She could still see the gilt-edged marble that had, mere months ago, been solid floor. She could read the words and phrases written there by mages who understood only a small portion of their meaning. Such words, the Gods might have spoken when they had dwelled, aeons past, upon the mortal plane. None spoke them now, not even Sor na Shannen.

She waited in the heavy silence before she dared to raise her head.

"My Lord," she whispered, when she deemed it safe, "your enemies become aware. The daughter of the Unnamed one has entered the field, and I do not believe she will leave it."

In the very center of the complicated pattern that was woven out of strands of silver, veins of gold, folds of marble, there was a motion that was barely strong enough to be noticed. But she felt its power as the darkness thickened and grew even more chill.

Demon-kin do not feel the cold, but Sor na Shannen shivered.

"I hear your will," she answered softly. "The mages who serve us will be summoned to your temple, Lord. We will work more quickly, more urgently. I have my spies in the land of your enemy."

She rose, her lips thin and taut as she pressed them together. Here, she wore no glamour, and called no power. For although the God was not present—not yet— the portal that had taken over a decade to bring to life served as an adequate conduit for his power.

She had no illusions. She was alive because he needed her to be alive. And she had enough time to prove herself before he arrived to once again walk the world in the fullness of his Night and the glory of his Shadow. Nothing else would go wrong. Nothing else could.

After all, the Horn of the Hunter—and at this, just a hint of delicate fang was shown to air—had not been found, or used, by any of the Hunter's followers.

"In months, My Lord, the gate will be open. The barriers will be breached. And you will be the only God who may walk upon the face of the world.

"Those who have not chosen, no matter how bright their souls, will be yours."

Hunter's Death

This is for Daniel, because as he discovers the world around him, he helps us to rediscover, relearn and remember the world that we grew up in—and because while so doing, we discover for the first time the world that our parents dealt with, day by day—all the visceral fear, the worry, the boundless joy.
Closed circle.

And this is for Daniel, because I am watching him sleep and he is the most beautiful child in the world, and he won't stay a child forever, except in perfect memory, and this is one.

Chapter One

21st Scaral, 410 A.A.
Averalaan, Twenty-fifth Holding

THE SINGLE DOOR TO the apartment opened silently into a darkened room. A small figure slid round the edge of the frame and across the threshold before swinging the door quickly and quietly shut. He stepped over the bedrolls that lay in a more or less orderly row between the hallway and the kitchen, and was only cursed once when he stepped on an outstretched hand.

"Sorry," he muttered out of the corner of his mouth. The apology was taken about as well as it was given, and he heard another sleepy curse at his back. He didn't really care. A lamp burned low in the kitchen, and he knew that Jay would still be at her work, whatever it was.

"Jay?" he whispered, as he pushed the kitchen door ajar and stepped into dim light made stronger by the shadows it cast.

She sat at a long, wide table that had been crammed beneath the window between two blackened walls. Her hair was shoved up and pinned in a messy, hasty brown bunch, and her shoulders were hunched. The lamplight played around her sitting form like a halo.

"Jay?"

"What is it?" The light caught her profile as she turned, sharpening an already slender, almost patrician nose, and a slightly pointed chin. "What is it?" she said again, the voice matching the profile.

As his eyes became accustomed to the light, he could see the dark rings under her eyes. In front of the lamp, just over her shoulder, he could see a slate, and beneath it, parchment. Inks were to the left, chalk to the right. She was practicing her reading and writing.

Jewel was the smartest person Carver had ever met. That was why he followed her and let her tell him what to do—there wasn't any problem that she couldn't solve.

Until now.

Jewel—called Jay by anyone who wanted to live out the week—was tired. The season had been uncommonly cold, and the living to be made off the pockets of the more wealthy—the truly wealthy never made it this far into the city—had been bad. She'd had to rescue Angel not once, but *twice* when his fingers had been slowed by the cold and his legs hadn't carried him away from the resulting trouble as fast as they should've, and she'd narrowly managed to avoid losing Jester to Carmenta's gang in the next holding. Which, of course, had cost her a lot of money.

Added to that was the worry of clothing—Arann's didn't fit him *again*, and Angel had lost halves of two sleeves, to name two—food and shelter. She had been taught numbers and rudimentary reading and writing by her father before his death and by Old Rath after it, and she struggled with both in the poor light, trying to figure out the best way to make ends meet. A sense of responsibility had been driven into her so sharply that even lean years living off the streets couldn't shake it.

Which was why she was the leader of her hand-chosen crew, but wasn't why she felt twice her fifteen years. *Don't do it, Carver,* she thought as she set the chalk aside and sat back an inch or two—just enough to give the lamplight play across Carver's face. His skin was ruddy with the chill air, and his hair, cut on an angle that leaped from his right cheek to his forehead, hung over his right eye like a black patch. He was thin and scraggly, as most of her boys were—only Arann stood out as the exception—but his cheekbones were high and fine; he looked like the urchin bastard of one of the patriciate's lords. When he was older—*if he survives to be older*—he was going to be damned dangerous.

Don't do this to me.

He couldn't hear her, of course, and had he been able to, he wouldn't have listened. It wasn't his way.

"You were out in the tunnels again, weren't you?" It wasn't really a question—more an accusation.

Carver's head dropped until his chin hit his chest. He swallowed. None of the bravado or the spit-and-fight of his usual expression was anywhere to be seen. He mumbled an apology—a sincere one.

When she heard it, Jay Markess became quite still in the darkened room. She was bright, all right, and it didn't take much to put two and two together. "Where's Lander?" Her voice was much sharper than she'd intended it to be. Worry did that.

Carver shook his dark head from side to side without raising his face.

Jewel was one year Carver's senior, and three inches shorter, but for sheer speed, no one in the den but Duster matched her. Carver didn't see her move, and didn't have a chance to get out of her way, not that he'd've been stupid enough to take it.

She caught him by the collar and the mane, and yanked his head up. "What the hells were you doing in the maze?"

"I—"

"Didn't I give you orders?"

"Yes!"

"Were they too hard to understand?" She shook him, hard. "Kalliaris' Curse! Why did I ever think you had a brain?" Tears started at the corners of his eyes, and his lip sank slightly in—enough to tell her that he was biting it. The anger left her in a rush, and she felt the chill in the air as if there were no fire in the grate. There wasn't much of one.

"Blood of the Mother, Carver," she said, as she released him and turned away. "Was this his idea or yours?" She knew the answer without having to ask the question, but she wanted to hear what he had to say.

There was a long pause before he answered, but he answered. "Mine."

She nodded as she stared at the tabletop, seeing Lander's face, and not the slate and chalk, parchment and quill. He was as pale as Carver, but his hair was the usual mousy brown of the street. It was also a good deal shorter, and usually tucked under a thick cap that rested just above the line of his brow. Made it hard to see his eyes.

She was certain that she would never see them again.

"Yours," she said quietly. Carver was telling the truth. It was the only rule she demanded of her den, that no one lie to her. He said nothing.

"How could you, after Fisher and Lefty?"

"We weren't even sure they got lost in the labyrinth," Carver began defensively. Then he saw her face as she spun on the spot. Her glare was enough to silence him. "We were being chased by Carmenta's gang."

"So what else is new?"

Carver shook his head, and this time there was a flash of real anger in his eyes. "This time was different—they were waiting for us in *our* holding. We didn't have a choice. They had us boxed in at Fennel's old space.

"Honest, Jay, we were just going to skim the edges of the maze. We weren't going to go deeper into the tunnels."

She took a breath, and then forced her lungs to expand around it. *Relax. Just relax. Carmenta.* Paying him off for Jester's release had been a risk, and it was clear that this year, at least, that risk had been a bad one if he now felt that he could just harvest the rest of her gang in their own territory. She forced her hands to be steady, but nothing could take the edge out of her voice. "What happened?"

"We got down into the tunnels and we hid close to the surface, but Carmenta's boys were really close on our heels. I told Lander to be cool—that they couldn't find us if they didn't know the way in—but they made a lot of noise, and he bolted."

Jewel nodded grimly. The streets hadn't been kind to any of her den—but they'd been damned cruel to Lander. He was an easy one to panic. "He ran in."

Carver swallowed. "I tried to follow him."

"And?"

"Nothing. He couldn't have been more than twenty feet ahead of me."

"Did you hear anything?"

Carver's hair swirled across the front of his face as he shook his head.

Jay exhaled.

"What is it, Jay? What's going on in the tunnels?"

"I don't know." She folded her arms tightly across her chest. "But it may be time to find out."

"What?"

"We've lost the maze as an advantage because we don't dare use it."

Carver nodded slowly.

"But I'll be damned if something that's preying on *my* den is going to get any use out of it either." She rolled her lower lip between her teeth and her brows gathered loosely above the bridge of her nose. Carver was familiar with the expression; he saw it often. "But I promise you this. It's time to get rid of Carmenta."

Morning. Sun across the table, through the glass of a lamp long guttered. In the growing light, the tired lines of a young woman's face, shadowed by fallen strands of hair and little sleep. Jay Markess was weary but too worried to sleep. It happened.

The labyrinths beneath the city of Averalaan were not very complicated once you'd traveled them for a month or two. But for that month or two, you wanted a guide, and a damned good one. There were places where the tunnels were patchy and badly worn—holes suddenly gaped up out of the shadows, and it was easy to break an arm or a leg, or do worse, if you ran into one.

The labyrinth was a dark place, set feet or yards beneath the surface of Averalaan's busiest—and oldest—streets. Parts of it were carved, smooth stone, and parts of it worm-ridden wood; like a giant web, it sprawled in shadow—and not even Jewel had a clear idea of where its heart lay or what was in it. Neither in nightmare or reality had she ventured that far in.

But she'd been brave enough to dare more than its edges, and she'd discovered that the passages opened up into all sorts of places—abandoned warehouses, yes, but also into the forgotten subbasements of buildings that merchants still used. They opened up into the debris of old alleys and the glittering streets of the merchants' market; they entered into the darkness beneath the silent crypts of all but the highest of Churches. The church crypts were the safest place to hide because the thought of all the dead didn't bother Jewel—it was the living she had to worry about.

No—that wasn't always true. Sometimes the dead came to haunt her. *Fisher.* She grimaced. Her den still clung to the faint hope that Fisher and Lefty were alive, but Jewel had none. She *knew* they were dead, with the same certainty that she knew that Lander was gone for good. There were times it struck her like that, so deep in the gut it went beyond mere instinct, so strong that it couldn't be ignored. She wasn't a fool; any time in the past that she'd tried to ignore the "feeling" it had gone the worse for her. She'd learned to listen to it.

Which was why she wouldn't let any of her den go off to the labyrinth to search for their lost brothers. There was death there. Maybe there had always been death there.

The maze was a secret that had been lost for centuries—if anyone had ever known about it—or so she'd been told; not even the oh-so-smart scholars in their white and gold towers had any clue that it existed. Jewel Markess had been taught about the labyrinths by Old Rath, self-professed gentleman thief, and one of the few people in the streets who'd managed to survive to be called old. Where Old Rath had discovered the maze, he would never say, and there were areas of the labyrinth that he had never shown her. Of course, he denied this strenuously, and he knew she knew he was lying, but there were whole branches of tunnels that he refused to explore.

There was a reason these tunnels were buried, he would tell her, his face a set study of deeply etched lines.

Oh? What was that?

If I knew, I wouldn't tell you, you little thief. You never listen to anything I say anyway.

It wasn't true. She listened to everything he said. She just didn't follow the parts of it that were obviously the products of superstition or age.

But she discovered that it wasn't all just age. She should have known better then. *That's* when she should've given the tunnels up for good.

There were crypts that weren't only Church crypts; there were tunnels, fine and grand, that led into dark places, old places. She shivered, remembering; she and Duster had wandered right into a crypt, but the statues atop the great stone coffins were no normal statues; the maker-born—maybe even an Artisan—had crafted their lifeless flesh. She should've known it, seeing them firsthand; they were of white stone, except where lines of silver and gold had been laid against their pale, chiseled hair; they were fine-featured and beautiful in a way that nothing in Jewel's life had ever been.

What lay beneath them? No commoner, and no common noble, either. Maybe Kings, although the faces of the ones that adorned the coins of the realm certainly weren't as lovely—as real—as these. It was hard to pull her eyes away; hard to remember how she'd come this way, and what, on the surface above, hid this crypt from sight. She'd known better, suddenly, than to try to touch 'em, but Duster— Duster's hand still bore the scar.

Here lie the Oathbreakers in no restful sleep, until they might wake to fulfill their oath and restore honor to the lineage of the First-born Houses. Wake them not, you who venture here to bear witness.

She hadn't understood most of what was said until months later, because she hadn't dared ask Old Rath what the words meant, except in ones and twos. He'd've known that she'd disobeyed him—and knowing it, he'd've refused to help her. But that had been a bad place. And she should have known that where there was one, there were many.

Dented tin plates and knives that had to be straightened every time they were used made an awkward pattern across the thick table as she pushed them to and fro, wanting their noise to distract her. Was it her fault that Fisher and Lefty were gone?

She pushed her chair back from the table and perched it precariously against the wall. Didn't matter whose fault it was, after all. Only mattered that it didn't happen again.

Lander. She closed her eyes and, in the darkness behind her lids, listened to the thrum of the pulse at her throat. The labyrinth had been their advantage, and she was now willing to give it up. Problem was that she didn't know who to give it up to. Not another den, and not another holding—that much was clear. Short of Carmenta, and maybe Hannes, there wasn't anyone that she wanted dead enough to give to the maze. Because she knew that the death was a terrible one. She just didn't know what caused it. That was the problem with "feeling." It gave you the truth without giving you anything you could show your friends—like, say, facts.

Don't ever tell anyone about your "feelings," Jay, Old Rath had told her, years ago, when she'd first managed to convince him that they were real. She remembered thinking that it would make him happy; it made him strange and intense instead. *Don't tell them. If you're lucky, you'll just be ridiculed as a young child with an overactive imagination. If you're unlucky, they'll know what it means, and you'll be pressed into service, or forced into it.* He'd caught her by the arms, and his grip was as tight as it had ever been. Frightened her, too—but back then, she was easier to spook.

Why? Why can't I tell them? What does it mean?

Just don't do it. You promise me, girl, or I won't teach you anything else. Don't tell anyone. She'd promised. Aside from telling her den-mates—who had a right to know the truth about who they were following—she'd kept that promise.

She could leave the holdings and try to sneak into the High City, maybe hook up with a member of the Order of Knowledge. She tossed her head in derision. That would be a great idea. Either she'd find an old, addled man who couldn't be pulled out of his books, or she'd find a power-crazed mage who'd be worse, in the long run, than the maze itself.

Her hair flew free as she shook her head. They wouldn't take her seriously if they listened at all. The same could be said of the Magisterium's sentries. Each of the hundred holdings was policed by three pairs of these guards; the merchants called them the magisterians, although it wasn't really an official title, and that had become their rank in the streets of Averalaan.

Well, in the common streets, it was.

And the magisterians weren't going to listen to a fifteen-year-old almost-woman tell them that three of her den-kin had disappeared into a mysterious maze beneath the city that they'd never heard of. They had more important crimes to worry about than runaways—and all of her den-kin were already that.

Even if they did listen, they weren't likely to be able to help. What real authority did a magisterian have? No. The maze needed someone bigger, or more able to deal with it. *Why?* She ground her teeth in frustration. She knew the answer, but not the question; it was always that way with the "feeling."

Sighing, she got out of her chair. She'd thought herself round in circles and still come up with no answers. It was time to admit that she needed a little help. And admitting that was harder than cutting off her right hand—it just wasn't harder than the idea of losing another of her den—or of letting the three that were dead go unavenged. She walked out of the kitchen into the big room; five pairs of eyes focused on her at once. Arann and Jester were out near the market edges bringing—one hoped—the evening's meal.

"Well?" Duster said, getting to her feet and squaring her shoulders.

"You and Carver come with me. The rest of you, stay put."

Duster rolled her dark eyes. "Look, Jay—what by the long night are we going to do about Lander?"

"There's nothing we can do. He's gone. Don't even think it, Finch," she added, as she caught a restless movement to her right. "He's *gone.*" She squared her own shoulders as she met Duster's steel-eyed glare. Duster had the most vicious temper of the den and wasn't above letting a violent impulse get the better of her. Luckily, she was balanced by a fine sense of where her loyalties lay. It was only at times like this, with loyalties pulling in either direction, that she was hard to manage. "If he'd listened to me in the first place, we wouldn't have to worry. Now, it's too late for him." She took in the silence, ground her teeth a bit, and then pulled her hair out of her eyes and rearranged her scarf over it. "Look, I've never given you bad advice about anything important. This is important. *Don't go to the maze.*"

Angel raised his head; a shock of white-blond hair was bound by spiraled wire into a long, tall spire. Jewel thought it made him look like an idiot, but at least he looked like a striking idiot. It wasn't an uncommon style in the street, and given that he was her own age, she couldn't treat him like a younger. "Fine. He's gone. But what are we going to do about it?"

"*We* are not going to do anything. I am going to see Old Rath."

"Wait for Arann," Teller said, speaking for the first time. He was small and slight for his age—thirteen, halfway to fourteen—and he spoke very rarely, which was why they called him Teller.

"Duster and Carver will do fine. Arann's got his hands full with more important things."

Teller's gaze was measured; she met it firmly and then looked away as she realized that he had been testing her choice, and that he'd taken out of her answer the information he'd been looking for. Of all of her den, only Duster or Carver had ever been forced into a position where they had to kill.

Old Rath lived in the thirty-fifth holding, a scant ten blocks from the holding that Jewel's den called home. But ten blocks in this part of the city could make a difference. Out of a hundred holdings, only three were considered dangerous to the wary passer-through—and the thirty-fifth was one of those. Rath liked it that way; Jewel was never certain why. Today, she didn't care.

Usually, when she wanted to reach Old Rath, she ducked into the safety and anonymity of the maze. That wasn't an option anymore, and it made travel much more interesting. Jewel hated it when life was too interesting.

Duster and Carver kept their attention on either side of the streets, where buildings that had seen better days gave way to the occasional burned-out husk. It was the duty of the various magistrates who governed the city to see to the leveling of such public hazards. Only in the thirty-fifth, thirty-second, and seventeenth holdings did the magistrates mysteriously turn a blind eye.

Not even the magisterians that were assigned here could be relied on; if they were good, they were transferred. Or at least that's what Old Rath said. Jewel preferred not to meet magisterians face-to-face, so she didn't have any basis on which to judge "good" or "bad."

Or she wouldn't have, had she not wandered the streets of the thirty-fifth. It told her all she needed to know about the magisterians in charge. The damaged buildings and the dirty streets, combined with the chill of the day and the lack of heavy traffic, gave the holding an air of subtle menace that the twenty-fifth didn't have.

She turned to see that Duster and Carver were just as spooked. They kept a close eye on the roads, and more particularly on the recessed doorways and long, flat steps that were peopled by men and women who fell silent as they approached.

"Great place Old Rath lives in," Duster said, trying to be jaunty. She failed, and she rarely failed.

Jewel didn't answer. Everything on the street had taken on the heightened crispness of form and color that danger always brought on. She saw the same doorways and stairwells that her den-kin did, but they were harsher, and somehow robbed of the shadows that usually pooled there. Standing out in this stark vision were men and women lounging beneath the mage-lights that lined the street in pairs. She could see their daggers and the bulges that signaled throwing knives; could see the scars across their faces or exposed skin; could even see the slight narrowing of eyes that indicated interest of a sort that she wanted to avoid.

She walked neither too slowly nor too quickly as she passed by them—this was a trick that Old Rath had taught her when she'd first met him years ago. *Too fast and you look frightened, too slow and you look suspicious.* You didn't want to stand out in the streets. *Of course, if you have to choose one of the two, choose suspicious. Frightened makes you a victim.*

Twice, when nearing a certain intersection or a certain alley, she was forced to make a detour, and it lengthened their journey by a good half hour. But Duster and Carver were used to her strange commands, and knew better than to question them in a foreign holding. Well, Carver did—and Duster wouldn't cause trouble in the thirty-fifth.

"*Real* nice holding," Duster said quietly, as they passed what must have once been a live cat. She grimaced as the smell hit her nostrils and stuck there.

"Shut up, Duster," Carver said, out of the corner of his mouth. Jewel had once again veered off the street, only this time with a look of intent purpose. Carver lengthened his stride and caught up with her. "This the place?" he asked softly as they came to an easy stop in front of a building.

She nodded. "I know it doesn't look like much on the outside."

Carver raised a black brow. "You can say that again." He shook his head as he looked at the flat, rectangular two-story building. It had once had windows, and those windows were—from the looks of the rusted bolts—barred from the outside. Maybe, before that, they'd had shutters; the paint around the windows didn't look the same as that around the rest of the . . . hovel. The wooden supports—they had to be wood from the way the building appeared to be dangerously tilted to the right—had seen better days. He hoped.

"Come on. We've—we've got to hurry." She could hear Old Rath telling her to slow down—but something a lot stronger than his memory and his teaching was telling her *speed up*.

"You okay, Jay?"

Her nod was curt and quick—and it was as much a "no" as she dared utter.

"What is it?" Duster whispered. "What's wrong?"

But of course she couldn't say. She didn't know. She walked down the small flight of stairs to a grimy, but obviously functional, door. "Down here. Quick." It was a tribute to Old Rath that the stairwell was empty.

"What are you doing?"

"What does it look like I'm doing?" Jewel said, as she bent down in front of the door and began to retrieve her limited equipment from her inner vest pocket.

"It *looks*." Carver replied smartly, "like you're going to try to pick Old Rath's lock. Have you lost your mind?"

Jewel didn't answer. The lock was a fairly simple one, if you knew what you were doing. She knew it as well as Rath had taught her.

"Can't we knock?" Carver spoke again, nervously shifting from foot to foot. Old Rath was old, but he wasn't weak, addled, or—more important—particularly tolerant, and Carver had been on the wrong end of his temper a time or two. "Jay, can't—ouch!"

"Shut up, Carver," Duster said, her words quiet and chilly. "And keep your damned voice down."

He muttered something under his breath about *girls*, and they both ignored him. Duster watched the road, looking as nonchalant as possible as she leaned casually back against the wall. After a few seconds, Carver joined her, but his nonchalance looked a shade petulant.

The lock clicked, cleanly and coldly.

"Come on," Jewel said tersely. "Get in." She took the precaution of locking the door behind them.

"This another of your feelings?" Duster asked, the minute the door was shut.

Jewel nodded almost absently as she scanned the hall. It was a short, narrow passageway that opened out into the room that Rath used for Mother knew what. His bedroom was the first door to the right, a kitchen of dubious cleanliness was the second, and to the left was the great room that he used for limited training. How he could afford this much space, when all of Jewel's den lived in something a third the size, Jewel didn't know. And she was smart enough not to ask.

She knew her way around; she'd been here often enough. There was a basement—a catch-trap beneath the training room—that led to a subbasement, and in that, there was an entrance to the maze. Wasn't easy to get to—it was two crawl spaces and a shaky platform away—but that suited everyone just fine.

Until now. "Carver, check out the kitchen for anything unusual. Duster, check the room to the left." She chose for herself Old Rath's bedroom.

Although the rest of his home was uncluttered and almost stark in its simplicity, his bedroom was the repository of anything that he considered worth keeping. It wasn't, given his age, that much, but it was cluttered enough that Jewel had to watch where she stepped as she made her way to the bed.

Old Rath could read, write, and force a pleasant tune out of hand-pipes; he could sew after a fashion, cook, and wield a mean long knife. He also owned not one, but two, swords, although she'd never seen him carry either.

Rath was a friend—probably the only one she had who wasn't also a responsibility. As such, he was highly valued, although she'd never have said as much to him. To anyone, really. Well, maybe on a good day she'd have told Teller. Didn't matter.

Rath understood her well enough. He was impressed that she knew how to read and write, and he'd done everything he could to encourage and foster those skills. He taught her how to manage her den-kin and their infighting; taught her how to handle the enemies that she'd made in the other holdings; even taught her how to use the long dagger she carried, given that she wasn't very large or very strong.

But he'd taught her a little bit more than that: He told her how the city ran— or how it was supposed to run—and, more importantly, who ran what. *Because,* he'd say, in that serious voice of his, *you can't stay on the streets forever, Jay.*

You have, was the first answer she offered.

She tried not to remember what he'd replied. *You think I'd stay here if things had worked out differently?* He laughed, and it was the bitterest laugh she'd ever heard. *This is all I've got, Jay. But I made it, and I'll hold it with everything I own. Still, there's no damned reason why you should. You've got potential, and you'll waste it or lose it here.*

The bed—it was years since Jewel had slept in a bed, and it pained her to remember the last time—was made; it was obvious he hadn't left in a rush. She smoothed a wrinkle out of the ice-blue counterpane, and then very gingerly pulled the covers back.

If you ever need to leave me a message, girl, leave it here. He'd very carefully removed the knob at the right side of the headboard of his bed, and retrieved a furled paper from the hollowed-out post. *It'll catch my attention, and I'll know it's important.*

She nodded, and he added, *I'll do the same for you. You can check it from time to time if you think it's necessary.* He trusted her intuition, although he'd only ever asked about it once. *Better not to know too much. But you understand that.*

The knob came off the post; she set it gently on the pillow, smoothing out the wrinkles left by its weight. Pausing to listen for signs of movement in the hall outside, she held her breath. When she was certain that Duster and Carver were still occupied, she reached in and pulled out a flattened, curled up set of papers. These she put on the bed as if they were too heavy to hold; she brushed the rounded surface of the post-knob and then replaced it carefully. There was something here. He'd left her words. Her hands shook as she started to unwind the string that held them together.

"Jay?" Duster's voice nearly sent her through the roof; it was tense and strained. She shoved the papers up her loosely fitted sleeve, straightened her vest, and headed for the door. "What's the problem?" It was open.

"I was hoping you could answer that," Old Rath said, as he stepped lightly into the room, one hand on Duster's shoulder, the other on Carver's arm. "What are you doing in my place?"

Jewel had never seen his eyes so dark or heard his voice so cold. She blinked, and his expression softened somewhat; the anger looked a little less icy.

"Came to talk to you," Jewel said, crossing her arms carefully.

"And it was so important that you had to pick the lock instead of waiting?"

She shrugged and then hung her head a bit. "Yeah."

His fingers were white against the dark clothing Duster and Carver wore. "And these two?"

"Look, you know the situation with the maze. I had to come here *on foot.* I don't do the thirty-fifth on my own. No one smart does." Their eyes locked; it was Jewel who, in the end, was forced to look away.

Having won the quiet contest, Rath relaxed. "What was so important?"

"Lander's gone as well."

Old Rath's lids were heavy as he narrowed his eyes. "When?"

"Yesterday. Early evening."

"And?"

"We—we think he was followed into the maze. Carmenta's gang."

"I see." Pause. "Were you there?"

"No. Carver was."

Rath looked down at Carver, and then at his hands. With a shrug, and a none too gentle shove, he released both of his captives to the care of their leader. "Carmenta's den is?"

"Twenty-sixth. They nest above Melissa's place, near the Corkscrew."

"There's no maze-door near the Corkscrew."

"You'd know," Jewel replied. "But it doesn't matter. If they know about the maze, they'll be in it like a pack of rats. We'll lose our advantage. And you know Carmenta. Word of the maze'll hit the streets like rain in a sea storm."

"I see." Rath was silent for a long time.

"Rath?"

"Go home, Jewel." She saw the smooth surface of his lids as he grimaced and closed his eyes for the briefest of moments. "I've kept out of the maze for long enough now. I'll find Lander for you. If he's injured somewhere in the maze, he'll have left some sort of trail. If there's something there . . ." He turned a dark eye on Carver. "Where did you say you entered the tunnels?"

"Fennel's old space. At the edge of the holding."

"The warehouse?"

"Whatever. It's not used for much right now."

"Good." Rath stepped into the hall, and very pointedly held the door to his room open. "Ladies, gentleman. If you'd care to depart?"

"What?" Duster said, but it was barely more than a whisper.

Rath still had keen ears. He turned his head slowly, pivoting it on a perfectly still neck. *"Get lost."*

They didn't have to be told twice, and if they didn't mob the door, it was only because there were three of them, and three made a poor mob.

"Where are you going?"

"You told us to get lost," Duster replied, hand on the knob of the closed door.

Rath sighed, and it was a weary, irritable sound. "Use the underground."

No one moved.

"Well?"

Duster and Carver cast surreptitious glances at Jewel. It was the only time they really looked their age. Jewel, on the other hand, who mentally squared her shoulders, seemed truly adult.

"We don't use the maze," Jewel said quietly. She couldn't have raised her voice if she'd wanted to.

"I'm not telling you to go very deeply into the maze. Jewel, don't let the events of the last two weeks turn you into a frightened child. The tunnels are the safest way through the holding. Use them."

"No." Very slowly, she let her arms unfold to hang loosely at her sides. "Carmenta's gang is probably wandering around all through it. I won't risk it. And I won't risk any more of my den-kin to it either."

"Carmenta's gang doesn't know the maze."

"They don't have to to get lucky." Her voice was very, very bitter. "Seems like they already have."

He stared at her for a long time, and then nodded tersely. "I'll meet you back at your den, either with Lander, or with news of him. Don't get yourself killed on the way back."

"Thanks, Rath," she said softly.

Duster opened the door, and she and Carver walked into the street. Only when they had crossed the threshold did Jewel follow; old habit.

She stopped with her back to the closed door for a moment, and then started walking with a crisp, measured step. Her head bobbed slightly as she nodded Duster forward.

"What was that about?" Duster said quietly, pitching her voice low, but keeping the sibilance of whisper out of it. "Carmenta hasn't come anywhere near the maze."

Jewel nodded with a half-smile that wouldn't have fooled a madness-taken simpleton. "Carver, are we being followed?"

He shrugged. They continued to walk out of the thirty-fifth holding, and three blocks from the east border, Carver's slanted hair bobbed up and down in time to his step.

"Who?"

The tone of voice that answered said clearly, *You aren't going to believe this.* "Old Rath."

"Kalliaris," Jewel murmured. "Smile. Smile on us, Lady." She continued to walk. "Duster, go home. Now. Take a route so twisted even your shadow couldn't follow you." Duster started to speak, and Jewel motioned with the flat of her hand. "Get everyone out."

"But—"

"Don't argue with me. Get everyone out! Take the iron box, and leave *everything* else. Find a place out of the holding to hunker down, and then send a message to us. *Send* it. Don't come yourself." She met Duster's brown eyes with her own, and Duster suddenly saw that Jewel's face, so well-controlled in expression, was ashen. The den leader turned away and began to walk again. Duster followed, her step easy and confident, her expression pale as light on water.

"Where?"

"The trough. If we're not there, or you don't hear from us again, the den is yours—and it's your responsibility to keep it safe. Stay out of the maze; *never* use it again."

"This have something to do with Old Rath?"

Jewel swallowed and nodded. "Yeah." She bit her lip, as if biting it could hold back her words. Then she bowed her head and stared at the cobbled stone as it passed beneath her moving feet. "I don't know who it was back there, but I do know that it wasn't Rath."

"What?"

"Rath's dead." Her voice caught on the last word. If not for fear, she might have cried, but she had no time for sorrow. "Now go on, Duster—or we'll all end up that way as well."

"This the Feeling?"

"Never stronger."

Duster veered to the right and was quickly lost to sight.

"Carver?"

Carver nodded again, his jaunty, cocky movements a stark contrast to his expression. Minutes passed; Jewel almost forgot how to breathe.

Then, "He's following us."

Kalliaris, please, smile on us. Mother, protect your children. Reymaris, give me the strength to make them pay for the loss of my kin. She smiled and began to walk in a direction that was almost, but not quite, in the opposite direction from home.

Chapter Two

21st Scaral, 410 A.A.
Breodanir

"WHY DO YOU ALWAYS come when it's dark?" Stephen held the lamp aloft; it further shadowed a face hidden by a midnight-blue hood. He spoke softly although there was no chance whatever that Gilliam would be wakened by his speech; Gil was not a light sleeper, and only when there was obvious danger—or when Stephen felt threatened—could he be roused once sleep had taken him. This was not one of those times, strange though the hour was.

"I don't know," his visitor replied, standing in the frame of the door as if anchored there. She never crossed the threshold without permission; like some wild wood-spirit, she lingered, waiting upon an invitation to enter as if it were the incantation that would free her.

The moon was at nadir; the lamplight seemed stronger for it. Stephen let her words linger in the air a moment, trying to get a feel for her voice. Was she old, this time? Was she young? Was she a woman in her prime, with a hint of mystery and veiled power cast round her like a shield that protected her from all questions?

"Come in," he said at last, lowering the lamp. He stepped back, granting her passage into a room that would have been silent if not for Gil's snoring.

Shadows flickered as the lamp bobbed up and down; Stephen very carefully moved two chairs closer to the fire. Wood was provided with the room, as was a servant to tend it; Stephen woke the drowsing boy and sent him on his way as kindly as possible. What the boy thought of the nocturnal visitor he was wise enough to keep to himself, but his regret at the loss of the fire's warmth was written clear across his features. It was cold, this eve; the winter had been unpleasantly chill.

She waited until the boy left, and then carefully took a seat. He watched her. Her shoulders were slightly hunched toward the floor; she placed her hands carefully in her lap, but they were stiff. He doubted it was with cold.

"Evayne?"

"I don't know," she said again, but each word was slower and clearer. "I don't know why the others come at night."

"And you?"

"Because that's when the mage sleeps."

"Truly?"

She didn't reply. But she raised her hands to the edge of her hood and carefully pulled it back. In the orange light and shadow, he could see her smooth, pale skin. Her hair, raven black, was pulled away from her face and hung at her back in a knot. At least, he guessed it did; she never showed him her back. Tonight, she was young.

And when she was young, she was easy to startle, easy to upset. Startled or upset, she was like a gorse bush or a brier; painful if not handled with care. He rose, so that she could see his back, and carefully lifted a short log for the fire.

"Do you mistrust Zareth Kahn?"

"Do you mean do I have a reason to distrust him? No. It's not just him, it's any of the mage-born. I don't want to talk to them. I don't want to answer their questions. Especially not when they're members of the Order."

He spread the leaves of the large cloth fan and began to wake embers. "I see." He could almost understand it; Zareth Kahn was both curious and deceptively ordinary in appearance. It was easy to relax and speak plainly and companionably with him—too easy, too quickly. "Why have you come?"

Her silences, when she came to him as an older woman, were things of confidence, and of confidences kept to herself. Or so it had first appeared. But a glimpse of her younger self, of this angry, tense, and fearful young woman, made of her silences an inability to communicate, a lack of common ground. Would she speak if she thought he could understand her? He was certain of it.

At last she said, as she often did, "I don't know."

"Do you know where we are?"

"On the road. To the land of the Twin Kings, the Empire of Essalieyan. To Averalaan, the capital."

"Well, yes. But do you know where on the road we are?"

She shrugged. "No." Her voice told him she thought it unimportant.

He knew that she had not always walked this strange road; that she had had a life of her own, in a village somewhere outside of Essalieyan, with friends of a sort. She could read and write, and she had learned much of this at the Mother's temple, aiding the priestess. He knew that her path was a matter of choice, a momentous choice, but a choice nonetheless. More than that—her age, the year that the village existed, the place, be it near or far—she would not tell him.

But he knew young ladies well enough, and he did not seek to fill her silence with words of his own. She wanted to be heard—even more, to be listened to— and she did not have much left over to hear or listen to others with. A half hour passed; the logs cracked and crackled as flames leaped up the grate. They sat together, Gilliam a noisy accompaniment in the background.

At last she asked, "Are you always like this?"

Stephen said nothing.

"I can't even see your face, with your back to the fire. But you might be a demon or a haunting." She looked down at her hands, and slowly turned them round in her lap; they were bare. She wore no jewelry at all, save for a clasp at her throat, a silver brooch of some sort. As it caught the firelight's glow, it seemed to be a flower of light. "What are they like?"

"They?"

"The others. Me. When I'm older."

"As different from you," he replied, "as I am from my eight-year-old self."

She smiled bitterly. "But you don't meet people who just spoke to your eight-year-old self yesterday."

"No, I don't." He turned and put another log very carefully into the fire. "I don't know what they're like, Evayne. If what you're asking me is are they like you, then I can't answer the question. I don't know who you are."

"You aren't supposed to," she replied, and again her voice was bitter.

"Oh?" He shifted to face her again. "And who made those rules?"

She was silent, and he waited, hoping that she would draw herself out of the shell of darkness that she sat in. But at length she rose. "I have to go," she said, but almost without rancor.

He didn't ask her when she'd return; he knew by now that it was a question that she was sensitive to—as she was to all else at this age. Still, he found it disconcerting when she began to shimmer in place. She stared at her feet, at something that he couldn't see, and then she took a single step forward that carried her out of his view.

What, he thought, as he left the room to search for the hearth boy, *made you choose this life?* He stopped, pressing two fingers to his lips, although he hadn't spoken the question aloud. There were things it was best not to ask because answers often had their price.

A chill crept into the base of his spine as he glanced up and down the narrow hall. He felt certain, quite suddenly, that he would have his answer.

Why do you always have to talk to her?

What difference does it make? You're busy enough as it is.

What in the hells is that supposed to mean?

Stephen sat on the edge of his bed, gritting his teeth. It had been a bad day, and while a bath and a good, hot meal had gone a long way to grinding down the edges it had produced, they weren't fully smoothed by any means. Gilliam, better than anyone he knew, could get under his skin and stay there.

If it weren't for the presence of Zareth Kahn, the argument would have evolved into something less wordy and more intense. As it was, Stephen's need to present as decorous a face as possible held his hand, and Gilliam eventually retreated to the company of his dogs and the wild girl.

Where once they had panicked her, their arguments were now a thing of curiosity to the feral child. She would sit and watch, head cocked to one side, black eyes unblinking. It was cold enough that she tolerated some mix of fur and clothing, but even then, she tolerated it poorly, and was likely as not to be seen running exposed at the side of the dogs. Her parentage protected her, one assumed, from the elements.

She was happy to be with Gilliam, and followed his commands—the ones that Stephen could hear—with more grace than the dogs that had been raised to it.

Gilliam.

What is Evayne anyway, a replacement for Cynthia?

Oh, it wasn't finished yet. Evayne at that age was hardly adult—if she was adult—and he wasn't attracted to her. How could he be? He'd started to pull his slippers off his feet when he heard the knock. Tonight, there was something distinctly different about it. He stood, grabbed the lamp, and crossed the room before he drew another breath.

He opened the door, and she stood in its frame.

He knew at once that she was the woman and not the child; the mage, and not the messenger. "Come in," he said almost meekly.

She stepped across the threshold. Lifted a hand, and sent a shower of gray and white plumes toward the window. The curtains fell with a crash, as if on a play that had come to an abrupt, and unexpected, end.

Stephen stepped back, holding the lamp in front of his chest as his only shield. He heard movement, and knew that Espere was awake; Gilliam, although affecting a snore, had roused the moment the sparks had gone flying to bring the curtains down. He could feel his Hunter's tension through their bond, as his Hunter felt his; their arguments were left to the light of another day.

Evayne turned to the fire and the frightened boy who sat, mouth agape, at its side. Her movement freed him; he grabbed an iron poker and held it like a club, while he braced his back against the wall. *"I mean you no harm,"* she said softly. The light at her hands became white, and whiter still, as the words, soothing and soft, left her lips. *"Sleep in peace; I mean you no harm; nothing will hurt you."*

The boy's lids began to drop as did the iron he held, each covering a gentle arc toward its destination. He slid down, inch by inch, until he sat, legs sprawled, on the floor. His breathing was deep and perfectly even.

Gilliam rose in that instant, but not to attack; he found his clothing in the scant light and began to put it on. "Go join the dogs," he told the wild girl.

"No." Evayne raised one slender hand. Command was in the single word, but no magic; Espere halted at the door and looked askance at her master. She was not uncomfortable in the presence of this sorceress; indeed, she seemed to be in high spirits at the sight of magic, as if magic's use was familiar to her. "I've come to guide you across the river. Send the dogs ahead; no one will stop them if they do not travel with you."

"I will not leave—"

"I cannot guarantee that any of you will survive the crossing; the dogs will most certainly not if they attempt it with us." As she spoke, she drew something from out of the folds of her robe; Gilliam caught a glimpse of the darkness within the robe's depths, and it seemed, for a moment, endless. "Do you recognize this? No, let me tell you. It is a seer's ball. Your dogs *will* die if they follow our road."

Gilliam met her gaze and held it. Then, grudgingly, he nodded. He closed his eyes, not because it was necessary but because it was fastest, and began to speak with his pack. They were already awake; the moment he'd known of danger, they'd felt it as well. Ashfel was standing at the kennel doors, growling quietly. He lifted his head, almost in salute, as Gilliam trance-touched him.

There was a boy asleep in the corner by the fire. Gilliam chose Connel, the smallest of the hounds, with which to approach him. Luckily, they were still in Breodanir, and the villagers that were chosen to tend the Lords' dogs were no ignorant or superstitious free-towners. The boy shook sleep from his eyes and rose as Connel tugged at his sleeve.

Salas, Marrat, Singer, and Corfel lined up by the door in a perfectly still circle. Ashfel, looking regal, growled impatiently.

"Aye, I'm hurrying," the boy muttered. "It's easy for the lot of you to be awake— you've got the beds." He hesitated at the kennel doors. "I'm not so sure I should let you out. What if it isn't your Lord a'calling?"

In answer, Ashfel growled again, and the six dogs turned, almost as one creature, to stare out, as if the walls did not exist. The boy shook his head again, said a quick, but very sincere prayer to the Hunter, and then opened the door. The dogs trotted out quietly into the night; Connel stopped to nudge the boy back into the warmth of the building.

Good, Connel, Gilliam thought, as he eased himself out of his trance. If he had the chance, he would have to talk to the innkeeper about that boy. A remarkable choice of guardian; one of whom Gilliam approved wholeheartedly. "It's done," he said quietly to the silent room.

The seeress nodded. "You are the pebble that starts the avalanche," she said softly and with no humor. "Come. The bridge has been burned to ash, and the family that collects its tolls murdered. They are waiting for you to attempt the crossing."

"Who are *they*?"

"Your enemies," she replied evenly. "We will travel a different route."

"We will—"

"Wake the mage."

"The mage," a new voice said, "is awake." Zareth Kahn stood, back to the closed door that adjoined their rooms. "And has been for some minutes." He stood in his journey robes, his arms across his chest, his gaze intent upon the newcomer. "You are Evayne?"

"We have," Evayne replied, "no time. We *must* leave, and soon."

"Evayne—" Stephen began, but the seer raised her hand and cut him off.

"Zareth Kahn," she said, her voice low and tense, "the date?"

"It's the twentieth day of the tenth month," he replied crisply.

"No," she said, "it's now the *twenty-first* day of Scaral." She watched his face, waiting to see the reaction that she desired. It came, but not quickly and not strongly enough.

"*Scarran,*" he said.

"Yes."

"What in the hells is *Scarran?*" Gilliam broke in.

But Stephen of Elseth was already throwing together the odds and ends that were absolutely essential to their survival: money, furs, the letters that Lady Elseth had written. All else was trivial. *Don't argue with her, Gil,* he thought, and the urgency behind his fear hit his Hunter hard. *We've got to run.*

Espere began to dance from foot to foot, her eyes darting from Evayne to Gilliam to the door as if they formed the points of a mysterious triangle that she was compelled to trace over and over again.

"*Scarran?*" Evayne said softly to Gilliam. "Do you know what *Lattan* is?"

"*No.*"

"*Lattan* is High Summer. The bright conjunction." She walked to the door, motioned Zareth Kahn to one side, and opened it. "*Scarran* is High Winter. The dark conjunction. The old power and the old roads are open this eve, and they will be used against us."

Zareth Kahn raised a dark brow. "The Summer and Winter rites? Not even the most diligent of pre-Weston scholars do more than a cursory study of their significance. There are certainly no mages who—" Then he stopped. "Ah. The kin."

"Indeed. No, don't use your magery here. I have studied the ways of hiding, and I've done what it is possible to do."

Zareth Kahn glanced at Gilliam and Stephen, then nodded. "It appears that we are all set to follow where you lead. Lead us to safety."

Evayne smiled grimly. "I can only lead you," she replied, "into the darkest night."

Night made of the world a quiet, sleepy place, a near-hidden landscape in which dream—or nightmare—unfurled. The air was crisp and chilly when inhaled, but there was no breeze. The moon was under a veil of darkness; to Stephen's eyes, it seemed that it had somehow shattered, and the shards, hard and cold, were scattered across the sky like a brilliant spill.

The shivery feeling at the base of Stephen's spine had little to do with the cold; Gilliam, Hunter Lord of Elseth, was calling the Hunter's trance.

Evayne said nothing, although Stephen was certain she noticed the momentary slowing of their pace, the stiffening of Gilliam's body, as he readied himself. She did not demur. Stephen unsheathed his sword, careful to make little noise. The stillness of the air, the silence on the snow- and ice-covered path, were eerie enough that he didn't wish to disturb them.

Evayne's hands moved briefly; she whispered a word that sounded vaguely familiar to Stephen, although it was in a tongue with which he was unfamiliar. He listened, trying to place the word, before he realized that he would listen long indeed, and with little result.

Magery.

Beneath his feet, the land changed. Where there had been a flat surface of ice and snow, a path appeared, limned with an eerie, pale light that wound its way into the heart of the darkness. She did not tell them to follow it; she didn't need to. They walked, two abreast, Espere bringing up the rear, the silence bearing down upon them more heavily with each passing moment.

Something's going to happen, Stephen thought, forcing himself to exhale as he strode across the night landscape. Although the night was clear, storm was brewing; the air was thick and heavy with it. He cast a surreptitious glance over his shoulder and met the gaze of Zareth Kahn. A flicker of blue light adorned the mage's eyes; they looked inhuman and unnatural. Stephen stumbled, and seeing this, his companion narrowed his eyes.

"What is it?" Gilliam said, instantly aware of his brother's unease.

Stephen swallowed. "Magic." Then, quickly, "Ours."

"No," Zareth Kahn replied, gazing at the woods they were approaching. "Not ours alone. Evayne—there. Directly north. Do you see it?"

The blue-robed seer raised a dark brow and then gestured; light flickered over her face like a mask before sinking into her eyes to lurk there like hidden fire. "*Kalliaris'* frown." The goddess of luck was, like the night, of dark aspect. Evayne raised her arms to either side; the command to stop was implicit in the gesture. "You're of reasonable power, Master Kahn."

"And you," he replied softly.

"The rest of us don't have mage-sight," Gilliam said tersely as he squinted into a row of trees that looked almost the same as any other row of trees did in the distance with night and winter to obscure it. "What do you see?"

"Spell," Zareth Kahn replied, his brow furrowed. "I don't recognize it. But it is either a very powerful Shadow magic or a very powerful *Scarran* rite. I don't know enough about either of those schools of study to say which it is with certainty." His tone implied that neither school was a magic that was friendly.

Evayne took a deep and weary breath. "This is ill news," she said at last. "I've done what I can to shield us from the sight of our enemies, but we can't continue to hide forever; it's a costly spell to maintain. I'd hoped that beyond the forest there would be some respite." She turned and began to retrace her path. "We cannot cross to the east; not tonight." They did not question her, but instead, followed as she led them west.

And in the darkness of the western woods, the same cold magic deepened and broadened the shadows of the night. Like a liquid, it pooled near the roots of the trees, waiting. Evayne would not tell them the spell's purpose, although it was clear that she knew it.

They walked to the north, and then to the south; in every direction, the danger was identical.

Evayne cursed, and then cursed again, more loudly, for good measure. "I am a fool," she said at last. "They never meant to wait for you to take the bridge; they only meant to prevent your flight should you make it that far." She lifted a hand to her lips, and stood, gazing out at the Northern woods. "Zareth Kahn," she said, after five minutes had passed, "give me some hope. Tell me that the shadows are not moving toward us."

"I never lie to a lady," the mage replied gravely. "But I had hoped that it was my imagination."

"What's wrong? What is it?" Gilliam reached out and touched the seer's draping sleeve. It pulled away from his hand, but in the darkness he could pretend it was the woman who had moved.

"Do you remember the demon-kin that you faced m the King's City?" Evayne asked quietly.

"Yes."

"Expect far worse."

Stephen's grip on leather and steel tightened out of habit; he no longer expected to be able to wield the sword to any advantage. He remembered the fight in the King's City quite well. He felt, rather than saw, Gilliam's painful wince; the Hunter Lord still bore the scars of that evening's work, and would while he lived.

Which might, Stephen thought, as the night began to deepen, *not be that much longer.*

Evayne cursed again. Stephen had only seen her thrice at this age, and on none of those occasions had he seen the weight of fear bear so heavily down upon her. She closed her eyes, and her brow furrowed as if she were already upon the field. Then she turned to the wild girl. "Espere," she said tersely. "Come."

Gilliam bridled, but the wild girl tossed her tangled hair and obeyed the seeress' command. She stopped mere inches away from Evayne's shaking, outstretched palm.

"Take it." A deep golden light suffused her hand, cocooning palm and fingers beneath the warmth of its glow.

Espere reached out and almost gently gripped the light. It surrounded them both, running from finger to finger, from hand to hand, until it was hard to see who it had originated from.

"Enough." Evayne lifted her head, and even in the darkness, Stephen thought her haggard.

"Evayne?"

But she waved him off. "Espere."

The girl blinked, and then, slowly, raised hands to eyes. Stephen thought the motion very odd, but not as strange as what she did next: she spoke. "Y-yes. I am—I am back."

"You won't be for much longer. I need your eyes. I need your father's ability. Test the wind, little one. Guard my back."

Espere nodded gravely, pushing a tangled curl away from eyes that were no longer black. Stephen's breath caught in his throat as he saw the change; she was golden-irised now, and her eyes had the peculiar brilliance of the god-born at work. Where had the wild girl gone?

Evayne reached into her robes and brought forth the crystal sphere that she had called the seer's ball. She cupped it carefully in her hands and bent over it; her dark hood fell forward, obscuring her face but not the ball itself.

Mists curled there, trapped beneath a glassy layer. Light sparked; shadows fled. Stephen took a step forward, as if drawn by the visions the ball promised.

And the wild girl stepped blithely between the future and the present, blocking Stephen's vision. She was not so wild now, and not so much the girl. There was a lift to her jaw, a strength to her features, that he had never seen there. He started to speak, but she shook her head.

"But—"

"No. If we talk, we may well pay with our lives for the discussion."

Wide-mouthed, he watched her as she left him, tracing some invisible circle around the seeress who gazed, transfixed, into the pulsing ball. He felt shock, surprise, even a little pain and bewilderment; emotions so strong, that it took him a minute to realize that they did not originate with him.

Gilliam. He spun lightly to see his Hunter Lord staring, almost glassy eyed, at the wild girl—at Espere.

"What's wrong?"

Gilliam shook his head. He was mute under the weight of what he felt; he had no words to describe it, or perhaps, no desire to bind the emotion with words. Stephen could feel some of it, but he could not understand it. What passed between Gilliam and his pack—be they the finest of the hounds, or a mysterious half-wit, half-god—was so private a communion that not even a huntbrother could comprehend all of it.

And what did it mean, to be bound in that way to a woman—to a whole, sane, rational being; to an equal? What did it mean, when the bond changed suddenly, shifting in place as if it had never truly been anything but illusory?

As if the question were one that he had spoken aloud, the wild girl turned and gazed at him, her eyes luminous in the darkness. He took an involuntary step back at what he saw there: grieving. Stephen of Elseth was a huntbrother, and therefore no stranger to grief. Although she met his gaze for only a second, he recognized it at once.

And then she lifted her head, testing the wind as if she were a scent-hound. It was almost a comfort to see the motion, because it was the only thing that she had done that seemed remotely familiar.

The comfort was a cold one, and the moment Espere spoke, it turned to ice. "They're coming."

"I . . . see them," Evayne replied. The light from the crystal shadowed the lines of her face, deepening them. "Oh, holy triumvirate, aid us. Goddess, smile. Smile, please." She bit her lip; her hands shook. Then she closed her eyes, and her face aged years. Slowly, carefully, she set the ball aside.

"Evayne?"

"Lady?"

"The tower was a game," was her pale reply. "They come in earnest. Look." And she cast her arm in a circle, scattering a spray of orange light across the snow and shadows. It melted the darkness, contorted it, gave it many forms. Each of those forms was moving toward them, linked in a series of concentric circles. Evayne stood at its heart, the center of a vast target.

"Well met," came a soft voice.

Zareth Kahn started slightly and then raised his own arms in a shield of coruscating light. It, too, was orange.

The demons—for there could no longer be any doubt as to what they were— slowed their stride. Twice, Stephen tried to count them and failed. He made no third attempt. He swung his sword round and held it level, glancing from side to side. *How?* he thought, as Gilliam became a wall at his back. *How did they get here?*

"Well met," Sor na Shannen said again, as she stepped from the darkness to the darkness, gleaming like polished obsidian. "We have unfinished business with all of you." She raised her arms and spoke three harsh words; the darkness fell from her shoulders like a cast-off cloak. Beneath it, her raiment was fire.

"High Winter makes you bold," Evayne said, her expression unreadable.

"No, seeress," Sor na Shannen replied. "It makes me *powerful*." Like a whip, fire leaped from her hands. The snow and the ice that she stood on were gone in an instant, as was the slumbering grass beneath them; the fire left red and white rock sizzling in its wake.

"Wild Fire," Evayne's whisper was a weary one.

"Oh, yes," the demon replied. "And now, before Winter passes, let us see an end to this."

The seeress nodded quietly. "Before Winter ends." And she, too, lifted her hands. In comparison, they seemed thin and frail, bereft of power or magic. She carried only a dagger, and it was a meager and pathetic weapon. A flash of purple in the handle caught the orange light and glinted softly above her head as she gazed into the moonless night.

The laughter of the demoness carried across the silent, winter landscape. "Did you truly think to stop us?"

Evayne tightened her grip on the handle of the dagger before driving it into the flesh of her right palm. Blood trickled from the wound onto her upturned face. Her voice was trembling, her complexion gray, as she began to speak quickly.

"We break the Spring circle. We deny the birthing." She shook her right hand; blood spattered on the ground and hissed there, as if alive and in pain. The ice beneath her feet gave way to a slick, sudden blackness.

Flame lapped at the perimeter of the first circle as Sor na Shannen gestured lazily.

"We break the Summer circle. We deny the living." Again she shook her hand, and again blood hit the ground as if it had become unnatural.

"We break the Autumn circle. We deny the dying." A third time, her hands flew. She cast a shadow in the orange light of Zareth Kahn's protective magery; it was a long shadow that fell over them all, deepening and chilling as the seconds passed. Even Espere stopped her circling, her soft growl, and moved quietly to Evayne's side.

"What are you doing, little seer? You cannot hope to escape us." But the words of the demoness had lost some of their grandeur, their glamour. She frowned, and gestured for the shadows that leaped up from the ground like eager counselors.

Evayne paid her no heed, for shadows of her own summoning now darkened the clearing. "We have come, free of coercion, to the hidden road, and we know well that we will walk it in Winter. I am Evayne a'Neamis; I have walked the Oracle's road, I have seen the Oracle's vision, I have made the Choice. The hidden path cannot be denied me. You ask for power and I speak with its voice. I bid thee: Open!"

"NO!"

The world fell away.

Sor na Shannen's cry of denial echoed in the hollows of the strange forest the land suddenly became. Trees, sharply defined even in the poor light, stood bare of leaves, and perhaps even of bark.

Are they trees? Stephen wondered.

"Keep to the road!" Evayne snapped. "Do not set a foot off it; do not even move down it without my guidance. Is that clear?" She opened her mouth to say more, and then bit back the words, shook her head sharply, and turned her back upon them. There was a curious finality to the gesture.

The demons were gone. They were safe.

But it certainly didn't feel that way.

Stephen swallowed and nodded. He expected Gilliam to argue, but Gilliam made no protest; he frowned, but the frown was turned wholly on Espere. She was pale, as white as the snow, and her eyes were wide, golden circles. The hair along her neck bristled; her gaze flickered from side to side as if she were surrounded by enemies that not even her nightmares conjured. The demons had not had this effect on Espere.

Stephen didn't need to be bound to her to feel her fear. It was palpable, another distinct presence.

"It is clear," Zareth Kahn said quietly, "but not necessarily acceptable." He crossed his arms and looked down at the curtain of midnight-blue that fell from her shoulders to the ground. "I may be mistaken," he continued, his voice soft and measured enough that one might think it friendly. "I confess my reliable knowledge of magery does not go back further than the dominance of the Dark League."

Evayne did not respond.

"But I have a cursory knowledge of the history of magery, and the branches of magery that have long since passed into disuse." He took a step toward her. "*Scarran* was called the dark conjunction, and if I remember correctly, only a Dark Adept could call its power."

"You remember correctly," she replied, bowing her head.

"I see." He took a step back. "I also seem to recall that the magic of the Dark Adepts often required a sacrifice."

Very slowly, the seeress turned. She cradled her crystal in the crook of her left arm; her right hand covered its surface, obscuring it from sight.

Stephen gasped and shook his head slowly from side to side. Zareth Kahn's power flared to life as he took another step away from Evayne. Or from the woman that had once been Evayne.

Her face was ice, her hair ebony. And her eyes, once violet, were now utterly black. All around her skin, hovering like a fine mist, were gossamer strands of darkness. She no longer appeared fatigued; she no longer appeared to be human.

"A sacrifice?" She laughed bitterly. "Oh, yes, Zareth Kahn. You do know your history. One of us will not leave the Winter road."

Chapter Three

22nd Scaral, 410 A.A.
Averalaan, Twenty-fifth Holding

THE SMELL OF SMOKE and burning wood made the stench of the trough bearable—but it was a near thing. Stale sweat and the sour smell of drinking gone bad clung to the air like lice to an alley mongrel. Jewel scratched her forearm and cursed the very thought of lice.

Carver was into his second mug of what Taverson cheerfully called ale. Jewel was into her second mug as well, but with one important difference; she'd been using her ale to help kill one of the two potted plants in the tavern. She was quite good at surreptitious movement, and only Carver, quite familiar with her dislike for alcohol of any sort, noticed the way she upended her mug into the soil.

Carver kept a dark eye on the tavern doors. They were old, but thicker than a drunk magisterian, and they were wide enough that the place could be cleared in a hurry. Lorrey, the barkeep who tended the trough during the daylight hours, was well protected behind the long, wide bar that stretched end to end across the tavern. To the far end of it was the kitchen and the infamous cellars; beyond that, the door to the alley. The alley was the place where garbage and unwanted human litter often ended up.

There was glass in the two front windows, but they didn't make much difference; when it wasn't raining, half of the tavern front opened into the nearby street, although you still had to walk through the doors to get in. Made as much sense as anything else did.

From his vantage point, Carver could see both the kitchen and the street, although they were sitting far enough back that those on the street couldn't easily see them. Jewel could see neither, but that was just as well; she was busy reading.

He wanted to ask her what she was reading—because, although he'd never have admitted it, he liked the stories she told them after she finished her "studying"—but he could tell by her expression that the only story he was likely to get was one that was a little too real for his liking. He kept quiet.

Old Rath. Dead. He couldn't imagine it. Rath was a son of Cartanis if ever there was one—who could kill Rath? He lifted his mug, swallowed, and lowered it again. And how could he be dead? They'd just *seen* Rath. Carver knew the old man well enough to know what he looked like, and he'd heard him shout enough to recognize the sound of his voice.

He glanced at Jewel, who was still absorbed by the papers she held in her lap. Jewel had never been wrong before. Well, not never—but never when it counted. He shivered.

Because if Rath was dead, and that wasn't Rath, then it only went to follow—

"Jay?"

"What?"

"How're we going to know if we're really talking to each other? I mean if Rath—"

"I know." The two words were curt, almost cold, but it was clear that she'd already thought of it. "I'll fix it, Carver. Keep your eyes on the doors." She went back to her reading, and then looked up a second or two later. "There were things about Rath that he didn't know. If he did, we'd already be dead."

Carver swallowed air, and then lifted the mug to his face. He looked at the black sheen of hair that was warped in the mug's surface, and shook his head. "Yeah." What he wanted to say was, *It's been two hours.* But Jewel knew it just as well as he did.

Hells, she probably knew it better. She was the den mother, after all.

Maybe they've already come and gone, he thought, as he used the bitter ale to get rid of the dryness in his mouth. It had taken a long time to lose Old Rath—or whoever it was; a lot longer than it normally took Carver to lose a single pursuer. *If,* he thought grimly, *we lost him at all.*

Carver wasn't one to pray much; it was a point of pride with him. So he bit the edge of his mug and stared around the tavern as if he were a drowning man in search of land.

Jewel, Old Rath had written, which meant it *had* to be bad news, *if you're reading this, I'm probably already dead. I should speak with you before leaving, but I'm not going to; I've got my own reasons for what I do, and I'm not about to explain them to a young slip of an overeager, over-intelligent, under-ambitious young woman.*

The most important news I have is this: The tunnels must be revealed. I know what it's meant to your den-kin, and I know what it's meant to me—but we were both living by the grace of Kalliaris' whim, and she's stopped smiling for good.

I've done some research in the last few weeks, and it's become clear to me that it isn't just your den that's suffered. All through the thirty-fifth, the thirty-second, and the seventeenth holdings, people have been mysteriously disappearing—for well over eleven years now.

And I don't think it's a coincidence that it was just over eleven years ago that I first discovered the tunnels. Nor a coincidence that no one seems to have discovered those tunnels before—or since. There haven't been any bodies turned up, so it's pretty easy for the magisterians to assume that people have just moved on.

That's what I assumed. At first.

For the first few disappearances—from what I've been able to piece together—it was a safe assumption to make. But there've been more than a few that can't be explained. People who were happy enough where they were, or who weren't involved in any of the trades that often lead to an untimely disappearance. I've written a list of their names for you to give to the proper authority.

The proper authority, in this case, is not the magisterians. Whatever you do, keep this information, or rather, the fact that you have it, from them. I've reason to believe that some, or all, of the magisterial guards are not to be trusted in this. It only follows that the magisterial courts may be suspect as well.

You never paid attention, so pay attention now. The magisterians report to the holding courts, which in turn report to the magisterial courts, which in turn report to the courts of Reymaris on the isle, should that be necessary. Magisterians may, therefore, be receiving their orders from three different sources. I know that the magisterians in the three holdings above have been turning a blind eye to the disappearances. But I cannot know whether they've been bought at ground level—which I find highly dubious—or they're in the pay of politically greater masters.

I told you never to explore the tunnels without me. You did. But I trust your instinct and skill; you didn't probe them too deeply or wander too far in their web. It's probably what kept you alive. Someone is using those tunnels to kidnap—and in all probability murder—citizens of Averalaan. I don't know why. I thought they might be slavers at first, but when you see the list of victims, you'll understand why that's unlikely.

Someone is going to have to explore the tunnels fully—but that someone had better be both powerful and well-connected enough to override, overrule, or overpower the magisterians—or their paymasters—who have done their best, over time, to hide the disappearances that have taken place within the three holdings.

Jewel looked up, saw that Carver's gaze darted between the two doors that led into the tavern, and looked down again to the scrawl of letters across fine, stiff paper.

Where was Duster's message? She heard the rustle of paper and realized that she was crushing the scroll. Without a change of expression, she forced her fingers to unfurl. *Come on, Duster, come on. Damn it, where's word?*

Carver set his mug to one side and stood, restless. "Jay?"

"No," she replied curtly. But she knew how he felt; she wanted to get up and scour the streets herself. "Have another." She forced her attention back to the letter and away from the den that was her life.

Reaching the right person is going to be hard at your station in life.

Jewel gave a mental snort.

But failing to reach the right person will kill you.

Thanks, Rath.

So I am going to break the oath that bound my life and made me who I am.

Which was, all things considered, a rather short-tempered, mean, but loyal sonofabitch. With a quick wit and good manners.

Go to House Terafin. Go quickly, and without delay.

"Jay? Are you all right?"

"Y-yes. Fine. Keep your eyes on the door."

Speak with The Terafin.

She might as well just cross the bridge to the Holy Isle and demand an audience with the Twin Kings themselves.

"Jay, are you sure?"

She nodded, but without much force. What Rath proposed was ridiculous. If she was lucky, she could get onto the grounds of a minor Terafin relative; the guards would skewer her if she set foot on the manicured lawns that belonged to The Terafin herself. All things considered, she didn't have clothing fine enough to pass herself off as one of the family's lowliest servants.

If as I suspect, you can't get past the guards, tell them that you've been sent with an urgent message. They're quite likely to be skeptical; only tell them that you've been instructed to speak with none save The Terafin. They will ask who sent you. Tell them Ararath Handernesse. If they will not carry the message, loiter until you can speak with a servant, and attempt to get the message carried in that fashion.

But on no account are you to discuss the text of this message with either guards or servants.

That was Rath, through and through. He liked to forget that anyone else in this city had a brain and knew how to use it.

She bit her lip and looked up, remembering an old admonishment to speak well of the dead. Remembering the voice and the words, but not the face, not the figure. Glimpses of early childhood. *Come on, Duster, where are you?*

Carver stared back at her. "Don't you have any 'feeling' about this?"

"I don't know when they're dying," she snapped back. "I only know when they're dead." It was the wrong thing to say, and she regretted it before she'd finished speaking, but she wasn't some sort of compass, to be pointed and read.

Carver slammed the mug down, attracting the stares of the nearby patrons.

"Tha's right, boy, don' let no chit of a girl give you trouble," an older man said, leering in Jewel's direction. He teetered to his feet, took a few steps toward the table, and then stopped as he looked down the length of Jewel's long dagger.

"Get lost," she said softly. "We don't want trouble, but we'll make it if we have to." She didn't want to stab him, but she was perfectly willing to—and it was only the last that was written across the fine steel of her expression.

She glared at him until he broke eye contact and retreated to a table that was not as close as the one he'd left. Then she sat with a thud.

"Carver," she began.

His shrug was his apology and his reply. His eyes went back to the door. Jewel could see the retreat of one black brow as his eyes widened; he was staring doorward.

Without thinking, she bunched up her papers and shoved them back into her shirt. Then she wheeled in her chair, her hand on her dagger.

In the open door, with a little sunlight lighting up currents of wafting smoke around his face, was Arann. He was unmistakable; at sixteen years old, not even in his full growth, he was a barrel-chested giant. The set of his jaw and the grim expression that he usually wore hid the fact that he was, of all her den, the most gentle.

Jewel might have been angry at any other time; orders were orders, and she never gave them without a reason. But she felt relief first and foremost, and then, as Arann staggered into the trough, concern.

She got up, crossed the crowded room, and stopped in front of Arann; this close, the bleeding and bruising was evident. His forehead had been gashed open, and the only thing that kept the blood from running into his eyes was his hair; it was matted and sticky with it. "What happened?" she asked quietly, as she put an arm around her den mate's waist. She couldn't reach his shoulders.

Arann swallowed and winced. He pulled away as a trickle of blood trailed out of the left corner of his lip. "The others—they're here. Duster told us where to run."

Jay closed her eyes briefly. All right. They were here. She'd have to deal with it—and at least they were all where she could see them.

"What happened to you?"

"Attacked," Arann replied. He started to say something else, and lost it to a fit of coughing. She gave him time to get his breath; gave him time to clutch his side and slowly straighten up. "Oh, Jay—Duster's gone—she made us leave—we ran—we left her behind—"

"Duster?" Jewel's voice was soft; she couldn't have put any force behind the word had she wanted to.

Arann nodded.

"Carver." He was already at her shoulder. "The others are outside. Get them in here fast."

He nodded grimly, all business.

As was she. She made a mental calculation, and then another, slower one. Swallowed. "Arann, does it hurt much?"

"No," he answered, and she knew he was lying. Angel, Finch, Teller, Jester, Arann, and Carver were all the den she had left—and she didn't intend to lose another.

But she didn't have the money for a healer, and she had a sudden strong feeling that she didn't have the time to wait for one anyway.

Carver came bolting into the tavern, and the rest of her den came at his heels, pale and drawn. Even Angel, ever flamboyant, was absolutely silent. "Jay," Carver said, throwing a glance over his shoulder. "We've got to run."

"I know," she whispered. She looked at Arann and swallowed. "Did any of you bring the box?" That box, small and gray, with chipped paint and enamel, was all that she had taken from her father's possessions. It held the entire monetary worth of the den. Didn't amount to much, but it was all they had.

Teller nodded; he was clutching it tightly under his left arm. Jewel shook herself hard; it wasn't like her to miss sight of something that significant. "Good, we're going to need it. We've got to get a carriage."

They nodded, each of them, looking at her as if she had all the answers. *I won't fail you. I won't fail you again.* But Arann was growing whiter by the minute. "Arann, can you run?"

"Yeah."

"Good." She nodded to the kitchen—which they all knew led out to the alley—as the front doors swung open again.

Standing in the frame like an impassable pillar was Old Rath.

Jewel looked up and met the eyes of darkness staring out from the subtle caricature of a familiar face. There was a clear path to the kitchens, but not much of a clear escape without a little diversion.

It was Duster who often caused their diversions. Jewel's jaw clamped around whatever it was her mouth wanted to say; she felt a rawness, and then a numbness, and then a fear so strong it was physical. Sometime later, she would have time for anger.

She looked up at Arann's pale face, and at the trickle of blood that still ran from his lips like a poorly quaffed drink.

Kalliaris, she thought, begging for the turn of Luck's lips. And then, *Mother, Mother, protect your children.*

"Carver, get going."

"No."

"I said, get going. I'll take care of this."

"No." It was always risky to disobey Jewel; she was undisputed master of the den. But if anyone was stupid enough to do it, it was Carver; he'd proved that many, many times. Rath began to thread his way through the patrons of the tavern, moving slowly but surely toward them. "Duster couldn't do it, you can't." His voice was flat and final. "You go." He grabbed her arm and pushed her back.

She saw the glint of his long knife as he steadied himself. She bit her lip; she knew it was true. Duster was the combatant of the den. And Carver was unarguably second to her. Second.

But Jewel would be damned if she ran away while a fourteen-year-old boy guarded her back. She would be twice damned if she left him to face whatever it was that was masquerading as Old Rath. And she would face damnation three times—a hundred times—over, if *she* lost another of her den. A scream was building up in her throat. She let it come.

"FIRE!" An electric silence filled the room. *"FIRE IN THE KITCHEN!"* Reaching out, she grabbed Carver's shoulder in a tight vise-grip as the room began to empty. Chairs and tables scraped the oaken floor. Some teetered, and some fell, sending mugs and glasses groundward. Jewel didn't wait to watch.

Because she knew that everyone was surging doorward; knew that Old Rath—whatever it was—was caught up in the crowd; knew that the path to the kitchen was clear, but not for very long. Carver was stiff; she knocked his right knee out from under him, righted him, and then spun him round. That snapped his resolution and his concentration.

Jewel, den as intact as it was going to be, led her chosen kin to the only escape route they had.

Kalliaris, smile. Smile and I'll worship at your whim for the rest of my life.

"You can let go now," Carver said, gritting his teeth. He inched forward on his stomach and peered down, over the edge of the squat, three-story building they huddled on. The alley was overlong, and Jewel had no wish to be trapped in it like a rat in a cage.

They'd climbed instead.

"Arann?" She kept her voice soft, as close to silent as it got.

"I'm . . . fine." He mouthed his reply more than spoke it. He was lying, and he was getting worse at it as the minutes snuck past.

Climbing had its price.

"Teller, who was it? Who attacked you?"

Teller stared at her, dark eyes wide. "It wasn't a who," he said at last. "Whatever it was, it wasn't a person." He shivered. She didn't need to hear more. Not now. Later, if there was one.

Carver waved frantically, and then stopped speaking. Hells, they stopped breathing, and most of them closed their eyes. He inched back, slowly and quietly scraping the roof with his chest. *It's Rath*, he mouthed to Jewel.

Jewel's brows drew together; she nodded, her jaws clamped tight. There had to be something to do; some way of escape. She knew, although there wasn't any reason to bring it up, that Arann's blood left a minute trail on the building's side. If this Rath had time to look around—and who was going to stop him?—he'd eventually discover it. They had to move. They had to do something.

She concentrated, fingers digging into the edges of the box that she'd taken back from Teller. She even closed her eyes, thinking, sorting it out, trying to come up with a plan that would save them.

Carver's curse brought her back. She saw him get up into a crouch at the roof's edge. He raised his left hand, and the long knife—the balanced long knife—that he carried went flying down. "Cartanis' blood."

Jewel had never seen Carver quite so pale.

"It's him," she said. "It's Rath."

"The knife. It—it *bounced.*"

"Everybody—north side. NOW." It led to the street, to the crowds, to the witnesses. Jewel had the sinking feeling that witnesses here weren't going to turn the tide. But at least it might count for something.

Angel and Finch scuttled down the eaves, clinging to an old trellis that was so covered it was nearly invisible. Teller followed, and then Jewel sent Arann down. Carver followed him; she left last.

And because she was last down, she was first to see the result of Kalliaris' smile: an empty, open carriage headed down the street at a brisk clip. Wind whistled through her hair as she scuttled down the building side; wind and a hint of something physical. She shivered with it, whispered a blessing in the name of the Mother, and then jumped the last ten feet, landing in a spectacularly bruising roll.

"Rider!" she yelled, waving her box high in the air, as it was the only flag she had. "RIDER!"

The two horses came to a halt as the bits hit the backs of their mouths. The driver pulled his carriage up, and Jewel's den were all over it like fleas on a dirty dog.

"Hey, you—" the driver began, the lines of his face stiffening into a glare. Jewel opened the box and emptied it out onto the carriage floor.

"It's yours," she said, turning to look over her shoulder for the first time since she'd hit the ground. "It's yours if you move *now.*"

He looked down at the coins scattered on the carriage floor, and then looked up at Jewel's desperate face. Shrugged and nodded curtly. "But pick 'em up." He put the horses to reins, and the carriage jerked forward with the rapid start. "Where are you going?"

"To the estates of The Terafin."

The driver snorted, but the sound was lost. Old Rath leaped from the top of the building and missed them by about three feet, landing with a crunch that was audible over every other noise the street had to offer. The ground caught him, hard—but Jewel wasn't surprised to see him stand. Nor was she surprised to see him begin to run.

She scrambled up the open carriage to the driver's side, her hands damp with sweat and shaking with effort. "You've got to *go faster,*" she shouted, trying to keep the plea out of her voice. "What kind of lousy horses are these? Look—a man on foot can keep up!"

"Don't get cheeky with me," the driver shouted back, turning to glare at her again. He stopped shouting as he saw the direction her hand was pointing in. There was a man, about two yards behind the carriage, who was keeping pace with his horses.

Now, truthfully, his horses were not the finest, but they were of good stock, and the man had pride besides. He doubled his glare at the girl who'd brought this humiliation to his notice, and then turned his full attention to the horses.

They began to *gallop*.

Jewel and her den discovered why horses pulling a carriage through city streets don't gallop. They were jarred and bruised and shaken by seats that weren't meant to be comfortable at a standstill. But they saw Rath fall farther and farther behind—although it was a slow process. Jewel would have bet on the horses, but she wouldn't have bet by a large margin. She threw in a hundred prayers for good measure.

As Rath became smaller in the distance, reaction set in; she felt giddy with relief. They had escaped. They were *safe*. She turned, hugged Carver, and laughed out loud. Angel joined in seconds later, as did Finch; even Teller smiled broadly.

But Arann, who was often quiet, covered his mouth and turned away. He wanted to smile, but he couldn't manage it, and after thirty seconds, he forgot what he'd hoped to smile at. He clutched his side, and it hurt, so he stopped, but that hurt as well. Movement hurt; even when he tried to keep very, very still, the ground wouldn't stop shaking. He tried to clear his throat, and then, when that failed, he sank slowly down as he heard the laughter of his den-kin grow muted and more distant.

"Arann, are you all right?"

"I'm fine," he heard himself say. He thought it was Jewel who asked the question, but he couldn't be sure; his eyelids were dark and too heavy to lift.

"Tell me if it gets to be too much."

"I will."

The carriage rolled to a smooth stop along the boulevard. Trees as old, Jewel thought, as the city itself grew in neat and even rows on either side of the stone road. Birds called to one another, and squirrels chittered in obvious displeasure, but those were the only noises the street had to offer.

She had never been this close to the High City before. Had never, in fact, had any reason other than curiosity to cross any of the three bridges that led to it. Curiosity alone didn't justify the cost of the toll—or cost of the ferry passage, although it would be marginally easier to stow away aboard the boats—and the guards who bore the emblem of the Twin Kings were unlikely to let her pass without paying.

Which was only fair, as she was likely to do her best to make her short visit worthwhile at the expense of one of the people that the guards were supposed to be protecting. She shrugged as the driver paid the necessary tolls, and gazed across the bay. Then she squared her shoulders and looked at the Isle of Kings, the home of the heart of the empire.

There were cathedrals here: three. Cormaris, Lord of Wisdom, Reymaris, Lord of Justice, and the Mother found worship and splendor on the isle of the Twin Kings. They were called the holy triumvirate, and it was a testament to the humility of the Kings that the cathedrals, each spired and perfectly built, stood higher, and more grand, man the royal palace.

Somewhere on the Isle was the home of the Order of Knowledge, where dusty old men and women clung to books and strange rituals. Here, too, was Senniel, the most famous bardic college in the world. There were rumors of a merchants' market so expensive that the streets were almost always empty. Guild headquarters were here, and here the maker-born dwelled under the eyes of the Kings.

But there were very few noble families who could boast the right to live on the isle. In fact, there were only ten, *The* Ten. They aided the Twin Kings in the governing of Essalieyan—or so Old Rath said—and warred quietly among themselves when the Kings were otherwise occupied. They had lands here.

The carriage rolled to a stop along the street beside a polished brass fence. The rails were wide and evenly spaced, and at their feet on either side were beds of flowers—some sort of pink and blue blossoms that seemed fine-veined and too delicate for a lawn.

"Here it is," the driver said, scratching his beard and staring with open curiosity at his passengers. "Home of The Terafin. You want me to wait?"

"No," she said curtly, knowing that she had no money for the return passage. "We'll be fine from here."

As she slowly climbed down from the side of the carriage, crouching at the step to find a reasonable handhold, her first impression was, oddly enough, one of disappointment. She had seen noble manors before, and she expected that the woman who ruled the most powerful family in the land—if you didn't include the Crowns—would live in something only a little less fine than the palace of Kings. But this—While it was a large building, it had no grand lawns, no fountains, no grounds.

Carver was staring at it with the same skepticism.

"It's the right place," the driver said, smirking. "There's not so much land on the Holy Isle that any noble can claim miles of grass and flower beds." He shook his head as he gently reined his horses round. "That's the guard gate."

Jewel nodded absently, and then she heard something fall behind her. She pivoted neatly on her right foot and stared down at Arann's back.

"Shit," Carver muttered. "Angel, get off your backside and help me move him." Jester was already there, hands at the small of Arann's broad back.

Angel nodded, and Finch and Teller quietly joined them. Arann was easily the largest of the den, and even awake and willing was almost impossible to move.

"What's wrong with him, Jay? Why are you looking like that?" Carver grunted as he shouldered a third of Arann's weight.

"It's nothing," she said.

"Jay?" It was Teller. "He's dying, isn't he?"

"Shut up, Teller." She looked down the walk to the guard post. It was maybe ten yards, but she measured each inch by Arann's gurgling breath. "Just shut up." She slowed her nervous pace, and caught Arann's slack right hand in both of hers. *I won't let you die*, she thought, searching for—and finding—a pulse. *I swear it by the Mother's sleep, I won't lose anyone else.*

"What's your business with The Terafin?"

Jewel had to give the guard credit. Whoever he was, he was completely neutral; if he thought she was an urchin from the worst part of town—which she was, practically speaking—he didn't show it at all. It made her nervous. She took a deep breath, glancing over her right shoulder to where Arann stood, propped up between Carver and Angel, with Jester at his back.

"I've been sent to deliver a message."

The fair-haired older man frowned slightly as his gaze swept over Arann's unconscious body, but that was his only change of expression. He held out his mailed hand. "You can leave it with us; we'll see that she gets it."

This was more along the lines that she expected. "I was told to deliver the message to The Terafin herself."

"You aren't ATerafin," the guard said, asking the question although it was clear that he knew the answer.

"No."

"Well, then, you probably don't understand the rules of the House. The Terafin's day is governed by strict schedule; if your message is a matter of emergency, you may deliver it to her right-kin, and he will see that she receives it."

"We can't." Jewel took another, deeper breath, and felt the sheaf of papers she'd taken from Old Rath's flat as they rustled against her skin. "Look—I've been told to tell you that the message is from—is from Ararath Handernesse. But I can't tell you any more than that. You just go and tell her—and see if she won't see us." She folded her arms, suddenly nervous, as Arann started to gurgle.

The guard stared down at her impassively.

The boy was dying; that much was clear the moment Torvan laid eyes on him. What had caused the injury wasn't completely obvious; it looked as if he'd gotten into a knife fight on the edge of a roof, had taken a few blows, and had been pushed off.

He looked at the girl who stood, arms crossed, lips drawn into a tight line, before him. He thought her seventeen at the very oldest, but in all probability younger than the age of majority. Yet it was clear that she, of this group of wandering urchins, was the leader. It was also clear that she had been told too many stories about guards and noble families, if she thought to force him to deliver a message to The Terafin. A message from the Kings themselves would have to be delivered—would in haste be delivered—to the right-kin, Gabriel.

He stared down at Jewel, at her folded arms, at her stiff expression. He almost thought her brave, to stand here in front of the personal guards of The Terafin. Behind her back, her den had formed up, and they watched her with trust and confidence.

It was a trust and a confidence that she did not feel herself; although she showed no fear, he was experienced enough to see the signs of it.

"I'm afraid," he said softly, "that the most I can do is carry your message to Gabriel ATerafin. Who did you say sent you?"

"Ararath," she replied. "Ararath Handernesse." Her brow folded in at the bridge, and her expression changed. "Look—if you don't carry the message to The Terafin, you'll regret it. She'll want to hear it, and she'll be very angry—"

He lifted a hand almost gently. "What is your name?"

"Jewel," she said. "Jewel Markess."

"But everyone calls her Jay," Finch added, from over her left shoulder.

"Jewel," he said, inclining his head in a gesture almost of respect. "I am Torvan ATerafin. The Terafin personally chooses the guards who answer the gates of her manor on the isle. She knows me by name, and I have some knowledge of her; she is the lord that I serve.

"If I choose not to deliver this message in the fashion you demand, it is unlikely to cost me much. There is trust between my lord and me." He didn't take his eyes from her face, and at last she looked away.

As did he—back to the boy.

The boy who was dying.

It was true, what he'd told her, although he didn't know why he'd said it. At market, he was far less patient with this sort of urchin, and more than likely to send the lot of them scuttling for cover should they come near.

"Wait here, Jewel Markess. I'll return."

She swallowed, and her eyes were darkly ringed. "I'll wait," she replied softly. He could almost hear the plea that she couldn't make in her voice.

He could never be certain why he did what he did next. But the words he had spoken to the young girl were true: There was trust between The Terafin and her Chosen. He should have taken the news to Gabriel—the most trusted and valued of The Terafin's advisers—and let the right-kin deal with it as he saw fit.

It was what he intended to do as he walked through the gallery on the second floor mezzanine. But he found himself walking past the hall that branched into Gabriel's quarters; found himself marching, and quite quickly at that, to the rooms that The Terafin used for her daily business.

"Torvan?"

"I have a request for the Lord," he said, looking forward as Gordon barred the doorway with his sword. Gordon was also one of the Chosen; he lifted his sword, nodded, and took two crisp steps to the side. All was as it should be in House Terafin. Marave cocked a dark brow, but she said nothing, as she was on duty. Guarding The Terafin's doors was perhaps the job which required the most dress discipline; Torvan rarely got assigned there.

The door opened into an antechamber that was both sparsely and finely decorated. There were four guards in it, but they allowed him to pass without challenge. They did not have a dress function as the guards at the door did; they were there as a precaution. Six months ago, an assassin had nearly ended The Terafin's life. Neither the assassin nor the hand behind him had been caught.

Still, he nodded at them as he made his way to the second door. Arrendas opened it for him, and allowed him to pass, lifting a brow in open curiosity. *Later*, he mouthed to his oldest friend, as he walked through the door.

The Terafin looked up from her desk. It was a tidy, almost severe affair; papers had been meticulously separated into neat piles of varying degrees of urgency. At her side were two secretaries who had been assigned the luckless task of sorting through the demands of the Terafin family and assigning them a relative degree of importance. Merchant matters normally rose to the top because, in matters that concerned money, voices were usually loudly and quickly raised in pleading protest.

"Torvan?" The Terafin said, the question in her voice soft. "Is there trouble?" She raised a delicate brow, and stood in a smooth elegant motion. Her pale blue skirts fell to her ankles. They were wide and quite practical, not at all the fashion of the current noble court.

But The Terafin, unmarried, was of an age where fashion did not rule. Torvan couldn't imagine that she had ever been at an age where it did. She was not young, but not old, and she wore her years like a fine and valuable armor. The analogy was apt; she also wielded her experience like a fine and valuable weapon, much to the regret of any who attempted to cross her. Her dark hair was confined by a glimmering net that fell just past her shoulders; sapphires glinted at her left ear and upon her right hand.

"Trouble?" He shook his head quickly. "No."

"Why," she asked, as she moved away from the desk, earning a glance of consternation from her undersecretary, "don't I believe you? What is it? Difficulty at the gate?"

He bowed his head. "Not difficulty, but not a normal occurrence. It seems that a street den has arrived and will not be moved."

The Terafin raised a dark brow and her lips turned up as she pictured it. "I see. Have they chosen my House in order to mark it for humiliation, or do they have a pretext for their trouble?"

"They carry a message that they will deliver only to you." She chuckled almost dryly, and folded her arms across her chest as she leaned back onto the lip of the desk. "I see. And what brought you here?" That she expected more was obvious.

"They say it is from Ararath Handernesse."

Her expression didn't change, nor did her posture, but The Terafin's Chosen were selected for their instinct and their intuitive ability, as well as their ability to fight; Torvan knew that the message meant something to her the moment the name left his lips. "I see. Well, then," and her voice was quite dry, "you had best see them in."

"As you will it, Lord," Torvan replied, without missing a beat.

Torvan ATerafin came quickly down the stairs that led to the narrow walk. His face was calm and his expression composed, but his stride was quick. He reached the gate—and his partner at arms—in half a minute.

Jewel couldn't make out what he said, but she could hear him speak. The gates swung open.

"Jewel Markess," Torvan said gravely, inclining his head slightly. "The Terafin has requested your presence. Please follow me."

Just like that. Jewel's knees refused to move; they felt weak and unstable. She looked over her shoulder and caught Finch's trusting relief. Swallowed.

"Arann?"

Carver shook his head. He took a step forward, as did Angel, but they both staggered slightly at the weight of their unconscious companion. Teller leaned toward Arann's white face, listened there a moment, and then looked up at Jewel.

"He's . . . breathing."

He's dying. She reached out—she couldn't help it—and touched Arann's face. It was cold and clammy. "Arann?"

There was no answer but the silence of her den. "C'mon Carver, Angel. Let's get him in. We can't leave him here."

He watched them struggle with the weight of their companion. Something about their struggle hovered at the far edge of his memory; it was familiar, but he could not recall where he'd seen it before. The younger girl was pale, and her eyes fluttered from person to person, lighting on anyone save the dying boy himself. The quiet boy did his best to help, but his spindly arms and legs were not up to the task. He could not take his eyes away from the unconscious young giant. The black-maned boy and the boy with a white spire for hair managed to support the weight of their companion as they followed their leader's directive, with the red-haired, awkward one struggling at their back.

And the leader herself? He watched her impassive face, and saw the fear alive beneath it. It was almost as if she'd seen too many deaths, too quickly.

He knew, then, where he'd seen the expression, and the struggle; the determination not to abandon the living—no matter how badly injured—because there were too many of the dead.

Those fields were years and miles behind him. He always made certain that they stayed there. But a slip of a girl and her followers suddenly brought them back, however distantly.

"Here, Markess," Torvan said gruffly, and his voice, deep, held the timbre of command. "Let me help you." He pushed her firmly to one side, stared down at Teller until the boy got out of his way, and then caught Arann under the arms and legs as the two who had been shouldering his burden stepped away at the quiet directive of their leader.

He strained as he lifted him, but he lifted him.

Jewel wanted to pay attention to the finery of the House. She wanted to notice the colors of the tapestries that covered the west wall, the deep hue of carpet beneath her feet, the paintings, limned in light, that hung in the galleries.

She wanted to pay attention to the unbarred windows, to the silvered mirrors that were taller and wider than she, to the crystal that hung, casting light against their shoulders, from a ceiling so tall it couldn't possibly be kept clean.

It didn't work; they faded into a pale, listless dream that passed around her without really touching her.

What was worse was that she knew she should be calculating each of the words and gestures she was about to make. She had to have her story straight, it had to be convincing. If she was clever about it, the den would profit—and there was no rule against making a bit of money while saving the world.

But she thought of Fisher and Lefty. Lander. Duster. Even Old Rath. Each of them had died. She didn't know what killed them, or when, or how. She hadn't seen it, and although she was responsible for her den, the responsibility for their deaths didn't have the viscerality that Arann's dying did.

Snap out of it, Jay, she told herself, as she saw the two guards at the end of the hall. *You won't do Arann any good like this.* She nodded to the right, and Carver came to stand behind her.

"Teller?"

The thin boy nodded.

"Keep an eye on Arann." *As if,* she added, but only to herself, *he can look anywhere else.* The halls were so long. "Can't we walk any faster?" she demanded sharply.

Torvan looked down and shook his head. If he found her tone annoying, he gave no indication of it.

She was acting like a nervous child, and she knew it. Torvan ATerafin was carrying—on his own—Arann's massive body; he was moving much more quickly than they would have moved had he not decided to shoulder their responsibility.

He's so white.

The guards at the end of the hall put up their swords in an X, barring the entryway. "We're here to see The Terafin," she said, before the clamor of their ringing had started to fade. "It's urgent. We've got to—"

"Marave, we're here by The Terafin's command."

The woman, her dark hair peering out slightly beneath the edge of her helm, nodded crisply and pulled her sword up. "You may pass."

The fair-haired, bearded man on the other side of the door likewise withdrew his weapon. "You may pass." Their movements had the feel of ritual, and Jewel had seen ritual so seldom in her life that it almost drew her attention away from Arann.

But Arann proceeded through the open doors in Torvan's arms, and she followed quietly, failing to notice that the eyes of what remained of her den looked to her for guidance or command.

The four guards in the next large room didn't speak at all; Jewel thought, for just a second, that they might be a trap. *As if,* she told herself, as her pulse returned to normal, *things could get that much worse.* She pulled at her sleeves as she crossed her arms, pressing the papers into her skin.

The papers.

"Don't stand on ceremony," someone said, and Jewel looked up at the sound of a woman's quiet voice. The woman was not speaking to her, but rather to the guard who held Arann's very still body. "I do not require you to kneel, Torvan."

She was, this woman, of medium height. Her skin was pale, almost milky white, and her hair was dark. It was probably long; hard to tell given that it was bound back in a net that cost more than Jewel's entire den was worth in a good year. She wore a simple dress, but Jewel thought it was silk; it was a pale blue that fell from shoulder to ankle without the interruption of a belt.

And, of course, the stones at her ear and finger were real. Had to be. Jewel found herself bowing awkwardly; she hoped that the rest of her den were doing the same. Bowing, that is; if they could get by without the awkward part, so much the better.

The room was fine but sort of empty; there was a single picture on the wall, and there was a fireplace—empty—beneath it; there were shelves of books—books!—to her right, and to her left, two grand windows with real glass. There were three desks in the room, and on each a large lamp was burning bright. It was clear that The Terafin had ordered her other attendants out.

"I believe," The Terafin said, her voice almost musical, "that you have a message for me?" She smiled, and the smile was warm, but the eyes behind it were hard.

Jewel nodded. She didn't trust herself to speak.

"Then I would have you deliver it."

The message was important to The Terafin. Rath had known it would be. Most times, she would have wondered why. But right now, the fact that it was important was enough. Jewel nodded again, pulled the papers that she held very carefully from their awkward hiding place, and then moved slowly forward. No one was prepared for her sudden lunge; she jumped to the left, grabbed the closest lamp, and held its casing against her chest as if it were a weapon or a shield.

"Jewel," Torvan said, his voice hard. "You don't have to do this."

Jewel shook her head; strands of hair flew out of her dust-covered cap. She felt dirty and grimy and poor and stupid and very, very desperate. "This is it," she said, waving the rolled vellum above the brightly burning flame. "This is the last message from Ararath."

The Terafin raised a delicate brow. "What are you doing, child?" She took a step forward.

"Stay right where you are." Jewel let the edge of one of Old Rath's precious scrolls skim the flames.

"Who are you?" The Terafin asked, acceding to Jewel's demand.

"I'm—I'm Jewel Markess. I'm the den leader here."

"And you've come to my House in order to extort something from me?" Her lips thinned. "I don't know how you found out about Ararath, but—"

"He taught me." She waved the papers over the fire. "He taught me about all of *this*. I—" She shook her head. "I don't want to do this. But you've got something I need."

"And that is?"

"Money."

If possible, the woman's lips thinned further. "You do realize that there are a roomful of guards in the antechamber?"

She nodded.

"Vellum burns poorly. I dare say that they'll have you in hand before even one of the scrolls that you carry is lost."

"Just try it," Jewel replied, but her voice was thin, and her words held no strength. What The Terafin said was true.

"Shall I call the guards?" The Terafin took a step forward, and this time, Jewel did nothing.

"We used all our money to come here," she murmured, so quietly it was hard to hear her. "And even if we hadn't, we'd never have enough for a healer." Then she turned to look at Arann's body, and she lost her voice.

For the first time, The Terafin looked at Arann. "I see," she said. "And this money—you want it for him?"

Jewel nodded. "He's my den-kin," she said.

"And what would you do for it, if I had it to give you?"

"Anything," Jewel replied, straightening up and lifting her chin. "I'll steal for you, if that's what you need done. I'll spy for you. I'll kill for you. I'll even—"

The Terafin lifted a ringless hand. "Enough." She walked to the fireplace and pressed her hand against a square of the stone wall just above it. The square shimmered very strangely in Jewel's sight, but even as she squinted to see it more clearly, it became ordinary stone beneath an elegant palm.

But The Terafin looked at Jewel very carefully before walking back to her desk. This time, she sat behind it, signaling a more formal interview. "Tell me about Ararath."

Jewel swallowed. "I—we didn't call him that. We called him Old Rath. He lives in the thirty-fifth. He's a . . ." She I met the older woman's eyes directly and held them for the first time. And as she did, instead of feeling lesser and more insignificant, she felt calmer; there was something in their depths, some coolness that spoke of shade and not shadow; shelter and not prison. "He was a thief there. The best. He was good with a sword—that's why he lived to be old. He knew how to read and write and speak like a gentleman.

"He didn't much care for the patriciate. He didn't much care for commoners either, when it comes down to it. But he was a good friend."

"Was?"

"We . . . think he's dead." She looked down at the curled papers with their extensive writings, their fear. She couldn't destroy them; not even for Arann. Her hands stopped their shaking, and she quietly set the lamp on the floor.

"I . . . see." The Terafin folded her hands and looked down at her fingers.

There was a knock at the door. Torvan very gently set Arann down on the floor. Teller waited until the guard stepped away from the body, and then knelt on the carpet beside his friend. He listened for a moment to Arann's breathing, and then quickly dropped his head to Arann's chest. "Jay," he said, swallowing, "I don't think he's . . ."

She pushed him out of the way with more force than she'd intended, and knelt on the carpet as well. "Arann!" Her ear scraped the fabric of his shirt as her cheek came to rest on a patch of crusted blood. She listened and heard what Teller had heard: silence, stillness.

"Arann, come on. We're safe now." She lifted his face in her hands and shook him, but not hard. He was cool and slack. "Please, Arann, please."

"Jay?"

She shook her head fiercely, refusing to turn around.

"Jewel, come. There's nothing you can do now." She felt hands on her shoulders and she stiffened; they were gloved and mailed. Torvan. She shrugged them off and crouched closer to Arann's chest. When had he gone? When had he slipped away? Was it while she was trying to bluff her way past the guards? Was it while Torvan—a stranger, an outsider—carried him? When?

"Jewel." The hands on her shoulders were heavier, the grip firmer. "Come."

She shook her head. Couldn't turn around. There were tears on her face and in her eyes, and she couldn't hold them back. She could stop herself from making any noise. She could control her breathing. But the tears, damn them anyway, were going to fall for just a few minutes. She couldn't afford to have them seen.

"Torvan, it's not necessary," someone said, and a figure distorted by the thin film of water that covered her eyes knelt beside her. It was a man, older than either Torvan or The Terafin—older even than Rath. His hands were callused and wrinkled, and his shirt—she would remember the cuffs of the sleeves for the rest of her life—was plain and simple white, except for the golden embroidery on the cuffs and collar. That embroidery was a sun symbol, a light symbol, in a pattern that repeated itself, dancing across a white field as if it were alive. He touched her right hand gently with his left hand, and with his right, he touched Arann's still chest.

She looked up, knowing that he would see her tears. But she was mistaken. His eyes were closed, although the fine skin, laced with blue and green veins, seemed to twitch at odd intervals.

This is magic, she thought, and knew it for truth.

"I'm Alowan," the man said, whispering.

"I'm Jay," she replied, before she realized that he wasn't speaking to her. She looked down at the hand that held hers, and very slowly covered it with her left hand.

"Come, Arann. Come home. I am Alowan. Follow me. No, do not be frightened. It is safe. Come."

There was no sound in the room save for his words; Jewel was no longer breathing. She listened for the sound of Arann's voice, but only Alowan heard it, if he heard it at all. He spoke again, calling, and again silence answered his words. But the silence had rhythm, private spaces for breath and pause; he broke it only to speak, and then, only to call Arann.

She wanted to join her voice to his, but she could not; instead, she mouthed the name. Arann.

And then the strangest thing happened. Arann's chest started to move, slowly but surely lifting their joined hands. She tightened her grip on Alowan, but Alowan didn't seem to notice. The old man smiled tiredly.

"Welcome back, boy," he said. Then he turned to the girl at his side. "Jay, you must release my hand now. It isn't safe for the healer and the healed to be too long joined."

She did as he asked, hardly hearing him. Arann's lids began to flutter, although his eyes didn't open. His lips twisted; he reached out weakly and grasped at air. Then he began to moan, and at last, his eyes opened. He was crying.

"Arann?"

"Jay?"

He reached out for *her* as if she were his mother. She froze for an instant, stiff as his arms encircled her neck and shoulders, and then she hugged him back, crying as well.

Teller came first, and quietly; Finch came last, and hesitantly. In between, Carver and Angel joined her at Arann's side. Jester rolled his eyes in mock contempt, grinning broadly and tapping his left foot as if to a tune.

"Torvan," The Terafin said, as she watched them, "escort Alowan and the boy—Arann?—to the healerie. If they're concerned," she nodded in the direction of the den, "take one of them with you. Anyone," she added, "save the leader."

"Lord." He stepped forward.

"Now," The Terafin said, her voice suddenly loud and distinct. "You will deliver your message without further delay."

"Carver," Jewel said, nodding in the direction of the door without taking her eyes off The Terafin.

"Me? But—"

"*Go.*"

"Yessir," he replied, obviously disgruntled. But he went, just as Torvan went.

Jewel Markess, feeling every year she owned as if it were insignificant and fragile, took a firm step forward and placed the sheets of paper she'd carried from Old Rath's flat into the hands of The Terafin.

The Terafin lifted them carefully in white, perfect hands, and rose, motioning for Torvan's attention. "Tell the secretary to continue without me for the moment; I can be found in my chambers if matters of import arise." She did not wait to see his open hand before she turned to Jewel. "Please wait for me in the antechamber."

Chapter Four

T HE SHADOWS LEFT HER slowly, lingering longest in the corners of her eyes, darker than coal where white should have reigned. They trickled out of her mouth, although her lips were pressed firmly together; they tinged her fingers and nails with a hint of darkness.

Watching her, Stephen thought she held them in somehow; held them back. He didn't know because he couldn't stand to look at her for long; the very wrongness of her magics—if that's what the shadows were—made him more queasy than any hunt he'd ever run, including the first.

Espere lost the gold in her eyes much, much faster. And that, in its own way, was just as disturbing. She still didn't speak very much, as if speaking—when she had the ability—was simply not her way. But it was clear that intellect was giving way to instinct as they shuffled along the cold, icy path. She stared at him once, with an odd, pained longing. He waited for the words that usually followed such an expression, but they never came.

Gilliam did instead, wrapping a protective arm around her shoulder even as he watched her uncertainly.

It was dark, but nothing was hidden by that darkness; Stephen felt more vulnerable, and more revealed, under the sharp sky, than he'd felt since he'd run the streets of the King's City as a hungry, desperate boy. He glanced at the empty road at their back, and then cast his glance forward to where Evayne's robes seemed to twist and turn as if they were alive and on fire.

He wanted to ask her what a Dark Adept was, but he couldn't bring himself to break her silence. Asking Zareth Kahn was an option, but the mage, once distrusted and now familiar, would not take his eyes off Evayne. He wore a patina of orange light like a hooded cloak. And orange, as Evayne had explained to him, was the color of protection.

Zareth Kahn didn't trust her. Neither did Gilliam. Even the girl bristled when she came too close. That left Stephen.

"Where are we going?" he heard someone say, in a strained and low voice. It was his own.

"You hunt, do you not?" she responded, and her expression, as she turned her gaze upon him, made them all shrink back a step. At their offered silence, she grimaced and turned again. "Listen for the horns, little huntbrother. Listen, and heed them."

She raised an arm, and gestured at the trees that surrounded the road they walked upon. "This is the forest in Winter. It is all that remains of the old rites. The forest in Summer is much safer, but no less mysterious." She stopped speaking suddenly, and doubled over. "No, don't touch me! I will be fine.

"If we are lucky, we will not see the Hunter and his Queen. Not in the Winter." But her voice was grim, if weak.

"There is no Luck on the Winter road," Zareth Kahn replied.

"Indeed." She raised her head, testing wind as if she were touched by the wildness of Espere, before she spoke again. "You know much about Winter rites for a scholar of little renown."

He grimaced at the mild insult, but did not take it to heart—she was living history, and as such, entitled to her scorn. "I have studied much, but I have no practical experience." He paused. "Were the circumstances different, I would welcome this."

"Then you are as much a fool as any cozened scholar-mage. Listen. Can you hear them?" She moved a little closer as she slowly turned to watch their faces.

Stephen closed his eyes and concentrated. As he did, he caught the quiet echo of a musical note. It clung to the air like a scent that is only bearable when faint and subtle. "Yes," he said. "Are they horns?" For they sounded distinctly unlike any horn he had ever heard.

Evayne paled, if that were possible. She reached for her crystal and then pulled her hand away quickly.

"Yes," she replied. "But they are horns made of flesh and bone, the undying and the unliving, and the note that they carry is the cry of the forever displaced."

Stephen bowed his head, and murmured a quiet prayer to the Hunter God.

Evayne's derision was harsh, but brief. "Did you understand nothing? We are forsworn while we walk the road in Winter. Not even the Dark God could hear your prayers should you choose to make them to him, Sor na Shannen knows the darkness and the rites, and she has the power to call them both; she travels with speed and impunity, but even she did not chance the road in Winter." She looked at Stephen intently. "The horns?"

"I don't hear anything," Gilliam said.

"It was pretty quiet," his huntbrother replied. "But it's getting stronger."

"I don't hear it either," Zareth Kahn said.

Stephen's brow furrowed. "Gil, does she?" A few seconds passed as Gilliam and Espere stared at each other. Then the Hunter Lord shook his head. "No."

"No one hears it," Evayne replied, "save you."

"But you said—"

"I've heard it once before, Stephen of Elseth, and I will never forget it." She shivered, as if with cold. "But rest assured. This is not your death."

She spoke with such certainty that he felt a moment's relief. And then he realized that she did speak with certainty. *What* is *my death, Evayne?* For he was suddenly sure that she knew.

"Death is not our concern," Zareth Kahn said. "There are many things that can happen to a man that would make death desirable and pleasant."

"Oh, yes," Evayne replied distantly, the corners of her lips twitching. "Stephen, is it getting any louder?"

"Yes."

"Is it at our backs?"

"Yes."

"Then come."

"Where are we going?" Zareth Kahn broke in, as Evayne began to hurry them along the thin stretch of road that disappeared into forest ahead, and yet seemed endless.

"Onward," she replied coldly. "Onward, before they catch their quarry."

Stephen swallowed, as he realized what the significance of the horns was. *He* was their quarry. What had Evayne said? One of them would not leave the Winter road.

The horns were winded again, and this time, their song was distinctly unpleasant; cold and clear but just off-key enough to be grating. He must have stopped moving as he listened, for Gilliam's hand was on his shoulder as the note died away. He met his Hunter's eyes, saw the concern in them, and felt the warmth return to his legs—although, until he felt it, he hadn't realized how cold they had become.

"Stephen," Gilliam said, shaking him. "Come on."

Stephen looked about him; his companions surrounded him in a half-circle. Evayne kept her distance, and her hood was drawn low so it covered the edge of her eyes. The wild girl was almost nipping at his heels in her unease.

"What is it, Evayne?" he asked, as he started moving again. "What is the Winter road? If no Gods reign here, who built it and who travels it?"

"A wise man," she replied, "wouldn't want to know. But as you may be traveling the road for a long, long time, I will tell you what I can. Come to me, Stephen."

He started forward and came to a halt as Gilliam's hand—still on his shoulder—

bit into his collarbone. "Not yet," his brother said, in a hard voice. "The darkness hasn't left her."

"Very good, Hunter Lord," Evayne replied, drawing the moving folds of her cloak tight around her body. "And wise. But I will answer your question. Come. Walk more quickly, but keep your distance."

Stephen watched her robe; it seemed both alive and trapped as it sought to escape her hands.

"Do you think that nothing existed before the Gods?"

Gilliam snorted. "The Gods created the world," he said, in a stiff, matter-of-fact voice.

"The Mother did," Stephen added, gently correcting him.

"And what created the Gods?"

"The Gods have always been."

Evayne lifted a hand as darkness fled her fingers, dripping like otherworld blood onto the hard snow. "Very well. They have always existed." She smiled at Zareth Kahn's exhalation.

"But they were not always so separate from us as they are now. They lived in our lands, and they warred in them; they ruled and destroyed us in their battles. Yet they also granted us great vision and greater power.

"They had children, God and God, upon this world." She lifted her head, but what she sought, they could not tell; they could see her hood ripple in the night. "And when they left this world, the children could not leave it; they are earthborn. They are First-born."

"Why," Zareth Kahn asked softly, "did they leave this world?"

"You are not the hunted here, mage," she replied evenly, "and I answer no question of yours."

He lifted a brow, but made no protest.

"Who are the First-born?"

"They are many, and unnamed. They have the power of their parents, and they live along the hidden ways, the old ways. It is the Winter turning of the old world, Stephen, and you walk in the kingdom of one of the First-born. If you are spared, you will not meet her."

He lifted his head and then turned slowly to look at the winding, narrow road behind him. The horns were crying, and above their blended notes, he could hear a distant baying. No dog made such a sound; no beast of little intellect. The night grew darker and more chill.

"Stephen!"

"What do you hear?" Evayne said.

"Baying," he answered, numbly.

"Dogs," Gilliam muttered.

Stephen and Evayne answered as one person. "Not dogs."

They began to run, and after a beat less timely than the heart makes, their companions followed, carefully cleaving to the road, or what little of it they could safely see.

It was colder, always colder. Breath came out in clouds and hung in the air like a shroud. The sky was the color of true night; endless and eternal. Running beneath it, Stephen could almost forget that he had ever seen daylight.

He heard the horns, if horns they were. They sounded like the call of twisted birds—something alive and unpleasant winded only to violate the air. He heard the baying, and as it grew louder, he forgot that he had ever been uneasy around Espere. Forgot that he had ever feared the death the Hunter God offered. His breath became sharper and harder to take; he felt his arms and legs grow sluggish.

"Stephen!" Gilliam's hands were under his arms. How they had got there, he didn't know. "Come on. She says we've got to move!" He shouted the words into Stephen's ears, but it did no good; they were tinny, like words spoken in a whisper into a late night cup.

Zareth Kahn's mage-light glowed bright white and orange, and Stephen felt warm for a moment. He shook himself, gasped for air, and began to run. The moment passed.

"They're coming," he whispered.

The wild girl pushed at his back. He did not often touch her, but he reached for her now, seeking warmth, familiarity. Her hands were strong, real enough that he could almost feel them.

"I don't hear anything!" Gilliam shouted back. But there was no doubt in him; he felt Stephen's fear and revulsion more clearly than words could express them. He caught his brother again and began to drag him forward. "Relax," he said, through teeth gritted with effort. "Don't fight me." He sent protectiveness through their bond.

"It is not you," Evayne said, "he fights." She faced them, and the darkness was a halo around her irises. It lanced out like lightning from her fingertips as she spoke the syllables of a night whisper.

Stephen cried out as the shadow touched him. He hurt; it was as if she had picked him up and slammed him against the ground at a very good speed. Coughing, he made to rise. Then he realized he was already standing.

"What do you hear? Evayne said, urgent now.

"Hooves," he answered softly.

She cursed in a language that no one else understood, and that only Zareth Kahn had any hope of identifying. "Then we have no choice." She smiled, but the smile was bitter and angry. "I understand, Father, why. I understand it all now. Nothing, truly nothing, was ever just for me alone."

"Come," the seeress said, addressing Stephen. She cast her arms wide and the darkness that was trailing to the ground ceased its flow. *"Come.* There are shadows to hide in, Stephen of Elseth." Her cloak flew in the roar and howl of wind, stretching from end to end like a cloth door suddenly revealed. Except that there was no wind, save that which came from the long, hidden drape of her sleeves.

Stephen hesitated.

"Do as I say," she commanded. The power of compulsion underlay her every word. And then she stopped, clenching her jaw as if to trap and change her words before they left her lips. Her mouth worked, she spoke slowly, and the darkness that gathered about her grew stronger. "Stephen, listen to me. You *will* surrender to the darkness; you have only the choice of master, and it may be late for that. You will serve her for Winter's eternity, or you will trust me. But you will choose *now.*"

He watched her struggle, and realized that what she fought for was the ability to give him the choice.

At his back, the sounds were larger, louder; he twisted in their direction like a leaf in a gale. Gilliam held him back; Gilliam, and the sense of his concern, his worry, his fierce possessiveness in the face of danger, kept him steady for long enough to take two steps.

Into darkness and shadow.

Evayne's cape wrapped round him like a serpent; he drew one sharp breath, but made no other noise, as he disappeared into its folds.

But Gilliam cried out in terror and lunged forward. Evayne lifted her hands, palm out, in curt denial, and he struck a shield that crackled with veins of orange across a black field. It was the first time that he had seen the color of her power as Stephen saw it, and it burned itself into his vision and memory.

He hit the ground, hard, and rose quickly, gaining both feet and weapon as he approached the seeress again.

"Do not make me injure you, Hunter Lord," she said gravely. "I know that you feel his loss, but he is not dead. He is as safe as he can be upon this road."

He attacked her as if driven, and once again, orange light illuminated his body and sent it shuddering back.

"He is not dead."

Gilliam froze and the stillness was enough; her words touched him and took root. "Where—where is he?"

Evayne met his eyes and held them. "I cannot tell you," she said softly.

"No. But you can—and will—tell me."

The Queen of the Winter road stepped out of the forest and onto the path. She moved slowly and carefully, and no motion was wasted, no gesture unnecessary. She wore plate armor across her chest and thighs, and down the length of her arms, but beneath that, gossamer, something bright and pale and cold. No padding, no gauntlets, no boots—but it was clear that she needed none. She wore no surcoat, although she was the only one in her hunting party who did not; she wore instead a tiara that seemed to be made of four fine filaments: earth and air, fire and water, twisted into one perfect shape. Beneath it, her hair was as white as the snow, but purer and clearer; it fell down her shoulders like a spill of light, brushing the ground in an end-knot secured by silver and obsidian. Her skin was white, and her eyes—

Gilliam looked away from her eyes.

There was much else to look at. He followed the length of her left arm, and saw a bow, strung but not readied, that gleamed in a perfect curve; followed the length of her right, and saw a halter. The halter was a simple, thin chain of gold and black; it might have served to contain a ferret, but not a hunting horse.

He looked away again, but he could not easily forget what the Queen led onto the road.

It wasn't a horse; nothing so coarse or so solid. It had legs like a stag's, hooves as delicate and perfect; he couldn't see a tail, but was certain that it matched the body. It had antlers, sharp as steel spears, tinged with a patina of brown at the tips, and a strong neck, a fine set of shoulders, a sleek and glossy coat.

And it had a human face, eyes the color of cornflowers, lips pale, cheeks reddened with the chase. Even that, he could have borne. But the expression that flittered across the face was the very expression a woman might have worn had she been trapped for an eternity of service on roads such as these, in hunts that Gilliam had never experienced in the darkest of nightmare.

Zareth Kahn stepped forward as Gilliam of Elseth and the girl that hovered beside him recoiled. He saw the Queen and her mount every bit as clearly as Gilliam but much more clinically. Blue light sparked across his fingers and his eyes. As the light cleared, a look of wonder transformed his expression; wonder, awe, and a hint of desire.

She saw it all, of course, and in the seconds that she spared him, she smiled a winter smile. Then it was gone to ice and shadow as she turned her gaze upon Evayne.

To choose between them, on this road, would have been easy. Where the Queen was tall and slender, strong and unbowed in her beauty and her cold, cold light, Evayne was bent and curled in, her face slightly marred by an expression of pain. Her eyes were black, her skin lined by sun and age, her clothing dowdy and ordinary.

Stephen had made his choice unknowing; Zareth Kahn wondered, if he had seen the Queen, whether his choice would have been a different one. Then he smiled grimly and cast a different magery about himself; it allowed him to look away from the Queen.

At her side, antlered and perfect as the Queen's mount, was a creature that was so much legend very little reliable description of him survived. He was taller than the Queen, and broader of shoulder, with arms and thighs as thick as any of the wrestlers who took the King's Challenge. His hands were human hands, but his feet were cloven and sat heavily upon the snow. He wore no clothing and no armor, and he carried no weapons, but on a belt at his side were a series of three horns. Standing behind him were a handful of tall, slender men who resembled the Queen, at least in superficial details; they were fine-boned and pale-haired, and their large, narrowed eyes were gray; they wore chain hauberks and swords, but carried readied bows. It was clear that they deferred to the Hunter and his Queen.

The great, antlered creature looked down. At his feet, silent but bristling, were the hounds of the hunt. The beasts' eyes were milky, almost white, with no pupil or iris to make the direction of their stare obvious.

One growled, and Gilliam, Lord Elseth, lifted his eyes. Zareth Kahn watched quietly as beast and man exchanged a long stare. To his great surprise, it was the dog—black and sleek and twice the size of any Breodanir hound—who finally looked away. A ghost of a satisfied smile twitched at the corner of Lord Elseth's ashen face, but that was all. The beast lifted its mighty head, baring its long dark throat. It howled, and any similarity between it and a hound was lost.

Gilliam touched his sword hilt, for comfort and for stability, and then joined Evayne, choosing a position at her back that was almost inch for inch the same as the one that the antlered Hunter took behind his Queen. Espere joined him, standing before him as if she were a companion, but growling as if she would, at any moment, test herself against the hounds of the horned man. Gilliam was suddenly very glad that he'd sent his hounds away. He closed his eyes and gently probed the darkness behind his lids, searching for any sign of them. They were gone. She remained.

The Queen came forward, her step light. She stopped ten feet away from the seeress and gestured. The ground beneath her feet broke in a crisp snap of frozen dirt and ice. A throne rose from the breached earth, one much like the Queen herself in seeming; tall and thin and perfect—but dark and cold and hard. She stepped back and sat upon it. The Hunter came to stand at her right, and to her left, the hounds; the small court that she traveled with formed a semicircle at her back.

Evayne's lips turned up in a smile that was as hard as the obsidian throne. "Your Majesty," she said, bowing as if it were her robes, and not her desire, that forced the gesture of respect.

The Queen smiled as well. "Seeress. You grace our road again. It has been many, many years. Had I known that it was you who occasioned the Winter hunt, I would have ridden your friend; I believe that he misses you."

"Ariane," Evayne said, and the word was a warning.

The Queen was not moved. "You have knowledge of something that I have claimed."

"You are not the only one to claim it," Evayne replied. "And the rules of the hunt are clear enough. I am not your quarry."

The Queen turned her smile to Gilliam. The blush that rose in his cheeks had nothing to do with the weather. He took an involuntary step past Evayne, and Espere was suddenly at his side. She pushed him back, and he skittered across a road made slippery by ice so smooth it was hard to believe that anyone had ever walked upon it.

The wild girl stalked forward, her golden eyes feral. Her dark hair was tangled and matted, and her skin covered with its usual patina of sweat and dirt—but she looked in her element here, as if the heart of her wildness was the only part of her that was true or real. She growled.

The hounds looked up at the sound as it left her lips. They rose as she placed herself squarely in front of her companions. The Hunter stepped forward; she snarled in defiance.

"Enough," the Queen said, lifting her chin. "Seeress, why have you come? It is Winter. Surely you must know by now that there is nothing for you here." There was no pretense of amusement in her dark eyes; she lifted her long fingers to her chin as she sat and stared.

"I am not required to explain my movements to you, be you Summer or Winter Queen," the seeress replied. "I know the dark devotions, and I have already proved my ability and my willingness to pay the price of travel." She straightened her shoulders, and her robes, rippling strangely, reached for the ground. She looked like a duchess approaching a queen; not her equal, but with power and station nonetheless.

"Indeed," the Queen replied gravely. "And yet we have chosen, by the rules of Winter, the quarry for the hunt." She sat forward. "Where is he?"

"It is called a hunt," Evayne said, no less gravely but with respect, "for a reason, Ariane."

"It is only in the mortal world that you may play your games with impunity. It is Winter, little half-sister, and I am waiting."

"Then send out the hounds, Your Majesty. Send the Hunter. Send the Court. Walk the roads yourself, or ride them. What you find there is yours for eternity. What you do not find you cannot keep. Winter is only Winter for the passage of a mortal evening, be it the hidden path or no."

"Very well, if you will play this game." She raised her right hand, and the dogs leaped forward, jaws bristling with perfect teeth.

The wild girl caught the lead hound by the throat.

"Hold!" Evayne cried. "Let them come—they are bound by their rules and their chosen game; let them come, Espere!"

*   *   *

Gilliam heard the panic in the seeress' command, but he still paused an instant before he forced Espere to release the hound unharmed. She battled him—tested him—every inch of the way. He had never heard her voice so wild or so frenzied, and although in the end he had to slip into her body to force her to carry out his order, he did not stay there. He forgot that she had been human, or almost human, scant hours past—because it was easy. Because it was natural.

He did not take his hand from his sword, but he offered the dogs—and their master—no violence. *Easy*, he thought to Espere as she strained against their bond. *Be easy. We're not in danger. Be still.* The hunting bond, however, was not a good place to lie, and she knew immediately that Gilliam didn't trust his own command, or the reason for it. Knew it better than his dogs would have known it.

The sleek black bodies of the white-eyed dogs slipped past them, crackling with energy. Their master, the antlered Hunter, came at their back, pausing in turn by each of the companions.

Zareth Kahn he had little enough use for, which suited the mage; as the Hunter drew close, he found himself both attracted and repelled by the being's presence—and Zareth Kahn was not a man given to either. He held his ground, confident in his magery, as the other drew near.

But the Hunter was not a creature of magic, nor a creature to be deterred by it. He was masculinity defined, but not a human masculinity—not a controlled, elegant strength, or even a brutish, vicious one. The very air around the Hunter was a wild, electric air; his scent filled it; his presence could not be denied.

As he had reacted to the Queen, so, too, did he react to the Hunter, but the latter reaction had a viscerality to it that the mage's daily life completely lacked. Only when he moved on, did the mage begin to breathe again, and for a few minutes, it was in uneven, shallow breaths.

The Hunter stopped next in front of Espere; she growled but did not open her mouth to bare her teeth. Gilliam felt her anger and her desire to challenge the Hunter, but beneath it, he felt her unease and her sense of . . . kinship?

She stepped back as the Hunter stepped forward, but she did not look away as the Hunter's hounds had done when tested by Gilliam of Elseth. He felt a pride in that, and then unease as he thought of what Stephen would say.

Stephen . . .

The panic started and he forced it back. Now was not the time. Not the place. The Hunter was coming to him.

As the Queen and Evayne, Gilliam and the Hunter were of a kind, but Gilliam would not have presumed upon the Hunt of this wild, deadly creature. He was not afraid to meet the Hunter's eyes, but when he did, he found that he could not look away.

Something in the gaze, in the dark green of the Hunter's eyes, felt familiar—as if a tune he'd heard throughout childhood was being sung in another language and a different key.

Had he thought himself a Hunter? Had he ever given himself the title Hunter Lord? The longer he was held by the Hunter's gaze, the farther away those memories became. What was a hunt with spear or mount? What was a chase if he could not *know* where the quarry ran, and how fast—if he had to stop and study the dirt passed over by hooves or paws or feet?

"Lord Elseth," someone said sharply, pulling him back to himself. He broke away from the Hunter and met Evayne's stern face. Squaring his shoulders, he remembered who he was.

It was easy, now; the Hunter had come to Evayne.

"Hello," she said, inclining her already bent head a little farther groundward before lifting her chin to meet his level gaze.

He did not speak—Gilliam doubted that he could—but he tested the air as if pausing downwind of a scent that had, until now, eluded him. His coat rippled, brown and sleek; her cape replied, dark and heavy. They locked eyes again, but Evayne's gave nothing away; she looked both bored and confident. Gilliam had never liked the older Evayne, and he was not certain that he liked her now—but he was very, very glad that it was the older Evayne, and not the young one, that had come to rouse them from their sleep in an inn a world away.

At last, the Hunter lifted his head, and the highest tine of curved antler gently brushed Evayne's cheek. It drew no blood and left no mark, but she shivered slightly at its passing. He smiled, a quick and subtle twitch of lips over teeth—but it was a victory smile, and he shared it with his Lady as he turned his head to face her.

"Oh, Evayne," the Queen said, using the seeress' name for the first time. "You are a sorry fool. You do not understand Winter, if you seek to hide my quarry from me in such a wise." She stood, and in the darkness cast a shadow; although there was no source of light to throw it upon the ground, it fell, dark and terrible. "You fight the Winter, and it will consume you. But before it does, you will consume the soul you shelter.

"You have won and you have lost, little half-sister. The road he has taken, I cannot take—as you well knew—without your leave. Nor would I. But he could not take that road had you not opened yourself to the Winter's power, and the Winter is the force that demands its price. Or have you forgotten?" Her expression said that the question was rhetorical—or that she was not particularly concerned with the answer. "By Winter's end, there will be nothing left of the sheltered soul."

"I am not you, Ariane," Evayne countered, her jaw clenched. "You could not shelter a mortal shard even if you desired it; nothing of mortality remains once it has stayed under your dominion, no matter how much you wish it otherwise." She spoke in anger; that much was clear from the tone of her voice and the livid flush in her cheeks.

"A challenge, sister?" Ariane raised a perfect white brow. "Very well. The Winter makes its demands." She gestured in the stillness and her Court, weapons drawn, encircled the still seeress and her companions. Her expression did not change at all, but it was clear that something Evayne had said had found its mark. "You think you can shelter him in safety, and I say you cannot. If I am wrong, the Hunter goes hungry. If I am right, the Winter bears fruit. We will stay until Winter's end."

Evayne's face bore a smile's ghost—something that lingered, flickering and lifeless, over cold lips.

"It is not Summer," the Queen continued, the softness of her voice a mockery of gentleness. "There are no rights of passage. Unless you choose to challenge?"

Zareth Kahn whispered something under his breath, but Evayne smiled bitterly and shook her head. "Do not call the fire here, mage," she said, in a tone so quiet that only Gilliam could overhear. "Nor water nor earth nor air. It is the Winter of the ancient world, and they are not your allies. If you must use magics, use only those that are your own. Make no attempt to manipulate nature."

He started to ask her another question, and then bit the words back as she met his eyes. He had seen, twice, the assault of the demon lord Sor na Shannen—but the darkness that he saw in Evayne had no match, no equal. He retreated before it, wondering what price a Dark Adept paid, and whether there was any soul left with which to pay it.

Gilliam understood that to stay here was not his death—it was Stephen's. But he also understood that to attempt to leave was Stephen's death as well, because for reasons that were not at all clear, the Queen felt bound in some way not to attack Evayne—her half-sister?—unless she met conditions that were impossible for him to fathom.

Stephen, where are you?

He reached, felt the nothingness that waited at his core, and recoiled from the question. Espere whimpered at his side; he could not hide his fear from her.

She prayed and she hungered; she hungered and she prayed. She could not help but consume the thing that she kept hidden, for this was the nature of the darkness, and few indeed were the Adepts who could avoid paying the price it demanded. Especially not now, with coils of power already wrapped around another life. She could feel the struggles in the darkness, but it wasn't clear to her whether they were his struggles or her own; she fought. She had always fought.

And she fought in silence, in stillness, her face a white mask, banded by shadow and darkness. She fought in isolation, because it was the fight she knew. But she prayed for a Winter's end less harsh and bleak than the only other High Winter that she had known.

Better to pray, she told herself bitterly, *than fight. Come, Father, if you walk these roads. Grant me a miracle.*

Her prayers were answered.

The air was alive with Darkness that whispered in an exultant gale. The trees, fine and hard and sharp, began to snap and tinkle as ice-covered branches collided. The dogs turned—as did Espere—their faces grown wild, the whites of their eyes a shimmery silver. Even the Hunter lifted his head and tossed his antlers in a wide circle.

"What is this trickery?" The Queen asked softly, loath to take her eyes from Evayne. "I did not think you had it in you, Evayne. This is grand." She lifted a mailed arm, and her fingers clenched in a fist.

"It is not I," Evayne replied mildly. "But it seems that more than one will walk the High Winter road this turning."

"I think it not possible," the Queen said cautiously, as she gestured her throne into nothingness and turned to face the road at her back. "Without your path, you would not walk mine; no mortal now exists who can walk this road in Winter."

"No," Evayne said, a fey smile touching her lips.

Out of the clear night air, a tall, slim figure came at a run. He wore a slender woven chain that jingled like silver coins in a shaking sack, and his hair, pale and fine, flew at his back. He threw himself at the feet of his Queen, elegant in his obeisance. Before she could speak, he pulled his sword and tried to bury it, beneath her regard, into the road itself.

The blade struck ground and shivered, but would not be driven home.

"What is this, Findalas? How come you to have drawn this blade?"

He made no answer, but his chest heaved as he gestured to the road behind. The Queen's back was perfectly straight as she gazed in the direction of his arm. Without turning—as if turning would deprive her of the vision—she spoke.

"I believe I understand why you chose to walk this road again, little half-sister."

"What is it?" Gilliam hissed as Zareth Kahn stared intently, in turn, past the Queen's back.

"We . . . were followed," the mage replied reluctantly.

Gilliam spoke in a fashion that would have been the humiliation of Lady Elseth. No one seemed to notice.

"It has been a very, very long time," Ariane continued, as she took a step forward and loosed her riding beast. "Winter has been a shadow of itself since the Covenant." She pulled a tiny horn, unseen until now, from her belt; this she lifted to her pale lips and winded.

The trees fell away in an instant, as if they were indeed mere shadows of a living forest. The road, gray and slick and hard, stretched out like a field of ice and snow over terrain that had never seen life. From the left and the right—east and west, north and south, seemed to mean little—the host of the Ariani came riding.

Their mounts were dark, with glistening coats, but they were no fragile creatures; they were like the soul of a perfect warhorse. Had they had fangs and claws instead of teeth and hooves, no one would have been surprised.

At the head of the host was a single rider, and he came toward the Queen, stopping at a respectful distance and forcing his mount to kneel. "You have called, and we have come. What would you have of us, Lady?"

"Who rules the road in Summer?"

"You, Lady."

"Who rules the road in Winter?"

"You, Lady."

"Has it always been so?"

"It will always be so," he replied, striking his long, kite shield with the black blade of his pole-arm. "What matter what passed before you? It is of no consequence. We are the Ariani. We will fight in the Winter."

She caught the white spill of hair in her left hand, pulled her long blade up in her right, and before the assembled host, cut a swathe through the one with the other as if it were fine cloth. The end-knot, still silver and obsidian, she bent and retrieved. Then she turned, her hair no longer confined by weight or ornament in the wild of the night.

"Come, lord," she said, and the Hunter came. "Come." The hounds as well. "Would you join me, little half-sister? Would you know the glory that your birth has robbed you of? You will never have the chance again!" She held out one hand, as if in welcome, all enmity forgotten, all anger buried beneath a tense excitement that—almost—made her seem youthful.

"If I could be assured of it, Ariane, I would join you forever," Evayne replied, and a quivering longing laced the words as the shadows filled her eyes. "But I believe that I will have this chance, or one like it, again before I die."

"I will not question you, or keep you further. Here," she said, her hand holding bound strands of her platinum hair. "You have granted me a boon, will it or no, and if the time comes that you require a like boon, bring this to my Court. You know the way."

"And your quarry?"

"I release it to you," Ariane replied, "and I release it now, by the Winter rites, that I might find another quarry before the Winter passes." She smiled then, but it was an odd smile—it spoke of youth, of youthful longing, of an innocence long dust. She waited, and it seemed that she trembled with the strength of her joy.

The demons came in a ring of fire.

At their head, Sor na Shannen, demon lord and servitor of Allasakar, entered the field. Her eyes were wide as her gaze touched the Ariani. She gestured, and the demons stopped in mid-stride.

Ariane stepped forward. "You are intruders in the land of the Ariani," she said, her voice clarion clear and matchless. "And all who travel the roads pay obeisance to their Queen."

Sor na Shannen stepped forward as well. "To Ariane?" She laughed, and the laughter was wild. Elemental. The darkness in her voice carried across the barren plane. "Ariane was a whelp when our lord ruled the elements! Begone, or you will know his wrath when he returns to claim them!" She gestured and the very heart of fire leaped to the sky. Wild Fire. The oldest of the forms.

The host of the Ariani murmured, a sound like a distant wave. "Oh, very good," Ariane replied. And she, too, gestured, and the fire met water in a crash and hiss. It was the signal.

The hosts moved forward.

"Come!" Evayne cried. She grabbed Zareth Kahn and Gilliam by the shoulders and dragged them back across the endless plain. "We are mortal in part or in whole, and we will not survive observation of this battle—let alone the battle itself. Come!"

Gilliam felt her fingers graze his skin as if they were sharpened; they stung as they drew his attention. He reached out and caught Espere as the wild girl stood, still as the ice beneath their feet, held by the opening clangor of battle. He felt it in her, then; the desire to stay, to fight—the desire for a freedom that not even he could imagine.

She did not test him. He did not test her. She came, as she had done and would continue to do, because he desired it, demanded it, lived it—for he was her Hunter.

Chapter Five

22nd Scaral, 410 A.A.
Averalaan, Terafin

YEARS, HE HAD WATCHED this woman. Months. Days.

She sat still now, as she always did, but there were subtleties to the stillness. Her hands lay palm down against the gleaming surface of her desk, and between them, sheets curled by sweat and rough handling, lay the letter that Ararath Handernesse had penned. She had finished reading it fifteen minutes ago; he knew it because although her eyes were fast upon the vellum, they had not moved at all.

Very few people understood the domicis, even among those who employed them, either short- or long-term. To the common people, they were glorified servants; stiff-lipped men—and the occasional woman—who, like the Astari to the Kings, served, protected, and did not question. They did not launder, they did not cook, they did not clean—but they arranged the day-to-day affairs of the powerful. They were even known to have given up their lives to save those that they served.

Service. He watched her unbowed head, seeing in the absolute absence of emotion, the emotion that must hide beneath the fine control she exerted.

The domicis were paid, of course. And they were paid well. Although almost no House did completely without their use from time to time, very few of the patriciate employed them permanently; it was costly. But the coin of the realm was not all that the domicis sought. They served. They made an art of service, of defining service. And they chose those masters who best fit their needs, and their abilities. For they studied in many, many fields, and mastered not a few. This was truth.

Years.

Morretz knew better than to offer her refreshment; knew better than to offer her companionship or comfort. She sat in an isolation of her own choosing, and she would not leave it until she was ready.

But he could wait; no one of the domicis could wait with better grace than Morretz. It was not, of course, one of the reasons he had been chosen—but it had served him in good stead.

When she looked up, she met his eyes in silence. They were master and servant here; more than title separated them. Because she wished it. She waited for him to speak; he waited for her. It was as close to a game as he dared play.

He was very surprised when she conceded. "Among the domicis, Terafin retains the service of three."

He nodded, intrigued; it was not at all what he had expected to hear her say.

"If you were to place an untried and ill-mannered young woman with one of these three, whom would you choose?"

"Is the young woman to remain here under your permanent protection?"

"Perhaps."

He thought it over carefully, knowing she expected no less. Caralas was too stiff, he thought; too intimidating. Morden was too soft-spoken, and definitely too attractive. But Parenal was a man who would not accept a master of little power— or little consequence; it was he to whom dignitaries of rank and stature were assigned while they sojourned at Terafin estates. He lifted his gaze, and read his answer in her eyes before he spoke it.

"It is as I thought as well," she replied. Her hands still lay against the table, and beneath her pale chin, the vellum. She looked across at him, and he thought her face a shade of winter, cold and clear.

"To whom do you wish a domicis assigned?"

"The street child and her kin."

Morretz raised a brow. "I do not think there is one among the whole of the guild who would willingly take such a lord." He should have been surprised, but he was not; The Terafin was a woman who had risen to her rank by making the unusual choice, the unpredictable gambit. Although these had lessened as she had gathered experience and power, she could never be glassed in.

"If I guess correctly," The Terafin said, "she will be a lord whose origins belie her import to this house."

"And your guess would be worth much. But I still cannot think of one—"

She waited.

"Ellerson," he said at length. "Not a name you would know, Terafin. Not a man who has served in many years. But I believe that he might be persuaded to take this service, at least on a contract basis."

"When can you have an answer?"

"When the offer is tendered," was Morretz's grave reply. "I will speak with the guildmaster immediately." He paused. "You realize that word of this is bound to travel?"

"I have considered it, yes."

"You realize that not all of the House Council retain the services of a domicis at the House's expense?"

"I know what it will mean, Morretz," she replied evenly, in the manner of one holding back angry words. "But in this case, the risk is justified. Do not question me."

"Terafin."

We serve, Morretz thought. *We do not question.*

Which was, of course, a lie. But it helped, in the early years, when one was learning the arts. Only as one gained experience and wisdom did one realize that mindless service was of little use to the master that one chose.

The halls of the domicis were stately and elegant, as always. Morretz raised his hand, palm out, as Akalia walked briskly by. She was one of the few who had chosen to serve the domicis as a whole, rather than choosing a single master, and it was under her keeping that the guild of the servitors flourished.

He had come here when she was old—or so he had thought her then; she was older still when he had been chosen as domicis by a young woman—Amarais ATerafin—and he had formally accepted service to her. In between, behind doors so closed that not even his master could cross their threshold, he had learned how to use his talents, hone his skills.

Power. He had chosen to serve it and to harbor and protect it; he knew it when he first laid eyes on Amarais ATerafin, although he had not acknowledged it until that day. Still, Akalia had selected Morretz for training in the delicate arts; she knew, before he did, how he would choose, if not who.

But not all men made such a choice.

Morretz crossed the wide foyer, seeking not the training rooms, but rather the libraries. There was only one man seated on the broad, low benches there.

"Ellerson."

"Morretz." Ellerson's voice was deeper, and his hair a little whiter—perhaps a little sparser—but time had otherwise been gentle with him, a thing which could not often be said of the domicis. "Akalia says you have an unusual request?"

"Very."

"You know I've retired from all of this nonsense."

"Of course."

"Which is why you had Akalia call me in, no time for more than a quick change of clothing and a hasty gathering of personal items?"

Morretz smiled. "Not precisely."

Ellerson raised a frosted brow. "Then tell me. Precisely."

"The Terafin wishes to hire you, for a contracted period, not for life." He paused, reading nothing at all in the lines of Ellerson's face. They were many. "You will have a wing of the house proper, and it will be your domain; you may choose your own servants, if those provided do not meet your approval, and you will, of course, be given a generous budget out of which to operate."

"Go on."

"You will be offered the sum of not less than two thousand crowns for a period which may be as short as two days and as long as two years."

At this, a brow did rise. "Two thousand crowns? That *is* rather a lot. Am I to serve a nefarious criminal of some sort?"

At that, Morretz smiled again. "Ellerson, The Terafin may not be aware of your particular choices in masters, but I am—I assure you that we would not house a nefarious criminal under your care. Or at all, for that matter."

"The patriciate is composed of them," Ellerson replied.

"However," Morretz continued, "we would certainly not shy away from asking you to serve a petty criminal."

"I beg your pardon?"

"A girl, possibly of age, but most likely fourteen or fifteen by her size and look." He took a deep breath. "She came in off the streets, quite literally—and they weren't the streets of *Averalaan Aramarelas*." He took another, deeper breath. "And she brought her den with her."

"This is some sort of a joke." It was not a question.

Morretz raised fingers to massage his brow. Obviously, this wasn't going to be easy.

Hours passed in the confines of the antechamber; guards changed shift not once, but twice.

They'd had no food this day, and little the day before, but Jewel and her den waited, fidgeting quietly as the sands ran. Arann was alive. No one wanted to ask why; if it was a dream or a spell, who wanted to be the one to break it? Duster was dead, and that was loss enough for one day.

Jewel nudged Teller with her foot, and he pried his lids open. Glancing up at the bright, high ceiling, he started before he realized where they were—where they still were. Angel was sitting, back to the wall, chin nearly buried into his lanky chest. She'd seen the posture a hundred times before, but only under this roof did it look . . . ridiculous.

What do they want? What do they want from us?

When the guards came, it was almost a relief. But what they said made as much sense as anything else that had happened in the last two days.

"The Terafin has granted you use of the guest hall," a guard said, without so much as a disapproving side glance. "If you will follow us, we'll escort you there. She asks that you await her word; there are matters of import with which she must deal before she can return to your case. She begs your pardon for any difficulty the delay may cause, and has taken the liberty of having a meal called for you. And," he added, "baths. You will find the large bath in the center of the hall is now full of warm water, and will accommodate you." Where Torvan was fair-haired and solidly built, this guard appeared almost feline; he was dark and slender and moved as if motion were a hard-won skill that only the favored few could truly learn.

Teller looked dubious at best, as did Finch; Angel said nothing, and Jester snapped his teeth across the words that he was about to foolishly say before he caught sight of Jewel's warning glare. "That'll be fine," she told the guard curtly.

Carver and Arann were still in the healerie, and Jewel didn't like to leave without them, but she knew a dismissal and an order when she heard it, and she was smart enough not to argue.

Where are they really taking us? she thought. She counted the six guards that joined them as they left The Terafin's antechamber. *Guest hall, I bet.*

Luckily, she didn't voice her sarcasm—because it meant that she didn't have to lose face when they passed between the tall, smoky columns that led to the wide sitting hall of the wing meant for visiting dignitaries.

Stories were made of halls less fine, dreams of rooms less vast and beautiful. No one spoke as they made their way beneath the arch and ran into the back of the guard when he stopped unexpectedly. Jewel thought she caught the faint trace of a smile around his lips, but it was gone as he faced them and performed a very formal salute: Shield arm across chest, weapon arm extended.

"In the name of The Terafin," he said gravely.

Jewel nodded. No one else spoke. They stared at each other for a few minutes. Then the guard did smile, but the smile was friendly and without the edge that often accompanied a smile in the twenty-fifth holding. *Soft living.*

"I am Arrendas ATerafin. We leave you now," he said gravely. "But if you feel the need for guards while you are under The Terafin's protection, don't hesitate to request them."

"Uh, right." She stared at him for a minute, and then stepped out of his way. She was already tired of his smile before he and the five who followed him bowed again and filed out of the room, two abreast. "Wait!"

Arrendas ATerafin snapped to a stop, as did those that followed him in formation. He turned on his heel, pivoting with the smooth easy grace that comes from birth and not experience. "Yes?"

"If I—if we—need guards, who do we ask for?"

"Arrendas," he replied. "Arrendas or Torvan." He waited until he was satisfied that she would ask no further questions, and then turned and led his guards out.

Finch waited until he was out of sight, and then threw up her birdlike arms and let out a squeal of glee. "Look at us!" she shouted, bouncing up and down. "Look at this!" She ran over to the west wall of what appeared to be a sitting room of some sort "If we took this with us, we'd have it made. This is worth a *fortune!*"

"Indeed it is," someone said.

Finch jumped ten feet and everyone else started.

In the inner door of the sitting room stood a severely dressed older man, watching the den with a mild frown. It was as close to disapproval as anything they'd yet seen—and that made it familiar and almost welcome. He stared at them for a few minutes, until he realized that they weren't going to speak. Then he cleared his throat.

"I," he said, "am Ellerson. I am the keeper of these rooms; if you will permit me to ask you a few questions, I shall see that your needs are fulfilled while you reside within them. I am called," he added, "the domicis."

"Does everyone have to talk like that?" Jester muttered under his breath.

As she'd been wondering the same thing, Jewel didn't snap at him. "Well, we want food," she told the old man.

"It has already been laid out, and is waiting for you in the dining room."

"Great!" Angel started forward. "Just lead us there and let us at it."

Ellerson raised a peppered brow and looked down his nose as Angel approached. "Follow me, sir." He led them—slowly—through the sitting room, past another room, and down a long, wide hall. Had they wanted to run down the halls, it would have been hard; there was something about his presence that was so imposing he couldn't be ignored.

When they reached a bare, pale room lined with towels and filled with the fragrance of some mix of flowers that Jewel would never have been able to identify, Ellerson stopped. "These," he said in an arch voice, "are the towels. Soap is with the bath. Those are pitchers and small basins, and there are two boys who will help you with your bathing needs."

"But we're hungry," Angel said, just before Jewel stepped on his foot.

"Of course, sir," Ellerson replied benignly. "And after the traditional bath, you will be seated in all haste. Unless," he added, raising an eyebrow, "you'd prefer the barbarian custom of coming to a table in your . . . current state."

Jewel recognized an order when she heard it. She wasn't even in the mood to be offended by it. "Bath first," she said curtly.

"But, Jay—"

"Now."

There was food for days; so much meat you could feed the den for a year if you could cure it all. There was milk and butter and cheese, but there were also fresh greens and sweeter things as well. They were served water, but if Angel and Jester hoped for a finer wine, they were to be disappointed.

Jewel stared down at the plates and the knives in front of her. There was also another tined utensil which she didn't often see—a fork. There was a spoon, no, two spoons. Three cups. She felt stupid not knowing what they were for, and then felt angry for feeling stupid. It didn't matter what they were for; there was food here, and she intended to eat it.

"Aren't you hungry, Jay?"

Normally, this would mean that Angel intended to eat whatever she didn't in-hale right that instant—but there was so much food on the table, that Jewel took it as an honest gesture of concern.

"Yeah, I'm hungry."

He looked at her mostly full plate, shrugged, and went back to shoveling food into his mouth as fast as he could swallow.

"Jay?"

"Just eat, Teller." She pushed her chair back; it made no noise at all as it ground itself across soft carpet. Frustrating, that.

"Where're you going?"

"To find Carver and Arann."

"You want company?" Finch piped up.

"No." It was exactly what she didn't want. "I want you to eat and rest up. We're probably going to be thrown out in a few hours, so we might as well get what we can."

Ellerson stopped her as she came into the sitting rooms, and after she told him where she wanted to go, he reached out and rang a series of chimes in a very dis-tinct pattern. A well-dressed young man appeared before the last of the notes had died out. He was attractive enough if you noticed that sort of thing; his hair was a burnished copper, and his hands were long and fine. His face, like his hands, was long and finely boned, his eyes dark.

"How may I be of service, sir?" he asked, standing with his arms stiffly at his sides.

"You may show the young lady to the healerie, and then lead her back after she's finished her business there."

"Yes, sir." He waited until Ellerson nodded his tufted head, and then began to walk at a crisp but leisurely pace. Jewel joined him.

"You work here?" she asked.

"Yes, ma'am."

Ma'am? She sighed. "I'm Jay. You?"

"Burton, ma'am. Burton ATerafin."

"B-but—"

The corners of his lips turned up in a smile. "Yes?"

"Nothing." She knew when she was being laughed at.

He knew what she'd been about to ask. "I have the honor of being one of The Terafin's personal servants. The Terafin's personal servants are *all* ATerafin, al-though the servants in other wings of the house are not. The title is granted for service—for service that The Terafin sees fit to reward. The title doesn't make us all-powerful lords. Most of us won't come near to the governing council. Doesn't matter. The Terafin's house wouldn't run without good men and women to see to it." He spoke with a natural pride that Jewel found odd. "I was born to a Terafin. I worked hard to show that I knew the value of serving, the value of service. Eventually, my father recommended that I be adopted by the house—and The Terafin herself approved it."

She might have sneered at him, but it would have been an empty gesture of resentment. He was obviously the better clothed, fed, housed, and taught for all that he was a servant. "Does it bother you," she said, giving him a sidelong glance, "to have to wait on us?"

"A guest," he replied, with even greater dignity, "is a guest. A servant who can't remember that is . . . well, common, really."

She'd always known that she'd never understand the nobility. She'd never realized that she wasn't even going to understand their servants.

"The healerie is coming up on the right." Burton looked straight ahead. "If you request it, we can arrange a tour of the grounds for you and your companions. If you'd—"

"Thanks. I'll keep it in mind." She veered off to the simple doors on her right. Burton cleared his throat at her back to catch her attention.

"That box beside the door, ma'am, is where your weapons are to be left."

"What?"

"That box beside the door is where you are to leave your weapons."

"I heard you the first time. What do you mean, leave my weapons?"

He blushed. "Healer Alowan will not have them cross the threshold of the healerie."

"But—but we didn't have to leave our weapons behind before we visited The Terafin."

"The Terafin is not so concerned," he replied gravely. "But it's hard enough to find one of the healer-born who will reside within a noble manor. Alowan sets many of his own rules, and if you wish to enter into his presence, you—just as The Terafin herself—must follow them."

Snorting, Jewel walked over to the box. She pulled open the lid—it was heavy—and saw that Carver's dagger and Arann's dagger were the only things in it. Sighing, she pulled her own out of her belt and gently placed it with the others. "You'll watch them, won't you?"

He nodded quite seriously.

"Good." She took a deep breath, put her hands on the latch, and gave the door a yank. It was deceptively heavy, but it came with a little work.

Jewel had never seen a healerie before, and she was quite surprised when she did. In the center of the room, where she thought beds should have been, was a grand fountain. In the center of that, like the grail of Moorelas, was a simple cup, held high by a thin, strong arm that rose from the water's depths. Liquid trickled over the brim of the cup, tinkling as it touched the pool beneath.

Light, from what seemed a hole in the roof, glinted off the moving surface of the water and the green, large plants that surrounded it. Jewel had no idea what they were; they were plants, and they were beautiful. That was enough.

"May I help you?"

She started, wondering for how long the fountain had captured her attention. "I'm here to see Arann."

"Arann?" The young woman's brow creased, and then her eyes widened. "Ah— you mean the young giant that was brought here late this morning?"

"That would be Arann, yes."

"Let me check with Alowan." The white-robed girl was gone as quickly and quietly as she had appeared. This time, Jewel watched her trace her path around the fountain and into a room on the far side.

When she returned, she nodded quietly—as she seemed to do all else—and Jewel followed her. Beyond the fountain, there were beds, although the beds themselves were arranged in small alcoves that gave them both light and air from open windows. Plants grew in abundance from hanging pots and trellises; Jewel ducked under their leafy vines and trails as she made her way to the only occupied bed in the healerie.

There, Arann, propped up by many pillows, lay quietly staring out the window. Carver was beside him, arms crossed, expression unreadable.

They were safe. Usually, she would have shouted something, but the healerie was so quiet, she felt that shouting would be some sort of crime. She padded silently across the floor and tapped Carver on the shoulder. He jumped, shouted, and fell out of his chair.

"Shhhhh!"

"Jay." He rolled his dark eyes. "What're you doing here?"

"It's fine. Everything's all right." She took the chair that he had vacated. "There's someone waiting outside the door for you. Tell him you're part of my den; he'll take you to where there's food. More food," she added, as he eyed her somewhat doubtfully, "than a den full of Angels could eat."

"I'll wait."

"No, you'll eat."

"I—"

"That's an order, Carver, not a request. *Do it.*"

He gave her a very sarcastic salute, but it was obvious that he was tired and hungry, and after another halfhearted attempt to change her mind, he left the room.

"Arann?"

He turned to look at her, and she could see tear tracks down both his cheeks. "Jay."

"What is it? Are you still in pain?"

He nodded, and then smiled weakly. "But not the side, not the ribs. It's—the Healer. He's—he's gone." Speaking the words brought the tears back, and he sank into the pillows in silence and sorrow.

Jewel shook her head slowly. "Arann? What do you mean?" Her voice gentle, she caught his left hand in both of hers. He returned her grip tightly, but shook his head and turned away.

What is it? What's wrong? "Arann, I want to talk to someone. I promise," she added, extracting her hand, "that I'll come right back."

She found the old man in a small room to the west of the fountain. He sat, legs crossed, on a flat stone bench that was surrounded on three sides by a profusion of greenery. Birds fell silent as she approached his back. She didn't even stop to wonder what they were doing inside.

"May I help you?" the old man said without turning.

Surprised, she stopped. Then she squared her shoulders. "Yes."

He turned as she spoke, and she was surprised at how frail he looked, how delicate. There were tears nestled in the wrinkles beneath his eyes; they caught the light and held it as if they were crystal.

"You are the young boy's friend," he said.

"I'm his den leader," she replied.

He nodded, as if the word meant nothing more to him than friend. Again, she was surprised at how frail he appeared to be. "What would you have of me?"

"I want to know what you've done to Arann."

The old man's lips turned up in the saddest of smiles. "I called him back," he replied. He unfolded his legs and slowly gained his feet.

Jewel quickly joined him and offered him the support of her arm. He shied away and instead pulled a gnarled old cane from out of the leaves of a nearby bush. "You don't know very much about the healer-born," he said softly.

She shrugged. "I've never been to a healer," she said, half-bitterly. "Couldn't afford one."

He grimaced. "There are reasons why the healer-born do not walk through the city on errands of mercy. Do not judge me harshly, young one. I do not judge the choices your life has forced upon you."

To her surprise, she felt almost ashamed. She didn't like it much.

"There are healers who will not call the dying back," he said, almost as if changing the subject. "To heal the wounded and the injured still has its cost in pain and time—but to call the dying is the hardest of the healer skills, and there are many who will not pay its price."

"What do you mean?"

"You know that we can mend the broken bone, and knit the ruptured flesh— but there comes a point when doing either is not enough. For your young friend, it was not enough. His injuries were too great. If The Terafin had not summoned me, he would have gone beyond the reach of even one healer-born.

"He was almost beyond mine." The old man closed his eyes, shook his head, and began to walk in the direction of the fountain. "Do you like the healerie?" he asked.

She shrugged, and he sighed.

"The young are always so impatient. I designed the healerie for myself. When I decided that I would serve The Terafin and her family, I knew that I would be called upon to heal the slightest of injuries on a daily basis. I knew also that, should the need arise, she would expect—and I would be in no position to argue—that I call back the dying.

"This fountain, these plants, these two rooms—they are my peace after the healing is done.

"Do you know why," he asked, as he came to rest at the marbled lip of the grail, "healers who do not choose to become Children of the Mother charge so much coin for their services?"

"Everyone likes money," she replied, almost flippant.

"True enough. But that is not what they seek. They charge money for their services because so few are willing or able to part with it, and it means that they will not be bothered by the injured and the dying every waking—or sleeping—moment for the rest of their lives. People understand that nothing is offered for free.

"You have not seen the things I have seen, young one." He closed his eyes and let the trickle of water speak for him for some minutes before he resumed. "I have seen healers who let their friends die, rather than summon them back."

Jewel had the uneasy feeling that she no longer wanted to hear the answer to her question. If she could have taken it back, she would have—because she knew, by the hunching of the old man's shoulders, that he was steeling himself to speak with her of something that still caused him pain. She wasn't always good at listening to other people's pain. *Well*, she told herself sternly, *you brought it on yourself by prying, and you'll damned well accept* it. Echoes of a lost voice.

"There is spirit—or soul, if you'd rather—and there is flesh, and the dying is merely the sundering of the two. But it takes the spirit time to divest itself of the rudiments of lung and heart and bone and muscle; time to relinquish the memories and experiences of a lifetime.

"No, I'm no Mother's Priest, if you're wondering where I get my understanding of theology. To me—to *any* healer who has called the dying back—it is not theology, it is truth, and no simple truth at that.

"We, the healer-born, can talk to the spirit long after the flesh has refused to listen—but we speak with the upper limits of our skills, the limits of our power, and we can only make ourselves heard if we shout into the threshold of the afterlife with all that we are. Do you understand me, youngling? *All that we are.*

"At that moment, our whole lives are focused and honed; our entire desire is aimed at the spirit that has wandered. And that spirit's body, still broken, is no home for it. No, if we are to catch the spirit, *we* are its body. We are its home. Do you understand?

"They return to us because we call them, because we can take them and hold them and comfort them against the pains that they feel and have felt. They return to us because they can see all that we are, and in that revelation of faults, of flaws, of aching and yearning and happiness, of weakness and strength, they see that we trust them, and in return, they give us trust that they have never given to anyone else—most of them, not even to themselves.

"And we need that trust to bring them from the darkness."

Jewel was silent because she could think of nothing to say. *Would I do that?* she thought, as the import of his words sank in and became real. *Would I let someone see everything that I ever thought or felt?* She took a step away from him.

He smiled, but it was a heavy expression. "And we see everything that they are, little one, just as they see everything that we are. We *become* one for as long as it takes to make the body whole. We belong together, for that instant. But once we bring them, once we have used this trust to keep them from the lands of the dead, we must snap it, break it, and send them away. There is no desertion," he added, although it wasn't necessary, "that will ever be worse.

"A part of me is Arann, and I know you, Jewel." He put a hand into the waters below his fingers, cupped it, and drew the fountain's clarity toward his face. It didn't matter; it didn't hide his tears. "I know you, and I expected that you would come, demanding your answers, and plotting some vengeance if the harm I had done your friend was irreparable. It is not.

"I am not sorry that I called him," he continued, and his face grew more serene. "But I cannot see young Arann, although I know it hurts him more than any wrong he has ever been done. For we are not yet separate, and there is a danger—although at my level of skill, it is a small one—that I could draw him out of his body once more, and hold him in mine. It has been done, but it is wrong, and in the turning, in the Hall of Mandaros, it will be judged so." He swallowed. "The pain that he feels—it fades with time."

It was then that she understood that the tears that Alowan had been crying when she'd first seen him were the same tears, measure for measure, that Arann cried. "Why—why do you do this? Why did you agree to serve the The Terafin if she demands that you—that you suffer this way?"

"Why?" He gazed out upon the surface of the water as he lowered his hand to its depths again. "Because she was the first person that I ever called back."

Jewel couldn't stay with Alowan—and it seemed that he did not desire company—but she couldn't desert Arann, even though understanding his loss only made it more difficult. Alowan was The Terafin's, and therefore The Terafin's business.

But Arann was hers.

She thought it would help if she explained what Alowan had told her, and she tried. But Arann turned to her, tears coursing down his cheeks, and said, "Never, never do this to me again. If I'm dying, let me die. Promise me, Jay. Never do this again."

So she held him, because that's what she did as a den mother, and after a few minutes, he suffered it, clinging to her as if he could somehow make himself part of Jewel the way he'd been part of Alowan.

I can't be what he was, she thought, thankful that she didn't have the choice, *but I won't leave you while you're like this. I'll stay until you don't need me anymore.*

She was wrong.

Two hours later, a pale and twitchy Carver came running into the healerie's bed room, followed by Torvan and an agitated young healer's assistant.

Jewel unhooked herself from Arann's sleeping grip—only in sleep did it relax enough that she could get clear of it—and rose to greet Carver. He was bad; she hadn't seen him this bad since—since yesterday.

"What's up?" she said, curt and to the point.

"It's—it's—"

Torvan gave her a low bow, but his gaze was appraising, perhaps even distant. "What the young man is trying to say," he told her in a slightly aloof voice, "is that we have good news for you."

"Good news?" She raised a brow and gave a sidelong glance at her den-kin.

"It appears that your friend, Ararath Handernesse, is not, as you feared, dead."

"W—what do you mean?"

"He's in Gabriel ATerafin's office, waiting for the opportunity to make an appointment to speak with The Terafin."

"Kalliaris' Curse," Jewel whispered. She caught Arann's hand in a tight grip and then leaned over and kissed his brow. When she stood, her expression was all business. She swallowed once, and then crossed her arms.

"That's impossible."

"What's impossible?"

"Ararath Handernesse isn't in Gabriel ATerafin's office." She forced her arms to relax, but her lips thinned. She knew she was doing it, but she couldn't quite help it. "It's not possible."

Torvan raised a pale brow. "Oh, isn't it?"

She nodded.

"Jewel—Jay, if you prefer," he added, as he saw her expression start to shift, "it can't be impossible. I led him there myself, at Gabriel's direct request."

"That's—that's not Ararath," she replied evenly.

"And how do you know this?"

"Because I—I know he's dead."

"Interesting. You didn't mention this in your interview with The Terafin." She licked her lips. "No."

"Jewel, if you're playing some kind of game, end it now. You weren't lying there—she would have known it—but I see now that you weren't telling the whole of the truth."

Jewel was terrible at trusting people—especially adults. She'd learned that it wasn't smart on the streets of the twenty-fifth; they'd take you for what they could, or just send you running like the pack of thieves that you were. And she remembered all that Old Rath had told her about her "feelings." Of course, it had taken her a little while before she'd decided to trust Old Rath, as well.

"Torvan," she said, and her voice was shaking, "you have to believe me."

"Make me believe you," he replied, and the distance gave way to a little bit of anger. "Tell me the *truth*."

"All right! But—but you've got to get help, and you've got to get it now. Call all your guards, get them together, have them ready, *please*."

"Why?"

"Because I *know* Old Rath is dead! No, I didn't see the body—and I couldn't tell you where it is—but that creature that looks like Rath and calls himself Rath is what killed him." And that, that was true. It hit her, hard. She saw his expression stiffen, and she raced onward. "Old Rath—that's what we called him—he made me promise never to tell." She swallowed, knowing that she was about to break a promise to the dead, and praying that the dead wouldn't become restless about it, because it was the living that mattered now. "But I get these—these *feelings*. And whenever I get them, they're always right. They're always true. They've always been like that." She saw his stony expression and started to speak more quickly. She knew she sounded desperate, and she hated it, but she couldn't keep the fear out of her voice.

"I don't know how," she said, swallowing. "But Old Rath is dead. And if we don't stop whatever it is that's pretending to be Rath, The Terafin—and the rest of us—will die as well."

"Feelings? What do you mean? Instinct? Hunch?"

"No—stronger than that. I *know* when something's true, but I can't control the knowledge. I can't listen to you and tell you when you're lying or telling the truth—it's not some sort of market trick. It's just—just feeling." She realized how stupid she sounded, how very, very lame. And then a thought occurred to her; she paled. "Did you—did you tell him we were here?"

Torvan looked down at her for a very long time before answering. Then, almost reluctantly, he said, "No."

Relief made her knees weak; fear shored her up again. "No? Why not?"

"Instinct." And for the first time, the crust of distance broke, and he gave her a very small half-smile.

"Can I say something?" Carver broke in.

"What?" They both turned to face him, speaking in unison.

Carver addressed only his leader. "You might want to point out that *this* Old Rath jumped off a three-story building and left a hole in the cobblestones, and then chased us down the streets and kept pace with a set of two horses at a gallop."

"You might want to say that indeed," Torvan replied, turning to Carver, anger replaced by a quiet fierceness that made him look, for the first time, dangerous. "What else can you tell me? Be quick about it—we don't have much time."

"No," Jewel said softly, with a faraway look in her eyes. "We don't."

They told him everything they knew, which wasn't much; Jewel kept it as brief and to the point as possible. Her early fear had guttered; she knew that Torvan believed her, although she didn't know why. She'd question it—or him—later.

"Why is he here?" Torvan said softly. "What does he want?"

Carver shrugged.

"To kill The Terafin if she knows too much," Jewel said. No one was as surprised as she was.

"Too much about what?" Torvan caught both of her arms; she shook her head frantically as Carver reached for his dagger. She'd forgotten, as he had, that he'd left it at the door, some guarantee of his behavior in the peace of an old man's rooms.

"I don't know—but I think it has to do with the papers that we took from Rath's."

"Mother's blood," he said, releasing her. "Come. Quickly." He left the healerie, turning at the door to make sure that Carver and Jewel were at his back. "Jewel, I want your opinion on something. I want you to clear your mind, and listen to what I tell you. Give me the first answer that comes to you."

She nodded. Swallowed. "Go ahead."

"If I gather the guards and we enter The Terafin's chambers, will she survive?"

"I don't know."

He closed his eyes a moment, and then nodded. "If we come in through the windows, or if we have archers prepared, can we save her?"

"I—I don't know."

"Will the imposter be using magic?"

"*Yes.*"

"Is he using it now?"

"*Yes.*"

Carver stared, openmouthed, at his den leader. He ran his fingers through his hair, pulling it back from his eyes—both of them—to stare at her more clearly.

"If we can get a mage here, will she survive it?"

"I—I don't know." She opened her eyes. "You don't have time to run someone to the Order of Knowledge and back!"

"Stop thinking!"

She swallowed. "Are we—are we finished?"

"Not yet," he said, lowering his voice. "I apologize for being harsh, Jewel. But The Terafin's life may hang in the balance. Please. Close your eyes.

"Is The Terafin in danger at this moment?"

"I don't know."

"Is the imposter still within Gabriel's quarters?"

"I don't know."

"Is the imposter a mage?"

"I don't know."

"Is the imposter human?"

"*No.*"

"Jay?"

Jewel's eyes snapped open as Carver called her. She felt queasy. "What?"

"How do you know he's not human?"

"How do I know what?"

Torvan looked down at them both. "It's as I thought," he said softly. He did not ask for her trust; he had it, and knew it by the answers she had given him, even if she did not. "But we've no time for it now. Come, both of you. If we're to save The Terafin, we have to enter the chambers of the Chosen."

The chambers of the Chosen were a series of three rooms that looked well-used, under-cleaned, and over-weaponed. There were swords on the walls, unstrung bows, quarrels and arrows and shields; there were helms and gauntlets and boots as well as metal-jointed leather armor. There was a great tapestry that depicted the Chosen at war, and three paintings, each lit by a source Jewel couldn't identify, that were larger than life on the otherwise empty wall they adorned.

"Later," Torvan told her, as she paused in front of a stern-faced young woman. "Follow me now."

Carver had his dagger readied, and Torvan did not demur. He did stop to ask if either of them knew how to wield a proper weapon, but didn't seem disappointed at the answer. They passed from the outer room to the inner room, and there they found six guards; two women and four men.

"Torvan?"

Torvan snapped a salute.

"What is it? What brings you here?"

"We have a hostile mage on the grounds. In Gabriel ATerafin's office."

Jewel looked up; she felt very, very cold as he spoke. "Torvan?" she said, and her voice was quavery.

"What?"

"He's—he's with her."

The six stood at once. "He's with The Terafin?"

She swallowed. "Yes."

"Let me pass, Primus Alayra," Torvan said to the oldest of the guards—a woman with graying hair and a deep, pale scar down the left side of her forehead.

"And what will you do?"

"I'm going to summon the mage."

"On your head, then," she replied, but the tone was one of ritual, not of disgust or abdication of responsibility.

"On my head alone." Then, belying the words, he caught Jewel's hand and dragged her past the guards in the chamber through another set of doors. These opened into a window-less room. A brazier burned at its heart, and lamps, one on each of four walls, flickered, alleviating what would otherwise have been complete darkness. There were no carpets here, no paintings, no tapestries or mirrors; in fact, there was nothing at all in the room save the fire and the lamps.

But as she looked at the stone walls, she noticed that each had an arch, carved in slight relief, that stood out. The arches were the height of a very large man, but no more; they were not grand, and had they been real, would merely have been functional.

Torvan walked three times around the brazier, and at the end of the third precise circle, he raised his hand and cut it. Blood sizzled as it struck the flames and sputtered there before becoming a dark, black smoke.

"In the name of The Terafin, we, her Chosen, summon you to fulfill your word and your bond." He raised his slightly bloodied hand and pressed it firmly against the wall, in the center of the western arch.

The wall came to life.

Stone became mist, and the mist swirled and eddied as if caught in a storm, although the room remained quiet and calm.

Too quiet, Jewel thought. Transfixed, she gazed upon her first true magic. The mist grew thin, and thinner still, as if layers of it were slowly being burned off by the thing that waited behind. And then the last wisps were gone; the arch was no longer stone relief. A door, fully formed and perfectly made, opened into the silent study of a tall, gray-eyed man with flowing white hair, a long, thin face, and a stern expression.

Angel, she thought, would have liked him on sight.

He did not wear the uniform of the Mysterium—the order within the Order that occasionally cooperated with the Magisterium—nor, in fact, any robe at all, save for a pale green bathrobe which had seen better days. His feet were sandaled, not booted, and his hands were in the middle of setting aside a quill and ruined parchment.

"What now?" he said, without looking up from his desk. "I'm a busy man, and I don't have time for insignificant interruptions. I've students, patricians, and merchants clamoring for attention; you'd best set yourself apart from them very quickly."

For the first time, Jewel Markess heard the voice of Meralonne of the Magi. "We need your help," she replied, although until she heard his voice, she had no intention of making herself known at all. "The Terafin is about to be—"

"We call upon you," Torvan broke in, motioning her to silence, "to fulfill your bond. I am Torvan of the Chosen, and I summon you to The Terafin's side."

The mage's expression changed subtly; his eyes were still narrowed and his lips thin, but the focus of his mood had shifted. He closed his eyes—those slate-gray, perfect eyes—and spoke three sharp syllables. Jewel had never heard a language so crisp or so definite; the syllables hung in her ears, teasing her memory, tempting her to repeat them.

"Torvan, what is the danger that you perceive?"

Torvan turned to Jewel, but Jewel was staring at Meralonne. The bathrobes were gone, and in their place was a gray material that seemed to shimmer in the poor light of the room he stood in; his sandals had been replaced by brown leather boots. He wore gloves that glinted with the same light his robes reflected. "Jewel," Torvan said.

She started and then swallowed. "My lord," she said, although she rarely granted that title to anyone, "we—I—there is an—an assassin on the grounds. He looks like a friend, but he—but he's not human."

"Not human?" The mage raised a platinum brow. "What is he?"

"I don't know," she said, meeting his gaze because there was no way she could look away. "But he—he jumped off the top of a three-story building and made a hole in the road."

"I see. I take it he then continued to move?"

She nodded.

He spoke again, and light flared at his fingers and around the rims of his eyes. Jewel opened her mouth to cry out, but only a soundless huff escaped. "You will wait until our business is done," he told her coldly. "For I wish to speak with you further."

She nodded, again because she could do little else, and then he looked back to Torvan. "I will come," he said. "Step back."

Torvan obeyed the mage's command, and pulled a near-paralyzed Jewel out of the way. The mage walked through the arch, and as the last inch of his robe cleared it, it shuddered and cracked. Where the mage's room had been, there was now ruined stone wall; a fine layer of dust covered the floor just in front of it.

Torvan called out two sets of orders and the six guards in the room just outside joined them, standing two abreast. They were tense; she could hear it in their breathing, see it in the way they held their drawn and readied weapons.

"You'd better be right about this," Alayra said softly.

"I know."

Meralonne gave them only this much time for chatter before he interrupted them. "Where is your intruder?"

"We believe," Torvan replied gravely, "that he is either with, or on his way to, The Terafin."

"Then let us repair to her quarters in haste." So saying, he walked toward the opposite wall, rather than the door.

"What is he doing?" Jewel whispered to Torvan.

"He made this room, these walls, and these arches. That wall, the one that he's standing in front of, leads through the fireplace into The Terafin's audience chambers. We must follow; wait for us here."

And the other wall? But she did not dare ask.

The wall began to undulate, and the mists that had marked the summoning of Meralonne began to roil again. The mage crossed his arms, impatient, and they cleared. Through the arch that was no longer part of a wall, Jewel saw The Terafin, standing rather than sitting, in the room that she used to receive her visitors.

It was a far grander and far larger room than the one that Jewel's den had been ushered into. There were no other desks; no assistants, no sense of business or bustle.

And save for The Terafin, the room appeared to be empty. The Terafin looked up and her eyes widened slightly as she saw who entered her room, and how. "What is this?"

Before anyone could frame an answer, the double doors opposite the magical arch swung open, a doorman on either side. Standing between them, well-dressed, clean-shaven, and unarmed, stood Old Rath.

Chapter Six

SHE COULD NOT BE certain that he had seen her, but she was by no means certain that he had not; upon sighting the open doors, she had all but leaped back into the summoning chamber. Carver—forgotten until this moment—was cautious in the face of the unknown; he'd obeyed Torvan's orders to remain behind. It was probably one of three times that he'd obeyed anyone's orders but her own since he'd joined her den. Smart Carver.

She cursed her own stupidity, lowered herself to the floor, and then lay there on her stomach, as close to the open arch as possible, straining to catch the words.

For the first minute or two, there weren't any.

Then, in a tone of voice that Jewel couldn't have managed had she tried, The Terafin spoke again. "Gentlemen, while it's been a pleasure to have your company, unless we can come to an understanding of circumstances, I will be forced to ask you to leave." Silence, and then, "I have, as you can see, a visitor who arranged to speak with me."

"If I've come at an inopportune moment, I can return at another time." It was his voice—Old Rath's voice. But the words were prettied up a lot.

"No," The Terafin said. "Gentlemen?"

Silence. Jewel hated silences like these, with no sight to guide her, no sense of action or movement.

"What are you doing?" It was Rath; his voice was sharp and grating.

A fan of orange sparks shot through the arch, fading from sight as quickly as a falling star. Jewel drew a sharp breath and rose instinctively to her feet. She crouched, dagger in hand, beside the arch as Carver gestured her down.

"Meralonne," The Terafin said, her voice almost twin to his. "Please. Explain your presence here *at once*."

"I am here," he replied, "at the behest of your Chosen."

"Obviously," was the icy reply.

"Please accept my apologies for the unannounced use of magecraft in your presence. And you, sir, if you would accept my most humble apologies."

"For what?" Rath replied, the edge once again smoothed out of his words.

Oh, shit, Carver mouthed.

"Indeed, Meralonne. For what?"

"I merely attempted to negate any . . . illusion that might have been present."

"Illusion?" Rath's incredulity sounded genuine. "Are you saying that I'm a mage?"

"No, my good sir. Please accept my apologies. Terafin, it appears that I have been summoned in error."

"Who summoned you?"

"I did," Torvan said. Jewel could hear the sound of an alloy knee joint hitting the grand carpets.

"We will speak of this later," was her cool reply.

"Lord."

The guards came in through the arch and eyed Jewel and Carver with anger and disdain. Torvan wavered a few moments more before also rising and retreating. He did not look at Jewel or Carver, but he didn't have to; his face was pale and stiff.

"I will take my leave," Meralonne said, turning in the arch so lightly and quickly that it caught Jewel by surprise, "but I think that I have not been summoned without cause." Jewel could hear the power in his voice. Shining brilliance came in through the arch; it was not so much a light seen as one felt. If someone had asked her its color, Jewel would have replied, *warm*. Not a color at all. She thought she could smell something sweet and wild in the air, some hint of a time and place that was safe and eternal.

A scream of mingled pain and surprise filled the room, turning to rage before it abruptly ended. Jewel was on her feet at once, shifting to take her second look into the room itself.

Old Rath stood ten feet away from The Terafin, his features contorted with pain. His hair was smoking, and his skin looked slightly singed. "My Lord," he began, facing The Terafin. "You can see that this—this mage bears me malice for reasons that I cannot begin to—" The words died abruptly as he met the eyes of Jewel Markess. His expression shifted, a subtle movement of muscle—a flag, just enough of a warning.

The wall exploded.

Torvan stopped two inches from the back of the mage. He shoved Jewel to one side, but he did not dare to jostle Meralonne APhaniel; he had the sense to understand that the only thing that stood between his Lord and her death was the mage. For he could see that, through some work of will, some magic invisible to his eye, The Terafin stood unharmed by the fire and rock fragments that filled the room like sunlight.

She had not shifted her position or her stance; even her expression was inscrutable. "Torvan," she said, without turning her head or taking her eyes away from her visitor, "I chose well, when I chose you."

Of course, she would speak these words when there was room for no other emotions but dread and fear.

Torvan said nothing; Jewel could see the tension and fear in the white line around his lips.

"Old man, do you think that you are a match for me?" Old Rath said. "Do you think that your magics and your pathetic human power will outlast mine? You've had decades, and I, eternity. But I will see you suffer before this is done." His voice was no longer the voice of her mentor and her friend; even the face, identical to Rath's, had somehow slipped, like a mask accidentally jostled at a nobles' masquerade. For that, she was grateful.

"Well, well, well," Meralonne replied, his voice so mild it was almost friendly. "It *has* been a rather long time, and I do admit that I'm rusty." He took a step forward and cleared the arch. Torvan practically lunged after him. A mistake; he crashed into empty air and bounced back, clutching his arm.

"Don't try it again," Jewel whispered. "Not yet." She watched the air between the columns of the arch, filmed and almost shiny but somehow still transparent. At her back, crowding her so tightly she felt her shoulders curl inward in reaction, were the rest of The Terafin's Chosen. "Carver," she snapped, "get out from underfoot!"

He was used to her temper in a fight and let the words—and the tone that conveyed them—slide off his back. He knew that if it were up to her, she'd've cleared the room of the whole damned lot of them, except for maybe Torvan. Maybe.

"What do you mean, not yet?" Torvan's voice was too tightly contained.

"He's keeping us out," she said, nodding to the back of the platinum-haired mage. "Or he's keeping that creature"—she was happy; she never had to call it Rath again—"in."

"How?"

"Mandaros knows," she snapped back. "Am I supposed to?" Then she bit her lip, and prayed that she not be sent to the Halls of Judgment—and Mandaros' sight—any earlier than lofty and ripe old age. She snuck in under Torvan's arm, pushed him—well, nudged really, as pushing a man in that much armor required more momentum than she'd managed to gain—to one side, and squinted fully into the room.

The sight of her seemed to enrage the creature. "*You* have caused me trouble, little urchin. My war is with you." Then, as if to contradict his own words, he gestured in a sharp, harsh arc. Hands that were human glinted in golden light as if they were made of steel, and something that seemed to be darkness made liquid spread from his fingertips.

Where it struck the ground, flames gouted; they traveled, hungrily turning the carpet to ash, to form a ring around The Terafin and her mage. Both remained untouched by fire.

Jewel jumped back and hit Torvan squarely in the chest; he'd moved again, and she'd been too absorbed to notice it. Bad sign.

The Terafin did not move. If she was afraid at all, the fear did not betray itself by showing its presence. No, to Jewel's eyes she seemed angry, but even the anger was a subtle thing. "Where is the real Ararath?"

"He is our prisoner," the creature replied, smoothly and swiftly. "But if I do not return in safety, he will be a corpse within the day."

"He's lying!" Jewel shouted.

For the first time, The Terafin's stare wavered. Both she and the creature turned to look at Jewel, and what Jewel saw in both of their faces—although the expressions were in no way similar—frightened her. She started, and Torvan's mailed hand caught her shoulder, both steadying her and keeping her in sight of the ruler of Terafin.

"How is he lying?" The Terafin asked, her voice level and gentle seeming.

"Old Rath is dead," Jewel replied starkly.

"He will be," the creature added. "But he is not dead yet. Do you think we would destroy so useful a bargaining tool, Terafin? This—" and he snarled as he gestured at Jewel, "has cost us much. We had hoped to take your House from within; it appears that we will have to accept destroying its leader."

"A poor consolation." But The Terafin's gaze did not waver as she studied Jewel's face. Jewel found it hard not to look away—but she knew that she must not, or else The Terafin would think her the liar. Held by The Terafin's dark eyes, she felt her fear give way to loss.

It was The Terafin who at last broke the stare. "Master APhaniel," she said, and her voice was steel. "Who—or what—is this . . . caricature?"

"I am your death," he replied, in a voice that was no longer Rath's or anyone else that Jewel had ever heard speak.

Time froze as they turned to stare at what had once been an old man. His skin seemed to melt into thinness over blood, and then even that ruptured as he grew in height and width. Slick and shining, his elongated jaws snapped shut and he lifted a vaguely reptilian head in a roar.

Jewel could have marked the second—the half-second—when that roar became a scream. Words escaped the sounds of agony, but they were spoken in a language that Jewel could not identify, and she had heard many in the streets of Averalaan. She didn't need to understand the words to know a plea when she heard it.

"Master APhaniel," The Terafin said, raising her voice so that it would be heard above the unnatural roar. "Cease this! We need information!"

A platinum brow rose. "I'm trying," the mage replied, through clenched teeth.

She fell silent at once and watched as the creature continued to writhe. It was hard to tell what was blood from what was skin; he looked like something newly birthed. Jewel turned her gaze to the woman who ruled, and kept it fixed there. Although this creature had been responsible for not only Rath's death, but Duster's and probably Lefty's, Fisher's, and Lander's, she could not watch his agony—it was too terrible. His death, yes. But cleaner somehow. In the end, although The Terafin stood firm, her gaze cool and remote as it rested upon the creature, Jewel's hands covered her ears, and her lids, her eyes.

I wanted to kill it, she thought. *He killed my kin.*

But even a dagger drawn slowly across an exposed throat, or one driven time and again into a prone back, were the most vicious of things she had actually considered; she could picture them in her mind, could almost force herself to *see*. Others were fantasies that had never gone beyond the feel of the words in her unspoken thoughts.

Nothing she had imagined was like this. Ask her and she would have said that the killer deserved the most hideous death that the Lady could offer. But its screams, like human screams, went on and on until she could no longer feel anything but horror and pity.

She opened her eyes to see The Terafin's impassive face, and it frightened her almost as much as the screaming did.

"Make it stop!" someone screamed. "For the Mother's sake, make it stop!" Later, from the rawness of her throat, she would realize who it was.

The mage was pale. Water ran from the corners of his reddened, unblinking eyes, but it was obvious they were caused by no emotion more complex than simple physical limitation. He took a step forward, and then another; a pure golden light cocooned his arms, his face, his chest. His robe crumpled; a knee hit the carpet before he righted himself. Then, at the last, he gave a cry, a snarl of fury— and the creature, limned in a darkness that was thin and hard and sharp, was gone.

Jewel slowly took her hands from her ears. Her arms were shaking with stiffness, but she brushed one quickly across her face. It came away wet.

"Jewel," someone said, and she forced her eyes open.

Shards of stone and a fine powder lined the furniture and the carpets of The Terafin's rooms. The curtains had been torn to shreds by the flying debris—except for the spot at which they would have had to pass through The Terafin; blue formed a perfect silhouette of her stance. Beyond it, the carefully beveled windows had been shattered; the lead-and-pewter frames had been twisted like thin reeds.

The damage was superficial, even pleasant to look upon, when compared with the room's center. What remained of the fine carpet was a damp, smoldering ruin, and the wet, dark stains across it would never be removed. But worse were the parts of flesh and skin stretched to breaking, of human teeth and the husks of human eyes, nails from hands and feet, matted, charred strands of hair.

Jewel was sick all over the good part of the carpet, but no one noticed. Meralonne, haggard but focused upon the task that he had started, crossed the room in safety, unconcerned for the dead that he might disturb. The Terafin watched him in silence as her guards emerged.

Torvan and Alayra immediately joined her, standing slightly back on either side. Their swords were drawn, and their shields, bright and burnished steel and wood, were across their chests. Torvan looked like stone, and Alayra, iron; they were hard and focused upon their duties to protect and guard their Lord.

But they were soft and yielding when compared to The Terafin herself. If such a woman had moved into the twenty-fifth holding to declare it—and all illegal traffic through it—her own, Jewel would have packed up and fled in a minute. As it was, she barely prevented herself from cowering to the side and ducking out of sight as The Terafin slowly approached the mage's side.

She looked down at the debris at his feet, and then raised her chin. In a chilly, quiet voice, she asked, "Is this human?"

He raised a pale brow, and then gazed at the scattered flesh and remnants as if seeing them for the first time. He gestured a green light into existence, and it touched them, twisting about them in a lattice of eerie spell-light. The light faded slowly as Meralonne let his arms fall to his sides. He turned to her without expression.

"Yes," he replied, no inflection marring the distance of the word. "These remains are human."

She nodded as if the question was as perfunctory as the answer was emotionless. But she turned to the ruined window, the shredded curtains, walking between her guards as if they were columns and not people. "Leave me."

"Terafin—"

"That was not a request. Leave me, all of you." The voice of command was so quiet that one had to strain to catch it—but once the words had been heard, they could not be denied.

Torvan and Alayra exchanged wary glances as they backed out of the room. Meralonne APhaniel finished his inspection, and then stood crisply, lifting the hem of his robes as he traversed the carpets. He paused in front of The Terafin.

"Terafin, I will repair to the Order and begin my report. On the morrow, I shall deliver it to you."

"You may return this eve," was her remote reply. "After the late dinner hour."

He bowed his acquiescence in near-silence.

"Jewel?"

Jewel, creeping along the side of the ruined wall, stopped short and fell to one knee. The edge of a stone chip cut into her kneecap; she bit her lip and waited.

"After the middle dinner hour, I would appreciate your company."

Jewel nodded.

"I will send someone for you in your quarters. Please be there."

She nodded again, and then scuttled out of the room as quickly as she could. She did not look back at The Terafin because she did not wish to meet her eyes or see her face again. It was too much like an invasion of privacy, an act of voyeurism.

Early dinner, middle dinner, and late dinner were not, as Jewel half-suspected, the different stages of noble repast. They were quite literally, as Ellerson pointed out, the hours at which civilized people were expected to—or allowed to—begin their dinner. In view of The Terafin's request, he ordered dinner for the early dinner hour.

That was not the only change he insisted upon; the second was a matter of clothing. The third was a matter of weapons, or rather, a lack of weapons. The fourth was a matter of language—but the fourth could not be supervised closely when she was no longer in the wing; Ellerson therefore concentrated on making her presentable. Presentability meant a dress; anything else was unsuitable for the dinner hours. Jewel wasn't even terribly surprised when he just happened to have a deep blue dress that was her size. It was not complicated, not frilly, and not restricting in movement. But it was heavier and finer than anything else she was used to wearing.

The sash, on the other hand, was worth more than the dress, and he helped her into it, tied it tight, and made sure she knew how to sit without destroying the lovely four-point flower he made of its length at her back.

"Nervous?"

"Shut up," she replied, scowling into Jester's smiling face.

He shrugged. "Hey. I was just going to say you look great."

She snorted. "I look like someone we'd try to rob, idiot."

"Given how hungry we've been this year," Angel added wryly, "that *is* great." He lifted the skirt and ducked as she whacked him soundly across the top of the head. "I was looking at the shoes! The *shoes*!"

Ellerson allowed them to continue their childish behavior for at least another minute before he pointedly cleared his throat. This subtle sound could probably be heard over the cries of merchants in the farmer's basket during a mild trade war.

"The Terafin has sent Torvan to escort you to her quarters," he said gravely. He said everything gravely, so it was hard to tell from his tone of voice whether or not he thought it was trouble. "You do not keep her waiting."

"Ellerson," she said, shoving Angel over and assuming a more dignified stance, "just because we're poor doesn't mean we're stupid."

"Of course not, ma'am."

Teller caught her on the way out. "Kalliaris' smile," he whispered. He was worried, which meant that it was obvious to him that she was. She didn't even try to hide it.

"She's straight," she said, taking his shoulder and turning him back toward the dining hall. "She won't do anything to hurt me."

"Then why can't any of us go with you?"

She didn't have an answer to that, and with Teller it was never smart to come up with an off-the-cuff lie. "Go on," she said, but he forced her to meet his gaze as he stared over his shoulder. After a minute, he nodded and let her go. Or rather, let himself be pushed away.

"What does she want?"

"I don't know," Torvan said, his voice neutral, almost officious.

"Can you guess?"

"Yes. I'd guess it has something to do with the events of the afternoon."

She rolled her eyes. "That's a big help."

The sound of his heels filled the arches above before he spoke again. "Jewel, she isn't a monster, and she isn't a magisterian; you don't have reason to fear her."

"She's one of The Ten!"

"She's the House, yes. But she's no threat to you if you haven't harmed the House."

"What have you told her?"

At this, he smiled. "The truth."

"All of it?"

"I'm hardly likely to lie to my Lord."

"I mean, did you tell her about the—"

"About my suspicions of your talent? Yes. She *is* my Lord, Jewel."

"Then what am I supposed to say?"

"The truth."

One of these days, she thought, as she hid a fist in the gathers of her skirt, *I hope I rule this House so I can hit you.* "Is she—is she upset?"

Torvan glanced at her. "Jewel." He stopped walking and turned to face her. "You may not know much about the Houses and The Ten. Let me explain, briefly, what I can. None of us—none of The Terafin's Chosen—were born to Terafin. The Terafin herself was not ATerafin at birth."

"I know."

"Do you?"

"Sure. If someone's good enough at what they do—and if it's a trade that's useful—then one of the Houses might sponsor them in. They get a home, a place to work, and the protection of the House—and they also get the name."

"Yes. And if you understand that, then you understand that many of us—most of us—have other families, and other parents, although we are adopted into this one. We aspire to greatness, to become a part of this House, with its history of nobility and strength in the face of forces that threaten the empire. And when we finally achieve that destiny, if achieve it we do, we owe our loyalty to the House. We have the family of our birth and the title of our House, and between them, were we forced to choose . . ." He shook his head almost sadly. "Coramis is *proud* to have its son be ATerafin.

"Not all of us are urchins, not all of us are bastards. Some of us come from houses of minor nobility, and some from houses of great riches. Some of us are artists, some warriors, some mages; some of us are farmers and merchants and carpenters. And a very few of us are leaders.

"The Terafin is a leader. But she was not adopted to be *The* Terafin; she was adopted to aid the house in its political course. She became the heir because she was our best.

"My name is Torvan Coramis ATerafin. Coramis was the family of my birth, and Terafin, the House of my choice. The family name will be mine until I die; the House name mine unless I commit an act of treason or disgrace myself in the eyes of The Terafin. The first is an accident, if you will, the second, an honor.

"Her name is The Terafin, but fifteen years ago, her name was Amarais Handernesse ATerafin." He turned sharply and began to march down the long hall in silence.

Jewel could think of nothing else to say.

The room that she was led to was not the first room that she had seen, and certainly not the wreckage that had been made of the receiving room; it was a small room on the uppermost level of the mansion itself, in a hexagonal area that jutted out almost to the edge of the street below.

Everything about it was clean and simple, but nothing was modest; the carpets were heavy, and the rugs upon them of the highest quality; the curtains were of a material that was not even sold in any of the shops that Jewel loitered in or around. The mirror—the single mirror along the wall of what looked like a sitting or dressing room—was gilded, although it was not ornamented; it was silvered perfectly and did not distort the face.

There were chairs here that seemed be to made of a single piece of wood, and that a heavy, dark one; there was also a table, low and long, that seemed to be grown, rather than carved, into an intricate flatbed with reliefs of wide, flat leaves to lift and carry it. The lamps on the wall seemed to contain the heart of fire itself, and the glass that restrained those flames seemed liquid caught in the motion of pouring.

Jewel recognized the artifacts of the maker-born, and she knew that she was looking at the end effect of more money than she had ever seen in her life, even if she added up every copper, half-copper, or lunarii that had passed through the hands of her den-kin as well.

"Are these her rooms?" she whispered to Torvan. He nodded, and if he was amused by her uncomfortable awe, he did nothing to show it. Instead, he came to the edge of the archway that opened, doorless, into the outer rooms of The Terafin's chambers.

As if his movement were a signal, a perfectly dressed man stepped into view. Jewel recognized him at once; he was Ellerson, only younger and a little less stuffy looking. His uniform was a study in simplicity; a long, pale cream robe with a gold-strand belt worn over house shoes. His hair was pale, more brass than gold; his eyes were dark. If he knew that he was under heavy scrutiny, it did not bother him at all. He bowed. "I am the domicis of The Terafin. She is waiting for you."

Jewel looked at Torvan. Torvan shook his head. "There are no guards within the chambers of The Terafin unless they are summoned in emergency. She will have no weapons and no hint of turmoil within her personal quarters.

"I wish you luck, Jewel Markess. I hope—" He stopped speaking abruptly and drew his forearm across his chest in salute. Then he turned and walked away.

"If you will follow me." There was nothing at all rude in the tone or the words, nothing forceful, nothing threatening. But Jewel knew an order, even if it was phrased remarkably like a question, when she heard it. She nodded, cleared her throat as unobtrusively as possible, unclenched her aching hands, and walked in his wake. He led her to a small library.

Above the room was a large, oval dome in which lead, like a web, held stained and painted glass. The sunlight was passing the horizon; by the end of the late dinner hour, it would be gone. Jewel almost wished it were midday, when she might see the ceiling in its full glory. She shook herself and looked down again.

There was no large desk in the room; there was a table as long and tall as a dining table, but darker and much heavier in build, surrounded by shelves placed along the walls. The Terafin was seated at it, book in hand; her hair was no longer bound, but hung at her back like a straight, dark curtain. She wore a simple shift, but again it was not inexpensive. Like the domicis', it was a cream color, with highlights of gold. She set the book aside as Jewel entered the room.

"Terafin," the domicis said.

"Thank you, Morretz. That will be all."

He bowed gracefully and gravely, and then stood, turning suddenly to meet Jewel's inquisitive gaze for the first time. She gasped, because his eyes were a blue that seemed too bright and shiny, and she had seen too much that was unnatural for one day. But the light faded into a trick of the imagination and he smiled, if a touch coldly, before he stepped out of her way.

Implicit in his gaze had been a threat; Jewel wasn't certain what it was, or why it was offered. She didn't have a chance to ask. He left her alone with The Terafin in the lofty confines of the library.

"Come, Jewel Markess. Join me." She raised a hand and pointed, palm up, to a chair that had obviously been arranged for the interview. Jewel approached it as if it were a cage.

"Do you read?"

"Yes. Some." It was hard to keep the defensiveness out of her voice, but she managed. She knew that something important was riding on the outcome of their interview. She didn't know what it was, of course—but she didn't want to blow it.

"Good. Have you done, or do you deal, with numbers?"

"Some."

"Have you handled a house, or the affairs of a house?"

She hesitated a moment before she answered, deciding on truth. Lies were complicated; Jewel had learned to use them sparingly, and to blend as much of the truth as she could into the mix. Truth had its own sound, its own special feel, and only a good liar could mimic it well. Jewel was not a good liar.

"No. I—I've handled the affairs of my den."

"Den."

She nodded.

"How long have you taken responsibility for these children?"

It was not the question that Jewel expected, but then again, The Terafin was so far from what she'd expected that Jewel was only a little surprised, and not taken aback at all. "For almost three years, by my count."

"Did you have to kill anyone to take your position?"

"Pardon?"

"In some holdings, and in some dens, leadership is decided by the demise of the previous leader."

Jewel was silent. At last, she smiled. "You know a lot about dens for one of The Ten."

"Knowledge is my business. You haven't answered my question."

"No. No, I didn't have to kill. I—I gathered. I found kids that were like me, people I could trust. I took them in, and organized them, and found them a place to live. Taught them how to avoid magisterians."

"I see. What did you do?"

She shrugged, uneasy. "What any den does when it doesn't have a lot of muscle. Steal what we could from the market or from people in the street."

"I suppose," The Terafin said, raising a hand to forestall any reply, "that you'll claim you had no other choice and no other way of surviving. I'll not dispute it at this time.

"But if you had another option, would you take it?"

It was a trick. Had to be. "Depends. We don't kill for money and we don't have experience robbing manor houses."

She raised a dark brow. "If," she said, her voice quite chilly, "I wished someone dead, I would not hand the task to a young woman who is barely adult with no experience and no . . . knack for the skill."

"Fair enough," Jewel said evenly, although the blush was in her cheeks. "We'd consider another job, yes. But we won't agree to anything without knowing what it is."

"Very wise." The Terafin placed both of her hands against the top of the table and rose, pushing slowly against it. She closed the book on the desk almost as if the action were an afterthought.

In the room's light, Jewel could see that the title was in gold inlay, with a leather relief that had been worn with the passage of time. But she could not read the words that she saw; they were not in a language that she understood—or if they were, they were in words so complex that she had never been forced to master them. And Old Rath, while he let her speak as she wanted, had always been a task-master. Old Rath . . .

"Did he teach you?" The Terafin asked.

Jewel looked up, aware of what could be read on her face, and not even con-cerned enough to hide it. "He was my second teacher. My father was my first."

"Where did you meet him?"

"I tried to rob him."

She looked very surprised.

"He was an old guy, walking slowly down the street. He was better dressed than any of the rest of them. He had what looked like a money pouch. I hadn't eaten in four days, or I hadn't eaten enough in four days.

"I was ten. We'd had nothing but rain for seven days. The rent my father paid had vanished, and I'd managed to lie low for two months in the old apartment until the owner found me out." She smiled, but it wasn't a happy smile. "So I was desperate, and not very good at being a thief. Most of the kids younger than me were much better at it—but my father had a real job, and I was expected to have a better one.

"Rath sort of took me under his wing—after he blackened my eye." That elic-ited a smile. "I told him about everything. Didn't realize how lucky I'd been be-cause I hadn't seen enough of the streets by then to know it. He told me. And told me. And told me."

"How did Rath occupy his time?"

"Not sure," Jewel replied evasively. "He'd done some time as a merc. He knew how to fight. Read. Write. Stuff like that."

"You aren't telling me all of the truth."

"No," Jewel replied.

"And if I wanted to hear it?"

"If I thought you wanted to hear it, I'd tell you." It was a risky answer, but it was true.

"I'm the lord of my House, Jewel. If I ask a question, I want the answer."

"But it isn't a matter of your House."

"Isn't it?" The woman's smile was cold and sharp. "Perhaps it wasn't; but the mage was summoned, two of my rooms are in ruins, my—Ararath is dead, and the cost to repair what has been done today will come out of the House books." But she turned her back to Jewel. "However, perhaps you are right. We had our differences, he and I, and I would not be surprised to learn how far back, and for how long, they extended." She paused. "There will be no funeral."

Jewel had already said her good-byes, and funerals were for the wealthy—or at least for those who could manage to scrape up enough money on top of what they needed to eat. She shrugged.

The Terafin turned again, her hair a curtain that slid slowly off her shoulders at the motion. "You showed a great deal of bravery, to come here."

"He told me to come here," Jewel replied.

"True." The Terafin's first completely genuine smile. "That he did. Have you read all of what you gave me?"

"All of it."

"Very well. This afternoon I sent out my own private investigators. I wished to be able to confirm some of what Ararath had written. It's quite extensive." She picked the book up from the table and walked over to one of the many shelves that lined the honeycomb walls. It was almost as if she could not—at this moment—sit still, or be idle. "They discovered nothing."

"Nothing?" Jewel furrowed her brow. "But what were they looking for?"

"Any of the entrances to these so-called tunnels of which Ararath wished me to be warned."

"But he didn't tell you where any of the tunnels were."

"You're wrong," she replied, and her voice was shadowed. "He did. In those lists, in the words that he chose, in the way that he put them on the page. Handernesse had its own hidden codes, and even after years away from that family, I have not forgotten them. Had I, I would not have learned what he wished me to learn—and I would not have known for certain that those texts were genuine. He told me much, Jewel. He even mentioned you, although not by name."

"Did he say anything good?"

"About you?" Another flash of smile. "Yes, or I would not have summoned you. But we have more serious things to discuss.

"I sent my people to the apartment that he called home, and explored the basement. There was no subbasement. Even using magical means, we were unable to detect one. In the end, my people were reduced to digging, both with magical aid and in the normal fashion. We worked with speed and as much discretion as possible. But there was no entrance into the tunnels of which he spoke. None.

"I do not believe that we will find any of the tunnel entrances to which he alluded, although teams of my people will explore those areas of which he wrote."

Jewel felt a tingling up her spine. "There was an entrance into Old Rath's place. I've used it. A lot."

"I don't doubt it," The Terafin replied. "But at this point we can only surmise that whoever it was who summoned the creature responsible for Ararath's death was also a mage skilled at gleaning information from an unwilling source."

Jewel waited for the rest, but the rest was long in coming; The Terafin's face was pale, except for the shadows in the hollows of her cheeks. Had she eaten or slept since the attack? Jewel was certain the answer was no. "Why do you think that?"

"Because the entrances are somehow disappearing."

"They might've done because they knew we'd escaped with that information."

A dark brow arched as The Terafin looked down. "Jewel, you were valued by Ararath, but the advice that Ararath gave you—to come to me—was sound. Ararath's enemies did not have much to fear from you. Who would listen to you? And who, in the end, would you have tried to speak with? You did not know who to turn to; you came at his command. His last act." Her smile was bitter. "Ararath sent you here—and one who was not familiar with Ararath, not familiar with the—with our relationship, would never have made the connection between him and me.

"He repudiated his family and his name. He would not mention our connection to anyone—not even those that he trusted absolutely."

Jewel was silent. Repudiation of family, even among the people that lived in the city holdings, was almost unthinkable. Family—if it was willing to claim you—was half of what and who you were.

"Do you understand now? The creature that became Ararath knew to come here."

"He might have followed us."

"True." She bowed her head. "But nowhere in the letter that Ararath left for you did he mention his relationship to me. He did not, I am certain, mention it to you—although he gave you the order to come here. No one who knew him as Rath knew it; I would swear by the spirit of the ancestor. Yet *this* Rath knew. I have a letter, delivered into the hands of my right-kin, that clearly states it." Her hands shook a moment; she looked down into them as if reading that letter again. Then the trembling stopped and the face tightened; Jewel was certain, seeing that expression, that there would be no trembling and no hesitance again. "If the imposter knew of our connection—knew that Rath was, in fact, Ararath—they must have coerced that information from him, and they must know much, much more. Therefore, any information which he imparted in the letter he left cannot be considered a secret." She stopped pacing very suddenly and turned to face Jewel, who remained seated.

"But not all of the letter was hidden; I read what he wrote to you. You explored those tunnels without his supervision—and against both his orders and his request—and I don't believe that you told him what you found, for possible fear of censure."

Jewel could add, even if what she was adding wasn't numbers. "Yes," she answered, her voice soft. "They don't know what I know. They don't know that we know the tunnel entrances to other places." She took a deep breath. "They'll probably guess that we know all the entrances in the twenty-fifth. If they know what Rath knew, they'd know most of the exits into the basin holdings—but not all. He didn't know 'em all."

"Indeed. Are you willing to work with my investigators?"

The big question, now. "And what do I get out of it?"

She did not bat an eyelid. This—although the language was far less formal, the nuance replaced by the subtlety of words poorly wielded—was what she did with much of her time. "For the duration of the investigation, you will need a place to stay; I will allow you to remain here. I will pay you at the same rate that the rest of my people are paid."

"What's that?"

"Two solarii a day."

Through a great effort of will, and the tickle of Old Rath's admonitions in her ears, Jewel kept her expression completely cool. *She's rich*, she told herself. *Two solarii might be more than we've ever seen for a day's work—but it's nothing to her. Hold out for more.*

"My den-kin?"

"They're your responsibility. They can remain with you—provided that you take responsibility for their adventures or misadventures while they are under *my* roof—or you can put them back where you found them."

She bristled. "They're *my* family. They follow my rules, they take orders from me. I don't throw 'em out anymore than you throw yours out."

The Terafin smiled again, and it was almost a smile of equals. "Very well. If you do as I ask, if you support me and show yourself to be worthy of *my House*, then I will make you—and yours—a part of it in name and in fact." It was clear from her easy acquiescence and the odd look in her eyes that it was an offer she had already considered—and considered Jewel worthy of.

Jewel could think of nothing at all to say.

"Morretz will see you out now. Consider my offer carefully; I will call for you after the hour of the first meal."

Morretz appeared like a pale shadow, moving so silently that Jewel was unaware of him until he appeared at her side. She followed him automatically, hardly aware of the carpet beneath her feet, and then a question rose to mind and lips before she could stop it.

"Why?"

"Why would I consider you as a possible member of Terafin?" The Terafin did not seem surprised by the question; indeed, she seemed to expect it.

"Yes."

"You wonder if it has anything to do with Torvan's report of your . . . special intuition."

"Yes."

"No, Jewel. In the end, it does not. A House is made by more than the ability of its members, and in only a few cases do we sponsor and adopt someone for the sake of his or her ability alone—and in those cases delicate political balances rule. You are not, because of your station in life, one of those cases, although I do confess that, when we have the leisure—and if I have taken your measure correctly—I would like to see your ability trained properly."

"But—but if not that, then why?"

"First: Because you have information that I desire."

"You could've bought that. I'd've given you what I had." Her eyes were very dark. "You know we need the money."

"Very good," The Terafin replied softly. "And if you had proved to be different, that is indeed what I would have offered you. But—" She smiled. "A family is made up of its members, no more, no less. You understand that; you show it to me, to all of us, by the way you lead your den, Jewel. Those children *are* your responsibility. Not your serfs and not the victims of your brutality; they are yours. I think—and I am not a poor judge of character—that they would die to protect each other. Because of you.

"There will always be room in my House for people who can instill that, and be worthy of it. You are worthy of your den, and if I am not mistaken you will be, in time, worth more."

"And if you are?"

"Then there will be no place in Terafin for you. It will not be the first time it has happened."

When Morretz escorted Meralonne into The Terafin's presence, it seemed for a moment an odd processional, where the master, white-haired, fair-skinned and richly attired, led the initiate.

The Terafin blinked and the image vanished; she was left with Meralonne APhaniel, looking slightly haggard and somewhat harried, as was his wont. He was a mage of the Order, and more besides, and she trusted him more than she trusted any other mage, which was little better than half.

He walked into the library without stopping to stare at the multiple shelves, the second story of which had been shadowed by the coming evening. He did not glance upward at the oval window, as Jewel Markess had done; he was an older man, and one used to power and finery.

Neither ever impressed him.

"Terafin," Meralonne said, bowing low.

"Master APhaniel." She gestured, and he took a seat quietly, rummaging in his sleeves a moment before looking up.

"Do you mind?"

"Not at all." It was a lie, of course; she hated the particularly acrid smell of pipe smoke. But she liked the look of the light in front of his lips when he gestured and the leaves, curled and dried, became slow-burning embers. And she liked the way that smoke, in a thin, gray-blue line, contoured his face and made of it an almost ethereal vision.

"I have taken the liberty of speaking with Morretz," Meralonne said. "Or rather," he added wryly, "Morretz has taken the liberty of speaking *to* me."

She smiled, but Morretz did not.

"As you suspected, the creature did not use illusion. He literally wore Ararath's flesh."

She nodded, and the smile was gone, consumed in flames darker and hotter than that which consumed the tobacco.

"Let me call it possession. I have done what research I can—and that research is severely limited for reasons which I will explain in a moment—and the most that I can tell you is this: Ararath was possessed and consumed by something that we know as demon."

She did not flinch, did not even feel the desire to do so. These were answers, and answers were all that was left. "How do you know this?"

"Because he was affected by a primitive branch of magic that is hardly practiced now. Historically, such a magic was used against the Allasakari and their allies."

Allasakari. The Terafin did not flinch, but she felt a chill wind take the room and make it a colder place. There were no priests of the Dark God in Averalaan, but history's lessons were dearly remembered by all who lived on the Holy Isle. "I see."

"Demon," he added, "is an old pre-Weston word; it means kin of darkness. Weston usage often called them 'the Kin' or 'demon-kin,' the latter of which is, as you can see, inaccurate."

This is why she usually stayed away from members of the Order. Bored lesson masters were less prone to odd—and inappropriate—conversational drifts than half of the Order's members. "It is quite clear that this creature was not a natural one. Very well, call it demon. What can you tell me of it?"

"Very little, I'm afraid. The knowledge and study of the kin, and their summoning, was lost centuries past in the great cataclysm. Research into this branch—and a few of the other branches—of magic is strictly forbidden to the Order's members, and the council of the magi also keep watch for the mage-born unbeholden to the Order who might stumble across its usage. You can understand why."

"Yes," The Terafin replied tersely.

"With that caveat, let me tell you what little I have been able to glean. The demons have their own phyla, and within those, a range of abilities. But from the old texts it is clear that there were a very few who were able to—absorb, I think, is the word we want here—the memories or thoughts of their victims.

"From Morretz's terse debriefing, I believe that that is the case here."

"You think he knew everything that Ararath knew?"

"Not everything, no. But much. Those memories that were long and grim, formative if you will, would be the easiest to reach." He stopped speaking for a moment, and then looked up. "I am sorry," he added softly, "for your loss."

"Don't be. He was lost to my family long before today." Her face was an ice queen's face; she rose and turned her back to him. "But you have answered my questions for the moment, and I wish to retire. I will call upon you tomorrow."

He left, led by Morretz, and she remained.

Chapter Seven

22nd Scaral, 410 A.A.
Free Towns

SHE WAS KILLING HIM, of course.

Evayne had sent Stephen, unprotected, into the darkness of High Winter. That darkness was the shadow of her soul, given strength and freedom. What it sought was the sacrifice that, invoked, it had been promised.

Once before—once before, when she had walked the Winter road unknowing, she had paid that price. The darkness gloried, and the brightness cowered, still.

You will not have again what I granted once. You will not have him.

But it was a struggle to contain the hunger. Darkness masked her vision; pain tried to cripple her. It grew worse as the time passed, and she could think of only one thing that would assuage it.

Not that, she thought, but felt herself sliding.

Stephen was screaming in the darkness of Winter, and only she could hear his voice.

"Lady," Zareth Kahn said, his voice the only sound to break the dark, pale chill of winter stillness, "where are we?" The Ariani and the demon-kin were gone, but the red of elemental fire was seared into the vision, held as it was in the hands of two who ruled in darkness. Although he had spent his entire life enshrouded in the study of ancient mysteries, he never expected to see them walk, who were so powerful and so cold they were truly beyond his understanding.

And the seeress—the magi—in her robes of midnight blue was the only bridge between the world he understood and the world, or worlds, he could not.

Evayne, bent and circled with thin wreaths of darkness, looked up, as if seeing the landscape—the exterior world—for the first time. The Winter held her, and held fast, but by the thin twist of her lips, by the shaking curl of fingers and fists, Zareth Kahn could see that she was fighting its hold. Possibly winning. She opened her mouth soundlessly.

Gilliam pushed Zareth Kahn aside. "Never mind that," he said, his voice cold but shaky. "Where in the Hells is Stephen?"

Espere, had she been a dog in fact and not just spirit, would have been running in anxious circles at his feet; as it was, she tried to butt his chest with her head while she uttered her soft keening whine. He pushed her aside, but unlike Zareth Kahn, she was unwise enough to return.

"Evayne, I asked you a question. Where is Stephen?"

But Evayne covered her mouth with her hands and turned away. Gilliam reached out to grab her shoulders, and Espere was there, in his way. It was too much.

Get back! His mental voice was a furious shout. *Get-out-of-my-way.*

Espere recoiled, and then, growling every inch of the way, she began to obey him. Her lips came up off her teeth as she met his eyes. She backed away, and he followed her with the force of his command.

How dare she interfere with his search for his huntbrother? How dare she try to stop him when Stephen needed him—must need him?

Stephen . . .

Gilliam stopped his sending; Espere lunged forward, free more quickly and more completely than either expected. She ran in circles around him, frenzied, as he covered his eyes with his hands. He stood because he was not a man to kneel to any but his leige.

He knew how Stephen would have felt had he seen Espere forced back so. He was not certain that he did not feel a trace of revulsion himself.

"Do you trust her?" he asked aloud. Espere quieted, hearing more than just the tone of his voice. "Then I will wait." But gnawing at his determination was the emptiness that seemed to be growing. He understood William of Valentin now—and he wished to understand no more.

Evayne seemed unaware of his struggle. She raised her head and looked beyond him to where Zareth Kahn stood in silence. "A hundred yards from here, no more, is a cabin that was once used as a way station for messengers from a lord who no longer rules. He had it crafted—as were all the stations, by Artisans of the maker's guild."

"By *Artisans*? It must have beggared him!"

Her smile was weak. "Indeed, it nearly did. But his wife was the daughter of the Artisan who ruled the guild at that time." She grimaced; a wave of pain—or something near it—transformed her features. "He was amenable to some of the Lord's plans. In the end, the stations were built before the beginning of the Baronial Wars. This one, and three others like it, survive unnoticed. The others have been destroyed, or have became, over time, inns or homes of particular note." She began to walk, and stumbled. Zareth Kahn stepped forward to offer her aid, and she shook her head. "Come no closer." The darkness made of her voice a cool and sensual threat.

"Why have you brought us here?" Zareth Kahn asked, as Evayne righted herself. "Why not deliver us to Averalaan? Why not Breodanir?"

"Because," she said softly, "this is where the road has taken us. Would you have walked another step in the Winter?" Her answer silenced him. It would not have, had he a better understanding of High Winter.

The title of Artisan was granted to very few of the maker-born. There were no Artisans in Breodanir, nor, in Gilliam's living memory, had there ever been. But according to Zareth Kahn, an Artisan ruled the maker's guild in the city of Averalaan. He was a rich and powerful man, and given to the odd comings and goings of one steeped in mystery or The Mysteries.

Gilliam shrugged. Stephen would have been impressed, but Stephen was not here.

"There," Evayne said. "Between the hillocks. It is not easily found, but once found, not easily lost. Come."

They followed her, Zareth Kahn with open curiosity, and Gilliam with growing unease. The snow was knee-deep except where the ground beneath made an unexpected rise or dip. Twice, Zareth Kahn had to be pulled up and dusted off. Gilliam and Espere had an uncanny ability to keep their feet. Evayne did not seem to need it; weightless, she brushed the snow's surface with the edge of her robes.

When at last she stopped it was in front of a modestly sized, wooden cottage. There was a door, and as she lifted a hand to knock at it, it swung open.

No normal building, without the care and attention of generations of owners, would have survived in this wilderness. But the Artisans made no normal things when called upon to use their craft.

"Come," Evayne said. "Here, we may shelter." She paused. "There are no rules save two: Enemies of the Baron may not shelter here and those who seek shelter may not raise a hand in violence against each other. The Baron is long dead, but the second rule is enforced in a particularly unpleasant fashion. Do not breach it."

They crossed the threshold, stepping into history. Above their heads, the ceiling was high and beamed in several places. The beams were stained, the ceiling around them a pale blue. There was a fire burning in the fireplace along the opposite wall; before it, in blues and browns that matched the ceiling, was a large oval carpet and four large chairs. Upon the carpet stood a squat, thick table, and upon it, glasses filled with amber liquid that reflected the flames.

To the right of the hearth was a hall.

Gilliam walked toward the fire, slowly removing his jacket. Espere followed behind him. "This place—it didn't look as big from the outside."

"It isn't," Evayne replied gravely. "There are rooms down the hall. Find one that suits you; it will be ready. I believe that after you have had a chance to bathe and sleep, food will be provided." She walked past them toward the hall.

"Where are you going?"

"To find Stephen," she said, without looking back.

"Let me come with you."

"No."

"Let me come with you," Gilliam said again, tossing his jacket aside.

"Lord Elseth, what I do, you cannot do. There is no help you can render me. Leave me be."

His cheeks flushed. He started to speak and then bit back his retort. Swallowed. "I can help you," he said. "I can help you call him back." Hard, to say those words to her. He didn't ask her where Stephen was; she didn't volunteer the information.

But she stood with her hand on the wall for long minutes before she at last nodded grudgingly.

Everything was wrong with her. Her scent was wrong, her shadow wrong, her gait, her voice, her movements. He needed no trance to sense it, although he was very close to calling Hunter's trance anyway. Her robe seemed to clutch at the ground as if it were a man clinging to the edge of a cliff.

She turned unexpectedly to the left, entering a room that, until the door swung wide, Gilliam had been unaware of. There was a small bed pressed against one wall, and one of the largest windows that Gilliam had ever seen made of real glass opposite it. There was no carpet, and no curtains; no chairs, no dresser, no desk. The only other thing in the room was a fireplace—but it took up the length of one wall; it was at least as large as the one in the great room. Dry wood was piled high and waited for the sparks that would start it burning.

"I am sorry, Lord Elseth," Evayne said. "But I can no longer spare you the pain."

Stephen came back to him, swept in like a leaf in a gale. There was no joy in the reunion, and almost no sentience.

Evayne's brief, cryptic comment had been warning enough; Gilliam, braced for it, managed not to scream.

Where is he? Where is he, Evayne?

In a place so dark, and held so close, that even Evayne could afford—while Ariane threatened—to ignore its existence.

And where is that? She felt her fingers lance her palms, but it was a distant sensation and almost a pleasure compared to the shadows.

The shadows held every lie that she had ever spoken; they held every death that she had caused, knowing or unknowing; every injury that she had inflicted—and, against the will of intellect, enjoyed inflicting. They held every second of her life that she had used her power, had called it, had stood, contained by it and containing it, a giant astride her world.

They held every hatred, every bitterness, every moment of avarice and envy.

Even contempt and bigotry had taken root and blossomed here, although Evayne never showed them the light.

But they also held Stephen. And in the darkness, they grew darkness, in the shadows, shadow. What was not to their liking, they consumed.

Fear makes of us all cowards. And cowardice is universal, predictable, malleable.

She forgot where she had heard it, but remembered the tone and timbre of the speaker's voice. It was true. And Stephen's darkness was, measure for measure, so like her own it was hard to separate it.

She cried out. Pain, of the devoured and the devouring, cut through her like sharp, wire mesh.

Against the pain, Gilliam threw up what shield he had. He staggered toward the window, although the landscape was still the night's, seeking stars or starlight's reflections across the snow. He found them in the window's length.

Stephen had a voice, but it was so distorted it was almost still. He began to press the ties that bound them, speaking in the language of the Hunter and his brother, in the cadence of Gilliam and Stephen, for which there had never been, nor would ever be, any equal. He took Stephen's pain, and offered his comfort in return, shouting it, whispering it, pleading with it.

Stephen was deaf.

The darkness could not be separated from the darkness, nor the fear from the fear. What was worse was that this part of her soul was one that was unmapped by her, unremarked on; she did not know it well, because she had refused to learn it. Which part was hers and which his? Did it matter?

She snarled, and it was a real sound, not a shadow sound. She felt it tickle her throat; as a prelude to violence it was welcome.

What does it matter? What is one life? One life, when yours has been surrendered again and again to the cause? He could never have done what you do, never have learned what you learned. What is one life, when if not for you, it would have been lost anyway?

What is one life, when, if not for me, it would have been lost?

She knew then that had it been Zareth Kahn, or Gilliam, or Espere—even Espere—she would have given up and let the shadows feed. She was not proud of the fact, but accepted it for the truth that it was. Because *it wasn't* Zareth Kahn, Gilliam, or Espere. It was Stephen.

Stephen.

Her robes twisted around her calves like cold snakes. Her sleeves shuddered and convulsed. In one second, hands that had been empty and clenched clutched at a shard of her soul made manifest: the seer's ball. Her crystal.

Now it is time for truth, she thought, as the blood from her hands smeared its surface. *Stephen.*

He rose before her, revealed in all nuance, all fear, and all sorrow. The crystal had once pierced his heart, laid it bare to the eyes of the seer. Had she promised not to use it? Had she promised to guard and to hide what was found?

The past was murky, thankfully obscured; it was the present that consumed her, consumed them both. She called him and looked upon him as she had not done since her youth. And she wept.

Stephen, she said, trying to rip her voice from the grip of the shadows, *come. It's safe. Come to me.* She pulled herself free of him, delineating carefully his beginnings and hers, his end—the end she knew—and hers. *Come quickly. Come while it is safe. Stephen . . .* But there was no movement in response to her call.

He did not trust her now. He was afraid of her, of what she had done and what she had become. He heard her voice and it was part of the pain and the ugliness with which he was surrounded. A trap. He was certain of it.

It was cold here, and the cold had teeth and fangs; it cut further into him, twisting and biting. But the numbness that came with cold never followed. Instead, images: thieving on the streets, tripping a den mate so that he might fall and distract their pursuers while Stephen escaped, lying, pleading with his mother when yet another man had left in the late evening, knowing that if he were better, somehow, she wouldn't have to have them—the things in his life that Elseth had taken, thankfully, from him.

Why had they returned?

The words came again; hers, but distorted and sharpened. He did not answer her because he was afraid that if she heard him, she would know where he was.

She had not foreseen this. She had forced her shadows back, but he could not sense his freedom, and it would not last for long. *Come, Stephen,* she said, more urgently. *There is little time left. Come!* She couldn't force him to leave, because in order to do that she would have to . . . touch him.

Hunger.

Stephen!

"He won't—he won't come," Evayne said, her voice a dry croak. "I'm calling him—but he won't come."

Gilliam felt just a twinge of smugness.

"If he doesn't come back to us soon, he—won't be able to." She stared into the crystal ball that her hands were clawing against. "I've given him the passage he needs. But he doesn't—I don't think he trusts me." Her voice was bitter and icy. "And if he doesn't, we've lost him."

As starkly as he knew how, Gilliam demanded his brother's attention.

Doubt came back along the bond—but it was Stephen's doubt. Fear.

I'm here, Gilliam thought, as he redoubled his effort. *I'm here.* He reached out, with both hands and the strength of his conviction. *Come, Stephen. Come back. There's hardly any time left.*

Self-loathing. Doubt. Shame.

Comfort. Belief. Trust.

Stephen answered, but as usual, there were no words to accompany the emotions.

The room, empty but for the bed and Gilliam and Evayne, became shrouded in a magical pall. The robes of the seeress elongated, rising like restless ghosts almost to the ceiling on either side of her.

"Look away, Gilliam of Elseth, *look away!*"

He did, obeying not her command but an instinct as old as the Hunter. He covered his ears as screams of rage and pain and terror buffeted him. Evayne had opened the gates. One voice in the storm of voices grew higher and thinner, but whether it screamed in rage or terror, in pain or even self-loathing, Gilliam could not say.

Stephen of Elseth, pale and thin and unblinking, stumbled out. The noise was cut off in an instant; the silence that descended was deafening in its suddenness.

Gilliam turned at once to see his brother prone upon the ground. Evayne was gone as suddenly as she had come.

"Stephen!"

Stephen did not move. Gilliam picked him up and carried him to the bed. He laid him down beneath the length of the window. The cold, for it was cold outside, did not chill the glass. But it chilled Stephen's skin.

Beneath the bed frame were blankets, heavy woolens, and lighter cottons. Gilliam pulled them all out and bundled them around and over Stephen's body. Then he rose to find food and water for Stephen's waking.

The dogs were at the door, and none too pleased to be there. Ashfel was in a foul mood, and was not above taking it out on the rest of his pack. Only Marrat, the oldest and wisest of the alaunts, had the intelligence to wait out of Ashfel's snapping range.

Gilliam nearly stopped walking when he heard their sullen voices pressing him. They wanted to know where he had been and why he had kept them waiting and if he had dared—dared!—to hunt without them.

He made haste to reach their sides, and after they had greeted him in their most enthusiastic way, he noted that among the paw marks his dogs had left along their path to the way stop there were footprints, faint and light, across the snowtop, accompanied by a sweep of cloth where robes might fall. He did not ask the dogs about it; Connel's acute sense of smell told him what he needed to know.

He did not understand Evayne.

He did not particularly like her.

But he owed her a debt, and he vowed quietly, as the night's grip began to crumble across a blueing sky, that he would not be in that debt forever.

The room was not empty when Gilliam returned with a tray of broth, bread, and warmed milk. Stephen was still in bed, but his wan face was propped up by several pillows, and his eyes were open.

At his side, sitting in robes of midnight blue, was a very young woman. Evayne the younger, as Gilliam thought of her. Her hood was arranged in a spill around her shoulders; her hair, dark as a raven's wings, was free. She started almost guiltily as he stepped across the threshold.

He wanted to ask her what in the Hells she thought she was doing here, but remembering his vow, said instead, "I brought some food." His tone was curt and grudging, but nonetheless, Stephen's approbation for his self-control was clearly felt.

And that made him smile.

"The sun is rising," Stephen said, ostensibly to Gilliam.

"Yes," Gil replied. "And I saw yesterday's sunrise as well. I'm hunt tired."

Evayne held out her hands for the tray, and after another minute, he let her have it. "I'll make sure he eats," she said, almost demurely. "I've—I've gotten sleep in the last several hours. I can take care of him for now."

"Stephen?" Gilliam asked brusquely.

Stephen's nod was not really an answer; his eyes were fixed to the window. The sun's disk was above the trees, but only by a hair's width. The sky was pink and orange and yellow; the darkness was gone, and the only shadows were those cast by the light.

Gilliam understood what Stephen did not say. He needed to see the breaking of day before he slept, or ate, or rested. Gilliam didn't. He could feel Stephen again, and Stephen was himself. That was enough.

"Wake me if you need me," he said, although he was certain that this young woman—so different in every way but uniform from her powerful, older counterpart—would die before she did so.

"I will," she said quietly.

When Stephen woke it was morning, but it was not the same morning that he'd witnessed the start of. The room was the same; a fire burned—he was grateful for its size and the warmth that the flames generated—in the wall opposite his bed. But there were deep green curtains, embroidered with browns and golds to look like a cloth forest, and beside the bed itself was a simple, cedar table that could, in a pinch, seat two. There was a chair as well as a bedstand.

It was the knocking that had pulled him from slumber, although he only realized this when it came again, faint but unmistakable, at the door.

He knew who it was, and who it wasn't.

"Come," he said. He spoke softly because he could not put force behind his words. The cold was in his spine, his bones; his chest ached from the bitter winter. Once or twice as a young boy in the King's City he had been racked with just such pain—but at that time it was accompanied by coughing and hacking.

The door swung open, and the young Evayne stood in its frame, holding a tray. When she saw him, she smiled almost brightly. "I wasn't certain if it would be you," she said. Then she glanced down at the soft foods she carried. "But I guessed it might be."

"Have you tended many other sickly people?"

"No," she replied firmly. "But I will." There was no doubt at all in the assertion.

"Oh?" He sat up, changing the configuration of pillows so they formed a brace at his back. Then he looked down and realized that he wasn't wearing his Hunter's garb. He blushed.

She blushed as well. "I—I didn't do that. Lord Elseth did. He—he said you needed cleaning."

Thank you, Gil. "Do you know who else you'll tend?"

"No."

"Then why are you so certain?"

"Are you hungry?" She put the tray down on the table and then pulled the chair up to the bedside. Her robes fell away from her arms, avoiding, as if by magic, the food beneath them. She saw him stare, and smiled with that odd mixture of bitterness, pride, and shyness that she only showed when she was young. "It was a gift," she said. "From my father. It's—it's magic. Made by an Artisan and, maybe—maybe a God."

"It's lovely," he said, meaning it.

Her smile was genuine and unalloyed. "Do you think so? Miramon said it was too dark."

It was too dark, he thought, for a girl her age; too austere, too severe. But he knew enough to know that a girl her age was not likely to want to hear that. If this Evayne truly knew how to be a girl like any other. "Very few could wear it so well."

"I don't get to wear much else."

"No?"

"No. Not even to sleep in."

He accepted the flat, shallow bowl she offered him, looking at its contour and shape as if it were an inverted shield and not a dish. There was a clear broth in it that smelled very strongly like chicken; it was thick and very hot; he could feel it warm his palms.

"It's an Essalieyan drinking bowl," she told him gravely, "In most of the inns in the flatlands, you'll find that food is served in bowls, with bread as a scoop."

"Ah. Ours are not so shallow." He drank, and she watched him.

"In Averalaan, they use all sorts of things to eat with. You'll see them when you get there." She fell silent for a moment; he glanced up to see her staring out the window. "Lord Elseth said I saved your life last night."

He stopped drinking his soup and shuddered; the cold gripped him tightly, and for just a moment he could not shake it. Then the waking nightmare passed. "Yes," he said.

"What am I like?"

"That," he replied dryly, "I would love to know. Who are *you*?"

"You'd know that better than I would," she said, the bitterness once again lacing her words.

"No," he said, setting his soup and his hunger aside as he met the violet eyes of a hurt young woman. "I wouldn't. The Evayne that I met last night is not you, no matter what you would like to think. You're different; you're your own person."

"Am I?" she sneered. "Am I really? Everyone knows that I'm going to be *her*. All of them."

"Everyone?"

"I can't tell you anything!" Her half-shout was startling because it was unexpected. Stephen watched her face in silence, and when he showed no reaction—no surprise or disappointment, she began again slowly and more calmly. "I'm not *allowed* to tell you anything. Everyone wants to know why I'm old and young and old and young. They want to know where I get my power, or how I use it. I'd tell them, if I could. But I can't. I gave my word, and more."

"I won't ask you those things."

"What else is there to talk about?"

"I don't know. I imagine that we'll find something. Or isn't that why you're here?"

She flushed and rose. Before he could speak again, she was at the door, and the door was open.

Stephen looked down at the cooling soup and smiled selfconsciously. It was not the effect that he was used to having, but then again, Evayne was in no way like the young women he was accustomed to meeting.

Four hours later—or at least he thought it four hours by the sun's position—she returned. Her cheeks were red with cold and wind and her feet showed the rare evidence of touching ground; snow was melting into the carpet at the door.

He rose—he was, by this time, dressed—and stopped as she stiffened. It was clear that she was still angry. "Evayne," he said, bowing slightly, "I didn't mean to offend you."

She shrugged. "You didn't."

"Will you join me for lunch?"

"If you want."

"I'd be honored." He offered her his arm, and she took it. It was embarrassing, really; he was still too weak to walk well, and the arm that was to be the gentleman's gesture ended up clinging to hers for support; she was deceptively strong. Yet that seemed to suit her, and when they reached the open dining room—with its long tables and tall chairs—she was once again calm.

"You aren't like your Hunter Lord," she said, as she found the table on which two dinners had been laid out.

"No." Speaking of which . . . Stephen glanced around the hall, but he saw no other places set. "Are these places for us?"

"Yes."

"Have you been here before?"

Her lips compressed into a thinner line, and he realized that he was asking the unanswerable. "Where were you born?"

She stared at him for a minute before she answered him, and the answer was heavy with the unspoken. "The free towns."

Every question he could think of asking seemed polite and trivial, and it was clear that if Evayne—this Evayne—had ever mastered either art, it was forgotten. Once again silence engulfed them, and Stephen felt it acutely. Parents? Friends? Home? He was certain that they were behind her, and that she could not return to them; perhaps that accounted for her bitterness, perhaps not—but was it wise to stir up things that were barely settled?

"You see?" she said.

"Yes," he replied, smiling wryly.

Silence again. And food. In her own way, she was like Espere; shy as wild creatures are, easily startled. He thought she might also be ferocious when cornered. But unlike Espere, he thought that Evayne was intelligent enough to be—to feel—lonely.

She said I was kind to her, he thought, feeling the weight of those words as a responsibility. *She was as old as Lady Elseth, and she still remembered it.* Somehow, because of this, he knew that he could help her, even if he didn't understand her. But the silence stretched out between them, lengthening and hardening.

He looked up to meet her violet eyes; saw the expectation that she would never voice, and the disappointment that was growing in its place. He could not think of a meaningful thing to say about her life.

Which left only his own, and there was risk in that. He could never say why, afterward, he decided to take that risk.

"I was a thief in the King's City when I was half your age."

Her violet irises were rimmed with white as her eyes widened. She didn't quite drop her bowl, but it was a near thing. Then her eyes narrowed; he could see her try to gauge his honesty. "Really?"

"Yes. For four years, more or less. I don't remember much of it—probably because I don't want to." He looked down at dinner, but he wasn't very hungry, and chose instead to lift a goblet of wine and rise. The chair was smooth and silent as he pushed it back. "But my mother was a prostitute in the city streets, and my father probably one of her clients; she wouldn't say, and that might be because she didn't know. I didn't understand it well then, and only as I got older was I able to put the pieces together. I remember her face; she was old by the time she was my age." Oh, it was cold now; the words brought the chill, and the shame. He almost stopped speaking.

But she asked the next question. "How did you end up with Lord Elseth?"

"It's—it's a custom of Breodanir. I don't know how much of it you know, or how much you understand. But by the time I was eight—or maybe nine; I was small for my age, so it was hard to tell—I was an orphan, and no one owned me but the den. Gilliam's father came to find a suitable commoner to live with his son, and I was his choice."

"You were an orphan?"

"My mother died when I was very young." Before she could ask, he added, "I remember very little about her. But when she left me—when I realized that she was never coming back—it was the worst of my nightmares made real. I searched for her. I ran through the warrens shouting her name. She never answered, and I was certain that it was because she didn't care what happened to me. I never found her.

"Later, someone told me that she had died." He swallowed. "But I remember the feeling of desertion, and knowing she had been killed didn't take it away; nothing did. I remember it still. Sometimes I dream of it now—that the people I've grown to love and value have discovered some terrible flaw in me, and one by one have deserted me."

The Winter had opened old wounds. But he was not alone in the darkness with them. Stephen could feel Gilliam, concerned, fluttering around the edges of his emotions. His brother.

"Why are you telling me this?"

"Why?" The surface of the wine was deep and dark as it caught his reflection. "I don't know." He lifted the cup and felt its cold edge between his lips. The wine was a good vintage—not sharp enough to sting the throat or leave a bitter taste in its wake. "I've never told anyone else this, not even Gilliam." He emptied the cup and then turned back to the long table, where she was now sitting motionless, staring up at him. "I'm sorry, Evayne. I thought we would speak of who you are, and instead, I burden you with the secret of who I am. Or who I was."

She continued to stare at him as she slowly pulled the napkin from her lap and set it aside in a crumpled heap on the table. "I used to think that my parents were Nolan a'Martin and his wife, Mary a'Graham. I was born in Callenton, in a different time.

"I've only been gone for a little while." Her eyes began to film, and Stephen did her the grace of looking away.

"I always looked different, but my father was a blacksmith, and everyone treated me well enough, except for the other children. When I was twelve, my parents told me that I wasn't really their child. I'd been left as a babe at the Mother's Hearth, and the Priestess there had been asked to find a suitable home for me. They had no idea who left me there, or why." As she spoke, her voice changed slightly, lilting in a cadence that Stephen had not yet encountered. "Then my father died, and everyone began to think I looked strange. Too pale and thin, and they didn't like the look of my eyes much.

"I only had two friends by the end of my fifteenth year. One was—" She bit her lip, hovering on the edge of a decision, taking, Stephen thought, risks of her own. "One was Darguar. He used to be a soldier, but he never would tell much about his life. He came to Callenton to forget about war, not to pretend it was glorious."

"He said that."

She smiled almost shyly. "Those are his exact words, yes. He said he'd been around enough that I looked exotic, not dangerous. He gave me this." She parted the collar of her robe and pulled out what appeared to be a delicate, perfect flower, except for the fact that it hung from a thin chain, and its petals, like the chain, shone like polished silver.

"It's lovely," Stephen said softly. "And unique, I think. It seems very delicate."

"But it isn't. It never breaks. It never bends. It was an adult gift." As she spoke, she looked down, and then cupped it carefully in two palms. He thought she would cry. But she swallowed, shook herself, and continued. "Wylen was my other friend. He was a year younger than I, and probably half as strange.

"I used to see them every day. I don't know if I'll ever see them again. I miss them," she added as she put the pendant away. "But if I see them, I don't know who I'll be, and I don't know who they'll be. I don't know if we'll be friends anymore." Her robes shivered as she spoke, and became tighter somehow.

"I never thought it would be easy," she added gravely.

He knew better than to ask what.

"But I thought, if I could save them, it would be enough."

Save who? Wylen? Darguar?

"And maybe it will be. Enough I mean. But I *don't know.* I don't know if I can save them from what—from what I saw. I wait, every day, to see if I return there. I wait to see if someone I meet can help my—my friends. And nothing happens. They aren't—they—" She lost her voice; Stephen saw a glimmer of gray light wreathe her lips, and wondered if a spell prevented her from speaking her mind.

Who would place such a spell on such a child?

Then he remembered the first time he had seen her. Dreams. Wyrd. Destiny.

"But I made my choice for them. And I don't know if the woman I'll become

will even have the time to care about one little village in the middle of nowhere."
She started to cry then.

He wanted so badly to ask her what she meant. *How could you not care?* he
thought.

As if hearing his question, she shied back, and then, when it remained unspoken, relaxed a little. But only a little. "You don't know," she said, her voice low and
shaky. "You don't know who I've met, and what they've said. You don't know what
I've started to learn, and what I have to learn. You haven't seen the end—" Again,
gray light shadowed her lips, and a choked silence descended. "It's why I want to
know who I am. What I'm like."

Evayne. He reached out carefully and caught one of her hands in both of his. It
was shaking. How could he describe the woman who had taken him on the Winter road and nearly destroyed his soul? How could he speak of the mage who had,
single-handed, fought off three of the demon-kin, buying his life, and that of
Gilliam and the wild girl? Could he tell her of the woman who casually stopped
time in order to urge them to travel to Averalaan to fulfill some mysterious destiny?

He could find the words, he thought, as he met her eyes. But he knew that they
wouldn't comfort the fear and the loneliness. So he chose different words instead,
and said a prayer to Justice and Judgment in apology.

"When she's twice your age, she seems much happier than you are, but more
powerful. She has more secrets, and she's not so frightened. She's also beautiful."

She blushed, and he smiled softly.

"When she's three and four times your age—it's hard for me to guess at ages—
she's quieter, but she walks like a queen, and she seems very much at peace with
herself."

"Peace?"

"Yes." He paused. "She's also very, very powerful."

"Do you think she—"

"I think she's probably already dealt with whatever problem it was that worries
you now."

"All of it?"

"Evayne, if anyone can, she can." He caught her other hand and held them both
tightly between his. "You can. I don't understand how or why, but you saved my
life when I was fourteen. You sent a man named Kallandras."

She started a little, and then smiled weakly. "It wasn't me."

"No, but I believe it's the person you become." He smiled gently. "And if the
person that you become can remember me—and make provisions to save *my*
life—surely that person can remember the friends that she wanted so badly to
save."

"I want to believe that," she told him.

"Then do," he replied gravely. "I do." That, at least, was the truth.

She pulled her hands gently out of his. "I—I have to go."

"But you haven't eaten."

"Neither have you." Her smile was shy and slight, but it was there.

"Why don't you stay?"

"I can't tell you," she answered, but not so defensively. "But I—but I hope I can return." She stood back, gave a half-curtsy, half-bow, and then walked rapidly from the dining hall.

That evening Stephen could walk and stand without aid. Gilliam's dogs had made of themselves a small court before the fireplace in the great room, and lazily rolled and yapped and played. It seemed that the designer of the way station had foreseen the need to take care of beasts other than those of burden; food—perhaps a little richer than what they were used to—had been provided in very generous quantities. Gilliam was as patient as he could be, considering Stephen's condition; he took the dogs out on a run so that they could all lose the nervous energy that had built up over the course of the last two days.

Zareth Kahn spent most of his time locked in his room. Stephen, having been apprised of the magical properties of this odd rest station, wondered what sort of rooms would be given to a mage. Common sense overcame his curiosity, but it was a close thing.

Which means I must be feeling better, he thought wryly.

She came to him, this eve, at a run. Unfortunately, she also came from around a corner, and Stephen had no time to get out of her way, let alone brace himself. They fell in an awkward spill of robe and tunic; Evayne screamed and then, realizing where she was, began to shake.

"What is it? What's wrong? Have I hurt you?" He righted himself quickly and put an arm around her shoulders.

She closed her eyes and shook her head. There were tears on her lashes; her skin was pale, with a slight green tinge to it, and her breath was short and sharp. Her body, stiff and rigid, made of itself a shield.

"Evayne," he said, speaking as if to a frightened pup, "it's all right. Wherever—whenever—you were doesn't matter now. You're here, and you will not find a safer place." He caught her hands and noticed that one was bleeding. He spoke two words that he hoped she would not understand; they weren't Weston, or Weston-based; they were of the eastern Breodani, the language of the streets. Then he swung her up, off her feet.

She was cold and silent and shaking. He knew that she was aware of him because she couldn't meet his eyes. And it didn't matter a bit.

What have you seen? he wondered as he carried her down the hall, waiting for a room to open up. His strength had not fully returned, but he swore to himself that it would not fail him before he had placed her safely down. *What are you running from?* A death. At the very least, a death. He looked at her ashen face, at the youth in it. She was too young.

He grimaced. How old had he been when he'd stumbled across his first corpse? Six? Seven? He hadn't the ability to count then, so he couldn't remember with certainty. What he could remember, as distinctly now as the day afterward, was the stench and the sight of the insects that had already made the spirit-fled corpse their home. And their meal.

A door opened to his left. It was a plain door that was the color of the wall; he thought, had it not been ajar, he might have missed it. Fitting, for Evayne. Nudging it open with his toe, he entered the room beyond. It was cool, but there was a fire that burned in a small grate. The room itself was not what he expected; it was a child's room. A narrow bed was covered with a patterned, pale quilt; there was a cloth doll and a battered sewn animal of some sort beside the pillows. On the wall, faded with sunlight and smelling slightly musty with age, was an old hanging that depicted the claiming of a unicorn. Across the free towns the unicorn was the symbol of childhood—that wild and mysterious realm of innocence and savagery, freedom and limitation. He wondered how long the hanging had been in the family—for he was certain that he had stepped into the room in which Evayne had spent her childhood.

She stilled as he crossed the threshold; he heard her intake of breath.

"No," he told her gently before she could ask. "This isn't your home." He could feel her shrink inward; her body gave a shudder, but she would not speak.

A lamp was burning on the small, nicked table beneath the shuttered window. Stephen set Evayne down as if she were a fragile piece of blown glass and then reached for the lamp. In its light, he cleaned her hands with a cloth and a basin which he found beneath the bed. And he found that the blood on her hands was not her own.

He did not ask. He didn't want to know. Instead, he put the basin outside in the hall, where some ancient magic would collect it and see to its removal.

"Can you sleep?" he asked her as he pulled the covers back and gently laid her down. She stared up at the ceiling, looking past his face as if she couldn't see him. The tears that she cried were a silent trail of water that fell from the corners of her eyes onto the pillow. On impulse, he handed her the doll and the animal, and she gathered them, one in either arm.

He hated whoever it was that had done this to her; had made her other than a shy young woman on the verge of adulthood. "Sleep," he told her.

But as he walked over to the lamp, she sat up, throwing the covers off. Her eyes were violet holes.

"Do you want me to leave the light burning?"

She said nothing.

"Evayne?"

She still said nothing.

The fire logs cracked in the silence, and Stephen looked toward them, almost thankful for the interruption. It was then that he noticed the large, dark chair in the corner of the room. It was not a child's chair, but rather that of a parent; it had rails and one could rock in it, or sit in it, through the hours of the night.

He pulled it out of the corner and set it down beside her bed. "Sleep," he told her, pushing her shoulders back toward the mattress. "Or rest. I will watch you. I will stay."

She did not speak but did not resist him, and in the end he stroked her tearstained cheeks; she clutched at these evocations of her past as if by doing so she could make them real.

In the morning, she was changed.

The curtains were open, and the room, flooded with light, looked somehow different. Smaller, perhaps. A little less cozy.

She lay in bed, staring up at his face, her eyes wide and lively. Where she had been sixteen, he thought her now eighteen or even nineteen, and those two or three years made a difference. "I thought you'd never wake up," she said, as she rose on an elbow.

"I thought," he replied gravely, inclining his head, "that you would never sleep."

She studied his face as if trying to absorb every line, every detail. And then, staring at the wall just left of his shoulder—the wall on which the hanging lay— she said, "I thought I never would either." She rose and sat on the edge of the bed. "We're at the way station. It's 410 in the year of our Lady Veralaan. It's the month of Scarran, four days after the longest night."

"Yes."

"Are you hungry?"

It was an odd question, but he was, in fact, starving. "Yes."

"Good. I think we can eat."

This Evayne was so unlike the young girl that he'd seen the previous evening that he wondered if they were the same person. Wondered, rather, how the one could grow into the other. This woman was full of nervous energy; she was happy. She was not afraid to speak of her life, even if she gave no specific details, and she was not afraid to ask Stephen about his. They ate alone.

"And so you started to study magery?"

"Yes." She smiled. "And with the grouchiest, touchiest, strangest of the mages at the Order."

"Who is that?"

She turned it over and over before she looked straight into his eyes. "Meralonne," she replied, and seemed surprised that she could. "Meralonne APhaniel. He has his own conflict with the darkness, and I'll find out what it is one day."

"And do you study history?"

Her face darkened for the first time, but she nodded again.

"Old history?"

"Some of it."

"Pre-Weston history?"

"You've obviously done studying of your own. Yes." She shook her head. "Most people would want to know about the magic, you know."

"I do. I just want to know about the magic that's history. I've already seen enough that isn't for *this* lifetime."

She laughed. He didn't.

"Have you been well?"

She looked at him oddly; the question hung in the air between them as if it were somehow unnatural. Then she smiled, but the smile was as strange as her stare had been. "I've been well. The last time I saw you was not the last time you saw me. You are such a strange man, Stephen, to be caught up in so much."

"Strange? How?"

"You are so very normal; even your decency is normal and not of the variety that topples great evil. Of all the people I've met, I think I understand the why of you least."

"The why of me?"

"Why I met you. Why I know you. I suppose," she added, still speaking mostly to herself, "there's a good reason."

"You mean besides the fact that the God of Darkness is trying to kill us?"

"Well," she said, as surprised at the interruption as anyone would be who spent too much time alone with their thoughts, "I suppose there is that." She frowned. "I think it's time for me to go. I really don't understand why I was allowed to come here at all." She stood in one easy motion, taking to her feet as if she seldom sat at leisure.

He stood with her. "Evayne—"

"Thank you, Stephen. If I never say it again, thank you for everything." She reached out hesitantly, and then stopped short of embracing him. They stood, awkward, and then Stephen caught her hand and kissed it lightly.

But he would remember this meeting, as he remembered all of his meetings with Evayne, old or young.

She came one last time before they once again took to the road. It was midday, and Stephen was alone in the great room; he was often alone, given who his companions were. Gilliam was out with the dogs—and Espere, who left his side less often than any of the pack—and Zareth Kahn was in his study; if they met for even one common meal, it was unusual.

But he did not think of them when they were not present; he thought of the fire's warmth as it brushed against the soles of his feet; the softness of the blankets and the pillows that he rested against; the color of the rug beneath his feet that, hand-knotted, depicted the delivery of a great and urgent summons—at least, so Stephen guessed.

But he knew when she arrived because the sound of her weeping filled the room. He stood and turned at once; she was only two feet away. Her hood had fallen from her face, and her eyes were red and swollen, as were her lips; her skin was flushed, and the strands of hair that usually adorned her cheeks were matted and tangled.

She was not the very youngest of Evaynes; he thought that she was the same woman he had seen yesterday morning—but it was not the time to ask, if there ever was one.

"Evayne."

She looked up, wide-eyed, and shook her head; open-mouthed, she took a step and then reached out to touch him. The touch itself was hard to bear; it was almost an act of desperation.

Think of her, he told himself, *as a child. She's a child.* He pulled her into his arms, and without hesitation, she came.

"F-forgive me," she said, between sobs.

"There's nothing to forgive," he replied, kissing the top of her head. "Wherever and whenever you were, you aren't there now; you're here, and here is safe. Here is always safe."

She cried, and he held her; he held her and she cried. Time seemed to stop around them, or else Stephen became unaware of it. The fire was at his back, and the room; there was no one else, for the moment, who needed his attention or his help.

At last her crying broke—but he thought it temporary, a lull in the storm, not storm's end. Still, he used the quiet to continue to speak of safety and shelter, until at last the words seemed to take root. She wiped her eyes on her sleeve—Stephen noticed that the sleeve seemed to absorb the moisture without showing it—and then pulled away. Her eyes were violet lightning; she was beyond being embarrassed.

From out of her sleeves, she pulled a rounded crystal ball. "Do you know what this is?"

He studied the luminous orb as if seeking answers within its murky depths. There was no surprise when they yielded nothing. "It's—it's a seer's ball." The words were spoken in a hush.

"Yes. But do you know what a seer's ball *is*?"

He knew that the answer was no, but looked at the expression on her face, and shook his head, wordless.

"It's a part of the soul of the seer-born," she said, holding it aloft. "It's that part made manifest by the First-born, once one has walked the path and made the choice." Light came from the ball in sharp, bright lances, piercing her palms but causing no pain. "It's the sum of the path that the seer-born will walk in her life, seen as the Oracle alone can see it. This is *me.* This is what I've chosen to become."

He waited, knowing that he was at the eye of the storm. Watched her, seeing in her youthful face a hint of the majesty and the mystery that she would wear in her prime.

"But it's also a part of my vision. It helps me to see clearly in the world that I walk; it strips away illusion, falsehood, and shadow when I bend my will to look through it." She lowered it slowly until it was held in both of her hands, level with his heart.

"What would you have of me, Evayne?"

Her eyes were like open wounds, and he could not meet and hold them for long; they made him ache so profoundly he felt, briefly, that he had never known sorrow.

"You were right," she said, her voice low and almost guttural. "This *is* safety— the only safe place and time. And I don't know if I'll ever return to it again. I want to keep it, Stephen of Elseth. I want to see it and remember it so well that nothing will take it from me. No matter what happens, I won't lose it."

What has happened? But he knew that he could not ask it, or that she wouldn't answer. Not with words. And he wasn't certain, anymore, if he wanted the answer. His hair stood on end as he lifted his right hand.

"What would you have me do?"

"Touch the crystal," she replied. "That's all. Just touch the crystal."

"That's all?"

"That's all." But the two words made it sound like the last task of Morrel. He came within a hair's breadth of the ball's surface.

"What will it mean?"

She had the grace to swallow, if not to blush. "It means that I will see you as you are. It means that the crystal will have your image etched into it, and I will always be able to call it up."

"What do you mean, see me as I am?"

She couldn't lie to him; he could see that, and also see that she wanted to. "If you permit it, I'll see the truth about you. How you feel about things. Who you are, and who you think you are. It'll be as if—as if there's a window from my soul to yours, and on such a window, there aren't any curtains."

"You've done this before?"

"No. Never."

Stephen wasn't certain that he wanted to be examined so closely by someone that he didn't really know. And he was certain that he didn't want her to know that he felt that way. He didn't want her to understand his relationship with Gilliam or his mother or his second mother or Cynthia; he didn't want her to know when he lied and when he was vain and when he was overweening in his pride. He didn't want her to know his fear or even to understand his hesitation.

"What if I'm not who you think I am?"

"Does it matter?" she countered, and he could see the storm returning to her eyes. "If you aren't who I think you are, you're still the person who comforted me the first time that I ever killed a man."

His brows rose.

"You're still one of the only people who's just talked to *me*, as if *I* mattered, not as if I were just the sum of my powers and my choice. If you aren't who I think you are, what does it matter? I know what you've done, and I'll remember it no matter why you did it."

"Why can't you just remember it the way anyone else would, and leave it at that?"

"Because I'm not anyone else." She swallowed. "Because this way, you'll always be a—a living part of me."

Does it matter? he thought, as her tears started again. *Does it really matter?* He smiled, although the smile was a very weak one. "Don't cry, Evayne. I can't say no to tears."

She cried harder, and the tears fell freely; she wouldn't lower the ball or put it aside to wipe them away. "I want to remember you as you *are*. I want to remember you as you. I don't remember my father well anymore. I don't remember Priestess Aralyn, although she was my closest friend when I was young. They're dead, and my memory isn't a good enough place for them to live.

"Please, Stephen."

He did as she asked, although his hands were stiff and his touch very tentative. He thought he would feel a shock, some pain, some effect of magic, but there was only a pure, radiant light, and it grew brighter and stronger as it flared in an aurora around the ball she held. He shielded his eyes with his free hand, but as the light grew yet again, he was forced to close them.

And when he opened them, she was gone.

Chapter Eight

23rd Misteral, 1st Corvil, 410 A.A.
Essalieyan

ONCE THEY WERE OUT of the mountain passes and beyond the foothills, their journey finally became pleasant and even enjoyable. The dogs had not taken well to the pass, and therefore neither had Espere and Gilliam; when Gilliam was miserable or ill at ease, it affected Stephen. Zareth Kahn was the only cheerful member of the expedition, and at that, it was a forced cheer that did more harm than good until he, too, lapsed into the near sullen silence that was only alleviated by the appearances of Evayne.

She came from around odd corners in the pass, from behind cliffs or rocks, from little outcroppings above or small crevices below. She ignored the prevalent mood of the party, and if no one else was happy to see her, the wild girl was. When she was not so young and not so powerful, she would snort something about men under her breath, just out of Stephen's hearing. Gilliam's more acute hearing, unfortunately, picked out the sentiment and the words that framed it.

But the Hunter Lord's mood broke as soon as the paths through the foothills were well underway, and not even the chilly rain could dampen Stephen's spirit thereafter. He knew that the mountain ranges were past the halfway mark.

They had traveled hard for three weeks and more; the snow was gone from the grounds as the Northern lands gave way to the flatter, warmer South.

Evayne, old or young, wise or naive, happy or grim, often joined them in the morning and led them along the roads, although those roads were very hard to miss. They were stone, or so it seemed, but wide and flat and smooth. A wagon could traverse them easily with little stress to the wheels or the horses that pulled it.

Zareth Kahn explained that the roads had been constructed hundreds of years previous, by the edict of the Kings, at the direction and with the intervention of the maker-born, in return for which the merchants followed certain rules and paid a tithe in a timely fashion for use and upkeep of the route.

That Stephen was impressed didn't say very much—but Gilliam was, too, and it was hard to attract Gilliam's attention to anything that didn't involve the hunt.

"It won't take nearly as long as we thought," Stephen said to Evayne. "Which means that Gilliam might still be Lord Elseth at the end of the journey."

"You don't know," she replied gravely, for she was older and more somber on that day, "how long your search in the city itself will be."

"But didn't you say you knew houses of healing there?"

"Yes, and I even said that you had the money for it, if I recall correctly; it was years ago from my perspective."

He nodded, used to this.

"I did not, however, say that the houses of healing were necessarily the cure that you seek for the wild one."

"Averalaan is the heart of the Empire," Evayne said quietly as she looked to the east. The sun was high, and the air warm; had they been in Breodanir, the snow would have barely broken. It was midday, and they had stopped to rest at a way station. Stephen marveled at it; it was designed for just such a stop, and not more, although in an emergency some shelter might be taken from it. He wondered at its upkeep, for it was obviously repaired on a semiregular basis, but Evayne seemed to take its existence as a given—and as she was familiar with the Empire of Essalieyan, and he was not, he did not question.

There was a pit for a fire, with benches beside it, and there was a lean-to made of wood in case of rain. There was a feeding box for the horses, although no oats or barley had been provided, and the river that ran twenty feet to the south moved quickly enough that not many insects gathered. The water was clear, and Gilliam and the dogs were at its bank sniffing around and testing their legs with the same ready impatience that the wild girl showed. She was covered—drenched—in clear water, and was mostly out of her shift. In the warm weather it was impossible to keep her clothed for a full day.

Zareth Kahn ate quietly and paid little attention to the food; he was absorbed by Evayne. Not her words, but rather her voice, her gestures, the way she carried herself when she walked, and even the way she sat.

Stephen was not so concerned. He knew that this woman was not the same woman who had led them on the Winter road; nor was she the girl who had come to him while he lay abed, recovering from that dark journey. She was in between; more confident and more powerful than he, but less grandiose, and therefore less mysterious, than Evayne the elder. She was also more friendly, and more at peace with herself. He found himself liking her very much.

"Do you know the history of Averalaan?"

Stephen shook his head. He had barely finished his lunch, and sat back against the rough-hewn wood to listen to her words.

"I know of it," Zareth Kahn replied quietly. "But I would hear it again; the teller of the tale often puts more into it than mere history."

She raised a brow into the shadow cast by the edge of her hood, and then nodded. "You know that unlike Breodanir, the Kingdom of Kallantir, or the Dominion of Annagar, Essalieyan is governed not by a single monarch, but by two kings?"

Stephen nodded; that much, and a little more, he did know. "They're the god-born kings, aren't they?"

"Yes." She smiled. "They make their home on the Holy Isle in the High City. The Isle is sometimes called *Aramarelas*. An old Kallantir word that means 'heart' or 'spirit.' *Averalaan Aramarelas:* The heart and spirit born of Veralaan. It is from Queen Veralaan that the empire as we know it was born; because of her sacrifice, the blood wars and dominion of the eastern wizards was finally brought to an end."

"Did you know Veralaan?"

"You mean, have I met her?" She smiled, and if the smile was a little grim, it was still genuine. She did not answer the question, however.

"The city is called Averalaan after the convention of the noble houses, but it is more than that; everyone in the city pays homage to her by living within it and abiding by the laws of the Twin Kings, for they are laws that wars were fought to uphold.

"I cannot tell you all of our history, but in these lands, long before they were the Empire of Essalieyan—which means Brightness in Kallantir—there was the Dark League, a consortium of priests and wizards who sought, and gained, control of these lands, and half of the lands to the south. You can imagine what ensued in the years to follow, but in the end, the Dark League fell."

"Vexusa," Stephen said softly to himself.

"You have studied," she replied. "Yes. In the end, the dominion of the League was so profound, the god-born joined forces across the breadth of these lands, and came to Vexusa. There, with the power of their birthright, they leveled the city. But it cost them dearly. Do you know the Priests' price?"

"They perished," Stephen said, "because they became conduits for power no more; when the power was gone, there was nothing but the body left. Or so the stories said."

"There was less left than even that," Evayne said, staring into the fire. She shook herself a moment, and continued. "But these lands, as well as much of the lands we will enter, were still held by the splinter groups that had once formed the backbone of the League. From out of this period came the Baronial Wars, in which wizards associated with the remnants of the older organization fought each other for supremacy. The Wars lasted centuries," she added, and again her gaze was distant.

"One man—Haloran ABreton—stood out in the slaughter, and he managed to cobble the Baronial states together into a kingdom. His was a long reach, given the time in which he lived, and his rule was not a kind one. But he did not trust the priests, and did not have the power of their support; rather, he played the churches against one another, and allowed the church of the Mother to flourish so long as the priests did not interfere with his soldiers or their work. Therefore, he did not have the power of the Dark League as it had once been.

"He had three sons and one daughter, by three wives. The first wife died in childbirth, and the second died at the hands of assassins, although whose, history still does not tell us. The third wife died in childbirth with a daughter. He had no use for a daughter at the time, and gave her over to the keeping of the Mother while he continued to consolidate his realm; at a later point in time, he would probably have used her to make alliance with political allies.

"But the sons who were to succeed him fell upon one another, and in the end, he had no heirs. He married again to preserve his dynasty, but that wife died childless, and the wife after her, in her pregnancy—both by the hands of assassins. It was, as I said, a bloody time. He held onto power until his death, and then the court which was left, rather than fall into a war which no Lord could easily afford, agreed that the crown should go to Veralaan, the daughter. They felt that, raised by the Mother, she would be a malleable child, and that the Lord who called her wife would rule. Each House with any hope of ruling set about her courtship, content that they might force her choice and win the lands that they had already struggled so long for.

"They were wrong, but not in the way that they envisioned. She was, indeed, almost a child—but she had traveled as a Priestess of the Mother, and she had seen the death dealt by her father and his minions. She had done what she could to heal the hurt to both land and spirit that he had caused, and she knew that should she choose any of the lords who offered her their allegiance, nothing would change.

"But she also knew that they would not accept her rule, for she did not have the power necessary to be anything more than a puppet. Puppets, unfortunately, did not live long enough to become anything else, and it was her guess that she would die shortly after her first child was born.

"Abdication was not an option, for she knew, as the Lords did, that a civil war would destroy the very fragile peace that existed throughout the land. So she did what she could to stall.

"Now at the time, the healer-born flocked to the banner of the Mother, and although the Priests and Priestesses of the Mother had agreed that they would not intervene in affairs of the state, no matter how unjust or brutal, they had their own rules to offer in return: that anyone of any House that raised hand against a Priest or Priestess of the Mother would never again be healed by her.

"So Veralaan was able to stall for some time, but she knew that the dictate of the Mother's church would not protect her—or her people—forever. A year passed, and then another half-year; at the end of this time, the council displayed an unusual cooperation and gave her this message: that the time for games was over, and she must choose should she wish to survive. In desperation, she prayed to the Mother, and the Mother answered, calling her into the half-world, the place between the lands of the Gods and mortals.

" 'Dearest of daughters,' the Mother said softly, 'why have you called me?'

" 'I need your aid,' was Veralaan's stark reply. 'For I am rightful monarch of the kingdom that my father gained by war's art, but I shall not be so for long without help.'

"The Mother was angry, but in the way that mothers are.

" 'I cannot leave the throne without starting a war that will never end. And I cannot rule among these vultures, for if I did I would have to grow cold and warlike to earn their respect, or to plot their deaths. There must be another choice.'

" 'Stay thus,' was the Mother's reply. 'Stay, and wait for my return.' "

"And the Mother left her troubled daughter in the mists of the half-world, and went to seek the aid of her sons, Reymaris and Cormaris. Reymaris and Cormaris conferred long, and at length asked the Mother's leave to accompany her back to Veralaan.

So did Veralaan first meet the two gods, and she saw in their faces all that she might have judged worthy, although the mists of the half-world obscured much.

" 'Let me leave my kingdom in your hands,' she said, 'For you will guard and guide my people in a way that I yet cannot.'

" 'It is not so simple, daughter,' Cormaris replied, 'and yet we might be of aid to you if you have the will for it.'

" 'What will is that?'

" 'Stay with us a while in the half-world, and you will come to understand. But you will have no company but ours, and while no time will pass in the world you have left behind, much time will pass here, and you will feel it all in isolation.' Thus spoke Cormaris, for he was the Lord of Wisdom, and he knew that mortals and immortals are, in the end, alien and unknowable to one another.

" 'So be it,' Veralaan replied.

"And when the Queen returned at last to the mortal world, she was much aged, and brought with her two young men; youths in seeming in every way but the burnished gold of their eyes. And one was born of Reymaris, the Lord of Justice, and he was Reymalyn the First. His brother, younger, was born of Cormaris, the Lord of Wisdom, and he was Cormalyn the First.

"Then the Queen went to the Holy Sister and bowed low, speaking as if she had been silent for decades. 'Holiest one, I come to present these, my sons, to you.'

"The Priestess looked long at the two who stood proudly before her. 'Ah, Veralaan, what have you done? For I see that these two are of the god-born.'

" 'Yes. God-born indeed, but they are of *my* blood as well. They will rule what

I cannot, and hold it in strength and justice. This is Reymalyn, justice-born, and this is Cormalyn, wisdom-born. Both are of the royal blood. They are the kings that will set this land aflame with all that it has sought to bury and defile.' "

Evayne fell silent as the last of the words died away.

"And?" Stephen said.

"And," she replied, gaining her feet slowly, "I believe that it's time that we were on our way."

"But what happened?"

Zareth Kahn grinned, for he knew the story well. "It's obvious that it worked out well, Stephen," he said as Evayne smiled. "Because there are still the Twin Kings, and they rule from the city of Averalaan." He pulled his pack up and tied it shut. "You, Lady, have a touch of the bard in you."

"I?" Her smile faltered, and then she regained it again, holding it tight to her lips. "No, it's just the influence of a friend in Senniel."

"Senniel? A talented friend indeed."

Kallandras, Stephen thought, remembering his first Sacred Hunt. But he did not mention the name aloud. Instead he wondered whether or not their sojourn into the city at the heart of the Empire would bring them together again.

"But I don't understand how it works. I mean, there are two kings *and* there are two queens—how does anything get decided?"

"Stephen," Evayne said, as the fire began to die in the grate, "it's a pity that you don't have a spark of the mage-born in you. You'd have made a wonderful mage. You could," she said, standing, "still join the Order of Knowledge. It exists for those who can't stop asking questions when the time for questions has long passed."

"Which means you don't know."

"Which means," she said, laughing, "that I don't understand it either, no. The god-born have spines of steel when it comes to the traits of their parents—I can't imagine either of the Kings being willing to compromise when it comes to those areas that most concern him. But I know there are situations in which wisdom and justice are not easy allies. I'm just happy I'm not either of the Queens."

He lifted his glass and drank the remnants of the oddly flavored drink that she had brought for him. He was happy for her company, although he could feel that Gilliam was not. This eve she was the same woman that she had been this morning, which was rare. "We're almost there, aren't we?"

"Yes. A few days and we'll be in the outer fields that surround the city; a full day more, and we'll be at the city itself. It's not walled in any real way, but there is the half-wall to mark its boundaries. You'll understand the lack of the wall when you see it." She smiled. "And you'll see the ocean for the first time, Stephen. I just hope that I'm here to see it with you. It has a feel and a call that is quite unique."

2nd Corvil, 410 A.A.
Averalaan

It was huge. It lay across the horizon like the scattered manors of giants, or the halls of the Gods beyond the half-world. At first, before the rising sun burned the misty gauze from the morning air, Stephen thought that he was looking at an unexpected mountain chain; he knew a moment of panic—what if they had taken a wrong turn? Followed the wrong road?—and then he realized that he was seeing the towers of Averalaan and the hills upon which they were built.

As they followed the wide road, wagons joined them in a longer train than Stephen or Gilliam had ever seen. Gilliam said nothing, but Stephen turned to Evayne. She was not quite the same woman as yesterday. He knew she was almost the same age, but whether younger or older, it was hard to tell.

"Is it festival season in Essalieyan?"

"No. Why?"

He looked over his shoulder, to his side, and then to the road that stretched, crowded as a market street, ahead of them. The wagons were of a different variety than those that were common in Breodanir—the wheels seemed thinner and the bases higher. They carried all manner of things—in fact, he thought he saw one that carried horses, and he could not understand why they were not made to walk.

Evayne tried not to laugh. "It's—this is normal for the time of morning, Stephen. Averalaan is the capital of trade along the seacoast; no city in Annagar can boast such a market, or such a selection, as Averalaan does. The merchants arrive by wagon and by ship. There." She lifted a hand and pointed. "Do you see the light flashing? Beside it, there are sails."

But her eyes were better than his, a fact which did not surprise him at all. His steps were quick and light. A situation of gravity and urgency had brought them to the heart of Essalieyan—but all wisdom and all knowledge could be found in Averalaan, or so the tales often said, and he could not help but be excited. Very few indeed were the Hunter Lords who could afford the time away from their demesnes that would have allowed them to travel to the city. Fewer still were those who would have any such inclination. And a huntbrother rarely left the side of his Lord.

Gilliam looked back and mouthed the word "Cynthia" and Stephen frowned. He took better care, thereafter, to conceal his enthusiasm.

The demiwalls that Evayne spoke of came into view, and as they did it became clear that they weren't walls at all; they were like the stone work fence that surrounded a few of the more pretentious manors in the King's City in Breodanir—but they stretched out to the horizon on either side, a thin, pale line whose division of the landscape faded quickly from view.

"We approach the city of Averalaan," Evayne said. "It is the city of the Kings, and the laws here are complex and more strictly enforced than anywhere else in the empire." She smiled wryly. "Of course that doesn't mean that you shouldn't keep an eye on your purses in at least half the hundred."

"Half the hundred?"

"The hundred holdings." Her eyes widened slightly. "The city is divided into a hundred holdings of theoretically equal size. No, they aren't visible divisions. In the King's City, there are different circles, and within those circles there are areas like the warrens."

"What do you mean by complex?"

She shrugged. "Actually, what I mean is be polite, don't steal, don't kill anyone who isn't trying to kill you first, don't run a horse to death and leave it in the road, and keep a tight grip on your dogs."

"Doesn't sound that complicated."

"Well, with luck you won't have to run into the complicated parts."

"Are there no guards and no gate?"

"No; they aren't deemed necessary. It's hundreds of miles to the border of Annagar, and hundreds to the free townships that buffer us from the kingdoms to the west. There are guards, but they watch the three bridges that lead to the Isle, and they man the ports to which the ferries travel with their goods. If Kalliaris smiles, we won't have to deal with them either."

"You don't think Luck is going to smile, do you?"

"This is what I think she'll do." She turned to him and made the most extraordinary face that he had yet seen her make. Then she laughed at his expression, sobering slowly. "No, Stephen, I don't think she'll smile, but if she doesn't frown, I'll make offerings to Reymaris for the rest of my life."

A horn sounded at their backs, low and loud, the captured voice of a cow. Evayne pulled them hurriedly off the road as four horses galloped down the stretch of road to the farthest south. There were no wagons along it, and the people that were there did not tarry either.

But the dogs barked angrily at the passing intruders and stopped only when Stephen made it clear to Gilliam that their anger was not acceptable. Gilliam's reply was subvocal, which was just as well. He was ill at ease on the road and the closer they got to the city itself, the more uncomfortable he became. Stephen had never felt such a lack of ease from Gilliam—not even when the most marriage-minded of ladies were attempting to ally their houses with his through their daughters and he was forced, by Elsabet or Stephen, to sit, smile, and endure. He could also tell that Gilliam was doing his best to subdue what traveled between them, but subdued or no, it grew strong, and stronger still, until the half-walls were at their backs and the heights of the city buildings began to cast shadows upon them.

It was hard to ignore it, but ignore it he did, although it took much of his concentration. Perhaps that was why he did not notice the shadows that crossed their path and stopped, weapons raised in swiftness and silence. Or why he did not notice, until he felt Zareth Kahn's sharp shove, the tall, pale stranger with eyes of fire behind four men in a foreign uniform.

But whatever it was that had webbed his mind and turned his thoughts so much inward that he did not notice his surroundings well was removed in that instant. As was Gilliam's unease—replaced by something akin to excitement. Excitement.

Zareth Kahn stepped forward. "May we help you, gentleman?"

"I believe you can. The young men you are with are wanted in connection with a murder that occurred yesterday."

Zareth Kahn's dark brows rose a fraction, and then he smiled. "Well, I can assure you that they could not possibly be involved in the commission of any such crime; they've never been to the city before they crossed the demiwalls today."

The man sneered; there was no other word for the expression. "I'm afraid that we're going to have to go to the magisterial holding courts, where the magisterial truthseekers involved in the rest of the investigation will decide that for themselves."

"Very well," Zareth Kahn said, with a snort that easily matched the sneer for contempt. "If you will insist on wasting our time in such a petty fashion, we'll follow."

"We will do no such—"

"Lord Elseth." Zareth Kahn touched his shoulder with the appearance of gentleness. It was only appearance; his grip was solid. "The customs of Averalaan dictate a certain amount of cooperation with the magisterial guards. We will, unfortunately, be brought to a hearing in which these charges will be summarily dismissed. At that point, we are well within our rights to question the competence of the truthseeker involved in our arrest."

Gilliam brought the dogs to bear and then stopped. "Stephen?"

Stephen was staring at the man that Zareth Kahn had called truthseeker. The man's uniform was not completely unlike those of the guards who surrounded him, but he did not wear the chain and plate that they did, and his insignia, that of two crowns above a crossed rod and sword, covered a white field, not a gray one.

"Stephen, what is wrong?" Evayne's voice was strained but oddly pitched; her words were a tickle in his ear.

"His eyes," Stephen whispered back. "Can't you see his eyes?"

The truthseeker leveled his gaze at Stephen, and then he smiled, and the smile was that of an executioner who revels in his work. **"These men are attempting to escape. Kill them."** His voice had the echo of a power that Stephen had only heard once before, upon his first Sacred Hunt.

The guards stiffened, and then their expressions changed. "Halt! Halt in the name of the Kings!" Even under the power of suggestion, the magisterial guards resisted the order to kill. "Halt!"

Zareth Kahn looked confused, but Evayne's features were harder and grimmer. She raised her arms and spoke three words; light flared from her hands. Stephen saw her limned with it, as if she were the Goddess at the birth of creation, offering the sun to the world.

The truthseeker screamed in agony.

The magisterial guards stopped as the fleeing suspects suddenly appeared, standing before them as if they had never left. "KILL THEM NOW!"

Evayne sent light in a fan of sparks, and the guards cried out, blinded even as their former leader. "Follow!" Evayne cried. No one gainsaid her.

She was afraid.

She was not the older Evayne; power such as her enemies possessed was still just outside of her grasp. But she recognized those enemies—that much was obvious to Stephen.

"Where do we go?" Zareth Kahn asked, looking over his shoulder, as he'd done every time they'd slowed their pace. He did not seek to accuse Evayne of causing trouble or breaking the much-loved laws of Averalaan; he knew her well enough by now to know that her reasons for it were unimpeachable—and more important, were not reasons that could be explained at leisure without some loss of life.

She looked around the streets, gazing at buildings and moving crowds as if to wrest some answer from them.

"There!" came a cry at their backs. "The men with the dogs! Stop them—they've murdered a magisterial 'seeker!"

Zareth Kahn swore.

Evayne paled.

And pale, she made the only decision that it was safe to make. She lifted her arms and cast a web of violet light across her group.

The people immediately around them gave a collective gasp and drew back, staring intently.

"What are you doing?"

"I'm doing my best to keep us hidden," she replied, speaking slowly and with some difficulty. "But I can't keep it up for long."

Zareth Kahn stepped forward quietly. "No, you can't. But I can. Let me, Lady."

She was not used to accepting help; not accustomed, judging from her expression, to hearing it offered. But she swallowed once and nodded.

"You will," the mage said softly, as his web seemed to settle over hers, dissolving and replacing the strands, "have to lead us."

She nodded. "Thank you."

"Where are we going?" Stephen hissed.

"Do you see the circle on the ground?"

He nodded.

"Don't step outside it. Tell Gilliam to keep his dogs, and Espere, well within its confines. We go to less traveled streets."

"Should we avoid going beyond the net?"

"The what?"

"The net. The one that Zareth Kahn has cast."

Her brows went up. "You can see it?" And then she shook her head. "Never mind. If you see me later, remind me. You are not a mage, and not mage-born, and only the mage-born have the sight. Or the seer-born." As an afterthought, she added, "And yes, avoid at all costs going beyond the net; if you pass your arm through it, it will appear, without the usual body attached, in midair in front of passersby."

Zareth Kahn knew that the invisibility that his magics afforded them would not be a blessing forever. Truthseekers were often also mages, trained in very specific and very narrow ways. Call a few, with the right guards to back them, and such a spell would prove not only useless, but actively harmful. Few were the people who dared to use magic openly in the city streets; the laws that governed magic's use—and the mages who enforced them—were the strictest of the laws in Essalieyan.

He was, of course, breaking at least one; Evayne, with the use of her light spell—a light that he had never seen before—had broken three. The truthseeker who had originally apprehended them had broken two, and if the guards had been quick and fast off the mark, would have broken three.

He was not a man who was readily accustomed to breaking the laws of Averalaan, although it had been many, many years since he had seen the city of his birth. He was, luckily, not a man who was inexperienced at the breaking of those laws, either. What had hunted them on the night of High Winter obviously had eyes here, and the niceties of royal law could be set aside for the niceties of survival.

It was not until they reached the bridge to the Holy Isle that Zareth Kahn realized where Evayne was leading them. He dispensed with a portion of his spell, freeing her to speak with the guards on duty while hiding the rest of his companions. It was difficult, this breaking and unfraying, but he was a past master at it, and if he had not used it recently, he was pleased to note that the old skills did not fade with disuse. She walked toward the guards, and then returned, nodding with obvious relief.

They had arrived before word from the magisterial forces—if the magisterial forces had considered the Holy Isle a likely goal—and were safe to pass. He let the last of his illusory protection fade from sight, sorry to let it go, but pleased that the strain had been lifted. He was not close to the fevers yet, but he would sleep well that night.

"We're going to the Order," Evayne said, and each word sounded grudging and slightly apprehensive.

"I haven't been there in years," was the older mage's reply.

"I—I want you to talk with Meralonne APhaniel."

"Member APhaniel? Why?"

"Because I think he's the only mage in the city who might be able to help us."

"You know him?"

She nodded into her hood, and then turned abruptly to face Zareth Kahn. Her dark hair hung in loose strands about her unblinking violet eyes. "I was his student for a number of years. We—we haven't spoken in months. Tell him—no, ask him—to aid these men; if he is reluctant, tell him that Evayne says they are part of her mystery." She smiled, and the smile had the feel of ash and shadow to it; Zareth Kahn had the absurd desire to reach over and wipe it gently clean. She was far too much the adult to deserve that gesture.

"I have my own friends in the Order," he began, but she shook her head.

"I cannot stay, Zareth Kahn. Already, I am being called away." She left him then, walking quickly to where Stephen stood. "I will only be with you for a few more blocks, and then my work is done for the moment. I was sent here because I—I was supposed to flee. And there is only one person that I dare flee to in this crisis, one person that I have relied on, and at Kalliaris' whim, will rely on again.

"Look carefully at him, Stephen—but never speak of what you see if you see anything unusual."

"At who?"

"Meralonne." She hesitated, and as she did, he reached out and caught her hand. Clasped it tightly between his own, and then, on impulse, kissed it.

"Good-bye, Stephen of Elseth. We will speak, I think, but not soon."

The manors that lined the roads of the Isle were not overly large, although they were all exceptionally tall. There was good masonry here, and very little wood or thatch to mar the sense of history and timelessness. Stephen had had little time to take in the view of Averalaan, and the High City was perhaps not the best place to start. It made him feel at once poor and ignorant, although the riches that were here were those that time had laid the foundations for, and that a generation alone would never dissipate. The roads were wide, the streets cobbled very prettily in places; there were gilded gates that sat no more than fifty feet from the mansions they enclosed. He was surprised by the number of columns that he saw; they seemed to adorn the fronts of most of the buildings that they passed. As he approached them, he could see engraved along their length, in a pattern that spiraled upward, runes in the Kallantir style. He could not read them all.

Zareth Kahn silently urged him on, and he went, trying to remember the flare of fire in the city beyond the bridge. But there was a hush on the Isle, a silence and a peace, that made him understand why it was called holy; he thought that whatever threatened them would not dare to come so openly here.

"What are those?"

Zareth Kahn sighed in resignation. "Those are the spires of the Lords Cormaris and Reymaris. They are the rulers of these lands, and their towers are the grandest buildings on the Isle. Not even the towers of the Kings' palace can match them; nor would either of the Kings try."

"But—but how can they stand?"

At that, the mage smiled. "More money than Breodanir sees in a year went into each day of work on those towers, and they were a long time in the building. This is Averalaan, Stephen. The guild of the maker-born flourishes here, and in some ways, even rules."

"Can we go to see the temples?"

"We may have no choice," was the cryptic reply. "But we will not see them today."

The Order of Knowledge in Breodanir was small and humble compared to the Order of the High City, and the building that housed the scholarly mages was rough and very common in comparison. There were pillars here that supported a roof four stories high; there was a courtyard of size and simplicity in which water ran from a fountain that looked like a suspended waterfall; there was a ceiling taller than any temple that Breodanir's finest city boasted. Light came down like spears, sharp and perfect through the glass above.

Zareth Kahn even stopped for a moment, almost as if to marvel. Then he shook his head and smiled. "I've been too long away, I fear. Come."

They walked between the columns and the arch, and into the grand foyer. At the far end, beyond a mosaic pattern of brilliantly colored marble and gold, was a large desk. The man behind it looked almost as pleased to see them as Gilliam was to see court balls.

"What," he said, in a voice sharp enough to cut, "are you doing with those *dogs*?" He lifted the metallic rims that adorned his face as if to see more clearly the outrage that was being perpetrated within the Order's sedate walls.

"Jacova, is that you?"

"What, is that little Zareth?"

"It *is* you." Zareth Kahn looked slightly uncomfortable, but very resigned. "I see that you're holding the desk."

"And I see that you've let this Breodanir nonsense infect your brain—bringing dogs into the building!"

Gilliam bristled.

"A matter of urgency, Jacova." He turned to Stephen. "This is Stephen of Elseth, and this is Lord Elseth. I'm afraid that we did not have time to kennel his animals before we crossed the bridge."

"Yes, well. Highly irregular, and I should have you thrown out on principle. I will if the dogs make a mess."

"I have control of my dogs," Gilliam said, from between clenched teeth.

Jacova gave him a severe look but declined to respond. "What brings you here?"

"I'm afraid it's not entirely social. You see, we'd like to make an appointment, if at all possible, to speak with member APhaniel."

"Member APhaniel?" He frowned. "Member APhaniel is currently involved in an investigation," and here he looked over his shoulder, scanned the foyer, and then lowered his voice and leaned over the desk, "with House Terafin. Under the direction of The Terafin herself."

"It's—it's very urgent that we speak to him."

"Impossible. As I said, he's—"

"Is he in the building?"

"He's making his third report of findings, and he's in a *foul* mood."

Zareth Kahn turned to Stephen. "I think we should delay, if at all possible," he said in a very hushed voice.

"What?"

"Master APhaniel is always rather, ah, temperamental. At least, he was known for it before I left for Breodanir. To say that he's in a foul mood . . ."

"We'll chance it. I think that the truthseeker was one of the kin."

Zareth Kahn smiled weakly and turned back to Jacova ADarphan. "We must see member APhaniel; we've important information that is part of the investigation that he's conducting."

"You have? Why didn't you say so? And why haven't I seen you around until today?" Jacova hated desk duty with the passion of any proper scholar, but he was not a stupid man. His eyes were narrowed with suspicion.

"Because I could not reasonably travel without being noted or remarked upon—everyone who knows me knows I'm in Breodanir," was the apologetic reply. "Do you think you might tell member APhaniel that we are here, along with a message from one of his former pupils?"

"That being?"

"Evayne."

Jacova snorted, but he rose and started his long climb up the stairs twenty feet from the desk. Zareth Kahn counted to fifteen—slowly and distinctly—and then turned to Stephen. "We follow."

"Shouldn't we wait?"

But the answer was obvious; Zareth Kahn started up the wide, marble stairs, taking them two at a time, but slowly enough that he never saw more than the black-edged hem of Jacova's robe. Gilliam and Espere were next, followed by the dogs that Jacova found so offensive. Stephen brought up the rear, as any good huntbrother usually did.

"I don't care if they carry a message from the Goddess herself—GET OUT!" Light flared into the hall from the open doorway in the tower room that member APhaniel occupied. The air had a prickly feel to it; Stephen thought, as he breathed it, that it should crackle.

Zareth Kahn cringed. "He *is* in a foul mood. Magics of that nature are strictly prohibited in the collegium. I really wish this could wait. He's a member of the Council of the Magi, and he's also an initiate of the first circle mysteries." Yet even as he spoke, he led them the rest of the way across the landing. Jacova, looking both harried and frightened, bumped into him.

"He—he doesn't want to see you," he said, but without any of the annoyed or irritated edge that usually accompanied these words.

"I can see that," Zareth Kahn replied mildly, "but unfortunately it's a matter of enough urgency that I will have to insist. Thank you for your diligence, but I believe I can handle things from here."

"And you believe incorrectly."

Stephen felt, hearing those words, that he truly heard the voice of Meralonne APhaniel for the first time. It hung in the air like a fog, discordant and yet somehow melodic. He looked up, and a man dressed in emerald silk bed-robes strode onto the overcrowded landing. His hair was white and long and wild, and his eyes, gray and pale, looked like steel embedded in a thin, fey face.

The robes that he wore looked wrong, so out of place that they were almost an obscenity. *He has to sleep sometime*, Stephen told himself, but he almost didn't believe it. He shied back as the mage's glare swept across them all. It was familiar, somehow; there was something about it that he had seen or felt before.

But those eyes did not dwell for long on him; they swept with anger and not a little contempt past Jacova and Zareth Kahn, past Gilliam, Stephen, and the dogs. It was the wild girl that caught and held them.

"And are you back again, strange one?" he said, and his tone of voice was altered.

Zareth Kahn cleared his throat. "She is," he said. "We brought her here because we hoped that we could find a cure for the condition that ails her."

"And that?"

"We do not know," he replied. "But Zoraban ATelvise bespoke his father before his death, and his father identified her as one of the god-born."

"Which God?" And then, before Zareth Kahn could answer, he added, "His death?"

"Word was sent," Zareth Kahn replied mildly. Jacova nodded at his back but chose, perhaps wisely, to remain silent.

"I've been otherwise occupied." Member APhaniel shoved his hands roughly into the wide, baggy pockets of his robe. "Very well, if you will interrupt me, interrupt me with intelligence. Come." He pulled out a pipe, and Jacova took the opportunity to return to desk duty; he had a great hatred of pipe smoke, especially of the variety that Meralonne preferred. "But I warn you, gentlemen—I am not in the mood to be bored."

Chapter Nine

MERALONNE LEANED AGAINST THE EDGE of his desk, pipe in hand, back to the shuttered window. "So Zoraban agreed to your request, and bespoke his father?"

Zareth Kahn nodded gravely. "Since the kin appeared to be involved, we all thought it wisest."

"A pity. I would have liked to be there; it is so seldom that any of the knowledge-born seek their parent's advice in the presence of . . . strangers. But do continue."

"The girl is god-born, although she bears none of the markings of such a child. Her eyes, for instance."

Smoke rings rose in the air as Meralonne stared down at her. When he was not asking questions, it was to her that he looked, as if, by staring, he could wrest answers from her.

"Teos told us that Espere was, in the more traditional sense of the word, Hunter-born. She is the daughter of the Hunter God of the Breodani." He expected there to be an outburst of some sort from the older mage; none was forthcoming. Instead, he received a curt, even brusque nod, which held the silent command to continue. "When we returned from the half-world, we were attacked by two demons."

"And you know for a fact that these were of the kin?"

Zareth Kahn looked slightly impatient. "I know it, yes. One was a blade-demon, and one a life-drinker. I have," he added, "made lost magical arts a major area of my studies."

The pale-haired mage raised a platinum brow. "I see."

"The life-drinker had the ability to wield mortal magics, as well as the magics of the Dark Lord. There was an aura to her magic use, a particular—and strong—signature. I believe her to be either a demon lord, or perhaps not far from becoming one."

"A life-drinker? Impossible!"

"As you will," was the cool reply. It was clear that the dark-haired mage, younger and less odd, knew enough not to argue with the older one—but it was also clear that, as the narrative progressed, he liked it less and less. "She killed Zoraban, and would have taken Stephen of Elseth, but she did not."

"She could not?"

"I'm not certain." Zareth Kahn's brow was creased with displeasure; now that he had entered the Order proper, he was once again impatient with any questions that he did not possess the answer to. "She called him, and he came—but when she attempted take him, she was repulsed by a power not her own. She called him oathbound."

"Oathbound?"

"Yes."

Meralonne stood and began to pace the room, trailing a cloud of smoke past his shoulder.

"What do you know of this, member APhaniel? I have come across the term once or twice in my studies, but only in a religious context—and at that, a religion long dead."

But Meralonne was clearly in no mood to answer another's questions. "Continue," he said, quite curtly. "I will make my observations on the full story, or not at all."

Zareth Kahn was not completely unused to this behavior from mages of the first circle, but he was not amused by it. His lips became a thin line, and it was Stephen of Elseth who adroitly stepped in to take up the tale.

He spoke of the blade-demon, and the fight with it; spoke of Gilliam's fall, the loss of the communication between them, and the sudden transformation of the wild girl into a creature out of legend.

And then, last, he spoke of Evayne.

Meralonne APhaniel's eyes grew very dark as he listened. "She told you to come to the city, and she left you?"

"Not exactly, no. She came to us five weeks ago, when the moon was at nadir; she called it *Scarran*. We'd been on the road for several days, and were in an inn along the eastern border of Breodanir. She said that the demons were gathering their shadows, and that it was not safe for us to remain as we were; she intended to lead us to safety."

He said nothing.

"And she—she led us along the Winter road instead. But—but she brought us back to the townships."

"All of you?" The pipe froze; a thin stream of smoke, trailing air, rose unheeded to the ceiling.

The eyes that Stephen met asked a question that he could not understand, and did not want to. He looked away, but nodded, shivering at a cold that was still too easily remembered.

It seemed that the mage might ask more; his lips were open as he stared at Stephen's fair face—and then at all of them, even the dogs. But he shook himself and lifted the pipe to his open lips instead. "I see. And then she led you to Averalaan, and told you to come to *me*?"

Stephen nodded.

"Did she bother to tell you that we did not part on the best of terms?"

"Yes."

"And?"

It was Zareth Kahn who replied. "When we arrived in the city—when we were only a few yards from the demiwalls—we were stopped by a truthseeker and four magisterial guards."

"And?"

"Evayne believed the truthseeker in question to be a demon. She cast a spell that I believe to be an old Summer spell, and the truthseeker was indeed affected. We fled, using illusion to mask the direction and the speed of our flight."

"Who did the truthseeker want? The girl?"

"Not apparently, no. He was interested in the Lord Elseth and his huntbrother."

"I see." Meralonne pulled a worn leather pouch from his robes. He set about emptying his pipe with care and caution—it was a delicate, long-stemmed object of obvious antiquity—and then, with just as much care, set about lining the bowl with new leaves.

"There is one other thing you might want to know," Zareth Kahn continued, although the words were edged. "I was summoned by Lady Elseth when a number of assassins, led by a member of the Order, were apprehended and destroyed. They wore the pendants of the Dark Lord."

Meralonne did not seem remotely surprised, but he seemed suddenly very weary. "Ah. Priests." He lifted the pipe to his lips.

Stephen started; memory made the words of Teos suddenly sharp again. "Yes, Priests," he said. "Member APhaniel—the Lord of Knowledge said something that I did not understand."

"Yes?"

"That the Dark God is not on his throne in the Hells."

"Not on his—" Smoke swirled around his face as if at a sudden breeze. The slender, pale mage turned to Stephen, his expression suddenly changed. He looked not man but ghost or guardian as he spoke next. "What else did the Lord of Knowledge say?"

"He spoke of the Covenant of the Lord of Man."

Pale lids closed over gray eyes; the mage lifted a hand to the wall as if he needed the support. "I see. This is . . . of import to us." He shook himself and his face slowly folded into its regular unfriendly expression. "Go, member Kahn. Eat, drink, and then await me in the Kallavar room."

"And my companions?"

"Turn them out in the street," was the sharp, sarcastic reply. "What do you think I intend? You brought them, they're your responsibility. Feed them and keep them out of trouble until the appointed hour of our interview."

"And that hour?"

"Get out."

Gilliam had only one argument with a man in the dining hall, but it was loud enough to attract the attention of a cluster of mages, who then began complaints of their own when they saw the six dogs that were sitting restlessly beside the wall. Zareth Kahn, still angry at his interview with Meralonne, was in no mood to handle the offended men, which meant that Stephen, stretched between an irritable Gilliam, an annoyed Zareth Kahn, and a bustle of mages, had to soothe any ruffled feathers. Only Espere seemed at ease, and that held until she decided that she had had enough of the restrictive clothing that she was wearing.

It was a disastrous meal, but at least the dogs got fed, although they ate food that they were not normally given; they were of the finest of the Breodani hunters, and as such, were quite restricted in diet. Gilliam was furious that so-called members of the Order of Knowledge didn't know how to feed a dog—but the dogs, to Stephen's eyes, were gleefully smug at the giblets and gravy that were finally laid out—in the thinnest and most perfect bowls that he had ever seen—on the floor in front of them.

It was when Espere began an angry keening and tried to knock Salas from his bowl, rather than eat the normal human food provided her, that things got rather messy. She snarled at Salas; Salas, of course, defended his food, and Gilliam, angry enough with the setting, nearly threw up his hands in disgust and let them fight it out. He didn't, but that was probably as much due to the fact that the dining hall mysteriously emptied, and that Zareth Kahn was sitting, food untouched, elbows on the table, face in his hands.

Eventually the man in charge of the hall came to speak with Zareth Kahn. His words were measured and slow, his voice calm and reasonable. But Stephen caught enough of the tone to know that if words were weapons, Zareth Kahn would have been slowly and evenly skewered.

They spent the next three hours waiting in the Kallavar room.

When Meralonne came to them, he was attired in clothing, and not in the casual emerald green robes that most of the mages of the Order were familiar with. The clothing was of an old style, although just what that style was would have been hard for Stephen to say; the fashions of Essalieyan were not the fashions of Breodanir among any but the most daring of ladies, and even then, only when the clothing was practical and everyday.

Cloth fell in a direct drape from shoulder to just below the knee; it was a shimmering darkness with hints of gold and platinum throughout—but no more than hints; to study the cloth too intently was to lose them as if they were the faintest of stars tickling the corner of the eye. He had sleeves, and they, too, were draped but gathered six inches above the wrist. The collar was high at back and squared in front; it was, in all, an unusual effect.

And Meralonne APhaniel carried it well, which was a surprise.

"I apologize if I've kept you waiting. I have been at some pains to conduct research in these pathetic libraries, and have come up with scant information. If you had a few months—if either of us did—I would have left you here. However," he added, raising a pipeless hand, "we do not have the time." He walked over to an unoccupied chair by the fire—there were several—and sat with his back to it. Shadowed thus, he looked almost like a ghost from an ancient past.

"I am involved in my own investigation under the command of The Terafin. It is connected to your case, although I am not completely certain of how. The facts, as I know them, are simple. Let me relate them to you.

"First: There are demon-kin in the city of Averalaan. There is no question of this fact; I was called in to an encounter with one, and while I do not personally recognize its type, I know it for what it was.

"Second: The kin seem to be operating in the holdings of the city itself. We are conducting investigations into which areas are possibly infested.

"The third fact is in dispute: that a mage, possibly a rogue, but unfortunately, probably not, dabbling in dark arts, has been hired to use these creatures to kill The Terafin—and quite probably to take possession of her form, and with it, her power." He saw Zareth Kahn pale immediately, and held up a hand before the younger mage could speak. "Krysanthos is a possibility, from what you've said. Let me finish."

"Fourth: The kin that I dealt with—and therefore, possibly others of its phylum—was able to wear the semblance and take on many, but not all, of the memories of the person it killed." Zareth Kahn ceased his attempt to interrupt. "Because of this, we cannot know who is, and who is not, an enemy. Not without the use of magics that most of the mages here have forgotten. Yes, Zareth Kahn. The Summer magics."

"You know them," the mage said, his eyes wide.

"Yes."

"And her—you taught her."

"I taught her some of them; she has obviously grown adept through teachers other than myself."

"Did you teach her the Winter magics as well?"

"Not I," was the soft reply. "But Winter and Summer are reflections; where there is one, the other is coming. There is balance," he continued, turning suddenly to pin Stephen of Elseth with his slate eyes. "Even if you do not see that balance addressed in a single mortal life, it is there, and it *will* be addressed. It is the law of the living Gods, and those that they left behind."

Zareth Kahn snorted. "Those who practiced the Summer magics did not learn the Winter."

"No?" A platinum brow rose. Then he smiled, but the smile was not warm. "But the use of Summer magics requires an intimate understanding of the strengths of the Winter. And more to the point, the only mage that has learned those arts in your lifetime has learned both."

It was Stephen who replied. "She may have learned both—but she learned them for a higher purpose."

"Oh?" He lifted a hand as Stephen began to speak again, waving him into angry silence. "Then think on this, young Stephen of Elseth, for I will not argue purpose with you. Many, many acts are committed in the name of a higher purpose, and a higher purpose has often claimed the lives of innocents as it rolls outward, so secure in the grandeur of its mission that it will no longer look at the cost to others."

"Maybe," Stephen countered, stung, "it's because there is no better choice. Grandeur has nothing to do with it—the course that saves the most life is the only one open."

Meralonne sank back in his chair and studied Stephen's face. Then he closed his eyes and shook his head. "As you say," he said, and the annoyance was gone from his voice. "But in all things, there are costs.

"Let me continue briefly. We have on our hands a young street urchin and her den. They claim to know something of tunnels that exist beneath the city streets— tunnels that Ararath Handernesse, the victim of the demon I fought, led them to. It is clear that the victim believed these tunnels to be of significance in the disappearance of a variety of people from the holdings in the central city. I have spent the last four weeks searching the city extensively for the whereabouts of just such tunnels. I have found nothing, no matter where these urchins have led me.

"Were it not for the death of Ararath, or rather, the manner of his death, I would have the lot of them turned out on their ears. But his death is his death, and we continue to search. And when I say that there is nothing, I mean exactly that; there is no trace of magic or magical concealment; there is no trace of newness or the newly hidden; there is *nothing* whatever to indicate that the so-called maze ever existed." He relaxed, placing his arms against the armrests and then lifting his hands in a steeple before his lips. "And now another mystery. The girl that you travel with—I have seen her before. Were the demons to be chasing her, I would not be surprised. But they turn to you, and to you, Lord Elseth, two hunters from the realm of Breodanir. Two lords who happen to be led to Averalaan by the ever-so-mysterious Evayne.

"If she led you here, you must have a purpose; that much I've been able to glean from her activity. And if she led you on the Winter road . . . that is not without its risks. Yet even so, I sense that you do not know her purpose, or your place in this larger game."

Stephen nodded warily. "She looked ahead for us."

"Ah. You know she is seer-born. What was her vision?"

"No vision."

"Did she speak?"

"Not so we could understand it," Gilliam broke in.

"I see. And what did she say?"

Stephen did not want to tell the mage of the prophecy that Evayne had granted them. But he knew that that had been her intent—else why send them here, to this Order and this cold, angry man? He took a breath, made it deeper, as if it could hollow out his lungs. Then he spoke in a steady, clear tenor.

"The Covenant has been broken in spirit.

"The portals are open; the gods are bound.

"Go forth to the Light of the World and find the Darkness.

"Keep your oath; fulfill your promise.

"The road must be taken or the Shining City will rise anew." As the last words faded, he opened his eyes, and only then realized that he had closed them. Slate gray met brown.

"She told you *that?*"

"Yes."

"And anything else?"

"That if we chose not to travel to Averalaan to help the wild girl—it was to help her that we wanted to come—she thought Breodanir might fall, and the empire as well." Stephen's glance, skittish and hesitant, only touched Espere briefly. "And if she is the daughter of the Hunter God, then I don't see that there's anything we *can* do to help her." But he remembered her very human voice, and he remembered the plea in eyes that were already becoming bestial. Something was trapped beneath the Espere of Gilliam's pack.

Meralonne rose swiftly and silent, and crossed the room to where the wild girl, impatient, sat at Gilliam's feet. Gilliam tensed, and Stephen sent his caution along their bond. But the mage made no sudden moves; indeed, the moment he was at the girl's side he ceased to move at all. "What do you know of this, daughter of the Hunter God that men have called no true God? If we return the gift of speech to you, will you answer my questions? Can you?" She met his eyes and did not blink or look away. He reached out slowly, and touched her chin with forefinger and thumb, lifting her face. She suffered it quietly. "You met her while she was being pursued."

"Yes."

"Did she bring anything with her?"

"No," Gilliam said. Stephen said nothing at all.

"Ah, mystery. It makes life interesting." He rose quickly. "Come, then. You have been delivered to the right man, whether or not you understand it. Zareth Kahn, if you wish to continue in your other duties, you may; the choice is your own. But I believe that the gentlemen and the lady that they travel with are best served by my companionship and guidance."

Zareth Kahn nodded almost blandly; he said nothing.

It was Stephen who asked. "What did it mean?"

"What?"

"Her prophecy."

"I am not certain what it meant. But the Light of the World is Averalaan, and the Darkness that you speak of is without question the power of Allasakar and the demons who serve him."

"And the Covenant? The Shining City?"

"About the first, little is known—but I will know more; about the second, I will not speak, except to say this: The Dark Lord himself ruled there in times lost, with magics most foul and most forgotten." He started to walk away, and then stopped, wheeling abruptly mere inches away from Zareth Kahn. "And those arts *will* remain forgotten." The younger mage met his glare as if he were fencing with his eyes, but although he had the strength not to look away, he took two steps back.

"Good," Meralonne said. "If we are to work together, it is important that we understand each other." He swept out of the room, then stopped, swung around again, and looked in. "I mean for you to follow," he said, as patiently as possible.

Gilliam urged his dogs out, and held on to Espere by the hand. Zareth Kahn made haste to walk beside, rather than behind, his fellow member of the Order. Stephen, as always, brought up the rear. As he closed the fine, solid door, taking care with the delicate brass handles, he looked down. At his feet was a small book, with a dark, blue cover and writing so faded that it was impossible to read. He lifted it.

"Sir APhaniel?" he said, holding the book above his head. "Is this yours?"

The mage looked back over his shoulder. "That? Oh, yes. Do bring it along."

Jewel was nervous. It was the cool season in Averalaan, but she was certain she'd never sweated more in her life. Four weeks and a day she'd been searching through the warrens trying to find any hint—any sign at all—of the labyrinth by which she and her den had kept themselves fed and clothed. She knew those tunnels like the back of her hand, and they were gone. Gone. Dirt and rock, uninterrupted by any trace of a tunnel, was all that remained, and if she hadn't known better, she'd have said that she'd imagined it all. But damnit, she *did* know. Somehow, in some way that not even the mage could detect, the demon had concealed them.

Which probably meant that there had to be more than one, because the creature that had become Rath was gone.

It was Rath's memories they were using; she was certain of it. And he'd said she'd explored areas that he hadn't—but what if that didn't end up being true? He was a canny old man, was Rath, and he always kept something up his sleeve in case of emergency. She cursed him with happy abandon in the relative safety of the den's rooms.

Ellerson appeared from around a corner. "You called?" he said blandly.

"You know damned well I didn't call," was her curt response. "So you can stop that stuffy, polite act."

"As you wish," he replied, in exactly the same tone of voice. "But may I point something out to the young lady?"

She rolled her eyes. "Like I could stop you if I wanted to."

"It is unkind—and inaccurate in some cases—to assume that the mannerisms and gestures of another person are assumed, rather than genuine. While you will never develop the same style that I have developed, you were also never exposed to the same influences. I do not assume that your behavior is an act."

She snorted. "If I was going to act, I'd probably choose something different to act like."

"Agreed."

"Ellerson, don't you have something to *do*?"

"I am your domicis."

The reply hadn't changed at all over the course of the last two weeks; nor had the tone. "I forgot," she said, her voice heavy with sarcasm.

"As you say."

"Did you come here for a reason?"

"Indeed. Suitable attire has arrived for you and your companions. I thought you might want to have your old clothing removed, as you will be representing The Terafin, and will therefore be expected to dress appropriately."

She knew better than to say no; she didn't even try. Instead she nodded and went back to her pacing. The room that she slept in was larger than the flat her entire den had occupied only weeks ago. The food was a bit unusual, but there was a lot of it, it came regularly, and it was good. The moneybox was still empty, but it didn't matter—while she served The Terafin, her den-kin were safe and secure.

But it's not going to last long, she thought, grinding her heels into the smooth, waxed floors, *if we can't find the damned labyrinth.*

Carver came sauntering into the room. Jewel looked at what he was wearing and sighed. Ellerson was wrong; if they were going to find those tunnels without being caught, they had to do it looking as if they belonged to the holdings they searched through.

"Carver, go tell Ellerson I've changed my mind about the clothing."

"Right, sir," he replied. "But I'll trade."

"Trade what?"

"The Terafin's looking for you. Torvan's outside."

"Why?" She heard the nerves make her voice shake and forced them out of it. "We don't have another meeting scheduled for two days."

"Teller says he saw the mage with a group of people. Three men, a really scrubby woman and a bunch of dogs."

"They've called someone else in?"

He shrugged, knowing the news was bad. "Looks like."

She said something extremely rude and left him by the door as she made her way—at a run—to Torvan's side.

The halls, with their almost cavernous ceilings and their width, would always surprise her; she was certain of it. Footsteps echoed strangely and words, even those spoken in near-silence, were caught by unforgiving acoustics. She fiddled with the sash that she wore; it was a shade of blue that Jewel couldn't identify because the dyes that were used in its making were not affordable to those who lived in her holding. Her hair was drawn back in a style that Ellerson had suggested—and while it was both simple to look at and practical, it was also a monstrosity of little hairpins and clips that she was constantly forgetting were there when she tried to run her fingers through it in her usual gesture of impatience or frustration. She hated it. The more she tried to fit in, the more ill at ease and out of place she felt.

But she'd worry about that later.

She had become accustomed to speaking with The Terafin in either her office or her quarters, and she felt slightly uneasy as she looked at the intricate doors five feet from the arches of the chambers that were used to address visiting dignitaries and people whose import to the House had to be acknowledged. "Isn't this where—"

"Yes. But the repairs have been done, and well; except for scoring in the stone, you would not know that a battle of any sort took place here."

Torvan answered so smoothly that she had to wonder how often such cleanups had taken place. It didn't ease her.

"Aren't you coming?" she asked, as he took up his place beside the doors.

"I wasn't summoned," was the wry reply. "There are other guests," he added.

"Which means I've got to be on good behavior, right?"

"The choice is always yours."

She snorted and caught the brass handles of the closed door. "Not much of a choice," she said to his turned back. "Starve, or jump through hoops."

"Welcome," he replied, "to the adult world." But his voice was actually very gentle.

She didn't reply because the open doors would carry her words to the woman she least wanted to hear them.

"Jewel. Good. Please join us." The Terafin was seated behind a large, elegant desk. It was not a match for the one that had been damaged when the wall exploded; Jewel knew it instinctively, although she couldn't say why. Still, the new carpets were a lovely deep blue with rose and gold embroidery and a pattern—an intricate circular dance of fire flowers in the first rain—that leaped to life from its center. There were sitting chairs here, and the fireplace wall had been cleaned and tended. If she looked, she could see where the demon's spell had done its damage. She did—but her gaze did not linger.

"This is Lord Elseth of the Kingdom of Breodanir. This is his companion, Stephen. The young woman with them is called Espere, but she is, unfortunately, mute—and they have traveled this distance to find a cure for her condition."

Jewel followed The Terafin's introduction and bit her lip to stop herself from speaking. Mute, in Jewel's opinion, was the least of the stranger's problems.

"Gentlemen, this is Jewel Markess. She is one of three people I've personally appointed to investigate the unusual occurrences in the inner holdings." There was a knock at the door—one that reminded Jewel that she, too, had been expected to knock and allow her presence to be announced. She blushed.

"Enter."

The door opened and a man whom Jewel had never seen before walked into the room. He was Torvan's age, but not like him in appearance; his hair was black with a sprinkling of silver, and his eyes were dark enough that they also seemed black. His face was long, his brow high, and his cheekbones pronounced. He smiled, and Jewel thought he had the most perfect teeth she had ever seen. "I'm sorry I'm late, Terafin."

It seemed to Jewel that The Terafin's smile was drawn out against her will. "I'd prefer that you were less often sorry and more often on time," she said, but she couldn't make the words as curt as they deserved to be. "Very well. You know Meralonne, more or less. The two gentlemen are visitors from beyond the Empire. This is Lord Elseth of Breodanir, and this, his companion, is Stephen. The young woman to your right is Jewel Markess; it is she that you will be advising.

"Devon ATerafin," she said to those that she had just introduced, "has been a member of my house for almost twenty years. He is absolutely trustworthy." Gilliam turned to Stephen, and Stephen shrugged. "Although his duties are to the trade commission, he has agreed to aid us in this difficult time."

And how exactly could someone from some trading authority help her? Jewel bristled slightly, but said nothing. As if she'd spoken, Devon turned slightly and smiled; she wasn't certain she liked the expression. Seemed a bit on the smug side. And his face was too pretty.

The fair-haired slender man named Stephen performed a very odd bow; after a minute's hesitation, so did Lord Elseth. Jewel was good at observing people; she knew that Stephen was relieved and that Gilliam was annoyed, and from this surmised that Stephen, of the two, was the one who worried about manners. What she didn't see was the signal between them that had forced Gilliam to his feet. Strange.

Did she know? It was a question that Devon often wondered when in her presence. He knew, of course, that she knew of many of his less well-advertised skills. Knew, too, that she considered him discreet enough to call upon them from time to time. But he did not know if she understood his position within the court of the Kings, and the rank he held there.

Very few did.

Devon ATerafin was one of five men who were considered trustworthy enough to serve one of The Ten while at the same time serving the Crowns; it had never, until three days ago, been a burden to him—but he was no fool, to wonder why so few House members were allowed to enter the compact that governed the Astari. He had studied his histories well, and he understood the lure of power for those who already possessed it.

His smile, smooth and convivial, made him a favorite of the younger Queen; he used it now to mask his concern and his worry. He was not certain it was enough of a mask to protect him from The Terafin, however. He took his seat, but even before he had pulled it into the circle, with a smile to either side, he had already taken stock of the people in the room.

The dogs seemed to sense what lay behind his smile—and indeed the dogs were the biggest surprise in the chamber. From what he knew of dogs—and he knew a surprising amount, for two of the Breodani diplomats often frequented the court of Queen Marieyan—they were of the best of the hunting stock.

"Isn't it unusual for Hunter Lords to travel?" he said, directing the question to the huntbrother and not the Hunter.

"It is very unusual," Stephen replied softly. "And we must not tarry; by the first of Veral, we must be in Breodanir, in the King's City."

"Or?"

"There is no or," he said gravely. "We are Hunters, and we abide by the Hunter's Oath. If we cannot achieve our goal—or yours, Terafin—by that date, we must set aside the goal until the passing of the Sacred Hunt."

Devon nodded as if satisfied, and in part, he was. He had never seen a Hunter Lord, but these two satisfied both his secondhand knowledge and his instinct. Nothing changed at all in his posture or his expression, but he relaxed slightly.

Until his gaze returned to Meralonne APhaniel.

Meralonne was an older mage with a reputation—what senior mage, he reflected dourly, did not have one?—and an overwhelming sense of his own importance. Unfortunately, from what the Astari could tell, his arrogance matched his ability very closely. That was all that the Astari had really been able to discover about the mage, and for that reason, he was still scrutinized.

He could not, of course, give any of the information that the Astari had gleaned to The Terafin. She had never pushed him to render any account of his day-to-day life to her; it was not her way. The people whose service she asked for she granted a large measure of trust; to this day, that trust had not proved ill-founded.

Do you know? He could not ask, and she never answered—not by word. But there was always suspicion. Especially now, confronted by two foreign lords and one of the Magi.

Why, Terafin, did you summon me if it solely involves the House? He could not, of course, refuse—not and remain a member of Terafin. But to see these foreign lords, that mage, and a young girl who had the aura of one not comfortable with the rules of the patriciate about her made him uneasy indeed.

"Devon, I must ask you one question. Do you know who holds the seventeenth, the thirty-second, and the thirty-fifth?"

He turned at the sound of The Terafin's voice and raised a brow. "Pardon?" Nothing about his surprise was feigned. This, this is why The Terafin ruled; she did in all things the unexpected. He held up a hand as she opened her mouth. "My apologies, Terafin. I heard the question."

"And?"

"I must confess that I leave that for the record keepers and the treasury. It's easy enough to find the three names if you require them."

"It's not necessary," she replied, in a tone that made it clear that it wasn't. "Meralonne?"

"They are not three names; they are one. Those holdings, as well as the seventh and the fifty-ninth, are in the care of Patris Cordufar."

"Two of the richest and three of the poorest," Devon said; the words had the quality of musing done aloud.

"*The* two richest and *the* three poorest," The Terafin replied.

"That is . . . unusual." More than just understatement; Families held a holding and its responsibilities; Houses might hold two or three. Devon would have sworn that no Lord in Averalaan could lay claim to three now—five was unthinkable. "Why is this of significance to this problem?"

"Because," The Terafin said, "we believe that the magisterial courts have been corrupted within those holdings."

It was all Devon could do to remain seated. "Oh?" he said evenly as he leveled his gaze at the woman who held his name. "By whom?"

"Either by Patris Cordufar, who leads one of the richest of the noble families in the Empire, or by those who have managed to take advantage of him. Devon, you've met Cordufar." It wasn't a question; she rarely asked them.

Damn her. Yes, he'd met Cordufar; the Cordufar fortunes had risen rapidly enough in the previous generation that they were worth watching—but Astari records indicated only that the previous Patris Cordufar was a merchanting genius with no real ambitions but a mind so sharp it could cut a careless man. In financial dealings, it seemed he had met many of them. The current Patris Cordufar was a tall and handsome man with just as little a sense of humor as his father before him and just as deadly an intellect. He could not imagine anyone who could take advantage of that Lord to such an extent.

"I realize that you would never make such a statement without proof," he said, "but I must nevertheless ask you why you've reached that conclusion."

"Of course," she said. "These," and she lifted a document from the edge of the desk closest to her, "are the names of people who have been reported as missing throughout the holdings in the last decade. These," she continued, lifting another document, "are a list of people who have gone missing within the three poorer holdings that Cordufar runs during that time."

He took them from her and browsed over the relevant numbers. Stopped. The second list did not in any way coincide with the first. Although there were officially reported disappearances of people in the seventeenth, thirty-second, and thirty-fifth, none of the names were on the second list. "If these were not reported, how do you know they've gone missing?"

"We have reason to believe that they were reported, at least initially. You'll want, of course, to read this as well."

He took the third report with a growing unease and a growing curiosity. It was a document, prepared by a clerk of the Order of Knowledge, which charted the missing person count reported and suspected, of the three holdings, and compared them with the rise in population in those centers, and with the economic conditions at the time of the reports.

The reported count had risen slightly over the decade. But the suspected count was spiked so sharply it nearly went off the edge of the document.

He was Astari. "You suspect that whoever has been suppressing these reports is also involved with the disappearances."

"Why?" Gilliam asked. His huntbrother's face remained serene, but for some reason, the Hunter Lord himself glared at him and then fell silent.

"Because," Meralonne replied, "it's perfectly clear that whoever has been suppressing this information knows which disappearances he, she, or they are responsible for, and which are random acts of violence."

Devon's hands were still as he set the papers aside, but years of training gave him that self-control. "Terafin," he said gravely, "I do not believe that this is House business alone. To imply that a Lord of the patriciate has somehow managed to subvert the magisterial courts is a grave accusation, and possibly worse. A matter of this nature should be reported at once to the appropriate—"

"Be seated," she said. "Devon."

He sat.

"There is more, and I trust that you will understand why I say what I say when you have heard it."

"Terafin, please. I—"

"You will *sit down!*" He had never heard her raise her voice; he sat because his knees were momentarily too shaky to support him. "And you will *listen.*" She stood now and left the protection of her desk. "Have you heard stories of the demon-kin?"

He nodded.

"Good. Because we believe that the people responsible for the destruction of the unreported missing persons are either demons or those in league with them." She paused. "Meralonne can attest to the fact that many of the kin feel a need to . . . feed. If a mage—or more likely a House—has a collection of these creatures, it is quite likely that they will require some physical sacrifice."

"The Terafin is correct," the silver-haired mage confirmed softly.

It was not what Devon had expected her to say.

"Further," she continued, "we know for a fact that some of the demon-kin cannot only assume the shape of a man, but also much of his identity and much of his memory. This is, of course, at the cost of the life of the one so imitated." She paused. "This is no illusion, Devon. Such an assumption is not magical in nature, and when looked for, no magic will be found."

Devon felt the blood drain from his face as the implications of what she was saying took root. "Reymaris' sword," he whispered.

"We do not know at which level the ranks of the Cordufar family have been infiltrated—but we know that, upon the staff of the magisterial truthseekers, there was one who was not seeking truth any longer."

"Then we must find the summoner of these creatures."

"Yes, we must. And we must do it with care and caution. I have already sent word, through all the channels that I have access to, that an assassination attempt was carried out, by magical means, against me. I have made it clear that there was a summoning of some sort, and have offered the usual reward for the mage who accepted the job."

"In other words, you've done everything you can to appear as ignorant as possible."

"Yes. But I'm not at all sure that it will work."

"Why?"

She shook her head, and then grimaced. "Because the man that they killed and replaced—the man whose partial memories they own—was once my brother. We did not love each other overmuch in our later years, but we knew each other well."

"Ararath," Devon whispered.

The Terafin smiled rather grimly; it was clear that she expected him to understand much more than one of his station within the House proper. "Meralonne APhaniel is one of a suspected half-dozen of the mage-born who can easily detect these creatures for what they are. But he must be looking for it. Needless to say, most people will not.

"We cannot allow this information to be known; if people know of it, and know further that they cannot detect these creatures easily, there will be panic. And the panic will be twofold." She no longer spoke to Devon, because she knew that Devon understood without the need for an explanation.

"First, people will begin to look for demons where none exist, and I fear that the innocent may well suffer from such a hunt, and second—and most important—if the kin are involved in higher levels of our councils, they may feel the need to prematurely move against us, our House, and our supporters. We must leak information, and that information must be true; we must let them know that we are stymied in our search, and that we suspect only the mage-born.

"To this end I have begun a 'private' investigation into the mage-born members of the Order of Knowledge. I have also sent my operatives into the lower holdings to search for foreign mages who may have been involved in this black art."

"And why do we need to involve our foreign guests in our internal matters?" Devon's question was pointed.

"Because," The Terafin replied serenely, "it seems that Stephen of Elseth—unlike Meralonne or any of the mage-born—can see the demon-kin without resorting to the use of spell. He does not need to search for the signs; if he can see the creature, we believe he will know it for what it is."

"And what proof do you have of this?"

Meralonne answered at The Terafin's nod. "For reasons that are not clear to me or any of us, the demons are searching for Stephen and Lord Elseth. They were waiting at the western demiwall for their arrival."

"Waiting? That implies that they knew they would be here."

"We met them first in Breodanir," Stephen added, speaking for the first time. "At the time, they were hunting Espere. She is not quite right, and we hoped to find both the answer to the question of why the demons hunted her, and the cure to her condition, if it can be cured, here."

"And instead you have found that these creatures are here and hunting for you?"

"Yes."

"I see." He trailed off into silence, absorbing the answers to his questions while preparing to ask more.

The Terafin interrupted his musing. "The demon that they met here wore the guise of a magisterial truthseeker. We have been able to ascertain which truthseeker; he has been in service to the courts for over fifteen years." She sat, then, and stared at her liege for a long time.

Devon was silent. The smile had deserted his face; his attention was focused inward with an intensity that he rarely showed. What was the connection between the demons, the girl, the foreign lord, The Terafin, Meralonne, and the urchin named Jewel? How many of these creatures were there, and how far up—or down—had they gone? If the power of the mage-born was at the heart of this problem, whose power, and what was their final goal?

He trusted The Terafin as much as he trusted any member of The Ten—but no more than that.

"Devon?"

The Crowns were his life, his sworn and his chosen life; and they *deserved* that loyalty and that dedication; they deserved it, and more, as no other rulers in any foreign country had ever done, or ever would. Against their well-being and their continued rule, the health of any House counted for little—any House save Terafin. *Ah, wisdom,* he thought, as he ran his hands his through his hair. *Where are you now?*

"Yes," he said softly. "I understand it."

"And you understand that *no word* of this is to leave the House?"

"Are you so certain that this is a House affair?"

"It does not matter if I am not," she said severely. "I gave you an order." Then, knowing to whom she spoke, she relented. But in the manner of Terafin. "Patris Cordufar owes his loyalty to which House?"

"Darias."

"Indeed. Do you see?"

Devon cursed inwardly. Less than fifteen years had passed since the House wars between Darias and Terafin had nearly brought The Ten to their knees. Forty-three men and women had died in the service of the two Houses, and not a few of them powerful, notable. The Kings had been forced to intervene, for only the second time in the history of Averalaan, and their intervention had cost both Houses dearly. Only in the last year had The Terafin finally brought the House back to its previous position of political power upon the council; Darias still had not recovered.

Darias.

"It may indeed be that this matter is not solely a difficulty which the House must face," she said. "But to bring it to the attention of the Kings, in the light of the assassination attempt, will cost us more than I wish to pay. If it comes to that, it is a decision that *I* will make."

He swallowed; he knew that she would never come closer to speaking of his rank within the Astari. If indeed she spoke of it. And he knew, too, that he could not keep this to himself for long, however he might try. If he tried at all. "I will remain ATerafin if you judge me worthy." The words and the tone were very grave. "But as a member of your House of little rank and merit, I must ask a boon."

"Ask, then."

"It is not, unfortunately, of you that that favor must be asked." He turned to Lord Elseth and his huntbrother, Stephen. "At court there are two women, Lady Morganson and Lady Faergif; they are of the Breodani, and they traveled here when their sons inherited the responsibilities of their demesnes. They are sharp and canny in defense of the interests of your kingdom, and they have become accustomed to all things Essalieyanese. But if they learn that a Hunter Lord has left Breodanir to journey to the Empire, they will wish to meet that Lord—and, of course, his huntbrother."

"You want us to go to court?" Lord Elseth said, with so much distaste that the huntbrother could not keep his disapproval from showing.

"What he means to say, Lord ATerafin—"

"Devon will do."

"Devon, then. What he means to say is that we are not attired or prepared for a court so complicated and unique as that of the Twin Kings and he does not wish to insult."

Devon did smile at that. "But he would come?"

"Yes, we would both be happy to accept your invitation."

"Good." Devon rose. If he could have the huntbrother for a gathering of the two courts, he could rest a little easier. He paused and met the eyes of The Terafin; he understood, then, why she had summoned him in the presence of foreigners. A gift, of sorts, to the Astari—guardians of the Kings. "Then I must prepare for your dogs—they will be properly kenneled and cared for in the style to which they are accustomed." He bowed—and it was the bow of the Breodani that he offered. Then he turned to The Terafin and brought his arm across his chest in salute. "Terafin."

"ATerafin," she replied. "We will speak again, Devon. You may have your day in the two courts, and then we must have your day in the streets of the city. We need to conceal what we do."

Chapter Ten

LORD ELSETH AND STEPHEN were escorted off the premises by Devon ATerafin, who was charged both with finding them a suitable domicile for their stay and extending the hospitality of Terafin to them. In normal circumstances, they would be housed in the manor proper at the very least, but The Terafin felt it too much of a risk to have all of the enemies of the demon-kin concentrated in one place, and although she did not voice this concern aloud, it was understood.

Jewel gave her report, and if she was nervous and a little terse, The Terafin did not appear to notice. Instead, she nodded. "You work well, Jewel. I understand the difficulty you labor under, and I must add to it; we will no longer send out crews to the various sites that Ararath mentioned in his letter. Instead, I will send you out with Devon, and only Devon.

"You are to follow his commands in all things; if you feel that his command exceeds my wishes, you are nonetheless obligated to carry out his word. I will take your reports in my chambers, and I will entertain any concerns that you may have at that time. Do I make myself clear?"

"Yes."

"Good. Dismissed."

Jewel's eyes flickered momentarily to Meralonne, and then away. She brought her arm across her chest and then stopped before the salute itself was complete. The Terafin smiled. "Indeed," she said softly. "You owe me no such respect yet; I have not given you my name."

Jewel nodded and walked away, and The Terafin watched her go. "She has temerity," she said softly, almost to herself.

"She has that," the mage replied dryly. "She also has a temper and a tongue to go with it. You've not been at the digs with us," he added. Then he inclined his head and held it, like a demibow, before raising his face.

"Well, then," The Terafin said quietly. "You have your own report to offer, I presume?"

"I, Lady?"

"Indeed." She leaned back and pulled the bell by the bay window. "Would you care for refreshments?"

"No, Terafin," he replied.

"A pity." She watched the doors swing open; a man walked through them, carrying a tray with a heavy decanter and three glasses at its center. The tray itself was ornate, a mixture of ebony and gold inlay that suggested great fragility while providing great strength. Not unlike the ruler of the House itself.

The servant set down the tray on the table between the desk and the mage; he proceeded to pour two glasses of a liquid that was cool and dark. Meralonne raised a brow.

"I may be persuaded to change my mind," he said softly.

"Good. Please." She lifted the blue liquid to her lips and then pulled it back, staring intently into its depths. She watched the surface of her drink, rather than her companion's expression, as she spoke next.

"Meralonne, everyone believes that you destroyed that creature."

He sipped the chill, bitter liquid and smiled as it fell down the back of his throat. "Everyone but you?"

"I heard you and saw you; I would guess that you were fighting not the creature but the darkness that enwrapped it."

"I see."

"You did not mention, in your report, the probable cause of the creature's death; did not mention whether or not you thought the creature dead at all."

"An oversight."

"Oh? But you did mention that you had dispatched it."

"There are games, young woman, that it is better not to play," Meralonne said, lifting his glass by the stem and staring through its facets.

"Indeed. May I give you the same advice?"

The mage stared at her a moment and then reached into the folds of his tunic and pulled out his pipe. "Do you mind?" She did not answer, and he took her silence as acquiescence. The slightly sweet acridity of pipe smoke began to fill the room by slow degrees.

"Meralonne, what you choose to withhold from anyone else is your business. I will not point out that you are in my employ, because it is of little consequence. I am The Terafin, and the battle occurred within the confines of *my* domain. I *will* know what happened."

"I'm not completely certain myself," he replied benignly.

"And yet, if I'm not mistaken, the magics used against that creature were of a variety that was once called Summer magic. Except that Summer magic was closely tied to stellar conjunctions."

"Obviously not completely."

"Obviously."

He stared moodily at the woman who was, next to the Queens, the most powerful in the Empire. "If only," he said at last, with a grim smile, "you were a man."

She raised a brow at his comment, and at the bark of bitter laughter that followed it, understanding neither.

"What would you have of me, then? I will tell you what I know."

"I doubt that, Master APhaniel. I doubt that very much."

As if she had not spoken, he continued. "There are always mages who study the lost arts, hoping for some glimpse of the powers that the mage-born once mastered in the past. It is," he added, in a darker voice, "a past that they do not understand, or they would not chase it so fervently and so foolishly.

"Understand, Terafin, that as you are the head and the embodiment of your House, so, too, am I responsible for mine; I am a member of the Council of the Magi, and it is under our guidance that the Order flourishes." Pipe smoke filled the air around his face like a thin veil of mist. "An incident of this like is by its very nature a matter for the Magi, and of great concern to the Order, for while not all of the mage-born are members of the Order, the Order *is* magic as far as most of the Empire is concerned."

She stared at him, impassive in the silence of her demands. He met that gaze without flinching, pipe in hand as if it were a ward against external influences.

But, significantly, it was Meralonne who spoke next. "Until we are certain exactly what it is we are facing, we are not at liberty to divulge what scant information we do have. In all honesty, we have not yet managed to argue our way into any consensus with regard to that information. I'm sorry."

Her eyes glittered like gemstones, cold and hard. "If the lack of that information costs this House, it will cost you, I promise it."

"Of course," Meralonne replied, smiling without a trace of humor. He lifted his glass to his lips and then raised it in her direction. "But let me say this, Terafin. For the sake of the Order, and your continued goodwill toward it, I will offer my services to your House, without interruption, for the balance of this difficulty. And I will do this without the usual fees that are involved in such a transaction."

"And if I choose not to accept this . . . generous offer?"

"You must do as you will, of course."

She watched him as he smoked his pipe; he was not in the least intimidated by her, nor she by him. They were both used to power and the subtleties of wielding it, and although they both craved information and knowledge, they were also used to making decisions based on instinct. At last, she nodded briefly.

"Very well, Master APhaniel. I accept both your offer and your service until further notice."

He knew a dismissal when he heard it, and rose quickly, but not hastily; emptied his pipe into the hearth, and then, turning, raised a hand in a gesture of both respect and partial fealty. He did not salute her.

After the doors had closed at his back, The Terafin lifted her glass. "Well?"

"He is lying." Morretz waited patiently until she had finished with her glass and then took it from her and placed it beside the decanter.

"You're certain?"

"Of at least one thing. He has not argued with the rest of the Magi, or even discussed the occurrence here with them. There has been no council called within the Order."

"And the rest?"

"I do not know. But it is obvious that he knows more—I would guess much more—than he wishes us to know."

"What is his game?"

"It is too early to say," Morretz replied gravely, "but were I to guess, I would say that it does not directly involve Terafin."

She smiled. "Is this your way of telling me that you would have also accepted his offer?"

"I believe it better to have him under our surveillance than otherwise. Besides which," he added, as he lifted the tray, "young Jewel seems to be able to work with him."

"A telling sign," The Terafin said, rising as well. "Probably *the* telling sign."

"I have already advised you," Morretz said, turning, "against relying upon one seer-born; the talent is wild and inefficient. You might recall the fate of Megan fair-hair."

"Megan fair-hair is—and should remain—a cautionary tale meant to guide children. And I have already said," she continued, in just as pointed a tone, "that it is not her talent alone, but my instinct, that serves me here. Now come. We have more important matters to arrange. I wish a meeting with Lord Cordufar."

"Out of the question."

The Terafin laughed; in tone and texture it made her seem bereft of both age and title. "Morretz, I believe you to be the most irritating and also the wisest of all the choices that I have made in this office."

3rd Corvil, 410 A.A.
Order of Knowledge

Sigurne Mellifas was a mage of no little power, which was not unusual on this, the Council of the Twenty-one, the Magi who governed the magical practices of the mages—and the mages themselves—who studied within the confines of the Order of Knowledge. But she was a woman of little temper and a spine of steel; it was an odd combination. One could not dislike her—she had no edges upon which to pin such a feeling—but one could not move her once she had decided her course of action. She could, Meralonne thought, probably run a man through while apologizing for the necessity of such an extreme course of action.

Or without apologizing at all, depending on the situation. Today, she offered no apologies as she spoke.

"There is only one course of action available to us. We must begin the mage-hunt. The information that young Zareth Kahn has delivered cannot be ignored."

The "young" Zareth Kahn winced slightly as he rose. "Master Sigurne is correct," he said, his voice strong and deep compared to hers, but somehow less forceful. "The Queen of Breodanir herself has made it clear that she expects a resolution. Were it not for the death of Zoraban ATelvise, the position of the Order would be untenable at this moment. The Queen realizes that, due to the loss of our leader, our House is in chaos—her words, not ours—and she waits upon our response." He did not need to add that she did not wait patiently. Reaching into the folds of his silver-lined, black and white robes, he pulled from them a rounded, wooden tube. Uncapping it, he reached in and removed the scroll that he had carried to the Order's council.

This he carefully handed to Sigurne Mellifas. She broke the seal, read it, and frowned slightly. She rarely frowned.

"Matteos," she said, lifting her chin.

"Sigurne?" He was a tall man; not a young one, but not a man to whom the passage of years had been unkind. Battle had etched a scar or two across his brow and cheek and instilled a wariness in his dark eyes, but his hair was still a dark brown, his shoulders still broad and strong, his arms still capable of bearing the weight of war's weapons.

"I think you had best send your boys out."

Matteos Corvel was, in all ways, Sigurne's protector—but he was more, besides. He nodded gravely because he understood—they all did—the danger that a rogue mage presented to the Order, and the safety of the Order.

A mad mage, especially one who practiced the dark arts, was remembered and feared long after he had met a particularly gruesome end. His name and his deeds became the measure by which all mages were judged and feared. Only by meeting the challenge of such magery openly did the mages of the Order protect themselves, and champion their own survival.

And they did so ruthlessly when the need arose.

"Put it to a vote, Sigurne," Meralonne APhaniel said quietly.

She turned her brown-eyed gaze upon him from the head of the table; saw the weariness in eyes that were lined with care. Meralonne's specialty was the study of ancient magics.

"Do you think Krysanthos could have summoned The Terafin's would-be assassin?"

"If you had asked me a month ago, I would have told you that Krysanthos couldn't summon a fly." Silver hair shifted as the mage shrugged a slender shoulder.

"He *is* a mage of the second circle, Meralonne," she replied, chiding in tone.

Member APhaniel shrugged again. "No, Sigurne. I do not believe that Krysanthos had the power to summon such a creature as I fought. But I very much believe that he is linked to a mage, or mages, that *do* have that power."

Silence, then, cold and still.

"Meralonne," Sigurne Mellifas said, the single word a rebuke. "If you wish to make an accusation, make it. If you wish to remain silent, remain silent. But you know as well as I that the only members of the Order who stand within the first circle preside upon this council."

"I know it," the mage said softly, casting a steel-gray glance around the long, heavy table. "But I have no accusation to give. No single mage here has fallen under such scrutiny, and no single mage—without exception—would survive it well. I have trusted this council as much as I have trusted anything—but I tell you, Sigurne, that the hand of the kin's summoner is a greater power than Krysanthos was capable of summoning.

"Send it to vote," he said again.

She did, although it was a formality.

Matteos Corvel bowed his head a moment and then placed both of his large, square hands flat against the table. He pushed himself out of his seat and rose. "I can try," he said, although no one had asked. "But you know as well as I that the risk to the civilians is increased a hundredfold if we have to bring him back alive."

They were silent, weighing the need for information against the need to minimize the possible consequences to the Order. Only in the Order of Knowledge would the struggle have taken so long, and been so close. But it was Sigurne's turn to preside over the twenty-one-member council, and no one thought to gainsay her when at last she spoke.

"Kill him," she said. "I will prepare the writ of execution and have it sent to the Kings."

3rd Corvil, 410 A.A.
Arannan Halls

Stephen of Elseth looked out at the cloud-shrouded sky before letting the heavy curtains fall once again across the window.

"What's bothering you this time?"

"Nothing," he said, over his shoulder. But he disliked the quarters they had been given; there was no glass in most of the windows, and no shutters either. Instead, like a veil or a shroud, heavy curtains on rods the width of his forearm hung across the open spaces.

There was a fountain of sorts that trailed into a cool bath—one that didn't see much use at this time of year, or so he'd been told—and all around their feet, inlaid marble and ebony, bits of gold and silver, and the occasional planks of darkly stained wood invited a soft tread. The heavy boots that had survived the rigors of the road had been exchanged for supple leather soles with straps and strings. Sandals, Devon had called them. He had also provided them with loose-fitting robes and belts that Stephen secretly felt better worn by the ladies—there were fine links of chain that formed a glittering web of sorts across the waist.

Gilliam, of course, refused to wear them. And Stephen, after a half hour of annoyed argument, gave in. But he wore the garments that Devon ATerafin provided him.

Devon was a mystery. Dark-haired and dark-eyed like the Breodani, but with finer features than most—a very handsome man. But also a man used to dealing with both power and the consequences of power; used to deliberating and then following difficult courses of action; used, Stephen thought, to killing if killing was necessary.

He did not know it for fact, but knew it for truth; he had met many Ladies and seen how they wielded their powers, and over the years he had developed a second sense for the mighty, no matter how demure or cheery, dour or grim, they appeared. But he found it disconcerting to see it so clearly in a man. Power for the men of the Breodani—for the Lords who hunted and died so that the kingdom could prosper—was a more immediate, a more visceral, occupation.

"What do you think he wants?" Gilliam asked, absently patting the head of a lolling Connel.

"I don't know."

"You're worried."

"I'm worried." Stephen laughed. "I'm not sure which is worse—knowing that we now depend on his good grace, or knowing that we're going to have to meet with Lady Morganson and Lady Faergif."

"Why?"

"You obviously don't remember Lady Faergif."

Gilliam seldom remembered anyone who wasn't a Hunter. He shrugged. Devon was not a threat, but rather a boon; the quarters—usually offered to official royal visitors and dignitaries from the South—were the first that had been set up to properly house and kennel his dogs. He was heartily sick of arguing with ignorant innkeepers along the route. The Terafin was much like the Queen, really; a woman with a great deal of personal power, but not one that he would distrust.

The same could not be said of mages. He pushed Ashfel's head off his lap and propped himself into a sitting position with his elbow. "You didn't tell Meralonne about the Hunter's Horn. Or the Wyrd. Why?"

"I don't know."

"You think the demons want it."

Stephen nodded. "But if they want it, maybe everyone will. I don't know what it's supposed to do, and I don't know why she gave it to me." Espere was asleep on the floor in the corner, having been given eight pillows, each the size of her back. "But they were hunting her for the same reason."

"Or because she's the Hunter's daughter."

"Maybe that's why she has the Horn." Stephen ran his hands through his hair. "I can't make sense of any of it. There are mages involved, or there wouldn't be demons. But there are priests of this—this Dark God involved as well as the demons." He frowned. "I don't know enough about Essalieyanese Gods."

"Can't be just Essalieyanese—not if it involves the Hunter."

"The Hunter is *our* God."

"Absolutely," Gilliam said with distinct pride.

"It's got something to do with the Dark Lord. Teos said that he was not upon his throne in the Hells. So where is he? Do you think he's trying to fight God in the Heavens?"

"If I were God and he were hunting on my preserve, there'd be war."

Before Stephen could answer, the chimes did. As there were no real doors, chimes, long and reedlike for all that they were made of some strange metal, were used in the place of door knockers. They were gently musical, almost like a contained breeze, and of all the strange things in the rooms they occupied, he liked the chimes best. "Enter," he said.

The curtains were thrown back, and Stephen had enough time to gasp and launch himself to the side before the crossbow bolt flew. It hit him, but not full in the throat; he cried out and reached for his shoulder as if to somehow damp the pain by touching it.

Someone cursed in a language that Stephen didn't understand; it was low and guttural, but it had a menacing musicality of its own. He looked up to see a thin-faced man with only half a head of hair—the left half—dressed very much like the servitors of the grand house in which they stayed. Damn the robes anyway; brown and long, they were ideal for hiding something as ungainly as a weapon.

Gilliam snarled; Stephen heard it, and realized that he had to keep the pain to himself for as long as he possibly could. Because, just behind the man with the crossbow was another one, tall and thin. And there was fire in his open eyes.

"Demon!" Stephen shouted.

As a warning, it was hardly necessary—their bond carried his surprise and his surge of fear more effectively than the word could. The Lord of Elseth turned as the first of the would-be assassins was lifted by the second and thrown bodily across the room to crash, hard, into Stephen.

The sound of flesh hitting stone—his own—softened the sound of steel against steel; it did nothing to drown out the rumbling growl of the wild girl. Stephen's ribs were cracked or broken; he'd suffered the injury before, and he knew what it felt like. It was a familiarity that he could well do without.

He did not, however, have to worry about the assassin. The dogs were there, and the man was stunned. It was not really much of a contest.

Stephen started to roll free of the dogs, and then stopped in mid-motion, cursing the stupidity of reflex. He crawled instead, lifting his head clear of Ashfel's back to see that Espere had bounded past Gilliam toward the door.

She was sleeping, he thought, but like a cat—not a dog—her sleep must have been an illusion.

The creature was smiling as he waited almost patiently for Espere's charge. And then, at the last moment, he threw his hands up, palm forward as if to repel her.

Flames gouted from the center of his hands.

Espere screamed.

Devon ATerafin looked up from his desk as he heard the horns winded and the bells—sonorous bells that were larger in diameter than the width of three brawny men—begin their steady, low tolling. He was on his feet before he had finished the count. Fire. And it was a fire in the Southerners' quarters. He had expected that there might be some difficulty—but not so soon, and not nearly so overt. It said much of him as a man that he did not even pause to think of what The Terafin would do should these two die in his care and responsibility.

The door to his chambers flew open and a young man in the gold and grays raced in, formality set aside—the servants here were too well-trained to merely forget or panic.

"Patris—"

"Fire in the Arannan Halls."

The fair-haired man nodded; the fact that Devon already knew what the calamity was seemed to take the edge off the youth's concern. "Gregor?"

"Sir."

"See that Alowan at the House Terafin is sent for at once, by my authority."

"Sir."

Her hair burned, and her charge was broken by the force of the blast—but she stood within its eye as if it were a passing storm. At her side, the curtains caught fire as if they'd been soaked in ale; the knotted rug was likewise consumed. For the first time, Stephen was grateful for her hatred of clothing.

He reached for his dagger—or tried to—as Gilliam charged in, leaping above the small tongues of flame that separated him from the woman who was part of his pack. Stephen's fingers felt strangely heavy; he fumbled a moment with the dagger sheath before he managed to grip the pommel. Levering himself to his feet was even more difficult; braced against the wall with back and hand, he found himself wondering where he was, and why.

The room was cloudy; the air quite heavy and hard to breathe. Fire, he thought, but although he tried to speak, the words came out as the faintest of croaks, ungainly and unheard.

Gilliam knew the feeling the moment it hit him: separation, an echo of the Winter void. Stephen was gone. He knew a second's panic, but not more; some instinct, something at a level that even the Hunter's bond could not reach, told him, *Keep fighting.*

He sent his call to Espere, reining her in; he sprang to the left with his sword, and she to the right, with no obvious weapons. He no more worried about the lack than he did about arming his alaunts on a hunt.

His trance gave him the time to examine things more closely than normal speed allowed. Espere was soot-tinged; her dark hair was an uneven crop of curled, burned strands that smelled not unlike seared flesh. But her eyes were both dark and light, blazing with things that by nature must remain unspoken. She looked like a creature out of legend, and at that, the dark wild legends that the cities had all but forgotten.

And the creature that Stephen called "demon" looked like a man—one tall and broadly built, with just a hint of muscle. He wore clothing much like the rest of the servants wore, with split burgundy sleeves and split skirts. He was in every way unprepossessing, but he carried his danger with him; the palm that had called forth flames still faced the farthest wall of the room. He stood, impassive, as Gilliam lunged forward first.

The demon caught the blow of the sword with his hand and grunted as the edge bit into the flesh of his palm. Illusion; Gilliam was certain of it; the last demons he had fought had been immune to the effects of steel.

It didn't matter; the blade and the blade's thrust were no more than a delaying action. It was Espere who was the deadly weapon.

He felt her anger and her eagerness; her focus and her strength. She was not like the dogs—not quite; there was an intelligence beneath the fire of her connection that made everything sharper and clearer. It also made things more dangerous; he had to work to keep away from the lure of seeing through her eyes.

The demon's cries of pain, he heard through two sets of ears; he smiled, and it was the Hunter's smile—feral and grim.

Gregor was a quiet aide, but he was both swift and efficient. His only weakness was his tendency to panic at times—but age would cure that. Or death would; to serve the Astari was sometimes a risky business.

Still, he began his job at once when they arrived at the Arannan Halls. The Kings' Swords were there in profusion, and they blocked Gregor's entrance.

"Have three foreigners, a dark-haired man of medium height and build, a fair-haired, slender man, and a rather unusual woman left the halls?"

The Kings' Sword thought for a moment and then shook his head gravely. "Either they left before I assumed this duty, or they are still within the halls."

"Then we need to enter," Gregor replied.

"No one is allowed to pass," the Kings' Sword said firmly—but politely. "There is a fire in the quarters, and the elemental masters are attempting to control it as we speak. If you reside in the hall, go to the Labaran Halls instead; there are rooms being readied and supplies that will see you through this difficulty." He bowed and then lifted his shield; it bore the twin crowns above the crossed rod and sword, but on either side were swords in the upright position.

"I'm afraid that my master's duties are within Arannan Hall itself, given the nature of the difficulty," Gregor replied carefully.

"Out of the question."

Devon stepped around Gregor; the eyes of the Kings' Sword widened and he dropped his head in a half-bow. "Patris," he said, his tone changing slightly.

"My aide is correct," Devon said tersely. "Our business is within Arannan Hall, and we do not have the time to dally."

"My orders are clear, sir. But Primus Cortarian is present, and I'm certain that he would make an exception for you. Please wait here."

"I will wait," Devon replied, raising his hand; he did not have to add that he would not wait long. On his left ring finger, he wore a band of solid gold that came up in the shape of a circle; within that circle was a sapphire, and around it, in perfectly carved symbols, was the name Terafin. There were few ATerafin who were given such a symbol and allowed to flaunt it so publicly; it made it clear that Devon ATerafin was a Lord with some influence in the upper echelons of the Kings' council, even if that influence was not official.

Primus Cortarian did not disappoint. He was a bronze-haired man only slightly older than Devon, and Devon knew him well, although they had met only once or twice in passing. The Kings' Swords were trusted with much, and those who rose in the ranks were scrutinized carefully by the Astari. There were also those in the ranks of the Swords who *were* Astari.

"Patris Devon ATerafin," the Primus said. "Am I to understand that you require access to the Arannan Halls?"

"Indeed."

"On whose authority?"

"My own," he replied. The reply was lost to the sound of thunder yards away—and on the ground. Devon started forward, cursing.

Primus Cortarian, under orders to protect the visitors and the civilians, let him go; were it a security matter, he would have argued it with the Queens themselves. But although Devon ATerafin worked within the office of Patris Larkasir—and that office was possibly the most important of the ministries of Essalieyan, as it was responsible for all of the royal charters given to the various merchants and their lines—he had an authority that that work did not convey. He had the name of one of The Ten. One day, Cortarian hoped to have exactly that—but he knew that that day was not yet close. To be offered a name, you had to have a lot to offer in return. Primus of the Kings' Swords was a start—but it wasn't good enough if you wanted to be a member of import in the House's council.

He wondered what Devon had had to offer so young and so early.

"That way," Devon said, and Gregor nodded, dropping the outer shell of his servant's garments in one easy motion. Devon did the same; they stood in the unrestricted leggings and tunics of the Royal Troupe of acrobats. They carried weapons, but the weapons were slight and of a hidden nature.

Thunder came again, and over the dying sounds of its rumble, a roar of pain.

Devon tested the wind with a hint of his trained ability, although it was more out of habit than necessity. *Magic. There.*

They ran.

Espere bled freely from a gash across her forehead. Her arms were likewise cut, and blood ran from her shoulder; the creature, human in appearance, had suddenly sprouted an elongated snout full of perfectly formed fangs. It was unexpected enough that both Gilliam and Espere were caught by surprise; had Gilliam been the target, he would have lost his face.

The creature fared a little better, but not much. Espere did not have the jaws of a beast—but her teeth were not entirely the flat, blunt chewing things that most humans possessed. She was also fast; faster than Gilliam in the depth of trance. The creature's fire came twice more, and each time Espere was the target.

Gilliam was vaguely aware that the fire had become too strong and too dangerous; he could smell the acridity of dark smoke as it began to fill the air with its poison. And he knew, too, that if he tarried for even seconds too long, the emptiness that was Stephen's place would never be filled.

But the creature would not retreat, and it would not die.

Smoke filled the arboretum, rising in black clouds to the open air. Devon knew exactly which windows were surrendering those clouds to the skies. He donned a thick mask, one designed by the mage Everem as a lark, which would protect him for a while from the effects of the smoke. Gregor, at his side, did the same.

Together, they crossed the wide, empty courtyard.

Half of the door coverings had been burned away; it looked as if someone had severed them with a sword of fire. Devon hated magery with a quiet passion. He pulled up to the side of a seat-window and then, swinging below the level of the smoke, tried to see what occurred within.

Lord Elseth and the odd—naked—girl were fighting with something that appeared to be almost human, except for the face and hands. The creature blocked the door, and the exit with which Lord Elseth was probably most familiar. There was no sign of the huntbrother.

It was not, of course, the only way into the room—but it was the best way to approach. Devon signed to Gregor, and Gregor signed back. They left, clinging to walls like silent, moving shadows cast by intense light.

Devon stopped down the hall that led to that door, and the demon's—for he was certain that the creature could be no other thing—back. Then, mouthing a faint prayer, he pulled a dagger from the sheath beneath his vest. It was not in any way standard issue, and in fact would have been the last choice for a man of Devon's skill; it was ornate to the point of ostentation—even the blade was engraved with intricate knots and elemental signatures—it was unbalanced, and it was far too heavy. Not only that, but the steel itself was soft, some fancy ancient alloy that robbed it of a real edge.

But it was not meant to be an ordinary weapon—it had been created as a ceremonial device for the Church of Cormaris, and then it had been consecrated by the rituals of the Church of Reymaris. The rituals were old and even dangerous, or so the Priests had said—but Devon's station and demeanor had convinced them of the need for both the rituals and extreme haste in performing them. He had not realized how little time he would have.

Devon smiled bitterly. He had spoken as openly as he dared—certainly skirting the edge of his oath to his own liege lord—with the Exalted of the Church of Reymaris; the Exalted was of the god-born, and the god-born could not be corrupted.

Let them be right, he thought, as he gripped the golden handle and stared down at the pommel into a diamond the size of a narrowed eye. He crept along the wall until the sounds of fighting were unmistakable; took a few steps more, until they were almost overwhelming.

Then, lithe and silent, he struck, seeing the creature's back for the first time half a second before the blade buried itself, as if pulled there, into the creature's spine.

The creature screamed.

For a moment he was angry, and anger was all that he felt. He knew a deathblow when he saw its effects, and knew further that it was not he who had dealt it. This was *his* hunt, and his alone to end.

But he was a well-seasoned Hunter Lord; the anger's moment passed as he watched the demon scream and turn his clawed, deadly hands to his back. Espere growled and tensed as if to leap; he called her to his side. She came, back facing him, eyes upon the creature.

The demon's cries were loud and furious as he rent his own flesh in an attempt to reach something that Gilliam couldn't see. Blood flew, and where it touched the sputtering flames of his mage-fire, it sizzled, forcing the flames up.

Almost mesmerized, Gilliam watched as the creature toppled slowly to its knees.

"Lord Elseth!" someone shouted. He looked up, coughed a little, and saw Devon ATerafin. "We do not have the time to linger here—come. Where is Stephen?"

Stephen. Gilliam wheeled suddenly, still caught in the speed of the Hunter's trance. There, against the far wall, standing in an almost protective circle, were his hunting dogs. He could see the sandaled foot of his huntbrother, but little else. Without regard for the fire that separated them, he crossed the room, bidding Espere to remain behind. The dogs parted at his unspoken, almost subconscious command.

Stephen's skin was pale—almost blue-tinged white. Gilliam could not hear, in the noise of the room, the sound of his huntbrother's breathing. Without a word, he lifted Stephen and bore him toward the door.

Devon was waiting, and with Devon a fair-haired man that Gilliam did not know. They both glanced at Stephen and then at each other. He didn't like the look that passed between them.

"Is he dead?"

"No."

"Good. Follow us, quickly."

The old man was not a regular visitor to the grandeur of the royal palace and its many outbuildings—but he was used to luxury and the finery that comes with rank and power. Devon knew it, but still found it odd to see Alowan, one of the most prized retainers of Terafin, dressed in his workmanlike and serviceable clothing, as if he were a mere servant with no pretensions of ever becoming anything more.

Alowan had, many times, been offered the House name, and each time, gently and firmly, had declined the offer. Other Houses had attempted to secure his services with similar—or greater—counteroffers. These, too, he declined. Devon did not understand him at all.

But he did understand that he was one of the very few healer-born who served a House. And he was not going to be the House member that offended or drove him away.

"Alowan Hanna." He dropped to a knee in the deepest gesture of respect that he could give.

"I believe you must be Devon," the old man replied. "I'm to understand that we have no time for pleasantries or even explanations."

"You understand correctly," Devon replied, straightening out and offering the healer his best smile and his arm. "Come this way."

Alowan returned the smile and accepted the courtesy. But as he walked, his smile dimmed. "These are Kings' Swords, and in great numbers. Tell me, Devon. What is the ailment that I have been summoned to tend to? The Terafin said we did not have time for explanations."

"There was a fire in the Arannan Halls."

Alowan winced. "Burns," he said, but mostly to himself.

"Not burns, at least, not to the outside of the body. We don't know how much smoke your patient inhaled, but we do not believe that that is the cause of his . . . current state."

"ATerafin—"

"Here we are." Devon ATerafin stopped in front of a wide oak door. The width of the door was covered by four men, each bearing the emblems of the Kings' Swords. "Primus Allarus," Devon said, lowering his chin in a formal nod, "this is Healer Alowan."

Alowan lifted his lined hand; the emblem of the twin hands, palms up to succor the needy, caught the light and held it for long enough that the Primus might identify it.

"I will personally vouch for him," Devon added gravely. "But his services are necessary immediately."

The Primus nodded his armored head and ordered his compatriots to grant them safe passage. The door swung wide on perfectly oiled hinges. To either side of the door, on the interior of the large room, there were also Kings' Swords—and there were two at the windows as well.

They relaxed marginally as their Primus gave them the nod that signaled safety.

"Lord Elseth," Devon said, for the fortieth time, "please. We have quarters prepared for both yourself and your pack. Do not feel it necessary to remain here; Stephen will be well-guarded. I give you my personal word, and the word of my House, that this is truth."

It was quite clear from Lord Elseth's response—an almost angry silence—that he did not appreciate the import of the vow that Devon was making, Devon knew it, and knew enough of foreigners and their customs not to be offended by it—but only just. "Very well. Please, stand aside."

"Who is that?"

Devon stiffened, but his smile never faltered. *Why*, he thought, because it had been a most difficult and long day, *could it not have been the Hunter instead of the huntbrother?* "This is a healer."

The healer in question touched Devon's arm and pushed him aside so gently that it took Devon a moment to realize that that was what he'd done. "I am Alowan," the old man said. "And I have come to see if there is anything I can do to aid your companion." He frowned. "You are wounded."

Gilliam nodded as if Alowan had asked a question about the weather; it was clear that the Hunter Lord was concerned about only one thing.

"What happened to him?" Alowan asked, as he took a seat by the injured man's bedside.

"He was hit by a crossbow bolt. But only in the shoulder. I don't understand it."

Alowan's face grayed at once as he placed first one hand, and then the other, against Stephen's clammy brow. It was quite clear that he understood. "Do you have the bolt, Devon?"

"Yes."

"Do you know what was on it?"

"No." He paused. "But the end is dyed or stained."

"Color?"

"We're not certain what the original color was. I'm sorry, Alowan."

"Not half as sorry as the young man is going to be," the healer replied grimly. "I am not much of a poison smith," he added. "And the study of poisons and toxins is an entire branch of the healing art." He drew a breath, exhaled forcefully, and then looked down at the unconscious man. "But I am all that you have, and I will do the best that I can."

He looked up as he finished speaking, and met the anxious Lord Elseth's eyes. "You may sit by me if you wish, but these others must clear the room."

"That's not possible," Devon began, speaking as gently as he could.

Alowan raised a lined palm, cutting off the rest of the sentence. "That wasn't a request, Devon. It was an order."

The guards were silent, as speechless as Devon was. Before they could find words, Lord Elseth had risen, and the dogs that sat at his feet rose also, in a single, almost eerie motion.

Devon was angry; it would have been obvious to any who knew him well. There were very few who did. He smiled smoothly. "Gregor, have the Kings' Swords double their contingent on the other side of these doors—and have them patrol the windows on the outside."

"Sir."

"The girl will have to—"

"The girl will remain with us," Lord Elseth said curtly.

Devon looked askance at Alowan, an open request for permission that a man of his rank did not normally make. Alowan, hands already on Stephen's bare chest, examined the girl closely and then, eyes flickering back to Lord Elseth, nodded almost grimly. "Go," he said, in an almost whisper.

Everyone who had not made the journey from Breodanir left the healer-born's side.

*　　*　　*

Devon repaired to the offices of the Royal Treasurer as quickly as decorum allowed. Gregor would return to him after the last of the tasks he'd assigned had been completed, but for the moment he was quite alone. He was glad for the lack of company, although even in isolation he was careful not to reveal too much of what he felt.

It was a trait that was being sorely tested.

The demon's body was gone; nothing short of summoning one of the Magi using the emergency protocols could prevent it from disintegrating—and Devon had no desire to summon any more of the Magi than were already involved in this affair.

The demon's ally had been badly savaged by the dogs. Devon had seen many different deaths before, but few quite so unpleasant. He wondered at these Western lords—for Lord Elseth not only seemed unconcerned, but even satisfied, at the man's grisly death. It was a type of savagery that Devon identified with the worst of the Southerners; he had not thought to see it in the heart of Essalieyan, so close to the court of the Kings.

But it was not just that that bothered him, for he was a pragmatic man; any of the Kings' Swords and any of the Astari would have thought first of capturing and containing the man for future questioning, regardless of where their personal preferences lay. Questioning a corpse offered very little in the way of satisfaction. For most men, it offered nothing.

But Devon knew from the markings around the man's wrists—faint and pale with time—that he was from the South. In and of itself that wasn't surprising; the Arannan Halls were used to house visitors—even those on extended stay—from the Dominion of Annagar, and where possible, it was staffed with Annagarians or those of Annagarian descent. He also knew that the man was not one of those servants.

But there was no telltale mark to give Devon proof of what he suspected, or if there had been, the dogs had savaged it into nonexistence. And without proof, he did not wish to raise the specter of the Allasakari among the Astari until he knew for certain that the Astari had not been infiltrated. Information was valuable; why give warning, where warning might serve an enemy?

Oh, he cursed, but silently, as he muttered a very real prayer to the fathers of the kingdom for the life of a lone Breodanir huntbrother. He sat back in his chair, surrounded by the trappings of a normal day, and began to formulate his report.

Stephen woke with a start to see an old man leaning against his chest. His mouth was dry and an odd, bitter taste lingered along his tongue.

"I told you," Gilliam said softly, and the old man's eyes opened slowly.

Stephen had never met one healer-born who did not wear the vestments of the Mother; he blinked at the lamp that the old man seemed to pull from nowhere as light shone off the golden emblem of twin palms. "Open your eyes, Stephen," the man said gruffly. "We're both tired, even exhausted—but I can't leave until I'm satisfied that you're safe."

Stephen nodded absently. He tried to remember how he'd arrived in this bed, but the memories were fuzzy and distant. He began to sit up and then stopped as a sharp pain in his shoulder buckled the length of his arm.

"Take his care," Alowan said softly to the Lord Elseth.

"I will." The Hunter Lord offered his arm to the old healer, and the old healer took it, unaware of the import of the gesture to Gilliam. "I owe you a debt," Gilliam said. "And if you call upon it, I will repay it."

Alowan's smile was tired. "I know," he said.

But once he'd left the room, he let his curiosity begin to really bubble beneath the placid surface of his expression. He had feared another near-death—and he was still recovering from the shock of the last call to life; Stephen had, in fact, presented no such dilemma. Rather, he seemed victim of both drug and magics in a very dangerous and unique combination—at least unique in Alowan's experience.

He was not dead so much as suspended, and in the end, that suspension was not proof against the healer's skill. Using a poison, for want of a better word, that was so easily dispelled by a healer's touch made no sense at all. There were no healers within immediate reach—but there were three that worked very closely with the Kings, the Queens, and the Princes, and not a single one of them would have mistaken that state for death once they'd begun the full examination.

And why magic?

Ah, too many questions for an old man.

He was troubled as he hurried down the long halls. It was dark; the carriage was waiting for the end of his task, and he would report to the Terafin upon his arrival at her estates. He had but to reach it, and he would be safe from political turmoil and the tensions that occasionally reared their heads in even the most stable of The Ten families.

Devon ATerafin was waiting for him in the shadowed open-air alcove that was the last hurdle. "Alowan," he said, as he stepped forward, blocking the way in such a genial fashion that it was impossible to see a threat in the motion. "I hear that I have much to thank you for."

"To thank The Terafin for," was the gruff reply. "And she's waiting for me."

"I don't mean to keep you from your carriage," Devon replied. "Let me walk with you." He fell gracefully into step beside Alowan; really, the comparison between their strides made the older man feel almost a mountebank. "You did well for a healer not schooled in poison arts."

Alowan nodded.

"What was the poison, or what was its family?"

"Simple enough," Alowan said, between pursed lips. "A heart medicine, common and of some beneficence when taken in the right time and the right season."

"I see. The name?"

"I don't remember it," Alowan said, and this at least was true. "But he'll be up and around by tomorrow; possibly by this evening if you've need of him. He will not be good for strenuous physical activity; his shoulder's stiff and will take more time to recover. Given the nature of the current difficulties, I did not think it wise to spend myself when I do not know how soon the next emergency will be."

Devon nodded; it made sense. But Alowan did not like the slight narrowing of eyes and subtle shift of lips that Devon displayed. Devon started to speak, and then fell silent. "Give The Terafin my personal thanks for the service you have rendered to the Crowns."

"I will, Patris." Alowan sighed inwardly. "And I will return in two days' time to see my patient once more."

Chapter Eleven

ZARETH KAHN WAS a pale and unbecoming shade of green when he stepped out of the golden circle onto the hard, polished wood. He saw his reflection, saw it waver, and saw—although it took him time to comprehend exactly why—its sudden approach.

Elodra Carlsenn caught his shoulders with the flats of two braced palms, easing his rapid descent. "You'd have to be face forward," he grunted.

Jareme Margon laughed, stepping into the range of Zareth Kahn's peripheral vision; he was dowdily dressed but handsome as always. He was a member of the mages' school because his curiosity, when it caught him, drove him hard. Unfortunately, he was adept at not being so caught; Jareme defined the word lazy. "He couldn't be guaranteed that you'd try to catch him if the only thing at risk was his thick skull."

Their voices were comforting, familiar, and slightly distant, the aftereffects of a spell woven by the combined powers of four members of Averalaan's Order. Four members, and the power of circles that had been carved into stone and wood by an Artisan whose name was history.

"Zar?" Sela stepped forward last as Elodra propped him up and skillfully wound an arm beneath his arms and behind his back. "You look awful."

"And you, Sela Mattson, look wonderful." He would have kissed her hand at the very least—although she hated the gesture—but he didn't have the energy to lift his own.

"We'd word that you were coming. It came half an hour ago through the crystal relays; nearly scorched the mirrored surfaces. I'd guess some first circle mage condescended to pass it on, with more thought to speed and less to power level. What's going on in the capital?"

"I'm not sure how much I'm allowed to tell you," he said stiffly. His lips felt numb. "But Matteos has sent the fire-mages out after Krysanthos."

Sela and Jareme exchanged a wary glance.

"What?"

"We've a missive from the Queen's representative."

"A message?"

"A missive. You'll want to read it yourself."

He doubted it. "Well, it won't be my problem for the foreseeable future." Straightening out as much as he could, while still leaning against Elodra, he pulled a creased scroll out of the length of his sleeve. "Elodra."

The slender lines of Elodra's brow drew up in suspicion. Suspicion which, quite frankly, was well-deserved.

"You're going to have to take it," Zareth Kahn said. "It's council writ."

"Elodra?" Jareme said, his voice rising on the last syllable as the member of the Order stared uneasily at Zareth Kahn's offering.

"Leave him be," Sela said. "He knows what it is, and if you'd half a brain, you'd know it as well."

Elodra Carlsenn straightened out a shoulder—the one against which Zareth Kahn wasn't leaning—and accepted the weight of the Magi's writ. "They've made me Master, haven't they?"

"Of the college in Breodanir, yes."

"But I'm not—but you're—"

"Zoraban wasn't either. Apparently, second circle mages of my age and dignity have a very good chance of achieving first circle if not bothered by the day-to-day travail of keeping an Order in one piece." He smiled grimly. "And look what happened to the only other second circle mage that Breodanir boasted."

Elodra swallowed. "But I *hate* speaking to the Queen," he said softly, to no one in particular.

"She won't bite," Sela said, smiling broadly. "Well, all right. She might a bit—but she's reason for it. Elodra, you *know* this is perfect, both for you and for the Order here. There isn't another man who could pull us out of this mess. Or any other mess, for that matter."

"Wonderful. So instead of finally forcing the lot of you to become independent, responsible human beings, I'm forced to give in and take over."

"It's not," Zareth Kahn said politely, "as if you don't already pursue that course. Can we move? My legs are about to collapse."

It was not just as messenger, or even diplomat, that Zareth Kahn was returned in such haste to Breodanir's lesser Order. He was a second circle mage, and his specialty was in the gathering of information. In a month—if, he thought grimly, they had a month—his brethren from Averalaan would join him in greater numbers. Krysanthos had dwelled a decade and more in the Western Kingdom of Breodanir. Evidence of his life, his dual life, lay waiting to be uncovered.

Or so Zareth would have said. But Krysanthos was a man who had hidden his arts and his practice for a long time against the admittedly poor vigilance of the

Order. Had he time to prepare? Had he known that he might fail in his assassination attempt at the Elseth preserve? Zareth Kahn thought it unlikely, for Krysanthos had always been an arrogant man. But he'd always been a cunning one as well.

The evening of his arrival in Breodanir, Sela quietly led him to the chambers of the Order which Krysanthos habitually occupied. Her demeanor was the only warning she gave of what he would find within; charred stone, ashes, shards of broken glass. Of his books and papers, very little remained, although evidence of ruined leather bindings that had been spell-protected lay fragmented among the ashes.

He hoped the Order's mages were up to the task of reconstructing.

4th Corvil, 410 A.A.
Averalaan, Senniel College

"Kallandras, are you all right?"

"I—y-yes," the golden-haired bard replied, with about as little conviction as Sioban had ever heard him use. His face was twisted in a momentary grimace, as if a spasm of extreme pain had unexpectedly come upon him; he used his long, golden curls as a curtain.

Sioban, her own hair peppered with time and drawn back in an unruly bundle, shook her head slowly to indicate her lack of belief. "What happened?" She straightened up, pulling her elbows from their perch on the sea-facing wall of Senniel College. The wind was heavy with the tang of salt; it was a brisk day, if a warm one. "Kallandras?"

Kallandras shook his head; his face was the white-gray of ash. He bowed, low and stiff, and then leaned onto the stone tops of the wall as if by doing so he could avoid her scrutiny. Sioban Glassen was a stern woman, the Master of Senniel, but also a very patrician mother figure for at least half the college. It was rumored—although she denied the rumors strenuously and severely when some youngling had the temerity to ask about them to her face—that she had served in the Kings' army during the skirmishes with the Dominion of Annagar; if she had, Kallandras was certain that it was as the representative of the magisterial courts. She had the voice and the demeanor for it.

He took a breath, and then another one, filling his lungs with the wet air and his mouth with the aftertaste of salt. Many argued that Senniel was not ideally positioned for the training and care of young vocal cords, but few indeed were those who, when offered a post or position at Senniel, refused it.

Senniel had been his home for the last ten years, and Sioban had been bard-master for all of them. He doubted that there would ever be another Master of Senniel; she seemed part of the pillars and foundations that stretched from the vaults to the heights.

"Kallandras, I asked you a question."

"I—had a momentary cramp," he replied.

She snorted. "I've seen you break your arm without grunting, young man. I don't appreciate a lie, and I've half a mind to speak the truth out of you."

He didn't even stiffen; he knew it for the hollow threat it was. Not that she couldn't do it had she the mind to, for although not all bards were talent-born, Sioban was. She had the voice—he had heard her use it precisely once—but he wasn't certain how strong the gift was.

At the moment, he didn't care.

The sea shifted along the horizon like murky water in the grand aquariums of the Royal zoo. He tried to grip the stone beneath his hands and felt it, hard and cold, refuse his hold.

"Kallandras!"

Her voice was in his ear, beside his face; her arms were around his chest. He felt them, but they were distant.

The screams were not.

She could not hear them; no one who had not been trained by and bound to the Kovaschaii could. But the dead were calling in pain and isolation, and somehow, for reasons that he did not understand, his brothers were not responding.

"Kallandras, go to the healerie. No, never mind. Amerin! Come, bring Tallos with you!"

The echoes of the screaming died; he took a deep breath and pulled himself away from the Master's awkward embrace.

"Stay where you are, Kallandras."

"I'm—fine," he forced out.

"The Hells you are." She looked past his shoulder at the sound of running feet; there were two, one heavy tread and one light. "Good. Help me with him."

"Amerin—"

"Shut up, Kal. Don't argue with the Master." A red-haired man six years Kallandras' senior caught his left arm; a dark-haired older master caught his right.

"Well, he's not feverish," Master Tallos said gruffly. "Out a little late last night, eh?" Then his eyes narrowed. "It's Kallandras, isn't it?"

"It is indeed Kallandras, as you well know," Sioban said curtly. "I wish him taken to the infirmary. I will be down shortly to see what the physicians have to say."

Both Amerin and Tallos nodded in unison at the commands of the Master of the college.

Kallandras did not argue further. Instead, he suffered himself to be steadied— to be almost lifted—and led away from the wall.

Kallandras was a mystery, and Sioban was too old to be attracted to the mysterious. She was, however, the bardmaster of Senniel, and it was her responsibility to

see that the college ran both safely and securely. It was Sioban who had first inter-
viewed young Kallandras when he was brought to the college, and it was Sioban
who decided that, past unknown, she would accept his word of honor that that
past posed no threat to her or her Order and allow him to take one of Senniel's
coveted positions as a student.

There was, of course, minor outrage, for Kallandras was considered young.
That outrage was both calmed and further incited—depending on which master
it was who had originally raised the uproar—when Kallandras proved an adept
and able student with concentration enough for five students his age and an ability
to remember that even Sioban found difficult to believe. Such focus, and in such a
seemingly normal youth was unheard of, but it was his song, his voice, that truly
made him special.

He was bard-born, there was no doubt of it.

He had graduated from the ranks of the applicant to the apprentice, and from
there, in six short months, to journeyman. He had traveled for a year each with
Amerin and Sorrel, and then, at the end of that second year, he had again outraged the masters of the college by taking the bardic challenge. He had emerged,
if not unscathed, as a bard.

It had not come as a surprise to Sioban.

If Kallandras sang it right, she was certain that he could call down the wind
and the rain from the heavens itself—that the Gods who were listening, who *must*
listen to such a voice, would grant him their blessing and their boon.

She shook her head, wondering if she had ever had that effect on those with the
ear to hear it. She wiped a tear from the corner of her eye, thinking herself maud-
lin, but not particularly embarrassed to be so. Kallandras was all angry youth,
and his song spoke to the heart, but there was little joy in it yet. She hoped that
one day, that would change.

Ah, but that was a matter of song, and this a matter of the college. *What are
your secrets, Kallandras?* She rose. As a bard, she knew how to listen, and in his
voice, in the few words that he had spoken as he began his collapse, she could hear
a horror so strong it had shaken her.

She was not a woman who liked to be shaken.

The screams returned, and in them, wordless, was the pain of a betrayal so vast
that it made Kallandras feel—for perhaps the only time since his desertion—that
his own crime had been paltry. He started to rise, and the glowering man beside
the pallet caught his chest with the flats of both palms and pushed him back.

It was the physician Hallorn, a man with the right disposition for a cook in a
very fine house. "This is the last warning you get, Kallandras. You *lie back*, or I'll
have you strapped down. Do I make myself clear?" His face was ruddy, and seemed
sweat-dampened; the lines in his brow were deeper and darker than usual.

Kallandras nodded, but the nod did not appear to placate Hallorn. He wasn't certain why; although Hallorn was known for his temperament, he was not often angry at the college's youngest bard.

He closed his eyes a moment, and then opened them again; he could hear them, distant now, although he was not certain they would stay that way. There were two voices; it was hard to identify them because they were so distorted in their despair and anger. But he knew why they were screaming.

They had died, but the dance was undanced; their bodies had failed, but their spirits, by compact, were trapped. The Lady could not come to them, come for them.

That will be me. He shuddered and then turned away from the thought as the screaming grew louder and more pained, calling all of his attention.

"That's it!"

It was Hallorn, and the voice was a rumbling growl. He felt arms against his chest; he stiffened in preparation for defense before he remembered where he was. Who he was, now.

"What are you trying to do?" It was not the physician's voice.

Free them, Kallandras almost replied. But he did not and would not. These were the rites of the brothers who had once been his, and whom he loved above all else, even dishonored as he was. He would not share them with any outsider.

But it was hard; the screaming grew, and try as he might, he could not feel the direction that it came from; could not *see*—as he had seen at every other death since his joining—the place of death. *Oh, my brothers.*

"Well?" Sioban's voice was about as soft as the rounded curve of her lute.

"I don't know." Hallorn, wearing the lines of years of service quite heavily at this moment, shook his head. "We had to restrain him; he's been in some sort of delirium. But it's not one I've encountered before—there's no fever, no vomiting, no widening of the pupils—nothing." He wiped his forehead with a rough cotton cloth, and then dipped it in warm water and began to wash his face down.

"Do you think it's magical in nature?"

Hallorn raised a dark brow and then turned to look at his patient. Kallandras slept, but the sleep was almost violently fitful. "I'm not of the mage-born," he replied at last, but with some reluctance. "I wouldn't recognize magic if it *had* been used. But if what you're asking is, are these the mage-fevers, than the answer is definitely no."

"What can we do for him?"

"We've got something that'll dull the senses some—but we don't usually give it unless someone's in great pain."

"He is," she said softly. "Go ahead."

He shrugged. Hallorn was not a physician who liked to overuse the herbalists, and she could hear his reluctance in every word that he spoke. That was right, and as it should be in a man of Hallorn's care and fastidiousness. She, on the other hand, felt no reluctance whatsoever. "How long?"

"How long until what?"

"Until it starts to have an effect?"

"It depends on the person," he said, and then, seeing her face darken, added, "probably an hour. Maybe half that."

"Good." She pulled up a chair—one of two, and at that, a rather rickety one—and took a seat beside the door. "I'll wait."

"So I gathered."

"Kallandras."

He opened his eyes. His tongue felt heavy in his mouth, but the voices were almost a whisper. If he tried, he could ignore them. He wanted to try, but it was too much of a betrayal. There were straps around his arms, his chest, and his thighs. He raised his head and saw his body as if it were someone else's.

"Kallandras, be still."

He nodded, groggy, and sank back into the pallet. There was something running through his system, some hint of heaviness or wrongness.

"We've given you seablossom," Sioban said, as if reading his thoughts. "You've been delirious, but it's not something Hallorn recognized. There isn't," she added, "much that Hallorn doesn't recognize."

Seablossom. *Niscea.* "Can I sit up?"

She watched his face for a moment, as if waiting for something to happen; when it didn't, she nodded and began to unbuckle the straps that Hallorn had, with such difficulty, put in place.

He sat, hating the sense of fuzziness, of heaviness—of otherness—but knowing that it was the seablossom that kept the pain at bay. Wary, he watched her as she watched him, aware that his facial expressions were on the outer edge of his control.

"What's wrong?" It was a question, but there was a demand in it.

Kallandras knew that she could hear the lie in his words, and without the screaming, without the viscerality of fear and the blind need to find and aid the helpless, he could think clearly enough that he had no desire to make the attempt. He said nothing.

Sioban waited. And waited. And waited. Finally she spoke. "We can't help you if you don't tell us what the problem is."

"I know."

"This has something to do with your past, doesn't it?"

He did not reply.

"Kallandras, you—"

"Bardmaster?"

Sioban turned toward the door; it was ajar, and the head of a young applicant peered around its edge. "Yes?" she said, in a tone that made it clear that she did not appreciate the interruption.

"There's someone here to see Kallandras."

"Oh?"

"Y-yes, Bardmaster."

"Kallandras is indisposed at the moment; I don't believe he's expecting visitors."

The young face paled but nodded and disappeared. The door closed quickly in its wake. "Good. Now we—" She stopped speaking as the door opened again. "Courtney," she said, in as severe a tone as she ever used.

"I'm afraid he's gone back to his tasks," was the reply.

Sioban turned at the sound of a stranger's voice, and saw a woman in long, midnight-blue robes. Her face was hidden, but her hands were not; they were smooth but strong; the hands of a woman in her prime, not her youth.

Kallandras smiled, but the smile was peculiarly bitter. "Hello, Evayne," he said softly.

"I cannot stay," she said at once, as she pulled the hood from her face, ignoring the bardmaster. She was thirty-five, he thought, or maybe a little older; her forehead already had soft lines, and her cheeks seemed hollow or shadowed. Her violet eyes were darkened. "I heard that you were unwell."

He said nothing, his lips turning down in the subtle scowl with which she—at any age—was familiar. She turned to the silent older woman who sat by Kallandras' side.

"Bardmaster, I believe?"

"Sioban Glassen," the bardmaster replied, speaking through slightly clenched teeth.

"We must speak alone for a moment, Kallandras and I."

Sioban glanced at Kallandras, surprised at the expression on his face; his lip was curled slightly, and his eyes narrowed enough it seemed his lashes might touch. In anyone else, the expression might be one of irritation, or even momentary anger—but coming from Kallandras, Sioban knew it for the open hostility that it was. Certainly very little provoked that reaction from him; she could not, offhand, recall a single other occasion. There was a song here, but it was probably an evening's work, and at that, one which required multiple voices.

"Kallandras?" Sioban said, although she thought she knew his answer.

"I'll speak with her," he said at last.

Sioban nodded curtly. She wanted to warn Evayne not to exhaust him or otherwise cause his condition to worsen, but she didn't want to reveal something that

Kallandras might consider personal or private. Instead, she stopped in front of the shorter woman and met her gaze, brown eyes against violet. She took her measure in that glance and was unsettled, although she couldn't have said why.

But she left them alone.

"Why are you here, Evayne?"

"I don't know," she replied, coming to sit by his side in the chair that the bard-master had vacated. Her robes eddied and then settled into perfect folds in her lap. "But Stephen of Elseth is now in Averalaan. The year is 410. Kallandras, do you have the spear?"

The bard started and then relaxed. "Yes. She brought it to me. The wild one."

"Good."

"Why?"

"I believe—although I am not certain—that you will have to deliver that spear to either Stephen or his Hunter Lord Gilliam."

"Stephen is the boy you sent me to protect."

"He is no more a boy," she replied gravely, "than you."

He nodded and then closed his eyes; his equilibrium had been damaged by the mixture that Hallorn had given him.

"Kallandras?"

"I am well," he replied, without opening his eyes. "Where is Stephen?"

"I believe he is at the court of the Twin Kings."

Kallandras gagged and then forced his body to bend to his control as it almost always did. He was fighting the effects of the brew, or rather, his body was; his mind knew that without it, he might not be able to function.

What happens to the rest of my brothers? he thought. *What happens to those who are already on the Lady's mission?* The answer was horrible to contemplate, but the Kovaschaii did not flinch from horror. Or at least, Kallandras reflected bitterly, he did not.

If he could find them . . . if he could simply *see* . . .

He opened his eyes suddenly and met Evayne's. They were guarded, as they always were in his presence. He started to speak and then fell silent; three times he opened his lips, and three times, the words would not come.

The screams, dim and distant, came instead. And, as before when he hovered on the brink of the choice that she had given him, he could not simply listen passively; he could not let his brothers suffer and die, even if to save them was to betray their edicts. He stared at her; she was perhaps ten years older than he at the moment, and more peaceful for the years.

I left my brothers for you, he thought bitterly. *What is one more betrayal?*

"Evayne, I have given you obedience, and I have served you in all things as you have requested since you first found me."

She nodded, waiting. Unlike Sioban, her wait was not in vain.

"I have asked you for nothing; I have done what *must* be done, measure for measure. If you walk your road alone, you have condemned me to walk mine in loneliness."

She nodded again.

"But now, I wish a return for my efforts. I wish you to tender a service to me."

She was tense, as he spoke, and that tension seemed to tighten her and hold her in place. "What would that be?"

"I need the aid of the vision that you were born to."

"Why?" One of the things he most hated about Evayne was the neutrality of her voice. Only young, with anger and pain, was it easy to read what she felt in her tone.

He swallowed.

He was surprised when she met him halfway. She reached into her robes; they parted for her, showing him a glimpse of silvered shadow. The light came out of shadow into her hands, turning into crystal-encased mist—the seer's crystal. With care, she settled the ball between her cupped palms and waited; her robes settled back into the folds that gravity—and not magic—decreed.

"Two of my brothers have been killed." He spoke quickly and then looked away. She had always been an ally, but a hated one, someone whose presence he bore out of necessity and a greater sense of duty. He, who needed no one but the Kovaschaii, had asked for aid from no one when his brothers had been forever denied him. Until now. "I wish you to find their bodies."

"I am not certain," she said, in an even tone, "that it is possible for me to do what you ask. My—my vision does not work on demand, Kallandras; what the crystal reveals is, in a way, part of me."

He was bitterly disappointed, and turned from her; he did not doubt her words, for he had never known her to lie to him.

"Wait," she said, and touched his shoulder with the curve of the glass. She flinched as he did; for a moment, they were almost reflections of each other. "If you—if you will tell me more, if you will touch the ball—if you will take the risk that I will see too much of you—" She pulled the crystal's surface away, and Kallandras was surprised at how cool the air against his skin was in its absence.

"And how much," he asked her bitterly, "will I see of you?"

"More than you ever wanted, if you choose to look." She held up the ball, and her eyes were very dark as she looked above its perfect surface to meet his.

He was not—had never been—stupid; he understood then that the risk she took was in some ways greater than his own—for he was cruel, and knew it. His cruelty, subtle and quiet, had only been reined in because he did not know how to hurt her. Did not know if he could ever hurt her as she had hurt him by forcing him to help her in her fight against the unnamed.

She waited, neutral and impassive, the sphere between her hands.

"Why are you doing this?" he asked at last, as he placed both hands across the warmth of the crystal. The sensation was profoundly disturbing; it was as if, for a moment, he had reached not crystal but something that existed beneath skin and bone and flesh. A heart. It pulsed in his hands.

"I am doing this," she replied, "because you asked. You only ever had to ask."

"Not true."

Her smile was a rare and genuine one. "No, then—I was young and far more angry, I think, than you know. But save for that first year it has been true."

"Do you know why I hate you?"

"I know." He watched the muscles in her forearms cord as she forced her hands to hold the crystal sphere where he could reach it. "But speak not of hate if you wish to aid your brothers. Tell me, Kallandras. Tell me of the Kovaschaii."

Silence then. The sound of three hearts; hers, his, and the sphere that lay between them, a bridge across the abyss. He did not want to tell her what she needed to know.

"I am of the Kovaschaii." He spoke without inflection, as if the words were too brittle to contain real emotion. "I was raised by them. I grew up in the labyrinths of Melesnea, learning the rituals of the naming, the killing, and the dance." He had desired little else for almost ten years, but to speak of it openly was wrong; he lifted his hands and his fingers fluttered a moment, like trapped butterflies, before he once again touched the crystal.

"I was bard-born, although they did not know it immediately. I came to the talent late in my training; I was small and grew slowly for my age.

"I learned to kill. Is that what you want to know? I learned how to kill quickly, and how to kill slowly, and how to kill secretly." His eyes narrowed as he studied her face; it was still and perfectly composed. He wondered if she was listening, and it stung although he could not say why. But he continued to speak. "We did not practice on our kin, or even upon the unchosen; the blooding and the death are sacred to our Lady, and all death is upon her altar.

"What life did you lead, Evayne? For I led the life of a brother. We ate together and drank together and practiced our rituals in the secrecy of the world that we created. While others were dreaming of love and work and a home, I was dreaming of the dance and the death, of the approbation of the Kovaschaii." He dreamed of it still, and once again his fingers convulsed as if they had a life of their own. *Are you listening, my brothers? Can you hear the wrong I do?*

"We are the servants of the Lady. We do not kill unless she blesses the killing: she chooses those deaths that she will accept." He closed his eyes and he did pull away, covering his face. "She chose yours."

"And perhaps one day you will give it to her."

He laughed bitterly, aware that in doing so he told her more than he usually did. "I will not kill you, Evayne; the time has passed." Swallowing, he forced himself to touch and speak again.

"We join the brotherhood when we complete our first mission in the Lady's name. She accepts us and anoints us, and we are suddenly linked or bound or woven into the very heart of the Kovaschaii; it is as if we become part of a single spirit. We know who our brothers are; we know them by more than sight.

"I'm sorry. What was I saying? Ah. That the Lady accepts us and anoints us and binds us. But the bonds are stronger than life or death, and when our bodies fail, or if we are killed on her mission, our souls do not leave.

"The threads she has woven with, only she can break. We *know* when a brother dies. We feel it, or see it, if we are close enough. And we go to the fallen, and about the fallen we perform her rituals.

"And then we dance the death. And when we dance it well enough, the Lady hears us and she comes. Only when she comes is the brother finally free."

For the first time since he had started his halting speech, Evayne spoke. "And you are still a part of the Kovaschaii."

"Yes."

"And when you die?"

He did not answer, but it was answer enough.

She stared at him, and her eyes were slightly rounded; she was shocked or surprised; he had achieved at least that much.

But it was not to do either that he had asked for her aid. He swallowed. "I can hear them, Evayne; I do not know how long it has been since their fall—but I did not *feel* the death. They have been trapped, and isolated; they are not part of us, but not free. They have been betrayed by the Kovaschaii—and that is not possible."

"You said you can hear them?"

"I—can."

"Then listen to them, Kallandras; listen, but do not lift your hands."

He did as she asked; he found it almost easy to follow orders. It was the drug, he told himself. But the crystal was warm beneath his hands, and as he opened himself up to the cries of the betrayed, he held the round surface as if he had never known warmth until he touched it.

They were crying now, with the wild anger that comes only from the deepest of wounds. He listened, trying to reach them; trying to find a voice with which to make himself heard. *Where are you? Where are you, my brothers? We are coming! We are searching!*

He opened his eyes and the light streamed in, hurting him. Tears ran down his cheeks as he stared at the seeress. She stared back, and he saw his own tears shining along her cheeks. "I'm sorry, Kallandras," she said, and her voice was shaky. "But I—I cannot see them."

The hope fled; his mouth became suddenly dry. "What do you mean?"

"I—I don't understand it. I should be able to find something—the connection between you is strong—but there's only darkness. There's nothing at all that I can see."

She rose and pulled the ball back to her chest as if to absorb it. Her face was pale. The neutrality was gone, and in its wake were guilt and confusion. She smoothed these from her expression, but it took time, and Kallandras still saw the traces of it in her eyes.

And then he, too, rose. Nausea pulled him floorward, but he held himself steady, fighting it. When the sensation had dimmed, Evayne was gone.

He did not know how he felt, and that was curious. A day ago, he would have been happy, because he knew that she was suffering for her failure.

And he knew that she had not failed. He wondered if he would have explained it had she lingered—if he would have attempted to ease her of her guilt. He did not wonder long. Instead, he began to make plans; he had to visit the court of the Twin Kings and seek out Lord Elseth and his huntbrother.

Which was the only thing that would be easy; his services had already been requested by the younger of the Queens—Queen Siodonay the Fair—at any time of his convenience; she was a bright and sunny woman with a hint of the bardic about her, and he was one of the few youthful things with which she surrounded herself.

Hands shaking, he rose; if he wished to attend court, he must send word, for even if one was favored, one did not presume overmuch upon the grace of a monarch.

4th Corvil, 410 A.A.
Breodanir, King's City

The glass shards were magicked, although they did not shine under the first of the three spells he chose to sweep over the remnants of Krysanthos' chambers. He might never have known their nature, except that the young men that Sela sent—juniors in every sense of the word, were overzealous in their attempts to categorize everything they stumbled over with their cloddish feet. One boy, Zepharim, cut his palm upon a long and slender sliver.

It had been a fight to preserve his life.

Vivienne, the much called and underappreciated Priestess of the Mother, came at once, and worked long into the night. Her hair had silvered with the events of the last year, but her face was fine and strong, and her eyes, golden, shone brighter than they ever had as she pursued her life's work. The Order's doctor had suggested amputation as a recourse; it was not done, much to the Priestess' relief.

"This is not glass," she told Zareth Kahn darkly, standing in front of the pile of splinters and shards that he now kept under magical confinement.

"What is it?"

"I would say—although I know it to be impossible—that it is very much alive. Dormant, as you see it now. I don't know what it was."

"I do," Sela said, her voice muted. "Vivienne—will you keep these events to yourself?"

"I have always," was the wry reply, "been a trusted confidante. And I have no great desire to see panic or fear among the people of my city."

"It was his mirror. He traveled with it almost everywhere. I thought him vain, but it was a fine, perfect surface."

"Oh?"

She blushed. "I remember thinking it maker-made because there was absolutely no distortion in the image it reflected. I assume he kept it with him because he could not—on his stipend—ever afford to replace it if it were broken or stolen." She grimaced. "That, and he was not averse to his reflection."

He would have waited for the mages from Averalaan. In truth, he looked forward to their arrival—for Breodanir had become his territory, and he felt, although he would have been loath to admit it, much at home there.

But *she* came, although it would be the last time for many a year that he would see her shadowed face. He lay in the shadows, and she stood wreathed in them. But it did not seem strange to him that she should arrive so.

"You are not sleeping," she said softly.

"No." He paused. "Nor you."

Her hood was low; he thought he saw the flicker of a smile across her lips, but he could not be certain. A smile was often a thing the eyes did, and her eyes, violet and strange, were well hidden. "I was not sent from Averalaan in such short order, at such a late hour."

"It wasn't my magic."

"No."

Silence. He was not certain if he dealt with the older or the younger woman; her voice was inflectionless and gave little away. Almost, he thought, as if she had no memory of their travels together—as if he were a stranger, or a near stranger. He did not ask. Instead, he said, "Why have you come?"

"To tell you—to ask you—to leave the Order. You will be wanted in Averalaan Aramarelas when the year is out."

He rose, casting just enough light to see by. "Why?"

"If I could tell you that, mage, I would, and be done. But I cannot. I ask it as a favor; there will be no earth-shattering consequences should you choose to deny the request. But I offer you information in return for this service."

"Information?"

She said nothing, waiting.

And he knew that he had responsibilities that should keep him in the King's City for months to come yet. But he thought he heard something beneath the smooth words that troubled him.

"Evayne," he said, calling her by name for the first time, as if she, like a demon or the First-born of old, could somehow be bound by the word.

"Yes?"

"Does this have something to do with Lord Elseth and his huntbrother?"

Her silence was long. When at last she broke it, she did not answer his question. Not directly. Instead, she said, "When you walk the road to Averalaan, please stop a moment at the eastern borders of Breodanir. Speak with Lady Elseth. Tell her of your travels, and the fate of her two sons."

It surprised him, although later he would realize it for the answer that it was. "All of it?"

"All of it. She is not a fool, and not a girl; let her understand that her sons have left her for no small reason."

"She knows it now," he said dryly, touching his shoulder as if the wound still stung.

"She knows it," was the quiet reply. "But time and fear erode the certainty of the feeling—and will erode it further ere the end. Tell her; you are good with words, and you have fought for your lives together. She will listen."

He nodded, then, thinking it wise for the Order's sake. Lady Elseth, of the Breodani, had been the noble wronged by the actions of the renegade mage. He took a breath, and silently began to enumerate the items that he would require in his travels.

"Zareth Kahn, your part in this game is at an end. What the mages seek here, they will find with or without your aid."

"Or they will not find, as the case may be."

She said nothing.

"I will travel as you request. But the information—I will require it as proof that this journey was undertaken as a method of barter, and not dereliction of duty."

"As you will. The shards of glass and splinters of wood that you have so carefully gathered are the physical body of one of the demon-kin. Blood will wake it, and the correct spell; nothing else." She turned from him. "It was a mirror, but more; it could speak directly to its master, no matter the intervening distance."

Chapter Twelve

T HE NIGHT WAS DARK, and the walls of The Terafin's manse were far enough away that they receded into shadow. Jewel sat up in bed, staring blindly ahead as she swallowed air and waited for her heart to stop hammering.

It was the nightmare again.

Ever since she'd made it out of the twenty-fifth with her den, all her dead came to haunt her. They walked, wounded and desecrated corpses, circling her in a silence heavy with accusation. They rose from the ground, pushing themselves toward her with unnatural strength through the tiled floors of the halls that she ran in. The grim relief of stone men, with their forbidding weapons raised and readied were her only companions as she fled. She could speak, but her dead kin did not answer, and if they had, she was certain she wouldn't like what they said.

She covered her face with her hands, and then reached down and used a corner of a sheet to wipe her forehead. She was sweating.

She didn't share her room with anyone—and that had seemed a luxury and a privilege when she'd first learned of it. But now, with only the sound of her breathing—breath too quick and too harsh—for company, she regretted it. She'd always had nightmares, and they'd always been bad. But when she'd been crammed into two-and-a-half rooms with the rest of her den, she'd always woken to the safety of their sleeping numbers. To the certainty that they were still alive, still there.

It's only a dream, she told herself, swallowing. *It doesn't mean anything.*

Yet.

She knew she wasn't going to sleep, although she tried for a while anyway before she gave up and slid out of bed. She needed space to stretch her legs, time to think, some company to help her escape Duster, Lander, Lefty, and Fisher. Ellerson was, thankfully, nowhere in evidence. She skirted the walls, keeping her touch light and sure; she knew the wing well enough by now that she could navigate it in the dark without tripping over every little table, chair, or stool. She only stopped once, outside of Arann's door, to whisper a little prayer to the Mother for his safety. The healer had said he'd recover, and she trusted him—but her den-kin wasn't the Arann she knew. Not yet.

It was strange. This big, old building was like a holding unto itself, with its multiple stories and half-levels. As far as she could tell, every wing that was like hers—and there were six in total—had its own kitchen, its own servants, and its own small courtyard. Ellerson told her that she had one of four "proper" baths; he was quite proud of it, although she didn't understand why.

Tonight, with the ghosts of the dead slow to fade, she didn't really care. She wandered the halls, seeing the occasional servant and the occasional pair of guards; she walked between pillars that were taller than any building she had ever lived in save this one; listened to the echo of her steps across wide courtyards; dropped the odd flat stone into the elaborate fountains that appeared in small alcoves throughout the first and second stories of the mansion.

Then, unsatisfied, she made her way outside, tracing the intricately tiled path to the four shrines that quartered the gardens. Each of the shrines was similar; small, with four pillars and a flat roof. There were glyphs carved beneath the edges of each ceiling, and in the stead of the statue that was often in the center of such a shrine was a brass plaque with a symbol.

The path from the manse followed a direction; it led the traveller, like a silent and dedicated pilgrim, to each shrine in its proper order. Jewel didn't usually like to have her way chosen for her, but the path had a hypnotic quality to it—she barely lifted her eyes from its surface to notice the trees or the vines, the flowers or the bushes, that colored the rest of the landscape.

She came to the first shrine in silence, and knelt a moment before leaving the path to stand in front of the brass plaque at its center. There, in a relief so good it must have been maker-made, was a sheaf of wheat held in two open palms: The Mother. "*Mother,*" Jewel whispered into the silence, "*save your son. Do not take Arann from me yet.*" She searched her pockets and left a coin at the base of the plaque; there was no altar, and no offering bowl. If it were her shrine, there'd be both.

The path took her again; she did not think of returning to the house, but rather continued her solitary quest into darkness. Night noises dogged her steps, but they were quiet and rhythmic; they held not the dead, but the peace the dead should have known.

The second shrine held a plaque with the sun rising over the horizon of a long sword. She didn't know whose this was, but she assumed it to be Reymaris: Justice. Here, she prayed, although she made no offering; Reymaris listened to the pleas of the wronged, and seldom needed another type of coin. "*Let me kill those who killed my kin.*" Duster. The prayer brought them back, but instead of guilt, there was sorrow and anger. She straightened out her shoulders, and changed her prayer into a vow. "*I will kill those who kill my kin. This is the law of Jewel Markess.*"

The third of the shrines was not made of marble, or at least not the smoky dark stone which graced the previous two shrines. No, this one was pale; in the rays of the garden's many lamps, tiny sparkles could be seen across the smooth surface of the pillars. There was a bowl here, and a plaque, besides; there was a small rail, which was obviously meant to help the kneeling rise. Of these three shrines, it was clear which was most important to The Terafin. Jewel knelt a moment before the brass relief of an eagle clutching a rod in its claws, and holding a servant's band in its beak. Cormaris, Lord of Wisdom, ruled here.

She gave him a coin, but not a prayer.

There was one last shrine, and Jewel visited it with some curiosity. All of the patriciate paid its respects to the three Gods that ruled the Isle. But there were more than three Gods; Jewel most often prayed to Kalliaris, and she occasionally whispered her guilty apologies to Mandaros as well. She wondered who The Terafin would worship on the side.

The fourth shrine, as she approached it, was better lit than the rest; it had torches on each of the four pillars, and a lamp that flickered beneath the roof, suspended by a brass chain. The roof itself was domed, rather than flat; as Jewel approached, she saw that the shrine was not square, but circular. The steps that led up to the dais were concentric marble circles. There were four.

She felt the air shift; a breeze blew through the pillars, testing the torches. She approached this last shrine as if it were a secret she was not meant to hear.

There was an altar at its center, albeit a small one; there was no plaque and no emblem. She searched the domed ceiling, but it was simple and smooth; there were no carvings and no painting across it. Almost disappointed, she reached out to touch the altar itself.

"Do not touch it unless you have something to offer."

She jumped and turned in the same movement.

In the darkness, torch in hand, stood Torvan ATerafin. His brow was shadowed, for he held his torch high enough that his helm shielded his face from the light. His face was almost impassive as he stared at her; she could not understand how she had not heard his approach, for he wore armor, bore arms.

But she relaxed nonetheless. Torvan was not a ghost, and not a man she feared. "If I had something to offer, who would I be offering it to?"

At that, Torvan smiled, and his smile was wry. He lowered his torch as he approached the shrine, and then set it into an empty ring meant for that purpose. "You would," he said mock-gravely, "be offering it to the spirit that guards Terafin."

She snorted, but when there was no answering laugh, she realized he was serious. "What spirit?"

"Well, rumor has it that the founder of Terafin watches over it still."

"Bet that's news to Mandaros."

"Perhaps, perhaps not. What we know of the Gods and the life beyond it is not perfect, Jewel." He walked to the altar and stood beside it. "Every guard who is

Chosen places his arms and armor here; they offer their service and possibly their lives to protect Terafin. If the spirit exists, he grants them his blessing in return."

"Why would he?"

"Why would he what?"

"Why would he want to stay here and watch?"

Torvan smiled, but it was a sad smile. "I don't know. If you died, would you not want to watch over your den?"

It wasn't the question she wanted to hear; she retreated into shadow, only to find that there wasn't any. "I don't know," she said gruffly. "I haven't done that good a job so far."

"You brought them here to safety, and you protect them while they are here. What more could you do?"

She shrugged. "I didn't bring them all," she said at last. "I lost Duster. And before that—before I knew what was going on—I lost Lefty and Fisher. Even when I had suspicions, I still lost Lander." She reached out and touched the altar, and this time, Torvan did not stop her, although he frowned slightly.

"Do you think that people in your service shouldn't die?"

"They don't *serve* me."

"They do," he replied. "They follow you, they obey you, and they trust you."

"All right! Yes, I think they shouldn't die. If I deserved their trust, they wouldn't have." She turned away from him, angry at everything. "I hate it," she added, for no particular reason. "I hate that they trust me and I hate that I failed."

"Then let them go."

"What?"

"Send them away. Refuse to take their service. Cast them off."

"I can't do that—what would they do?"

"What did they do without you? They survived, and I imagine that they will survive again."

She snorted, but this time the anger was gone. "I know what you're trying to do," she said softly. "And you don't have to do it." Rath used to play this sort of game—provoke her one way and then turn it around, just to get her attention and make her *think*. But Rath was dead as well.

"No? Jewel, do you think they hold you responsible for the deaths of their den mates?"

"No."

"Good. But you hold yourself responsible."

Weary, she sighed. "Yes."

He surprised her. "Good." He smiled at her expression. "You aren't," he added, "and you are. You did not kill them, but had you not chosen them from the streets—and chosen, I think, well—they would not have died at the hands of demon-kin."

"Thanks." The word was sour.

Torvan didn't stop. "Remember this feeling. Because to The Terafin, the House *is* her den. You don't understand her—or so you think—but you have more in common than you know."

She was silent; he had complimented her, but she wasn't certain why—or even why he had mentioned The Terafin. In the light, his face was an odd color.

"Why did you come here tonight?"

This, she could answer. "I'm having nightmares. I've been having them a lot recently. All of my dead kin come back to me; they surround me and try to take me with them." It wasn't all of the truth, but as close as she wanted to come.

"Ghosts?"

"No—walking corpses. Ghosts, I think I could live with."

"Corpses?"

"Yes."

"You are certain that they are dead?"

"Look—they're *my* dreams."

"Interesting. Do you always have such morbid nightmares?"

"Only when I've lost over a third of my kin," she snapped back. Then she sighed. "I'm sorry, Torvan. I know you're trying to help, and I know what you've told me is true—but it—it makes it harder."

"I know," he replied, and his voice was gentle. "Stay at the shrine, if you will. Don't let me disturb you. But, Jewel: Trust your instincts."

5th Corvil, 410 A.A.
Averalaan, The Common

Jewel was nervous, and not a little angry.

She wasn't used to being out on the streets alone; hadn't been used to it since she'd gathered her den so carefully a couple of years back. Carver was her shadow, and Arann her shield; Duster was her dagger, and Teller her voice; Finch was her hidden self, her little joy, Jester her ability to laugh. And Angel? She grimaced. Angel was his own.

Duster's gone, she told herself grimly. And, truthfully, Arann still hadn't recovered from the healer's touch. But he was speaking and eating properly and Jester could coax a smile from him sometimes. It was better than she'd hoped for when they'd first arrived at The Terafin's, but worse than she wanted now. That was the way of things.

She started to fidget with her belt, which was fine and heavy and not at all the customary wear of the Essalieyanese. Gold-plated chains hung from her lowest rib to just below her hips, and across these were hooked small pouches and a wineskin.

Devon ATerafin frowned at her with his eyes and the lines in his forehead. She'd been subject to that frown for the better part of two days, and was heartily sick of it. Unfortunately, she was paid in part to endure it, and she had no intention of giving up the fortune of her den by refusing to cooperate with a member of the House. But the moment this was all over, she was going to deck him. Or push him into the bay. She wasn't sure which.

"Jasmine, dear, do pay attention."

She smiled with what she hoped was the right amount of simpering stupidity and narrowly avoided the flap of a wagon which had just been lowered for business. This was a farmers' market, but it was also the foreign market, and the streets were crowded with bodies, wagons, horses, and the occasional ring of trees.

The trees were old and grand, and they were Jewel's favorite landmark in the twelfth holding. She wasn't certain what kind of trees they were, as she seldom ventured this far into the quarter at a time of day when the leaves and bark were clearly visible, but they were four times her width at the base, their leaves were shaped like flat, white hands with green borders, and they towered over most of the buildings in the web of old streets that met at the common, providing a bower of sorts that could be seen at a great distance.

The common itself was huge, but its size was never felt; it was always occupied with one caravan or another, and there were permanent stalls and buildings that always had wares to sell, even during the off-season. It was guarded, sort of, but the merchants themselves watched like hawks, and in this area, with foreign tempers to contend with, thieves were known to have fatal accidents.

It was a good area to pick through—but Jewel didn't consider it worth the risk to her den. As she swung her hips round to the side, flattening to a profile with just enough speed to avoid getting the pommel of a large sword in her rib cage, she remembered why.

Southern tempers.

And she knew enough about them; she had one. Her mother's. She also had the language, although it was rusty, and she knew how to inflect Essalieyanese like a true Annagarian. She rarely did it, but it did come in useful; people tended to treat foreigners like idiots if they didn't have a mutual language.

Unfortunately, Annagarian was known to about a quarter of the people in the city—or in the city that she knew. Maybe not on the Isle, although on the Isle some people also spoke Weston. She felt a pang of envy and let it go. When she'd established herself firmly as ATerafin, she'd learn whatever she damned well pleased.

But she had to survive her own temper, and her work with Devon. He could be such a charming, friendly man, it galled her when his mask dropped; it was as if he put on the effort for everyone else but didn't consider her worthy of it. Luckily, they were out in the streets and he was all jaunty smile. Maybe he'd even be attractive if she didn't know what he was really like.

He had a Southern air about his features, but it was subtle—so he used a bit of color to highlight the contours of his cheeks and the shadows beneath his eyes. He worked quickly with what looked like ash, and the effect was astounding. Another thing she wanted to learn.

Her own features would pass, but he worked his facial art on her as well. Then he gave her something that smelled, well, musty and told her to bathe in it. She didn't ask why. But that was only because she wasn't getting much in the way of answers to the questions she did ask.

Devon is in charge. Listen to Devon. Follow his orders. She swung to the side again, lithe and easy, as a small palanquin, with its attendant guards, pushed its way through the crowd. Her belt jangled; it was an irritation, a distraction.

It'll be over soon, she told herself. She twisted her fingers in the gambler's prayer, hoping to catch the attention of Luck's smile.

In the last two days, they'd been to well over eight sites—each, according to Jewel's memory, an entrance into the maze under the city streets. They found dirt, or solid rock, or solid wood. Nothing else. The mage, who had accompanied Jewel on previous excursions, had been left behind; if he hadn't found evidence of magical concealment so far, there was unlikely to be any. According, of course, to Devon.

Devon's word obviously carried weight; the mage was gone. Jewel was glad although she kept it to herself. The mage swore like any member of her den, and had a similar temper; he also had quirks and odd bits to him that made him interesting. He rarely used his magic, and when he did, it was always quiet, not at all like the use of great magics in the old stories. But in spite of all this, or perhaps because of it, he made her very uncomfortable. It was as if he were wearing a mask that didn't quite fit.

"Jasmine, dear."

She was tired; the nightmares robbed her of sleep. Jewel often had a sharpness that gave her an edge over other people, but that was blunted now. She grimaced, knowing that she deserved his disdain, and hating it nonetheless. She mumbled an apology and he nodded curtly.

They passed beneath the shade of another ring of trees, and stopped to rest there, pulling their skins, as many of the other market goers sitting in the ring had already done, and drinking deeply. Then, having finished, Jewel smiled weakly—and falsely—at her companion, and began to lead him toward the market's center. There, in a building as old as the city, the market authority ruled the merchants, taking its tariffs, setting its exchange rates and, on occasions when difficulty was suspected, searching the cargoes of the traders who traveled the Kings' charter routes to see that they complied with their majesties' laws.

The market authority was a hive of business, of barter that Jewel herself did not fully understand, and of guards, dressed in the standard livery of the Crowns, which Jewel understood quite well. These guards were not magisterians, but rather guards who directly served the market authority; they were not as severe as some of the magisterians because they were quartered with foreigners whom the market authority did not wish to offend. Still, when they caught a thief, they weren't gentle about the handling.

She relaxed a little as they approached the open arches that led to the courtyard of the authority. Here, there was such a buzz of traffic that she felt unnoticed and unnoticeable. The stone of the walls, defying the midday sun, was cool; she used it to guide her steps, remembering the two times that she had seen the market authority from the inside. The first was upon discovering the exit from the web of exits that made up the tunnels beneath the city. The second was upon discovering that Southerners took poorly to thievery, especially when the thief was almost within their grasp. There had been no third time.

A bird chittered, high above the press of people; Jewel looked up to see its bright blue breast. Its wings were a fan of green and gold; it was out of season, she thought, to be looking for a mate—but it must be a male, for it was lovely and not a little showy. She smiled up and whistled at it; it was high enough, on the courtyard walls, that it could look down without fear at this intrusion. And then there was no time for birds, or even passersby.

Something was wrong.

Jewel froze, her hand on the brass rails at the side of the broad flat stairs that led into the great hall. The sun was on her hair, her neck, her back—but she was cold, as if daylight had been suddenly denied her. Devon's back—red-shirted and embroidered—receded; before she could find voice to call him back, the market crowd surged around her and he was lost to sight. Very little stood still this close to the market authority.

Gritting her teeth, she shook her hair; something in it jangled—a bit of golden chain or net. She slid her hand into the pocket, deep and open, of her skirts. Beneath it, skin and a dagger strapped to her thigh. Devon had insisted on it. She was grateful.

She took the steps slowly, as if remembering with each step how to walk; she moved with the crowd, using each passing back as a small wall or a shield. Then, aware of how much like a nervous thief it made her appear, she relaxed and once again took the stairs in a jaunty—even an insolent—way. But it hurt to enter the building.

The merchant authority was a towering great hall with a floor that was open to the three-story ceiling above. Two galleries overlooked the vast majority of the crowd that came to the authority as they milled about making their deals, arguing for their concessions, and seeking authority witnesses to finalize contracts and commission statements. Framing the hall were the wickets and offices at which most of the day-to-day affairs of the market were decided.

Each market in Averalaan had a market authority, but none so well-guarded or so officially watched over as this; this market dealt with all manner of foreign coin and foreign custom, and the Crowns felt it important—or so it was said—to keep an eye on the foreigners' affairs.

Which was why, Jewel reminded herself, as her grip around the handle of her knife tightened, the hall was so full of guards. There were market authority guards, there were four magisterians, and there were any number of privately hired guards in the livery of the nobles who paid them. Private guards were always the big risk, especially if they were Annagarian; you didn't cross them if you didn't want to wind up under the wheels of a passing wagon.

But it wasn't the guards that made it so hard to breathe. Something was wrong; something almost as bad as the feeling she'd gotten when she'd first laid eyes on the Rath that wasn't. She backed up against the central pillar of the north half of the hall; the stone at her back was cold, but it was a comforting cold, a certain hardness, and using it to guard her back, she began to look for Devon.

He found her first, coming in to the side just at the edge of her vision. His forehead was creased and his lips were turned slightly down in as much of a frown as he ever showed her. One day, she was going to push him into a real display of something—and she'd probably regret it, at that—but not today.

"I've been waiting for you," he said lightly. "Come on."

The rings clipped to her ears jangled as she shook her head doorward. His brows went up slightly in question, and then his color darkened. He caught her wrist, and a few of the people to either side looked askance at them before placing them as both Southern and a couple.

"We don't have time for this," he said, and pulled her farther into the hall.

"Something's wrong," she said. The two words were forced, and they were the first that she had spoken aloud since she'd entered the halls. He started to reply, but she lifted her hands to cover his lips. Her arms were covered in a fine nubble of little bumps, and her hair looked as if she were caught in the center of a storm before Reymaris' lightning found its target.

She covered his hand—the hand on her wrist—with her own, and pulled him suddenly to the side, to the wickets, already crowded, that housed the money-men who dealt with foreign coin and writ.

The chest plate of a guard caught her left shoulder, and the guard snapped out a surly warning, raising a mailed fist in her direction. Devon, righting himself like a cat, broke into fluent Annagarian, and apologized for the wayward temperament of his young—and new—wife. The guard said something to make Jewel's cheeks burn, but they didn't; they were pale.

Devon stopped and stared at Jewel and then his expression changed. He smiled, although the smile was one that occupied his mouth and the corners of his eyes, not the eyes themselves, and let her draw him away from the great hall's center. He signaled to the door, and then, tugging her into his arms, whispered, "Should we leave?"

She shook her head, no. It was too late for the doors.

Devon pulled her into an embrace that brought scorn or amusement from those close enough to see it. Her eyes were to the wall, and his to the doors, when the crowd began to stir slightly. He whispered a ten-word string of invective into her ear and then did what he could to still her trembling.

She wanted to ask what it was that was happening at her back; he knew it, or if he didn't, knew better than to keep her in ignorance. He said two words, and the words rang in her ears like the curse of the Queen of Night. "Patris Cordufar."

Patris Cordufar was an important merchant; arguably the most important within the foreign market. His merchant-lines traveled directly to the heart of Annagar, returning with spices, incense, and the gems of the Southern mines. The gems, unworked, usually went to the guilds, to return South—but not always; there were rare stones with reputedly unique properties that were sought by less mundane professions than that of jewelsmith.

Still, the Lord was a rich man, having continued in the tradition of his father before him, and he was feared. Devon ATerafin knew that fear to be justly held. He had met Patris Cordufar three times—each at court—and he did not trust him. Of course, he trusted very few of the patriciate; he was Astari, and the Kings' safety demanded that vigilance be kept in all things.

He cursed inwardly and took care to pull Jewel as far from the wide bank of steps as possible, for it was there that Patris Cordufar appeared to be headed with his sizable entourage. Voices began to dim the sound of the guards' lock-step; the merchants and their followers returned to their daily business.

Devon smiled and stepped briskly toward the easternmost wicket to do the same. Then he stopped and very gently pried Jewel's fingers from his wrist. Her hand was white, and her lips so pale they were almost gray. She was afraid—no, terrified. He knew the signs of it well enough by now.

But she straightened her shoulders and lifted her chin, shaking or no, and then she straightened her belt and forced her lips into a shaky smile. The cascade of golden rings that caught her lobes captured the light as well; her determination, seen as it was through a layer of fear so thick it could almost be tested, made her striking, even beautiful.

She would make the Astari proud, if she were trained and schooled well. And if, he thought, grimacing, she could be pried from The Terafin's service.

They approached the wicket, and Devon removed a curled scroll from the swath of blue cloth across his chest. The wicketeer looked down the bridge of a narrow nose and then started to speak Annagarian without the slightest trace of accent. Devon made the switch with ease, following the flow of syllables as if the language were his first. It was supposed to be, after all.

They spoke of exchange and exchange rates, and Devon made it clear that the amount offered was nothing short of robbery; this much, the wicketeer expected—enough so that he carried on his end of the curiously flat argument with a yawn and a look of ennui that might have been annoying or even condescending in different circumstances.

"That isn't even an offer," Jewel broke in, as the wicketeer announced his figures yet again, "that's theft. Or isn't our gold good enough for the likes of you?" Her dark eyes narrowed into a curious mix of ice and fire. "You're Voyani."

The wicketeer nodded as if he had no neck to speak of.

"And you would do this to your own? Have you so forgotten yourself that you've sold all your honor to those foreign lapdogs?"

Ennui was burned away in a flash of crimson.

"My love," Devon said, interrupting what was certain to follow—although he half wished to hear it, as his ability to curse in Annagarian was not what it could be. "I think you react a little too strongly. It's not as if—"

She yanked herself free of his hand and stared at him; her cheeks were flushed. "So, you start this again?" Before he could answer, she raised a hand and slapped him; the sound resounded in the small alcove. "What kind of a man are you that you choose *him* over me? You've done nothing but bow and scrape since we crossed the cursed border!"

Devon's face was red with both anger and a handprint; this was not exactly as they had planned. "Jasmine," he began, but she snorted, tossed her hair—looking very much like a furious, prize mare—and stamped off into the crowd. People who had witnessed her display—and they were many—made a clean and easy tunnel for her passage, although it was quite clear that she, in her anger and her foreignness, had no idea where she was going.

"This," Devon ground out to the wicketeer who was already sinking back into a calm stupor, "is what you get when you marry a woman of the Voyani! Jasmine!" Looking very much the embarrassed and furious husband, he pursued the young woman, moving quickly enough to catch up with her, but not quickly enough to stop her from walking. As he walked, he could hear amused murmurs, and even one or two suggestions that were, in Essalieyan, quite illegal.

And then they were free of the crowds, and just as suddenly, free of the posture. Jewel's sash was already off her shoulder and half unwound in the shadows of the small stone alcove that stood to the left of the wagon dock. She stripped down quickly and wound the sash around her waist to prevent the belt from making noise; likewise, she pulled the long earrings from her ears—and hair—and shoved them deep into the dark leggings beneath her skirt.

Devon also rearranged his attire, but it was so much routine by now that he could watch her out of the corner of an eye. She was still pale, and her breaths were short and shallow. Her hands were shaking.

"Jewel?"

Her hair flew, much as it had done when she had displayed the temper of a spoiled young Southerner, but this time there was no fire in the movement. "We don't have time," she said. But while the words were curt, the voice was faint. It was a strange combination.

He started to ask her why; they were alone, and no one, so far, had noticed them. But she caught his hand and began to run—to scurry, much like the mice in the merchant authority's vast halls did—between places that offered shelter from prying eyes. She knew where she was going; it was he who now had to follow.

To get to the basement under the authority wasn't very difficult as long as you weren't stupid enough to try entry through the offices of the authorities' officials; there was a wooden hatch close to the wagon docks, near the offices that were occupied by inspectors who were usually too busy to stay put. The only risk you ran was that someone had boxes piled over it; it really did look like part of the floor, and at that, a well-constructed part. Jewel said her prayers to Kalliaris as she ran and ducked, peered out from the nearest box, and then ducked and ran. She no longer held on to Devon; she trusted that he, as ATerafin, was at least as competent as she—that he could keep up and stay hidden at the same time. If he couldn't, they were both dead.

And she was certain it was death she was afraid of; certain that if they were caught—although she didn't know by whom—they would only appear again as the corpses left over from some suspicious accident. She swallowed as the fear swept over her, momentarily paralyzed by it. Then she took a deep breath and continued to move.

Because if she didn't move, she would never complete her task, and if the task were not completed, there would be no home for her or her den in Terafin.

Kalliaris, she thought, although she couldn't make her lips form the name, *please, Lady, smile.*

They found the hatch easily enough; it was where Jewel had said it would be, and there was very little blocking their entrance—although they had to wait fifteen minutes for an argument between an overseer and an authority official to move past them before they dared approach it. Devon provided the muscle necessary to move the hatch; there was no lock and latch to it, but rather a simple embedded handle that looked like a short wooden slat until it was pulled up and twisted crossways.

Jewel slid down the hatch, and whispered a warning to Devon; he heeded it and as the hatch came down, jumped into a darkness that was almost complete. The ground here was hard, even rocky; it felt uneven, as if the basement had only been partially dug and then abandoned.

"Come on," Jewel whispered. She caught his hand after three attempts, and then tied a thin line around both his waist and her own. He waited until she had finished before he reached into his sash and pulled out a small, perfect crystal.

There was light at its heart—a light that was bright, intense, and still quite easily hidden in the palm of a closed hand. Jewel gasped as he lifted it, and then lifted her own hand in response, reaching for it as if the light compelled her and she could not do otherwise. He closed his palm and darkness returned.

"Lead," he whispered, and he watched her shadowed outline nod. The string at his waist grew taut, and he followed the pace she set, choosing his steps with care as he once again let the light glimmer in the darkness.

It was eerie, to walk like this beneath the authority building. But the walls, uneven and barely carved, became much flatter and smoother as they progressed. The ceilings became higher, and to either side, in brass rings that had not been cleaned for decades, were torches waiting the touch of fire.

"We're under the main hall," Jewel said, looking up.

Devon could hear nothing, but he didn't argue; it wasn't important. He watched her as her eyes narrowed; she spun to the side and then turned back, and her eyes were wide, dark circles.

"The light!"

At her tone, he wrapped his hands round the crystal; darkness fell like storm, and they stood in it. He listened for a moment, and realized that she wasn't breathing. Before he could ask her why, he heard footsteps; a set of footsteps. He caught her hands, as she reached for him; together, they retreated, flattening themselves into the corner formed by the wall and the floor.

He knew, then, that she was waiting for something, although he didn't know what; knew, too, that she was terrified. He could feel her heart as if it were his own—in fact, he could not feel his own so strongly.

He started to speak and her hand found his mouth, pressing his lips together. The footsteps drew closer, and closer still, but there was no accompanying light; whoever it was who approached was familiar enough with this basement to forgo torches.

There was no voice, no spoken word; nothing but the sound of even steps in the darkness. The shadows seemed to pick up the noise, to wrap it in velvet and yet strengthen it. Devon thought of praying, and he was surprised by it; he was not a man to leave his fate to the Gods, and he was not a man to incur a God debt—the Gods had their own games, after all, and not all of them coincided with the good of the Kings or the empire.

But Jewel's tension was like a disease or a poison; he had been exposed to it, and he could feel it settle into places that he had thought long since outgrown. He cursed her, and himself; and he counted the steps and their growing volume with the same dread as she.

And then, the unexpected; the steps grew no louder. Instead, carried by darkness, they grew quieter. He felt relief weaken his hold on Jewel, but even as it did, he was calculating. They must be at a T-junction, and the people who had passed must have continued on the straight. Very slowly, and very carefully, he began to rise.

With him, came Jewel.

They stood in darkness; Devon clutched a source of light that he dared not release for fear that it might be seen. Time passed, or perhaps it did not; he began to count his breaths, making them as deep—and silent—as possible. At last, he spoke.

"They are going where we wish to go."

He felt her nod.

"Then we must follow." He began to walk, and she caught his arm.

"We can't."

"We can. Or I can."

"Devon—"

"That's not a request," he added. "But if you fear to go, I will go alone."

"We can't see what they're doing. They travel in darkness. They work in darkness. If we bring light, they'll know who we are, and they'll destroy us."

But he was Devon ATerafin. He intended caution, and he moved in silence, but there were answers to be found; he was certain of it. He was not willing to lose the opportunity.

They waited fifteen minutes and then turned the corner. Devon needed the light to see by, although Jewel would have preferred to scrape the wall or the ground in a slow crawl. The basement was on a level; there was, beneath it, a subbasement— one flat and low enough that not even Jewel could stand at full height. This crawl space was not easily found, but it extended well beneath the merchant authority in a small web, and if you followed it south—at least she thought it was south—it came to the collapsed ruin of a door's arch, another hole—and an entrance into the maze itself.

It was obvious. In fact, it seemed to Jewel that the basement had been built above the subbasement, and the floor had collapsed over the years, slowly sinking into the maze the way glass, over centuries, pooled toward the bottom of the Churches' lead frames. At that, it had only sunk in the one spot, and it was not a large one; big enough for a person, or maybe two. If it were in an area that was used at all, it might have been pursued; instead, it was tucked away in a moldy corner like a forgotten secret. There were boards above the hole, but they had been eaten away by time and moisture—it was these slats, hoisted out of place by Carver's slender shoulders, that had signaled the exit from the crawl space into a larger building.

It had never occurred to Jewel to wonder how it was that she and Carver had found the entrance where no one else had noticed; had not, in fact, occurred to her to wonder how something as useful as the maze had remained such a well-kept secret for so long. But she wondered now, and any answer that came to mind wasn't one that she liked.

Lefty and Fisher died for this.

Lander died because it wasn't serious enough.

Duster died because she was the only real killer in the den, Carver notwithstanding, and against what Rath had become—or rather, what had become Rath—only a killer could stand.

And now Jewel was on the threshold. She grabbed the thin strand that bound her to Devon and pinched it tightly between two fingers; in her palm it felt insubstantial, and she wanted a sense of another person's physical presence, even if he wasn't the ally she would have chosen. The hole loomed closer, and closer still.

Devon periodically lifted a finger from the crystal's surface, listening first for the confirmation of safety that silence brought before releasing a thin beam of light. That light caught the wall and the floor, illuminating them so briefly they seemed a still painting over which a protective cloth flickered in a heavy wind. It was a risk, but it was one that he felt necessary; neither he nor Jewel had sight for the darkness, nor the training to move well within it. That was not the case for all of the Astari—but Devon had not been born to the compact.

Each time the light came, Jewel tensed; her breath cut across her teeth as if at a sudden, sharp pain. The ray itself she both used and avoided—he had seen such behavior before, but only in very shy animals. He had no desire to offer her comfort; this was, in some ways, the testing ground, and on it she would prove her worth to Terafin—or to no one.

Still, he watched her when he could see her; he listened for her, when he could not. She moved with caution, even with fear—but she moved. Fifteen minutes passed, or perhaps more; it was hard to tell, deprived of the sun's light and the shadows by which time made itself most obviously seen. Time ceased to matter as the floor began to slant toward old, worn slats of soft wood.

Fingers tightened around crystal; sharp edges bit into his palm and the undersides of his knuckles. Now, he felt the danger that Jewel was paralyzed by. For the slats were pulled back, and there was no branching tunnel down which the unknown others could travel. They were here; they were in the crawl space.

Jewel lay across the ground, inching the side of her face over the hole in the stone. She paused there a moment, and then drew her knees up slowly, gaining her feet. Only when she tugged on the rope to signal the beginning of her descent did Devon step in.

He did not speak, but instead pushed her firmly and gently to the side. She had a dagger or two, but she hadn't much experience using one; she had no magics, and no skills to speak of that would serve her in a tight fight in an enclosed space. He did not expect her to give her life foolishly in Terafin's service; his test was a test of courage and resolve.

You pass, he thought, knowing she couldn't see his smile. In the darkness, the rare smile was what it was, not less; in the shadows, Devon was hidden enough to feel comfortable revealing what he wanted no one to see. It was odd, this juxtaposition; but he had long since discovered that people *needed* to express what they felt and what they believed they knew, even if they wanted no one to have possession of so dangerous a knowledge. He was no better a man than most, but he had no fear of the darkness.

Jewel spoke softly and with great strain. "Devon—I *must* go first. I know the tunnels."

Of course. He nodded, and the nod was grim. But he held her arm as she lowered herself down into the crawl space, and he followed immediately, staying as close as possible.

He lowered himself into the crawl space, wishing for Jewel's height and Jewel's build. As it was, he was uncomfortably close to wall and ceiling, where they were distinct enough to be distinguished; the ground beneath the basement was an odd patchwork of worked bits of stone strewn among rough or jagged surfaces. He crawled, following her closely. Because the space was so limited, and Jewel was in front, wending her way in a darkness that the tunnels—and their unknown visitors—demanded, he had no need to call upon light; indeed, he knew it for a danger here. He slid the crystal into the darkness of heavy cloth and skin and let it go.

Time passed; he scraped his head across low-hanging stone and likewise bruised his knees. In one or two places, the ceiling rose. Jewel did not, and Devon chose to follow her lead. He did not, after all, have much choice.

But at last, when he'd lost any true sense of direction, Jewel stopped. She had started and stopped several times during their navigation of the tunnels, but there was a quality to her lack of motion, a stiffness, that told Devon more than simple words would have done.

Fear had a scent of its own, and it affected different people in different ways. Some found it exciting, some arousing, some disturbing, and some disgusting. Devon did not judge it; he acknowledged it as an element of the landscape through which he might have to fight. But her calf was stiff beneath his hand as he used her body to guide himself into a position where he might be the first to react should reaction be necessary.

He was almost surprised when she reached out and gabbed his shoulder; her grip was hard and surprisingly sure as it sought to hold him in place.

Before he could react—and his reactions were swift—he heard speech; the tunnels carried and distorted it slightly, but the words were clear.

"I said *all* life."

"It is done, Lord."

"You are certain?"

"As certain," the second voice replied, "as I can be."

"Good. Your existence depends on it. Now, stand out of my way."

"Lord." The word was layered with a variety of emotions; Devon wished to see the face of the speaker. He looked into the darkness; there was no light for his vision to adjust to.

And he wanted the light, suddenly; he had an irrational urge to pull it from its safety and let it burn away at the darkness that surrounded him. It was unexpected, the impulse, and strong; he forced it back, and then brought his shoulders in line with Jewel's. She'd told him, as much as she could, to wait. He waited.

As he did, he began to realize that he was wrong. There was light here, but it was slow to grow, slow to find its way to his vision. Jewel, beside him, stopped breathing; he reached out slowly, touching first her shoulder and then the side of her neck, before he brought his fingers up to her face.

Her mouth was wide, her jaw slack.

He knew then that she saw something in the darkness that he could not see. He was not even very surprised. Damn The Terafin anyway, for sending him out—as always—with only half the available facts. He waited, as the light flickered; it was just enough to frustrate, not enough to illuminate.

Jewel leaned into his hands, and then back; her body began to tremble with the tension that held it in place. He did not know how long they sat while she watched in darkness. But he knew when it was over; she shook her head and suddenly started, as if waking; she scrambled back on her knees in panic.

Time to leave.

He caught her, took the risk of whispering one word, and that, her name. Then he pushed her forward, and took the rear. It was hard, of course; he expected this. The possibility that they were being followed, and by enemies who could see in the dark, was high.

Don't let fear make you slow or clumsy; don't let it make you careless. But of course he couldn't give her this warning; he had to trust her. Devon ATerafin, raised within the patriciate's lower ranks and sponsored into the Astari, had made a career out of trusting no one.

He grimaced, thinking of her fear and of his own, one so visceral and one so . . . intellectual. All of his senses had sharpened; were there light, he would see by it more clearly than either Jewel or their pursuers; he would notice the variation in shadows, the subtlety of motion, the shifting of expression that warned of imminent attack.

If he had the time to turn and let the light shine.

He followed Jewel's breath, the sound of her knees shuffling against rock, even the sound of a staccato gasp when she hit something that hurt. He was aware of the passage of time, but not aware of whether or not enough of it had gone by. He followed and listened.

Are they demons, Jewel? Are they mages? What did you see?

But at his back, nothing; no sound, no shuffling, no spoken words. He wanted to ask Jewel what she had seen and why she had chosen her moment to leave, but it would wait.

And then she stopped; he could hear her struggle to stand in the enclosed space. Her fingers brushed rock and then something else—the planks. In the silence, their creak sounded like the movement of an old mast on a ship no longer seaworthy.

For the first time, he heard a sound that neither of them made; it was at his back, but how far away or how close, he could not say. He cursed, but wordlessly. Sliding to the side, hands outstretched and flattened, he caught Jewel's knee and then took the weight of her feet. She was surprisingly light.

He followed as quickly as he could—which was very quickly, and then reached into his clothing. His hand closed round the crystal as if it burned; he pulled it out, hand shaking, and lifted a slender finger for only a second.

The pale light washed all color out of Jewel's face; her eyes were wide and seemed completely dark. She stood as if frozen, as if waiting; he caught her hand in his own, locked their fingers together, and then began to run. There was no choice left her but to follow, and that was just as well; there were times when choice was prized too highly.

He let the light flicker as he ran, retracing the steps that they had so quietly and painstakingly taken. Darkness grew behind them; he had seen enough of it to spare no backward glance.

Jewel's cry told him that she had not chosen to do likewise. He did not catch all of what she said, because half of it was wordless, midway between gasp and whimper. Instead of trying to catch a glimpse of what she saw, he ran faster, taking the corner of the junction that would rob any pursuer of immediate line of sight.

Light flared down the stretch of corridor; light and heat, a fierce redness. He forced a scream out of his throat, hoping to buy time; the heat lingered at his back even though he did not stay.

Up ahead, the walls were roughening; there was a pale and indistinct light, a hint of escape. Jewel stumbled, but his grip was so sure she was forced to right herself, forced to follow, half-dragged, where he led.

There. Air burned his throat no matter how even his breaths were. He pulled Jewel round and shoved her up against the rough rock of the half-dug tunnel. She began at once to try to lift the hatch. Cursed, twice, sharply—but her hands remained steady; she was free of the panic that often destroyed deliberate motion.

Light; early evening coming in at a slant from the wagon docks. With a grunt, Devon half-pushed, half-threw her. She was gone; darkness remained, and in it, danger. His hair stood on end with something other than fear—although fear was there, and strongly.

He gripped the edge of the hatch and launched himself in a full circle that would have done an acrobat in a festival troupe proud. Only his hands remained on the lip of the entrance when the fire erupted at the end of the tunnel.

This time, Devon bit back a very real scream and yanked his hands away. They were blackened and bleeding; useless. Tears blurred his vision as he crouched in the basic defensive posture. He almost rolled away from the small hand on his shoulder before he realized that it was Jewel. Fire *hurt*. He knew it, of course, but it was hard to control his momentary reaction to the pain.

Jewel did not grab his hand as he had grabbed hers; she caught his elbow instead. But she ran, just as he had done, pausing only long enough to unwind her sash and wrap it round his hands in several layers. Smart thinking, really; it would stop his blood from becoming a telltale trail that they very much wished to avoid leaving.

Jewel didn't know the market well, and the crowds had thinned greatly; only a few stalls were still open, but they would not remain so for long; their flaps were slowly folding and their flags were being pulled down from the poles that announced their wares and their presence. There were guards, mostly private, waiting to escort the merchants—and their day's coin—to safety.

Still, if she didn't know the market well, she knew enough about dodging pursuit. It was evening, although it was not yet dark; she wound her way between the stalls, taking care to avoid the overly cautious guardsmen.

Once or twice she paused to look over her shoulder; Devon shook his head tightly and urged her on. She saw nothing following, but she would not stop running until she was safe within her rooms.

It was a long way to the Isle.

Chapter Thirteen

THE OVERHANG OF CRIMSON curtains caught the light and held it at bay. Beneath the slight shadows, The Terafin stood, face to the window, back to her study. Although she wore a pale, light turquoise, she looked a shadow, thin and wraithlike—the body, not the woman. Morretz, standing a respectful body length away, bowed quietly. The panes of the window cut his shadow, and the blurred reflection of his body, into precise rectangles. She looked beyond them.

To The Terafin's eyes, there was little movement; the hour was late enough that visitors and gardeners alike had retreated for the day. Only her guards adorned the fences, light flickering off their polished helms; they were so much a part of the manse and the lands that surrounded it that she did not notice their presence.

Ah, the path was being lit; she had been mistaken. There were gardeners yet, working in the new night. There, a torch being lifted to the glass lamps that lined the tiled walk. There were patterns within the tiling that had taken a decade to produce; her contribution to the shrines that quartered the gardens in their quiet simplicity. If one sought solitude, and one's purpose was internal and true to those that one sought, the path brought quiet and peace. Such was the way of pilgrims.

But it was not as a pilgrim that her attention was required. Morretz had been patient; would continue to be patient should she choose to keep him waiting, half-bowed, for the duration of the evening. It was not a kind use of the man she most trusted in Terafin.

She turned.

"Terafin." He bowed fully, and then rose, showing no sign of discomfort at having had to wait. "Jewel Markess and Devon ATerafin request the privilege of your audience."

"Granted," she said at once.

"In the library?"

She nodded. "I will join them momentarily." Watching him leave, she wondered what training it was that he had undergone, what vows he had taken, what abilities he had hidden to become the domicis of The Terafin. It was not the first time she wondered it; it would not be the last. The domicis were essential to the running of almost any noble House; she could not think of a member of The Ten, except perhaps the lowest, that did not possess at least one. But there were rules that governed the servant and the master—rules of privacy that she did not choose to breach.

Her predecessor had disliked the domicis—but he was a man who had insisted that control of his own environment be his own, regardless of circumstance. He never said that he distrusted them, but Amarais wondered, privately, if that was his worry.

Had there ever been a case of betrayal? She thought not. But she could not, of course, be certain. If there were one, who better able to carry it out than a trained domicis? He or she would have access to everything—every bit of personal, private, and public information—necessary to insure that discovery would be unlikely at best.

She shook herself, and stared down at the shrines. It was an ill use of time, this meandering, this gloomy imagining. There were far more real threats to worry about.

Devon was standing when she entered the library. Everything about him, except for the torn and dusty state of his clothing, was strictly formal. The salute he offered, however, was not. His hands were bandaged in a brilliant swath of blue silk; there was a spatter of blood across his shirt, although the color, rust against red, stopped it from being immediately visible. She knew Devon reasonably well—he was in pain. He did not show it.

She nodded her acknowledgment immediately, and watched his knees fold into a sitting position. The chair at his back caught his full weight with a creak. It was not a graceful movement, but it was probably a necessary one.

Jewel, still uncomfortable with the formality of a salute—and painfully uncertain of when to use one—remained seated.

"Terafin," Devon said, before she could speak.

The Terafin raised a brow, but did not demur; they both knew that her meetings with Jewel were to have been private. "Why have you come?"

"We have news," Devon answered, and it was clear that Jewel did not even resent the intrusion.

"Then give it."

"I believe we've uncovered the first evidence of the tunnels that Jewel claimed existed."

The Terafin raised a dark brow; she straightened her shoulders very slightly, and her eyes narrowed. Again, the shift in expression was slight, subtle; Jewel, watching, did not notice it. But Jewel was tired. "You found the tunnels?"

"No, Terafin." Devon bowed his head, an admission of failure. But the gesture, while perfect, was empty; the failure was to the letter of her order, not the spirit.

"But today we believe that we've discovered the reason why no entrances to the maze itself have been found."

"And that is?"

"They are unmaking them."

"Unmaking?" She sat back in her chair, favoring him with a frown as she brought her hands together. "Speak plainly, Devon."

Devon's brow rippled. "Would that I could," he replied, and turned to look at Jewel's profile. Jewel was silent, as if Devon's words hadn't penetrated her musings. Morretz, watching as always, caught The Terafin's eye; The Terafin nodded almost harshly. In the darkness cast by the shelves beneath the oval dome of a window above, Morretz left the room. Devon did not appear to notice, but she knew it for an act; he noticed everything. He continued to speak; recreating the events of the afternoon's search, and ending with the voices in the darkness.

"What do you think they meant by 'all life'?"

"I don't know. I imagine exactly what they said."

"What life is in those tunnels?"

Devon shrugged.

"And then?"

"And then, darkness. Silence. I did not see what occurred—but young Jewel did. She has a very keen . . . vision."

"Jewel?" The Terafin chose not to respond to Devon's comment. She covered the back of her left hand with the palm of her right, but no more.

Jewel shook her head and swallowed. "I couldn't see them," she said faintly. "I couldn't hear them as well as Devon did. But I saw—I saw the entrance."

"What do you mean by unmake, then?" The Terafin's voice was gentle.

"There was shadow," Jewel said, as if she hadn't heard. "And darkness—it was darker than the lack of light. And there was the door, the entrance to the maze. Some of the entrances aren't well kept, and some are bloody dangerous. They—they're old wood and they rot, or the stones fall and try to kill you. But not this one. This was real stone—it was broken because of some accident, I think—but it was pretty solid. It—" She fell silent.

"Yes?"

Swallowed. "It started to—well, the edges of the entrance, they *shimmered*. And then they started to change—to get solid. It was like the air was building rock to replace the stone that had cracked."

"And you never saw the creature casting this magic?" She didn't ask if it was magic, and Jewel didn't deny it. What else, after all, could it be?

She shook her head: No.

"And then?"

"And the stone got sharper, harder even; it—there was more of it—and then there was cracked and splintered wood—and then just wood. It was a door, and the stone arched over it like it does in the great hall here." She closed her eyes. "And on the arch there was writing, at least I think there was—I couldn't read it."

"And you read." It wasn't a question.

Jewel nodded.

"And then?"

"And then the door vanished. It just—there was a minute when it seemed to flicker, and then there was nothing there."

"I believe," Devon broke in, "that you will discover only dirt there now. It seems almost as if—and I am no mage to judge well—the entrance of which Jewel speaks wasn't destroyed. It was literally unmade." His gaze darkened.

The Terafin was silent, absorbing the description, the words in which it was cased. At last she favored Devon with a brief smile. "I believe I understand your frustration. But if I had to guess, I would come to the same conclusion that you have: Jewel saw the door's making as if time's sands were running *up* the glass."

"And that," another voice said, "is impossible."

The three turned to face Meralonne APhaniel as he stood in the open door, Morretz at his back.

Morretz was pale but calm. The Terafin raised a brow in his direction, but it was a tribute to his skill—and his past service—that she showed no sign of anger; that, in fact, she felt none. She did not trust Meralonne, but that distrust was in large part due to Morretz. If Morretz felt that it was best to summon the mage, she would countenance that independence.

What surprised her, as she studied the haggard face of the mage, was the speed with which he'd arrived. The construction necessary to repair the calling room, and the magics necessary to activate it, had not yet been completed—the only way the mage could arrive with such unseemly haste was by his own power.

The Terafin did not know much about mages, but she knew this: It was rumored that in history only a handful of the mage-born had learned to travel great distances in no time with the use of their power. It was also rumored that such travel had killed two.

"Master APhaniel, please. Be seated." It was not so much an order as a request; the mage's usually pale features were all but white, and his skin shone in the lamplight with the glow that sweat brings.

He nodded almost absently, but he took the chair; she watched him to see whether or not the tremors had set in. But he walked slowly and deliberately, denying her the answer that she half-expected; it was only upon sitting that he seemed to slump with exhaustion. And even that weariness was in body alone; he turned to look at young Jewel as if his eyes had edges.

"What you suggest is impossible," he repeated flatly.

Jewel, wary, met his gray eyes; they looked silver in the low light. "It wasn't my suggestion," she said. She spoke stiffly and kept her chin level; The Terafin thought she was trying not to bristle. It was a brave attempt but not a successful one.

Meralonne raised a brow and then almost smiled. "Very well. It was not your suggestion, but you were the only witness. Tell me, slowly, what you saw. Describe it in detail. I will aid you where I can."

He lifted his fingers in two complicated circles and then lowered his head; his smooth brow bore the lines of concentration, and his eyes, shut, were a sweep of platinum against alabaster. Before him, clouds formed. They were dark and fell to look upon.

The Terafin disliked them, and Devon shied back—but Jewel did not seem alarmed at all. She had started only once, and at that, before the mage began his motions. Now she stared, as intent as he, at the image that had formed.

"You have the sight," Meralonne said, his voice low.

Jewel looked askance at him and then turned to look at everyone else in the room. Slowly, her gaze came back to rest upon Meralonne's face.

"No," he said, as if it were an effort merely to speak, "they do not see as you do. But come. Describe what you saw."

She did. And as she did, he brought it to life, allowing her to correct him. This time, however, Devon and The Terafin were privy to the vision that Jewel's sight had granted; they saw, unfurling in the clouds, darkness and more; the outline of the crawl space that led to the gaping entrance to the tunnels themselves. That hole became a door, and the door became nothing. It was as Jewel had described it: an unmaking.

"And?"

"And then I knew it was over," Jewel said, the hush of the words making a monotone of them.

There was silence as everyone absorbed what was said. At last, Meralonne exhaled. "What you described seems much to me as The Terafin supposed it. But it is not possible."

Jewel said nothing.

The Terafin raised her head. "Meralonne, a question."

"Ask it, Terafin. I shall endeavor to answer."

"Why would they wish to destroy all life?"

He froze. "Pardon?"

It was Devon who answered. "There was a short conversation before the spell was cast. We did not hear it all, but one sentence stands out."

"And that?"

" 'I said *all* life.' "

"Are you certain?"

"That," Devon said, with a wry and deep inflection, "was what he said next. After the second speaker assured him that it was done."

"Jewel," Meralonne said, leaning back into the rest of the chair, and gripping the arms with his hands, "you said there was darkness, and I have captured what I can of it. What did it *feel* like?"

"I—I don't know."

"You felt nothing?"

"I don't know."

"What do you mean you don't know?" The edge of irritation that he often showed had crept, unbidden, into the words.

"I—I don't know. I was, I was already nervous." Her glance slid to The Terafin and then away. The girl, The Terafin realized, had been terrified. That fear lingered in the words and the way she spoke them; Jewel was usually much more aggressive. *But you served me,* The Terafin thought, as she watched Jewel struggle with shame and the need to speak the truth. *You served me well.*

"I was frightened. I—the moment we reached the market authority, everything felt wrong. And then, in the tunnels, it grew worse and worse. It wasn't until we reached them that I realized we were going to die." She swallowed and then reached for a glass of water. Morretz held it, although he had offered no refreshments to anyone else. "The darkness was worse than darkness, and it was cold. I had to watch it; I was afraid to move. That's why I saw—what I saw."

Meralonne nodded, but there was ice in his gesture. "Yet you managed to escape."

"Yes," she answered, and her voice was so quiet, The Terafin had to strain to catch it. "But the darkness wasn't looking for me." She swallowed again. "Only at the end."

"At the end?"

"I thought it—it was trying to guess my name."

"You heard it?"

"No—I *felt* it."

Meralonne whispered something in a voice too low to be heard. The Terafin, having heard enough of Meralonne's colorful invective, was thankful for his near-silence. "Master APhaniel?"

He stood, swayed, and sat again in a single awkward motion. Morretz was at his side at once. "Terafin," he said gravely, as he touched the mage's forehead, "we must find him a place to rest."

"What?"

"He is the throes of the fever."

Her face paled; she rose quickly. "I see. Very well. Take him at once to the healerie."

"Terafin?" Devon raised the bundle that was his hands. "With your permission, I would like to adjourn to the healerie as well."

"Very well. I will expect a report, Devon."

He started to salute, but she stopped him with a swiftly raised hand. "Do not stand on formality. And the next time you are this severely injured, you *will* visit the healerie before you attempt to speak with me. Is that understood?"

"The injury was not severe enough to—"

"There is blood on your lap, and on my chair."

He looked down and raised a brow in faint surprise. "Terafin," he said, acknowledging her order, as he did every order she gave.

"Good." She rose. "Jewel," she added, in a voice much less harsh, "you have served us well today, whether or not you know it. Go back to your den; I will call for you after the late dinner hour."

Jewel bowed, awkward in the motion. The door opened and closed with unseemly haste as she fled the room.

Jewel caught up to Devon as he walked down the long hall that led to the grand stairs. To either side were the rooms of the minor functionaries whose entire life was to see to The Terafin's various needs; there were paintings, most old and elaborately framed, and there were two long tapestries, although what they depicted, Jewel didn't know. Nor did she much care.

"Devon, wait!"

He stopped at her command and then pivoted on his left heel, standing exactly between the alabaster sentries at the top of the stairs. He was smiling, but the smile was both strained and sardonic. "At your command, lady."

She snorted and held out her arm; it wasn't an offer so much as a demand. This was Jewel Markess, den leader and guardian; he saw her rarely. "I told you, healer first, Terafin after," she said crisply, in a tone of voice which took for granted that he would be smart enough to listen next time.

He was grateful for her aid, and halved his weight between her arm and the railing.

"Devon?" she said, when they were halfway to the foot of the stairs. He turned to meet her gaze, and found that it wasn't possible; she was staring at her feet. "I want you to know—"

Had his hands not been wrapped in folds of silk, he might have lifted them to her lips to stop her words. Instead, he shook his head. "Jewel, you did well today. You would have done so with or without me." He made a point of raising an elbow, and she favored him with a half-smile. "I'm not so very certain that it's not I who owe you thanks." The smile left his lips slowly, but when it was gone, she knew it. "But perhaps thanks, like congratulations, will have to wait. We're not finished yet."

"No," she replied. "But *you* are. Until the healer says different."

He started to speak and then laughed. He knew, from the sidelong glance she gave him, that she didn't understand why.

*   *   *

The Terafin sat quietly in her chambers as Morretz applied a cooling balm to her shoulders and her arms. Her eyes were closed, as if in meditation, and her arms delicately folded; her hair was drawn up above the nape of her neck to better allow Morretz to do his work.

"What did Alowan have to say?"

"Bow your head," Morretz replied. The smell of something cool filled the air as he broke a scented wax bead against her pale skin.

"Morretz?"

The domicis sighed. "You will not be pleased."

"Oh?"

"Meralonne refused our aid most emphatically; he would not even suffer the healer to examine him. To make his point more strongly, he cast a protective circle around the bed we managed to force him into."

"Cast a protective circle? In the midst of the fevers?"

"Terafin, please."

She struggled to find her quiet and relaxed again under his ministrations.

"He is, even now, struggling through them. What we can offer him, we have offered."

"We can't afford to let him—"

"Terafin," Morretz said gently, "the mage-fevers cannot be hastened or lessened by the healer, or have you forgotten?"

"I've seen a healer aid a mage who was suffering from them."

"No," he said, equally gentle in his correction. "You have seen a healer contend with the physical damage the fevers left behind. And even then, there is no guarantee of success."

"Morretz."

"Terafin. Devon is resting well, and will be able to continue his activities in your service without interruption."

"Good." She sighed. "But it was not Devon's opinion I wished; it was Master APhaniel's."

"You had it," Morretz replied evenly. "He has said that what Jewel described— what she saw in her vision—was impossible."

"But she saw it."

"Yes."

"And it was not illusion."

Morretz was silent a moment. Something fragrant and slightly bitter trailed down the back of her neck; another wax bead, another exotic oil. "No, Terafin. Neither I nor Master APhaniel believe it to be illusion." He paused. "She has the sight, and illusion would have left telltale traces to her vision."

"Then if she saw it, how can it be impossible? Why is it impossible?"

Morretz' hands stilled a moment; she felt their warmth, but felt their stiffness as well. At last he said, "I do not know." It was an admission he hated to make. "But everything I have ever been taught agrees with what Master APhaniel said."

"And you think he understands more?"

"Yes."

She cursed. "How long?"

"I do not know," he replied gravely. "Terafin, I had no idea that he could travel thus. And after such travel, he still had the power to play out young Jewel's vision that we might see it and he might clarify it for his own purpose. I cannot think of another mage who could do the first, let alone survive it to continue to the second." He was silent for the space of five seconds before he once again began his massage.

"Tell me, Morretz."

"Very well. I summoned him, but did not expect his immediate arrival. It worries me. Meralonne keeps his secrets well; indeed, he is known in the Order for no less. He is powerful enough to be feared—just how powerful, I did not know until this eve—and he has few enemies, although he has few friends."

"But tonight, for reasons that he has not—and in all probability will not—state, he came in undue haste; it was as if he was afraid of what he might hear. Or, perhaps, afraid that he might hear it too late. The thing that can put that fear into Meralonne APhaniel must be terrible indeed."

The Terafin was silent. Morretz slowly worked his way down either side of her spine; she curved her back beneath his fingers, sinking slowly into the bedding. She thought to pretend to be relaxed, but Morretz knew her too well.

"Who are they?" she asked him, seeing Ararath behind the closed lids of her eyes. "Who are they, and why do they seek to take Terafin?"

"Why?" Morretz echoed. "One month ago, you would not have asked that question."

It was true. But one month ago, it was perfectly clear who her enemies were both within and without Terafin. Within Terafin, they sought control of the most powerful of The Ten, and without, they sought to damage Terafin enough that Terafin would lose its rank among The Ten. The idea that controlling Terafin would not be an end in itself was so foreign it had taken time to gather strength and become deliberate question.

She shivered, suddenly cold; Morretz, expecting this, wrapped heated blankets around her shoulders before moving to the fire. He paused by the brazier and very carefully broke a small cone into its flames. Smoke eddied briefly in the rising currents; in minutes the air carried the scent of sandalwood.

"Sleep," he said softly, as he placed kindling into the hearth. "I will wake you when it is time."

*   *   *

Ellerson found her in the kitchen, with a lamp on the table and a slate beneath her shaking, chalk-covered hands. Beside her was the box that carried every coin the den owned.

"That is not," the elderly domicis said, "a wise use of oil."

She looked up at him, the shadows under her eyes cast by more than the round light. "I'm studying." Her lids fell halfway shut, and she forced them up.

Ellerson lifted his own lamp and brought it to within two inches of Jewel's face. "To bed," he said, in a voice that brooked no argument.

To her surprise, she found her feet and even managed to stay on them. "I—"

"To bed, *now*."

It seemed very childish to tell him that she was afraid of sleep. To point out that, three times this eve, the nightmares had forced her, screaming and sweating, to wake. Jewel Markess was the leader of her den, and guardian besides. There were certain kinds of fears you didn't own up to unless you wanted to be thought of as weak.

But she couldn't go back to her room. It was too big and too cold and too empty; the ghosts were waiting for her before her lids were properly closed. She lifted her lamp and held it aloft, some sort of unfortunate shield against the rigors of natural night.

Ellerson's expression was not what she had feared it would be; the severity of the day was softened somehow by the hour and the isolation.

"It's not often," he said, as he lowered his own lamp, "that a domicis finds his master in a kitchen."

"Back at the den, it was the only empty room. Wasn't even a full room." Lamplight skittered off the walls and the wide bank of flat, perfectly clean windows, softening the bare walls. "Our whole place was smaller than this."

"But you miss it."

She looked up, for Ellerson was quite a bit taller than she, but there was no accusation in his eyes, and no contempt. "Yes," she said. "I miss it. It was mine. I knew how much it cost, I knew when I had to pay rent, I knew how to clean it and break into it when I had to.

"It's stupid," she added, almost forlornly. "I couldn't dream of a better place than this."

He said nothing.

"But I don't see my den-kin anymore. I go out early, I come in late, and I'm forbidden to speak about anything I do in The Terafin's service. It's not what I thought it'd be."

"No," Ellerson said. "It never is." He pushed her lamp across the table, setting it aside as if it were no longer necessary. "Come, Jewel. It is time to sleep."

His voice reached for her, although he kept a respectful distance, as station and rank demanded. Not very many people told Jewel what to do anymore—at least, not like that. She found herself following where he led, and was almost disappointed when the journey ended at the door to her rooms. Like a well-dressed doorman, he opened her door and held it while she slowly crossed the threshold from the wing into her private quarters. Then, lamp still bobbing in his hand, he stepped over it as well.

She stared, openmouthed, and then remembered what little manners she had.

"Jewel," he said, his voice less stiff than she remembered it, "I am a domicis. I have been trained for most of my life to serve. I take pride in it; all of our number do. I was brought here to serve you; it seems that you did not—or do not—understand this." He walked up to her and reached out for the lamp in her hand; her nerveless fingers let it slide. She was tired and weary; exhaustion made her stare although her eyes weren't really seeing.

"Come. It is time for you to sleep." He placed a lamp on either side of her bed, one on the low, flat set of dressers, and one on the tall, narrow table that was meant for a vase or a pitcher. Then, satisfied that both were full and secure, he stepped back.

The room was lit, and the shadows cast by the lamps were small. Without darkness to hide them, the walls did not seem so far away or so barren. Ellerson quietly pulled up a chair, choosing to place it halfway between his mistress and the door.

"I will watch the lamps," he said quietly. "When they are low, I will fill them."

"But the oil—the cost—"

He smiled, and the smile was a rare one. "Sleep, Jewel. You are not the master that I envisioned when I was called to serve—but I understand now why it is I who was sent."

She wondered what he meant as she slid between the covers and then struggled to kick her sandals out the sides. Wondered, but didn't have the voice or the wakefulness to remember to ask.

Devon ATerafin stared at the moon. The sky was clear, and the luminescent orb was almost full—although whether it was waxing or waning, he could not remember. In a darkness so lit by the scattered glow of moonlight and the brilliant spill of stars it seemed hardly dark at all, his hands looked whole. The skin was tender to touch, but no one touched him, and it was unlikely that the injury would be remarked on, even were one to be looking for it. Alowan's touch was potent, Alowan's skill without equal.

But Alowan was also old, and wont to look and act his age. Time ran across his brow with ungentle feet, and sat upon his shoulders with increasing weight. *See us through this crisis, old man,* Devon thought. Then he grimaced. There was always one more crisis to last through.

Always.

With genuine regret, he left the balcony, with its cool, stone seat and its thick, overadorned rail; with its exposure to moonlight and starlight and the crisp, soothing breeze. Devon was a moonchild, not a sunchild, and the light that he preferred was one that accented shadows without stripping them of power.

He turned and pushed the curtains back, holding them long enough to enter into the office from which he served Patris Larkasir in the overseeing of the Crowns' trade routes.

On his desk were reports and paperwork, and the paperwork at this time in the season was unusually heavy. Trade with Annagar was still opening up, and many were the merchants who clamored for permission to bear the Crowns' seal along the various routes. Patris Larkasir had been most patient about Devon's comings and goings, but judging from the size of the small mountain on his aide's desk, Devon thought that patience would soon wear thin. It was unfortunate; an impatient Larkasir was rather like an impatient bull.

In the small, middle drawer above his lap was flint and tinder; he pulled them out, navigating his way around the quills and brushes that work demanded use of without making a sound. Almost, he lit the sole lamp that stood, full, on the right corner of his desk. Almost. But there was a shadow, and it was wrong.

He froze at once, but before he could arm himself, he heard a voice he knew quite well.

"Devon ATerafin," it intoned, "the Astari summon you."

Water trickled out of the cupped palms of a kneeling, alabaster boy. He was blindfolded, and his hair was cropped very short; there was nothing at all around him but still water. Stephen found the fountain vaguely disquieting, and wondered if that had been what its maker intended. It was hard to say; there was so much in Averalaan that seemed to defy sense, reason, or beauty.

He was well enough that the night no longer exhausted him; well enough that, during the day, he could begin to pen long letters to Cynthia, as was his wont. He was not quite well enough that he was willing to venture into the Kings' court—or the Queens, as they seemed to be two separate things—to meet with the Ladies of Breodanir.

On the morrow, however, he would have no excuse; guilt and a sense of duty, even in this foreign place, conspired to rob him of peace as he stood alone in the silence. Gilliam was someplace in the eastern courtyard, with his dogs and Espere for company—but Stephen could sense his Hunter's unease and restlessness. They had come to Averalaan for a reason, but that reason was Evayne's to dictate, and she had not seen fit to visit again.

Or rather, the path had not seen fit to bring her.

He tried, at a distance, to calm his brother, and felt the hint of Gilliam's annoyance in return; it was familiar, and he missed the familiar enough that it made him smile.

Come, Stephen, he thought, as he stood and left the fount behind, *don't tire yourself. Tomorrow, you must fulfill your word to Lord Devon.*

"Am I interrupting?" The voice was soft and faint, but Stephen would have recognized it in a crowd that roared. He turned at once, dropping into a bow of genuine respect and gratitude at the feet of the healer-born Alowan.

Alowan's smile was genuine but tired. "I've come to see the patient, but I see the patient is well."

He found himself nodding; found himself trying to square his shoulders enough that he might look the picture of perfect health. It drew another smile from Alowan; that of a father who knew what the son was about.

"I'm well," Stephen said, and then added sheepishly, "well enough to visit the Queen's court on the morrow."

"On the morrow? Well, that *will* be the occasion. If I'm up to it, I may see you there."

Stephen raised a brow, and almost asked the healer what he meant—but he set it aside. Alowan looked his age at the moment; Stephen felt guilt for being the cause of his venture into the palace and the Arannan Halls. There was a cadre of guards at every entrance and exit, and running their gamut bred a type of exhaustion that was unique.

Almost, he sent the old man away, but as he led him to the door, he hesitated. And then, quietly, he called to Gilliam; Gilliam's concern came back, and Stephen calmed it as he could.

"After all you have done for us, Healer, I know it would be ungrateful to ask you for more."

"But?" A white brow rose, skeptical, at Stephen's graceful words.

"But indeed," Stephen smiled, as one caught out, "if I might trouble you to answer a question of some urgency to myself and the Hunter Lord Elseth? We can pay," he added quickly, and then, seeing the lines in Alowan's forehead, fell just as quickly silent.

"What question is this?"

"It concerns—ah, Gilliam. There you are. Did you bring Espere?"

Gilliam's suspicion was immediate, as was Stephen's annoyance at it. They glared at each other a moment as Espere very neatly stepped round her Lord and into the open courtyard.

The old man looked down at the girl. "Is she the matter of concern?"

"Yes."

"No."

"Gil—"

The Hunter Lords of Breodanir were not known for their tact or their lack of temper, but Lord Elseth did what he could to bite back the words that he knew, on some level, he'd regret later.

"Espere is . . . she's . . ."

"Yes?" Alowan knelt in front of Espere and waited, his hands on his knees. He did not move, although he did continue to speak. "Are you saying that she's simple?"

"Not quite."

"Not quite?"

"We believe her to be god-born. No, we *know* it. But she cannot speak, as you see her now."

Espere was very much like an intelligent dog; she knew well who was the center of attention, and while she hovered around Gilliam, she let her attention stray to the old man who knelt so oddly before her. After a few minutes she tilted her chin in Gilliam's direction; a question. He nodded grimly.

Very slowly, wild dark hair a tangle as she shook her head, she approached Alowan.

"Do you have reason to believe that she can speak?"

"Yes. We've heard her talk—just as you or I do—and I believe that when she speaks, she knows that she should be more than a—more than a—" He glanced almost guiltily at Gilliam. "More than a beast."

"Beast?" Alowan's white brows rose. "I see."

"It was to aid her that we were to come upon this road. I believe that, in aiding her, we will somehow help your lord—but I do not know it for fact."

Alowan's curved fingers were upon either side of the wild girl's face; he patted her cheeks with his thumbs, as he might have a tamed pet. But he did more; he spoke in a rhythmic chant, in syllables that Stephen could feel, although he could barely hear them.

Time passed; minutes blended together in the hypnotic sway of his voice. But at last, with the moon a little higher in the open sky, the healer bowed his head and gently released her captive face. "You are right," he said, and if possible his voice was weaker than it had been. "She is god-born. But she is healthy, she is whole, she is what she is. If you came to have her healed, if you thought her behavior some sort of physical affliction, I must disappoint you. She is exactly as she should be."

"I see." Stephen nodded almost ruefully. "But we *have* heard her speak. There are rumored to be houses of healing. Might they—"

At this, Alowan looked genuinely annoyed, and he was not a man who was given to irritation. "Stephen, the houses of healing are peopled with the healer-born who charge in crowns for the service that I have just rendered. If *I* cannot aid the young woman's complaint, there is not a healer in Averalaan who can."

"I'm terribly sorry," Stephen said, and it was quite clear that his embarrassment was real. "I don't have much experience with the healer-born, and I didn't—"

"And you didn't know that you might sting the pride of a testy old man." Alowan ran his hand over his eyes. "I'm sorry, Stephen, Lord Elseth. That was completely uncalled for." He smiled wanly. "But as you are well, and as the young lady is beyond a healer's skill, I believe I will return to the healerie of Terafin.

"I hope you won't misunderstand me when I pray that you have no reason to call upon me again."

If the affliction was not physical, Alowan could tell them nothing else about it. Nor did Stephen have any desire to press him. Gilliam, satisfied and also ashamed of that satisfaction, had once again retired to the east court. Stephen chose to retire to his room.

It was the fifth of Corvil, and if Lord Elseth was to retain title to his lands, they must leave by the fifteenth of the month in order to arrive in haste, and with a smaller pack than usual, for the calling of the Sacred Hunt. That did not leave much time, although if they traveled hard—as they undoubtedly would have to—things would be well.

They had to be well.

Lord, Stephen thought, invoking the image of the Hunter God, *smile on your Hunter and his huntbrother. Our spirit has not faltered; bring us home in safety; bring us home in time.* Then, unbidden, he thought of Evayne. *You had a purpose*, he told her in the silence. *We cannot cure Espere; there is no means to do it.* But even thinking it, he knew that their task was not finished. *Tell us what your purpose was.* But he knew, should she come, that she would tell him little or nothing. He trusted her, but that trust was fast becoming a burden. And one he was too tired to carry this eve.

Stephen navigated his way to his sleeping room by the lights of the courtyard and the near-full moon. There, he found his sleeping silks and removed his sandals; he opened the curtains wide to let the night breeze blow in; he placed his sword and his dagger aside, and removed the hat that he had half forgotten. Weary, he sank back, and felt the edge of something hard beneath him.

It was a book.

Books were rare and expensive enough that he didn't travel with them, and for a moment he wondered who it belonged to. And then he remembered Meralonne APhaniel. He had forgotten, in all of the events that had occurred, to return the tome to the mage; it was another task, and one that he did not relish, for he also found the mage an enigma that he did not like.

Still, he was curious; there was no book upon the Elseth Estate that had been proof against his curiosity. Had the sun been high, he would have been tempted to read. *It's a sign*, he told himself, as he set the book aside. *I'm not a child, to be ruled by curiosity.*

*   *   *

Duvari waited for Devon in the silent library of the Kings' palace. Moonlight cast long shadows through the two-story windows, bending them across desk, chair, shelf, and man. The light was poor, but it was not by light that Devon knew who had summoned him. Who else but Duvari had the authority?

The doors swung shut at his back; he could not tell if they were closed by the hand of Duvari—for Duvari was many things and possessed talents that not even the Astari had cataloged all of—or by another member of the compact. Nor did he dare to look around. Instead, he assumed that he was not alone; there was at least one man at his back, possibly two.

He walked to within ten feet of Duvari, and saw the shadows beneath the master's eyes. They were like scars as they rested beneath his unblinking gaze. He knelt then, resting his forearms against his left knee. "Duvari."

"Devon."

"You summoned me."

"Yes." Duvari did not move; it was as if all of his attention was bound up in the intensity of his stare. "You failed to make a report."

Inwardly, Devon cursed. "Arannan Halls," he said; there was no point whatever in playing the fool.

"Indeed."

"I have not gathered enough information to make the report formal." Devon tried very hard to pierce the darkness, but Duvari wore it like a gauze mask—not enough to hide his face, but enough to obscure nuances of expression.

"And when will you have enough information?"

"By the end of tomorrow, Duvari."

"I see." The shadow stood, rising to full height in the moonlight. He left the chair and table behind, and also left the distance. "You remember your vows, Devon."

"Yes."

"You remember that you are not ATerafin in the service of the Astari."

"Yes."

"Tell me of Arannan Halls. Tell me of the two who stay there. Tell me of the work that you have been doing at the behest of The Terafin."

Are you a demon? Devon thought it, but the words would not leave his lips. "Are we alone?"

Duvari stared down, again cloaking his face in shadow. Then he raised his head and nodded. The door creaked very slightly; Devon heard no footsteps, but rather, the small scrape of metal against metal—the latch. "Speak."

Devon did not pray, but his spirit withered. Duvari was the master of the compact; there was no option but obedience. And yet, if he were not who or what he seemed . . . He cursed the young huntbrother's illness, and cursed the lack of time with which to use him in court. He met the eyes of the man who had taken his oath, knowing that he had only his own judgment at this moment, and nothing more.

Swallowing, Devon ATerafin made his choice. "There is an element of magery involved," he said. "One that I have not encountered previously. There is a mage, or possibly a group of mages, who set an elaborate trap for The Terafin. Had they succeeded, Terafin would now be ruled by a demon."

"Continue."

"I cannot say more at this time—not of that; she demanded my oath, and I swore it: that I would not speak of the investigation's particulars unless I was certain that it involved more than Terafin." He waited for Duvari to speak, knowing that the master of the compact had little patience for the foibles and the secrecy of the patriciate. He was not of the nobility, and not even his family name remained to him; Duvari *was* the Astari. He knew no other loyalties and was bound by no other duty.

"You have always had some loyalty to the House that gave you its name," Duvari said at length. "I am aware of this—and I have never distrusted that loyalty until now. Why did you not disclose the full particulars of the attack in Arannan?"

"Because there is a magic loose which, carefully used, could destroy the Astari—perhaps even the empire." *Choose your words carefully, Devon. Speak them softly.* "Not only can the caster assume the appearance and likeness of another, but he can also assume the memories. He *is*, to all intents and purposes, that person. Or he is in part. I could not make such a report if I—"

A hand was raised in the shadows; the call for silence. Duvari did not speak a word, which was either a good or a bad sign. Devon knew that the full import of what had been said was already obvious to the master of the compact. The shadows between them lessened, although the light did not grow. Duvari stepped back and with a gesture, bade Devon to rise.

"You have a method of detection," he said. It was not a question. "You intend to use it before you make your report, unless your findings indicate otherwise."

"Yes."

"And you can trust it?"

"To be accurate, yes."

"Does it involve magery?"

"No." The sound of Devon's breath cut the air. "We have reason to believe that most available forms of magery would not detect the imposters, if they are there."

Duvari inclined his head; there was an anger and tension that seemed to ebb out of him, softening the line of his jaw and shoulder. "Continue, then." There was no apology for the suspicion, nor would any be forthcoming. "But if your findings indicate infiltration, do not make the report."

Devon nodded grimly. Stephen of Elseth would be in court on the morrow unless he was dead.

Chapter Fourteen

O F ALL THE LADIES in Breodanir, the one that Stephen had most dreaded as a child was Lady Faergif. She was sharp-tongued when she spoke at all, and wont to be severe, and she made age seem the very pinnacle of power, where in others it was an unfortunate consequence of time. She dressed in a manner to match her character, and she neither ate much nor drank much; it was perfectly clear that it was her hand that ran Faergif's responsibility.

Still, Lord Faergif was, for a Hunter, jolly, and his huntbrother—what was his huntbrother's name?—more so; it was clear that Lady Faergif had not managed to ruin their lives by her grim and dour disposition.

Of course, to be charitable, Lady Faergif was only Lady Faergif for two years of Stephen's life as a huntbrother—his eighth and ninth—and his memories were tinged with the absolute harshness of unforgiving youth. He hoped, almost prayed, that time would take the edge off those memories and replace them with something more pleasant.

On the other hand, he did remember Lady Faergif, whereas the memory of Lady Morganson was not so clear.

Gilliam's mood was sour; he had been told to leave his dogs behind—which was acceptable, as dogs were not usually to be taken to a court that involved Ladies—but Stephen had also made it perfectly clear that Espere was to remain behind with the pack. The very idea that a young woman in the company of a Hunter Lord might suddenly turn and remove all of her clothing—or those bits that were possible for a single person to remove—had made the very idea of her presence anathema.

Gilliam turned a stare upon him that might have wilted strong stalks of corn; Stephen ignored it. Gilliam never worried about the Ladies, but then again, that was not the duty of the Hunter. It was the huntbrother who was expected to smooth the way, with manners, tact, and as much grace as possible. Of course, the Ladies would expect minimal grace and manners from a Hunter, which meant that Stephen's task, at least in terms of keeping Gilliam out of trouble, was not so difficult.

Therefore it was not Gilliam but Devon who worried Stephen. Devon had such a placid expression, such a pleasant disposition, such a grace and surety of movement, that Stephen should have found him charming. And perhaps he might have—but Gilliam's hackles rose, as if at the thought of a rival Lord poaching in his demesne, whenever Devon came too near or stayed too long. Gilliam's instinct was a Hunter's instinct, and Stephen had learned to trust it, even if he lamented the way in which it was handled.

"Stephen," Gilliam finally said, through clenched teeth. "Stop pacing."

Stephen grimaced. He was pacing, as accused. It was several hours to the meeting with Lady Faergif, but he was already nervous. The proper clothing of the Hunter's court was heavy and cumbersome when compared with the wear of the Essalieyanese; it was also very formal and seemed, when compared with the clothing of a man like Devon, overdone.

Overdone.

Stephen stopped pacing, closed his eyes, and took a deep, deep breath. The green, the brown, and the gray were the colors upon which the entire kingdom prospered; they were the colors by which the Lords fulfilled their responsibilities to their people and their lands; they were the colors by which they fulfilled their promise to the Hunter God, and the colors in which, in time, they died.

He had been long away from the courts of the land, and far too concerned with pleasing foreigners, if he could forget that, even for a moment.

The exterior chimes sounded and he turned as their high tinkle faded into silence. "Enter."

The heavy door-curtains were folded to one side as Devon ATerafin stepped neatly into the room. He bowed quite low—and in the custom of the Breodanir commoners to their Hunter Lords; Stephen was both surprised and impressed. Gilliam was suspicious.

"Lord Elseth," Devon said gravely, showing no indication that Gilliam's obvious lack of grace had been noted. "Stephen."

"ATerafin," Stephen said. He was rewarded by a glimmer of a smile—one that was both fleeting and genuine.

"Let me again apologize for the lack of proper security within the Halls. I trust that you have not been troubled again?" Devon said.

"Not once," Stephen replied graciously. "And the rooms are not what we're accustomed to, and for that reason quite welcome."

"Do you mind if I take a few moments of your time?"

"Not at all," Stephen replied. He motioned to a chair, and Devon took it; they were both crisp and formal.

Devon sat. For a moment his gaze was appraising, and in that appraisal quite distant. Then he leaned forward, and his eyes were a bright darkness, his gaze intent. He looked, Stephen thought, like a falcon free to hunt.

"I do not know what your part is in all of this," Devon said quietly—and unexpectedly. "I don't even know if you know it. But it can be no accident that these creatures—these demons—are hunting you. We have a common enemy, Stephen of Elseth. And I require your aid in the hunting of it."

At this, Stephen felt the current of Gilliam's curiosity shift. The Hunter Lord, not addressed, nevertheless came to stand a discreet distance from his huntbrother's side. He was listening keenly.

"What aid do you require?"

"Your vision," was the quick reply. "Not even the mage APhaniel can see as quickly and clearly as you seem to.

"I have invited you to court—or rather, you have been so invited; Lady Faergif and Lady Morganson will be in attendance at the request of Queen Marieyan. You will no doubt be waylaid by these two fair Ladies, and no doubt they will wish every bit of news that you can possibly bring them about their distant home. But I ask you to discharge your duties with both grace *and* speed; I have need of you in the palace, if you will consent."

Stephen cringed; he knew what Gilliam was going to say a fraction of a second before it was said.

"We will." Any excuse to be free of the niceties the court forced on him would do—but Devon ATerafin proposed a hunt, of sorts, and that was to Gilliam's liking.

Seeing the expression upon Stephen's face, Devon smiled, and the smile almost reached his dark eyes. "I realize that I've not set an easy task for you, and I apologize. The women of Breodanir are sharper than Annagarian daggers, and more determined. But I must, of course, ask you to say nothing at all of what has befallen you."

"I understand." Stephen rose. "But, ATerafin?"

"Yes?"

"What do you wish me to do if I see another of the kin?"

"A wise question," Devon replied, and ran a hand through his dark hair. "And one, of course, I assumed you would know. Forgive me, Elseth huntbrother; it has been a long three days. If you see such a creature, say nothing; do nothing to indicate that you recognize it for what it is."

"And if it attacks?" Gilliam broke in.

"If," Devon replied, his smile no less friendly, "it attacks, you must naturally feel free to respond in kind."

"Then we need Espere," Gilliam said.

"Very well."

Stephen sent as strong a surge of disapproval as he could to his Hunter, and received only smug satisfaction, and the keen desire for a hunt, in return.

Devon rose. "I am not, unfortunately, the man who will guide you to court, but I will be present as quickly as I can discharge my other responsibilities. I shall meet you there."

"Of course."

Stephen waited until the curtains' circular pattern, with its bold gold lines and red, red center was once again whole, heavy with the weights that kept its halves straight. Then he turned on his Hunter. "We can't take her," he began.

"We need her," was the reply. "Without her, we'd have died during the last attempt, and you know it." Gil's expression dared him to disagree, but Stephen was not so foolish; he knew that his Hunter was right. "I can keep her under control," Gilliam added, his voice taut as wire drawn across a lute's bridge.

Stephen said nothing at all. Espere glanced apprehensively at Gilliam, and then swung her wild, tangled hair toward Stephen. Nervous, she pranced back and forth between them, butting Gilliam in the chest, but stopping short before she touched Stephen. She was willing to mock-fight with the hounds, but Stephen she did not touch. Which was just as well.

She's not an animal, Gilliam. She deserves to be treated like more than a running hound.

He didn't say it aloud; he was half certain that Gilliam wouldn't even understand what he meant by it: After all, what was more important than the hunt and the hounds?

A servant came to escort them from their rooms to the palace proper; for some reason, she came very much earlier than the sun's shadow indicated, and Stephen would have worried had something about her nature not been so calming. She was young, but tall and supple, and her hair, like burnished bronze, was drawn back in a complicated crisscross that Stephen had not seen even in the Ladies in the King's City. Her face was not beautiful, but rather striking; her eyes were deeply inset and her nose fine, long, thin; her cheeks were high and her chin almost too delicate. She wore a white shift that hung from three braided straps across her shoulder; it was edged in gold, and across its back, in full display, was the emblem that Stephen associated with the Twin Kings: The crown and the rod. She introduced herself, but quickly, and Stephen missed her name, which was just as well; he found her striking.

Gilliam knew it at once and snorted; the servant was good enough that she did not seem to notice this unexplained expression. Or perhaps she was used to foreigners.

The air was brisk, almost chilly. It caught Stephen's green velvet cape, and the servant's white robes, and tangled them a moment in the air.

"It's a sea wind," the bronze-haired woman said. "At this time of year it can almost be cold." She smiled softly, showing her teeth; she had all of them. "I've been told you come from a land of winter."

Stephen nodded. "In Breodanir the lands are still covered with snows, and in the North, the storms are strong." He stopped a moment in the open courtyard to gaze skyward; there were clouds across the sun's face, but the breeze pushed them aside, forcing Stephen to squint or look away. "But you could almost forget that winter existed in a place like this."

"Almost." She smiled again, staring skyward, completely oblivious to the sour grimace on Gilliam's face. "But occasionally the northern winds have a stronger hand and the cold blows in from the mountain chain. Then, it's often dangerous. We aren't a people prepared for bitter cold. They say that when Averalaan sees even a glimpse of the winter, the darkness follows—but I don't believe it."

"No?"

"No. How can it, with snow so white and so brilliant?"

Gilliam snorted loudly enough that it was clearly meant to be a contribution to the conversation. The imperturbable servant looked up, waiting. "It's pretty clear you've never seen a real winter," he said dourly. "Nothing grows; there's no food. Only the predators and the sleepers survive it."

"And, of course," Stephen added smoothly, "the people of Breodanir, who know the winter well enough to prepare for it, and who also honor it with their games. There's little harvesting to do in winter; little work. If you know the winter well enough, it's no more a danger than the spring." He stepped between Gilliam and their guide; the point was not lost on the Hunter Lord.

"They have snow in the South, beyond Annagar, or so I'm told," the guide said. She smiled at that, and her cheeks dimpled; there was a sparkle in her eyes that spoke of a secret memory.

"And none in Averalaan. You must have a growing season that lasts forever."

She shook her head. "It's not that simple—but I must admit that matters agrarian have not been my field of study. Come; the Queen and her Ladies will be waiting." Her stride widened slightly, although she never once appeared to be hurrying. Stephen followed her from the carved, stone courtyards of the Arannan Halls to the open quadrangle that seemed almost a small forest. He could hear water running, but he could not see its source, and he almost stopped to search for it.

Their guide was at his side in an instant. "Averalaan Aramarelas is like this; it has its hidden pockets of life and light. Will you be staying here long?"

At that, Stephen returned to his duty. "Not long, no." His smile was shadowed, although it did not leave his face entirely. "We must depart by the half-month of Corvil."

"Why?"

"Because," he said, "it is the custom of the Breodani. You might ask Lady Faergif or Lady Morganson to explain it. I'm sure they're most curious to know why we're here in the first place."

"Oh, indeed," she replied, with just a touch of sardonic smile. "Leave the dell, then. Come—the doors to the palace are just beyond the footpath."

To call it a footpath was to call the gown of the Queen's coronation, with its multiple layers of jewels and colors and textures, a frock. But with a city that the maker-born called home, what else could one expect? Stephen walked as if a dream had opened up before him, one in which time and urgency retreated like any other daytime squabble. There were flowers that lined the simple, but perfect path, shadowing it with their leaves and petals, of a type and kind that he had never seen; plants of a texture that made them seem dangerous, yet still hypnotically beautiful with their deep indigos, their fuchsias, their magentas. There were birds that stopped at their feet, staring up at them in haughty pride as if they knew they belonged at court more than the intruders; there were small creatures that hung from the trees, fur-covered and round-eyed and altogether magical.

The servant stopped again and again, but she did not interrupt Stephen's reverie, and indeed, after a few moments, Gilliam allowed himself to be pulled into it as well—a testament to the achievement of the maker-born of Averalaan, although they would never have known it.

When at last they entered the palace and left the dell, as she had called it, behind, a hint of its peacefulness and its vibrancy remained with Stephen. His step felt lighter than it had since he had first placed foot upon the Winter road; he smiled at Gilliam, and Gilliam surprised him by returning it.

Yet the hall was no less splendid than the dell had been, and no less wild; the stone itself seemed to be alive with the pageantry of history. There were fountains, small and large, and places where water might be drawn; there were statues and tableaux of men and women, in armor and in robes, in contemplation and in action, that seemed to breathe, to whisper, to plead. There were tapestries, long and tall and deceptively deep, wherein one might take a step and be lost. And the servant, immune to the effects of so much grandeur, merely waited as they stared at the artifacts of the Twin Crowns.

Then, at last, she brought them to the end of the hall, to an arch that was oddly shaped. As they approached it, Stephen saw that, in the center of the arch's peak, a young woman stood, her face turned toward the city. Her hands were open, whether in offering or in supplication it was hard to tell; she looked peaceful. Her dress was not the dress of Averalaan, nor the dress of Breodanir; it was simple and unadorned, as was she.

Beneath the arch, to either side, a man knelt, head bowed, crown upon the perfect stone strands of hair. Bearded, and girded for war, dressed in heavy plate, they clasped their mailed hands. To her.

"It is Veralaan," the servant whispered. "To her right and below, with the sword, Reymalyn; to her left, with the longbow, Cormalyn. They are returned from war to keep their promise to her." She paused and bowed deeply, the hem of her robes dusting ground so clean it almost gleamed. "Through these arches, you will find the Queens' court. They will be expecting you."

"You—you're not coming with us?"

"I? No, alas. Although I would dearly love the company of the indomitable Lady Faergif, there are tasks which call me, and to which I must attend. I am Miri," she added with a dimpled smile. "If you wish my aid or my services as a guide, you may ask for me and I will be summoned."

Stephen bowed very low, in the manner of the Breodani. Gilliam stepped on his foot.

Miri smiled deeply, but it was a smile that contained many things that could not be put into words. "You are not of Averalaan, and it is said that the lands of the Breodani were somehow proof against the predation of the wizard lords. But it is said that only in Essalieyan and Breodanir do the courts of the Queens surpass the splendor of Kings. We have little in common, our people, and much. Remember it." The smile grew deeper still. "We are ruled by Gods in Essalieyan; the Queens intercede for us where intercession is necessary."

At that, she turned her gaze to Stephen, and he realized that she knew exactly what a huntbrother was, and respected it in a way that the Hunter Lords they served could not. She bowed, and it was a Breodanir bow, but somehow deeper and more supple. He did not tell her that Ladies seldom bowed to either Hunter or huntbrother.

Instead, with almost a sigh, and Gilliam's muttering at his back, he turned and walked beneath the arch over which Veralaan presided.

There was another hall that started immediately after they were through the arch, and it was quite clear that it was not the same hall, not only by the arch which separated the two but by the construction of the hall itself.

Where at their backs the very past of the Empire seemed to loom, ready to embroil the unwary stranger, ahead of them there were great windows that seemed to reach from beneath their feet—although that was illusion—to the heights of the vaulted ceilings. They were immense in width, if possible, wider than the construction of the walls themselves, and in each of these windows, standing to one side that they might share the view and the warmth that light provided, were single statues.

The statues were the work of the maker-born, as was the hall, and the stones upon which they walked, the heights which dwarfed them. They were of stone, these statues, and yet more. When Stephen met their eyes, he had the curious sensation that something living looked back, appraised his passage, and then returned to the aloof material from which it had been chiseled.

The first of the statues was a man in his prime, armed and armored, with a helm in the crook of his left arm and a great sword, point to the ground, beneath his mailed right hand. His hair was cut and bound, and his cloak was still, as if he were at the eye of the storm of battle. There were, at his feet, a shield, a ring, and a crown.

"Cartanis," Stephen said softly. "Lord of War."

Gilliam knew the name, but little else; it was not of concern to the Hunter Lord, who did not worship other Gods; he barely thanked the Mother for her harvest, never prayed to Luck, and never gave a thought to what Judgment might say.

But it was the stuff of the stories those scholars and bards had brought forth from Essalieyan when they traveled to the West, and Stephen knew them as if they were written upon the backs of his eyelids.

He turned his gaze to the right, and saw there a man with a wreath of fine leaves and branches. Closer inspection showed both blossom and thorn across his brow, although he knew peace. He was not a young man, yet he possessed that peculiar androgyny that some do in youth, and in his left arm, held as if it were a child, was a small harp. He wore robes, soft and simple if made of stone, and his feet were bare against a small knoll of grass. His lips were open, but whether in song or speech, it was hard to say.

Omaran. Lord of music, of poetry, of art.

Next, opposite each other, were the Lord and the Lady; they had no other names, but in the Empire of Essalieyan the Lord brought sleep, and with it dream or nightmare, and the Lady brought death. The Lord was tall and regal and gentle, but there was an edge to his eyes, a surety in his stance, that spoke of cruelty. The Lady, robed in a simple gown, looked almost like a maiden not yet free from childhood; simply clad, she gazed out as if at a vast landscape. And there was nothing at all in her eyes that Stephen could understand. He pulled back and bowed, almost self-conscious in the gesture, as if by appeasing her, he might avoid her a little longer.

Only one of the Gods was seated, and Stephen knew him at once: Mandaros, called the Judge in Breodanir. He wore the robes of an ancient office, and beside him to the right were the scales by which he measured the soul's choice; in his right hand, the gavel by which he pronounced his judgment. And to his left, at his feet, the beginning of three paths: one rocky, one smooth, and one almost insubstantial.

Opposite the Judge was the oldest of all men present; he had a beard that ran down his face, and then his chest, like a snow-covered icicle, but his eyes seemed sharp and clear. He, too, wore robes, and he carried in one hand the staff, and in the other, the book.

Stephen would have recognized him had he seen him in the street, and not in the Hall of Gods; he was Teos, Lord of Knowledge, and he had promised Stephen the answer to one more question—and only one—should Stephen choose to call upon him.

Kalliaris was next, and she, Stephen did recognize, for although the Hunters and their people worshiped the Hunter, the thieves and the poor prayed to Kalliaris. The Breodani called her merely "Luck" or "Lady Luck." She was not as he imagined her—but then again, recently, he had not seen her smile as much as he'd hoped—but he knew her by the two masks she held in either hand.

She was opposite a young child who huddled in a corner, trying to cover its face with its hands. It did not quite succeed. This God, Stephen did not recognize; there were few tales of it that he had either read or remembered.

But he recognized Laursana and Karatia—Love and Lust—immediately. As a child, he had always thought them stupid, and sometimes, as an adult, the same—but as a child, he had been immune to their whims and their effects. They were not female and not male, and yet, being neither, they were attractive each in their own way. They had hair that reached to the ground and twined around their ankles like bracelets, or chains. Karatia was often depicted without clothing, but the maker-born who had chosen the God's form here had covered it, hidden it, made of it a mystery.

They were almost at the hall's end when he saw the Mother; she held in her arms a babe, and over her shoulder, in the slings that were so common among the Breodani field-workers, she carried stalks of corn and wheat and barley. She was not a slender woman, not a child; she was full and solid and certain of form. Around the corners of both her lips and her eyes, there were lines—she was smiling gently, and it seemed that those lines were etched there by the combination of time's passage and that smile.

He knelt at her feet a moment, whispered words of thanks. Then he rose, for across from her, as if no other window could hold him, was the Lord of the Hells.

Allasakar.

Stephen could not believe that here in this hall there would be a place for such a creature, and he froze a moment beneath the God's gaze, as if the God were indeed about to pluck him from the safety of Averalaan. Yet nothing happened, and after a moment, the hackles that had risen fell. He faced a tall and lordly man, one of perfect features. But in his left arm, tucked there in terror, was the twisting face of a man in torment; in his right hand was a scepter upon which a small, living creature with fangs for half its face, perched. The God wore a crown, and the crown was dark; upon its side were closed lids, but not for human eyes.

He wore wisps of shadow like a robe. The sculptor who had fashioned him must have been a master without parallel. There was something about the face of this God that was more seductive, more compelling, than even Karatia had been. He almost could not pull his gaze away.

And then Gilliam's annoyed grunt—which might have contained a word or two—broke the spell; there was no majesty, there was only perfectly carved and formed stone.

Only the Mother could love you, Stephen thought, as he found and kept a smile. *No other God would suffer you so closely.* But he wasn't certain anymore if that were true.

There was only one other window, and it stood alone, and it was not so grand or tall or perfect as those that preceded it. It was also empty.

He stopped a moment, and then gazed out of the window. As he stood directly in front of it, he saw that the window framed not the port, as he had first thought, but a building that lay on a hill in the basin across the water. At the height of that building was a statue of a man with a raised sword; his cape was caught in a fierce wind, and his shield was raised in defense. He wore, Stephen thought, greaves and plate armor, but it was hard to tell from this distance.

Moorelas, he thought, although he could not be certain; he cast a long, slender shadow. Then he looked away from this last window, for the hall had become another arch, and through it, he could hear the strains of strings being made to dance and shiver in air by the hand of a bard. They were almost upon the rooms in which the Queens, by day, held court.

There were two things that surprised him.

The first was that, although there were guards at the very end of the hall, their livery was fine to the point of ostentation, and Stephen thought them more for show—as were the paintings and the delicately arranged flowers—than for practical purposes.

The second was that there was no page-herald to greet them; no one to announce their presence or even to ascertain that they had indeed been summoned into the presence of the Queen.

In Breodanir, the Queen had her cadre; they were not Hunters, of course, but they served her in the capacity of guards with a severity and seriousness that would not bear this sort of display. And, of course, there were announcements; to enter the presence of the Queen was indeed a serious thing, at once a request not to be made lightly and an audience which, once granted, was not to be wasted.

The Queen's court was a matter of severity and of beauty, but not of frivolity, for, along with those very rare Judgment-born Priests, the Queen sat in Judgment in her demesne—and also sat in Judgment in those cases where a noble had been accused of a crime.

However, that was Breodanir.

Averalaan was a very different place, as his walk through the hall had shown him. The very Gods seemed to live in every shadow on the Holy Isle.

Stephen looked up as they entered the first room; it was huge; larger than any single room that he had ever seen. It was tall, and gave the illusion of being open to the air; light streamed down in broad, straight beams to touch the mosaic upon the floor beneath it. The mosaic was the crown and rod, the sword and the staff, and above it the eagle, beneath it, the mare. There were other patterns nestled among these things that Stephen knew he would not understand were he to study them carefully. He did not. Instead, he looked up.

There were galleries above—two, in fact—and recessed into them were chairs. Some were occupied by small groups of two and three who were obviously engaged in conversations that ranged from pleasant to heated, but the galleries themselves were so large they seemed, for the most part, empty. Toward the end of the room, there was a single throne; it was vacant, and because of that, he could see the detailing carved into the height of its wooden back. The dagger and the ring, surrounded by a wreath of thorny roses—an emblem of faith and oath in adversity. Stephen waited, and held Gilliam in check, but after five minutes it became clear that no one would approach them.

Almost embarrassed, he began to cross the room.

People looked up from their conversations and then raised a brow; the dress of the Breodani was unique in the halls, and to add to that, Espere was already chafing at the collar of her dress.

And then he saw her: Lady Faergif. He felt relief, which was exactly what he had least expected to feel. She was a good deal older than he remembered, and perhaps that age had softened her, for her eyes lit with a warmth that recognition of the blessedly familiar often brings. She was dressed not as Breodani, but rather as Essalieyanese; she wore their loose-fitting robes, soft and silky, and shoes that were meant for easy weather and little outdoor travel.

But the robes were not the usual pale colors that Stephen saw everywhere; they were instead a deep and royal green, and they were edged in brown and gold—for the gold had been the rank achieved by her late husband, and it was hers forever should she choose it. A wide gold net was pulled around her waist like a belt, and her hair was pulled simply and securely from her face.

He had thought her old when he was eight or nine, but now he thought her simply strong and in that time of life where age and power in a woman mix to great advantage. His bow was immediate; it was low and extremely formal, as was his dress. He did her the homage not only due a Lady of her station, but also due one whose husband the Hunt had taken. Then, chagrined, he nudged Gilliam into doing the same.

It made her smile.

"Lady Faergif," Stephen said, rising slowly. "It is an honor to meet you here."

"And, I imagine, a bit of a relief?"

He almost blushed, but he nodded. "There aren't any—"

"Pages? Yes and no. They do not, however, announce their guests in these rooms. These halls are the Queen's halls, and for her guests and chosen friends; she does not entertain those who petition her for royal business here. As you can see," she added, nodding to the empty throne, "she is not present at the moment.

There is the day's business to attend to, although it is not heavy by Breodanir standards."

"But we—"

"Stephen of Elseth," Lady Faergif said, in a tone of voice which he much remembered, "do you think you would have walked that hall were you not expected? Come, think before you speak."

This was much more the Lady Faergif of his childhood. But he was not a child, and the nervousness of hours past began to fade. She was a Lady, and one who spoke strongly and sharply, but she carried the heart of all Ladies who lose to the Hunter God the things they love best, and like those Ladies, she endured it for the good of the lands.

"Come, if you will. Lady Morganson is waiting by the fountains." So saying, Lady Faergif turned—but Stephen stepped up beside her and carefully held out his forearm. She almost missed a beat in the next step she chose, and then she smiled, yet it was with that strange mixture of happiness and a deep and abiding sorrow that Stephen had seen many times in his life but did not fully understand. She placed her arm delicately over his, folding her fingers over his knuckles. And she allowed him to escort her, as she was once escorted in the court of the land by her Lord's huntbrother.

"I've been long away from home," she said, as if to explain her slight misstep, "and there are niceties of custom that the Essalieyanese do not preserve. But you will find them a canny people, although there are far too many merchants to make one want to relax one's guard." She looked up. "Ah, there she is. Helene, look who's arrived."

Lady Morganson looked up from her seat by the edge of a very grand yet very quiet fountain. She was, charitably, a short woman, with hair the color of iron but eyes the color of cornflowers; she was rounded by the years, and perhaps even softened by them, although it was hard to tell—she was not in her native setting.

Stephen escorted Lady Faergif to her, and then looked at the fountain itself. There were fish in it—not large enough to be eaten well, but not small enough to be used as bait should it be necessary—and anyway, these were not fish to be so used. They were brilliantly colored; he thought they must be mage-changed, somehow.

All around the fountain were rocks, and the rocks themselves were not carved; there were plants and shrubs and oddly shaped trees that crept up between them. There was no look of planning to the garden, but no look of wildness either; it was strange, but in the strangeness oddly peaceful.

Or perhaps that was due to the two Ladies who sat within it, waiting. He turned and bowed very formally to Lady Morganson, and she nodded.

"We received word," she said, "from Lady Elseth. She thought you might be in need of our assistance, and asked that, should we come across you, we offer it."

"I assure you, Lady Morganson and Lady Faergif, that we have—"

"Already been attacked within the Annagarian guest halls," Lady Faergif said sharply. Her eyes were narrowed. "Don't assume that because we are no longer in Breodanir, we are in an august, witless dotage."

This was the Lady Faergif of his youth. He took a step back, bumped into Gilliam, and bowed his head, more to placate her sudden temper than to hide the reddening of his cheeks.

"Leof," Lady Morganson said softly. As Lady Faergif fell silent—or rather, did not continue her tirade—Lady Morganson began. "We do not know what brought you to Averalaan—what, indeed, forced you to cross the Breodanir border. We are curious, but Lady Elseth was most emphatic, and therefore, in deference to her wishes, we will not ask you to speak more than you will.

"But word of the incident in the halls has passed from servant to servant and noble to noble; although very few now know who the targets of that attack were, we can safely guess that it was you. Do you know why you were so attacked?"

Stephen shook his head.

"Very well. Our sources here are not as good as we might hope." She rose, leaving the stone ledge that overlooked the fountain and the fish swimming in its rippling basin. "We have been able to gain an answer that satisfies neither of us. You are currently under the protection of Terafin. Are you aware of this?"

Gilliam said no and Stephen said yes; the Ladies exchanged wry glances.

"Are you in the service of Terafin?"

Gilliam said no again, and this time, Stephen remained silent, unsure of how to best answer the question.

Lady Faergif's brow rose a fraction, but that was all; she lifted a hand, forestalling her companion, and began to speak in her stead. "Terafin has many enemies among The Ten, and few friends—it is the most powerful of the seated Houses, and it has, in the person of The Terafin, the Kings' ears. Morriset, the second House, disputes much of the current merchanting holdings of Terafin, but more besides; the current Morriset is sly and crafty and not to be trusted. He is an older man, with the cunning and experience that that implies—but his House is divided. The other House that will openly take sides against Terafin, and bitterly so, is Darias.

"Neither of the Lords spend much time at court, and it is unlikely that you will meet them unless you are here at the first and half-month. We counsel you to avoid those who are ADarias or AMorriset, for we believe—although there is no certainty in this belief—that one or the other of these Houses is involved in the attempt."

"Why?"

"Because it is through the auspices of The Ten that the assassins, dressed as servants, gained entrance into the grounds." Her eyes narrowed as she started to speak, and then she shook her head. "I forget that you do not understand Avera-laan and its customs. Lord Elseth barely understands Breodanir."

Lord Elseth refrained from comment, but only because he was trying, with what dignity he could force, to stop Espere from jumping into the small fish pond.

"The Ten are part of Averalaan and its history; if not for The Ten, the Twin Kings would never have taken the rulership of the land. The Hall of The Ten is a part of the palace, a court unto itself in many ways. There are rooms and meeting halls within which The Ten and their members may meet; there are libraries of documents pertaining to The Ten, and there is a special court, at which crimes involving The Ten—and there are very, very few—are tried.

"There are servants provided by The Ten to man and staff the halls; guards, however, are provided from the ranks of the Kings' Swords, for reasons which I should think obvious.

"It has become clear—don't fuss, Helene, this is not a court and we are not the arguers; we don't have to have solid evidence to present—that the two who made their way to the Arannan Halls came through the Hall of The Ten. We believe that someone either AMorriset or ADarias let them in."

Lady Morganson was slightly uneasy, but she nodded as Lady Faergif finished. "What we don't understand, Stephen, is the *why* of it. You've been in the capital for four or five days, which is certainly not enough time to gain the confidence of The Terafin—and we would know," she added, with a rueful grimace, "but you've gained the enmity of another House, which certainly implies that you *are* impor-tant. Why?"

"If I knew the answer," Stephen replied, "I would most certainly say it." But he hesitated over what he did know, seeing before him the practical Ladies who were the backbone of the kingdom that he loved. Finally, he bowed, and the bow was low and long. "There are mages involved, Lady Faergif. More than that, I do not understand." Without meaning to, he glanced at Espere; she was fidgeting in a way that suggested her clothing was not long for the world. "But let me introduce Espere."

Espere, hearing her name, scampered forward, just as any dog might have. Her eyes were sharp and clear, but they also had that peculiar vacancy that the dogs did not possess. Her hair, wild, was already breaking free of the combs with which Stephen had—barely—managed to bind it. He felt Gilliam's annoyance, and saw the girl tense before falling into a sullen stillness.

Lady Faergif raised a brow and looked down her nose. "And she?"

"She is the daughter of the Hunter God."

Silence, long and loud; a flickered meeting of eyes, the hint of raised brows. Then, "I see."

"And the assassins were hunting not only Lord Elseth and me, but Espere."

But Lady Morganson and Lady Faergif were no longer listening; instead, they were staring at Espere intently, a look of curiosity, fear, and an unexplained pity upon their faces. "Is this well known?" Lady Morganson asked at last.

"No. But by someone, possibly a mage. We found her while she was being hunted, and in some ways that hunt has never stopped."

"Does she speak?" Lady Faergif asked abruptly.

You could not hide a thing from the noblewomen of Breodanir. Not one thing. And a wise man, Stephen reflected rather ruefully, did not try. "No, Lady. Although we know that, in the right circumstance, she is able."

"I don't suppose, during that 'right circumstance' you thought to ask her why she was being, hunted?"

He reddened at the sting in her words. "We did not have the time."

"No, of course not. Helene?"

Lady Morganson shook her head, looking rather dour. "Hunter's business," she said at length, "and it's probably best left to Hunter Lords."

Lady Faergif's sour expression made it clear what she thought of that, but she held her silence for all of a minute before she began again. "Well, there you have it then. Hunter's business." She took one last look at Espere and then shook her head as if to rid herself of that glance. "There are other rumors in court, much harder to come by, and much less substantial.

"One of those is that there was an attack upon The Terafin, a nearly successful one. Do you know anything of it?"

"Not really. We—"

"Because it's said that Darias hired a mage, through the auspices of one of his linked lords, and that mage attempted to assassinate her. The name of that member of the patriciate is not, unfortunately, in circulation."

"Lady, we've spoken only once with The Terafin. We know very little about her affairs, and—"

"You've spoken *with* The Terafin?"

Stephen took a seat by the fountain, drew a deep breath, and then nodded. He expected a rapid barrage of questions but was disappointed; there was silence again, and it was almost as long, and contained almost as much surprise, as their first silence. But this was *not* Hunter's business; not as they understood it.

Lady Morganson's eyes were clear and sharp as she took a seat beside Stephen and turned to face him.

Before she could speak, however, someone came into the small clearing in the quiet stone garden. Although he did not talk, he did not come in silence; the song of his strings stirred the air and announced him more effectively than mere words would have.

"I hope," he said, with a perfect smile and an equally perfect bow, "that I have not interrupted anything of import?"

Stephen looked up and saw a face that he recognized, although eight years lay between the man that he was and the youth that he had been the last time he'd seen the bard. Kallandras. He wore a pale blue and lavender jacket, rather than the loose-fitting robes that many of the men wore as a matter of course, and his boots were of the variety that were used for traveling. He wore no hat, and carried no obvious weapon; he seemed gaudy, for all that the only unnecessary item he wore was a complicated ring with a diamond that seemed entirely made of light. It didn't matter; Kallandras was still youthful, still beautiful, and still slightly haunted.

"Kallandras," Stephen said, rising and bowing in a single smooth motion. He was grateful for the interruption; a Lady on a quest for information that she believed to be her province was not unlike a Hunter on the trail of his quarry. "You do not interrupt but, rather, honor."

"And that is very well," the bard said, smiling broadly. "Lady Morganson. Lady Faergif. It has been far too long since I've had the pleasure of your company." So saying, he bowed again, and golden curls fell from his shoulders without once touching and muting the song that he continued to play in the background.

Lady Faergif looked singularly unimpressed, but Lady Morganson returned the bow with a good-natured smile. "Kallandras, you are always welcome at the Queen's court, and know it well. What are you in search of this time?"

"You wound me, Lady," he replied, "but as you expect some motivation, I shall endeavor not to disappoint. The truth is that I had heard a rumor that Lord Elseth and his huntbrother had come to Averalaan."

"And that has something to do with you?" Lady Faergif's question was sharp.

"Oh, indeed," the bard said, gravity coming suddenly to his features. "For it was at the Sacred Hunt that I first met Lord Elseth and Stephen; I joined the drummers for the Hunt's start, and I sang the Hunt's close." He bowed then, very low, to Lord Elseth, and Gilliam, stony-faced, returned the bow.

"You sang the Hunt's—" Her words trailed off, for she knew which Hunt it was, then, and what the significance was to both Lord Elseth and his huntbrother. For it was not a custom of the Breodani to have bardic song at any time during the Sacred Hunt, and on only one occasion could Lady Faergif remember reports of such an occurrence. A young bard, of Senniel College no less, sang the death lay of Averalaan for a fallen Hunter. Kallandras. She rose stiffly.

"Lord Elseth, Stephen." She bowed. "We hope that you will be able to attend court again before the day of your departure."

"As do we," Stephen replied. He frowned slightly. "But that must be before the half-month of Corvil, if we are to return to the King's City for the Hunt."

"We will look for you, and we will keep our ears open. What we hear, we will pass on. We expect," she added severely, "that you will do no less."

"Lady," Stephen said, nodding. He bowed once more, and she accepted it with good grace and a touch of melancholy. And then, Lady Faergif and Lady Morganson departed the garden; Stephen, Gilliam, and Espere turned to face Kallandras.

It was silent. The strains of calm and quiet music disappeared as the bard's long fingers came to rest against the strings.

Only then did Stephen realize how pale he was, how fatigued; his eyes were lined and darkened, and his shoulders slightly bent. All youth fled, running down his face as if it were water. What remained was haggard and almost fearful. He took a step, and then another. The ledge of the fountain provided support as he gently set his lute in his lap.

"Hello, wild one," he said, and although his voice was quiet, there was an intensity to his gaze that was more frightening than any shout or cry would have been. "I have need of your aid."

Gilliam was at her side, and slightly forward, before the last words had died into stillness. His hackles were up, and his teeth on edge; his whole body was taut. "What do you mean?" he asked softly, his words no less intense than the bard's.

The bard's pale brow rose as he glanced from the wild girl—the dressed and combed and bathed wild girl—to Gilliam. His own gaze was cold and measured; there was no violence in it, but there was no fear at all of any violence that Gilliam might offer. "I have met the wild one before," was his grave reply. "We traveled together for a short while."

The answer seemed to dull the edge of Gilliam's ire, but Stephen knew that that was not the case. Gilliam felt threatened by a past that he did not know of and did not understand. Because, of course, he owned Espere, even if that was not a word he would acknowledge.

"I have need of her company again," Kallandras continued, when Gilliam said nothing. "I need her to lead me to the darkness."

Chapter Fifteen

DARKNESS.

The word hit Stephen like a long, thin needle; he was unaware of how much it bothered him until the damage it caused welled up in the silence and began to spread. This Kallandras was not the Kallandras that he had met in his youth, or rather, he was not the bard. He was the man, glimpsed only for a second, who had forced Stephen to run from the sight of a would-be assassin with a voice that could not be denied.

"Did she send you?" The words sounded tinny as he spoke them.

"Yes." A long pause, as if the word had been weighed and found wanting. "And no." He lifted his lute and began to strum it absently. His fingers slowly relaxed against the strings, playing a tune as if the act of playing, and not the music that came from it, was necessary. "We cannot speak here."

"No." Stephen cleared his throat. "But we cannot leave." He felt Gilliam like a pressure at the back of his thoughts. Sighed. "Kallandras, where did you meet the wild girl? Why do you think she can—she can lead you to what you seek?"

"Where?" The bard's eyes were distant, almost colorless. "I met her in Averalaan. *She* brought her to me, or brought me to her. It was long ago, and not far enough away." Then he shook himself, and seemed, for an instant, to have his old edge, his old clarity. "Lord Elseth, your pardon. I was given something that I have kept for some years; it is yours, although I did not know it until a few days ago."

"What?" The word was curt and short.

Kallandras continued to play, filling the silence with peace rather than responding to Gilliam's one-sided rivalry. But he did not answer directly. Instead, as any Breodanir Lady would do in the face of such poor behavior, he turned to the huntbrother, showing no signs of concern or even irritation at Gilliam's brusqueness.

"I would like to speak with you at the earliest hour of your convenience. If you will permit, I will visit you in your quarters."

The hair on Stephen's arms stood on end; he felt the lightning before its strike, although the occasional clouds tossed briskly above were not storm carriers. He wanted to speak with Kallandras, for the bard knew much, and Stephen's curiosity was keen, almost painful. But at the same moment, he wanted to shy away, to somehow avoid the conversation to come. He glanced at the wild girl, and she at Kallandras; there was a tension in the air, and they were the four corners of it, pulling at each other invisibly with their desires and their fears.

And then Stephen realized that the bard was singing, and he knew why he thought of storms; Kallandras' words were like thunder over the chords of the lute, for all that his voice was soft and well-modulated.

"Before the wars that won the land,
before the time that birth renewed,
before the measure of the Twins was taken and found true,
There rose above the dark'ning sky,
a spire grim and glorious high,
that many saw and many fled and those survived were few.
The Shining Lords, they called themselves
And light was on their comely brows,
Who lived within the darken shroud that lay upon the land
And in the name of light unholy
Serving Lords of evil glory
The Shining City lit a pyre 'pon which the very Gods might stand."

There was no sound in the small garden, if it was not Kallandras' voice.

"You are bold as always, Kallandras."

"And you are stealthy," the bard replied as the song left his lips. "Master APhaniel."

"Why sing you so dark a lay?" The mage-born master was tall and slender, and Stephen saw him as if he had never seen him before. There was a shadow about him, and a silence that held the hush before an ambush. He wore his usual robes, and they glittered in the hide-and-seek of sun and cloud. He carried his pipe, and its smoke wended its way into the garden's air, scenting it with a mildly bitter, burning herb. His hair was long and drawn back in a braid that nearly reached his feet; his free hand, fine and slender, was clenched, fistlike, against his chest.

"Dark?" Kallandras replied, and his fingers touched strings again, quickly and lightly filling the air with melody and counterpoint. "Your pardon. It is an old lay, and only the very young or the very old require it of us. It is merely myth and legend, Master APhaniel."

The mage's smile was grim indeed as he bowed his head. "Mere, is it?" he said softly, as his slate-gray eyes met Kallandras'. "But then again, who among us would not lend credence to the most scurrilous of lies if it were carried by your voice?"

Even his voice sounded strange to Stephen's ears, richer and deeper than it usually did; not a match for Kallandras' bard-born tones, but a counterpoint to it, with a strength of its own. One of the most powerful of the mage-born members of the Order seemed suddenly out of place in this court of the highest nobility in Essalieyan.

And where was his place? The small, isolated tower room of the Order of Knowledge? The crowded, argumentative gathering hall of the Council of the Magi? As if he could hear Stephen's musings, Meralonne turned his head slowly, leveling his eyes as if they were readied weapons.

Espere growled, and Gilliam came to stand at Stephen's side; Stephen wasn't even certain if Gilliam's maneuvering was conscious. There was something between Kallandras and the mage, and something about Kallandras and the mage, that set them apart from not only the court, the city and the land, but from her people.

At last, Meralonne turned to Kallandras. "You are a fine bard, but still a young one. Be careful of what you invoke." He lifted his pipe.

Kallandras smiled, and the smile was flawless, but it did not touch his eyes. He swept into a low—an exaggerated—bow and then began to sing again.

"*Earth and air; fire and water*
long before the Mother's daughter
graced the land with turning season
gave to us the Gods of reason
Wild the ways, and wild the wise
before the dawn of mortal's rise
Who could hold the captive spark
of four, interred, against the dark?
'Twas Myrddion of fatal flower
working to the foreseen hour
Who captured each in stone and ring
Who forced the elements to bring
Their power and their ancient guise
To fools, heroes, and the wise
And then in darkness sowed the seed
in blood and death, for greatest need
But whose the hand that taught the mage?
Which the wise and wildcraft sage
steeped in lore of ancient choice;
the light and dark and First-born voice?"

"More of your children's lyrics? Kallandras, if you continue, you will bore us all." Meralonne blew rings of smoke into the air. Watching him, Stephen was reminded of his own childhood stories. And in them, boredom was not the threatened end.

"Perhaps," was the quiet reply. "And perhaps not. Shall I continue, Master APhaniel?"

The sage was quiet. "Continue?"

"Ah. Yes, continue." He turned to Stephen and Gilliam, speaking to them, and yet pitching his words so that the mage might clearly hear them. "You see, what I have sung so far is what the children sing in their drawing of the quarters in the streets of the city. It is a game they play, and if they cross the lines that they have quartered—or rather, touch them—they must 'dare or die.'

"But they know only a fragment, and at that, a small one. Do you have the time to listen? For I am certain—"

"Enough, Kallandras."

Kallandras smiled, and the smile itself was fey and troubled. "Enough? But I—" He stumbled suddenly; his hands gripped the lute and pulled it close to protect it. The fabric of vest and shirt stilled the song and silenced it as the bard slid to the ground.

Stephen was at his side in an instant. "Gill—go at once—send for a healer."

"Send for a physician," Meralonne said, overlaying it with the tone of command. "In Averalaan, healer means one healer-born, and there are few of those." He set his pipe on the stone beside the fountain.

Gilliam hesitated for only a second, and then he was gone—but Espere remained at Stephen's side, growling fiercely.

Stephen raised a hand in warning as the mage approached. "Stay where you are." He touched Kallandras' pale, sweaty brow—no fever. As he listened, as breath struggled in and out of the bard's slack jaw, a word escaped him, a single word.

"I will not harm him," Meralonne said, almost wry in his inflection. "It is not due to me that he has fallen."

Stephen looked up as the mage spoke; he caught the bard's shoulders and pulled him into his lap, raising his head above the flat flagstones. "What is *niscea?*"

Meralonne's eyes narrowed as he studied the lines of Kallandras' still face. At last, after some thought, he spoke, and his words were measured. "*Niscea*, also known as seablossom, is a blend of herbs, mushrooms, and saps. In strong doses, it is death."

Stephen paled. "Poison," he said softly.

"In weak doses, it is a fool's pleasure," the mage continued, his expression remote, almost calculating. "But Kallandras has rarely been called a fool."

There were physicians within the court of the Queen, but there was also a healer— in the Essalieyanese use of the word. He was a much younger man than Alowan,

The Terafin's healer, but he had about him a quiet and a calm that was uncannily like the older man's. His hair was pale and long, but it hung at his back in a practical braid that was otherwise not seen at court.

At his insistence, Kallandras was taken to the healerie. Twice, the bard stirred, and twice he struggled; his movements were sharp and hard, even dangerous. The healer had him strapped into a pallet before he was lifted and moved, but even so, he was not easy until Kallandras was safely within the healerie's confines.

And the healerie of the Queen's court was not at all like Alowan's healerie; it was a much more practical place—a long, rectangular room, with beds against the wall that faced the windows and the balcony. The beds themselves were as fine as the one in which Stephen slept, but they were legless and rested against the flat, smooth stone of the floor. There were cupboards and bed boxes which held needed supplies, and there were two young men who served the healer, attending his commands and words.

It was from their gentle and unobtrusive questions that Stephen learned the healer's name: He was Dantallon.

Master APhaniel did not love the healer, or so it seemed; he kept a great distance from the young man at work, although it was clear that that work interested him. But it was the mage who told Dantallon about *niscea.*

The word caused the healer's face to cloud. "Are you certain of this?"

"I? No. But the young diplomat may well be; it was he who overheard it. He does not understand its significance."

At that, the healer turned his intent gaze. "Your pardon," he said. "But I must ask you to confirm what the member of the Order states."

Stephen swallowed and nodded, wondering if by doing so he was condemning the bard to whom he owed his life. He started to speak, when Kallandras spoke instead.

The words were not Essalieyanese; nor were they of the Breodani. It was clear that the healer could not understand them either, but he did not need to; the pain in them was obvious, and the wildness beneath them frightening.

One of the restraining buckles snapped as the bard drove his shoulder through it.

"Mother's blood." The straps were a thick, cured leather, harder than court shoes, softer than armor; they were meant to hold a man twice Kallandras' size and strength during seizures or fits. From the paling of Dantallon's face, Stephen guessed that one had never been broken, until now. They froze, staring at Kallandras until the second strap snapped.

"Cadrey! Lorrison! Grab his legs—I'll take his arms!"

Stephen stepped in to help, as did Gilliam.

"*Stop.*" Meralonne's voice was quiet compared to the healer's shouts—but it carried, filling the hollows of the room completely with its command. "Back away. Do not touch him."

Dantallon gave the mage a withering glare—but to Stephen's surprise, he followed the command; they all did.

Kallandras snapped the last restraint, and rolled out of the bed; his feet touched the floor first, and then the tips of his fingers. His hand touched his thigh, his arm, his waist, and then his eyes narrowed. He looked up. Sweat matted his curls to the side of his face; his eyes were wide.

"Evayne," he said, his voice a hoarse whisper. He took a step forward, reaching into the folds of his vest. His hand came out empty.

"Cadrey," Dantallon said softly. "Call the Kings' Swords."

"Sir," was Cadrey's taut reply. He was closest to the door, and lingered a moment on the threshold, as if afraid to leave his master behind.

"Cadrey!"

He did not, however, wait to be told a third time. The heavy tread of his steps could be heard rapidly diminishing in the hall. Once he had chosen to move, he moved quickly.

"Dantallon, your leave?"

Dantallon stared intently at his patient. Kallandras took a step forward, his eyes focused on something that no one else in the room could see. The bard pivoted neatly and then cried out in pain, clutching his ears, the side of his face, his hair. His knees folded like stiff cloth as he crumpled to the floor. He should have made noise as he struck the ground, but he was silent.

"Dantallon?" Meralonne's hands were static in midair, prepared for motion and the gathering of power, but not yet in the dance.

"No."

"*What?*"

"No. You will not use your magics in *my* halls." He spoke to Stephen without once taking his eyes from Kallandras. "You said that he mentioned *niscea*. These effects—this delirium—are not caused by *niscea*." The bard stopped his shouting as suddenly as it had begun; the healer's voice, barely heard, became a booming tenor. "I don't know what's causing them," he added darkly, "but I believe the bard was asking that *niscea* be administered."

At the word, at the sound of the word, Kallandras turned to face them. It was the first time that Stephen had met his eyes since he'd collapsed in the stone gardens. No words accompanied the glance; they weren't necessary.

"Yes," Stephen heard himself say. Then he straightened his shoulders. "Yes. I will take responsibility for the administration; I will accept the burden of the cost."

"Good. Will you take the risk of attempting to feed it to him?" There was just an edge of humor to the words, and Stephen thought he caught the hint of a smile—perhaps it was a grimace—across the healer's face.

But he nodded as if the words were serious.

"Dantallon." Meralonne's voice was charged. "Don't be a fool. I tell you now that—"

"And *I* tell *you*," Dantallon replied, "that your magics are not acceptable to me in my halls; by compact of King and Crown, you *will not* use them here."

"You don't know what you're facing," the mage replied gravely.

"And you do?"

Silence, and one more telling than words. The mage folded his arms across his slender chest and looked down at Dantallon, and only in that gesture made Stephen realize the difference in their heights.

He was suddenly very tired of tension and conflict, Kallandras rested in the balance; let the two men argue as they might later. "Lorrison?" he said softly, and the healer's assistant looked away from his master.

"Sir?"

"Do you have *niscea*?"

"Sir. But very little; it is not used commonly, and only in cases of—"

"I don't care what its normal use is; we need it now."

The golden-haired shadow that lay writhing across the floor stopped suddenly. In a movement so quick it was hard to follow, he was on his feet by the window. Light streamed in, making of him a white, deathly wraith; light flickered off his hand. Something shone there, against his finger, nestled tight; something glinted and flashed in his palm as he traced a small arc in the air.

Beside him, and beneath the window's lip, was a long, flat table. On it, rolled and spun, were strips of loose cotton in narrow, even rows. And seconds ago, beside those strips, had been a thin and narrow set of shears. Kallandras had found his weapon.

Brushing the wet curls from his face, he became a study in concentration; he stared, calming as he did, into the room's center. He mouthed a single word. *Evayne.* For a moment his face was so peaceful it seemed at odds with the shears in his hand.

And then the peace was gone; his teeth clenched, blocking but not silencing the scream behind them. His body spasmed twice, and he folded in the middle— but his grip on the shears did not lessen.

Stephen heard the sound of keys and a door; he heard the rustle of robes or linen; he heard steps coming up behind him. He held out his hand, watching Kallandras, and Lorrison placed a stoppered ceramic container into his outstretched palm.

But before he could take a step, the door to the healerie flew open and smashed into the far wall. Kallandras heard the noise from wherever it was his mind had gone; he blinked, looked up, and then *moved.* He came to rest, back against the wall farthest from the Kings' Swords that filtered into the hall, weapons readied.

* * *

The steel of armor and steel of sword glinted in the daylight, but there were bows as well, longbows, strung and readied. Stephen saw a sea of helmed faces above shields and weapons; he glimpsed surcoats of royal blue and white, bearing the crest of the Crowns bounded on either side by a long sword.

At the head of the Kings' Swords was Miri.

She was armed with a drawn sword, and her easy, cautious stance made it clear that she knew how to wield it to good effect. Gone was her dress; in its place a tunic and something that looked almost like practical breeches. Her hair was bound tight in a pearled net and pulled fully from her face; it made her seem more severe, but no less striking.

Dantallon and Meralonne made to bow, and she shook her head, forestalling them. "What has happened here?"

Her voice was not the voice that Stephen remembered; there was a coolness to it, a harshness, that made it seem quite remote.

Dantallon pointed to the back of the room. "It's the bard, Kallandras," he said softly. "He is in delirium, and we fear that he may harm himself."

"Harm himself?" Her eyes darkened as she narrowed them and stared at the bard. He was breathing heavily and loudly, and his face was obviously gleaming with sweat; his lips were a thin, white line. "I see. And this required the presence of Master APhaniel?"

"No, ACormaris."

"Good." Turning, she faced the Swords. "Fan out, be ready, do *nothing* without my leave." The man at their head nodded and rapped his chest with his mailed fist. The surcoat muffled the impact.

"And you," she continued, turning to the pale-haired mage, "will also follow those orders. Or you will leave."

"I will, of course, abide by the orders of one—"

"Good." She left them behind and walked silently across the tiled floor. Stopped in front of Stephen and met his gaze for a moment, searching for something. She found it—or she didn't—for her face softened and he saw the hint of a rueful smile. Just the hint, though.

"We need to give him this," Stephen said, although she'd asked nothing. He held out the stoppered container, and she examined it. *"Niscea,"* he added.

Her eyes widened as she stared at the flask without touching it. "Is this true?" she asked loudly enough to demand the healer's attention.

"Yes, ACormaris."

She swore softly under her breath in a language that Stephen could not quite understand, although its cadence felt familiar. "Very well." She lifted her hand and motioned; six men stood forward at once, although three had to step around Gilliam to do so. "Catch him and hold him down. Don't injure him."

"ACormaris," Meralonne said, and again, although the word was not shouted, his voice filled the room. "I do not believe that to be the wise course of action."

She lifted her hand again, so sharply and precisely that Stephen thought her sword superfluous. Her eyes were glinting as she stared ahead, at Kallandras, crouched low against the wall. But she did not demand further explanation from the mage; nor did she even bristle slightly at his interruption.

"Stand back," she told the six. And then, to Stephen, "Give me the flask."

He looked at it, at its unadorned simplicity, its stone stopper. He looked at the smooth and slender hand in front of him, and then let his eyes focus beyond that, to Kallandras. Something shifted in the bard's expression, hardening like water turned suddenly to ice.

Without thought, Stephen pushed Miri to safety—and nearly fell as he discovered that she was no longer standing by his side. Kallandras was, but briefly; the shears in his hands struck cloth and split skin.

Gilliam cried out in shock and surprise—both his own and Stephen's—as Kallandras attacked the bronze-haired woman who was obviously not the servant they had assumed her to be. He started forward, hand on hilt, and was immediately apprehended by Kings' Swords—two on either side.

"What are you doing?" Gilliam took another step forward and four more men closed off his path; he could no more enter the fray than walk to the room's center. "Have you lost your sense? The Lady needs—"

A mailed hand covered his sword arm and then withdrew. "The Lady needs obedience, no more, no less." The man who spoke was grim and slightly pale; he was perhaps four years Gilliam's senior. A helm obscured the color of his hair and he wore no beard, but his shoulders were broad and he was tall. He had seen at least one combat; that showed across his forehead and the upper bridge of his long, fine nose. "She's given us no word; we're to wait." He paused. "I'm sorry, Lord Elseth; you are not under her dominion, but I must ask that you follow her counsel."

Gilliam could smell the fear that lay behind the man's perfectly composed face. But he was not afraid of the Hunter Lord—that sort of viscerality, Gilliam could not have mistaken. No; he was afraid of—or for—the bronze-haired woman.

What was her name?

Looking to the side, and then to his back, Gilliam could see that all of the men in the room were watching; they breathed across the edge of their teeth, and their hands were slowly curling into metal-jointed fists.

Not one of them broke ranks. Not one raised a bow or nocked an arrow. They were crazy, these foreigners. They were just going to sit and watch. And he was going to stand and join them. Because he could feel Stephen press against his anger and his concern, trying to shape it or calm it. Stephen did not want him to interfere.

He called Espere to heel, pulling her in and trying to douse the fury that made him want the fight the Swords would offer. "She's not even armored," Gilliam began again.

"Neither is the bard, sir," was the even response. "And I'd put her sword against his scissors any day." He met Gilliam's eyes—or tried to; the Hunter Lord was staring first at Kallandras and the bronze-haired acrobat, and then at his hunt-brother, who stood isolated and immobile in the room's center, palms cradling a ceramic flask.

Espere whined softly, and he caught her shoulders and pulled her close, touching the top of her wild thatch of hair with the tip of his chin.

She was bleeding; Stephen saw the bright gash appear across her torso, made wider as cloth absorbed blood. It wasn't a deep wound, and he thanked the Mother for it; he'd seen torso wounds in the Hunt before, and they were almost always fatal—worse, the fatality was lingering, fever-ridden and painful.

She jumped again, followed by Kallandras; she seemed a leaf to his gale, but she moved ahead of him, in silence, always landing close enough for his strike or his swing, and always—save for that single first blow—being a hair's breadth ahead of it. He was pale, and his face was awash with the sweat of his efforts; his breath, heavy and labored, belied the agility and the grace, the ease and the accuracy, of his movements.

But he stopped almost in mid-stride, the guards now along each of the four walls, and he and Miri doing their dance of death in the center of the healerie. There were beds to either side of him, flat on the floor; facing him, the window. Miri was a yard away, knees bent and lips slightly parted. She, too, was sweating, but her cheeks were flushed with effort, where his were pale.

He held the shears in a tightening grip as he slid floor-ward, drawn as if by web and force, and not by weakness. By slow degree, he curled in on himself, writhing, his face taut and terrible with pain. The shears, like an afterthought, fell, but only when his hands shook too much to bear them.

Stephen did not wait for Miri's command; he darted forward immediately. Someone shouted a warning at his back; later, he would realize that it was Meralonne, and that the warning was, word for word, the warning he had offered Miri—and she had heeded.

But he needed no warning; he knelt before the writhing bard, one hand cupped round the bottom of the warming flask, and the other palm out and empty. Many, many times on hunts too numerous to count, Stephen had seen dogs injured. When in pain, the alaunts and mastiffs were most vicious, and often least aware of their surroundings. They could be approached with safety by their Hunters—but if the Hunter was injured—and this, too, happened—the huntbrother was often left with the task of tending to the wounded beast.

He's not a running hound, Stephen thought as his hands shook. *He's a man.*

Gilliam was in his mind, calming and steadying him; there were Kings' Swords to either side of the Hunter Lord, and they refused him passage. He was not so much the young Hunter that he challenged them, but his fury was obvious.

Thanks, Gil, he thought, and very slowly, very quietly, began to speak with the bard. His words were simple and short; he said them over and over, in a tone just above a whisper.

Kallandras' head snapped up; his eyes were wide and pale; tears streamed down the side of his face. Stephen flinched. Tears, he saw often, and he was not a Breodanir Lady to disavow them or find them upsetting—but he had never seen them from Kallandras, and he knew, without knowing why, that he never should have. Biting his lip, he unstoppered the flask quickly.

"Drink," he said, his voice calm and quiet. "Drink, Kallandras."

The flask disappeared; Kallandras had reached out and taken it before Stephen could begin to react. The Breodanir huntbrother tensed, prepared to leap left or right should it be necessary.

But Kallandras knelt instead, staring through Stephen, and then, by dint of will, *at* him.

"Niscea," Stephen whispered, as if the word were a benediction. "Drink, Kallandras. Drink."

"Evayne?"

"She is not here. She cannot harm you."

At that, Kallandras laughed, and the laugh was wild and loud and angry. But even as he cut it off and brought it under control, Stephen could see the bard's sharp eyes staring out at him clearly as a glint of sun through roiling clouds. His tears were gone, but their tracks remained.

Shoulders hunching inward, Kallandras pulled the flask to his lips and tilted it up. He drank soundlessly but quickly and then set the small, pale ceramic bottle aside. It was done; there was little but waiting left before the potion took hold. Stephen came in quickly and kicked the shears aside; they went skittering loudly across the floor to where Miri stood. The bard said nothing; did not move to react to the intrusion or the possible danger. His fine jaw clenched and his hands slowly crept up his face, but he did not speak and he made no move to attack.

"Leave me," he whispered, although his lips hardly moved.

Stephen nodded, his fair face pale as he stood and began to edge, cautiously and deliberately, away. His movements were sure and slow, and he made no sound that was not soothing, even, quiet.

"Stephen of Elseth," Miri said, voice cold as steel in winter. "Stand by your Hunter and do not interfere again."

Stephen bowed, his stiffness his only display of irritation. He took his place beside Gilliam, and the Kings' Swords closed in around him like a wall.

They waited, watching Kallandras carefully and neutrally. Stephen was reminded of those days in his youth, when the storm clouds were almost black in their density, and he stood, with Gilliam, beneath the cover of the kennel's out-roof, watching in silence and awe as the rain came thundering down.

Miri's tunic clung to her back, but her hair was still secure. Squaring her shoulders, she sheathed her unblooded sword, and walked toward Kallandras, taking measured, cautious steps. He made no move toward her; indeed his head remained so bowed that the edge of his hair touched the floor.

She did not speak, but rather, at a yard from his crouched body, knelt herself, resting her elbows across her knees. Kallandras stiffened; his neck jerked up, but his hair hid his face from all but Miri's view, and what she saw she did not speak of.

Fifteen minutes passed, and then, at last, he slowly raised his face. He rose, as if movement were unnatural, and waited until Miri also gained her feet. Then he bowed.

"ACormaris," he said softly. "I beg your forgiveness for my intrusion upon the peace of Avantari." His eyes narrowed, and then widened, as his glance strayed to the reddened edges of a tunic that was no longer white.

"Kallandras of Senniel," she replied. "The Queen Marieyan an'Cormalyn conveys both her concern and her wish for your speedy recovery."

He looked down at the empty flask in his hands; they were steady now, the hands of a bard and not the hands of a madman. "Where is she?"

"I believe," Miri replied gravely, understanding him at once, where Stephen did not, "that she is in the keeping of the healer. Dantallon?"

At the sound of the name, motion returned to the room, lending it the color of surcoat, the sound of speech and question. The healer appeared immediately, his robes brushing the ground as he approached Kallandras. The bard suffered his attention in silence, and almost, it seemed, in shame.

Cadrey handed Miri an old, perfectly waxed and polished lute. Across a perfect bridge, strings were tautly pulled; as his sleeve brushed them, they sang. Miri took the lute quietly, and held it as if it were a newborn babe.

"Dantallon?"

"As before," the healer replied quietly. "Kallandras, these fits—this episode— when did they start?"

"Three days ago. Four. I'm not certain."

"Who prescribed *niscea*?"

"Hallorn, the physician at Senniel." The bard's blue eyes vanished beneath the heavy, gray pallor of his lids. At once, Cadrey and Lorrison were at his side, following Dantallon's silent directive to lower him into a bed. This time, however, the healer did not bother with restraining straps.

"I know of the danger," Kallandras continued, without opening his eyes. Cadrey jumped back, like a startled child. "But *niscea* has properties which make it valuable to my current state." He swallowed. "The bardmaster of the college has requested aid from the Order, but it is not yet forthcoming."

"From the Order?" It was Meralonne APhaniel who spoke. Miri raised a hand, silencing him. The gesture did not appear to surprise him.

"I—I am not used to dealing with such potions. I did not realize that I had not taken the appropriate dosage."

Dantallon shook his head. "You probably had—but it was the right dosage for four days ago. How much have you consumed, and how often do you require it?"

Kallandras, eyes still closed, sank further into the mattress beneath his back. He seemed heavier, and without the animation of motion, almost cadaverlike. "Less than the contents of the flask that you gave me."

"How much less?"

"I do not know the full measure."

"How often?"

"Three times a day. Maybe four, if I am not to sleep."

"Miara's curse," Dantallon whispered. "And how often did you intend to continue with this?" A high note had crept into his otherwise calm voice.

"I do not know," Kallandras replied, his words faint. It was almost as if the bard-born voice had deserted him utterly, and he was just another exhausted man, with no strength, no talent, and no hope. It was wrong.

Stephen started to speak, but his words were lost as the door to the healerie burst open.

The Kings' Swords turned almost as a man as the doors swung wide. Two more of the Kings' Swords stood abreast in the doorway; they stared straight ahead, and entered the room without once looking to either side. Behind them was a man in slightly different dress; he wore the markings of the guards, but not their surcoats. A sword, sheathed, hung by his side, but he wore no helm, no gauntlets, no real armor. Instead, he wore a deep blue jacket, with the crest of the Kings' Swords emblazoned over his left breast. There were markings above and beneath it: four golden quarter circles, lined up across invisible diagonals.

He was tall, this man, and older; streaks of gray mingled with his brown-black hair. That hair was long, although exactly how long was hard to say; it was pulled tightly back, and twisted in a single knot before it spilled down the folds of the cape he also wore. He was beardless; indeed, he was unadorned by any marking, scar or otherwise. He had the bearing of a man who was accustomed to power.

The healerie was filled with the sudden, single noise of two actions repeated by thirty men at once: mailed hands striking mailed breasts, and soles of heavy feet being planted an exact distance apart.

It didn't matter; Stephen would have stared anyway. In the easy light of the healerie's sparse confines, the man in uniform surveyed those that stood before him. His eyes did not stop or come to rest on any but the mage, but in the single quick and almost dismissive pass that he made, Stephen saw his eyes.

They were the color of trapped fire.

Miri tensed slightly and rose, leaving both Kallandras and Stephen as she turned to see who had entered the healerie. Stephen lost sight of her face but could see the line of her shoulders tighten further.

"Verrus Allamar," she said softly.

"Princess Mirialyn." He bowed respectfully. "You are far from your duties at court."

"Not today," she replied. "One of Queen Marieyan's courtiers was injured in a fall. He struck his head, and suffered some slight delirium after the fact. Dantallon was not certain of the protocol involved in treating a respected visitor; he sent for the Kings' Swords, and I, upon hearing of the difficulty, took charge."

"I see." He turned to one of the Kings' Swords. "Report."

The man rapped his chest crisply. "It is as the ACormaris states, sir."

"And the mage?"

Meralonne raised a silver brow. "It appears I am to be the lord of afterthought," he said wryly. "I am not here in an official capacity, either for the Order or for the Crowns. I was in the courtyard where the bard had his fall. I tended him until the healer arrived, and then chose to accompany him to the healerie. I trust this does not break any of the rules the Kings' Swords enforce?"

Verrus Allamar tilted his head slightly; his eyes met the mage's. He did not reply, but he was clearly not happy to see Master APhaniel within his jurisdiction. "I did not ask that question of you," he said coldly. "Sentrus, report."

"The mage was here when we arrived. He has done nothing, sir."

"Nothing?"

"He is under the command of Mirialyn ACormaris, sir."

"I see. Continue."

The man who had been called Sentrus—and from the sound of the word, it was a title, not a name—fell silent a moment. He glanced at Miri, and Stephen saw Miri's hands slide behind her back, where they became solid fists. But she said nothing.

"The courtier was delirious when we arrived, sir. He injured ACormaris in his thrashings before the delirium broke."

"I see. And the gash across Princess Mirialyn's abdomen?"

"He was—he was holding bandage shears, sir."

"Holding them?"

"Yes, sir."

Allamar's expression sucked the warmth out of the room. It was clear that he did not believe the Sentrus—but equally clear that he did not wish to openly challenge the Princess. *Princess.* "Very well. Has the courtier been confined?"

It was Dantallon who replied. "The bard is my patient. He is being tended and is not fit for travel."

"ACormaris?"

"I am only superficially injured, and will be tended to here."

"I see." He paused. "And these three?"

"These are visitors to Queen Marieyan's court. This is Stephen of Elseth, and that, his Lord—Gilliam, Lord Elseth. They hail from a great distance, and seek to visit the court of the Queens for reasons of trade."

"They were present for the incident?"

"Yes."

"And they cannot speak for themselves?"

"Verrus Allamar, I realize that—"

"ACormaris, your business is the court. My business is the protection of the Crowns. I must ask you to step aside."

"Verrus Allamar," Miri replied, "might I remind *you* that visitors to this court are considered diplomats and therefore the priority of the *court* and not the Swords?"

"You may," he replied coldly. "But I will see it for myself. I do not believe that this has been the only incident involving these two foreign lords." He turned to Gilliam; Gilliam met his eyes without flinching. But Stephen saw the hardening of his Hunter's jaw, and the squaring of his shoulders; preparation for combat.

No, Gil, he thought—but he did not say it. There were times when he had to trust his Hunter. He hated every one of them, of course; but he was huntbrother.

"You are Lord Elseth?"

"I am."

"And this woman?"

"She is my servant."

"I see." Pause. "Her name?" He reached out for Espere's chin, and she snapped at his hand, growling suddenly in a voice that could be heard down the length of the room.

Stephen turned white as chalk; he scrambled to his feet as six men suddenly surrounded Verrus Allamar, swords bristling like spines at Espere and her Lord.

He doesn't know, he told himself, as he walked briskly toward the Kings' Swords. *He doesn't know that we know what he is.*

And how the Hells do you know that?

Miri was at his side like a pale shadow. "HOLD!" she cried, and the Swords ceased their movement as if frozen in place by bardic voice. "Verrus Allamar, this is not a matter for Swords."

"You are trying my patience, little Princess," he said, without looking back.

Her eyes grew round and then, quickly, very narrow. This was not a new fight or a new confrontation, and Stephen did not want to be the terrain over which it was fought yet again. He fell to one knee in a Breodanir bow, exposing the back of his neck.

"Verrus Allamar," he said softly, "you must forgive the servant. She is simple and does not speak."

"And the Lord?" was the icy reply.

"In Breodanir, the Hunter Lords are above question," Stephen replied gravely. It was truth.

"This is not Breodanir."

"No, Lord," he replied, equally grave. "And we have come to realize that it is a very different world. But we ask your pardon. We are not used to so many strange and different ways."

"I had heard that the Breodani men stayed at home; I have never seen a Hunter Lord travel. Why are you here?"

Stephen swallowed. "We are from the eastern edge of the kingdom, and we have done some trading with the border towns and the empire itself. My Lady was injured in a riding accident this autumn, and she is not yet recovered enough to travel. But we came in her stead to seek the grant of—of trade route through our demesne." He looked up. It was a mistake.

Fire caught and pinned him, kneeling and helpless, to the ground, casting a shadow that was very dark indeed.

"And have you found what you seek?"

He swallowed or tried to; his lips were moving, and not of his accord. The room had become a well of darkness, through which only the light in the eyes of Verrus Allamar shone. He tried not to answer, but the words were burning his throat; he needed to speak them.

They were not words about diplomacy—of which he knew little—or trade routes. They were words about the Hunter, the Horn, the wild girl, the darkness.

And he knew them for his death.

Chapter Sixteen

THEN, AS IF FROM great distance, he felt Gilliam's concern and solidarity; Gilliam, Hunter Lord, who wished only Stephen's unspoken permission to intervene.

The feel of the bond was rarely so strong or so solid—only at times like this, with the trappings of the real world peeled away by either force or unusual circumstance, was the Hunter-bond, the brother-bond, laid bare. Stephen understood, again, why the Hunter Lords found stark things beautiful.

He felt the bond as part of himself, and then *as* himself. He had no choice but to answer the question that Verrus Allamar had asked; the need was visceral, stronger than any hunger that he had ever felt.

But he did not have to speak to the Verrus. Instead, he spoke into the silence of the trust that ceremony had made solid; to Gilliam, Lord of Elseth. And he looked up, in the silent saying, to meet the eyes of Verrus Allamar.

"Ah, Verrus," someone said. Stephen could not turn until Verrus Allamar did, but once the man's gaze was broken, its power was gone. The green-clad hunt-brother rose as Meralonne APhaniel approached with an unlit, but well-stuffed, pipe in his left hand. "You really should know better than that. I'm almost shocked. Dantallon, you don't mind, do you?"

"Of course I mind," Dantallon replied, but it was quite clear that he held the dangers of magery to be greater than the dangers of acrid pipe smoke, for he did not press the issue.

The tips of Meralonne's fingers shone with a pale orange light as they hovered above the bowl of the long-stemmed pipe. Embers caught and flared, and he nursed them along with the pull of his breath. Then, smoke trailing the corners of his mouth as if he were some ancient, wizened dragon, he looked up.

"Meralonne," Dantallon said, voice heavy with warning, "you try my patience."

"I did not bring a tinderbox; really, the manners of the court are far more . . . courtly. But we can apologize to each other at a later date."

The healer snorted and tossed his long, pale hair. They were almost like brothers in seeming; fine-boned with pale, long hair, narrow faces, slender limbs. But

Stephen thought that Meralonne was like winter and Dantallon like spring; the end and the beginning.

"Do not interfere, APhaniel," Verrus Allamar said. His lips were thin with annoyance.

"I merely wish to see the much-vaunted laws of the Crowns respected by the more powerful of their enforcers."

On the verge of speech, Verrus Allamar lapsed into silence. "Very well," he said at last, speaking quietly. "I would ask you, young man, to accompany me voluntarily." He caught Stephen's gaze again, and fire burned. "**Come with me to your quarters.**"

"Nonsense," Meralonne replied, gesturing indolently through a fine web of smoke.

"APhaniel, I warn you—your interference in this affair will not be tolerated. If I must, I will—"

"You will do nothing," Mirialyn said quietly. "You are bound by the law you uphold, Verrus. Never forget that."

He looked as if he might argue further, but thirty of the Kings' Swords stood between him and Mirialyn, and of the two, it was clear who they felt they owed their loyalties to. "Very well." Verrus Allamar turned back to Stephen, the flames in his eyes burning coolly. "Where are you going, where will you be staying, and who will you be seeing while at court?"

"I believe that I might answer that," someone said.

It was Devon ATerafin.

They were made to attract trouble. There was not a place they went for any length of time that danger and death did not dog their steps. Safeguarding the Kings themselves was a less difficult and less onerous task than watching over Lord Elseth and Stephen.

Devon was tired and not a little hot; he wore full court dress, with its many layers of fine fabric, dyed in shades of brilliant blues and greens. He had waited an hour for Stephen at the Queen's court before discovering what had happened, and when.

Opening the door to the healerie in silence, he saw the middle of a day that had already begun poorly. First, there were the Kings' Swords, in far too great a number to be an honor guard to lesser foreign dignitaries. Then, the hint of sparkling robe that signaled the presence of Meralonne APhaniel—although if the robes hadn't given him away, the stench would. Dantallon looked in fine fettle, which was to say, he looked angry, and at his side, the redoubtable Princess Mirialyn, who, were she not ACormaris, would have been known as the flighty royal. But she was ACormaris, and treated with the respect and the obedience that was due that title. She was not in court dress; she looked as if she were prepared to go riding anonymously. Except, of course, for the gash across her abdomen.

He hoped that it had nothing to do with Lord Elseth or his huntbrother, because if it did, there was little he could offer in the way of intervention.

Then, to make matters as difficult as they possibly could be, a Verrus. And not any Verrus, no; it had to be Allamar. Allamar had never had much of a sense of humor, and it had gone downhill as he struggled toward what Devon ill-humoredly hoped was a painful and tiresome dotage.

Unfortunately, it was a long hill, and Allamar was nowhere near the bottom of it. Devon pulled himself up to his full height and smiled pleasantly, showing nothing to the world but the relief that he felt at finding his charges.

"Verrus Allamar," he said, inclining his head as formally as possible. "Let me apologize. These two young men were to appear at court for a short interview with members of the Queen's entourage, after which they were to be directed to Patris Larkasir's offices."

"ATerafin," Verrus replied.

"I was sent to meet them—the palace is large, and unfortunately difficult to navigate—but when I arrived at court, no one knew where they were; it took some time to find answers."

"I see."

"They will not be returning to the Queen's court after this day, and they will spend the rest of the day in the company of myself and Patris Larkasir. It is possible they will return to the palace on the morrow or the day after; we have some terms to negotiate that may prove to be delicate.

"Unfortunately, I am not permitted to discuss them further until accommodation can be reached."

"I see. Very well. I will send a man down to your office if that proves the wisest course." He turned a baleful eye on both Mirialyn ACormaris and Meralonne APhaniel, and then he stared at the kneeling huntbrother with a gaze that Devon could not interpret.

In silence, he turned sharply and left, followed swiftly by his two attendants. It was clear that he was in a foul mood.

"Miri," Devon said, bowing like a man who is courting. "What in the hells was a Verrus doing here? Tell me it didn't have anything to do with the mage."

The mage in question blew thick rings up into the beams of the ceiling. "Of course, it's *always* got to be something to do with a mage. Devon, your suspicion does your House no credit."

"I'd like to know why a Verrus thought this relevant myself," Miri replied coolly, ignoring Meralonne's interruption. "And I'd also like to know who informed him. If it was Cormeran, I'll have his hands."

Stephen rose slowly, his face ashen. "ATerafin," he said, lowering his chin and raising it again. "Please accept our apologies.

"ACormaris, our thanks."

She smiled a little sadly. "ACormaris, is it? Very well. I accept your thanks, oh foreign dignitary. But I did not come for your sake. Kallandras is widely known and widely admired." She walked back to the bedside and knelt against the cool, smooth stone.

"Princess Mirialyn," Dantallon said, choosing to set aside the more formal ACormaris. "You *are* my patient."

"Yes," she replied quietly. She did not move, and Dantallon delicately raised a hand to massage his temple. Devon knew exactly how he felt; he had had, in the course of both of his duties, to deal with Mirialyn, and it was almost—but not quite—as much a difficulty as dealing with the Breodanir Lords was turning out to be.

"Stephen, Lord Elseth—come. We must depart here. I believe that what we planned we can no longer carry out." Devon knew Allamar well enough; he would no doubt have his Sentrus' spread out across the grounds, taking reports to him to satisfy his pride and his curiosity.

What did you say? he thought as he glanced at Stephen. *He rarely reacts this personally.* And then he fully took in the stillness of the Elseth huntbrother, the paleness of his face, the thin sheen of sweat across his brow.

Fatigue was burned away in an instant.

"So, this is *your* office?" Meralonne, pipe still trailing pale, acrid smoke, looked around the neatly kept and polished desk as if he knew it almost never looked like this. He wandered over to the rich spill of dark curtains that brushed the floor. "You don't mind, do you?" he asked, drawing them wide to reveal the full, arched window that overlooked both balcony and treed grounds below.

"No, of course not," Devon said, sounding as if he meant it. "Our presence here is not a secret."

Meralonne's slender form was outlined by the high afternoon sun; his shadow, solid against the intricate work of lead bars and glass, was short but still graceful as he stood, staring out into the height and the distance. "This is such an unusual land," he said softly. "Come, let us dispense with this foolishness."

Before Devon could stop him—if Devon could have stopped him—he lifted his left arm in a broad, wide arc; it was a lower half-circle, centered just below the line of his brow. There was magery, unseen, unfelt, and unheard, but nonetheless present, in the offices of the Trade and Charter administrator.

Meralonne raised a sardonic brow. "If, of course, my interference is acceptable to you, ATerafin."

"Master APhaniel—Meralonne—I have never criticized your use of magic. You are not one of the young hotheads who charge out of the Order filled with the zeal of The One Answer—that is, of course, whichever answer intellectual fashion considers popular at the moment. The Council of the Magi takes your counsel; you are considered one of the wise."

"Well said," Meralonne replied. "Do you mind if I sit?"

"No. Sit and be comfortable—but do what you came to see done."

"I have."

"Good. Lord Elseth, forgive me if I seem rude. I address your brother because he often speaks for both of you, but should you have anything relevant to add or to say, feel free to interrupt." He turned to face Stephen, and the light, pleasant smile that had occupied his face fell away like a mask. "Tell me."

It was not bardic; there was no compulsion in the voice. But Stephen did not wish to be the man who refused to follow the ATerafin's command. "Verrus Allamar," Stephen said softly. "Verrus Allamar is one of the kin."

Devon lifted a hand and glanced at Meralonne. "Did you notice this as well?"

The mage raised the stem of his ancient pipe. "I? No. But I was not looking for it, and had I been, I think the outcome would have been more devastating."

Devon was silent, staring at the smoke wreaths above Meralonne's silver brow as if to wrest answers from their ethereal passage. Finally, he turned back to Stephen. "Does he know?"

"That I know? I tried not to show it. I don't know."

Devon was happy, if such a feral satisfaction could be called happiness.

The Verrus was their link. Had to be. He had access to the information about each of the visitors' wings; who was staying, when they had arrived, what their servant detail—if any—was to be . . . the list went on. There was no need to employ spies further; Verrus Allamar had always been a very thorough man, and there wasn't a report that crossed his desk that he didn't eventually read. He was not now, nor had he ever been, a joy to work for or with—but that eye for detail served him well and furthered his career, where a lesser man might have been hampered by it.

"How long?" he said aloud; silence answered him. He rose swiftly and walked to the window; stepped out onto the balcony and stood beneath a crimson canopy, shadowed by and shaded from the sun. There, beneath the office, were two Sentries; in the grounds, in a formal marching pattern, another eight. There were, he thought, Sentries in the visitor's gallery as well.

He knew himself to be above suspicion—until now—but the mage and the visitors were obviously under the glare of Verrus Allamar's watchful eye. He shook himself; it was going to be hard to think of Allamar as a demon, even if demonic was an adjective that had often been applied. Hard or not, he would do that and more; he was Astari, and the safety of the Kings depended on it. Without a word, he returned to the office.

Stephen was exhausted. A day spent at the King's Court required all of the control that he had been trained to, but not born to, and he was often fatigued by the end of a day spent doing nothing more strenuous than merely speaking with the Ladies of Breodanir. He had not, until now, considered a day of that nature to be easy.

But the Kings' courts, Queens' courts, the House of The Ten and the Civil Offices—although why they were called that, he didn't know, given the obvious tensions between the various nobles who worked there—plus the knowledge that he was being followed at every step by the eyes and ears of Verrus Allamar, were far, far worse than any Breodanir day could have been.

Still, he felt certain that Devon had shown him every quarter, every nook and cranny, of miles upon miles of palace ground; that he had viewed every living creature, with the possible exception of a few mice, who lived within the confines of the grounds—and that only Allamar, of all of them, had eyes of fire.

It would be good to get back to the halls that had become a substitute for home. A poor one, but better than nothing. Espere was whining softly; hunger, he thought, but he couldn't be certain.

As they approached the Arannan Halls, it became clear that the dogs were upset about something; Gilliam's mood shifted suddenly.

"Is there a problem, Master Stephen?"

He gave the mage a sidelong glance. "You mean besides the fact that we're being dogged by kin, assassins, and probably worse? I don't know." He looked askance at his Hunter, and the Hunter's expression changed. He was smiling.

They paused a moment outside of the smooth, wide wall, that bore a plaque that named the wing—one that neither Stephen nor Gilliam could read. Gilliam reached for his sword and then shook his head. Instead, he entered into his chambers in the Arannan Halls before Meralonne could insist on taking the lead, which was just as well. The dogs were growling—no, snarling—loudly enough that they could be heard without being seen.

"Who is it?" Stephen said.

"The bard," was Gilliam's reply.

Stephen's brows disappeared into the line of his hair. "Call them off!"

The Hunter Lord bristled slightly, but before he could answer, Meralonne did. "I wouldn't be so quick to forgive were I you. I would counsel against."

Stephen kept his smile at the mage's mistake to himself, and even kept the feeling behind it from Gil; of the two, he was better at masking his feelings. The huntbrother always was.

Gilliam, bristling, turned to the mage. "I know how to handle my dogs, and I know a threat when I see it."

Only a silver brow rose at the tone that Gilliam took. "I see," he said quietly. "Very well. It is your decision and I, of course, bow to it. Shall I stay," he added, in a much more biting tone, "to make certain that you don't suffer for it?"

Stephen intervened at once. "Master APhaniel," he said gravely, "although you may not be aware of it, we have met the bard before, and he honored us by honoring our dead. It is rare," he added, "that anyone who is not Breodani understands so much of our custom."

Meralonne did not appear to be impressed, but he kept his silence.

The dogs came to the entry hall at their master's unspoken command, growling and yipping almost at the same time. They were pleased with themselves; one didn't need a Hunter's bond to see that. Ashfel shouldered Marrat and Connel out of his way, and then bounded up to Gilliam, planting his ash-gray forepaws firmly in the center of his master's chest.

His master was unimpressed, and after a few seconds, Ashfel sighed and fell back to the ground to sit at the front of Gilliam's small pack. He did, however, nudge Gilliam's palm with the top of his broad head until Gilliam acceded to the unspoken demand and began to pat him.

"You can come out now," Gilliam said, raising his voice.

A minute passed, but not more; the unruly golden curls of the bard Kallandras could be seen as he peered cautiously around the corner. Singer and Corfel—at the rear of the pack—turned suddenly and snapped; Kallandras disappeared as Gilliam roared.

The dogs, Stephen saw, were not in the best of form. It had been days since they were allowed their run, and longer since they were allowed their hunt; they were restive and not a little frisky. Gilliam understood it well—but it was no excuse for disobedience; Stephen could feel his Hunter's anger as clearly as if it had been directed at him. He was thankful—and not for the first time—that he was not one of Gilliam's pack.

"Is it *really* safe this time?"

"It was safe last time," Stephen called back, his words carrying the tone of his smile. "They're playing a game; you happen to be the bone."

"You'll pardon me if I don't find that comforting." Kallandras appeared in the doorway. His jacket was askew and his hair somewhat wild, but his smile was genuine as he bowed, Breodanir style, to Stephen and Gilliam. "Meralonne," he added, straightening out. "You appear in the strangest of places." His lute was strapped across his chest, and it appeared to be unharmed.

"I should think," the mage replied, "that it would be I who would say that to you. It's not often that welcome guests feel the need to sneak about in such a fashion."

"Sneak? You wound me. I was told that Lord Elseth and his huntbrother would repair here, and I thought merely to wait until they did." He threw a rueful glance at the pack of dogs. "And, in fact, I did wait. It's a good thing the armoire here is four feet shorter than the ceiling."

"Kalliaris was smiling on you," Stephen said, "if you could climb that before the dogs could reach you."

"It had nothing to do with Kalliaris," the mage replied darkly.

Kallandras stared at him, and the mage returned the gaze. Stephen knew it for the contest it was, although he found it less interesting than Gilliam did. Piercing gray met piercing blue and held fast. A minute passed, and they continued to glare unblinking. Another minute.

Espere whined and nudged Gilliam; he caught her by the arm and held her back.

They're not going to stop, Stephen thought with wonder. Neither man had moved a muscle; it appeared that neither needed to draw breath; the conflict was enough, silent and still as it was, for either.

And then he realized where he had seen such behavior before, and it brought a quiet smile to his lips. Gilliam felt his amusement, and the flash of remembered emotions, the tangle of youth, that went with it. He smiled broadly as well.

"Kallandras," Stephen said softly, "when you are ready to speak, we will be by the fountains in the smaller courtyard."

The words did what pride would not; Kallandras immediately looked away, and even had the grace to flush slightly. "Your pardon, Stephen. And yours, Lord Elseth. I forget myself, even here. Might I accompany you?"

"Please do."

"Your pardon, APhaniel, but I fear I must ask that this meeting be conducted in private."

Meralonne smiled grimly. "Indeed, I thought as much. Let me just say that if you truly wish privacy, you will not dismiss my aid. Think of that what you will." He paused, and then added, "Kallandras, whatever else you may know—or think you know—about me, you must know this: that in this conflict, we are not on opposite sides."

"It is never just one conflict or one battle," Kallandras replied, equally grave. "The knowledge that you have now, and that you may gain, will be carried forward."

"And likewise for you," was the reply.

They were silent again, regarding each other; Stephen was worried that it was about to degenerate into a staring contest. But it was Kallandras who at last nodded, all business. "Follow if you will."

"I wouldn't miss the opportunity."

Stephen sat, his back to the blindfolded, kneeling boy. The water that fell from the child's cupped hands made an instrument of liquid. Stephen half expected to see Kallandras take up his lute and begin to accompany the broken stillness.

Salla was in the bard's lap, but she was quiet; his fingers rested very gently against her strings to still them. "You understand that Meralonne's loyalties must lie with the Order of Knowledge?" he said softly.

Stephen glanced at the mage, who was as still as the fountain's statue. "I'm not certain," he replied at last. "Evayne led us to him before she vanished. She must trust him in some measure." He paused and once again looked at Meralonne.

Kallandras closed his eyes at the name and bent his head. When he raised it minutes later, his face was shining slightly. Sweat.

"Are you ill?"

"If you mean, will I lose control as I did this morning, then no. But I am not well, and it is because of my . . . ailment that I've come to court to seek you out."

"You said you had something to give me?" Gilliam interrupted.

"Aye," was the soft answer, "I do. But it is not easily reached, Lord Elseth, and better not discussed until it is finally in your hands." He turned to look at the girl who sat, alert but still, at Gilliam's feet. "The wild one must know of what I speak."

"What can we do to aid you?" Stephen asked, speaking as if Gilliam had not interrupted them. He did it out of habit; many of the discussions between a Lady and a huntbrother were broken by the Lord. Norn had explained it thus: the conversation is a stream or a river that passes between the Lady and the huntbrother; the Hunter Lord is the large stone and small pebble over which it must pass, unimpeded.

"We must speak," the bard said at last. "And we must have our words kept here." Kallandras stared into his hands; they were cupped and empty. And then, as if deciding, he straightened his shoulders and looked up. The face of the bard—amused, bemused, or composed—was gone. In its place was something at once cold and desperate. He lifted his left hand and held it aloft; he spoke a single word and the breeze blew his hair from his face. It touched only Kallandras; in every other corner of the courtyard, had anyone thought to check, there were only shadows and stillness. But it was hard to see anything else; there was a light upon the third finger of Kallandras' raised hand that shone like sunlight encased in ice; it was bound by something that glittered palely. The breeze became wind, and the wind's roar was a song, wordless and primal.

"Blood of the forebears," Meralonne whispered, as he stared.

Stephen knew that what he saw was a Work, some artifact of the maker-born, something ancient and possibly dangerous. It *felt* old; older than the palace and the Isle, older than the city and the reign of Kings.

He had never seen such an artifact before, although Averalaan was rumored to be alive with them—but he had read about them, even dreamed about them, in his youth, yearning for their power and their mystique to somehow elevate him from the ordinariness that plagued a huntbrother.

What he had never read, or perhaps what words could not convey at a distance of time and remove, was that these Works were beautiful; that they could, with no context, pierce the heart and move it. He said something, and the words were swept up like so much dust, and cast aside without being heard.

Light limned the arm of the bard; light contoured the gaunt edges of his up-turned face. And that was a strange thing, for the light itself was unnerving in its beauty, but it did not bring beauty to what it touched; it was harsh and rendered all visible.

"Enough! Enough, Kallandras!" Meralonne's voice was tinny and small compared to the wailing of the wind—but it was heard.

Kallandras, bard of Senniel, slowly lowered his arm. He was sweating, and his eyes were dark; he cradled his ring hand a moment with his free hand as Salla lay unsupported in his lap. He breathed in, as if to catch and hold the last whisper of dying breeze in his body. And then, quietly, he began to strum the strings of his lute, filling the silence with a music dark and somber, but gentle nonetheless. A dirge. "We can speak," he said quietly. "The words, the wind keeps."

The mage was as pale as his hair; he moved stiffly, like a very old man, and then took a seat beside Stephen at the foot of the blindfolded, kneeling child. "Do you know," he said quietly to the huntbrother, "what the statue behind you is named?"

The wind had taken Stephen's voice for the moment; he shook his head dumbly.

"Justice," Meralonne replied. "It was created by an Artisan who managed to flee Annagar during the forty-year Clan Wars. You will see its like in many of the homes of those of Annagarian descent. A bitter testimony to a dark time and a merciless rule."

"An Artisan? But isn't an Artisan a—"

"Maker-born, yes. But of the highest skill; they are rare."

"Was it an Artisan who made—"

"Don't speak of it, Stephen," Meralonne said softly, and Stephen found it easy to lapse into silence. The mage began to fill his pipe in the newly still air. "No Arti-san made what you saw," he said at last, lighting the leaves with a flicker of his fingers. "But three hands lingered over it. It is almost time," he added softly, as if he could not believe what he was saying. "So much is explained. So much."

"Time for what?" It was Gilliam who spoke; Gilliam, who had the soul of a rock and the romantic notion of a dog. But Meralonne merely shook his head and looked to where Kallandras sat, telling a wordless tale with Salla's song.

"You found Vexusa," Meralonne whispered, and the words, although quiet, held a mixture of horror, awe—and pity. There was no question in them. "You've found the cenotaph of the Dark League."

"I was there," the bard answered in a hushed voice that hardly carried. "But I did not find it, and I could not find it again, no matter how much I desired to do so."

Silence. Then, "*She* took you there." There was envy, even anger, in the statement, but there was no surprise.

"I *am* transparent today," Kallandras replied. "But no, in the end, although she was with me, she did not take us; I do not know that she could find it either."

"Then how?"

"The wild one began to lead us," he said softly, nodding to Espere, who sat composed and watchful at Gilliam's feet, as if the light and the bard that held it were of little interest.

Both Gilliam and Stephen turned to stare at her, and she smiled; there was the curious air of a comfortable cat about her.

"Began?" Meralonne said.

"Yes—we encountered the kin, or rather, they encountered us. Magic was used, and of a power that I have not personally encountered before; we were taken from the streets of Averalaan to the foot of an ancient cathedral."

"Taken?"

"Yes. Evayne, the wild one and I—as well as the caster."

"Was it—"

"Yes," Kallandras replied quietly. "The shadows came, and the skies faded; light did not return."

"And there?"

"There, we were captured by two of the kin, using magics that not even Evayne could counter."

"That would not be hard," Meralonne began. He stopped himself, narrowing his eyes. "Or would it be?"

Kallandras averted his gaze a moment, then continued. "It was there that the wild one disappeared; she alone could not be held by the powers that were invoked. I do not know why, and Evayne did not choose to enlighten me. I do not even know *how* she escaped the citadel—but she did, for some many years later, she found me again, and gave into my keeping an item."

"What item was that?" Stephen heard himself saying.

"A simple spear. It has no magic about it that I can see. Nor was it maker-made. But because it came from the wild one, I accepted it, and I have kept it hidden these many years." He turned and bowed slightly to Gilliam. "It is to Lord Elseth that I will give that spear.

"But it is also of Lord Elseth that I will ask my favor. The wild one knew where she was going—or so I believe; if she would, I would have her lead me there again."

"No."

"Gil—"

"No. If it took her years to come back, it could be anywhere—and it could be dangerous. I won't allow it."

Meralonne raised a hand to forestall the argument that was about to begin between the brothers. "Gentlemen, please. It may not be entirely necessary to worry about distance traveled. I begin to see the pattern here, and I understand it. For I have been pursuing a different investigation at the behest of The Terafin, and now I see that they are not different at all.

"The lays—and they are old and fragmented—that survive both the Dark League and its passing say that the city was leveled by the combined will of the god-born and the remnants of the Dawn Rose. I will not name the city's Lord, but we have already had confirmation that his priests are at work here; they killed Zoraban in Breodanir, and attempted to kill the wild one there as well.

"But now, I do not believe that the city was leveled; I believe that it was *swallowed*. There is no magic now that could raise it—but were I to guess, I would say that Averalaan is literally founded upon the ruins of that evil place."

"Then what of the kin?" Kallandras said softly, speaking into the chill silence that stretched out around them as if it could barely be broken. "For they were there, Meralonne. They were in Vexusa."

"So you said, but what of it? They cannot raise the city, even if they choose to dwell within the tunnels and empty streets below; they have not the power. Although," he mused softly, "they *have* power, and of a like that has not been seen for a very long time. It is still a shadow of what it was."

"A dark shadow," Kallandras replied. "And they draw it, I think. From a gateway, or a door, something large and magical."

"Well? Door?" The mage frowned slightly and lifted the stem of his pipe to his mouth.

"It was," Kallandras said, closing his eyes as if the closing required a great force of will, "tall. An old, eastern arch, with a glowing keystone. I saw it, and she as well; I believe I asked her what it was. She did not answer. But she was afraid," he continued, musing. "She never shows me her fear; she showed it because she couldn't contain it. I was younger then. The kin drew power from this arch by calling upon their Lord."

"What did you say?"

"They called upon their Lord for the power that came from the gate."

"Then they must have been god-born."

"They were of the kin; there was nothing about them that was human." Kallandras' eyes narrowed. "You know your history as well as I—it would be impossible for a human to carry a child darkness-born to term. They were demon lords."

"That is *not* possible. I assure you, Kallandras. You know your lay-lore well. There is no possible way that—" And then he stopped speaking and turned to look full upon Stephen and Gilliam and the god-born girl who sat unruffled at her lord's knee. The ancient pipe clattered to the stone. Meralonne drew a quartered circle in the air before him, and then rose jerkily as if clumsily pulled by a rope. Turning, he gripped the lip of the fountain's basin with two fine, shaking hands.

"Justice," he said bitterly to the silent, blindfolded boy, "is weaker than your maker could have possibly imagined." He stood, picked up his guttered pipe, and bowed very formally to his three companions. There was no hint of antagonism left between him and Kallandras.

"This is not a matter," he said gravely, "for any one group. I cannot remain here, although your safety may be in question. I will summon you all; should you choose it, respond to my summons. It will not be long in coming."

Before they could stop him, he was gone.

6th Corvil, 410 A.A.
Cordufar Estates

"They know that we've spies in the palace." The words were sharp and crisp in the silence of the chambers that were reserved for the use of Lady Cordufar. The sun was coming down from the full heat of high noon, but the heavy curtains with their fringes of lace and lilac remained closed, denying the light.

Shadows, however, filled every possible corner.

"They do not know."

"I tell you," the man in the pale blue day-robes said, as he leaned forward and placed his elbows against his knees, "they know. Or if they do not, they will." He looked fatigued; his hair was streaked grayer than it had been mere months past. But he did not look terrified, and even surrounded as he was by the personal servants of Lady Cordufar, he did not feel threatened. He was, after all, Krysanthos of the second circle, and although the magery of the demon lords rivaled his own, it did not surpass it. Still, he wished that of the three, he could deal with Isladar—*that* Lord was subtle and had an understanding of human nature that dwarfed many men's.

Lady Cordufar rose angrily; she was, in all things, passionate. Her lips, thinned, were still a glistening curve, and her skin seemed to glow like a satin that demands the hand's touch. Even so cloaked and so disguised, the true nature of Sor na Shannen could not be completely suppressed. She turned to her entourage. "Get out."

They fell at once into the submissive posture and held it long enough to pay homage to her rank, but with enough brevity that they did not appear to be failing to comply with her command. It was clear that her wrath would be played out against something soon.

When they had cleared the doors, and she had secured them, she turned to Krysanthos and raised a dismissive hand. At once human guise fell away—as did the diminishment of human clothing. Her dark hair fell like shadow across her breasts. That was the only concession she granted him.

"You have not secured the return of the Spear or the Horn." He saw her eyes flicker with a deep, red glow, and he stopped himself from smiling at her expense. It was enough to know that he was right, and that she knew it well. "You have also failed to rid us of the threat that the Breodani bring to the heart of our master's dominion."

"If we speak of failure," she said, and her tone was an icy purr, "then we must speak of the attempt that should have been successful within the Hunter Lord's demesne."

This was not to his liking; he frowned and straightened out. "Sor na Shannen, whatever your regard for humans—"

"You have no more regard for *your* food and sustenance," she said softly.

"You must acknowledge that we are in danger here," he continued, as if she had not interrupted him. "This is not a mere city—it is *Averalaan Aramarelas*, and all of our foes dwell here in their greatest strength."

"And they will die here, and that strength will mean less than nothing—as it did in the days before humanity infested the realm; in the days before the Covenant of the Meddler."

"They will only die if our spell is completed. We are not now near completion. If they know that we have a demon in the palace, they will know that this is widespread. I tell you, they will make the connections that the beggar girl brought them."

Her smile was one of the most sensuous that Krysanthos had ever seen; he could not help but respond physically to it, as she intended. His facial muscles did not shift at all. "We are mere years away, mage. Decades and more have gone into this casting; it is a matter of two human years—less, now. Surely even one of your limited lifespan can appreciate that."

"I tell you that we will not have it. What we've kept concealed is no longer concealed. The maze has been discovered, and soon, the undercity—"

"Will never be found." She rose and brushed her hair back, walking toward him like a dream or a dare. "Did you think that we would just leave the maze to be discovered once we detected the breach of our magical concealments? We have been closing the Ways."

"You cannot close them all before—"

"We are almost finished with our task." She stopped, her bared breast a hand's span away from his bearded face. "The ways have been unmade; they are returned to the time before they were created."

Krysanthos paled instead of flushing. "With what power?"

"The Lord's," she replied sweetly.

"But the cost—"

"And then," she said, ignoring, as she often did, his words, "let them know of the undercity. Let them try to flee or try to discover it. We are safe; they cannot find what does not exist. In all of our time here, there have only been two seers who attempted to find us; they flickered on the edge of our concealment, and they gained no answers."

He was silent, absorbing what she said. Victory, of sorts. But then he added, "it doesn't matter if they find the city. If the Hunter Lord and his kin have the Horn—"

"I *know* what will happen," Sor na Shannen snarled, losing the edge of her sensuality.

"Good. Then you know that we have no choice. We must abandon our original plans; they have failed us. If we are not to fail our Lord—"

"We have begun to gather the living," she said, grudgingly. "Before we seal the last of the entrances, we will have the sacrifices we need to give our Lord his anchor here."

Krysanthos nodded grimly. "That many victims over so short a period will be missed," he said softly. "But better so. If we start with the last summoning now, it will take a month. Maybe two."

"Longer," she replied, casting off her glamour and assuming once again the drabness of human aura. "For the Lord's power has been much used and tested in the sealing of the city."

"Then when?"

"The middle of Veral."

Krysanthos frowned, but the frown smoothed itself out as he considered. If the maze was completely sealed away from the discovery of those who dwelled in Averalaan, the ceremonies could be conducted with the very earth itself as a fortress wall between Allasakar and his enemies. It was probably worth the power.

"Very well. Let me continue my own surveillance of the Order of Knowledge. There are two there that are of sufficient worry that they may have to be removed."

She nodded. "And I," she added, "have a report to make to The Darias. I think it may almost be time to reap the rewards of serving under his banner." Her smile was a dark radiance.

The Terafin studied the missing persons reports that lay across her desk. Morretz stood by her side in silence, unmoving. She knew that he, too, read the lines of words and numbers that made the loss of the living so impersonal.

It had not been easy to gather the information from the magisterium, but ease had never been the case in crisis, and she had not expected it. She had also not expected the numbers that she saw before her, and she could well understand the magisterium's reluctance to make public—if acceding to the *personal* request of The Terafin was considered public—the findings here. There would be panic, at the very least.

Almost two hundred people—spread out over the holdings of the basin—had disappeared within the last three weeks. The ages varied, as did the walks of life; there seemed no rhyme or reason. Here and there, whole families had simply "gone missing." It could not be a coincidence.

"These creatures—they were never after Terafin," she said, musing aloud. "Did Ararath discover them by accident? Or was the hand of the One behind it?"

Morretz said nothing, but moved quietly to pull her chair out as she made to rise. "Terafin?"

"I am going to the shrine," she said softly. "I do not need the company, although if you fear for my safety, you may accompany me."

He shook his head. "As you wish, Terafin. You did not take the late dinner— may I have something ready for your return?"

"Not tonight," The Terafin replied quietly. "Put the reports away, Morretz. I've seen enough; now, I must make a decision."

It was not yet dark; the sky was an orange-pink, bordered by a deepening blue that stretched up into eternity. Faint stars began to tremble in the wake of the sun's passing.

The lamps were aglow near the flowers and bushes that followed the winding path of the Terafin manse. The Terafin followed them in the silence, hearing only the steps of the small night guard somewhere in the distance. Here, for the moment, there was a curious peace; the gardener worked well to maintain it.

Find tranquillity in the quiet of nature's beauty, he would say. And she would reply that this much work on such foliage as Terafin possessed could only barely be considered natural. But he smiled because he knew that in the gardens that contained the shrines, she did find some small measure of peace.

She passed by the shrines of the triumvirate, nodding to them at a distance in the darkening sky; the shrine of Terafin waited for her, and it had been too long since she had last visited it.

But as she walked the last leg of the tiled path, she saw the flickering of an orange light, the dim glow of a glassed lamp. Someone had come before her. A momentary irritation flared; her hands became ivory fists, and the stillness of the gardens deserted her. She called it back slowly and took a deep breath; any who were ATerafin were free to place their offerings here.

Yet as she approached, she saw the back of the kneeling young woman who rested with her forehead against the edge of the altar, and she knew that it was no ATerafin that robbed her of privacy: It was Jewel Markess. The dark, slightly wild hair of the younger woman was half-wrapped in a wide swath of twilled cloth, from which strands had escaped into the night breeze.

The girl was praying.

And how long, Amarais, has it been since you last prayed? she thought ruefully. *Come. Join her.* She walked up to the flat, marbled dais with a light and silent step and came to stand beside the kneeling young woman.

Jewel looked up, opened her mouth in a silent o that reminded The Terafin very much of the fish that summered in the garden, and then blushed. "T-Terafin," she said.

"Jewel," The Terafin replied, all annoyance vanished. "We have come here, no doubt, for the same reason—although I confess I'm surprised that you found the shrine so readily."

Jewel said nothing, and in the lamp's light—which was brilliant and harsh compared to the light in the rest of the garden—The Terafin saw that the young woman's face was pale and shining with sweat. And the evening was cool.

"What troubles you, Jewel?"

Jewel shook her head slowly, and then once again assumed the prayer position, although she covered her face with her hands instead of holding them out, palms up, in supplication. Into the silence, she began to speak.

Perhaps it was because Jewel was tired and the hour late—The Terafin could not be certain—but she knew that Jewel had never spoken so freely in her presence.

"I don't know how you do it," the young woman said softly, speaking through the cracks between her fingers. "I don't know how you can be responsible for so many people. I don't know how you can choose your Chosen. It's not their oath—I understand that—it's that they uphold it all. Torvan says they die. For you."

"They die," The Terafin replied remotely, "for *Terafin*."

"They die for *you*."

And then The Terafin understood why Jewel had come. In some ways, although her own motivations were more complicated and far more political, she was often moved to the shrine for the same reason. "Jewel."

"We don't even have the bodies. I mean, not that they'd've meant much in the twenty-fifth—but here, here where everything's decent and we've got anything we ever wanted—here, it matters."

"Jewel, you cannot continue to think about the dead. Think about the living."

"I do," Jewel whispered and, if anything, her voice was more intense. "I think about them all the time. Because if I make a mistake, they might not be alive to regret it." She ran her hands up her face, pushing her hair away from the edge of her eyes. It was unruly, that hair; much more so than The Terafin had initially feared its owner would be.

"Then if you ever desire rulership, remember this," The Terafin replied. She softened her voice before she continued. "How do they haunt you?"

Jewel started and then slowly relaxed. "At night. It's always at night. I haven't had a single night's sleep in the last three weeks where I didn't see them. They're dead. They rise out of the ground, out of the stone—they reach for me and there's *nothing* in their eyes but death. They blame me." She laughed a little shyly—or at least, to a less perceptive woman, it might have sounded shy.

But The Terafin heard the fear in it, the skittishness. And she remembered again that Jewel was seer-born, and her dreams and visions were not the same as those without talent—such as The Terafin herself—might endure. "Are your dreams usually significant?" she asked softly.

Jewel, pale and wan, swallowed and nodded. "If they happen all the time." Lamplight flickered as a breeze too strong to be kept at bay played havoc with the wick of the burning lamp. "They aren't—they aren't the Wyrd," she added. "They're different enough each time."

The Terafin didn't need to ask the obvious question. "Raising the dead in such a fashion is an art long lost," she said at last. She knew it for bitter consolation. Because she knew that first among the practitioners were those who called themselves the Allasakari. They were already involved to some extent; Devon said that of the two who had attempted the assassination of the foreigners, one had probably been a servant of the God whose name was never spoken aloud.

She began to bow her own head, and then she stopped. "Jewel, how long have you been coming to the shrine?"

"I don't know. A week, maybe a little more. Why?"

"Who taught you the customs of the Terafin shrine?"

"Torvan."

"Oh?"

"He was on duty in the gardens the night—the first night—that I came here. He said I wasn't allowed to touch the altar unless I had something to offer the House. And I do," she added, her voice tinged with defiance. "Myself and my service."

"I see." The Terafin nodded gravely. "And that, in the end, is all any one of us has to offer; no more, and no less. Come; if you take comfort from this, then join me. For I, too, have had my nightmares. This force that we are searching for—it is not the province of Terafin alone; I do not have the resources to combat the kin, wherever we may find them, and to uncover the source of their summoning."

"But you're part of the Kings' council," Jewel replied. "You have the ears of the Kings. You can go to them and tell them and they'll listen to you."

"Yes." The Terafin looked at her younger companion. "But it would be much as if you went to the magisterial guards when you had difficulties with your rivals in the twenty-fifth."

Jewel snorted, and her eyes sparked as she tossed her head. "No—they'd never listen to me."

"Then it's not the same. But there are similarities. The Ten are not like brothers and sisters; they do not serve the same House, or the same purpose, although they serve Essalieyan in their particular ways.

"Among The Ten, there is a hierarchy, an understood measure of power and influence. Terafin is a seat which holds power. And I will weaken Terafin in the eyes of The Ten if I go to the Kings for aid, no matter how justified that request might be. Among The Ten are two who are our enemy, and close enough in rank to take advantage of any sign of weakness.

"But if I do not go to the Kings, there may be, in the end, a far greater price to pay than momentary political power. I don't know what form that price will take, but I believe that it has already started." She bowed her head into the edge of perfectly smooth stone, closed her eyes, and began to pray.

Guide me, she thought, her lips moving over the words as she held out her hands in supplication. *I am only Amarais. I am not the embodiment of Terafin.* The answer that she sought came, but as often happened in such a supplication, it was not the answer that she thought—or hoped—to receive.

Jewel cried out and fell back; The Terafin heard the young woman's hands hit the marbled stairs before she tumbled down them. She turned at once, the hypnotic and desperate stream of her silent prayer broken. "Jewel!"

Propping herself up on one elbow, Jewel rose. Her eyes were wide, her mouth round. "Don't do it," she said softly. "Don't do it or they'll kill you."

Chapter Seventeen

STEPHEN OF ELSETH lay awake in the shallows of the night, thinking of sleep. It eluded him, and each time he pursued it, other images slid between day and night: Kallandras wearing a ring that could summon the wind itself, and Meralonne recognizing the ring for what it was in a voice that carried the hush before battle; the light, white and sharp and harsh, the heart of the element, unshadowing the hidden things in Kallandras' expression. Snatches of the lays that the bard had taunted the mage with came back to him in bits and pieces, each phrase dark and cold.

In Breodanir he could pride himself on his knowledge of things historical, but here, in Averalaan, it seemed that history lived, and in living, defied all explanation and understanding. He knew little, if anything, and felt that he understood less.

Kallandras was in the west sleeping room; he was asleep, or so Stephen thought by the sounds of the occasional sharp cry that sleep should have muffled. The healer had given him something to help him sleep, and after some argument—civil and polite, but quite steely—Kallandras had reluctantly agreed to its use. It was clear that in Averalaan the healers were used to being obeyed, no matter who they dealt with; Dantallon was unbending in his demand, and showed no hint of surrender. Connel and Singer now watched the sleeping bard with both curiosity and the vigilance that their master demanded.

Espere slept at the foot of Gilliam's bed, on the thick rugs that had been brought for the use of the dogs. Stephen wasn't certain that she would stay there, which meant that Gilliam would spend another sleepless night, walking the line between desire and self-loathing. It was a dark line, and his huntbrother did what he could to dull its edge without blurring it.

Stephen rose and reached for the odd bed-robes that Devon had provided; in the shadows they were soft and fine, and the richness of their colors, the detail of their embroidery, were no longer intimidating. The rooms were not dark; even during the cloudy nights here, they never became so. Light from the courtyard's many torches mingled with the glowing stones that Stephen had once thought so remarkable to keep the deepest of darkness at bay.

He could not sleep, and at last gave up trying. For light at night was rare in Breodanir, and the use of candles, while not forbidden, was seen as a luxury that set a poor example for those servants and villagers who were forced by circumstance to be much more restrained. Why not make use of it?

He was halfway out of his room when he remembered the book. He wavered on the threshold, the door hanging heavy against his shoulder, the smell of sea salt lightly tinging the air. It was not, after all, his book; he had meant to return it to Meralonne, but in the confusion, had forgotten.

Or had he? He was curious about it, and as Gilliam slept fitfully, he let curiosity have full reign. This book, small and obviously very old, was a book that a mage—and more important, a member of the Order of Knowledge—had found of interest enough to carry on his person. But when Stephen had gone through the effort of pointing out that he had dropped it, Master APhaniel had seemed unconcerned.

Still, it wasn't his business. It wasn't his book. And he remembered well the old stories about attempting to pry into the affairs of mages. He stepped out of the room. Turned. Stepped back in. There was light, there were no onerous Hunter duties, and there was something to read. They were a potent combination.

The book was old, and not well-kept; the blue-stained leather, once fine and soft, was now cracked and chipped with age; the back cover was creased to near-breaking and the pages—made of a substance that Stephen did not recognize to touch—were crumbled at the edges and brittle with time.

There was a title, but only two of what Stephen supposed to be several words were now readable, and they were pressed in a style that made them seem almost a different language. It wasn't, quite—but it was stiff and formal and often oddly phrased. Stephen grimaced; he had seen similar works before, and they always made his head ache with the effort of concentrating.

But they were almost always worth that effort.

The front cover, like an unlocked door, was turned; he saw the frontispiece of the book, pocked slightly and faded with time. But the words that the cover had lost, the page retained: *The ceremonies of Oathbynding, the various methodes and reasons for so doing, and the effects upon the Oathbounde.*

Oathbound.

The air in the courtyard was chill, and the lights seemed somehow harsher. The scent of the lilies that floated above the carp in the long, oval ponds built into the rock of the grounds mingled with the scent of dust, of things so aged that the freshness of the turning time and season could no longer have an effect. He trembled, although he did not know why; there was an instant of fear, and of something buried beneath it, that stabbed him cleanly between the left ribs. His hand froze on the book's cover, but he knew, even as the intellectual part of his mind considered, that the deed was done: The door was open, but it could not be closed again.

He turned the page.

Know it for truth, whosoever readeth this tome of slender weight, yet significance beyonde compare, that these are the words of Our Lord, who is above all Gods the most trustworthy; who demands above all things the honor of his followers, and the honor of their oaths, both to Him and to their compatriots. You who are His followers, follow not lightly, and under- take the Oathebynding with gravity and with the understanding of the consequences that the Oathebynding shall work.

Do not seek to coerce those who will not understand the full measure of the action they take and the words that they speak, for the Oathbynding is beloved of God, and once made, it cannot be broken, save at his will—and He does not countenance Oathbreakers, and his wrath is Great.

But if you have those who indeed wish to swear their Oath and have it witnessed, and take the sacrament, and be Bounde, realizing in full that which will befall them should they fail in their Oath and become Oathbreakers, then you must follow the path set by our Lord, Bredan of the Covenant in the Heavens, he whose powers keep even the Gods from warring.

Stephen stared at the name on the page as if it, alone of all the words so far, was written in a foreign language that defied his comprehension, and yet at the same time spoke to a part of him that existed without language, or before it, it was so deeply buried. Bredan of the Covenant. The formal address made it clear that this Bredan, this keeper of Covenants, was a God.

Except that there was no such God in Averalaan; none in Essalieyan. Only in Breodanir was there one whose name was close, and he was the keeper of no Cov- enants. Bredan. Breodan.

Surely, Stephen thought, as the words gathered and blurred, losing all meaning as words will if stared at and repeated long enough, the Order of Knowledge would have known, would have seen the similarities? Surely if this Bredan were somehow connected to Breodan of the Breodani, they would have made those connections? Maybe they did; they had sent members of the Order to study the Breodani for decades past—to somehow prove that the God was either a true one or a false one.

He had to speak with Meralonne APhaniel. He made to rise, but it was a feeble attempt; the book lay open in his lap beneath the rounded glow of the lamp that lit the small alcove in which he sat.

. . . and of the various effects on the Oathbounde, there is one of note: that the soul of the Oathtaker is Bounde in truth, and cannot be ensorcelled or otherwise trapped by the priest of another God, or the fell creatures that inhabit the Northern Wastes. Nor by the kin of the Darkness, nor again by the First-born who is called Calliastra, nor by . . .

His fingers felt as if they belonged to another man as they moved the pages, turning them gently and dwelling on the surface of their words while shying away from the depths. He paused at last at the book's fourth and final section, titled simply, *Oathbreakers*.

Gilliam woke in the darkness, tossed off the plenitude of fine, soft silks that hampered his movement, rolled across the floor, and grabbed his sword. Before he had come to a stop, he had slid into and out of the vision of six sets of eyes, spinning between them a web with which to capture a limited feel for the surroundings outside of his immediate senses.

Stephen was frightened, and he could feel that fear as viscerally as if it were his own body that contained it. Still, there was no obvious sign of attack.

As he got to his feet, he found Espere at the door; she was alert and watchful as she shouldered aside the hanging and waited for her master; no trace of sleep remained with her. Moonlight, or what he persisted in thinking of as moonlight, illuminated her face, her shoulders, her body. Still, he was barely tempted to touch her, although her scent, musky and familiar, drew him as it often did.

Shaking his head, he crept stealthily into the halls, using shadows for scant cover as he made his way to Stephen's rooms. He liked these halls and quarters because they were so sparsely decorated and furnished; there was nothing to trip over, nothing to worry about breaking. A long stretch of hall, punctuated at the end by a mirror and a squat, flat stool, lay before him.

The hunt shifted, or so it felt; he stopped moving, his hand against the smooth, cool walls. Stephen was not in his rooms. But where?

Espere whined softly.

"Not now," he whispered, pushing her firmly to one side. "We need to find—" He stopped as Stephen's fear was swallowed by a silence deafening in its totality. His own fear replaced it. He pushed at the bond, forcing it as much as he had ever done. Something broke through the silence, like water rushing up between the cracks in the surface of a partly frozen lake.

Fear and fury; anger, pain, loss. Betrayal.

He cried out and stepped back. The dogs, all six of them, began to bark and howl in a frenzy; he heard and felt their acknowledgment of his momentary panic. They came, as if at his call, abandoning their posts and places.

Stephen was gone again.

Stephen, back pressed firmly into the wall, closed his eyes and did all that he could to pull back from the Hunter who was both his Lord and his brother. The book lay closed and flat between his shaking palms, as if it were part of an elaborate prayer.

He waited in silence until Gilliam and Espere entered the courtyard. Gilliam was dressed for sleep, and Espere was not dressed at all.

"Stephen?" The single word was intensity itself.

Stephen rose and bowed stiffly, sliding the book into his pouch as he did so. "Gil, don't ask," he said, and the words were distant. They had to be. He lifted his head and met his brother's stare, and it was Gilliam who at last looked away. Gilliam, who had never been good at speaking about emotion.

"Where are you going?"

"To my room," Stephen replied softly.

"And then?"

There was no point in lying. "To the Order of Knowledge."

They both knew that the city contained almost as many people as the entire country of Breodanir; that their enemies, hidden by darkness, knew the city better than they, and that they were, in all probability, watched by those who waited for the opportune moment to strike. Knowing it, they did not put it into words; not now. There was no need. Stephen was going to the Order, and he intended to travel, if not alone, then without Gilliam of Elseth.

And it hurt them both, to know that, and to be forced to accept it.

Gilliam nodded stiffly, and Espere whined, crossing the courtyard suddenly and freezing ten feet away from where Stephen stood. She looked back at Gilliam and growled; her voice was low and angry. Gilliam's brow furrowed as she took a step forward, and then another; his cheeks flushed. But she was not a dog, and in the end, she came to stand before Stephen of Elseth.

Her eyes, as she met his, were a black-brown that seemed devoid of whites.

"Did you know this, wild one?" he whispered, as he cupped her cheek in the palm of one shaking hand. He could not ask more, not only because she would not answer, but because he could not control what came with it. And he was the hunt-brother, he reminded himself bitterly; the responsibility of control was his.

Her eyes, dark, were still luminous; they glimmered with reflected light as they met his, unblinking. Stephen wondered if the tear that gathered, unshed, in the corner of her eye was a trick of light or a lack of blinking—or whether it was the only answer she was capable of giving him. He was moved, as he had not expected to be moved, and he lowered his hand gently.

"Take care of him," he told her softly. "I will return."

"Yes, you will. I give my word to Lord Elseth that I will see to your safe passage."

They all turned to stare at Kallandras.

The streets were shadowed and empty. They reminded Stephen of Gilliam, of what he felt in Gilliam through the bond that they shared. And they reminded him, as well, of the life that he had led before Soredon of Elseth had called his city hunt so many years ago.

It had been a long time since he had hidden in the cover of shadows and darkness, since he had walked the city streets with a very real desire to go undetected. As an eight-year-old boy, he had never been very good at it, but better a little experience than none.

And besides, these streets, so well appointed and so perfectly made, with their wide, stone roads, and their perfectly planted trees, their "Avenues" and their "Boulevards," were nothing at all like the warrens in the lower city. He had left them behind, whether he willed it or no, fourteen years ago, and they would not come back to him now.

Kallandras was a good deal better at the silence of movement than Stephen thought he would ever be. Although he dressed like a bard, and still carried Salla—in a case that he strapped lightly and quickly to his back—he moved with a precision and a grace that was astonishing.

"What were you before you became a bard?"

Kallandras said nothing at all, and Stephen let the question die into stillness and silence. He had the sudden feeling that to tell Kallandras that he, before his service to Elseth, had been a thief would neither impress nor distress the bard; they had pasts which did not connect or touch, and never would.

But Kallandras surprised him. "I was happy," he said softly, "learning what it is to be . . . a soldier." He looked at Stephen, his face hidden by darkness. "Were you happy before she came to you?"

"I don't know." It surprised him, to say that. "I think so. I was young then."

"And do you know what she wants of you? Do you finally know what it is that she will cost you?" The words were sharp and intent—used in a way that only a man trained to words could use them.

They demanded a truth that Stephen did not wish to—was not yet able to—part with. But he could not turn away from the bard either; he was compelled to speak, although whether it was Kallandras' desire or his own, he could not say. "Why does she do what she does?" he asked softly. "Why is she young today, and old tomorrow; foolish at one moment and wiser than anyone I've ever met the next?"

"She is trying to prevent the world's end," Kallandras said, as if he were seeing into the future that Evayne was trying to prevent. "And you and I are pawns to that game." He turned and walked a bit, surveying the street and listening as if he were testing the wind for the slightest carried sound. Lifted a hand a moment, and then nodded Stephen forward.

"But I have seen the Darkness, I understand the desperation, and one day, I think I will no longer hate her."

"You hate her?"

Kallandras' smile was bitter. "Stephen, she took me from everything that I had ever been and ever loved, and then forced me to continue to use it. There is no way for me to go home; those who loved me once hate me now, and with just cause.

"And you—do you not feel anger? Resentment? I'm curious, you see. She does not come to many, and of those, you are the only one I know at present."

But Stephen shook his head softly, seeing the past and the present as things that were lost to him, and seeing the future as a darkness without end.

"I heard you," Kallandras said quietly. "In the courtyard."

Stephen nodded.

Meralonne APhaniel himself came down to the desk to greet Stephen and Kallandras. Of course, he had no choice; the hour was poor and the guards on duty would not see fit to release the two visitors until a member of the council had deemed them safe. The huge foyer of the Order of Knowledge showed starlight through the canopy of glass, filtering its color without losing its flickering brilliance. It was only upon seeing this that Stephen realized that the glass was not glass, but some form of magery. He was not surprised, but he felt a tickle of awe and wonder as he stared at the night sky.

"Gentlemen," Meralonne greeted them softly, seeing the two who waited. He bowed, and the bow was an unusual one; he bent one knee, although he did not fall to the floor, and his back remained straight, but his neck was bent.

Kallandras raised a brow, and Meralonne stepped smoothly out of the bow. "It is late," he said softly, "and dark enough. Come. Let us repair to my study."

"Why have you come?" Meralonne asked, breaking the uneasy stillness that had settled in the room only after he had picked up his pipe and made certain it was well lit with burning leaves. He did not sit, which was not unusual, but he stood with his back to the open window, staring into the room's center.

"I've come," Stephen said quietly, "to return to you a book which you dropped."

The mage nodded, his gaze unblinking and eerily like starlight—flickering with light in an endless darkness. "I see. And?"

"You meant for me to read this."

"Did I, young Stephen of Elseth?" Smoke rose to the ceiling in a thinning cloud. "And did you understand what you read?"

"Yes."

"Yes?"

"And no." He walked to the mage's desk and gently placed the book, cover down, upon its wide, flat surface. It was odd, that the desk was so uncluttered; he couldn't remember if it had been so the last time he had been shown to this tower room. Or perhaps all was becoming uncluttered and unfettered; the illusions were falling away, and the truth, terrible and simple, was all that remained. A window was open somewhere, although he could not see it; the smell of the salt-laden winds, cool now with night, mingled with the scent of burning leaves.

"You have come to me for explanation."

"Yes."

"And I have precious little to give you. The book that you hold was a book written just before, or perhaps just after, the last ride of Moorelas, called Morrel, or Moorel in lands west of these. Very few such tomes survive, and we are not able to authenticate most of them; this is a rare exception. It was written—or so I believe—in the time of Moorelas and his fellowship."

"Fellowship?" Any question. Any way of avoiding the answer that was fast becoming the only answer.

"The Sleepers, Stephen," Kallandras replied.

Stephen was quiet as he tried to remember all of the stories that surrounded Moorelas. They seemed to change from region to region, as if each country, even each dale, remembered best the events that marked his coming to that locale. At last, he shrugged.

"But who—what—are they?"

"They are the renegade princes of the First-born," was Meralonne's cool reply.

"They are," Kallandras said softly, "the heroes of a very different age."

"Perhaps they are both; Moorelas was many things to many people." The mage blew rings into the air and watched them rise and fade. "But they are not the subject of this evening's discourse. Stephen, the answers that you wish, I cannot give you. But what I can tell you, I will.

"The wild girl is the daughter of the Hunter God—the first proof, after decades of study and more, that the Hunter God is, indeed, a God. There is a second proof, but for that, I must delve a moment into a history that most—that even Senniel College—remember only in lay and children's game.

"Because in some measure, Kallandras is correct; there was a different demeanor to the earlier ages. There was the Wild Age, and then the Age of The Powers; there was the Age of Gods—and it is of the Gods that you must ask, for the Gods were, in some manner that we cannot understand, fashioned by men and the dreams of men, even as they fashioned them.

"There were wars," he continued, staring into the rings of smoke blown parallel to his face, "and dead without number. It was thought that the race of man would perish under the weight of their devastation, for where a God walked the land, *nothing* was impossible." He reached for a small bowl and began to tap the ashes from the pipe into it. "But humanity survived, greater and lesser in number, and they served the Gods.

"The God that is written of in the book that you possess—he was Bredan, of the Covenant. We know that he sanctified sworn oaths, and made of the breaking of them a fitting and unpleasant death. But we also know, through oblique references, that his powers affected man and God alike, although few indeed were the oathsworn Gods.

"Very little else survives about Bredan. When the Teos-born questioned their

Lord, they discovered only that Bredan was no longer within the Heavens; more than that they could not learn, for the God did not possess the knowledge that we sought. Yet Teos assured us that in the Heavens there was no Hunter God—nor had there ever been."

Teos-born. The word, said so casually, brought back the striking and singular image of Zoraban, calling upon his father in the half-world. Stephen stared into the pale darkness, seeing the very God.

"Nothing is learned in vain. When you came to me, you said that the succubus called you Oathbound. You said also that the wild one was Hunter-born. What can we then assume? Either that you have somehow met both the Hunter God—whom you worship—and the Oathbinder, whom you had never heard of, which is unlikely; or that the Hunter God *is* Bredan. And that he is no longer in the Heavens."

Stephen was silent as he absorbed what Meralonne said. His words filled the room as if he were the Bell of Truth and Stephen had struck him thrice—and yet somehow, Stephen felt that he was not telling all that he knew. But he had said enough. "In Breodanir, we speak of the coming of the Hunter," he said softly, in a room lit only by the glow of a new-lit pipe and the embers of an old fire. "He was our Lord, and we His people. It was a dry and cold winter, and a dry and hot summer; the Breodani had wandered the lands, searching them for food. The old died, and the young; the weak fell, and the strong became weak. We were starving. At the last, the sons of the Hunter gathered, and together, joining, made a plea that our Lord could hear in the Heavens." Stephen's face was like the desert as he spoke words which this evening had changed the meaning of forever. "We were His people, and He our Lord, and we had served Him in all ways faithfully, where all others had disappointed Him.

"He came to us in our need, and taught us the lesson of the hunt, and when He had taught us all we needed to know, He granted us Hunter Lords, like unto Himself, and bade them return to their people to feed them and succor them. To them, He granted also the Bredari, the first of the hounds; to them, He showed the ways of the land and the creatures that inhabited them.

"In return for this gift, there was a price: that once a year, we who were the most cunning of His creations would become, as any, hunted; that we would know the effect of our power upon the lesser of His creatures. And every year, at the appointed time, one of our number has faced the Hunter's death. None have ever survived it." He closed his eyes as he spoke and sank further into the chair, allowing the arms and back to shore him up in their wooden embrace.

"Stephen," Meralonne said, and his voice was surprisingly gentle in the darkened room, "you swore an oath, and you are bound to it with your life. Yet when I called you oathbound, you were surprised. Do you even know what that oath was?"

"Oh, yes," Stephen said, bitterly and quietly. "There are only two meaningful oaths that I have ever sworn. One, to a woman of my choice, but never, because of our situations, of my choosing." He stopped speaking then; it was hard to tell if his cheeks were pinkened by the declaration.

But Meralonne spoke; softly, softly. "There are secrets this room has heard that it will never release; they are hidden, as even Vexusa cannot be. If you will, I would hear the other oath."

"There is no secret in that," was Stephen's strained reply. "It was spoken, with the Hunter Lords of Breodanir as my witnesses, when I was eight years old." He continued, his voice trembling with anger and fear, "I swore that I would hunt, as my Lord will hunt, without use of his gift. That I would be the bridge between this son of the Hunter and the people whom he must succor." His eyes grew opaque as he stared into a young boy's past, understanding clearly all the fear of his youth. He had *known*, somehow, the truth of the words, when no one else had understood them. The Hunter's Death had always shadowed his life. But the words were impossible to say softly; they had formed him, and informed him; they were the foundation upon which—until this evening—he had stood with pride. "To guard him and protect him and see all dangers by his side; to face the Hunter's Law so that we may remain strong. To remind the Hunter, always, of the people he must defend."

"It sounds . . . innocuous."

Stephen shook his head as he raised it. "Yes," he said. "It does. Because I don't think that we—the Breodani—understand it any better than I did when I said it. For I must face the Hunter's Law, called also the Hunter's Price—the Hunter's Death—*so that we may remain strong.*"

"You all face that," was the quiet reply.

"Yes. But . . . but I believe that it is the huntbrother, and not the Hunter, who is meant to die in the Sacred Hunt." Norn's face, ashen and empty, returned to him, as it often did, death already writ large across it, although he was still walking among the living, and would for some months. *It should have been me*, he had said, and Stephen had never forgotten the anguished guilt that he heard there. And now he understood, fully, that it was more than guilt that spoke—it was an absolute understanding, after too long a time, of a sanctified oath.

"Why do you believe this?" Meralonne pressed him.

"Because," Stephen answered, raising his face to meet the silver gaze of the man across the darkened room, "after the Sacred Hunt, if the Hunter Lord has died, the huntbrother follows months later. They linger in loneliness and guilt, and then they pass away."

"Does this always happen?"

"Not always," Stephen continued. "But not all oaths sworn to the God are sanctified." He made to reach for the book, but Meralonne waved him back. "I am not guessing, Meralonne. I *know* it."

"And yours?"

"I told Gil that I would face the Hunter's Death for him. After I had made my vows. After I swore, as the Priests would have me swear. I—I added that vow of my own. Because I felt, at eight, that it was the truth. It *was* the truth," he added, his voice low. "And I knew it because I felt it, here.

"Corinna, the village wisewoman, spoke with me years later about it. She remembered it because Norn had, during *his* first vows, said almost word for word the same thing. It's not so uncommon among the young huntbrothers—especially the good ones. The villagers were so pleased with Soredon's choice of a huntbrother for their young Master Gilliam, because it's believed that a show of loyalty that spontaneous must come from the Hunter Himself."

"Norn?"

Stephen started to speak, but the words were too heavy to contain even the slightest trace of the man that Norn had truly been. He tried a second time, and then a third; but there was no fourth attempt. Let the dead rest; let the sorrow still felt at death, sleep. He said merely, "Norn was the huntbrother to Gilliam's father," and then dropped his forehead into the palm of his waiting hand.

"And I believe," Kallandras added softly, "that Norn died of a wasting illness some six months after his Hunter Lord was taken in the Sacred Hunt."

Silence.

"Does Lord Elseth know?" The question, coming from Meralonne, was unexpected. Stephen did not hesitate. "No."

"And will you tell him?"

Again there was no hesitation. "No."

Meralonne nodded quietly and sat back in his chair to ruminate. But Kallandras leaned slightly forward. "Why?" he asked gently. "Why would you keep this from him?"

"Because he's my brother," Stephen replied.

Kallandras stiffened a moment and then smiled sadly. "He would die for you."

"His oath is the Hunter's Oath; to fulfill it, he *must* join the Sacred Hunt. What choice would he have? To refuse the Hunt is unthinkable, but if he knows what I know, to take part in it is almost worse. Gilliam *is* a Hunter. It's all that he is. He's good at it; in time, he'll be the best. I won't take that away from him."

"And you, Stephen?"

"What of me?"

"Will you die for him?"

Bitterly, Stephen laughed. "If the Hunter demands it, it looks like the only choice I have is the manner of death, not the fact." His eyes narrowed, becoming streaks of darkness in the room. "You will not tell him," he said.

"I? No. Nor Meralonne, I think." He looked to the silent mage. "But why, then, are the Allasakari involved? Why are the kin involved?"

"I do not know," Meralonne replied. "I have been thinking on it, but I do not know enough." It was obviously not an easy admission for a member of the Order of Knowledge to make.

"And do you know the right questions?" Stephen asked.

"Pardon?"

"If you ask the right questions, there are always answers." The young hunt-brother rose, pushing his chair back with a shove, a fey expression about his face, and a dangerous light in his eyes.

"Stephen," Meralonne said cautiously, rising as well, "I think perhaps you have had—"

Stephen lifted his arms and his face, looking not to the roof of the tower room, but to the space beyond it, above it. *"Teos!"* he cried, and in the single word a plea, a demand.

His two companions froze as the word hung in the air, resonating as if it had been picked up by a distant chorus and now echoed in the timbre of a thousand—a hundred thousand—voices.

"What is this?" Meralonne said softly, all warning forgotten. He set aside his pipe as the room began to dissolve into mist as thick as smoke. The floors vanished first, and then the walls; the chairs melted into distance, as did the window with its waft of sea breeze.

Clouds grew, like foliage in a jungle, all around them; Stephen could see Meralonne and Kallandras, but poorly, as if they were obscured by the veil of distance. Light touched the surface of the eye-level clouds, and at his feet, a path opened, arrowing toward the unseen. There was no human architecture here, no trace of human structure. Only cloud and then, miraculously, sound and sight.

"Well met, Meralonne APhaniel. Well met, little brother; it has been long since last we met, and I hope you have fared well."

They looked up at once, into the eyes of a man both young and old, slender, tall, and fair, who was girded as if for war. His hair, where it could be seen beneath his helm, was fair and his eyes, brilliant; his face was bearded with fine-spun gold.

The half-world took the shape and substance of Teos, the Lord of Knowledge. Stephen saw the face, and knew it. But where there had been a book, finely bound and heavy with the knowledge of man, there was a shield, and where there had been robes, there was a breastplate and greaves of perfect manufacture. Only the Sword remained as it had been, and it was wielded.

"And well met, Kallandras of Senniel. Well met, Stephen of Elseth." At the last, he bowed, and the gesture was so perfect that Stephen almost forgot how to speak. "I have been waiting for your call."

Chapter Eighteen

"TERAFIN." Morretz's voice. Quiet, in deference to the hush of the hour. He brought light with him, trapped in crystal and gold: a fitting illumination for The Terafin. Dawn was not far; the sky was the blue of early evening or early morn, pale and cold.

She sat so still, her cloak heavy and stiff around her slender shoulders, that she might have been sleeping. But Morretz knew well that sleep was not what she sought here, and doubted very much that she had found it. He gazed skyward a moment, and then set the light aside on the roof's flat. Her feet were bare, and her legs; she wore a sleeping shift and a simple, brown wool cloak, which was older than she. It had come from the estate of her maternal grandfather shortly after his peaceful death. Very few knew that she possessed it, and only Morretz knew that she had requested it; her departure from the family fold of the Handernesse clan had been difficult, and she had taken very little with her when she assumed the rank ATerafin. Even after the family had reconciled itself to her rapid rise through Terafin, she had allowed herself to take little from it. Just an old man's worn cloak.

But she wore it seldom.

The Terafin had at her disposal the wealth of Terafin; she owned this mansion, a summer estate to the northwest, several smaller guest houses throughout the city, trade missions through the Empire, and at least one diplomatic estate in each of three cities in the Dominion of Annagar. She could, at her whim, fashion out of any of these a private space, a personal retreat—a place of safety, wherein she could discard, for moments at a time, the weight of Terafin.

Had she, she would not have been The Terafin to whom Morretz had sworn life service.

"Terafin."

She nodded, almost imperceptibly lowering and lifting her chin. This, this rooftop seen by those who tended the cisterns and saw to the repair of the manse itself, was her chosen retreat, the aerie of her fancy. Beneath her bare feet, the grounds were waking slowly; dew was on the grass and the leaves of the low-lying Southern flowers. The gardeners of Terafin were about their business and she watched them calmly.

"The plants in my rooms always die," she said softly, as she watched the men and women at their work. "I forget to water them."

"The servants would water them if you would let them."

"Yes." She lapsed into silence, knowing that he knew that the growing of a plant, to The Terafin, was also the owning of it; having the servants water them would make them servants' plants, and not her own.

He said nothing, knowing it better to offer her the comfort of his silence. In silence, many things could be said, and many things hidden.

Wind came to punctuate the stillness; her hair flew back from her pale cheeks in dark, fine strands—loosed, as it seldom was. Unfettered by the severe and perfect finery that she chose for her rank, she seemed young; the slenderness of youth, the coltishness, lingered in the slim frame of her body; the defiance, behind the surface of her open eyes. She had been a girl once, although it was only at times like this that he could see even a trace of it in her.

He was the second man to see it, and the only man living; he felt a slight twinge—envy?—as he saw her curl the cloak more tightly about her shoulders, taking comfort from the ghost of memory, the false safety of childhood.

She brought her chin to her knees and stared bleakly ahead as he studied her profile. At last, he asked, "Will you eat?'

"No."

"Amarais," he said softly.

"Morretz, go away."

He started to speak, stopped, and retreated to the edge of the roof trap. There, he watched her, holding light in his palm which the sun's ascent made less and less useful.

It was hard to touch her when she was like this; hard to know how to be careful with her. She seldom needed care; she was hard and cold, although not cruel and not unjust. She knew power well, and understood its uses, but understood better than that the responsibility involved in invoking it. And he knew her and admired her for what she was.

Yet it was at moments like this that he found her most fascinating. He had chosen to serve Terafin because Terafin was a House of power, and such a House needed a domicis of his capability; he had chosen The Terafin because she was strong, and in this passage, he desired to learn the ways of strength. Weakness had a different lure; that of necessity, of being irreplaceable, of walking the very farthest edge of the life that service—that the honor of serving—demanded.

It did not attract him.

And yet, in her . . . He shook his head softly, closing his fingers over the light. Perfection was something to be striven for, but not to be attained; it was the flaws that were the blood and flesh of a living person.

Is love a strength or a weakness? he wondered, as he watched her fingers ruffle the edge of her grandfather's worn cloak. As a child, the answer was simple; as a youth, simple as well, although the answer was different. Now, with youth and childhood behind him, he had lost the confidence required to make of anyone's life a simple statement.

She looked up, as if hearing him; she was uncanny that way. Her eyes were wide and unfocused, staring through him as if she had no sight to speak of. But the vulnerability that he had seen moments before was already sinking quickly beneath the surface of her face. She was steel and stone as she rose, pulling the cloak from her shoulders and making of it a bundle of cloth.

"Morretz."

"Terafin."

"Please send for a messenger."

"Terafin. To?"

"The Kings."

"At once." He bowed. "May I also arrange for—"

"Summon Jewel Markess, if she is within the grounds. Have her meet me after the messenger has been sent, and only then."

He bowed again. "And may I—"

"And *after* Jewel and I have finished our meeting, you may, if it pleases you, arrange for the midday meal to be served in my personal quarters."

"Terafin."

"I will join you shortly," she added, as she took one last look at the grounds of Terafin from the mansion's height.

"Where in the hells have you been?" Angel vaulted from the ledge of the low, long window in the courtyard, turning easily in midair to land on both feet with a solid thump.

"Getting sloppy," she said. "I'd've heard that a block away." She reached up and pulled the servant's kerchief from her hair and face.

Angel shrugged. "The way you've been lately?" His derisive snort was enough of an argument.

The blackening on her teeth came next, and the "shadows" beneath her eyes. Her hair, on the other hand, would remain the russet color that the dyes had decreed. "What's up?"

"Where've you been?" Angel said again, falling into step beside her as she marched past him. "C'mon, Jay."

"Out. Why?"

He frowned; ran his hand through the bangs of his otherwise monstrous shock of platinum hair, and then gave in. "Carver's looking for you."

"Great. What happened?"

"So's The Terafin."

That got her attention. She stopped, doffing the last of the heavy towels that added weight to her midriff and arms. "Terafin can wait," Jewel told him. Angel's brows disappeared into the line of his hair. It made her smile, although the smile was less than kind.

"I want you to gather the den," she told him, not giving the surprise a chance to lessen any. "Have 'em meet me in—in the kitchen."

"Why?"

"I'm not going to go through it all more than once—you can hear it when everyone else does."

"But—"

"Angel?"

"Yes?"

"That's an *order*. Do it."

He met her dark eyes with his slate gray ones, and then a slight smile, crooked but sharp, twitched at the corner of his lips. "You've got work for us," he said softly.

"Maybe," she said, relenting a little. "But *go on*."

He didn't wait to be told a fourth time—which was just as well. Jewel wasn't a monarch, and she wasn't one of The Ten—so she didn't demand that her den obey her the first time she spoke; Hells, the first time she said a thing, it usually barely managed to get their attention—unless it was a matter of life or death. But she only repeated an order three times. There wasn't a fourth, and they knew it.

Ellerson stood stiffly at the door. Jewel had asked him to leave, and he had patiently explained that he was *her* domicis for the nonce, and that it was *his* duty to make sure that anything that she required be taken care of to the best of his abilities. He did *not* serve The Terafin; nor did he spy for her. He served Jewel Markess.

She told him that if he truly served her, he would never have insisted on the courtly clothing, the mannered manners, and the bathing every time she turned a corner—but he took it in stride, and waited patiently until she had finished her tirade before quietly pointing out that as he served Jewel, he insisted that she do what would best serve her interests.

In manners of the House, Ellerson knew what would serve her interests best, of course.

"Of course," was the grave response.

The funny thing was that if Jewel ordered Ellerson to leave—instead of asking as she had—he'd do it. She couldn't. Wasn't certain why, either, but didn't want to push it.

Carver, last to come as always, took a seat and then glanced uncomfortably at the domicis.

"You can trust him," Jewel found herself saying. "I do."

"Yeah, great." Carver brushed his hair out of his eyes and slouched into his chair. "We're supposed to talk *work* around him?"

"Carver."

He subsided, but his expression was just this side of mutinous. Jewel sighed and looked around the table. It was a lot larger than the table at home had been, which made her den look smaller than it ever had. But at least the table wasn't warped, the legs were all level with the ground, and the smooth, gleaming surface meant that no one dared to fidget by carving their initials—or worse—into the wood.

Arann was looking good. It surprised her, to see him look so well; she'd been so busy digging around the ground beneath the city that she just hadn't noticed. That was going to change. He smiled almost shyly at her, and if there was a trace of pain in the expression, they both chose not to notice it.

Jester was still, well, Jester. Teller, beside him, cupped his hand round Jester's left ear and whispered something behind the curve of those fingers. He rarely spoke at meetings like this, and when he did open up to the whole group, it was always with something worth hearing.

It was Finch who piped in first. "Angel says you have work?" She had lock picks dancing between her slender, tiny fingers, and light dancing in her eyes.

In fact, they all looked excited in their own way. She realized, with a shock, that this easy life, with more food than any hundred people could eat and more clothing than any two hundred could wear was just as hard on them as it had been on her—maybe worse. She was out in the streets, taking the risks she always had. They were in here, and they belonged in Terafin like The Terafin belonged in the streets of the twenty-fifth.

I only wanted to protect them, she thought, but the words sounded hollow as she looked at their eager faces. Then the words took on strength as she thought of the den members who weren't here. And why.

"Jay?"

"Hmmm? Oh, sorry. I was thinking."

"Share it with the rest of us?" Finch again. "You've been real busy."

"Yeah. Maybe too busy to be smart." She leaned slightly into the table as she spoke; they all did. "We've got trouble."

"What kind of trouble?" Carver's slender dagger, well-oiled for a change, gleamed in the brightly lighted room.

No point in playing her hand close to her chest; no point at all. "Demon trouble."

"You mean like Old Rath?"

"Yeah. Probably worse." Her gaze skittered off Arann's very quiet expression and then came back to rest on it.

"Tell us," the oldest member of her den said. "Tell us what you know."

"First: I can't find any of the old entrances into the maze. Not a single one. But we do know that they're closing them."

"The demons?"

"No, the magisterians, Angel. Don't interrupt me."

"Sir!"

"Second: The Terafin knows more than she's telling me."

Carver snorted. "Big surprise."

"Carver," she said, warning him. "It boils down to this, though. She thought maybe Old Rath was killed because they were trying to get at *her*—and even if it wasn't true, she thought she could take 'em."

"Take who?"

"Don't interrupt me. Now she thinks it's got something to do with the whole damned Empire."

Silence. Then Teller said softly, "So she goes to the Kings and gets them to fix things."

"Right the first time," Jewel said, smiling just as softly as Teller spoke. "And none of that is our problem—we couldn't help the Kings if we wanted to; couldn't get near the damned palace."

"So?" Both Angel and Carver were practically flat out against the tabletop in frustration. "What about us?"

"They're going to come here."

"Who?"

"Not sure. Either demons or people who work with demons. And we're going to stop them."

"*We're* going to stop them? Jay—The Terafin's got about two hundred guards. Even if we wanted a piece of the demons, we can't take what those guards can't."

"That's what I thought, too," she replied. As she spoke, her eyes found the center of the empty table; she stared at it quietly.

The den fell silent as they watched her expression; they'd seen it before, and they knew it well. "What is it? What're you looking at?"

"A battle," Jewel replied, her voice curiously flat. "Dead all around. Armor. Swords. A lot of blood." She swallowed, staring as she paled. "And The Terafin, staring; standing. I don't understand it—but behind her, behind her is her death. It strikes, and she falls."

"*What* strikes?" Carver demanded.

"I don't know. I can't see it at all."

"Is she dead?" Teller asked.

"I—I don't know. I thought she was dead last night. She may well be dead—but *I don't know.*"

Finch looked unconvinced. "Sounds like you're trying to sell us something you're not sure you believe."

"Maybe. Maybe I am. But I'm tired of feeling helpless. This—it's a not-happened-yet thing. It's not like Lander or Fisher. I *knew* it was too late for them." She pushed her chair back and stood. "But I think it's up to *us.* We're not important, you see. You, Carver, Angel—the rest of us; we're not important. Everyone knows that we're thieves and ne'er-do-wells."

Ellerson cleared his throat.

"Shut up, Ellerson," Jewel said, without looking over her shoulder. She was quite surprised at the silence that followed, but not so surprised that she wouldn't use it. "So that's what we are. We're used to having to hide from armed men. We're used to trying to hide in plain sight, and we're used to being watched if we're noticed."

"So?" Angel said again.

"So we don't have armor, and we don't have fancy weapons. So what? Never did. We were the *best.* We're still the best. We've just got to change the rules a bit. Look—we can't stand up to the guards in a fight—and we can't stand up to anything that can kill half the House guard. We don't have what it takes. Doesn't mean we don't have anything.

"There's going to be a fight. It's going to be aimed at The Terafin. And it's going to go crashing through the guards trying to reach her. That's not our problem.

"But there's also going to be a different attack; I don't know what. And *that* one's a sneak. I think. And that's the one we might be able to help with."

"So why don't you just tell her this, and let her deal with it?"

"I'm going to," Jewel said softly and with utter certainty. "And she will. But not well enough."

"And we're going to be able to do better?"

"Count on it," Jewel said, with no less certainty. She reached into the sash at her side, and pulled out a sheathed dagger. It was fancy, the handle so ornate and so perfect that it looked like it should be fenced. Her solemn expression told them that it was more important than that. She handed it to Carver without a word.

"Where did you get this?"

"I found it." She didn't add that she'd found it in the private quarters of Devon ATerafin, one of four such knives. "It's special, Carver, real special. Worth more than your life. Don't screw around with it; don't take it out of its sheath until it's needed. Got it?"

"Why?"

"Because I said so," she replied sharply. Then, relenting, "And because I'm not sure what it does, and I'm not sure it'll work more than once." Swallowing, she took a deep breath, and once again surveyed her den. She wanted Duster, missed her sharply. Was surprised at how much it stung, to start a fight without her. "You know what's at stake," she told them solemnly. "We've already lost four. Vote."

Carver placed his right hand, palm down, on the table's surface. "I'm in," he said, without hesitation. Made her wonder if he really did understand what was at stake.

"Me, too." Angel also reached into the table's center with the flat of his right palm.

Jester plunged in with both hands, meaning he was committed if they all were. Finch came down with the flutter of a right palm, as did Teller a second later. Arann took the longest to decide, but in the end, he, too, chose the right hand. As his fingers unfurled to lay flat against the smooth wood, he looked up into his den leader's eyes.

"No healers if things don't work out," he told her softly.

"No healers," she replied, not certain whether or not she was lying.

"Uh, Jay?"

"What?"

"That only applies to Arann. If I'm not dead, I don't want to be left to get that way." Carver's grin was cocky. Always was, really.

"Got it."

"What's the plan?"

Jewel smiled. "First: We don't tell The Terafin. We don't tell any ATerafin either. This is *ours*. We know our own, and we know how to make sure no outsiders get in." She took her chair slowly, turning it back to the table and sitting with her legs astride it as she usually did in their war council. It felt good. It had been a long time since they'd done anything other than be afraid—or be quiet.

Ellerson very loudly cleared his throat at her back.

"What is it?"

"The rest of your plan, while I'm sure it's laudable, requires that you be on the *inside* of Terafin—if I may be so bold as to guess."

"Yes, so?"

"The Terafin has been expecting you for five minutes, and I do not believe that even her right-kin, Gabriel ATerafin, keeps her waiting longer than ten."

Verrus Allamar sat in the sanctuary of his office. The hour was late, but he was known as a hard-working soldier; indeed, perhaps the most dedicated of all the Verrus. His lips thinned into a smile that would have chilled the men who served with the Kings' Swords. "Enter."

A young woman, dressed in the livery of Darias, made her way across the threshold, walking neither too quickly nor too slowly. But she made certain that the door at her back was closed tightly before she turned.

The light around her body shimmered and flared; her voice became deeper and heavier as she chanted softly. Her body blurred, as did her uniform; her face changed, chin elongating into a frosted, black beard, shoulders broadening, waist thickening. The livery was still of Darias.

Verrus Allamar's eyes narrowed. "You took your time."

"We did not have the choice," Krysanthos replied tightly, as he unstooped his shoulders and clapped his hands in front of the door's keyhole. "After your failed attempt at delivering the Breodanir hunters to us, security has grown . . . diffi-cult." He turned back to the Verrus. "You were supposed to see that the Hall of The Ten remained relatively free of interference." It was an accusation.

"You did make it in," Allamar replied coldly.

"Yes. And at some personal cost. This had better be important."

"It is." The Verrus planted both of his hands on the flat of his immaculate desk and rose, placing the weight on the tips of his fingers. The desk creaked beneath the force he exerted. "Mirialyn ACormaris has requested the use of the Kings' Swords three days hence for a meeting with an un specified personage. She did *not* route her request through the regular channels."

"This means that you've no idea what the meeting is about?"

"It means that I was not even supposed to know that the meeting existed." He smiled at that, the very wolf of a smile. "And I find that rather odd. It seems that my position here has been compromised, and it will probably be of little use in the very near future."

"Agreed," Krysanthos said, almost absently. "What else have you discovered?"

"Both of the Kings—and the Queens—are to be in attendance."

Krysanthos swore. That meant—it could only mean—a personal request from one of The Ten; no one else could demand and receive an audience with the four Crowns on such short notice. And only one House might consider the affairs of the city to be in enough of a state of emergency to do so. "Terafin," he said softly.

Verrus Allamar had the grace to look surprised. His confirmation was unnec-essary, but he gave it anyway. "How damaging will this be?"

"I'm not certain." The mage took a chair and sat heavily, brooding. "Sor na Shannen is loath to part with information about her activities; I only know that the work in the labyrinth is not yet completed."

"That would make us vulnerable."

"Yes. But not by much. Remember that none of the people who lived by the maze had full knowledge of its workings."

"Depending on the ignorance of our enemy has always been folly."

"Tell that to Lord Karathis," Krysanthos replied, with a shade too much bit-terness.

The Verrus smiled at the sound of the grating in the mage's voice. It was a hint of food to a man starving. "Very well. How much time is needed to seal the maze completely?"

"As I said, I don't know."

"Your best guess?"

"More than three days."

Verrus Allamar flicked his finger and the desktop cracked. He smiled, and as he did, his lips grew thinner and wider until they opened fully upon a row of teeth that could never belong in a human mouth. "Only give me the word, Krysanthos; give me the word of my Lord. I will see to the rest."

Krysanthos' eyes snapped open; his expression became crisp and clear of worry. "You will do *nothing* until you have that word. Your position here as a Verrus is of import to us, as you well know."

"My position here has already been compromised."

"We have no positive proof of that—your squabbles with the Princess are well known, and a slight of this nature would not be beyond her." He paused. "However, we assume that you are being watched; it is why I was sent."

Verrus Allamar's face shrank back into the confines of a human expression, and at that, a sour one. "Very well. I will wait your word. But do not delay. I do not relish the fate of Akkrenar."

"Agreed," Krysanthos replied. "But were I you, and I wished to avoid such a fate, I would not challenge APhaniel directly. He is more than your match. As," he added softly, "am I."

Stephen bowed low, his face wreathed in the curling mist at the God's feet. He felt humbled by the aura of the Lord of Knowledge, but not so humbled that he could not speak. For he had come to ask his questions, have his answers, and have done with the Gods for as long as he possibly could.

Before he could speak, Meralonne did, and his voice, in the muted surround of the half-world, was stronger, richer, and deeper than Stephen had heard it before. "Why are you dressed for war, Master of Lore?"

"Because there will be a war," Teos answered without preamble, his voice a thousand voices. He lifted his sword arm and pointed; the tip of the double-edged blade touched Stephen's forehead. "This one has ridden at the front of that storm. And I foresee that it has not yet finished with him."

"Bredan *is* the Hunter God," Stephen said with certainty.

The Lord of Knowledge gazed at him a moment, and then gave a measured nod. "We did not know, although we suspected it to be so. My sons and daughters are not among his kin, and his powers are not what they were."

"I have come," Stephen said softly, stumbling over a ritual that he only half-remembered, "to offer you information and, if it pleases you, to ask of you the question that you granted me."

Teos' eyes glimmered with a smile that did not reach his still face. He nodded gravely. "Your information?"

"The demon-kin have found Vexusa, the home of the Dark League."

The golden eyes of the God closed as he bent his head in acknowledgment. "And?"

"We believe it to be beneath the ground upon which we stand." It was Meralonne again. "And worse; the Allasakari and the kin are *unmaking* the ways that lead to it."

"Unmaking?"

"Indeed. They use power as if there is no end to the power that they can summon. They use power as if—as if the Covenant of the Unnamed One had never been made."

"What *is* the Covenant of the Unnamed?" Stephen said, surprising himself. It was not the question that he had thought to ask, but he asked it, and it hung in the air as if the words had become physical, tangible.

The God stared at him a long time, and then at last, said, "that is the right question, Stephen of Elseth, although you yet may regret the asking of it. Will you hear the answer?"

"I will."

"Very well." He nodded and the book fell open in his left hand; pages, thin and supple, turned as if at the behest of a strong wind. "We are the Lords of the Heavens, and the Lords of the Hells; we are the Gods to whom you look and from whom you receive direction, should you choose to ask it. We are the gatherers, and we are the judges.

"But in the time of the Shining City, we were more than that. We walked among you, in the Age of Gods." He looked up, and his face was the very face of youth; what he remembered, Stephen could not even imagine—for what could make a God feel young?

"You are the last-born," he said softly. "And you are the strangest of the creations. Your bodies are weaker than we could have imagined when first we encountered you, but your minds are quick, and you are, of all the creations, most curious." His smile was fond. "But you did not survive much."

He looked up. "The Gods warred in their youth. The mountain ranges to the west of Averalaan were created in an afternoon's battle, and might just as easily have been unmade.

"But not the humans. It was Mystery who showed us their truth. For the souls of the mortal kin were little shards of light too beautiful to be cased forever in dying flesh; and when the flesh was stripped away, the shards remained, colored by the brevity of the life led.

"Mystery said to the Gods of the Heavens and the Lords of the Hells: Here, within each mortal, is the best and truest test of your power; no more will your battleground be earth alone. Each mortal is infinite in possibility, and finite in time. Do you call yourselves powerful?" At this, the God's expression darkened, but he continued to speak. "Behold: the changes that you have made over land-scape are already healed; for all your rage and glory, they might never have been. Yet your influence here, with these mortals, might be lasting and felt forever.

"And we saw what he showed us, and we saw what might follow; we saw the truth in the words that he spoke—although we did not comprehend all of his motives. There were the Heavens, and there were the Hells, and to these, in the end, those souls of man would go; and when the Mother at last was appeased—for it was hardest to part her from the children she had known, but that is another story—the gods withdrew to let the last-born flower.

"But Mystery was not content, and wisely so; he went to Bredan, and asked him for a binding that the very Gods could not break, and Bredan bound us by our words and his being: No God could come directly to the world again and wreak their power upon those too weak to bear it. And Mystery sealed the bar-gain, and there was the Great Change, that closed the world of the last-born to us forever. Bredan was the Oathholder, and Bredan the guardian of the divide.

"Yet there were three who did not swear the binding oath: Bredan of the Cov-enant among them, for he is the holder of the oath, and he enforces it."

The air was alive with the last words of Teos, Lord of Knowledge. His sword sparked, and the book slammed shut, as if a final judgment had been pronounced.

Meralonne cursed in the silence.

"But it doesn't make any sense!" Stephen cried out. "If—if he's *here*—why would the Hunter God not tell us this? Why would he hide his true name and his true nature?"

"Mortal life is short," the God replied gravely, "and mortal memory shorter still. The ages pass and change it. For my part, I do not believe that Bredan lied to his people. It is not his way.

"For there is more, Stephen. The Covenant bound us, but it was *not* the only binding; the Great Change sundered us from the world, and the world from us. We are not as we were, and we can never be so again, and just as we have sought to change you, so you have, in some remote way, touched us. There is a divide between us and within us, and the crossing of it would be perilous even if the binding were not in place. Not one of us knows—not even I—what might happen to a God who makes that crossing."

If there were a chair, or ground that he could see, Stephen would have let his legs collapse beneath him. He did not. "He's here," he said softly. "He's always been here."

The God made no reply.

Stephen paled, and then, wind taking his hair, he raised his face, lifting his sky-blue eyes to meet the warmth of golden ones. "If the Lord of the Darkness is not on his throne in the Hells, where is he?"

*   *   *

Teos lowered his helm and lifted his great sword. "War will come," he said softly, "and I pray that war can be contained in the Hells.

"Find Bredan. Find our brother, and return him to us." He bowed to Stephen, the full bow of the Breodanir.

"What? How?"

But the Lord of Knowledge did not answer. "I fear that we will not meet again, Stephen of Elseth. At least not in this world." He rose, and then nodded to Kallandras and Meralonne as they stood in silence. "Perhaps," Teos said to the mage, as the mists began to grow and thicken between them, "you and I will meet again in future. You have but to ask any of my children in the Order."

Meralonne nodded gravely.

"You know what is at stake, Illaraphaniel. Do what must be done."

"Have not I always?" The words hung in the air as the walls of the mage's tower study became substantial, became real. A crack of pink light, straight and thin, peered out from the edges of the shuttered window. Time passed strangely in the half-world, or in its lingering aftermath.

Stephen looked up into the pale face of the slender mage whose gray eyes were focused on a distance that none but he could see. "Meralonne?"

The mage looked down, as if from a great height, and a cold one. "Yes?"

"He's here, isn't he?"

"I think not," was the quiet reply. "If I read the Lord of Knowledge aright, then he is neither here nor there. Were he here, in fact, we would know it; and not just us. The continent itself would be re-formed to the vast wastes of his desire." Absently, almost as if by drill and not conscious desire, he reached for the pipe that he had set aside. He lifted it, empty and cold, to his lips, and inhaled. "Yet he is not on his throne in the Hells. He is somewhere *between*."

"And we must stop him," Kallandras said, speaking for the first time since the half-world had taken him into its fold. "I saw the arch. The gate," he added. "I saw it, but I did not know it for what it was."

"If you saw it and you escaped, he was weak indeed, and his grasp upon the world was poor. When?" As the bard hesitated, the platinum brows of the mage drew into one thin, long line. "Kallandras, we have no time for foolishness. *When?*"

"Eight years ago. Near Lattan."

The mage smiled softly to himself, but the smile was bitter. "I see." The smile withered. "Where?"

"By Myrddion's final resting place. In Vexusa. I would not have escaped, but *she* sent me away; she used her magic to move me from the coliseum to the streets of Averalaan Aramarelas."

Meralonne turned to Stephen. "He thinks that you are capable of finding Bredan of the Covenant—of finding your God. Do it."

"I—" All protest died on Stephen's lips as he met the mage's eyes. Winters were warmer than what he saw there. He swallowed. But before he could speak, the mage spoke again, and his tone was softer, although his face was no less bleak.

"I understand that if you find your God you may well face the fate to which you were bound. But that fate was your choice, and if you did not understand all of what you were swearing, you swore the oath nonetheless, and you have bene-fited from it. If you do *not* find your God, then it is not only Breodanir that will suffer, but the Kingdoms of the West, the Empire of Essalieyan, and the Domin-ion of Annagar."

"I don't—I don't understand."

"Bredan was the keeper of the Covenant, but he was also the guardian of the 'divide.' It is that unknown divide that the Lord of the Hells is crossing as we speak. If we want any chance of hindering Allasakar—yes, *Allasakar*—in his pas-sage, we *must* find Bredan."

Ashfel saw Stephen first and bounded up to him, taking long easy strides that ended with two gray paws splayed out against the breadth of Stephen's chest. Were it not for the intervention of the wall, Stephen would have fallen, and he lost no time in telling Ashfel exactly that.

Ashfel's response was unacceptable, and he knew it; he also knew the exact moment that Gilliam was about to cross the threshold, for he bounded up and off, and sat with delicate good grace at the disheveled huntbrother's feet.

Dogs, of course, were usually rather stupid when it came to lying, and Ashfel was no exception. The idea that Gilliam had already *seen* the end of Ashfel's paws planted firmly against Stephen's chest just didn't occur to him until Gilliam caught him by the snout. At that point, he realized that he'd been caught out, and struggled between defiance and pathos; pathos won.

Or at least it might have had Stephen been the Hunter Lord. Gilliam was un-amused. Stephen thought it strange—he almost always did—that these dogs re-vered Gilliam, that they would die for him without hesitation, yet that it was Gilliam who was most severe and rigid when any of his rules were broken.

"You're late," Gilliam said, although his gaze was on Ashfel, who lay belly to ground in the entry hall.

"Sorry."

"What happened?"

"We're in trouble."

"I'd guessed," was the quiet response. He caught Stephen by both shoulders; the huntbrother tensed, but met his Lord's gaze.

Don't ask, Gil, he thought. *Just don't ask.*

Gilliam was not good at asking questions; he was not well-versed at the art of starting a dialogue with little help. He also had his pride; Stephen felt it prickling the edges of their bond. He knew that Gilliam was hurt, and knew better that Gilliam would never admit to it. Just as well. Anger, he could deal with.

"Messenger came," Gilliam said gruffly, as he let go of Stephen and turned away.

"What?"

"A messenger."

"At this hour?"

Gilliam nodded. "From The Terafin. She wants us back."

"Why?"

"How should I know?" He turned to walk away, and Stephen went after him.

"Gil—"

"Don't bother." He walked to the flat surface of an unused desk, and picked up a curled scroll. "This is the message," he said, turning, his face dark.

Stephen took it, looked at it, and saw the perfect brush strokes of a person well-versed in the art of writing. More than that would have to wait. He curled the message up and slid it into the hip sling that he wore. "Gilliam, I won't lie to you." He couldn't; a lie required the building of far too many walls, and the bond would not allow them. "But I won't tell you things that are too personal either. You've said nothing at all about Espere, and I've only ever asked the one time."

Gilliam grudgingly met Stephen's gaze.

"This—it's personal to me, and it's going to be personally very costly, very painful. But in the end, it has *nothing* to do with you."

"How can it have nothing to do with me? You're *my* huntbrother!"

"Yes. Not one of your hounds." He pulled the Hunter's Horn from the sash at his side. Held it gingerly, the way one might hold a dangerous poison; he couldn't hold it any other way, for he was suddenly certain that his life and his death were notes that the Horn, when winded, would sound. "This is *my* Wyrd."

"And that means you have to face it alone?"

"No. And yes."

"You were—"

"I was afraid. I'm not anymore." He lifted the Horn, searching its simplicity for some rune, some marking, some hint of its maker's purpose. It was easier than meeting Gilliam's eyes. "We have a task, and I don't know how to do it."

"What task?"

"We have to find the Hunter God."

The silence, although short, could not have been more complete.

"And then, when we find Him, we have to return Him to the Heavens." He looked up then, to meet his Hunter's eyes. They were slightly wide.

Before Gilliam—who had never been good with words—could frame a reply, Espere appeared at his side; how she'd crossed the room unnoticed, Stephen didn't know. She placed a small hand on Gilliam's chest, drawing his gaze downward; then, when she had it, she nodded solemnly and quietly.

"She's afraid," Gilliam told his huntbrother, as he cupped her face in his hands. "But she knows that you're right."

"You're back," Meralonne said softly as he stared out of the shuttered windows into the early morning street below. The wagons were rolling into the Order, carrying from the farmers' fields the food with which the members would be fed their day's meal. They disappeared quickly from his line of sight, taking the route that the merchants and servants were to use.

"You're awake."

"Did you hope to find me sleeping?" The mage turned, his smile both sharp and sardonic.

"You? No, Master APhaniel. I never expect to find you asleep." The bard gave a low, deep bow. The movement was precise and crisp; it was also silent. What he wore was dark and simple; his hair was caught and pinned into near invisibility. He did not carry a visible weapon, which was not terribly surprising—but he also did not carry his lute, which was.

Meralonne started to speak, and then shook his head softly. "I weary of this game. Speak, Kallandras; you have come for a reason."

"You know what I was, once." There wasn't even a trace of question in the sentence.

"I know," the mage replied evenly, "what you are."

"And that?"

But Meralonne smiled thinly. "The youngest master bard that Senniel College has ever produced. Were it not for your elusive past, I believe that you might become the youngest bardmaster as well—Sioban favors you. It is well known."

"And you," Kallandras said gravely, "are a mage-born member of the Order of Knowledge. You were born in the South—or some say the West, and you have resided here for twenty years or more." He paused. "So that we understand each other."

"What do you seek? For it appears that we will walk this road together for the time."

"We will walk it and be damned," Kallandras' voice was barely a whisper, but it carried; a bardic whisper could make itself heard down a city block without losing subtlety or nuance. He bowed again, and then stiffened; his skin was as pale as the mage's hair. "I need you to carry word to those who protect the Crowns."

Meralonne's eyes became steely slits so narrow they seemed a weapon's edge. "What do you mean?"

"I cannot carry the word myself, or I would do it; you can."

"Kallandras—we have not the time for this. Speak plainly."

"Two men were to be hired to assassinate the Kings."

A silver brow rose, hovering. Meralonne did not fill the silence with questions.

"They refused the kill."

"Very wise."

"They died for their refusal." Blue eyes iced over as he spoke.

"I see." Meralonne reached out and closed the shutters. "When?"

"Ten days. Two weeks. I cannot be certain."

The mage turned. The room, without natural light, was darkened and gray; there were no lamps burning, no magestones glimmering. A crack of light traced the shutters, as it had already done once this morn. It was enough to see by, if one knew how to look. Kallandras knew. And he stared into the face of Meralonne APhaniel, seeing in it a surprise that was already dying and being replaced by an expression of understanding, a sympathy that could only be born of experience.

"What killed those two," Meralonne said softly, "must be dangerous indeed. Where did they fall?"

But Kallandras could not answer; his tongue was suddenly thick with the horrible truth that it had uttered. *This* was truly an act of betrayal so profound that the Lady Herself would damn him for eternity with serenity. The killers had already condemned themselves to death by the hands of the Kovaschaii; but the target, the victims—*that* was information that had never in the history of the brotherhood been spoken aloud. There had never been a need, until now.

He thought to explain it, but the mage lifted a hand. "I am sorry, Kallandras. I will not ask further."

And yet, because he had come this far, he felt he must at least excuse himself somehow. "The Coliseum," he said, his voice so alien it was not the voice of a bard.

"When?" Meralonne said, so softly that the question should not have carried urgency. It did.

"The deaths were to occur during the month of Veral, mid-month, at a date that was to be made precise as the time drew near." No bard's voice this. And no brother's. Yet it held its story, its music, its dread.

"I will go," Meralonne said quietly. "I will go in haste to the Crowns. And you?"

"If Sioban can manage it, I will be in attendance until this affair is resolved."

The mage nodded quietly. What he did not say, and what they both knew, was that two of the brotherhood lay dead at the hands of their enemies; how difficult would it be to kill one more?

Chapter Nineteen

7th Corvil, 410 A.A.
Terafin

"**R**EPORT."

Carver nodded quietly. "She's surrounded by her Chosen all the time now. Had two appointments today, but she canceled them. She's not taking dinner in the dining hall with the rest of the House Council; she's staying in her private chambers.

"But there is one interesting thing. Apparently—and I didn't see them myself—two foreigners and a bunch of their dogs arrived here under heavy guard just half an hour past dawn."

Jewel's brow furrowed slightly, and then she smiled. "Where are they?"

"Not sure yet. I should know in an hour or two."

"Good. Angel?"

"Pretty much the same. Her food's being prepared by the ATerafin on staff, and none of the cooks or servants are new. This started today. They're all talking about it, and they're all worried—but I don't think she's in any danger there. If Carver can't find out what we need to know, I think I might be able to dig it out of the cooks' servants if I eavesdrop for long enough."

"Better." Her smile deepened. "Teller?"

He shrugged. "Nothing much."

"Which means?"

"Guards are antsy. They've doubled patrols and started overlapping shifts. But they're not great about it. As long as they recognize you, you're okay."

"They can hardly be expected," Ellerson interjected, "to turn the entire building into a prison. That is not their function."

"Finch?"

Finch's naturally pale cheeks reddened slightly. "Well, I'm not sure. I don't think there's much danger from the valets and the personal servants—but you should hear them talk! I don't think anyone here's got a private life that anyone else doesn't know about."

"And we don't need to hear about it either. Well, not now." She looked at Arann. Arann smiled almost shyly. "And you?"

"I don't think there's anything wrong with the House Guard. But I can't really tell. None of 'em trust me yet."

"Well, no. They wouldn't; it's your first day." She stopped to really *look* at Arann; he was still wearing the armor that had been laid out for him as part of his pay. He filled it; he had always been big. At his side was a long sword, with the crest of the House in brass as a pommel. It was to be kept clean, Arann had said; everything was.

He was to report for training in the early morning, along with the rest of the new guards—of which there were, she thought wryly, three—and then, the rest of the day was his. Apparently, the new recruits were always put onto the latest shift.

"Are you still all right with this?"

He looked down at his mailed fist and then carefully removed the gauntlets. They were heavy, and overly warm. Everything was.

"Arann?"

"You should see the old man in the drill yard," he said, staring at the tabletop rather than his den leader. "He's older than Rath. And meaner. I think he almost broke Claris' arm."

Jewel grimaced. "But you're okay?"

"Me? Yeah. *I* didn't tell him I knew anything about using a sword."

"Good. You don't." She reached across the table and caught his unmailed hand; it was sweaty, and not, she thought, just from training. "Was he surprised?"

"About me? I think so. But it was The Terafin's order, and he doesn't question 'em." He looked up and met Jewel's eyes; there was something in his expression that she wasn't sure she liked. "Jay?"

"What?"

"You told her you wanted me in with the guards?"

"I told her," Jewel said, "that I thought you would make a good House Guard; you've the size for it, and the strength—and what you lack in training, you make up for in loyalty. Even I didn't think she'd react so quickly." It wasn't the truth, but it was truth of a sort. "Why?"

"They'll count on me," he said quietly. "To stand and fight if we need to. To protect the House at all costs. Stuff like that. And they don't care what I used to do. They don't care where I come from. They didn't even ask. They just asked me—asked me to take up arms and take the—the oath."

"So?" Angel said. "Take the oath."

"Shut up, Angel. You wouldn't know an oath if it kissed your—"

"Carver. Angel." They both subsided as Jewel's grip on Arann's hand tightened. "What do you want to do?"

"I don't know," he said again, and again he dropped his gaze. "But—but they said, if I serve well, and if I—I distinguish myself, I can *be* ATerafin. And more than that—if I serve the House well enough, I might one day be one of the Chosen."

Angel snorted in disgust. "When the Sleepers wake!" He slapped the table with both palms, hard.

Teller drew a sharp breath, and everyone else winced. They knew that Jewel didn't like the phrase; something had happened to her and Duster a year ago. Wouldn't say what, but she'd made them stop using it. Angel flushed, avoided meeting the gaze of his den leader, and continued. "Like any one of us is ever going to be ATerafin. Use your head."

"Angel, *shut up.*"

"Well, what's the problem anyway? Take the god-frowned oath and—"

"*Angel.*"

Silence. "Do you want to take the oath, Arann?"

"I don't know." He looked strained by the question; it was obvious from his tone that he'd done enough thinking and more. "I can't take it if I can't keep it," he told her quietly. "But if I take it—"

"You don't serve me anymore."

His shoulders slumped as she said it—as she said what he—and no one else in the room—had already considered.

"All right," she said softly, but not to Arann. "Get out of here—go back to watching. I have some things to think about myself."

Everyone stood quietly, and everyone stared at Arann, who in turn stared groundward with a fixed determination.

"Oh, I forgot. Finch and Jester."

"Jay?"

"Put them back. *All* of them. Now."

"Put what back?"

"Don't give me backtalk, just do it. We can collect household items later, if we have to fly the coop. But it's *later*, and only at my say so. Understood?"

Jester pursed his lips and made a very wet sound; Finch kicked him in the shins. "Yes, Jay," she said meekly, but there was a twinkle about her eyes that said more. "You know what they say."

"No. What do they say?"

"You can take the girl out of the street, but you can't take the street out of the girl."

"Out."

"Well?" Ellerson said, when the room had been emptied for five minutes and it became clear that Jewel had no intention of moving.

"What?"

"Can you take the street out of the den?"

"Why don't you do something useful?" she said softly.

"At your command."

"Get lost."

He cleared his throat. "I will of course, give you privacy should you desire it. But might I also say that there are members of Terafin who serve other organizations, just as The Terafin herself serves the Crowns?"

Jewel nodded quietly. After another silent moment, Ellerson left the room, letting the doors swing on well-oiled hinges in his wake. When she was certain he was gone, she finally let her elbows collapse and slide along the surface of the table. Her cheek touched the cool, waxed wood, and her eyelashes brushed her cheek; she was tired, and the night to follow didn't look like it was going to be any more restful than the last had been.

Arann wanted to take that vow.

He knew what it meant, and he didn't want to ask her for permission—but he *wanted* to take that vow and be counted as one of the fancy-dress guards of Terafin. And why shouldn't he? Why shouldn't he want to be part of guards that used real armor, real weapons, and served a real purpose? Why shouldn't he want to be shoulder-to-shoulder with people he could trust, people who would serve the same cause that he did?

He'd never have to steal again, that's for sure. And he'd never have to fight in the middle of a den war, with nothing but a few coppers and half-coppers as a reward for survival.

Isn't that what you wanted? He'll be safe. He'll be safer here than he ever was with you.

But she felt a terrible pang, and worse. Arann was, of all her den, the most loyal—the most protective. He wasn't simple, but he was direct; he protected his friends, and he followed his den-leader. Carver and Duster always argued, and sometimes, in the heat of it, things could get dicey. Angel was just as likely to disobey you after he'd agreed to whatever it was you demanded. But Arann—he was special.

It's your own fault, she told herself, balling her hands into fists and then forcing them, slowly, to relax. *I told her I wanted him in with the House Guards for a few days.*

Still, she felt betrayed by The Terafin, because no matter what her decision, things with Arann would never be the same; she would always know that in his heart he wanted to serve a different cause, a different master.

A few days.

What had Rath said, years ago, when she thought him crazy and addled? It was always the honest ones that would break your heart.

The door swung open again; it was Ellerson. He was quiet. "Go away," she said tonelessly. Then she stopped. "Ellerson?"

"Jewel?"

Funny. All her life, the name had been a joke. Only her father had ever used it seriously. But in Terafin, the only people who called her Jay were those she'd pulled from the streets and dragged here. She should've minded it more. "You said that you serve me."

"That is my function."

"But you said that you were chosen by The Terafin?"

"Indeed."

"And if The Terafin chose to order you to cease your service, would you do it?"

"I? No," he said gravely. "But The Terafin understands this well enough. The only choice I have, besides the choice of vocation—that of service—is whether or not I will take a given master. I believe," he added, with a rare smile, "that I underestimated both the master and the difficulty when I chose to accept you.

"However, once I have made my decision, it is made—and it is only unmade in the event of my death, your death, any unusual change in circumstance or the expiration of any contractual period of time."

"What?"

He smiled obliquely. "Some people will ask for the service of a domicis for a period of time—say, three years—and at the end of that time, I would then be free to leave."

"What about the change in circumstance?"

"If, for instance, you were somehow to become Terafin—or rather, to become *The* Terafin, that would warrant a shift of service."

"You mean, if I became *more* powerful, you'd leave?"

He nodded, and his expression was if possible graver. "To serve a person with power is a difficult task, and it often requires power. Few of the domicis understand the nature of power, or great power; it is brutal, gentle, and subtle. *I* do not, nor would I claim it."

She was quiet a moment, and then her shoulders sagged again. "I don't have any choice, do I?"

"You always have some choice," he replied.

"What?" The single word was bitter. "I can't keep him. I just can't. He doesn't want anything that I don't. He wants—" She laughed, but it was a choked laugh. "To be ATerafin."

"Many, many boys dream of joining one of the great Houses." There was something odd about Ellerson's tone, and Jewel looked up for the first time. His eyes had a faraway expression, part wistful and part something else that she couldn't identify. "You don't have to lose him, you know," he told her as he turned for the door.

"What do you mean?"

"Many, many are those who dream of joining a great House. How many truly dream of leading one?" He was gone.

*   *   *

Magic had a certain feel to it, a slight wrongness, a quiet discordance; it had a scentless smell, an unseen shade—something. Devon was not always aware of it; he was not mage-born, nor in any way talent-born. He recognized it when he saw it in use, and he knew how to fight certain branches of the art—but only rarely could he detect it when it had no visible component.

He rose from his desk, nonchalant; he walked across the stretch of open carpet that led to the fireplace and the window bay. His muscles corded, shins tensing and shoulders curling slightly inward as he reached for the door to the balcony.

A Terafin.

He froze and then slowly turned to view the empty room. An aide ran in and out, looking harried; Patris Larkasir was preparing for a three-week river journey to the city of Cordova in the Valley Terrean of Averda, and the strain of meeting his deadlines showed on the staff of young men and women.

I have word for you, and it will not wait.

Magic, indeed. Something about the faceless voice was familiar, but he could not immediately place it. "Go on," he said softly.

It concerns the brotherhood.

At that, Devon turned and deliberately spat to the side.

The voice continued; it was clear that whoever spoke did not, and could not, see him. *An attempt at their hire was made recently. They refused the kill they were offered.*

I wish you to know that the kill they were offered was no less a target than the Twin Kings.

"I'm listening," Devon said, his voice measured and calm in the waiting stillness.

The deaths themselves were to occur during the month of Veral; I do not know why, although it has become more of my concern than you can possibly imagine to find out. I believe that it is no longer safe to travel so openly to you, and besides that, it is not efficient.

"And why do you not take this to the Kings?"

I expect, the voice continued, *that you will know what to do with this information; one way or the other, it will get where it needs to go. I would advise you to keep as much of it to yourself as possible, excepting perhaps Miri, whom you should trust.*

It was Meralonne. It had to be. And not only could he not see Devon, but it had become patently clear that he didn't particularly care if he could hear him either.

Devon was not a man to be irritated by such apparent lack of grace or consideration. The message was all that mattered, and as the words sank in fully, they became the focus of his world—and his world grew smaller and sharper and clearer with each passing second.

The middle of Veral. Why?

There was much to be done.

He did not wish to contact Mirialyn ACormaris; not at this juncture. If Verrus

Allamar was indeed the weak link in the enemy's forked plans, he no doubt had the solitary Princess under a fierce watch. Such a surveillance would not cause much more than the raising of an exasperated brow—they were not known for their friendly feelings toward each other. But they were—they had both been—considered above reproach and above suspicion.

"Morretz," The Terafin said, as she looked up from her business, "I've known you for years, and I do not think I have ever seen you this uneasy. Please stop." Colored by sunlight poured through the stained glass dome above, she looked an artist's skewed vision of The Terafin, and not the woman herself.

"Might I correct The Terafin?" he said, without otherwise acknowledging her complaint.

"If you must."

"I have been exactly this uneasy in the past. It was during the House war with Darias and Morriset. You may recall it," he added.

"Indeed. But I suppose I was young enough then to feel as uneasy as you did. Only one assassin made it past my guard."

"Only one was required," Morretz replied, rather sharply.

"Yes. Well. She didn't make it past you."

"No. And that," he added, as he looked down the bridge of his nose at the woman who ruled Terafin, "is because I was vigilant."

"If that's what you're calling it," she said wryly. "You make me feel like a coddled child." She paused and then frowned. "I hate to be coddled. Cease."

"If there is any particular aspect of behavior or service that you wish me to stop, I will be pleased to do so. Only specify it, Terafin."

Which was, of course, the problem. Nothing in his routine had changed noticeably; he was just on edge. As, she reflected ruefully, were her Chosen. The words of the seer-born girl had electrified them all; they were waiting for the heart of the storm to descend upon them.

"Delores is pressing for a full session of the House Council," she said, changing the subject by lifting a sealed letter and letting it hang a moment in the air.

"His concern is . . . touching. How does he justify his demand? It is not the time for a Council meeting."

"It appears that he has heard rumors about a possible danger to The Terafin." Her smile was icy and thin indeed. "The man has the best spies in the Empire. I wish he were working for me." She let the missive drop to the table.

"Shall I respond?"

"I've already regretfully declined both his suggestion for the Council and his request for a personal appointment."

"Risky."

"Yes." She closed her eyes for a moment and raised a hand to delicately massage her brow. "But there are risks that we've no choice but to take; this is one. I've set Gabriel against him; I believe that Gabriel can hold him long enough."

"Long enough?"

She shook her head. "It's in the air," she, said softly.

"Yes."

"Morretz."

"Terafin?"

"What we can do, we *have* done. There is nothing to do now but wait."

Gilliam hated The Terafin's manse. Although in style it was superficially akin to the palaces in Breodanir, there were guards of all stripe and color in constant evidence, and servants underfoot at every turn. The dogs were just as like to be shooed away as gaped at, and they were testy to the point of being difficult.

Stephen knew it, watching his Hunter; he paced, just as his dogs did, very much the wild force in the pretty cage. He felt it a little himself; the Southern style of the Arannan Halls, while very strange, was also comfortingly free of pomp and ritual. Here, in the manse of the woman who ruled the most powerful family in the Empire, pomp was obvious in the sparest of details. She was a power, and one couldn't help but feel it.

As well, Gilliam was put in the unwelcome role of follower; it was Stephen's unusual gift of sight that The Terafin required—requested—and therefore Stephen was both busy enough not to feel the stab of homesickness that struck his Hunter, and deferred to enough that he felt his own stature was undiminished by his stay on the soil of a foreign nation. Gilliam had been too long away from home.

But that would change; it would have to.

Yesterday, Stephen had toured the grounds, and then joined an inspection of the household staff, the guards, the Chosen; after this, a meal had been served and he had been allowed to retire to the privacy of his chamber, where Gilliam paced in annoyance and frustration.

Be easy, Gil, he thought; he could almost feel Gilliam's teeth grinding. *We'll be returning home soon.*

It was, as he counted back, the eighth of Corvil, and no matter what the state of affairs in Averalaan, he, Gilliam, and most probably Espere had little choice but to begin their trek back to Breodanir by mid-month at the very latest. Henden was coming, and upon its heels, Veral.

No Hunter Lord failed the call to the Sacred Hunt. Nor any huntbrother.

8th Corvil, 410 A.A.
Terafin

Jewel woke to darkness with a cry.

For the first time in weeks it was not nightmares of the walking dead, the waking dead, the vengeful dead that forced her to flee sleep. It was worse.

"Jewel?" Ellerson's voice; Ellerson's calm, still face cast into harsh relief behind the white glow of lamplight in darkness.

Beside her bed, strewn across a chair like castoffs, were a sleeveless shirt and dark leggings. Shielding her eyes from a glare that was already diminishing, she threw off her blankets and reached for them. The servants had tried—how they had tried—to have the clothing taken away; she'd fought with them over it for just such an emergency. A fierce smile folded her lips and was gone.

"Wake the others," she told the waiting domicis.

"What should I—"

"Tell them it's now."

He paused at the door a minute, wavering like the flame in the lamp that he held. She thought she saw appraisal in his glance, but that was all; he lowered the lamp so that its glow touched the underside of his chin, rather than illuminating his face. But he did not speak, or even begin to; his face was as impassive as she'd ever seen it.

She lost sight of him as she pulled the shirt over her head; when the soft ripple of fabric had cleared her face, the room was empty again, but the light remained, swaying slightly as it hung on a brass hook mounted in the wall. She did not stop to wonder where he'd gone; she knew he was waking the den.

The sea air was carried by a strong wind; the night was dark and cool, the air sharp. She closed her eyes, shutting out the details of her room, her sparse life in Terafin. In the distance she heard raised cries and the sound of metal. Nodding, she opened her eyes and grabbed the lamp, hurrying through the door, into the antechamber, and then into the hall.

Adrenaline shook off the physical effects of sleep and made of the world a sharper place, but there were things that only wakefulness brought back; it was only when Carver and Angel trod lightly across the threshold of the kitchen that she remembered whom she would not see this night: Arann. He was on his rounds as a House Guard.

The cries that she had heard, however faintly, in the distance could be his.

"Jay?" Finch. "What is it? What's happening?"

"Listen," she said softly. "Listen well."

Carver looked at Angel; Angel shrugged. Finch's eyes screwed up and she pressed her lids tightly together, but when she opened them, she, too, shrugged. "What are we supposed to hear?"

Thunder. She rose, toppling the lamp; Carver cried out in a panic and righted it, mindful of the heated glass.

It hadn't happened yet. "Ellerson!"

"It is already done," he told her quietly. "If you can be, be at ease."

It surprised her; she had no words to offer, not even those of thanks. How had he known? How had he known what she, in her sleep-fogged state, had not? The cries were those not yet raised; the clash of steel a conflict not yet started. She shivered, feeling the chill in the air; it was cool, and early in the season for it. It had been twelve years since she had heard the sounds of an event before it had occurred—and that single time was a sweet memory compared to this one: the dance of the bears and the huge cats to the jangle of hoops and rings and bells.

No, not so sweet; one of the bears had been maddened, and a death had occurred there, beneath the closed pavilion of Southern delight.

Thunder and lightning, her granddam had called it.

"What's already done?"

"The guards and the Chosen have been alerted; they are all awake, and they are preparing for intruders. Jewel?"

There was only one man in the room who ever called her that; out of habit, her den wisely chose the more familiar Jay. She looked back, into the broken shadows. "What?"

"I believe that now is the time to decide upon your course of action."

She hated it, to need the reminder, but she accepted it without demur. "Right. Carver?"

"Got it," he said, lifting the edge of his shirt to show an ornate dagger hilt.

"Good."

"Why don't you take it?"

"Because next to Duster, you're the best person we've got with a knife." The words faded into an uneasy stillness. Jewel cursed inwardly, wondering how she could forget the death, and knowing at the same time that it was the most natural mistake in the world—for it was during moments like this when Duster really had become the second in command. All her angles became edges, and all her edges became honed and sharpened.

They'd never had a big dust-up without her.

Angel broke the silence. "Yeah, well. What about the rest of us?"

"The rest of you are to listen for the key words we spoke about. You hear 'em, you get the Hells out of the way. Got it?"

"And?"

"And if you don't hear 'em, let the men in armor take the brunt of the fighting, but help as you can." She rose. "Now, follow me."

"Where?" It was Teller, with his slightly rounded eyes and his knowing little smile. What he knew was this: Jewel had no idea where she was going; she was running on instinct, and praying that it worked.

"Just follow."

The halls were darkened and heavily patrolled, but the guards had their orders, and when the dark-clothed den of The Terafin's most unusual young visitor slunk past, sticking to the shadows they could find, the House Guards tensed but did not seek to act. There were few servants in the halls; the hour was late. The only noncombatants that seemed in evidence appeared at the front and the back doors of the manse, carrying torches and oil for the lamps. There were glowstones as well, although not many, and they were almost always in the keeping of the leaders of the clusters of guards.

Jewel walked quickly, her very way of movement a type of speech with rhythms and cadences familiar to those who followed in her wake. They did not speak, not even among themselves; they could see in the hunch of her shoulders and the stiffness of her quick steps the fear that she always took care to keep out of her voice. They followed, in the order they often kept; Carver at her back, and then at his, Finch and Teller; behind them, Jester of the keen ears and poor vision, and Angel pulling up the rear. That had been Arann's position until this night, but at least he was still alive to fill it again, should the need arise.

She could feel the dead at her back, and occasionally glanced into the shadows to catch sight of them if she could; she saw the living, and the spaces behind or beside them where the dead would once have walked. But she felt no fear and no guilt, no terror or horror; the dead were sleeping peacefully this one night.

She would strike a blow for them if she could.

"Can you not remain here?"

"Morretz," The Terafin said, her voice as cold and sharp as fine steel, "the discussion is at an *end*. You will not raise this point again, now or in the future. Is that clear?" She did not choose to wait for a reply, but instead turned to face Arrendas ATerafin. "How long has it been?"

He gave her a full-armed salute which was both exact and fast; it was the answer she wanted, not the patina of drilled respect. "Not more than twenty minutes, Terafin." A fine sheen of sweat made his skin, around the dark bristles of close-cropped beard, glow.

"The Chosen?"

"Readied."

"Good. Has the mage been called?"

"Torvan has been sent to summon the mage," Arrendas answered.

"The guards?"

"The House Guard is being led by Alayra."

The Terafin nodded grimly. "Morretz?"

Morretz' bow was grace personified, but his eyes were darker and more troubled than they had yet been. He stepped forward, hands outstretched and carefully balanced beneath the sheath of a long, curved sword. Gold inlay, jeweled by the hand of a maker, declared the motto of Terafin: *Justice shall not sleep.* Each of the Chosen had seen this sword once, but only Alayra, in the grounds below, had seen it twice. Until now.

Jewel, The Terafin thought, as Morretz dropped to one knee and raised the sword like a priest offering the sacraments, *let your sight be true; I am committed.* She lifted the sheath, and with deliberate care, girded it fast. There it shone like a promise; it was the soul of Terafin, and she, as The Terafin, was given the right and the privilege of wielding it. But never in vain, and never with vanity.

The hilt of the sword was remarkably cool beneath her steady palm. "It is time. Let us repair below."

Alowan hated the night, although he would never have thought it could be so in his youth. The night held stars and the hidden wonders of love and desire; it held the stillness of the sea, the voices of the insects, the silence of a city that was always too noisy, too busy. But it was never for these that he was awakened, and never for these that he held the vigil of the healer in the tense silence of the healerie.

No; if anyone had the temerity to waken him in the dead of night—with no patient that needed immediate attention—it was The Terafin, and it was not her intent that he witness the beauty of the shadows. It was the carnage that she asked him to wait upon. There was battle in the air.

Who is it? he thought, momentarily angered. *The House wars ended a decade ago; who dares to renew them?*

The physicians were also awake, and they busied themselves with the beds in the alcoves, adding stretchers and floormats where there was space for them; it destroyed the carefully designed illusion of privacy and quiet, but Alowan was enough of a healer not to resent their eminently practical choice. His personal assistants were laying out bandages and shears as well as the herbal remedies that would kill the infections that started in gut wounds. No one spoke, and he hated the silence.

Who dares, he thought again, *to attack the House itself?* For of a certainty, the Kings would notice—could not help but notice—and where there was such a war, they could *not* turn a blind eye and leave the Houses to deal with their own. Oh, it would damage Terafin, there was no question of it.

But he didn't give a damn about the House and its politics. It was the ravaged flesh of the individuals that worried him, and that would do more than that by the dawn.

*   *   *

Claris, bruised but otherwise whole, was shifting his weight from left to right foot so rapidly it seemed a sort of dance. His red hair was cropped short and all except a shock of curl was hidden by the helm that he clearly didn't like. That helm topped Arann by a good six inches, and Arann had never been small.

"What do you think's going to happen?" Claris whispered. "Why do you think all the guard's been mobilized?"

Arann shrugged, wishing that Claris could shut up for five minutes in a row. Holloran, the sergeant on duty, glowered in their direction; he was not with them, but rather, with one of the Chosen. Receiving orders, no doubt.

"It's got to be something big," Claris continued, as Arann tried to shrink into the fancy boots that went with his armor and his uniform. Holloran was well-named, and Arann was afraid that they were both going to get the lash of Holloran's careful scorn. Again.

He was almost right. Holloran crossed the tiled floors, his step firm and completely regular. He stopped five feet from Arann's chest as both he and Claris attempted to look reasonably watchful. They weren't very good at it, especially when compared to their eight companions, who fell into the attentive pose immediately, and awaited the word of their commanding officer.

"Cartan, Morris," Holloran said, looking distinctly un-amused, "I'm this close to suspending you for the action. You are here to *watch* and *listen*—and if necessary, to fight—not to jabber like dress-servants off-duty. Is that understood?"

"Sir!"

"Good." But the answer didn't appear to entirely satisfy him; he stared for a long, uncomfortable moment at Arann before he spoke again. "Cartan."

"Sir?"

"You didn't come to Terafin on your own, did you?"

A brief hesitation.

"Just answer the question; when I want you to think, I'll tell you."

"No, sir."

"I see. And the person or persons that you traveled with also remain within the grounds of Terafin?"

"Yes, sir."

"What can you tell me about your . . . leader?"

He felt ten pairs of eyes on his face, burning a deep blush into the sides of either cheek. The silence stretched out, and this time Holloran didn't deny him the time. "What—what do you want to know?"

But Holloran shook his head in mild disapproval. "You've told me most of what the guard needs to know," he said, the words sounding very like a threat—although almost every word he spoke did. "Tell me this, then. Can we trust her?"

"Yes."

"You have no doubt?"

"None, sir. If she—if she's the one that says something's happening, then that's the way it is."

"Good. Because it doesn't appear that we have any choice." He turned to his small troop. "Deploy," he said softly. "Sound the alarm at the first sign of any unusual movement." He stepped back, lowered his arm, and watched as his men—eight of them, at any rate—smoothly shifted position.

Battle was in the air, carried by the sea wind and the ghosts of old memories; a hint of Southern fires, a hint of the Western borders. The Terafin made her way down the staircase of the giants, leading her Chosen. She was diminutive in her armor, but the shield and the sword that she bore were unmistakable, and even the servants, rushing in haste and fear from one corridor to another, stopped to gape as she passed them, the very ire of a grand House made real.

She made her way through the ivory hall into the grand foyer, and there she stopped, waiting. She did not wait for long.

Alayra, wearing steel and sweat in what seemed equal quantities, brushed her chest plate with her fist and then lifted her chin. "Terafin."

"Report."

"There are men in the west garden, near the House shrine."

"Ours?"

"No," was the grave reply.

"And?"

"And down the road, perhaps half a mile, there's a large procession moving toward us. It may be coincidence, but they carry torches and not lamps, and the light cast is glinting off steel."

The great hall was on fire, had been on fire; unnatural flames had cracked the stone floors as if they were timber, leaving splinters for the unwary foot. He was bleeding; the flying shards had struck his forehead, his arms, his hands.

His hands.

He looked down, and he saw that beneath the sticky film of drying blood, they were wrong; they were a boy's hands, a youth's hands. The hands, he thought, of an oathsworn huntbrother untested by the King's Forest. The Sacred Hunt.

He knew who he was.

Stephen of Elseth.

And tomorrow, tomorrow was the first of Veral.

Tomorrow, the drummers would beat their steady rhythm against the skins of previous years' kills. Tomorrow, the King would take to the forest's edge, divesting himself of all rank but the one that the Hunter knew: Master of the Game. Tomorrow, the Ladies would gather, in their brilliant dresses, their perfect sashes, paying obeisance to their Queen—and to the men who fulfilled their oaths.

The Hunter's Death was waiting.

He heard the screaming; the splintering of wood—or stone—the cries cut short, and worse, the cries that lingered. They were coming. They always came.

Shadows flooded the great hall; the wall shattered. In the ragged hole that broken stone and mortar made, she stood. Hair of midnight, eyes darker, bruised lips. At her back were men, women—Priests of the God that no one gave name to.

Allasakar.

He ran.

Three times he had made this trek. This fourth time, he thought it should somehow be different. But the narrow, perfect halls became shadow forms at his back; fire brushed his ankles as he turned corners; lamps doused themselves in the wake of his passing. Pain became his only companion; his side cramped, and he clutched it, knowing there would be no relief. How could he stop?

She laughed. Her voice was velvet, desire, death. He thought, a moment, that he might stop and just accept the death that she offered—the fear was that strong, and the weariness. But his oaths were his oaths. His feet beat a path across the cold stone while his mind numbed.

He knew the way, although the building itself was less than a memory to the Breodani. Had there been no torchlight, no blue light, had there been shadows and darkness not just at his back, but all around, he would still have known how to reach it.

The Hunter's Haven.

There, the door; light gleaming beneath it. He reached for the curved handle, but before he could touch it, the hinges creaked. The door swung open.

There, spear in hand, dog at his side, was Gilliam. But not Gilliam the page; it was Gilliam the Hunter.

"Stephen!" he said, his face folding into familiar lines of both danger and relief. "You made it! Get behind me. We'll take care of her."

He was so exhausted. So relieved. The giddiness made his last steps light as he crossed the threshold and stood behind the man that he had followed for almost all his life. He felt liquid coursing down his cheeks; he thought, in confusion, that the wound across his brow had opened up again. But no. Tears fell, the first of the tears he had yet cried in this history, this dream, this place.

He stepped back as the darkness reached the mouth of the Hunter's Haven. His back hit something; he turned, and saw the Hunter's relics laid out as they had always been laid out; but they were all gray and lifeless. Save one. The Hunter's Horn was a soft, warm ivory, with a simple mouthpiece. Carved in a continuous turning line, the symbol of a vow that not even death could end.

No. He would not take it. He would not take it here.

He looked at the reassuring sight of his Hunter's back. *Felt*, for the first time in this terrible, Wyrd-ridden place, the bond between them. Looked down at his hands, and saw that they were the hands of his adulthood, and not the hands of his youth.

And then he looked at the dog, wondering; it wasn't Ashfel, but it was familiar somehow. The proud alaunt turned, swiveling its black-masked face toward him. He lost breath then, and heart.

Corwel.

"Stephen."

The voice carried darkness, was part of the darkness; there were no lights in the room that he could see by. No, not no light; there was a silver glow, fainter than distant starlight, that took form and shape as his eyes accustomed themselves to the gloom—a glow around the form of a young woman.

Evayne.

The cry died in his throat as he glanced wildly about the room's darkened walls. The dream was gone. But she was here. She *was* here.

Stephen sat up in bed, tossing aside both sleep and blankets that were there more for comfort than warmth. He had guttered the lamp's flame, and there was no fire in the hearth; still he squinted into shadows, trying to discern her age. Her breath was rough and heavy, as if some physical exertion had only just ended. Running, perhaps.

"Stephen?" That she called a second time told him she was younger.

"Evayne," he said softly.

He heard her sigh of relief; it was loud. "You've got to get up," she said, the words beginning a headlong rush out of her mouth. "You've got to wake Gilliam."

"What? Why?"

"Because they're coming for you."

He stood, and after a moment, there was light in the room, harsh compared to shadow, but weak compared to day. Stephen lifted the lamp aloft to better see Evayne's expression. Midnight blue framed her face; her cheeks were flushed, her eyes wider than they'd ever been. And there was no line or wrinkle at all across the smoothness of her skin; she was fair and pale, and her hair was perfect darkness. Only her eyes themselves—not the lids of the skin around them—were unchanged by her youth.

The door opened; Espere crossed the threshold. She saw Evayne, and came up short. The younger woman smiled, but fleetingly. "Wild one," she said softly. "I think it time to rouse your master. We must flee."

Stephen touched her shoulder gently, where he might have grabbed the arm of any other speaker. "Evayne, *who* is coming for us?" He asked because he did not want to know, to acknowledge the fact that he *did* know.

"I—I don't know," she whispered. "I don't know who they are. But they're coming to Terafin; I heard them speak. They're looking for you here." She turned fully to face him. "Stephen, please. Trust me."

She was young, was Evayne. Her lip trembled as she made her plea. The older woman would never descend to such behavior—because the older woman had lost all sense of vulnerability in her isolation. "We'll trust you," he heard himself saying as he left his room to rouse the Hunter who was already waking. "You haven't led us poorly yet."

She watched him leave, taking light and warmth with him as he sought to rouse his Hunter Lord. Lord Elseth was already awake—she had looked into the night that contained the sleeping city, and found them both. She drew the crystal, rounded and yet imperfect as any life was, and ran her fingers across the stability of its cool surface.

Images flickered in the silver mists, silent and distant, yet also distinct. There were tales in the ball's depth; whispers of other times and other places imposed one on top of each other like layers of ghosts—or perhaps, more practically, onion. What lay at the heart? Was it the final step on this thrice-cursed path?

Stephen did not understand all of Evayne's life, yet he knew the cause she pursued was a just one, at this age or any other. What he did not know—and what she, at this age, would not tell him—was that the path took her places without direction or directive; that she had to guess, from her time and her surroundings, what her purpose was to be.

Sometimes the purpose was hard to know, harder still to fathom; sometimes, times like tonight, it was simple and clear.

Evayne, called a'Nolan in the free towns of her birth, had the fear and the confidence of youth. But she was not known—not yet—for infallibility.

Chapter Twenty

THE MOMENT THE FIRST of their enemies set foot on the grounds of Terafin proper, Jewel knew. Her skin felt as if it were the surface of a large bell tingling at the stroke of the clapper. Behind her, Carver pulled up short; he took one look at her face as she glanced over her shoulder, and closed his lips firmly on the question he'd been about to ask. It was dark in the halls, but not dark enough.

Not dark enough.

She shivered; the chill grew piercing.

Then, swearing none too softly, she lifted a hand in a pitched signal and began to run.

The halls were grand and smooth and glorious; taller than any but the cathedrals of Averalaan could boast. The ceilings were simple, although the height of the columns folded into a fanned pattern directly above them; the windows were full and long.

Yet as he stepped into those very halls, every hair on the back of his neck rose. Something struck him from within—a thing almost too forceful to be what it was: memory, however warped and twisted.

"Stephen!" Gilliam was at his side in a second, all irritation at the young Evayne—at Stephen, at The Terafin, and at the Empire—forgotten in the urgency of his huntbrother's fear. Ashfel joined him, growling uneasily, ears flattened against his broad skull.

Evayne glanced sharply up at them both, Stephen's white face and Gilliam's slightly flushed one. "What is it?" she asked, perhaps a bit too quickly. "What's wrong?"

Stephen raised an arm. It shook; there was a weight across it too heavy to carry for long. But he managed to point, his single finger tracing a downward curve until it met the floor in the distance of the fountain alcove.

They all looked, then. The dogs were silent, staring at something their master felt to be an enemy. Only Espere tossed her wild, tangled mane and snarled in angry defiance; her eyes, dark, still seemed to carry a spark within them that left no space for fear.

Evayne drew a breath so sharp it cut the silence.

"What? What are you all looking at?" Gilliam said, his frustration held in check by his concern.

"Look through her eyes," Stephen said, speaking for the first time. Only Gilliam was surprised to hear his voice—even weak and shaky though it was—because only Gilliam knew how paralyzing his huntbrother's fear was. He did not quibble or even hesitate. Instead, he did what came so naturally it was easier than making a verbal reply: he slid into Espere's eyes, seeing for a moment as she saw. No more, and no less.

The hall was as his own eyes made it to be: pretentious, grand, foreign. But the floor, tiled and etched and rugged—the floor was different. Shadow crept like living mist gone mad across every nook and cranny—a shadow cast by no light that he had ever seen. As Gilliam watched its slow progress, he wondered if anything that it obscured would emerge whole and unchanged. And if it did not, what change would the Darkness decree? For there was Darkness here.

Like Espere, his response was immediate; as Espere with her growl and her teeth, he drew his bright, long blade with a cry that was wordless and defiant. There was no room in his heart for fear—excepting only the space that Stephen claimed and crossed.

He stopped a moment, and then looked at Evayne, saw her as Espere saw her. Friend. Pup. There was nothing of a rival in her fine, porcelain chin, her high cheekbones, her fragile expression. Nothing of Cynthia, nothing of Maubreche. He owed her a debt for the saving of Stephen's life. He owed it, and if possible, tonight would be the night that she was repaid in full.

He closed his eyes a moment, denying the darkness as he slid back into his self, his full self. The dogs were there, at the edge of his awareness, and Espere, like them to the very core. Only Stephen was closer, and Stephen knew better than to interfere with a full Hunter who chose, in haste and need, to call the Hunter's trance.

Time changed, slowing; he could hear and identify the timbre of Evayne's unfamiliar breath, the shuffling of his wild girl from foot to foot as she stared intently into the shadows, the growling of his pack. He could smell their sweat, each scent resolving into something distinct.

His hand found his horn, trembling with a type of excitement, but although he could not have said why, he stopped himself from winding it. There was a hunt, yes—but who the hunter and who the hunted had not yet been defined enough.

"Come," he said, his the voice of command. The stillness shattered as the dogs pulled into a loose formation in front of Evayne and Stephen. Ashfel at their head looked a fifth again his size as his fur rose along neck and back. There was no thought that was not obedient. They were at war, they were in danger, they were hunted—and Gilliam was their unquestioned leader.

And he ordered them quickly away from the alcove in which shadow pooled—but not so quickly that they did not hear the shattering of stone that was older than the city itself; nor so quickly that they did not see the outer wall fall, crushing the fountain's delicate structure, and making of its tinkling water's fall a final gurgle.

Dust rose, a cloud shunted this way and that by the downward rush of the fallen wall. Gilliam did not give the dust time to clear; he forced his people away from the enemy as fast as he could.

But Stephen knew what had destroyed the wall; Gilliam felt the tension of that knowledge, the welter of the fear that Stephen could almost—but not quite—conceal from him.

I'll protect you, he thought, and the thought was so forceful, the intent so true, that Stephen's fear ebbed a little.

From the grand foyer, at the foot of the stairs, The Terafin felt the building shake. Ornaments—vases and plaques, framed paintings and free-standing sculptures—shuddered; some fell, and some held their ground. A silence more profound than panicked cries and shouts descended upon them.

Then Alayra spoke, and her voice was a quiet, gravelly sound that didn't quite fit in. "It's got to be the western wing."

No one gainsaid her; they all had ears.

Silence again, and in it, the questions were gathering. The Terafin watched her Chosen; in some ways, each of them, woman or man, *were* Terafin to her. She had handpicked them from a number of supplicants almost too great to remember, had added to them over the years as a candidate proved himself or herself worthy of the honor. There was no better place to make a stand, surrounded by these, and honored by them.

And silence, she knew, was an unacceptable offering to their loyalty. "Where is the mage?" she asked.

"The mage," came the silver-toned response, "is here."

He was, standing in the glow of a light so bright it was hard to gaze upon. His raiment was almost practical—a dark cloth tunic, laced with silver or platinum, but collarless; leggings, not the fancy dress of the Order, in the same material.

"Where is Torvan?" The Terafin said sharply, perhaps too sharply.

"He could not travel in haste," was the grave reply. "Not armored and burdened as he was. I chose to travel ahead to the rendezvous. If," he added, "that is acceptable to The Terafin?"

"It is acceptable," was the brittle reply.

"Good. What, by the Dark Court, is happening?"

"Torvan didn't brief you?"

"He said it was urgent that I meet you in the foyer as it was where you would be directing affairs. Or something similar; I confess that I don't remember his exact wording. When I attempted to discover what, exactly, it is that you intend to be"—and here he stopped to take in the full, and functional, armor and armaments that the Chosen and their leader wore—"fighting, he didn't have a satisfactory answer."

"No," she replied. "But I hope you do. If I'm not mistaken, our enemies—and I believe they are at the very least Allasakari—have just attacked our walls."

"Walls?" he said sharply. "The manse doesn't have walls—it barely has gates."

"Ah. I meant, of course, the walls of the mansion itself."

"Interesting," was the soft reply.

The Terafin looked at his suddenly neutral expression more carefully. She had known Meralonne—in a manner of speaking—for years. But she had never seen him look quite so . . . luminous. Or, for that matter, so anticipatory. Or was it just her imagination? His face, as usual, gave nothing important away. Oh, he played with emotion, blustered, made the right sort of noise—but it was a mask as much as perfect composure could be said to be one. Perhaps, tonight, she might get a glimpse of the real man beneath the mage's face.

She took a little comfort from the thought—because beyond it, there was only cost. To the House, at the very least.

There. In the foyer, of course, where just about anyone could sneak around her and get a good shot. Jewel snorted, ground her teeth in frustration, and then stopped. No point in it, not now; if someone could sneak in, then so could the den; if someone could hide in the shadows, unseen, then so could her own.

She flinched as she stared at the mage; he was bright and pale and tall—and his hair was unfettered by anything smart. Like a braid. What did these people think a fight was?

"Jay?"

Of course, there wasn't much in the way of shadow here.

Yet.

The clangor of armor—light armor—came in from the east. A guard, wearing the surcoat of Terafin. Messenger, from his dress, although he wore two swords and a shield slung over his back. He fell at once to his knee in front of The Terafin, slid an inch or two, and hit his breastplate hard and fast.

"Report."

"The gate's being attacked. It won't last long. I think there's at least one mage out there. Probably two."

"Who?"

He looked up, his eyes seeing new death, sudden death, before they saw her. Who was he? Kevin, she thought, or perhaps Kalvin—he was a newer guard. A young one. He swallowed. "It's—it's Darias."

"Darias?" She could not keep the surprise and the anger out of her voice.

"Darias colors," he said, holding his ground even as he averted his gaze. "Captain Jed'ra confirmed it."

"But that's *insane!*" Alayra said, speaking for every member of the Chosen who knew better. Alayra had never been selected for occasions of pomp and rarely stood on ceremony. "They—they must be fighting under false colors."

"They aren't our friends, and never have been," the young man shot back. He paled as he remembered where he was, and with whom. "Captain Jed'ra—Captain Jed'ra recognized some of the guards. The officers. Three of them. He says they're Darias all right. There are a hundred and fifty men, maybe two hundred. And that's only at the gate."

"Go back to the captain," The Terafin said softly. "Resume your post. Alayra."

Alayra saluted, her face etched into dark and angry lines. "Terafin."

"It's not just two hundred," a new voice—a tired one—said. Torvan ATerafin came, from the small hall to the south, into the foyer. "They've about forty men in the back. None of them are wearing any colors; they're in dark clothing. We spotted them early, and the archers were keeping them at bay."

"Were?"

He swallowed, raising a mailed hand to wipe the sweat from his brow before he realized how futile that was. "There's some sort of magery at work out back. Shadows," he added, his eyes wide. "Darkness."

And then, the last blow: the sound of the bells in the gardens; the sounds of metal alloy being struck and struck again. Fire.

Stephen ran down the hall. At his side was the young Evayne, not nearly as frightened as he; at his back, taking the rear line of defense—the only important line— were Gilliam, Ashfel, and Singer. Gilliam had taken the lead for as long as their absolute safety required it; he took the back when it was clear that the worst of the threat lay behind, on their trail. Espere and the rest of the dogs were ahead, the vanguard of the small group. He should have felt safer, to have them all there.

But he felt alone. The darkness had pulled from his waking mind the memory of nightmare; he could see, more clearly than the lovely Imperial architecture, the rough-hewn stone of an old Breodanir church with its empty, shadowed passages. Death was behind him; the screams had just faded. Only his bond with Gilliam touched him at all, and he clung to it while at the same time trying to hide from it.

"To the left!" Evayne shouted, and Stephen shifted down the hall that opened to his side instead of continuing down the straight path.

"Where are we going?" Gilliam shouted back, although he shifted his pack to accede to her sudden command.

"Deeper in!" was her response. "There were guards—I saw them—many—maybe they were—ready for this!"

Stephen felt Gilliam's momentary territoriality give way to practicality as he ceded command to Evayne, but kept the responsibility of their protection for himself.

Jewel knew, before she started, that there was no good ground position to occupy. Problem was that there didn't seem to be much of a mediocre one either, and poor didn't cut it. The foyer, while it seemed a stupid place to make a stand—it was far too exposed—was, in fact, very hard to launch a sneak attack from. There were no alcoves, no little halls, no servants' supply closets—there was barely any furniture. There were long, slender ovals and one mirror that trailed the length of the staircase from the door to the lower hall; there were plants, of a tall and thin variety, that were good at hiding nothing.

"Jay?"

She shook her head and Angel subsided. "It's either here on the landing or there."

Carver looked at the "there": the stairs themselves, wide and grand, with cold, polished marble beneath a fixed layer of woven and hand-knotted carpeting. "You're crazy," he said flatly.

"Good. You come up with a better place. Now."

At that, he fell silent, scanning the area just as she had. Then he shrugged, which was his version of a graceful surrender.

They crouched below the rail, out of habit and not because the spindles provided any cover, and then began to quietly crawl down the stairs. On impulse—an impulse that she didn't bother to question—Jewel took the southern rails and began her vigil; The Terafin stood at the foot of the stairs below. She had to be careful; the steps of her home had been short and high, and the rails close enough together a mouse would barely fit through. These, a mixture of stone and brass, were spaced as the steps were; there were gaps between them wide enough to fall through if she turned sideways.

Wide enough to push someone else through, if it came to that.

Don't look up, she thought, although at whom she didn't know.

"Your pardon, Terafin," Meralonne said gravely, as the bells ceased their clanging. "But I believe that you will find there has been some interference in the duties of your guards."

"Shall I?"

"Yes. I thought it best, after speaking with Torvan, to stop at the gates a moment." His eyes were steel in motion, flashing as if at reflected light. "The fire that your servants are ringing is not exactly as it seems."

"What?"

But he laughed, fey and wild; a younger man. "I believe that my duty is at the gate; your young Sentrus seemed to feel that there was a 'mage or two' present— and it is strictly forbidden, by edict of the Magi, to practice magic of this nature in Averalaan Aramarelas without a writ of approval, signed in full.

"Which reminds me. Terafin, I give this to your keeping, as it may become necessary if I am not in a position to defend myself after this eve." He handed her a rolled scroll; it was not sealed.

"And this?"

"A writ. Signed in full by the council, of course."

She laughed; it was the first laugh of an evening that had given her, as yet, no cause for mirth. "Alayra," she said, sobering quickly. "Accompany the mage."

"Is he to be in command?" Alayra said stiffly.

"He is to be an adviser. A *valued* adviser."

The older woman gave a gruff snort, but her shoulders were slightly less stooped than they had been. "Come along, then."

He drew his sword, cut a lattice of colored light in the air, and then bowed as they stared. "At your service, ATerafin," he said gravely.

Jewel noticed it at once, because her only role on the stairs was that of observer. The sword was silent. The scabbard from which it had been drawn vanished into cloth and air. The blade was long and fine and slender—like a razor more than a sword—but she knew it was not for show and not for dress.

And she knew that the mage knew how to wield it; how to use it to best advantage. She did not question how she knew it; she never questioned that feeling.

But she did wonder why a member of the Order—a member of the mythic Council of the Magi—would resort to such a weapon when he had so many more at his disposal. The blade danced in the air, glittering like ice. She shivered and tried very hard not to wonder anymore.

The Terafin took the luxury of a few seconds to watch Meralonne, light and lithe in his movements, leave the hall. Alayra seemed stocky and heavy beside him, but at least she was a known and trusted quantity. Then, without turning, she called, "Arrendas."

His dark-bearded chin bobbed as he bowed his head and made the salute.

The sound of mailed fist against plate brought her back to herself and her duties. She turned quietly. "The second rank of archers?"

"Hidden, as you requested. Ready."

"Good. I believe that the moment is now." Her gaze was intent.

He saluted again, bowing stiffly as he turned to relay the orders to a waiting messenger in the mouth of the southern hall. He stumbled as the building shook again. This time, they heard the sound of falling stone and knew it for what it was.

Wordlessly, the Chosen began to form up, the majority of their numbers placing themselves between their Lord and the southern halls.

Stephen wiped the sweat from his brow, surprised that sweat could exist in such a cold place. His single backward glance took in shadows that the lights did not cast and could not dispel; the shadows were closer now, the pursuit faster.

The wall collapsed behind them, sending shards of stone into his calves and his back. He heard Gilliam curse, and felt his Hunter's rush of fury as the dogs yelped.

He ran, knowing as he did that the lamps at his back were being guttered, one by one. His hands were bleeding; he furled them into fists and felt a dull ache, followed by a rush of a warmth, of too much warmth. Opening them, he glanced down.

Saw his feet; saw the rough-hewn stone beneath them. The dead were at his back—all the dead. And before him . . .

"Left!" It was his voice. He knew, or thought he knew, where he was running. Knew, or thought he knew, what he would find. And then he bit his lip, and the fog of memory cleared slightly. This was no dream; the waking world knew itself, and he knew it. The sanctum of his wyrding was a sanctum to a Hunter God, not to a mortal lord, and besides, the Horn of the Hunter was already his.

And he would not wind it.

He swore, in the silence of heartbeat and raw breath, that he *would not wind it.*

Blue light lanced past—through—his shoulder. He screamed, grabbing at it, the world rushing up to meet his face. By his side, another scream, a foreign one, and inside, in the darkness that only one other person could touch, fear and anger. He clutched the anger as he clutched the blue mage-light, fighting it as if it were a serpent.

"I am Oathbound!" he cried, throwing it, writhing, into the darkness. "You have no hold over me!"

And the darkness answered with a voice he had heard once before. "Have I not? A pity, little mortal, for you are young and not unpleasant to look upon."

With the darkness as wreath and robe, Sor na Shannen stepped out of the shadows, leading her followers into battle.

The Allasakari were part of legend and part of history; priests of a God that no civilization, save one, had ever openly allowed the worship of. They were mad, or so she thought them; for in time, their minds were devoured by the activities that the darkness spurred them to; they became pale imitations of, and dwindling servants for, the kin that they were ordered by their Lord to summon.

And that, The Terafin thought, was one of the reasons that she—in any situation—would never be Allasakari. To serve, for Amarais Handernesse, had never been enough. It never would be. And to sit at the feet of something that claimed with ease what she could imitate but could never truly attain—to spend her life being nothing more than a *mockery* of a demon, or any of the horde beyond, for that matter, was death. Worse than death.

What did they gain for it? Power, of a sort.

But at a price far too great to pay: all pride, all dignity. And, she thought, with a wry grimace, all humanity. It would not do to forget what the Allasakari actually did in their attempt to better be like the kin. If they realized that that was what they achieved in their sorry tenure.

The hilt beneath her hand was warming; she waited, knowing that these thoughts were idle, but thinking them just the same. The attack on the gate was an attack, but she was certain that it was not more; it was diversionary. The real enemy was within the manse already, hunting beneath the arches of her halls—killing her kin in the smug surety that the bulk of her force was occupied.

Terafin fought you, she thought, and then smiled, realizing where the thought was going, and how best to use its truth and its defiance.

Lifting her sword, she gazed at her Chosen. "Terafin fought the Allasakari and their mage-born followers," she said, her voice the steady, strong force that it had almost always been. "And became one of The Ten, revered above all others save the god-born." The pitch of her tone changed as she faced the southern hall and the shadowy tendrils, tentative and barely visible, that slowly crept along the base of the walls. "*Come.* Your enmity began our road to greatness; let it continue that road, unhindered. We are ready!"

Behind, there was darkness; ahead, there was light. But for how long? How long? The halls of the manse were terrifying in their length and breadth. At any moment, Stephen thought their enemies might step from the sides or cut off their escape at the front. He prayed, as he had not prayed in years, the words a silent mantra, said so often they lost the edge of their sense, but not their intensity.

His chest hurt; he realized, with a start, that he had almost left Evayne behind and began to reach for her wrist, wondering when he had dropped it. But the color of her robes, the way they twisted at her feet as if they had a mind and will of their own—they reminded him of dreams. Wyrd.

No. There had been no escape in his dreams; no true light. And ahead of him, past Espere's steady shoulders and bowed head, light streamed in, cast in shards by the chandelier above and the beveled lamps that lined the walls. He smiled, but the relief was short and quickly gone; these lamps were finer than those behind him, but no more magical, and no more proof against the shadows that sought to engulf everything.

Or were they?

Light defined itself into a sharper glitter than he was used to seeing, and as Espere continued to shift and move in front of him, he saw why: The grand foyer, large even in the distance, was full of armed and armored men and women. Steel caught the light and sent it scattering; they stood their ground, firm and fearless, a living fortress. A testimony to Terafin.

Jewel watched in silence from her perch on the stairs. Carver was above her, and Finch below; Jester and Angel were higher up. Teller, flat against the ground with daggers in either hand, was on the landing; he didn't trust the stairs to provide cover, and besides, it was always useful to have an attack from a totally different vantage point.

They had all heard The Terafin speak her high and fancy words—and they all, with one exception, felt a yearning to *be* one of the men or women that she spoke to. Just for a second, of course; after that, the practical demanded attention.

"What the hell?" Carver whispered. His leader elbowed him sharply in the thigh, and his jaw snapped shut.

Jewel watched.

The dogs came first, running to a halt and skidding slightly across the shiny, smooth floors. They were bigger than most dogs she'd seen—of course, that wasn't hard, given that most of the dogs she'd known were alley scroungers, same as she'd been—with broad, flat heads, ears turned down to skull, and short, glistening fur. Brown; black and white; black and gray; gray and brown. The minute they stopped, they turned and stood, growling, four perfect sentries. It was almost frightening, to see dogs behave so unnaturally.

An almost entirely naked woman came next, but she could have stopped on a banker's heart, she was so quick and light on her feet. She glanced up the steps, narrowing her eyes as she met Jewel's. They were brown, her eyes, and odd, although Jewel couldn't have said why she thought so; they flickered slightly and then looked away.

Back to more important things. Jewel grimaced, tightening her hold on dagger hilt and rope.

She recognized the man who came through the arch next; she'd met him once before in The Terafin's public office. Stefan, Stephen—something like that. The foreigner. He was red with exertion; she could see his sweat beneath the harsh glare of too many lights. He stumbled, righted himself, and stopped in the front of the line of the Chosen, all the while holding fast the wrist of a slightly built woman in dark blue robes.

She, too, looked up the length of the grand stairs to meet Jewel's gaze—and this time, Jewel looked away. There was something in the violet stare, distant as it was, that was uncomfortably perceptive.

Last to come was the foreign Lord; the obvious master of those who waited. He brought two more dogs, each flanking him—a gray one, bigger than the rest, and a white and black that seemed to be preoccupied with the halls it had just stepped clear of.

"Terafin," the fair-haired Stephen said. "We're—we're being pursued."

"Let them through." The Terafin's voice was steady and calm. "Let them through and close ranks around them."

Her Chosen moved at once to follow her commands, maintaining as much of a defensible formation as they could while opening their ranks to allow the Breodani free passage.

Stephen stumbled in, as did his young companion—but the Hunter Lord, Gilliam of Elseth, chose to stay outside of the protection her Chosen offered. He did not look exhausted; nor did he appear frightened. He was on edge, but even the edge was a strange one—it was as if he were aware of every element of his surroundings, without being affected by any of them.

"Lord Elseth," The Terafin said, slightly irritated. "Please."

But Lord Elseth did not respond. Instead, he motioned, and the wild girl—the unkempt and unknown danger—came running to his side, flanked by the rest of the Hunter's pack.

"Terafin," the flushed huntbrother said, striking his chest with the flat of his hand and kneeling in the deferential posture.

"Speak," she replied, watching him carefully, impressed in spite of herself at his ability to maintain this much composure in the face of his obvious fear.

"We—there is a demon-mage in pursuit."

"Demon-mage?" she said. "What do you mean?"

"She—it—calls herself Sor na Shannen. She is a very powerful mage, but also one of the kin. The darkness follows her; she is its lord here."

"Who else?"

He seemed nonplussed. "Who else?"

"Besides this demon of whom you speak. Who else follows her?"

His brow furrowed, fair and gleaming; at last he looked back to his very young, and until now silent, companion.

"The—I think—the Allasakari," the young woman in the dark robes said softly.

"You think?"

She swallowed, and then caught the breath that Stephen of Elseth was struggling with. Although her movements were still tentative, she had decided something, for she thrust her hands nervously into the depths of her robes, and from them pulled out a single, large glass sphere.

Except that it was not glass, and within it, trapped as if alive, were roiling mists and the ghosts of swirling images. The Terafin's eyes widened in genuine surprise. The young girl's eyes, luminous and violet, held a hint of smugness as she met The Terafin's. Then it was gone, as the silver mists demanded—commanded—her attention.

There were so many questions that Amarais wanted to ask, for she had only read tales about the seer's crystal, and in her adulthood, discounted the veracity of them. Until now. For the girl's robes rose about her with a magic of their own; there were shadows that had nothing to do with the darkness and everything to do with the hidden depths of a young woman's private tragedy that gathered in the grim lines of her face, her carriage; she had seen much, and at The Terafin's unknowing request, was willing to see more.

Amarais knew that the nature of the seeing would not be pleasant.

"Allasakari," the girl said, speaking without inflection. "They wear the pendants; they bear the scars." She took a breath, her eyes narrowing so much they appeared almost to close. "They carry the darkness, Terafin; they barely contain it, and it will consume them if it does not find release."

The Terafin could hear the drawn breath of her Chosen; the rising tension. "Numbers?" she demanded, her voice cool.

"Thirty. Maybe a few more or less. There is one other mage with them and his signature is powerful."

She cursed, but silently. "Put it away, child," she said, turning. "We have no more need of your sight now."

It was true. Shadows burst out of the southern hall like black fire gone wild, lapping at light as if it were mystical kindling.

"Stand back!" Evayne cried, as she realized that the men of Terafin intended to stay their ground. "Get out of its way—it's deadly to you unless you're shielded!"

But they listened as if they were deaf—which is to say, they moved not at all. Only The Terafin could command them, and she chose to hold her place as foolishly as they.

"Evayne," someone said, and she turned to see Stephen's pale face. "The Terafin is no fool. Trust her."

"She doesn't know—no one does—"

"Trust her," he said again, catching her trembling shoulders and stilling them. But he watched the growing shadows with the same dread fascination that she did, wondering the same thing.

The mistress of the darkness, limned in ebony that somehow glittered and shone, stood out like the jewel at the peak of a crown. If there were Allasakari at her back, they were momentarily forgotten; she was the obvious power,' and she was due the full force of Terafin's attention.

Her hair was a dark fine glory that lay in a barely concealing web across her body; she was fair, and her lips were very, very red. The pursuit had not ruffled her, or even tired her; she paused to look at the Chosen of Terafin before her lips turned up in genuine pleasure.

"This is almost a worthy welcome," she said, her voice so perfect it was hard to listen without being stirred. "A fitting beginning for what is to follow."

"Lay down your arms, turn over to me those three who are my rightful quarry, and you will come to me in peace. Fight me, and you will come in pain."

"That is not," a new voice said—a voice that seemed as strong as hers was warm, with tones as pure and as demanding of attention, "much of a choice."

Sor na Shannen's expression shifted as she stared into—and past—the Chosen as if they were suddenly so much chaff. "What is this?" she questioned softly.

A man strode across the foyer, coming from the northern halls. His hair was loose and long, as hers; it shifted in a breeze that touched no other man in the room. Where Sor na Shannen was the velvet of endless darkness, the promise of pleasure and pain in the shadows, he was not day—but starlight shone about him like raiment, the bright face of the night.

The Terafin drew breath; held it. The sword, which she had seen for the first time this evening, was more easily recognized than the mage who wielded it. But if she stared long at the clarity of his features, the intensity of his expression, she could see enough of the familiar—barely—to recognize Meralonne APhaniel.

There were others there who should have but could not; Evayne a'Nolan, young and terrified, who stood this eve on the edge of magics which would form the whole of her life. She watched, lips parted slightly, as this tall man—this slender giant—strode past her with purpose. He turned, once, to see her youthful face, and she blushed, although she wouldn't later remember why; his gaze was cool and saw much in the second he spared before he turned his full attention upon the only other creature in the room who equaled him. Sor na Shannen.

He raised his sword and swung it in a wide, whistling arc; light lanced out from its edge, cutting the fingers of shadow that clung to every crevice in the foyer.

Dark eyes widened; she raised both of her arms, lifting them in either command or supplication. Shadow surged forward, but slowly. "I do not know how you come to be here," she hissed, the velvet of her glamour cast aside like refuse. "But this is not your battle. I have chosen these as my own. Remember it, and you may walk from the field."

"It is not for one such as you," he replied, "to choose my battles for me. And as for these—surely they will decide their own fate." He laughed then, and the laughter was wild and not a little bitter.

"Very well," she said softly. Her left hand fell like the sudden stroke of an executioner's deft blade. The shadows parted, and a man unmarked by the worship of the Allasakari stood at her left side. He was taller than she, and older; his face was framed by streaked dark hair and a dark beard. He wore robes, simple and light in color, a contrast to the shadows that surrounded him; there were no obvious weapons at his side.

She turned to this new companion. "Kill him."

He nodded, and then raised his head, seeing the enemy against whom he was to be set. "Well met, Member APhaniel," he said, his voice just shy of contemptuous.

Meralonne APhaniel frowned. "Krysanthos," he said at last, shifting his stance. "Indeed."

"I believe you barely made second circle at the last ordination."

Unruffled—barely—Krysanthos shrugged. "Should I have revealed more of my powers to the council? It was only barely worth the effort I did put in. But I am curious, APhaniel. Why do you play with the sorry sticks of lesser men when you have the power of the mage-born?"

Meralonne APhaniel stared at him in silence. After a moment had passed, it became clear that he did not intend to dignify the question with an answer.

"Very well. Let's get this over with." Krysanthos raised his hands in an intricate, almost hypnotic dance; the air responded with the music of flames and the cries of those who stood, suddenly, in its midst.

Challenge offered.

Chapter Twenty-One

MERALONNE APHANIEL SMILED and nodded almost gently. He was ice and winter; so distant and so removed from the flames of the majestic and sudden summoning that it seemed the fire itself feared him. In a radius of ten feet, it burned nothing, touched nothing, changed nothing.

Called out by the enemy's challenge into a known and despised arena, the mage stepped forth, his light feet crushing the flicker of fire wherever he trod. He carried his sword, flat across his left shoulder, as he approached the waiting shadows.

Krysanthos frowned. The flames leaped and struggled under his dominion, but they did not threaten Meralonne; if they snapped too closely, the silver-haired mage sliced at their odd limbs with his bright and shining sword, and they drew back. His blade was a chill and icy thing.

The fire guttered as Krysanthos turned his effort to a different form of attack.

The earth shuddered beneath the feet of Meralonne; the Chosen of Terafin faltered as their landscape suddenly shifted, breaking away into joists and stone and dirt along the thin, narrow line that Meralonne walked. But his feet did not seem to touch the ground, and what occurred beneath the surface, invisible but sure, that they did touch did not concern him.

Lightning strove groundward, fizzling feet away from Meralonne's unprotected head; blood-rain fell, turning to water as it reached the ground. Krysanthos was a learned and powerful mage, and he had studied the arts of attack well; many were the forms that he tried that had no visible signature—but these were least effective of all. For Meralonne resisted the magical purchase that Krysanthos struggled to gain as if the shadow-sworn mage were no more than a ghostly visitation.

At the last, Krysanthos brought the chandelier that was the pride of the grand foyer down. Meralonne walked, unheeding, toward it. Several voices cried out in warning and in fear—but an inch above his head, gold and crystal flailing, the chandelier stopped its rapid descent. He passed beneath it, touching it gently with the very tip of his fine, sharp blade.

Gingerly and carefully, it lowered itself to the ground at his heels.

Behind the lines of battle, beyond the center of the foyer, Sor na Shannen waited in repose, her smile couched in velvet silence. There was no fear in her, but her eyes looked almost fevered, and the fire that burned there burned high and bright. "So," she said, as she noted the pale, sweaty brow of her companion. "Even this is beyond your ken."

"I would appreciate," Krysanthos snapped, through lips that barely opened, so rigid were the muscles of his face, "your assistance."

"You will have it," was her answer. "And it will cost you. *Never* question me again, little mageling." She stood, lifting her hands in supplication. To them came two things, out of the folds of dying fire that laced the ground in a magical pattern: a sword, curved, with an edge that bore teeth, and a shield.

Krysanthos did not question her choice of weapons. He stepped back, grim in his fury and his humiliation.

But Meralonne only smiled as he saw her step down from the shadows that held her onto the reality of The Terafin's floor. He snapped his right hand, and to it came a shield, silver and fine and ringed all round with runes that glowed white. She waited as he approached; he neither tarried nor hurried. They did not need to take each other's measure; they knew it.

"This man is mine," Sor na Shannen said, pitching her voice into the shadows behind her as if they were alive. "But now is the time. Take the others, leaving only the quarry that I demand as my right."

The shadows surged forward, and the darkness that Meralonne's presence had dispelled grew strong indeed as his attention turned to Sor na Shannen. She leaped up, using the air to turn and angle the sword from a vantage no human could have used unless they were winged.

Meralonne was not there when the sword singed the air.

Challenge met.

In the wake of the dying fire, the Allasakari came, caught and hidden in the bowels of the shadow until they were almost upon the Chosen of Terafin. The sheath of their blades was darkness; their faces were hidden by shadows so deeply etched that natural light could not disperse them. But worst of all were their eyes; for beneath their lids, and behind them, was a darkness so complete that it showed nothing, reflected nothing.

They crashed into the defensive line of Terafin with a thundering . . . silence.

There was no noise; no clang of steel striking steel, no sound of the impact of bodies as men were driven back several feet, no battle cries.

Let loose, the darkness seemed intent on devouring all. And soundlessly, the Chosen of The Terafin began to die.

Blood ran.

From the edge of a sword raised and swung wildly, it splattered Stephen's cheek and chest. He felt it, but there was no *sound*, no comfort of sound. Not ten yards away from where he stood, rooted in marble as if he had grown there, a man in armor was screaming with his last breath—he could *see* it in the contorted lines of the man's unrecognized and unrecognizable face. But he could not *hear* it. The very wrongness of the theft stilled his breathing.

He felt a hand at his elbow and cried out—but the cry was stifled. Turning, he saw Evayne, the folds of her robe raised high over her shoulders like the protective wings of a Guardian. Her eyes were wide; she spoke, but he could not make out, in the semidarkness, the words she meant him to hear. Deaf and mute, he tried to follow her gestures.

Gilliam.

There, in the darkness. He turned, but in turning was already too late. At the feet of his Hunter Lord—at the feet of the man who was brother and more—was the broken body of Singer. Cut nearly in two, his blood seeped into the darkness of the shadow-covered floor as if it were being drunk. Gilliam reeled with the shock of the sudden death.

Loss was not unknown to the Hunter Lords, and those well-trained were able to bear the severing of a life bond under the duress of battle. Gilliam was well trained. He kept fighting. But Stephen could hear the keening that began to mount in the wilds of his soul.

Something was grabbing his shoulders before he realized that he was trying, desperately, to get through the lines; to stand at Gil's side. His sword was unsheathed—when and how that had happened he could not have said. With an angry shrug, he freed himself; the grip wasn't a strong one.

But in the time it took, Corfel was gone, his black and white body vanishing into darkness as the Allasakari continued their chill approach. Gilliam cried out again, and Stephen *felt* it, although everywhere there was silence. It was almost unreal, this death unfolding before him; the fallen to either side. It was cold in the foyer, and dark; he wondered if death's lands were not enshrouded in this very fog.

But Gilliam was real; Gilliam bridged the distance of silence, of darkness, of death. He knew the instant that Gilliam was wounded. Felt the darkness latch on to the open scrape, a dangerous and unknown poison seeping into the blood. There was no scream; not to be heard, not to be felt. As always, physical pain only made Gilliam more determined—it was the dogs that were lolling him with their deaths.

Stephen struggled forward, and this time the grip on him was *strong*. He tried to tell them—the Chosen, he thought—that he *must* go to his Hunter, but not a single sound escaped the tortured, silent rush of his lips. They were large men; Stephen had never been large. And he did not wish, not in this darkness, to turn his sword upon them—for such a division in the face of such an enemy was too grave a wrong. Helpless, he stared into the fighting, watching it unfold in silence.

The lack of sound made his hair rise; he wondered what else was being stolen, what other parts of the world were being devoured by the shadows the Allasakari carried. If he could somehow be heard—if he could give voice to the fighting Chosen—the battle's lines would be changed in an instant. For it was clear that the Allasakari were not fully in control of their actions; they did not seem to work from plan, and they were not working together. They were vessels, and only because of the thrall of the darkness did they carry the advantage.

The hair along his arms began to rise. The dreams returned, because they were also nightmares, and what better to carry them but darkness? His hand slid, nerveless, to the folds of his tunic; to the pouch that rested against his skin; to the thing therein.

There was one act that he could perform that would shatter that silence.

Gilliam! he thought, as he raised the simple, bone horn to his trembling lips. He swallowed air, drank it into his lungs as deeply as he could.

And then, on the ninth day of Corvil, four hundred and ten years after the return of Veralaan with the Twin Kings, Stephen of Elseth winded the Hunter's Horn.

There was no grace in the note; it was loud and short, more like the honking of an angry, giant fowl than a musical call. But his hands were shaking, it was all that he could manage—and it was *heard.*

A ripple went through the ranks of the Allasakari; a shiver through the fog and cloud of shadow. The Chosen of Terafin seemed to straighten slightly, although they did not turn to see what had caused the sound.

Nothing else happened, and after a moment, the shadow grew stronger and thicker, redoubling its effort as if speed were suddenly of the essence.

It wasn't enough. Stephen swallowed air; forced his shaking hands to rise again. He knew what he had to do; knew what call he had to make. Years, he and Gilliam had studied these. But it was the Hunter's duty to call the Hunt, and although Stephen knew the call, he had never made it.

Such a simple call; the easiest of all to make. Three long, loud notes in a rising sequence, held to the end of the caller's breath.

One note, and he could hear Evayne's pleading; the tenor of the fear beneath her words stronger than he had ever heard it. Two notes, and he could hear the cries of the Chosen of Terafin, free from the bondage of shadow, issuing orders and calling point. Three notes, and he could hear the panicked shouts of the Allasakari and the angry snarl—loud enough to fill the curved ceiling—of a demon lord in combat.

"You did it!" Evayne shouted, her violet eyes round with relief and wonder. "Whatever you did, it's—"

Her words were lost to the roar of thunder; the voice of the storm; the death of the Breodani. Stephen turned his pale face toward the west wall, where the shadow was beginning to buck and writhe like a living thing in agony.

"What—what's that?" she cried, her words a frightened echo of the dismay The Terafin's Chosen showed.

Stephen took her hand numbly. "Nothing that you need fear," he said, pitching his voice so that it would carry above the din of the fighting around him.

"But what is it?"

He watched as the shadow grew frenzied; watched as a shred of it suddenly flew back. Shedding darkness as if it were colored water, it rose, scaled and furred and fanged. What its shape was, Stephen could not say; it writhed and twisted, shifting from beast to beast, death to death.

"It is," he said softly, as even the Allasakari fell silent in awe and terror, "the Hunter's Death."

The next screams that filled the hall were the last that the Allasakari closest to the western wall would ever utter.

Gilliam knew the Hunter's Death at once; his entire body resonated with recognition. With a wild cry he drew his horn and winded it, loud and long, calling the hunt Stephen had called, but without the timidity of the huntbrother—acknowledging his Lord's price with the defiance, marred by only the smallest of fear, with which the Hunter Lords had always approached it.

"Terafin!" he shouted, suddenly in his element in the damaged halls of an alien land. "Order your Chosen to retreat!"

The Terafin stiffened at his command—as did her Chosen—but she saw the look in Lord Elseth's eyes, and knew that he knew what he dealt with. She did not; her mage was in a combat that was hidden by the folds of shadow and darkness, and she could not reasonably turn to him for advice or counsel.

I can well see, she thought, as he gathered his wounded beasts around him, *why the demons feared you.*

She turned to Torvan. "Signal a retreat to the Hall of the Lattan Moon."

Bloodstained and wearied, he nonetheless saluted sharply and carried out her command, his voice filling the air where hers did—and could—not. And then, as the Chosen began to form up, fighting their way into retreat position, Torvan ATerafin pivoted neatly and lifted his arm. Its shadow, short and squat, fell upon The Terafin's exposed back.

Jewel saw him and froze. Torvan's helm caught the light and threw it up in shards as his hand came down. The knife that he carried found its mark easily in the exposed back of the woman he served.

Not Torvan, she thought, her hands sliding from the rails that she'd gripped during the onslaught of the Allasakari. *Not Torvan.*

Carver wasn't beside her; she spun to give orders as her voice made its way up the closed walls of her throat, and found herself talking to air. Angel tapped her shoulder lightly before he bounded down the stairs, taking them three at a time and barely touching down before he was off again.

"Stay where you are!" she told the rest of her den, feeling failure and fearing it. Using the rails as a guide, she tore down the stairs—too late, already too late. The Terafin's body sprawled, in a half-turn, across the floor. A flash of crimson lay beneath her, running through the supple plates of her armor to cool against marble.

Carver was there, dark hair and shadowed visage a contrast to the light reflecting off Torvan's glinting armor. He was armed with daggers, a long, thin stiletto in his right hand, and a thicker, cutting knife in his left. Of the special dagger that Jewel'd gone through so much trouble to borrow, there was no sign.

Had there been, Torvan would not have noticed it. His movements were stiff and jerky; his face had the appearance of thickness, of heaviness, that made it look as if he were wearing a mask.

A flesh mask.

Some of the Chosen cried out—those who were in a position to see what had happened. Swords, already drawn and blooded, were turned back, retreat was forgotten.

Not for the first time, Jewel understood just how special, and how honored, the Chosen felt in their service. For where they had shown no fear at the onslaught of the darkness and its terrible silence, their expressions now were those of open horror. Like Jewel, they were momentarily frozen and silent.

The silence dissolved in a roar that filled the hall with loss, with a keening wail that spoke of betrayal and failure so large that it made Jewel's guilt seem—for as long as the cry lingered—paltry. Torvan turned to face them, casting his sword and his dagger aside, arms wide, lips trembling.

And she saw his face.

She *saw* his face.

Shadow parted where the Hunter's Death tore it free from ground and alcove, from wall, mirror, and painting. But it did not give ground easily, and it did not give ground without making the gains of the great beast costly.

Had there been blood before the Hunt was called? Stephen couldn't remember it. The darkening splatters on his clothing were pale evidence; easily forgotten as he watched the progress of death itself across the width of the foyer.

Savaged bodies lay aground like shattered vessels. The hand of night was lifting, and Stephen could see, behind the roving frame of the beast, the clash of swords that were more magical than physical: Meralonne and Sor na Shannen. Light arced around them, in pale twists of different colors; light the offense, and light the defense. On such stuff as this, he had first learned to read, to dream, to remember the glory of ages past.

He never, never wished to see it again.

For here, in this hall, power spoke with such savagery that the conflict behind it was almost forgotten. Where at first he thought the bodies in the wake of the called Hunt were due to the Hunter's Death, he realized now that they were also the casualty of the battle between the two mages. Neither mage seemed to care what cost they exacted from their surroundings; the columns that framed the southern halls had crushed two of the Allasakari in their fall.

He looked away with a lurch as Gilliam reached out to grab—and hold—his attention.

Saving only Sor na Shannen, there were no more of the enemy; the last had given up its feeble struggles with a screaming wail that made Stephen long for the silence the Hunter's Horn had destroyed. The great beast of the Sacred Hunt roared in triumph—and then it turned its wide, feral jaws to the retreating forces of The Terafin. To Gilliam, Espere, and Evayne.

To Stephen of Elseth.

"Call it off!" someone shouted. Stephen turned to see the ashen face of a lithe and lean guard. "We can't retreat—The Terafin's been injured. It's done what it was summoned for—call it off!"

He stared at her helplessly, and she repeated the words, loudly and slowly, as if she were speaking to an imbecile. What answer could he offer her?

"CALL IT OFF!"

Call off the breaking of the earth; call off the wail of the sea's retribution; call off the wind-tossed storms that ravaged the eastern plains, or the fires that claimed the forests, or the mountains that surrendered their snow in a rush that buried whole villages. Sooner that than the Hunter's Death.

"We don't—we don't control it," he shouted back. "It's—you've got to flee!"

It wasn't like Rath.

With Rath, at first sight, she'd *known*. That knowledge drove her here, with what was left of her den under wing—to Torvan. To Torvan, who had carried Arann, dying, in from the streets where any other guard would've probably given them the heave. And that man was there—she knew it just as surely as she'd known that Rath was not.

Problem was that he wasn't alone. Something was in there with him.

"Don't kill him!" she shouted, and her voice reverberated in the clamor below. Too late—was it always to be too damned late? Lightning lanced down from the ceiling above, speeding unerringly by in a crackle of magical blue light.

Torvan didn't move; struck where he stood, he faltered, stumbled, and then righted himself. He looked up, scanning the mezzanine until he found what he sought. Morretz. His lips turned up in the rictus of a smile, and Jewel knew that Torvan was still there—but whatever was in there with him had just gained a whole lot of ground.

"Stop it!" she shouted to the domicis. "Stop it—you're just making it worse!"

Lightning, called by the unseen other, lanced up from the floor, drawn in a circle of gesture and fire. Morretz leaped off the landing before the rails were made kindling and smoldering brass.

The Chosen closed.

As did Jewel.

She knew that her part was a small one. No one would listen to her, and she didn't blame them—or she wouldn't later when she was thinking clearly—but she had to do something, and she lit upon the only idea that made any sense. Carver.

It was easy enough to reach him; he hadn't a chance at getting past the armored men and women who were trying to reach The Terafin's body.

"Where is it?" she asked, as quietly as the noise allowed.

He jumped five feet and spun, daggers point out; relaxed a bit when he saw who it was. His face was pale beneath the darkness of his hair; wasn't hard to guess how much he wanted to toss the knives and run. But he hadn't. She caught his left forearm, squeezed it, and nodded, a weary smile dimpling her cheek. Carver and Duster had killed before they'd come to her den, but Carver hadn't killed since. She was suddenly glad, in the midst of this slaughter, that he wasn't going to have to start now. "Where is it?"

He reached into his shirt, pulled hard, and handed her the sheathed dagger. She was surprised at how heavy it was.

"It's not Torvan, is it?" Carver asked her.

"It's not just Torvan—but he's there. In there."

He spit to the side. "What do you want us to do?"

"Nothing." She unsheathed the knife. "Nothing at all. Just get the Hells out of the halls, and take everyone else with you."

"*What?*"

"You heard me. Get out!" Lightly and quickly, weaving around the rigid bodies of moving men and women, she began to hunt her target.

Salas' brown coat was matted and sticky; his legs were cut, and blood clotted the wounds slowly. But he stood at his master's side, growling, his ears so far back against his skull they might as well have been missing. Connel, young and light on his feet, was limping. Hard to tell whether or not that meant a break. Stephen might have prayed to the Hunter God for better fortune, but he knew that right now, no one was listening.

Ashfel, the largest of the alaunts, iron-gray and iron-hard, stood in the front, bristling. He knew the Hunter's Death, but he did not fear it; he was Gilliam's liege, and that was his only cause. Marrat's body lay where it had fallen beside him.

The beast roared, and Ashfel growled back, lips curled up over sharp, white teeth. Gilliam, sword blooded and readied, stepped forward. Espere whimpered, and Gilliam's jaw set in a tight, angry line.

He was trying to send her away. She refused to leave. And Stephen knew that Gilliam was dangerously close to the end of his reserves; he would not waste them on struggling with the wild one. The wild one.

She turned and roared at the beast; the beast pulled up on its hind legs and roared back. Stephen thought—for just a moment—that she might somehow be able to speak with the creature. Something flickered in its multicolored eyes; something that seemed almost intelligent.

Then it was gone, and the beast continued to stalk a quarry that barely moved.

Jewel.

She looked up at the sound of her voice, even though she knew at once that she would see no one calling.

Jewel.

No time for it; not now. Or maybe there was, curse it. The Chosen were determined to end this in their own way—and as fire lapped up from the ground to sizzle their legs, she wondered if she would have any chance to reach Torvan before she, he, and they perished.

Jewel, listen carefully. Raise your right arm if Torvan is of the kin. Raise your left if he is not.

Something about the voice was familiar. She couldn't place it. Didn't matter. She lifted both her arms in a quick sweep and then lowered them again.

In the silence of her private ear, the voice said something extremely curt and extremely rude. So it was odd that she would recognize his voice only then: He was Morretz, the domicis—the most trusted servant that The Terafin had.

"Morretz!" she shouted, hoping to catch his attention. "I need your help!"

Up ahead, the clanging of swords answered her. She shuddered because she knew that Torvan no longer carried one.

We don't have a choice. We have to kill him.

"We have a choice, curse it—get me *to* him!" The words had barely left her lips before she remembered the old Valley proverb that her mother's mother had often quoted after the end of her long and magical tales. *But be warned that you'll get what you ask for if you ask it of a mage—and it won't be what you expected, because the mage-born are like that.*

Jewel had never thought to meet one mage-born.

When the ground peeled away from her feet, she was so shocked not even a squeak came out of her mouth. Like a drunken bird attempting to wing its way to the safety of a familiar perch, she lurched in the air, spinning slightly as she tried to get a grasp on the events beneath her feet.

At your command, the voice said.

Silence was her best weapon, and she kept it—but she promised herself that Morretz was going to get an earful when this was settled, one way or the other.

Stephen had never loved the dogs, not the way Gilliam had. It wouldn't have been possible, and besides, it was not one of his duties. But he did love Gilliam, and he knew that the dogs—those that remained alive—were the vessels that carried Gilliam's heart. Such as it was.

Although he knew it was foolish—knew that to approach a hound in pain was the act of a madman, or a Hunter—he grabbed Connel's small body, taking care to catch his head and confine his jaws. Connel twisted and whined, and then, miraculously, became still.

Ah. Gilliam.

Keep him quiet, Gil, he thought, as he handed the dog to Evayne. She blanched and stumbled a bit, but righted herself, carrying the injured alaunt like the burden he was.

"What are you—"

"Take him. Leave. Now."

"What about—"

"If I've earned the right to ask any boon of you, let it be this. Take the dog to the healerie."

He turned, hoping she was safe.

The great beast was upon them.

The dagger began to glow. At first, Jewel thought it was reflected lamplight, but as she lurched and spun—held by some invisible string, rather than magically steady hands—it became clear that the fire was coming from within. The dagger was golden, and as she moved it seemed to drink light from the air, capturing it for its own use.

She prayed, as she flew—if flight it was—although she did not know the words or the ceremony that the dagger demanded. Beneath her hand were the joined symbols of the trinity; the dagger had been blessed at the highest altars of each of the three Churches in the Holy Isle. But the man who had accepted their blessing had also partaken of the sacraments of the three. She hadn't. Prayer would have to do, and if fervor counted in the fields above, the Gods would have no choice but to listen and acknowledge.

She positioned the dagger carefully, gripping its hilt tightly with both hands; no other choice of movement was given to her. Morretz was the fighter here; he made all decisions except the thrust of the dagger itself. She wondered, briefly, why she hadn't thought to give him the knife—but as the strings were suddenly cut, as weight returned to her body, dragging it downward in a rush of air, she knew why.

The man that was, and was not, her friend, turned at the last moment, crying out in a language that she didn't understand—and, judging from the tone, just as well. He had time to react, he was so damned fast. His palm sprouted a blade of flame, and he slashed out at her.

No, not at her—at the dagger.

The heat of the flames seared her skin, singed her clothing—but the blade continued to fall, untouched by the magical attack. The pain was enough to jar her, but not enough to force her to forget what the purpose of *her* attack—not Morretz'—was.

Jewel's teeth pierced the skin of her lower lip—when the Hells had she started biting it?—as the dagger plunged into Torvan's left shoulder, slicing through chainlink and underpadding into the flesh below. Blood weltered up—blood and blackness, crimson and night.

She heard two things simultaneously: a grunt of pain and a scream of agony. Torvan stumbled and doubled over, scratching at his shoulder in a frenzy. More blood, and more shadow. But the blood that reached the ground beneath his metal-jointed knees remained as it was, wet and sticky; the shadow began to smoke.

"Chosen, in the name of The Terafin, stay your ground! Hold your arms!" Morretz' voice.

Pulling the blade back, Jewel crouched over Torvan's bent body, staring wide-eyed at the Chosen who were, once again, still and watchful. The dagger was no longer glowing; its fire was quenched in the cold darkness. They had, she thought, consumed each other.

"Jewel—what has happened?" It was Arrendas. Torvan's friend. White face framed by dark beard and halved by a thin, red line an inch below his eyes, he watched her warily.

"It's not his fault," she replied evenly, waving a dagger that wasn't even much of a dagger, it was so unbalanced and ornate. "You sent him to get the mage alone—and he did—but he was—"

"The shadows were waiting." It was Torvan's voice. Cracked and dry, as if he'd spent the last hour screaming as loudly as a throat could allow. "Arrendas, The Terafin—"

Avayna pushed Arrendas aside and knelt beside the body of her Lord. Silence, terrible with its weight, the uncertainty behind it. She did not raise her heavy head, but said only, "I don't know. Call Alowan, *now.*"

"We've—we've got him," said a voice that Jewel recognized too well. Finch, followed by Alowan and Teller, appeared from the north. Her hand was firmly entwined in the wrinkled grip of the older healer, whether for her comfort or his, she wasn't certain. Finch always looked young because she was small; she even looked helpless most of the time. Jewel smiled a little. Wasn't what she'd ordered, but it'd been the smart thing to do.

They'd answer for it later.

"Alowan—The Terafin—"

But the old healer had already firmly taken Avayna by the shoulders and pushed her aside as if hers was the lesser weight and the weaker body. He knelt, touching The Terafin's throat; bowed his white head, closing his eyes. All around him, silence—and beyond that the growling of dogs, the roar of the beast.

"Let's move her," Avayna said, looking over her shoulder. "We're about to lose the line."

But Alowan, eyes still shut, said softly, "She cannot be moved. Do not interrupt me. Do not allow *anything* to separate us."

With a renewed energy, the Chosen turned to face the Hunter's Death.

All but two.

"Go to the north. You're injured, you can't fight here."

"I cannot leave. If not for me—" Torvan retrieved his sword without really seeing it; he had eyes for the vanishing darkness and the beast, wild and furious, that had destroyed it. "If not for me—" He stumbled. Stared long at the two men and one woman who, with nothing but dogs for comrades, held the beast at bay. The young girl in the dark robes hung back, cradling what he assumed to be a dog's corpse. All around them, like the refuse that they were, the Allasakari lay. "Arrendas."

"I won't do it. I'll ready my weapon for battle, but not murder."

"Is it murder?" He turned to look at Jewel, and was surprised at the way she stared back; her eyes were round and shining; he could see the tears more clearly than he could see the color of her eyes. *Why didn't you just finish it?* "You should have . . ." but he could not say it, not to her. And it wasn't to her that it needed to be said. "We swore our oaths, Arrendas ATerafin. We are the Chosen. We pay the penalty for dishonoring *her* choice."

"And *she* decides whether or not that penalty is to be paid. It is not up to you—or me—to decide that for her."

Their jaws were clenched in anger, and their words forced and heated, but as they turned to see her body laid out like death's handmaiden against the floor, they fell silent. Bristling, Torvan stepped out, into the front of the line. Around him, the Chosen murmured, but they did not deny him. Still, he flinched.

Then, there was no time for flinching. The beast roared and charged.

*　　*　　*

Perhaps he knew his own flesh, his earthly blood. Perhaps he did not wish to harm her, although there was no recognition in the glint of his eyes. But the beast leaped *over* Espere. The ground shook with his landing, and the Terafin's Chosen were once again under attack.

But the Allasakari had been human—imbued with darkness, driven by shadows that Stephen did not understand, but human nonetheless. The great beast was not. Someone vanished under the weight of its claws; silver and steel snapped between its jaws. There was a scream, high and terrible—but it was not uttered by the dying.

Only the living had anything to fear.

Transfixed, Stephen watched the carnage, thinking, *knowing*, that this was his death. The hall's light was oddly colored; he thought he saw the ripple of windblown leaves in the shadows above, but there was only torchlight across barren stone. This was not the right place, not the right time.

Gilliam cried out a warning; Stephen felt it, but did not hear it. His world was a place of the dying and the newly dead. Leaping lightly over slick stones to join that vision was Espere, hair flying wildly behind her. She wore the shreds of clothing and even these seemed out of place; she was the wilderness, as the beast was the Hunt.

Impact.

Gilliam screamed.

Stephen wanted to shout out a warning, but he had no voice for it. His Hunter raced deftly past the fallen Chosen, the standing Chosen. He had, in his hand, his boar-spear, although when he had loosed it, Stephen could not remember. During the fight with the Allasakari?

Gilliam!

The wild girl reeled back, bleeding; the bone of her forearm had been laid bare, and the skin across her collarbone was missing. She stumbled, gained her feet, and then froze as Gilliam bid her stay with such force that Stephen could hear it although no words had been spoken aloud.

The beast reared up, coat rippling with scales and fur and a sheen of otherworld magic. Gilliam braced himself and the spear, waiting for the attack. Was there fear there? Oh, yes.

Stephen swallowed voicelessly; his breath was short and shallow and harsh. Gilliam was afraid that *they* would die: the wild one, the dogs, Stephen. His own death stared him in the face, roaring, jaws ever-widening in the crest of its face, and he had no fear for it.

"Stephen!" he cried. "Take them to safety, now!"

Almost gladly, Stephen obeyed. He pushed Espere to the north, grabbed Ashfel and Salas, and began to herd them between the base of the stairs and the Chosen who gathered there.

And then he froze as he heard the jaws snap. Turned, his legs moving of their own accord, his eyes unblinking. The snout of the beast was closed, but Gilliam was not trapped between the sharp rows of teeth.

He'd thought he could do it. He really had.

"Evayne," his voice was shaky.

"What?"

"Take care of them."

"What?"

"Take care of Gilliam and Espere and his stupid dogs." He turned back to her, and she wavered in his eyes as he realized how close to tears he'd come. "Promise it. Promise that you'll watch them no matter what age you travel in."

"But I—"

"Promise it."

"I—I promise, Stephen. But—"

"Swear it by Bredan. Swear it in his name."

"I—" she swallowed. "I so swear. But—"

He ran, then. But not to the north. The south, with its crumbled walls, shattered crystal and guttered torches was the only safe place to retreat to. His conditioning was good; he could, for brief bursts, maintain the speed and the pace of a Hunter in trance. He called on that skill now, although it was hard to breathe, hard.

Breath was required. His hands, nerveless, gripped the Horn as he reached the theater of his choice; he dropped it once, and forced himself to right it. The beast, snapping and growling, had not yet killed his Hunter. He could see Gilliam, darting back and forth. A crimson slash spread itself across his chest, but he was whole; he didn't seem to notice the wound.

Gil, he thought, *I love you.* And then, because he knew that Gilliam couldn't hear the words, and wouldn't make sense of the emotion in the complex thrill of the trance, he shouted it, that the world might hear. And remember.

The mouth of the Horn in his trembling lips was cold. But he blew it, somehow. And this time, there were nine notes; two long, two short, two long, and three of a length that only the huntbrothers used, and only during the Sacred Hunt.

And the beast wavered, stiffening suddenly as it caught the scent of its quarry. Stephen dropped the Horn because his hands hadn't the strength to bear it. Dressed in Hunter green, in the rank that he had sworn his service to, Stephen of Elseth fulfilled the Hunter's—the huntbrother's—Oath, and alone, faced the Hunter's Death.

It came, bearing down too swiftly for flight. He had time to swallow, time to inhale, time to scream once—and he had time to bind himself so tightly that the pain and the horror could spill out without driving Gilliam mad. It was his last gift.

*   *   *

Gilliam of Elseth screamed. The Chosen surrounded him as the world slid out from beneath the sureness of the Hunter's trance. He saw weapons—theirs—and knew, for a few seconds, that they were trying in some way to protect him.

He said something, or maybe just roared. But the roar that left his lips was a thin, terrible sound. He could make no denial.

He *knew*.

Silence reigned. Where a moment before, the beast's voice had filled the hall, there was stillness now. The Hunter's Death had chosen among His people, and having satiated the desire to hunt—and to kill—it honored its victim.

Beneath the cracked facade of the southern arch, surrounded by the broken, shadowless bodies of the Allasakari, the great beast began to unmake the body in the way that the wild beasts do. And then, as the Hunter Lords did upon the completion of the Sacred Hunt, it began to feed.

Chapter Twenty-Two

L IGHTNING STRUCK THE FEEDING BEAST.

Sizzling against iridescent scales, sparking off claw and fang, it began an intricate, complex dance along the length of its body. Fire flared, surrounding the beast with a heat so sudden it was almost white. It joined lightning sparks, melting the fur and the skin of the creature. Light came next, and with it the shaking of earth, the falling of water; all things happened at once, joining in a dance that seemed to sculpt the very flesh.

Slowly, the beast lifted its head; slowly, that head began to shrink in on itself, warping and twisting beneath a multitude of lights and seasons.

The hall was silent as the mystery unfolded within it.

Only two in the foyer were not surprised by what they saw; the wild girl who did not speak, and the Lord that she followed, who could not.

The hall had been blackened by fire and lightning, drenched by elemental rains; blood darkened the floors; shards of crystal and twisted gold carpeted body and marble alike beneath the feet of the Hunter Lord.

Gilliam had thought He might come in Hunter green with spear and arrow, sword and shield. He thought that dogs should attend him, that birds of the sky-hunt should perch upon his wrist, that the pelt of the offered kill should ride upon his shoulders in a place of honor.

There were none of these things.

And yet this was the very Hunter God; Gilliam knew him by the tines that forked from his pale and perfect brow, rising into the air like a stag's in season. No blood stained his hands, his lips, his chest; no wound marred his features. His eyes, as they scanned the silent, gathered crowd, could not be met and held for long—there were sights reflected in them that mortal eyes could not see, nor should.

He stepped forward, and simple white robes gathered like cloud out of air around him. At his back, there was darkness and death. Stephen lay there, unmoving.

"Hunter," the God said, and his voice was the voice of the multitude.

Pale and grim, Gilliam stood forward. It wasn't necessary; the Hunter Lord knew well that only one of his followers was in the great hall. He watched, unblinking and silent in his regard as Gilliam of Elseth dropped to one knee and lowered his forehead.

Carver fell to his knees at once, glancing with comfort at the broken and trammeled bodies on the floor—at anything but the God; Angel dropped to one knee. Finch, Jester, and Teller reached the floor, staying behind the stiff knees of the Chosen of Terafin. But Jewel did not bow. She bit her lip, kneading it between her teeth; she paled as she inclined her chin, but she did not—would not—bow.

Evayne held her ground. Hands covering her mouth as if to keep the breath in her body, she stared beyond the Hunter's shoulder. She knew what he was, and knew who—better than anyone else in the foyer except perhaps Espere.

The Chosen of Terafin did not bend or bow—but they stood in that formal rigidity of posture that spoke of respect as they formed an outward-facing circle around Alowan and The Terafin. Alowan alone did not pay heed to the God's visit.

Espere never left Gilliam's side. As he stepped forward, so, too, did she; but when he knelt, she stood proudly by him. Her eyes were golden, although it was hard to tell if it were color or the reflected light of the God in the tears she shed. They were Gilliam's tears; Gilliam's loss; he was so empty of purpose that he hadn't the strength to shed them.

The Hunter Lord stared for a long time into the silence of anger and pain. Of a sudden, he raised both arms skyward, his hands clenched in fists. The mists rolled in around them, becoming a thick, heavy wall. When they stopped, Evayne, Espere, and Gilliam stood within them; without, the rest of Terafin.

"The Breodani were starving." The Hunter Lord spoke to Gilliam of history, but slowly, as if the passage of time made remembering difficult. "Of all the human tribes, they had chosen to follow my edicts; they are a people of honor, whose word and deed are entwined.

"When first they called, I would not leave my throne to make the journey across the divide; was I not the keeper of the Covenant? Was it not my rule and my binding that kept the Gods from journeying back to the mortal fold? In the half-world, we met; my silence was my answer.

"When they called a second time, when their pleas could be heard across the Fields, I again undertook the journey to the place of meeting, and rebuked them for their summons. For the freedom of man the Covenant was joined; man had prospered by it—would they have me break it? Their silence was their answer.

"Thrice they called; but this last time, they did not ask for aid. They had become, at the last, a people of pride and strength. In their failing, in their twilight, they sought me. I came in anger; they met me in silence. And then the leader of the people that you once were knelt in the mists and plunged his spear into the half-earth.

" 'Why have you called me thus?'

" 'We have followed the ways of the Lord of Truth all our lives; as did our parents before us, and their parents, and theirs. Those who have failed have been cast out in accordance with the severity of their breach.'

" 'This I know,' I told them, waiting.

" 'But we have failed. We are few, and our children succumb to the harvest of the Lady. The land is barren; the hunt yields nothing.'

"Now it comes, thought I, for this is the way of man. 'Why have you called?' I said again.

" 'To the East and the South—from a great remove—there are a people who do not know the Ways. They do not hunt, and they do not honor the seasons, and they do not keep the covenants that they have made, for they will not seal them with their lives.'

" 'I know of these people,' I said, for I did, and with misgivings.

" 'We have come, Lord, to lay before you the rings of your binding and the spears of our adulthood. Our land will not bear fruit, nor any to the North that we have searched, and to the South and West, there is death. But in the East, we have been offered food and shelter for our children.'

" 'We would have died for you, and in truth, we may still. But many of our children are not of the age to make the Choice that you have decreed, and we cannot in honor sacrifice them when a haven remains.'

" 'You have honored us in our life with your wisdom. You have strengthened us with the Code. We thank you, Lord. And we bid you farewell.' They stood, leaving their spears in the gray ground before me. 'But we vow that in our time, we will return to you if we are able.'

"I did not take that oath. These people were *my* people, and while I had fashioned the Covenant's binding, I was not subject to it. Were they to be lost to the whim of the Southerners? Were they to become a people without honor, without oath, dwindling in time to a shadow of their former selves?

"I came. You know this.

"But the divide was not meant to be crossed by one such as I. The world that the Gods once knew, the world that we once walked, was strangely, subtly changed." His eyes grew distant. "This city is not the city that it was; not so grand, and not so terrible. And humankind is not what it was." He shook his head. "They have changed, but so, too, have the Gods.

"We cannot walk here without paying a price." He lifted his chin and his eyes were very, very bright. "You walk to the Hall of Mandaros, to be judged and to choose, but if you return to walk in flesh again, you have no memory of the past for which you have been judged. Yet if you have no memory, it does not mean that you have not been born before, that you have not died; it means that you cannot *know* what has gone before until your return to Mandaros. That is the nature of this new world: That the essence of the divinity is absorbed into the flow of mortality until it wanders unknowing to remake its choices. It does not die, but it does not live as it was.

"I did not know this when I came." He bowed his head. "I spoke with the Maker of the Covenant; he was cool to my cause, and angry. Be wary of him.

"But he explained much to me. And much was bitter. A mortal cannot know the before, but a God can—because the power of a God is vast and deep. It is not endless.

"I came to my Priests—my children—and between us we fashioned a magic to hold the land; we brought life to the vast and empty wastes. The body of the earth is an ancient thing, and not easily appeased; not in a day or a month, a year or a single mortal lifetime, could such an undertaking be finished.

"Such was the power that I used, that during the fifth year, I could no longer remember the Fields; during the sixth, I could no longer remember my brethren; during the seventh, I could no longer hold the shape of the magic that we had built. I succumbed to the nature of the World of man because I had no power left.

"The land began to die. I knew it; and knew that there was nothing further I could do. I was not in my dominion. There was no power to call upon; no thing that was immortal and everlasting."

Evayne's drawn breath was so sharp it cut off the voice of the God.

"You see much," he said softly, "as you were born to. There was one thing upon which I could draw."

"Them," she whispered, horrified.

Her horror did not offend or perturb. He turned quietly to the silent Hunter before him. "They would not offer your strong; but your weak, your sick, your crippled—those could still be of use, when they could no longer aid your people in their struggle to feed their own.

"It was not so simple for a people of honor; while the Priests and the Hunters understood our need, they could not ask the Breodani to murder their mothers, their fathers, their children—it was too high a price, and too dark a stain. Days, we spoke on this, and weeks. And yet, in the end, the choice was not our own.

"I remember him still, the man who began the long tradition. He had been a Hunter for all of his young life, but in the prime of his days, he was struck in the thigh and the leg by a wild beast. The bleeding did not kill him, nor the infection thereafter—but he could not hunt again, and he fell in upon himself and grew old in a space of years, shadowed by the light of his former glories.

"His name was Jerem, and he offered his life as sacrifice—his life and more— that his people might live. His only request was that he once again be allowed to accompany the Hunters; that he die in the Hunt.

"He died as he lived. Bravely, and with honor. That much I could still do, then. I took his spirit as it lingered for the Three, and I made it a part of my own, that

I might draw upon its brief light to remember, to retain what I knew. It was not enough, this single life, yet it was something, and after the ceremonies and the silence, we gave his blood to earth. And there, too, came the unlooked for.

"The Old Earth answered: *a life for life.*

"It was an offer, Lord Elseth. And we were failing in our power. We accepted. It is to the Old Earth that the blood of the Hunt still falls; it is the Earth that punishes you when the Hunt fails, and only when the ancient ways are a shadow of memory, forgotten even in child's play, will the land—and the Breodani—be free of that binding; for the Breodani and the Old Earth are Oathbound."

He paused, measuring the Hunter who knelt before him in angry silence. And then, so softly it might have been a single voice speaking, he said, "The soul of Jerem still resides within me, trapped until the moment of my ascension."

"And Stephen," Evayne whispered, when she could speak at all.

"Even so," the God replied.

Gilliam of Elseth said nothing; it was Evayne who cried out wildly, savagely, "Let him *go.*"

The antlered God was not troubled; he spoke. "I cannot; I do not have the power. These are not the forests of Breodani; not the lands of the Leoganti, and even there, the choice is not mine. Under a different sun, I was a Lord of the Wild—and not for the sake of a soul, not for hundreds, would I unleash that upon this earth."

It was to Gilliam that he spoke, but it was Evayne who shook her head numbly.

"This is not the time of renewal." The tines of the Lord of the Hunt angled up, and up again, as he stared at the curvature of the ceiling that was now hidden in the darkness of the chandelier's demise. "But you have called, I have come. The price has been paid. You are Lord of the Elseth Responsibility, and I deem you true to your Oath." His face was impassive as he spoke, but something in his eyes shifted when the daughter of his earthly flesh stepped forward, shielding the man who was—and was afraid to be—her master.

She did not bow as she stood; instead she tossed the wild tangle of matted dark hair defiantly, angrily. Gold eyes met eyes that had no earthly color; blood-spattered lips opened upon a single word. "Father."

He flinched as she spoke it, and then bowed his head. "Tell me," he said, the softness of the words in no way masking the command they contained.

Not even Kallandras could have told a deeper—or a truer—story, but no one in the hall could know it, for the language that she spoke was not a human language, and the throat that uttered it, not a human—not quite—throat. Her voice was the rush of wind, the twisting of ocean current, the slow growth of forest—a roar that spoke of time and change and more subtle things beside.

His voice was the beast's voice, but robbed of the wilderness that was death;

and in timbre it matched hers, but in glory far outshone it. He called her once, and she would not come. A second time, and she stepped forward but held her ground. A third and she snarled back, pain mingled with defiance.

And then the God smiled, and the smile was light. "I see," he said softly. "Very well. It is your choice to make now." A youthful seeming was upon him as he turned to Gilliam.

"Your history has been lost to time. But my child tells me that you are still a proud and honorable people. That you wield your power as the sword and the responsibility that it is; that you bring nobility to being noble-born. The lands are green, the game is plentiful, the magic of the sacrifice renews all in its human season."

Gilliam looked up bleakly.

The God's smile vanished as he met his follower's gaze. Gilliam pulled back as Espere whined—for in the eyes of the God was a terrible longing. Almost a fear. "It is time," the Lord of the Hunt said. "I have fulfilled my oath." He lifted a hand and a trail of gold-edged light pierced the darkness. "Fulfill you now your people's." The Horn came to him. "Take this, and wind it on the Day. Call me, as the Hunters of Breodanir have called throughout time."

Gilliam struggled in the silence a moment before he spoke a single uninflected word. "Why?"

"Why?"

"Why should I obey you?"

A glint of red beneath the tines of the antlered God; a glimmer of simmering anger. Then, "Because you have given your oath to my service."

"I'm not a Priest."

"There are no true Priests left. *Allasakar* saw to that." As he spoke the name of the Lord of the Hells, the air snapped and crackled with his anger made manifest. "But I will tell you this, although your boldness displeases me. With the spear that was hewn from the Fields of the Guardians, you shall hunt me.

"For it is my time. Kill the body of the beast, Hunter Lord, and I will no longer be wrapped in mortal flesh, or trapped in mortal lands. Hunt, as you have been trained to hunt, and you *will* find your quarry."

"And if he does as you ask?" Evayne said. "If he frees you from these lands, will there be no more Sacred Hunts? Will his death be the final death?" She did not name him; she did not need to.

The God turned then to Evayne as she stood with her burden: a quiet, injured dog. "While Breodanir exists, the Hunt will be called," he said. "The earth will take its due, or in the Hunters' lands, there will be no spring."

Grim but satisfied, Gilliam nodded; if there was relief at the Hunter God's reply, it did not show. He held out his hand, and the simple Horn came to it as if called.

"Daughter of my kin, you know what is at risk here. Lead him, if you can.

Guide him. For there are no forests in this small and crowded space, and we face the twilight and the darkness is almost nigh. It is in Averalaan that the Hunt will be called." He lowered his chin to meet her gaze. "For the Hunter, the Hunt is all. But you are not a Hunter."

She stared beyond him, to the body that lay unmoving in shadows. She even nodded, and as she did, the hood of her robes fell away, revealing her face. Her eyes were reddened, but her smooth, young skin was very, very pale.

"You do not understand," he said; it was not a question.

She did not answer. Instead, she walked steadily and quietly toward him, holding the dog as if he were a shield. He was. For Evayne knew little, but she knew this: Only she could walk the Path, and it would not take her if she carried any other living thing. She was not ready to leave, not yet.

The words that the God spoke made a dim and distant sense, but they did not touch her. *The soul still resides within me, trapped. . . .* She could not look at him, so she looked at the dog's head instead, at its flat, triangular gray and brown fur, at its floppy ears. It was heavy, this dog, but not so heavy that she couldn't hold it for just a moment longer.

Don't stop me, she thought, and he didn't. She walked past him, past the light that he shed, and into the shadows.

There, kneeling slowly and carefully, she came to rest beside the body of Stephen of Elseth. Huntbrother. Friend. She'd brought him to this, somehow; she was certain of it. Kallandras was right; he was always right. She was like death, but less merciful.

I didn't mean it, she told him, looking into his still face. His body was rent like so much thin fabric; blood, sticky and red, was cooling everywhere. But his face was untouched. Pressing the dog firmly into her lap with her left hand, she reached out with her right one and touched his *cold* cheek.

The body was nothing. She'd heard it before from any number of priests. Even the one who called himself her parent said this over and over, as if it was supposed to render death meaningless. As if it did away with loss.

Angrily, she shoved the dog aside and sat beside Stephen, pulling his head into her lap; trying to give him a place to rest.

She cried out once in pain and anger and denial, and then cried out in surprise. When she rose, gingerly lifting Stephen's head and setting it once again against the cold floor, her face was the face of a woman of power, not a tortured girl. But her lips still bore the faint twist of a pain renewed.

She saw the God, and he her; he turned to face her.

"I hoped never to see this place again," she told him gravely.

"Perhaps you never will. But that was a child's hope, and this is not a children's war."

"Children will die in it," she answered softly, "and most certainly," she added, staring through the wall of mist as if she could see through it, "they *will* fight in it. But I believe I understand why it is I who am here."

"I cannot remain here long," the God said. "The forests of Leoganti provide some protection against the ruin of the world, and I must return to them— already, my time is dwindling and the pull of forgetfulness and the wild is growing." He stopped a moment, staring into the mists as if they were a seer's ball. "Allasakar seeks to break the Covenant. He will; it can be done."

"It is to stop him that I have labored," she replied, but she did not meet his eyes.

"The Hunt will be called in this city, Evayne a'Nolan, for I believe that our enemy is here. Call the Hunt in the proper place, and before I ascend, I will fight him."

"And will you win?" she asked coolly. "Will you take an oath to end his threat forever?"

"I take no oath I cannot fulfill, as well you know." He paused. "It is dangerous to judge a God, little one."

"It is dangerous to have anything to do with Gods." She lifted a proud head, and the robes that she wore rose to frame her face. "Especially if you are not one." Her gaze touched darkness, and skittered shyly off Stephen's body. His corpse.

"Evayne," he said, "if it were not for the ability of the mortals to choose, what threat would any of us be? The Covenant—"

"The Covenant was not enough!"

He stared at her oddly, the light glimmering in his eyes like sun at midday. "Not enough?" he said softly, the voices a whisper. "Perhaps. Perhaps not. You are mortal; you are of this world. Make of it what you will. Come the first of Veral, if you wish to have a world that is not an extension of the Hells, you will call the Hunt."

"Oh, the Hunt will be called," she said bitterly. "For Gilliam of Elseth *is* a Hunter. The Gods will continue to have an even field on which to play their games."

"Games?" The tines of the Hunter God began to fade, dissolving into air and nothingness. The pale, scarred brow of a slender, ageless man remained. He was tall, this man; taller than Meralonne APhaniel; taller than any mortal Evayne had ever met—and she had met many. "I pity you," he said softly. "For you do not understand all that is at stake. Our power is not like the studies of the mage-born; not even like the compulsion of the healer-born to the hurt. It is older than time, and stronger; it compels us, and it will not be denied.

"And now, I have truly said enough." He turned very carefully, and before anyone could stop him, gathered up Stephen of Elseth's limp body, cradling it as if it were a child's. "The earth," he said sadly, "demands its due. We shall return home, he and I."

Gilliam bore it proudly, lifting his chin as he stared with a terrible longing at the Hunter's burden. And then, before the tears could start, the Hunter was gone, dwindling in the sight as if a great distance had come upon them unawares. He waited until he could no longer see a thing; until even the afterimage of bright light against his vision had faded completely into darkness. Then he turned to Evayne.

"Get me the Spear," he said. Dreams of death. Of vengeance. Of killing.

She nodded, seeing death as it hovered about the lines of his face. Like a bruise, the marks took a little time to darken; he was in shock. Her face was well-schooled; she offered him no pity, and even the horror of her youth fell away before the shadow of his loss. It was one of the few things they shared, although he could not and would not admit it yet. And she would not ask.

He turned to walk away; his knees, and not his feet, hit the floor. Behind him, someone gasped; he flipped over, reaching for a dagger, as Espere approached.

"G-Gilliam," she said, as if the name did not come easily, "you are hurt." She offered him a hand, and he stared at it—at her—as if he understood neither. She pulled back, hurt, and he pulled farther away, gaining his feet clumsily.

"Lord Elseth," Evayne said darkly, "this *is* Espere. She is bound to her father's life, and while he lives upon this world, she is bound to his season. For a week or two, she is as human, but over a space of days, the wilderness that binds her father destroys her as well.

"She is *not* an animal, no matter how much you might wish otherwise."

He bristled and began to speak, but Espere raised a hand to his lips. It surprised them both. "I am not human either," she said. "And will not ever be." She stared at her Lord, her eyes gold and brown. "But help me, and I will be all I can be in your service."

"Well said." Evayne looked faintly chagrined. "My apologies, Espere. You are not an animal, but you are also not a child. You were sent to choose, and you have chosen well." She bowed, her robes fluttering above the ground like trapped butterflies. "I shall see you both; Corvil is not yet finished, and Henden must pass before the Hunt is called."

Chapter Twenty-Three

BLACKNESS.

Not the darkness between lid and eye that vanishes with waking, but darker and deeper; the blackness between the living and the dead.

Ashfel's gray head rested against his ash paws; he licked the ground and looked into the shadows. Salas, made gray by an evening uninterrupted by torchlight or lamplight, stood to the side, whining softly. Connel rested in his master's bed, his leg bound by a splint and wrapped round with heavy, padded gauze. The air did not carry the familiar sounds or scents of the rest of the small pack of dogs that had followed Gilliam to Averalaan; they lay on biers of an elaborate and foreign design, although the man—the domicis—had taken great pains to treat the fallen as they would have been treated in Breodanir.

Espere was nowhere to be found. Nor did Gilliam wish her to be there; she could interrupt his silence with the unfamiliar sound of a voice that did not bark or growl or whine—with a voice that reminded him, measure for measure, of the God that had fathered her. The Hunter Lord.

He should not have let the God take the body.

But was he to let Stephen be forever buried beneath foreign ground? Was he to be laid to rest in a land where he would not be honored, his death at most a curiosity, and at the least, something that no one—not a single person here—could fathom the importance of?

He stood in the darkness, asking questions in the silence that there were no answers for; repeating them over and over as if, by doing so, he might finally receive an answer he liked.

His arms ached; the wound across his chest, the gash below his rib cage, throbbed. If they had hurt a little more, if they had been a little deeper, Stephen would not have had to die.

Bowing his head, he twined his fists beneath his chin in a gesture that was more accusation than prayer. The fact of a death did not bother him; the fact that the Allasakari had, in numbers, died without effect came as little surprise. The Hunter Hunted the Hunters. That was the law.

But it was Stephen who had died.

I'll protect you.

I'll protect you.

And Stephen was stupid. Always had been. He'd been *comforted* by the lie.

He could not sleep. He had tried. But in his dreams only death had any viscerality; he longed for it, and in the privacy of a space that not even his dogs could touch, he hated Stephen for being the one who had passed into the Hunter's Wood.

Because he knew that Stephen had chosen that death.

He cried out, although no sound escaped his lips. Ashfel whined and raised his nose, but Gilliam could not—would not—respond. They held him back, these two. Pulling his hands apart, he spun, crouched and ready to face anything.

Nothing was there.

I'll protect you.

Stephen was dead.

Papers gathered dust on the table beneath the grand window of The Terafin's library. She had sent for them, had laid them out with great care that she might study them further. But those that were important—death writs, and writs for the proper funds to be sent to the bereaved families of her fallen guards—had already been dealt with, and what remained was far too workaday to command her greater attention.

Morretz was nowhere in sight, at her command; there were no servants, no attendants, no one carrying trays of food, dishes of water, changes of clothing. Here, there was privacy, and it was as much as she could hope for. It would not last long.

Her slender fingers furled into shaking fists; she forced them to relax, studying her hands as if they belonged to someone else. They almost did.

Ah, Cormaris.

But she was not Arann of the young Jewel's den; she would not deny Alowan's power to be free from the pain and the loss that followed it. She wondered, for the hundredth time, where the healer was—but at the same time knew that she had but to walk to the healerie and she would find him, white-haired and bent, in the pursuit of his duties and his responsibilities. Perhaps his hair might be a little whiter, if that were possible; his face a bit more lined. He knew who he was.

And she?

The Terafin, of course. And The Terafin was the strength of the House.

Her eyes were not dry as she rose. She wore black and gold; the colors of respectful mourning. The dress itself was thin and plain in line, but it had been made by Allerie of Courtis herself, and cost dearly. Her hair, tended to by dry-eyed silent valets, was beaded with ebony and drawn tight in a fine-meshed net that glittered under light. No other adornment was necessary.

Silent, she rose; silent, she crossed the room, squaring her shoulders before she opened the doors and walked into the world again.

Jewel waited in a tense and weary silence. Torvan was still alive—how, after the attack of that creature, she didn't know—but she wasn't allowed to see him. He was under some sort of fancy house arrest, and it was very hard to get more information than that.

Which wasn't, of course, why she was tense.

"Heard anything yet?" It was Carver, jogging her left elbow.

"Not since the fiftieth time you asked, no," she snapped.

Angel sauntered into the kitchen, dragging his left hand through his bangs as he took up his spot against the wall. They both turned to stare at him. "Well?"

He shrugged. "Bad night," he said. "For all of us."

"Then the gates—"

"You've seen the grounds, right?"

"We've seen 'em," Jewel replied tersely. The gardeners were out in beleaguered force, and most of the other servants stayed well enough away from the charred and burned ruin of the flower beds and the shrubs. The trees had been singed; heavy branches had come down in at least three places but the trees themselves looked as if they would survive. "Mage-fire?"

"Yeah. But not as bad as that—*our* mage killed most of 'em at the start."

"And?"

"Darias men, all of them—at least by their colors. Pretty well-run show; they were supposed to attract most of the House attention up front while their boys in the back did the other stuff."

Other stuff. Jewel snorted. Angel had such a way with words. "And?"

"They outnumbered the guards at the gate at the start, but the gates were sealed somehow by the mage. Got through 'em anyway, by destroying part of the wall."

Enough, Jewel thought. She jumped up and out of her chair, walked over to her den-kin, and grabbed him by the collars. *"What about Arann?"*

Carver started to laugh before Angel could get out another word.

"Did I forget to say he was all right?"

Meralonne APhaniel sat under the open sky in the empty amphitheater. Waves lapped at the seawall a hundred yards to the west, but the gulls were quiet, and only the insects disturbed his peace. He sat on a hard bench in the cool night air, cradling his arm absently.

There were stars; beneath the farthest edge of the canopy, their light danced in absurd glory from a distance that time had done little to diminish. Watching them was soothing now, where once it had been painful.

There were things that gold could not buy; peace was one. Wincing, he shifted position. Dawn was hours off, but it would come, and he did not wish to witness it. For with the dawn, there would be questions, answers, legalities, *rules.*

He did not know if he had won. And for one fragile moment, he didn't care. To be tested in battle—to be tested and to pass—was enough. Or it had been, in his youth. The chills that shook his body were deep; to escape the summoned beast he had used what remained of his power, and more besides.

The sky was a winter sky, dark and cool.

Mage-fevers racked his body. His lips were cracked and dry, except where blood moistened them; the seizures were severe.

The room was dark and shuttered. Cracks of light glimmered between the uncurtained wooden slats; this was a haven of last resort, and as a last resort, it had not been chosen for finery or appointment. Above, there was the sound of argument; beneath, the sound of moving chairs and tables that might indicate someone actually cleaned their home in this sorry tenement.

The thirst came on again. It was weaker this time; he was glad of it. With no power at all to spare—with too much borrowed too close to the source of his life—he hadn't the ability to force a stranger into temporary servitude.

Sor na Shannen, he thought, although that took almost too much strength, *I will pull your name from the bowels of the hells.*

If she remained upon the world. The kin were like their Lord; they wore flesh and form decreed by mortal lands. To kill their bodies sent them home, devoid of the power they needed to rule. A grisly fate, that.

He did not know, not yet; in his weakened state even an imp would be able to feed off his eyes with impunity. He did not dare return to Vexusa. The rules of the Hells were remarkably simple: the strong preyed on the weak. It was not an end he wished to risk.

He coughed, pulling the blankets close and wrapping them round his body. The ways to the undercity were closed; to arrive there at all, he needed more power than most of the mages in the city would ever know.

He would have it if he survived the fevers.

The tenth of Corvil dawned beneath a shroud of wind and drizzle; the tang of the sea touched lip and tongue. The Priests of the trinity had come, but not to lay the dead to rest; they attended the Exalted, with ceremony, with conviction, with dedication—and with a hint of nervousness.

If you wished to gain an audience with the Exalted, you traveled to *them.* You

paid your obeisance, you made your offering—at that, usually a generous one—
and you waited a gracious and appropriate period of time while the god-born
rulers of the Churches extricated themselves from their responsibilities.

You did not, upon a single day's notice, request the presence of each of the three
and *receive* it for any less a death than that of the Kings or the Queens. And yet, in
the sparse gardens of Terafin, upon a hastily constructed pavilion, not one, but
three of the Exalted stood, practically shoulder to shoulder in grim silence—to
preside over the First Day rites, not of The Terafin herself, but of her servants.

Brother Mayadar, ceremonial officiant, clerk, and general gadabout for the Exalted of the Mother, paled further—if that were possible—when he saw the elaborate and graceful biers, circled by white-flowered wreaths, that contained, of all
things, *dogs*. It was *outrageous*.

The sniffs of a few other members of the large delegation told him clearly that
he was not the only Priest present to feel so. Really, The Terafin's power had obviously gone to her head—such hubris, such arrogance, was *not* to be encouraged.
The Exalted of the Mother had little tolerance for self-aggrandizement; she would
put The Terafin in her proper place, she would.

He knelt stiffly, as did the brothers and sisters chosen to attend her at this function. They formed the Mother's Circle and then waited while the Priests of Cormaris and Reymaris joined them upon the dais, in smaller circles to either side.
Acknowledgment that the Mother was the source of all life.

Surrounded by their servitors, the Exalted stood.

As one, the Chosen of Terafin knelt before their Lord in three unbroken lines.
The House Guards were already kneeling, and Brother Mayadar noticed that there
were servants in attendance. An older man was obviously hissing instructions at
them—they were so poorly brought up they didn't know how to behave in the
presence of the Exalted. Outrageous.

The Terafin, last of all, fell to one knee and bowed her head.

Which left a lone man upon his feet.

He was broad of chest and dark of hair, but too fair of complexion to be a
Southerner. At his feet, standing almost at attention, were three more dogs. One
was an even and perfect gray, one gray with brown markings, and one brown with
white boots—and a splinted leg. They looked unnatural, even magical; they did
not move at all.

All eyes fell upon this stranger and his entourage. If stares alone had weight, he
would have crumpled to the ground at once, planting his face in embarrassed
obeisance into the nearby dirt. But he met all glances with pride and thinly veiled
anger; after a minute it became clear that it was not ignorance of the custom that
kept him on his feet. He had no intention of showing the proper respect for the
Exalted.

Brother Mayadar chanced a stray glance at the Exalted of the Mother; she was staring past him, and past the standing stranger, to the biers upon which the dogs had been laid to rest. Satisfied, she nodded.

The Terafin rose. "Exalted," she said, speaking first to the Mother's Daughter. "You grace us with your presence."

The Priests shuffled to the side to allow the Exalted free passage; when she had broken the perimeter of their circle, they were free to stand. "Terafin," the Exalted said. "It has been long since you have graced *us* with your presence. But we have received your word, and we will do what we can to lay your kin to rest." She walked to the biers, the hem of her robes trailing the crimson carpets that had been placed above the wooden planks. Stopping at the first body that lay against linen and silk, she bent and touched the forehead with a slightly bent hand. The frozen rictus beneath her fingers seemed almost to shudder.

Pale, she lifted her head and signaled to her followers.

A burning brazier, hung from a brass pole by a slender chain, was lit; fire flared a moment as she spoke over it, and then a sweet, thick smoke wafted landward in the breeze. She lifted the tiara from her forehead, and with great care removed the finely detailed and embroidered overrobes that were the symbol of her office; these she handed to one of the brothers.

Unadorned, she would still not have been mistaken for a woman like any other; her eyes were glowing with a golden brilliance that could not be met.

"It is as you feared, daughter," the Exalted said. "Brother Mayadar. Sister Taralyn." They began to walk in step across the dais at her command. Her lips folded in a frown. Mayadar missed a beat. "Bring us the dagger," she told them, patiently but tersely.

The dagger was part of the First Day ceremonies, but it was seldom called for until the dead were to be interred. Mayadar retrieved the box from the young Priest-designate who had been chosen to carry it. With unseemly haste, he returned to the side of the Exalted, bowing low. She nodded her thanks, but her attention was already upon the dagger. Without preamble, she lifted it and slid its wavering edge across her palm. That was not part of the usual ceremony. Blood.

No one spoke as she touched the dead man's forehead before that blood had cooled or ceased its flow. His muscles slackened by slow degree as the shadows left his face. Paler, the Exalted stood. "As you feared," she said gravely to The Terafin, "and worse."

"Daughter of the Mother."

She did not turn to look; only four in the city could call her by that title, and only one would feel the need. "Son of Reymaris," she replied. "The Terafin has seen truly. This is the work of the Allasakari, this rictus; but its hold is stronger and surer than any shadow that I have yet felt."

"And may we help?"

"You may."

The Exalted of Cormaris did not feel a like need to gain her permission, and, as she, he divested himself of the symbols and the finery of his office, save one: the power behind the Church. In silence they worked their blessing against the darkness of their parents' eternal enemy.

Chanting quietly, the Priests formed up behind their leaders, holding braziers, burning incense, whispering over and over the phrases that centered the Exalted in the mysteries of their parents. The Terafin had seen such effects before, but she had never felt they were necessary; today, for the first time, the ceremony of the First Day had a very practical, very pragmatic meaning.

Is it true? If the shadow is not dispelled, will the bodies of the dead rise at the end of the Three Days when the spirit is at last free? But it was a scholar's question, an earnest youth's, or even a child's. She was The Terafin; curiosity did not force her speech.

In the end, the work was done. The Terafin watched the Exalted, sweaty and fatigued from their labor, as they retreated to the circles of their attendants. The air was heavy with the combined scent of three braziers and the perfumes and oils in which the dead were bathed.

The Exalted of Cormaris stood forward, and bowed very low. "It is done," he said gravely. The Terafin bowed in return, but before she could speak, Lord Elseth did.

"My dogs," he said softly. "My dogs were killed in the same way."

The Exalted of Cormaris raised a dark brow. His face was pale and finely boned, with high cheekbones and brow. He was not a young man, but then again, no son of Cormaris ever truly seemed young. "The dogs," he said gravely, "burning will save."

Before anyone could stop him—and that wasn't difficult as no one in Averalaan could conceive of any sane person behaving in such a way—Lord Elseth grabbed the Exalted's left arm and swung him around. He was the heavier man.

The Exalted of Cormaris raised a brow, but did not struggle.

"My dogs died fighting your enemies," Lord Elseth said, teeth clenched and lips barely moving. "They will be given to earth; they *will* be honored."

Priests of Reymaris quietly joined the Exalted's side; they were armed, and although their weapons remained sheathed, their meaning was clear. The foreign Lord stared at them a moment, as if weighing his chances.

A young woman came, moving so quietly that she was noticed only as she reached his side. She touched his arm, caught the white, white knuckles that rested against the pommel of a sheathed sword. He turned to her and opened his mouth.

She said, "It will not bring them back."

"Go away."

"Do not do this. It will not bring *him* back."

He paled; his hand slackened. If his feet were not so firmly planted, he might have stepped back. *"Leave me."*

She did, vanishing into the crowd with the same ease with which she had appeared.

The foreign Lord released the ruler of the Church of Cormaris. The Exalted turned immediately and continued to walk away from the dead.

The dogs at Lord Elseth's feet began to snarl, although their master was silent and still. As if the ruler of the earthly dominion of Cormaris had set the standard for the behavior of the rest of the gathering, people began to melt away, giving wide berth to the stranger and his creatures without offering obvious disdain. Not even The Terafin chose to have words with her visitor, or to grace him with her support; not here, and not after his breach of conduct.

And then, as the growl of the hounds turned to a soft, high whine, as the Lord Elseth turned to face the biers upon which his pack were laid, one person stepped out of the flow of the crowd, moving cautiously and confidently. She had, after all, little to fear.

The Exalted of the Mother approached quietly, gesturing her attendants on either side to stand back. The growling of the beasts grew as she came near, but she offered them a frown, and after a few seconds, they fell silent. Only then did she smile and reach out—and the largest of the dogs began to trot across the platform to greet her. His tail was wagging, his ears were up.

But he did not reach her.

Brother Mayadar had never seen a dog stop in mid-stride before—but these dogs were unnatural, so it didn't really surprise him when this one did. He thought the Exalted might say something, or do something, which would *finally* put this—this pompous, ignorant barbarian in his place. But when she spoke, it was to the dog.

"Ashfel," she said quietly. "You must tell your Lord that we mean him no harm. We have traveled to his country, to visit her Holiness in the King's City; we have witnessed the Sacred Hunt." As she spoke this last, she looked up from the dog's cocked head to the master's impassive face. "We do not understand the mysteries of the Breodani; we do not understand their Hunter God. But we do know that the earth and the hunt are tied in ways that we, daughter to the Mother, cannot fathom.

"Your people are true to your Lord and to ours; and the dogs that you honor above almost all else are part of the Hunt that, in the end, feeds *our* children, our followers. We know that you are without your huntbrother," she said gravely, the seriousness of her expression saying more than the words. "And we know that the huntbrother is the one who would be versed in our customs. We do not take offense at your request, Lord Elseth." She paused, and lowered her head a moment, as if gathering her strength. "And it pleases us to grant you what you wish."

He stared at her, and the impassivity slowly drained from his face. That left him with words, and he would not speak them; he had never been good with words, and it was suddenly important that he not offend this woman.

She knew what he had lost.

Her eyes were bright as she waited for the acknowledgment that would not come, and then, realizing it was there in the openness of his expression, in the suddenness of vulnerability, she said, "Come; we fear that our blood has been thinned by the ceremonies. You must provide that which we cannot."

10th Corvil, 410 A.A., evening
Hall of Wise Counsel

The screaming was distant now; like the tide, it was low and high, and at times such as this he might almost forget that it existed.

His body had accustomed itself to the *niscea*. A bad sign, but he was more aware of its effects than the untrained would be, and he did what he could to limit the dosage. If the dead were not laid to rest, the cure would become a curse of its own.

"Kallandras." The voice was quiet, softened by enchantment into an otherworld whisper. He was trained to listen to all manner of speech and song; he knew at once that the words to follow were meant for his ears alone, and would reach no others.

Still he glanced at his companion to see if her presence had been noted—for it was Evayne who spoke, and at that, the older woman, not the child. Devon ATerafin, on edge, had noticed little out of place; Kallandras swept the chamber with the eye of his early training. She was not immediately obvious.

"What is it?" Devon said quietly, pitching his voice low.

Kallandras shook his head. Devon's sensitivity had nothing to do with magic or ritual or training. A most unusual man in many ways. He tried not to remember the brotherhood, and failed—for Devon was like, and unlike, the Kovaschaii.

"Kallandras?"

"Kallandras."

"Nothing is out of place, ATerafin," he said, and then, using the talents for which he was known, "Evayne. What tragedy have you brought this eve?" No one who was not Evayne could catch the words, but one bard-born and trained would know that there was speech, and that it was private.

"You're looking for something," Devon said tersely, his blue eyes icelike in the chill of his face.

Evayne was silent, and when she spoke again, he lost the drift of her words to Devon's continued accusation. Luckily, it didn't last long; Devon had made the chamber his first concern, and could spare little time from watching over it.

In the annoyed silence that Devon offered as he turned his vigil back to the Kings' Swords who stood at the doors that led to the Hall of Wise Counsel, and thence, to the interior rooms that the Kings occupied in the winter season, Kallandras sorted out the words that had been Evayne's. They were curt and brief.

"Carry the spear that the wild one brought you to Lord Elseth."

He nodded, knowing that she would see it, and accept it as his pledge, no matter where she stood. She was seer-born; little was hidden from her sight when she chose to look.

Twenty-four men—on the ground floor—made the chamber itself look small, although a dozen of those men and women were tucked away near servants' entrances. Another two dozen lined the gallery above, patrolling the three doors that had been locked and barred for the evening. There was not a young man or woman among them; Devon had, with the aid of the Princess, chosen only those with experience. And skill.

It was odd, though, to see four Primus and a Verrus serving in the role of night watchmen. Kallandras risked a sidelong glance at his dark-haired companion. The ATerafin had pulled in many favors for these evening shifts—and they would not last long. The bard did not wish to see Devon's fears made real, but he knew that, should nothing happen, it would cost Devon his credibility.

Folding his arms, he relaxed into the edge of the basin by the wall. And what should he care, if Devon failed? Moody, almost grim, he stared into the chamber, aware of every movement within its walls.

"It seems," Evayne said, "that I've made an error in judgment." Her inflection was wry but cautious. "Having given you the message, I thought the path would take me where it must—but it appears that I am already there.

"I should have guessed," she added. "Why else would I come upon you here, surrounded by evening and the Kings' Swords, if there were no . . . difficulties?"

Before he could answer, a door in the upper gallery drew his attention. Someone was on the other side of it, banging loudly. He turned to Devon ATerafin; Devon was rigid but silent.

"Mailed fist," Kallandras said, sweeping his hair up and catching it so firmly with a long pin and net that the curls lay flat. Salla was in his temporary quarters, and he wore no sword—but he was armed, and armed well. Shaking his wrists with a distinctive snap, he armed himself with stilettos.

Devon raised a dark brow, and for the first time in three evenings, he smiled cautiously. "Meralonne said you were . . . more than you seemed."

"Meralonne," Kallandras said, almost bitterly, "said no more than he needed." He paused. "Arm yourself. There is danger."

Devon nodded and looked to the door.

Primus Cortarian came from beneath the gallery, walking briskly toward the ATerafin. He bowed, making of the gesture something perfunctory and quick.

"Report."

"An urgent message. From The Terafin. The Kings are to be informed at once."

"Of what?"

"The man will not say—the message is to be delivered to the Kings." He paused. "The message is, apparently, not written; it is verbal. There is no seal to verify. We do not know who the carrier is; as per your instructions, we have not opened the doors."

"Ready your men," Devon said softly. He turned swiftly. "I will deal with the Terafin messenger."

Primus Cortarian bowed again.

Before either man could reach the galleries, the doors flew off their hinges, splintering against the rails opposite them. The two men who had been standing in front of those doors had no chance to cry out; the force of the impact drove them over the rails to the ground below. They lay there limply.

In the semidarkness, in the doorless frame, stood a single man: Verrus Allamar. He wore no armor, and carried no shield, but in his left hand he held a great sword as if its weight was of no more consequence than a dagger.

And at his back, in numbers the light made difficult to judge, were Kings' Swords.

"What is the meaning of this?" Verrus Sivari stepped forward from his position by the doors to the Hall of Wise Counsel. He was a younger man than Allamar, and smaller of build, but he had thrice been Kings' Champion; he was a man who not only knew how to command, but also how best to use the minutiae of the swordsman's life.

Verrus Allamar stepped into the gallery in silence, ignoring the challenge posed by the only man in the room who might be said to outrank him. He lifted an arm, and waved the men at his back forward; they came in like a tide made of something thick and heavy.

A *twang* cut the silence, and a crack; Verrus Allamar smiled broadly as he glanced down at the quarrel in his right fist. With a twist of fingers, he snapped it in two and tossed it aside.

Devon cursed and lowered the crossbow; Kallandras felt a twinge of surprise; he hadn't noticed the older man arming himself with the weapon, and he was not given to missing much. Fire flared from Allamar's hands, singeing the wall where Devon wasn't.

Devon ATerafin could *move.*

"It has started," Allamar said, with a grin that was literally too wide for his face. "Shall we dispense with pretense?" He gestured in a wide arc, and his skin began to fall away, peeling down the sides of his face even as it burned. Throughout it all, his grin grew wider—and the teeth in his mouth more pronounced, more fanglike.

The men at his back and side, dressed in the two crowns above the crossed rod and staff, bore quiet witness to the transformation.

Devon swore as he gained the ground two inches from Kallandras. "Not one of those men are ours," he said.

"Then we have our work cut out for us," was his companion's inflectionless reply, "for there are seventy-seven of them." He paused. Then, "ATerafin, what do you know of the *Allasakari?*"

Devon ATerafin's low, vicious curse was all the answer he needed.

The Kings' Swords regrouped in front of the doors to the Hall of Wise Counsel; there were forty of them now. Devon ATerafin joined them. Kallandras did not, for he was in need of shadow more than he feared it, and he was not trained to work with such obvious soldiers.

Meralonne, curse him, was nowhere to be found—and from the gathering darkness that centered upon Allamar—upon what had once been Allamar—he would be missed.

With hooks and grappling ropes, the enemy began to descend from the gallery; the two sets of stairs, delicate and narrow, were barely wide enough for one large man in good armor.

Their leader came as well, stepping out into midair and finding, in the thickening shadow, a platform that slowly descended. "We will kill you quickly, or we will kill you slowly," the creature that had been Allamar said. "But this is the only chance you will have to choose. Choose swiftly."

"Why have you come?" Devon asked, gaining what time he could.

Allamar's teeth flashed; it was clear that he understood the gambit. "Why, to kill the Kings, of course. The Queens are already dead."

Silence, deep and profound.

Then: The clang of swords against shields in the dim hall, a metallic cry of despair.

"No quarter!" cried Verrus Sivari.

"No quarter?" Allamar replied, incredulous. *"No quarter?"* He lifted his arms, throwing them wide; fire flared like a fan from the arc he traced in the air.

There was no time to brace for the fire, but the men that Devon had chosen were fast enough to respond, raising shields in a line against magics that they did not understand. If Verrus Sivari had only a few seconds to speak—if he had the choice of only two words—he had chosen well. The men and women sworn to the service of the Crowns did not falter.

Not even when the fire splintered their shields.

Behind the Allasakari and their leader, the shadows grew, leeching the chamber of color, and then, of light. In a mockery of the uniforms they wore, the Allasakari paused in ugly salute and then drew their weapons—not swords, but daggers. The blades did not glint or reflect light in any way; they were like pieces of the shadow itself, made hard and sharp.

"Your souls will feed our Lord," Allamar said. "The first of many so reaved. Take them!"

"Bold," a quiet voice said, "and as ever, a liar. We know well that the Gods alone may take such a sacrifice."

"What is this?" Allamar looked into the galleries above. His eyes narrowed, and then he grinned broadly, for around the galleries, against each of three walls, was a thin line of shadowed figures. "Do you think to menace me?"

The reply seemed to come from all around, above and below; it was colder than the darkness of moonless winter in the northern wastes. *"Kevellar-arrensas,* I bind you by the power of the trinity made one. Your name, the Hells have surrendered."

The creature cried out, and its followers shifted, shying like horses made nervous by sounds of unexpected battle.

"And no," the voice continued, coming now from the center of each of the four chamber walls, "the darkness shall not take what we have labored to capture; this is *Averalaan Aramarelas* and when the Lord of Darkness himself walked upon this world, his city still fell before the trinity."

The shadows that had filled the room ceased their upward struggle.

"Reymaris," a deep voice said, as a man stepped forward into a light that had no source. He was dressed in the simple robes of the Church, and girded round with a single, sheathed sword; he wore a small shield strapped across his chest from shoulder to waist, but did not seek to ready it.

"Cormaris," another said, and he, too, came forward, bearing the staff of his office.

"The Mother." This third voice was the only voice that was tinged with regret, and yet the woman who spoke was stern in seeming. Her hair was golden, but drawn and bound tightly, and she wore a shift that would have been more appropriate on a well-muscled farmwife.

"Think you to bind me so close to the source of His power?" Allamar was incredulous, and yet beneath the scorn of his words was the first hint of doubt. "He stood against the trinity until the coming of the cursed rider—He has nothing to fear from you!" Once again, fire gouted from his fingertips.

"Forgive me, but I fear you misunderstand me. The trinity *is* the power that will bind you—but it is not the only power present." The first voice to speak was also the last, yet no figure came to stand out of the darkness and the shadows. The demon's fire went out so suddenly it might never have been called. "For I represent the Covenant of Man—the Covenant and its maker." The voice changed in tenor. "Lord of the Hells, bear witness: We are the sons and daughters of mankind, and these lands are ours. We have worked our lives against your dominion, and we declare ourselves now. Behold!" And the shadows were devoured in an instant, snapping and shattering into a welter of light—and at that, no cold light, but the light of spring dawning, the light of summer day, the light of autumn's harvest. The light of the trinity.

"This is not possible!" the creature cried.

Night itself shrank from the Exalted as they stood at the edge of the gallery: East, South, and West. They looked down, the hidden power of their heritage unveiled for a moment as the creature named Kevellar-arrensas struggled against a binding not visible to the naked eye. But his struggle diminished as the binding grew; in the end, not even his eyes were free to move.

Bereft of the shadow and the demon that led them, the Allasakari did many things. Some fled toward the doors to the west, and some to the galleries; some drew weapons other than the daggers that had, with the shadow, evaporated; some formed up into a loose, defensive line; some attempted to draw upon the power of the God they worshiped, pulling out their ebon amulets and holding them aloft in angry defiance.

But they all died.

For in the galleries, behind the Exalted, waited the shadowed forms of the Astari. Masked and clothed in a uniform that was a simple, dark ash, they leveled crossbows—or longbows—and fired into the Allasakari below. No one spoke to stop the slaughter.

Devon waited until the last bowstring quivered into silence before he looked up at the gallery. The Exalted—the three!—stood as they had when they'd stepped forward; they were serene in expression, but to his eye pale, and all of their attention was focused upon their captive.

To either side of each of the Exalted, the Astari were putting up their weapons. A few left the gallery, no doubt to rummage among the dead and the dying to ensure that their work was finished.

Devon did not speak, but waited. The knives of the compact were sharp and quick—more merciful than their victims deserved. They rose and fell thrice in the lights, glinting; there was little struggle.

At last, a lone figure detached himself and came to where the Kings' Swords kept their vigil. He bowed, very low, to Verrus Sivari. "As you commanded," he said softly. It was hard to place the voice, and hard to guess the age of its speaker; the Verrus did not bother to try.

"You knew of this in advance," he said coldly, "and you passed no word to the Kings' Swords."

"The Kings' Swords are not our responsibility," the man replied, but smoothly and almost deferentially. "The Kings are. Between us, we have ensured their safety. Had there been time, we would have warned you."

The Verrus said something rude, but not at all unprofessional; he had been, after all, a soldier. "You had the time to roust the Exalted," he said coldly. "You had the time to inform us."

"Although I owe you no explanation, Verrus, I will say this: The Exalted were ready and waiting for us; *we* did not go to *them*. Had that been necessary . . ." He shrugged; they both knew what the lost time would have meant.

There was a long pause before either man spoke again. When one did, it was the Verrus. "The Queens?"

"The Queens," the Astari said, with infinitely more regret in his voice, "are also not our responsibility."

Silence.

Verrus Sivari said nothing to the Astari. Instead he turned and began to give orders; there were few to give. His men left with haste in a grim and orderly silence that was punctuated only by the sound of armor moving. He led them.

Devon stayed behind. "The Queens?"

"There is fighting in their quarters," was the quiet reply. "You did well."

The ATerafin glanced at the bodies of the fallen, and then, at the solitary figure that remained standing in the room's center, a twisted statue that paid homage to the power of the Three. The demon.

"The Exalted had the foresight to bring a seer with them," the Astari said softly, noting where his companion's glance strayed. "Together they will question the creature before they return him to his dominion." The smile in the words could be heard but not seen; Devon was glad of it.

"You took a risk," he told his leader.

"There are always risks," was the soft reply.

Devon nodded absently as he looked the room over, and then smiled oddly. Kallandras was nowhere to be seen.

11th of Corvil, 410 A.A.
Royal Healerie

Princess Mirialyn sat in the healerie with a serene impatience that the healer, Dantallon, found far more frustrating than the usual argumentative demands that injured royalty—or worse, the injured Swords officers—usually displayed. It was clear that she wished to leave, and it was also clear that she took to heart his missive and remained abed, where disinfectants and feverweed could be readily administered by his overworked apprentices. She offered no resistance, but her eyes burned holes in the closed doors, and her people came and went, in and out, out and in, with the same annoying overpoliteness that their leader herself showed.

She had taken three wounds, and it was the last—an abdominal wound that had pierced the stomach wall—that had the best chance of causing her death; he had tended it with the skill he could spare, but it was not severe enough to demand his full attention—not now, with so many close to death. The other two, a thigh wound and a grazing of the skull, were messy but easily dealt with by Cadrey and Lorrison.

The infirmary was lined with beds, and the overflow room with cots and bedrolls; three of The Ten had donated the services of their healers in the cause of the Crowns. They were sorely needed.

"Well, Miri," Dantallon said gruffly, "I don't suppose this will teach you to wear proper armor." The bandages beneath his hands were reddened, but the wound was clean and cool.

"No." She stared at the wall, her eyes reflecting light that poured in through the unshuttered wide windows. "In two days, I may rise?"

"Two days, yes."

"Thank you." She turned as the door swung open, tensing slightly. The golden-haired, golden-tongued bard of the Queens' court sauntered in, lute in arms, hat askew.

Dantallon studied the younger man's gait, and then, as the songster drew close enough, the lines of his face, the color beneath his eyes. He remembered the last time he had tended Kallandras. As if aware of his appraisal, the bard bowed ironically, strumming the chords of a melody at once familiar and unknown.

"Healer Dantallon?" Cadrey was at his sleeve, his sleepless eyes darting in the direction of Verrus Sivari.

This, Dantallon thought, as he turned away, *is why a Verrus is never supposed to see action.* And this was what he expected from the ACormaris. People in positions of responsibility did not look at near-death as a good excuse for dereliction of duty, and they usually thought of the interference of the healer-born with little more love than they did the injury that had brought them to the healer. Verrus Sivari, an able-bodied man with a razor-sharp mind, was unfortunately also a *doer*.

"Verrus Sivari," he began, as he nodded poor Lorrison away from the Verrus' side. "It's good to see you awake."

"Don't start with me," the Verrus replied shortly. "I've business to attend to, and I don't have the time to laze about like a mewling child with a scraped knee."

"The report that has come from the Kings' Swords—and from the office of the Kings themselves—has indicated that you were instrumental in winning the battle in the Chamber of the Graces; my commendations."

"Dantallon—"

"I have, however, taken the liberty of addressing the Kings personally about the nature of the injuries sustained by their officers in the battle."

"*Dantallon—*"

"And the Kings have ordered you remanded into *my* custody until *I* deem you fit to return to duty. There will, unfortunately, be a debriefing; the Kings will come shortly, and you will be removed, for a time, into the ready room. You will then be returned to the infirmary, where you *will* follow the instructions of my apprentices. Is that clear?"

"Perfectly." The word came from between teeth closed so tightly Dantallon wondered if the jaws would survive the pressure. They'd better; he'd enough work to do as it was without adding spoonfeeding a man with a broken jaw.

"Good."

"Healer?"

"Yes?"

"The Queens?"

Dantallon smiled softly, and let the edge wear away from the exhaustion and the irritation of the day's long labor. "The Queens are safe. Queen Marieyan ACormalyn was injured, but recovers well." Her recovery, unfortunately, cost the healerie their most powerful healer; she had been very close to death. "Queen Siodonay AReymalyn was among the Swords that your men joined in battle. She accounted well for herself, as befit her former House."

The Verrus sank back into the bed and let the fight go, at peace. Dantallon knew it wouldn't last, but he was willing to take advantage of it for as long as it did.

Kallandras regarded the Princess as she sat against the wall behind the narrow bed that was to be her home for the next two days. She was fair; the color had been leeched from her by the wounds she'd suffered. But her hair was still glorious, still bronze, although it had been sheared by a careless healer in order to add a few stitches. Her eyes were darker than usual.

"You look lovely as always," he said, bowing.

"And you speak smoothly as always—but one hopes a little less accurately." She smiled ruefully. "I hate it here. Give me word of the court."

"The court?" Kallandras laughed and began to absently coax a peaceful collection of notes from Salla's strings. "The court is in a state of what could politely be called chaos. The Ten are in session, and the session is, from the sounds that can be heard *outside* of the Great Doors, quite grim. Accusations are flying of a less than delicate nature."

"How . . . interesting." She watched his fingers play against the strings as if the movements, and not the resulting sounds, were the art. "What other news, Kallandras? Does Sioban send word?"

"She is quite occupied," he said. "The tales of the Allasakari are more legend than history to all but the trinity, and even among the Churches, it seems that knowledge of the known rituals are limited to a few. The Exalted, for example, learn them as part and parcel of the antiquities."

"You speak that word lightly."

"Antiquities?"

She frowned. "Exalted."

"Ah, Mirialyn. Your looks and bearing are wasted upon you; you should have been born old." The smile, light and playful, fell from his face; his eyes darkened.

"What word?" she said, leaning forward.

His reply, when it came, was in tone and timbre a private thing; the bustle of the healerie did not touch or weaken its whisper. "I chanced upon a member of the Order, summoned to the Kings' Council." He paused. "We are . . . friends, of a sort."

"And?"

"ACormaris," he said, all playful flirtation gone, "Sioban and the Bardic Order now rifle through every bit of folklore and child's wisery looking for answers to an old and dangerous riddle."

"Riddles," she said softly. "You speak them. Be blunt."

"*Vexusa*," he replied, and the sound of the word was ugly.

She sank back. "I . . . had heard rumors. What of it?"

"It is upon that place that Averalaan is built."

She said nothing, her face set in an impassive mask. "History," she said at last, the word neutral, "hides much when the cataclysm is great."

He shrugged. "In this world, a simple bard does not judge the likelihood of the information he receives; if the counsel of the wise says it is so, he believes it."

"A simple bard." Her eyes flickered impatiently. "Then we must be about our business."

"Not we, ACormaris. *I.* Your business is healing."

"Kallandras—the rest."

He sat upon the side of the bed, leaning close to her as if the bardic voice did not guarantee him the privacy he desired. She made no protest. "They captured the leader of the assault upon the Hall of Wise Counsel."

"The kin."

"Yes."

"And?"

"He is gone, but before he was banished, he told them this: That the ways to the Shining City have been unmade."

Her face was whiter than the sheets upon which she lay. "The Shining City," she said.

"You know your legend. It would appear that Vexusa was not built upon this spot without reason. There is a darkness that waits."

"And there were roads . . . to this place?"

"Which were unmade."

"Unmade?"

"A technical term. Erased from existence as if they had never been. It *is*, according to the Council of the Magi, quite possible—if theoretically so—when enough raw power is available."

"Meaning," she added, "that no member of the Order could do it."

"Meaning that no member of the Order would confess to such an ability, no."

Her brow arched as she studied his face. "The Shining City—if such it is—has been sealed off beneath us?"

His smile was sympathetic—and false; she knew him well enough to know that the news disturbed him greatly. Or rather, she knew him well enough to know that he had never seemed so ill at ease as he did by her bedside in the healerie. "Yes," he said, gazing past her to a point beyond the wall's plain surface, "it's like being on a boat with a very thin bottom while the dragons of the deep circle at their leisure." He shook himself. "The mage—the member of the Order—has been out with the most powerful of his brethren, digging—if you can call such destruction mere digging—through the ground upon which the city stands. They go so far, and no farther—a barrier is there that *cannot* be breached by the full extent of the power they can summon. In combination." He paused. "The Exalted have been summoned, but they must hoard their power; the questioning of the demon was not lightly undertaken."

She paled, and then paled further, clutching her side. "It's worse than that, isn't it?"

He nodded gravely; even injured, one did not condescend to Mirialyn ACormaris. "The undercity is protected by the very power of the God himself. Not his followers, not the kin, but the *God*. The Lord of the Hells—whose name we will not speak—has set one foot firmly upon the mortal land—and if we cannot find a way to breach the barrier that divides his Shining City from our own, he *will* walk the world again."

Chapter Twenty-Four

12th Corvil, 410 A.A.
Council of The Ten

THE COUNCIL OF THE Ten was never peaceful; called once a quarter at most—and often only once a year—it consisted of posturing, politicking, the veiled threats that are often exchanged as pleasantries among people of power. Trade affairs were sometimes ironed out—when a foreign power such as the Dominion of Annagar was involved, The Ten usually underwent the effort necessary to achieve a semblance of unity—but the minutiae of the affairs of the Kings' Councillors were usually conducted in secrecy among the Houses involved.

The Council of The Ten, of course, was called in privacy, but not in secrecy; it gathered in the Halls of The Ten upon the Holy Isle, and anything said in a wing of the royal buildings was said for the royal ears, or worse: the Astari. But it had been privately agreed—among The Ten—that such a gesture, in a state of such emergency, was of the utmost necessity.

The Terafin sat quietly in the chair reserved for her use. It was not at the head of the table, but in the Council it was considered to be the seat of power; it was held, after all, by Terafin. The Morriset, replete in the elegant pomposity of his office—it could be said that Morriset and Terafin were not friendly—stood speaking in a corner with The Berrilya; they were not bantering.

The Korisamis sat in silence, observing her as she observed him, and then moving on to watch the rest of the room.

This was the second meeting of the Council of The Ten. The first meeting had had a most unsatisfactory conclusion for The Terafin—for the Council—and in the end, a recess had been called. Now, nine of The Ten stood or sat, waiting upon the final member: The Darias.

He had much to answer to Terafin for; the graves of the dead were still fresh, and the scent of broken earth reminded her, as she kept the Three Day vigil, of all that Darias had cost her House.

He claimed his innocence; she was not, in the end, a poor enough judge of character to fully disbelieve him. But if innocent, he was ignorant, and in his ignorance, he had failed in his responsibility both to his House and to the Crowns.

To fail either duty in a minor way was the privilege of the powerful—but to fail either in a noticeable way was almost always the end of that power.

The Terafin had had only an enemy's respect for Darias; he was clever, if deadly, and had always played his game well, even if, in living memory, he had played it against Terafin. The rules that governed The Ten, unwritten and unspoken, had been the razor's edge over which he had balanced with such precise care. Until now.

What she wanted—if it could be gained without cost to the kingdom in such a perilous time—was blood for blood spilled.

Time passed; The Darias had still not arrived. The nine sat. It pleased The Terafin little to wait upon her enemy, but pleased her greatly that the other eight were subject to this insult as well; any leverage at all that she could gain in her case against Darias—especially when it was an outright gift—she would take.

But when the doors opened and the tenth man entered the room, it was not The Darias she had known for all of her tenure. This man was stooped and fair, and obviously of a more sedentary bent than the tall and dark Darias. He was younger, perhaps by fifteen years, and his face was round and bearded, where The Darias' had been lean and long.

But he wore the family crest, and although the coat fit him poorly, it was obviously his right to bear it; no one, especially not so nervous a man, would dare to enter this hall in that crest otherwise.

He came to the seat of Darias, and stopped behind it, closing his eyes a moment as if to gather himself. And then, shaking his head and squaring his shoulders, he stood to his full height—which was not, after all, so insignificant.

"Forgive me," he said, speaking out of turn and with a shaking voice. "I am Parsus ADarias." He bowed.

It was The Morriset, eyes gleaming, who raised his chin and brow at the same time. "ADarias?"

"The Council of Darias has sent me to take the seat of Darias at this time. Were circumstances different, the seat would be left vacant."

"What game are you playing?"

He turned to face The Terafin, and his cheeks were slightly pinker, although he would not meet her eyes. "Terafin," he said, bowing very low indeed. "We play no game. The nature of your accusation was made clear to us after the Council of The Ten met yesterday." He raised a hand, forestalling her speech—which was dangerous in and of itself. "We do not doubt your word. What you state must have happened the way you stated it did; you are The Terafin—you know the cost better than any of The Ten and you would not have brought news of this House altercation into royal play were the threat not so great.

"There is no defense that Archon ADarias can make for his actions."

There was a shocked hush in the room.

"Yes," the man said, although he did not look around to see the faces of The Ten. "Archon ADarias resigned in disgrace from the title of Darias, and the seat." He lifted his face then, and it was clear to all who saw it that the speaker felt the loss keenly. "His wishes for the disposition of his lands and his title have been set aside; there is no longer an heir to the seat, and until such a time as one can be chosen, I will rule as regent."

"And the—and Archon ADarias?"

"The First Day rites have been observed by the Priests of the House chapel." Parsus ADarias seemed to curl in on himself, losing the height that he'd momentarily gained. "Terafin, the assessment of your claim against Archon ADarias is under review. The House will reach its decision shortly."

14th Corvil, 410 A.A.
Cordufar Estates

"ATerafin?"

Devon looked up from his earthen perch, and set his handglass aside. Jewel Markess stood quietly before him, waiting for his attention. How long she'd stood, he didn't know; she was not usually given to being so quiet.

He well understood why, however.

Cordufar was a gutted ruin. What had once been among the finest of the city estates was gone to blackened wood, stone, and ash; twisted strips of lead and shards of crystal from the towering windows of the great hall had been flung as far as the ring of trees that marked the midpoint between the front gates and the manor itself.

Jewel stood outside of that ring, her hands behind her back. Crossing the gated threshold onto Cordufar lands had quieted her in a way that he did not like, but knew better than to ask about.

Still, quiet or no, she was company of a sort that he rarely had; companionship was not a part of the nature of his calling. At the gates, the Kings' Swords were gathered in a thin line; gawking spectators were politely ushered about their daily duties as quickly as possible. Unfortunately, the citizens of Averalaan had much to stop and gawk at; such a ruin, in so short a time, without the fires and their attendant warning plumes of smoke, was a thing of wonder, no matter how ugly.

"What have you found?" he asked calmly, rising from his crouch at the base of an old ash tree.

"You'd better look yourself," she said, her eyes wide and unblinking. Then, as if to prepare him for what he might find, she added a single word. "Bodies."

"Show me," he told her, hastily wrapping the shards of glass that he'd cut free of the bark and sliding them into his shoulder sling. Silent, she nodded and led the way, treading carefully and quietly across the short grass. He watched her back, as he watched the ground, the walls, and the shadows at play, thinking her too quiet.

I shouldn't have brought you here. He was surprised at the thought, and then wry: it made him realize the difference between their ages. Jewel had proved herself more than a worthy ally; she was necessary. While he was deliberate, analytical, and deductive, she was more often the successful one when it came to unraveling mystery. She could stumble across things of great import while daydreaming.

No, that was unkind.

She could—

He stopped as she slid into the wreckage of what appeared to be a large closet at the base of the stairs. A servants' supply of some sort, wooden, shattered by the fall of the ceiling above. "What are you doing?"

"There are stairs," she said softly.

Stairs. He wanted to ask her how she had chosen this, of all the piles of debris to search, but forbore. He knew her well enough to know she had no answer. But if there were stairs here, they were not a part of the plans that the Lord Cordufar had registered with the city officials.

Without another word, he began to lift wooden planks and slats; she was smaller than he and better able to slide into nooks and crannies. At last, the darkness opened up before him, alleviated only by the flicker of a small torch.

"Get a lamp," he told her as he looked at the steep angle of the very narrow flight of stairs.

"You won't need it," she replied.

"Jay."

But she shook her head, and even in the poor light she looked pale. "I'll get the mage to meet you."

"I don't want the mage yet. Get me a lamp and follow." She hung back, and after a moment, he realized that she had no intention of obeying his order.

Not even in the subbasement of the market authority had she hesitated, and she had had a clearer idea of what they faced there than he. "All right," he said quietly. "Get Member APhaniel." He took the torch and made the descent into darkness, the rough texture of hewn stone against the palm of his left hand. Halfway down that narrow flight, he stopped.

Bodies, she had said, in a peculiar, subdued voice. The stench of the unburied came up from the hidden ground with a force that stopped movement and even breathing for a moment. These were not newly dead, these bodies. He turned to look up the stairs, but she was already gone.

14th Corvil, 410 A.A.

Lady Leof of Faergif was in her element, thanks to the quiet intervention of the Princess Mirialyn ACormaris, and in her heart of hearts, she cursed the younger woman for bringing the duty to her—and for being three full days late in her report.

She knew why, of course; Mirialyn carried word privately and personally, and trusted it with no messenger; she had been abed after the mysterious battle near the Hall of Wise Counsel; she spoke against the wishes of the Astari, which was never wise; and she demanded secrecy and silence until the Crowns themselves agreed that the information—any of it—was safe to convey. But three days were three days. And in that time, no proper respect had been paid, by the Breodani to the Breodani, for the death of Stephen of Elseth.

Stephen of Elseth.

Her hands were clenched and whitened; she opened them slowly and watched as they shook. It was not the first of Veral; the year—and the Hunt—had not been called. But the sketchy report that the Princess had, in her concern, delivered was every mother's nightmare. Every Breodani mother. The Hunter's Death had been in the Terafin manse.

Finding a dress of the appropriate color had been very, very difficult—for the Essalieyanese did not wear mourning in the fashion of the Breodanir, and black was considered too dour for anything but the most sophisticated of events. And today, although it was after the fact, she was Breodani; nothing—no physical distance, no passage of time with its gentling of memory—separated her from the home of her youthful dreams. Her broken dreams.

There were some wounds that never healed; they became scabrous, but they bled. How, she thought, as she girded her shoulders with the black, plain wrap that she had ordered made—and quickly—had it come to this, here?

There was a knock at her doors. She looked up, and then rose; she had sent her servants away for the day because she could not bear to have them at her side, with their stiffness and their perfect manners and their complete lack of understanding, no matter how well-intentioned they were.

Lady Helene of Morganson stood in the open door. She, too, wore black, but her eyes were red in the pale stillness of a slightly puffy face, where Leof's eyes were dry.

You've had enough of my tears, she thought, the anger waking slowly.

"Here," Helene said softly, holding out a long length of black lace. A veil.

Leof shook her head.

Helene smiled for the first time that day; it was a joyless expression of strength. She herself had chosen to openly give God her tears as the accusation that they were.

"How could this happen?" Helene said softly, in the quiet of a room they hallowed with their grief.

But Leof shook her head. "The carriage is waiting," she told her compatriot. "Or it had better be."

They were expected, of course; Lady Faergif understood the social necessity of appointment. She also understood that, as a foreign dignitary, she was granted leeway in her demands, be they reasonable or no. The right-kin of Terafin had been reluctant to have visitors so soon; the Lady Leof of Faergif had been most insistent.

In the end, The Terafin herself had intervened—although why, and why in favor of the Breodani over her right-kin, Leof did not know.

But she understood why Gabriel ATerafin had been, in his quiet and determined way, so complete in his desire to avoid the company of diplomats. The front gates were in disarray, and although there were men and women who toiled upon the grounds removing timber and stone and glass, one wing of the manse looked as if it had been crushed by a God's mace.

And the God, their God, did not wield a mace.

She frowned. "Helene?"

"I don't know what damage He might do to such a place," Lady Morganson replied softly. "When has the Hunter ever left his forest?" But she stared at the gates and the broken walls a long moment before shaking her head. "Fire," she said, pointing.

"I saw it," Leof replied. "I think it unlikely that it is His work." In spite of herself, she felt curiosity come, keen and unlooked for. The rumors at court were fierce.

But Helene saved her by catching her arm and walking them both toward the guards at the gate. They were stopped—given the state of the manse itself, it was not unreasonable—but when they gave their names, the guard bowed quite formally.

"I am Arrendas ATerafin," he said gravely. One of The Terafin's Chosen. "We were expecting you. If you would follow me?"

The Chosen rarely acted as guides or escorts for visitors of little import. Leof and Helene exchanged glances and then nodded quickly. He led them through the main doors into a foyer that stretched to a height that was uncomfortable to look at—and undignified, which neither Lady could be said to be. But they were not, as they had been on previous occasions, left to wait in the sitting rooms to the east or west of the foyer; they were taken into the manse itself.

They thought little of it; the foyer was obviously being rebuilt from the ground up, and it was no place to leave the men and women who had power enough to request, and receive, an audience. But as they passed door after door, following a long hall; as they passed mirror and fountain and open sky; as they stopped at checkpoint after checkpoint for a cursory inspection, they realized that they were not being taken to wait.

Ah, Leof thought, and the thought was bitter. *You are cruel, Hunter Lord.*

Because she knew, the moment before six of the Chosen moved into two small rows of three guards each before a closed door, that she was on the verge of realizing a long-held goal: She was about to meet The Terafin for a personal audience. And this one day, this one occasion, neither she nor Helene could do anything political or financial at the behest of the Breodani.

The Terafin was a younger woman than either Leof or Helene—but she was used to wielding power; more power, financially, than the entire Kingdom of Breodanir. Yet she was standing as they entered the room, and she nodded quietly, holding her head down a moment in respect.

"Lady Faergif. Lady Morganson."

"Terafin."

"Please, be seated. I know that you have come to attend Lord Elseth, and I do not wish to keep you longer than I must."

They sat; what else could they do? But Leof of Faergif felt a chill that the ruins of the manse and grounds had not put there. The silence was profound and awkward.

"I have always found the women of Breodanir to be perceptive, perhaps because Breodanir only chooses to send its best," The Terafin said at last. "How much do you know of what has occurred upon these grounds?"

The two women, Helene and Leof, glanced at each other out of long habit; it was Leof who replied. "Why?"

"I have been studying what little we know of Breodanir," was The Terafin's quiet reply. "Lord Elseth will not speak to anyone, and although he has been seen on the grounds, he leaves his dogs. He will take his meals, but he eats poorly."

The glance that Helene and Leof exchanged was longer and more painful. "That is . . . as it often is."

"Always is," Leof said.

The Terafin nodded. "So we understand. But I owe Lord Elseth—and his huntbrother—a great debt. I cannot repay Stephen of Elseth; we do not even have his body." She rose, turning to stare at a painting that was windswept sky and open plain without the clutter of any moving life; there were no windows in this room. "And I confess, Lady Morganson, Lady Faergif, that by my understanding of the law of the Breodanir, I will owe Lord Elseth and his family far more than I can ever repay them. We all will."

Silence.

Then Lady Faergif spoke, her voice a hush of cool, cool words. "You do not intend to allow him to return." It was not a question.

The Terafin's brows rose a fraction, and then she smiled, the expression at once rueful and mirthless. "I will offer you honesty. If it came to that, no." She turned her face to the painting again, as if to find some solace in isolation. "But it will not come to that; Lord Elseth knows what is at stake."

Leof snorted. "He's a Hunter Lord. He cannot know what is at stake."

"Leof. He knows—as all Hunters know—that he will lose Elseth if he does not return for the King's Call at the Sacred Hunt." The set of Helene's lips were grim.

"He is," Leof replied, "wild with grief. He does not see his duty or his responsibility clearly."

"Leof—"

"No, Lady Morganson. Lady Faergif is correct. He *is* wild with grief. I think he knows what he will—what he must—lose, but he does not care. I have rarely seen a man so close to his own death before." The Terafin was silent a moment, and then she said, "At night, he keens like an injured animal. He will not see Alowan, although he was wounded. No one touches him. Even the mute companion—the girl—he shuts out."

"And you are so concerned with his welfare that you risk exposing secrets to us?"

"Yes," The Terafin said flatly. "Because I believe that he is necessary. The battle that began here a week past has in no way ended. I am sorry, Lady Faergif. But the risk that we face is graver than you know. You worry about the sorrow of one man; I worry about the lives of the entire city.

"The entire Empire." She paused. "You sat, each of you, in judgment. You made decisions that profoundly affected the lives of the commoners in your demesnes." Her voice was softer, but only slightly. "I make no apology to either of you; you know how power cuts.

"But if you, upon that hallowed seat, had the choice between the death of a man and the death of the kingdom, can you tell me, honestly, that you would not choose the man?"

"A child's question," Leof replied tersely. "For there is no situation—" She stopped, suddenly.

The Terafin's eyes were a very dark color, some trick of the light perhaps. Grudgingly, so grudgingly, Leof of Faergif bowed her head. "We do not choose the Death," she said at last, her voice faint. "The Hunters and their brothers make that choice when they take their oaths."

"They take their oaths when they are eight," was The Terafin's cool reply. "And Lord Elseth is no boy of eight."

"Stephen of Elseth—according to those of my Chosen who were in a position to see it—chose his death."

"The Hunter chooses," Helene said, correcting The Terafin gently.

"That is what I read, yes. But Arrendas ATerafin—the man who escorted you to these rooms—says otherwise. The Hunter Lord faced the Death; he ordered his companions to run, and they did. But not for very long, and not very far.

"Stephen of Elseth left his companions, and his Hunter; he traversed the ruins of the foyer, and there set the horn that he carried to his lips. That horn brought the Death; it seemed clear to Arrendas that that horn summoned its attention.

"I do not pretend to understand the bond between a Hunter and his brother. But it is clear to me that Stephen of Elseth died to save his Hunter's life. It is equally clear to me that the Hunter, thus abandoned, lives only to Hunt his brother's Death." She gestured, sudden in the motion, her hand rising and closing at the same time. The painting, wild cloud and windswept grass, began to shift in its simple frame, contorting and changing in a swirl of pale color until it contained a seascape: the mild waves lapping against the walls of the harbor city. And centered there, sword lifted in a salute or gesture of defiance, stood the cenotaph of Moorelas, the last of the heroes of the past age.

Leof and Helene gazed at the picture almost in awe, aware only now that its handiwork was that of an Artisan.

"His enemy," The Terafin said starkly, staring at Moorelas' graven visage, "is our enemy."

They both knew of whom she spoke, and they paled, and they did not demur again. But Leof of Faergif rose. "Terafin," she said. "We will see Gilliam of Elseth now. I ask that you clear a space on the manor grounds, leaving only the green grass and the tall trees. We are not Priests; the Priests do not travel. But bring an unadorned altar, and leave it where we might approach."

"This cannot be done in a day."

"Then do it in two. We will wait."

"My sources believe that half the family council was destroyed before suitable intervention arrived. The Darias—ah, forgive me—Archon, had put out a call for members of the Order, but those members were delayed for reasons that are not clear."

The Terafin closed her eyes and leaned into the high back of her chair. "He knew his council was infiltrated."

"He must have—but he must have reached that conclusion only yesterday, after the Council of Ten began discussions on the Darias affair." He paused. "There will be no threat from Darias to any House for at least three years—but if the damage is as I suspect, it will be closer to thirty. There's only one man who can rule the House, but he was Archon ADarias' choice. The House will do everything it can to avoid the stigma of choosing him heir."

"Good."

Morretz fell silent as he watched his lord. "Amarais," he began, his tone greatly changed.

She raised a slender hand. "Don't." She rose. "Have Devon and Jewel returned?"

"They are cleaning up, and will report within the two-hour."

"So we know what happened to the missing servants," Devon said softly. "We suspect that the slaughter started a week ago—not more, but certainly not less." The set of his face was grim and pale. Jewel Markess did not speak at all.

"There were day servants who did not reside within Cordufar proper. We've spoken with those that survived the fall of the estate at length, and we can ascertain that both Lord and Lady Cordufar were not among the dead." He paused. "Their children were, and recently dead."

"The fires?"

"Killed no one. The deaths occurred before the manse was destroyed."

She regarded him in the silence of the unsaid. He returned her gaze unsteadily, and at last looked away. Jewel had still not spoken, which was unusual.

"Jewel, what do you think?"

The younger girl did not start or jump; she did not blush or otherwise show any embarrassment at her stony silence. Instead, she met her lord's gaze with an impassivity of her own. "I think," she said, in a hushed whisper, "that they have to be stopped. They *all* have to be stopped."

Devon reached out and caught her hand; she gripped his a moment and then relaxed.

"And that," The Terafin said, rising from her chair to signal an end to the interview, "is just what we cannot do. Were you not what you are, Jewel, I would not tell you this. But I value any insight that you might have, however and whenever it might come, and I wish you to feel free to interrupt any meeting that I might have, should any insight of relevance arise.

"*If* we can make our way into the maze that your den used to travel, the mages of the Order—guided by Teos, Lord of Knowledge—believe that we would be able to stop the enemy from completing his ascent. But we have searched, and searched again for a way into the undercity; we have the entire Order, from the fourth circle and up, attempting to break the barrier that the—that our enemy has imposed.

"Not even the combined power of the Exalted has been able to achieve the smallest rupture."

"Can't they call their Gods, the same way the Allasakari have?"

"They can," she said, her expression remote, "but at the best guess of the Lord of Wisdom, it would take twenty years for the Gods to answer in a like fashion. And He believes that if we have twenty weeks before the Lord of the Hells takes Averalaan, we are very, very lucky."

Torvan ATerafin waited by the shrine of the House. He sat, kneeling stiffly in the cool breeze, his hands palm up across his lap, and in them, the scabbard of his partly unsheathed sword. It was not an easy position to maintain; his legs were bent around a scarring wound, and his shoulder throbbed in the wet air.

So many of the Chosen lay dead, their faces shielded by caskets from the up-turned earth. To his bitter regret, he was not among them. Marave, dark-haired and hawklike, was gone, her sword snapped at the hilt, its blade lost; Gordon, Chosen a month later than Torvan, had been accepted into the Mother's arms. Alayra fought death successfully, but it was rumored that she might lose her leg; after the battle, the healer was in no shape to heal; he had called The Terafin back from the path the dead walk. From a path that she would never have touched that eve had it not been for his own weakness.

And Torvan?

A cut in the leg an inch above the knee, a dislocated shoulder, a scrape across the cheek, a broken rib. A gash along the right shoulder. The memory caused him more pain than these.

At his back was the shrine, lit for the coming evening. Leaves and late-falling petals, blown wayward by salt-laden wind, collected upon the altar where Torvan had once laid down arms and armaments. Where he had picked them up again, with pride and quiet confidence, and offered them at once to The Terafin herself, eight years before he had been Chosen.

The Chosen . . .

He had been kept in confinement for three days, the first of which had been spent speaking with the mage, the second with the Exalted. The third day, he had spent in isolation, speaking only to Arrendas, and at that briefly. The rest of the Chosen did not know how to speak with him or to him—and he couldn't blame them. His was the face of the man who had almost assassinated The Terafin.

Jewel had come; he had heard her angry voice through two closed doors. The Chosen that she spoke with remained calm in the face of her anger, and also re-mained adamant: there were rituals and rites to be followed by the penitent, and speaking to the servants—speaking even to the guards—was not among them.

She hadn't liked that much.

He could almost pity the Chosen who had had to deal with her. Ah, he felt the knots in his neck and realized again how tense he was, how stiff. The sun was falling groundward in its daily descent; the color of the landscape was being al-tered by slow degree. Beneath it all, he sat, as he had sat since mid-morning. Waiting upon The Terafin. If The Terafin chose to come.

And if not?

He looked down at the blade in his lap. Looked up at the gates, beyond which lay the city of Averalaan, with all of its possibilities, all of its open futures—none of which included Terafin.

The grass grew darker, and the sky redder; the wind stilled although the air was chill in the dusk. He watched the mosaic of the path, maintaining his posture, his thoughts slowly calming. Did he pray? No; what was there to pray for? Death? Absolution? He could not be certain which of these two would be the easier thing to bear. But he had not spoken with The Terafin since before the battle for the manse; he knew she had survived because Arrendas was kind enough to tell him so.

Wait. There, beyond the low hedge, a faint glow in the darkening sky; the halo of light around a lamp. Someone was coming toward him; someone dressed in simple robes, who walked the path alone. Breath grew scarce as his chest tightened; he bowed his unhelmed head and sat, legs folded, face pale.

"Torvan."

He looked up to see The Terafin. She wore a great cloak, and at that, a fine old one that was far too large for her shoulders. The hood must have hung down her back almost to her waist, and the hem of the cloak itself trailed across the grass except where she lifted it. It was odd to see her so, who always looked so perfect; almost, he thought of a child dressed in a parent's clothing.

Almost. But she was The Terafin. And he was the man who, sworn to her service, had almost killed her. He dropped his head again. "Terafin."

"We have spent the Three Days in our own vigils. Why do you wait here?"

"I wait," he replied gravely, "upon the will of The Terafin, and the will of Terafin."

"Look at me," she said softly, in a tone of voice he had never heard before. It broke something in him, to meet her gaze, but he had never disobeyed a direct order. Her eyes were dark and wide, unblinking, the essence of the coming night. "What am I to do with you?"

He did not offer an answer. It was to receive one that he had waited this day.

"Fully half of my Chosen are dead or dying." The cloak, she drew tight around her shoulders with both hands, curling the collars inward as she did. "And were it not for the creature that possessed you, they might be standing with me today."

He did not flinch as she spoke; these were the very words that he had told himself, over and over again, during the Three Days vigil. But they hurt to hear.

"Shall you be held responsible for the Lord of the Hells? Shall you be held responsible for the reavers? Shall you be held responsible for the Allasakari? I have been to the Shrines that quarter my gardens; this is the last one. At the Shrine of Cormaris, I knew that I must lose you—whether in disgrace, or by your own hand in honor. The Chosen *know* what you did. They know what drove your hand, but just as you, they believe that fighting harder might have somehow spared them your fate. To have you in their midst—"

He lowered his head again, and she snapped, "Look at me!" She let go of the cloak; her hands fell to her sides, curling slightly. "What they believe is wrong. It is simply not true. Were *I* to be met in that darkness, that darkness would have consumed me. Meralonne might have had a chance against it. And even he is not so certain.

"Understand what I am saying, Torvan. I know that what you did was not your choice; I find no fault with you." Her smile was bitter indeed when she saw the look that transformed his face. "But knowing it doesn't necessarily change the wise course of action." She raised a hand.

"At the Shrine of Reymaris, I knew that I must keep you; that the action of the enemy should not deprive me of a man I *know* to be loyal—a man that I chose, and in choosing, did not fail.

"This is what the Kings face," she said softly. "This terrible choice—between the wise and the just. If I keep you, it will weaken the Chosen who are the backbone of my House, and if I condemn you—and we both know that it is death I speak of—I weaken myself."

But he knew, then, what her choice would be, for The Terafin had always chosen to adorn the shrine of Cormaris; of the trinity, it was Cormaris to whom she paid the highest tithe, the greatest respect.

"What would you give for the Chosen?" Her voice was hard. "Would you die to keep them whole?"

In answer, he lifted the sword from his lap, and in a single awkward motion, unsheathed it. He was glad that it was growing dark, because in the dusk he could pretend that her expression never wavered, that her eyes were not reddened. She was The Terafin; the House. In time of war—and such a war as he had never conceived of—she could not be seen so.

The Terafin bowed very low, turning her face away. "You have not failed me," she said softly. "And I will remember it well when this is over. I will send Arrendas to you for the aid that you require." She stepped forward slowly and touched his forehead with the tips of her fingers, pulling away as he looked up.

"No!"

They both turned at the sound of the single, forceful word, the man on his knees, and the woman, in her own way, no less abased. At once, The Terafin drew herself in, her features darkening with a glimmer of real anger.

Jewel Markess stood at the foot of the shrine, hands clenched in angry fists. She wore nightclothing, as if she had jumped out of bed and rushed headlong to the shrine. Except, of course, that the garden was closed and guarded against intruders.

"What-are-you-doing-here?" The Terafin's voice had never been so precise and so even. Jewel took a step back, stumbled, and righted herself.

"I'm here to save him." Her hand shaking, she pointed to Torvan ATerafin.

"He doesn't need saving." It was Torvan who replied, steadying the flat of the naked blade. "Jewel—Jay—"

"Don't talk to me like that." She cut him off, her voice intense, almost gravelly. "Don't look at me like that. How can you *do* this?"

"I serve Terafin," he replied softly. The young woman, unlike the woman in her prime, wore her wildness across her face in a splash of angry color.

"No, Goddess curse you, you serve *The* Terafin." She turned, her hands curled in shaking fists. "You're his leader," she said. "He follows you. He would die for you."

"Jewel, leave. This does not concern you."

"The Hells it doesn't!"

Torvan was shocked. Never once, in all of his days of service either to Terafin as a guard, or to The Terafin as one of the Chosen, had he ever heard anyone speak in that tone to his Lord. He almost rose and drew his weapon, as automatic outrage followed shock. But he did not.

The Terafin was white.

Jewel had the grace to drop her head a moment, and when she lifted it, her voice was even, the anger now beneath the surface of the words rather than riding it. "I'm not ATerafin, Terafin. I am not under your command."

"No, you are not."

Silence. Then Jewel drew a deeper breath, a freer one. "I lost my den-kin to the demons," she said, and every word was sharp and clear. "But I never *gave* any of them up."

"Terafin is not a small den in the middle of a poor holding," was the bitter reply. They both knew that The Terafin had but to walk away to end the conversation—and more. Torvan ATerafin was still of the Chosen.

But this was not the first time the two had come to the Shrine of Terafin in the evening, with much on their minds. This was not the first time that they had discussed the responsibilities of power. The echoes of the past made of the garden a hallowed place within which the truth could not be dismissed.

"No. Terafin is a great House," was Jewel's equally bitter reply, "in the middle of *Averalaan Aramarelas*. Much too good for the likes of me, of us."

"Jay." Torvan again.

Neither woman looked at him. Then Jewel dropped her eyes briefly, and muttered an apology. The Terafin nodded her acceptance—but they both held their anger and their tension, their fear and their guilt, as shields bright and shiny. "You can't let him do this."

"I can't see the Chosen weakened."

"It's not her choice," Torvan said. Again, neither responded.

"You *will* see the Chosen weakened," Jewel snapped back. "Sure, maybe most of them think that Torvan should've been able to stop the demon somehow—but Arrendas, at least, knows the truth. Maybe Alayra knows it now, too. You think those two won't be hurt by this? You think they won't know that you've just given up on him?"

"I think," The Terafin said, speaking as softly as she ever did, "that they will not question me."

"They won't." Jewel's face was set and grim. "But I will. I understand that you don't want your den to look weak. I know that you can't afford to let the outsiders know what you've lost. You call it wise. Sure.

"But I also know that this isn't about just a stolen loaf of bread—it's a *life*, and it's *his* life, and he'll throw it away because you don't want to take the risk." Tossing her wild, dark hair, she walked over to where Torvan sat. Before he could move, she lashed out with her foot and sent his blade skittering into the well-tended grass. "I'm tired to death of being polite and deferential and *political*. You don't want him? *I'll* take him."

"It seems," The Terafin said, in a distant, icy voice, "that you have a champion, Torvan."

Torvan's silence was the muteness of shock.

"Why this one, Jewel? Why Torvan?"

The question surprised him, but it did not surprise the young den leader who, in the end, knew very little about House politics and House power. "Because," she said, "I owe him."

"Oh?"

"When we first came here, he could've thrown us out. He didn't. We'd've lost Arann without him—because we'd have had to play games with time that Arann didn't have."

"Is that all?"

"Yes. No." She looked up and met The Terafin's eyes unflinchingly. "Because he made me understand, at my very first visit to the Shrine of Terafin, that *I* had something to offer the Houses—and that I did understand power. Your power.

"And it's because I understand it that I can't let Torvan die—even if he wants to, even if you think it's best for the House."

The Terafin drew the large cloak tight about her shoulders and turned to face her unarmed Chosen. He was not looking at her; instead, he stared quietly at Jewel. "You must be mistaken," he said at last, although he hesitated in the saying. "My rounds do not bring me to the Shrine of Terafin; The Terafin does not come here with any of her guards except, on rare occasion, Morretz."

"W-what?"

"I've never spoken with you at the Shrine of Terafin."

Jewel stared at him, openmouthed, as the darkness grew.

But The Terafin looked beyond them both, to the Shrine itself, her eyes wide with surprise and sudden understanding. She walked past Torvan, and past Jewel, placing her feet deliberately and slowly upon each flat step as if she walked in a ceremonial procession. Her cloak she lifted gingerly around her. When she reached the altar, she knelt at it, bowing her head into the cool stone.

When at last she stood, she stood taller somehow, as if the prayer had relieved her of a burden.

"Jewel," she said softly, "you were right to come. It has been a long time since things were as clear for me as they are for you. A long time since risk was the only way of life, for me. I want safety; I want certainty—I had almost forgotten that in ruling there is neither.

"Torvan, I Chose you, and I Chose well; you have never disappointed me. If I have—almost—disappointed you, then you are free to leave; any dishonor or disgrace will be mine alone to bear."

He was silent at her words.

"But if you would, I would have you remain as one of the Chosen of Terafin. You know well how difficult it will be; you know the distrust that you will suffer, probably better than I."

She watched him, seeing his answer clearly in the stiffening lines of his face: That he would, as always, bear any difficulty in her name, and for her House. As he stood, he grimaced, unfolding his legs as if they had locked in position; they probably had. It had been a long day, and a cool, damp one.

His sword lay in the grass where it had fallen; he walked over to it, bent, and then looked up at Jewel. His words, The Terafin could not hear, but she could see the embarrassed nod that Jewel gave. It was only a nod; Torvan had already turned to The Terafin. He walked to the foot of the shrine, and she met him there; she opened her hands, and he placed the blade, by the flat, into her palms.

But he stumbled slightly; the edge of the blade cut her hand, and blood welled there.

The Terafin met his horrified stare with a wry smile. She carried the sword as if it were a burden. It was. But as much as he would have liked, he could not take the blade back until she had given him leave, and she did not, but the cut did not deepen or worsen.

"Pride is such a necessary thing in power, and such a dangerous one," she said softly, although it was almost to herself that she spoke. "What you have offered, I accept."

"Your hand," he said softly.

"I know." Very carefully, she returned the sword to its wielder. "It is . . . Terafin. Reminding me."

The question was in his eyes, although he would not speak it. Very quietly, she answered anyway. "I bleed. I don't need to be more than I am; I only need to be all that I can.

"Now go back to your post, but attire yourself appropriately first. I would speak with Jewel a moment in privacy; tell the Chosen."

He bowed very low as he accepted the sword—and what it signified—in silence. This woman, this Terafin, was not one he had seen before; and neither knew if, after this evening had passed, he would see her again.

But he was her Chosen; he stepped away from the shrine, saluted sharply—or as sharply as stiff arms and a broken rib would allow—and then followed her order, leaving the shrine, and the two women, behind.

"His name was Jonnas," The Terafin said, when only the sound of swaying branches remained in the wake of Torvan's passing. "He was, of all things, a cook, and at that not the cook to The Terafin himself, but rather a cook to those who tended the affairs of the House in this manor. Common wisdom dictates that cooks are either too large or too thin, but he defied common wisdom in many ways; he had lived his early years in the free townships, and retained many of their mannerisms. I'm not sure why he elected to serve at a big House.

"He kept the kitchen staff together as if it were a family, and he an uncle distant enough to be allowed to dispense wisdom without the resentment that it usually brings. Dispensing wisdom was one of the things that he did.

"I met him on my eighth day in Terafin, and I liked him. We had little in common—I, noble-born and bred, and he a commoner with no ties, until Terafin, to the nobility, and little enough respect for it. I asked him once why he served a noble House—one of The Ten, no less. His answer was this: It's The Ten that're most uppity; they don't *know* how to get anything practical done. They need me. And a man's got to be needed, he's got to be useful." She shook her head ruefully. "I wasn't," she said softly, "The Terafin then. And not destined to become The Terafin in his lifetime either." She turned to face the shrine, with its bare altar, the darkness of night beyond it now complete.

"I discovered the shrine on my own, when difficulties in Handernesse—the family of my birth—arose. And Jonnas would come to me here, to speak with me and offer me advice on the responsibility of both the House and its Leader. Of family one is born to and family one chooses. Of the ties to either. He was known for his common wisdom, and it comforted me to hear it, because I respected the old man, even if I never told him so in so many words.

"When he died, I was already struggling with the three other possible heirs to the title; there was politics, and in one case, a very messy death. Assassination was not the way that I wished to take Terafin, and I would not use it; I was not involved in it, yet it still left me one less rival.

"But the divisions in the House caused by the death of the man in question— and his young son—were terrible; the manner of death could not be kept from the Crowns should it occur again, and the other Houses were beginning to crowd like vultures at our step.

"And I came to the shrine, as I did when troubled, for it seemed to me that I was going to lose my bid for the House—and possibly my life—to the man who was most ruthless in his quest for power.

"And as I prayed, Jonnas came to me as he always had, and sat, just there, cross-legged and at ease, waiting for what I had to say. And I said, 'But you're *dead.*'"

She walked to the shrine, beckoning Jewel forward. The steps she took one by one, until at last they stood in front of the altar; there, she placed her reddened hand firmly down. "He said, very gravely, 'No, but I will be, if Hellas becomes The Terafin.' Ah, I'm sorry. Hellas ATerafin was the man considered most likely to draw victory out of bloodshed. And most likely to cause bloodshed. We do not speak these names to outsiders.

"I realized then that he wasn't Jonnas, that he had never been Jonnas, and I understood at last what Jonnas—what this one—had said about Terafin, about the spirit of Terafin. I was his Chosen, and I was to rule Terafin . . . with honor." She bowed her head softly to the stone, and then raised it; turning, she caught Jewel's gaze and held it.

"Do you understand?"

Jewel nodded. "Do you still speak to him?"

"No," The Terafin replied, her eyes dark. "I have not seen him in many years. But if Terafin needs his guidance, and no one else can fulfill this role, he comes. Tonight, he called you."

Jewel was silent for a very long time, and when she spoke, it was only partly to The Terafin. "I'm already ATerafin, aren't I?"

"Not yet," was the quiet reply. "For I am The Terafin; the living rule here, and not the dead. Come. It is dark, and we have missed the early dinner hour. Dine with me, if you will."

The fifteenth of Corvil.

The day upon which Stephen of Elseth had planned his departure, in haste, to the King's City. The day by which their safe, if hurried, arrival could be guaranteed, and upon which the fate of Elseth—Maribelle, Gilliam, and Elsabet—rested.

But no passage had been booked or arranged, no horses bought, or wagon for the dogs. And they would not be, Leof thought, as she stood beneath the face of the watching sun. They would not be.

It was not the Hunter's green that either Morganson or Faergif knew. It was neater, warmer; the grass was older and thicker. No spring mud weakened it, no heavy rain, no melting snows. The altar that stood in its center was a flat, stone tablet laid out atop two plain pillars; it had no history, no family of women who came, before and after the Hunter's short season, to pray, to mourn, or to offer silent thanks.

But it was a quiet, private place, and the words that they spoke here, or murmured, the press of warm forehead to cool stone, would hallow it and make of it a space where the Hunter's people might go.

Gilliam of Elseth stood at the periphery of the circle. His dogs were nowhere in sight, and it pained Leof greatly to see their absence. The Hunter's daughter was likewise absent, but she felt she understood that: She was kin to the one who had taken Stephen of Elseth. What Hunter could bear that knowledge, and not resent the fact?

Lady Morganson crossed the green first, carrying the kneeling mats in her arms although they were largely symbolic. Leof hesitated. Gilliam, Lord Elseth was hooded; he wore black, although where he'd found it, and when, she didn't ask. She couldn't see his face, and wasn't certain that she wanted to.

Because she knew what it looked like.

Turning, she saw Helene kneel and touch the altar. The shadows lengthened as the woman who had once ruled Morganson paid her respects to the dead. Gilliam did not move; he stood erect, his hands locked behind his back, his legs planted firmly against the ground. Bearing witness, Leof thought. For Stephen.

It occurred to her, as she crossed the green in her turn, that he was angered by the lack of villagers, the lack *of family*, that followed the Sacred Hunt. That these two women, each offering a woman's respect and the depth of a private grief, could not compensate for the ceremony that Stephen, dying upon foreign soil, had been denied.

She acknowledged, not for the first time, as she knelt and pressed her head firmly against the stone, that there was a reason Hunter Lords accompanied the dead on their final journey from the King's City; that they formed an honor guard and watch against carrion eaters; that they came, by Hunter's Law, from the surrounding demesnes, with their entire families, to pay their final respects. Their grief was a commonality and a binding for the Hunter Lord, or the huntbrother, left behind.

And as she lifted her face, turning it a moment at just the right angle, Leof met the eyes of Lord Elseth. She looked away at once, but not before the image of his face had burned itself into a memory that had never failed her.

She let her forehead sink into the comfort of stone again, and she wept, as she had promised herself she would not do. Because Gilliam of Elseth needed to see tears cried for his brother, and he would not—could not—cry them himself.

But she heard, in the distance, the howl of the hounds, and she knew that they, too, offered a voice to their Hunter.

15th Corvil, 410 A.A.
Vexusa

The screams of the dying were constant.

In the darkness, they did not falter and they did not fade; the kin were adepts at the art of pain, and they kept their victims awake and aware for far longer than any mortal torturer might have. Nor did they dabble in the merely physical, for pain was their vocation, and the causing of it no base thing.

The coliseum of the cathedral was lined with the bodies of the dead—and the bodies of the living, made spectator to the work below. Men whimpered, and women; the children were silent in the face of a terror so large they could not give voice to it. But they knew, for they had seen the truth of it, that their parents would provide no protection at all from the reaving.

The demon that had passed as Lord Cordufar for far too long breathed in the scent of fear-laden darkness, content—or more than content. For *these* souls, these unstained little bits of divinity, had not chosen their final place of rest—but they would not go free; they would know no peace. The Lord of the Hells was close enough to the world that he needed the sustenance of their spirits to continue his journey.

These souls were trapped in Allasakar for eternity.

Sor na Shannen was licking her wounds in the undercity; she was his promised victim when the Gate finally opened fully and the Lord of the Hells walked the earth as freely as his servitors.

"You take your time."

The demon lord turned his head slightly, and then frowned. "Isladar. I would think your work here done."

Isladar came, shrouded in human frailty; only the glint of eyes in the darkness were truly powerful. "Oh? Why?"

"There is *nothing* the humans can do now. We've sealed off the city. The Lord will come; he cannot be prevented."

"I see."

Cordufar hated that tone of voice; Isladar commanded nothing in the Hells; no demesne was his. And yet the Lord valued him highly, and he was not without his power. Power always ruled. Power that did not was incomprehensible. And what you did not understand was always dangerous.

"We were careful before because we needed to take these sacrifices in secret. Now, we have what we need."

"You underestimate, *Karathis*, and you always have."

"Mortal months, and each passing day our Lord grows stronger. Listen well to the upper world; their mages and their Priests cannot pierce the barrier that our Lord has built."

"That barrier delays the Gate's final opening."

"What of it? I tell you, it cannot be breached!"

Isladar was silent a long time, and when he spoke, his voice was a whisper that the screaming almost drowned out. "Remember the Shining City," he said softly. "Remember Moorelas."

Snarling, the demon spat.

"Mortal legend says that he will return to ride again against the dark host when the need is greatest."

"And only you would spend the time necessary to learn what mortal legend says. He is dead," Karathis replied coldly. "Mandaros has long since sent him on his way. And such a one," again a snarl, "is long beyond the confines of *this* world."

"Ah. Then remember, Karathis, the Oathbreakers."

Distant screaming, the warmth of it suddenly vanished.

"Why have you come?"

"To see that your arrogance does not doom us all," was the smooth reply.

"It is clear to me, Isladar, that you do not rule."

"No. Nor do you; we both serve Allasakar."

They stared at each other a moment, Karathis very close to the edge of a challenge that could spend his precious power. But it was Isladar; his game and his purpose were unknowable.

"Bredan could still pierce the barrier," the lone demon said, staring into the roiling darkness of the gate.

Karathis nodded, but grudgingly. "The Oathtaker was called once by his followers, and he did nothing. If he did not assail us when we were weaker, he will not assail us now—and if he does, he will not succeed. Not without warning. These last few days, our Lord has grown strong in his hold here." He listened a moment, gaining a measure of peace from the proceedings below before he spoke again. "The servants of the Oathtaker will find no passage here. Sor na Shannen failed us," he added, with quiet pleasure, "but it matters not; the Spear of the Hunter was meant to kill the Oathtaker's form. It will avail our enemies nothing against the Lord."

Isladar nodded quietly. "But they are working against us," he told Karathis softly. "Let us distract them, brother."

Chapter Twenty-Five

MIRIALYN ACORMARIS RARELY TRAVELED. The Halls of the Righteous Rule were her home, and even when the courts removed to Eveicve for their brief Summer sojourn, she remained behind, watching halls that had been hallowed by history, and seeing to their safety.

Outside of those halls, she almost felt she had no identity; the world, even *Averalaan Aramarelas*, was a place where the lives of others unfolded—others who did not require her protection, her guidance, or her ability to assume responsibility. Or so it had been.

The dirt was loose and lightly packed in piles about the roadway; the cobbled stones had been removed either by soldiers' hands or dubious magic, and lay scattered about as well, across the broken landscape. The gate of the manse protected the site from idle curiosity—it was the ideal place to begin excavations of a magical, and dangerous, nature. Especially since it seemed that it was in Cordufar that the threat to the lands originated.

Three shattered bodies lay beneath a heavy shroud in the early morning sun; they were newly discovered this day, and no one could say with certainty that they would be the last. All other bodies had already been interred by the cooperative power of the Priests of the triumvirate. Such a slaughter as had happened here had never been seen in living memory; even the stories of the grim rule before the Advent were not so terrible in fancy as the dead here had been in fact.

Allasakar. It had almost become a name to frighten small children with; a threat to keep them well behaved, while youthful fancy conjured demons hideous beyond imagining. And now, they were all as children before the threat of the God's return; they bore a fear that was palpable, those who worked these grounds, a fear that was hard to reason with.

Mirialyn was ACormaris. But she still felt the edges of that irrational fear tug at her as she surveyed the grounds. Meralonne worked diligently with members of the Order in the bowels of the house; Devon and his small staff sifted through the artifacts that the mages declared "safe." They were trying to reconstruct the events that had led up to the destruction of the House and the slaughter of the family.

But, privately, Mirialyn had been told that three of the mages trained in delving into such events with the use of magic and an understanding of time that bordered on gibberish had already retreated to the farthest edge of the investigation that the Order would allow.

"Miri!"

The sound of that alto voice was familiar; turning, the ACormaris saw the broad shoulders and tilted, strong chin of a woman known widely throughout the kingdom. "Bardmaster." Mirialyn bowed elegantly.

Sioban Glassen smiled, but it was the smile one offers when in pain, a tightness around the lips and eyes that passes into nothing before it's finished. "We didn't expect to see you," the older woman said quietly.

"Nor I you," was the equally quiet reply.

"I've brought the bard-born," Sioban said. "Kallandras was here yestereve." She paused. "He said that they—we—were needed. If you want him, he's with Devon."

"Devon? Interesting." Miri stared into the harsh clarity of the cloudless sky. "When will it start again?"

"There isn't a set time," the older woman replied, unconsciously wringing her hands. "It just—starts."

"You're certain it's human?"

"Well," Sioban said tightly, "screaming is not a discipline we teach at Senniel, so there might be some small chance that I'm wrong." Pause. "Apologies, ACormaris, it's—"

It came, clearest from the bowels of the manse, but not confined to it. The ground trembled, the ground *spoke*. And it spoke with a child's voice, attenuated, high—the sound of a child, who could not yet speak, pleading and crying. Another voice joined it, a woman's voice, low and loud and hoarse; terrified. They screamed together, woman and child; the one being slowly killed, and the other, forced to watch it all.

Miri turned her face to the heavens in white rage; in a mix of emotions that she could not even name. The air carried the sounds; the people in the streets beyond stopped, as frozen as she.

It went on. And on. And on. And then: a voice.

Ah, I fear she's dead. Come, little mother, you can hold what's left if you like—your son is waiting his turn at the altar.

Silence. Pain too profound for weeping.

Mirialyn ACormaris was white, except where her nails had pierced her palms. She met the eyes of the bardmaster in horror.

Sioban Glassen's eyes were so dark the brown seemed dissolved into the blackness of pupil; it was almost as if she stared into the deepest of night, with no light at all to guide her. Her face was gray, her hands were shaking; the horror that Mirialyn felt seemed suddenly weak by comparison, although why, the ACormaris could not say.

The bardmaster's lips moved, deliberately, slowly, but the sound that left them was taken by breeze, by bardic will, by the working of talent; Miri heard no word.

Jewel's fingers didn't fit into her ears, but she tried to put them there; her hands, cupped tight, were not enough to stop the voices. But once heard, the silence wasn't enough either; memory played them again and again, demanding some response, some action other than cringing or crying or screaming in chorus.

She hated Devon ATerafin, for he worked, and continued to work, all the while the child died—and the dying was long.

"It isn't real," he said, through teeth clenched so tightly his voice was unnatural. "It's an illusion, a delusion—don't give in to it." His face, pale, was beaded with sweat, and his shoulders hunched as if against a gale—but he continued with his work, clinging to it.

But it *was* real. There was nothing illusory about it. She knew it for fact, and the knowledge, harsh and terrible, would not let her slide into Devon's beliefs.

The first time, two days ago, it had not been so bad; the cries had been distant, and only when working in the stairwells and underground was the full force of the torture made evident. Yesterday, it had grown loud enough that it could be heard no matter where in the ruins of the manse you were—and today . . .

"Put it down, Jewel!"

She looked up at the sound of her name—at the sound of the name she despised—and saw Devon's face.

"Put it down," he said again, but not so frantically.

She held a shovel. There were clods of grass and dirt all round her feet, and a shallow hole before her. When she had started to dig it, she didn't know. But it wasn't big; hardly large enough for a small squirrel, let alone a child. A child.

I'm not a child, she wanted to tell him, but she couldn't speak; her throat was full of words and fear and the self-loathing of helplessness. He took the shovel from her hands and threw it to the side without bothering to see where it landed.

I lived in the streets, she thought. *I saw worse than you could ever imagine, you pampered lordling.* But she looked up into the collar of his shirt, the rolled edge of his cloak, and she wasn't so certain anymore; she felt the curve of his arms around her as the world blurred. The boy was whimpering; he was calling his mother. His mother was trying not to scream, trying not to terrify him.

"They have to be stopped," Jewel said. "They have to *pay*."

"They will," Devon answered, his lips close to her hair, her ears. "I swear it by the turning, and by every life I ever have." He lifted her, swinging her legs lightly over his arms, although he was not an overly tall man. "Come. This is not the place for you."

She threw her arms around his neck, not in an embrace, but rather in the sudden abandonment of responsibility that marks childhood, and not until she heard the new sound did she raise her head.

Devon stopped walking, although he did not put Jewel down. They both looked toward the ruins of the gutted manor. There, in a thin line around it, stood men and women of indeterminate age; they wore different styles of clothing, and different colors, but it was clear that they served a single purpose here.

Sioban.

"Who are they? What—what are they doing?" It was Jewel's voice, but so quiet and so tentative that it hurt to hear her speak.

"They're from Senniel," he told her, bowing his head to answer.

"Bard-born?"

He nodded, although he didn't know it for fact. The Astari did not have many connections in the bardic college—the bards were notoriously poor at keeping information to themselves. No matter who it was given to there, the truth, embroidered by song and a change of name or two, always seeped out in song. And in song, there were none to challenge the master bards that Senniel produced. None.

As if to prove the truth of this, the bards began to play, their fingers against the strings of their varied instruments a quiet resistance.

Jewel gained her feet almost shyly, but held on to Devon's arm; together they made their way across the broken ground, listening to the music that in no way masked the screams of the dying.

"What can we do?" Gilliane's voice was strained, although her playing never faltered. She was an elderly woman who had done her traveling apprenticeship on the southern border during the Annagarese campaigns; it had hardened her, in some ways—but not so much that she couldn't feel horror.

"We can drown them out," Tallos offered.

"We could," Sioban said, her bard-voice strained from overuse. "But for how long? They grow louder by the day, and if all of the bard-born singers in the Empire were gathered here, we couldn't sing them to silence for—" She stopped as her words caught up with her. For how long? How long?

"You've an idea," Alleron said, testy as was his wont. He had a reputation to preserve, after all; he was the most feared master in all of Senniel, and it was to him that the youngest and most prideful of the newcomers were sent.

"Not a good one," she answered softly. The screams grew in the silence, wrapped around words that were still recognizable.

"It's better than nothing."

"We can Sing them to sleep."

"You're right," Alleron snapped. "It's not good."

"Then come up with something—anything—else."

There was no silence to think in, no silence in which to gather thought. And then, the youngest of the master bards spoke, his voice cool and measured.

"Sioban Glassen has the right of it. If we drown out the screams, we aren't ending their pain, not even for a moment."

"And Sleeping them will end it? They'll be woken again, sure as sunrise—it'll be that much the worse; the hope, and then, more torture."

"Alleron." It was Tallos—and he, AMorriset. The master subsided. "We do not think clearly. Kallandras, Sioban—forgive us. This is not the work that we thought to do when we first arrived.

"Let us weave a song of Sleep, and let us make it strong. We have fifteen voices here; it will not be so easy to wake the Sleepers while our voices still have strength. And after?" His face grayed. "And after, we will know that we have done all that we can. The triumvirate does not ask for more, and if we are to continue, we *must* not."

He spoke with the voice, and the voice was heard. It reminded everyone present—any who needed the reminder—that to become AMorisset *meant* something.

"Alleron," Gilliane said softly. "You tell this to your students time and again: The voice cannot force a man to do much against his nature. The voice cannot order a man to die. These, we cannot save; accept it."

"I'd give them death, if I could," the master said, his voice as quiet as it ever was.

"Then you would study the lost arts. The dead arts. And you would make of us something other than what we are—if that possibility exists in the here and now."

"I know it," Alleron said, speaking through teeth that would hardly open. "But it must be better than allowing *that*." Pale, he dropped his head into the edge of his harp. "Sioban, forgive me. I—I will speak Sleep."

"It's already done. Come. Let us begin."

Some of the men and women who had been playing set their instruments aside; some did not. The use of the voice did not require music; it did not, in fact, require song, although many of the bardic masters had been taught with song as the medium.

What it required was will, and the peculiar focus of talent, of self, that only the bard-born could call upon.

The members of the Order of Knowledge came first from the bowels of the building that was their study; they moved with the skittish nervousness of fear, of strain. Only Meralonne was calm as he approached the bardic masters, and he bowed stiffly and formally.

"The field is yours," he told Sioban, for all that she was no longer listening. Her face was turned inward, toward the burned ruins, her brow creased in concentration and sorrow. She was the bardmaster; she spoke first, fashioning with her voice the essence of sleep, of the desire for sleep, of a weariness so all-encompassing that not even pain could stand against it.

Tallos joined her, speaking second as was his right; he whispered of dreams, the hidden fount by which the night ruled, the landscape of the impossible, where horror could at any second turn into familiarity and beauty.

Alleron sang; his was the voice of a stern and wise parent pointing the way to bed and sleep, by turns threatening and cajoling.

And when Gilliane sang, she sang of deserved rest, of the softness of sheet against skin, of the comfort of arms against back and shoulder. Of the end of war, when finally, and fully, one could take one's rightful rest.

We are with you. We are watching. We stand guard.

Sleep, precious children, sleep.

One by one the bard-born took up the chorus and verse of the command, weaving into it, as they must, the parts of it that were themselves and their own experience.

So when the youngest, and the last, of Senniel's bard-born masters spoke of endings, he did not speak of sleep.

Into the darkness, he sang of darkness, and his voice rose above the voices of the bards of Senniel College as if they were sparrows, and he the matchless eagle. He called power, his voice was the very thunder; all who spoke shuddered a moment as they heard the force of his words.

He spoke of killing.

He spoke of claw in eye, of sword through heart, of the snap of bone at the back of the neck; he sang of deaths in endless number—quick and rapid, sudden; he told the assassin's tale, not the torturer's.

Behind each word was force, for those to hear it.

The master bards of Senniel College spoke to the humans who were waiting to die or worse, contained by chain or spell or barrier in untold, unseen number. Kallandras spoke to the kin who presided over the ceremonies.

Each found their audience.

The pleading stopped in mid-word, first child and then mother, never to be resumed. A great beast howled, loud and long, with a voice that contained the wildness of forests at the dawn of time, forgotten except in nightmare. A cacophony of human voices erupted, abruptly broken by the sounds of wings, some great bird landing.

Abraxus-karathis! Stop!

The roar grew louder, and the cries fewer; among them, one or two voices were raised in a wail of song, a tremulous giving of thanks, a terrified peace.

STOP! I COMMAND YOU!

But the bardic voice passed into darkness, just as the sound of the dying passed out of it, magnified by the unknown and unseen. The creature that heard its call heard little else; the voice of an angry Lord did not have the command that Kallandras' determination did.

The beating of wings grew louder; thunder clapped air in the storm beneath the barrier. A snarl, a growl; the utterance of a challenge so old words could not contain it.

And beneath it, quiet but distinct, a chuckle.

Very clever.

Mirialyn ACormaris watched the bards as they tended to Kallandras. The youngest—and easily the most attractive—of the master bards lay upon a thin pallet, his eyes wide and unblinking. The land was once again quiet; the bards of Senniel had paid their price and done their duty. For now. The members of the Order were assembled, waiting upon her instruction; she nodded, and they departed to once again comb through this emptied den of changeling nobility. All save one: Meralonne.

"Bardmaster Glassen?"

Sioban shook her head wearily. "I've never heard his voice so strong." In spite of herself, she shuddered. "No, Kalian. Lie back. That's an *order.* You'll catch the fevers if you don't rest now, and you're no mage to handle them well."

"No mage handles the fevers well," Meralonne said gravely, staring at the wan bard. "Might I speak with him?"

"He needs rest, not—"

"Sioban."

She met Kallandras' piercing eyes and then shrugged, wilting as this last responsibility was removed from her. Standing, she winced; she'd almost forgotten what her knees were like in this kind of air. *Who are you, Kallandras?* She looked at him a moment, and he met her gaze unflinchingly. Better not to ask, not now. Later would do, if there was one. She stood back and gave his care to the mage.

"You did well," Meralonne said, kneeling.

"What happened?"

"What you intended, if I heard the voice correctly. The torturer descended upon his intended victims and slaughtered them outright. No torture, no games; just the death. And the death does not provide the God with all that he requires."

"You . . . heard the voice." Kallandras smiled quietly, and then the odd smile dimmed. "They will not stop," he said.

"No. The creature was not allowed to kill them all before he himself was destroyed; the game of sacrifice will continue. But not, I think," he said, looking toward the silent house, "today." He caught Kallandras' hand in his own; the movement was unexpected. "The bards are weary, but at peace for the moment."

"I heard them," Kallandras whispered. "I heard them so clearly I had to shout to hear myself." He closed his eyes.

"We do not understand the nature of the barrier," Meralonne said quietly, for perhaps the hundredth time. "We do not know how it was made permeable to sound, but not light, not spell, not any other physical intrusion. The barrier is not a magic that *we* use."

Mirialyn and Devon ATerafin listened quietly; there were two other observers in the audience chamber, but they observed from the shadows, unremarked on by the three. And each of the three knew who they were and why they were present: Duvari of the Astari, and his boy, come to seek the information that would protect the Crowns.

Devon spoke softly. "They magnified the sounds they wished us to hear."

"It was not only those on Cordufar that they wished to speak to," Miri said. "You were occupied, Devon—but I came through the front gates. I was close enough to them when the noise started that I could see the reaction of the people passing by on the streets." She grimaced and dropped a small sheaf of papers onto the room's only desk. "These are the reports that made it to the magisterial guards. Because of the nature of the reported crime, and the severity of it, the reports were passed immediately to the Courts of Reymaris, and through them, to the Kings' Swords." She ran a hand over her eyes. Before either Devon or Meralonne could ask, she said, "There are just under fifty of them."

"Cormaris' blood," Devon said softly, sitting on the desktop.

"I spoke to the members of the Order involved in the excavations—your pardon, Meralonne, but you were in council with the Exalted at that time—and the screams were growing in volume almost hourly. Sigurne believes that at the end of less than two weeks, a third of the city will be able to hear what the demons are doing in their pits, should they choose that method of . . . attack again."

Meralonne raised a platinum brow. "You managed to get that definite an opinion out of Sigurne? I *am* impressed. Oh, you most certainly can trust it; in fact, she is wont to be conservative when she estimates." He smiled softly. "Matteos Corvel—a mage of the first circle as well—calls her the dormouse."

"That sounds like Matteos. But Sigurne's of the first circle, isn't she?"

"Yes—and part of the Magi as well. But she is unassuming to the point of invisibility at most times; she rarely states an opinion, chooses no side of a debate or argument—but she is meticulous in her honesty. And yet, of all the Council, Sigurne has been the one most diligent in her duties at the ruin of Cordufar, the one least put off by the feeding of the God."

"Of all the Council save one," Devon said quietly. "But we stray. The ploy of the bard-born is unlikely to work a second time. From what I understand of the bard-born, I'm surprised that it worked the first time."

"True."

"Do you think they'll try again?"

"This may surprise you, ATerafin, but I'm not so well-versed on the strategy and tactics of the demon-kin that I can readily answer that question."

"My apologies. I believe that the kin are a summoned creature—and only the mage-born would have that ability."

Meralonne bristled at the implication. "It is a forbidden art."

"Then the Magi have not been vigilant in assuring—"

"Gentlemen." They both looked up at the cool, impatient word. "Let us assume that the demons will pursue this attack; it costs them little—"

"It costs them greatly," Meralonne said. "But yes, they have much to gain. If our efforts are diverted to containing the panic—and the ensuing possibility of chaos and violence that panic will breed, they are that much closer to the safe completion of their task."

Devon stood. "I will speak with The Terafin."

"And she?"

"She," he said, with just a hint of the pride of the House, "will mobilize The Ten."

"Good," Mirialyn replied. "For the Exalted have mobilized their priests and the noteworthy among their congregation; Meralonne has taken the Order in hand; Sioban has called the bards from every town and college within a week's hard ride, with orders to spare no horses."

"And all of that," the mage said darkly, as he stared into the distance of the Hall of Wise Counsel, "will avail us nothing if we cannot find a way to break the barrier down before the creature walks."

The dreams meant something.

"Jay?"

She looked up from the glow of wasted oil in the otherwise darkened kitchen. Carver. "What?"

"You're up again."

Sarcasm took energy, so she nodded instead. "So are you. Couldn't sleep." She paused. "Seen Arann lately?"

"At dinner—he came here." Carver was snickering. "Covered in a dozen bruises bigger than my fist. Says he's learning how to use a sword." Pause. "He asked about you. He thinks you're mad at him."

"What'd you tell him?"

"That you were out chasing one of the ATerafin."

"And?"

"Nothing else."

Carver couldn't lie worth a damn. "Look, how much does everyone know?"

He spread his hands out, palm up, in the shadows. That much. "We're your den-kin," he said, defensively. "It's our business to know."

"It's your business to know what I think you should know. And where the hells did you hear it, anyway?"

"One of the servants told me. The redhead with the gorgeous—"

"Carver!"

"Yessir." He was quiet for a long time. Then another voice chimed in. "Jay?" Finch.

"All right," she said, turning up the oil and brightening the kitchen considerably. "Get your backsides in here." She watched as, one by one, her small den joined her in the kitchen. All of their important meetings were held there; it was a habit that she didn't think they'd break, because she couldn't.

Last came Ellerson, but no one seemed to mind; in fact, if it weren't for the flickering of the light, Jewel would have sworn that Finch actually winked at him. They dragged chairs across the smooth floor, propping them up against walls and the table's edge. She looked at them in the darkness. Saw Arann there and actually felt better about it. Angel, Teller, Jester. Her den.

"It's like this," she said, and haltingly began to describe the days she'd spent working with Devon. Described what she'd managed to eavesdrop on. Talked about the Lord of the Hells without ever mentioning his name. She was no Priest or Exalted; she had no way of protecting herself from his attention.

If anyone in Averalaan did, anymore.

"I can't leave here," Jewel told them softly. "But the usual offer is open." A minute passed, and then more, before she finally exhaled into the welcome silence. They were, by the Gods, *her* den.

"Is there anything that anyone can do to stop him?" Teller. He never walked around the tough questions.

"*Yes.*" The word was out of her mouth before she realized that it was the truth. She *knew* it. Maybe she'd known it all along.

Her den relaxed visibly—as did she. There *was* something. After another minute, she realized that her den was waiting, and she gave them an apologetic smile. "It's the feeling," she said, shrugging her shoulders. "Don't ask me *what.*"

"Well," Finch said, with a false bravado that surprised no one. "Look at the bright side."

"What?"

"If things get much worse, we'll all be here when Moorelas rides again."

"Moorelas is a story," Angel said curtly. "And we're going to need a hell of a lot more than stories to save us."

"Well, Allasakar was supposed to be a story, too! And if he's here, Moorelas can't be far behind."

But Teller said, "Jay?" and they all turned to look at him; his face had that stillness it got when he was thinking—and at that, thinking about something he didn't much like.

"When the Sleepers wake." Jewel laughed a bit weakly at her own humor, and then continued uncomfortably when no one else got the joke. "When Moorelas rides again, the Sleepers wake," she whispered. "'To fulfill their broken oath and restore honor to their lines.'" Her eyes widened then. She pushed her chair back as far as it would go, balancing on two legs while Ellerson frowned.

"It's the crypt," she said. "Mother's blessing, it's the crypt."

"The what?"

But Jewel was already off her feet in agitation. "We were there," she said softly, so softly her voice didn't sound like her own. "That's what they're trying to tell me."

"Can you explain it to the rest of us?"

"Back when we first started exploring the maze, Duster and I—we found one old tunnel that was, well, like a manor hall. It was made of big, wide cut-stone blocks—real high ceilings, pretty frilly engravings, stuff like that. There were mage-lights in the walls. We thought it'd be the perfect place for the den; we'd never have trouble with turf wars again, and we could live in style."

"But something was already living there."

"You never told us about it."

"If I told *you*," she said sharply, "you'd've dragged Lander off on some crazy search for—" She bit her lip as Carver's face paled. Lander. He and Carver had always done point together. "Sorry," she muttered.

"Doesn't matter. Tell us now."

"You remember the old crypt in the Church of Cartanis?"

"Yeah. Plaques on the floor, engravings on the wall, bits and pieces of stone."

"Not those. The big, stone boxes, with the statues on top. The ones the really important people get."

"I believe," Ellerson said, clearing his throat in exactly the way he did when he was about to offer a helpful correction, "that you are speaking of the sarcophagi. And it is not necessarily people of import that receive such treatment, but rather people whose generosity to the Church is measured in appropriate funding. Usually after the fact of their death when their last testament is made public in the Halls of Omaran."

"Ellerson," Angel snapped, "do you have to turn everything into a lecture?"

The domicis subsided with a sharp glare, but Jewel smiled. It helped, to hear him so normal in such a terrible time. "Do forgive the interruption, Jewel. Continue."

"We didn't know what they were. We thought they were just statues, same as always. I didn't think we'd come out beneath a Church—but you know how hard it is to figure out how the underground and the above match up. Anyway, we went to grab a torch—the room was lit—but there weren't any." She smiled bitterly. "It was magic, of course, and magic makes me nervous. Made Duster nervous, too."

Angel swore.

"Right. You *know* what she was like when she was nervous. We had our own small lamp, and we went into the crypt. You couldn't see the ceiling. I don't understand why. It was like—like walking into another world. But you could see these three tombs, and on them, these three statues. The floor was stone, same as the walls, but around each of the three were three thin, black circles, and in each of the circles were words. At least I think they were words. Couldn't read them."

"Did you recognize the alphabet?" Ellerson's voice was slightly sharp.

"No. It was more like pictures than anything else.

"But the words, or whatever they were, were in gold; Duster thought we could pick them out, maybe sell them. I thought we could try tracing a couple, maybe find out if Old Rath could read 'em." Jewel shook her head. "Duster got there first. She bent down, touched the first circle, and *snap*, she was flying across the room."

"That's where she got that burn!"

"That's where." Jewel's smile was bitter again. Mention of the dead was still too painful. "They were *alive*. The one that she'd gotten near—he moved." She swallowed. "They were—they were asleep."

"The Crypt of the Sleepers," Ellerson whispered. "Blood of the Mother. You do not know how lucky you were, young Jewel; there is a God that watches you. I have heard stories . . ."

"Yeah. Me, too. Like about where the Sleepers supposedly fell."

Their silence was—for the den—profound.

"I thought they couldn't be—they couldn't be *the* Sleepers—but they weren't human, Ellerson. They weren't like anything I've ever see. They were taller and thinner and paler; they wore armor that only an Artisan could've made. And—and—they were so *beautiful*." But she shivered, saying it.

"You didn't like them."

"How would I know? They were sleeping."

"Jay," Teller said.

She sighed. "No, I didn't. I don't know how Moorelas could have chosen them to make his final stand with—Moorelas was as close to a god as any man's ever going to be, but even *I* wouldn't take 'em for my den." She glanced sidelong at her domicis. "What is it, Ellerson?"

"Tell The Terafin," he said quietly. "Tell her all."

"But we don't know what it means yet."

"Trust your instincts," he replied.

Trust your instinct. The guardian of the Terafin Shrine had said no less to her, that first night when the dreams had driven her out of the manor.

"Do you know where it is?"

"Could I reach it again above ground, do you mean?"

He nodded.

Jewel glanced nervously at her den and then at the table-top. The silence, not of uncertainty but rather of fear, grew.

"Jewel?"

"I think so."

He raised a brow. "This is unlike you," he said gently, although each word was a rebuke. "Where?"

"Beneath the Sanctum of Moorelas." She said it defensively.

The eyes of the den grew wide, and wider still as they watched her pale face.

"I wasn't aware," Ellerson said at last, "that that was possible."

Carver and Angel were still staring at Jewel. It was Carver who spoke at last, and his words were a muttered prayer to Kalliaris. "You fell under Moorelas' shadow."

Ellerson snorted, and there was a very real anger to the sound. "You speak like children at street games," he scoffed. "Will you also not step across the cracks of the cobbled stones?"

"Duster died," was Teller's quiet reply.

20th Corvil, 410 A.A.
Terafin

"Lord Elseth."

At the sound of the voice, Gilliam looked up into the face of Kallandras, the bard of Senniel College. His was an almost welcome face, because Kallandras was one of the few Essalieyanese who still had a connection—however tenuous—to his huntbrother.

Kallandras was not the type of man that Gilliam usually spoke with: He was not a Hunter Lord. But there were no Hunter Lords in Averalaan, and only three of his dogs. Ten days had passed; he walked the edge of anger and an emotion that he did not wish to name—but the anger, like some thin veneer, was cracking. He could not say it, but he did not wish to be alone, and that surprised him, for he had been alone most of his adult life.

No, not alone. Never alone, until now.

Ashfel whined; his master snarled, and Ashfel, subdued, sank back to earth. It was enough that he was there, but it was hard, both for alaunt and master. Espere was nowhere in sight. She came for short periods, and he took comfort in some small measure from her presence—but he always sent her away again.

Because, of course, Stephen would be angry. Disappointed. Maybe disgusted. And although he was dead, it *mattered* what Stephen would think. It was the only respect he could pay the memory.

"I'm sorry if I'm interrupting your practice," the bard said quietly, as he noted the wooden stick that Gilliam held in a sweating hand. It was long; not a sword, but a spear; weighted at the front with iron, the midsection was cut across with a bar intended to keep the gored animal at as safe a distance as possible. It often didn't work.

Gilliam grunted and put up the spear; it was as much a reply as he usually made. But then, because he didn't want the stranger to leave, he added, "No. Nothing to hunt here yet." His voice sounded strange to his own ears.

Kallandras held Salla—at least, Gilliam thought that's what Stephen called the heavy, rounded lute—in his arm. She was quiet.

They stared at each other for a moment, and the moment lengthened; neither man—the friendly, courtly bard, nor the taciturn, grieving Hunter—knew how to start to bridge the gap that silence—and privacy—made between them. Not surprisingly, it was Kallandras in the end who found the words; it was part of his calling.

"I was—unable—to attend the rites." He paused. "Were it not that the safety of the Kings themselves required my presence, I would not have missed them." His ice-blue eyes met Gilliam's dark ones. "We are tied, you and I, at least in this part of the battle. If you would grant it, I would ask a boon of you."

"What?"

"I sang your father's death at the end of the Sacred Hunt. If you would, I would be honored to sing your huntbrother's death."

He didn't know how to say no, and he didn't want to. Stephen's death was one of many to The Terafin and her people, and it wasn't special; there were customs and niceties observed by the Ladies and the villagers of Breodanir that Gilliam finally understood the need for. Song, oddly enough, was not really one of them— but Kallandras' offer was an offer to honor, and Stephen *needed* to be honored.

So Gilliam, Lord Elseth, nodded. "There is no bier," he told the bard solemnly.

"Ah, but there is, huntbrother's brother. You carry it here." And he pointed to the center of Gilliam's chest. "And no fire will raze it, no earth will open to swallow it, no water will carry it upon the eastern boats into the arms of the open sea." As if realizing that he had spoken too intensely, Kallandras began to strum his lute.

He sang.

He sang as he had spoken, but with an emotion beyond even the words. He sang with *understanding*. Gilliam had lost his brother, and the word brother, to a Hunter, meant more than it did to any other men or women; the great Houses could not conceive of its depth, and even the petty nobles, with their hopes of continued lineage, could lose their best and brightest heir and never know the loss that Gilliam felt.

Did mother lose child, who could feel such a void? No. There had been Stephen, and there would never be a man to take his place; Gilliam of Elseth had been cut in half, and would wander blindly through life, for Stephen had been his eyes, his mouth.

Stephen had been his soul.

Gilliam cried out, and it was a type of song, a keening, the wildness of the grief that he felt, expressed in the only way he knew how. Yet even uttering such a cry gave him a measure of peace.

Because Kallandras understood.

We will hunt them, you and I, the bard sang. *We will kill them, you and I.*

Peace.

Two days later, in a silence heavy with the unspoken, Kallandras of Senniel— Kallandras of no other name that Gilliam had ever heard spoken—brought the simple, unadorned spear that had in the days of the Breodanir's youth been the centerpiece of the Hunter's Temple. It was long in shaft, and slender, with no knots that the eye could discern, no flaws; it was oiled against the damp and the dry, but it was not colored. The tip of the spear was made of a metal that might better be suited to jewelry, it was so shiny—but it was sharp enough to cut the finger on, as Gilliam found out.

He started to ask the bard questions, but Espere growled low and backed away as the spear came to her master's hand; nor would she approach him again while he carried it. And when the spear rested in his palms, Gilliam of Elseth felt a jolt, some shock of knowledge, that rendered all questions meaningless.

This was the very Hunter's Spear. He was meant to wield it on the Hunt, and not for anything, not even safekeeping, would he relinquish it now. For with it, Stephen's death would be avenged. Stephen and every other huntbrother who had ever given their lives to the Hunter's Death.

Meralonne APhaniel sat in the office of The Terafin as if it was the only civilized room he had seen in the last month. His hair, fine and long, was braided tight and held above his shoulders; his hands were callused, and dirt, black and rich, clung to the undersides of his chipped nails. He, who never looked tired, seemed exhausted.

And that did not bode well for the interview.

"Terafin," he said, nodding his head instead of performing the required, socially correct bow, "I realize that I am a mage in the employ of your House. But at the moment the Crowns demand my attention and my diligence. It is not easy to come here, and my presence will be missed."

"I would not call you for a message of little import, and indeed I expect that you will see this information to the source that it will best be served by." Her words were brittle.

He sighed, stood, and formally bowed. "Your pardon, Terafin."

"Accepted."

"How may I serve you, Terafin?"

The smile that touched her lips was cold, but it was genuine. "It has come to my attention that there is a colloquial phrase used among the general populace. 'When the Sleepers Wake.' It is used to mean—"

"That something will never come to pass. Yes. I've heard that phrase."

"Good. It is not a phrase that is used in my presence, and not one that I am familiar with, perhaps because I have studied some of the history of the Sleepers."

"You have studied childhood lore," was the sharp reply.

"And yet, you would agree that the Sleepers do exist."

Utter silence, and then Meralonne smiled, and the smile eased the exhaustion and toil of responsibility from the fine lines of his face. "I would agree, yes. But I would not necessarily say that the bardic understanding of the Sleepers and the actuality meet in any meaningful way."

"Are these Sleepers dangerous?"

"Who would know?" The mage lifted a silvered brow. "They have never woken."

"Yet it is considered an act of treason to interfere with them at all—to even, if I understand the law correctly, attempt to see or study them." She lifted a sheaf of papers from her desk's surface and let them fall again. "A very old law," she said softly. "Upheld when the Kings took power. It is not in the records of the current magisterial courts, but rather the historical ones. Four hundred years ago. When the Sleepers were, in fact, considered myth."

"How—"

"I wished plans, some lay of the ground, that would indicate that the Sanctum of Moorelas had once been part of a building." She paused. "Have you heard the phrase 'under Moorelas' shadow'?"

Meralonne's face paled, and his brow rose in the most open display of surprise that The Terafin had ever seen from him. Then he smiled, and she recognized the smile for the concession it was. "Yes," he said softly. "It means, colloquially, that someone is doomed."

"So much history," The Terafin said softly, "beneath the ground of Averalaan, of what was once AMarakas, and before that, Develonn. And before that? Vexusa, I think." She saw the cool shift of Meralonne's eyes, understood well his dislike of the name, and continued. "Yes. The Dark League. I did not know how old these lands were, or how much history they contained; I feel, almost, that I walk in legend." Abruptly, her tone changed. "The Sanctum," she said softly.

He said nothing.

"It is a shrine to the memory of Moorelas; a monument to the forces of justice, of courage, of sacrifice. Each year, upon the four quarters, wreaths are placed at the foot of the statue that guards the city's bay. There *are* no doors into it, no windows—until today I did not realize that it *could* be entered, although perhaps I should have; it *is* called the Sanctum of Moorelas. Few, if any, know what lies beneath its facade.

"You know." In the last two words, everything.

"It is an edict," Meralonne replied, with a guarded expression, "that was decreed by Cormaris, Reymaris, and the Mother; those who serve Cartanis have also upheld the law, and I believe that the Mandaros-born do so as well. In fact, if you take the time—"

"I will find that there is not a single God who does not wish the Sleepers to remain undisturbed."

"Indeed."

"In fact, I will find that there is not a single God who will even make reference to the Sleepers without indelicately applied pressure."

Again he bowed his head, lifting his hands in a familiar steeple.

"If you'd like," she said softly, "Morretz will bring you a pipe."

"He will not bring me *my* pipe," was the mock-grave reply. "Terafin, you put us in a difficult position."

"How much does the Council of the Magi know?"

Silver-gray eyes grew distant. "The Council? I cannot say for certain. Krysanthos knew, although he was not one of the wise. The Kings know. The Exalted. Certainly the Astari."

"But not The Ten."

"It is not relevant to The Ten." It was, of course, the wrong thing to say.

"It is relevant to The Ten now," she said sharply. "It is relevant to all of Averalaan."

"What do you mean?"

"It is through the Sanctum—and the secret that the Sanctum contains—that we will find our way into the undercity." There was no doubt in her voice.

Meralonne's pale face grew ashen, his silver eyes wide. "Of course," he said softly, but his voice held only apprehension. "We should have known it."

"Tell me, Meralonne—why do the Gods fear the Sleepers?"

His expression grew remote, almost cold; his eyes touched the distant wall as if it were a thin veil drawn over a history that could be seen if one stared hard enough. "I . . . do not know," he said at last, after some thought. "And I will not venture to guess; it would take years, and a better understanding of the relationship between the Gods and their followers than you or I possess."

The answer was not to The Terafin's liking, but she let it pass, granting Meralonne the respect that was his due as a member of the Council of the Magi. "And is the fear of the Gods for the Sleepers greater than the fear of *Allasakar's* coming?"

He bowed his head slowly, and then rose. "I believe it is time to answer that question," he said gravely. He walked to the door, paused, and turned. "Terafin."

"Yes?"

"If you worship those Gods, you might wish to pray that the Sleepers do not awaken."

Before she could demand an explanation, he was gone.

Chapter Twenty-Six

JEWEL KNELT AGAINST THE GROUND, pressing her forehead into the stone for perhaps the hundredth time that morning. She was heartily sick of it, but Ellerson had been quite strict in his admonitions—the Exalted were only second in rank and power to the Kings themselves, and they were to be treated with the same respect, measure for measure, that one would give the Kings.

She no longer had any desire to ever meet the Kings in person.

Or, she thought sourly, she had no desire to meet the Kings until she was ATerafin—for it seemed that The Terafin and her Chosen did not have to bow, scrape, bend, and kneel at every change of position the Exalted made. Luckily, she was enough of a commoner that the bowing and scraping was pretty simple; total abasement left very little room for mistakes.

Devon nudged her sharply and she looked up into the grave face of the Exalted of Cormaris. His peppered hair was drawn back from his forehead; nothing hid the piercing glow of golden irises. Who would have thought gold could be so icy?

"Describe again the halls you traversed to reach this supposed crypt." He motioned the Exalted of the Mother forward; she was the only one who had not yet heard Jewel's full story. At once, the former den leader bowed her forehead—again—to the ground and left it there until she was told to raise it. Then she described the hall to the best of a memory that didn't seem to satisfy either the Exalted of Reymaris or the Exalted of Cormaris. In fact, it didn't seem to satisfy the Exalted of the Mother either, which disheartened Jewel.

When she got back to Terafin—if they ever let her leave the palace grounds again—Ellerson was going to pay.

The Terafin said nothing at all; her Chosen said nothing—in fact, the only friend she seemed to have in the entire hall was Devon. Certainly the warrior-priests who attended the Exalted looked upon her—when her eyes were raised enough that she could see their expressions—with a cool distrust. It was a crowded hall; there was a lot of suspicion in it.

Tell them, he'd said. *Tell them all.* Oh, Ellerson was going to suffer somehow for this.

It was when a door that didn't even look remotely doorlike opened, and two men and two women, attended by eight strangely uniformed guards stepped in, that Jewel truly understood how miserable she could be.

Because even though she'd been born and raised in the twenty-fifth with no hope of ever reaching a noble rank, she recognized the Kings and the Queens when she saw them.

The Queens came first: Marieyan the Wise, robed in simple midnight blue, and Siodonay the Fair, in morning white. But the materials were of a kind that Jewel had only seen The Terafin wear, and at that, seldom; they glimmered, catching a subdued light as they fell. Queen Marieyan wore a slender tiara through hair frosted white, and she wore a wide belt into which was embroidered the rod and the crown.

Queen Siodonay was called the Fair as a play on words; she was both fair in her dealings, as was demanded of the Queen of Justice, and fair in complexion as the Northerners. Her hair was a platinum spill of light, pulled back and twined in a braid upon her head; she wore no crown, but carried instead a sword with jewel-encrusted scabbard that told the tale of her rank. It was said she knew how to use it, and well.

King Reymalyn came next, his golden eyes narrowed, his face cast in a grim light. Fire-haired and fire-bearded, he was the tallest man in the room; across the breadth of his shoulders he wore an emerald cape, and beneath it, simple attire. But he, too, carried a sword, and his wrists were banded with an odd metal that caught the light and seemed to absorb some of it. Jewel would have taken a step back, but she was kneeling. Not to King Reymalyn would she go for mercy, if mercy were ever required.

But perhaps she might plead with the wisdom-born King: Cormalyn. Dark-haired and golden-eyed, he was younger than his Queen, but no less regal. Of the four, it was King Cormalyn who drew the eye and held it longest, although he wore no heavy mantle, no jeweled crown, no emblazoned crest. He carried the rod of his office, and the color of his eyes was sunrise; there was a sadness to his face, and an air of peace, that made one want to trust him.

And Jewel badly wanted to trust someone here.

"And what makes you think that this . . . this crypt is located beneath the Sanctum of Moorelas?"

Because you're giving me such a hard time about it—where else could it be? But she bit her lip on the words as Devon applied a gentle pressure to the small of her back— a pressure that could not be seen by her questioners. "I don't know it for certain," she told the Kings' questioner softly. The man glanced beyond her shoulder—at Devon, she thought, since they seemed to know each other well.

"Yet you've told your Lord that this is the case."

"Yes." That was said through clenched teeth. Couldn't be helped. Something about the man made her edgy.

"Why?"

This dark-haired, pale-eyed man was so intense it was almost easy to forget that there were other people in the room: the Exalted, the Crowns, The Terafin. "Because I couldn't think of where else it could be. The Sanctum stands alone. The library closest to it doesn't have a crypt."

"Who else have you told about this?"

She was silent, weighing the question; weighing the decision that would be made by answering it.

"I asked you a question."

"I heard it." Devon's hand was at her back again; she stepped an inch or two forward, denying it without exposing his support. If support it was. The guards moved in at her sides, but she ignored them, as if they were no more than common beggars, and she the Queen.

"Terafin," she said quietly, the softness of her voice masking its lack of strength.

The Terafin stood forward. Jewel was not certain what the older woman would do; here, she was outranked by seven people, or eight if you counted the man who questioned. But her Chosen—Torvan among them—stepped forward as well, subtle in their protectiveness. The Exalted made way before her, polite but cool; the Queens paid her the respect of a slight nod. Only the Kings were remote.

"Jewel," The Terafin said.

"Terafin." She bowed quite low. "I've told them everything I can tell them. I serve the House."

"You have not," the questioner said, rising from his chair in a quick and supple motion, "told us everything we wish to know."

"I have told you," Jewel repeated, her voice more strained, "all that I *can*."

"It is not for The Terafin to decide that; it is for *me*. The Crowns are not yet satisfied with your response. We would ask you to resume your place." Jewel had heard death threats that contained less menace.

She did not move. Because she understood—although it had taken the better part of two hours—that the Exalted and the Crowns' inquisitioner were not questioning her because they did not believe her; quite the opposite. They were *afraid* that what she had to say was truth.

Jewel knew that it was dangerous to know too much. In the streets of the thirty-fifth, Old Rath's hunting grounds, it had often been the death of some hapless young thief, at least until the magisterians had done their work. There were no magisterial guards that could protect her here; she knew too much, and she knew it in front of the people who *made* the laws and could change them to suit their whim. But she'd be damned if she'd speak the names of any of the rest of her den. She'd be damned to the fires, thrown out of the Hall of Mandaros without so much as a second chance. She was their leader, after all.

"Jewel Markess." The man's voice was ice. *"Sit."*

"Hold."

The Terafin frowned at Jewel, but the expression that molded the contours of her jaw was distinctly cooler when she looked at the Kings' servitor. A moment passed; The Terafin's expression deepened, as did her annoyance. At last, she spoke. "Astari," she said, measuring each syllable, "the girl is a member of my House. She answers to me by the covenant between The Ten and the Crown, and I do not choose to press her response."

Silence. Then:

"We were not informed that this was the case."

"I was not aware that the permission of the Astari—or the Crowns—was required. Nor was I aware that prior knowledge was a legal imperative."

"It is—"

"It is not, of course, required." It was Queen Siodonay who spoke. Her voice was softer than her expression, but strong for all that. "But as a courtesy—both to ourselves and the young ATerafin—it would have been appreciated."

"It would," the Astari who was responsible for questioning Jewel said coldly, "have been impossible."

"Lord of the Compact," Queen Marieyan said quietly.

The Astari turned to face her; his face twisted a moment in frustration and then eased into a remote neutrality which fooled no one. "As you say, Majesty." He stepped aside to give Jewel room to move, and then turned lightly on one foot. "But, Terafin, you understand your responsibility in this matter. If this young girl's information were openly known—"

"Then what?" The Terafin's voice was, measure for measure, as clipped and icy as his. "I have heard nothing today that indicates—to me—that you have any idea whatever of what will happen. If history—that remote and sullied record of events past—is to be trusted, these Sleepers have existed as they are now for eternity; they have not once woken, they have not once been disturbed. And there have been wars, and worse, that have played themselves out above them and around them since the dawn of time. Vexusa fell around their ears—and such a fall as that city faced woke the very dead.

"Therefore, unless your purpose is to intimidate a young girl, I believe your interview here is at end. Is that clear?"

"Terafin." It was Queen Marieyan. "Lord of the Compact. Our grievance is not, and must not, be with each other. Terafin, you must forgive the Lord of the Compact; his purpose is the protection of the Crowns, and he is zealous in his pursuit."

"And arrogant. And ruthless."

"It seems to me," the Exalted of Cormaris said quietly, appearing from the far end of the hall without warning, "that history, both ancient and recent, plays its hand. Terafin. Lord of the Compact. You do not serve your best interests, or ours, by this. Cease."

The Terafin bowed at once, low and proper in her respect; the Astari grudgingly gave way as well, but with an obvious lack of grace.

"Who knows now matters not; more will know than we could possibly deal with before this matter is closed. This does not grant dispensation for any further spread of this tale by anyone in this room—or in House Terafin." He turned to Jewel, the full weight of his ceremonial robes trailing across the ground. Aside from the warrior-priests, he had no attendants—and the warrior-priests did not lift or carry a train, even if it be the Exalted's. "Young one, we believe your story, although we wish it otherwise." He turned to the Exalted of Reymaris. "Son of Reymaris?"

"I concur," was the short reply.

"Daughter of the Mother?"

"I also concur." But her full lips were turned down at the corners, her eyes narrowed. She turned to the Kings, who had remained silent throughout. "Your Majesties," she said, bowing low. "I speak for the triumvirate."

"As is your right," King Reymalyn said.

His voice was a shock. It was low and deep and musical; it filled the hall as if it were a shout, yet it was soft in tone—almost gentle.

"What would you have of us?"

"If there were another way, we would ask nothing," the Reymaris-born King replied. "But it seems to us that the Crypt of the Sleepers must be disturbed if Allasakar is not to walk again. We would ask that you open the Sanctum to our forces."

She lowered her head a moment. "It will not be an easy task, and the triumvirate alone cannot accomplish it; we must bespeak the Church of Cartanis and the Church of Mandaros, and their leaders must be in agreement." She paused. "There are reasons why the very ground would deny a making or an unmaking, such as our enemies have done, that did not have the keys of the Gods behind it." She paused. "All keys."

"Let it be done," the King replied.

"As you command."

Devon was stiff and weary. "You took a risk," he said, as he sank back into the wide, high-backed chair in his office.

The Terafin raised a dark brow before accepting his lack of formality; it had been a most trying morning. "*I* was not the author of that risk." Glancing at Jewel, she smiled; the young thief sat meekly on the window ledge, attempting to hide in the very scant shadows.

Jewel had the grace to blush under the scrutiny. "I'm sorry," she offered at last. "But thanks for covering for me. I owe you."

Devon and The Terafin exchanged glances.

"I don't think you understand," Devon said quietly. "Did you think that she was merely trying to save you some time at the hands of the Lord of the Compact?"

Jewel stared at him blankly.

"The name ATerafin is not offered lightly." It was The Terafin who spoke. "And it is never offered in jest or in subterfuge. You *are* ATerafin, Jewel. This is no game."

Speechless, Jewel gaped; it caused Devon to laugh, and the mirth was genuine, if somewhat edged.

The Terafin waited patiently for the sound to die out; it did not take long. "Why do they believe it?" she said to Devon, as if the interruption—and the slight to her House—had not happened.

"Because," he said soberly, "the Sleepers *are* history, and they have slept, unchanged and unchanging, forever. I do not believe that our enemies somehow missed this entrance into the undercity; I believe that they unmade it—as they unmade the rest.

"But the Exalted believe that unmaking was rejected, as all known attempts to change the Sleepers have been—in a slow and subtle reworking that a mage in haste would miss completely. It is almost as if time itself guards them."

"They unmade the way," Jewel said softly, "and the protection around the Sleepers unmade their unmaking."

"Yes."

"Then . . . they don't know."

"That is our hope," Devon agreed softly. "And we believe," his voice grew into a thin whisper as he shaded his eyes in the darkness, "that it is our only hope."

"No," a new voice said.

Devon threw himself from his chair, and when he rolled to his feet, his hands were shining with the glint of metal in the poor light. He threw them; they stopped an inch from the hooded face of the intruder and then fell with a clang to the ground.

Jewel gaped for a second time that day—and not because of the magic; she'd seldom seen a throw that good—he'd've hit both eyes if not for the spell. She was certain of it.

But the spell was there; the daggers lay, cold and flat, against the floor. "Well met, Devon ATerafin," the figure said. "I come in peace; I mean no harm." So saying, she reached up and pulled the folds of the hood from her face.

A woman slightly older than The Terafin stared out at them, her eyes violet, her hair still dark, although time had frosted it slightly. Her chin was strong, her nose prominent; she was not lovely in the way the delicate are—but age and power lent a depth and beauty to her face that she could not have possessed in youth. "I am Evayne," she said softly.

"And I," The Terafin said, rising to greet an equal, "am The Terafin." She paused. "I do not recognize you."

"No? But we've met. A long, long time ago. I was a youth, Terafin, and you were a combatant."

The Terafin's frown deepened. And then her expression changed. "The robes," she said. "Seer. You are . . . much aged."

"Yes. I am." She nodded quietly to Jewel ATerafin. "Jewel. You have not yet made the pilgrimage, but if I am not mistaken, and my memory does not fail me, you will." Jewel stepped back, hit the wall, and stopped self-consciously, for she saw in this woman the girl who had come running into the foyer, all darkness in pursuit, the two foreigners close behind. "You are young; younger than I was when I was left upon that road. But enough.

"My time is brief; if the Lord of the path is willing, I will meet you ere this battle's fought."

"Put it away, Devon," The Terafin said, although she barely caught the slight movement with the corner of her eye. "I believe that if the seer wished us dead, we would be."

"I am no threat to the Crowns you defend, Astari," Evayne said remotely.

The Terafin's eyes widened, as did Devon's.

At last, Devon ATerafin spoke. "How did you know that I am Astari? It is not common knowledge."

"I've met you many times, ATerafin, and in many situations. This is one of the most peaceful, and it may be the last; it is not given to me to know *my* future."

"I've never seen you before in my life."

"No. You have not." She turned from him to Jewel, and reached into her robes. What she drew out shone in the room like a living crystal laced with shadow, cloud and lightning. "Jewel—or Jay, if you prefer—I know who you are. Look at me carefully, and look at what I hold. Then tell them what it is."

"But it's a—it's a seer's ball," Jewel said.

"Very well. But what, exactly, *is* a seer's ball? A crystal? A globe blown of glass for use by charlatans? Come, Jewel."

Jewel looked to The Terafin; The Terafin nodded quietly.

Thus granted permission, she turned the focus of her attention upon the orb the mage held, but she did so uneasily. She did not fear danger, not precisely; did not fear for her life. But her chin shook as she leveled her gaze, and her eyes darted toward the wall and windows—not this unknown woman's face—as if they could anchor her somehow.

"Jewel."

She swallowed. Nodded.

Seconds blended into minutes; time froze as the young thief's dark eyes slowly widened, absorbing the light. Devon and The Terafin glanced between Jewel and the mage, waiting for some word, some sound, some reaction. And there were minute signs of it: the young woman's shoulders, tense and curled downward, relaxed; the line of her brow lost the creases that had not yet been etched there by age. Her mouth opened slightly, in wonder, but not even a whisper escaped.

At last, Devon cleared his throat.

Jewel started, flicking a glance in his direction as if she'd forgotten that there was anyone else in the room. Even Evayne's face, inches above the globe, seemed a bit of a shock to her, judging from the expression that crossed her face. She came back to herself slowly, remembering first who was with her, and then where she was, and last, the question that had set her staring into the roiling light.

"It's her heart," she told them hesitantly, as if afraid of their mockery.

"And you can read it?" Evayne asked.

Swallowing, the young den leader said to her companions, "I—I'd trust her." She looked up, and found that she didn't have to; she and Evayne were of a height. "I already do. This—it was made by you."

"No, Jewel," Evayne replied, her voice almost sad. "It was made *of* me. I walked the Oracle's path; I passed the Oracle's test. And she," the seer added, with the flash of a grim smile, "passed mine."

"The Oracle," The Terafin said, the two words distinct yet hushed, as if they were a secret. "You walked her path. They called this a soul-crystal, a soul-shard. I remember my grandfather's stories," she added, as the seer raised a dark brow. "Is it like all the stories? Does it lose its romance and power as you approach its reality?"

Evayne's smile turned sharply inward, although it remained upon her face, changed in tone and texture. "It loses none of its power," she whispered, "and all of its romance." Her attention turned to Jewel again. "I thank you, little sister. And I hope—although in truth, I fear there is little chance of it—that you will not bear a like burden in your day." She lifted the stone one final time, and then shuttered its light with the folds of her cloak.

Drawing herself to her full height, she spoke to The Terafin. "You have in your dwelling a foreign noble."

"Yes," The Terafin replied. "We believe he is of import."

"He is. But he is the weapon, not the swordsman; know how to wield him, and when to let him fly. It matters little who else is chosen, but Lord Elseth *must* be sent to the Sanctum when the way is open." She turned her attention to Devon. "And you have, at court, a young bard. Bring him as well."

"I see," Devon said. "She is to *send*, and I am to *bring*? You do not know The Terafin."

Evayne shrugged. "It will not be easy, and it will not be simple, but the ways *must* be opened, and the path must be walked. Jewel, you and I will meet again ere this long battle is over. But time," her lips quirked up in an odd smile, "is of the essence." She stepped forward, toward them; the air swallowed her, leaving no sign of her presence.

25th Corvil, 410 A.A.
Senniel College

"We can magnify the sound of your voice," Sigurne said quietly.

The bardmaster looked back out of eyes rimmed black with sleep's lack. "If it were that easy," she said softly, running a hand over those eyes, "wars would have been fought and won with the use of a single mage and a single bard."

Sigurne raised a pale brow. "I confess that I've studied little of the bardic voice. The bardic colleges are not—"

"Open to the study of the Order," Sioban finished for her. It was a complaint that she had dealt with, more or less directly, for the duration of her tenure. "Some magnification is helpful, but we cannot increase the effect of the voice without using our personal power. I don't know why," she added quickly, as she saw the question flash through Sigurne's dark eyes. Talking to the Magi was an exercise in frustration; they were always wont to ask questions that, while of interest in the long, idle hours after a tavern's jig, drew attention away from the immediate and the necessary.

On the other hand, a break from the immediate danger—and its attendant responsibility—was something that Sioban desperately craved; it had been a hard week, and by all accounts of the Council of the Wise, it was only going to get worse.

The demons in the undercity had returned to their work carefully; the voices below were not so distinct as they had been, and not nearly as strong—but the power in their despair and terror was growing daily. The bards could not contain it.

The Priests of the Church—the god-born Priests—had joined their efforts to the bardic colleges'. Sioban privately believed that the answer to their dilemma lay with the Gods—for it was through the power of a God that the barrier had been created. But the Gods were disappointingly silent in their conferences with their half-blood children, and the power that the god-born could channel did not meet or scratch the surface of the power that . . . she shook her head, weary. Fear did that.

The members of the first and second circles of the Order of Knowledge were also struggling daily with the question of the blackness below: what it was, how it functioned, how to contain the cries that emanated from it, how to control the panic that was beginning to sink deep roots in the heart of Averalaan.

"Bardmaster?"

Sioban found herself on her feet, staring into the waves that rolled against the break below Seahaven. Here, in the heart of her small dominion, she could not make out the screams unless she called upon her training and her power. She did not.

"We can't keep it up forever," she said softly.

Sigurne was quiet a moment.

"I don't know how you do it."

"I?" Sigurne rose to join the weary bard at her place by the window. "What choice have I?"

What choice, indeed. "How long will it take?"

"Until the voices can be heard by the entire city?" The mage shook her head. "I can't say with certainty. But if it follows its current growth curve, four weeks."

Lady Mother, Sioban thought, pressing her forehead into her hands, *help us all*.

11th Henden, 410 A.A.
Avantari, Kings' Palace

"And *I* tell *you*, Verrus Sivari, that there's no possible way that we can evacuate any more of the city. The Cordufar Estates are situated in an ideal locale—most of the neighboring families are noble-born and can afford to retreat to their alternate homes. But *this* area," the red-faced magisterial guard said, stabbing the map with his finger, pausing to swear when he hit a marker pin, and then continuing, "is packed to the roof with people who won't be pried out without an army. It's their home—they've got nowhere else to go."

"The army is available," the Verrus said coldly.

The magisterial guard sputtered a moment; he hated dealing with the Kings' Swords. He started to speak, and Verrus Sivari placed his own pointer—a brass stick of some sort—against the contour lines of the map. "We received the reports from the magisterial courts this morning," he said, his voice growing quieter as the magisterial guard's grew louder, "and in the last two weeks, in areas that have not been properly depopulated, the increase of violence—and violent death—has become unacceptable to the Crowns."

"It's nothing compared to what you're going to get if you try to force an evacuation."

"Major Capren," Verrus Sivari said, grinding his teeth slightly, "there is no guaranteed evacuation; it is an *emergency* plan. Now, if you have nothing further to add, I believe I have business—"

The door burst open; both men looked up.

An ashen-faced Sentrus forced his arm across his chest in a sharp salute as he stood just this side of the heavy door. "Verrus, forgive the intrusion. You are needed at once."

The Verrus reached for his sword. "Report."

"It's Queen Siodonay and the Princess." The Sentrus swallowed. "They've been arguing with the Lord of the Compact."

Sivari paled. "Enough." He turned to the magisterial guard, who looked somewhat queasy himself. "You will excuse me," he said. It was an order.

When he passed beneath the arch that led from the Hall of Gods, he was immediately greeted by Primus Allarus.

"Sivari—thank the Gods." It was not an auspicious start.

"Why in the name of Cormaris would Queen Siodonay be arguing with the Lord of the Compact?"

"It's not in Cormaris' name that she's arguing," the Kings' Sword replied. "But she's got Mirialyn on her side."

"Queen Marieyan?"

"Nothing. Not a word. She says that this is not a matter of common sense, or a matter of right and wrong."

"Enough, Allarus. Tell me."

"You won't like it."

"I dislike it already. Tell me."

"Queen Siodonay intends—with Princess Mirialyn and the Kings' Swords under her command—to ride the streets of Averalaan." He paused as he watched the words take root in Verrus Sivari's imagination. Then he added, "Until the crisis is over."

"Impossible," the Verrus said flatly.

"That," Primus Allarus replied, "is what the Lord of the Compact told them." He smiled briefly. "And this," he said, as the Verrus made his way into the court rooms, "will be the first time I think I've ever seen you argue on the same side."

It was clear from the nonresponse that Sivari did not find it as amusing as the rest of the Kings' Swords did.

Queen Siodonay stood beside her throne. Hanging at her side was the sword belt for which she was famous in the North, although she wore it rarely now. Ceremonial breastplates and greaves were being fitted to her by her attendants; she stood, arms out, like a cross, her dark eyes cold as any winter night.

They brightened slightly as they caught sight of Sivari, and then narrowed. "Verrus. To what do we owe this honor?"

"Sanity," was his clipped reply. With the Crowns, a certain etiquette was required—except when one was dealing with Siodonay of the North. "You cannot mean to ride through the streets of the city." That she would not know the full extent of the crisis was not a possibility; in times of crisis, the Queens were involved as a matter of necessity.

"I seldom don ceremonial garb for any other reason."

"Your Majesty—Siodonay—we cannot afford to lose one of the Crowns at a time like this. The streets are—"

"Not yet in chaos."

The Verrus turned at the sound of the voice, recognizing it at once. "ACormaris," he said, bowing stiffly, although privately he thought the title undeserved at this particular juncture.

The Princess smiled, and the smile was almost rueful; she knew well what he was thinking—it was etched across the lines of his eyes, his mouth. "There is a wisdom to the human heart that follows no rigid logic, and no common sense. Yet there are rules to the heart's sway, and I argue that it is folly to ignore those rules under the guise of 'rationality.'"

"Do you know what a blow it will be if the Queen is lost? She is the warrior of the city's heart."

"Oh, yes," Miri said softly, her eyes focused beyond his shoulder. "And it is precisely because of who she is that she must do what she must do. Excuse me, Verrus."

Sivari stepped aside as a swordbearer in robes the color of rust—or dried blood—stepped forward to the dais, kneeling reverently against the wide arc of the stairs. In his arms, cradled against ivory cushions, was a long, slender scabbard, one jeweled with three large stones, and lit with gold inlay. Nodding, Mirialyn lifted her arms to the side, and the swordbearer carefully girded her with the sword that was her birthright.

He stared at her hips very carefully and then proceeded to make all the necessary adjustments. "You will not have the rest?" he asked her.

"No. Just the shield and the sword."

Regretfully, the man bowed as low as, or lower than, he had the first time. "ACormaris."

Grinding his teeth, the Verrus waited respectfully until the man was out of sight. "What exactly is it that you think this will do?"

"A moment, Verrus. Jordan—the horses?"

"The stablehands are readying them—but you may have to go to the stables yourself to see Thunder armored."

"Very well."

"Miri—"

"I think," she said, adjusting the sword slightly, "that you already know what we intend. It has been two weeks, and Averalaan is filled with dark murmurings and the screams of the dying. We have held up little against them; but it is to the Exalted—or to the Crowns—that the people will turn for comfort and for succor."

"And when you can't provide it?"

She was silent. "There is a risk," she said at last, her voice quite cool. "But I believe that if we go now, and in haste, if we make our rounds, and touch the earth of Averalaan instead of hiding in the relative safety of Averalaan Aramarelas, we can turn this from a terrible unknown evil, into a terrible, known war—a war between the triumvirate and the Darkness.

"And we can make clear that to fight *is* to remain calm; to *win* is to show the enemy that we *cannot* be broken by this—this magical illusion." She pulled her sword, and the sound of steel against steel silenced the hall. "It is Henden, Verrus Sivari. The month of great darkness, during which Veralaan and the Mother's Children stood alone against the assemblage of the Baronial Wizards and their followers. Our people were slaughtered, whether for magical power or as examples. Our children were starved. Our lands were fired."

Verrus Sivari fell, slowly, to one knee.

"They knew that if they could break the spirit of the people, there would never be war; Veralaan would be married and then murdered, a footnote to her father's history. Remember the Six Dark Days."

He bowed his head. She spoke of the history of the Empire, and its founding. "ACormaris," he said at last. "I remember. And I remember what followed: Veralaan's return with the Twin Kings."

"You are not the only one who will remember it," she said softly. "They will. But they will only remember it clearly and sharply if we ride."

He brought his hands across his eyes, as if to clear them of webs.

"Against this, we measure the risk as small. If we can reach our people, they *will* listen." She looked up at the approaching Kings' Swords, and nodded sharply. "Sentrus, escort the Queen to the courtyard; I will join the stable detail and meet you there." Barely noticing the sharp salute, she turned once again to the Verrus. "I hope you understand why we will not be deterred."

He raised his arm across his chest in a sharp, perfect salute. "If you would accept it, I would be honored to serve beside you."

"And not under?" She smiled. "I would accept it in a minute, if only to convince the Lord of the Compact that we will be duly and appropriately guarded."

The Queen rode, and the Princess at her side; behind them, in the regalia that spoke of the games of the summer quarter was Verrus Sivari: Kings' Champion of a bygone season. Everyone knew what the wreathed leaves of gold meant as they adorned his brow and caught the light in liquid reflection; in his prime, he was the best combatant in the arena of the summer games. Better than any of the Annagarians; better than any of the free towners; better than any of the Westerners from their tiny, isolated Kingdoms. And he had met and matched them all.

Vanity was such a terrible thing, but he gave in to it a moment as they crossed the bridge that led to the city around the bay, leaving the Holy Isle behind. Salt-laden wind touched his face, pushing his cape back over the ornate shoulder joints of the Champion's ceremonial armor. The sun was shining, high and bright; the nightmare seemed a passing conceit.

But the moment passed; the horses made their way into the wide, flat streets of the city. They shied back, as if the bridge were a safe haven, and the road before them fraught with peril—but they were animals trained for war, and after a moment, they were forced forward.

"Can you feel it?" The ACormaris asked him quietly.

He nodded.

"It gets worse."

He didn't ask her how she knew it—although it was clear by her tone that she spoke from experience—because he didn't want to know. What he didn't know, the Lord of the Compact could not find out.

The standard of the Queen uncurled with a bang.

"This is war. Sound it. Make our intent known." Mirialyn gestured, and the horns began their lowing across the open bay. He listened to the notes, long and lingering, as if they spoke truth in a language that he had been born knowing.

Beneath him, Warfoal relaxed—because it was a language that he, too, understood.

And all across the Holy Isle, the preparations for festivity, for the rites of Return were taken up at the call of Queen Siodonay the Fair. Hesitantly, timorously, the nobles and their servants brought the shrouds and pennants out from their stores, and began to prepare for the Six Dark Days.

They sang their songs of freedom and of fear, of courage and of loss, and in the singing—with the bard-born scattered among them like anchors—brought themselves a measure of peace: These were days of darkness, and Averalaan had survived the darkness before.

But on the mainland, the fight was harder, and where the wreaths were laid, they were laid over a fear so deep it could be tasted. But they were laid, and they were more of a weapon than a dagger or a sword in the shadows.

Chapter Twenty-Seven

28th of Henden, 410 A.A.
The Sanctum of Moorelas

A N HOUR OFF MIDNIGHT; the twenty-third hour. Moonlight, lambent
glow beneath the wispy cover of night clouds. The cries of the dying, ghost-
like yet visceral, drowning in the slap of high waves against the seawalls that
dotted the bay. Towering above in darkness, the statue of Moorelas, grim-faced
and determined as he must have been before his final ride. Beneath him, octagonal, carved reliefs of ancient history—Moorelas' history.

Starlight reigned; the little lights of the city were doused as was the custom for
the Six Dark Days. Six days, each named for one of the Barons who ruled before
the Kings. The Terafin bowed her head in silent prayer, feeling the wind's sharp
sting across neck and cheek. She drew her cloak in around her shoulders, tightening it; it didn't help. The chill she felt had little to do with the weather.

Beside her, Jewel shivered.

"You feel it," The Terafin said quietly.

Jewel nodded. "When I was little—when my parents were alive—we followed
the Six Day rites. I know the prayers." She shivered again. "Makes me feel old, to
need them."

A dark brow arched in response. "When my grandfather was alive," The Terafin said at last, "I hated the Six Days. I hated reciting the names of the Blood
Barons; I hated giving up almost all food in favor of scraps that not even our servants were forced to suffer through during the rest of the year. I hated the lack of
lights, I hated the sobriety—" She laughed ruefully. "I was a child.

"But he explained that these days were our history, and that we must suffer
through them as our ancestors did to understand all that Essalieyan means now.
Because, he said, if we did not learn to understand what the Empire is, we would
be doomed to lose it." She did not smile as she spoke, although there was a thread
of affection in the whole of the picture she wove. "As I got older, and I better understood the custom of the Kings and their birthing, I realized that he was
wrong—that we could not so easily lose the kingdom that the Kings had founded.
We argued."

She bowed her head again, her fingers sliding over the smooth, carved surface of opal prayer stones. "If he has not returned from the Hall of Mandaros—if he still watches us now—I hope he knows that I understand, in every way, what he meant."

Beside her, Morretz stirred; she turned her head and met his eyes before they flickered back to the Exalted. *I rarely speak so, do I?* she thought, although she did not feel the need to say it. *But these are the Dark Days, Morretz. And my grandfather also said—and I didn't appreciate it either—that in the days of darkness, in our horrible desperation, we sought solace in each other and we accepted that that solace was for, and of the moment.*

Jewel stared up at Moorelas' graven face. "Your grandfather was worse than my mother," she said at last. "My mother used to tell my father that even in the darkness, children were loved, and mothers still did what they could to comfort and protect them." Jewel paused as her gaze was once again drawn groundward, to the Exalted. "My Mother was Annagarian. From the Valleys," she added in defensive haste. "My father felt that she never understood the customs of Averalaan."

"No. But she wasn't wrong; it's why the birthdays of children under the age of four are still celebrated when no other festivities are allowed. Because even in the darkness, we celebrated life."

"Especially in the darkness," Morretz said. It was the first time that he had spoken. He was not used to being away from the manse; indeed, The Terafin had all but forbidden him to accompany her to this tomblike place. But he would not be left behind, and in truth, it made her feel more steady to have his quiet, obdurate presence at her back.

"Shhh. They resume."

"What are you doing?"

"What does it look like I'm doing?" Finch, struggling with a wreath made of white blossoms, pale orchids, and tiny thorns, cut across the open doorway, scowling slightly at Teller. Wasn't like him to ask stupid questions. But it had gotten bad, these last few days.

Her hands were shaking. If she listened—and not very hard—she could hear the dim cries carried by wind across the bay. It made her wonder what people were doing in the twenty-fifth.

Lefty and Fisher. Lander. Duster. They were the edge of the storm—and who would remember them, when all this was over? Would there be anyone alive to remember them at all?

Teller fell into step beside her; the wreath was large and yet delicate. "It's early," he said at last.

"Yeah." She knew it, too. The wreaths didn't go out until dawn. If. Jay told them that it was tonight, or never. She stopped. Started. Stopped. "Teller?"

He stopped and stood beside her, waiting for her to gather her words.

"I want to go to the bridge. The twenty-fifth is—" Finch swallowed and shrugged. "I don't miss it," she told him softly, "but it's still home somehow. I can't ask Carver or Angel, and Arann's busy with the guards." Pause. "Jester's coming."

He didn't ask her why she couldn't ask Carver or Angel; he didn't have to. They'd laugh. "Can I follow?"

"Yeah, sure. But help me with this—I'm cutting my hands ragged on the stupid thorns."

The Exalted stood around the monument with the Sacred of the Churches of Mandaros and Cartanis. A member of the Order of Knowledge, golden-eyed and aged in appearance, was also part of the circle—he represented the interests of Teos, Lord of Knowledge. Both of the Kings stood with them, arrayed in full armor, their swords sheathed and girded round. Together, the eight began their supplication, joining hands to close the circle, filling the air with their plea.

But they spoke no words that those without god-blood recognized, and as their chant grew longer, it also grew more complex. They had been thus joined for all but five minutes of each of the last twelve hours; the next would tell all.

Kallandras stood by the edge of the retaining wall, leaning against its upper edge for support. It was cool against his forearms, and he concentrated on that sensation a moment, as if surprised he could feel it.

"Kallandras?"

He glanced to the side, the wildness in his eyes the motion of water beneath the stillness of gentle waves. Sioban was staring at him with open concern. He hated it. But the drug's sway was waning; he could hear the voices of the dead more clearly than the song of the Exalted, the Kings, and the Priests. Mixed with their despair, the despair of the dying beneath the earth.

And to lay either to rest, the way had to be opened.

"I'm fine," he told her curtly.

She shrugged, withdrawing the unspoken offer as she shouldered her lute.

Her lute. His was safe in his small, cramped quarters in Senniel College. He almost never traveled without Salla, but tonight, with darkness all around, was the first time he truly missed her.

Gilliam of Elseth stood by himself, keeping his own space as well as his own counsel. With him were Ashfel, Connel, and Salas; they were edgy, but the cries of the humans in the ground beneath their feet had become, over the days, simple background noise like any other. Now, they started at the sound of silence—for the creatures underground would stop an hour here or there, to give the city a hope it could then dash when the cries began again.

He watched, impassive, as the circle of eight began to chant anew; they were a tool, but they were not, in and of themselves, compelling to him. No, the only figure of so-called power here that drew his attention—and his admiration—was Queen Siodonay the Fair. The streets were alive with whisper and song as they spoke of her passage through them; she was the bright and shining moment that had kept the worst of her people's fear at bay. Such a Queen could stand in the same hall as the Great Queens of the Breodani.

He wore a sword, but aside from a supple leather shirt, no armor to speak of; he expected the Hunt to be a long one, and the weight of armor would significantly cut the length of time that he could maintain the Hunter's trance.

The spear was a weight in his hands, unexpected in its heaviness. Espere, not ten feet from where he stood, seemed isolated; she fluttered around him in a circle as if the spear prevented her approach. He felt her distress keenly, but also thought he felt a distinct yet subtle satisfaction. Her eyes were drawn to the monument, and then away, to and then away, as if the motion were as necessary as breath.

This was not the forest of the Sacred Hunt. This was not any land that had ever been Breodani. Smooth, hard ground beneath his feet, the constant smell of salt, the lap of waves longer across than large villages—these were foreign. And on foreign soil, he stood—his lands forfeit, his title disgraced. When the Hunters gathered in the Kings' City, he would not be counted among them; he would see no ascension, be party to no celebration, test his hunting skill against no other Lord, no peer.

He knew he should feel something.

And he did: pride. For even though his peers could not know it, he faced the Hunter's Death—and he faced it alone, with certain knowledge. This time, this one time, it would be different. The afterward, Stephen would have worried about, but Stephen was not here.

The waiting was harder than it had ever been.

Meralonne sat in a silent crouch beside Sigurne. She was calm, almost preternaturally so. Of all the Magi—and the Council was, with three exceptions, assembled here—she was the one he least understood. She was slight of build, short, and quiet to the point of being passed over at all but the most crucial of Council decisions; if any were to be left behind, he would have assigned her one of the positions. She had been offered a berth, and she refused it.

"Cantallos is older than I by thirty years," she'd said quietly, "and Alene by eighteen or so."

"Cantallos," Cantallos said brittlely, "has at least had the advantage of seeing previous battle."

Sigurne made no reply, but the set of her jaw, the slight tensing of her shoulders, made Meralonne wonder if Sigurne, in a past that had not unfolded before him, had not herself seen war. In the end, her power and her quiet argument could not be ignored; she sat before Moorelas' grim-faced statue looking very much as if she were merely waiting for dinner, and not death.

Matteos beside her, broad-shouldered and overbearing, glared at any and all who came near; he was her self-appointed protector. If this annoyed her, she kept her annoyance to herself as she almost always did. Matteos did not take a seat, as most of the Magi did; he stood.

"Are we ready?"

At the sound of the voice, Meralonne turned. A young member of the Order—a promising student in the arts of war, and one pledged to the Magisterium after the full course of his studies—waited his response. "No, Torrence," he replied. "But either we will be in the next half hour, or we will never be." He nodded toward the circle of eight.

Torrence Briallon bowed. "We await your order," he said softly, withdrawing.

Devon ATerafin stood beside the Lord of the Compact, watching the Kings as if his life depended on it. It did.

But even had it not, he would have watched. The Kings were in their power, if not on their thrones; as they chanted the rites, as they spoke the key not meant for mortal ears to hear or voices to utter, they seemed to grow in stature, in height.

No food had passed their lips, no water; they did not sit or stretch their limbs or in any way relax—nor had they this eve. Yet they did not seem to flag or suffer for it, and their eyes, when their eyes could be seen, were like the golden moon.

That moon shifted across the sky; he could mark its position only by the spires of the Churches upon the Holy Isle. Without meaning to, he began a silent prayer, his lips forming words, although to which God, and with what supplication, he did not know. A young girl's pleading sobs caught his attention, held it, deepened the force of the words that he spoke. What threat could the Sleepers pose, he wondered, that could be worse than this?

He, who was trained to imagine any possibility, could see none. And so he continued his makeshift, inexperienced prayer.

The moon at its height; the final hour.

The voices of the eight stopped the interwoven chant that had occupied their energies in turns and cycles for the last several weeks. The harmonies and melodies of their song-speech suddenly converged in a rush, rivers seeking the ocean. The eight most powerful men and women in the Empire spoke with a single voice—a poor imitation of the multitude—the barest hint of what a God's voice must feel like to mortal listeners.

The witnesses—and there were many—tensed as one man, drawing in on themselves, becoming at last fully attentive and fully silent. The moon, high and full, illuminated the sea, the seawall, the armor and drawn weapons of the gathering.

Eight words were spoken.

Eight times the words died into the silence between the lightning and the thunderclap. The last time, only silence prevailed. The circle lifted clasped hands and raised stark faces toward the heavens.

Above, on the platform that stood over historical relief and graven statuettes, the heavens answered. The statue of Moorelas *moved*.

The face of the statue was harsh, graven in stone that had worn and weathered over the centuries. No fleshly tone transformed it; no glint came to armor, or color to cape or boot. Yet it turned—he turned—in a large, slow circle, sword raised, to view the supplicants. First, the eight. The Exalted of the Mother. The Exalted of Cormaris. The Exalted of Reymaris. The Sacred of Mandaros. The Sacred of Cartanis. The son of Teos. Cormalyn. Reymalyn.

To each, he nodded, and as he did, they stepped out of the circle, breaking it. At last, unbound, he turned his cold, stone gaze outward. There he saw the warmages gathering in a grim and expectant silence; he saw the Kings' Swords and the Kings' armed defenders amassed to the North. To the West, he saw the paladins of Cartanis, who made a religion of the sword raised in just cause; with them, stood the Priests of Reymaris and the Priests of Cormaris—for in either Church, weapon skills were not uncommon. The Mother's Children were not armed to fight, but they brought to the battle their skills and talents at healing, and the Mandaros-born brought the talents of their parent to the battle as well.

"Well met," he said, his voice the very thunder.

Almost as one, they fell to one knee.

"Follower of Bredan," he continued, seeing through the darkness as if it did not exist.

The lone Lord of Elseth looked up.

"Free your Lord, and you will have peace."

Then the foreign Lord lowered his dark head.

"The time is not yet," the statue continued, speaking again to the assembly. "But the ways will be opened. Touch not what you see, and seek not to disturb it—or you will break the Compact which your Lords—and mine—have made." He knelt upon the small, raised platform that had borne his weight for the ages, and would bear it for longer still. His sword, he lifted, one hand on either side of the long, flat hand guard, point to the ground. "Fare thee well," he said softly. "For ere this night is past, many of you will walk upon Mandaros' fields and in his halls. Walk in honor." Without another word, he drove the sword point groundward, into the wide pedestal upon which he stood.

Light flared around him as he knelt before the hilt of a buried sword.

Beneath his feet, the octagonal reliefs began to undulate, changing in shape and texture before the watching crowd. Where historical carvings had once told the tale of the great acts of bravery—of honor—that were Moorelas' life, only a shimmering clearness remained, like glass but thicker and somehow more liquid.

"Pass through," the statue said, its voice already dying. "And quickly. The time is short."

The Kings began to issue orders, girding themselves—at last—for war. Queen Siodonay stood at the head of the Kings' Swords that were her personal guard and escort. She had seen the streets of the city for weeks on end, but she was denied the conclusion of the battle. The Kings would go. If the Kings fell, it was to the Queens, and the young god-born Princes, that the Empire would turn.

Siodonay raised her chin slightly and smiled. The smile was the wolf's smile, a Northern legacy. She raised her sword, held it high a moment in salute, and then brought the side of the pommel crashing into the width of her kite shield.

The Kings' Swords at her back were silent, except in the ranks that contained men from the Northern climes; they, too, began to strike their shields with their swords. A send-off. A warrior's salute.

The Terafin stood her ground as the small army began its descent into the literal darkness. Whether they would rise again, she could not say—nor could Jewel, who stood in somber silence by her side. They had no skills to offer the Kings; they had responsibilities elsewhere in the city. Neither would set foot in the maze below.

But only Jewel was bothered by it.

They killed my kin, she thought, as a dark shame dimmed the moment. *I owe them.*

But instead, she would let these others—Priests, mages, and warriors all—fight the battle that had started as hers. Some part of her was glad of it, too, which only made it worse.

But Jewel was no master at keeping her thoughts from her face; The Terafin noted the young woman's expression in the unnatural light that emanated from the monument.

"We would not have come this far if not for your intervention," The Terafin said unexpectedly. "No dream would have led us to this place, and if not for this, we would have no chance at all.

"You are ATerafin, Jewel. You must learn to think beyond the fist that strikes or the dagger that draws blood. Instead of one hand, you have called upon many. Where you have no hold on the fires or the elements, the mages have come, where you cannot heal or offer succor, the priests, where you cannot fight and stand against the force of demonic skill, the warriors." As she spoke, The Terafin drew her hood above her shoulders. "Come."

Jewel nodded quietly, hoping that one day she would understand The Terafin's concept of honor and duty. She did not realize how much she already did.

Although they appeared to be of living glass, the walls gave no hint of what lay beyond—no darkness or light escaped. One had to walk through them to gain that knowledge, and the act was not a simple one—for each of the soldiers assembled here could see the man before them swallowed whole without a backward glance. Many of the soldiers closed their eyes or held their breath at the moment that they lifted foot or pushed arm across the threshold. But not a single one refused to follow where the Kings themselves—to the great distress of the Lord of the Compact—led.

To pass through the walls was a sensation that was at once many things: quiet, loud, pleasant, jarring—it was as if the walls themselves were the repository of the lives of the people who had come to place wreaths at the foot of Moorelas' statue—or to kiss there in the darkness that young lovers make light. But the walls that they had passed through, of glass, of light, of standing liquid, disappeared at their backs. In their place, long musty shadows that reached out to touch the half-height of what had once been towering walls. The very giants must have built the room, and assembled in it, for the hundred men and women here were dwarfed by its dimensions. The ground at their feet was marble, and gloriously worked; it had weathered the centuries with no loss to its dark luster, and the golden inlay glowed faintly with a light strong enough to see a short distance by.

"How do we leave?" one young Sentrus whispered.

No one cared to give the obvious answer.

"We will have more light," someone said, and a new voice answered.

"NO."

At once, swords were drawn; the gathering of the mages prepared; the Priests began to burn their braziers and murmur their low chants. But no one moved, for the figure herself was made clear as she approached.

She was not a young woman—perhaps older than Queen Marieyan—for she radiated a sure confidence, and a power, that the young rarely have. To the foot of the Kings she came, and there, at a distance of thirty yards, she knelt, dusting the ground with the hem of a cloak that seemed to make way for her knees. A trick of the light, perhaps.

The Kings glanced at each other a moment in silent conference, and then King Cormalyn spoke.

"Rise," he said, his voice carrying in the hush of the room. "Rise and identify yourself."

She obeyed his command quickly, unfolding her knees as if they seldom bent so. "I am Evayne," she said softly. "Evayne a'Nolan."

"Who are you, and what are you doing within these walls?"

"I am waiting for you, Majesty. For I have walked the hidden path, and in so doing, I have learned enough to be of service to you while our paths converge." So saying, she pulled a shining orb from her cloak and held it beneath her chin.

"And why should we trust you?" It was the question in almost everyone's mind. Almost.

"Because, my Lord, no one living, no one sane, seeks the ascent of the darkness. Those who call themselves Allasakari have already been devoured, and those who delude themselves into thinking they will have power . . . But it is not to speak of that that I have come. I am seer-born, and the way to the undercity is treacherous. Will you accept my aid?"

"And who is Evayne a'Nolan that we should know her to be sane?" The Lord of the Compact spoke in his sharp, pointed voice.

"A friend."

"But friend to whom? It is a matter of ease to claim friendship—and often a matter of deceit."

"I will not force myself upon you," the woman said quietly. "I cannot. If you will not have my aid, I will leave you."

"No," the Lord of the Compact said, "you will not."

"And will you detain me?" Evayne's smile was a crack of ice between thinned lips.

To the Kings' side, from nowhere, came Kallandras the bard. He knelt in the posture of abasement before King Cormalyn's feet. "Majesty," he said, interrupting the royal interview, "I am Master Bard Kallandras of Senniel; I have served the Crowns' circuit for my tenure. I bear this woman little love, but I will speak for her. You may trust her."

The King raised a streaked, dark brow.

A second man came, struggling through the still crowd, and he, too, flattened himself against the floor, his white hair a spill against cool green. "Majesty," he said, "I am Member Meralonne APhaniel of the Order of Knowledge, and of the Council of the Magi and of the Wise. This one was once . . . my student. I, too, will speak for her."

And before the King could speak, a third man came, but he did not abase himself. He knelt, on one knee, his animals standing at rigid attention at his back, a long, plain spear beside him. "Your Majesty," he said, speaking as if words were not his strength, "I am not Essalieyanese, but I have fought the demons and the darkness in my native lands—and you have granted me permission to hunt them here. If my word means anything to you—or to the man who speaks for you—I give it as well: I speak for Evayne."

"I do not speak for the King," the Lord of the Compact said, in a voice as thin as Evayne's smile had been.

"He speaks," King Reymalyn said, his voice light with just a hint of amusement, "for the Kings' safety. We will accept your guaranties, gentlemen."

The dark-robed woman stepped forward as the three men rose to greet her. She stopped first in front of Kallandras and met his eyes gravely. They were darkly hollow, where once they had been the sky of high summer. She started to speak, but he turned away from her; her eyes flickered at the slight, but her expression did not shift.

To Meralonne APhaniel, she also offered her silence, but in that silence was the hesitance that a student might offer a master years after the relationship has been severed. To see them, the powerful woman and the powerful man, face-to-face, made the man seem almost ageless.

"I have not forgiven your silence," he said at last.

"I know," was the soft reply. "But mark it well: The time is coming when my silence will be broken at your behest, and then we will both wish for the years in which I sat at your feet learning the arts."

"Is this a seeing?"

"Yes," she replied, already beginning to move away. "But not of the gift. Of the heart."

Last, she came to Gilliam of Elseth, and before him—only before him—she bowed low, bending both knee and head. He caught her arm, little realizing that he was the first man to touch her in many years, and pulled her roughly to her feet. "Don't," he said, releasing her as if she burned to the touch. "I didn't save him either. He always said the Hunter would take him. I always said—

"But tonight," he finally added, hefting the spear, "it will all be over."

"Hunt well, Hunter Lord," she told him quietly. "And you, little sister. Hunt well."

Then, schooling her face, she went to the Kings, and stood before them as a respectful peer—a Queen—might. "Your Majesties," she said softly, bowing once. "It is not safe to use magic within the great chamber. It has . . . unusual effects, and not all of them pleasant. However, if someone should be so foolish, it will almost certainly be survived. But below, in the chamber where the Sleepers lie, any use of magic will destroy the caster. Once we are in the tunnels proper, the protections wane."

"Very well," King Cormalyn said coolly. "Member APhaniel, you had best impart this information to your mages."

Evayne led them through the half-lit great chamber to the remnants of an old door frame, crossing a floor that was tiled with letters too vast, and too foreign, to be easily read. But every so often, a member of the Order of Knowledge would stop in a shock of recognition before his brothers and sisters ushered him on into darkness. Twice, the hint of magic flared in the chamber; once, it fizzled, and the second time it turned into a moving, noisy display of fire-lights. There was no third time, and although the Priests and the soldiers ground their teeth in annoyance, the mages at least lent their sympathy to one whose specialty of study had suddenly, dramatically, taken on new life—and one who was never going to be able to wring answers from the discovery, to examine it, or to learn from it.

At last the gathering stopped in front of a door through which ten men might easily move abreast. Or rather, a frame; the door was missing, although the hinges and joints were still there. As the walls did, the frame disappeared into the darkness above, but it was clear that the doors had been much, much taller when this hall had last seen light—if it ever had.

"Here," Evayne said, staring into the darkness, "we begin our descent. Light your lamps, if you have them, or your torches—but *do not* rely on magery to guide your steps."

As if she were a stone in a pond, word rippled in an ever wider circle at her back, and with it came the meager light of torches; lamps were carried by the Priests who attended the Exalted, and the Astari who attended the Kings. She waited, arms crossed, violet eyes seeing into the shadows that blanketed the landing. At last, the Kings' men gave their ready signal, and she began to lead them toward a large set of stairs.

In width, the staircase was at least the match of the door frame to the great chamber. But its finer detailing had not been lost completely to time and accident, and when foot was placed upon the foremost step, a hollow chime sounded. There was a momentary panic, but Evayne lifted a hand.

"It is the song of approach," she said, "and of departure. The stairs were built to chime it, by some magic or some craftsmanship that has long been forgotten. No one could approach by stealth those who waited above. No one could leave in secrecy."

"Then they'll hear us below."

"I do not know," she said. "But I think not. For the chamber of the Sleepers lies between us and our enemy."

"Lead," King Cormalyn told her quietly.

"As you command."

The music continued, but it played as cacophony; this many men were not meant to approach or depart in so disorderly a fashion. Or perhaps it was meant to be discordant; what had dwelled in this citadel in the mythic past no one could say for certain except Evayne, and she would not name it. Whatever the reason, many were the soldiers who, on their descent, stopped a moment to tie their sword knots and ready themselves fully for combat.

Yet what greeted them was an empty hall, and a long one; it was fashioned of plain stone, but of larger blocks than were used anywhere else in the city. There were no windows—had this part of the building originally been underground, there would have been no need—but there were also no torch rings, no lamp hooks, no provision for the light.

The halls were high, the ceilings, where the light carried by the servants of the Kings or the Exalted was strong enough to make them visible, vaulted in an odd, fanned lattice. To the side, left and right—east, west, south, and north seemed for the moment to have lost their meaning—were narrower exits from the main hall they traversed, darkened branches into the unknown. Evayne kept them to their course; any difficulty was again with the Order's members, many of whom were accustomed to pursuing their studies with a single-minded purpose that occasionally bordered upon the irresponsible.

Yet if curiosity drove them to stare into the ruins of doors and halls as they passed them by, it also drove them forward, and at last, after a time that was only measurable by the lowering of the oil in the lamps, the hall ended in a forbidding set of doors that stretched from floor to unseen ceiling.

Set across the closed doors was a large seal with runes emblazoned in a closing spiral from edge to center; it seemed to be made of gold, and in the darkness of torch and lamplight, it radiated light like a bonfire.

"These are the last of the doors," Evayne said softly. "There were three, but two have already been breached by the breaking of the earth and the sinking of the city. They were magicked once, but the source of their power has long since fled this world."

"Magic," Meralonne told her, "does not flee when the caster dies."

"No," she nodded, taking his correction as quietly as she had always done. "But it *is* weakened when the race dies. Or when the race leaves." She smiled slightly. "And if I gave you the impression that no magic remained here, please forgive me—for the magic is not one that you or I could easily break." She turned and bowed to the Exalted, and they came.

"It offers warning," the Exalted of the Mother said quietly.

"And promises danger," Evayne added.

"You read the oldest tongue?"

But the seeress did not reply. Instead, she said, "Exalted, grace us; open the door that your ancestor barred. We have so little time."

People seldom saw any of the Exalted hesitate; they thought it merely a trick of the light, for with surety and purpose she approached the wide doors. Lifting her arms, she began to speak, her tone quiet and reasonable, her words incomprehensible. Minutes passed; the sound of flames lapping oil and air, of breath being drawn, formed a stage for her voice.

The doors dissolved.

And with them, the darkness.

*   *   *

Silence, blessed silence. The cries of the dying, the pleas of the soon to be killed—they did not touch the Sleepers' Crypt at all. It was hard for the men and women assembled without not to rush headlong into it. There had been little peace in the last few weeks. But they were well aware of their duties.

No lamps shone that were bright as the light in the crypt; day ruled there, framed on all sides by darkness and earth. Upon three stones biers, arranged like the petals of the trifold flower, lay the Sleepers. Their feet pointed inward, heads to the round, curved gallery sculptors had made of the walls. Above them, stellar vaulting, beneath, concentric circles laid into the fabric of the stone itself.

Yet it was not the architecture which drew and held the attention; it was the Sleepers themselves.

"Do not approach them," the Exalted of Cormaris said. His voice while not sharp, was hard. "And be wary of crossing any circle's path."

The Kings nodded, and word, as ever, was sent through the ranks. Yet no man or woman passed the biers who did not stop a moment to gawk. Even the knowledge of the darkness that waited in the halls beyond this chamber did little to still the Sleepers' spell, for they were beautiful and they filled the heart with a deep longing, and a cold one.

"Did you always know where they were?" Meralonne asked Evayne quietly.

"Not always."

"Did you know of it while I taught you?"

"No."

The mage stepped past her; she raised a hand to his shoulder reflexively, and then let it drop before she touched the heavy darkness of his robes.

"Mage," the Son of Cormaris said.

"If I could, I would not wake them," was the low reply. "I understand what you vowed, Exalted, and I would not force you to defend that oath while there is a greater enemy—a mutual one—to face." He bowed slightly, and then stepped carefully around the periphery of the widest circle to better see the light of a Sleeper's face.

He—if he it was—was both tall and slender, with hair that fell around his face like a spill of pure silver. His lashes were white, and his skin pearl-like in its luster. He wore a golden breastplate, and a shield, with a design that denied the light yet did not claim the darkness, lay below his folded arms. Blued and gilded greaves he wore, and gloves, and beneath his chin a long and flawless gorget. His helm rested beneath the steeple of his hands.

Yet he held no sword, nor was one laid at his side.

"What—what are they?"

Meralonne turned at the sound of the voice, meeting the gaze of a young man before that man was swept past him by the movement of his fellows. Still, knowing that the answer might be carried by the room's perfect acoustics, he answered.

"They are the Princes of the First-born."

"And what was their crime?" The Exalted of Cormaris asked.

"Did your Lord not tell you?"

The Exalted frowned. "Only that they were guilty of betrayal."

"But not what that betrayal was?" Meralonne's smile was bitter indeed. "It was manifold, Exalted. And for it, they have lost their swords and their names—see, you cannot glance upon the device that was once the pride of their kin." He lifted a slender hand and pointed to the shield.

"You know much, Meralonne."

"Legend lore is one of my specialties," the mage replied. "Come. The darkness is waiting, and it will wait neither peacefully nor long."

Chapter Twenty-Eight

DARKNESS AND DEATH; the cries of the dying a glimpse of what eternity in the Hells must be like. Every man, every woman, tensed as their feet crossed the threshold from light and silence into the footpaths of the undercity.

Beyond the cavern of the Sleepers, in a twisted, broken tunnel that might never have seen the day, the torches began to flicker: a change in air currents. The army shifted uneasily, but Evayne was unconcerned; she followed the winding tunnel until it once again reached a flat, worked place. The ruins of a hall, broken gargoyles, the bases of statues that had once lined the ways—these were blanketed in shadows that grew heavier and heavier with each step taken.

Those steps were silent, a gift of the mages who now walked slowly behind their compatriots and ahead of the main body of Priests. Anyone with the sight for it would see them coming; the lattice of magical light necessary to blanket such a large group had a distinct and unavoidable signature. Still, that signature was less obvious than the sound of a hundred—and more—booted, heavy pairs of feet. Any advantage, no matter how slender, would be used.

The Kings led again, but this time, the ranks of their Swords and Defenders were broken by the presence of war-mages. Mandaros' Priests also walked in the forefront, judging the shadows, looking for any signs of life, natural or no.

They did not see as keenly as the woman who walked in midnight-blue robes; they did not have the hidden eye. But if she saw danger at the start of their descent, she did not speak its name: They journeyed into darkness to destroy a door through which a God was stepping. Danger enough.

The first creature to come out of the darkness swept in from the side, through a tunnel that was rough-hewn and recessed into the hall along which they had chosen to walk. It was not humanoid, and in the end, not sentient enough to realize that a small army was bearing down upon it.

It was fast enough, however, to claim first blood—first death—before its victory celebration was brought to a messy, and magical, end. For one brief second, the cries of its dying agony eclipsed the suffering of those below.

There was no body to study.

The mages fanned out into the side tunnel, but they found no other such creatures on the prowl. Fifteen minutes, perhaps less, and the army was once again on the move.

Another demon, hunting Gods only knew what, fell to the mages. A third.

The fourth came down from above, casting a dark and fiery web upon the unsuspecting Priests at the rear of the group. Although the war-mages joined the fray as quickly as they could, the maze and the updrafts in the large, abnormally shaped cavern were the territory and the strength of the beast. The fight was long and hard, and in the end, fully twenty men and women lay badly injured or dead.

But the seeress brought worse news than that.

The enemy would soon be warned of their presence. They would have time to prepare a defense.

Karathis-errakis erupted into the coliseum like the living flame that he was. He spun in air a moment before guttering; the ground approached his knees and the heels of his multiple hands as he rushed to abase himself against it.

"Lord." His voice was muffled by dirt and the sound of the dying, but it was clear enough—barely—to be heard.

Karathis' gaze, where it met the back of the prostrate creature, literally burned. But Karathis-errakis knew better than to scream or attempt to protect himself; to interrupt a lord while he presided over the damned was never a wise course. But to do nothing, this time, was even less wise. He waited, hoping to survive the wrath of a demon lord in the throes of the Conviction and the Contemplation.

It was not Lord Karathis' even temper which saved errakis' existence upon the mortal plane. "Enough, Karathis." The fire burned less fiercely; the smoke of charring flesh gave way to the simple stench.

In the Hells, such interference would be an open declaration of war, and such wars, in a landscape where power and rulership meant everything, were common fare. But there had been no rulership challenges upon the mortal plane in millennia, perhaps because there was no easy dominion over the souls of those who had not yet chosen. Or perhaps it was merely because a demon lord rarely walked the plane; two were almost unheard of. Karathis turned his gaze upon Isladar, and Isladar raised an unfettered hand, one quite human in seeming.

Karathis did not know the limits of Isladar's power, for he had never seen Isladar use it to its full extent. Isladar ruled no terrain in the demesnes, he forced no lesser creature to bear his name and do his bidding, he chose to absent himself from the ducal struggles, when the hierarchies of the Hells underwent their radical changes—and yet, absent, he incurred the wrath or enmity of no Duke.

It was almost as if he existed outside of the realm which had birthed him.

And in that realm, the unknown was the greatest danger of all. Karathis frowned openly as his surroundings lost the edge and the clarity that the Contemplation brought on.

"Speak," he said.

Karathis-errakis did immediately as bid. "Strangers approach from the southeast."

"What is this?"

The creature swallowed, and the last of its protective flame went out completely. "We think—we think at least one hundred, at most three. Humans."

"Impossible," Karathis said, folding his arms while his claws grew darker, longer, and harder.

"From the southeast?" Isladar asked.

The creature did not respond.

"Answer him."

"Yes, Lord Isladar."

"Interesting. Were they armed?"

"Yes. But—the armed men have not been fighting in the tunnels. They move with speed, and in complete silence."

"How were they discovered?"

"Arradis-Shannen was destroyed in the seeker's cavern. Before he died, he sent word."

Arradis-Shannen served Sor na Shannen as lieutenant. He was not the most perceptive of creatures—but he was one of the more powerful; had his intellect ever matched his ambition, he would have been a threat.

"They have mages," Karathis said coldly, no question in the question.

"Yes, Lord."

Karathis seemed satisfied, but Isladar was not. "Karathis, do not be a fool. Arradis-Shannen was *Kialli*. If he were brought down in battle by mere human mages, we would have felt the ground breaking beneath our feet." The demon lord turned to stare into the darkness at the mouth of the coliseum's southern doors. "No, they have Summer magic," he said softly. "They think to bring the light with them into the Winter's haven."

At this, Karathis smiled; his teeth gleamed a moment before his lips once again covered all but the longest of them. "Let them bring light," he said softly. "We lost many to the cursed bardic voices—let them supply the final sacrifices that our Lord requires."

"We cannot afford that," was Isladar's steely reply. "Think: the one who carries the Hunter's Horn may lead the human pack."

Silence.

And then the darkness began to fold and fray as Karathis raised his voice in a roar and a summons.

* * *

"This is not possible," Sor na Shannen said, her voice a sensual growl—and a furious one. "Karathis—"

"I closed the tunnels personally. I *saw* each unmaking. Or do you challenge this?"

She said nothing; it was a small enough council that she did not dare to stand her ground. In a fight at this range, Karathis was assured a victory—with a lord of his stature, she could not even be certain it would be a costly one. "We cannot hold that tunnel," she said at last.

"We have no choice."

"Look at it. There are no crawlways above it, and none below; it is too low to properly shadow. If Isladar is correct, the strongest of our number will not be able to wield full power."

It was Karathis' turn to snarl. "You are not required to hold it indefinitely. A few weeks—"

"You will not have weeks," Isladar said quietly.

Karathis turned a dark, dark ebony; his eyes burned orange, a glitter of sparks. Yet he did not argue with Isladar's words. Instead, he spoke two of his own. "How long?"

"Hours, I think. And at that, few."

The demon lord looked to the Gate that stood at the center of the coliseum, its iridescent keystone shining above a mass of roiling shadow. The altars were before it, and around them, piled like the refuse they had become, bodies. Not enough of them.

Karathis turned, wings unfurling from between the span of his shoulder blades. He gestured, and an ebony blade came to his hand, slick and wet from use.

"Isladar," he said softly, the fine ridges of his wings flexing at each syllable, "you know what must be done. Do it. *I* will attend to the intruders."

They felt the first tremors as the ground beneath their feet began to shake. Rubble from the walls came trickling down, as if the firmament had become, for a moment, a dangerous liquid.

The Lord of the Compact barked out orders before the rumbling stopped; the Kings pulled back, or rather, the Astari advanced, surrounding them in a slender protective shield. They held position as the ground trembled again.

"What is the cause of this?" the Lord of the Compact shouted.

"Some sort of magic," Sigurne replied, her brow furrowed.

Were the Lord of the Compact a less literal man, his sarcasm might have reverberated in angry echoes down the length of the hall. Instead, he said through clenched teeth, "Can you counter it?"

"Not if we don't know its type, no," she replied, her tone ever more serene.

There was reason that she often performed the function of liaison between the Crowns and the Order. "But if the Magi cannot discern it—" Her words were broken by the ominous shifting of rock; the ground shook and the ceiling creaked as if, having borne the weight of the earth for millennia, its strength was finally giving out.

Evayne, the crystal ball of the seer caught between two pale hands, looked into swirling mist, her pupils so large her eyes seemed blacker than the shadows.

"Evayne?"

She looked up at the sound of her name—a bad sign. When her sight was keen, and the vision clear, a storm raining down upon her exposed head could not distract her. Kallandras knew it for fact; he had seen it happen. Now was not that time; her eyes were already resuming their violet shade, and the ball was dimming—cooling, he thought—between her palms.

"I cannot say for certain," she said at last. "I feared it might be the elemental magics—but it seems that they are too wild for our enemies."

"They are not too wild," Meralonne APhaniel said softly, "but they are not appropriate here. If what you have said is true—if what you have seen is true—we are on the road to the Cathedral that once stood at the heart of Vexusa. If you look at the ground here, and here," he pointed very carefully, "I would say that we are almost upon it. Call the elemental earth magics, call the Old Earth, and it is quite likely that not only the tunnels, but also the Cathedral, would be destroyed." His smile turned grim. "And the caster, for that matter, if old tales are true.

"Never bargain with the Old Earth when you have nothing of value to give it." He paused a moment as the tremors stilled. "The demon-kin have nothing at all of interest to the earth."

"Not to the earth, little brother," a voice said in the darkness. "But come. Let there be *fire*."

Orange light, white roiling heat. Framed by it, fanned by it, a creature half the height of the halls, with wings of dark flame, and a sword that shimmered as it cut the air. It stood, manlike but not in any way human, its eyes of fire, its tongue of flame.

"This is ill news," the platinum-haired mage whispered softly. He gestured and the hall, yards away from where the creature stood, was suddenly illuminated by a shimmering opalescent wall.

"You know what it is?" Evayne's voice, tighter, smaller somehow.

A lift of a brow answered her question; a glimmer of arrogance. "Oh, yes," he said, master to student, as if for a moment that relationship had never been broken. "He is—or was—one of the Dukes of the Hells." Meralonne lifted a hand, and to it came a blade that only Evayne and Gilliam of Elseth, of the assemblage gathered here, had seen him wield. It was blue ice to dark fire, thin and hard and uncompromising. "Tell me," he said to Evayne, although his gaze did not leave their enemy. "You learned the Winter rites—did you ever learn the wild ones?"

"No mortal can contain the wild ways," was her curt reply. "How can you test me at a time like this?"

"It was not a test," was the equally curt answer. "It was a very, very strong hope. I do not know everything about you or your kin—and those mortals born of immortal blood, no matter how tainted, can sometimes bear the wild weight a moment or two." He turned to look at the men and women at his back: the Kings, the Astari, the Defenders, the Exalted and the Priests, the mages. The dogs. "How important is this mission, Evayne? At what cost must we succeed?"

Fire casually began to bore a hole through the transparent wall that Meralonne's magic sustained. He grunted. "Answer me; we do not have much time."

Her violet eyes narrowed as she glanced at her back, seeing what he saw; then they widened as she understood what he asked her. "Not at that cost," she said sharply.

"We will never reach the Cathedral if a price is not paid. Do you not understand what you have seen this day? This was Vexusa, yes, but before that it was something far worse, far darker; the Sleepers fell at the heart of a God's dominion. There are places upon the world that still hold the ghosts of the things that have passed within them; there are places, dark and deep, that hold more. This is one." Meralonne spoke from between clenched teeth; his knuckles, where they gripped the sword, were white. Fire had worn the shimmering wall to a clothlike thinness; before the wall snapped, the mage cried out sharply—a three-word command in a language that contained only magic. The wall shuddered, shrank, and flew to his outstretched hand, becoming a shield of the same substance as his sword.

The creature's large eyes narrowed into edges. "Well met," he said, almost pleased.

But there was no wildness to Meralonne, no exultation. He was pale—although he was always pale—and his eyes were the color of steel. "Evayne," he said softly, "tell the mages to use spells of defense—and only those spells."

"But—"

"*Do it.*" He stepped forward.

"You are already too late," the creature said, stepping farther into the hall.

"If we were too late, we would face the God and not the lackey," the mage replied.

The words cut the smile from the demon's long mouth. "You will wish, before this is over, that you had." His fire shot out like a whip, flaying the surface of rock and dirt. Where it struck, the rock grew red and white—above the heads of the army that waited at Meralonne's back.

Meralonne's magical shield-wall had given the war-mages the time they needed to react to the attack; molten rock dripped down in a glow of angry heat, and stopped in midair, congealing upon the invisible barrier hastily erected against it.

"You will wish it," Meralonne replied through gritted teeth. "Your lord is not known to suffer failure gladly."

"You are beginning to bore me."

Fire.

Strike and counter, strike and parry, strike and miss. The demon's sword cut a deep gouge in the face of the solid stone wall; the act did not slow his blade at all.

Perhaps the others did not note it; perhaps they did—but Kallandras was trained to observe in just such a manner. The demon's height gave him the advantage, as did his weight; the size differential did not slow him. Curious that; he would have expected Meralonne to last scant seconds against such an opponent.

But the silver-haired, slender mage, with no obvious spell and no obvious defense, gave ground slowly and grudgingly. Ah. That was close. The ground thundered with the blow of the demon's sword; shivered with the touch of his fire. Kallandras looked up at the crack that had appeared in the abutment. They could not stand here for much longer. The mages did not have the power to deny the demon's attacks.

"Evayne," he shouted; she turned, the edges of her cloak swirling wildly. She was the older Evayne; the woman of confidence and mystery. But he saw the fear in her eyes as they met his; the uncertainty shook him. Still, he lifted his hands to his mouth to mimic the call of the horn.

She knew which horn he referred to. "Not yet," she said through clenched teeth. "Too early, and we have come this far for nothing."

"We cannot—" He stopped at the sound of a terrible cracking, and swung round in time to see the shield of Meralonne APhaniel splintering into shards of cold light. The mage's cry reverberated throughout the sudden silence in the hall.

The demon's smile was a chill and terrible thing.

There were archers among the Kings' Defenders; they were assembled in haste and brought forward along the tunnel's width. But they were few, almost an afterthought to the battle plan, and not a conscious tactic. The light was poor in the tunnels, and the ceilings not always so high. But the demon was a target of such size that only one new to the art could miss—and there were no fledgling archers here.

Arrows, steel tips balanced by perfectly designed flights, were nocked and aimed. King Cormalyn, against the urgings of his brother, saw fit to test a single arrow's flight before giving the order to let fly.

So it was that he lost a single archer, and not the group—for the arrow turned in flight to find its target at the center of the Defender's eye. The archers were commanded to stand down in a silence heavy with uncertainty.

A Duke of the Hells gave them laughter in return for the offered death.

* * *

Fire ruffled the earth, transforming everything about it. Meralonne raised his blade against its onslaught, but without his shield it seemed clear that he had no defense. Clear, at least, to Kallandras.

He was no loremaster, to understand the niceties and subtleties of what he saw—but he was a bard, and the bardic colleges were built upon songs that were ancient before he first drew breath. The shield was riven, the fire stronger for it.

Can you wield the wild magics? Meralonne had asked.

But he had asked Evayne. Evayne's answer was not Kallandras'.

We need you, he told himself, meaning his trapped brothers and he. In the darkness, he raised his arm and called. Searing in the shadows and the dim light, the answer came: the ring upon his left hand flashed, illuminating him. He spoke to air, and air answered, pulling at captive curls and tugging at the seams of his dark clothing—an invitation to play, or worse. Pointing, he spoke again. To fire went wind, and around it laid its binding.

Kallandras' will was strong, but the demon lord was in his element. The fire banked but did not gutter.

Gilliam could see the fighting clearly because of the light the magical fire and ice shed in the hall itself. He could hear the grunts of the mages who kept the army protected, could hear the whispered, desperate prayers of the Priests, and the murmuring of the Exalted. That murmur was the only strong sound in the room, and it spread, growing louder and stronger in the saying.

The demon lord looked up as the darkness surrounding the army gave way to a golden light. His smile, if anything, grew broader. "Summer magic. How quaint. But you face no mere Winter."

"No? We faced one of the *Kialli*, and he fell, taking only a handful with him." Meralonne rose from his crouch; his shield arm dangled awkwardly at his side, but he did not favor it or attempt to protect it. The Summer magics seemed to strengthen him, if they did not weaken his foe.

"You did not face one of the Ducal Lords," was the cold reply. "I do not know why you chose to interfere in this battle—but for you, it no longer matters."

Meralonne opened his lips to shout a warning as the fires grew wild and uncontrolled. All that left him was a scream.

At his back, three of the Astari were ash in mere seconds, their armor and their swords a stream of smoking, white liquid.

Gilliam started forward, whether to aid or to flee even he was not certain. At his side, Ashfel growled; he brought a hand to the dog's head and held it there a moment, steadying both himself and his pack leader. His pack. Fingers white where they gripped the Hunter's Spear, he stared into the darkness, fumbling at his side. Evayne told him that he would *know* the right moment to make the call.

He'd missed it; he must have, but he'd make up for it now. His hands found the small, smooth Hunter's Horn.

Espere stopped him, her hand on his. Even here, it was hard to be touched by her.

Her eyes, he saw, were very golden and in the darkness almost luminescent. She opened her lips quietly; he thought she might whimper or growl. Instead, she spoke.

"Set me free."

He stared at her as if the words were incomprehensible.

"Lord," she said, tightening the grip she had kept on his hand. "Set me free."

He could not speak. He felt her anxiety, saw his expression through her eyes; he knew that she was afraid of what she asked.

"I would stay with you," she told him. "But if we are to fight, we must be equal—and we must be separate. Please."

He didn't even know how to do what she asked; the Hunter Lords built their invisible and necessary bonds, but only death broke them. And yet . . . her fear was not for him, and not for herself; it was an unnamed fear. Her fingers were curved and hard; he pulled his hand free of them and stepped back. Took a look at her, from the outside, as he would have to do with no Hunter's bond to guide him.

He was lying to himself; he knew how to let her go. He could feel the stretch and stress of the bond between them, for it was thinner than that which bound Ashfel to him. And he had made it so, distancing himself from Espere, this strange, half-human creature, this daughter of Stephen's killer, this—*say it, Gil*—the only woman for whom he had ever felt such a visceral desire.

Set me free.

He had distanced himself, but never completely.

The smell of charred flesh was carried down the tunnel by the howl of an unexpected wind; he froze in its chill and turned. She turned as well, and he saw the creature—the demon lord—through her eyes. But it was not as a human that she looked, not as a human that she saw.

Swallowing, closing his eyes a moment against her, and seeking instead the waist-high vantage of Ashfel, he cut her free, as cleanly and as quickly as possible.

It didn't hurt nearly as much as he had once feared it might—but it left an emptiness. She filled it with surprise, with wonder, and with a little fear. Because, the moment she was lost to him, she found a different anchor.

Espere began to *change.*

Stephen had told him about the first change. But Stephen's words were thin and weak compared to the reality of the child of the Hunter's Death. Her arms sank to the shaking earth, and her knees; her head she bowed down to her chest as she began a guttural keening that grew lower and louder and lower still. What had once been skin became harder and took on a sheen of reflective gold. Scales, he thought. He stepped back, to make room for her.

"Don't panic!" someone shouted. "She's one of ours!" He did not know for certain, but he thought the voice Evayne's.

Her face was the last to change, but if you looked upon her eyes, it was not so disturbing as all that. Yes, her jaws thinned and stretched, her teeth grew sharper and longer, her neck became almost the length of his arm from fingertip to shoulder joint—but her eyes were still Espere's eyes. Only larger.

Was she taller than the demon? It was hard to tell. Was she longer? Her tail flicked up, tearing a chunk of the stone from the side of the wall.

She had no wings. There was no need for them. With a roar that shook the ceiling no less than the fires had done, she leaped.

From out of the darkness of the tunnels, gilded and shining with Summer heat, hope came. It howled in wordless rage, its teeth crashed shut on empty air, its tail struck ebony thigh. Where seconds before a demon the color of night's despair fought a slender, injured mage, he now faced the Hunter's scion: Bredan's daughter.

Kallandras froze a moment in wonder—something his training should never have allowed—before he saw his opening. Without a word or a backward glance, he took the only chance he had to reach Meralonne APhaniel's side. The mage was propped to near-standing in a crevice that his battle had made in the wall; he cradled his arm against his chest, although he did not drop or put up his sword.

"Meralonne," the bard said softly.

The mage's eyes were slow to focus, and when they did, his slender features twisted in a bitter disappointment—as if, for a moment, he had expected to see another face, a different compatriot.

Kallandras said nothing, but offered him instead the use of a strong arm, a strong back—and a silence in which to gather the pain and bury it deeply.

"What a pair we make, we two," the mage said softly, his voice carrying over the thunder of a battle of giants.

"Yes," Kallandras replied. But his attention was focused upon other things: fire, falling rocks, the movement of stone plates beneath his feet. The mage was not, after all, a light or scant burden—but he was not immobile either, and together they reached the line of the waiting army. The Astari opened the ranks to let them through as if even they knew there was no danger in it. The battle was between the demon lord and the beast.

"Will it be enough?" Kallandras heard himself asking.

Meralonne grimaced. "I am no seer," he said, clenching his teeth. "But the Oathbinder is very near, and while he is here, his half-blood child is in her element. I would not choose this battle."

"Kallandras."

The bard turned to see Devon ATerafin's pale face. "Take him to the healers."

Wordlessly, Kallandras nodded; together they began to make their way down the eastern side of the hall.

But the bard stopped well short of the healers, seeking the shadows that fell between the radius of priestly lights.

Seeing this, understanding what it meant, Meralonne slumped against stone that was, for the moment, hard. "They cannot help me," he said softly.

Kallandras nodded.

"The shield was riven."

The bard again offered his silence. He had heard the cry that Meralonne gave as the shield splintered; had he not been watching, he might have mistaken it for a death cry. Might have. But he knew that Meralonne's death, when and if it came, would occasion no mortal cry.

The vision of the Kovaschaii was still sharp. What had divided them, unspoken, bound them together now in the silence.

"Bind my arm, and return me to the front."

"They will know that the healers have not tended you."

Meralonne's grimace was wry, and pained. "Yes, they'll know. And I'll give them the sharp edge of my tongue if they question me. Let the healer-born use their resources on the fallen they can help." He fumbled in the darkness a moment, his smile growing less fragile as he saw the disapproval in Kallandras' expression.

In the midst of a battle that would decide their fate, and the fate of Averalaan, Meralonne APhaniel lifted a long-stemmed shallow pipe to his lips with his whole hand. The aroma of burning tobacco made of the towering halls a familiar place.

He did not know what she was feeling, did not know what she was seeing, could not taste or smell or hear the sounds of battle as she did. As her tail cut a swath through fire and air, as the ground once again shuddered and heaved beneath the blow of demon blade, he made his way toward the front line where people stood at the ready as if they were uncomfortable just watching, but had no other choice.

Evayne caught his shoulder as he stepped past her, unseeing; he started and brought his spear around, but the space was too cramped to bring it to bear, which was just as well. He knew what she wanted to say before she spoke; her lips moved as the Hunter's daughter roared in angry pain, drowning out sound and warning to underline her point.

This was not his battle.

There was no hunt here, no quarry that he, and his pack, could bring down. There was only ancient war. Stephen would have appreciated it. Or maybe not;

maybe he would have been terrified because he understood all of its ramifications. Probably both.

He could bring himself to feel neither.

Either Espere would fail and he would perish here, in flame so hot and final that he probably wouldn't have time to feel pain, or she would succeed, and he would be one step closer to the time when the Hunter could finally be summoned.

Unblinking, he watched as the demon and the beast circled each other. They were both, he realized, strangers to him. Neither spoke, although it wasn't clear to Gilliam that the Hunter's daughter could; such a serpentine head was not built for the nicety of speech.

He cringed when the demon's sword struck home; she roared. A whip of flame caught her tail and held it a moment, but it did not burn or singe the flesh. Cascading sparks of pure green light fanned across her skin, and where it struck rock and stone it exploded; she was unfazed. At his side, Gilliam heard Evayne murmur, and although the words were indistinct, the surprise beneath them was not.

But the demon was also scraped by fang and claw, and forced back by the strike of tail, the ridge of skull that was almost hornlike. There was no easy victor here, no sure victim; where Meralonne had been overmatched, the beast fought upon an even field. It was not to the demon's liking. Pressed, he called upon the shadow, and it came; he was close to the power of his Lord—closer than she to hers. His wings spread like the swan's—deceptively lovely, ultimately deadly. Borne by the undercurrent of the Lord of the Hells' power, he rose to take the advantage that height offered. The blade that fell against her upturned neck drew blood. Red blood.

But she was not alone.

The air grew cooler, and the shadows less; light, not sharp or harsh, but bright nonetheless, began to make headway in the long halls. Incense masked the stench of fiery death, and the strongest of the burning braziers filled the air with the scent of ash and a hint of cedar, the smell of fire in the hearth. Many were the months in Averalaan when that scent was foreign—but to Gilliam, Lord of the responsibility of Elseth, Hunter of the Breodanir, it was life; the winters were long.

I am Bredan's follower, he thought, hating it less as he said it, over and over. *She is Bredan's daughter. We are the Breodani, we two.*

He brought the spear up, shrugging Evayne's hand from his shoulder. Then he stopped, thinking, *I am a Hunter.* The Hunters chose their quarry and they felled it with their pack—or they failed—alone.

But was she a Hunter? He hesitated; the moment seemed long. The demon's blade fell again, finding its mark across her flank. Crimson followed in its wake.

"Lord Elseth," Evayne said, her lips almost pressed to his ear, "this is not the Sacred Hunt."

He lowered the spear.

And then, sudden and swift, he raised it with a guttural cry of anger and denial. The Sacred Hunt had already claimed its victim. He did not have to stand by; he *would not* stand by to watch and linger like a helpless child, afraid to raise hand or weapon.

He called the trance early, and it came to him with an ease that it never had. The light became bright and exact, the darkness hard and well-defined. Around him, like mist or fog, the floating whispers of the foreign Lords tweaked his ears. He saw Ashfel, proud and alert, saw through Salas' eyes, caught more keenly the scent of the Mother's hearth.

Grabbing his horn, he winded it, long and loud—but he called only the ground hunt, and not the great one.

The lowing of the horn reverberated throughout the hall, louder even than the sounds of combat. Before it died into stillness, the eyes of the demon lord sought the eyes of the Hunter Lord.

Recognition.

The nature of the battle changed in that moment. Unlooked for, unrecognizable until the instant the horn was winded, the miserable Hunter Lord had revealed himself—carrying, in his folly, the single item that was a threat to the Lord of the Hells.

Karathis had been in the Hells when the Horn was first taken, but he knew it on sight, and knew further that no simple spell, whether born of wild magics or darkness, could destroy it; the Horn's destruction was not his intent. But the human bearer's was.

Could he but retrieve the horn and retreat, the war was theirs to win at leisure. Gathering his power, he struck the ground with sword and flame-touched invocation. The rock shattered and melted beneath the human's feet, fanning upward in a spray of heavy liquid.

But his target had already moved. Cursing, Karathis raised his blade as the beast roared and struck.

Gilliam pushed the trance to its limits, taking the speed and the strength that it had to offer and using them. The demon was faster than any quarry that he had ever hunted—and no quarry had proved so dangerous except the Hunter's Death. The shaft of the spear felt too thin as he turned it in his hands, gripping it tightly.

The ground buckled beneath his boots; he felt it break as he rolled to the left, gaining his feet without a backward glance. This time, he did not stand for long; the spear became a vaulting pole as he thrust himself up from the rock a second—less—before it, too, splintered.

As he landed, he heard the demon snarl in pain, and his lips folded up in a vicious smile. Espere could strike where Gilliam could only flee; she could stand upon the demon's summoned fire just as easily as the demon himself.

The smile dimmed quickly.

For as Gilliam looked hurriedly around, he realized what the demon's intent was. The ground, inch by inch, was becoming a red and white patch of heated, melted rock—rock upon which Gilliam could not stand, let alone fight.

Sor na Shannen's hands were slick with blood, and she stared down at the liquid with both distaste and fascination. Of the kin, she was a subtle creature, and her torments were not of the body, but of the mind and spirit. To kill in such a physical fashion, when her victim was helpless and waiting, was almost anathema to her. It did not show, however; the altars were blooded quickly and efficiently.

The Allasakari presided over some of the slaughter—a point of contention among the kin, but one that would be addressed later—and Isladar stood at the foot of the Gateway that had been so long in opening, kneeling so close to the tentacles that the God anchored himself to the world with that if he moved a hair's breadth, he might be devoured. He did not move.

Above the arch that opened into the void and the darkness, the keystone glowed a pale green, pulsing like an irregular heartbeat. Not a living creature, save for the Allasakari, remained in the coliseum. Those who had been kept in the pens for the weeks to come were led out in herds, driven to the arms of the kin and the Allasakari, dedicated to the darkness, and destroyed by it.

But would they be enough?

"Lord," Isladar said as the earth trembled beneath the coliseum, "all life and all light that can be found in your city has been offered to you. The Gate, we will hold while we can, but your ancient enemy stalks the streets of the city."

The darkness turned in on itself in a twisting convulsion, and then it grew still for the first time in decades.

Be prepared, it said.

Isladar watched in utter stillness and silence, as the darkness began to coalesce. Above it, the keystone began to dim.

"What is that fool doing?"

Evayne, staring at the patchwork the demon lord made of the stone floor, made no response to Meralonne's incredulity.

"The beast is weakened," Kallandras said, in her stead. "Perhaps he thought to help."

"Why thank you." The mage's voice was heavy with sarcasm. "That much is obvious. I merely hoped that the mysterious Evayne could tell me—tell us—that the young man's ability matches his intent." He drew upon pipe smoke as if it were necessary breath, and then blew it out in a huff. Teeth clamped together, he handed the pipe to the bard. "Take care of her," he told the younger man, as he gritted his teeth.

It was Evayne's turn to stare. "What—what are you doing?"

"What does it look like I'm doing? Your powers of observation have obviously dimmed over the decades." Again, he grimaced; the expression of pain didn't stop him from summoning his sword. It was slow to come, but when it did, it glittered in his hand like sharp, cold ice.

"Meralonne, this is not your fight."

"No?" Of all things, he laughed. "Evayne, it is not for the student to choose the master's battles."

"I am not your student, nor have I been for—"

"Evayne."

"What?" She did not turn to look at Kallandras, but she acknowledged his interruption.

"If Lord Elseth dies, who will wind the Horn? And if the Horn is not winded, who will face the God?"

For the first time, he saw the older Evayne angered as she turned to face him; her eyes flashed and hardened into something as cold as Meralonne's sword. "I have lived my life in this cause," she said though clenched teeth. "Do you think to remind me—"

The demon roared in agony.

As one, the three looked up to see Gilliam, Lord Elseth, dangling from the haft of a spear buried halfway into the demon's back. Buffeted by the thrashing of powerful wings, he clung blindly. His struggling body cast a shadow above the fires that rippled and stretched as if to reach him; to fall was death.

"Meralonne," Kallandras said urgently, surprising himself. "Can you save him?"

But Evayne said only, "What of the Spear and the Horn?"

The mage had no chance to answer, whether by word or deed, for as the demon struggled with the weight at his back, the beast struck, great jaws snapping so quickly they could be heard more easily than seen.

In a moment, the demon's cries were cut off as the beast's teeth worked their way into his throat.

"It seems," the mage said softly, "that this discussion is at an end."

It was too soon. Another two months would still be too early—but form would be easier for the Lord to assume, and the Gate easier to breach. Sor na Shannen felt the rumbling grow stronger beneath her feet. There was nothing she could do to stop it, and nothing she could do to bring her Lord closer to the plane; she looked inward instead.

Centuries ago, her name littered about for the idle and the foolish, she had been summoned to the plane by a young, long dead mageling. He was naive enough to believe the words of a demon, and talented enough to be able to teach her to manipulate the magic of the form; she had learned much from him before she had finally emptied the font of both his knowledge and his life.

It was Sor na Shannen who discovered Bredan's presence. It was Sor na Shannen—succubus, not demon lord—who had made her way to the Allasakari, and thence, to the meager and ill-protected Priesthood of Bredan's ignorant followers. It was Sor na Shannen who had in glory and power taken the Spear of the Hunter, and the Horn. Because it was Sor na Shannen who understood that if Bredan could somehow, in some way, walk the plane, so, too, could Allasakar.

If Allasakar began his ascent, Bredan would notice. If Bredan could notice, Bredan would interfere. Oh, it had taken years to understand most of the customs of the intricate and futile Hunt—and even now, she did not understand why Bredan chose not to feed upon the surrounding countryside to maintain his power and his sentience. But she knew that Allasakar would have no such difficulty.

It was a mark of genius, really, to destroy the priesthood. Ignorance descended upon the enemy's followers in a generation or two. And Bredan? The God was barely intelligible. The kill that he took was enough to keep him from being claimed by the wildness, no more.

She had visited the forest. Sought the crippled God.

Her first mistake.

But her name had still lingered upon the mortal plane, and her plan, interrupted, still flourished. Licking her wounds, hiding in the Hells under the guise of mere succubus and not demon-mage, she had waited. And waited.

Davash AMarkham, member of the Order of Knowledge, finally dabbled in the dark arts, and on his twenty-eighth summoning, managed to reconstruct her name from forbidden scribblings and ancient texts. He was an older man, and quite a powerful one, but he mistook her, as so many did, for a mere succubus. Within six months, she had her freedom from all but the most tenuous of control. Two years later, having learned what he could teach, she summoned Karathis, offering Davash—and his master, Lord Cordufar—as fitting sacrifice.

Karathis had almost destroyed her then and there. But her Lord protected her, and in the end, a Duke of the Hells was forced into an alliance with—as he called her—one of the least of its demon lords.

For almost four decades she had labored upon this plane—labored as a servitor to the Lord of the Hells, and not as a free demon seeking the momentary pleasure of flesh and form, the idle torment of those who have not yet chosen.

She was the architect of Allasakar's return.

Or she would be, once he crossed the threshold. And what might she ask for then? A return of the ancient, wild days, replete with shadow and suffering, with mystery and the magic of the unknown. Her lips were dry as she watched the arch in silence.

The keystone began to flicker.

When its light was dimmed completely, the door between the Hells and the world of the free would finally be pried open wide enough—and for long enough—that the Lord of the Hells could step across the threshold to claim the world as his dominion without the interference of the rest of his brethren.

"Master Gilliam," a voice said softly.

Gilliam looked up into a shadowed light to see the familiar face of a healer. Recognizing him, he relaxed and turned away.

In his arms, Espere stirred. She lifted her head a moment, and strands of matted hair clung to his leathers, wet and sticky where blood had not quite dried. Tensing, he watched her eyelids; they flickered but did not open. He did not know what she felt, could barely guess; she was no longer his. Yet they were not free of each other. If she was not part of his pack, she was part of his responsibility, and he claimed her for Elseth with a sense of quiet, fierce pride.

"Master Gilliam." The healer, Dantallon, spoke again, his tone strangely gentle. "The Kings are waiting."

Let them wait, he thought, but to his surprise, he looked up.

Dantallon's eyes were an unusual color. "Let me take her," he said softly, gazing down at Espere. "If she'll be safe anywhere—" He stopped, straightened his shoulders, and looked carefully at the man who sat upon the ground cradling an unconscious god-born girl. "I give you my word that I will watch over her."

Gilliam's arms tightened; he bowed his head a moment, resting dark hair against dark hair, filling his lungs with the scent of sweat and blood and ash. "You'll take care of her?"

"While I have breath," was the grave reply. Dantallon was not a large man, nor a particularly well-muscled one, but he was strong enough. To be a healer, to take the talent one was born to and temper it, to give everything that one was, and when that failed, still find something left to give—that took a strength that Stephen of Elseth had barely understood, and Gilliam of Elseth had not. Until now.

Quietly, Gilliam gained his feet, balancing Espere's body against his chest and the crook of both arms. Dantallon's sleeves were rolled up and buttoned to the edge of his plain shoulder seams, and his arms were stained with blood. Their hands met a moment as Espere passed from one to the other. Of the two, it was the healer's that was the surer grip. He smiled, his brown eyes ringed with lack of sleep and hollowed with care.

Espere stiffened and raised her head; Gilliam tensed, prepared to take her back should she wake and call. But she did neither; instead, her expression relaxed into something that was almost a smile. Dantallon shifted automatically, juggling her weight so that her head rested beneath the point of his chin.

"We both have our battles to fight," he told the Hunter Lord. "I envy you your prowess, Master Gilliam. It is upon your shoulders that the fate of the Empire rides. Do not envy me."

Oh, the vision of the healer was sharp.

Gilliam stood, feeling a mixture of comfort and, yes, curse him, envy.

"The Kings," the healer said, turning from him.

Lifting the Spear and girding himself once again with his sword, Gilliam of Elseth called his pack and strode toward the Kings of this foreign land. His leathers were singed, but miraculously whole, and the three burns across the length of his legs had been tended to by Dantallon himself. Gilliam would accept no other's intrusion.

The Hunter Lord returned to the Hunt; it enfolded his vision once again, drew him into its purpose.

Espere would not Hunt further with him this day, and perhaps that was best; after all, what kind of a Lord would force his liege to kill her father?

The mages had cooled the rock, but the once fine floor now resembled a fallow field after first thaw. The army began to pick its way across the uneven ground, avoiding the wells of unnatural shadow that lingered where the demon had fallen. Of the demon itself, no other trace remained.

The order of march altered as the shadows grew stronger; the Exalted joined the Kings, followed by their priestly attendants. Their braziers now burned bright, and the chanting of the Priests, low and even, filled the halls. This was their battle hymn; there would be no other. The darkness was so pervasive it demanded silence from those that walked toward it.

The landscape changed abruptly; the halls ended, as they had once before. But this time, there was no turning back or turning aside. Earth hemmed them in, tight in places and loose in others; above them, wooden joists, great beams or rock wet with mildew and time.

No normal formations, these.

Meralonne, arm bound tight to his chest, walked the tunnels in quiet thought.

"Meralonne?" Sigurne's voice, soothing in its ordinariness.

"Look," he said, pointing to the earthen formation above their heads. "Roots. There."

She nodded. "I noticed. But the tunnel walls, the roof, the ground—none of these have weathered time in any normal fashion. I fear the power that sank the city did not foresee such . . . resistance."

He shook his head. "No."

Her plain eyes were almost cutting as she cast a sidelong glance in his direction. "What power sank the city, and when?"

"It was never made clear," he replied neutrally. "Do you feel it?"

"Yes." It was as close as Sigurne would come to acknowledging the darkness.

Her eyes sought the earthen roof once more, as she lifted a lamp aloft. "Are we walking on an upward slope?"

"A gradual one."

They drew closer to air and sky, closer to Averalaan. The thought should have been comforting. "How long?"

"Sigurne, this may surprise you, but Vexusa was not my specialty of study."

She smiled as smoke eddied up in a slow moving cloud. "Everything is your specialty of study, Meralonne. Give me an educated opinion."

"Very well, but I won't be found at fault if I prove incorrect." He paused a moment, lighting dried leaves with a flicker of personal flame. "I would say that we are not fifteen minutes away from the main thoroughfare of the city."

Like a falcon loosed to sky in search of earthbound quarry, Kallandras could suddenly see. Imposed upon the rocky twisted wall that was this tunnel's surface, flickering as if it were the fire of a glass lamp in a gale, a vision of the dead came to him. His dead; the brothers that he had left.

"Kallandras?"

They lay stretched and broken in numbers too great to count, heaped like scraps of peel and core—the unwanted portion of a meal. Pressed thickly together by weight, he could discern among these corpses no face, no mark, no uniform.

"Kallandras?"

The vision altered as he searched; he could not hold it long.

The stretch of Kallandras' mouth, the intensity of his gaze, the way his shoulders curled in told Evayne more than she wanted to know and less than she needed. "Kallandras," she said for the third time.

"They're in the coliseum."

She didn't ask who, and as someone—she thought perhaps the ATerafin—began to, she lifted a slender hand, demanding, by gesture, silence.

"We're too late," he continued, his voice a curious blend of flat monotone and earnest desire. "The prisoners are dead. They've slaughtered them all."

Her hand rose again, and again questions gave way to silence, albeit annoyed.

"Something's happening to the arch."

Evayne turned absolutely white.

"The keystone is flickering." He did not ask her if she remembered either keystone or arch; neither of them had forgotten, nor could. "I think it's going out." Blinking, Kallandras glanced over his shoulder, surrendering the finding vision to rock and shadow.

Evayne had already turned away. "Your Majesties," she said, in a voice that carried weight because it also carried fear, "we are almost upon the Cathedral. Follow me now, and *quickly*."

*   *   *

The tunnel twisted to the left in a sharp, awkward angle; Evayne did not even pause at the branch to see if the enemy was waiting for them. The time for caution had passed. She moved at great speed and with great silence, unarmed and unarmored as she was; they lost sight of her almost immediately as the darkness began to eat away at the lamps and the torches they held.

But they had enough light to see the walls fall away into blackness on either side; whether they knew it or not, they stepped across a threshold. Above, there was darkness, and at their feet, shadows; they knew that they were no longer in the tunnels because their voices carried higher and farther.

The Exalted paled and began their chant, but Evayne waved them to silence. Pulling her hood from her face, she turned to the Kings, back to the darkness, arms raised high as if in supplication. "So that you will see and remember," she said, "*Father!*" Her cloak roiled at her feet as if her body itself were changing in shape as Espere's had done. From out of the folds of a midnight-blue so dark it seemed black, the seer's crystal rose.

Cascading down from the heights of a cavern that seemed—that *was*—too vast to be natural, came sparks of angry orange light. They traced a path in air, burning it into the vision not as a band of green afterlight, but rather as a swath of color. Like the brush of a crazed painter, these bands of light grew, ribbon by ribbon, until the whole of the cavern was revealed.

The dusty ruins of old stone buildings lined rubble-strewn streets. Brass railings and verandahs that looked down with suspicious ease on the grounds below were still intact. Doors, where doors might have once been, had long since rotted away; shutters were nowhere in evidence. But here and there, bottom-heavy glass work had not been shattered by the city's descent.

And the city must have descended with speed and a terrible force. At the edges of the tunnels, halves of buildings stood, their rotted, snapped joists revealed as if a dull sword had cut from roof to basement in one stroke.

"My Lord, they are in the city."

Sor na Shannen's glassy eyes took in the keystone's flickering light as if by doing so she could drain the last of it into her private darkness.

"Lord Isladar, should we—"

"No. Stand ready. He is almost nigh."

"What brought this here?" King Cormalyn's hushed voice.

Evayne pointed. At the center of the city, darkness lay like a formless cloud. But it rose almost to the cavern's height, and it was wide and long.

The King nodded to the seeress; at his back, his men began to form up. Where light could not go, they would. The air was heavy with things unspoken.

"Now is the time," she told them, seeing their apprehension and their determination. "Kings, Exalted, Sacred; Members of the Order of the profound; Astari, Defenders, and Priests—to the heart of a history that you could not have made, I have brought you.

"The darkness rises; beneath the shadows that light cannot pierce, the citadel is waking. *Allasakar* takes the last steps upon his path to this world. Let us meet him, as Moorelas met him; let us tender no less an answer."

There was silence, and then from the men of the North—and there were few— the sound of sword against shield. Tentative at first, it grew louder and surer, and the cavern caught its tumult and echoed it. Then a single voice joined it, raised in a rough and uneven bass. King Reymalyn was singing *"Morel's Final Rider."*

As if his unaccompanied chorus was a command and an invitation, others began to join him, searching memory for the words that most had not sung since they were very young. The song that had eluded them in their march through the tunnels finally gave them strength now.

"Lord Elseth," Evayne said, grave but loud, "the time has come. It is the first of Veral. The sun is breaking across the horizon in Breodanir." She lifted her crystal high enough that he might see it; it looked for a moment as if the sun had been cupped in her hands. "Call the Hunt, Hunter Lord, and join it."

Gilliam took the simple, unadorned Horn in his large hands and raised it, shaking, to his lips. He had come this far for only this reason: to Hunt the Hunter God, and have peace. But here, at the very threshold of an ancient, nigh forgotten city, his lungs faltered; he could not draw breath.

Isladar raised his head from the position of supplication to stare, not at the keystone, but at the darkness itself. To either side, the tentacles that had form and substance began to uproot themselves, taking great clods of dirt and flesh as they rose.

The shadows were omnipresent, but the darkness was not yet complete. With a mere gesture, Isladar doused the pathetic human lamps and plunged the coliseum into night. If the Allasakari objected, they did not give their anger voice—and in that, they were much like the kin in the face of their Lord.

The keystone was so pale it was almost simple stone. It flickered once, twice. Almost. Almost.

Was it fear?

Evayne watched his face as he pulled the Horn back to study it. "Lord Elseth?"

To his shame, his hands shook. Could it be that he was *afraid* to test his skill against the Lord of the Hunt—the very God who had given the trance, the bond and the hunting art to the Breodani? Angry, he gripped the shaft of the Spear and brought it down upon the ground in time to the beating of the shields.

Lifting the Hunter's Horn, he drew breath as if it were blood. And half a continent away, at exactly that time, on exactly that signal, the King of the Breodani stood at the edge of the Sacred Forest, surrounded by the sound of the beating drums, the heightened awareness of breath and heartbeat filling his ears, the smell of his chosen quarry coming from eight different noses, the drive to be gone, be running, be *hunting* not quite driving away the sure and certain knowledge that by the end of this day one of his valued Hunters would lie dead at the hands of the Hunter.

The King of the Breodani lifted his intricate, ancient horn to lips as Lord Elseth—the lone Hunter Lord in the King's lifetime to miss the call at the edge of the Sacred Forest—tipped smooth bone upward.

As one man, as one spirit, they called the Sacred Hunt, winding the Horn in its dance of three notes.

In the ancient city of Vexusa, in the heartland of his greatest enemy, the Hunter Lord answered.

And in the center of a Cathedral lost to shadow and magic, before the waiting eyes of demon-kin who stood at rigid, silent attention, the darkness finally became *perfect*.

Chapter Twenty-Nine

IT WAS NOT THE Hunter's Death, but the Hunter, who came to the call of the Horn. Limned in light, wrapped in robes that no human hands had ever touched, Bredan, Lord of the Covenant, stepped into the streets of the undercity. He seemed at first a ghost, some remnant of a forgotten, long-dead man—but he walked, gaining form as his bare feet traversed the cracked and rubble-strewn ground.

Gilliam felt his chest constrict; words, always a weakness, deserted him. Sinking to one knee, he clutched the Spear as if it were an anchor. The anger and the pain that Stephen's death had left him had been nursed into a cold and bitter thing; he had thought it could grow no worse. He was wrong.

For as the God took final form, his hair was fair, his features fine; he was neither short nor tall, neither broad of chest, nor stripling boy. If a God could be said to be any age, then he was a young man, near his prime. Were it not for the color of his eyes, he might have been Stephen.

Until Evayne gripped his shoulder, Gilliam didn't realize that he'd brought the Spear to bear. "Lord Elseth," she said softly, "peace." But the hands that rested upon his shoulder were as sharp and tight as the words she spoke. He looked up to see her face; it was turned toward the God, lips pressed white and thin.

Together they waited in silence; they did not wait long. As the God neared the body of the army, he began to move quickly and surely toward his single follower: Gilliam of Elseth. He ran as Stephen ran, with the same gait, the same rhythm of running step, the same awkward flap of arms. His expression melted into a pained exhaustion, just as Stephen's would have done at the end of the exertion of the Hunt. He wore a slender, unadorned scabbard across his back—for running, this, and not for some fancy Lady's ball—and at his hip, glinting with unnatural light, a horn.

It was too much.

In anger, in outrage, Gilliam of Elseth gained his feet. At his side, Ashfel, growling; to his left, Salas and Connel.

"Lord Elseth," Evayne said again, her face as pale as his was flushed, "now is not the time to use the Spear."

No. He knew it well—this was no Hunt, this steady, fleet race *to* the Hunter. But his arms ached with the visceral need to heave the Spear across the vanishing distance and have done.

As if that thought were loud enough to hear, the God stopped fifteen feet away and let his arms fall to his sides. "Gil?"

He spoke with Stephen's voice.

Stunned, Gilliam offered silence as a reply.

"I told him this was a bad idea. I told him you'd think it was an insult. Did he listen?" Snort. "I can understand why he's called the *Hunter* God."

"Stephen?" Fifteen feet disappeared in seconds.

Ashfel was uncomfortable; Stephen didn't smell like Stephen, even if everything else but the eyes was right. The anxious dog grabbed the back of Gilliam's cape between a generous set of teeth and pulled, hard. Gilliam snarled, but would not let go.

"Gil," Stephen said—for it was Stephen, it *had* to be Stephen—"I'm not—I'm not alive."

He knew it, of course; knew it because there was no bond—except for this physical embrace that he had forged—between them. But if he could not feel what his brother was feeling, he could hear it in his words, and the words, the sound of his disparagement, were sweet as any Hunter's call.

"But He—Bredan—told me I should speak with you."

"Where are you?"

Stephen's laugh was shaky. "I don't know. Not here. Not there. I—I don't like it much."

"I'll get you out."

"I'm not the important one," Stephen said, although the intensity of his relief belied that. "I was the last one taken; I still have some . . . solidity." He turned, then, to face the darkness. *"He's* stepped across, Gil—but he came too quickly— you forced him. Bredan asks your leave to Hunt once more before—before you do."

"My leave?" Gilliam's tone was bitter.

Stephen reached forward, forming a knot of his hands between Gilliam's shoulder blades. Then he shook his Hunter soundly. "This isn't about your loss—or mine—Hunter Lord," he said, his voice a mix of emotions. "This is about the fate of man. If Bredan doesn't kill the Avatar of the Darkness—"

"I know," Gilliam said, the words a low growl. His grip tightened; he held fast for five seconds, counting each one slowly and deliberately. And then he let go; he was Lord Elseth of the Breodani; he had called the Sacred Hunt; he was prepared to die so that Breodanir might continue. "Stephen, I—"

"I know." The huntbrother smiled, and then the smile vanished. "He doesn't have much power," he told his Hunter gravely. "The fight with the enemy will drain it all—and more."

"What does it—"

"It means that all that'll be left is the Hunter's Death. The beast, and not the Oathtaker." He paused. "That's when the Hunt starts. But, Gil—He says that it will be as if the Hunt hasn't been called in years."

Gilliam blanched and then nodded stiffly.

"We—He—" Stephen shook his head. "In Mandaros' Hall," he said.

"Swear it."

"I swear it." A crackle of blue light laced the air as the God behind Stephen's eyes witnessed—and accepted—the oath. Time did not allow for any other words, any other regrets or arguments.

As Stephen turned away and began to run toward the darkness, his body lost shape and substance, dissolving into an ethereal, moving mist, and resolving—in the distance a burst of great speed made—into a great, pale beast, a thing of light. That beast lifted its head and, opening its mighty jaws, roared its challenge to the cavern's lofty heights.

Lifting Horn to lips, Gilliam blew a long, loud note in response. A call to arms. It was the only signal that the army of the Kings needed. As one man, they surged into the streets, following the trail that the Hunter God had cut into the ground by his passage.

"Lord Elseth, what did he mean?" Meralonne APhaniel seemed to appear out of thin air, much as the God had done.

"He meant," Evayne said, choosing to answer for Gilliam, just as Stephen might have, "that the Hunter's Death will kill anything in sight until its need is satiated."

The silver eyes of the mage narrowed into a dagger's edge as he met the stony gaze of his former pupil. For they both knew that only one sworn to the Hunter could satiate that hunger. But all he said was, "Hunt well, Lord Elseth."

In perfect darkness, the subtle senses came into play.

A moment, and the eyes were forgotten; another, and the fear of the loss of vision was eclipsed by the quiet wonder of true night. Listen, and one could hear the sound of breath being drawn, or more significant, the lack of it; then, as the hearing made its adjustment, the sound of nails scratching palms, the rustle of hair, the licking of lips rough with dryness.

But there was more.

Without the intrusion of sight, the smell of blood, of ruptured skin, of human corpses newly made—these became stronger, fuller; laid beneath, the musky odor of human sweat, the scent of dirt, of stone, of rotting damp wood. Even the fabric with which the living and the dead were clothed had a distinct aroma.

Isladar stood, listening; he held himself perfectly, rigidly still, withdrawing from the world that he studied.

There—the sound of chitin scudding gently across the dirt. At its side, the twist of scales, and the pad of soft feet. Perhaps the click of hooves. The air began to turn and move; in minutes a wind with no natural beginning circled the coliseum in a magically contained gale. The other sounds were lost to the storm; Isladar sighed, giving himself over to the movement, the things of the flesh. The Lord was taking form. And what that form would be, no one could predict; the ways and the anchors of the world were strangely changed since the Covenant of the Meddler.

The Lord of the Covenant. He bared his teeth in contempt; that one had no subtlety, no true understanding of the ways of power. Direct, he was foolish; no other Gods would trap themselves so thoroughly on a plane not in their control. The Lord of Wisdom was a more interesting enemy, but even he was not of interest to Isladar. No.

Will you show your hand here? he thought, as he waited. *Will you, nameless one? Come then. The Covenant was witnessed by your lackey, but it was not his creation and not to his purpose. Do you think I do not understand the target of your maneuvering? You have waited long; here at last is my Lord's opening move.*

The shining beast reached the clouds of darkness first, but instead of disappearing into the beads of black mist, he drove them back as if they were alive and they could not bear his touch. He cut a path through the shadows that the army could follow, a wall of normal seeming, a curtain of light to either side of the magnificent, smooth streets. Into the heart of darkness he ran, and when at last the shadows were unraveled, the army stood mere yards away from the building upon which Vexusa had been founded: The Cathedral of Allasakar. There were no outer walls to protect it, no gates, no guards; in Vexusa, the arrogance of the Dark League had been exceeded only by its power.

Pausing at the foot of the black marble steps that reached into the depths of the Cathedral, the great beast shook its hoary head and roared.

A man in dark robes appeared at the top of those stairs, standing beneath the first of the five recessed arches that formed the complicated doors' architrave. In the shadows to his left and right stood two tall creatures that in poorer light might have been mistaken for gargoyles. As if aware of that, they flexed long, thin wings that stretched from triple-jointed claws to delicate, three-toed feet. Their eyes were an unblinking brown, their faces pointed, their ears very large for their faces; if not for the fact that they stood eight feet tall, they might have been deformed bats.

But when they opened their mouths, teeth glinted across the distance, and when they exhaled it was clear that their very breath was the darkness.

The man laughed; his voice, laid above the hiss of the demons to either side, was undeniably a human voice, even if one heavy with Allasakar's touch. "You are too late," he said. "Our Lord has come." He raised an ebon staff in the light, and called darkness, icy and chill. "Prepare, sacrists. Prepare, exultants. Allasakar—" The rest of the sentence was lost with his throat as the muscled hind legs of the beast coiled and then sprang, propelling him up the stairs in a single, powerful leap.

The demon-kin to either side leaped up and away, but they were not fast enough to avoid the shining glory of a forgotten God. Shreds of their wings and limbs fell to ground as the beast, unopposed, raced into the long hall that wound itself through this monument to Allasakar's fallen glory.

All this, the Kings took in as they reached the foot of the grand stairs that formed a graded semicircle. The Exalted girded at last for war; the braziers that had burned by chant and dint of magical grace in the winding tunnels of the maze to the undercity were now lit in earnest. No breeze or gale or mage-cast shadow would dim these lamps; nothing but the touch of the god-born or the God. And of the Lord of the Hells, there was no human-born offspring; it was well known that the very taint of the darkness was death, and if there were women who survived the start of such an engendering, there were none in all of history who had survived the term of the pregnancy to bear living offspring.

Many of the soldiers said a prayer—and many of those prayers were rusty with disuse, but all the more fervently said for it. Those who had not yet tied their sword knots did so now, taking care to knot the cords tight enough that sweat— or worse—couldn't loosen them on either wrist or haft. They hadn't chosen the field of battle, but they knew it for what it was when they saw it; this was their last chance to prepare.

The Astari stood guard over the Kings. They did not move, or speak, or pray; the time for these things had passed before the monument—the cenotaph—of Moorelas had been opened to them.

All of these things and more Kallandras saw as he stood at the foot of the shadows. He, too, knew that this was the last breath before the dive; once inside the Cathedral, the only certainty was that there was no safety. Quietly, he pressed his hands together and bowed his head, his lips moving to form words that he couldn't give voice to.

Would she hear him? Would she listen? Did she know that he alone, of all the Kovaschaii, could dance the dance and call her to the meeting place? He touched his ear a moment, his fingers following a pattern that had been magically pressed into the soft lobe. It was prayer, of a sort.

His hands shook; he had to lower them.

For the first time in years, his mission was not one of disgrace, not one of indifference. It mattered, all the more so because the death that he danced was not a death that he had caused. *It doesn't matter,* he told himself. *You will never be forgiven; the backs that are turned to you will not be turned again.* He believed it with the terrible conviction of dispassionate intellect; it was true.

Yet beneath that belief was another truth.

While the soldiers readied their weapons, he readied himself. *Do not,* he told the Allasakari, *stand between a brother and his fallen.* But he both knew, and hoped, that they would.

Darkness closed around them like a velvet glove as they took the stairs and passed beneath the recessed arches of the doors; the lights of the Exalted burned more brightly for the lack of any other visual distraction.

Evayne led them.

The vaulted ceiling of the grand hall was hidden by unnatural shadow, which was just as well; it was a grand and glorious sight when given the light of day, a testament to the aesthetic sensibilities of the Dark League's guiding members. Having seen it once before, at the height of its power, she would not forget—but she would pay dearly to avoid having to view it again.

She was tired; sleep had eluded her these past three days, and this was not the first battle—in those scant hours—that she would at least see the start of.

Be honest, she told herself wryly, as the mists shuddered and thickened within the crystal sphere. *It is not the battles which exhaust you. It is the hope of an end to them.* Could history be cheated? That was her folly; that she could, after all that she had seen, believe the answer was *yes.*

"Seeress." It was the Lord of the Compact.

She nodded coolly in reply to the question he did not ask. "The halls round here," she said, "into small apartments, and offices for lesser dignitaries. Ignore them; follow the hall to its end." Speaking as if she had not already given these directions several times, she added, "The Cathedral here has no nave—it has a coliseum. The halls that we are traveling form the interior wall to the pens. The coliseum itself is four stories high, and in its day—" She stopped speaking. "We must enter as the—as the combatants did."

The halls trembled as the beast roared in the darkness; they shook as the darkness answered.

Sor na Shannen heard the beast's roar, and she knew it for what it was: the cry of Bredan, Lord of the Covenant. Centuries, she had worked so that she might hear that cry on her own terms, and in the fullness of a power that might see the God brought low. She realized, listening to cries of the enraged multitude rebound in the hollows of the coliseum, that that had been a futile endeavor. Spear or no, this creature was a *God.*

Had it been so many millennia that she had forgotten what it was like, to stand on the darkened field and wait for the charge of such a creature? Had it been so full an existence that she had forgotten that deep and perfect joy that came of standing by the armies of her Lord in the battle against His ancient, eternal enemies?

For her Lord was One, but they were many—and they had never succeeded in laying him low, no matter their numbers or their advantage. She threw back her silken, flowing hair and laughed, loud and long, as Allasakar made his response; as the multitude spoke through the masque of darkness and shadow. Fire she called, and it came, wreathing a face so fair, and so painfully lovely in its newness that no soldier could dare to strike it without at least pause for concern. She gestured, and her clothing dissolved into a patchwork of artfully bloodied shreds, revealing less than desire would have and more than dignity declared. Her lips were pale, her chin weak, her hands small and soft.

Ah, the battle, let it come, let it come soon. Of all the things that she desired, it was this: to fight again across the length and breadth of this world, with all its visceral pain and pleasure, its weakness and strengths, its savagery and its unutterable beauty.

As the voice revealed her Lord in His glory, she began the dark dance, both as homage and for her own pleasure—for she was a creature of the later abyss and understood well the value of both. Her power was a spiral of times forgotten as she called it fully for the first time in the last four decades. Only in the presence of the Lord of the Hells could such a dance *be*. How could she have forgotten it?

He spoke her name—her true name—and she shuddered with delight to be so noticed, so set apart, raking her claws in simple spasms across the legion of the dead. *Lord I have served and served and served; I have graven Your name across the mortal night. This is all that I desire.* Almost, she thought He smiled; she could not know for certain as His form was not yet whole.

It was the enemy who answered her prayer.

Light, harsh and alien, shattered the doors that led to the coliseum.

Dancing in the fires of the void, Sor na Shannen bowed to the ground as her Lord took His first steps across the firmament. The Gods warred among themselves as equals; they were beyond even the greatest of the demon lords in stature and power. But at the back of the beast, in the tunnels beyond, her enemies were hurrying to witness her dance—and their deaths.

There was no meeting of heralds upon this field; no observers to watch the standards of the great waver and fall, no bards to keep lists of the dead. No parley was initiated by either side, no lines drawn, no terms—however ludicrous or inflated—offered. These were civilities placed upon the face of battle, and that mask—for better or worse—had been removed. Only the killing remained.

These were the killing fields, these chaotic mounds of dirt and flesh beyond which the darkness swirled. They stopped here, those who followed the Hunter's

Death, banked as if they were fire and this a width of river that tongues of flame could not cross. The dead, faceless, had faces for those who could see them; each one, slack or rictus-touched, spoke in silence of their failure.

Too late.

Despair was sharp and swift, anger swifter still; across the darkened ring of the coliseum, the Allasakari readied for battle.

"No quarter!" a voice cried, from deep within the Kings' ranks. "Accept no surrender!"

"None will be given!" the Allasakari cried back, voices so laden with their Lord's power they seemed almost demonic.

The pale beast shed a brilliant light that should have illuminated the coliseum. Instead, it cast a longer, darker shadow for all its power. Into this shadow, with a hunger that could be felt if not seen, the Lord of the Covenant charged. The Lord of the Shadows roared as they met.

Thunder and lightning.

"Jewel?"

The Terafin sat upon her rooftop haven, the newest—and most unceremoniously declared—member of her House to her left. She heard the trap as it rose and fell in a hush that spoke more clearly of Morretz than his words.

"Terafin."

"Is it time?"

"It is. The servants have gathered, and the family. They are many this year."

The older woman turned to gaze at the younger woman's pale profile. "Are you ready?" she asked softly.

Jewel Markess ATerafin swallowed, and then swallowed again, as if for breath. Her dark eyes were wide as she gazed across the bay. She spoke, but the words were a movement of lips with no sound; The Terafin had to lean forward to catch them as they came again.

"Not yet."

"What is it, Jewel? What do you see?"

The younger woman lifted a shaking finger and pointed to the heart of the city across the bay. She opened her lips again, but this time, The Terafin lost her words to another sound: the trembling of earth.

The land shook.

"Terafin."

The Terafin nodded once and rose, snapping into a thin, straight line. "Jewel, come. We must attend the Family."

Jewel rose as well, and they stood a moment, these two, beneath a shrouded sky. It was no longer night, or even dusk, but although the sky was a deep, deep crimson, they saw no sun.

*   *   *

Gods met; earth shook, wind roared. Where the arch had been, there was now a column twined and braided with magic and pattern that defied the understanding of human eyes. Around the packed dirt, empty seats rose into the darkness, inviting the followers of either God to watch, to observe, and to raise no hand.

False promise.

Meralonne APhaniel stepped over the crushed forehead of an elderly man, planting his toes against an oddly angled arm, the balls of his heels against clear dirt. He raised his whole arm and pointed into the darkness; light seared a trail across the air. Piercing, clear and loud, a shriek responded to its passage.

Sor na Shannen stood above flames sustained by no earthly fuel. Lips soft and pale as a young cherry blossom gathered above her teeth in the beginning of a snarl; they rippled into a smooth silence as her eyes met the mage's.

"Again," she said, her soft voice reaching the highest of the coliseum's empty seats. "Again you trouble me."

"Oh, yes," he replied, calling his sword from the folds of darkness as his voice failed to meet hers in either volume or majesty. "And this time, there is no turning back."

She stared at him a moment, and then her smile returned, deep and sensuous and oddly innocent. "You have no shield."

"Against you, I do not require it."

"And if you do not require it, you will not use it?" She laughed.

"You fled our last meeting, drinker, not I."

The laughter trailed into an abrupt silence. "At our last meeting, mage, you were not so eager for speech and nicety. Did I not give you what you desired?"

He did not answer her with words, but the lines of his face became so coolly neutral it was hard to believe there was a living man behind it.

"You are too human," she said, drawing the fires around her into the form and shape of a red crescent saber. "Come, then. Come and dance."

He stepped toward her as if compelled to allow her the choice of field. Something beneath his foot *snapped*. Leaping up, he brought his sword down, severing hand from arm at the wrist. A dead hand. A dead arm. "Surprise," she said softly, and launched herself.

They heard the crying as they made their way to the top of the manse's wide stairs; The Terafin lifted her chin, and did not drop it again. She was slender and hard, like a blade; Jewel remembered her as she had been the night the foyer had been destroyed.

And she remembered the darkness. Today, it lingered in the small pockets of room not exposed to light, waiting. Morretz was as neutral in expression as she had ever seen him, and she had come to understand that this was the face he wore to battle. Both he, and the master he had chosen to serve for life, were preparing for combat.

She did not understand why until they reached the stair's height and she could look down.

There, gathered in the foyer as if seeking shelter—and they were, they were—were the servants and the men and women who bore the name ATerafin into the world beyond the gates. She had never seen so many people gathered in the manse at one time. They huddled together, a press of bodies, their uncertainty and their exhaustion writ clear across their faces; women carried children, crying, in their arms, and men cried, too; some in the crowd carried bags.

"Terafin!"

"TERAFIN!"

"Amarais." Morretz pitched his voice above the crowd's voice, although he would not be able to do so for long. He knew his master well; better than Jewel, it seemed. For The Terafin did not hesitate at the height of the stairs. Instead, regal, she began her descent as if such a descent were as natural as breathing. There was about her both power and determination, and her expression was serene.

She wore plain cloth and no jewelry; she bore no shield, no sword, and carried none of her possessions. It was First Day, yes, but each and every man and woman here knew that the Dark Days had not yet passed. But what she did carry was enough to silence, for a moment, the panic of her people. Pride. And strength.

One man caught her arm, and the crowd seemed to stop breathing, for on this day, this First Day, there were no Chosen to stand between The Terafin and her Family. But she turned, and said simply, "Come to the shrine." And his fingers fell away, as if nerveless.

She led them out, into the uncertain morning.

And Jewel knew, as the doors opened before this woman, and she gazed out into the unnatural shadow that lay across the bay, that she would follow The Terafin forever.

For The Terafin did not blanch, or blink, or bow.

Instead she turned to her people, and spoke into their shocked horror, their terrible silence.

"This is First Day, as we have never seen it and we wait—as our ancestors waited—for the coming of the Kings."

The dead rose before the ranks of the Allasakari like a shield-wall, forming a line three deep. Naked, disfigured, partly dismembered or jarringly whole, they were as they had been at their death—but this time, unarmed, they were not weapon-less.

In the third row, nestled around the Allasakari, the dead linked arms, planting their feet into the earth as if to take root there. But in the second row, and the first, they moved forward, awkward in their gait where limbs were broken or missing, but no less determined. Unseeing, they saw.

They know our weaknesses well, Devon ATerafin thought, as he watched the lines shuffle into two distinct groupings: the men and the women fell back into the second row, the children and the elderly stepped into the first. Dispassionate, he wondered if the smallest of the corpses had even possessed the ability to walk—or if this macabre shuffle represented its first steps. At Devon's back, the intake of breath was sharp, and words of horror unmuted; he was afraid that the Kings' Swords would disgrace themselves by some further show of weakness. If they did, they were mercifully silent.

The Exalted were committing to light and shadow the First Day blessing. Their power was strong; the God's was stronger. The dead barely flinched before they continued their shamble.

"ATerafin," a voice said to his right.

Dark hair rose and fell, a subtle flick of chin and forehead. He threw his hands up into the air; from a distance it might have been a gesture of despair, because at a remove one wouldn't be able to see the cold, grim line of his mouth, the set determination of his eyes. The hands that he lowered held knives, each heavy and unairworthy. Worked in a metal that seemed at once to glimmer with three different sheens, the hilts of each dagger were traced in gold, with opal, diamond, and aquamarines to set off runes that Devon ATerafin did not pretend to understand.

It was enough that he knew their effect.

The dead, he noted, did not walk quickly—although perhaps they would if they were substantially whole. Men and women—the corpses of men and women—could easily be dealt with when the need was clear. But the younger corpses were a thing of nightmare, their faces contorted into expressions of fear and helplessness that demanded justice for the failure of the powerful to protect them in their need.

And the worst part was that the guilt was absolute; the accusation just. They *had* been failed. Never had he understood so clearly the old Weston saying: Failure is the forge in which a man is tempered.

Do you understand what the Kings are, and what they stand for? At times like this, the first question that he had ever been asked by the Lord of the Compact returned to him, made more cutting by events just on the inside edge of his control.

Creeping forward, he thought the world both slowed and darkened. Shifting his position and his stance, he dared a glance at those Kings. Justice. Wisdom. But more: Courage, compassion, conviction. The empire *was* the Twin Kings. Oh, he knew it well.

Understand that any act of brutality, any cruelty, any injustice or folly on the part of those who serve the Crowns injures the Crowns.

This, too, he understood; no one unworthy could aspire to the Compact, because the Kings trusted more than their lives to its members.

Behind the Crowns, the Swords and the Defenders were forming up, but their lines were patchy and fragile. Before them, Duvari stood like a thin—and arrogant—shield. The Magi were also there, a collective council of arrogant and powerful people; they set light against darkness, choosing shields of subtlety and power as a defense against magical attack, known and unknown. Still, he was not alone. The rest of the Astari joined Devon in ones and twos, choosing their positions with as much care as they could afford.

What would you be willing to do to protect the Kings?

Gritting his teeth, he crouched—not to hide, but rather to face the enemy of his choice. Devon had no children, partly by luck and mostly by choice; he wondered if this battle was easier for him than for Delana, who mothered three. Hoped that he would never have the chance to find out. The daggers he lifted before him in a tilted cross. In an almost leisurely fashion, he invoked the names of the triumvirate.

A boy with no lower legs reached him at the same time as a young girl with a head tilted at a horrible angle. Breaking the cross, he swung his arms open as if to catch them in his embrace. It was a lie; the blades struck them cleanly, opening bloodless gashes over their tiny hearts. Their fingers convulsed, gripping air. He spoke the names again: Reymaris, Cormaris, the Mother. Almost, he could see the fine layers of darkness that shielded them, the threads that jerked them forward; he cut them one by one, thinking as he worked to stay clear of their broken hands: The demon had not died so slowly.

They wailed piteously.

This could not be happening. The dead were just that; dead. It was a trick of the enemy, with darkness so strong and so sure that any lie could be forced out of a dead child's lips. He told himself this, who did not have the time to ask the Exalted.

What would you do?

He struck them again, and then again, and at last they fell before the power of the blessed and anointed daggers. He wanted to bow his head a moment, to murmur First Day Rites, to take a breath—but he could not. For the worst of the dead was already before him, wobbling and struggling to reach him. First steps.

So he knelt forward, crossing the knives again, setting his jaw. At either side, he was aware of his compatriots, and he took what little comfort he could from them; he knew that for the next few minutes he was perfectly safe in his task. They were felling their own dead.

The darkness here was powerful. He could taste it, and it was bitter, almost metallic; a cold and lonely thing. He could barely shake it—no, could *not* shake it—so he stopped trying. Because he was Astari, he knelt. And because he was only Devon ATerafin serving as Astari when the baby's corpse finally reached his knees, he opened the cross that he'd made of the daggers and held his arms wide, offering, this time, no lie. The corpse—the child—walked into his arms, little fingers preternaturally strong as they reached for his throat and pressed against it.

Holding his breath, grunting against the unexpected pain, Devon ATerafin closed the circle of his arms, bringing the daggers to bear through the child's back as many times as it took to still its movements.

Anything.

To either side, he heard the clatter of armor, the scrape of greaves against greaves, the cries of the Northern scouts. Lines that had held for the falling of the dead children surged forward, holding a very loose formation. They passed him by as he knelt in the dirt. Rising slowly and stiffly, he lifted his face to better see the conflict.

A fleeting glimpse of shimmering air, the blue light of the flashing storm, the red of elemental fire were jarring in their unexpected beauty. Gods, it seemed, whether at war or in council, were destined to attract the regard of men.

His first mistake, to look upon them there; his second, to attempt to take, in the midst of joined battle, a moment of peace. Instinct pulled his ear, his hair; he turned to see a creature leap out of the darkness directly toward him, long claws gleaming with someone else's blood. His own hands, heavy, were full.

Without another hesitation, Devon threw the small corpse into the demon's path and rolled to the side. Survival had its own imperative, its own rhythms. It did not allow for grieving, for horror, for hatred; it demanded, and received, undivided attention. Mercifully. Thankfully.

Gilliam and Evayne crouched within the second circle of what had once been a crowded amphitheater. Evayne knew that the fine, well-crafted chairs and benches that had seen use at the city's height would not have survived its fall. She did not speak. Her hands were white ice against the surface of her crystal, although the mists therein did not move or part. She did not search them; her eyes were upon the arena and the drama unfolding beneath them.

Protected by a spell of her weaving, Gilliam felt curiously removed, as if the battle's muted sounds and effects were the backstage maneuvering of a talented troupe. The darkness did not fill him with horror, nor the light strengthen him. He heard a whisper, a murmur; turned to see Evayne's lips moving near-silently. She was praying, he thought, but to whom he could not say.

Kallandras heard the cries on the left flank of the Kings' Defenders; surprise and silence, surprise and silence, spreading in a widening sphere. Putting the voice into his voice, he forced a warning cry through a thickened throat and began to push himself through the opening ranks.

Extended from the line of walking dead, he found them: Allandor and Kyria, one of the oldest of the brotherhood and one of the youngest. Kyria's long hair was bound back in a dull and dirt-streaked tail; sallow hollows were all that remained beneath cheekbones that had once been high and fair. His eyes, time had already taken.

He could not dally with the living, for, oathsworn, he had nothing but his own death to offer them. It was to the dead that he offered all the things that he knew could no longer be rejected.

He had no words to give, and had he, he could not have spoken them. Ten yards from his outstretched arm were the two whose cries he had hoped to silence with the comfort that only one Kovaschaii-trained could offer. The motivation was not a pure one, and he knew it well; this was as close to the life he desired as he could come, this dance of death, and he would give it where his former brothers could not. Or he would have.

But he could see *them* as they battered against the confinement of dead flesh, moths against the contours of a lamp's glass, and in that moment, he only wanted them free; who danced, and how, no longer mattered. Time had left its mark in the tone of their skin, the texture, the scent. Kyria's body was unmarked by the torture and violence that had disfigured most of the other corpses, but Allandor's was terribly broken, as if the heat of battle had decided his fate and the victor had continued to worry the fallen in an unstopped frenzy.

It was, he thought, with a grim practicality, for the best; of the two, it was Allandor that he would have had trouble stopping. He was not so certain that, broken and bent but still moving in an awkward parody of life, Allandor would be easy to lay to rest now. A leap carried him out of the way of Kyria's sudden strike.

At their feet, the newly dead lay broken, their fine armor no proof against the assassin's strike, their weapons useless. Kallandras saw and passed over them; they were nothing to him now. Only Kyria and Allandor mattered.

He wrapped their names in the secret voice, protecting them from the ears of the uninitiated, before he called them, loud and long. Did Kyria's blind head shudder? Did the line of his shoulders waver? The answer was bitter, the hope too thin to bear the weight of delusion for long. The dead did not hear or see.

And yet, blind and deaf, the Kovaschaii were more effective than the demons at laying their inadvertent enemies low. Kallandras leaped, and leaped again, keeping the distance between himself and Kyria great enough that no death strike could reach him, and small enough that he presented the best target.

Ah, death had its advantages. He grimaced, drawing sharp breath as sweat trickled from the tightly drawn line of his hair. They were slow, these two—but they would not be slower forever; they did not tire. Kallandras did.

Rolling along the arena's packed floor, he struck out at Kyria's leg, hoping to snap it; Kyria, dead, was too fast. He was also in the air a hair's breadth before Kallandras struck.

How did one dance a death when the dead were trying to kill one?

No, she wasn't praying; he saw folds of her robe snap into place as her hands left the crystal sphere floating untouched in the air before her. Her lips stopped moving, but her expression was just as distant, just as focused, as it had been since they'd entered the coliseum.

What is it? he thought, his grip on the Spear so tight he could no longer feel his fingers. He did not dare interrupt her by asking; instead he turned his feral attention to the battle below, seeking answers there.

Dead, Kyria was still fast enough to push him, and to push hard. Allandor, a shadow that loped beyond their struggle, broke the ground with his oddly angled arms, his uneven, grinding stride. Had either been armed—or worse, both—the battle would already be over.

As it was, Kyria's body was now marked and gashed by the wide sweep of Kallandras' steel—to no effect, of course. The only way to stop the dead was to dance for them; to call the Lady to the meeting place and ask Her for their peace. It was a peace only She could grant.

He knew it well.

Look long, he thought, as he jumped over Allandor's outstretched arm. *This is your fate.* Sweating, he put up his sword. Kyria struck without regard for the edged parry, slicing himself from fingertip to elbow without actually losing the arm. Gritting his teeth, Kallandras brought the sword around and up in a sudden, vicious arc to claim what, dead, Kyria was still not foolish enough to surrender: His arm.

The loss did not slow him.

Something had to. Because the dance itself took strength, and Kallandras was slowly giving his over to this painful and necessary combat.

Sing, Kallandras.

Evayne's voice. Of all the voices he wished to hear, the least. He made no reply; had he wanted to, he would not have. Allandor's fingers, almost separated from his hands, were trying to snap the bard's ankle.

Sing, she said again.

To what? He wanted to cry out in frustration, but his training prevented that show of weakness.

The dead were not affected by the voice.

Sing!

Levering the fingers from his boots with the sword's point, he froze a moment. Because while the dead could not hear the bardic voice in any way, the *deaf* could.

And the Kovaschaii were not dead until the dance. Hope came in a sharp and painful breath—a breath that no other bard, locked in mortal combat, would have been able to draw. This skill was a gift of the Kovaschaii; fitting, then, that it be used in their aid.

He did not tell them who he was. Instead, he told them what: a brother, come finally to dance their deaths and give them the peace that they were promised. He filled his voice with the longing and the love that only the Kovaschaii felt for one another—and that was no artifice; had he wanted to, he could not have kept that from them.

Did they stop their attack? Did they freeze a moment and actually look *at* him? He thought so, but could not be certain, and the faltering of hope was bitter indeed.

Evayne cursed and bowed her head a moment. When she raised it, her skin was paler than it had been, her eyes darker. For the first time, she spoke, the words as polite and noble as any that a hunter on the trail might speak to a fool who had dared interrupt him.

"Guard me."

Kyria's arm snapped to a stop; Allandor's teeth, opening to bite, froze as if in mid-snarl.

Dance, Kallandras.

Sweating, bleeding, bearing the dirt of the coliseum in hair and clothing, he plunged his sword into the ground. These two would not slacken and fall; there would be no cleaning of the corpses, no artful arrangement. These, he would not miss. But the final embrace, the resting of the head in his lap, the whispering of words that only the dead would listen to—they haunted him as his feet touched dirt and leaped clear, touched down and leaped clear.

The song that he had been singing shifted and deepened as he traced the first five points of the Kovaschaii star. Mind. Heart. Soul. The brotherhood.

The Lady.

The hidden star came next; he danced two, quick and light, singing the birth names, the brotherhood's names, and the hidden names of the two who stood in magical thrall before him. And then, again, the two points of intersection between the man and the Kovaschaii. The brotherhood.

The Lady.

The arena tilted beneath his feet; his ankle rolled gently, refusing to bear his weight. The fine fabric of his tunic clung to his skin in damp, darkened folds as his knees bent beneath him. Sweat trickled into his eyes, rolling down the tip of his nose, his chin; he could not lift a hand to wipe it clear. Never in his years with the Kovaschaii had he ended a dance so poorly.

802   ✦   Michelle West

Never, in all those years, had the Lady's answer been so forceful. Mists which had always been a gentle, subtle presence roiled with the force of a storm; where soft, pale glow illuminated her coming, the air now crackled with sharp shards of light, too harsh to glance at for long. Ah, it hurt to cover his eyes, to lose the glimpse of the Lady that he had sworn to follow—and that he still, in his fashion, served—but instinct forced his hands up and bound his fingers into a tight shield.

"What is this?" she asked, her voice the very thunder.

They answered her with their cries, insensate in their relief, all ceremony forgotten.

She called them to her, and he heard their babbling, their tears; he could almost feel the circle of her arms closing around them in the half-world.

"Where," she said, speaking again in fury, "were your brothers?"

Kallandras forced his hands away from his eyes, wincing and squinting against the angry radiance. "Lady," he said, calling her attention to himself although he could not prevent reflex from curling his body inward.

"You," she said coldly. He could not look upon her countenance, enshrouded as it was in a bitter light, although the tone of her voice forced his head up.

"Lady," he said quietly.

But when she spoke again, the great anger was gone from her voice. The light dimmed enough that Kallandras might open his eyes to behold the faint luminescence of raven hair in the half-world. Her dark cloak swirled as if caught by wild wind, and at her side, clutching folds of fabric in their unbunching fists, two men. Each bore a delicate, long-fingered hand upon the shoulder closest to her. "Who calls?" Ah, ritual. "Who wishes to meet me in the half-world?"

"I do."

"And you?"

At once, he bowed the head he had raised. "I am Kallatin of the brotherhood, Lady. You hold my name." That name was a tremor of shaking lips.

"You are no longer Kallatin," was her reply. "But, yes, I hold your name."

He waited in silence, his face the perfect Kovaschaii mask; he was no longer a youth, to have it crack so easily.

The corner of her pale lips turned up in a slight smile; she nodded—approval?— before looking away to the taller of her two companions. Height, rather than age, differentiated them; he was no longer aged, no longer lined with care and the toil of years.

"You have served me well," she told him, "and I have come to return to you the name that binds us, Allandor nee Eadward Parakis. And you," she turned to the slender, shorter man, "have earned your name in my service. I return it to you as well, Kyria nee Calavin Warran."

Tight-lipped, he watched them both as they relaxed in the cover of the Lady's night. He was not a youth, no, but the mask slipped a little.

"Come," she told them softly. "The path is waiting, and we will walk it together, you and I."

Kyria turned at once, but Allandor's gaze went not to the mists, but to the man who stood as outsider at their edge. "Why?" he asked softly.

"You saw the Darkness," Kallandras said, with a bitterness that not even pride could contain.

Allandor nodded grimly.

"None of the brotherhood knew where you were, although they could hear your cries."

"And you?"

"*She* brought me," he replied.

Allandor's face darkened. "She who—"

But the Lady raised a delicate finger to Allandor's lips. "Hush," she told him quietly. "Speak not in anger when that anger is my right." Turning to Kallandras, she said softly, "you have served me well this day, and I shall not forget it. Speak if you will; I will not prevent it."

"Allandor," he said softly, "I would die for the brotherhood." He paused and smiled bitterly. "But I alone of all of the brotherhood would do more than that: I would *live* for it, and without it, in pursuit of that service."

"The brotherhood," Kyria said coldly, speaking for the first time, "*is* the Lady's will. The Lady decreed—"

But the Lady raised a regal hand to stem the flow of his words. "You are young," she said softly.

And he would never grow old.

Allandor bowed as if Kyria's interruption had never happened. "I have seen the Darkness," he said, and his fine features twisted in a shudder. "And it has seen us. You are not my brother," he added harshly. The eyes of the dead met the eyes of the living, and the harshness was lifted slowly as he continued to speak. "And yet we are bound. Or we were. You danced our death, Kallatin. And although you have earned it, I would no longer see you trapped undying upon the plane." He bowed, touching finger to forehead in a gesture of respect.

Kallandras let nothing show.

"Allandor. Kyria." The Lady wrapped her cloak tightly about her shoulders. "It is time." Mist rose, curling in a spiral that began at her hem, streaked with shadow and a hint of the worlds that waited on either side. At her feet, a footpath shone gently, leading into a distance that Kallandras could only guess at; it was not for his eyes.

Raising a finger to forehead and away, he bowed to Allandor, masking his face in a different way. He did not wish to see them leave.

"Bard," the Lady said. It hurt; it always hurt. For she had his name, and she would not speak it. The years had not gentled the desire at all; he knew then that they never would.

But he lifted his gaze at once. "Lady."

Anger darkened her eyes and thinned her lips, although it took no grace from her. "I have had no quarrel with my brother; he is but one of many things that brings an end to life, and all life must end." She paused and the ice reached her voice. "But I have quarrel with him now, for the sake of my chosen. To kill them, if he was capable of the act, was his right. But to keep them from their brothers—and from *me*—was not." She raised a slender arm, releasing Kyria a moment to point. As he followed the direction of her hand, he heard the sound of battle growing louder, nearer.

"Between you and me, there is no bridge. I know of the wrong that you have done." Her eyes were cold; she spoke truth, but not to wound him, and if it wounded, she did not care. But she held his name; she knew what the words meant. "However, if you desire it, I give you my blessing; kill the Allasakari in my name."

"Lady," he said. "In Your name." For the first time, a hint of color traced his cheeks. She would not forgive him and accept his return to the only home he desired, but out of the back door she had thrown him scraps from his brothers' table—and to both his gratification and his humiliation, he was hungry enough to joyfully accept them.

For they would know.

Chapter Thirty

STEPPING INTO THE WORLD again, Kallandras called the wind, raising his hand so that the light of the diamond bound there might burn the darkness from his vision. The bodies of the Kovaschaii now lay upon the ground, limp and empty; they had been purified by the Lady's anger, and they would not rise again, not even if the Lord of the Hells himself pulled the strings. Burial, if there was one, would wait. The dance had been danced; all else was illusion.

There were no cries to haunt him, no accusations of betrayal from which to hide behind drug effect and sleep. He—and his brothers—were *free*.

Wrapped in the eye of the storm he stood, seeing for the first time in far too long with the assassin's vision. There were those whose only threat lay in the fact of their death; there were the kin who hunted between the cracks in the army's defense; there were the forms of great light and great darkness, of terrible beauty and danger, that he did not look at for long, precisely because they were all of these things. And there, at the farthest remove the arena allowed, behind the cover the dead provided, the Allasakari.

A chill went through him, bracing in its clarity. Although so much divided them, none of it quiet and none of it still, the face of the First Priest of Allasakar was absolutely clear. Black-bearded and dark-eyed, his lips formed words out of the shadow itself as he made himself a conduit for the power of a God locked in combat. *Marius.* Beside him, tall and slender, a pale-haired Southerner with perfectly chiseled features, a beautiful mouth. *Karnassas.* And beside him, pale and fair as well, a lithe and slender girl. *Loriel.* There were more. He looked at each one.

Their names came to him, and as he collected them, he felt his body resonate as if he were a bell chiming a perfect, high note. What he did not know, he could not kill; the names settled into that part of his soul that the Lady owned.

Kill the Allasakari in my name.

His feet were light against the arena's even floor; had he been a dancer of anything but death, he might have crossed to the theater and back in a light and happy step. He *felt* their names travel down his spine and curl there—and he knew that far and away, in the streets above the undercity, hunting their own kills or wrapped in personal contemplations, the Kovaschaii felt every name as clearly.

There were no rules to the kill, although each brother often developed his own. There was no stricture, no law of how or when—what mattered was the death itself, for the death was the Lady. Senses heightened, he watched the army of the Crowns battering against both the dead and the demons; the Allasakari were far enough behind their lines that they could not easily be reached. Not by the Kings' men.

And not by Kallandras, a lone brother on the field.

Kill the Allasakari in my name.

Was it the drug that made the words so powerful? Was it the *niscea* that made the sting of fear so enticing? He struggled to mask apprehension, to swallow it with the neutrality of cool indifference. But his throat was dry and his tongue thick with the taste of a familiar bitterness. Ten years ago, the dream of the Lady's favor had been beyond him; to bask a moment in her glory, however much of an afterthought it was, was more than he had ever hoped for.

They were beyond his reach. No—let him think, let him only think a moment; other deaths had been more difficult—

He called upon calm in this dark and noisy place, and it eluded him as the names of the Lady's chosen, unspoken and unspeakable, twirled like ascension lights before his darkened eyes. It was unthinkable that these not be his; that some other hand might fell them; that this one bridge to the brothers who would never be his again should be crossed by one who could never appreciate the privilege.

Shuddering as if they contained the fear he would not acknowledge, his hands curled into fists. A chill descended upon him, and then a sudden heat; his breath, as it left his open lips, came short and sharp.

What form of attack was this? His vision doubled a moment; he spoke the words of focus, but instead of speaking them in the high, sure tenor for which he had become known throughout the Empire, he spoke them in a guttural, harsh burst, as if they were curses. Sweetly sounded or no, they served the purpose they were meant to in the labyrinths of his childhood, revealing to his inner eye the form and shape of his body and the lines that bound it to earth.

There was no magic. No poison.

But a need drove him from within, slowly consuming his body with a desire that had nothing to do with the mind or the heart. *Niscea.* Siren's song. He thought as clearly as he could, but no matter how he considered it, the timing was wrong; over the weeks, he had become used to the ebb and flow of the drug's demand, and not at such a crucial time would he make so foolish a mistake.

It was very cold in the arena.

Steadying himself, he forced air down his throat, swallowing it as if it were too thick. At his side, in a slender pouch that conformed to the curve beneath his rib cage, were two stoppered vials; he had not known, of course, that he would need them, or they would already be empty.

Reaching for them, he knew a moment's panic. The pouch was flat and slightly bloused, although it had not been opened. His hands shuddered as he lost his focus; he forced them—forced himself—to stillness. His chest rose and fell, sweat beaded his brow; these two things he had not the strength to prevent.

They were gone.

Not broken, for there would have been shards of glass and pungent liquid as evidence. They were simply gone, as if the deliberate efforts taken to store them there had been the delirium of a cautious man. He spoke a single word, but it held no power; it was a man's word, not a bard's or an assassin's, and it held only the pain of the helpless.

Had he thought the Lady neutral? Had he thought her anger diminished somehow by time or event? Had he truly believed that he could *speak the name* of even one whose death she had refused to sanction to those who were not her chosen?

There were no stories among the Kovaschaii of her cruelty. And even if they knew of his plight, there would still be none: Justice administered, however severe, was not a matter of malice. Time passed strangely in the meeting place, and if one delivered oneself to the will of the Gods, many things might happen there. He passed his hand over his empty pouch numbly.

She had said he might kill in her name; was it mere mockery, then? But no. No—for the names of the living had burned themselves deeply into his center, linking his fate with their own inextricably. What she offered, she offered; if she chose to force him to fight without the weapons he had honed in her studies, she so chose. Who argued with the Lady's will?

A bitterness turned his lips at the corners, although whether up or down, it was hard to tell; they trembled. Curling his hands into fists to still their shaking, he turned once again to face the Allasakari—the men and women who, bound to their God, were now so far from his reach they might never have been named at all.

And then he saw, beneath his hand, the edge of hard, white light that burned away darkness. Diamond, trapped in a delicate platinum lattice, called him with a wildness that he had never heard before. It was the song not of breeze or wind, but of gale, and it roared along the length of his trembling arm as if he were but a leaf caught in it.

But he was the bearer of Myrddion's ring, and upon its altar, that ancient mage had perished in ignominy and defeat so that the elements might be bent into weapon's shape and form against the Lord of the Hells.

A tickle of words played at his ears; he thought he must understand the language, but the meaning eluded him. A hunger far stronger than that which *niscea* caused forced his hand up in defiance.

Here, in this musty and ancient place, buried so far from sun, rain, and wind, he called what had never been called: the full force of the ring's power.

Brothers! he cried, but the roar of the wind took the words.

That, and more.

To force the crystal to release its vision of the here and now was grim work; hard enough for a seer of power that it required focus, concentration, strength of both body and mind. To search for the glimpses of the future that made the seers both feared and respected—to search, and somehow wrest answers from the half-seen, shadowy glimpses of events that might never come to pass instead of waiting for those glimpses to wander across the vision like lightning before the storm took arrogance, a hubristic self-delusion.

Or desperation.

She had not yet entered the battle, although she had been fighting the war for all of her adult life. Scenery flickered before her eyes in a silvered mist, a blurred glow. Glancing up, she saw what she most feared: Bredan was weakening.

He had the power that any God might have should he walk again in mortal lands, but the will—the ability—to use that power was diminished by the wielding. He had chosen, wisely, to attack Allasakar and press him closely enough that sheer physical strength, the instinct of the beast, would serve him best.

She had thought it would be enough, but watching the sands drain, she knew it for a fool's hope. The dead that walked upon the stage set by the Allasakari were a testament to their foresight; the God was well fed.

To interfere was death, and it wasn't even a good one; where Gods walked, very few could challenge—and no matter how learned she was in the ancient ways, Evayne did not count herself among that number. The Sleepers, yes. She cursed, wondering what tragedy would bring about their hour of waking if this did not.

The mists roiled, pulling her gaze and repelling her vision at the same time. A fleeting glimpse of one, where two now stood locked in combat, emerged from beneath the veil; it was gone before she could glean anything but the terrible sense that the battle was over.

Carver and Angel worked their way through the crowd; Jewel could hear the muttered curses as she watched the bobbing of a shock of white hair.

"Jay?"

She was glad, fiercely glad, that they were with her. Finch, Teller, and Jester were nowhere in sight, and Arann was on duty.

"We started this together," she told Carver grimly.

"Yeah." Pause. "How's it going to end?"

"Wrong question," Angel said sharply. "Are we going to win?"

But Jewel offered no answer to the question that everyone was thinking. Instead, paling, she pointed. The land rumbled; the waters shook. In the heart of the old city, the shadow was coalescing into a tall, dark shape.

Listening, she thought she could hear screams in the distance.

"What—what is it?"

"*The Shining City,*" she said. "*It's rising.*" But she said it softly, and the words only carried to her den, The Terafin, and Morretz.

Angel and Carver knew that voice.

"Lord Elseth," Evayne said, through lips so white they seemed bloodless, "the time is coming." Suspended in the air inches before her unblinking eyes, the seer's ball spun in an even, slow circle. What it showed the seeress, he did not know.

Lord Elseth stood in the silence of the coming Hunt. Evayne had let him play no part in the battle below; he had become audience to the arena, mere observer. His eyes, human, were drawn again and again to the complex struggle of giants—a struggle that at last seemed to be reaching its end. At their feet, the ground was liquid fire, frozen rock, melting dirt, shadow and light; the air was sparks of storm and summer heat. Where they met, the warcries of the battle surrounding them became, for a second, meaningless.

Hunter, he thought, and drew breath on the word. The darkness seemed stronger, fuller, richer, the howls of the Death that he had faced yearly for all of his adult life, weaker.

He had thought of nothing but the Hunt since the moment Stephen died. He thought of it now, for if the Lord fell here, there would be no Hunting. No vengeance.

No life.

He felt the rustle of midnight-blue fabric an instant before he heard the sharp intake of breath. Turning, he saw the profile of the seeress cast in fleshly alabaster as she stared, her lips parted slightly over two words. "Kallandras, no!"

Kallandras? Gilliam's eyes narrowed as he tried to find the lone bard in the chaos below. No sight of the golden curls and dark clothing on first pass—but he did not search for long. A howling, as if from the throat of the beast that coiled at the earth's heart, began. Wind rose, wild and chill; dirt and stone formed a flailing curtain.

Evayne did not speak again; instead she lifted both hands and grasped the sphere, although whether to wrest answers from it, or to protect it, he couldn't say. The edge of raven hair brushed the smooth, curved surface as she bowed her forehead a moment.

Light, glimmering and tenuous, shot out of the crystal's core, growing and changing as it unfurled in flight. It was not so vast or so dramatic a calling as the unveiling of Vexusa, but her fear made it more intense, although only Gilliam could sense it.

The army of the Kings, buffeted by wind and the sting of sand through helmet visors, held their lines; the mages at their back attempted to calm the wind, to somehow shield the Crowns—and their followers—from its effect. But it was no normal wind; it was Air in wild fury.

The lightest of the corpses that lay sprawled across the ground began to shudder and roll.

"Kallandras!"

"What is he doing?" Gilliam had to shout to be heard—and if the wind grew much stronger, even that would not suffice.

But Evayne did not answer; her robes rose on either side like dark, layered wings. She pulled the crystal sphere to her breast, and the cloak's folds swallowed it. "Lord Elseth," she cried, hurling her words against the wind as if she, too, realized that the time for speech had almost passed, "join the fighting below. Stay as close to your Lord as you dare." She opened her mouth to say more, but fell silent instead, searching his eyes intently.

"And you?"

Her expression became curiously flat, almost cold. "Kallandras must be stopped."

Light to be seen by. Light to sing by. Kallandras' voice was wild as the wind, carried by it, harmony to it. He had never sung a song such as this, and he marveled at that lack; it was as if music, *true* music, had always been absent from his gift. But no more.

He did not like the arena; loathed the ceiling by which the coliseum was covered. There were no open spaces here, only ratholes, nooks, and crannies in which darkling spawn might hide and play their games. He would see an end to that. There, one of the so-called kin. Fine rock whipped around it in an air-borne frenzy, abrading scale and skin as if the creature were pressed, struggling, against a carpenter's sanding wheel.

Fire flared and the gale tore through it, carrying shreds of orange and white as if they were brightly colored ribbons. Only the great flames were dangerous, and to the air, least of all.

Meralonne APhaniel felt the rush of the wind before he heard its keening. Platinum strands of his hair were caught in elemental fingers, lifted as if at play. Close his eyes, and he could almost feel the turn of a new sun under a sky deeply, perfectly blue.

Open them, and he could see fire.

Shadow fled Sor na Shannen's otherwise perfect skin where his blade had scored it; blood darkened his own. The sight of both disturbed him for reasons that were not, after all, so different. Fatigued, he took her measure and she his; stroke and counter, stroke and parry, cast and counter.

But the wind's voice grew stronger; he saw the flames of her calling shift and weaken, shrinking inward as if to avoid the touch of water or heavy earth.

"What is this?" she asked softly, her eyes narrowing.

Meralonne made no reply, but put up his sword, watching her carefully. Where his hair was light, hers was midnight and reflected fire. It, too, felt the wind's caress.

The wind's wildness.

There was only one man in the arena—one being—who could call the wild wind with such force. Meralonne smiled softly as Sor na Shannen's expression grew apprehensive. They both knew the voice of the air, but it had been a very long time since they had heard it speak with such strength.

Only when the stone balcony that overlooked the arena splintered against the far wall did Meralonne's smile dim. For if it was as he suspected, and Kallandras had called the wind, he was dangerously close to losing control of it; the balcony, the bench, the splintering of rock—these were acts of destruction that were too wild to be entirely the bard's.

And what of it? What of it?

Wordlessly, he leaped into the swirl of dust and dirt that made the current visible. He heard Sor na Shannen's voice, saw her spin beneath his feet.

It was almost exhilarating to ride the wind, and the desire to remain in its grip was strong—but that way lay a madness that Meralonne was not willing to face again while he lived. He fell, heavy and earth-pulled, toward the demon lord. Strike.

Her counter was slow; the wind tugged her arm, delaying her parry.

Shadow.

And blood.

They heard the roar of the darkness upon *Averalaan Aramarelas;* they heard it in the streets, where the New Year wreaths trembled palely and the waters began to leap above the seawalls.

Victory.

The statue of Moorelas shuddered against the horizon; the ground buckled. Word, in several languages, took to the air: the Kings would not return. The city was lost.

Marius. Karnassas. Loriel.

Names. None of them his own. And yet . . .

They were his intended. They were his responsibility, his duty.

He spoke their names with the wind's voice. That wind rose over the paltry shield of rotting corpses, drying sticky blood in its passage. Light as empty egg shells, the Allasakari rose in the grip of the gale, shattering beneath the confines of flesh where they struck stone.

The last one, the frail one, the air kept a moment, at play with the half-tones of her screams. And then, bored, it dashed her into the height of the only freestanding structure in the arena.

The arch.

Unlike the stone balconies, the brass rails, and the rotting timber of wooden benches long past their time, the arch did not buckle; the wind's sway, as it battered the pillars upon which large, heavy stones curved was the breeze's flutter, no more. These were no normal stones to withstand such an assault—especially not built as they were into such a flimsy arch.

Nothing stood against the wild winds. Nothing.

Wheeling, turning so perfectly the flight of the eagle was clumsy and awkward in comparison, the wind uprooted a column near the combatants' pen. As if it were a javelin, the column flew on currents of warm, rushing air to the height of the arch: the keystone.

He had to be stopped, and she knew it; knew further that in some distant time, in her youth and in his prime, they would meet again, had met—whatever it was she would have to do did not involve his death.

But it was not death that Kallandras feared, and it was not death in the end that could wound him as she had already done so many, many times. It was always thus when she walked upon the path. Nothing could be left alone; she was sent to act—and by her actions, the war took shape in subtle ways that even she could not fully appreciate. At least she was no longer a girl, to weep and mourn the actions she was forced to now, whatever those actions might be. There was very little that she would not sacrifice to achieve her goal, and she had come to realize that grief only exacerbated the pain; it did not stop her from raising the hand to strike.

Before she reached Kallandras, she heard the cracking of unnatural stone; the sundering of a union forced by magic. The air carried the sound to the heights as if in celebration of its achievement. Kallandras was her target, but she stopped a moment, wide-eyed, as the arch began to shiver, to almost shudder, before her violet eyes. There were no shards of dark marble, no falling stones, no cracking columns—and yet she *knew*, as only a seer could, that the arch was about to fall. There was a magic invested here, a power, that should have evaporated when the Gate had served its function.

She forced breath, measured and slow, from her lungs. The Gate *would* have lost its power.

Her face paled and then flushed oddly; she searched the grounds for sign of

Kallandras, pulling her lower lip between her teeth as if she were, for a moment, quite young. Was this why Kallandras called the wild wind with such force? Had he understood that the arch was not yet finished, that it played a role—unseen, but felt—even now? Her hands furled into fists, her cloak closed round her like a shield to keep debris away. She wanted to believe it.

But she saw him, standing, legs planted as if at ease, his hair a mass of unruly, perfect gold, his head tilted back as if the song he sung had become far more important than the audience for whom he sang it. There was a wildness to the cast of his delicate features, a fey joy, that she had never seen there.

Wind continued to buffet the arch.

Evayne watched, frozen between two different imperatives.

Sor na Shannen heard as well the strike of the wind's victim against the mighty keystone, the foundation of the Gate. She cried out a warning, and the wind let it pass, filling the coliseum with her sudden fear.

At another time, in another combat, Meralonne APhaniel would have been shamed to take advantage of the distraction. But that time was far removed from the arena in which the darkness sought to gain the only foothold that it would need to conquer these lands. He did not pause as she did; he did not hesitate as she opened her lips over exquisite teeth to utter her cry of warning to the Lord of the Hells.

His sword cut a path through air that ended with her throat, and he did not flinch from the delicate and helpless startlement that played across an expression of innocence abused. It was her last chance to wound him, and he took it as part of the battle, no more.

Her sword of flame flickered briefly; the ground absorbed what remained of her perfect body. He hoped the Hells had opened its embrace to her, for she had chosen her place and her plane long before this battle, and she deserved the home that she had made there.

His own sword did not dissipate; into the howl of wind, Meralonne APhaniel turned its edge, slicing a clean path through the gale. The wildness did not fight against his passage; it was wrapped around the arch that he, that they, had all assumed was a closed door.

And it was good, for if the Air were not occupied, it would know a danger, however slight, and against the wildness, here in this place, with too many battles just behind him, he had little chance.

At the heart of the arena, the balance of power began to shift. A roar, louder and deeper than the wind's voice could ever be, shook the heights and the foundations of the coliseum. All who heard it knew it for the voice of Darkness; Allasakar in anger.

Where shadow had formed a dark blanket over the dirt and the stone, the marble and the foundation of the coliseum, he called it in, wrapping it around himself like a mantle as he turned his full attention to the wind, to the arch itself.

The last line of the walking dead faltered and suddenly toppled as the power animating them withdrew; the kin who had been capable of withstanding the wind's onslaught—and there were not a few—regrouped and banded together. Their Lord's power had been summarily withdrawn, but without it they were not helpless; what they lacked was a leader. Sor na Shannen was gone, as Karathis before her, and Allasakar spared them no thought.

Swathed for a moment in his full glory, he stood out like a beacon—proof for those who had always doubted that un-sullied Darkness could be glorious and beautiful, a thing beyond compare. He gestured, and the shuddering columns at the Gate stilled; gestured again, raising both of his arms as if to catch the wild wind and hold it captive.

As he did, his darkness grew, and the shadow he cast, with little light behind him, was dark and long.

Gilliam made his way down the steps, feeling, as he approached it, the heaving of the ground upon which the coliseum stood. There was no huntbrother to steady him, but instead of denying the loss, he let it come, let it in. His pack was as safe as it could be in the streets of the outer city; he had had no desire to lose them to this battle, when he had already lost so much, and he had chosen to leave them in the care of the Priests of the Mother.

But in doing so, he crippled himself. He had one set of eyes and one set of ears, instead of the many he normally used to gain his vantage. Espere was with the healers; she would not come to him before he came to his Lord.

The Horn was at his side, secured there by Evayne; the Spear was in his hands. He gripped it tightly, as if it were alive and might at any moment evade him.

As he approached the coliseum's floor, the voice of the wind lessened; he could hear the clash of metal, the scrape of sword against unnatural skin, the cries of victory and of warning. He could see the fallen; they were all the Kings' soldiers, or subjects. The kin did not leave corpses.

But he did no more than glance at his surroundings; the Hunter Lord drew his attention and held it. For he was the Death, and every beast in the forest that hunted, every creature that killed, was a part of his body. Just as the God did not speak with a single voice, but rather a multitude, a single form could not contain him. Fur glinted, and fang; claw and horn, muscles rippled beneath hide and the flash of iridescent scale.

The Lord of the Hells roared in fury. Gilliam tensed, willing himself to inch forward, toward them.

And then Allasakar did, of all things, the least expected: He pulled back from the Hunter and turned away. Stunned, Gilliam of Elseth watched the muscles in the hind legs of the beast as they rippled perfectly, tensed for the leap. Where they touched ground, claws sparked against the flat stone tiles upon which the blooded altars stood.

Did the Lord of the Hells understand his danger? How could he, and turn his back? Gilliam's mouth went dry; breath was almost painful, and he could not force it deep into his lungs, although he tried.

The Lord of the Hunt drove himself forward into the broad, black back of the Lord of the Hells. Unfurling like a dark eruption, great wings grew out of the shadow with which Allasakar was cloaked; a great wind rose out of the hollow of those wings as they descended and rose, descended and rose.

Gilliam had heard that the swans of the Western Kingdoms were deadly when confronted in their lair at the wrong time, and he had always thought the rumor a lie that only a gullible child would trust. Seeing these wings, he knew that he'd been wrong.

But the Lord of the Hunt had a grip on his prey, and like the broad-headed, strong-jawed alaunts of the Breodani—like the finest and the truest of the *Bredari*—his hold was not easily shaken.

The wind howled in rage; the corpses of the Allasakari and the Essalieyanese soldiers were torn from the ground, along with chunks of marble and stone and dirt, twisted in wide and swift aerial circles, and thrown like blunt javelins at both the arch and the Lord of the Hells.

The Hunter did not let go.

She could see it now: The Lord of the Hells was somehow gaining in power as he fought on two fronts against the wild air and the Lord of the Covenant. And in the warped and twisting light of a God-battle, the lines of his shadow became sharp and hard.

He had stepped clear of the Gate and stood upon the mortal plane—or so it had first seemed, and still seemed if one had no way of shaping, of altering one's vision to fully understand the darkness. Evayne a'Nolan had twice walked the road in Winter; she could shape her vision, her interior sensitivity, if she let the darkness in. And that itself was a danger.

There *was* a link between the God and the arch. And it was not so tenuous as all that; it was a part of him, a tentacle, an extension. A fierce smile touched her lips, a vicious one; it was the first and the only smile she would offer this battle. They *had* arrived in time. He was not truly free. Bredan—Lord of the Covenant— had more control over the shape of the land than he.

Her eyes glanced over Kallandras, flitting past him as if he were a wound that she could not bear to acknowledge. The wind, the wind was necessary. The Lord of the Covenant was necessary.

And Evayne a'Nolan, god-born, mage-trained, adept of the Summer and the Winter roads, was also necessary. She knew why the path had brought her here, and with a quick step, a terrible, sudden hope, she darted across the arena, the hem of her robe skirting a half-inch above the bloodied dead.

She raised her hands in a high arc, mirroring in the movement the shape of the arch itself, and ending with a clap where the keystone was. Many were the spells she might have called, but none were so devastating as the light that flared in a single, fist-sized ball, blinding in its radiance, painful in its intensity. Everything that she was, that she had been, she put into it; there was no reserve of power left in the line of her shaking, quivering arms. Her knees gave messily beneath her, and her hands, clasped as if in tremulous prayer, fell to her lap. Let it be enough; let the combined weight of the wild wind and the Lord of the Covenant pry between them a crack for her meager power to slide through.

The God roared; she heard the screams of the multitude—anger, despair, fury, hatred—and better than that, much better, the sound of cracking stone. Oh, the wind raged, whipping at her hair, her face; beating at her back. Sand stung her eyes, and tears coursed down the sides of her cheeks as the wind grew wilder and wilder still.

She had no power left to deal with Kallandras; none left to deal with the kin. But if she died here, if somehow she died having changed history, it would be enough, more than enough.

The shadows were weakening and faltering; the God's strength, split so evenly between two forces, buckled. She raised her head as an odd light began to gather to either side of her exhausted body.

No, she thought, although she hadn't the strength to utter the word. *Not yet! Not yet!*

The arena dissolved into rolling, silver-gray mists, and Evayne a'Nolan covered her face with dusty, bloodied hands.

It was hard to see in the sudden storm; Gilliam was close enough to the pull of the wind that he forced himself to ground. But sight or no, he could hear the muffled growl of the Hunter God give way to something louder: a triumphant roar. He had heard echoes of savagery before, but until this moment he had never realized how weak the viscerality of his experience had been.

That thought would have humbled Stephen; it didn't slow Gilliam down at all. Because if that had been weak, this was his one chance to prove that he was not. He could not fail; to fail was death.

It will be as if the Hunt hasn't been called in years.

Stephen's voice. He gripped the Spear in both hands and stood, leaning forward into the gale, testing it. For the Lord of the Hunt was now winning the contest.

*   *   *

Meralonne bowed his head a moment as the wind moved round him, pressing tightly to the sides of his body without picking him up and tossing him, so much flotsam and jetsam, into the cyclone. That much, he could still prevent. He heard the roar of the darkness as the Gate to the Hells began to crumble.

Only kill it, he thought. The God's half-formed and ill-prepared avatar would be no pure vessel for its divinity; crippled, it *could* be dispatched.

Wind roared, gaining speed; the eyes stung at its passage. He turned away as he heard the Lord of the Hells speak in the voice of the multitude in a language that only Bredan could understand. It was still a battle that the Gods would decide; he had his duty now, to the Crowns and to the Order, although neither would know it.

For the wind was too wild, and its call too strong. Just a moment, he thought, as he tested its currents, its lovely eddies. Just a moment. As if it could hear him, a cool breeze, gentle in the face of the growing cyclone's brutality, slid across his upturned cheek.

Gritting his teeth, he shouted a single word.

"Kallandras!"

Singing with the voice of elemental air, he paused, lifting his head. Golden curls bobbed on the eddies of a warm up-draft, tugging at his face; his arms felt like wings as they floated at his sides. There was darkness beyond him, and light—but they were distant.

The voice was not.

And whose voice was it? Who called him in the gale, who interrupted his song? His eyes narrowed as a fine layer of silt brushed his cheek in caress, pulling his attention from a sound as significant as the bump of tree against roof in the night.

Kallandras.

It was a thin voice, a reedy one; the wind almost swept it away. Was it imagination? He glanced around again, and this time gold obscured his vision, the breeze in his eyes becoming a stronger force, but still a gentle one. There was no ground beneath his feet; he noticed it as if for the first time, thinking it odd.

Or right.

The standing arch was dust now; it alone defied him, and it had paid the price. He gazed up into the darkness of earth's hollow in distaste; there was no reason to remain trapped here when beyond this fragile layer of dirt, stone, and wood the open skies were beckoning.

Kallandras.

But the voice—he thought he should know it. Answer it before his ascension into the world above. His lips were soft and dry as they opened around words, a phrase of breeze and wind, a hint of gale.

He asked his question.

* * *

Meralonne heard it; the fluting of woodwind, air through instrument. There were words to its peaks and valleys, but even he could barely discern them from the element. Curiosity, yes. Confusion. A desire for the sky. The air had the strength to rip the dirt from the cavern's magical roof.

Upon that roof, the oldest parts of the city of Averalaan rested. And within them, the heart of the city: its people. Meralonne spoke urgently of them. And then his lips turned up in a bitter smile as the gale grew; who was he to speak of the sanctity of life to one whose life had been dedicated to ending it?

He cursed Myrddion in the silence of thought and will, gesturing himself onto the banks of the wind as if they were solid steps, feeling air trace his ankles, his soles, his thighs. Oh, it would be good to feel the open plain again—to see it as it was truly meant to be, windswept and empty.

But it would not be windswept and empty; it would be littered with refuse— tracked stone, splintered timbers, broken bodies. Again he spoke, and again there was no answer, although it was clear to him that the bard heard his words.

You cannot reach him, he thought, steeling hands into fists. His sword came as he called it for the final time in this battle. The ground beneath his feet was already a swirl of dirt and debris; if he listened hard, if he directed the course of the wind's passage, he could hear the wailing of the Kings' men, the cursing of his brethren.

And louder than that, carried by nothing but the force of its own wildness, another sound: the triumphant howling of the beast.

Until he heard the roar, Gilliam had been afraid that he would somehow miss his moment; that the Lord of the Hunt's victory cry, obscured by unnatural storm and the cries of the men of Averalaan, would never reach his ears. An odd confidence buoyed him. He *was* Hunter-born. The God was his God, in all its primal fury. They were linked; they understood each other in some measure.

Breodanir, Lord of the Hunt, had been called to the Sacred Hunt by the Master of the Game and his peers; to the Hunt he now came in frenzy.

The Terafin's manse.

The gardens, green and still, as if the air itself had been robbed of the movement of breath. No one spoke; prayer, if there was prayer, was silent.

But Jewel ATerafin's dark eyes widened and she raised a hand. "Wait," she said softly, gazing into the darkness that seemed to claim the bay. "Look."

There, in the cloud cover above, a glimmer of sunlight.

Meralonne's hair streamed out behind him like shining, white liquid; his eyes were shining silver as he held the flat of his blade against his palm. He wore no cape, no armor, bore no shield; he was not broad of chest or large in build. But majesty was there for those who cared to see it. Or those who could.

They met in air, the bard and the mage.

Kallandras offered no resistance as Meralonne brought his weapon to bear; indeed, he hardly seemed aware of the mage at all. The sword rose, and it fell, but it fell slowly and without striking.

For Kallandras was not merely a vessel, although a vessel he had indeed become; he was not slave, if he was not master. His arms were lifted to either side, and his clothing billowed like raised sails, but the song he was singing was his *own*. For the moment.

It should not have been possible, but Myrddion's rings were crafted by a man with a talent and a glimmer of madness; who among even the Wise could predict the full force of their effect? There, upon the binding finger of Kallandras' left hand, the ring glowed a brilliant white; it was hard to look upon.

"Kallandras!" he cried.

There was no answer. The air shook with a voice that was neither bard's song nor mage's cry; Bredan's frenzy. Meralonne clutched the haft of his sword tightly, deciding. He brought it up, and as he did, it dissipated. Quietly, he reached out to touch Kallandras' outstretched hand—the right one; the one which bore no ring.

There were spells of elemental force, and spells of vision; spells for gathering ancient lore and spells for travel; there were the forbidden arts, whose scions—kin and corpse—they had fought this very day, and there were spells of illusion, of misdirection, of negation.

But there were other magics, deeply personal, prying, intrusive; they were arts that touched a soul the way a thief's fingers pry into pockets, lifting bits and pieces of things valued but not tied down. There were edicts against the use of such spells, and the penalties for breaking these edicts harsher than any offered save those for murder by magic.

Meralonne APhaniel was one of the wise, the most learned of their number. He hesitated, but only a moment, before he began to speak the binding words. He touched Kallandras' life, and he was not gentle—but he was not thorough either; he had not the time for it, even if he had the curiosity.

Beneath the song and the yearning it held, burning like a beacon that the wind could not—quite—douse, was a single word that held all hope and all desire. Releasing his hand as if it burned, Meralonne trod back on air, eyes slightly wide, lips pale.

And then he lifted his head, his expression unreadable. Twice he started to speak, and twice he stopped, but the third time he spoke a single word.

"BROTHER!"

Kallandras turned his pale face.

Gilliam was not closest to the beast when it turned from its task; the kin were. Thankful for it, grateful for it, Gilliam bowed his head into wind and began to struggle against it. The Lord of the Hunt, he thought, would need no such effort. His hands shook, part gale, part excitement, and part tension; he was Hunter-born, the trance was on him—he felt no fear. Either he would kill here, or be killed. That was the rule of the Hunt, and no coward, no man afraid of either the first or the second, became a Breodani Lord.

His only regret was that his pack was not at his side. It had been wrong to attempt to protect them by leaving them behind; wrong to deny them their chase and their hunt—to deny them the law that creatures who hunt live by: kill or be killed. He vowed as he struggled that he would not make that mistake again; the sentiment had been Stephen's, the fear a weakness brought on by the madness of the Hunter's loss.

Something struck him in the forearm; he grunted as the blunt curve of a metal helmet disappeared into the storm.

Meralonne knew that the word would draw Kallandras' attention; he did not know what his reaction would be when he realized who—or more importantly, who had not—called. Lifting his arms, he mirrored Kallandras' stance; the wind sung through his hair, his robes.

The bard's eyes were blue-white, a frosted, unnatural color. His lips were turning in wonderment, in joy; they froze as his face became still.

A wise man, Meralonne thought, as he waited in a silence that rose above roaring wind and primal growling, would not tempt the pain of an assassin. Yet he felt no fear; for the first time since he had passed through the chambers of the Sleepers, he was calm. "Kallandras," he said, neither raising his voice nor muting it.

The golden-haired man did not reply, but he lifted a hand in denial of the words that Meralonne might speak. His flickering eyelids closed, his lashes forming crescents against his white, white face. And then, of all things, he smiled, and if the smile was bitter, if it was embroidered with loss and longing and hunger, it held joy in part, no matter how fragile.

The mage was no member of the brotherhood, to call him or to hold his attention; he knew it almost before he turned, but he could not ignore such a cry, in such a tone. The wind song died on his lips, although around him the gale grew stronger.

As the Lady commanded, he had done: the Allasakari were dead and scattered about the grand cavern for carrion. But their names had not been spoken, and only in the speaking would the Kovaschaii know. How could he have forgotten? Why had he delayed? They would know that he served, that he served still.

The ground was far beneath his feet; the bodies of the dead were not in sight. He listened, but the wind carried no sound to him; looked, but the dirt and pebbles, the fine dust of stone and broken wood, were a swirling, dancing veil. He could not pierce it.

What had happened?

"Kallandras!"

It was not Meralonne's voice that he wished to hear, but it was the only one that carried; he opened his eyes to meet the gaunt, gray gaze of the mage.

"Call the wind back! Call it, or you will do the work of the kin!"

The kin were no part of his song, and no part of his desire. They were—but, yes, they were a part of this, for they served side by side with the dead, the Allasakari who were the Lady's show of mercy. And he had fought against the Allasakari—he fought—

Eyes wide, he looked at the ring upon his finger, at its brilliance, at the vortex that spun in its center. Curling that hand into a fist, he met Meralonne's gaze across the divide. His nod, slight but distinct, was his salute.

He watched as Kallandras closed his eyes, planting his feet apart in the wind's hollows as if he were standing upon firm ground. Air was not his element, but no more was earth, water, or fire; he was a creature of light and shadow, touched on all sides by the weakest of wildness and its stirrings.

And he sought to deny what he had unleashed.

Beauty was found in such unusual places; not for the canvas or the sculpture, the song or the poem, was such a moment. This, this was why wars were fought, and had been fought, for as long as he could remember. Close to death, life yielded its finest moments, its best.

Meralonne flinched as Kallandras cried out in pain, breaking the delicate image. The Kovaschaii were trained to silence; it was either the bard who spoke— or the intensity of the pain. The ring was pulsing as the gale grew; the wind's voice was now like the God's.

Storm-called, ring-wielded, the elemental air was in its glory; Meralonne smiled grimly and bitterly as he, too, bent his strength—what little remained of it—to the bard's aid. And what way, what other way, was there to fight?

Opening more than his arms, Meralonne let the wildness in.

Struggling through a forest made of moving wind and debris, Gilliam listened for the roar that moved counter to the wind. The Lord of the Hunt was not canny; He made no attempt to hide His presence from His follower. Gilliam's smile was grim. Why should He? For years upon end, this *was* His day; He was not victim but victor, not hunted, but Hunter.

At his side, a man struggled through the gale toward him, speaking— shouting—in Essalieyanese. It was the court tongue, but not the Hunter's tongue, and Gilliam almost brushed him off in anger. But he did not, and because he did not, the man drew close enough that Gilliam might recognize him. Devon ATerafin.

His face was bloodied by a grazed forehead; the set of his jaw was grim, and his pallor was gray. He was a court noble, but he offered no finery and no fine words, and in his expression, Gilliam saw the hunted.

"Lord Elseth! *Lord Elseth!*"

The Hunter roared.

"What?"

"The beast is at our flank." He opened his mouth to say more, but the words fell away as Gilliam's expression made his understanding clear.

"Get out," he shouted. "All of you, get out!"

"We can't," the ATerafin shouted back. "The wind blocks the exits—we've lost four mages against it."

"Then stop the wind!"

Devon's brow furrowed in confusion and then grim understanding. He offered a ragged bow as Gilliam waved him back and struggled forward again.

He was empty, empty, empty.

His brothers were lost.

The Lady was a glimmer of past power and undying anger. An oath had been given, and an oath broken; the life that he had built had been shattered against it, and no service, no act of contrition, would build it anew.

Essalieyan was his home, and within it, Averalaan. He had grown accustomed to the foibles of the men and women whose company he could not avoid, and over time, he had grown fond of them in his fashion. The ache and the anger had dulled; he had been lulled into a false sense of self, an uneasy compromise between the past and the present.

Evayne's coming had broken that, rupturing the mask of self-deception he had placed across his drama. Even that he could bear. But his shield was riven, and to remake it was the work of decades; without its protection he was vulnerable in ways that no other mage could comprehend.

And without it, he faced the wild winds, hollowing himself into a tempting vessel, whispering the promises of open sky and ancient sacrifice. The smell of singed flesh swirled briefly past his upturned face.

He opened his eyes, wondering when he had closed them; Kallandras was yards away, his curled hand the only difference between their stances. *The fight will kill him*, he thought dispassionately. It didn't matter.

No?

Then why was he drifting forward, why was he extending himself, daring the storm and the wind's rage? Bitterly he realized that his facade was not entirely self-deception; in inhospitable soil, the mask had grown roots.

Brother, he said again. But this time he listened to his own voice and understood why Kallandras had turned, blindly, toward it. Knew, uttering it this second time, that Kallandras would not ignore it. Lifting a fine-boned, empty hand, Meralonne reached out.

Kallandras mirrored his movement, lifting his left hand, his curled, burned, ring hand, toward the mage. He tried to open his fist; the fingers shuddered, but would not unlock. Meralonne could see the blistered, reddened skin before he reached out to cover the knuckles with the palm of his hand.

Contact.

Chapter Thirty-One

THE KINGS' MEN WERE DYING. Against the gale, they had some protection, but against the beast, none. Gilliam of Elseth cursed the wind, the dirt, and the dead; he cursed the kin. He could not reach the Hunter in time to stop the slaughter—the Hunter Lord was hungry, and in hunger, merciless.

It should not have been his concern, but it was; Stephen's ghost rode him harder in these few moments than he had at any time other than his dying. Was he never to be free of the conscience, the responsibility, the distraction? Was the full depth of the Hunt never to be his again?

Calm returned to him, and a sadness.

He would never be the same again, because to be the same was to deny Stephen of Elseth—the best huntbrother that Breodanir had ever known—his due. No one would grant it, if Gilliam did not.

Stephen of Elseth was responsibility personified. Stephen of Elseth was willing—*had*—given his life to the only death that he had truly feared, so that these strangers, these foreign nobles and their kin, might live. No, he thought, grimacing; it was not so that *they* could live.

I would not have taken your oath. I would not have accepted your death in my stead. But I am alive, Stephen—and I promise your death will mean something.

He knew, then, what he must do. Wondered why he hadn't thought of it earlier, and knew at the same time.

Gilliam stopped his struggle against the wind. As Stephen had done, he stood his ground, although he overcame no terror to do so. Holding the Spear upright with his left hand, he reached into his vest with the right. Cold and smooth, the Hunter's Horn came to his hand.

They practiced their calls together. All huntbrothers did. Although the calls for the huntbrother were different than those the Hunter employed, no Hunter escaped his early training without learning both. Tilting the Horn to his lips as if it were a flask, he raised it, inhaled, and blew the three notes; they were as wild, as raw, as the voice of the beast.

Would He come? Would the call of the Hunter, and not the brother, invoke the ancient oaths?

They could not be together, but having joined hands, they could not be separated; they were not brothers, but they were more than comrades.

"Its voice—" Kallandras said, his own a croak.

"I know," the mage replied gravely. "Hold tight, little brother. Hold long. The wind is about to realize that it is angry."

"Meralonne," Kallandras continued, swinging his uninjured right hand over Meralonne's and holding there, "I don't know how to let it go—I don't *want* to lose it—" *Because I did not miss them. I did not remember.*

False words came to the mage, and false words died before they left his lips. "I know," he said. "But we are fated to have and to lose, you and I. Walk the path bravely." He brought his left hand to Kallandras' right, bracing the arm with what remained of his mage-power. It hurt, but there was worse pain. There had always been worse.

Together, they began to call back the gale.

But the wild wind was not a mage's breeze, to be called and lightly dismissed; it had a will of its own, and in a fashion, a mind; the skirmish that had begun with Myrddion's ring became a battle. Meralonne brought the wildness home, containing it as he could; he spoke its name with a voice that no one—not even the bard—could hear. The breeze that had been warm and soft was chill and biting in its fury, for it knew betrayal.

Accuse me, Meralonne snarled into the wind. *Accuse me—you will not be the first.* But Kallandras cried out in denial, wordless; he offered no anger, and the wind struggled harder for the lack, seeking purchase in guilt and pain that anger did not allow.

As if they were two points on a wheel whose center was their joined hands, Meralonne and Kallandras began to spin. The earth rose to greet them in a deadly rush, peeling away at the last moment as the mage brought his will to bear. His grip on Kallandras tightened; their fingers twined; around their hands grew a halo of sparking light.

Blood trailed from the bard's lip up the side of his cheek, tracing his fine features. He was prepared enough for pain that he did not surrender to it. Fingers gripped and knotted his hair, pulling it back; his throat, pale and unadorned, was exposed a moment before he could free himself. Two arm's lengths away, Meralonne's eyes widened a moment in surprise as Myrddion's ring seared his flesh. But he did not release Kallandras.

It was the bard as much as the assassin who saw the pale-skinned, platinum-haired mage, his eyes shining as brightly as—or more brightly than—the ring, his expression taut and pale. In seeming he was no longer old and wise and learned; his power was youth's power, youth's certain belief in immortality.

It was the wind's power.

The two—wind and mage—seemed inextricably linked, the binding between them no less pervasive, no less necessary, than the binding that held the Kovaschaii together. Kallandras sang with the wind's voice; Meralonne *was* the wind.

Pain brought him back to himself; pain and determination. Lifting his chin, he sang, his voice the bard's voice, a counter to the wind's anger. Myrddion's ring burned at his flesh; the air reddened his cheeks with chill. Again, the ground rushed up, and again it stopped, but his shadow was inches from his cheek before he righted himself. Or was righted. His toes brushed the earth and remained there.

Meralonne's face was twisted, his lips thin; the pain that was writ across his features looked as if it might never leave, it was etched so deep. He held fast to Kallandras, and in the light of his eyes, the bard saw a glimmering. If they were tears, the mage would not let them fall.

The tenor of the wind changed abruptly; the storm ceased its buffeting chill. Curls flattened against forehead by sweat and blood were lifted again, ruffled; the sweet smell of open sky teased his nostrils. He could see, more clearly than the death and the darkness, the perfection of sun across a crimson horizon, the whisper of nodding leaves, stalks of grass; he could feel the caress of feathered wings along his forehead.

In the wind, innocence, wild joy, perfect beauty. A place where pain and loss had no meaning, and never would.

It hurt him, to deny it.

But he had already denied so much for the sake of this battle, it came naturally to him. As if the things he could have, rather than the things he could not, were the illusion or the trap. What had Meralonne said? To have and to lose.

He sang the wind home, and the wind, crying, came.

Silence.

Meralonne caught Kallandras as his grip slackened and he fell. Had there been no breath, no pulse, he would not have been surprised; the bard weighed no more than a child, albeit an older one; his cheeks were hollowed as if by long years of privation, his eyes ringed darkly. His hand—the hand that had borne, and still bore, Myrddion's ring—was blistered, and in two places blackened to bone. Without the aid of a powerful healer, the talent for which Kallandras was known would fail him; no hands so injured could bridge the strings of a lute.

And the other hurts, time would heal. Or nothing.

As the mage cradled the bard's limp form, the air returned—gently—to earth the things that should have remained upon it: bodies; the weapons and armor of the fallen; jagged rocks and other fragments of what had once been altars, columns, and arches.

I hear you, Meralonne told the wind. *I know what you desire. But it is not the time, not the place; you have done damage enough with what little freedom you were granted.*

He received no answer, but expected none. Long ago, he would not have spoken. Grimacing, he realized that even in this, time had changed him.

At his back, he heard the roar of the beast; it was distant enough for the moment that he did not seek to flee it in desperation. Instead, he turned in its direction, cradling the bard to his chest as if his weight were negligible. Remembering that his arm, braced by magic, would suffer the weight only so long, and not longer.

The beast was in its fury; beneath its open jaws, the savaged corpse of a dead soldier lay sprawled at an angle that even in death should have been impossible. He could not think of this creature as a God; such a primal force had its roots in things older and wilder than the Lords of man. Yet it was compelling in its rage and hunger, and beautiful in the way that creatures of power are. Like the elemental air. Yes, very like it.

The Kings—he could see their standards, broken and twisted by wind, now raised by the shadowy lattice of magical hands—were alive; their soldiers, what remained of them, regrouped around their monarchs. The standards of the Exalted were likewise borne, but the daughter of the Mother was busy; the healers had been left in the streets where the fighting could not destroy them and no one sought to summon them yet.

There should have been a breeze; a wind across a plain whose silence was the aftermath of waged battle. Some sun, dying light, the flight of birds in the high skies above, waiting. There should have been horns, trumpets, pipes; there should have been heralds, those who told the battle's tale to the families and the countrymen who waited behind the lines the generals had drawn.

There were none of these things.

Instead, all eyes were upon a lone man who stood, Spear to one side, Horn slowly falling from steady hands. Meralonne could see his back; he did not know what expression played across the face of Lord Elseth of the Breodani, but he knew, as the beast's great head swiveled, as it roared again, that the Horn was the Hunter's Horn, and by it the beast had been summoned.

But the beast was canny in a feral way. It did not charge.

Nor did the waiting Lord.

This will decide all.

Meralonne stepped back, carrying Kallandras from the field. To his great surprise, the bard lifted his head; his curls, sticky and matted, clung to his face. He tried to speak, but his voice was a ruin and it formed no words.

"What is it?" Meralonne's voice was gentle.

Reaching out, Kallandras clutched the mage's robe. His lips formed words that his voice could not carry, not yet.

There was a danger here, and Meralonne knew it—but the battle had not yet left his blood. Softly brushing the hair from the dull blue eyes of the younger man, he nodded. He thought that Kallandras might relax, but instead he pulled himself up by the mage's collar until he was almost sitting in the cradle of his arms. His eyes became opaque; he lifted his hands in a shaking, jittery motion that meant nothing to Meralonne. His mouth moved; cracked lips split further as he carefully, delicately, formed thirteen words.

Curiosity was the very heart of the Order of Knowledge, but even so, Meralonne granted Kallandras as much privacy as he could, holding him without watching, allowing him to struggle without superfluous offers of aid.

He knew it was over when Kallandras began to weep, and almost against his will, he held him a while, watching the battle.

Silence.

No gale, no clashing of arms, no dying cries. It was as if the huntbrother's call had stopped the world; as if the mystical meeting place of Gods and men had been bridged so that the two, Hunter's Death and Hunter, might meet here for the last time. His arm shook as the Horn's final note resonated into stillness.

He wore Hunter green, the dark rich weave that was the emblem of his rank; he bore a sword across his back, a sheathed dagger for the unmaking across his thigh.

Death stalked him, moving across the bloodied, even sand; Death roared twice, an answer to the call of the Horn. The Horn lay at his feet like so much refuse. By it, Stephen had called his death, and Gilliam would not allow it to be winded again while he lived.

The Hunter's movements were graceful, powerful; they spoke of the kill, of the freedom of the kill, of the end to hunger. Waiting, he listened for the third roar—there had been three notes. When it came, he knew that the Hunter's Death would spring on coiled hind legs, cover the distance between them; force him to stand against superior strength, speed, weight. A calm descended on him as the beast raised its head.

At his back, he heard a murmur break the silence, and then, louder than that and sweeter by far, the baying of the dogs. Three. He knew their voices, heard the reproach in them before it gave way to joy, to fear. To the Hunt. He could not stop himself; he caught their eyes, their ears, their noses, shifting his stance subtly as the information became a part of him; as the Hunt became *real*.

He heard his heart beat, felt theirs and, more, felt an inexplicable joy, a perfect well-being. Had he thought, had he even doubted, that he could stand against this creature? Why?

Around him, like columns in an ancient ruin, ghostly trees cast their shadows and offered their cover; he heard the rustle of leaves and undergrowth, the snap of dry twigs and dead branches. This forest was the Hunter's mantle, and Gilliam felt no surprise as it unfolded around him. The Hunt that the Breodani had been given was not a hunt of air and wing, nor of open plain, nor of rocky mountain face; it was a forest Hunt, and in the forest, all things could be hidden.

Stay! he cried out, as Ashfel howled and pulled away, arrowing toward the beast as if the beast were not his death. He caught Connel and Salas—long-snouted, white-booted pup—before they could join their leader. *You wait*, he told them, *for me*.

There should have been fear. But the dogs did not have it; indeed they might have been chasing a rabbit or a fox for all the caution they showed. He looked at them closely, seeing them through his own eyes—and each other's. Like pups, they bounced on the pads of their feet, anxious to be gone, but willing—barely—to obey.

A smile turned his lips up; he reached for a horn—his own, and deservedly so—and blew the harboring of the beast. They joined him, baying, as the beast came.

Spear became an extension of arm. Gilliam heard the beast roar, saw the glint of fur and fang as it leaped; he was not there to greet it. The shadow passed him, clawing at air and cloak. When Gilliam turned again, he brought the Spear to bear.

Through his hounds' acute senses he tried to penetrate the mystery of the creature. All things had a definitive scent, some mark of sweat and musk upon the air by which they could be identified. But the Hunter's Death *was* the forest scent, and no part of it could be pared from him. It was almost as if . . .

From death, life.

The moment of wonder held him still almost too long. The creature's lunge caught his cloak and shirt; he heard the snapping of a brittle, fine clasp—his mother's gift—seconds before claws traced a path across his thigh. *From death*, he thought, drawing painful breath across teeth as his leap proved the muscles hadn't been slashed. First blood.

But the death—the Hunter's Price—had already been paid. And paid. And paid. At once, the forest's shadows were harsher, sharper, longer. The dogs had come to stand at his side, but Stephen's place was empty, and would remain so. The beast roared, or so he thought until he felt the rawness of his throat as he drew breath.

Bringing the Spear to bear again, he backed up slowly; the shadow of a great tree crossed over his shoulder. Crouching, he tightened his grip on the Spear's plain haft, wishing for a boar-spear. The world slipped into shades of gray as he caught Salas' view of the moving beast's flank. It was coming for him, quickly.

*   *   *

"Stand your ground."

At the curt command, the Kings' Sword—the Verrus Sivari—glanced up. His eyes became darkened, wary slits. "It is not our way to stand idle while our allies face death."

The slender, platinum-haired mage frowned at the tone of the man's voice. "And it is your way, of course, to commit to death your own people. Stand your ground."

"The Kings' Swords," he said curtly, "take their orders from the Kings."

Meralonne raised a pale brow and then bowed very low.

"Member APhaniel," King Reymalyn said quietly. "What would you have of us?"

"I would have you," Meralonne replied, his voice a study in neutrality, "save the lives of your servitors. They are gathering to intervene in the struggle." He paused and spoke again only when it became clear that the King was waiting. "There is only one weapon in the city that can affect the creature you see before us. That man wields it, as he is oathsworn to do. Neither he, nor the creature, would benefit from the aid that you seek to offer—but neither he, nor the creature, would be injured by it either. Your men will break like a single wave against the seawall."

Verrus Sivari bristled.

The Lord of the Compact, dirt-stained and bleeding but utterly unfazed by either, said, "My Lord, heed him." No more. It was not to Verrus Sivari's liking.

King Reymalyn raised his hand and gave the order.

The beast moved slowly, stalking toward him like a giant cat as he shook the forest with his growling. Inches disappeared under the quiet fall of footpad and claw; Gilliam held the Spear before him as if its shaft were a shield behind which he might weather a strong attack. Hunters dreamed of such a moment; were, in their Hunt in the safety of the Sacred Forest, dreaming of it now.

Ashfel came from the left, seeking purchase in the shoulder haunch of the beast, at a safe remove from reach of its heavy head or jaws. But Ashfel was alaunt, and the beast was God; almost before he made his leap, he was flying in the wrong direction. Gilliam grimaced as he felt the impact, aware that the act of disposing of the slight threat had distracted the Death.

Ashfel rose from his bed of twigs and dirt, growling; had he hit tree or rock in his fall, more than dignity would have been injured. Gilliam caught him and held him back, weaving invisible couples around him and Salas. Connel was the wisest of the three—and, not coincidentally, the oldest; he was willing to wait upon the word of the Hunter Lord.

Looking up, unblinking, Gilliam stared into the eyes of the beast. A mistake, and almost his last, for the God stared back. Men give a hint of their intent by the shifting of their eyes, by the narrowing or widening of their lids; the Hunter's Death was intent incarnate, and when he sprang, there was no change at all in the lidless depth of his gaze.

But perhaps there was something else; some spark of Godhood not consumed by the Hunt; perhaps the lives that he had already taken in the first flush of his victory had had their effect—although that should not have been possible—for the leap was heavy and fell short; jaws that should have snapped shut over the forearm and elbow cut grooves into flesh and slid free.

Old scars would be buried under new ones. Gilliam grunted in pain and then let the pain wash over him as if he were stone and it, liquid. This was why Hunters did not use bow and arrow; they did not wield crossbow; they did not throw javelins or ride—as was the custom in the West—after their dogs at a safe distance.

Mighty head coiled on muscled neck; the beast growled as Ashfel, Salas, and Connel joined the fray, harrying it at a vantage that teeth and claw could not easily reach. Gilliam willed the beast to turn, but the beast knew who the leader was. And knew best that to kill the Hunter was to destroy the pack. Had he not fashioned that truth and given it to the Breodani at the dawn of time?

His muscles were not severed; as the beast raked claws across Connel's side, Gilliam gritted his teeth and lunged forward with the Spear.

To the parish, to the village, the stag was the best kill; the largest and the one that provided for most. But to the Hunters, it was the boar that was the test; even the bear, cornered, was not so dangerous.

Gilliam had been tested. And he had passed that test because he *was* Breodani; he *was* Hunter Lord. The Spear's fine, unadorned tip found a home in the beast's throat an instant before its great jaws descended again.

The earth left Gilliam's feet, but his hands held fast to the haft of the Spear as the beast reared up on two legs, seeking to dislodge him.

Connel watched for him, seeing the whole event as he could not; Connel's eyes saw Gilliam's body as the beast sought to scrape him off on the bark of a great tree. He reacted to what the alaunt saw, as he had always done, bringing his feet up at the last minute to use the tree for leverage. To push the Spear farther home.

The beast roared, but the roar was a gurgle of anger and pain; he snapped his head to the side, and Gilliam once again held on to the Spear, nothing more, as he swung in a wide arc. Ashfel sought purchase in flank; Salas harried the beast's back.

Twice, the beast struck out with claw where fang would no longer reach; each time, he scored flesh, drew blood. This struggle was at the heart of the Hunter's dance, the Hunter's Death. They both knew its cadences, and its pain, and they knew its goal: One would weaken and die; the other would survive.

But Gods live forever.

Gilliam's hands were slick and sticky with wet blood, with drying blood; he slid an inch down the Spear's pole before his grip tightened enough to hold on. The beast dropped to all fours, suddenly pressing him to ground when he least expected it. Connel's vision was blurring; Gilliam knew that soon, the contest would be over. He could not hold his link and trance for much longer.

The Spear bit deeper, swallowed by fur and blood, but it was not deep enough— he knew that now.

Claws raked his chest, his stomach; he closed his eyes a moment and felt the heaviness of lids, the physical reluctance to see—to watch—his death.

And perhaps it was because his eyes were closed, perhaps because he could not see the physical world so clearly and so brightly, that he felt a glimmer of a familiar presence. It offered comfort, sent him strength. In the darkness of lidded eyes, he felt ghostly hands around his shuddering grip; they were gentle but firm as they closed around his knuckles, holding them in place.

He should have been surprised, but he couldn't be. The hounds, he had sent away, and they had returned because their place was the Hunt; Stephen, the Hunter God had taken, and his return, no matter how limited, no matter how slight, was no less right. He had never faced the Sacred Hunt without Stephen. This was their final Hunt together, a gift unlooked for. He wanted to hear Stephen's voice again, but he knew he never would—not outside of the Halls of Judgment.

A calm descended upon him, easing his pain a moment as he opened his eyes and stared up at the throat and upper chest of the Hunter's Death.

Stephen's confidence buoyed him, cutting through pain and exhaustion. Lips moving, Gilliam of Elseth spoke his huntbrother's name as he used the last of his strength to drive the Spear home.

Wind filled the arena; trees, or the shadows they cast across Gilliam's upturned face, dissolved into earth's night. But this wind did not roar, and as it traveled across the breadth of the coliseum, it touched everything with a subdued light.

The Lord of Elseth felt the shock of the sudden silence as he stared into the still, stiff face of the Hunter's Death. He expected a roar, some denial of the Spear that had finally found its mark, a final frenzy—but there were none of these things. Instead, a stillness, an odd quiet. The beast's eyes widened; it lifted its head blindly as if catching a scent on the wind that Gilliam couldn't detect. Then, slowly, that head came to rest, falling like an unbearably great weight to the broken ground.

He was gone.

The breeze came down like a summer shower, and everywhere that it touched the Hunter's Death, the creature was transformed. But it was not transformed into flesh of a different kind; it was dead, and the need for body was beyond it.

Instead, a pale light grew, like a halo, around each part of the great creature. That body faded slowly from sight, as if consumed by light—or returned to it.

The unmaking, Gilliam thought absurdly, of a God.

He did not speak; he had nothing left to say to a God who had, in the end, deprived him of the only person who meant anything. Or if he had, it was not particularly pious. He tried to rise to one elbow, and felt Ashfel's nose against his bloodied cheek.

Idiot, he thought, as the dog jumped up on his chest, flattening him. He coughed and winced. Then he noticed that the Spear was gone with the God. He imagined that the Horn, as well, had vanished. He had no proof that he had Hunted this day at the behest of the God of the Breodanir; nothing to take to the King and the King's Hunters.

Was it worth it?

The wounds across his chest and thighs burned; he knew he was bleeding profusely.

Was it worth it, to lose every honor, to lose land and title and name?

A grim smile touched his lips.

Now, Meralonne thought, music. And so it came, although Kallandras was too broken in body and spirit to play the bard. There were no harps, no lutes, no instruments but the human voice, but these voices were enough. King Reymalyn started, for his voice was easily the better of the two Kings, and he sang "The Return of the Queen."

Above them, high, high in the streets of Averalaan, upon rich and poor, upon powerful and weak, the sun's rays were breaking the shadow's grip. It was First Day; it was the New Year. Blessed be.

The Kings' Swords joined him in ones and twos, testing their voices in the silence of the coliseum's height. Even the Astari offered the cadences and harmonies of their choosing.

Only the Exalted of the Mother raised a dark brow at the song. Gathering her fallen cloak, and motioning her attendant—the one that remained standing—forward, she began her trek across the arena. When the young man stumbled and gained his feet, struggling all the while with her standard, she stopped.

What was said was not clear, but to Meralonne's amusement, the young man's face slackened into lines of horrified propriety that could easily be seen by any who cared to observe. The standard wavered a moment, and she spoke again. Glancing over his shoulder, the man reverently, even sorrowfully, laid the pennant down.

The battle was won; there was, in the mind of the Exalted of the Mother, no more need for heraldry if the choice was between that and the dying who waited upon her ministration. Although he had only met her a handful of times, and during that handful she had never been more than civil, Meralonne watched her back fondly as she marched across the sand. The dead did not call her, but the living—no matter how slight or dim their spark—would; the patina of crusted blood and broken bone could not fool her blood-born instinct.

Meralonne looked down at Kallandras, thinking of healers, of the healer-born. The battles were always won—by one side or the other—and in their aftermath, the dead, the dying, and the injured remained. But there were some injuries that the healers here could not deal with, and some that healers, aligned, should not be privy to.

For to be healed, of course, was to be known.

But there were other ways. Older ways.

Gathering Kallandras in untiring arms, Meralonne APhaniel summoned what remained of his power, gathering its gray mantle around his slender shoulders. The bard was light enough to be little encumbrance, but even had he been a real weight, Meralonne APhaniel thought he might expend the power that he did not have to carry him to the open air of the city above.

"Sigurne," he said, casting the words, with spell, to her distant ears, "I must depart. I will see you above."

Gilliam of Elseth recognized the Exalted of the Mother when her face appeared in the periphery of his fading vision; when her torn and dusty robe gathered in folds at his side as she knelt there. Her hair, once a golden, severe knot, escaped to frame her face in loose, wavy strands; she looked younger somehow, although he wasn't sure why.

"Well met, Lord Elseth," she said, and her voice was the low music of the horn, deep and earthy.

He wanted to speak, but his lips barely moved; she pressed her slender fingers against them, calling for silence. "You are wounded," she told him, although that much was obvious to both. "Ashfel," she added, "you need not clean his wounds; trust me. I will tend him."

Gilliam wasn't even sure that he wanted to be tended; what reason was there for it? His lands, he tried to tell her. His lands—the life that he had been born and bred to—they were already gone. He had missed the King's call to the Sacred Hunt, only the second of the Breodani Lords to so fail in their pledge. Worse still, he had lost the purpose behind which he had hidden his loss; the God that had killed his huntbrother was dead and gone. But it hadn't brought Stephen back; instead, it had taken the very last of Stephen's voice away. Without it, the Hunt and the huntbrother, he had no life that he wanted.

But meeting her eyes, he knew that it would do no good; he could tell her to let death take him, and she would become stern-lipped, matronly, the voice of the Mother's determination.

"Have you been with a healer before?"

He nodded, remembering Vivienne of the Mother's Order, although it seemed decades, and not months, past.

"Then you understand, Lord Elseth. You are . . . badly injured." She placed her hands very gently against his chest. "But you have done the Mother a service that you cannot know; live to benefit from it."

Incense began to burn; he could smell it keenly, although he could not see its source. She began to heal him, and as she did, she came perilously close to touching the open wound of Stephen's loss, for she became a part of him. Had he been stronger—had he been Stephen—he would have warned her; he was not, and he could not.

But she was the Mother's daughter, and the Mother's voice in the Empire, wise beyond her years, and strong in the quiet and enduring way of the women of the Breodani. She felt his loss as personally as he felt it, and more, but she did not pull away from the open pain.

She called him back, and who could ignore her voice in the darkness?

Chapter Thirty-Two

DAY. Light across the roads and bridges, the waterfront and the thawing grass. What shadows remained were shadows cast by sunrise over the streets of a silent city. Silence, blessed and anointed by the ghost of Veralaan, held; there were no screams, no hint of demonic torture. Henden had passed, and with it, the darkness.

From out of their small homes and large manors, from balconies on the Isle and window casements on the mainlands, the citizens of Averalaan rose to greet the sun. Some slept, and were wakened by the tugging and pulling of young children; others, who understood better what the ride to Moorelas' Sanctum had meant, greeted the New Year with no sleep to break that longest of sleepless nights.

And as the city rose, as the merchants made ready to brave the First Day—and the First Day festival, for which so little preparation, this one year, had been made—they heard the lowing of the horns, loud and clear: victory on the field.

Finch, Jester, and Teller, of no family but Jewel's den, heard the lowing as it carried across the channel. They sat at the foot of the bridge, behind the statue of the founding fathers, part of the shadows that slowly fled the lands. Their hands were locked in fists, clenched to shaking; they waited, and heard again the call of horn in the blessed silence. Finch rose first, uncurling her stiff legs and knees. Then, carefully, she walked to the statue of Cormalyn the First. At his feet, laid out to bear witness to the sacrifice of Veralaan, was a lovely garland of white roses and orchids; it was clearly the gift of a well-moneyed patron, but during the Dark Days, even the rich and lofty nobility worshiped in secret for fear of their lives. She smiled, touching the orchid's fragrant petals; Ellerson had paid for them.

Lifting the wreath carefully, she nodded to Jester; he rose at once, while Teller watched their back. Cupping his hands, he knelt; she placed her foot against his palms, and he lifted her up while she balanced with her other foot against the statue's carved greaves. Then, struggling to balance, she laid the flowers around Cormalyn's neck.

1st Veral, 411 A.A, evening
Averalaan

Jewel Markess sat on the ledge of a window twice her height. Teller sat quietly at her feet although there was space—more than enough—for both of them. He was quiet, which, in Teller's case, meant nothing. If you didn't know him. If you weren't the one who had picked him off the streets because he was too small—and too plain—to be of use to anyone else.

It was over, one way or another; they all knew it. The servants, having heard the blessed—yes, *blessed*—sound of the royal horns, had dropped to their knees to offer thanks, and to begin fully and completely their celebration of the end of the Six Dark Days. There should have been song and ale and noise; there should have been dancing and wild revelry. But there was silence; for if this was the first day of the New Year, it was also the First Day that the dead could be properly mourned. And, Jewel thought, the first day in many, many days that sleep would not be interrupted by the sounds of the dying, except in nightmare.

And who would have thought nightmare a blessing?

Still, when the horns blew on, and became more solid in their presence than the memory of darkness, joy took root and held, and it was the joy of a victory earned in the most just of battles.

The Terafin had dismissed her family with the same certainty and ease with which she'd addressed them, but even in her very proper and confident demeanor relief and joy had shown in equal measure. Carver and Angel were out on the grounds somewhere—she had a sinking feeling it had something to do with the young women who served in the kitchen, so she hadn't asked; Arann was with the guards. Finch and Jester were out by the bridge that led to the Isle, waiting for sight of the Kings. The Return of the Kings. Ellerson was in her wing, cleaning meticulously. Cleaning, in fact, as if he were a welcome guest who wouldn't be returning for a while. She wondered if that had anything to do with the fact that, when this was over, she wasn't going to be needed here anymore.

That left her Teller, and the window, and the sun sinking into the horizon of tall buildings and clear sky.

Word had come, carried by a boy little older than she, and certainly no more finely dressed. He would bear his message to The Terafin, and The Terafin alone, and judging by the set of his face, he meant it. The Chosen let him through when he showed them something that he carried in a clenched fist, but they watched him somberly, as if he were more of a threat than all of her den combined had ever been.

That was an hour ago, and the boy, ushered to The Terafin's personal chambers, had yet to emerge.

"Jay?"

"Hmmm?" She lifted her chin from the knee it was propped against.

"Isn't that Torvan?"

"Where?"

Teller pointed and Jewel cursed the colored pane closest to her face. Getting down, she stuck her chin onto the window seat and squinted, tugging strands of dark, unruly hair out of her eyes. "Yes. And Alayra." She'd recognize that hawkish woman's face at any distance. Alayra's anger at Torvan had only barely subsided, and it was clear that she did not trust him yet. If she ever would again. But at least Alayra was forthright about it.

"Is that the messenger?"

Jewel snorted. "Sure. But he's aged ten years, grown eight inches, and dyed his hair." Pressing her face further into the window, she watched them cross the courtyard. "He's going up," she said at last.

"Yes," a voice said from behind. "And so, if you've finished, are you."

Blushing, she turned around to see Arrendas. He stood with three of the Chosen whom she did not immediately recognize, two women and another man. They were clearly on duty, and even Arrendas, who was usually one of the few friendly members of the elite guard, looked unnaturally grave. "You are requested," he added softly, as Teller made to rise, "to come alone."

The domed, stained glass of the library ceiling let in the lengthening shadows, the reddening sky; lamps, oil, and wick, were lit along each of three walls. The Terafin sat behind the austere surface of a large desk, her hair drawn tight, the shadows beneath her eyes deepening and lingering as the day stretched into night. Neither woman, The Terafin or Jewel, had slept the evening, and it showed.

To the right of The Terafin, as dependable as a shadow, was Morretz; if worry had deprived him of sleep, there was no sign of it across his neutral expression. Torvan and Alayra stood a little distance off; Jewel's escort joined them in a silence that made them—almost—invisible. To Morretz' right, seated, was the man Jewel knew as Gabriel ATerafin. Ten years her senior, he was The Terafin's closest counselor, and in House affairs, her staunchest ally. His lined face was a study in concern.

To the left of The Terafin, standing almost insolently, arms folded across his chest, was the stranger. His hair was coal black, and his eyes dark enough that it was hard to tell where he was looking; he wore red and black, and although the lines of his robes were simple, the material was very fine. Bloused sleeves caught his wrists in perfect bands, and beneath the edge of a black hem she could see well-kept leather boots.

She disliked him immediately.

As if aware of her appraisal, he raised a brow.

"Jewel," The Terafin said. "Please. Be seated."

While he stood? But The Terafin's words weren't a request, and there was no way to pretend they had been. Swallowing, Jewel chose a chair closest to the shelves of books that formed The Terafin's private collection.

The door opened and, unescorted, Ellerson, domicis of Jewel Markess, walked quietly into the room. He looked at Jewel, and then away, his face very grave.

Her heart sank, if that were possible.

"Ellerson," The Terafin said. "Please, be seated."

He nodded his acquiescence and chose a seat a suitable distance from The Terafin—but also from Jewel. She was surprised at how much it hurt, because she knew before he said it that he was going to leave her.

She *knew*.

The Terafin's smile was serene. "Yes," she said, granting Jewel the foreknowledge.

But Ellerson turned quietly; he looked aged. "Jewel," he said.

She didn't want to embarrass herself in front of all of these people—the Chosen, The Terafin, the arrogant stranger. But she had to speak, so she kept her voice as quiet as possible. "You told me—only if you died, or if I died—"

"Or if the contract expired. Or," he added quietly, "if there was a great change in circumstance."

"But there hasn't—"

He raised a hand with a certain imperiousness; she was used to it and fell silent. "I am not your lord," he told her. "It is not my place to tell you things that you obviously have not considered carefully enough for yourself." But he cleared his throat. "Think, Jewel born Markess; think carefully."

Before he could continue, The Terafin raised an unadorned hand. "Ellerson of the Domici, you have served well; the House of Terafin is pleased with your effort." She turned to Jewel, and her expression was unreadable. "Understand that it is not at my request that Ellerson has removed himself from your service."

"But why?"

"Because," Ellerson said, breaking his own edicts by interrupting The Terafin. "I am not the right domicis for a young woman who will—someday—be a person of great power. Remember what I told you," he added, softening his voice. "To serve a person of power, one must *be* a person of power. I am not that. I have never been that. And to serve in that capacity would be, ultimately, a failure of service so profound that I could not contemplate it seriously." He paused. "You are not what I thought you would be, young Jewel, and I have served many in my time. Had circumstances remained what they were, it would have been my honor to serve."

He rose, then, and Jewel realized that he was just going to leave. And that there wasn't anything she could do to stop him.

Numb, she watched him, wondering exactly when it was that she had decided not only to trust him, but to rely on him. A mistake that, and as she watched the doors close on his back, she promised herself she wouldn't make the same one again in a hurry.

It was the stranger who broke the silence that was left in Ellerson's wake. He turned his head slightly to The Terafin and said, "This is the one?"

"Yes."

"Good."

Jewel was out of her seat before the light that flared up in the stranger's hand had a chance to leave his fingers; sparks erupted in her wake as the mage-light broke against—and splintered—the chair in which she had been sitting.

Morretz cried out; light again flared in the study as The Terafin's domicis unveiled his power. But The Terafin, seated, did not react at all. Her Chosen, weapons drawn, froze as she raised a hand and waved them back to their posts; Gabriel picked himself up off the soft pile of her carpets. Jewel rose as well, using the weight of the bookshelves as a support.

"That," The Terafin said coldly, "was unnecessary."

"For you, yes," the stranger replied, his voice quite neutral. "But it is not you who will devote your life to the service of this one." He raised his head and met Jewel's stare. "My apologies," he said, as if he'd done nothing more than accidentally spilled a cup of water.

Morretz was still bristling. "Avandar," he said softly, "you go too far."

"Oh?" Their eyes met, and they stared, grim-faced and angry, more behind their words than just this meeting, this day.

Jewel watched them carefully for a moment, and then she smiled; it was not a pleasant expression. As they stared, as they watched each other, she very carefully pulled a slender tome from the shelf beneath her hand. She moved slowly, so as not to attract unwanted attention. So far so good.

Noiselessly, she pulled her arm back and let the book fly. It struck the mage low—hitting him, corner first, in the shoulder rather than across the side of the face as she'd intended.

The stranger turned, jaw clenching, eyes widening.

Jewel stood forward, arms crossed tightly, lips pressed tighter.

"It seems," The Terafin said wryly, "that you are not the only one to test, Avandar."

"No," Avandar replied, as his face lost anger's edge and became once more quite emotionless. "Just the only one to fail." And at this, he bowed quite low, sweeping the tips of his fingers across the carpet. "Your pardon, little one."

She bristled.

"Terafin, I accept your contract. I will serve this one."

Serve? Jewel looked blankly at her Lord. The Terafin's smile was slightly pained. "This," she said to the young den leader, "is Avandar Gallais. He is of the Domici, and he has come to fulfill the obligation that Ellerson felt he could not."

"W—what?" Jewel's arms fell to her sides.

"I am," Avandar said gravely, "your domicis."

"I won't have him!"

At that, Morretz smiled, and the expression was a shock to Jewel; she realized with a start that she had never seen him smile before. Given the edge to the smile, she wasn't certain she wanted to see him smile often.

But The Terafin rose quietly. "You will," she said coolly. "This interview is at an end." Gathering her skirts, she left the long, fine table and made her way to the door. The Chosen, four of them, followed her.

Bitterly, Jewel swallowed. It was clear that she either accept Avandar or leave Terafin—and she balanced on a fine edge for a moment as she considered both options carefully. "*You* serve *me*, is that clear?"

"Oh, absolutely," Avandar replied, with a trace of sincerity. Just. Then his expression darkened. "And *you* will listen to *me* in emergencies; you will do as I say, and you will allow me to protect you as I see fit."

Mutinous, she glared at him; he returned her gaze with a forced indifference. She really wished that the book had hit him in the face.

But before she could speak again, Torvan did. "Might I speak with you privately, Jewel?"

She nodded and he left Avandar under Alayra's watchful gaze, retreating to the muted quiet of the farthest shelves. There, he found a stool and sat her down.

"Understand," he said quietly, "that to speak to Avandar as you did was an insult to The Terafin. She is not pleased, and has every right not to be."

"But I don't—"

"Nevertheless, while she is not required to give explanations, you must trust that what she has done is for the good of both the House and your place in it. Think, Jewel. You are seer-born. There is no doubt left in the minds of anyone on the House Council. You have proved your value to The Terafin, to Averalaan, and to the Crowns. They all know of who, and what, you are. But if they know, you are no longer a secret. The other Houses will know.

"There have been no seers in the service of the great Houses for at least two generations that we're aware of. The talent is rare, and it is not without risk. You didn't fight in the last House War—but if Darias had known of your existence, he would have spared no expense to have you removed. Yes," he added, as he saw the shifting lines of her face as understanding came, "assassinated. The Kings are above such games, but the Houses . . . the Houses are only human."

"You have a future with this House—and The Terafin, by honoring you with a domicis of Avandar's ability, has indicated that you will be among her most valued advisers—if you survive, both physically and politically." He looked beyond her to where Avandar stood. "You are no longer a den leader. The rules of the street are poor protection for the life you have embarked on. I know what you think of him." He smiled. "Everyone in the room couldn't help but know it." The smile dimmed. "But Avandar Gallais was chosen for you by The Terafin. If anyone can guide you into your majority in this House, it will be Avandar.

"You don't have to like him, but trust him." He paused. "He is your domicis. And unlike Ellerson, the only thing that will part you is your death or his."

His, she thought churlishly. She was wise enough to say nothing.

"Now come." He offered her his hand, and after a moment, she took it. His smile was gentle, and although he did not offer her more comfort than that, she took comfort from his presence. "You will be assigned your own guard," he added softly. "They will not be many. But if you would have me, I would be honored to serve you."

Jewel was dumbstruck for the second time in an afternoon—and that didn't happen often. "But—but you're one of the Chosen!"

"Yes. One of the Chosen of The Terafin. It was my request, and she saw wisdom in it; if you will accede, she will allow it, and I will retain my rank." His smile deepened. "And as the ranking guard, I may choose the men under my command."

She knew what he was offering her: Arann.

"Let him—let him make the choice, all right?"

At that, Torvan smiled. "You really don't understand military service, do you? Very well. If you so request, I will let him decide his own future." He looked down at her hand, still twined tightly around his.

"There is always loss," he told her softly. "And gain. Come, ATerafin." He paused. "If you haven't been informed, the battle is over. We won."

She couldn't think of a single thing to say—or perhaps she could think of too many. "Devon?"

"Alive. With Alowan."

"He's here?"

Torvan caught Jewel's arm before she could bolt out of the library. "No, Jewel. I didn't say he was here."

"Then—"

"The Terafin sent Alowan to the palace with the young . . . runner. We won, but not without cost."

Cold, unlooked for, reached beneath her skin, where warmth could easily dislodge it. She paled; her eyes widened. Avandar appeared at her side at once, although how he knew, she couldn't say.

"What has happened?"

She forgot to distrust him; forgot, for a moment, that her dislike of the cool, self-assured man mattered at all. An ice that made him seem warm, a darkness that made him seem light, put her once again into the tunnels beneath the market authority, sole witness to the unweaving of reality. Eyes wide, she stared into an uncertain distance. "Tell me," she said softly to Torvan ATerafin. "Tell me what happened."

1st Veral, 411 A.A.
Breodanir, The King's Forest

She had thought never to attend another Sacred Hunt in her life; too much of her heart's blood had been spilled by the Hunter's Death to make these hallowed, ceremonial grounds bearable. But Elsabet, Lady Elseth, stood in all her finery at the forest's edge listening to the muted thump-thump of the drums. Remembering.

At her side, tense with waiting, and pale with unspoken fear, was her daughter Maribelle. This year, at sixteen, she was to have been introduced with quiet pride and a certain triumph to the Queen's court. This year, at sixteen, she was to have begun her search for a suitable husband—or rather, she was to entertain the offers of those that Elsabet deemed suitable. Maribelle had been trained and raised on the Elseth Estates, and she had handled them with grace and responsibility, proving her worth.

Elsa glanced down at her daughter's hair; it was pulled tight and held up with plain pins and a silver net. Gone—or hidden—were the curls and ringlets that had marked her youth. She wore a spring dress of pale green, pale blue, and a deep violet—all colors that had cost dearly—beneath a cloak the color of Hunter green. At her throat, a clasp that was an heirloom of Elseth, one fine and old and delicate, held her cloak in place. Her head was unadorned.

Lady Maribelle of Elseth. Lady Elseth.

They were titles that they had the right to use until the last call of the Hunt was sounded. Elsabet glanced at the Queen's Dais. The Ladies of the court, the wives and the daughters of the Hunters who risked everything for the land as they waited, gathered by or about the throne—or upon the green, near the great, empty altar, in small groups.

She could not bear their pity—or worse, their stunned silence, their incomprehension, their horror—and so she waited alone with the daughter who might have no future. Even her rivals, those women with whom she had made her struggles over trade, barter, goods—took no joy in her misfortune; it was too grave a loss for that.

They were dead, she thought numbly. She knew her sons. They *had* to be dead. If she only had their bodies . . .

Her petition was before the Queen, and the Queen was aware of the state of affairs—of the reasons for the departure of her two sons. But the laws of the Hunt were not decided by the Queen, and perhaps not by the King either. And if the Hunter knew mercy, it was not on *this* day, when he wore the face of death for the nobility of the land.

Oh, the air was cold. She was too old for it, although she had scarcely seen her fortieth year. *Not for my sake,* she thought, as she glanced again at her daughter's stiff, proud face.

Lady Faergif had written to Elsabet after meeting with Gilliam and Stephen in the court of the foreign Queen Marieyan. The latter had impressed her, and the former—well, she thought him a very fine Hunter Lord. That had brought a smile to Elsabet's lips, but it was brief and easily broken.

The rest of the letter had offered little in the way of information, and although Elsa had written quickly and spared little expense to ensure that her message was received in haste, Lady Faergif, an old friend and an old ally, had in the end returned her a reply that was cryptic and—to either worried mother, or a woman in danger of losing title to her life and her life's work—of little use at all. *Tell me,* Elsabet had written. *Tell me that they're living, that they're on their way home. Or tell me that they're dead.*

Twelve days ago, on the eve of her departure for the King's City, she had received her answer.

It is, Lady Faergif had penned, in her stately, delicate form, *in the hands of the Hunter, Elsa. I wish you well.* And later in the letter, toward the end of unusually idle superficialities, she had said, *You have raised Breodani sons.* Only that, no more.

But the Breodani did not miss the Sacred Hunt. Gilliam and Stephen had not arrived to join the King's call; they had not come to the forest to renew their pledge to the Hunter God by joining in the Sacred Hunt. They were dead, she thought, too raw to remain numb.

They *had* to be dead. Because if they were not, the stain they had brought to the Elseth name could never be removed.

Her hands curled into fists before she forced them to relax. The air was heavy with chill although the sun's warmth softened the bite of this cold first day of spring.

The sun sank slowly; the light cast by its western face lengthened the shadows of its fall. The pits were being cleared and readied by the servants, and the altars were tended to by the Priests who, not nobility, were not required to serve as sacrifice to the Hunt itself. There were not many.

Chairs and benches had been provided for the use of the Hunter Ladies, and many of these were occupied when the first strain of the horn's clear call could be heard. Oh, the horns had been singing their call throughout the last hour as the Hunters found their quarry—but *this* call, this elegiac note, no Lady could mistake for anything other than the sounding of the Death. In ones and twos, as the sound traveled throughout the wood, other horns joined in. Not all Hunters would hear the call; some were busy with their quarry, in the heat of their trance.

But those who had either completed their kill, or who had not yet caught their beast at harbor—they made of their horns a mournful, a respectful, chorus.

Elsa, ashen, bowed her head a moment into the tips of her fingers; she took a deep breath, squaring her shoulders unconsciously as she raised her chin. Her daughter, to her pride, did likewise; they looked very much kin, these two. The Hunt was over.

Gilliam of Elseth had not returned.

Elsabet looked down at her hand; at the signet ring that had been given her by Lord and Lady Elseth upon her rites of joining to their Hunter son—their only son. It was an old ring, and although it had been sized to fit her hand, no other work had been undertaken upon its detailed, golden surface. Hands shaking, she quietly removed it, holding it in the cup of her palm as she drew her cloak tightly across her shoulders.

"Mari," she said softly, using a name that she had not used since her daughter was a child. "We must go."

Maribelle gathered her slight train in hands that were steadier than her mother's. She nodded wordlessly, but threw a backward glance over her shoulder at the Queen's pavilion and the women gathered there. They had been—and would have been—her peers and her worthy rivals.

If Elsa thought to protect her child, if she thought to somehow be the strength for both of them, then she was mistaken; Maribelle at sixteen was tall and proud, a woman of strength and conviction, if not all of the wisdom one could hope for. It was Maribelle who offered an arm, and Elsa who, after a long pause, accepted it.

To walk away was harder than she had ever dreamed.

"Lady Elseth!"

Hope was such a strange thing. She heard the cry, and out of habit she stopped. It was not, after all, a mere name or title; it was *who* she had become over the years. Curling her fist tight around the ring, she bent her head a moment, for the voice was a voice that she vaguely recognized.

Ah. That was it: Iverssen. The King's Priest. She straightened her shoulders and gently released her daughter's arm—her sole support—before turning. But it was not Iverssen that she saw first; it was Corwinna—Lady Valentin. And Lady Valentin's face was pale—an odd mixture of relief and profound empathy.

"Elsa," she said softly, and Elsabet knew it was not good news—although what news could be harder, she did not know—for Corwinna was wont to be more formal in public circumstance.

"I heard the King's Priest," Elsa said softly. *Calling me by my title.*

But Corwinna shook her head softly. "Maribelle," she said, as strands of graying hair slid free from the fine, jade comb that had pinned it just above the gathered folds of her hood. "You must come to the Queen's Dais now." She paused, and then said softly, "I am sorry."

Together they crossed the green, passing the first group of returning Hunters who had already set about, in grim silence, the work of the unmaking. Their sleeves, blood-splattered, were rolled up and pinned to their shoulders; their cloaks, drawn back, were a heavy and mud-stained green—Hunter green.

Braziers burned in the cool spring afternoon, lending blackened smoke to the twist of the breeze's current. The hearts of the great stags were burning in ones and twos, freeing their spirits from the cage of earthly flesh.

As they looked up, the Hunter Lords saw her passing, and they recognized in her Soredon of Elseth's wife. The youngest of the men here had never hunted with him, but the oldest had. His death, more than his life on this single day, made him a part of the Sacred Hunt. In respect, they bowed their unadorned heads, and in respect, she nodded in return, feeling the ice lodge at the base of her heart so completely she wondered if, offered to fire, it would burn.

Because as she passed them, she knew that each and every one of them— Hunter Lords and huntbrothers all—would know that Gilliam of Elseth had failed to answer the summons. What respect would they then have for his house? And why?

To the clearing she walked, Corwinna at her side, the light of the sun dying by slow degree. There were more Hunters, green clad, struggling with their burdens as the forests released them. She saw their Ladies, brightly, gaily, stepping across the reeds and mats placed over damp dirt to greet their Lords' return. And then over the hushed whisper of work and private words, the sound of the drums.

Corwinna did not touch her; instead, she stepped back so that Elsabet might see the path to the altar that rested upon the Hunter's Green, before the Queen's Dais. The Hunter's Priests, robed in green-edged grays and browns, began to line that path like a wall. The oldest of the Priests carried the banner of the King: the stag on green field over the crossed spear and sword, the crown above it. It was heavy; the breeze did not move it as it hung like a sentence above the forming procession. The younger men carried the tautly pulled skin of the drums. They were here to honor their dead. Here to give thanks for the sacrifice of the Breodani noble who, by his life's blood, ushered in the spring.

Iverssen stood at the altar, waiting quietly by the King's side. His face was lined with care and sorrow, like unto a Hunter's Lady, and not a Hunter Lord. So, too, was the King's. The King's title was the one title in the land that Elsa had never envied. For he was expected to be the strongest and the swiftest of the Hunter Lords, the most canny of their number—yet he was also expected to hold court with the Ladies as if he were the Queen's equal; to dispense wisdom in the making of those laws that affected the Breodani; to lead, always, the Hunt in which some of his closest friends were taken, year by year.

She bowed her head in genuine respect, pity pushing fear aside for a welcome moment. And then, raising her chin, she met the King's eyes and flinched. They were dark, those eyes, and she thought them reddened, although it was hard to tell at this distance, with his face so composed.

"Lady Elseth," he said gravely, his gentle voice carrying across the open clearing as if it were the wind. "Lady Maribelle. Come."

She knew, then.

She knew before the procession of Hunter Lords—five—came down the human aisle, bearing their precious burden. Knew before she saw the body clearly enough to recognize whose it was, who it had once been. Knew before she heard Maribelle's little scream, choked at once into silence but uttered nonetheless for all of the nobility—the silent, somber nobility—of Breodanir to hear.

She raised her head, lifted her chin, let the water film her eyes without letting it fall. The men might weep—were weeping—but the mothers, with the witness of servants and commoners and strangers and rivals, should not. For this sacrifice, this loss—this was what the Breodani *were*. Yet when they came, bearing Stephen's body, when they placed it down, as gently as she had ever seen Hunter Lords do anything, the tears fell.

This was her shame: not to know whether they fell from the sorrow of his loss or the relief of it, for Stephen's presence—and his absence—were clear proof that Elseth had not failed in its duties.

"Gilliam?" she said, her voice quiet because she had not the strength to speak loudly. She could not tear her eyes away from the face of her son; the Hunter had left her that.

"Lord Elseth," Iverssen replied, "is not in Breodanir."

"But that's not—"

"Here, Lady." He touched her shoulder, where no one else would have dared, and pulled her firmly around. "This is yours; it was found with Stephen of Elseth." Into her hands he placed a soft, supple piece of hide—deer, or rabbit, she thought—before he edged her away from the altar. The body had yet to be tended; to be wrapped and cleaned as it could be before the last of the ceremony was performed. It was not often done in the presence of kin.

Elsa let him push her away, fighting the desire to cling, to stay and bear witness.

In shaking hands, she unfurled the soft hide. It was long, and across its length, in large, perfectly formed letters, there was a message:

Lord Elseth has fulfilled his duties to the Hunter Lord. He has called the Hunt, and joined it, upon soil that the Hunter deemed Sacred.

The price has been paid; the promise has been fulfilled. Honor his name.

At the bottom of the message was a complicated insignia that Elsa recognized at once: the seal of the Hunter's Priests. But there were differences in it, subtle and odd, that she thought no less than a month of study would reveal. She would not give it a month, or even another minute, for it was clear enough that to Iverssen this was the will of the Hunter made manifest.

And perhaps, she thought bitterly, as she gently rolled it up, it was; for there was no mention of Stephen of Elseth, and he, her son, was the one who had paid the Hunter's Price.

Word rippled around her as if she were a stone; she heard Stephen's name in hushed and fading whispers as it carried beyond her reach. And then she heard a single cry, wordless as if words alone were poor containers for the depth of loss. And that cry went on and on in memory, speaking for Elsa, for Maribelle, for Gilliam, where these three could not.

Cynthia of Maubreche crossed the green, shaking herself free of her mother's hand to do so.

Cynthia, Elsa thought, *you injure your future.* But she said nothing; it was not her place to say it; Cynthia, at eighteen, almost nineteen, was woman enough to decide her own fate and abide by it. Instead, Elsa moved to one side, and when Cynthia approached the bier, let her pass as if she were Stephen's kin.

Cynthia pushed Iverssen to one side; the older Priest stumbled and took three steps back before righting himself. But he had seen grief of all nature at this altar, on this day; he was prepared for it, and did not judge it as harshly as Lord and Lady Maubreche would later in the privacy of their manor. Instead, in silence, he allowed the young Lady to reach out to the slack, still face; to touch dead cheeks with living palms, to stroke eyes closed that would never again be opened.

She cried, the cry was an open one, and in her tears, Maribelle found the company that she sought, and began to cry as well although she would not touch the body. The drums began their roll; the fires were lit.

Oh, Stephen, Stephen, Elsa thought, as she clenched her hands into fists in the folds of her skirt, that no one might see them. *Did we save you from starvation in the streets of the King's City to feed you to the hunger of the Hunter?*

Yes. And that was the worst of it. Knowing his end, she would never, given the choice, change his life. Only his death, and his death had never been in her hands. But was any death, really?

Gilliam, she thought, *where are you?* For she knew, of a sudden, that her living son needed the strength of the Breodani; he was without his huntbrother, and quite alone. She thought of William of Valentin, of Lorras of the Vale, of Lord Browin, of Hunters without number who had lost their huntbrothers to this Hunt, in this fashion.

Would he live? Would he want to?

Maribelle came to stand at her side. She said nothing, but Elsa saw, in the redness of her daughter's eyes, the wakening of knowledge and the beginning of wisdom; for in just such a way, upon the death of her brother so many years ago, had Elsa begun to understand the price that the Breodani women paid for their choice—for their lack of choices—in the men they raised.

Corwinna came also; they stood, these three, as the Priests tended to Stephen, until the shadow of a fourth woman joined them: the Queen. And then, quietly, they allowed themselves to be led away to the dais upon which the thrones were.

But Lady Cynthia of Maubreche would not leave.

4th of Veral, 411 A.A.
Averalaan

Her hair was dark and sleek, bound back by comb and pin in such a complicated way it might just as well have been magic for all she understood. Gone were tangles, brambles, and the odd bit of food—and they would likely never return. The Hunter had ascended, and with him, much of the wildness. What remained was a young woman named Espere who had no family, no home, and no Lord.

No Lord.

A loose-fitting robe, one warm and soft as the fur closest to a rabbit's skin, had been gifted to her by Mirialyn ACormaris. She wore it now, pausing a moment to stare at the light reflecting off a sheen of dark, dark blue. Gold edged the hem of the skirt and the sleeves; she disliked the feel of the embroidery against her skin.

At her back, a fountain trickled a steady stream of water into a smooth, wide basin; she knelt a moment to drink, forgetting once again the pitcher and goblets set out in the cool air.

Men and women had come—and gone—for the last few days. Three? She thought the word, lifting her fingers to count it. One. Two. Three. The rest, she did not know, or did not remember. There was very little that she did remember.

Ashfel's scent drifted downwind; she straightened and turned to see him gambol across the open courtyard with a very superior, but very friendly air. Galling quietly, she waited for him to come, wondering if his master would stop him. But no; Ashfel wet her cheek with his nose and then laid his jaw across her shoulder, wuffling into her tightly bound hair.

Ashfel whined softly, prodding her grave face.

"He won't speak to me," she told him, catching the underside of his great jaw in her hands and scratching it. "Why?"

"He won't speak to anyone, Espere."

Looking up, she saw Mirialyn, her bronze hair caught neatly in a long, braided tail that draped over her right shoulder. "I know." She paused, and her voice grew softer; she could not explain to Mirialyn—to anyone—how she felt about his distance. His absence. Since the end of the Hunt he had been so distant; he had given her freedom to fight, but not freedom to return. She had tried and tried and tried, but it hurt, and so she stopped. "It's Stephen."

"If I understand the Breodani."

"Does he blame me?" She did not keep the fear out of her voice; she was not in the presence of an enemy—why was there need?

"I don't know." Mirialyn did not lie. She had no scent of fear about her, nor did she have the nervous, quick movements, the sudden jabbing of finger or raising of voice, that seemed so common; it was why, of all the people gathered in these crowded, busy buildings, Mirialyn was the one she most trusted. "Lady Faergif and Lady Morganson have been with him for the last three days. He eats little, and he does not speak, but both Lady Faergif and Lady Morganson seem satisfied with his progress." She looked down into Ashfel's brown eyes. "Hello," she said gravely. "And you, Lord Elseth, if you're watching."

"He's not," Espere told her.

"Not?"

"Not watching."

Ashfel whined softly as Mirialyn shifted her gaze. "What will you do, wild one?"

"I don't know."

"There is a home for you here, should you desire it; there will always be a home for you while the Twin Kings reign." She watched Espere's face; watched the trembling lines of her lips, the turning of her newly intelligent eyes. Gently, for she found she could speak to this woman-child in no other way, she said, "What do you want to do?"

"I want to go home." Espere paused a moment, lifting her head as if testing the wind.

"Home?"

"With him. Where he goes." She looked up at Mirialyn, at the glimmer of sun that peered over the courtyard walls, at that shadows of her face. Then she shook her head. "He won't speak. He won't speak to me." Drawing her arms across her chest she stared at the flat stones across which Mirialyn's shadow fell.

It was hard to wake up in the morning. Hard to eat, get dressed, make plans. Ashfel, Connel, and Salas whined and whimpered at him like hens worrying the corpses of their chicks no matter how strict his orders were. He hated it. And he hated these halls, this overly warm weather, the prying eyes of the foreigners and the visits of the Ladies Faergif and Morganson.

Clenching his teeth on a growl, he twisted in a sudden spasm.

Stephen was gone.

There was no body, no ceremony, no farewell; there was no honoring of the dead, as if that could make a difference. Stephen was gone, and he knew now that not even the death of the Hunter could assuage that pain.

The gong clanged in the outer hall; he rose swiftly, casting off thin sleeping silks.

A slender, dark-haired man stood in the entry hall, waiting quietly. When he saw Gilliam, he bowed quite low. "It has been a long time since we walked the Winter road," he said gravely. "Although it was my desire, I was not chosen to join you in your battle." His expression darkened as he spoke, a momentary ripple of muscles across an otherwise calm face.

Gilliam said nothing although he recognized Zareth Kahn quite well; the Winter road had been part of a different world, a different life. The mage did not seem surprised by this. "I will not offer you condolences, Hunter Lord," he said gravely, as he pulled a rolled and sealed scroll from out of thin air. "But where I can, I will make it known that without the intervention of Stephen of Elseth, there would be *no* Empire." He bowed again, and handed Gilliam the scroll he carried. "It arrived," he said quietly, "an hour ago. From Breodanir's Order."

Gilliam took it without any display of curiosity, but his glance strayed to the seal and stayed there. It was the seal of Elseth. "This—when did you get it?"

"An hour ago," Zareth Kahn said again, his voice calm and quiet. "A message of this nature can be sent magically, but it is not usually done except in case of grave emergency; the cost to the sender is quite high because it—" He lapsed into silence as he realized that Gilliam of Elseth was not, probably could not, listen. "Lord Elseth," he said, and then, after a few minutes had passed in silence, "Lord Elseth?"

Gilliam's gaze rose from the seal reluctantly. "What?"

No huntbrother, this Lord, but Zareth Kahn had lived in Breodanir for many a year; the lack of finesse, of manners, of civility's little guises did not bother him. "Should you require it of us, we will return a message in the fashion in which this was received."

"I—I don't know."

"Send a runner to the Order of Knowledge if you have need of my service. Ask for me personally, and I will come for your letter." Gilliam of Elseth could not know that this message was the first such one carried for an outsider—including the Crowns themselves—in the last decade.

Gilliam nodded gruffly, pulling the sealed letter closer to his chest before he thought to offer thanks.

"Do not thank me," Zareth Kahn said gravely. He started to speak again, to offer his condolence or his gratitude, to praise the dead—and the living—but Gilliam of Elseth, very much the Hunter Lord, had already turned his full attention to the scroll.

And Zareth Kahn well knew why. Lord Elseth had missed the call to the Sacred Hunt in the King's Forest, and by Breodanir law—a law more ancient than the founding of Averalaan—the Elseth name should be no more. It was Zareth Kahn who had insisted that a message be sent to Lady Elseth, and in haste; it was Zareth Kahn who had supplied the power necessary to bring her response back. It was the only gift he had to offer.

Because in Averalaan, death on the First Day was merely a death, perhaps even a blessed one; because, in Averalaan, the festival of lights would go on for two days yet, and the bards were filling the common streets with song and story and embroidered, simplified history. Nowhere was the somber respect, the sense of mutual loss, that the Hunters had grown up with; nowhere was there the weeping, the mourning, the gratitude that came from the common peasants to the noble families who year by year fulfilled their duty by sacrificing one of their own.

"If you would have it," the mage said softly, uncertain as to whether or not he was heard, "I would be pleased to travel with you when you return to Breodanir."

"If," Gilliam replied, but the there was no bitter force in the word, and his fingers traced the unbroken seal as if he was afraid that to break it was to destroy the last vestige of a family he had thought lost.

Zareth Kahn withdrew quietly, to give the Hunter Lord peace, thinking how very changed they had both been by their windows into each other's world.

She knew the sound of his footfall; knew it better than the sound of her own. The air was still and carried no scent, but she turned her head to watch the heavy door hanging as he moved it to one side and stepped out beneath the open sky. She was afraid to move; curling her arms around her legs, she rested her chin on the rounded shelf her knees made.

He came not in the robes and silks of the Essalieyanese, but rather in the dark, deep green of the Breodani Hunters. His eyes were red, and his hair a little wild; the lines about his jaw were tense. But his hands hung loose as he looked into the midday sky.

Ashfel appeared from the north, followed in short order by Connel, by Salas. They were frenzied in their greeting, making enough noise to be heard in the streets beyond the palace grounds. He let them come for the first time since the Mother's daughter had called him back; even let them leap up and place their large paws on his shoulders, chest, back—anywhere they could find purchase.

Oh, she wanted to join them. She wanted to jump up and run and leap about his feet in their dance of joy, to butt his chest with her head and listen to his thoughts and know that she belonged to his pack, that he loved her, that above all people—if not Ashfel—she was valued. She had known that once, but she was not the same.

And because she was not, he could not be.

You are not an animal, Espere, Stephen had told her—and he was right. She was the daughter of Bredan, and without his presence as anchor and influence she was no longer chained to the ebb and flow of his will, his season; the two weeks of clarity that followed the Sacred Hunt, the two weeks in which he, as father and not Hunter beast, had taught her speech and oath and honor, could continue for the rest of her natural life. Her father would no longer descend into slow forgetfulness, and thence to wild hunger, dragging her down in his wake; the Heavens held him.

I wanted this.

But as she watched the dogs, as their scents rolled into each other, becoming one, she knew that it was not enough. Because if she was not animal, she was not human either. On the day that she had first found Gilliam—and Stephen—in the streets of the King's City, she had found the only Lord she wanted; pack leader, Hunter.

Her cheeks were wet; lifting her hands, she touched them. Curiosity stayed her fears a moment as she stared. And then another's hands touched her very gently.

Before he could pull them back, she caught them and held tight. She was Espere, and knew no guile, no pretense of strength or independence. What she wanted, she wanted, as unfettered in desire as a child.

Still, she was afraid to meet his eyes, so she pulled his hands close to her face, and cupped them round her cheeks for warmth; the tears had cooled her skin. "I didn't mean forever," she said, into the palm of his hands. "I didn't mean you to set me free forever."

He did not speak, and she did not expect it; he had rarely used words with her and she didn't want them now. But he pulled her face up, and because she rested in the palms of his hands, her gaze rose as well. His eyes were all pupil, and hers, the night; they met, as they had in the streets of the King's City at journey's beginning.

Contact.

More. He lifted her into the curve of his arms, and she came, releasing his hands long enough to throw her arms tightly around his neck. His chin touched the top of her perfect hair.

"Ashfel," he said, "come. It's time to go home." His arms tightened. She felt what he did not say, and her tears fell again.

Epilogue

13th of Veral, 411 A.A.
Breodanir

THE MASTER GARDENER TOILED in the heart of the Maubreche labyrinth, beyond the roses and the flower beds and the ancient trees that wore spring's first colors. The Sacred Hunt had come and gone, and life had taken the land in its strong grip; only winter would loose it.

But winter was not the gardener's concern. He labored, as he had always labored, in the green, alone. Many were the people who had marveled at the gardener's art, but few indeed were those who had seen him at his work—and of those, each and every one had been born to the Maubreche responsibility.

He was a watcher of life; over the years, his understanding of its physical nuance outstripped the inborn talent of the Makers, and to his private satisfaction, among the most ardent of his admirers had been Ovannen the Artisan. But it was not for the regard of strangers that he worked now.

For, having completed the foundation for this season's living sculpture, he now approached the tapestry. Hands shaking, he set aside his tools a moment to better examine the hedge that never wintered. His gift kept it alive, when so much else had withered and died at time's march, or worse.

The past glory and tragedy of the Maubreche line had been detailed here by his hands from its beginning; it was time—at last, time—to draw that story to a close. To fulfill an oath, and have peace.

Was it dawn? Had he looked so long, worked in such distraction, that he had failed to note sun's rise? Yes, he thought, picking up his shears and watching the matted reflection of early light on the leaves. But he had hours yet before the grounds were no longer his canvas. Quietly, as he did all things, the master gardener began to clip.

This season, Cynthia of Maubreche was to have accepted the suit of one of four Hunter Lords; to have brought that chosen Hunter, and his huntbrother, into the heart of Maubreche, where both might serve her family's name and duties. She had decided upon Corwin of Eralee, the third son of a shrewd and capable mother, a man known for honor, if not intellect. His huntbrother, Arlin, was a soft-spoken, quiet man six years her elder, who understood her well enough to know when to leave be and when to press suit. Or perhaps it was Lady Eralee's advice that guided Arlin. It mattered not—for the ability to take good advice was also both rare and an asset. His hair was dark where Stephen's was fair; he wore a beard, where Stephen's chin was smooth; his face was long and perhaps a little plain, where Stephen's . . . Stephen.

Of the four suitors, it was Arlin who best understood that her heart, not in the match, was elsewhere. He did not speak of it, not to offer comfort, not to chide or show largesse, not to pity; duty was duty, and she by birth, he by young boy's choice, were Breodani.

But not even Arlin could ignore her outburst at the end of the Sacred Hunt, and although the suit and offer still stood, Lady Eralee thought it best to bide the year, and to come again in the spring.

As if time could somehow make whole what the Hunter had broken.

Cynthia wore black, edged in Hunter green; she covered her hair with the hood of an ancient robe of mourning that had been a part of her family for generations; it was taken out and worn by the Lady of the manor when the Hunter's Death cast his shadow upon Maubreche. Lord and Lady Maubreche said nothing at all when she had ordered the keykeeper to bring it out of its place of honor. She almost wished they had, because she had a great desire to fight for Stephen—for his name, his honor, if not his life—and no one at all to fight with.

She sought solace in the garden, following the labyrinth out of habit, searching for peace although she was quite certain she would never know it again. In the isolation of the new green, she let the facade crack, and the tears—for they never seemed to stop—came. Yesterday she had almost thought she could survive his loss; the morning was bright, the sun warm, the sky clear. She heard birdsong, the buzzing of early insects; she felt the life of the estate in spring buoy her.

But this morning, it was gone; this morning she could not stop saying, over and over again, all of the good-byes that his death had precluded. At last, drawing her robe about her, she left the house.

Left it to stand in front of the still back of the master gardener at the end of the tapestry that his hands had made of Maubreche history.

"Lady Cynthia," he said, without looking up.

She did not know his name—and it had been years since she had asked it, for he never answered, and as she left childhood behind, she came to understand that he never would.

"What are you doing?"

He said nothing, and she watched him in the silence. Then, as her eyes focused on his hands, on the clipped and perfect curve of the hedge beneath them, she said, "what are you making?" For she saw that his shears were shaping the wild hedge, and suddenly, although she could not say why, she was afraid.

"Lady Cynthia," he told her softly, his back still toward her, his adept hands still clipping and trimming and changing the hedge, "go to the God."

But the God had taken Stephen from her, and she did not wish to see His graven face. She moved quietly, stepping across the early grass to better see what the master gardener had shaped.

And she saw her own face in the leaves, emerging from nature to take her place with her forebears. She did not speak, but only because she could not.

"Cynthia," the gardener said, turning from his task. His eyes, steel-gray, seemed almost silver in the early morning light. "Go. Now."

She stepped back, stumbling on the hem of her robe. Righting herself, she made haste to the heart of the maze without another word. She had never been afraid of the master gardener before; she had always considered him the quiet, re-clusive bringer of life. Yet there was death in those eyes, and not a little of it— how could she have missed it, all these years?

Her feet carried her automatically to the center of the labyrinth, for she had come to it, time and again, all of her life. It was in the fountain beneath the God's eye that she had first been washed after birth.

And it was beneath the eye of God that Stephen had sworn to return to her.

The morning mist that often crossed the lowlands was thick and heavy, some-thing almost unseen in the high city. Looking up, she realized that clouds had rolled in—although from where, she could not say—to turn the sky a hazy shade of pale gray. Slowing to a walk, she began to listen for the sound of birds at the fountain.

But silence reigned instead, and it was such that she was afraid to break it with the sound of her voice. This was not the labyrinth of her childhood games or adult musings. The master gardener had sent her on—but to where, and for what pur-pose, she did not know.

And then she heard it for the first time, although it would not be the last: the voice of Bredan, Lord of the Covenant. Her memories did not hold the multitude of voices, but her heart did, and before she could stop herself, she had folded at the knee in the deepest of the Breodani bows, drawing a cloak-draped arm across her chest as she lowered her head into the smoky mist that lapped like dream's waves at her feet.

"Cynthia of Maubreche," He—they—said, and although she was afraid, she lifted her head as if the words were a command. The God's eyes were luminescent, but of a color, of a brilliance, that she could not even name. Yet she found that she could meet them, and trembling, she did.

"Do you know me?"

How could she not? He dressed as a Hunter Lord, and not the robed statue of the God in the garden; He carried a bow across his back, a sword at his side, and although no pack attended him, she felt that, in the distance, the *Bredari* waited his will. "You are the Hunter," she said.

"Ah, yes," he said softly, if a hundred thousand voices could be said to speak softly. "But I am more than the Hunter, or I was, and when the Breodani remembered, Maubreche was the family that served me best."

She felt pride, fierce and sudden, at his words, and swallowed as the blush rose in her cheeks. Where was her anger now? Where was her sorrow?

As if he could hear her thoughts, he smiled sadly. "You will have cause to remember it throughout the years to come. As will I." He held out a hand to her, and after a moment she took it, rising.

His hand felt like a man's hand, no more. Looking again into his eyes, she felt her awe diminish, although she could not say why, for they were still the essence of divinity. And then she noticed that beneath the heavy green cloak he wore, his tunic was slashed.

"You're wounded," she said, eyes widening.

"Yes," he said. "And the recovery will be long and difficult. If I could, I would tell you that it is not of your concern." But his eyes lost a little of their light. "I have never lied to Maubreche, nor it to me."

"Why—why have you come here?"

"A thousand years and more have passed since my worship was practiced in the world of man," he told her gravely. "It is said that Gods, unworshiped, die—and this, at least, is false. But Gods unworshiped have no power to influence the course of the world of man."

He raised his face, looking into the cloudy distance as if a storm was on the horizon. "A darkness has entered the world, just as I have left it. Measured against the strength of a God, it is weak and crippled—but measured against the races of the Covenant, it is strong." Lightning arched in the skies above. "Had I understood the need, I might have asked for more, who had already taken too much from my people. I did not see—I could not understand—" He paused, and lowered his gaze to once again meet Cynthia's.

"My Lord," she said, touching his shoulder softly, "what would you have of us?"

"Of Maubreche? Tend my sanctuary, follow my ways."

"And of me?"

Like a Hunter—the very Hunter—he answered bluntly and without guile. "A child.

"Through my children, my influence is strongest; they are the vessels for some part of my power." He paused, turning away from her paling face. "If I listen, Cynthia, and my child speaks, I will hear him across the divide. And if I speak, and he listens, he shall hear me."

Minutes passed before Cynthia spoke, and when she did her voice was laced with bitterness. "Is there no one else you can ask this thing of?"

"If there were, I would. And if you had the time, I would wait—for I know the price that you have paid." He turned back to her, his face grim. "But you are Breodani. Understand what it is I ask of you, and why. Because when you make your oath, I will take it, and it will be fulfilled."

When, Cynthia thought. Not if. The shadows beneath her eyes deepened as she opened her mouth and paused in silence, weighing caution against growing anger. At last, she gave in to the desire for words, although her voice was a Lady's voice, quiet in its sharpness. "You accepted Stephen's oath."

"Both of them," the God said gravely.

She made fists of her hands, and held back the tears that threatened to fall. "No," she said, the word a low growl in the back of her throat. "He promised to return to me. He gave his life to you instead."

"He was no oathbreaker," the God said sharply. "Nor would he have returned to you had he been." The storm in His eyes ended abruptly as he stared down at her; He had grown in stature, although when she did not remember. "But I knew what his end would be, and I accepted his oath.

"Cynthia, when my cloak of flesh was destroyed, the souls of my dead were free to walk the Halls of Mandaros, to meet him, to be judged, and to return to their birthworld if that is their fate."

His hair began to soften, his shoulders to shrink in. Even his height dwindled as he spoke, and the voices of the multitude began to fade and dim, until only two voices remained.

She raised a hand to cover her mouth.

"But one soul alone, I did not release, nor would he have it any other way."

She reached out to touch the face of the God, stopping a hair's breadth from the contours of his cheek.

"I will not lie to you, little one," the Hunter said, although she was barely listening. "The spirit alone is the man that you knew; the flesh that is wrapped around it is my own."

All the words made sense, but dimly and distantly; she began to cry in earnest, and the tears obscured his face, his blessed face.

"I can return nothing else to you," the God said. "Except this: the knowledge that Stephen of Elseth is no oathbreaker; nor was his Lord. Or Lady." And as he spoke the last word, the two voices became one.

And that voice was Stephen's.